TRIPTYCH

Born in Donegal, Ireland, of a Devonshire family long settled in that part, Joyce Cary (1888–1957) was given for first name – according to a common Anglo-Irish practice – his mother's surname of Joyce. He was educated at Clifton and Trinity, Oxford, and studied art in Edinburgh and Paris. Afterwards he fought with the Montenegrins in the Balkan War.

Later he studied Irish Cooperation under Sir Horace Plunkett, and in 1913 joined the Nigerian Political Service. He fought in the Nigerian Regiment during the First World War and was wounded at Mora Mountain. On returning to political duty, as magistrate and executive officer, he was sent to Borgu, then a very remote district. His health, however, had never recovered from war service and in 1920 he was advised to retire from tropical Africa. He then began to write, and his first novel, *Aissa Saved*, was published in 1932. *Herself Surprised*, the first volume of this trilogy, was published in 1941, and was followed by *To be a Pilgrim* in 1942, and *The Horse's Mouth* in 1944. Each part is complete in itself. The trilogy was designed to show three characters, not only in themselves, but as seen by each other. Of *Herself Surprised*, L.P. Hartley said, 'There seems to me more truth of human nature, a profounder understanding of the springs of action in *Herself Surprised*, than in any novel I have read for a long time', the *Observer* wrote of *To be a Pilgrim*, 'Its excellence lies in the great skill with which a character is drawn in all its variety, in the minor portraits of members of his family, with their subsidiary stories, and in the unhesitating and illuminating detail of half a century of English life', and of *The Horse's Mouth* Ivor Brown writing in the *Observer* said, '[It] has the kick of ten stallions. Mr Joyce Cary writes at top pace, at the top of his voice, and the top of his form . . . for the argot and aroma of its bars and doss-houses – and for a lively parade of gross and roaring Bohemian humours – this book is a nailer and a knockout.'

Joyce Cary's other books are *The Captive and the Free*, *A Fearful Joy*, and *Mister Johnson*, a comic masterpiece set in Nigeria, the trilogy comprising *A Prisoner of Grace*, *Except the Lord* and *Not Honour More*; and *Spring Song and Other Stories*. *A House of Children* which was awarded the James Tait Black Memorial Prize 1942, is partly autobiographical.

Joyce Cary

TRIPTYCH

Herself Surprised
To Be A Pilgrim
The Horse's Mouth

PENGUIN BOOKS

Penguin Books Ltd, Harmondsworth, Middlesex, England
Viking Penguin Inc., 40 West 23rd Street, New York, New York 10010, U.S.A.
Penguin Books Australia Ltd, Ringwood, Victoria, Australia
Penguin Books Canada Ltd, 2801 John Street, Markham, Ontario, Canada L3R 1B4
Penguin Books (N.Z.) Ltd, 182–190 Wairau Road, Auckland 10, New Zealand

Herself Surprised first published by Michael Joseph 1941
Published in Penguin Books 1955
Copyright 1941 by Joyce Cary

To Be A Pilgrim first published by Michael Joseph 1942
Published in Penguin Books 1957
Copyright 1942 by Joyce Cary

The Horse's Mouth first published by Michael Joseph 1944
Published in Penguin Books 1948
Copyright 1944 by Joyce Cary

This collection published as *Triptych* 1985
All rights reserved

Scanned and phototypeset by
Datasolve, London
Printed and bound in Great Britain by
Cox & Wyman Ltd, Reading
Typeset in Photina

Contents

Herself Surprised

To
Mary Ogilvie

1

The judge, when he sent me to prison, said that I had behaved like a woman without any moral sense. 'I noticed,' he said, and the paper printed it all, 'that several times during the gravest revelations of her own frauds and ingratitude, Mrs Monday smiled. She may be ill-educated, as the defence has urged, but she is certainly intelligent. I am forced to conclude that she is another unhappy example of that laxity and contempt for all religious principle and social obligation which threatens to undermine the whole fabric of our civilization.'

When he spoke in this way I was upset and wanted to tell him that I had never been against religion; far from it; but the policeman stopped me and afterwards I saw that I had no right to be angry with the judge. Perhaps I had smiled when some of the lawyers brought up old stories about me from years back. It is strange to stand in that box and hear yourself taken to pieces by strangers.

At first I could not believe that I was anything like the woman they made me out to be. But the chaplain tells me that nearly all the women who come here to prison have the same story, that the lawyers were wrong and made them seem worse than they were; and I couldn't deny that each little bit they brought against me was true; or nearly true; and that some things they did not know were worse.

I was shocked by the prison clothes, and the way I was treated, as if I were a criminal. Now I see that I am a criminal just like the others, and that perhaps some of the others became so in the same foolish way, without knowing what they were doing. So perhaps some who read this book may take warning and ask themselves before it is too late what they really are and why they behave as they do.

'Know thyself,' the chaplain says, and it is true that I never knew myself till now. Yet I thought I knew myself very well, and that I was humble enough, and I remember the first time I saw myself in my true body. It was on my honeymoon, in Paris, in a grand shop, the grandest I had ever seen. It had big mirrors in the showroom, between the pillars, like glass doors, and I was walking to the stairs in my new hat as big as an Easter cake, and feeling the swish of my new silk petticoats and the squeeze of my new French stays. I seemed to be looking into the next saloon, and I thought: 'Look at that fat, common trollop of a girl with a snub nose and the shiny cheeks, jumping out of her skin to be in a Paris hat. Wouldn't you bet she was out from Dartmouth fair last week? You can almost smell the cider on her lips. What a shame to expose herself like that and her nation to these foreigners.'

But in the same flash I saw that it was me. It stopped me dead with the blow. I knew I was not a beauty, but till that hour I had not seen myself with the world's eye. I had made a love of my nose, snub and broad though it was, and my eyes which were nothing but brown. Are not any eyes wonderful if you will look at them alone and forget the rest? I had praised the shining of my hair and even the shape of my big hands and every bit of me at one time or another. So I had made a belle of myself when I was nothing, as they used to say at home, but maiden meat. My husband Matthew saw me stop and said: 'What is it, love, is it the hat? I thought perhaps it was a bit bright for your complexion.'

I was going to say, 'Yes, indeed,' but instead the words popped out: 'No, it's not the hat – it's the glass. I never saw one so big.' So I kept the hat, and if people looked at me I thought: 'If I am a body then it can't be helped, for I can't help myself.'

So I would think in those days; whenever I wanted to please myself; even against my husband. Yet I meant to be as good as my vows and better. For I could not but wonder that he, a gentleman and rich, had taken me, an ordinary country girl, neither plain nor pretty, with none of the advantages he might have expected. I would think that perhaps it was only a fancy in him; for I knew that nature made men mad now and then, when they would catch at the nearest woman, but when they were tired of their play, they waken up and wondered how they had been taken in.

So I was in terror that Matt would wake up, especially when I mistook in conversation. For though I could speak very well, like any farmer's daughter in those days, I knew very little of geography, or music, or languages. I remember in my first month I asked a lady who had been on the Rhine about the Russian food, thinking she had been in Russia. But the worst thing was when I saw Matt turning red, I went on to mistake things which I knew quite well, and said: 'Oh, I didn't know Russia was in Germany,' and so on; trembling at my poor Matt's feelings and yet going on with my nonsense, only to make the woman think me more ignorant than I really was.

I knew, of course, that all the ladies of Bradnall Green, which was where we lived, were studying me and telling the news 'a month ago she was a servant.'

2

For that was how I began with poor Matt. I had been cook to his mother, Mrs Monday, who was a widow. It was true that I had come from a good home, for my father was a freeholder and working foreman, and my mother had been a teacher. I myself had prizes from school for recitation and scripture, and a certificate for sewing; and afterwards I had a very good training as kitchenmaid under a man cook in a good religious house with a very rich brewing family, who never allowed so much as an ounce of margarine or custard powder or any made-up stuffs in their kitchen, even for the servants. My mother wanted me to be a first-class cook fit for the best service; and so did I.

Indeed, even so long ago as the Diamond Jubilee I had a pick for my first place, as cook. I could have gone to a General. But I chose Mrs Monday's because the house was not so big, or the family; and it was not too far in the wilds. I liked to stay South, too, and Bradnall, though it is fifty miles from the sea, is still south feeling. It stands in a valley among orchards, which I liked, from the cider orchards out at home; and yet the downs was not too far.

It is true Bradnall town was nothing much except for the Cathedral and the close; just shops and streets as dirty as you please; but Woodview, which was the Mondays' house, stood two miles out at the Green. It was not too quiet either, but right on a main road, with carts and carriers passing all the morning, and in the afternoons always some good carriages. I could see the coachmen's hats from my kitchen window, coming up the hill; then I would often go down to the back gate to see them trotting past on the level. I always loved a good carriage and pair, with its shining horses going up and down like rockers; and silver on the harness; and spokes twirling like an egg-beater; and the coachwork so bright that you could see the hedges and the sky in it.

Then the village was close, and it was a good village with five or six real shops and a real draper, I mean one that sold only drapery and could find you a draw-ribbon or match your wool, at the last minute.

The house was very pretty, too, all covered with trellis in front, for roses, and creeper behind. It reminded me of a picture out of *Mrs Ewing*, with its high chimneys and trellis roses, except that it was not really old. But then again, if it had been old, it would not have had such good sinks and hot water laid on, and a porcelain bath that cleaned with bath brick; and looked clean when it was done.

Woodview had a good garden, too, and especially a good kitchen garden. I always like to see a kitchen garden in a house, to know that my vegetables are fresh, and to walk in. For servants can use a kitchen garden, and what I feared to miss most, in service, was a garden. All my friends in service said the same, that they had no garden. You might say that country girls do not set much store by a garden when they have one, but then, country girls at home have the lanes and the fields. But a girl in service can't run about the lanes in her kitchen print or her uniform. Everyone can recognize her a mile away and say: 'There's Minnie or Millie again, running after young So-and-So,' and it will soon come to the mistress. The very names of hay cock and housemaid, put together, will terrify any mistress. But in a kitchen garden a maid can walk and look at the world, I mean the growing world, and sometimes even bring out a kitchen chair and shell her peas or shred up her runners, and feel the open air, a feeling which you don't have walking in a road.

I'll own I soon found a corner in the kitchen garden at Woodview where no one could see me from the house, and where I was well away from the rubbish heap, with a sweet briar hedge at my back and the cabbages in front; and beside the cabbages, a great bed of larkspur, which they grew there for cutting; and then I would often bring out my chair and read all afternoon between luncheon and tea. It was at Woodview I first took to reading. For though I had been a prizewinner at school, I never knew how to read for myself and get the sweet pleasures of a good book until I came to Woodview. They had books there, put in the servants' rooms, religious books. So I began with them, with missionaries to the Kaffirs. Their name was Moffat, and I have never forgotten their goodness and bravery; for truly they offered their lives to God.

Then, too, it was in that happy, quiet time at Woodview, before I was married and while I was still a sober maiden, that I first read Charlotte M. Yonge. Of course, I had heard of her fame before, because my mother had the *Young Stepmother*, and my teacher at school taught us that she was as great as Shakespeare, and truer to life. But it was only now, when Miss Maul asked me if I would like a good book, that I remembered the name and asked her for a Yonge. And Mrs Monday had the *Pillars of the House*, which Miss Maul lent me, and it gave me such pleasure I was quite made for reading and could not eat or sleep for thinking of it. I was glad that being cook I had my own room, for I read often half the night, and, I'll admit it, so excited that even in my work I would be thinking of that poor family, thirteen children left without a father, and the noble Felix who gave up his education to support his mother.

My own daughters laughed at Miss Yonge's books and at me for upholding them, but I told them often and I believe it still that great books should tell of good, noble characters and show them in the real trials and sorrows of life, for God knows there are enough in every life, and everyone of us wants help to face them. I know that Miss Yonge did me much good and gave me strength in adversity, and I have often thought, in my bad times: 'How would Violet Moss have borne this – she would have made nothing of it'; or 'What would Mr Underwood have said, though he was dying of consumption and leaving a sick wife and all those children behind him in poverty'; and then I got courage again and cheerfulness.

But even when I was still in the Woodview kitchen, the Moffats and Miss Yonge did me good. They made me ashamed of my comfort and my spoilings. For now when I look back on that time it was not only good religious thoughts that came into my head. I say I was a sober-sides, and I was certainly shy in strange company, but I know I had begun to spoil myself. I always had my fingers in some sweet thing, and often, even from that same quiet corner in the garden, with the *Pillars* in my hand and tears in my eyes, I would jump up and rush to the back door, only at the sound of the milkman's voice. Because he was a good-looking boy, and a charmer. Indeed, I let him flirt with me, though I know he was a philanderer and had misused several poor girls, and, what was more, I used to forgive myself afterwards, saying: 'I'm only young once', or 'That's the way I'm made.' Indeed, I think if I had not been sober brought up by a good mother, I might have gone to the bad in my teens. But my mother was a good woman, one with a conscience. She never minded giving me a hard smack now and then where it did me no harm (for she never boxed my ears and would rage against any parent that did, saying it was dangerous to the drum), and when she saw me lolling and lazing and skimping my work about the house she would tell me so in plain words and say: 'You can do your work properly, my girl, or you'll get nothing from me but bread and water and sackcloth.' So indeed she has given me bread and water only for my breakfast and, when I sulked, told me that I was a fool to spoil my temper as well as my welcome. 'For if you want to get a husband,' she would say, 'you'll have to do it on your temper and your character. Your face and your shape will take you no further than the workhouse.'

3

I knew my luck at Woodview, and, indeed, I did not know how there could be such delight in the world, and especially in service, even good service. So when Mr Matt began to wait about the back stairs and to come upon me in the attic landing, I was angry with him for bringing me into the fear of losing such a good place.

I could not blame the poor man himself; he was so held down and cramped by his good mamma and his older sister, Maggie, or Maul as they used to call her. It was Matt, Matt, all day; and where have you been and what do you want in your best suit. It was a shame to see a man already up in his forties so hampered and hagged, like a child, and kept from his rights as a man. All we girls pitied him.

But I had been well brought up, as I say, and I asked him to leave me alone.

The truth was that though I pitied him then for his poor creeping life, I did not greatly like him. I thought him a poor thing, with his long neck and long nose, his bulgy eyes and his bald head. He would look so startled as a hare when I told him that it was not honest of him to lie in wait for me; and then when he looked at me through the kitchen window, from the garden, his eyes were so sad as a wounded hare. And that, God forgive me, made me want to laugh. He was a joke to all of us girls, for we were a young, careless lot, always ready to laugh.

He kept away from me for a time, and then he began to be more than ever in love. I could not stop him. He came breaking into the kitchen whenever he thought I was alone and then he would take me by the hand or arm and falter out: 'How are you, Sara?' or 'What a nice girl you are.' Never a word of love. But his face would grow red all the way up his baldness.

I could not be too angry, for I saw it was nature working in him. Yet I was frightened and so sharp enough. 'Mr Matt,' I said, 'have you no shame behaving so in your own mother's house? If you want a girl, go and take one in your own class and don't pester servants who have their own way to make.'

When at last he wrote me a note, proposing that we should go off and get married, I could not believe him. As I say, I didn't like him then; he seemed too old and serious; besides I was afraid to marry a gentleman, with all their rules and manners. But he would not take no. He kept on asking me every day; and one day, when he asked me if I could not like him enough, though I meant to say no, yet the words came out of my mouth that I would try.

I don't know what was in my mind, for though in our parts girls did sometimes try a marriage with a man and marry him after, I can't have thought that. I wouldn't have thought it with my religion, and I know, too, that Mr Matt wanted a marriage at once.

All that evening I was surprised at myself. Yet it seemed to me that I could still draw back, and that it was all a kind of play.

But not a bit. For now I was caught up and couldn't get out. He brought me the ring that night and how could I say no then, with it round my neck? It was the ring on Monday and the registry office on Thursday and London that night and Paris on the next Tuesday. In one week from that idle word my whole state was changed as much as if I had been made over into another woman. I could not believe it myself and still it seemed to me that I was play-acting, or that the world was more like a play than I had thought.

You will say that was just what a flighty girl would do, marrying for a whim. But I was not flighty then. I was a sober-sides. If I had been flighty, I would not have been so surprised at myself, as I was for many a day, until I had no time to think of anything.

4

Matt had left behind a letter for his family, but you can guess how I was in terror of them. I hoped, indeed, that they would never forgive him, only that I might not have to face them again.

But Mrs Monday, though stiff and proud, was a noble soul and a true Christian. She called me daughter in her first letter and summoned me home. Miss Maul, indeed, was another mould, for though she was polite enough when I came, she soon found how to quarrel. She was a cross kind of woman and I think she suffered from losing her power over Matt, who had been like husband and son to her from his babyhood.

I could not blame her for being cross and she had one reason to find fault. For as it happened, no sooner had I reached home than my friend, Rosina Balmforth, came to visit me.

Rosina was two years older than me and my mother had never liked her. She had always been a bold girl, talking broad and dressing in a way that gave a wrong notion of her. For though she had little enough religion, she never allowed any freedoms with her nature.

Rozzie and I had lived at the two ends of one double cottage in Rackmill where we were both born, and though we were different, she was my best friend. She had such spirits and she never let anything put her down. Yet she had no luck and no prospects. She came from a bad poor home. Her father used to knock her about and she was always in rags. She had no proper education. Her looks, too, which might have been her hope, were spoilt by a bad skin, and in those days a girl could not powder and paint to give herself justice.

Yet Rozzie had made her own way. She had got herself, at only fifteen, a good place at The Case Is Altered, which was then a rough enough house, though free, and doing the best business in the village. And once she was there she made herself respected by the worst. She would fight off the men with her fists and her tongue. So, before she was eighteen, she was the real manager and married the landlord, Willie Balmforth.

This was a good match, for, as I say, Rozzie had nothing but her health and go, and a good bust. And Willie owned the house and fifty acres of good land beside. He was a striving man, too, who meant to make his fortune. The village all wondered at his taking Rozzie. But I thought it was Rozzie who had taken him and I admired her for the way she had fought herself up out of dirt and rags and ignorance.

But it did well. Rozzie stayed behind the bar, and managed that side of the house better than any man. She would throw out a drunk with her own knee. She made the Case so respectable that the Vicar would come there, yet consumption went up by barrels a week. She would fix a man

15

with her eye in such a way that he dared not hang over a pint for more than twenty minutes, or a quart for half an hour.

Meanwhile Willie built out a wing in iron, bought secondhand, and took cycle clubs and Sunday schools and Buffaloes. He had summer visitors and sent them out by char-a-banc to the beaches.

The only trouble at the Case was that Bill could not hold his drink, nor Rozzie her tongue. They were cat and dog and Rozzie would write and tell me never, whatever I did, to marry a man, for they were all hateful.

5

But though I admired Rozzie for her character, I could have wished she had not come to see me quite so soon after my marriage and I had great harm from it. Yet it was not Rozzie's fault, but my fault. You might say, I had reason to be flighty; a young girl, I wasn't yet nineteen, just married to a gentleman with his strange nervous ways, and never knowing whether they were Matt's own ways or proper rules of the class I had come into. But it was not that I was flighty, but that there was a bad spirit in me ready for mischief and for any temptation, and I would not fight it.

Yet now I was growing in love with my Matt. No girl could have helped loving a man so kind in himself and so loving to her. So it was the last thing I wanted to upset my poor Matt and when Rozzie came I went to meet her at the station to warn her that the Mondays were a strict family and that Matt was a shy man and a true gentleman, easily put out of countenance among women.

But Rozzie was full of confidence. 'Don't tell me,' she said. 'A word to the wise. I'll butter them all up like a sore tail. What about the costume? It's the one I use for customers' funerals, old ale colour.' It was true she was in a dark brown cloth dress, very quiet and respectable, but her first words to Matt were: 'So you're another of them.'

'I beg your pardon,' Matt said, all eagerness to make my friend welcome, especially because his mother and sister were looking at her already as if she was dirt on the carpet.

Rozzie knew as well as I did that she was going wrong. She turned purple and stuck out her big chest. But do what she would, she looked bolder and fiercer than ever and fairly shouted at Matt: 'I meant husbands, not pigs. I respect pigs.' So then she turned to old Mrs Monday without being introduced and gave her a nod and said: 'We know men, don't we, mam – hogs by night and monkeys by day.'

Matt tried to laugh but could only move his lips and I was in despair for him and the Mondays. But I couldn't blame Rozzie, for as soon as I had got her out of the room she stopped and said to me: 'You can kill me, Sara;

16

go on, give me a good smack in the mouth'; and she asked me: 'Whatever did I do that for? – a nice beginning, I must say. But curse me if I let out another fly word. From this lamp post to round the corner, I'm a lady in both legs.'

But though Rozzie tried to hold herself in, she couldn't do it. She told Matt at dinner not to kick her under the table. 'If you have enough for Sara, it's as much as your life's worth'; and she said to me: 'Don't be jealous, Sara – I wouldn't have him for a back scratcher, in spite of his nose.'

Poor Rozzie was in as much agony as I was, and when I went to her bedroom I had to console her and tell her that nobody minded. But she was no fool and she would say: 'Of course they mind, Sara. And I'm doing you a lot of harm. I wish you could just give me a good kick in the stomach – it would make me feel better. But I'll go away tomorrow and never come back.'

Of course, I could not bear that. For the truth was I was glad to have Rozzie. I had been feeling lonely with no woman to talk to.

So Rozzie did not go, and on the third day she came out in a pink silk with a green sash and she had a green hat with ostrich feathers almost to her waist.

She was a little ashamed of it and yet I could not tell her it was on the loud side. For even Rozzie could be touchy when she knew herself in the wrong.

When I went out with her, people turned to look at us in the streets. Then Rozzie would stare at them and say in a loud voice, to be overheard: 'What's wrong with the mump heads – or aren't they used to seeing a lady in these parts?'

But I think Rozzie liked to be stared at, and I couldn't blame her, for it was all in her bravery and her go, which were what I admired.

But the worst was this: that I went shopping with Rozzie and bought the same kind of clothes. Then not to waste them I had to wear them and we gave Bradnall a fine spectacle. This in my first six weeks when I was on my trial, and I thought myself so dutiful.

Poor Matt did once try to make me wear something more ladylike, but I pretended that I did not know what he meant. 'I like a little colour,' I said. But I knew quite well that I was making an exhibition of myself and that everyone was saying: 'There goes the girl poor Monday married – she was a cook and doesn't she look like it.'

6

Rozzie wasn't gone a day before Miss Maul was at me about the clothes. 'I think,' she said, 'that you'd better not wear that new pink to Lady So-and-So's.'

'It was my own choice,' I said, for fear she should abuse Rozzie, and then I should be cross.

'Oh,' she said, 'I only noticed that it was like that terrible dress Mrs Balmforth was so fond of.'

So then, of course, I had to say that Rozzie was considered to have very good taste, and Miss Maul answered that it was not a suitable taste for young married women, at least in Bradnall.

Of course, she was quite right but I could not allow it, and so I had to go out in the pink dress and shock another party and make Matt wretched. For though he never noticed for himself what I wore, Miss Maul soon showed him that it was vulgar and such as only a common woman would wear, and so he was in agony for me.

I tortured him so and suffered for him, but so it was. It seemed I was two women; and one of them a loving wife and the other mad and wicked. I did not know how to manage myself, any more than a filly foal running about the field with her tail in the air and pretending to bite the trees, and to kick at her own mother. And as I say, I was frightened too, for I thought: 'This luck can't last. Think of all the girls prettier than me, and ladies, too, that never get husbands at all.'

So I was reckless, too, and it's a true word that the reckless are meat for any devil.

7

The worst battle with Miss Maul was when she told me, in anger, because I would not change my style of dressing, that I had set my cap at Matt and caught him. This made me angry, too, and I was going to tell her how I had fought against him, when it came upon me that perhaps it was true. For though I had run away from him and told him to let me be, and kept out of his way too, all these could be for leading on as much as putting off. Hadn't I played that very trick on the village boys, when a girl, running off from them, when, God pity me, my aim was only to drive them mad and take them away from their own belles; and to be caught at last and kissed. But what before all confounded me with Miss Maul was that at that very moment, I was playing upon my poor dear man. For the more I loved him, and I had never loved him so much as then when he had to stand up for me before the world, the more I held away from him, and pretended to be nice and ticklish. Day and night I held him away, making him dancing mad for me and to fall down before me in worshipful gratitude for what was his by right and justice and all the time I wondering at my own luck and the sweetness and goodness of that dear soul, which I tried so much.

So, indeed, like the young fool I was, thinking all men hot knives to a woman's butter, and never to be hurt or blunted by them, I did him great harm for which we both suffered and which still comes up on my conscience, when I least expect it. For men are far more delicate in their ways and feelings than many girls, and so girls should be taught to be helping and not hindering with foolish tricks. I do not mean that the girls are bad by nature, for I would not blacken my sex; but only that they are simpletons as I was and ready for bad as good, just upon the way of the wind. But men are not so innocent and so they are more particular and more delicate in their nerves.

So though I told Miss Maul it was a shame of her to say such things to me, especially to my face, and to hurt me, I felt a terrible sinking in my courage. Indeed, I never again was easy on that point; to think that perhaps I had played so meanly upon my poor Matt. For make no mistake, he suffered by marrying me. No man can marry a servant and live on in the same place without a stab, even unmeant. Poor Matt would change colour if anyone in the room should say the words cook or saucepan. Stove or kitchen would prick him like a gad. Only kettle and trivet were safe, because kettles can belong to a drawing-room; so I would always say, if I wanted to run out to the kitchen, I think the kettle must be boiling, though it was the soup or the milk that I had on my mind.

Miss Maul gave him a hundred stabs a day. She could make him scarlet only by looking at my dress or my big hands. But to me she was as good as a sister. For if she blamed me and abused me for catching her brother (as she thought) with wiles, she was not the woman to bear resentment or keep up a quarrel. She was a Christian, too, like her mother, and she had a mannish manner of mind and face, able to feel hot and think cold. She gave me good advice about cards and visiting and conversation among ladies, which, except about the clothes, I took; and it saved me from making a fool of my poor good Matt when all Bradnall was watching for my slips.

Yet with all my faults and Rozzie's visit, there were only two ladies that closed their houses to us. Our only trouble was that the better people, such as Matt ought to have known, always had engagements when we asked them to the house. But as I say, Matt had lived quietly and given no parties for himself, so we had no right to wonder that Bradnall did not flock in to us.

8

It was a great trouble to me to find how Matt had been put upon and lost his rights as a man. It was waste of both our pleasure, for he was always saying that we could not do this or that, only because his mother and Maul would not like it. But worse, he felt his own injury. He told me once, in our first weeks, when disappointed in the way you know by a failure of his nature, that he was too shy. 'It's my great fault,' he said, 'and a very bad one, for it makes me unsociable. I ought to have asserted myself more,' he said, 'and had my friends to the house.'

'How could you,' I said, 'when your mother and sister would allow no drink and no late hours? You can't have men in without offering them something.'

'No, no,' he said, 'it wasn't their fault, but mine. I was afraid of it. I was always shy and I've given way to it.'

So I said that at least he would get his rights with me and he could bring in his friends. I would be very glad to see them. For we had our private sitting-room and I meant to have whiskey there for men, and port for the ladies.

'You have only to ask your friends,' I said, for I did not know then that he had none. I had thought, like other foolish young people, that everyone had friends, and it was only when I grew into the world that I found out how many people had none, to call friends, but only daily acquaintances. Matt truly had no friends, and when I said: 'But what about so-and-so?' giving names, like Mr Boler, his partner in the foundry, and Mr Hickson, who did business with him, he cried out: 'Good heavens, not Boler – and Mr Hickson is a millionaire.'

'But why should you not know millionaires?' I said.

'You don't understand, my darling,' he said. 'Mr Hickson looks upon all Bradnall people as provincial people, and bumpkins. His real home is in London and his country place is a hundred miles away, almost in Devonshire. He uses his house here like an hotel and only keeps one because he likes to be on the council and to have his finger in every pie.'

But I thought that a cat may look at a king and so I plumped for a stall in the Church Bazaar, in June, when I was a six-months bride. The Mondays had always had a stall. And when the Committee, whose chairman was my chief enemy, said all the stalls were given out, though I knew they were not, I went to sell at Miss Maul's, for she couldn't refuse me. And when Mr Hickson came over to the stall, for he went to everyone, I looked at him with a friendly eye.

Of course, all the ladies did as much; it was their duty to give kind looks for the men's money; but I'll own I put that in my eye which, among us village girls, had meant: 'I have a soft place for you.'

As well, I liked Mr Hickson at first sight for his sad eyes; and perhaps for knowing he was a sad man. Although he was not yet at the middle thirties and married for the last four years, his wife was a gadabout, neither to cherish nor love, nor even to give him a home to make his friends welcome and hold up his position in the world. She was only a shame to him. I was told that at all their houses, in London and the west and at Bradnall, where she was never seen, she had her own rooms and her own bed and never came to his and gave him no comfort even in duty. It seemed very wrong that so rich a man, who had worked hard for riches, should get so little for it, not even so much as any ploughman with a simple woman to his bed and his table.

Yet he was not so bad-looking a man; neither crooked nor bald. He was on the short side and his head was on the big side, with a very big face, and big nose. But he had very good eyes, brown and clear, and a handsome chin with a cleft. His teeth, too, were beautiful; too good for a man and nearly as good as my own. As for his complexion, true, it was rough and brown, like coffee, and full of holes from smallpox because he had been born and brought up in Africa, but that did him no harm in my eyes. I never liked pretty boys. A man's face should be for use in battering at the world, and show the scars of it.

Now whether it was because I was a bride, or so much talked about as the cook who married upwards, Mr Hickson stayed chatting for ten minutes and showed by many signs that he was ready to know me better. He said, too, that he had known my husband for many years; and was delighted to know me.

All this, I admit, was a triumph to a silly young girl, for Mr Hickson was the greatest man in Bradnall; and as Matt said, he used to go among us, especially at bazaars, with a face of duty. He was affable as any prince, but you saw that you were of his daily work and not of his pleasure. And there he was talking to me with his hands in his pockets and his eyes jumping about, and standing on his heels and laughing with all his teeth, like any boy that has just picked up a belle at I Spy corner. All the other ladies, and especially poor Maul, were smiling one way at their customers, and looking the other, with their eyes, at poor me and my conquest. And so it was. For to my great surprise, while I was still planning how to bring great Jack to the jug, as they say, and trying to get Matt up to a garden-party, which would not fix Mr Hickson to an hour and which would bring in all the doubting ones to see him, he walked in to tea, all by himself, as cool as you please. Imagine Matt's surprise when he came home at half-past six and found me talking art with Mr Hickson, and Mr Hickson hanging upon my words as if I had been his doting-piece these four days.

Now I know nothing of art, as I told Mr Hickson, who was a great collector and had his houses full of pictures; but he made me talk, all the same, of what I liked, such as Marcus Stone and Raphael; and also of my young life in the country and that sweet land where I was reared.

Matt, as I say, was amazed. Yet I was glad to see how, shy as he was, he came out when Mr Hickson used his fascinations upon him, and talked and laughed. I had been afraid of Matt's fumbling and stumbling with him. But no, and this was the advantage of his good education, for though he was shy, he knew himself Mr Hickson's equal, and could say, 'when I was at the varsity,' to which Mr Hickson would answer that he had been there too.

He asked Matt to luncheon, on some business which he said he had for him; but I believe he invented it. And after he had gone, Matt was in such a state of wonderment and joy, and pride in himself, and pride in me, that he seemed quite comical. He talked about it all the evening and half the night and said a dozen times: 'The truth is, my dear Sara, you've bowled him over. What a joke and what a slap in the eye for the Upper Road,' which was that part of Bradnall where the best people lived, like the colonels and the knights.

And so it was. For when I got Matt at last to give my garden-party, though he would give me no band and no strawberries, only in the plates four at a time till they ran out, yet because Mr Hickson brought the county member, who was a lord and a famous cricket player, I could have had all Bradnall, and those that were not asked were ready to hang themselves.

And afterwards Mr Hickson stayed to a little supper, just the three of us, in our own sitting-room, not to trouble the Monday ladies, and was so sweet to Matt that he was touched to the soul; and said afterwards that Mr Hickson was worthy to be rich because he was a noble-minded man, and set the things of the spirit above the body.

9

So it came about that Mr Hickson called in almost every day and had tea with us; or if Matt could not come home to tea, with me alone in our own sitting-room. And he talked to me about everything and listened to my words, as no one had ever done before. I thought that this was in compliment and only to flatter me. Mr Hickson was a clever man, I knew, and though still in his thirties, a man old in the world; he would know how to fiddle all tunes which women dance to. But I found now that he truly pondered my words, and gave them back to me, many times, with improvement. As when I was disappointed of a party by the children being ill and said, after my good mother's words, that 'life was a gift that Solomons miss; and none so plain but the sun will kiss,' and he came back the next day and answered that life was not only a gift, but to him, a very real gift; for he was blessed with riches and some very dear friends. 'No,' he said, 'I ought to be a very happy man, and you have made me ashamed of my grousing.'

For Mr Hickson did often complain to me of his sad life, without home or wife or children; and indeed I thought he might well be envious of Matt and me. For though, as I say, I had made things hard for Matt, in his nature, and my own ignorance, yet it was not fourteen months before we had our first child, a girl Belle. She was a lovely girl from the cradle and never gave me any reason for those fears which every mother has.

And in only eleven months after, I had another daughter, Edith, who though small and frail seeming, was always the healthiest and most independent of my children. Even as a tot, she kept herself close and made up her own mind, so sweet-tempered as she was sure of herself.

Yet though I was so much in the nursery, Woodview was already another place. For Hickson brought friends to tea and we went out to dinner. And Matt joined a golf club.

10

It was Mr Hickson who got Matt to play golf; and just as I had hoped, that led to a golfing suit and at last, after another year, to brown shoes. He would not buy them for me, but when Mr Hickson told him of his own bootmaker who made the best brown shoes in the world, then he got a pair.

I could not say thank you to Hickson for anything so private and so small, but I told him how I was grateful by my handshake and by a joke about my going to the new shoemaker. I was indeed grateful; who but Mr Hickson would have guessed that I wanted anything so little and ridiculous as for my Matt to wear brown shoes on Sunday afternoons, and to have a knickerbocker suit like other gentlemen. I was ashamed to say it to anybody, knowing that women are named for just such littleness. Yet that clever little man knew my wish mind only by the way I had admired his own breeches and said that they were good for the long grass; and by the way I had only looked at his brown shoes and then at Matt's city boots. I believe he knew the map of my whole soul better than myself.

On that first day when Matt went out in his new suit and brown shoes, Mr Hickson came back early from golf, having got a twinge in the wrist, and when we went into the garden before tea, he held me by the top arm the whole way round the rose garden. I noticed, too, how he mentioned Matt, saying: 'He's coming out a bit, isn't he? We'll make a prime minister of him yet.'

I did not know how I liked his pressing my arm especially where Maul might see, and saying that we would do so-and-so for Matt, who was worth ten of Hickson, in spite of his riches and cleverness. And then he began admiring my frock, which was a Russian blouse all ruffled down the front, lifting the ruffles and pretending to see how they were sewn to the bodice, but really to touch me. I did not think I liked it, and yet I thought, what harm if he enjoys it, poor little man. I owe a great deal to him, I thought, for he has got for me much I could never have got for myself. How could I have gone to golf clubs and county clubs and shoemakers and tailors or made Matt do it? In all my life Matt would never take my advice about anything except a menu or the kitchen crockery. A woman can do as little for a man in a man's world as a man for a woman in hers.

But since Mr Hickson had flirted so with me once, touching me, he had to do it again. And this is the great difficulty for a woman. How to put an uppish kind of man into his place, without hurting him more than he deserves. For, after all, it was no great crime in Mr Hickson, to be a man and like me as a woman. Or if it was so, then providence must answer for our shapes.

Yet, as I say, since I did not know how to stop the man, he ended by going too far and bringing upon Matt and myself a great misfortune.

11

The first time this friendship with Mr Hickson brought our happiness to danger was just after Edith was weaned; and I was coming down to a reasonable size, and going back also to some outdoor gaieties. For I nursed all my babies nine months and could have nursed them for a year, I was so strong and healthy.

Now Mr Hickson had bought a car, the first in Bradnall, and the dearest of all to my memory; for in it he gave me my first airings after all my first four babies. It was an Argyll, green with brass lamps like trumpets; and what I liked, very high in the back seat, so that you could see over the hedges. Not like your modern motors, with windows like cracks in a door; and so near to the road, you see only half men and half women, trousers and skirts, much less the fields. But what a delight to go bowling along in the old Argyll and look once more on the fields especially about harvest-time when Edith was born; and the corn as ripe brown as a duck's egg and the barley so white as a new-washed hair-brush. And three larks at a time trilling and tweeching as if the sun had got into their brains and made them glorious.

Oh, that joy, to feel the open again and to see the lovely world and know that your nine months are over, when you felt like a parcel coming out of its string; and to have a new baby at home. Matt and Mr Hickson would laugh at my spirits and my calling out 'There's the Green Man, or the Blue Posts,' as if I had never seen them before; or driven along that road.

So, as I say, I loved the Argyll, and I was delighted when Edith was weaned at last, the most difficult to wean for the obstinate thing meant to have my milk even with six teeth, biting holes in me; that Mr Hickson proposed a long trip, to his great house at Addingley. It was shut up, as nearly always, since Mrs Hickson did not like country; but we would see the pictures and gardens and have tea and supper there, and stay the night and go home next day. A good holiday without taking me too long from the children.

So we drove through plenty of dust, I'll admit, but what was dust then to a motorist? and got to Addingley for tea. All the furniture in covers; and no footmen or grandeur, only a caretaker and Mr Hickson's own man, to see about our meals.

But such rooms and pictures that made you say: 'Oh, to be rich!' Here I saw for the first time pictures of women quite naked and Mr Hickson was amused when I was shocked. I had seen that one before, of a girl with a water-pot, but she was sideways, and besides, not in colours. But it seemed to me, and does still, a queer thing that for a girl to go naked would be shocking; but not her picture done from life, on the wall.

The house outside was not so much, though big and old; a great square block like a box, with stone railing round the top and statues all along; as if someone had opened the box and left the nails sticking up. But the gardens were a wonder; and to beat Babylon, falling down by terraces, and fountains in every one, to a lake, and on the other side of the lake, rising grounds with woods and single trees and Jersey cows as fine as deer, and pale as lemon, grazing and drinking. It was about sunset with a sky like a kitchen fire, all sparkles below and blue ash on top; meaning perhaps a storm tomorrow. But the air as warm as new milk and still as water in a goldfish bowl. The water was as soft and bright as sweet oil; it seemed that you could have put it on your tongue and tasted its luxury.

There were many islands on the lake, one with a bridge to it, like a willow pattern; but the bridge in white stone and the temple on the island like a little Royal Exchange, with pillars; but all white and clean, as if from a wedding-cake.

There was a boat waiting as if by chance and Mr Hickson said shall we go for a row. But of course the boat was prepared, with cushions ready.

We said we should be delighted and Matt said that he had rowed at his college, though in the second boat. But just then Mr Hickson's man came down with a message, on the telephone. Matt and Mr Hickson went to the house and Mr Hickson came back alone. It was urgent business, for them both, at the Hickson works, thirty miles away, but Matt had said he would see to it alone; and the car would take him.

How like Matt, I thought, not to want to spoil my day. For Matt was the most thoughtful man I ever knew, to give another pleasure. So that was how Mr Hickson took me out alone in the boat.

I always loved to be rowed on water, for the feel of that wonder; all that weight of boat and people floating upon the air as you might say, for it seems but thicker air; and so smoothly as an angel might slide in the air; and I liked to watch the splash of the oars coming upon the trees turned upside down in the water as still as sleeping princesses; and making them shiver and wriggle and stretch themselves as if the prince had touched them with his finger.

Even the knock of the oars I liked, because, on the water, all sounds are like music and make you feel that joyfulness in the body which would be like dreaming if it was not so lively, and sometimes bad. For every knock was closing the eyes of my soul and opening the thirsty mouths of my flesh.

So when we came to the little temple and found there all kinds of lemonade and wines and sandwiches and sweet cakes laid out upon a clean cloth; and garden chairs with silk cushions, I was very ready to drink some sweet wine, and eat and compliment Mr Hickson on his water party. 'You spoil me,' I said, but he answered No, he could never do enough for me in return for what I had done for him, and so on. He had often spoken so and I did not greatly attend to it. And at the same time, I admit, he would take and press my hands and even kiss them, and once or twice he had even kissed my cheek and squeezed me a little.

Why had I not stopped him? I can't tell except that he was my friend and Matt's and I did not want to hurt his feelings.

So now in the temple, what with the water and the stillness of everything, even the aspen leaves seemed to be asleep, I did not notice Mr Hickson or what he was doing, but only felt the joy of the evening, until I came to myself and saw that he was going too far. Then I was so angry that I hardly knew what I said. I told him, of course, that I would never see him again, and he apologized a hundred times, and blamed my beauty and his own love and so on, as they always do.

Yet I insisted on going back to the house at once and I wanted to telephone for Matt. But Mr Hickson asked me if I wanted to upset my poor Matt and I saw how wrong that would be.

So I shut myself in my room till after supper-time. Then Matt or no Matt, I had to come out and I could not snub Mr Hickson with his own man behind my chair. So we chattered and not to spoil so good a supper, I let myself be a little gay.

The upshot was that Matt did not get back that night. The car had broken down. But I took care to lock my door, and Mr Hickson was wise enough to let me alone.

But it came out in Bradnall, I daresay by Matt's own innocent talk, and made a scandal, which Miss Maul brought, all hot and peppered, to me first and then to Matt. She was too honest to go behind my back, but she took care to see Matt before I could catch him. She told me that I was imprudent and I would come to disaster unless I was careful. For Matt was a jealous man and if he was once made jealous, he would tear down the world for his revenge.

What she told Matt I don't know, but he was in such a fury that I heard him from three rooms shouting. And I quaked to my bones. For though I was not truly guilty in my soul, yet in the world's eye, which does not look at the mind, but only the flesh, I had gone far to break my vows.

Yet all Matt's raging was at Maul. For he said that Bradnall had a mean mind and so had she to repeat it; and he came into me straight and told me that I was not to let myself be hurt by any of their vile gossip which attacked me and Mr Hickson, only because we were above such meanness ourselves, and provincial prejudice.

And when I said, that all the same, I would like to be more careful in future, Matt said no, he would have no truckling to meanness. For friendship was innocent and a noble thing, and should not bow down before idle spite. And as for jealousy, he said: 'I know my faults, I hope, and they are plenty, but I hope jealousy is not one of them. For it is the most contemptible of vices.' A very good true speech, and what was better, all meant. For Matt was good all through, without a bad bone anywhere.

The end of it was that Maul left the house and took another small one of her own. I was sorry for her, and we were always good friends; yet I was glad too, because she could not help thinking that she knew best for Matt. Even though she saw him so happy that he was a different kind of man, yet she would make herself believe that happiness and gaiety were bad for him. If it wasn't his liver, then it was his character and religion. And I was rattling him into his grave.

12

So all was as before, and I forgave Hickson; not, I mean, by words, for words would have brought it all up for talk, and talk is dangerous in such a case. But it was understood that he was not disgraced, and in a week, he was holding my hand as before and telling about his sad life and his need of me.

But now Maul was gone and Mrs Monday had died the year before, we began to give more parties. There were luncheons and dinners every week. For Matt, with his clubs and his knickerbockers, and his Homburg hats, like Mr Hickson's and the new King's, was fast coming out of his creeping ways that the Monday women had put on him. He had begun to be bold on all sides; not only in clothes, though they are always the beginning. He had even turned against the church and criticized the sermons and the prayers and even Heaven and Hell. I was sorry for this change round in Matt, but I could not be sorry to see him acting the man and the master of the house; and sending the port round his own table, as a gentleman should; and calling the men out from the drawing-room after tea, to have a whiskey with him in the library. The first time he did that, I could have hugged him; not Mr Hickson could have done it better. For he looked as if he enjoyed the very idea of it; and poor Mr Hickson, for all his polite easy ways, never looked as if he enjoyed anything except what he should not, philandering with me.

And I'll admit that I was too careless and too easy with him. A woman grows easily coarse as she is made for the rough work of child-bearing, and so things that would have shocked me as a bride were so little to me now that I did not even notice them at all.

But then, my boy Matthew was born and died of croup in the first month. I had had no fears for him, as for the others; nor for myself. I was so well and gay in my carrying, and he so fat and strong and greedy. But he died in ten minutes when I was only gone to choose a chicken for Matt's dinner, and even before he was dead, and when I saw the maid running for me, I knew that he must die. So, I thought, God strikes when you least expect and His wrath is terrible.

I could barely cry and Matt wondered at me. He was afraid for my health and my looks too. For though my breasts were sore and running with milk, I grew so thin in the face that my friends would have me take tonic and oil and my enemies rejoiced and said: 'At last that fool Matt Monday will have his eyes opened, and see that he was caught only by the girl's country colours, and that she is really a plain common lump.'

'It has come,' I thought, 'and it is just what I might have expected, for as my marriage was far beyond my due, so out of my marriage comes my punishment and my destruction.'

I remembered then all my provocations, and Hickson, and that I had put off my blacks for my poor mother after four months, only to go to a garden-party. For poor little Matthew I wore them like a widow, and the coarsest linen and wool stockings that made my legs itch. I would not let Matt near me and mortified my life. I trembled for the next stroke, for Belle and Edith and for Matt himself.

But at last poor Matt was fretted into such a state that I could not hold him off. Only I took care to take no pleasure myself and to think meanwhile of my grief and danger. However it was, within another two months I was carrying again and full of terrors.

But my girl Nancy was a kind baby from birth, and never a day's illness. Not so pretty as Belle, or so clever as Edith, but the sweetest affectionate nature to make up for it. So God struck the balance for the child.

28

Here was I then, not yet twenty-four, with a house of sixteen rooms, and five servants in and three out; and my landau and my victoria and my governess-cart; and my at home days; and three children; and another started; Mrs Matthew Monday of Woodview on the county nursing committee.

You may say that it was no wonder I forgot those warnings and gave myself up to the sweet world; but the truth was, that at my very worst, and when I least expected it, the fear would strike me like a cold shiver, and I would say God is not mocked. Then, indeed, I would wonder at my lightness and folly.

13

But now I was in the fury of my life when a woman has no time to know herself or anything else, unless she is strong in remembrance of her religious duty and can fend off the world. I had never less than two thoughts jumping in my head, if not a dozen, and the telephone as well. Our telephone was not a year old, but it was already as much as two more children.

I gave myself no time to think, except of trifles and vanities, arranging the dinner guests or paying a call, or altering the girls' frocks, or giving them their medicine. I don't think I ever read a book in those years; not really to read it and feel it; for even when I opened one of my old favourites, I would find my mind wandering off upon some rubbish. Though my eyes would be reading of Violet Martindale with her husband going to the bad and not knowing how to stop it, my mind would be noticing the children's voices in the garden and saying: 'So they're back already. I wonder has Belle changed her stockings.'

And this, though I knew my books as well as my kitchen and could open *Heartsease* at the very page where Miss Yonge says of Theodora Martindale: 'Many thoughts floated through Theodora's mind; but whether the better or worse would gain the advantage seemed rather to depend on chance than on herself.'

It might have been written for me.

Yet even in that page, though I saw the words, I did not feel the truth and the meaning of them. What was worse, I would be deceiving myself. I would think I had been spending my time seriously when I had only been fritting it away, just as before.

But what took up more time even than the children was the parties and the calls. For Matt had come right out from his timid ways and we were as gay as the rest. Indeed, looking back at that time before the war, in the nineteen tens, it seems to me that the world was all gaiety; delights crowding together till there was no room between. For it was parties, parties all the time; in summer, croquet and tennis and luncheons and teas and pageants and plays and regattas; and in winter it was dinners and balls, and such balls. Even in our Bradnall balls we had the cotillions and prizes for everybody; good prizes. Matron as I was, I won so many favours that I didn't know where to keep them. It was a heaven for girls in those sweet days, for the men had not lost their manners and at all dances there were chaperones to see that they danced with even the plainest. So they did too, for they knew their duty as gentlemen.

Then there was Henley too, and Wimbledon and the Eights at Oxford. Matt had been to Oxford and he had a cousin there, a professor. So we always went to Eights and then again to Commemoration. I would dance all night, three nights running, for though Matt could not dance, his cousin would find me partners and come himself. But what was sweeter than dancing and the lovely waltzes of those days were the gardens gay with paper lanterns, and the trees as green as lettuces over the fairy lamps; and the smell of the limes and the night stocks hanging on the dark, and the lovely girls in their trailing skirts walking under the old walls, like the ghosts of queens. Then we would go out in the early morning, all as we were, but wrapped up in furs, and take breakfast on the river; so sleepy and lazy that the noise of the water sent us to sleep.

And not only at home in England did it seem that life was nothing but joys and new dresses; for when you looked in the illustrated papers there was nothing but gaiety abroad. There you saw that the Emperor of Austria had given a great ball and that Paris was mad about the new dances from Russia, and in Germany the Kaiser and the Tsar had had a great review and a yacht race and more luncheons and dinners and balls. Of course, all this gaiety meant plenty of work, too. As I say, I spent half my days making up parties and some of the ladies at Bradnall village were busier still. For we were not the gayest, as we were not among the rich, as riches went then. Yet we lived in glory and luxury. I don't know how it was but everybody seemed to have money then; and money seemed to go further.

You may say that such a life was bad and trifling. Yet I think people were no worse then than now, and perhaps better. For in all our happiness there was more religion, and no one in Bradnall, however gay, would have thought of tennis on Sunday, or of not going to church. If I went to the bad at last, it was not the fault of the times, but of myself. It was not because I loved the parties and the gaiety and even as a mother and a matron up in the thirties, danced through twenty pairs of shoes in a year; but because I did not remember my weakness and study my faults, and because I forgave myself too easily for those evil deeds which always took me by surprise. For many were as gay, who were also good, and happiness was a grace to them, as it is God's most precious grace; they lived with God and never forgot their gratitude. So I have thought, even in a ball this sweet pleasure is provided for me, and felt the wonder of God's providence and my own special luck.

This was a happy time for Matt, the happiest in his life, before his troubles began. He would groan indeed that he had never peace in his own house and make a terrible outcry about the bills. He would say that it was me, only who liked the parties and that he bore all the noise and expense only for my sake; but I, who heard him talk afterwards of what he had said to this man, and how he had set that other right, knew well his gaiety on party nights and the good to his natural spirits, which indeed made him so lively and boisterous that he often left the proof upon my skin; I say I knew differently. So I did not argue with him but was content. I was a foolish woman enough but I knew that what a wife may lose in justice comes back ten times in kindness.

14

But our chiefest joy was Matt's new glory when they made him a councillor. After that, no one could say I had dragged him down. And this was through Mr Hickson, and through a mere hint of mine that Matt, though he laughed at the council, would not be against it, if he could be sure of getting in.

Mr Hickson said only that it was an easy thing, and sure enough, he had Matt in within six weeks; and nothing said to him of our private chat. Yes, I may reproach myself for being too free with Mr Hickson, over so many years; allowing him so much that I can't believe the eyes of my memory, or its feelings; yet he did me great services, and was a good close friend.

For you may say that a married woman cannot be close friends with a man without wrong. But wrong is not a steady thing; and if I did wrong with Mr Hickson so often, I can't believe I did but right.

He would come sometimes to supper, just with us two; when he was most cast down. Then Matt, seeing his grief or his need, would say: 'Take Sara out for a walk – she's had nothing but children all day and she needs some peace and fresh air. But please excuse me – I'm too busy.'

So I would put on a shawl and we would walk out through the lane and the fields, which were being built over so fast that every day there was a new tree down and a new stream turned into a drain. Indeed, by daylight, Bradnall town, with a new motor and a new cement works, had come out to us, so that we were built in on three sides. If I had seen Woodview now, when looking for a place, I would not have called it a country house, but a villa in a suburb. Out of my own bedroom window I saw not fields and willows and the stream winding away to join the Thames, but rows of little houses like kitchen fenders, with blue roofs, and, beyond them, a gas works.

It had become an ugly place where no one cared to live, and already some of the big houses were sold and their grounds built over. I don't know how it was that in so gay and sweet a time, such ugliness came into the town and the country; but wherever we went we heard the same tale, of villages spoilt and parks built over, and rivers turned into sewers, and the country paths stopped up. It puzzled my daughter Belle, who was a clever girl, and when she asked me how it was, I asked Mr Hickson and Matt and several more councillors and public men. But none of them could help me. It seemed that it was something you could not stop, like mould in a bread bin, without cleaning everything up and starting again. Which, of course, is nonsense in a nation.

But on the one side there were still some meadows and some poor old willows, bald and broken, and a clear stream; and here Mr Hickson and I would walk and he would think himself so well off as in that beautiful land around Addingley.

So we walked about the lanes until dark fell thick and the fields were so black-green as well-moss and the trees quite black except at the top; and the sky like the water when you wash an ink bottle; as black as blue can be in the middle and paling away to skim-green at the edges; and the owls calling like ship horns as I used to hear them from Rackmill, on their way to America. And the cows breathing in the dark so quietly that you thought it was the field itself, until they heaved up and trundled away. Then Mr Hickson was at his truest and best; his soul came out of him and I could no more have set him down than if he had been a child. And to be fair to him, he never thought of me then as flesh, but as a friend and a woman's ear; to listen and understand what men could not: his loneliness, and his wonder. For he too would wonder how he had missed his happiness after working for it so hard. He knew it was not all his wife's fault, for he had asked me often should he be divorced, and then he said: 'No, what good? Another scandal among the rich, all for nothing.' But I thought he thought too much about himself, and what was due to him in joy, to get any. So I have hinted, but he never heard me, to understand.

I do not say this, that there was true friendship between Mr Hickson and me, to excuse myself for what was more than only friendship allowed, but to show that it is hard to judge people as all of a piece.

For Mr Hickson could not only be a true friend to me, but to Matt, and he gave us both happiness when he brought on Matt, in business, to be richer, and in the council, to be more known. Matt was the best of men but had no push, and so he owed all his success to Hickson.

And a successful man is a comfort in the home even when you are not thinking about him. Indeed, I always thought the house itself looked brighter and the fire drew better on a day when Matt had made a good stroke in his business or asked a question in the council and come out in the paper. Success was good for Matt if it was bad for me. It took away the fret of his nervousness. Even after quarter days when the bills came to light, he would no longer cry out that he would be ruined and really fear it. He would only shout a little, as indeed he had a right to do, and then remember himself as a man acknowledged in the world, and say only: 'But goodness knows, Sara, I hate all this fuss as much as you do. It's so undignified. If only you would keep some check,' and so on, and then saying: 'Well, my dear, I suppose I'll have to pay it,' and paying it and giving me a kiss and telling me not to look so upset. Which more than anything made me swear I would reform. For God knows I would catch myself looking upset when my mind, knowing that the worst was over, had flown on to the children, or the larder, or even another new frock.

15

Now I come to the time of my meeting with Gulley Jimson, who was the turning-point in my downfall, and, I dare say it, the instrument of providence, to punish my prosperity and forgetfulness.

I say that Bradnall village was now joined on to the town, so that people even wondered why we lived there any more; and many poorer families had moved out. But we would say, since Matt was a councillor, he must live in the town. And the new building made it the more interesting. Always new schemes and new committees. We had already a new Union workhouse, two new hospitals and an asylum, and now there was to be a new town hall.

So we told people, and it was quite true, that Matt took great pleasure in the council work. He had always been interested in architecture, especially Tudor architecture, which the new town hall was to have; and both he and Mr Hickson were on the building committee.

They had planned a fine lobby for the entrance and Mr Hickson proposed that it should be painted with a decoration or scene by an artist called Gulley Jimson, who, he said, was going to be famous, but who was still cheap.

No one had heard of Jimson except Hickson and Matt, who only knew the name through Hickson, and the committee asked to see his work. Mr Hickson showed some photographs, but no one liked them. So in the end, not to offend Mr Hickson, they proposed to put up the wall for competition.

Every artist was to send in a coloured drawing, eighth size of what he would do on the wall.

Then he asked Matt if he would give Jimson a room while he came to measure the wall and to make his first sketch. He said the man was very poor and besides needed care and comfort.

'Only starting, is he?' Matt said.

But Mr Hickson said that Mr Jimson was not very young and had been at work for many years. He was a true genius in his way but poor because no one would buy his pictures and the critics despised them. 'I wonder he has gone on,' Mr Hickson said, 'he has had no encouragement to do so.'

'He's had a bad time,' Matt said and I could see he was coming round to Mr Jimson. For being himself so open to be put upon, he hated all oppression and tyranny. I saw how he felt and willing to bring him out in this new way, I said that we had the pink room with a good window and a lovely view, which any artist would like.

'We have several rooms free,' Matt said, 'and I should be delighted to put the best at Mr Jimson's disposal. Delighted,' he said, 'it's a privilege,' and then he said that it was a duty to support artists and especially original artists. It was the fault of our democracy that it neglected art and culture. Mr Hickson said that he was quite right and then he asked if he might bring Mr Jimson at once to introduce him. So he did, for it turned out that he had him waiting in the road.

16

Mr Jimson was a little bald man with a flat nose and a big chin. His head was big and hung over so that his face was hollow in the middle. He was much older than we expected, getting on for forty; very shabby too, and had a front tooth missing. He said that he would bring his painting things next week and all he wanted besides was a room with a good light from the north.

We had never seen an artist before and though Mr Jimson was not my idea of an artist, he was better because he was so simple and gay, never minding his own shabbiness or his lost tooth. He smiled away as if he had no thought of it. I thought: 'You're not one to care what the world thinks,' and so I warmed to him at first.

When he had gone again to fetch his luggage, Mr Hickson told us of his struggles and his poverty and how hard it is for a genius to make his way against the ignorance and jealousy; and how he had been a gentleman before he took up art.

This, I thought, made it still worse for him to be a failure in life, and homeless, especially by the spite of others. But then, as Mr Hickson said, he had no push and a man who takes up art needs push before all things, or money, or he will be trampled over. Both Matt and I were sorry for Mr Jimson and thought that he should get a chance at last. 'It's a scandal,' Matt said that evening, to a party we had, 'that such a man is still almost unknown and can't even make a living. I don't agree with those who say that our industrial civilization is bound to be selfish and materialist, but we have to admit that it has very grave faults and the chief of these is its neglect of original art. That indeed is a blot upon our recent history.' This was from a speech Matt was going to make next week, at the prize-giving in the girls' school. He had it on his mind for he was always very nervous before a speech, so he brought it out now.

I loved to hear him speak so, and it seemed to me that our own lives, running so sweetly, were a temptation. 'God knows,' I said, 'we might be ruined tomorrow and homeless and not so ready for it as Mr Jimson. The rich grow soft to sorrow. That is God's own plan for their punishment.'

'We have much to be thankful for,' Matt said, 'but we mustn't forget our luck. No, I shall give every word of that speech even if it does get me into trouble with the agent, and I'll send it to the papers tomorrow in case I can't be heard properly or forget some of it.'

So he did, though luckily the papers did not print the strong parts on account of the big election that year; it must have been about 1910 because I remember a mourning dress I bought for King Edward.

I was glad in myself that the speech was not printed because I was always afraid that Matt would make enemies who would play some mean trick on him. Indeed, for a long time I thought my downfall would come from that side, since that was my glory.

But Matt himself grew more fearless every day, and more happy and more easy in his mind, so it seemed that what little we had done for Mr Jimson was coming back to us.

17

We were so excited on the day that Mr Jimson came that Matt stayed away from business to receive him. But Mr Jimson made little of that. He did not even say how do you do, but only: 'I'll just look over the rooms and see what you've got.' Then he darted over the whole house, even in the servants' rooms and the schoolroom, where the girls were doing their homework, and said that the only room he could take was the morning room where we sat when we were by ourselves and where I did all my accounts and sewing.

I was afraid that Matt would say no, but not a bit; he answered Certainly, he was very glad there was a suitable room; would Mr Jimson like any changes in it? Mr Jimson said only to take all the pictures out of it. So we went at once and stripped the walls. It was like a holiday and it made me laugh to see us pulling down our own things which we had picked so carefully, just at a word from a stranger. Indeed, Mr Hickson, finding out how Matt was giving Jimson all he asked, warned us not to let the man be a nuisance. 'Don't spoil him,' he said. But Matt said it was a privilege to assist Mr Jimson and spoke of a great poet, Coleridge, who had been taken in to live by a doctor.

18

The next thing was that a party got up in Bradnall which said that they would have none of Mr Jimson. His pictures were indecent, because he painted men and women naked. I knew now that this was nonsense and both Matt and I told everybody we knew it would get Bradnall a bad name because artists had always been allowed to paint naked. Yet when I saw Mr Jimson's first coloured drawing I was startled and so was Matt, though he did not confess it. It was not the nakedness of the people, but their shapes and colours. They had very short legs and big heads and especially very big eyes. The women, too, were all in red and the men in green.

This began our first trouble with Mr Jimson, not because either of us thought at any time of criticizing his way of painting, for, as Matt said, we were learners only. But that when we tried to understand the pictures, he laughed at us or put us off. I did not mind this for myself, but I minded for Matt who was very sensitive to snubs. I never admired poor Matt more than in the way he would face up to Mr Jimson and try to get something out of him, in spite of terrible snubs.

He would look at the canvas a long time and say at last: 'I think I see what you mean.'

'It's more than I do,' Jimson would answer, turning and grinning at me. When he grinned like that, the gap made him look wicked.

Matt would grow pink, especially his nose, by which I could tell that he was hurt. But he did not give way. He said that it gave him the feeling of poetry and the secret influence of nature. The green men were like trees and the red women like flowers.

'More like mud,' Mr Jimson said, laughing.

'Our human clay,' Matt said.

'I'm not a poet,' Mr Jimson said, 'I'm a painter.'

'But you must have a reason for painting your figures in that way.'

'I paint 'em as I see 'em, Mr Monday.'

When I saw Matt turning scarlet, I thought I would change the subject and I said that everyone saw it differently.

But he only laughed in my face and said: 'That's right, Mrs Monday – they do. Different is the word. But excuse me –' and he put down his palette and walked out.

After the first week, every time we looked at his picture he said: 'Excuse me,' and walked out, so we gave up looking at it. But we both felt we were right in encouraging Jimson. And when I puzzled over our troubles with him, as I did many nights, and wondered if, after all, we had been tricked by Mr Hickson who was using us to push Mr Jimson and to take the risk of looking great fools before the world, I thought that no, for at least Mr Jimson is not in the plot. For what does he get out of it? Nothing but poverty and misery. It must be that he is chosen for it and so we must be right to keep him.

19

Though Jimson was so hard on Matt, he was very friendly to me and even on the very first day he began drawing he opened his door when I was going through the hall and called through the hall to me. 'Give me your hand a moment, Mrs Em –'

I was surprised. But it turned out he wanted only to draw my hand. And the next day it was my arm, which he pretended to admire. I had been ashamed of my great thick arms but one night at a party, given for him, he took hold of my arm, all mottled as it was in the cold weather, and lifted it up before all and asked them to admire it. I did not know whether to be angry or not. But there was Matt looking very serious and saying: 'Yes, yes, I see – I always thought so myself'; and as for those who were laughing and saying to themselves: 'A regular cook's arm, got them pounding steaks and whisking soufflés,' I could laugh at them too.

But Jimson was always calling for an arm or a hand or a neck or even a leg; though he did not get it; and while I sat, he would make talk and so we were howdedo friends, and had some private jokes. As I say, what I always liked in Jimson was his gay spirits, little enough as he had to keep them up.

So one day I dared to ask him why he was so scornful of Matt. I told him that Matt admired artists and wanted to help them.

'Oh,' he said, 'I suppose Hickson has been talking to him. Hickson tells everyone about my genius.'

'So he does,' I said, 'and isn't that a good thing for you?'

'And for him,' he said. 'He's invested in me, you know. I painted about twenty-five square yards of his hall wall at about forty shillings a yard. He wants to push up the stock.'

'So much the better for you,' I said.

Mr Jimson said nothing to that but kept on laughing at me. He never paid any attention to my words, like Mr Hickson, and he thought me a fool about art, as indeed I was.

Yet I did not dislike him for that, but for something much worse. After he had been with us about three weeks, he went away suddenly and stayed away two months, so that we gave him up and put back the pictures in the morning-room and hung a curtain over his picture. For Matt would not have it touched and yet he did not want the children or visitors to see it.

But no sooner had we got back the use of the room than Jimson walked in, one afternoon when we were all out, and brought a wife with him. When we came back late for tea, there they were having a high tea in the dining-room. At first we were both glad to see them because though Jimson was a nuisance, he livened us all up; but afterwards we could not bear the way he treated his wife. He made her a slave; and as we found out afterwards, would even beat her.

20

The wife was called Nina. She was a little thin thing with a long neck and a very big forehead. Her nose and chin were small so that the forehead seemed out of proportion, especially with the style of hairdressing at that time, all on top, with rats underneath to puff it out, and a bun behind. Nina had blue eyes, not big, but a very pretty colour, like forget-me-not. She was dressed very badly; a kitchenmaid in a good house would have scorned to go in such dowdy clothes; a flannel blouse, a black skirt all down at the back, and long cracked boots.

But she was so gentle and sweet that we both liked her at once, and Matt asked her to stay as long as she liked and complimented her on her husband's genius. He made her blush with pleasure and I must say I was delighted with him.

Nina was no trouble to anyone, always neat and clean and punctual, very quiet and serious. Indeed, she saved us trouble, for she waited on Jimson hand and foot, as he demanded; and kept their room beautifully clean and tidy and tidied him up too.

Now I don't know what it was but I fell in love with Nina almost from the first day. You would say we were very different and when Rozzie once came for a week-end, while the Jimsons were with us, Nina could not bear her and Rozzie despised Nina and said she ought to be in the Salvation Army.

It was true that Nina seemed very religious. Yet she was not a Christian. On Sunday she behaved as on other days, waited on Jimson, and sat with him while he drew or painted. Her sewing was beautifully fine and she took commissions for work on trousseaux and she would embroider initials and monograms. Then every afternoon, wet or fine, and this was January, she would go for a long walk alone. For Jimson never took any exercise. He would either work all day, or stay in bed till tea-time and then go to a public-house, where I heard he would cut jokes by the hour and drink beer.

When I knew Nina better I asked her how she could bear to walk alone and she said that she liked to go out alone every day, as a duty. 'If I don't go out to see nature every day, I forget what it is like, and how beautiful the world is.'

I thought that nature was not very beautiful in January, except in snow, but then I knew that I was country bred and that townspeople like Nina often thought more of trees and fields, even when bare and dirty, than I could in full summer. It is like a religion to them, and I'm sure it is a good harmless one, though, like Nina, they don't know an elm from an oak, and think that all corn is wheat and all green, grass.

Mr Hickson used to laugh at Nina to me and call her a romantic soul, but I knew she was better than either of us. She accepted her hard lot with so sweet a mood, better than patience, for she set no value on herself as a patient sufferer. Then when she went out to walk so seriously, she was full of delight and thanks even for the dirty fields round the village. I never knew anyone who took such happiness from so little.

I don't think Nina ever cared much for me. That was natural; for I was now getting full blown in the rushing tide of my worldly delights. Matt had given up trying to control my dress and Bradnall was used to it. But when a little while ago I looked at old photographs that Jimson had kept and saw the woman I was in my thirties and early forties, frilled and flounced and laced and thrusting myself in front and behind, I can't believe my eyes. There is no doubt that in those days I outdid Rozzie herself. I seemed a very bad kind of woman, worldly, common and worse.

The wonder was not that Nina drew away from me but I had still the sense to like her and know my need of her.

21

Mr Hickson was always trying to get portrait commissions for Mr Jimson and so did we. We gave two big parties for him and showed two of his portraits. But no one liked them. At last Matt ordered a portrait for fifty pounds.

I was against the portrait and yet I was for it. I knew that if Matt was not painted now he would never be painted at all, because he would think it too conceited to order a portrait of himself, except as a charity; but then I was afraid, too, of how Mr Jimson would paint him.

I was quite right, for first he would not paint him, as we both wanted, in his golf suit, with grass and trees behind, to make a picture of it, but he would have him in a black coat and a stiff collar. The next thing was he made his nose so big and his forehead on a slope and his chin so little, that he looked like a goose peeping out of a jug.

As soon as I saw how the portrait was coming out I knew we should have trouble with Jimson.

So the next time Mr Jimson wanted my hand, I said to him that his portrait might be good but it wasn't my husband.

'Oh,' he said, 'but he's not my husband. He's Mr Monday and that's the way I see him.' And he would make no change.

I knew it was no good to ask Nina's help, for she would never interfere with her husband, and as for Hickson, he was away in London, and besides, we were not then good friends.

The truth was that Mr Hickson had given me a great surprise by warning me against Jimson; in a way that I could not brook. For he seemed to say that I was too much with Jimson, and had shown him too much for his drawing. Which was false, and what was worse, unfriendly.

This quarrel with Mr Hickson was another cause that brought up my reckoning. But I must not say it was a cause either; but rather all my indulgence that went before, to him and to myself, which spoilt my modesty, and his manhood. For to hear him in our quarrel you would have said he was a little spoilt boy with a pain, that is told he mustn't have any more sugar.

22

Now, all this time, I was complaining to Matt and trying to get him to suggest another position, with his head more up and a winged collar. But Matt only laughed and said that he did not mind how he looked. 'What does it matter,' he said, 'if he paints me like a baboon – those who know me won't mind, and those who don't know me, can think what they like. After all, Sarry, I never was a beauty!'

Yet I knew that this was only his bravery, because he would go in to look at himself often six times in half-an-hour, when Jimson was at his bar, and when you saw his face coming out, you could see he was troubled. And one day, when I caught him coming out from the room, God forgive me, like a fool, I burst out at him and said: 'You're not going to let him hang that up in an exhibition.'

So Matt was taken off his carelessness and let himself out, and said: 'Well, Sarry, it's not for myself but the children. Perhaps there is a ridiculous side to me or at least my face, but it's not what I would like to be remembered by.'

Then I was angry with him, for I knew this was a sore place with Matt, that people might laugh at him. Indeed, I had got a picture, bought from a curiosity shop, only because it was Matt's image, and hung in the bedroom corridor, General James Wolfe, victor of Quebec, saying I had my sister in

Canada, but really to show him that a delicate chin and a sharp forehead could go with a general, and who had once been a famous man.

So I told him that long faces are among the highest dukes in Europe, and considered to be the mark of the blood.

'If only my face were long,' he said, 'but the whole is squat – it's the shortness at the ends throws out the nose. You'll never make me into a donis with all your fussing about my clothes and my shirts and my shoes.'

I told him the truth, that it's not the face that matters but the spirit, and a man that carries his features like a first prize will make them a model.

But Matt shook his head and I thought he looked smaller and older. 'No,' he said to me, 'he's seen me as I am – and he's brought it out in the portrait. That's his genius – to put a man's character into his picture.'

I argued with him and I got him round to saying that it was not really himself in the picture, not the one who got on the council and made the speech against civilization, not my Matt, but only a little bit of Maul's Matt. But I felt frightened, as well I might have been, and so I took the bull by the other horn and went to Mr Jimson with a photograph of Matt. It was by a very good man in London who had brought out the distinction of his character by electric lights. So first I made myself as nice as I could to him, and, as it seemed, more than I need have, for he rose like a fish, and I was in terror that Nina would come in or Matt himself. He surprised me then, the nasty little man, but I dared not put him down too hard. So I took out the photograph as quickly as I could and said: 'Mr Jimson, you say we are friends and that I have helped you at your work, and you have done a lovely picture of my husband. But yet it is not quite the man I know. For how could you see him as we see him and know his fine character and his courage in standing up to corruption. This is the Matt we would like painted.'

Mr Jimson looked at me laughing and said: 'You say we are friends, Mrs Em, but you want me to destroy one of the best things I ever did.'

'No,' I said, 'only improve it.'

But he said only: 'Tell your husband that if he doesn't want the portrait, he needn't pay for it. I'll keep it,' and he opened the door to get me out.

'At least,' I said, 'you won't show it.'

But the very next week it was in an exhibition in Bradnall town, labelled 'Portrait of a Gentleman.'

Of course the opposition paper put Matt's name to it and besides everyone recognized it. Though Jimson had taken an inch off the forehead and put it on the nose, clever as he was, he had made it the devil's likeness of my poor Matt.

Indeed, everyone who knew Matt recognized it and all our friends came to sympathize with him and with me and to see how we took our misfortune. Now if the devil had contrived such a trick, he could not have found a better to drive my poor Matt mad. For it hit him in his two sorest places at once, his great modesty left over from the creeper days, and his decent pride, new got in the clubs and by being master in his own house. It had him between two irons like a lemon squeezer and it squeezed the life out of him. For pride would not let him complain that he minded what face he was given, and modesty could not bear the exhibition of his weaker parts and the laughter of the very workmen in his own foundry. It gave him no peace. All night I would feel him wriggling there beside me, and when I asked him, had he a pain, he would answer in a despairing voice that there was nothing the matter with him and tell me to go to sleep.

I could not bear it so I went to Mr Jimson and told him that it was a wicked thing to show the picture. 'Not that my husband minds,' I said, 'it's a trifle to him. But I mind.'

'You don't appreciate my masterpiece,' Jimson said smiling.

But I was angry and lost my temper and said that even if he was a genius, he had no right to do a cruel thing.

Then he was furious too, and said that it was not cruel to paint a fool in his own colours; for how else could fools be painted. So I answered him that he was mistaken in Matt, who was worth ten artists, and twenty Jimsons. I always hated meanness, for it frightens me. So I went out for fear I would take the man and shake him.

It happened we were out to tea, and I was glad to be out. But still I knew that I had been foolish to quarrel with a man like Jimson. You never know what an artist will do. I came home early to apologize to him and win him over again. But I could not believe it, he had packed already and gone off, in two cabs, and nothing left but a letter from Nina, thanking us for our great kindness and saying that the insult to her husband could never change her gratitude to us.

I was shocked, but Matt suddenly changed over and said: 'Good riddance.' He said that Jimson was not even a true artist, for the true artist was never spiteful or cruel. It was impossible because, if he was inspired, it must be by God.

Then, too, I had to confess that I had quarrelled with Jimson and might have been the cause of his going. So he raged against him and said that he would like to kick him. I had to smooth him down.

I was glad to see Matt take it in this style, with spirit, but I think now I was wrong and that he was giving way to himself more and more.

23

The Jimsons took a room in the village, over the stable in the Swan yard; not half a mile from us. Matt was afraid that he would meet the man and never went through the village. He was still in a fury against Jimson, and I think he was afraid of what he might do next.

'Keep away from the Swan,' he said, 'he might get hold of you and worry you. I don't want him to upset you again.'

But even then I had seen Jimson, in this way. The first market day I saw Nina at the fruit stalls and the moment I set eyes on her, I knew how I had missed her.

She was looking serious as ever with her head in the air. Her nose was red as usual in a wind, but no one ever minded poor Nina's nose; she did not mind it herself. She despised looks. Her hair was in a bun so neat that it might have been carved on a stair knob.

There was no one like her, so neat, and yet dowdy. You would have thought her a Christian except that she never preached and never thought evil. It was a pleasure even to think about her.

She had a big bruise on her cheek and I asked her how she had hurt herself. But when she said, an accident, I asked no more. I saw she did not want to speak of it. I had no notion then that Jimson beat her.

I asked her about her room and the picture. She said that the room was a good light but Jimson had not gone on with the picture. It was still lying on the floor, rolled up, and he would not touch it.

'But there's only a fortnight before the sending-in day,' I said.

'I know,' Nina said, 'and so does he. But it's no good trying to make him paint if he has lost his inspiration.'

'Inspiration is all nonsense,' I said. 'He told me so himself. He only wants to be put at it.'

But she looked grave and said that Jimson often talked like that but it was not true. How could he paint without inspiration?

'This competition is the biggest chance of his life,' I told her. 'If he wins it, it will give him a real start. They are going to have a royal prince to open the Hall and unveil the picture.'

'I know,' she said, 'and he was painting so well even on Monday – but he has not touched a brush since.' She said it in such a way that I knew what she meant and I said: 'What, it's not me who's upset him.'

'He was very upset,' she said. 'You know he looked upon you in a special way as his friend.'

So I was astonished to think that I could have upset anyone so much; especially a gay, brave man like Mr Jimson; with a few words. But I was put about too. For, I thought, if he loses the competition, it will be my fault.

He *must* finish it, I said. He simply must send his picture in. He *musn't* miss this chance if he dies for it. So then I told her that if the picture was sent in it was sure to win, for Mr Hickson had just got a grip on the third vote on the committee. I could not help telling her but I made her promise not to tell. 'So whatever you do, see that the picture goes in.'

When I met her the next day she told me that Jimson would not even look at the picture. But I could not sleep for thinking of how little would save them both and change their whole lives.

The end of it was that the next day, happening to go past the Swan yard, I had a sudden idea and went up to their room. There was Nina sweeping the floor and Jimson on the bed, smoking. He frowned at me but I paid no attention to him. I said I had come to help Nina. 'The first thing,' I said, 'is to get the picture up – there's no time to waste with that.'

'What picture?' Jimson said.

'Your cartoon, as you call it,' I told him, very short. 'You only have ten days to finish it.'

'I'm not going to finish it.'

I said nothing but I began to unroll the papers and look for drawing-pins.

'Where are your pins?' I asked him.

He stared at me as if he would bite me but I knew that he would not behave like a fool before me, after his philandering. So I said again: 'Here or there. Which is the best light. Even if you don't finish it we want it out of the way.'

'Where you like,' he said, 'the pins are in my big box.'

I began to pin up the sheets and asked him which was the middle one. He stared again and then he laughed and came to help me. 'Are you going to take me up?' he asked. 'I suppose you're tired of bridge parties and want a new toy.'

'Maybe so,' I said. 'I don't know. But you will look foolish enough if you throw away the chance of your life when you have it in your hand.'

'A chance of making money,' he said, 'and being taken up by snobs.'

He kept on laughing at me, which I thought a good thing. He said at last: 'You're like a train – nothing will turn you when you get started. It's a good thing you're not my wife or I should have murdered you long ago.'

'Maybe,' I said, 'but I am not your wife and if I were perhaps I should do the murdering.'

This was the kind of thing he always made me say, pert and foolish.

When we had finished putting up the sheets of paper, I began to admire the work and say that it would be sure to win the competition. But he put on his hat and excused himself and went out. Nina was still cleaning the room. She said now: 'Never do that again, Mrs Monday – interference drives him mad.'

But I thought only that her interference might drive him mad. Indeed, next day when I called, I found him hard at work on the picture and when he saw me he cried out: 'You see, Mrs Monday, the result of your influence.'

But I knew that he was trying to stab at Nina so I said: 'Nothing of the kind. You would have started today in any case.' She said only in her serious way, that she had never liked to try at inspiration, in case she might do harm.

I said she was right, but I thought it might have been better for them both if she could have laughed more and enjoyed what little, poor thing, she had to enjoy. There's not so much happiness in the world that anyone can afford to waste it.

Yet she made me know my own wastefulness too. For one day when I stepped out of my carriage to ask if I could do some shopping for her, in Bradnall town, she said no, but she would like to drive the other way, into the country, to see the spring. 'I'm missing it,' she said. 'I haven't seen any of it except in gardens.'

'I would like that too,' I said, 'if I had only a moment. I lost last spring in the children's whooping cough and this year in parties. And now today I have to meet Nancy at the dentist's. He's a man from London and this is the only time he could give me.'

But Nina asked me what I had to do after the dentist and proved that I could find time by going home late for tea.

I liked my tea in time but I did not like to admit it to Nina. I was especially anxious to do anything Nina asked, on that day, because I had just been told in the town that Jimson beat her. I thought I could see a mark under her left eye, like a bruise, and I was horrified to think of the brute hitting that saint in the face. So I could not say that I liked my tea better even than spring.

'It would be good for us both,' Nina said, 'to look at the trees and forget our stupid selves.'

'You can't forget a child's teeth,' I said, 'when she's a girl and has no advantages. Nancy's are going already at thirteen, and she's growing plainer, too. Belle has everything, looks and brains, and Edith has brains; and Phyllis is the world's darling, but Nancy has nothing.'

'You must forget them,' Nina said, 'it's a duty – you can't enjoy the spring while you're thinking about teeth.'

For Nina, of course, trees and grass were holy. Indeed I think everything was holy for her and I suppose, if God made the world, that she was right. But whether right or wrong, it was in her character and it made her different. And I looked forward now to my drive with her, for I thought: 'I've been getting too fond of my tea – I'm too fat too, which is just God's rightful punishment for indulgence. It will do me good to see nature and enjoy it in spite of not having tea till five or even none at all. It's what I need, to clear all the rubbish off my soul.' So I prayed that if I went without my tea and drove out to see the spring instead, the man would give me a better report of Nancy's teeth. My idea was that if I could save them till she was twenty-five or six, I would have six or seven years to get her married. I was determined to marry Nancy to make up to her for all her disadvantages, and I had begun already to tell Matt how I would like to travel some day and see India where, Mr Hickson told me, a girl with some money would always get something.

But the dentist gave me no comfort. I did not deserve it, perhaps, with the life I led; but it was a terrible blow to be told that the child had been neglected. She should have had a plate, he said – two of her teeth had been killed.

It was no good me telling him that we had gone to the best dentist in Bradnall. He looked into the air over me and pressed his lips together as if I were not fit to speak to. He would make me no promise even to save her front teeth.

I could see he was the kind of man who thought women were fools to think so much of looks, and I was in terror that he would pull our Nancy's front teeth only to triumph over me. I could not even be nice to him in case he thought that I was trying to charm him. He was the kind of man who would have turned spiteful to a charmer, and even as it was he kept looking down my figure and my dress as if to say: 'a common cheap woman who might as well be on the streets.'

Yet I had put on my best dress and powdered to please him, not knowing that a London dentist was almost the same thing as a doctor or a clergyman and that I ought to have dressed down for him, instead of up.

So I came out with Nina feeling like a murderess who had killed her own child by her follies. I felt such a weight on my breast that I wanted to cry out.

Nina did not even ask me about the child's teeth. She began at once to look about her, even at the trees in the gardens, and to breathe through her nostrils, trying to smell the blossom, so that I wanted to tell her that laburnum had no good smell and was a town tree.

I was angry with her for not asking about Nancy, and even when we came out into the real country, I would not listen to her talk about the lovely day, or sniff at the air. But all at once she said to me that it was a day when God seemed so close that you could hear Him breathe. Then, I don't know why, my heart opened from its bitter clench and my anger against her changed to love. For Nina had great religious power so that though sometimes you hated her for her taking no notice of your troubles, the next moment she said something that went straight into your soul. She made you remember God and the shortness of your time on earth and your own littleness.

So I said: 'Yes, indeed, you do,' and took her hand in gratitude, and looked about me to make the most of spring. For the truth was, since my difference with Mr Hickson, I had not been out so much as usual in the country. It was Mr Hickson more than anyone who used to take me away from the children and tea parties, to be quiet for a little and to admire beauties.

And this was indeed a lovely day, to make anyone religious. The apple trees were just budding with new leaves, and the sky so pale blue and clear as a baby's eye, and the air blowing fresh as if straight off a sea; and some little thin clouds floating high up like muslin sleeves on a washing day; and I could smell the new hawthorn leaves in the shiny hedges, like a warm iron when you try it on your cheek. What with this sweet beauty that was there for me to take and would be gone in no time, and my pain and guilt and wondering what would happen to Nancy with her plain face and Belle with her obstinate perverseness, I was in agony.

'Oh dear,' I said at last, 'why don't I come out every day? Once in a way is making too much of it. I can hardly bear it.'

'That's true,' Nina said. 'It's what my husband says – we ought to live in God as familiarly as in a lodging, dining-room, drawing-room, bedroom and kitchen. He did one of his best pictures about it for Mr Hickson. But he would not take it.'

'Where is it now?' for I was mad to see this picture and know Jimson's religion.

'I don't know – we had it when we were in London – it was in our lodgings, but we had to leave and the landlord kept all the canvases until we could pay the bill.'

I asked her why Mr Hickson would not take the picture. For I wanted still to know what it was like.

Nina hesitated a moment and then she explained that it was because the picture showed the plumbing – there was even a W.C. with a man in it. 'But it wasn't Mr Hickson, though I think he thought it was.'

I said I didn't call that religion, and then the words jumped out of my mouth: 'Does he really hit you?'

But Nina, good soul, answered me as simply as if I had asked the time, that Jimson never hit her unless she exasperated him. 'I am not a very good housekeeper,' she said, 'and besides, think of all his discouragements; no one understands what he's doing.'

'But why need he paint like that, Nina?'

'It's the only way he can paint. But I think sometimes he would like to stop.'

I said that he seemed quite mad, but Nina answered me: 'Oh no, he's very sane – the other people are mad – to live as they do without happiness or God.'

Then, again, I felt her goodness and I asked her how she could bear to live with a man who beat her. She said she had two good reasons. One was that she couldn't live without him and the other was that he needed her.

I said: 'I suppose he is your religion.'

But Nina was shocked. She said: 'No, how could any man be your religion?'

47

Still I thought that if Jimson was not her religion, he was most of it, and perhaps the beatings were part of it too. For she hated to indulge herself and I know she always despised me.

24

I thought that I should not bear to see Jimson again after knowing that he had hit Nina, but I was wrong. When I went back with Nina to their room for tea, I stood off from him, but I saw he did not notice it. It was never any good to disapprove of Jimson because he did not care. So soon we were laughing again at some joke, and the next day I ran in again, between the shops and luncheon, to see how the work was going on.

I couldn't do without my visit, and if I had been a great church woman, like Maul, I would have thought I went there to be out of my tearing life in Bradnall, and out of worldly cares.

I was glad, too, when Jimson would call out, just as before, in my own house: 'Give me your hand, Mrs Em,' or 'your neck,' and draw me for the picture.

Nina herself would ask me to sit and once she telephoned from the Swan for me to come and be drawn. She would have liked me to sit naked. It seemed nothing to her, I suppose, and when I refused to strip, she would look sad and say: 'That's what he really wants, but he doesn't like to ask.'

'I should think not,' I said.

'Don't you think it's a pity when you could help him so much? He thinks you have the finest figure he ever saw.'

'It's only a fancy,' I told her. 'He is a fanciful man and he likes fat women.'

But I will confess that on the last day before sending-in day when we were all mad to get the picture done, she and Jimson so persuaded me that I sat for him down to the waist. I could not believe it was myself, sitting there, half-naked, but there was my dear Nina in the room, as calm as you please, sewing a shift; and Jimson painting and humming and looking at me as coldly as if I had been a statue.

It seemed to me then that I had been a fool to be so prim before and yet I wondered at myself. I could not tell whether I had done a religious thing or a bad one. When I went home again, I was in wonder and dismay all the evening. I thought: 'What will I do next – there seems to be nothing I wouldn't do.'

25

As it happened, Matt had been very busy all that fortnight and with the children at school I had had plenty of free time, but on the sending-in day, Saturday, he came home early from the office, before lunch. I saw there was something wrong, but I could not tell what. I thought perhaps he had had a letter from some lawyer about some bill. That had happened before and made a terrible quarrel.

I was in a great difficulty, for I had ordered the landau at three to take the picture to the town hall. I dared not let Matt know that I was going to the Jimsons', but I could not disappoint Nina and risk the picture missing the competition. The man's whole life depended on it.

So I went round to the stables to get into the carriage there. But Matt threw up the library window and called out to me:

'Where are you going?'

'To make some calls.'

'On the Jimsons, I suppose.'

'No,' I said, for I was not calling on them, only to fetch the picture.

I drove in the opposite direction to the village and left cards on some people. Then I went back to the Jimsons'. I had feared the picture would not be ready, but it was ready, only Jimson had not troubled to finish any of the faces.

He said: 'Here you are – take it away quickly. But if I had not promised you, Mrs Monday, I would much rather burn the thing.'

I dared not ask him to touch the faces. We were glad to get the picture away from him. 'It won't matter what it looks like,' I told Nina, 'for Mr Hickson has the committee in his pocket. He has just given a big contract to Mr Jones' son-in-law and Mr Jones was the only doubtful one.'

When we had left the picture safe, I was so happy that I almost cried. Nina, too, was pleased and when we came back to the Swan I suggested we should have a celebration tea. So I ran out to buy cakes and Jimson to get some port wine. Jimson was in his most outrageous spirits and I could see he wanted to flirt with me. He looked at me now with a different eye from the day before when he had drawn me. But, as I say, I was wild too, and I admit it, I didn't mind for anything, not even for his squeezing and pushing me on the stairs, or his risky jokes. I felt as I did with Rozzie and if he had asked me to drink in some public-house, I might have done it, in spite of all Bradnall.

Luckily he did not. He was satisfied with his jokes and his eyefulls. So we made tea and we were joking and using all our private jokes, like Jimson's with me: 'Your hand, Mrs Em', or mine with him: 'Your ear, Mr Jimson,' meaning not that I wanted to talk into it, but box it; when a girl came up from the Swan to say there was someone on the telephone for me.

Down I went in wonder and fright. And it was my nurse, a nice little thing from my own village and my good friend, to tell me that Matt had just set off to find me, and seemed to be upset about something. 'And I thought if you were at the Jimsons', mam, you might like to know in case the master could not find you.'

The clever little thing meant to tell me that Matt was coming to catch me at the Jimsons' and that he was in a terrible rage with me.

I felt so bewildered I didn't know what to do, but while I was standing there Nina came down and asked me what it was. So I told her, and she said I had better go home at once and she would swear I had never been there. She didn't want any scenes between Matt and Jimson, I could see that.

I had sent away the carriage, not to betray myself to all the town, and so I had to walk home. But I was glad of it to give me time to get my senses back. And as I got nearer to Woodview, my feet began to drag as if they would never bring me there, and as if the weight of guilt was bearing me down to the ground.

For now, all at once, I saw myself, with Maul's eye and the world's eye; and I could not believe how I had been so bad a wife. Now all my debts and my philanderings came down upon me in one thump and crushed me.

Yet I could not make out even then how bad I had been, or how guilty. For I knew I had always loved Matt with all my heart and never thought wrong to him for one moment. And people use words so that you can never be sure what they mean. When the preachers used to speak of adulteries, it would turn out after all, in the thirdly or fourthly, that they were thinking of silk stockings, or women's bicycles, or mixed bathing; and again, for some it was devil's work to play beggar my neighbour, with your own children and nurses, in your own nursery. Then one will say the act is all, and another, the bad thought. So that a cross word is as good as murder, but a kind man could kill kings and still be holy if his heart was pure.

'Oh,' I said, 'if only I had a glass door in my heart, like the new ovens, to see what was really there, and whether I am the worst of women, or just the common run of ladies in rich houses, with friends, who are guilty indeed of worldly living, but not of deadly sin.'

But suddenly I heard Matt's voice, which scattered all my wits again. It is strange what a coward I was before that little man, but not so strange, for I knew him good and honest, when I was neither. The landau was at the kerb and he jumped out and said: 'You have been at the Jimsons' again.'

'Yes,' I said.

'Were you alone with him?'

'No, not today.'

'But other days you were. Come, get in, we can't stand here.'

I was glad to see the carriage was open, because he could not shout and wave his hands at me before all Bradnall.

But angry as he was, he saw that himself, and stopped and asked the groom to close it.

'But Matt,' I said, 'it's so hot.' He would not listen. I could see his trouser legs shaking with rage, and my own legs were trembling. Yet I had to bow to several people and smile while the footman was shutting up the landau. I had to look even more friendly than usual to quite ordinary acquaintances, because Matt saw nobody. He would not have taken off his hat, at that moment, to the Queen. His rage terrified me so much I could hardly get into the carriage when at last it was closed, and he was so furious against me and impatient that he gave me a great push behind which nearly threw me down. It was the first time Matt had ever handled me rudely.

'Why did you tell me lies?' he said. 'What have you been doing with that man?'

'I only took his picture to the committee.'

'You've been there every day for three weeks – don't contradict – don't tell me any more lies.'

So it turned out that somebody at the Swan, probably the landlady, Mrs Fogg, who never liked me, had told him about my visits. I saw that the man was quite mad with rage and that he believed I was in love with Jimson and had done wrong with him.

And now he began to talk about Mr Hickson too, and even some man I had forgotten. He said that I had flirted with them all. 'But it's my own fault for marrying you – I was warned about you, but I didn't listen. I suppose you were deceiving me with that fellow under my own roof, and laughing at me.'

I was horrified at his thinking such things, but I could not say anything. It was not that I was frightened but I felt that all this had been prepared and that nothing I could say would be any good. So I sat like a fool and looked at him while he raged and screamed, and threw my arm about.

'You have always laughed at me,' he said. 'You have never cared one farthing for me, an old bald fool marrying a servant-girl twenty years younger than himself. You and your friend Mrs Balmforth think me the best joke you've ever seen. And nothing but lies, and bills and robbery and men ever since. There was that garden-boy to start with and Hickson all the time.'

The sweat was running down his face and he gasped as if he were swimming. 'And now this wretched painter – I suppose he sent his wife to fetch you. Hickson tells me she gets any woman he fancies – he fancied you from the beginning. Why, I caught you together, when he was pretending to draw you.'

26

This was the second time he spoke of Hickson and it made me wonder. And afterwards I found out that it was Mr Hickson had put the whole thing into his head that I was going to the bad with Jimson, and he had even given a hint of the freedoms he had taken for himself. All, I suppose, out of jealousy and spite.

And what a warning it is to us all, against jealousy. For here it made the clever Hickson do a mean trifling thing, which lost him my better friendship, and drove Matt mad. Yet I suppose those that are born jealous or envious will never be cured, for if you gave them a million in a bag, they would still be afraid of it bursting.

As for Hickson, I was sure even then he had told, because when Matt went on he said that he had always known about Hickson, and never spoke, for the children's sake. And that I must not think him jealous. 'I don't mind what you do – a woman like you – why should I? I'm not such a fool as that.'

He grew worse and worse, and when we got to the house, and I went up to my room so that the servants could not hear him, he followed me and began again. He said that this was the end and now he would summons me into court and expose me; and Hickson and Jimson. He would divorce me and keep the children.

I wondered if he could do that. But I knew that the evidence would be black against me and that if I was appointed to have a fall it was no more than I deserved. It was no good my speaking to him so I took off my hat and went to go out. But he held the door and said: 'Where are you going to now?'

I said I had to see about dinner.

'Dinner!' he shouted. 'Do you think I can eat?'

I said I could not eat either, but dinner must be cooked and sent up or what would the servants think.

'And what are you going to do next?'

I said that I supposed I would go to Rozzie. She would always give me a home.

'And you will leave me and the children without another thought?'

I said that, of course, I would never leave him until I was turned out.

Then he stared at me and said: 'If I let you stay, it will be the same thing over again. I can't trust you an inch – your whole life is a lie.'

'I can't trust myself,' I said, 'I never meant to deceive you.'

'And you expect me to believe that,' he said, 'that you're a weak, helpless woman, when after fifteen years you still do exactly what you like? Not one word I say has ever had the least effect on you.'

'I don't know what I am,' I said. I was too miserable to argue with him. I begged him to let me go to the kitchen.

But suddenly he sat down on the couch and burst out crying. I was always shocked to see Matt cry. He only cried two or three times in all those years, once when I refused him, and once now, and once when he was dying. So I sat down to ask him what I could do. But he jumped up again and told me to go to the kitchen.

I went and arranged for dinner, but when I came up to dress, I found Matt in my room. He said that he had thought things over and it seemed to him that he had been at fault too. He had left me too much alone, and as for Hickson, it had been his fault to introduce such a cunning philanderer into the house. Jimson, too, was not a fit person to know me. 'Yes,' he said, 'I ought to have considered the difference in our ages. How could I blame you even if you did like the garden-boy better – not to speak of Hickson?' So he blamed himself for everything; and I, seeing that it was to be peace between us, was glad, like a fool, and only tried to say that I, too, was greatly to blame.

But he would not let me speak and kept on crying: 'No, let's have the truth – or I'll go mad. I can't bear any more pretending.'

So I saw it was better to let him believe what he liked; even in the garden-boy, and indeed, so he believed for the rest of his life, and gave himself peace.

And now I know that it was a bad kind of peace and that it brought our downfall. Not a great scandal or the loss of my home and Matt, as I had feared, but the ruin of the whole, which was the true punishment of luxury.

For Matt said that he had neglected me too long and that he could not bear to do business any more with Mr Hickson, who was his greatest customer. So he retired from business and resigned from the council, and took me away to Paris to forget our quarrel.

All I had to do was to let him spoil me as much as he liked and so he did, buying me all the newest clothes and a diamond bracelet.

Yet even then I saw how he was changed, and how he went back upon himself to the creeper time. He would scarcely cross the street without holding my hand; and never take any but the middle carriage of a train, in case of collisions front or back, or sleep above the second storey in case of fire. He became as timid as a child, the poor lamb, and could not bear me away from him. So when the war came, it nearly killed him as it finished our destruction. For he sold out all his investments in the first week, for anything he could get, and we could barely scrape enough after to send Phyllis, our youngest, to school.

The war was truly a bad blow to Matt, for he had always been one for abolishing the Army and Navy, thinking that they were too warlike. And now he found that it took but one to make a war, and as we used to say: 'One dog will drive a thousand sheep.'

I had promised never to see the Jimsons again and this promise I kept, only sending Nina some work now and then for her fine sewing, when she gave me her address at a box number.

As for the competition, when the councillors saw Jimson's picture and found out that the committee was bound to accept it, because Hickson, even without Matt, had a majority, they called a full meeting and put off the decoration of the lobby on the grounds of expense. Mr Hickson made them pay the artists a few guineas each for their waste of time, but no one got the order. This was the end of all my struggles to get the picture finished, yet so it was that when the news came out a week after, I thought nothing of it. I agreed with Matt who said that if Jimson had no success it was his own fault.

As for Mr Hickson, I did not see him for a long time. Matt could not bear the sight of him and said even that he had cheated him in business.

But I met him one day at a party and after we had looked at each other, I could not help smiling to see him so nervous. He looked like a little boy afraid of a smacking. So we talked a little and afterwards we would meet now and then, when I went for my hair, or for afternoon shopping, and walk across the new park. It was on one of these walks that he pulled out his pocket-book and showed me the drawing of a woman. I did not recognize it until he said: 'It's one of the best things Jimson ever did – because he did it for his own pleasure, I suppose. I show it to you only to let you know it's in safe hands. I'll destroy it if you like, and I promise you it won't be shown to anybody without your permission. But I hope you'll let it live because it is a little masterpiece – a master's drawing of a magnificent subject.'

I was shocked and said it was very ugly. I hoped he would burn it. But he smiled at me and spoke of false modesty. It was always his idea that I had liked Jimson's flatteries and that Jimson had made me value my shape. And so, perhaps, it had been true, at the first surprise to have an artist admire me.

But I insisted that the drawing be burnt. I feared like fire it might come round to Matt.

So at last Mr Hickson put it back in his pocket and made a little bow and said: 'It shall be as you please.'

But he did not burn it. He even lent it to some publishers who brought it out in a book of drawings where it was called 'English Portrait, from the Hickson Collection.' He showed it to people, too, for even ten years afterwards it was thrown at me by an enemy.

27

Matt would not forgive Jimson and would not even speak of him. From the year of the war I had no news from Nina, and I had forgotten the Jimsons, when one day the maid came to me in the kitchen and said a Mr Jimson was at the front door. She had been afraid to let him in because he looked like a beggar. So I said: 'Bring him round to the back.'

For Matt was already failing then, and I did not want him upset.

Mr Jimson was certainly very shabby, but gay and smiling.

'Don't be afraid,' he said, 'I won't come in. So he's still alive?'

'Of course he's alive,' I said.

'I heard he was dying. He must be getting pretty old.'

'Only seventy-two this year.'

'But he was old for his age.' So he went on as if we had not parted a day. He kept eyeing me too, and said: 'You haven't changed, Mrs Monday – I think you've improved.'

'I'm fatter.'

'Yes, you've improved.'

I was afraid he would press me to sit so I asked him what he was doing. 'I've got a commission to paint a Mrs Bond.'

'And where are you living?'

'I'm going to Bidlee for this commission,' he said, which was a village not three miles away. 'But I'll have to get some materials and clothes.'

'How's Nina?'

'Dead,' he said as if it was nothing. ''Flu.'

I was shocked and said that he didn't seem to mind very much about his wife's death.

'I miss her a lot,' he said. 'I haven't done any real work since she died. She kept my time free and managed the housekeeping.'

Then he asked me to lend him thirty pounds, so that he could buy materials and clothes for his visit to Bidlee. I said I had nothing to lend.

'I thought the place looked run down,' Jimson said.

'I do the cooking. We have one maid for the house.'

'I don't know what I'll do,' he said. 'I was relying on you. It's only for a few days till they pay me.'

I had a soufflé in the oven that needed watching like a young child on its first legs so I gave him ten shillings to get rid of him. But he was back in three days. This time he let himself in by the back door and came into the kitchen before I noticed him. He made me jump when he said: 'Good evening, Mrs Monday.'

But there he was and I couldn't tell a friendly visitor to go out of the house.

He sat down and kept looking at me, without speaking, while I was rolling out some scones. At last he said: 'Mrs Monday, I suppose it's no good asking you to marry me.'

He said it so quietly that I did not feel the shock of it for a little while. So I could not be angry. I said only that I had a husband already.

'I meant, of course, after he dies.'

I thought that this was a shocking thing to say and if Mr Hickson had said it, I think I would have been disgusted. But the way Jimson said it, I felt that it would be silly to be angry. Because the truth was that poor Matt was dying. So I went on with my work and answered him that Matt might live a long time yet. There was good hope of it.

'I'll wait as long as you like,' he said, 'if you agree to take me in the end.'

'The last man.' I said. 'Why, Mr Jimson, have you forgotten that I was Nina's friend? Do you think I don't know how you treated her?'

'You don't think I would ever hit you, Mrs Monday?'

'If you did,' I said, 'it might be the worse for you.' For I was a head taller and my arm was as thick as his neck.

I thought he would laugh at this, but instead he looked very serious and said that I had not known Nina. 'I may have given her a little slap,' he said, 'but she was a maddening woman. You mustn't think I'm a bad-tempered man. I'm very easy to live with.'

'Mr Jimson,' I said, 'I hope you won't go on like this, because it won't do either of us any good. Even if I were free to marry, I would never dream of taking you.'

He went away then, but he was back again in a few days and though he did not propose, he kept looking at me as if summing me up. But one good thing was, now he was courting, he sometimes talked in quite a new way, seriously and quietly, not laughing at me all the time.

So he told me a great deal about himself, how he had been the son of a doctor, and sent to a good school. But his father had died without a will and all the money had gone to the eldest son, who gambled it away on horses in no time. The schoolmaster had give him free schooling until he was sixteen and then he had gone into an office. Then when he was twenty-six he had suddenly begun drawing and painting and couldn't stop. He gave up the office simply because he couldn't bear to leave his drawing to go to work. 'Luckily,' he said, 'I had some money saved – it kept me alive till I got married and then my wife kept me.'

'Haven't you ever made any money?' I asked.

'Oh yes,' he said, 'I made a hundred pounds this year – and I could make much more than that if I liked. Hickson will always get me commissions for portraits.'

I could not drive the man away so long as he behaved himself. He was so pleased to come.

Betty, the housemaid, an old woman that had been the char before I was married, was my good friend and I knew she would say nothing in the house; and neither Matt nor the girls ever came near the kitchen. Matt, with his bad heart, could not leave his room and I did not like the girls in the kitchen, getting in my way, or spoiling their clothes and their hands. Nancy specially, who would have liked to help me, had a very nice young man who was interested, and I wanted her always to look neat and fresh for him and to practise her music. He was very musical and shy, and though he was plain and rather short, so that the girls despised him, he was in a very good business as a lawyer and very religious, and I knew he would be a good steady husband to any woman.

But Nancy hated music and so I would drive her to the piano, and Belle was too clever and proud for housework. She had always plenty of young men and she had been engaged already to one that was killed. And Edith had just taken up her hospital training, and even when she came home at weekends, she would work at her books or learn at Chinese. For she always meant to go into the Chinese missions.

As for Phyllis, we had got her to boarding-school at last, and there she was still, though doing no good with the books. So Betty and I had the place to ourselves and when Jimson came, Betty would go to the scullery.

I say I did not like his coming, but though I never liked the man, I liked his chatter and his jokes.

He was like a piece of the old happy gay times before the war, and he brought Nina back to me when I had forgotten the world at Bradnall.

28

I thought very much about religion in those days, for God had punished me at last for our prosperity, and I was suffering very much with poor Matt. He kept quarrelling with the girls, which was very bad for him and for them. He was all for me chaperoning Nancy with her young man, though I had no time and I knew the only hope for the poor child was to be alone with the fellow so that he might forget his shyness with her and talk about himself. So I would tell Matt that chaperones were out.

But he would shout: 'What's that got to do with it? You used to be particular enough and you change because of a fashion. You don't seem to have any idea of right or wrong.' Then he would say that I was teaching Nancy to behave like a Jezebel and he made me ashamed, for it seemed to be like the truth; yet I could not bring myself to spoil the poor girl's chance, a great piece of luck for her at last, by rushing in, and perhaps at the very moment when the young man was warmest.

And since Matt was at home now all day, which is not natural for a man, he grew difficult and quarrelsome.

He quarrelled with Belle for her politics, because, like all young people with natural spirits, she did not agree with him and took up a little communism to have something of her own; and he complained of Edith because she was so set on leaving home. But why not? Thank God for the ones that know what they want and want something sensible. As for Phyllis, he said I had ruined her, and perhaps I had, for she was too like me in her love of pleasure.

But quarrelling was bad for Matt and for the girls too. Nothing worse in a home, for it destroys all joys even among the richest. So that just when Jimson told me that I was happy by nature, I was at my wits' end with worry to know what would become of us all. It was no good warning Belle and Edith that a quarrel might kill their father. And if you think them hard then you don't know what girls can be in the twenties, and yet ready to throw away their lives for any revolutions, or the Lord.

And when I tried to find out Jimson's religion, since he was so gay under all affliction, he answered me only: 'Don't worry, it's bad for your figure and your hair.'

And then again, and he seemed to mean it too, he said: 'You're Mrs Em and I'm Gulley Jimson and that fly on the wall has its own life too – as big as it likes to make it, and it's all one to God as the leaves to the tree.'

But another evening, when all the girls were from home and Matt was asleep with his draught and we were sitting over the fire with some toasted ale, as Rozzie used to like it, he seemed to be more serious and open as people are at that hour of a winter's evening, and especially before the kitchen fire. Believe me that is the sweetest fire in the house, for confidence and for lovers, and for consolation, and for religion too, I mean facing the world.

A kitchen fire is just the right height to look at, without going to sleep, and then it is a useful fire and not just luxury; and it is so made that it drops its coals and tells you, with every fall, that life burns away, and it has the stove top for a kettle to remind you that, at the worst, there is always tea, and that the best comforts are at everyone's hand.

So Jimson and I had at last some good serious talks by the fire, from time to time, in those sad months; and once when we had been talking about the war and its terrible weight upon artists, in stopping the sale of pictures, he said: 'But what can I do? The great thing, Mrs Em, is not to give a damn for all that kind of thing. Yes, to be all serene.'

'Like Nina,' I said.

But he said no, that Nina was always holding herself up and following a rule. 'No,' he said, 'you need to live in serenity there where it grows. To be at home there, and not to swear.'

58

Then I remembered that I had never heard Gulley swearing and from all I knew I think that this was Gulley's religion. Not to trouble about his ups and downs. But to get on with his work. And I liked him for this, too.

29

Of course the girls soon found out that Jimson was coming to see me and Nancy made a great fuss. She said that I had encouraged the man. It was strange how these young girls would abuse me, but the truth was, I had spoilt them. Belle, when she came into the kitchen one day and found him there, would not even shake hands with him or speak to him. She spoke only to me that she wanted tea early, and went out with her nose in the air.

Jimson was very angry with the girl. He said that she wanted smacking. But I told him that it was my own fault if she had no manners and that I could not complain if she thought little of me because I was not her class. She was a lady in all her feelings and it was no good pretending that I was one.

'Better than any of them,' he said.

But I knew very well that I had failed to be a lady, even for Matt's sake, because I was too weak. I had gone back instead of forward and now sometimes I would talk broad, even to the girls. Only the week before, when Belle had a crowd of her friends, talking about literature, I had said that the old books were the best for the new ones had no religion. But I spoke broad and said 'bestest' and 'they'm'.

I could see everybody looking at me and afterwards Belle said that I had done it on purpose to make her look like a fool. But it was not so. I was quite as surprised at myself as she was. I could only think it was my own nature coming out.

So I could not complain if Nancy was ashamed of me before her young man, who was very polite and nice, or if Belle despised me.

At last Nancy came to me in tears and asked me not to have Jimson to see me. She said it was making a scandal and she was afraid it would reach her Geoffrey and put him off. She did not like me being so much in the kitchen either, or coming into the house with my sleeves rolled up and floury hands.

So I promised her to take more care with my appearance and to send Jimson away. But as it happened, before I could do so, while I was still wondering how to do so, Geoffrey proposed to Nancy. The engagement was printed in the paper and so I did not need to offend poor Jimson. Only I gave him the hint to come when the girls would be out.

30

Yet I, too, would have been glad to see the end of Jimson because he had begun to pester me. He would not talk any longer. He would only sit and stare or follow me about the kitchen. He was as stupid as any man in that state, quite hang-dog with love.

It drove me distracted because Matt was then at his worst. The poor man had gone behind all sense now and he was like a child, afraid of the dark. He would wake up at night, and say that he was smothering and catch hold of me and cry out that I must save him from hell. He said that he had done such wickedness that God could never forgive him. All this, so the doctors said, because his heart was weak and could not put enough blood into his poor brain.

I told him a thousand times that he could never have done anything bad enough for hell, but he said I did not know the great evils in his mind. Then I said that according to science there was no hell, as he had often told me so himself. But he answered out of the Bible that he had spoken as a fool, for now he could see it opening for him; it was dragging him down by the legs. It seemed to me a cruel thing that Matt should suffer so in his conscience, who had never done any harm to anybody and only for the weakness of his body. But when I told Jimson of it, he said: 'He is not suffering for his miserable sins, but for being a coward and losing his serenity. That's a certain way to be in hell.'

It was true, of course, that Matt had always been a timid kind of man, but then again, it was not fair. For it wasn't his fault that he was born nervous, and kept down by his mother and sister – and I still cannot understand why the poor man was made to suffer so terribly in his last days.

The worse Matt was, the more Jimson pestered me till I lost my temper and told him if he proposed again, I should turn him out and keep him out.

Then he went away and I did not see him for nearly a year. But when he had finished the portrait of Mrs Bond, he sent me five pounds by post to pay his debt. He owed me much more, but I don't think he knew how much it was. He was always a man who counted shillings as nothing even up to thirty or forty shillings, but thought of five pounds as a big sum.

31

Matt died in the spring of 1919, and it turned out that he had lost even more money than I had thought. And great debts. He had left two thousand each to the girls and the house to me. But the house had a mortgage on it and the lawyer told me that when the debts were paid, there would not be much left for me except the furniture. And he advised me to sell it and buy an annuity, however small, to have a regular income. I said: 'No, I'll open a boarding-house. For I can make double the income that way and keep out of investments.'

But the girls were all against the boarding-house. Nancy, of course, had to think of her husband and his grand relations, and Edith was sure I would lose all my money, feeding up the customers, and Belle was afraid she would have to live at home and help me.

'But what will I do?' I asked them. 'I can't sit down and twiddle at thirty-nine, and the only thing I know is to work about a house.'

'I'm sure you want a rest,' Nancy said. 'You can live very well on an annuity in very nice places.'

'I see, you'd like me to be out of Bradnall,' I said. Then the girl turned fiery red and said: 'You're always saying things like that, mother, but you know they're not true. If I were ashamed of you, I ought to despise myself. But I hope I'm not such a common snob.'

'I never said so,' I said, 'and I wouldn't say such a thing. All I say is that you would be happier if I were away from the place so you didn't have to be anxious for me not to say the wrong thing.'

'You can say what you like, mother,' said she, 'and I'll never be ashamed of you and never was.'

'Not of me,' I said, 'but for me and why should you not?'

But she would not listen to me and we had another quarrel and did not speak for a week. Perhaps I was never tactful enough for Nancy. I never found the word to get past her school manners. But the truth was, she was too delicate in her mind. I couldn't complain of that – it went with her good heart. But those who said that my daughters had been spoilt with their good school education, were foolish. Belle had a better education than Nancy, but she and I never had a tiff. 'It's better for me to go,' I told her, 'because I don't fit in with your young friends and I'm too young for the sect of widows in the Upper Road.'

' I think you're very wise, mother,' she said. 'You'll be lost among those snobs and tabbies in the Upper Road. Of course,' she said, 'there's old Mrs Benger and her literary circle, but I don't quite see you in that galley.'

'No, indeed,' said I.

'And that reminds me,' said Belle. 'Why did you plunge into the conversation yesterday when young Tonkin was here – about the new poetry?'

'Did I?' I said, and I thought: 'That's a new young man,' and I thought, 'what a pity it is she doesn't stick to one, and fix him, instead of dodging about all the time. But it's no good telling her that there are no perfect men any more than a perfect woman. She wouldn't believe me.'

'You did,' said Belle, 'and why on earth did you say your favourite poem was "Now avening tawls the knell of parting day," trying to imitate my broad talk.'

'I don't know,' I said, 'unless it sounded more solemn.'

'My dear mother,' Belle said, 'it's all very well with me but it does make things awkward for strangers.'

'Of course it does, my darling,' I said, 'and that's one reason why I'm going away. To give you a chance.' Then I asked her about young Tonkin. But she would never tell me how she was with a man. Belle was close and hard. She hadn't Nancy's tender heart. I often thought: 'If so be Belle does get a husband, and I pray God she may, he'll have to toe the line. She'll make him or break him.'

32

So it was settled that all should be sold, house as well as furniture, and Belle would set up a flat where Edith could come at week-ends, and Phyllis spend her holidays between Aunty Maul and me. But I thought her Aunty Maul would keep her away from the boarding-house and so would her sisters, bless them.

For I was to set up house with Rozzie, who had been left pretty well off, nearly three years before, by Bill Balmforth. Rozzie had got a flat in Brighton and was longing to have me, and what better place for a boarding-house?

But on the very day before the sale, when the house was like a second-hand store, full of upturned chairs, carpets with the tickets on them, and a lot of things brought into it that we had never seen before, in walked Jimson. He was terribly ill-looking, just out of bed from the 'flu, but gay as a bird. 'My fortune's made,' he said, 'and what is more important, I've got a wall without conditions.'

I hardly listened to him, for all I had to think of. It was my first house and I thought it would be my last true home. Every last day was like another root pulled out of me. All was to be sold, for Nancy and Belle, if they agreed in nothing else, agreed that our good new furniture, which Matt and I had hunted for beauty and goodness through every shop in Bradnall and a special trip to London for the drawing-room suite, was not worth having. Belle laughed at it and Nancy hated it. 'Vulgar yellow varnish,' she said of our golden oak. She and her poor little manny would have nothing but antiques.

And as for the old Monday stuff, the few good pieces that Maul had not carried off, Nancy and Belle quarrelled so bitterly about dividing them, that I wished they were sold, too. For Nancy, who had just had her first baby, said her milk would be spoilt if she did not get the mahogany bookcase; and Belle, who was jealous of her for getting married, even to a man she scorned for herself, would not give way one inch. And as for me, I only wished I had milk myself for the poor baby who was really suffering in his stomach.

Old and new, all gave me pain; the cracks and cobwebs that shamed me; the dirt I had never seen before and jumped up now, like old sins in the angel's book, to cry down all my housewife vanities. They made me feel worse, for I felt: 'Poor house, you are to be despised by those who did not know your true character all these striving years.'

So though I was glad to be busy, clearing out the rubbish and sorting the crockery, I was not so pleased to see Jimson and I showed him no great welcome. I wished him well away.

But on he went about his wall, fifteen by twenty, in a new village hall at a place called Ancombe, on the Longwater, not twenty miles from my old home in the south. 'A hundred pounds,' said Jimson, 'and no conditions – free living with the old woman who's giving the hall. She doesn't know a picture from the bath mat, but Hickson put her on to me. I'll do it in six weeks and then I'm off for the grand tour.'

His coat sleeve was ripped at the shoulder, and I saw that it would be out tomorrow. But I wasn't going to say a word about it, for I didn't want to show my interest in him, now that Matt was dead and I was a real widow, without natural protection.

Talk away, I thought, but I won't ask you to tea. I'll give you no encouragement. But he went on talking about his great chance and the hole in his coat kept catching my eye until I said to him as coldly as a stranger: 'Excuse me, but your coat seam is ripped.'

'Oh, yes,' he said, 'it's been like that a long time,' and he started again on his wall and his travels. So I said to myself, If you will ruin a good coat, you will, and nothing can stop you. Wives or coats, you're a born waster. But the coat kept on nagging at me. It was opening its mouth like a baby crying to be taken up and at last I could not bear it, and I said: 'Mr Jimson, for poor Nina's sake, let me sew up your coat.'

'No, no, my dear Mrs Em,' said he. 'Why should you take all that trouble? I'll do it myself. I can sew very well,' and then back to his wall and how unlucky it was that he had sold all his paints and brushes.

So I went and got my work-box and threaded a needle before his eyes and said: 'Now, Mr Jimson, excuse me, but I can't bear to think of your poor wife seeing you in that condition.'

No, no,' said he. 'Really, it's too much –'

But what with the thought of Nina, poor helpless dead woman, and the hole, and my scorn for that poor feckless being, I fairly laid my hands upon him and took off his coat and sewed it up for him. Not only that, but two of his trouser buttons, which were dangling from him like a fool's bells.

Now when I found myself sewing his trousers and he in his sleeves, I thought: 'This is not fit for a new widow,' and I looked severely enough. But he took no advantage then. but chattered about his wall and he was in a difficulty because he had no clothes and no materials and his last landlord had seized even his canvases.

'I've been sleeping in fourpenny dosses, Mrs Em – till I remembered all your kindness.'

'Oho,' I thought, 'so he's going to beg.' True enough he asked for an advance of ten pounds on the price of his wall. And he brought out letters and a newspaper picture of a village hall to show me how he would be sure of getting the hundred pounds. But I would not look at them. I was not to be caught.

'I haven't ten pounds,' I said. 'We are very badly off. Where is Nina now?'

'Where is she?' He was surprised.

'Buried,' I mean.

'Oh, near London. Mrs Monday, do you realize that this is the great chance of my life and I may lose it for lack of a pound or two? I haven't even the fare to go south and claim the job.'

But I thought of that bruise on Nina's cheek and I would give him nothing. 'No,' I said, 'I have my poor girls to think of, and the lawyers are not done with me yet. I am a poor woman – ask someone else.'

'There's no one else, Mrs Em. Come now, only a pound – I'll go part way in the train and walk the rest.'

'Why did you beat poor Nina?' I asked him.

'What's that got to do with it?' He was angry at me and went away. I felt ashamed, but still I said to myself: 'Don't you encourage that one. He'll stop at nothing. He doesn't know the meaning of shame or common decency either. You're well rid of him if he does have thoughts of you.'

33

But Jimson, if he was not a worldly man, was, for that same reason, an abashless one. And back he came on the evening of the sale, all among the moving and the packing-cases, and a winter rain of straw and dirt that made me sneeze so much I could not tell whether I had tears in my eyes for grief at leaving my home or only from the straw dust.

You don't believe in my wall,' he said.

'I don't know what to believe,' I said.

'Then come and see it,' he said, 'it's not so far – two hours by train.'

'What nonsense,' I said.

'Mrs Em,' he said, as serious as a condemned man, 'it's life or death to me.'

'Then you must die,' I thought, and yet I knew it would be easy enough to see his wall and put him off my conscience, after the furniture sale and before the house sale and fixing with Rozzie, when I knew what money I should have. In that week I had nothing to do, except I was meeting the lawyers in London and having luncheon with Rozzie, just to see each other and not for business.

For after all, I thought, I have seventy pounds loose money for the furniture, and the house is to come. It seemed a mean thing, with Nina's memory before me, to make that poor struggler lose his best chance for lack of a few pounds ready cash. And I knew he would pay me back if he could.

So the end of it was I gave way to him enough to say I might make enquiries if I had time, and I took the address. And so I made time, and ran down to the old country before London and saw some old friends in Rackmill, and dropped in at Ancombe on my way to the station.

I had written to Miss Slaughter, the old lady who ordered the picture, to be sure she would be in. No wall, and no hall yet and Jimson had never been there. But the commission was true. Miss Slaughter had engaged him by letter. She told me she had subscribed two hundred pounds to the hall on a bargain that she should have the end wall for a picture.

She was a little pink-faced woman with a fichu, like granny in a song, white curls all round her head and blue eyes, with a sweet voice and sweetish ways. But I could see that she had a will and so I noticed how she said twice that the picture was to be paid for when finished. She said the 'f' so plainly, I knew that she meant it, and that she knew artists, or perhaps Mr Hickson had told her that Jimson was a slippery customer. She showed me the room she had for him, all white muslin and pink bows; and she told me that she would like punctuality at meals, but if Mr Jimson could not manage it, then he must say so, and she would arrange for him to get them by himself at his own convenience.

The more I saw of her the more I thought: 'This one is no fool and not so soft as she looks.' But then few old maids are. They can't afford to be soft.

I wondered how she would like Jimson's wall if she ever got it. But it came out that she had seen Mr Hickson's wall, and he had told her that it was the latest thing and a great work.

She said to me: 'I wanted the best for my hall' (she always called it her hall, though she had only given two hundred pounds for it out of a thousand

it was to cost) 'and if you want the best you have to take the best advice.
I always consult experts. It pays in the end. I got my lease here done by
the Lord Chancellor's own lawyer and I went to London for that electric
fire. You won't see another like it west of Bristol. My roses too – I wrote to
the President of the Rose Society and it cost me nothing.'

It was spring and raining, so I could not judge her roses. But I liked old
Miss Slaughter, for old maid as she was, she had branched out and kept
alive. But I thought, too, that I would not like to live with her for she would
have been the brass pot to any delf.

So I went away to Taunton, pretending that Gulley was to get his
luggage, and come back at the end of the next week. But the fact was, of
course, he had to buy paints and brushes, shoes and a suit, even pants and
vests and a tooth-brush. He had nothing except the rags he was in.

I wired his fare to Gulley that afternoon and down he came next day,
and we fitted him out. It was strange to see that man of nearly fifty, already
bald and grey, strip off his coat at the tailors and show his bare back
through the rags of his shirt. I blushed for his shame and my own folly in
not thinking before how he would be bound to have new holes. But he did
not blush. He was laughing all the time and making jokes with the shopman.
'I've lost my wardrobe and run a bit low,' he said. 'It's the great advantage
of being a duke that you need not mind appearances.'

I never saw a man in such flowing joy, or so sweet in it. He could not
say or do enough for me. While we were sitting in the loose box waiting
for them to bring suits to try on him (for he asked for ready-mades, to be
easy on my pocket and quick) he took my hand, gave it a little slap, and
said: 'I see you mean to make a good job of me while you're about it,' he
said.

So I said that he knew very well he had it in his power to be a well-
known artist and quite in the first rank, of country artists, at least, if he
would stick to his work, and not quarrel with his friends.

I dared to say so much because I saw he was in so sweet a mood, he
was open to a hint. For he only laughed and said I was quite right. He
could have been in the Academy if he had liked to keep up with the right
people and especially the right ladies, and tickled the freaks.

I asked him what he meant by that and he laughed and said: 'What did
you think of Miss Slaughter and her idea of being immortal?'

I said I hoped especially he would not quarrel with Miss Slaughter, who
seemed to me a very sensible woman, and would give him a nice home.

'Oh yes,' he said, 'I'll be good. But why do the freaks always run after
painters? I mean all painters, good or bad.'

I thought it might be because artists were also a little bit in the freakish
way, but I did not say so. I wanted to get Jimson in a good frame for settling
down. So I went on giving him advice, and looking very coolly on his smiles
and his philandering.

66

We stayed that night at Taunton in a temperance hotel, though Jimson proposed to me again, in the coffee-room, with six commercials in the room, using the hotel paper. I set him down so hard, he was serious for all the next morning. I locked my bedroom door that night, but it was never necessary. So all well. But I had been going to meet Rozzie next day in London for our lunch, and when I saw the trains would not suit, I sent her a wire, also wrote, giving the Taunton hotel for her answer. I wired: 'Kept on business, writing.' But the next morning, when Jimson and I were at lunch, waiting for his suit to be altered and the trousers turned up, who should walk in but Rozzie, as if she owned the place. Rozzie walked into all hotels like that. She could never forget that she had been in the trade.

Now though I loved Rozzie, she could not have come at a worse time, for she not only set me off, but Jimson. As soon as he saw her, he seemed to take to her ways, and began to make his chaffing jokes. Rozzie, of course, scorned him as she did all men, only more so, because he laid himself open and he delighted in it. He began to be so free with her that I thought she would box his ears, but she only glared at him and pushed out her front and said: 'My God, you make me sick.'

I could see she liked him, and both of them were at their best. Yet I was downright ashamed; a widow not six weeks, all in my blacks, and giggling till I choked. I knew it was wrong and that I oughtn't to laugh, but it was just as though I had a button in me, and every time Rozzie or Jimson touched it I had to laugh, if it hurt me. So it did hurt me. For I hate to laugh against my will.

There we were after supper in a little kind of snug behind the billiard-room, with some bottled beer Rozzie had got in from a public; all of us in a row on an old horse-hair sofa with its springs burst. First it was when the springs made noises under us that Rozzie made remarks, and do what I would, she set me off. Then Gulley was such a queer sight, the little spindle, between us two big women, bulging out over him, that it made us laugh to see him. Rozzie would shoot me a glance over his bald head and roll her eyes over him with a face that made me laugh till I cried.

Then he, quick as he was, would chirrup 'Mahomed between the Mountains' or the 'Widow's Cheese Mite' and Rozzie would fill up his glass and say: 'You're getting warm, Mr Rat – it must be the heat, I suppose,' and 'Take one, Mr Gulley, your temperature's going up. Don't burst anything.'

It was true that the man was hot. He was fizzing between us like ginger beer. He could not stop laughing and chattering. He squeezed us by the arms and said: 'The best pair in England and the finest four.'

'Four,' Rozzie said. 'He's seeing things.'

'I wish I could,' he would say, for as I say, he had just caught Rozzie's note and, indeed, he always had that side to him.

Rozzie was bigger than ever since the war, and her clothes worse. She was all in crimson and mauve that day and when she asked me what I thought of her dress and I said it was striking, at least, she answered me that it was a mistake. 'I got it on Monday in a fit of the cheerfuls, and I knew it was awful. But at least it makes a splash. And so ought you, Sally. What are you glooming at, you silly girl? Mind those blacks don't work into you and rot your guts. I'll never forget the time I was in my black. They ate into me till I was nothing but a dish-rag; no appetite, no spunk, no nothing. Why, I couldn't even think and was a regular cry-baby. You know, my dear, it wasn't for grieving over my Bill after his being paralytic nine years – a happy release for all. No, I cried because I was so fallen away and come down with those blacks. I tell you, when I went into magpie even, I picked up half a stone. But I never had my senses and my life again until the year was up. Colours are my religion, and I always say, Sally, people had better stick to their own religion for it always sticks to them and if they try to throw it off, as often as not it will turn back on their stomach and come out in spots. Well, believe it or not, the only time I ever had spots was in my blacks. And the doctor himself told me it was because my blood had taken a turn.'

Rozzie would say anything for a joke and she was free and bold. It was always a wonder to Matty and the girls how I could like Rozzie Balmforth; and often when I was away from her, it was a wonder to me. For she often made me angry as now when she pretended to think the worst of me and Jimson. She would say: 'I wouldn't blame any widow for getting a bit of fun. Hasn't she had enough trouble with her husband?' or 'It's never too soon to be happy.'

She would never give me the chance of telling her that I would scorn to live with a man, and when I said I shall be glad when I can get the man fitted out and well at work, she would look at me with her bold eyes, which stuck out of her head like a pigeon's, and say: 'I'll bet he's good at the work. The little ones are. The sap is tighter packed.'

It would have done me no good, but harm, to be angry with the woman or to go on my knees and swear that Jimson and I were no more to each other than brother and sister. What she wanted to believe, so she would think and say, and she always liked to think the worst. If she had had her way she would have talked only that, and a few music-hall jokes, like those ones about the sofa springs, and a little about drinking. And yet I was always glad to see Rozzie and to hear her roaring voice. It wasn't that she made me laugh, for often it hurt me to laugh at the way she put things, but she warmed me up with her go.

I don't know how it was, but to do anything with Rozzie, even to buy a packet of pins, was a living pleasure. She made the sun warmer and colours brighter and your food taste better; she made you enjoy being alive. When I was with Rozzie, I would watch myself laughing or drinking or eating or cutting a dash and I would say to myself: 'What a time it is.'

If my poor Nina made me remember God and brought up my soul when it had fallen flat, Rozzie was the one to make me thank Him for being alive.

34

Yet I was very cast down when the house was sold and the time came for me to leave Bradnall for ever, and join Rozzie at Brighton. The house sold better than we had expected, for they were going to pull it down and build over the garden. I had twelve hundred pounds clear, over the mortgage, and good hopes to get well started in my new life. But I always misliked changes and I knew that from that time the children would go their own ways, and that it was time for them to try their wings.

For even Edith was all in the air and never thought of me unless she had washing or sewing to be done quickly, or talked to me of anything but Chinese diseases, which horrified me. True, it was partly from affection, for she wanted to make me feel her value, but it was scorn too, to triumph over my nerves. Edith had plenty of bravery and I often thanked God for her backbone and her true religion, which had given her life a hope, in spite of her plain face.

So though I was broken-hearted on the platform seeing Bradnall for the last time; and Nancy cried, and Belle and Edith, God bless them, both came to see me off, in spite of all their work and parties, and did not, for once, scorn Nancy's softness before me, and end up with a quarrel; yet I knew it was God's will for parents to lose and suffer in the forties, and perhaps His meaning is to harden them off for the terrors of the grave.

So though I was down when I got to Brighton, I knew I mustn't give way to it; and the first thing I said to Rozzie was that we must get to work and find our hotel. For Rozzie and I had agreed to take on a little hotel together, for superior visitors, and Rozzie was very keen on it. With Rozzie to manage the guests and the bar and me to keep an eye on the catering, I thought we would make a fortune. But now I made a discovery. So true it is your best friends have three sides in the dark to every one you see. For Rozzie always had an excuse from coming to see a place and when I dragged her to it she would always find some fault with it. It was too big or too small or a tied house or no proper snug or no room behind the bar; or too much room and half a mile to walk for a double Scotch. It went on till I saw she didn't really want a place; she only thought she did, but when her brother-in-law, who was a sergeant-major, and one of the finest men I ever saw, came down to see us, and I asked him to give Rozzie a little push, he said: 'Me! I might as well push at a corporation bus. Bill could do it. Bill was the only man who could push Rozzie into taking a chance. But it took even Bill six months to get her into a motor, when motors came in, and she wouldn't telephone now to save her life. She's nervous, Rozzie – she doesn't like responsibility.'

So that was the end of our hotel. For who was I to push Rozzie if that man couldn't? Then I was indeed cast down, for how could I ever take an hotel or even a boarding-house by myself. I had been leaning on Rozzie to play the man with agents and all those widow-eaters.

I wondered now how I would live with nothing to do. But Rozzie and I had already got into a kind of holiday life, and though my conscience would prod at me, yet I was enjoying it. It always seemed to me that we were busy and it was not till you took thought that you saw that you were busy with pleasures only. We got up late and ate a good breakfast. Then we went out to breathe the sea air and catch an appetite, to do our shopping and look at the people. Then we ate a good lunch and rested till three. Then we walked in the gardens and looked at the people and got an appetite for tea and dinner. Or we had tea out and got our appetite on the way home. Then we had a good dinner and afterwards we went to a cinema or we played bridge with some nice ladies in the boarding-house and we knitted and talked. Then we went to Rozzie's room and drank a little port for night-cap and had a long good chat. Then we went to bed and slept till morning.

All this was a great pleasure, the sleeping, the eating, the walking and looking, the having nothing to do. I liked it so much that I thought I would never be tired of it.

The only fly was Jimson, for it turned out that after I left him at Taunton, he had got after Rozzie. He had tried to make Rozzie marry him and chased her all the way to Brighton and stayed a week pestering her.

'Yes,' said Rozzie, 'and he wanted to know my income too, to see if we could both live on it, and if my money was tied up. Talking of your widow-eaters, how's that? And no bones about it, the rat.'

Rozzie had got rid of him only the day before I came, not wanting to have me bothered.

But I hadn't been there a week before he came to see me too, and lay in wait for me at the pillar-box, not to let Rozzie catch him. I told him then I knew he had been after Rozzie, and he said that it was out of desperation because I wouldn't have him. And he would hang himself if I went on refusing him.

So I lost my temper and told him that if he did, it would be the loss of nothing but a rope, unless it could be used again, for hams. So he said yes, he deserved the worst I could say. But he did go off at last only begging me not to tell Rozzie he had been.

I had been angry with Jimson, but now when I heard nothing of him, I wished I had not set him down so hard.

35

I could not write to Jimson, for the one thing I feared was to bring him back to spoil my peace, especially in the fine weather we were having.

But he did begin to spoil it for me, only worrying if he had gone back to his work, and how he would live if he hadn't.

The upshot was I wrote to Miss Slaughter and asked her for a scarf I pretended I had left, saying that if she had not found it, then I had left it somewhere else and not to bother, and in a P.S. I wrote: 'I hope your wall is going on well.' Not a word about Jimson in case she told him she had heard from me.

When I had posted this letter then I said to Rozzie: 'That's the last time I'll bother my head about the fellow. I've done my duty, I should think, and more.'

'How much more?' Rozzie asked me.

I never knew a woman like Rozzie for turning everything. Yet she made me laugh and that was all I asked for. I suppose I laughed more that week than ever I did in my life before, and again I nearly laughed my hat off. I had to stop in the public gardens and lean against a tree. People must have thought I was drunk. So I was drunk, with laughing and something else; I don't know what, it was a feeling underneath like a big hiccup that wouldn't come up. It worried me, too, that feeling, and made me the quicker to laugh. I would laugh whenever Rozzie opened her mouth.

Even Rozzie laughed in those days, though not out. I never saw Rozzie laugh right out in her life but once, and that was when she lost all her money and her left leg in the same week. The best she would do in an ordinary way was a smile that came out just at the ends of her mouth, and you could see even that much was against her will. She would never do it unless she had had a couple of quarts. But in those days when we were both mad for some reason, with the sun and the great crowds and Rozzie had a new frock that fairly made the people point at her and call their friends, I saw her laugh three or four times. She would try to stop it, but up it came with a kind of choke. Indeed the first time she did it I thought she was going to be ill and I said to her quickly: 'Rozzie, I told you the port wouldn't lie with the chocolate,' so that she came back at me and said I'd called her drunk.

It was Rozzie's great pride that she'd never been drunk in her life. That and her foot and her hair and never being taken in or giving herself away, were all her pride.

I think she was ashamed of laughing and that's why she picked a quarrel with me about my hasty words. But she laughed again two or three times at the wild things we said and thought of, before the Monday when I came down for lunch and saw Jimson waiting for me in the hall.

Then I knew what the hiccup was lying on my chest, for I nearly turned and ran upstairs again. But I was the last to do a thing like that. I never had any presence of mind, so I just let manners carry me on to destruction and I went up to him and said: 'What, are you back again?'

He said nothing, but he looked so wretchedly at me that I felt guilty and asked after the work. But still he was silent. And nothing could have worried me more; it was such a change in him. I took him out to the Pavilion, not to see Rozzie, and then we looked at the iron palm trees which we both liked, and had a long quiet walk. He said he would never be fit for anything if I didn't marry him, and I said how could we be happy if he went on wasting his life.

So he said he would not waste it if I took him, and after all he had done some not bad pictures. 'There are Hickson's and Bond's and the dealers have some more.'

And I asked him what was that for thirty years of a man's life.

'What, indeed!' he said, looking sidelong. But I knew what he meant. 'You blame that on the people,' I said, 'but why should they buy your pictures if they don't like them?'

'No reason at all,' he said. 'I quite agree – I agree with every word, Sally.'

'Yes, but you think,' I said, 'that it's because they're too good for them, something new. But you could do them in a new way and still please them. It's like the fashions. A hat may be as new-fashioned as you like, but it must stick on a woman's head. You know very well my poor Matty would have taken that portrait if you had made it like. It wasn't because of the style he wouldn't have it but because of the bad likeness.'

'I've got a commission for a portrait now,' he said.

'But you won't do it or you'll twist up the poor man's face to look like a goose or a toad.'

'That's true,' he said, 'I might. This one looks very like a Yorkshire White. He's even got the eyes. Yes, I might bring it out.'

'But why will you do it?' I said. 'Everyone says how clever you are. Don't you want to be a success, or is it just to amuse yourself?'

'That's perfectly true, my dear Sall,' he said, 'to please myself.'

'Mr Jimson,' I said, 'I'm sure I've no business to give you sermons, but if there's one thing sure in this uncertain life, it is that no one can afford to please himself. I know it may seem to pay in the beginning, but where are you in the end? – without a friend or a crust. Especially for anyone in the arts. Because an artist lives only by giving pleasure.'

'Perfectly true,' he said. 'No doubt about it. Would you marry me, Sally, if I got another picture in the Academy or painted a royal portrait?'

I could see he was chaffing me, so I said: 'If it's a joke to you, it's nothing to me. A man who can joke about his own waste and ruin is not worth crying over.'

'That's true,' he said. He was surprised and kept looking at me as if I had pulled out a new feature on my face. 'That's very true,' he said, 'and it goes deep.'

Then we said no more for some time, and I saw that I had talked too much and abused him too much. For to abuse a man is a lover-like thing and gives him rights, which Jimson felt very well. For now he said that he would not press me, but at least would I come and stay over the week-end at Rose Cottage as a friend, and perhaps give him my hand and my arm again. Miss Slaughter wanted me very much, and she would be my chaperone.

And the upshot was, how could I refuse? For I was doing nothing at Brighton. Though when I told Rozzie, she said: 'You are done for, Sall; why, if you couldn't do without a man to fuss over, you must take that rat, beats me flat, which is another wonder in itself.'

Now whether I knew that I was going to my fate at Rose Cottage, or I had brought it on myself, I can't tell now, for since that boarding-house fell through I seemed not like a woman, but a truck, which goes where it is pushed and knows not why.

For, of course, the week-end turned into a week. And Miss Slaughter was at me every day, saying that I would be the making of Jimson, and what an honour to marry that great man. And Jimson was as good and sweet and serious spoken as any man in love. Nothing too much for me and all truly meant, because of his state. And then we could have our own rooms at Miss Slaughter's, or take a half house across the road where, as Jimson said, there was the latest stove for hot water, and a new porcelain bath.

So at the end of a week we were engaged. And yet I could not say I wanted it, but that it had come upon me.

36

We were going to be married at the Queensport Registry Office. Only Rozzie was to be there and Jimson didn't want even her. But I said I must have some real person at my wedding, if it was only in front of a counter.

I wrote to the girls, but only so that they should get it on the day after. I knew the trouble Nancy would make if it wasn't too late.

Now when at last the day was fixed, Jimson lost all his serious airs. He was so excited I had to laugh at him. He even looked different, you would have said he was full of clockwork, and when he walked his legs seemed to jump about as if he had St Vitus.

The same night that we posted the notice, he came to my room at one or two o'clock and tried to get into my bed. I was surprised at his impudence and told him to get out quick. So he apologized and said he had only come to say good night. The next night he was half in before I waked up, and I had to jump out and take him by the shoulders and fairly put him through the door. We made a bit of noise between us and Miss Slaughter came out of the bathroom. But she pretended not to see us. She was a sly one and meant Jimson to have me, like meat to a lion.

So I asked her next day for the key of my door, not that I was afraid of Jimson, but I wanted to show her that I wasn't giving way to his nonsense. She said there was no key. Yet I'd swear there had been a key a week before.

All that day Jimson was as black as night. No more smiles and jumps. He wouldn't come near me. He wouldn't eat either, and he never went near the hall. Miss Slaughter was in a twitter and kept looking at us as if to say: 'What have you done to my genius?' It was a miserable day and I thought: 'A nice lookout for a wedding.'

But I put a chair against my door. I was having no more nonsense. I stayed awake till two, for I said: 'I'd rather look like death than begin a serious thing like marriage and a holy sacrament by laying myself open to a villainy. My complexion will always come back to me, thank goodness, but not my self-respect, and this marriage is quite risky enough without beginning on the wrong side of God's law.'

And I paid no heed to Jimson's sulks. But in the afternoon I saw that the weather was clearing and I thought: 'There's no good in spoiling the whole day, especially when it may rain tomorrow.' So I said to him: 'I hope that's the end of your madness until we're man and wife. Then you know I'll never stint you of your rights.'

He swore it and I forgave him, and we were happy again just in time for the afternoon sun. We picnicked at the Point and bathed and lay in the sun. Westerpoint is a lovely place under the cliff by the lighthouse, but not where you can be seen, and the sand lies among the rocks so that you can have your private place and make a back and sit in comfort. It was June, before the trippers, and hot enough for August. The sun was so bright as a new gas-mantle – you couldn't look at it even through your eyelashes, and the sand so bright gold as deep-fried potatoes. The sky was like washed-out Jap silk and there were just a few little clouds coming out on it like down feathers out of an old cushion; the rocks were so warm as new gingerbread cakes and the sea had a melty thick look, like oven glass. I love the heat and lying in the sun and I know it makes me lazy and careless so I don't care what happens. So that my mind was laughing at little Jimson when he held my hand and told me he could make me so rich and give me furs and jewels; yet my flesh delighted in his kindly thoughts. So it grew sleepy and I forgot myself and he had his way, yet not in luxury, but kindness, and God forgive me, it was only when I came to myself, cooling in the shadow, that I asked what I had done. Then, indeed, I felt the forebodings of my misery, and punishment, and I was weighed down all the evening.

But though I jumped out of bed the next night when he came in to me, I thought it was not worth while to keep what little decency was left me, and to deny him what he thought so much of. So I got back again to him, as sad and mild as any poor girl that has no right to her own flesh and let him do as he pleased.

So it was every night. I even made it seem welcome to please the man, for I thought, if I must give him his pleasure, it was waste not to give him all that I could.

37

So on the Thursday week we went off by the early train to Queensport. The time of the wedding was eleven, and the train got in at half-past ten. Rozzie was with us and as we walked along together, arm in arm with Jimson in the middle, we girls both noticed that Jimson was very quiet and pale and Rozzie kept on making jokes about the young bridegroom and his virgin fears. But poor Jimson could not even laugh. Suddenly he asked us to come in with him to a public-house and take a drink. He looked so pale and queer that Rozzie said: 'It's not a bad idea. We don't want him to swoon on my bosom, and cut his face open. We'll all go in.'

'Not you, Rozzie,' he said, 'I just meant Sall.'

'Gooseberry,' Rozzie said, 'the giant gooseberry in his silly season.'

'Just a quick one,' he said, 'to put some spunk into the ceremony.'

'Go on,' Rozzie said, 'I'll pop into the public bar.'

So we went into the saloon bar, and Jimson asked for two double brandies. Then he pushed along the counter till we were at the far end and said: 'Sally, I've got a confession to make.'

I thought he was going to tell me about some more debts or some of his models. Not a bit. He said: 'I'm afraid there might be trouble about this marriage. You ought to be warned.'

'What trouble?' I asked him.

'I may have a wife already.'

'Do you mean Nina isn't dead?'

'Oh, yes, poor thing – but I had a wife before that, oh, a long time ago. In Glasgow.'

'But you married Nina, didn't you?'

'No, we weren't legally married. We just said we were. It's quite easy. If you like to do that.'

I was furious with him. I called him all the names and said that he had deceived me.

'I'm afraid so,' he said. He was looking quite green in his misery. 'My conduct is as bad as anything could be.' And so he went on begging me to forgive and saying how his only fault was loving me so much.

At last Rozzie put her head in to tell us we'd be late. 'There'll be no wedding,' I said, 'he's married already!'

'So he told me,' Rozzie said, as cool as you please. 'Well I'm glad it's off. I congratulate both of you,' and she began to make jokes about Jimson taking her instead if he would wait six months, saying she didn't mind bigamy in the winter.

I was too angry to laugh. I said we'd better get back to the station.

'You're not going to leave me,' Jimson said. 'You can't leave me, Sally, when all my fault is loving you so much. I told you I'll marry you.'

'And get seven years,' Rozzie said.

'I wouldn't mind.'

'Why, how can you talk so?' I said. 'Prison would kill you – you wouldn't be let draw there.'

That made him think and he said: 'Why should anyone find out?'

'I'll tell 'em,' said Rozzie, 'if Sara's such a fool as to take you on. All you want is her money.'

We went on arguing, and presently Rozzie said that if we were going to make a parliament out of it, we'd better sit down, and take something. So we went to a table and ordered some more brandies. Now, in talking, the thing got to look more ordinary and Jimson was proposing, as bold as a pie, that we should call ourselves married. 'No one ever questioned my marriage to Nina,' he said, 'and even her own parents never doubted that we were married. People don't ask to see your certificate – they take you on trust, unless, of course, you've got another wife or husband going about making trouble for you. And mine won't do that because she's pleased herself elsewhere.'

'Why didn't you divorce her?'

'Costs too much money and too uncertain.'

I said that if he got a divorce, I might think of him after all. For though I had not wanted to marry Jimson, yet so it was that I didn't want to go back to Brighton either, and that trolloping life. I felt let down as far as I have ever been.

They turned us out at last and we went to the hotel for lunch and had some beer with it. So we talked all day and kept on drinking till all at once I found myself so muzzy I was afraid to stand. Jimson, too, was quite drunk and kept on mixing up his words. Only Rozzie was solid as a rock, though her face got redder and redder and her voice louder. But though we were all shamefully drunk, we were sad and serious. Jimson kept on saying that he was a brute and a beast but that I was his star and his angel. He saw all the difficulties and the terrible position he had put me into, but he couldn't do without me. 'Of course,' he said, 'I know I'm no good – and you've every right to say that I'm not worth saving. I couldn't blame you. No, I should only thank you for the joy you've given me already.'

So Rozzie shouted that if I had given him joy, she hoped I had had some too, for that was all I would get out of this silly mess, and she kept on saying that all this love business made her vomit and that all lovers ought to be pole-axed. Love was the source of all the trouble in the world and she wished God had left Adam and Eve plain and not stuck the odd bits on to them.

At last they put us out and we went to look for an hotel. So Jimson went into the first. He jumped in so quickly that Rozzie said: 'He's up to something. You look at the register.'

We went in and sure enough he'd registered 'Mr and Mrs Jimson' for a double room and 'Mrs Balmforth' for a single one.

I began to protest, but the clerk looked queerly at me and Jimson said quickly: 'Rozzie and you can have it if you like.'

But I was dog-tired and said at last I did not care what happened. So we went up to bed as man and wife and Rozzie said only that I was a bigger fool than I weighed.

38

So we went for our honeymoon after all, not to Brighton, but Bournemouth, and it was a great success. Jimson had said that he could make me happy and I never knew any man so clever and pleasing when he chose. It was wonderful how little he needed to make me laugh with his stories and imitations.

'It's all nonsense,' I thought, 'to say he's difficult, and if he did beat Nina, she said herself it was only when he was driven mad with troubles. And no wonder with the way he's been treated by the world. All he wants is a little success and respect and money, which is every man's right, to ease his mind and take it off the stretch and please God he will have it now.'

I was bold, therefore, remembering that Mr Hickson was always the man of business, to write to him about commissions, and he wrote me a very nice letter arranging a meeting and saying that Gulley must have an exhibition. So I told Gulley one night when he was gamesome, and he laughed and said: 'Go on, my dear, and make my fortune. I appoint you managing director and subscribe myself yours truly.'

So he made a joke of it, but agreed with everything too. He warned me only that the last exhibition had been a failure.

'What?' I said. 'Did you have an exhibition?'

'Why,' he said, 'of course I did – in nineteen oughty four – it was the biggest joke of the year.'

I saw that he did not like to remember that exhibition, so I said that his art had been new-fashioned then, too new for the people, but now everyone was painting in modern.

'You're quite right,' he said, laughing, 'and if they laugh, let them laugh. You shall have your exhibition.' He proposed even to paint some portraits. 'I can always make money at portraits and they take no trouble – not the kind of portrait people want – and you and I could live like millionaires on five pounds a week and a couple of gallons a day – I mean we should have all we want.'

'So we could,' I said.

'And so we shall,' he said. 'I put myself in your hands and if I begin to get on my high horse and talk about art, give me a slap on the nose.'

It was true that he never talked about art with me, or religion either. Except to chaff me for mine and especially for going to early service. For he always said I went to seven o'clock service only because I hated getting out of bed. 'Like a woolly savage that cuts off his nose to please his idol.' God knows it may have been true, but I did not think so. For though I hated getting out of bed, yet I was never sorry when I was up and out, at that early hour, when the whole world looked as if it was new washed and waked and going to service itself; so quiet and calm. Even the sky, I thought, was like church windows. I mean the plain ones with glass like tapioca. And then, what an appetite for breakfast afterwards. Bacon and eggs is my favourite dish, but I can never eat it except on a Sunday when I have been to service.

I would have liked to take Gulley to service, for I thought a little steady religion might be good for him. But Gulley never talked seriously to anyone unless the fit took him. Then he would start off to any chance-met, in the train or a public, and often he would start a great argument. At Bournemouth he nearly had a fight in a public bar with a bus conductor, who held up the Government. I must say I agreed with him, for Gulley was quite against all governments. He thought all the badness and misery in the world came from governments, and that there would be no peace or comfort anywhere till we all went back to live like Adam and Eve in the Garden of Eden.

This seemed so mad that at first I thought it was one of his tricks, because he wanted us to play Adam and Eve when we were bathing at the Point. Just as poor Matty gave out the idea, and believed it when we first married, that children should be begotten in the early morning, when their parents were refreshed with sleep. Because the truth was, Matt's nerves were so upset in his first months that he could do nothing at all with me, poor darling, unless he had been asleep first, and took his nature by surprise. So that he would be scornful of nature and say that it was a nuisance and a trap, and he would do the thing in a rough way that hurt me, snorting or grumbling as if he hated it, only because he had to be quick before his nerves spoilt him again, and shamed him. For he would almost cry with shame when he had to shuffle off and pretend that he had meant nothing but good night or good morning.

So I thought that when Gulley talked of going back to Adam and Eve, he meant only to get me to go naked before him, making his wish a religion. But I found out I was wrong, for he would talk in the same way to anybody, and get excited and shout against the laws. What I wondered at, after only three days with Gulley, was why he had not been locked up long ago. Not that he was mad with me. But he was mad to the world. So I noticed what a lot of mad people there were and what a lot of nonsense talked, quite as bad as Gulley's, and no one troubling their heads about it. Go you about with a man like Gulley and you will see what nonsense people listen to, as calmly as you please, and swallow every word, and then bring out some nonsense of their own.

Yet Gulley, though he always laughed at me before and after, as he laughed at the world, did sometimes speak seriously to me on our honeymoon. 'Look how happy we are,' he would say, 'Why? Because we don't care a damn for the law.'

And little as he was, and thin, Gulley never seemed to flag; you would have taken him for a young boy in his first hot youth, and the fiercer he was, the gayer and the more full of ideas. He would keep me awake half the night and have me up with the birds to bathe, or really, I think, to draw me. For though I hated to be seen naked, even by Gulley that was professional, almost like a doctor, and though I always refused to be his model, except for the head and arms and as much as a decent woman would show, yet he was always sketching at me and always inventing new tricks to spy on me and draw me.

Sometimes indeed he would rage at me when I would not sit and shout that I was a vulgar middle-class woman full of silly prejudices, still I felt that modesty was not given to a woman except for some good reason.

Yet at that time we had few fights and made them up soon and then we would be astonished at ourselves, so that I caught myself laughing and thinking: 'Well, whatever is coming to me of trouble, I am the luckiest woman to have such gaieties and a new loving husband, at my age.'

So trouble did come, in full measure. But I shall never forget our happiness at Bournemouth. For if Gulley and I agreed in anything it was in the same enjoyments, in laughing at nothing, in eating well, in bathing and sitting in the sun; we even agreed in liking to drive in an old landau they had along the front to Boscombe and back. I had always loved, from my rich days, the swing and jiggle of a carriage, and the clop of the horse and the back of the coachman and the shine of his hat, but I never enjoyed anything so much as driving there by the sea. For the sea itself, though gloomy from a boat, is always lively from the land. Even if it should be flat, on a hot day, yet it always has a sparkle. It never stops winking sunshine. But when it has waves, then it is like a whole ballroom full of heads bobbing up and down, and you would think the waves falling on the sand were the swish of skirts in the old grand waltz, not too quick, but always turning. The Blue Danube. But even at night we had to walk along it by the sand and Gulley would model corpses or lions or dead horses. Then we would sit down against the horse or lion, between its legs, and watch the sun going down like a hot penny through green and yellow like snapdragon fires; you could see right through them into the sky behind, and above the sky was like a Dutch bowl, blue delf. Then the waves seemed to come up suddenly all glittering with hundreds and thousands, like cakes for Easters and birthdays, and try to go on for ever, and only get so far and break themselves to pieces with a mournful noise, and fall back with a long sigh. It made me feel sad to see such waste of their work and to think of it going on for ever, but then it was a comfort too, to think that they would always be there, whether anyone was looking or not; such is the bounty of providence, to pour out pleasures.

I daresay only looking at the sea was one of our great pleasures in that month, which was, I think, the happiest in my life. And I shall always owe it to Gulley. Not that Matt was not worth six of Jimson and not that he did not make me happy, but that we were young together and did not know how to relish the sweet joys of only walking and talking and looking about us, and eating and sleeping, in amity and kindness. Neither did we store up the memory of our pleasure, whatever it was, so that I have still but a confused notion how I felt as a bride, and how we passed a whole three weeks together with so little to talk about and so little to do; whereas Jimson and I caught up every moment, every bright day, every laughing face that passed, and every calm night, and rejoiced in it to each other and put it away in our minds. Even years afterwards when we were at peace, we would bring out some trifle of that short time and admire it and enjoy it again, and live again by it in the time of our innocence.

39

My daughters would tell you that Jimson took me for my money and robbed me of it and then left me on the streets without a penny, but it is not so. It only seemed so. Rozzie was shocked because I paid the hotel bill at Bournemouth. But Jimson had no money then. He said that he would owe me, and if he forgot, it was only because his head was so full of his work that he never thought of bills and debts. Even on our honeymoon, though he made me so happy, I knew his eye was always picking something up and his mind was always turning over colours and shapes. So in the last days, when I began to ask if we would take rooms at Ancombe or board with Miss Slaughter, as she proposed, he would answer: 'Just as you like.'

'What will suit you best?'

But his eye would be on somebody passing, or on a tree in the gardens, and he would say: 'Did you see that old woman – she had one eye half an inch higher than the other, and twice as big,' or 'You could do something with that pine – the red and green are the same tone as the sky.'

But though, to be honest, up to the last day of that month, we were both on fire, and would even walk hand in hand like the children on the piers; yet as soon as we got in the train, Jimson seemed to forget all about me. Out came his book and he was drawing all the way. When we got to Queensport, he was still drawing, and I had to get the porter and find the luggage.

It was comic to see the change in him between one night and the next morning. For one day he had not been able to keep away from me and the next day he did not notice me at all. So he went on all that week, drawing all day, and whistling to himself, or at the Hall, measuring, and trying new kinds of plaster to see how they would take paint. He would often draw all the evening too and come to bed at one o'clock yawning like a dog, and fall in beside me and snore all night like a horse, without so much as saying good night. The bolster was not less to him, something to lean against, or push into some other shape, as he wanted.

I was surprised but pleased, too. For it was as it should be. A honeymoon is one thing, and life is another. I was only surprised when I looked at it, because Jimson had turned so sensible and ordinary.

But as he couldn't bring his mind to look for rooms, we stayed on at Miss Slaughter's, and in the end we agreed to her plan and boarded with her.

40

I did not like beginning another life in an old maid's house, who thought that an arm-chair was anything with arms; and though I had liked the idea of Ancombe since it was in my own country, I had never liked the look of it.

A long twisted street on a high road beside the shore of the Longwater. Plain brick houses and a tin chapel; the church small and ordinary, and only two shops. Then it was close to the Greenbay and Westerpoint and Bluerock sands so that from May to October there was nothing but buses and cars, taking the summer visitors. Indeed when I first went to Ancombe the dust stood up all day so high you could see it from the fields, over the roofs, like a fog, and even at night when the moon touched it, you could see it like a fine smoke. But when the cars got worse, they brought one advantage, that the roads were tarred. Indeed, the tarred roads did good in all the country because the hedges were not smothered, as they used to be, as soon as the leaves were out. Even the may, in those old days, for all its glitter and sparkle, would look like dirty flannel long before it put out its flowers.

So in Ancombe we blessed the tar, in spite of its smell, which got into the very tea, for it meant that we could open our windows sometimes, even in the hottest weather.

Miss Slaughter's house was right on the road between the new Hall, which was still going up, and the doctor's. But though I did not like the first look, I thought better of the last, for there was nothing behind the houses except the garden and Miss Slaughter's was on the south side, so that her garden ran down to the water. I have always loved a big peaceful view and I think this was the best I ever knew; first the garden, which was nothing but a few rose beds and then a strip full of gooseberries and cabbages. And then a slope down across a piece of meadow, which belonged to the garden; and then the water which was half a mile across, and on the other side good arable fields in all their colours, changing every year. I could see out of my back window just how it went with each of them, in roots and wheat and barley and oats, round again to the ley, and I could guess which was the better land and which was the farmer's favourite and which never got its rights, being too far off from the road or having awkward gates.

Morning, midday, and evening, except in a sea mizzle, there were the grandest skies you ever saw; and sometimes, even in a mizzle, if it was thin, I loved the view of clouds melting into it like suds in water, and the sky coming through on top like a touch of blue, and the Longwater like frosted glass, and the fields on the other side as bright as jellies, strawberry on the new plough, and gooseberry on the swedes and lemon on the barley. Then if you had it thundery over on the south next towards the sea, and the morning sun behind, you would have thought Longwater clear glass and the fields bits of coloured glass, in a black wall, with a light behind. They were as bright as my lampshade in a dark room.

The other thing I liked at Ancombe was the yachts going past, often to race and often with girls steering. It was pleasant to sit and wonder if they were being courted by the men, and if such girls, with their manly knowledge and their sports, would make better wives than us old ones. Belle's tennis, I thought, had done little enough for her, and Nancy was the happier woman, for all her silliness. But then Belle had been too choosy, and Nancy, for all her silliness, had never valued herself too high.

82

Then, too, though Ancombe had no shops, to call shops, there was a daily bus to Yeovil; and what was better, every year great steamer yachts came to Ferry for the regattas and brought ladies in the newest fashions. It was better than a visit to Paris to see them in the little village streets, coming and going from some party on shore. I never saw such beautiful coats and skirts as in that small place, fitting like a coat of paint. I knew of course that they had been measured by a man over a special foundation, and to fit the stays, and I daresay some of those smart women dared not eat butter, and I'm sure they could not lift their arms. But it was a great pleasure to see such a beautiful cut, and women turned out so smooth and polished that they had not a hair turned up, not the least speck on their shoes. You would have thought they had a new pair every day and ordered them by dozens, which perhaps was the truth. I liked to think it so, for I always liked a thing well done.

41

Yet in all the peace of the garden at Rose Cottage, I never had much time to sit down and think of myself or what I was doing. I did not read either, for I had forgotten to bring away my books and somehow they were put in the sale, or perhaps thrown away. I never liked any others but my Woodview books which I had from Miss Maul or which I bought for myself.

But I wouldn't have found time to read then, for, apart from the curtains and cushion covers, I was working up the exhibition. I had to write to Paulson and Robb, the landlords who had kept poor Jimson's pictures; and also arrange dates with Mr Hickson.

I saw Mr Hickson one day by appointment and he was very pleasant. But he had grown very old since the war and all the fire was out. He was like a father or uncle to me now, and liked only to be kindly and to gaze and talk, in his own sad way.

I asked him one question that had troubled me. 'Was Jimson a genius?'

'Of course he is,' Mr Hickson said. 'No doubt about that.' But Mr Hickson was one of those men who are so honest about some things that even business ideas and politenesses will not quite skin them over. And he was always honest about pictures.

So after thinking a minute, he pulled himself up and said: 'To be quite honest, Sara, I don't know and I can't tell. I don't think anyone can. We're too close to him. In a hundred years perhaps or even fifty it will be quite obvious.'

'Fifty years,' I said. 'But we'll all be dead. What good will it do him to be famous when he's dead?'

He smiled at me and said: 'From your point of view, I suppose it's no good at all.'

But I wasn't to be laughed at even by Mr Hickson, and I said that I was thinking of Jimson himself. For it was very hard for a man to be happy in his work if he got nothing at all from it, not even a decent living.

I put it as low as I could because I knew Mr Hickson, honest as he might be, had a business eye, and took but a cold notice of religion or people's rights. 'I'm not too old,' I said, 'to be tired of my life and I mean to enjoy it if I can. But how will I enjoy it if my husband is always in misery and wasting his talents?'

Mr Hickson liked that very well. He said: 'You're a very sensible woman still, Sara, and I'll do anything I can to help you, that is, your husband, to establish himself and have a successful exhibition.'

This agreement made me very happy because I trusted Mr Hickson. That kind of cold man nearly always does what he says, and besides, I remembered what Jimson had said, that Mr Hickson had invested in him and would like to see his stock rise. One way or both, I thought, Mr Hickson would give us a push in the right direction.

42

But the money I had meant for the exhibition went elsewhere. Now on the very first day we came to Miss Slaughter's, she began to get after my money. She said what a pity it was the builders hadn't finished the Hall yet, and that the subscriptions were so slow in coming in. Then she looked out of the window and said: 'I believe you did subscribe to the Hall – do have some more cake.' Knowing, of course, that I had not subscribed anything.

The next thing was she left a subscription list in my room, and an appeal, and then set the vicar at me.

Miss Slaughter was mad about the Hall; that is, she was mad to get her picture done and it could not be done till the Hall was finished. I don't believe she ever thought of anything else. I thought it was wonderfully kind of her to take us in, with our own bedroom and sitting-room, and all board, for only fifty shillings a week; but I believe she would have taken us for nothing only to have Jimson well in her grip till the picture was squeezed out of him. She had heard that artists were sometimes very slow to finish a work; and so she was running after him all day. How was the design going; had he everything he wanted?

Of course Gulley said that the picture was going to the devil and what he wanted was a nice desert island with five thousand a year.

The poor body took it like a rock. She was ready to bear anything. But she tried a new plan. She said that she wanted the rooms in six months, for a married niece, so the picture must be finished then. The Hall would be finished in a month and Jimson would have five more to put his design on the wall.

The next thing was she offered what she called a premium, of twenty pounds extra, if the picture was finished within three months after the Hall was ready for it.

I used to dodge her to keep away from her hints and questions. Yet I was sorry for her too. She was old and she had nothing to show for her seventy years. Now somebody, perhaps Mr Hickson, had put this idea into her head and it had changed her whole life round; she had got a fancy for doing something big and important after all. So she had come out of her shell, and pushed and schemed till, only for her two hundred pounds, she had got the right to put up a Jimson picture in the Hall. I admired her for it. I know I could never have done such a thing, against the will of the churchwardens and all the parishioners. But I suppose it is true that old age is a kind of madness in itself which either sends you wool-gathering like a child, or makes you run after some crank as if there was a hornet behind you. Indeed, so there is a hornet, for you know you must die soon, and perhaps get nothing done after all. So I admired Miss Slaughter and pitied her too, while she fretted about Jimson's whims and the builders' strikes, and the subscribers who would not pay. I was told that she was going madder and that only a year before she had still kept up the garden and given tea-parties to other old ladies. Now the garden was going so much to waste that she was glad to let me dig it and cut it, and prune her roses, only to get the flowers.

I say Miss Slaughter got after my money from the first day. But I told her that it was all in stocks and bonds, and that even if I wanted to sell them out the lawyers would make such a fuss that my daughters would come down upon me and stop it.

Then I saw another side to Miss Slaughter, for she went at me like a dog at a rat. 'I'm surprised at you, Mrs Jimson,' she said, 'that you don't think more of your husband's work. No Hall, you know, no picture.'

'But Miss Slaughter,' I said, 'if I pay for the Hall and you pay for the picture, we might as well both keep our money.'

'I'm not suggesting that you pay for the Hall, but advance some small sum to keep the builders at work.'

Miss Slaughter was always a tiger after loose money. She would even watch the corn merchant's lorry go up the road to some farmer, and call on him the same day for a subscription.

She caught me at last on Oldport fair day, where so many girls have fallen. She was at me all that day, knowing I had drawn five pounds that evening for our expenses, and a car to and from, not to be squeezed in a bus which we both hated. But we dodged her then by going from the public-house at the corner.

Oldport fair was always our favourite. For first the town is so pretty between the high Oldport hill, hanging right over it, and the creek. Then it has a garden full of trees in the middle as well as trees all along the promenade. And always some yachts and often some navy ships, small ones, in the creek; and on fair days they dress themselves with lamps. That year the navy ship had lamps from the very tip of the front, over both masts and down again to the stern. The promenade was gay with lanterns and there were hundreds of lanterns among the trees in the garden.

On the promenade it was quiet, only the couples walking and whispering together, and if you looked over the wall the water was quiet, rolling up and down against the wall just as usual, and not a sound from the yachts or the ship. Just one spark where a sailor was smoking his pipe on one of the yachts. Then you went through the trees and the crowds got thicker and in the middle there was a dance; young men in their shirts and girls in their new muslins and prints, dancing seriously and carefully as they do in the country. No romps. Even the drunks were keeping their bodies sober and you could see the madness only in their eyes, and the beer only when it poured down their cheeks.

So you came to the fair itself and the darts and the roundabouts and the shooting-galleries with their pretty girls. There, of course, it is allowed to romp, and even the sober were bumping and tickling each other with feathers, or screaming on the horses. Five or six organs playing different tunes and all the boys blowing whistles and trumpets. It went to your head and made you mad. It's no wonder, I thought, that nine months from Oldport is the time for sudden babies and hasty marriages. Had I not screamed and romped myself, as a girl, and been squeezed and kissed too, and felt myself go careless to all but joy. Was it not luck, or only my mother chasing me home, that saved me, on fair days, from my nature? But then what I loved at Oldport, when feeling so mad and joyful, and on that night with Gulley we had both been drinking beer too, was to stand among all the music and lights, and to raise my eyes to the hill behind and see the hedges against the sky and a cow nodding along; and behind them the sky as deep blue as sugar-paper, and yet as bright and clear as the water in a chemist's sign.

I said to Gulley as he hung on my arm, with his hat falling off the back of his head like any labourer's: 'How quiet and peaceful it is – the cows don't even turn their heads at the rockets. You ought to paint it for the exhibition.'

But Gulley only laughed and carried me off to the Noah's Ark, which was the fastest of all the roundabouts. It nearly shook my clothes off. So when we were coming home up the village street arm in arm, it seemed to us both that the world was not big enough for our joys. Gulley kept on laughing and squeezing me and calling me his fair girl, and my head was so full of lights and faces, and the quiet boats and the sky, and my flesh was so full of the dust and the warmth and the beer and the shaking, that I was like another person in my own dream.

So when we saw Miss Slaughter's light, Gulley said: 'The old freak is sitting up for us.'

I was angry and said that she would be coming at me again about the cheque. 'She says if the builder doesn't get a week's wages by Saturday, he'll have to pay the men off.'

'Well, why don't you let her have it?' said Gulley. 'It's only fifty pounds.'

'And she's only giving you a hundred for the whole picture.'

'And if there's no Hall, I won't get that. All right, you're the business manager. Come on, old girl – I'd rather push a horse uphill.'

Indeed I was hanging back for fear of Miss Slaughter. I did not want my happiness broken in half by her mad look. But Gulley dragged me in and she came out in her blue dressing-gown, with rabbit fur round the edges, and said: 'Oh, Mrs Jimson, I wanted to tell you there's another note from the builder.'

'Go on, Sall,' Gulley said with his hat still on: 'Sign on the line and come to bed. It's all right, Miss Slaughter – she's just getting her cheque-book.' So, I don't know how it was, I went in and signed for fifty pounds. And yet I know it did not seem like weakness at the time, for I remember laughing as I wrote and thinking 'So much for you' and signing my name with a dash. So I don't believe I gave it another thought, neither that night nor the next day, till I had a letter from the bank and another from my lawyer. Then there was a great fuss about selling out some shares. But the thing was done and I was not going to be pestered to death. I got upon my high horse and I told the lawyer to sell the shares and to pay the bank, and the bank to pay the cheque. I believe I was too happy to bother my head about money.

43

Now the exhibition came on again. Mr Hickson, seeing I could not take a gallery, offered to have the exhibition in his own house. At the same time, he got us a commission to paint a general called Foley, medals and all. But when next day I asked Gulley to fix dates with Hickson and for the exhibition, and a sitting with Foley, he always forgot. Yet he was mooning about again and doing nothing. Seeing that he had stopped work, I thought, here was a good chance to get him to attend to business. But not a bit. When I spoke of this at breakfast, saying: 'Heavens, I've forgotten that letter again,' he only stared at me and said nothing.

Then he began to follow me about. When I went into the kitchen he followed me there, and when I went to the village for stores he came after me into the very grocer's and stood staring at me.

I was buying a few sweets for myself, and I thought perhaps that annoyed him. I was still eating too many sweets, but I always found it hard to stint myself of sweets.

So I said to him: 'You see, I still have a sweet tooth – what a monster I shall grow unless I take care.'

'Go on,' he said, 'eat the shop.'

So when we came out I said: 'What have I done?'

'Nothing,' said he.

'Why are you angry at me? Tell me what's wrong, at least, for I can't bear dumb bad feelings. They spoil the whole day.'

'I'm not angry,' he said. 'Are you trying to pick a quarrel?'

'Good gracious,' I said, stopping in the street, and the words popped out: 'That's what it is.'

'What what is?'

I had thought only that here was the flaw. For I had thought that Jimson had fallen out with Nina, angel as she was, because only she was not the type for him; too flat and too religious. But now I saw that I had been too conceited. It wasn't Nina, it was Jimson.

'What is what?' he said, so I answered him only: 'I'm not going to quarrel about nothing – I have better things to do.' For Miss Slaughter's cook had gone off and I was doing the work.

But he was determined to have his quarrel, and as any wife knows, it takes only one to do that. He followed me to the kitchen and tried this and that, my doing the cook's work, my being put upon by Miss Slaughter and so on. I said that I liked cooking and that we owed so much to Miss Slaughter that we could well overlook a little cleverness in taking small advantage.

So then, suddenly, he began on the portrait painting and said: 'That was pretty clever of you to get me tied up with old Foley.'

'You aren't tied to a day,' I said, 'there's a whole month for it.'

'Yes,' he said, 'a good idea. Why shouldn't it work?' and he began to walk about the kitchen and say how he could paint a family portrait in three sittings. 'Forty guineas a time – two or three a month – say, fifteen hundred pounds a year – and three weeks in every month for my own work. Do it all the better perhaps for coming at it with a fresh eye. I'm not one of those half-baked amateurs who thinks he has to wait for inspiration. Inspiration is another name for knowing your job and getting down to it. I can paint anything you like any time, and why not. I've learnt my job. I'm a painter, a working man, a tradesman. Do you know, Sall, I wish the very name of artist was abolished. It's simply a bad smell, it's not even good English. Painter is the English word, or limner. Well, I'm a working painter. Tell me what to paint and I'll paint it.'

So he went on until he carried me away and I forgot my doubts. I knew he had started in a bad mood, but I thought that he had talked himself round as anyone might, especially when his mind is in a loose quarrelsome state, not knowing what it wanted.

'It's not that we need the money just now,' I said, to keep him smooth, 'but it's always something to know where to find it if one wants it.'

'I think I'll write to old Foley now and ask him for a sitting.'

'But there's his own letter waiting for an answer,' I said, 'I'll get it for you.' Floury as I was and the oven waiting, I ran into the sitting-room to get the letter out of the table drawer.

Then I felt Gulley behind me and a feeling coming out of him; I did not know what kind. So I jumped round and then he was grinning in my face. 'You brought that off pretty well,' he said, 'you and Hickson.'

'But it was you said you wanted to write.'

'My dear Sall, you've never had any other idea but to turn me into a money-maker with a balance at the bank and two motor cars. Well, I give you warning – stop it and stop it now. That's all I ask. Not to be nagged.'

So then I lost my temper and said: 'That's one thing I would never do. I'd scorn to nag – and I scorn a nagger.'

'On the contrary, you've never stopped nagging at me – why, you nag me even when you're asleep. Your face says: "Go on and make some money and be somebody in the world." That's the word, isn't it? That's the way you think. Well, stop thinking. I won't be thought at.'

'And I won't be talked to like that. I'll not stand it.' I tried to walk out, but he got across the door. We looked at each other and I could see that he was blue and green with rage and shaking all over.

I tried to push past him and at once he hit me on the nose with his fist. I was so astonished and so furious that I could not say a word. I caught him by the wrists and pulled him from the door. I wanted to shake him and box his ears. But suddenly he jerked away from me and walked out of the room. I went upstairs in a rage. When I looked in the glass my nose was bleeding and I was afraid I might have a black eye, too.

'That's enough,' I said, 'no more of Mr Gulley.' So I packed a bag quickly to get away before he came after me with his apologies or before Miss Slaughter came to make the peace.

44

You may say perhaps that I brought it on myself by interfering with Gulley. Now to interfere with any man of set ways is dangerous and stupid and I never did interfere with Gulley, for he himself wanted that exhibition and the portraits. He himself wanted to be known and to make money, for he had admitted that very thing at Woodview when he said he wanted to be in the Academy. And as for nagging, he invented that for an excuse.

'No,' I said, 'I'll never go back to be called a nagger.' And as soon as my bag was packed, I went downstairs to catch the bus. I meant to send for my boxes.

I had half an hour to wait for the bus and all that time I was in a fever that Gulley or Miss Slaughter would come after me. But they did not. So I went to Queensport and took a room for that day at the King's Arms.

Queensport was a pretty little town going up on a steep hill with a church at the top and the Longwater at the bottom. There are quays there and lamps and some squares of grass; a ladies and gentlemen, and a cinema. A few ships bring coal to the pier. I liked Queensport and I thought that I might spend a day there while I decided what to do; whether to go to Rozzie or visit the girls, or to make some new plan. But I woke up so miserable that though the day was beautiful and the hotel better than most, I could hardly even bring up a smile for the girl that brought my tea and I ate nothing for breakfast. I don't know how it was, but I felt as if I had no business to be there alone in Queensport. When the bell rang in the hall, I jumped as if someone might be coming for me; not, of course, a policeman, but somebody from a church or chapel, a curate or a minister perhaps, to ask what I was doing there, as if I was a runaway from vows.

I went to send a wire to Rozzie, but when I had written it I thought: 'Rozzie will say, I told you so and then how she will abuse Gulley. He's bad enough, I daresay, but not so bad as Rozzie makes out. She can never be fair to any man.'

I thought too: 'And I can't go to Nancy's either, for what will she say when she knows that I have broken with my husband after six weeks. Of course, she will take my part, the poor darling, but she will wonder at me.'

But the worst of that terrible day was walking about and wondering what I would do. Every minute my mind was hopping back to the kitchen at Rose Cottage, saying: Now's my chance to get a new colander, or, perhaps they will have a bain-marie in this place, or, I must try Jimson with salmon in pastry. For though Jimson was the kind of man who could live on happiness and mouldy crusts if you let him, he had a great taste for good food. He would even sit in the kitchen till a soufflé was ready, to eat it before it began to lower its head and sink from the height of its glory. It had been a pleasure to cook for Jimson. His senses were as quick as a girl's and he loved the art of it. He would admire my touch with the pastry and say that I ought to be a chef. Whereas my poor Matt had never liked to talk about cooking in case he might hurt my feelings or call to the girls' mind that I had been a cook.

But now when I saw something in a shop and said I'll give him lobster tails, or, what about a bombe surprise if I had a thermos to keep the ice in, I would be stopped at once by the thought that I had left the brute.

Then when I thought backwards of those two letters lying in my drawer, and all that might have come from them, Jimson's success and happiness, and the use of his talents, I could have knocked my head on the walls.

Yet I hated Gulley. I hated his cruelty and spite. I was still raging at the man, and the very thought of his striking me in the face when I never even expected it made my bones freeze.

I made up my mind to go to Rozzie, let her be all-wise as she liked and use her nasty tongue on Gulley. I wired to Miss Slaughter for my trunks and went to get my ticket to Brighton. But it was a lovely afternoon and suddenly I felt gay. I said: 'I'll stop till tomorrow and take the early train. It's a better one. No fear of Miss Slaughter catching me because she can't catch the bus today and I'll be gone before the bus comes tomorrow.'

So I had a good tea and afterwards I walked on the quays. The seven lamps were lighted and there were about a dozen boys and girls walking up and down, in twos and threes, the boys together and the girls together, in their best clothes. They pretended not to see each other and when they passed they put their faces close together and laughed or talked loud, just like the boys and girls at Brighton or Bournemouth. But they were quieter-looking, and had thick boots instead of fancy shoes, and they seemed happier too, in themselves and more enjoying. I suppose they had less amusement and did not expect so much, more perhaps than anyone could get.

There were three old men on one seat under a lamp, looking at the water and talking about fishing, and the old woman who looked after the ladies' lavatory had her arms crossed over the rail and kept looking at me as if to say: I'm ready for you. I was the only visitor. It was like a real sea front, only so quiet and small it made you want to laugh and cry.

I didn't want to go into the hotel; I felt so full of this strange kind of happiness. My feet trod on air, and yet I was fearfully sad, as if I was saying good-bye to my youth. I said: 'It's the boys and girls playing round each other as I used to play when I was a village girl.' But I knew it was not.

45

At last I went back to the hotel, and there, sitting in the hall waiting for me, was Miss Slaughter. The moment I saw her I knew that I had really as good as sent for her and if she had not come, I would have waited till she did.

Of course, she begged me to go back. She said that Gulley had been nearly mad when they found I had gone and she was terrified of what he might do to himself. She had brought a letter from him, but it was short and flat. It said nothing about hitting me, but only that he wanted me back and that he would have come for me himself if it hadn't been for an important engagement with the architect to discuss a new plaster.

'Pretty cool,' I thought, swelling, and I made a great to do. But, of course, I knew I was going back, and so did Miss Slaughter. Yet I'll say of her: She was a lady and knew what was due to me. Though she saw (as I saw) from the first minute that I was longing to be home again, and knew perfectly well that I had sent for my trunks only to get her to bring me home, she went on apologizing for Gulley, and telling me that I had every right to leave him, for the next hour. She considered my pride and I needed it, for I felt low and mean. I am not a crying woman, but all the way back in the bus I was flooding with tears. They did not come out of my eyes, but my whole blood was swimming with their bitterness, and my heart was drowned under their salt. For I felt that I was leaving behind me the last of my youth and all good hopes before I needed. I was wasting my poor self, so healthy and strong and full of life, so ready to enjoy that my whole flesh would often seem waiting to laugh at nothing at all, only Rozzie putting on her stays or a man in a street with a long face and a pork-pie hat.

So I sat feeling like a martyr going to the torturers and slow hard death, and all for what? There was nothing religious nor any sense in it. God knows, I thought, you're a floating kind of woman; the tide takes you up and down like an old can.

I promised myself, at any rate, to put master Gulley in his place. But not a bit of it. For when I came in, there he was sitting at his table ruling little squares all over a new drawing. He did not even get up for me, but called out: 'Hullo, old girl! There you are, at last. You gave me a fright, but I felt sure you wouldn't do anything silly. Just a minute while I finish squaring off this sketch.'

'So ho,' I thought, 'is that his line. I'll show him,' and I answered in a sulky kind of voice: 'No hurry at all.'

He began to hum and swing his foot. He was full of his drawing and he always hummed ruling off squares. So I said: 'I see you've got started again – perhaps that will improve your temper.'

'Started!' he cried. 'I never stopped.'

'Isn't that a new drawing?'

'I put it down today, but it's an old idea of mine.'

But I meant to take a strong hand and I said in the same voice: 'And what about Foley's letter? I suppose you never answered it?'

He gave me a look as if to say: 'She dares to bring that up again,' then he laughed and said: 'To be honest, I forgot about it – but you're the business partner, aren't you?'

'It must go off now.'

'There's no post.'

'It must catch the eight o'clock tomorrow.'

'All right – tell me what to say and I'll say it.'

'And the letter to Paulson.'

'Won't that wait?'

'No, it won't. That's more important than the other. How can you have an exhibition without pictures?'

He went on ruling and said nothing. He had a kind of smile and I knew that he meant to get out of the letters if he could. But I was hard and bitter still. I thought: 'If I'm to be hit, at least I'll stand no more nonsense. If he treats me like that, I'm not going to treat him like glass.'

When he drew the last line, he jumped up and came to me where I was leaning against the wall and threw his arms round me as far as they would go. 'Welcome home,' he said, but he was still laughing at me and he kept looking at my nose and laughing at that, too.

'Yes,' I said, 'but things are going to be different.'

'How's the old potato?' he said.

'If you mean my nose, it's no better for being punched, and it won't be punched again. That's one of the things that is going to be changed.'

'Punched,' he said, 'who punched you on the nose? Where is the brute that raised his hand against a woman? But I thought you might have knocked it against something when you rushed into me like that. I felt a distinct blow.'

'It's not a joke,' I told him, 'as you'll find out if you do it again. I'm a great deal stronger than you are and I have a temper too.'

'The elephant never forgets,' he said, laughing.

'How could I forget?'

'You won't, anyhow,' he said. 'Trust a woman to keep her mementoes. Come, Sall, aren't you going to be nice to me. I've missed you fearfully. I couldn't sleep last night with the draughts all round me.' So he went on half chaffing and half serious. He could not make me laugh because I was too sad, knowing what was in store for me. But he went on buzzing about me with his compliments and his jokes till I could not go on using a sulky voice, for it would make me ridiculous. He insisted on helping me to undress and when I was at the dressing-table brushing out my hair, he perched himself on my knee.

I knew what this meant and I was in two minds to refuse him what he wanted. But he was so clever, so gentle, so quick, that he made it seem that I would only be a sulky kind of fool keeping up a quarrel for the quarrel's sake. So I had to do as he wished, and since to do so without kindness and kisses is a mean dirty thing, I let myself be friendly. And when I had no guard on myself and no dignity, the words popped out: 'Why did you hit me?'

'Because you asked for it,' he said, and that was all he would say. And he would never admit that it was because he was stuck; still less that it might be his liver. For Gulley was a yellow man and took no exercise, and I always believed his sticking and his tempers came from his liver. But that was a great and bad difference between my dear Matt and Gulley. Matt lived upon the honest ground and you could say anything to him, except about the bills, and he was never shocked by the quirks of his own nature. He knew that constipation made him cross and so when he was cross and I said: 'Perhaps you need a pill,' he would receive it as a good idea and thank me and say: 'Yes, I don't believe I did my duty yesterday at all. No, I missed it running for the train,' and he would take a pill and wait to see if it improved his temper.

But if I had said to Gulley: 'Next time you are stuck and feeling miserable, why not try a pill or a tonic,' he would have laughed at me and raged at me. For he was up in the air always, and I don't think he ever asked himself, all his life, what our poor souls may owe to the flesh or how often the greatest heroes must dance to its comical fantods.

I caught him again at the good moment, the next evening, after the Scotch salmon in pastry, and he wrote off the Foley letter at last. But the exhibition contract he would never sign. He said he had no pictures good enough to show.

I did not try to bring him to a better idea, because he was working again, full steam, and so in full happiness.

But though all seemed peace and comfort, and I found myself singing over my pots, delighted every day to be back in my own home, I knew very well that I had given myself up to a bad, uneasy life. It was no good my telling myself that Gulley had learnt his lesson and would never strike me again. I had seen and felt his cruelty, and I knew he would always beat his women. He had beaten Nina, gentle as she was, and he had beaten me.

A beaten woman that goes back to be beaten again can never know the same happiness or hold up the head of her soul. She feels a disgust at herself that works into her flesh. I was a worse woman for going back to Gulley. But who knows if I had gone to Rozzie I might have taken to her way of life and thinking, which would have destroyed me altogether. For I was not made of that battering stuff. I never had Rozzie's art not to care for anything and to keep myself going on, like a horse, without any kind of happiness or hope or proper object in life.

46

Now I don't know whether it was a reward or not, but Gulley was so pleased to see me again that he said, all by himself, he would agree to the exhibition at once. 'It won't do any good,' he said, 'but Hickson will have to buy a few quids' worth because it's in his house and we'll have a binge on it – good old Brighton.'

But I think it must have been a reward, for the same week I got a letter from the man Robb, who had kept Gulley's old pictures. He had changed his address, but he had the pictures still and Gulley's bill was only nine pounds and a few shillings. So I paid it and had the pictures sent straight to London, to be framed and taken at once to Mr Hickson's house in Portman Place, in case Gulley should mislike them and say they weren't to be allowed.

Mr Hickson arranged them in the drawing-room, and advertised the exhibition in the papers. Though he charged me with the cost, that is to say, I owed him for it. Also he got a famous writer to write a notice in the catalogue explaining why Gulley painted in new shapes. He and I did all the arrangements. But I could never get Gulley to fix prices, and then when the catalogues got sent to me, I found he had put mad prices on them, no painting under a hundred pounds, two more three hundred, and one was five hundred. But when I went to tell him that he must be mad, he said only that the National Gallery had just spent fifty thousand pounds on pictures much worse.

'Yes,' I said, 'old masters that are dead and famous.'

'Why shouldn't I be famous when I'm dead?'

It must have popped out by accident, but it was a giveaway too. Because Gulley always made out that he scorned fame. I saw him turn red and furious, so I said quickly that, of course, he would be.

'Not that I care, for I won't even be here,' he said. 'Dead men can't read the papers.'

I said that he would be famous alive too, if he went on giving exhibitions. But five hundred pounds was too big to start with. 'My dear Sall,' he said, 'you won't sell them anyhow, so why not put a fair price on them. Those people have no other standards but money. If I put down fifty pounds they would say these pictures can't be much good. I wish now I'd told Hickson nothing under a thousand pounds.'

So I thought: 'I'll have to tell people that I'll take less.' But when I went up to town, the week before the exhibition, I got another great shock. I had not seen any of the pictures before, and all the ones from Mr Robb, eleven in all, were of the queerest kind, with the red women and the green men and purple trees, and the flowers like buttercups about three times their right size. But what was worse for me were four great new pictures that he had done from me myself, though I never knew it. Mr Hickson had got them from him without telling me. It was a plot between them. It gave me such a terrible feeling to see myself naked on those walls that after one look I ran out of the room. I felt that God would strike me and at first I said that I could not bear such a thing. So I went to find Mr Hickson and I wired to Gulley himself. But Mr Hickson was not at home and Gulley did not answer my wire. It was all in the plot. Then I told Mr Hickson's servants not to open the exhibition until I saw Mr Hickson. But when I went in next afternoon, it was open and there were a hundred people in the room, drinking tea and making such a noise you couldn't hear yourself speak. And there was a crowd of men round my pictures, staring with all their eyes, as they well might.

Then suddenly Gulley stood before me. He was laughing and I thought he was laughing at me. So I said: 'It's no laughing matter. Those pictures have to come down.' But he answered: 'No, why, let them laugh. Why shouldn't they?'

'They're not laughing,' I said. 'It wouldn't be so bad if they were – look at them.'

'Oh,' he said, 'I didn't mean the nudes – they don't matter. I meant the pictures from Robb. Look at that woman over there – she's laughed so much that the tears are coming down her make-up. I'm told she's a duchess too – Hickson has spent a month trying to get her.'

'What should a duchess know about pictures?' I said. 'I think she's laughable herself, old fowl dressed like chicken. I think that the exhibition is a great success.'

'You bet it is,' he said, laughing. 'Look at that old man over there shaking all over. It's the joke of the year.'

It was true that people were laughing, and that they seemed to be laughing more and more. 'Well,' I thought, 'I've heard a lot about London people and their great knowledge and up-to-dateness, but I think you are no better than a lot of silly children and well behind the fashion, too.' And as for the crowds still round the pictures of myself, I was disgusted with them, for if the others were children, what were these, well up in years, and gentlemen from the best part of the town, staring and staring at a fat naked woman. For that was all those nudes were. I could not have stayed in the room with those pigs of men if it had not been I was so anxious about Gulley. For though he was laughing, I could not forget that other exhibition, when the people had laughed him out of the room.

I knew that, however he might laugh and keep up a bold front, he had suffered then so much that he had never wanted to show his pictures again, or perhaps even sell them; and that he was suffering now. No wonder. The people were getting worse and worse and I could see the exhibition was a terrible failure. I could not keep my temper and I said to him: 'Come away and leave them, dear. I can't stand them another minute. A lot of silly children and worse.'

But Gulley was never so grand. 'Go on, Sally,' he said. 'What's wrong with you? This is nothing. Better they should laugh than cry. Come on, you're in the profession now, you must learn to take it on the nose. This is nothing.'

And he said over and over again, what was true, that we couldn't expect people to understand his pictures. They were a new idea, and just because they were new, they surprised people and made them laugh.

'No, my dear Sall, I can't complain that people don't understand me – I ought to be damn glad that they don't hang me or shoot me. That's what a lot of them would like to do.'

This was really true, for one man wrote to us and called Gulley a Bolshevist and said that if he dared to exhibit again, he would beat him up. 'What we want in England,' he wrote, 'is a few blackshirts to deal with scum like you.'

But Gulley laughed at him too, and said that it had been the same with William Blake, some people wanted to put him in gaol, and after he died one religious man burnt nearly all his work. And now Blake was in all the poetry books. 'It's only that some people don't like anything till it's a hundred years old,' he said.

Gulley was always reading Blake, who was a poet about a hundred years ago, and illustrated his own poems. I think Gulley agreed very well with Blake when he told me Blake used to play Adam and Eve with his poor wife, and draw her too. Once he threatened to take two wives and he always claimed the right, and this was like Gulley, who used to argue that it would not matter to me if he had another woman so long as she did not interfere with me or my pleasure. So I would tell him that if he meant Rozzie, he might try, but I didn't think he would succeed, and if he did, it would be the end of him. For Rozzie was a man-killer and had killed her own husband.

47

The exhibition, as I say, was a failure. Only one critic wrote about it and he said that Gulley was not an original artist at all but an imitator of two other artists, French artists, who were not only old-fashioned, but quite different from each other. The nudes were like one and the other pictures like the other. Gulley only laughed and said that the critics always wrote so after they had stopped abusing you. 'If they can't say you are bad, they say you are not original.'

But I was very cast down. There were only two people in the rooms the whole of the next day, and none on the day after. I sat there moping at my little table and when anyone did come in, I kept my head down and my chin in my hand, and pretended to be writing, so that they wouldn't recognize me on the walls.

But as if to show me how wrong I was to complain about my luck, the exhibition took a good turn. For on the day before the last, a very nice young man, with a little fair moustache, came in and looked at the pictures. I was sure he was an officer by his beautiful suit and his shoes. Then a little dark woman came in too, older than he, but very pretty and lively. You could see there was plenty in her. They met behind my back and I think they kissed then, because I could feel it on my skin. I felt too that it was a true case. So I went out and the woman gave me just a glance through her veil to say thank you. But the great surprise was when I came back there was a note left to apply for one of the pictures of a hundred pounds. It was one of me, the best, as I thought myself, and what was still better, with my face bent down and not well seen. The note gave an address at the Albany. So I telephoned and I had a cheque the next morning. I could not believe my eyes. A hundred pounds out of the air, for nothing. Then the next thing was, on the last day, two dealers came. One was a dirty little man with a grey beard who had been there on the first day, laughing and joking. I hated all those who had laughed, so I was very cool to him. But all at once he offered me a hundred and fifty pounds for the exhibition, the whole lot as it stood. I was just going to say: 'Yes, indeed,' when we both heard someone else coming through the hall. I thought it was the young man back and I thought, perhaps he wants another of the nudes if that's his taste, which it might well be. I didn't mind so nice and clean a young man having the pictures of myself. For I thought that it was all in nature that he should have that taste.

So Greybeard, seeing me hesitate, said: 'Take it or leave it, Mrs Jimson. I have to go to Paris today and I couldn't repeat the offer, because I shall spend the money over there.'

But I held out till the other man came in, not my officer, but another dealer, a tall dark man, who as soon as he saw Greybeard burst out: 'I hope you haven't sold the nudes, Mrs Jimson!'

'No,' I said.

'Because I want them,' he said, 'if we can agree on a price.'

'But I've got them already,' said the other.

'No,' I said, 'you have not. You made me an offer only!'

'How much did he offer?' said the other.

'Two hundred,' Greybeard said quickly, 'for the whole show.'

'I'll give that for the nudes alone,' said the other.

I thought they were going to have a great argument and put up the price and so I said quickly that of course the real prices were much higher and I did not know if I could take less without consulting the artist. But to my surprise, they did not say another word. They just looked at each other. Then Greybeard walked out of the room and the other, after looking all round, gave a sniff so loud as a pig and followed after. I was so cast down, I went to Jimson and told him my folly and said 'Now hit me as hard as you like.' But he, good man, said I was a hero and bought me pearl earrings out of the cheque. 'You see,' he said, 'I can make money with the best. Now for dear old Brighton.' And when Greybeard wrote and offered him a hundred for the whole exhibition, he took it and thank you.

I saw I didn't know how pictures were sold and, after our holiday, I went to ask Mr Hickson, for I thought he at least would know the business part. But he repeated my question: 'What is the value of a picture, my dear Sara, nobody knows, not even the dealers. A picture has a price but not a value. The price is anything you can get – the value is a mystery, like all the things of the spirit.'

So I asked him if he thought Gulley's nudes were things of the spirit and he said: 'Yes indeed – don't you make any mistake, Mrs Jimson. They're his best things,' and he tried to persuade me to get Gulley to paint only nudes. But I could see he knew very well who the model had been, and so I thought: 'I know why you like them,' and I didn't encourage him to go on.

When I told Gulley of what Hickson said, that a picture is worth what you can get, no more or less, he was delighted and said: 'He's quite right, and there you have him to the life, the dirty little money-changer.' Gulley did not mind even when two days later we saw one of the pictures of me in a Bond Street window with a ticket: 'New works by Gulley Jimson,' and inside there were four more pictures at a hundred pounds each. What's more, we found out that the dark young man, who had no gallery of his own, had gone shares with Greybeard, and then sold his share to other dealers, at a profit of about ten times, especially for the nudes. One of them was bought by a rich newspaper lord and Hickson said he had paid five hundred pounds for it.

I own that when I heard this I cried from pure mortification, for this was a year after, when we were so poor that we didn't know what to do for money, and when my poor Gulley was in despair with his work, and when, to tell the truth, he had beaten me so cruelly that I thought I could not bear another blow. For he had broken my nose and loosened my teeth, and though I never cared for my nose, which would have been vanity for a woman of my age, yet I valued my teeth, for my health's sake. But what was the worst, when I tried to have another exhibition, even Mr Hickson said it would be no good; and when I even went to Z., that is Greybeard, to sell something, he would not buy even a nude. For he said that no one would buy Jimsons and the old ones from the first exhibition were still on his hands. 'If Jimson would only paint some modern pictures,' he said, 'it would be different.' So I asked to see some modern pictures and he showed me a thing like a patch-work quilt, with a piece of a fiddle worked into it.

I told him Gulley would never paint like that. Yet I did suggest to him once that it would be easy to paint a few patchworks for Mr Z. But he only laughed and told me that he was too old-fashioned. 'I'm out of fashion,' he said, 'before I was ever in fashion. But don't worry yourself, Sall, even if I did paint quilts, no one would buy 'em. It's not the quilt they pay for, but the name.' Then he began to laugh, for he was in one of his good moods, and said: 'Do you remember the time when I was going to make our fortunes?' and he began to tell the story of that exhibition. He acted Mr Hickson, and the young man buying the nude, though he had never seen him, and the duchess, and the dealers; even imitating their voices and waving his hands about; and then himself and me cashing the cheque at the bank and going off to Brighton to stay at the Albion. Gulley never forgot that we had stayed at the Albion, with two lords and a cabinet minister, and paid a bill of over seventy pounds at the end of our holiday. He would tell it to everybody and make a joke of it and say that I had flirted with the lords and that we had sat two nights in the bow window, for all Brighton to admire my dress and my figure. It was one of his pet stories, part true and yet all made up. He told it differently every time. Sometimes the dealers were Scotsmen and sometimes they were Jews. Either it was Lord Lonsdale at the Albion who complimented me on my figure or sometimes it was the Prince of Wales. But he could always make me laugh with it, and yet I wanted to cry too. We had been so happy then, and I had really thought that our fortune was made, and that we should have many such holidays, in the best hotels, with the best of everything. For I had thought even if the dealers caught me this time, next time I will know better and charge proper prices.

And Gulley knew my feelings, for if any of his friends were in the room when he told the story, he would imitate me in the bow window, pushing out his chest and patting himself in front and he would say: 'And Sally there, you should have seen her playing-up – she spread herself over Brighton like a million pounds. Poor girl, she thought she'd caught a real money-maker.'

'Well,' I would say, 'it was good while it lasted. I'm sure you enjoyed the food too, and the champagne.' For the truth was that Gulley had been the spender at Brighton. It was he who had said that we must go to a good hotel and live like millionaires, and he who had ordered champagne for dinner, and all kinds of expensive dishes.

What I wonder at in my life with Jimson was how much happiness we had, with all our ups and downs. For it was not only that I lost all my money at Ancombe, and got my nose broken, but that we never had a day's full peace from the picture. And let me tell you it took five years.

100

There was always some new hitch; either the plaster was wrong or the paint wrong or no money.

Miss Slaughter said the Vicar was against us, and hated him. But I always put my hopes in the Vicar. It was not only that he was a good man, and preached good sermons, but that he admired poor Gulley's work. First he helped us with the churchwardens when they wanted to write to the Bishop against us, and then he would say often: 'Yes, Mrs Jimson, you may count me among your husband's admirers,' or 'the colour is really excellent.'

Gulley would laugh at him and say we were a pair of devil dodgers, but Gulley laughed at everything, and the vicar did me much good, especially his sermons. Because they were aimed always at selfishness and self-indulgence.

Every week he would tell true stories about those who had given way to their faults and come to ruin and misery by them. 'For the desire of the body infects the soul,' he would say, which I knew well to be true. His name was Rodwick. He looked always sleepy and I was told that he did not like the country. He had been a famous slummer in some big town and his health had given out. He lived with his sister who was a little square woman with a red nose like a finch, a great visitor and gardener. She was gay and lively and she would bounce on Miss Slaughter's sofa so that the springs sang and Miss Slaughter would draw herself together like a cat at a dog-fight. She could not bear Miss Rodwick's strammaging ways.

Miss Rodwick was a good soul. She would bring me daffodils and tulips, and if they were the short ones or the little ones, as Miss Slaughter said, why should I poison a gift with looking beyond it, especially in the country where, God knows, a bad thought about a neighbour is as good as grease in your own soup. Miss Rodwick gave many a start of pleasure and asked nothing in return but a few recipes and now and then a day's helping at the vicarage, when she was giving a party.

Miss Slaughter said that the Vicar was worn out; and that the Bishop had thrown him upon us only to die. 'They think any rubbish is good enough for us in the country,' she said. But I thought it must be hard enough to be a clergyman in these days, when for all you do, the people care more for the newspapers than the gospel; and people get sober and clean in spite of you, only because they have better houses and better wages. It is a hard time for all clergy and I used to feel sorry for the poor Vicar, with his wasted life.

And even if he had pushed harder at the architect and been firmer with the builders, so that the Hall had been finished, Gulley would never have got on with the work. For he would give himself a holiday as he wished it, and make me sit for him. 'Come, Sall,' he would call, 'give me your back.' And he would say it was like a holiday to paint my flesh.

So it was, for when he was happy, so was I; and then, as I say, we had great joys. We would go up on the moor perhaps, and bathe in the dam, where the waterfalls poured down on your head, and you could stand inside them and see the sky itself melting down like blue copper flames. Then the water was like gold, with the peat, and when I sat in it, my legs were like ivory, like that old master of Hickson's. I was always surprised to see my beauty in that golden water.

But it was cold and we came out as pink as cochineal; and so hungry we would eat a dozen scones apiece and a whole plum cake. Then, if the day was warm, we were sleepy and Gulley would put his head on my stomach and go to sleep and I would think of sleep too. But I did not want to sleep, either, because it seemed waste to sleep away such an afternoon, with the sky full of clouds like old pillows, gone yellow, and the smell of the grass like new cider and the waterfalls ringing like a peal of bells, from the little one high up to the big one at the dam. And a waste, too, of the memory of our sweet bathe and the good tea; and the weight of Gulley's head, enjoying his peace, poor manny, while he had it.

48

It was hard to come back from the moors or the beach and find Miss Slaughter in a new fit about the Vicar, or the builder wanting a new cheque, or only in terror that the picture would never be finished. She would speak to me sometimes so madly that I thought she would soon forget herself in the village and be locked up. She would say she was ruined with our keep and that Gulley was cheating her. 'He promised me my picture in six months and it's not finished after four years.' It was always her picture. She would say to visitors: 'Yes, my picture is going on very well. It is going to be finished by next month. A wonderful conception, don't you think, the Garden of Eden?'

Of course, all the people in the place were disgusted at the picture. Ugly was too good a word for it. It was an outrage, an insult to decent folk, a bolshevist plot. Why they thought it bolshevist, I never could find out, because it was only naked men and women in a kind of garden with queer flowers and trees, and some of them speaking words out of their mouths, written on coloured puffs. None of the words were to do with bolshevism, which Gulley hated like poison because, he said, the bolshevists tried to make artists paint for the government.

One of the women, with very short legs, was saying in pink letters on a blue puff: 'Love is my name, on death I stand.' A tree with white flowers was singing out of one of the flowers: 'I sleep in this joy, do not wake me with admiration.' A goat was saying in white letters on a green puff: 'Chain me or I shall eat the world bare.' An old man with no ears or arms or legs was saying: 'You do not speak my language – I can't hear your voice.' A big strong black man with his legs like tree roots was saying in black letters on a big white puff: 'I am death, from life I grow. Maids, take my seed, and bear.'

No one liked the picture, not even Miss Slaughter, who was shocked by the puffs. She was terribly upset when she saw Gulley painting them on, in the very last month. I heard her catch her breath. But as I say, she was tough, and she always stuck to her principles, which were that Gulley was a genius and that a genius is always right. So she even praised them to him. But all he said was: 'I think they look silly.'

So I thought too, and I hoped he would change them. But he never did. For one day he came in and told me that the picture was done; he never wanted to see it again. He agreed only to stay for the opening day, which was to be after harvest Sunday.

Miss Slaughter couldn't wait even so long as a month. She turned us out as soon as the picture was finished. Not that she was rude. She said that her niece was coming, but no niece came and it was only to get rid of us. I don't blame her after five years. But as it turned out, we had no money, at least till Gulley finished a portrait down in Queensport; so we had to take the cheapest room, over the blacksmith's.

It was small, but that was no drawback when Gulley was happy. So he was, glad as always to be finished with a picture; and full of a new one, for Mr Hickson's drawing-room, twenty feet high and forty feet long. Mr Hickson had not ordered it and we both knew he would never take it; but it kept us both happy in that week. For as I say, when Gulley was happy then we were both gay.

49

We were laughing together, I don't know why, and I was only in my petticoat, when Miss Slaughter came to us with her white hair blowing like fleece on a bush and her eyes red like the windows of a house on fire, to tell us that there would be no opening day for the picture. No one would open it and the Vicar would not take down the stage. Now the Vicar had put a stage against that end of the Hall for the Dramatic Society to rehearse, and a curtain over the picture, till it was opened, and to keep it from harm.

But now, according to Miss Slaughter, the stage was to stay and the curtain was down, and holes knocked in the picture already. It was all a trick, she said, to get rid of the picture. 'But they won't get round me like that,' she said, as fierce as a snake. 'I've written to my lawyers and I've warned the Vicar that he will have to pay the damage.'

So she wanted Gulley to come and patch up the holes. Gulley, I say, was in a good mood. So round we went to the Hall. There, just as she said, was the stage all fixed and bolted to cover the bottom of the picture, and a piano stood against it, and piles of chairs and ladders leaning against it; and a hole knocked in the woman who was saying: 'I am love – on death I stand.' Her nose and half her forehead and a bit of her balloon had been knocked off with a ladder. There were nails, too, driven into the black man.

Now I'll own that though I had never liked that queer picture, when I saw those nails, and how they had been driven in malice, I broke down and cried. I went beyond even Miss Slaughter in denouncing those murderers. 'It's a wicked thing,' I said, 'and God will punish it if the law won't.'

But Gulley was looking on with his hands in his pockets as cool as you please, and even whistling to himself.

'Don't you be sure, Sally,' he said. 'Perhaps God is on the other side. The Vicar would tell you it's a wicked picture.'

'But he got his Hall by allowing the picture.'

'He would say that he has brought good out of evil.'

I could not help being angry with Gulley, taking so coolly what was his own ruin and the waste of five years. So I said to him: 'It cost you enough, at least.'

'I suppose I enjoyed it while it lasted,' he said. 'At any rate, I'm sick of the sight of it now.'

We both begged him to fight, and I was going to run for his colour box that he might patch up the woman's face and the nail holes. But Gulley caught me by the arm and squeezed it so hard I knew he was determined. 'Don't trouble yourself, Sall,' he said. 'It's not worth me doing anything to it. If I started on it, I'd never stop. You can't fight against the whole village.'

'I'll fight them,' Miss Slaughter cried, 'if I have to shut the Hall. Such creatures are not fit to have a hall.'

'You can't shut the Hall because it isn't yours. It's vested in the parish.'

'But I have the Vicar's signed letter to allow the picture to be painted.'

'He didn't say he'd let it be seen, did he? Besides, it's not the Vicar only, it's all the churchwardens and the whole parish. Why, Miss Slaughter, don't you see that what between you and me and the churchwardens, the Vicar was in a nice jam. But he's got out of it very well. He's a smart chap, the Vicar, though he does look half-asleep. Yes,' said Gulley, 'I admire that chap. I'm ready to bet that there won't be anything left of my picture within a year, and no one responsible.'

'I'd die first,' said Miss Slaughter.

'Yes, perhaps you will,' said Gulley. 'I daresay the Vicar counted on that, or his sister put him up to it. That's more in a woman's line.'

The poor woman looked shaken at that, as well she might, for I suppose it was true that her whole idea was to be immortal, which was why Gulley always despised her and pricked her on that score. And there now was her immortality with a big hole in it before the first week was out. She turned as red as if she had a stroke and it was half a minute before she pulled herself up again and said that her lawyers would take care of the Vicar, if only Gulley would mend the picture. 'I know you wouldn't like your masterpiece to go down to posterity in a damaged state,' she said.

'Posterity will have plenty to think about without me,' Gulley said, 'and to tell the truth, I don't think much of that picture. If I had to do it again, I'd do it differently. My ideas have changed a good deal in five years. The balloons are not bad, but all the early part is rubbish.'

Then when she went on at him, he said: 'Paint it yourself, Miss Slaughter. Anyone can slap on a piece of plaster and rub a little paint on it.' So he came away, whistling.

I say I was more upset than Miss Slaughter. So I stayed to promise her that I would help her and do anything she liked to save the picture and get it properly opened. For it was only Gulley's due to have an opening. A wall picture, as you know, might as well be thrown into the sea without an opening, for you can't send it to an exhibition. It never gets in the papers, or even known, without an opening, and a party.

I was resolved to have my opening if it was only by Mr Hickson; and I promised Miss Slaughter, too, that I would bring Gulley round to mending the holes.

Now I daresay I was so angry and so upset that I didn't pick my words, or consider how Gulley might be feeling. For he might whistle and make light of the thing, as he had made light of the laughers at his exhibition. But no man can see his life and work thrown away without a pang, and Gulley was already grey. All this I should have thought. But whatever I said or did I upset him, for as soon as I began about mending up the holes, he told me to say no more. 'Don't pester me, Sall – the picture's done for and you know it as well as I do.'

'It's not done for if only you will fight for it.'

'I'm not such a fool,' he said. 'Fighting is a fool's job for me. Painting is my job, not fighting, and if I start fighting, I won't be able to paint. That would be one up for the churchwardens, wouldn't it, to smash the picture and stop me painting too – and worry myself to death on top of all.'

So I said if he would not fight, I would.

'That's the same thing,' he said. 'If you get into fighting and bitterness, then so do I. The only thing for us, Sall, is to keep serene and spit on the lot of them. Come now, old girl, you don't want to get grey hair and wrinkles from knocking your head against a wall. You did your best on the Vicar. Well, then, let it go.'

I said I was not going to let us be ruined and wasted, all for want of a little spirit.

So then he turned savage and told me that if I said another word, he would hit me. And I daresay I said the word, for he gave me the worst beating of all. I was so obstinate, indeed, that even while he was punching me with all his might, I was full of bitterness and anger against the Dramatic Society and the village and the churchwardens, and all the world; and I kept on saying that he could never knock me out of it. So I drove him mad. The upshot was that he knocked me out against the bed-post so hard that I cut my head open and put me into a faint, the first time he had ever succeeded in such a deed. And when I came round he was gone, and I didn't see him again for years.

50

At first, of course, I didn't know that he had run off and I hurried up to get lunch, for he had made me late. I was giving him for a treat, and at our worst I never gave Gulley cheap food, a snitzel and a cheese soufflé which he greatly liked and though I say it, I would cook either of them against the Ritz. But I would not start cooking the soufflé till I had him under my hand, and so I waited for him. Then I put on my garden hat to cover the cut and went out to see if he was at the Brethren. But no. And then the smith told me that he had seen him jump on the twelve o'clock bus with a bag and a colour box.

The smith was goggling his eyes at me as if he was full of news. The smith always knew when I had been beaten. He would hear our feet shuffling and me falling, through the floor. So though he had been my friend, I had come to hate him, and I would not speak to him now or ask him why he looked at me so tellingly.

I went in and waited and when Gulley did not come I put my veal away and the bowl of eggs for the soufflé and made myself a cup of tea for lunch. I never could be bothered cooking for myself, and then having to wash up my own plate and my own pans.

When he did not come back that day I began to think perhaps he had run off, and I remembered there was a girl in Queensport he had been painting in a portrait, a big buxom girl, his very type, who was playing at art too, and made a god of the poor manny.

Sure enough, in came the post girl with a telephone message from this girl to ask for me. I went to the phone and the girl's mother, so calm as you please, said that the girl had gone off with him. She had just wired from such and such an hotel in London. Would I go up and take him away from her?

How could I get him back if he wanted to go, I asked. I was told: 'You have great influence over him, Mrs Jimson, and I feel sure that this is only a passing infatuation on my daughter's part.'

I thought that even if I could bring Gulley back, I would not, to beat me again. But I said only that I was afraid I hadn't so much influence as that.

Then I went back to my room. I was in a great rage at Gulley and I think if I could have got at him, I would have beaten him. Though indeed I might have been afraid of doing him a real injury, for I am a very strong woman and he was so light built that the wind of my skirt would make him stagger.

I raged at him all that day and the next. I could not sleep, and what was the good of eating? I think that next day was the worst in my life yet, for I was full of hatred against him and the girl, and hatred is always bad for me. It makes my head split. So I thought: 'I mustn't go on in this rage or I shall do myself an injury and perhaps turn my hair grey and have a stroke from the pressure of my blood.' But as soon as I tried to turn my mind from Gulley and get on with my work, I found there was nothing reasonable to do. For I did not want to cook and so there was neither cooking nor shopping; and why should I mend for a man that wasn't there?

So I was putting the room straight and the shelves, and smoothing out the covers on Gulley's canvases and portfolios, which he had left all behind him, to worry me with wondering what to do with them, and dusting and cleaning and washing, for no purpose at all but only as a duck will kick after its throat is cut; when I felt something wrong. I wondered if it were milk left in some bowl, but my nose, if ugly, has always been good for its work, and I soon tracked down my feeling to the meat cupboard. So I opened it and there was the piece of veal, bread-crumbed as I had left it, two days ago ready for Gulley's lunch. But when I opened the cupboard the stink came out with the door as if it had been a coffin lid. The thunder weather had been too much for it.

I took the plate up to throw the meat away, when suddenly it carried me back. When I remembered the busy day when I had gone into Queensport by the bus, to get the meat and been so happy to find just what I wanted, tender and prime, and then getting it ready and thinking: 'This is going to be a grand success.' Suddenly I began to cry. And I threw it in the dustbin and banged the lid enough to bring the village running. For I did not care though all saw me there bloody and weeping.

It made me cry and it made me rage when I threw that lovely piece of veal into the dustbin. Waste and nothing but waste. I thought: 'I have wasted five of my best years, and I hope I'll never see him again.'

But, as they say, the worse the grief the better the heart to bear it. When the ball hits the floor, it must bounce or burst. I was knocked so low I couldn't go any lower and there was nothing to do but get up. So I got up and no credit to my quality or my religion, for God forgive me, I had not been to church since Christmas, and I had my hair curled over the cut and I went to a little public in Queensport where I was known and put down my name at a registry office for a cook's place.

I left all Gulley's things with Miss Slaughter and she was my reference, and she agreed to say that I had been her cook-housekeeper, as indeed I had been. For the last four years of the picture I had done the whole work of the house for no wages.

51

I was lucky. There was a place waiting for a cook-housekeeper at seventy-five pounds – good wages in those days, and I would have got it if it had not been for my trouble with the police.

This was my first police trouble and it did me so much harm at my other one that I must say it never seemed to me so bad as they made out. It happened so. When Gulley left Ancombe, the bills were falling like may flowers in June, unlucky to all they touch. But I had nothing except my fall back, that is, nine gold sovereigns sewn up in my stays, which Rozzie had told me to put away at the time Matt died. For, she said, a widow never knew when she might need gold, if only to bury herself.

Now I would not touch that money, for the rule with such a fall back is that you must pretend it isn't there and count it nothing, for bills. So I had only cheques, and I paid with cheques, though I knew we had nothing at the bank except a debt; and got a few pounds change for ready cash.

Now I cannot tell why I did so foolish a thing. I could not believe how I had done it when the policeman came to the hotel and took me up. 'You surely don't think me a robber,' I said, 'for you see I haven't run away.' It was true that the bank manager in Queensport was a friend of mine; indeed he had often come through his counter only to see me and chaff me and pat my arm. So I had thought perhaps he would cash my cheques, and let me owe him for a little. For goodness knows he had had plenty of my money.

So I may have thought, but the truth was I was in such a hurry to be away from Ancombe, I did not care what I did. So I was had up before the bench and it was a near thing I did not go to assizes and prison. There was still a lot of feeling about the picture and bolshevism, and somehow, I don't know how, it was known that Gulley and I had not been married. Then the cheques had come to seventy pounds and that was a big sum. I was lucky indeed to get off with a probation order, and a promise to pay as I could; and a word to my character from the Vicar and Mr Hickson. Mr Hickson, too, took back his own debt which I owed him for the exhibition frames, thirty pounds, and he paid the bills at the colourman's, only for a letter saying that I owed him so much.

I was lucky in my friends, and I was lucky, too, that they never searched me and never found the gold in my stays.

I was lucky, too, in getting a place, having lost my character. For when I went back to the registry office the other place was filled and the woman shook her head at recommending me, unless, she said, I would go to Tolbrook Manor.

'Why not?' I said.

She shook her head again and said that it was not really on her books, for she could not recommend it to any respectable girl. But perhaps it was all I would get. When I heard this I felt myself turn over within. It was the first time I was made to feel like a criminal, not just to the police, but to the world, and to know what it is not to have a character.

Yet I was due for a check too, not only from the police. For I had gone down hill with Gulley, not only from his beatings but his spoilings, which had brought me to pamper myself. I had grown soft to my sins.

52

When I asked the registry woman what was wrong with Tolbrook, she told me as if it pleased her. A big country house, with only two maids indoors, no gas or electric light and three miles from a village or even a bus. And it had a bad name, too, that is to say, Mr Wilcher, the owner, had a bad name, deserved or not. He had difficulty with keeping servants, specially female servants, and once or twice he had nearly been had up with his goings on.

When I heard all this I said I would never go to such a terrible place and I held out two more days. But I saw I would get nothing better from the registry office with my character, and I had pawned even my clothes to live on at the Crown.

So I took the place at Mr Wilcher's. For I thought, 'If it is bad, perhaps it is meant for me. And bad as it may be, it won't kill me.' For thank God, I had my health and my strength, all my teeth, which, though I say it, were the wonder of every dentist that ever saw them, only to clean them, for I never had a stopping, and not a grey hair. No one would have taken me for forty-six, nor yet thirty-six. For if I was plagued by my heavy body, yet I had this for a come-back, that my fat kept my skin tight and firm. My skin, which was always my consolation and my best friend. Indeed, when I gave the police my true age, they were surprised and the sergeant said that I had the complexion of a baby. So I might have called myself less and saved myself another fall if I had not feared to keep anything back from the police, in case it came out. But I found that I was down for thirty-five at the registry, and so when my true age came out in the papers, Mr Wilcher's agent spoke to me about it as if I had been telling lies.

He ought to have known, I thought, that just as twenty-five in a cook means nineteen, so thirty-five or forty means not her years, but that she is strong and fit for heavy work. As middle-aged means doddery and fit for no work, except eating and sleeping, poor things, if they can.

53

Tolbrook Manor was a rambling kind of place in a field with a ha-ha fence. It had no park to call a park. The gardens were behind and the field in front, and outside the ha-ha there were meadows and hedges. The house had good rooms and very good furniture, but in sad repair, both up and down stairs; holes in the roof and the floors and half the windows with no cords. I was surprised to find a good double sink in the scullery, and the range gave all the hot water we could ask. Rats and cockroaches, yes; but a girl who is frightened of cockroaches had better not hope to be a cook in the good old places. The Tolbrook rats, I'll admit, were something special, as big as jack rabbits and as fierce as boars. I used to tremble at them galloping in the passages and jumping on the stairs.

The house, too, gave me shivers, for it was all under the trees, and even in broad daylight there was a green shade over everything so you would think the kitchen table had the green sickness. The fields were small, and the hedges full of great elms and oaks, the sun never could get into them except by streaks like the gold on a green tomato.

It was a lonely place, too; only the two other indoor servants and a daily help, the gardener's wife, who slept at the lodge, and two outdoor men for the gardens in their own village half a mile away. The head keeper had a man under him, too, but we never saw them at the house. They took their orders from the agent. The first nights at Tolbrook, lying all alone in that dismal place and listening to the rats, I thought I had been a great fool to come there. For though it might be my deserts and a fair punishment for so many years of luxury and gaiety, yet I thought it would do no one any good if I went out of my head. I was always a good cook, and though I say, a good servant, and I set that value on myself. Our Lord himself claimed the name and gave it for an honour. Martha, too, was praised in the Bible, and I always thought that she was perhaps a better woman than Mary, if we knew the whole.

As one who has been both mistress and maid, I will say that both have their tasks laid upon them and their rewards; and I could not tell now which I had liked better. For if the mistress has more glory, the maid has more peace in herself. She always has her profession. Then, too, the ladies, if they are better clothed, have great trouble to get husbands, while a good servant is never without her followers.

Yet in those first days at Tolbrook, for all that I knew I could not have got a better place, after the loss of my character, I pitied the waste of my talents. I will admit that when I stood in my bath and looked down upon myself, I have cried to think that I was done for, and thrown away upon a living tomb, pitying my flesh as well as my skill.

So I was surprised at myself when, after a month, I had a letter from Gulley saying that he wanted me to come to him in London, and I found that I did not want to leave Tolbrook. True, I was in the middle of the biggest house-cleaning I ever did; a job that still gives me satisfaction, and I had been to the agent about the roofs and I was expecting a plumber and the plasterer, tradesmen that you can't get in the country when you choose, but only when they like. I scarcely left the house for a fortnight, so fearful I was to miss them when they came and not fix them for the jobs I had waiting. Gulley couldn't have chosen a worse time to send for me, as I told him. So I looked into my mind and I saw that the truth was my grouses against Tolbrook were just a habit from the first days. So I stopped them. I always hated a grouser, for one of them will spoil all the pleasure in a house and spoil you too. If I ever loved Gulley, it was for his never grousing and never spoiling a joy in hand with yesterday's grief or tomorrow's fear. And if I have called him a sparrow for heat and the fidgets and his stick legs, I say he had the pluck too, and nothing would put him down. I'll own I nearly packed up and ran to him, like a wet hen into the coop. But I thought to myself: 'I can't go now with the cleaning here and the agent's letter coming, and the sink ready to flood the whole kitchen storey.' So I sent him three pounds advance on his commission, which was all he asked, and half a ham, to be sure he had food in the house. For I thought that woman must have left him already, if he was wanting me so soon.

54

So I found myself quite grown into the quiet of Tolbrook, and even the shade. I thought here was the very place to remember my faults. I had had a great fright to find myself in the hands of the law: a warning to stop in time, and seek grace. So at Tolbrook I first took to saving, as a religious duty, to keep out of extravagance, and of giving cheques, and put money in the Post Office.

And though when I first came I thought Tolbrook a poor sort of house, I grew to think it the sweetest of all with its old gardens full of yew hedges and old statues of the women goddesses. When I saw them I knew why Gulley had called my figure good, for they had just such thick waists and wrists and ankles, and heavy chins. Not that I was so cocked up by that, for I had known a hundred country girls with the same limbs, and the boys used to call after us all: 'Beef to the ankle.'

But the sweetest sight of all was from the scullery window across the fields in front, which should have been a lawn, and the ha-ha, into the meadows with the high trees in the hedges, elms and limes and chestnuts; and the Devon cows grazing, as red as port. The meadows were so shaded that you would say the house was gloomy, but I never minded a shady garden or a shadowy field so long as it was green. So at Tolbrook I liked to see out of the scullery windows when I was washing up, the banks under the trees so fresh green as angelica, right into June, and the elms rich like cucumbers half way through August. Then there was a pond in the first meadow that they called the fish pond, and from the housekeeper's room I could see the tops of the trees in it hanging down in a row as clear and sharp as a plush valance on a looking-glass, except when it was raining or blowing or the cows went in to drink. But I liked it just as well then, when it was covered with the rain like sequins or crinkled up with wind like a watered silk, or trod by the cows into great smooth rings, like slices of watermelon, green and pale green and clean gold and dirty gold.

Everywhere you looked round the house you saw nothing but peaceful harmless things, like the trees and the cows, and if the fences were rotten, then you felt at least they had been left in peace to go their own way.

Inside the house was another thing, for I was shocked to see the dust and the cobwebs. It was plain that Mr Wilcher had been badly served, just like all bachelors, for the top of everything, furniture, panelling, tallboys, door frames, was like a chimney flue.

But it was a real pleasure to rub up that furniture, and indeed I felt angry with Mr W., old bachelor as he was, that he had let it get in such a state. Furniture like that had a right to be properly looked after. And when I asked Aggie, the housemaid, if he was the kind of man to let things slide, so long as he was easy, she said no indeed, and poked his nose in everywhere, and his fingers too, she said, giggling. But I pretended not to notice this last turn. Aggie was always hankering to tell me tales about Mr Wilcher's philanderings with girls about the place. She would throw out a hint and giggle till she was swelled like a boiling tomato, ready to burst.

It was Aggie who told me about the last cook but one, Mrs Frewen, who had, so she said, let the master come too near her. Then he had turned round all at once and put the police on her box and run her into gaol.

'I daresay she got too cheeky,' I said.

But Aggie said it was only because she sat down one day in the drawing-room when the master was there. 'He's a funny one,' she said, ready to go on for a week. But I thought that I was the cook and in charge of the house, and I had no business to hear tales against the master. It would do no good to anyone, him or me or Aggie. So I cut Aggie short. Besides, I knew all the story from the gardener's wife, which was that Mr Wilcher had sometimes squeezed one of the maids a little or pinched her, or perhaps shown her something that he had better have kept to himself, and that he had been warned by the police, more than once, magistrate and church-warden though he was, to let the girls be. And as for Mrs Frewen, she had flouted herself in the village and said that Mr Wilcher was going to marry her and that she would make him. 'So no wonder he ran her into gaol,' I said, and the gardener's wife, though stupid enough with a duster, had plenty of woman's sense, and she agreed with me that if a gentleman like Mr Wilcher, who was so strict about church-going, went so far with the girls that it came to the police, then he could not help it and ought to be pitied, or, if mad, locked up, or married.

Not that I didn't feel the wrong of it in a gentleman like Mr Wilcher and the foolishness too, but I thought country people were more uncharitable than they used to be and less reasonable in their thoughts. The schools gave them too many books and not enough Christian sense. Yet, I admit it, I was all on fire to see the new master, when at last he came down, in the latter end of September.

55

He was not at all what I expected. He was a little man with a bald head and round black spectacles. His nose was very short, just like a baby's, and he had a long blue upper lip, like a priest, which made me say: 'You're one of the arguers.' He had long thin red lips and the under one stuck out and curled over, which made him look obstinate and sulky. His chin was blue as if it had been shot full of gunpowder and it had a very nice split in the middle. His neck was blue too, and there were scars on the back and I could see, too, that the poor man, like Matt, had suffered terribly from boils. His face was pale yellow all but a little mauve, rhubarb colour, over the bones of the cheek. I thought with these colours and lips and something in his eye, he had hot blood still, and sure enough within the month the poor man had a boil on his behind which gave him no peace. But he wouldn't lie up and he would just sit on a rubber cushion and bear it. I don't know why men should be so afflicted in this way; perhaps it's because of the hotness of their blood which my mother used to say was an affliction God gave them to balance that stupid thing which is such a trouble to women and which nearly frightened me out of my soul when I was a child, not knowing to expect it and thinking it was God's punishment for some sin. And indeed I suppose it was for the sin of Eve and if so, she was fairly caught, as I was, for I too was one of those who can put their conscience to sleep when they like, just to please themselves.

As for those who said Mr W. was a hypocrite to make so much of church and then run after young girls, I thought of his boils and his hot blood, and I thought, too, of my past deeds. And it seemed to me that I might have been called a hypocrite, when I was going to church in my best, knowing that Hickson and several more men were looking upon me with lickerish eyes. So that I could not have told you whether I was laced and dressed and scented to an inch of my life, for the honour of God, or the lusts of the flesh.

I thought, too, how often I had gone to church only to repent of some sin, and to keep myself from another as bad. If Mr W. is even as bad as they say, I thought, he may be better than most, having greater temptation and a harder fight.

56

Now, from the very first I'll admit I took to Mr Wilcher, and he seemed to take to me. Whether it was because I was sorry for the neglect he lived in, or for his pain, I felt quite a flutter when he first began to send for me, and to ask about the larder and arrange the dinner.

Above all, I liked him keeping up family prayers, and the way he read the Bible, as if it had been about real people. He said the prayers, too, better than anyone I have ever heard, and on Sundays, when he read the lessons in church, it was as good as a play. I never enjoyed anything so much before in any church, and I thought: 'Oh, that some would take example from him and then there would be no more sleepy heads in God's house.' For he would read like a lion and change his voice, too, in the speaking parts. So, indeed, when he spoke like Ruth in the corn-field, he made his voice so like a girl's that the tears came into my eyes. For I had always loved that story and, indeed, it is easy to know how poor Ruth felt, so low one day and so raised up the next. Boaz, too, you can see him, the good manny, doting on his nice young wife. Yet she would not mind his being so much older, in those days, for girls were brought up differently, to value a husband, however old. I often wished to know how many children Ruth had and how happy she was with Boaz, after that good beginning.

Mr W., as I say, seemed to take to me too, for he would send for me often to do little things for him, and he complimented me, too, on my good work in the house, and thanked me for bringing the others to church, even Aggie and the gardener's wife who had not been for a long time, and he found out, too, that I was a reading woman, and he would talk with me about the books.

For at Tolbrook I found books again and time, and my reading came back to me. I must not say that I would have come back to that duty of reading good books by myself, but only that it came back to me, or God brought it back by way of Mr Wilcher.

For one day when he had gone out to tea, and came back earlier than we expected, he found me sitting in the little patch of garden behind the kitchen with a book. It was only a paper book, that I found in the kitchen, about a girl that had come into millions and left her poor lover for a rich one; but even a poor book will give you good ideas.

Now Mr Wilcher, going in at his own little back door into his study, was so surprised and shocked he did not know what to do, but stood on one leg beside the door and pretended not to see me, until I had gone away, which I did quickly enough, for, of course, I had no business to be in the garden while the master was at home.

But the next morning when he called me in about a luncheon party, he asked me if I liked reading, and what books. So I said Yonge was my favourite. Then he was very pleased and cried: 'You could not do better, Mrs Monday. She was my father's favourite.' Then he told me how his father, who had been a colonel, had taken *The Heir of Redclyffe* with him to the Crimea, and been shot in it. 'When you come to London, Mrs Jimson,' he said, 'I'll show you the bullet. It went right through to Chapter Sixteen.'

'Is that where the young baronet is suspected to be a gambler?' I asked.

Mr Wilcher was surprised to see I knew the book so well and said that he did not remember. But that if I wanted to read, I could always sit in the garden, even when the family were at home, unless I thought it might upset the staff.

'The best place I think for you to be quiet and undisturbed is in the corner by the yard well. No one will trouble you there.'

The corner near the yard was behind some laurels, so I thought his real idea was that I should not be seen, should anyone call, and his slyness made me laugh. He was still a regular old bachelor, full of his tact. Anyone could see through him. Yet I mustn't say he was sly, for I daresay he didn't know why he did just so.

But then, when I had put my chair in the patch, he came to me and asked about the book. And I said: 'It's nothing of a book, sir – but it makes you think – and I haven't got my own books here.'

'Nothing has a better influence than a good book,' he said. 'I must look you out some.'

So he did, and filled a shelf with good old-fashioned books, some on religion, and some by Yonge, and Braddon and G. Eliot and J. Austen; some from his own library, though not in leather, of course.

57

Now this was one of the kindest things he could have done for me, and what I can never forget. For perhaps if the good books had not been brought to me, I would have gone on with Aggie's paper books. It is easy to read bad as well as good, when you get the habit, and please yourself. But the good books take hold of your mind, too, and in the end, you have double the pleasure and twice the profit. Going back to my Yonges was like going back to my first service and the time of my sober conscience. For the thoughts that came to me out of the pages were the same thoughts, as if they had been pressed between the leaves, only to remind me of my simple days, when my highest joy was a ribbon or a half-day to the fair.

Yet I was wiser too. I knew more of the world and its temptations, and how much better off I was, in this quiet corner, with a good place and a good book, and the afternoon to myself, than the richest in the land, who have no time to feel or think or wonder at themselves, wasting their days like flies on a cow pat.

It is easy to say so much, but not so easy to know it, or believe it. For what is deceiving is that the rich are often gay and happy. So was I at Woodview; I would not have changed places then even with Nina Jimson for all that I loved her. I pitied her poverty.

But my gaiety was not the happiness I had at Tolbrook, in the garden corner, nor yet what I had left, when I married Matt. So it was really waste of my days and their proper delights.

58

The next week was the first of the shooting, and the London staff came down, Mr Felby, the butler, Mrs Felby, the housekeeper, and three maids. Mr Felby was the finest man you ever saw, like an archbishop, as clever as a lawyer and a beautiful waiter. But his eyes swimming in drink and a bad sly tongue. He made game of Mr Wilcher's boil and said: 'Serve him right, the dirty little swine – I wish it was a carbuncle.'

'Why?' said I. 'That's a cruel wish for the poor man.'

'Poor man,' said Felby, 'he has a million if he has a pound, and look at the way he lives – meaner than a rat that eats its own tail.'

'That's right,' said Mrs Felby, who was a sharp cross little thing with a hump on her back, 'with all his locks and his double locks – the one thing gives me a happy feeling when I get my pain and can't sleep is that he's going to be shown up.'

'Not a bit of it,' said Felby. 'He's got off before and he'll get off. He'll buy himself out of it. A rich man can get away with anything.'

Indeed, they both hated him, but I think they were the kind that hated anybody unless those that were only fit to be scorned. Felby hated the world because he was not a millionaire himself, and it was true he was born for it. A man like that, so handsome and strong and clever and well-mannered. I often pitied him in servitude and married to that wasp who would stab him so that you could see him swell up weak and blue like a sting on your neck.

'To hear you talk,' she would say, out of nothing at all and like a hornet on a summer day, 'you'd better tell people how I took your trousers down last time and gave you toko, yes, and made you kiss the stick and say thank you, mamma,' and she turned to me: 'If a man behaves like a dirty little boy I say I'll treat him as such – drink is no excuse.'

Sometimes she brought Mr Felby so near tears that I couldn't look at him, and I was in a hurry to change the subject. I daresay it was her back made her so mad at him, but no woman has a right to bring her husband to public shame; it is too easy, and my mother used to say: 'Never spoil a man's dignity, for he's a poor remnant without it, and don't think yourself so good a wife either if you do so much. It's only common sense and your own best interest.' My mother was a true Christian woman and I never forgot her teaching. It was in my blood, the best part of me, and, I daresay, the only good part I had, so it was shocked by Mrs Felby's cruelty.

But she hated all men, not like Rozzie for the joke, but in good truth.

'You know it yourself,' Mrs Felby said. 'Men are rubbish and dirty to boot.'

So I said that we couldn't do without them and that God had his purpose for them, trust him, as for the worst of us.

But Mrs Felby was fierce and careless. 'Oh, that God!' she said, rubbing her hump. 'Poor thing, don't bring him in. I've no patience with him. But it seems that he was a man too, or he wouldn't have stuck his image into the world to be an everlasting pest to a decent woman. We never asked for him and only want a little peace and quiet.'

So I dared to remind her that if there were no men in the world there would be no babies either, and no girls.

'Good riddance,' said she.

'Well,' I said, 'you wouldn't have the world come to an end?'

'Why not,' she said, 'it'll last my time and what then. It won't be anything to me either way for I won't know.'

I was shocked at this at first that anyone should care so little for the whole world, but then I thought: 'Ah, the poor thing, she hasn't children to carry her spirit forward.' So I turned back and said: 'If we don't need men, they need us, and I wonder Mr Wilcher has never got him a wife. With all that money he could have had the pick. And they say he needs one.'

'You be careful,' she said to me. 'I hear he's throwing an eye on you already. Has he been pinching you?'

'Good gracious, no,' I said. 'How could he?'

'And what was he doing in the upper passage last night, when you went to bed?'

'I never saw him,' I said. For the truth was that just when I was going up to bed, I had seen the master come out of the attic with a candle, and with only a towel round his neck, as if from his bath. So he walked towards me, but as if not seeing me. And I had pretended not to see him and turned my back to go into the linen room. But I wasn't going to tell Mrs Felby that tale with her bad mind. For I thought still that if the master had that whim, to show himself, it was no harm in the world, except to idle heads and bad tongues. If he had been a drunkard, or spiteful or cruel, then I might have misliked him, but not for being simple, like any lad in his teens.

But Mrs Felby had nothing to do but nurse her rage and feed her pain. She went on at me: It was as much as my place was worth to give way to the master. 'You know what happened to Mrs Frewen.'

'I hear she tried to frighten him.'

'And so she could have, the fool. But he's a bold one, the master, I'll admit. He told her she could send it to the papers if she liked and when she spoke of the police, he sent for them there and then and put them on her box.'

'Had she taken anything then?'

'She said no, that the master had given her the things. But then she began to howl and wouldn't say anything more. She was quite beaten flat, the silly sheep. She got eighteen months and serve her right for being such a fool. To think she could have brought the master into court and shown him up before the whole county. May she rot.'

Taken all round, I was more shocked by the Felbys than any couple I can remember. To think how they lived in daily bitterness. You wondered they did not die of the poison. And I thought: 'I wonder did my servants when I had them talk about me so,' and thought: 'Ah, my girl, you don't know how well off you are back in the kitchen with the good honest flags under your feet.' For a drawing-room, comfortable though it be, may only be stuck on the roof of envy and backbiting and no real peace in the whole mansion. See how I live now without an enemy in the world to poison my sleep, and good food and fires of sweet-smelling wood, and it seemed to me that it was providence himself that had taken me by the hand and led me back to the kitchen. For where could a woman find a better life, I mean in a good house with a good draught in the chimney, and double sinks and really hot water, as I always had at Tolbrook. Then it came back to me about what poor Jimson had said about my true home being in a kitchen and that I was a born servant in my soul and my heart gave a turn over and I felt the true joy of my life as clear and strong as if the big round clock over the chimney-mouth was ticking inside me. 'So here I am,' I thought, 'mistress of my own world in my own kitchen,' and I looked at the shining steel of the range and the china on the dresser glittering like jewels, and the dish covers, hanging in their row from the big venison one on the left to the little chop one on the right, as beautiful as a row of calendar moons, and the kitchen table scrubbed as white as beef fat and the copper on the dark wall throwing out a glow to warm the heart, and the blue delf bowls like pots of precious balm. And then beyond where the larder door stood ajar you could see bottles of oil and relish and anchovies and pickles and underneath the lid of the big flour-bin as white as its own lovely flour, I call it a treat for queens to sink your hands in new wheaten flour. And next the larder, the dark scullery door with just a wink within of the brass taps to say: 'Your servants, madam,' and a slow drip from the one or other to tell me: 'We are ready this minute and never will fail,' and next the scullery, the kitchen pantry. I could not see its glass-fronted cupboards as fine as the British Museum, or its china and glass in thick heaps like the treasures of Aladdin. I could not see them, but I felt them like kingdoms in my charge. And, indeed, I felt bits of myself running out from the grand kitchen into pantry and scullery and larder and beyond into the passage and the still-room and even to the wood cellar and the boot-hole as if I was really a king or queen whose flesh is brought up to be the father of all his countries, and not to forget the little bye-lands even when they are on the dark side of the sun. You would say I was putting out in buds like a shallot with my big kitchen heart in the middle and my little hearts all round in the empire of those good faithful offices, all fitted up as they were, even the cupboards, in the best of country materials. The very shelves in the boot-hole were oak, and the fruit-racks were sweet apple.

'How many women,' I thought, 'can sit before a fire like this one among such a noble property of bowls and pots and cups and plates and knives and forks and whisks and pestles and colanders, bottles and kegs and jars.' 'Why,' I thought, 'the mustard-pots alone would make a regiment,' and a kind of awe came on me at all these many things put into my sole charge. 'Well,' I thought, 'if you tied a knot of all the roads and railways and pipes and wires in the world it would come to a kitchen in the middle of it.' And so close and neat, there wouldn't be room in it for a single piece of useless nonsense or vain furniture. For the great beauty of my jewels was that every one of them was needed and of my treasure-chests that all this silver and gold was new-minted flour and fresh-baked cakes and my shining armour was to keep dinners warm and my regiments were to cut up chickens and ducks and to stick their bayonets in chops and steaks for the glory only of conquering hungry stomachs and bad tempers. It's after a good dinner, I thought, that the lion and the lamb lie down together and let out their top buttons (as poor Mattey would do) and put their feet on the hob.

So I looked round me that night and many more afterwards in the Tolbrook kitchen, and prayed: 'Let me only live cook in this dear place and not die too old for the work, and I'll never want another heaven.'

This was my prayer and it seemed a judgement on me for making it when not three months after I was sent for to come up to town in place of Mr Wilcher's town cook.

This was the first work of my chief enemy, though I did not call her enemy then, and she meant to do me good.

59

The name of this woman, when I first knew her, was Blanche Hipper. She came to Tolbrook that year in September, with her elder sister Clarissa, when the first party was made up, to play tennis with Mr Loftus Wilcher, the master's eldest nephew. Mr Loftus was a soldier, a pretty man, fair as a girl, but sleepy. He would often dawdle about the kitchen at Tolbrook for mutton-fat for his boots, or oil for his flies, or only for something to do, and though he spoke little, he was easy and friendly. I liked him well and wished him joy, which I thought he would have, for the girls were mad for him, with his looks.

This Blanche was nineteen, daughter of the vicar in the next parish, plump and pretty enough, though too short in the neck and high in the shoulder. Her prettiness, to tell the truth, was only in her skin and eyes.

Even then I liked Miss Clarissa better, for though she was not so pretty, she always treated us servants like human beings with souls, and Miss Blanche was hoity-toity even to the butler. Yet I could not feel angry with Miss Blanche because she was so gay and full of life and ready to enjoy everything and to make things go. Indeed, I always felt a liking for her and I could never be her enemy. I thought then that as she came from a poor family she had not learnt how to treat servants, and had not enough sense, like Miss Clarissa, to think it out for herself. Miss Clary was three years older and working in London at an office for a whiskey company. She and Mr Loftus were childhood friends and we were all sure they would make a match of it, a good match for both, for he had money and beauty and she had brains and kindness.

I wished for the match more than anything in the world, for, as I say, Miss Clary was friendly with us all, and from the beginning she was my special friend. Of course, she came to me, at first, to get something out of me, special sandwiches for her lunch in the train, to save her pocket, or coffee to dye her stockings, but she did it so sweetly, it was a pleasure. Then to reward me and make all seem friendly, she would always talk, and she talked so freely, I was surprised. I had not known how the new girls that had come up in London since the war would talk about anything to anybody. It shocked me at first to hear Miss Clary, mentioning Mr Wilcher's boil, speak of 'poor old bottom' and say that Aggie behaved as if she were in the family way again, and she hoped not because the girl was so careless in choosing her sires.

But though we servants could never have talked to each other as Miss Clary talked to me, and some were offended, I saw it was only the new way. For the new ways always begin at the top and go down; so I remember, when poor Rozzie went to the workhouse at last, she complained there was an old woman in the next bed who called her a Jezebel because she tried to powder her nose with plaster off the wall and tooth-powder. As Rozzie said, she would rather have died before the war than paint, but now even the vicar's wife powdered. And the poor-law nurses, as grim a set of crows as ever picked among old bones, painted and rouged; for all she knew, so she said, they dyed themselves pink behind like the monkeys.

I never could get used to paint, and, thank God, I never needed powder except in the time with Gulley, to hide a black eye or a swollen nose. But they were in fashion, even for ladies, and I saw that Miss Clary's free talk was all in the fashion too. So I did not mind it, for I thought: 'The world must move.' I even got to like it, for, as I say, it made me friends with Miss Clary, and I saw very soon how it was with her and Mr Loftus. For she did not speak freely of him, or if she tried, her voice would change and her colour come up. So she would say of a dance which Mr Wilcher didn't want because of the expense: 'I'll get Mr Loftus to ask him – he'd do anything for Mr Loftus.'

It is true that Mr Wilcher liked Mr Loftus and it was said, too, he wanted him to marry Miss Clary and often asked her out, in London, to meet him.

Not that Mr Loftus was so certain to be the heir and to get Tolbrook. For though he was the true heir, the only son of Mr W.'s brother, Mr W. liked better another of his nephews, who was the son of his elder sister. This was Bobby Brown, who was still a boy at school. His mother was dead and his father was married again, in India, so he often went to Mr W.'s for his holidays.

I say Mr W. looked upon Bobby almost as a son; yet whenever Bobby came here, he always managed to fall out with him. He would come to me and say: 'Mr Bobby will be here tomorrow, Mrs Jimson – his favourite pudding is suet with jam and we will have a goose for dinner. He likes goose.'

Master Robert was just sixteen, but small for his age, and not needing to shave except once a month, with scissors. He had a young voice still and he would call out like a child. But he would talk at anyone like an old man, about anything you liked. He was at the age when boys begin to read and think they know everything because the books make it seem easy. I suppose they must, like a cookery book, for how could they put the hard parts, like real life, which are different every time; your cream all turned that morning, or a hole in the stock-pot; or the kitchen boiler to be cleaned. I dearly loved Master Robert, who came to me the very first day of his holidays, to make toffee in a soup-plate, and abused me for not knowing how to cook.

'Now then,' he said, 'come along, and I'll show you.'

But the toffee stuck to the plate which broke in getting it out; one of the best china service. 'Oh lord,' he said, 'what will uncle say?'

'Perhaps he'd better not know,' I said.

'Oh, I must tell him,' Bobby said, putting out his lip just like Mr W. 'Oh lord, aren't I a fool not to remember to butter it? I could kick myself. Oh, well, come on, what's the next thing? Get a move on, old lady. We want our tea.' And he would take me and push me round the kitchen like a bath-chair.

That was when Mr W. was not at home. For Bobby, having no home and no place to go, often came to Tolbrook for his holidays, and was alone there for a week or more. Of course he had his friends and would go off fishing or sailing most days. But he was often in the house too, and then he would always be in and out of the kitchen, chattering or whistling, or watching me work, and picking it up too, in a wonderful way. He always made the coffee and he could turn off a sweet omelette, too, to beat the French. And it was always: 'Come on, old lady, what's the next item in the programme?' He was as familiar to me as if I had been his own nurse; and so I felt to him. For all his roughness was the kindness of a good young soul that had nothing to spend it on and did not know how to come close to those he loved except by running into them or slapping them, by hand or word, as little children do.

Bobby even wrote to me from school, though it was only to send his cricket trousers, or some toffee. But he would put in his love and remain your affectionate.

Mr W., as I say, loved Bobby well and I'm sure he knew the lad's true goodness. Yet I dreaded their coming together in the holidays, because it always meant putting the master out, and upsetting him, including his appetite.

It upset him to be so upset over arguing with a boy, and because he would often find himself turned right round, as arguers will, and arguing against his own mind. So when Bobby would say that the coal-miners ought to have better pay because it was a dirty job which he wouldn't like, Mr W. would smile and answer: 'Perfectly true.' But, of course, the matter was not quite so simple, for what about this and that, the steel workers and foreign competition and so on.

But then, Master Bobby would say: 'Wages come first,' and Mr W. would say: 'Not so. What if the country were ruined? then Wales would starve too.'

So then they would argue until Mr W. would be telling Bobby that his pets, the miners, only wanted to ruin the country, so that they could start a revolution, having begun by saying they were good fellows, as all know, and only sometimes misled.

Then he would send away his plate and eat nothing more for dinner, nor even breakfast. For Mr W. took everything to heart and didn't get over his troubles like the lighter kind, all in a moment.

60

Miss Clary and Bobby were very good friends and Clary often made peace for him with Mr W. Mr W. really loved Miss Clary for her gentle ways and her good sense. We all hoped for the romance between her and Mr Loftus to have a happy end, as soon as might be.

That September, Mr Loftus and she came down together by the same train and we were all sure that he was going to propose. Indeed, the housemaid found a new ring-box, done up in tissue, in his collar-box, a lovely sapphire with diamonds. Sapphire was Miss Clary's colour, to bring up her eyes, which were blue, a far better blue than her younger sister's, but not so strong. She wore spectacles for work and she could not play tennis.

But just when Mr Loftus was going to propose and they had danced one evening together to the gramophone, Miss Clary being a beautiful dancer, her aunt fell ill in London and there was nothing for it but she must go back to nurse her, because Blanche would not. Indeed, her own father said she was not fit to nurse anybody, being too noisy and selfish. For so the post office told us, which was the Hippers' post office, too, and knew all about the family.

Miss Clary went off on Monday and Mr Loftus drove her to the station in the trap. We were told she was in tears on the platform as if going to a war, to throw away her life, and saying good-bye to all the joys of this one, and so she was, poor child. Mr Loftus came back looking very cast down, and did nothing all that day. He was a young man very easily bored, like many horse soldiers, when there's no hunting or races or horses either. For we had none at Tolbrook then, but trappers and the cart-horse. So Mr Loftus was quite worn out with nothing to do, and having to make talk with Mr W. who, talkative as he was, could never get up a real conversation with Mr Loftus. He would speak about the Army and about the lessons of the last war, and Mr Loftus would say: 'Yes, Uncle,' and 'No, Uncle,' and hardly be able to open his eyes for boredom. He was a young man who hated conversation.

Then Blanche came along for tennis, and when Mr Loftus said it was too hot, that he had no things, that the court was not fit, she said: 'Nonsense.' So she made him roll the court himself and tie up the net with string, and she borrowed the agent's trousers for him and lent him her second-best racket; and she showed him new strokes all the afternoon and fairly abused him when he could not do them. I heard her myself call him an ass, the very first day. Of course she had known him for some years too, but not since her hair had gone up, for she had been at school until the last two years. And I'm sure she had never been familiar with him before.

So she bullied him and made him run about, and the next day it was riding in the field, because she wanted to practise her riding. Mr Loftus had despised riding about on a cob, but he did not mind when Miss Blanche made him take her out. Then it was picnics to Longwater, and sailing, and the end of it was, after only a week, that they were engaged, and she had on her finger the ring that poor Mr Loftus had bought for her sister.

It was said that she proposed to him; but I think it more likely she only led him up to it, after a little kissing and perhaps only one kiss. For to do her justice, she was very particular and no flirt. Perhaps she had set out to catch Loftus, but if she did, it was not by philandering with him; never more, at least, than putting her cheek close in front of his eyes, in a gate or a gig. Any girl who knows that her complexion is her chief beauty might do so much, without knowing her own artfulness.

So Mr Loftus married her and she had Clary for a bridesmaid. I never saw a girl so green at a wedding, and I thought she would faint. We all thought it the cruellest thing that she had to stand up there and hear her man say that he would love and cherish her sister. Some blamed Miss Blanche for it and said it was a piece of her spite, because she was jealous of Miss Clary's brains and goodness and her being loved more by their father. But I thought it was only the way it happened. Miss Clary could not stand out, or people would have said that she was bitter and unforgiving, in her sister's time of joy. I think it had to be and that Miss Clary was to suffer that cruelty. But she did not faint, and when that night she wanted to go to bed early, because she said her head ached, but really I think it was because she could not bear daylight any longer, she asked me if I could make her some tea. And this was the beginning of my friendship with Miss Clary. For when I said the tea must not be too strong, to keep her awake, she said that she did not hope to sleep 'this night of all nights.'

It was a slip and she coloured up when she had said it. But the truth was that she had got, even then, into such a way of chattering with me, that she never thought before her tongue spoke. Then she looked at me and smiled in a way that almost made me cry, and said: 'I've shocked you again, Sara,' for she always called me Sara. 'But you shouldn't be so comfortable to talk to.'

I thought then that she might be going to cry but if she might cry for joy, she was not one to cry for grief, and it was just as well, seeing her appointed fate. For she never stopped suffering from that disappointment and the ruin of her whole life; and if she had been a poor spirited girl, she would have gone to pieces and turned into a misery, fit for nothing but to drag upon other people. But not at all. Miss Clary never dragged on anyone and stayed what she had always been, her father's right-hand and so Mr W. told us, the prop of her whiskey office in London. It was my only consolation when Mr Wilcher, that November, sent for me to London, that I might see Miss Clary there.

61

The Loftus Wilchers had used the town house in a part of their honeymoon and the cook there was to make arrangements. But it seemed that the new Mrs Loftus, full of her wedding ring, had found the place dirty and quarrelled with the cook.

So the cook went out at a day's notice, which was always Mr W.'s way. He would never keep a discharged servant in the house one night, but handed her a month's wages and a bit over and sent her off. 'A regular old bachelor,' I thought, 'who can't bear to sleep on so much as a crumb.' But the Felbys, of course, had another tale. That the woman had something against the master and gave Mrs Loftus some hint of it. And that she went off with a hundred pounds to keep her quiet.

I thought I would break my heart going from Tolbrook to London; and to make me feel it more, it was snowy weather. There was no place prettier under snow than our Tolbrook with its old garden walls and the yew hedges, its small fields and big trees, and the pond and streams. When I went out for the eggs, before breakfast, by the cart lane, the fields were like icing sugar and the pond so grey as eels with the snow water; the sky was like new cleaned window glass full of its own shine, the very weeds and old docken were like silver and velvet cut for a wedding. Then when I was going away, the sun was up and all was like a pearl, pink and blue, and you saw the snow at the roadside full of bubbles like white of egg beaten up, with rainbows in every one. The air, too, was so clean with all the dust brought down that you couldn't believe that there was such a thing as dust in the world, to spoil all, and waste our lives away, only cleaning it away.

And then to come to London, as dim as a cellar in mid-afternoon, with a sky like a coal-hole ceiling, even to the black cobwebs, which were their clouds, and the roads like cold gravy, and the snow like marzipan piled in the gutters, and the trees in the gardens weeping down black as if their sap was only soot.

The town house, No. 15 Craven Gardens, was what you would expect; a slice of a house, seven storeys from basement to attic. I felt squeezed sideways as I went in and going down to the basement was like going to my grave. A real old-fashioned basement with long passages and dark holes off them, a great low kitchen with the ceiling hanging down as if it would fall on you; a fog of blacks and gas and smoke like the old underground, and a cold smell of cockroaches and mould and mice. If it hadn't been for the other servants I would have sat down and cried.

My bedroom too, I would never have put my own kitchenmaid in such a place. A cupboard with the ceiling down the floor on one side, dirty matting eaten away by rats, an iron bedstead with a tin jug, one chair with a hole in it, and when I had a fire lit, the chimney smoked me out. 'No,' I said, 'I'll go. I can't bear it and I have no right to bear it, with my quality as cook and housekeeper. I'll give in my notice tomorrow. I know that with my nine months' character, I could get a better place.' I could have picked and chosen.

Now why I did not give notice, I don't know, for I certainly meant to, or get my lot bettered. But I think it was only my rolling way. For when I got up there was the breakfast and then the looking over my battery and the larders, and then the cleaning, and before I could think of notice again, the master sent for me.

62

Mr W. put me on a chair in the corner. He looked so queerly, jumping about the room, I remembered all the stories I had heard and went cold with fright. 'Well,' I thought, 'if I don't struggle he won't kill me and the worst of such wickedness is only the thought of it.'

Then he sat down and drew up a chair till his knees were nearly touching mine and said in a voice, like his church voice, that seemed to pray in my mind: 'Mrs Jimson, I am at your mercy.'

I was too frightened to speak. But he was too excited to notice it. And the whole thing was that he wanted me to be housekeeper instead of Mrs Felby. He was going to put out the Felbys, and I was to manage both houses.

When I said it was above my degree, he said: 'Mrs Jimson, you have been mistress of a household much larger than my modest establishment, and as the wife of a distinguished artist, you cannot plead that the housekeeper's room is above your degree.'

Then I begged for Tolbrook only. But Mr Wilcher was one of those who will not take a no. Hadn't I seen it in his lip and his nose too. 'Mrs Jimson,' he said 'I mustn't press you but as you see I'm in a terrible difficulty. I must get rid of the Felbys and they'll have to go at once. Who is going to run this house? I could go to my club, but I can't leave it with servants only – you know what they are as well as I do. They'd be up to mischief as soon as my back was turned. And I have my work to think of, important work. It's waiting for me now, at the office. How am I to work when things like this go on happening? Never settled for a moment. The place is like a madhouse.'

He was so excited with his wrongs that he jumped up and ran about the room as if he were really mad. I could see indeed that the houses were a perfect pest to him, as you might expect, in a wifeless man.

'Mrs Jimson,' he said, 'if you desert me, I don't know what I shall do. You understand the Felbys are going today. I had to give them notice in case they heard anything from other sources.'

'Mercy me,' I thought, and I wondered at the poor man's faithlessness. No wonder, I thought, he's half-mad with it.

So I thought, I could do with extra money, especially if Jimson should write for more advances, as I expected, and I agreed at last to be house-keeper, town and country. But no sooner had I said it than Mr Wilcher was up again and crying out, what could he do for cooks – two cooks. Where could he find them? And he asked me to do the cooking too.

No, no, I thought. It's too much – it would be killing work. Then he was in despair again and when I said I could get cooks, he said that he only wanted my cooking. But if I went on as cook, who would be housekeeper?

'Of course,' he said, 'I'll consider it in your salary.'

So he went on at me till I found that I had agreed to all. Only I held out for a kitchen-maid. And he said I could have one, if I didn't give more than sixteen. It was all he could afford. But where could I have got a kitchen-maid, at that rate, in 25?

When I went out, I was to do four women's work, for less than the wages of one. For I knew Mrs Felby had seventy-five for her own part, and he was to give me sixty-five.

Of course he was full of his thanks and compliments. I did not know quite how I stood, until I was downstairs again, in my own place. Then I was angry, for I thought I had been done out of my deserts. But I would not say now that Mr Wilcher meant to take advantage of me. He was a man so worried and pestered by everything in his life, by the houses and the nieces and nephews and the times and the world, and I suppose his own nature, too, that he was like three men tied up in one bag and you never knew and he never knew which of them would pop out his head, or something else, or what it would say or do. True, all of him was of a saving disposition, as I was; though he had given away thousands, too, as I heard, to missions, and he had doubled the seating in Tolbrook church.

So I came to see that if I had been done, it was my own fault, for giving way to him, and as for my deserts, it was what they say:

> If I had my deserts, I should ride a King's coach
> With bows to my back should the courtiers approach,

Flogging and whipping as court shall devise
And coach to the gallows to give me a rise.

63

And the place was easy. In London Mr Wilcher lived like a clock. It was a pity to see how little he had of a life, with all his money and his houses. Up at seven, cold bath, a cup of tea and a walk round the gardens; then house prayers in the dining-room and breakfast in his own room, and off to work.

It seemed that he was a lawyer in a very old firm, which had been in the family since George the Third. Every evening except Saturday he came back to tea at five, drank a cup of tea and read the evening paper. Then a long bath and dinner at seven. After dinner he often went to a concert or a theatre. But often he read the whole evening, heavy big books from his own library, so quiet you would not know that he was in the room. His room was a small study next his bedroom and bathroom on the fourth floor. He really lived there, for he never went into the dining-room only for prayers and dinner. He had that in style, with four candles and flowers and plate, and dressed for it; but he ate very little and did not stay long. He drank only soda water or one glass of port.

On Saturday he had a turkish bath and tea at his bath; and he went out to dinner with an old friend and often stayed till two or three in the morning; or all night. But he always came in to No. 15 early to change and bath before he went to the office. On Sundays he went twice to church, often to early service too.

Not much entertaining and always at dinners, which I prefer. A party of five or six about once a month, and much talk and sometimes cards after. But they talked at cards too, and I don't think Mr W. cared for cards. He would rather talk, especially to clergymen. There was always one or two clergymen at our parties, which I liked too, for the rich ones are always so pleasant and the poor ones could always do with a good meal.

When the captain came with his new wife, we would have young people, but these were always the quietest and saddest of all. The only one to talk was Mrs Loftus, and if she did not get anyone to talk the talk she liked about tennis or golf, she just ate. The footman, Billy, who waited, said they would all sit mum like corks on a wire, waiting for a wind to make them sing.

As for giving Mr W. satisfaction, that was easy enough. He wanted only simple food and he never noticed how the house was kept up, except now and then when his fidgets took him into some shut-up room and he would find dust on the mantelpiece and ring and say to me that no doubt the housemaid had forgotten the mantelpiece and he had no wish to worry me with trifles, but look at his finger. This to show he was keeping his eyes open, when he had not seen the great black cobwebs which the Felbys had left on every cornice.

But I liked him for trying to do his duty by the house, although it was not his born work. He tries to keep things up, I thought, and give them their rights, when he might let them down and let himself down.

64

I had been afraid of a town life; that it would drive me mad, boxed up among houses; but not a bit. It was true I still liked Tolbrook best; but I got to love No. 15 too. I loved the peace and quiet of town without hens and calves waking you up at four in the morning; and the company. For I had many friends and went out to tea or to cards two or three times a week. There was my first cousin married to a grocer in Ealing, and my two old aunts at Penge. I went to them and they came to me in my own room, which was prettier than any of theirs. Then I would walk in the park, which is better than the country for company. I would go often to sit by the Round Pond where the nurses take their prams and the children sail their boats. I can't tell you the pleasure I had there, all for nothing. For first there were the prams and the babies and I always knew some of the girls, so that when they sat down to rock the pram, I could talk with them about their babies and mistresses, and their young men. Then there were the little boys and girls running about mad with the water so near, for water always goes to a child's head. And the other people enjoying the sight and the children, such people that you know are a good kind of souls; and then there was the breeze, and the open sky, and the trees full of the breeze and the water itself glittering and jumping like a child's sea, as gay and happy in itself as any child. And the boats, and the wonder would they get across; and last but not the least by long ways were the grown men with big expensive boats and long beautiful brass polished hooks to catch them with. There was one there, quite old and bald, with fat weak legs, who would run after his boat and pant until you were afraid for him, and if he had been a child you would have told him to wait and gone to catch his boat for him. But since he was a man, in a very good suit too and gold watch chain, you could not help him; you could only hope the boat would not turn away from him before he ran himself into a fit. I don't know why to see this man so anxious about his boat, made me feel so pleased that I would be gay all the evening, as if I had been a young girl coming from a party or from the Communion; not knowing yet my own self or the traps of the world.

I remember the feeling because I needed it just then. It was the first time we all noticed what a grip Mrs Loftus had upon poor Mr W. Now her husband's regiment was in London, she came round almost every day and used the house like her own. Indeed, it surprised us all how that girl had changed in one single year from a lumpish sort of kitten into a touch-me-not kind of cat. She walked as if the floor was hers, and spoke as if the rest had only ears. Especially after her boy was born, she would tell Mr W. himself how the law was and what must be done. As for us servants, she treated us like dirt; even me whom she still liked. She told me that when her husband got the property, she would continue with me as cook at the Manor; for though my cooking was not up to London standard, it was good enough for the country. But she would do her own housekeeping. 'For I hate waste,' she said, 'and I never allow perks.' She was not yet twenty-one and had engaged her first servant less than a year. 'They're quite unnecessary,' she said. 'I don't mean that you would ever take anything, Mrs Jimson, but then you're an exception.'

She meant, of course, that she was sure I did take as much as I could get, and that I had better stop it, before she caught me.

But what troubled me and Miss Clary was to see the power she had over Mr W. We had seen how she swallowed up her poor husband, so he could not blow his nose without her. Not that she was rough with him. She was never out of temper and always ready for anything. But that was it. She was always with him, whatever he did, shooting, or hunting, or sailing; they say she had gone to the parade ground with him till the Colonel gave her a hint, through his own lady. She was like a slave to him and yet she was his master too. For he could not do without her. At Tolbrook, it was 'Where's Blanche?' all day; or if he was asked to shoot or fish or ride, he would say: 'I don't know what we're doing today. Ask Blanche.'

She kept him on the go, and I never saw him bored, but I never saw him laugh either in his old way and sometimes I thought he would have liked to dawdle again and talk nonsense with Miss Clary.

But how was it that Mrs Loftus had such power over Mr W. that it seemed she would take anything out of his hands and rule his house, and get the property for herself and Loftus, in spite of all he could do and his natural feelings towards Robert? Miss Clary said it was because Mr W. was so shilly-shally in himself that any woman could do what she liked with him. She said that Mrs Eeles, who, it seemed, was his Saturday friend, had always turned him round her finger; and it was lucky for him that she was so stupid and lazy she did not think of marrying him or robbing him of all he had. 'She takes hundreds because she can't think in thousands,' Miss Clary said; 'and besides, she doesn't need jewels or clothes because she hardly ever leaves her room. She used to go out on the streets and take pick-ups to the park; but now she gets the drink sent up and won't be bothered with men.'

130

But I did not think it was all shilly-shally with Mr W., because he would often refuse to take Mrs L.'s advice. He would come to me about a dinner party. 'I'll ask Mrs Loftus – she understands these things.' But he would change her plans too and cut off half her guests and all the champagne.

He used to say of Mrs Loftus, like Miss Clary: 'She's young – and it's a young world. Perhaps it takes youth to understand it.' But though he often took Mrs Loftus's advice, he never listened to Miss Clary. She was too free and too much for politics, or too much for Bobby's and my Belle's kind of politics, which I would have thought young. But Mr W. seemed to think the other old Blue kind could be young too, in Mrs Loftus.

65

I had not heard from Gulley in three years except when he wrote for five pounds and offered to sell me all the pictures left behind in Ancombe, for a hundred pounds, paid in instalments. I said nothing to that. Where was I to get a hundred pounds, even if I had thought of buying pictures with it? But I sent him three pounds and after that he had written only once more for another three pounds. And put in a kind of account showing that I had paid six before.

When one afternoon at Craven Gardens, the footman Billy came down to say there was a gentleman for me in the drawing-room. 'He says he's your husband.'

'In the drawing-room,' I said. 'Why did you put him there?' Billy was only a boy, not yet seventeen. He said that he had pushed past him, and wouldn't be stopped.

It was just time for Mr W. to come home from the office; so I ran upstairs as fast as I could, and asked Gulley if he wanted to lose me my place. But he answered only that I looked younger than ever.

I thought he looked much older and shabbier. He smelt of whiskey too. But he would not tell me anything about himself or where he was living. I knew it was in London, somewhere near Finchley, because he had given his box address there, at a tobacco-sweet shop. But he would not say the address, or come downstairs.

'At least if you came down, I could clean your shoes,' I said, 'and save that coat button.'

'No,' he said. 'I want to see this Mr Wilcher.'

I saw that he was in a bad mood and I was terribly frightened. 'You don't want me back,' I said.

He didn't answer but looked at me more slyly than ever. I saw he was in a bad idle mood and I was frightened. For I thought I could not bear any more beatings. 'Pretty comfortable,' he said. 'Housekeeper to a single gentleman, all found and bed and board. Especially bed.'

'It's a lie,' I said. 'Mr Wilcher would never do such a thing.'

'That's not what they say about him at Queensport,' he said. 'So you don't mean to come back to your lawful husband.'

I was terribly cast down, for I knew I would go back if he asked me, and be beaten and lose all my comforts. I dreaded it and yet I knew he had only to say the word. For cruel as he was, he had yet a hold on me. I don't know how it is but when you've lived with a man, and cooked and cleaned for him and nursed him and been through troubles with him, he gets into your blood, whoever he is, and you can't get him out. Besides, there was no doubt Gulley was the most of a man I ever knew. For he carried his own burden, which was a heavy one; and even if he was cruel, it was only when driven mad.

'The only thing is this,' I said. 'If I come back to you, how will I be able to pay you your instalments?'

'I don't care about the money,' he said, eyeing me over. 'My God, Sall, I believe you've improved in these years,' and he caught hold of my front with his hand and squeezed me. 'Just as firm as ever. By God, Sall, we had some good times, hadn't we, and what a model you were. Some of those drawings were first-class, though I say it. Well, so you'll come back to me. Better clear out before Wilcher arrives. I'll order a cab, shall I?'

But he did not order a cab. Instead he kept on looking at me sideways, in his wicked mood. I thought that probably he had been stuck and suddenly had the idea of coming after me.

'That reminds me,' he said, 'Where are the drawings? I sold you the canvases, not the drawings.'

Now Gulley had written of the drawings, the time he asked for the three pounds, but, of course, I knew nothing of them or the canvases except that I had left them with Miss Slaughter, and when she died, Mr Hickson had said that he would take care of them; and pick out two canvases in exchange for our debts which he had paid. I had signed a paper to put me right with him, and glad I had been to throw that weight off my conscience, in exchange for pictures that no dealer would look at.

But I dared not so much as speak the name of Hickson to Gulley, who would rear up at the word; he had so made it a hobby to hate him.

So I pretended to look stupid and said: 'What drawings?'

'All my drawings,' he said; 'about five hundred of them. Come, be honest for once, Sall, and own you've pinched them.'

I denied it for I was in terror of his picking a quarrel. But Gulley could always see through me and now he said: 'What will you bet your box isn't full of my things? – I know your old cook's box with loot twenty years old.' For he had always laughed at me for keeping some old things from my first place, only in memory of it, a velvet ribbon someone had thrown away and a trumpery bangle, a fairing from the man cook there. Then he took me by the arm and said: 'Come on, Sall, where's your room? Show the bridegroom into the wedding chamber – and welcome him with sackbuts.'

Then I was in terror, for the truth was I had a few of his drawings at the bottom of my box, and one pinned up on the wall, a head only. I had packed them at Ancombe in the hope some dealer would give a pound or two for them, since I could not pack the canvases; but Mr Z. had offered me only five shillings each; and I said I would rather keep them. For one thing, they were all of me and I did not want to see myself naked in a shop window, only for five shillings. It would have been a sin to bury a lot of money in my box; but if only shillings, it was better not to expose myself and risk the master seeing me, and knowing me, by the name and the figure.

Besides, I did not want to take him up to my room, for I was afraid of him, in his wicked mood; I had got too soft for Gulley in my comforts. So I began to say that my room was too untidy and that Mr Wilcher was just coming in.

So he came close to me and said: 'Are you coming back to me, Sall, or aren't you?'

'Of course,' I said, 'if you want me – haven't I always been ready?' But I knew it was my death.

'You think I can't support you,' he said.

'For God's sake,' I said, 'if you want me, call your cab and let me go and pack my box. But don't go on worrying at me.'

'Worrying at you,' he said.

So then I lost my hold on myself and said: 'I suppose it's only because you're stuck and ready to quarrel with your own shadow.'

'Stuck,' he said. 'I'm never stuck. Thank God I'm never short of ideas. What do you mean, stuck?' and he came at me. So I told him not to dare to hit me, for I wouldn't bear it. I was too old.

'Stuck!' he said. 'What do you mean, stuck?' and bang, his arm came out so quick, you couldn't see it. It was like a snake striking. And so hard the blood flew over his own face. I saw a drop on his own forehead.

He called me names, too; names I couldn't write; and I never saw him in such a rage. But though I was in such terror, my bones were melting, yet I would not run away, or give ground, but stood there and took his blows and told him he was a brute.

But suddenly we both heard the front door open and steps in the hall; Mr Wilcher, and Billy come to take his hat. 'There's the master,' I said, and flew out of the room and past Mr Wilcher, and up to my room, to put my poor nose into cold water.

So I heard no more till I came down to make the dinner and Billy told me that Jimson, all bloody as he was, had come into the hall and introduced himself, and shaken hands with Mr Wilcher. And then they had talked about art, Mr Wilcher complimenting Jimson. Mr W. had even asked him to stay. But he would not, and went off. And Mr Wilcher had even gone down the street with him, talking all the way.

Now I think that if those two had begun about art, they ended about me, for though Mr W. never said a word to me, and only once looked sharp at my swollen nose, yet he began to show me new little kindnesses from that day and told me I could spend a pound on the garden patch behind the house where I sometimes sat, if I thought I could improve it. He even sent a pot flower.

But I hardly noticed the change at first because I was in such terror of Gulley coming to take me away. I was grown such a coward I would lie awake at night in a sweat to think of his beatings. I could not believe how I had been so happy with him, and I wondered at my strength in those days and thought how I had fallen off, and was the more exposed to a let down in my old age. Savings in the Post Office were something, I thought, but the better ones were in the soul. For even the rich are wretched without them.

It was from this time that I began to pay Gulley instalments every week, but whether to keep him in some comfort and please my conscience, or only to keep him away and please my flesh, I never could tell.

66

But I know I was glad when he did not come, and indeed my only troubles in the rest of that year were my weight and sometimes cook's eye from living too much over steam and smoke; and of course Madame Loftus. But for two years about the time that skirts began to get longer and figures were coming back, she never came to us at all because of a great quarrel with Mr W. about his Saturday friend.

Now, though I rejoiced that Madame Loftus left us alone I was troubled, too, about this friend of the master's. He was not growing younger and every winter he began to have lumbago. He did not sleep so well either and would often fidget about the passages half the night; or read, not in his room, but downstairs in the library, as if he could not bear his own place.

Now I happened to know that this Saturday friend of his was also getting old, and she had been growing into drink; and with one thing and another, she was a great nuisance to my poor master, and had been so for years. Miss Clary also told me that she had never been good to him and had caught him young and kept him only because he was too polite to hurt her feelings and break with her.

This was what Madame L. and he had quarrelled about. For she always wanted him to give the woman up. And even after two years, when they were friends again, Mrs L. kept at him. To do her justice, she never considered her own interests when she had something on her mind. She would have called down an archbishop before the whole county, to please her conscience.

Whenever Mrs L. had another wrestle with the master, he was upset for a whole week and fidgeted till we were all on pins and needles.

Now he had got into a habit, which pleased me very well, of coming to the housekeeper's room every Sunday evening to look over the bills and tell me his plans for next week. Then he used to say: 'Sit down, Mrs Jimson,' and make me sit down by the fire, and he would say: 'You don't mind if I smoke,' and he would light a cigarette and sit on the other side of the fire and smoke it out and talk about the great cost of everything since the last war, and the changes in the world which we had both seen.

So we went on till it was a settled thing; our talk by the fire, and I think he would have missed it as much as I did. After two or three years, we got so far he would smoke two or three cigarettes and stay an hour; and sometimes he got off the changes in the world to his own changes. He spoke even once or twice of Gulley, respectfully saying that he did not understand modern art, but showing to me, too, that he thought I had been taken in and misused, that he knew my story. Now one Sunday night, when he was only just over the fidgets from a quarrel with Madame L. about his woman friend, he sat so long with me, and so quiet, that I wondered what was coming. He sat till nearly one o'clock, never speaking. Till all at once he said: 'Mrs Jimson, how long is it since you came to me? It must be nine years.'

It was only seven, but I myself was surprised at the time; it had gone so fast, but I thought, if he makes it nine, then he has something to say upon that, so I did not gainsay it.

Then he said: 'I hope you have been as comfortable as you have made me.'

I said that I couldn't ask for a better place.

'In fact, I don't know what I'd do without you.'

I said it was very kind of him to say so, but he answered: 'No, yours is the kindness; you've made a home for me that I never expected to have. For when I decided to be a bachelor, I knew that I should have to make some considerable sacrifices.'

I said I was sorry for any bachelor that had to be at the mercy of his servants.

'And not that only.' He stopped a moment and then he said: 'You are a woman of the world, Mrs Jimson, or ought I to say Mrs Monday, I have never known exactly which was right. Not that I would dream of hurting your feelings by recalling anything painful to your memory. Yet may I ask if you are free from that unfortunate entanglement with Mr Jimson.'

I said that, to be honest, I had never been married to Jimson.

'So I understood,' he said, 'and I admit that it is a great relief to me to have it confirmed from your own mouth. That you are free. But now I have my own confession to make. I believe you probably know that I have had an arrangement in a certain quarter that takes me out now and then in the evening, often till rather late. Now that's all very well for a young man, though I'll tell you in confidence, I never liked it. It means going out on wet miserable nights which make the whole thing a perfect penalty. And now that I'm getting older and have a touch of rheumatism, it is really quite ridiculous. To undergo such a disturbance and such misery just because one has made a certain arrangement, and to pay a considerable sum for it, and on top of all, to risk lumbago, is a perfect humiliation.'

When Mr W. said this, I felt quite delighted. For it was really what I felt myself. So, though I knew I was on delicate ground, where I might easily offend his manners, I said that I would be very glad indeed if he didn't have to keep such late nights, come all weathers.

'I'm very glad you do,' he said in a pleased voice, 'but I thought you would, and if it could be avoided, by any possible way, I will gladly stay at home. So the question is, how can it be done.'

It had been on the tip of my tongue to say that he only had to pay the woman off and stay at home, but I knew in that last minute that this would be just the very thing that would upset him. So I said nothing.

'How can it be done?' he said again, looking at me.

'That's the only point,' I said.

'If you could help me to answer it,' he said, 'I should think myself a very lucky man and a completely happy one.'

Now when he said that, all at once I had the feeling that he was going to propose marriage. I couldn't believe it, for I knew that Mr W. was not the man to marry his housekeeper, and yet for all my surprise, I felt it was coming. But before I could think, he went on: 'You and I know, Mrs Jimson, at our age, that the really important thing in life is living together in amity and mutual respect and we have that already. Anything more is not really of great importance. As they say, those that have it think nothing of it, and those that have not, think much too much of it. So if you feel that you wouldn't like to go any further in the matter, you'll never hear any more from me. We'll forget that we said anything about it – I'm not going to throw away the solid good fortune I have with you just for the little extra. Pleasant as it would be and convenient, since we do inhabit the same house, and I won't hide it, a great addition to my comforts, I'll think no more of it. What do you say, Mrs Jimson, shall I drop the subject?'

So I, still thinking that he was making a proposal, and that he was only not wishing to give me too grand ideas about his feelings, I said to him he knew very well how much happiness it gave me to be with him.

'And you think you could give me this other addition to it? Of course,' he said, 'I'll see that you don't suffer. I'll see that your position is secure. Though, if you wouldn't mind, I'd rather not have any settlements for family reasons.'

I thanked him very much and said that he was very generous. And then he said: 'Very well, we'll shake hands on it.'

So I shook hands with him and then at once he said that it was time we were in bed, and went off.

I thought all this was very well done; a very dignified kind of proposal. Only I was sorry to feel that he did not like me better than to make it all so much a matter of business.

What was my surprise when I was brushing my hair for bed, when he knocked at the door and walked in.

'So here I am,' he said, 'my dear Sara.' Calling me Sara for the first time. I was so confused that I did not know what to say. I went on brushing my hair while he walked about impatiently. At last he said: 'Come on, my dear. I don't want to be too late. I've got a board meeting tomorrow.'

So then all at once it came upon me what he meant and that his whole talk had been nothing to marriage. Indeed I had been a great fool to dream it, for I knew what he knew about me. So there was I brushing my hair and wondering what to do.

For I thought: 'If I turn him out, he'll be bound to be hurt. Whatever he says, he's a man and though I've no doubt he is not so delicate as my poor Matt, he has a great sense of what is proper, and is easily hurt by anything unexpected. Here he is now, so sure of himself and if I tell him it's all a mistake, won't he feel like a fool?'

So after I had waited so long as I could bear him waiting, I said: 'You don't think it's a little soon.'

'Why, Sara,' he said, 'if you think so, it is so. This is my usual day, you know – but I'm not so tied to routine, and I wouldn't for the world do anything to hurry you, or bother you. For I know when I'm a lucky man and have got a woman that I certainly never dreamed of. Yes, my dear,' he said, putting his hands on my shoulder, 'a good woman.' But then he was taken with his manners again. For he jumped away from me and said: 'Tomorrow, then,' and went out of the door. But when he had half-closed it he put in his head and said: 'Or when you like, my dear Sara, for it's for you to say. Remember that I am fully aware of my extraordinary good luck.'

He did not come the next day, or the next, and he behaved as if nothing had happened. I might have thought he had given up the whole thing. I almost believed it, but I knew in my mind that he had not. I knew very well that he was holding to his word and that it was for me to say.

I'll own I found this a terrible difficulty. It was bad enough to take him but worse to ask him. Yet I don't know how it was, but I felt that I must. Again, I thought, if I don't have him it will be, at the best, some late nights, more of that coarse rough woman, and more lumbago too; and at the worst, a chill and double pneumonia on top of it. For a man is always more exposed to chills after it, and indeed it is the most natural thing for him to stay warm in a double bed, and that, I always thought, was why nature had suggested that kind of bed till the modern unnatural customs were brought in.

Now I have to confess that I was quite confused between my conscience and my duties, and indeed I prayed one night, and cried over the whole thing, since I thought that even if mother could have been alive, she wouldn't have been able to guide me, yet all the time I knew I would give way. For I liked my happiness in Craven Gardens and my comforts and my peace and my dear Mr W. himself far too well to do anything to lose them, or do them any injury. So that (I'll confess) more than half my grief was simply the perplexity how to tell him that I would do what he liked, without making myself ashamed, and without giving him any offence. For goodness knows, it is easy enough to offend a man at these critical moments.

So while I was puzzling one night, after dinner, it came to me in desperation that I couldn't wait any longer. So I took in the savoury myself and put it on the table and said: 'I'd rather you said, Mr Wilcher.'

'Said what?' said he, surprised to see me in the dining-room, and not too pleased.

'When you wanted to come to me.'

So I blurted it out and I was fearful at once that he would be put off for ever; as Matt would have been. But there was the difference in the men. I couldn't have done a more sensible thing with my honest Mr W. if I had studied him like a skeleton leaf under the magnifying glass. He answered me at once: 'Very well, Mrs Jimson, as you wish. But, of course, you must turn me out if it's not convenient.'

So he came along that night, and what was strange and unexpected, he was most gentle and respectful. Though I should not say so, yet I must be honest and confess his way was a real pleasure; he was so thoughtful and attentive.

Now although in the next years I often suffered in conscience, and wondered at myself, while I walked in the gardens and thought: 'How is it that I can go about like this, like an ordinary person, and not be found out, or sink into the ground with shame?' yet the truth was that I was very happy.

So we went on three years without a single cross word, and the most perfect understanding. The only thing that gave me grief was that Mr W.

would never allow me to show him any kindness, or rather, I saw that it upset him. I must never allow a dear to slip out, and if I had to touch him for any reason, I must do it as to a young nervous creature, with a quiet movement and a steady still hand. For if I seemed to pet him, he would jerk away and say something cool and businesslike. 'Come now, it's late,' or bring in some conversation about the house. At first I thought he kept me at a distance for fear that I would grow conceited and make myself a nuisance to him, as I daresay other women had done. Afterwards I saw that he was nervous of kindness; and perhaps indeed he was afraid of women. He had learnt one way to deal with them and so he could not risk any other. For I know he was happy with me; he told me so many times.

67

Now it was said at the trial that I got Mr W. into my clutches and drove away his own family; and did what I liked with him and robbed him of everything. It was made out so, or nearly so, by the evidence, but it is very hard to get truth into evidence, as I think it is hard enough to get it in life, about human people, or even yourself. It was Mrs Loftus's evidence went against me; and she believed every word of it, for she was always very truthful. Yet I think she was wrong. She took a dislike to me and could never get over it.

The first time she quarrelled with me was at the time of the great slump. Bobby Brown had finished school that year, and he had won a prize at Oxford, forty pounds a year. So, though he had not meant to go to college, now he was eager. Mr W. was pleased about this, and delighted about the prize. But then it turned out Bobby's father would not pay for him. Mr W. would have to pay.

This, coming on top of the slump, upset Mr W. very much, and this was the first time he talked to me in a private way, about his affairs and told me his troubles. Even then I don't think he would have forgotten his manners, if it had not happened one night that he fell asleep in my arms; our first night that year, at Tolbrook.

Indeed we had both been very sleepy and both of us fell asleep. I don't know how it was, but waking up like that in a strange bed at a strange time, for it was dawn and the birds were singing, he seemed to forget himself and instead of getting up and going off, as he usually had done all these years, with a polite 'Good night, I hope you will sleep well,' or 'It's very good of you, Mrs Jimson. I hope I haven't disturbed you too much,' he began to talk freely.

'Is this Wednesday?' he said, and when I said it was, he burst out: 'Then it's the day of the lawn meet here.' So I said yes to that too.

Now the hunt had always upset Mr W., for he did not hunt himself. Indeed, he had meant to be a clergyman, before his elder brother was killed in the war, and he had to look after the property and the nephews; and this was another reason why he hated all the burden of the houses. He said they had spoilt his life.

'A perfect nuisance,' he said, 'and more expense. I'm sick of it. It's a damnable life.'

I was surprised to hear him swear in my presence. For though he had burst out at Bobby and even Mr Loftus, he had never forgotten himself with a servant. So I said that so long as he didn't let too many of the hunters into the house and kept the whiskey back and pushed the three-shilling sherry, I hoped it would go off under five pounds.

'Five pounds,' he said. 'Twenty guineas subscription and the chicken fund. It's the life of a convict – a life sentence.'

'But you see the neighbours and they like to come.' So I said how everyone admired Tolbrook.

'I wish I'd never seen it,' he said, 'or No. 15 – a couple of white elephants that are eating me into the bankruptcy court. And now I'm to pay out a thousand pounds for Master Bobby, because his father has some crack-brain prejudice against the universities.'

Now here comes in what they said was influence. Miss Clary and I were both fond of Bobby and we wanted to see him get his rights. Miss Clary had been at Mr W. already, many times, to get him pocket money, or clothes, when, poor lad, he had grown out of his suits like a charity boy, and now it was my turn. For both of us knew the poor boy was looking forward to Oxford like a birthday party. He was expecting wonders from Oxford, not only enjoyments, but discoveries, about the way the world really worked and what he should do to help it on. Of course he wanted to row too, and to drink beer, like any boy out of school, and why should he not while he was young? But he truly wanted knowledge, which is like a boy too, of that age. I really loved Bobby at eighteen. He was little and ugly, but good all through, not a speck of meanness in his whole body. If he was noisy and sometimes seemed to be rude, it was only that he did not stop to think, or know what it was like for old people to be old. Why should he know the pains of that state, not only the rheumatism, and the not sleeping, but the great heavy cares and the wondering: 'What shall I do in this or that,' and 'Have I done right or wrong,' and also all the memory of all their mistakes and sins to confuse them about their duty.

If Bobby was sometimes rude to Mr W., it was not out of unkindness, or socialism, but only because of what he could not know, which makes all the young ones impatient with our old dilly-dally.

So finding Mr W. in so soft a mood, I spoke to him about Bobby's hopes, and I said also how much he looked to Mr W. as his father, since his own father was so unnatural.

140

Mr W. was surprised, and perhaps I made a little more of it than was true. For I was carried off by my hopes. And he agreed that Bobby was a good lad in spite of the nonsense he picked up at school.

Yet as for influence, no sooner had I got him to that, than he fell away again and said that good lad as Bobby was, Oxford might spoil him. For as Mrs Loftus had said, it was full of socialists and playboys, a disgrace to their class.

Then he got quite furious again, and when I had turned him off Bobby, he cursed at the hunt, at the farmers, at the Tolbrook roof, which was leaking in twenty places, and even the collections. He meant all the things collected by his grandmother, china and jewellery and stamps and medals, which were in glass cases about the house or packed away in the attics.

He said it cost him two hundred pounds a year only to insure them and they were nothing but rubbish. So I got up my courage and said that I thought Captain and Mrs Loftus were wanting him to sell No. 15 and let them live at Tolbrook.

'Captain Loftus is a very useless person,' he said. 'Why, he's a rich man at the rate he lives – doesn't need to spend anything. But of course he's a regular miser.' So he went on to the Captain for ten minutes or more, that he was a disgrace to his order, and a parasite on society, till I had to stop him for fear he would say too much and be ashamed before me.

'It's quite light,' I said.

'So it is,' he said, surprised. I think he must have had his eyes closed before. Then he noticed that he had his arm round my neck, and he gave a little cough and after a moment said: 'Bless me, where's my handkerchief?' for an excuse to take the arm away without hurting my feelings.

Then he blew his nose and said in his old voice: 'I'm afraid I went to sleep, Mrs Jimson. I hope I haven't been a great nuisance to you.'

'Oh no, sir,' I said.

'I didn't keep you awake?'

'Oh no, sir. I slept very well.'

'Then perhaps I had better be going. Good night, Mrs Jimson,' and he went off. But his voice had been getting more and more polite and I thought that I had been too late after all in calling him to his recollection. I was quite right, for he hardly spoke to me for a month and never came to visit me at all. On the other hand, he was very kind in his messages and would send down after every meal to say he had appreciated it.

Now, of course, I had a new idea of Mr W. and I saw how the poor man had cause to be troubled about expenses; for whether reasonable or not, he felt them a burden. So I went to him and told him some ways he could save; on the coke, for instance, and on the laundry, by doing away with the table-cloths which he used in the dining-room, cloths three yards by two, three times a week, for his own use only. He thanked me very much, and we cut down the coke, but not the table-cloths, because the Loftuses

141

hád done away with theirs and he could never bear to follow them, even if he took Mrs L.'s advice. For she got her way, for all our economies, and Mr W. said he could not afford Oxford. And Bobby was to go into a bank.

But the poor boy would not go into a bank. And the end of it was the Queensport Estate Agency, which, indeed, I advised, to get him used to managing property.

Then Bobby liked the work so much and did so well that all were delighted with him and Mr W. began to consult him about the Tolbrook property.

Now when, next year, Bobby was to come of age, it seemed he would be made heir. We gave him a hint of it, to mind his arguments with Mr W. and make no trouble about names, if Mr W. wanted him to change his. Miss Clary said it was snobbery to take any notice of names at all. The thing was to study what was right and what was wrong. And he was the only man to do right at Tolbrook.

Miss Clary was always my stand-by with Bobby and Mr W. She could bring them round to things I dared not touch. She was clever and besides, she was a lady and understood the minds of that class, as I never could. For one minute you would think it was all religion with them, and money nothing; in the next, money was all and religion nothing. But, of course, money for them often comes out as duty, and so religion, while for the poor, money is always money only, because there is not enough of it to be duty. So Bobby agreed that if he had the property, he would be Wilcher Brown, and yet, as I said, it was not against his religion, because the property was so big that it was his duty to get it and improve it.

68

But then he got out such a plan for improvement, as he called it, at Tolbrook, as frightened Miss Clary and me into fits. For half the house was to come down, or be turned into barns and byres; and all those elms and oaks in the shady fields were to be cut and sold; and the little fields themselves to be drained and turned into very big fields for the tractors.

But we knew it was no good talking to Bobby about the look of things, so we went at him about Mr W. If he saw such a scheme as that, we said, turning Tolbrook into a farm, all among the smell of cows and pigs and manure, with the fleas hopping out of every man's trouser-turns, as soon as he came into the house, and the flies blackening the ceilings, then good-bye to his hopes.

'Get the place first,' I said, 'and then try your improvements – a little at a time. For you know Tolbrook is as much your uncle's home as 15, and he loves every crack in the plaster like the face of a friend.'

'I wouldn't take the place,' Bobby said, 'except on my own terms. As it is, it is good for nothing and doesn't even pay its way.'

And I told him he was an obstinate, foolish boy. 'I'm sorry, Sara,' he said, a bit put out, 'but what else can I do?'

So we told him again to keep his scheme back for a while for all our sakes and his father's too. That made him think, and he pondered for a moment or two, but then he gave a sigh and said: 'No, it wouldn't work.' Then he pinched my chin as he loved to do and said: 'It's no good, Nanny, you can wangle your way through a brick wall but you couldn't wangle me out of this. If I took Tolbrook on your terms, it would soon come to a real split with uncle, and I don't want that, for after all, he does mean well – though he is such a footling old fossil.'

So he sent in his scheme. And what was our surprise when Mr W. said it was just what he wanted.

'Tolbrook will be a real manor again,' he said, 'the centre of country work. Making its own bread and its own beer, and the squire of Tolbrook will be a real country man, as in the old days of Doomsday, when lords could not write their name.' And he said how wise he had been not to send Bobby to Oxford.

So off he went to the West, to see Bobby and go over the place with him. For Bobby was to do what he liked. No money spared till it began to come back again. Bobby was to be the manager and bailiff so that when he came into the property, he would know all about it.

69

The next thing we knew was that Tolbrook had been let for seven years to a rich young man called Fewless, who had made a fortune in wireless sets. He was to pay a very big rent and put the whole place in order, and a new floor in the ballroom.

It was Madame Loftus who had found the tenant and made the agreement. As for Bobby, he knew nothing about it. He had not even quarrelled with Mr W. who still liked the scheme greatly. But he had said: 'Now this tenant has turned up, who will mend the roofs and put the gardens in order. Perhaps we had better see how the old place shapes with plenty of new money before we undertake any new big change.'

Bobby was disgusted and I don't blame him. He went off next year to Canada and worked his own way up to a farm and we did not see him again for years. Mrs Loftus was in triumph. And in the same month she took Tolbrook rectory for herself, and her husband out of the army, to have her finger in all pies there and to get the poor captain into playing the squire. Indeed, she was like the squire from that time, for Mr Fewless, not being born for that troublesome work, could not be bothered with it, and never learnt even the names of his own workers.

And when Mrs L. next came to London, she walked into my kitchen one day and said: 'Let me give you a little piece of advice, Mrs Jimson, to mind your own business. You fancy yourself as having influence with your master, but a woman in your position had better be careful, or she may end in very serious trouble. I believe you have been in prison once already.'

I was going to say that this was not true. But then, I thought that perhaps it was not worth making so much difference between the dock and the prison, and besides, I was so startled by the woman's fierceness, for I didn't know how I'd deserved it. So I went on with my ironing, not looking at her. I was ironing Mr W.'s suit, which I had cleaned too. I saved ten pounds a year on cleaning.

Now whether she thought I was being rude in not answering her, though it was only that her tone of voice took my breath away, she burst out again and said I had better give in my notice. 'If you had any sense, you'd get out while you can do it quietly, without a scandal. And if you think you have Mr W. so much in your clutches that he can't escape, you'll find yourself very much mistaken there, too. Mr Wilcher may have his faults, but he is a very religious man at bottom, and he always comes round to his religious duty. Remember that he was with that other wretched creature for more than thirty years, and left her in the end. And he is turning against you already. I know the signs. As for money, if that's what you're waiting for, I've seen to that. There's not going to be any settlements this time. That was his mistake with Mrs Eeles, as I told him. And he quite agreed. After she had nothing more to expect she did just what she liked and treated him abominably. No, he's had his lesson. You will never get your settlement, Mrs Jimson or Monday, or whatever your real name is.' And out she went, quite raging.

But, I thought, what is my influence worth, when Mr W. drives away Bobby to Canada and lets Tolbrook, with my kitchen and my garden, so that I can't see it again for seven years?

None of that came out at the trial. But how could it? There was no room.

70

But as for my robberies, that was another thing and I still wonder at myself. For at this very time, when I was helping Mr W. to economize, and cutting down even his own dinners, I was still cheating him. How I came into this double way of life, I cannot tell, except that I got used to my pickings; and that I was bound to send something to Gulley; and I had made an agreement with myself never to use my savings.

You may wonder how I got any money from Mr W. when he went through the bills every week and counted the legs and wings of the chickens, but I had a dozen tricks. I must have been a born rogue for I was never at a loss. For I told Mr W. it was a great economy for me to have money in my pocket to get bargains when I saw them, of fruit and dusters and cleaning stuff and brooms and mats. So I would take a pound a week and spend five shillings or less, and bring up to Mr W. a bundle of dusters and say: 'Isn't this a bargain?' To be honest, the one bundle did for six bargains. For how was the poor gentleman to know how long a duster lasted, or a drying-cloth!

Then I would bring him a broom and he would feel the handle, and raise his eyebrows, and look down through the hairs and say: 'H'm, that's the weak part, in brooms, but I admit this one *seems* all right,' as if he knew all about brooms. But, of course, he had no idea if they cost a pound or a shilling.

So I cheated the poor man. And yet I was always in debt. A pound a week was the least I could send to Gulley, who never asked much from anyone and could fairly have asked for my life, and though I was getting, then, seventy pounds a year wages, I was expensive in clothes. Nothing would fit me from the cheap lines, and the truth was, I could never bear cheap stuff anywhere near my skin. I believe my stockings were often as good as Mrs Loftus's, though, of course, I did not show them. Mr W. liked his servants in the old long skirts, and I was very willing to wear them, for they gave me height and took off from my hips, but I always loved to have some yards of good silk dashing round my ankles. So I made a bargain with my conscience by telling Mr W. he could take something off my wages to cut his staff expenses. And he was so pleased and so grateful and so respectful of my goodness, that I nearly confessed to him the truth. But I did not, thinking of all the trouble it would make, and he took off five pounds, which gave me some comfort in my conscience for that time.

71

That was just when Bobby had gone to Canada and Mr W. was still so upset I thought he would lose his wits. I was upset too, for the boy came to say good-bye to me, one afternoon, without warning, and I was out, so when I got his note, I had to take a taxi to Victoria station and run all the way down the platform, and I was in such a state of heat and worry, I hardly knew how to speak to him. Then, too, with the excitement, I lost hold of myself and began to cry, which I never did before, on a platform. So I forgot all I had to say and only hoped he had said a proper good-bye to Mr W.

But he said no. He had only wanted to see me, who had been so good as his mama.

I said nonsense, he mustn't quarrel with Mr W., who was his only friend in trouble, having the capital to set him up; and he must write a very kind letter that day and explain that he had not been able to see him in the rush. He promised me, and so we parted. But I was upset for a week after, fearing I would never see the poor lad again and perhaps didn't look after Mr W. as well as I should have, especially in his time of trouble. I had noticed, indeed, that he was restless in the house, that he did not come to see me as usual. But I had thought it was because I kept on speaking of Bobby, and how good he was, to make his peace with Mr W. Perhaps too much. But as I say, I was upset and not myself.

However, it was one afternoon, I think it was the Saturday after Bobby left, for I know I was having a good clean-up of the kitchen copper and the brass, which I usually did on Saturday, to be bright for Sunday, when I looked up through the area grating and saw a policeman turn in at the door with two girls, and one of them making a hullabaloo.

Then my heart fell into my stomach and I thought: 'It's come at last, the poor unhappy gentleman. But what have I been thinking of?' I ran upstairs as fast as I could go, to answer the door myself.

The policeman asked if there was a gentleman in the house with a white face, a bald head and spectacles, in a grey suit and spats. I said no. But the girls began to scream that they had followed him and saw him come in at this door. The policeman asked who owned the house and if Mr Wilcher answered to the description given. I said no, but he asked if Mr Wilcher was in.

I said no again, so he said that he must examine the house. He came in then, and left the girls in the hall to watch the door, and looked through the whole house. But he found nothing, and went away, saying only that when Mr Wilcher came in he had better report at the police station. I couldn't make out where Mr Wilcher had gone till I was shutting up the attic and heard a noise on the roof. So I put my head out of the window and there the poor man was, down behind a chimney-stack, only his head looking round and terrified to move. It made my heart turn over to think how he must have crawled along the parapet to get to the stack. So I said: 'I beg your pardon, sir. Shall I get the cleaners with the ladders? I could see you were looking at the broken slates.'

'No, no,' said he, 'I will come back if you will kindly hold out a stick – I believe there is a curtain-pole which would reach me.'

So I pulled out the curtain-pole and jammed the end behind the parapet and he crept along again and I helped him in. You never saw such a state he was in, dirt and blacks from head to foot and both knees out of his best suit.

But he was trembling too, and pale as china. I didn't say anything about the policeman for I thought: 'He knows I wouldn't be here if they were here, and as for going to the station, I'll say I forgot it and so it will be my fault.'

'I thought I would have a look for that leak,' he said, 'but it was not so easy as it looked.'

'Good gracious,' I said, 'no indeed, you might have been killed.' I felt so sorry for him then, trembling like a frightened child and so brave, too, in keeping up his dignity, that I could have cried. 'I hope you'll never do that again, sir,' I let out. But he gave me a sharp look as if to say: 'Mind your own business, my girl,' and answered drily enough: 'Perhaps you'd better bring me up another suit, I don't want to be seen in this state.'

So he changed in the attic and told me not to say he had been on the roof.

But he was summonsed and there was a paragraph in the paper; and though luckily they had the address wrong, the family were all in terror. They went to lawyers and Mrs Loftus was for putting him in an asylum, if he would not go abroad. Miss Clary was the only sensible one of them all, as usual, and she came to me in the kitchen and said: 'What he wants is a wife. It's what he's always needed. Why don't you marry him, Sara, or couldn't you stand it?'

'How could I marry the master?' I asked her.

'You could make him if you liked. He's terrified of scandal.'

I was shocked at that. 'So am I,' I said, 'and I have too much respect for Mr Wilcher to think of such things.'

'And you used to be a lady,' she said, 'if you forgive the word – you're quite equal to the part, you know, more than many.'

I told her no, that I had never been a lady, and though Mr Monday had been a gentleman of very good family, he had been a simple good kind of man too, and easily satisfied in everything.

'If you don't marry him,' she said, 'he'll end in gaol. It might even come to murder – the old idiot is so tied up in himself that he's not safe. I can only thank God that it's not children he gets after, or he'd be there already.'

So I said that Mr Wilcher was a good man and a natural man in all ways, given a natural life.

'Well,' she said, 'I'm not married and I don't feel any necessity to run about the streets and exhibit myself with pocket torches or tickle women in Hyde Park.'

'It's different for women,' I said, 'because of the build.'

The poor child said that it was, very different. For a man could always get a wife if he wanted one and a girl never be sure of a husband.

'They tell me it's a time of confusion,' she said, 'when the young people are so muddled with nonsense they don't know what they want or what to believe; but I don't see any confusion. I know what I want and what I

147

believe but I can't get what I want and it doesn't make any difference what I believe because the papers are making such a silly noise.'

She meant about the young. For as she always said to me, she never saw anyone like the young in real life. Miss Clary hated all the papers.

'Well,' I said, 'the papers must live and they say the competition is terrible. So they have to make a bigger noise now than they used to.'

'I wish it wasn't such a silly noise,' she said, 'because poor old mummies like Uncle Wilcher swallow their papers whole and think we are a terrible lot, and that the country is going to the bitches.'

That was to shock me. So I was not shocked. I said only that Mr W. was no mummy, but a living man and living men could often change their whole minds. Just as Mr W. had surprised us about poor Bobby's scheme.

'Men can do a lot,' the poor child said. 'It's a man's world and so it will be until we have polygamy, like the Africans, and we can all live at peace in our own families and just send for a good husband when we need him. Then I could borrow my flower among men for a day or two.'

'Perhaps it would be enough,' I said.

'Of course it would,' she said, 'I know I'd be tired of him in the house. But that's no consolation as you ought to know if you've ever been in love.'

She was laughing at me; but almost crying too. And so we changed the subject.

I was always heart-broken for Miss Clary and the waste of such goodness and sense, and indeed for all the waste of nice sensible girls going on everywhere. For, of course, there weren't enough men at that time for these girls born to be wives and mothers, and wasted in singleness. Not that I agreed with Miss Clary's plan, which was half a joke. But I remembered the old country ways, where I know if there were not enough men, still the girls managed to find babies, and to bring them up too, and to make a home. As widows must do; and often the best of homes.

72

The summons was put off for a week by Mrs Loftus who got a medical certificate that Mr W. had a heart-attack. Mr W. promised to stay in the house, to save the doctor's face, but he seemed to take no interest in the case. He said it was all nonsense and a mistake. And he did not even obey the certificate, for at night he went out into the gardens or the streets and walked about. But I could see that he was shaken, for he came to me all times of the day and night and we had long interesting talks. It was then I really got to know the master and his true religious heart. For true religion is in the heart or it is nowhere. Of course, we never spoke of the summons, but sometimes of new savings, which Mr W. was always thinking of. I encouraged him indeed, for whether he needed to save or not, it was a hobby for his mind, and kept him out of mischief. Or he would talk of books. This was the time he began again to speak of reading. For one evening I went out to the garden to find him, seeing by the lamps that there were some nurse-maids still there, and I saw him on a seat, doing nothing. And before I could slip away, he saw me and asked me to admire the sky. 'I often see you in the garden,' he said. And I said that I always liked these gardens because the elms reminded me of Tolbrook.

'But you won't see such a sky,' he said, 'except in London, because only the smoke in the air can give that colour. It's like old varnish, and makes every London view into an old master.'

It was true that the clouds were like old fiddles and the blue between so dark and rich as ammonia bottles, full of light too, because still soaking in the sun. I always liked that time when the gardens were in shade and the shadows of the chimneypots on the odd side fell on the evens; but the tops of the trees were still like African islands, in the warmth.

It was late October, but some leaves were still hanging in the top branches, twiddling in the breath of air as bright as new sovereigns. I said I wished all that gold could pay the taxes, but he was not in that mood. He answered that beauty was a jewel beyond gold just because it had no price. 'Any poor outcast could enjoy it, perhaps better than we, having no worldly cares. But you understand that better than I do, Sara.'

It was always one of his ideas since Tolbrook, that I was a very religious woman, and I think he always had the idea that the poor were nearer Heaven than the rich. In prayers he would always read those bits about the rich man and the camel and the needle's eye, or the young man with great possessions, who turned away sorrowfully, with a very strong voice. He would even pause after them, as if to let them sink in. And would say to us: 'How could the rich, with all their comforts safe, feel God's mercies; and without feeling, how could they remember providence?'

So, too, he would pick up some country word of mine and improve it, like:

> Grace and disgrace
> Are twins in every place.

or:

> The first breath
> Is the beginning of death.

Then he would say to me that it did him good to talk about religion with me because of my good, old-fashioned training. 'You believe that we have souls to be saved or ruined and so do I. But you have kept your soul alive and I have nearly smothered mine under law papers and estate business

149

and the cares of the world. Under talk too, for I talk too much about religion and forget that it is not a matter of words, but faith and works and vision.'

I thought that he did not know my soul. But I did not say so, for it would have done no good. Mr W. was a truly religious man, but he was also obstinate in his own way.

73

So tonight I saw he was in a religious mood and not ready to talk about the bills. And sure enough:

'How is your reading going?' he asked. 'I was looking into one of your favourites only today, *The Pillars of the House*, where poor Underwood dies leaving a sick wife and thirteen children.'

Then he said that no modern writer would dare to write such a book; people would laugh at it. 'They laugh at everything good, or noble or unselfish. They don't seem to understand what life can be like, and that people really did feel and do fine things and lead noble lives or try to lead them, when that book was written.'

So then I was delighted and said that was what I had always told my girls, and believed. That it was not Miss Yonge's fault if the men in her books seemed too good or the women too gentle, but the world's. Because I knew from my mother that in her time, before the old Queen lost her Prince, there were many good clergymen, who tried to be saints, and that many girls were brought up just so soft and forbearing as Violet Martindale or Amy Marville. It was the fashion then for good men to be saintly and girls sweet and dutiful, and so they had been, many of them.

Mr Wilcher was so eager to agree with me that he would not let me finish. 'Yes,' he said, 'exactly. Just what I tell Clarissa,' and 'People are what you make them. They may laugh at Underwood, but he wasn't a drifter, at any rate.'

Now I have always thought that in real life I mightn't have been so patient with Mr Underwood, having a child every year; but still I'm sure it was better for a clergyman to be a saint, even if difficult in life, and to obey God's law as he thought it, of multiplying, than stay just an ordinary man and make nothing of himself or of life either.

So I said. And Mr Wilcher answered me that it was the big clergyman's families made the Empire when it was a great thing, with a Christian purpose. 'My own father,' he said, 'when he went to India as Colonel of his regiment, would have no subaltern that did not go regularly to Communion, and he had prayer-meetings for the men too, and taught them how to fight the good fight. For it is a fight,' he said.

So he was so interested that when I went in to begin the cooking, he followed me to the very kitchen, to go on about the fight. We had only one maid and a daily woman then, in our saving time, and luckily both were out. So while I was stirring up the fire, for we had no gas stove yet, except a ring, he walked round the kitchen table like an admiral on the deck and said that life was truly a battle, a terrible battle, 'and the trouble is the enemy goes on changing his uniform and his plans. Now, in my father's day,' he said, 'a country gentleman knew what he had to do and felt his responsibility – so did a lawyer like my Uncle John, who was my father's eldest brother. They always worked together and fought cheap corn and tried to keep up the country life and the country ways and parsons.'

For Mr W. loved the old ways, as I did. When the parlourmaid came in, he pretended to have come about the dinner, and went off and had his dinner like a gentleman, dressed and bathed, with candles. But at night he was up with me from ten o'clock almost till morning, talking, till, indeed, my head went round. For though I could sleep while he talked, especially since all our lights were fused, on the top storey, for the last six months, and he would not waste candles by keeping them alight; yet if he heard me breathe a little loud or snore, it naturally put a damper on his spirits, poor gentleman. For he was too polite to wake me, except by fidgets or coughing, as if he did not mean it, even to himself.

74

All this time the family were having the greatest trouble with him to get him to defend himself in court, or even to put off the case. For there was a hope that if the case was put off, a little longer, the girl would cool down and perhaps come to a settlement privately. But Miss Clary told me it was regular diplomacy to do it, for if she should get an offer and change her mind again, then she would have a fine tale to tell and the case would be lost. So the thing was to go through a friend of hers, and first by hints.

But Mr W. would do nothing and even I could not get him to see the lawyer or the doctor. Yet the summons was put off, and the next thing we heard, the girl would say she had made a mistake; and the police had caught somebody else who had a title, and the case would make a bigger noise than Mr W.'s and so do the government good, in Wales.

We were all delighted and Mrs Loftus, I'll own, had won a great triumph. For it was her go and her contrivance that had done it all. I always admired Mrs Loftus for her great backbone and her never letting go. You couldn't beat her down.

But Mr W. went really very queer, at least for a while. I must confess it for the truth's sake and to cover myself. I have said that he had been strange all that week and more talkative than ever before. It was Mrs Loftus telephoned in the evening that 'it would be squashed or not come on at all,' meaning the summons, for Mrs Loftus had given orders we must never write or telephone the word summons in case it got to the police; and I took the message, being alone in the house. Then I ran out to the garden to tell Mr W., but he was talking to the estate gardener, a great friend of his, about the new bulbs to be planted. And when I said: 'Oh, sir, Mrs Loftus has rung up to say that it's all off and you needn't trouble,' he only looked at me and said, after a minute: 'Thank you, Mrs Jimson,' in a flat kind of voice.

I thought him queer then. And what was queerer still he ate no dinner to speak of and did not come to see me till two in the morning. It gave me a fearful shock to see him then, in his long nightshirt, like a ghost; and without his spectacles, which made him screw up his eyes in an unnatural way.

'Mrs Jimson, Sara,' he whispered, 'are you awake?'

Then I waked quite up and said: 'For gracious' sake, sir, don't stand there in the draught, with your bare legs.' For as I said, my room was as cold as an ice-house, all winter, with only matting on the floor, and no fire able to be lighted, because there was a brick fallen across the chimney. The ceiling was in holes, too, where the plaster was down and the draught, not to speak of the rain, coming through the slates on the roof.

I was always in terror that Mr W. would catch pneumonia in those bitter winter nights and, indeed, he had noticed the cold himself, and had said more than once the room was a disgrace, and he must get an electric-fire and a plug. But he had always forgotten or perhaps found that they would cost too much and now the wiring was found so rotten that the electric company wanted us to renew it. I was glad only that at the time of his many troubles, he took to staying the whole night and keeping warm. I'll own it at once, I liked the feel of a husband again, though it was only to talk about bills.

Now I begged him to jump in quick, and opened the clothes for his poor shaking legs. But he did not seem to listen. He came over to the bed and put down the candle in the middle of the floor, and sat down on the chair with his head in his hands against the bed. I thought he was going to say his prayers, as he did sometimes in my room, though only when he came at his usual bed-time; and I wondered if I had better get out and say mine too, for company. For if he was early, and before I had said my prayers, we would have to say them at the same time. Indeed we had often said our prayers at the same time, though, of course, I would keep a little distance. Our prayers were still our own business, not being man and wife.

But then I heard him talking aloud and I could not believe my ears; he was asking me to save him. And he said all he had said before, in little pieces, over years, about my influence, and my being his help and stay and a messenger from providence, to save his soul alive. The upshot was, he was going to give himself up to the police, and go to prison, and afterwards, if I would have him, he would marry me and live in a poor way, in some quiet place.

I saw now the poor man had gone mad with his nerves, and I knew it was dangerous to contradict him, so I said: 'Yes' and 'Yes,' and of course I would and could do anything if only he would get into the warm out of the draught. For I knew for a certainty that if he did not he would get his lumbago, or perhaps sciatica, and be laid up; and Mr W., for all his goodness, was a misery to himself and to everyone else, ill in bed, especially on the third storey, with only two servants to bring up his meals and his letters.

But he would not get in. He said he was not fit. And he confessed that he had done all the girl had said, and worse to others, for years, out of pure wickedness. He had given way to the devil all his life, and the worst was he had known all his life his real duty, which was to put off worldly things and follow God's commands.

I saw that he was well started, and nothing would turn him, so I put the eiderdown over him and tucked it over his shoulders and round his thighs as well as I could.

Then he asked me again if I would take him, after the prison, and I said of course I would. But he would not get into bed until he had told me a lot more about his crimes, and how he saw nothing would save him but a public confession, to break his evil pride and put him right with God.

I thought that there were as many traps in humility as pride, and that the devil's best hook was baited with confession. For I had found out even as a child that a quick confession could save me a slapping and a bad conscience too, and so, back to the jam. But, of course, I did not say so to Mr W. in his wild state. I agreed with everything he said and so got him at last into bed and he was as frozen as if he had been out of a refrigerator. I fairly got to work and rubbed some life into him. Not that he paid any more attention than a hospital patient, but went on talking about the badness of his life and the need for a new start, from the bottom.

But I was too late, for he did get his sciatica, and a nice job it was to get him back to his own room before the housemaid found him in mine. Luckily he was a light-weight and so in the end, I took him up, master or no master, and wrapped him in the eiderdown, and carried him downstairs like a baby. Then I rang up Miss Clary, early as it was, to give her a hint that the poor gentleman was shaking in his mind, and might yet do something foolish.

75

Mr W., when ill, as I say, was troublesome. And now he would not let me out of his sight. I got the hot-water bottles for his leg and slipped away to get breakfast; but he would have me back, to confess, and to talk. They say mad people must either eat or talk, and if so, I thought, the master was certainly mad.

For now he had got on to religion again and a new wobble. He changed right round from what he had said only yesterday, that the old ways were the best. Now he said that old ways were done and just as a rose will go bad and stink out a whole room, so the old religion, beautiful as it had been, was a poison to the world. We must go back again to the beginning and be as little children learning from our father without book; or like the early Christians, who lived together and had everything in common.

Of course I agreed with all and, indeed, I often thought that you couldn't go back on a fashion. For say what you will, fashions never do go backwards, and now if we had saints again, and good family women delighting in children, they would be a different brand from the old, just as, though figures have come in again, since the slump, and now woman need not try to make herself look like a bicycle pump, only for fashion, yet the figures are new, with big waists; a good thing, I daresay, for those that like their food.

So I said to Mr W. that it was the wine and the leather bottles, and he said: Yes, and the wine was still good; it was only the bottles were rotten.

76

The next thing was that when I came in from shopping all the family were there, Miss Clary, the Captain and Mrs Loftus who was with Mr W., and Miss Clary came to warn me Mrs L. had heard about his offer to me and was getting him round.

'Don't stand any nonsense,' she said. 'Make him marry you. It's the only way to save him.'

'How could I make him?'

'Bring an action. Breach, or something. He's terrified of scandals. They all are. You'd have thought that summons was the end of the world. You've got to fight, Sara, or she'll turn you out. That's what she's driving at.'

I said I hated scandals too, and I had to think of my family. Besides, I did not really believe that Mrs Loftus could get me turned off, till I went up to change his bottles while the Loftuses were at luncheon, and he began to say that I mustn't mind Mrs Loftus if she seemed a little impatient at times.

'She's young,' he said, 'and she's had a great deal on her shoulders. She's done wonderful work round Tolbrook, with the Sunday school and the institute and the flower show and the market stall, and now she's going to have a harvest home, quite in the old style. The place is really alive again. She and the Captain have given it quite a fresh start of usefulness. All it needed was a little fresh capital and faith.'

Mr W. was always saying that what he admired about Mrs Loftus was her faith. She really believed in the good old ways and that was why she made them work again.

So the poor man excused himself for his weakness and for not being able to make up his mind quick enough for Mrs Loftus, who, though perhaps I oughtn't to say it, never had one to make up.

He had talked so before, as when he had let the manor and thrown poor Bobby over, but now I thought he looked more queerly. And when I said something about the case, he answered that it seemed he could not do anything more without bringing the girl into it and spoiling her character.

'Well,' I thought, as I went downstairs, 'Mrs L. is a wonder to turn that poor manny round her finger.'

But what a wonder I did not know till after luncheon when she came down into the kitchen and gave me a day's notice, with a month's wages. 'I'm taking over the housekeeping,' she said, 'from tomorrow, and I shall make my home here and a home for Mr Wilcher. And you will kindly not attempt to communicate with him. He does not wish it and I will take care it does not occur.'

So out I went next morning, after thirteen years, with my box and my clothes, thankful only that she did not have me searched, like Mrs Frewen. For be sure she would have made out that I had taken something; and I was always in terror of the police. I know they had my name in their books for the old trouble about the bad cheques.

77

This was on Monday, and on the Wednesday I was going to see my daughter Nancy at Bradnall, who was ill. So I spent one night in a servant's room at Miss Clary's hotel, where she lived then, and went on to Bradnall on the Wednesday morning.

Poor Nancy was now my only daughter at home, for Belle was always travelling the world seeing sights, and Edith was in China, and Phyllis married in America, or so I hoped. For when she had gone away suddenly from Bradnall, at only seventeen, as travelling nurse to some American children, she had stayed over there and written to me that I was to address her Mrs Monday. Not a word of husband. But I thought: 'Why shouldn't she have married a man of her own name?' However it was with her, I knew she was happy and well, for she sent me presents every Christmas and always a note: 'To my darling, with all my love,' or 'Dearest mum, from her best lover.' And the best notepaper. Only a new address every time and she never answered a letter.

For many years, indeed, I had missed my girls. Even Nancy, though not far away, had never found it easy to see me, because her husband and his family had been so upset by my going off with Jimson, and being had up for writing bad cheques. I do not mean she did not have a proper feeling for her mother, but only that my visits would have been a nuisance to her. So we wrote and sometimes met in London, for shopping and news.

But now Nancy was getting well into her thirties, and her children were all at school and away from home and she began to feel her affection and to want to see me. She wrote every week, letters which surprised me with their love, and often begged me to come and see her.

So I would go sometimes on a Wednesday when her husband was away from home and see her and let her have a good talk about the children, who, she said, were very unloving and ungrateful, and she was tired of them, and then I would catch the milk train and be back at Number 15 in time to see the master's breakfast on the tray. He never had but a tray to his bedroom, and only rolls and coffee, but yet if everything were not just so, the butter properly rolled, with a shaving of ice, and the coffee just the right strength, and the clean napkin folded round the rolls, he could not touch a morsel.

I had to be back to make sure of his breakfast, or he would go to work famished, and ready to faint.

So on this Wednesday morning, when I came out of the tube, I forgot that I had been sacked and turned into Craven Gardens. It was habit. And I could not make out what had happened. It was not yet half-past seven and the streets were empty and strange, as streets seem on such a morning when the sky is already light, but no one moving; but Craven Gardens full, and two policemen at the corner.

Then I saw fire-engines and I asked where the fire was, and they said: 'At fifteen.'

I almost fell down. 'Oh,' I said, 'that's my own house and I must get through at once. I must know about the master.'

An inspector came along then, with Miss Clary, who was in trousers like a man. She told me that Mr W. was safe and lying down in one of the neighbours'. The fire had started at the top and he had got out by the stairs. But it had been such a quick and bad fire that almost nothing was saved. An old trunk and hat-boxes from the box-room, thrown out by the housemaid, no one knows why, for they were empty, and some of the collections from the glass cases, which the firemen and Loftuses had saved. The Loftuses had taken all the snuffboxes and gone off to their flat. As for Mr W. he had brought off only some miniatures and stamps, which he kept under his bed.

Miss Clary said that he was in such a state that the doctor had put him to bed, and no one was to go near him. I could do nothing. So I went back with Miss Clary and had breakfast and afterwards we went to see the ruins. But the salvage men would not let us near.

We did not see the master for three days. But he did not see the Loftuses either. Indeed, he had broken off with them, but Miss Clary said it was really because Mrs Loftus had gone at him till he couldn't bear it any longer.

Instead of going to Mrs Loftus he came to Miss Clary, but so shaky and worn down, I scarcely knew him. He would jump at a sound, and when he saw me for the first time, he said only: 'A clean sweep, Mrs Jimson – I can't believe it yet.'

Then the insurance people came and nearly drove him and all of us mad with their questions. About the wiring of the house, and why it had been neglected, and when the fire was first noticed, and even why I had been away that night from my room, which was next the attic, where, it was said, the fire started. You would have thought they were accusing the master of setting fire to his own house.

Yet I had a fright too, for when I met the housemaid, a girl called Halley, who was in a new place, she told me that the master had been in the attic that evening of the fire only a little while before he knocked on her door and asked her if she smelled smoke. 'He went up three or four times before dinner, and it's my belief that he started the fire by tinkering at those wires – and not just all by accident, either.'

I thought perhaps Mr W. might have had an accident with the wires, trying to put in a fuse, and that was why the insurance company made him so angry, fearing it would not pay him. So I told Halley, the master was the last man to burn his own house, where he was born. 'No,' I said, 'you've been reading about the fire-raisers in the paper.'

'So has the master,' she said, 'and if it was his home, perhaps he didn't want Mrs Loftus to take it from him. He wanted to keep on in his own way.'

She meant to keep on with me, so I answered her pretty sharply:

What nonsense, a gentleman like Mr W. didn't go in for fire-raising and she'd better keep such scandalous talk to herself. 'The fire was a fire,' I said, 'like any other, and we had been due for a fire anyhow, with the bad state of the wiring, and that old house full of treasures, and no other fire or even a robbery since it was built, eighty years.'

'Of course, I wouldn't say a word,' she said, 'except to you. Didn't you see how I answered the insurance man. As if I was going to save money for the insurance, with their millions, when they take sixpence off my wages every week.'

'What a providence,' I thought, 'to send us a girl that was a very good maid and clever enough to see so far into her master; and yet so foolish that she mixed up all the insurance together, and thought a gentleman's company, like Mr W.'s, was all one with the Government robbers.'

78

The master was so ill that we thought he would die. But on the Saturday he took a better turn and on the Sunday he got up and carried me off to early service. Not a word about my notice nor the Loftuses. Though I knew he had quarrelled with them about my notice, of course he could not well say anything against Mrs L. to me. But when I was going to a separate pew, he took me by the arm and turned me into the same one with himself. Afterwards he seemed very cheerful and spoke of the great consolation of the church; how it gives the same comfort to all, good or bad, if only they will receive it. I saw he had taken a good turn and I told Miss Clary to see that he had the best dinner the hotel could give, and some wine, even if she paid for it. The good girl did give him wine, though she had to pay for it, and though he had given her only a ten-shilling note for her birthday; and it did him so much good that he came to me afterwards up the back stairs, among the servants' rooms. Luckily I heard his step and slipped out and warned him that the hotel was very strict with servants and that the walls were very thin, and he might be reported, if he came in to me.

So he went down again. But the next day, when I was coming up the back stairs from our breakfast-room, which was in the basement, he popped out from the dining-room floor, where he must have been lying in wait for me and said: 'Put on your hat, Mrs Jimson, we're going out.'

He looked so excited that I knew he had some new scheme and, sure enough, he took me straight to a registry, and before I knew whether I wanted to marry him or not, he gave in our notices. And from there he went straight, by the same taxi, to a place called Ranns Park, all new built, rows of little houses, red and green with pink roofs, like pastries in a shop window. We went to the office and out came a young man who took us to see one of these houses, to be finished next week, and for sale now.

Mr W. went jumping on the floors and trying the windows and sniffing at the drains and he said to me: 'You'd better look at the kitchen, Mrs Jimson – that's your province.'

'But are you taking it?' I asked.

'Why not?' he said, 'I must have somewhere to live and this is clean and new, and I'm told the firm is moderately honest as builders go. But, of course, if you don't like the kitchen, we'll try somewhere else.'

Since he had given the registry notice Mr W. was like a boy, full of briskness and mischief too. But he was not so polite to me. He said: 'Do this,' and 'Do that,' as if we had been married for years.

The kitchen was good enough, though no proper larder and a cellar like a boot-box. But I hardly looked at it, I was wondering so much at Mr W. coming to live in such a place, like any clerk. Yet he took it there and then and went and bought a house full of furniture the next day and sent me for new pots and pans. I was settled in before the electric light was joined up or the plaster dry. But Mr W. was mad to get the carpets down and the garden dug.

He himself was not going to live there until we were married. For he said he was not going to start his new life, in a new place, with a scandal. So he went back to his hotel every day and only came out to Bellavista, as the box was called, in the afternoon. But then he worked like six men, laying carpets and arranging the furniture, and hammering nails in the new plaster.

If Mr W. still talked about his ruin, he was quite a new man from what he had been latterly at Number 15. I don't think that I ever saw such a change in a man. It was something that Miss Clary and I never stopped wondering at. I thought it was because Mrs Loftus never came to see us and so never troubled him, for she had been so furious about his engaging to marry me at last that she said she would never speak to him again or come to the house while I was there. Only the Captain came, as was his duty, but he never wondered at anything, he was too sleepy. He followed his uncle about while he was shown the garden and the kitchen and the bathroom and drawing-room with its new furniture, and said only: 'A bit poky.'

Mr W. was angry with him, and then he laughed and said that he had forgotten already how the rich felt. What most surprised me was how Mr W. could like the furniture. I thought it was an ugly cheap lot, but he kept on saying that it was wonderful what they could do at the price. Then he bought tools and began to dig in the garden and set me to dig too. He would say in the evening before he went: 'Sara, don't forget to try that new polish on the drawing-room floor,' or 'Don't forget to dig the front bed – it will need double trenching.'

It was a great pleasure to see him lively and interested. Miss Clary would laugh when she came out and found us both cutting or digging or staking, and say: 'I wonder what Higgins would say of your efforts.'

Higgins was the head gardener at Tolbrook. But Mr W. never bothered to answer Miss Clary. They were very good friends, but I don't think he ever thought of her as more than a little girl whose talk was no more to

159

him than a window rattling, or less. 'Here,' he would say, pushing a hoe into her hands, 'can you hoe? – Don't cut down my new roses. If you hoe the whole bed, I'll give you a glass of sherry.'

But he did not say when, and indeed he had no sherry in the house. For if we had lived carefully before and saved, we counted every penny now. The insurance people were still fighting Mr W. They even sent a man out one morning early to ask me about the electric wires on the top storey and why they had not been put in order, and if I had ever touched them or seen Mr W. touch them. I said, of course, that both of us had put in new fuses several times, until we found that it was no good, because they always blew out the first night.

Mr W. was so angry when he heard of this peeping work that he wanted to bring an action for defamation of character, but the other partners in his office would not let him.

So, as Mr W. said he had no money, I had to live on kippers and margarine, and scrag end. I don't know how I would have managed for some extra expenses with Gulley if I had not had two lucky strokes in the same week. First, the salvage came in, and Mr W. told me to throw away some old rubbish saved in a cardboard box. But I found some old brass chains in it which were a curiosity and which I sold for three pounds to an antique shop. The second was that Mr Hickson, when I wrote to him for a loan, gave me fifty pounds for the drawings which were stored in his house all these years.

79

Now I must explain how I came to be having more expenses with Gulley. About two years before the fire, I met him in a strange way.

I hadn't seen much of Rozzie for the last years after Jimson and I took up together. She would never come to see us at Ancombe and we went only twice to see her at Brighton, where Jimson and she kept digging at each other all the time, and meaning to hurt. But just after the slump was at its worst, I had a letter from Rozzie saying she was ill in hospital, and would like to see me. I got leave that very day and went straight to her, for I was frightened. I wondered then at myself for not keeping up with her better. The truth was, I was never a great letter-writer and she was worse, and so, though she was often in my thoughts, she had become a stranger. For the one in your thoughts is not the real one; and no loving thoughts will ever keep up a friend in the flesh as duty commands, and your own good.

I could not believe my eyes when I saw my poor Rozzie in the hospital, gone to skin and bone. She was not sixty, and she might have been eighty, with a folded face like an old worn-out shoe.

She had been knocked down by a lorry and lost her leg at the thigh. 'And the same day,' she said, 'I heard that all my money was gone in the Mortimer Hotels crash. I heard at breakfast and the lorry got me at half-past ten, going over to the Three Crowns for my morning drop, and when I woke up in hospital, I had my best laugh for years.'

'Nothing to laugh at,' I said, for I was almost crying. But Rozzie gave a heave and a kind of laugh and said: 'You wouldn't, Sall – it wasn't your money and your best leg. I've still got the bad one.'

The end of Rozzie was very sad. For when they got her well enough to go on crutches, she was still not fit to be about; and she had no money left. There was no place for her but the workhouse infirmary. Her only relation was her brother-in-law and he was in India and had his own wife and family. Besides, Rozzie would never be a burden on anyone. So there she was and there I went to see her three more times, before the leg broke out again and she died of blood poisoning.

'A good thing, too,' she said, when they told her she was going. 'I've been a fat lot of good, haven't I? I wonder why I was ever born – but I expect I was an accident – one at the start and one at the finish.'

I told her how I respected her for the fight she had made, but all she said was: 'I was bound to be tough and so you, too, had better be tough – the world being what it is.'

But I thought that I could never go by Rozzie's way, for with all her fighting, what good did it do her. She was fighting for nothing.

I was shocked by the waste of her and I wanted to say a prayer for her or read her something from St John, especially the Revelation, which the old squire had been used to read at death-beds. But she would not have it. 'No consolations,' she said, 'I may be a good-for-nothing, but I've got my pride. And if I can't die happy, I won't go out howling. Don't break me down with your Bible stuff, Sall, or you'll make me sorry for myself. And I've no right to it.'

So she still kept joking in her old style, saying: 'If only they'd let me have my stays. They were always my best support in time of trouble and I wish I had them now to meet what's coming.'

I asked her did they treat her kindly and she said: 'Yes, but no allowances. Human nature can't be happy without that, as you know, Sall, and I tell you this place has more human nature to the pound of bones than you'd get in a stone of steaks, anywhere else, cut where you like and duchesses not barred.'

Poor Rozzie, she wouldn't let me read to her or say a word of kindness, and she held herself up like a soldier, only to the last breath, when her face gave way, as if she was going to cry. But thanks to God, she had no time for it, her jaw fell, and she began to settle in. It was only then that a little water came out in the eyes.

80

I went to the funeral, and indeed I paid for it. There was no one else and I couldn't bear to leave Rozzie in a pauper's grave behind me. I could never have slept in peace. But who should come to the funeral, the only other mourner, but Gulley. I didn't know him at first when I saw him in the chapel, among all the chairs turned wrong way up. The light was bad, and I thought him only one of the paupers. For he had a regular pauper's face, with his nose come right down to his lip, and his chin sticking out under it, and his eyes gone back into his head. I was crying too and could not notice anything except the miserable place, like a cellar, and the bearers yawning in their hats, while they pretended to be serious; and the clergyman gabbling, a mortuary clergyman paid by the piece, I suppose. It seemed so miserable an end for any human, let alone Rozzie with her great go and jump, with strength for two men and a heart like a lion; I was torn in two and fairly sobbed.

I must have looked quite drunk at the graveside with my hat crooked and my red eyes and nose and my hair coming down with my hat. I knew it, but I did not care, when I thought how I'd neglected Rozzie, all for a quarrel about a man like Gulley, who was not worth a day of her life.

It was only when I threw some Parma violets, Rozzie's favourites, into the grave, that I saw another bunch go down and I looked up, and there was Gulley, full face, looking up at me across the grave. He grinned at me and I got such a jump that I said, right at the grave's edge: 'It's not you!'

'Oh, yes it is,' he said, grinning still and looking at me as if he would bore me through. He came round the grave and said: 'And how are you, Sall?'

But my heart was full of Rozzie, and I could not think of myself, or him. So he took my arm and we went towards the gates.

'Poor old Rozzie,' he said. 'Poor old horse.'

'How did you know?' I said.

'Oh, I used to write. We sent cards every Christmas, and I heard about her accident. I meant to see her, in the beginning, but I never had time.'

'I'm glad you made it up,' I said.

'Yes, we made it up,' Gulley said, still looking at me and grinning. For his idea was that I had been jealous of Rozzie. And perhaps I had been. For God knows I never knew myself.

Then at the gates he said: 'What about a half?'

'Oh,' I said, holding back. I had not been into a bar for ten years.

'They're just open,' he said. And then I thought there couldn't be a better place to see Gulley, for none of Mr W.'s people or he himself went into bars. So we crossed the road to a public-house and had a pint of bitter. It was a regular town bar with little tables and red plush seats and we sat in a corner and had a good talk. It seemed that he was full of an idea for a picture of God like a glass man, with the people running about in His veins and nerves and some of them fighting and giving Him a pain in His stomach.

It was to be done on canvas ten feet high and fifteen feet wide, and Gulley had his eye on a kind of shed at Hammersmith, which would be the right place for painting it.

'Is that where you live now?' I asked him, for I had always sent his money to a box address, at a sweet shop.

'Why?' he said, grinning at me and thinking I was curious.

'Because if you were alone, I'd like to see it,' I said, 'and see if you're comfortable.'

'Oh yes,' he said, 'quite comfortable, thank you.' But I knew he had some woman with him, for the top button of his coat was a safety-pin. And by that pin I knew she must be a slummock; and I pitied him, poor manny.

But he would not tell me his address. He only went on about the picture, and at last, just as I had feared, he asked me for money to buy a canvas. Ten pounds to buy an old Academy picture, which would be half the price of new cloth.

I said I couldn't afford a big sum like that. And Gulley did not say another word about it or pester me. He simply grinned and called for another drink and said: 'Well, Sall, I've got to thank you for keeping up the instalments – the best patron I ever had. I've often lived on nothing else, for weeks together.'

This was Gulley's good side; he never pestered or groaned or pitied himself. And his coat green as cheese-mould, and that pin winking at me as if to say: 'We live in pigsties.' So when the time came for us to part, suddenly I said that perhaps I could find a pound or two towards that canvas.

I never saw anyone more delighted. For Gulley had two smiles, his smile of keeping up, and his smile of joy, which was like any street child's with a sugar bun. It went through your very soul. So the next thing was, I sent him his ten pounds.

I thought myself foolish at the time and I said: 'This will bring him down on you every time he has a new dream.' And so it did. But not for some new mad picture, only to mend up his clothes and get him settled.

81

He was living with a girl called Lizzie, and just as I had thought, she could neither sew nor cook nor clean nor contrive. He was in a nest of such. For I found him in a slum and his flat in the dirtiest of the row, with a dozen bells and a string of blowsy trollops labouring in and out like sick bees in a rotten skep.

And the pity of it was that he had got his start at last, if only he had known how to use it.

For as Lizzie told me at our first meeting, he had a picture in a public gallery, at last. She told me, in the National Gallery, which I could not believe. And sure enough, when I took a day off to go to Trafalgar Square only to see it, it was not there at all, but down on the Thames side, in a place called the Tate; Mrs Bond's portrait.

But even though it wasn't in the National Gallery, it was something for an artist to be proud of. So I told Gulley but he laughed and said: 'The portraits are the winners, you told me so.'

I was angry. For I had not told him so; I was not so stupid. What is the good of saying so to any man, for it does you no good with him, and him no good at all. But he kept on laughing and the end of it was, he gave me a little squeeze as if scorning my brains, but I easily held him off, and told him that I would not come to see him if he did not behave himself.

And so he did. Never once had he struck Lizzie, so she told me, and was surprised to know that he had ever struck anyone. And as for me, he would only take me by the nose, now and then, and pinch it a little and say: 'Don't you stick it in too far into my affairs, Sally, or I'll have to push it back again,' which made us both laugh. This, of course, at the very time when he was calling out for me to do this or that, to pay the bills for Lizzie, or to get his boots mended. More than once, in spite of my warnings, he telephoned to me at Craven Gardens, only to come and clean him, because Lizzie was too ill, or bring him some colours.

So the first thing was to move him to a better address, where, if portraits came his way, he might do them. And we found a very nice flat down west, near Hammersmith Bridge, and quite near his shed which was in a builder's yard. The poor man's idea had been to go across London, morning and night, only because Lizzie could not think how to get a better room or to move their few sticks from east to west.

She was a queer girl, a lady by her rights and as pretty as a supplement, though gypsy in her colour, but as helpless as a sheep on its back, turning up its eyes at the sky and bleating for the moon to drop grass into its mouth. She could sit all the morning in her pyjamas, smoking cigarettes and reading an old magazine. When Gulley came in for a meal, he would open a tin for both of them. As often as not, Gulley made the tea and even the beds and emptied the slops, which was only when the pail was running over.

When first I knew Lizzie I thought she was a drugger or a drinker or worse, to be idle all day, and though not too dirty in herself, yet living in dirt. But no, she was only a dreamer, the worst I ever knew. She would walk about for half an hour smoking and dropping her ash over my clean floor, for the first thing I did, every time I went to see the Gulleys, was a general clean and wash for everything; and then she would say in her soft voice: 'Do you see, Sara, there's a million people drowned in China. Did you see, Sara, that skirts are going to be longer again, to use more stuff.' And though her voice was soft, it was never sleepy. You could tell she was full of her news, however useless.

She had been an artist herself, and thought Gulley the genius of the world. Also she was musical and she used to go off a lot to concerts, and come back in such a state of dreams and excitement that if you had put soap into her mouth, for dinner, she would have eaten it and said: 'Thank you, Sara – you're too good.'

I grew so fond of Lizzie she was like a daughter to me; and I believed she liked me better than my own daughters, except for poor little Nancy. She always had something for me to do, either to wash her stockings or let out her dress. For she was in the family way, and no more fit to be a mother than Gulley a father. Yet there was a child with them too, a boy called Tom. Now I knew when I first went with Gulley that he had one child by his wife, which she had kept. But I'm sure he had others and this was one of them. He would never tell me the mother except that she had been his model. Tommy was nine, he said, though he might have been younger, by his looks, and older by his knowingness, a regular slum boy, and a demon for noise, dirt and wickedness. Nothing he did not know or wouldn't do.

Lizzie, of course, could do nothing with him, and did not try. Gulley would sometimes take him down to the shed, which he called the studio, to keep him out of mischief, but Tommy was away into the streets as soon as he chose. And Gulley would never correct him. He said it was bad for children to be checked, or even taught.

82

Now Tommy was thrown upon me too. For though Lizzie would say that the child was spoilt from never going to school, and that he was very gifted, and Gulley too would say that he was a clever spark, they never did anything for him or to get him brought out. Not that I believed it then, for he seemed to me only wild and bad, and I knew that for Lizzie, all geese were swans or ostriches, and for Gulley, all children were marvels. He was one of those who believe that any child's scrawl is art, and that it is nothing but schools which make fools.

So all I did for Tommy was to take him off their hands, when Lizzie, poor thing, was green with sickness, and Gulley wanted to get on with his work. I would take him to a cinema, or to tea in a shop, which was what he loved, and we would walk along by Strand-on-the-Green and look at the river, and the barges going up with the tide, or sometimes an eightboat, rowing like a toy. Tommy, I say, was a devil, and so Gulley and Lizzie would wonder that he always came out with me and stayed with me. They invented the tale that I had great influence over him, which was to excuse them making me take him off their hands.

Now it is true that on my Wednesdays, young Tommy would run down the street to meet me and hug me and dance on my toes. But that was because I always had a chocolate bar, or a paper of bulls-eyes in my pocket. And if he was good with me when we were out, it was because I let him chatter, and he knew, too, that if he stayed by me and was good, it meant a cream bun, or an ice, or a sixpence. It was all cupboard love in that young monkey, though whether children have anything else before they are twelve or thirteen, I might doubt, and for all I know, one love may be as good as another, to lay hold of a limb.

'Aunt Sara,' he would say, while we were walking, and I was longing only to cool my feet or to run into the Black Lion for a draught: 'Are there any pirates now?'

'Indeed,' I would say, 'I don't know, but if not, it's not for want of people ready for any villainy.'

'Yes,' he would say, 'there are privateers in China. Did you ever hear?' of some bay or other.

'No, Tommy, I never did.'

So then he was well away telling me about the Chinese pirates and Chinese tortures. It was a wonder what horrors that child carried in his head and he loved to talk of them. But my rule has always been, let a child talk and tell all, and though they say I spoilt my children, I think them not so poor, with one doing God's work among the heathen, like a hero; and two wives, and the fourth, though she has not seemed to do anything, yet, when you know her, an upright and honest woman, afraid of nobody.

So Tommy talked about how the Chinese pirates would cut a man into mincemeat or drop water on him in little drops till he went mad, and I would go along under the trees and look at the water, as bright as a new knife, and at the pretty houses which looked all as if they were made for runaway couples, or wicked baronets or good people who have renounced the world and come to their senses, in their old age. I liked the Brighton houses for the same thing and my favourite hotel there was one with mahogany doors, that had been built for George the Fourth, in his gayest time. But Strand-on-the-Green was dearer to my age, for it was more quiet and unfashionable. You could walk there in your old easy shoes and let yourself wag; and if you spoke to someone in the street, to ask the way or the time, it was odds they would stop and chat. You might have been in the country. So I liked my walks with Tommy in spite of his chatter, and thought what I pleased; Mr W., poor little Lizzie, or often, I'll confess, my tea. For at fifty-seven I was growing to think a great deal of a sit-down, and a good tea.

But I'll say this for Tommy, pest as he could be with his dirty finger-marks all over my best silks, and trampling my skirts and shouting in my ear to make me jump, which I hated most of all, he had a sweet heart at bottom, and never bore malice. He would give my hand a great jerk and shout: 'You're not listening, Aunty!'

'Yes, indeed I am, my sweety,' I would say.

'Then what did I say?'

'Something about torturing pirates.'

'No, it was about wireless. I knew you weren't listening. I was telling you how wireless worked.'

'Yes, of course you were, my dear – that's what I meant, and it was very interesting. That's just what I want to know, about valves and waves.'

And then he was off again. For he wanted to tell me. He was ready to teach the world, at that age. Just like my dearest Bobby, in his. But Tommy bullied me more, because I was older and he younger.

83

I say I didn't think so much of Tommy's brains, that they were beyond ordinary. Until one day there was a summons from the school officer. The Jimsons were always being harried by school officers and mistresses and even masters about Tommy, for he was a devil to play truant, and I think Gulley encouraged him.

So this day Gulley said he wouldn't go to court if they gaoled him and Lizzie said she couldn't because she was too big. She had no suitable clothes for the wife of Gulley Jimson. She was worried to death, poor lamb, when I got to the flat at nine, and Gulley was nowhere to be found. So the end of it was I went and answered the questions. At first they were going to arrest Gulley, but I said he was very ill. So one thing led to another, till I was Lizzie's sister, and she was an invalid like her husband, and I was the only responsible person to look after the boy.

Then the magistrates gave me a good talking to about the way I'd neglected the child and warned me to be very careful in the future.

I got off easily enough. But just as I was coming out of court, a tall thin man with a big nose like the fiddle of a spoon came up to me and said: 'Mrs Jimson, I believe.' So I said: 'Yes,' for I didn't want to bother him with names, and he answered: 'I'm afraid I was too late for the court or I would have seen you before. I'm the headmaster at –' I didn't take the name, 'where your son will be coming on Monday.'

'I'm afraid he is a great nuisance,' I said.

'He is a very great disappointment to Miss Stoker,' he said. 'I don't know if you realize that he is exceptionally gifted – quite exceptional, Mrs Jimson, Miss Stoker put him down long ago as a certain scholar. You understand what a scholarship would mean to your boy, Mrs Jimson?'

So he went on telling me that a scholarship would take Tommy to a secondary school, and to Oxford or Cambridge. He might be a doctor, or a scientist, or even Prime Minister and sit down with the King at Buckingham Palace.

I saw that he threw in the Prime Minister and the King to catch my fancy. For he took me for the kind of slummock that would let her son go to waste and dress up in her best only for the court, and I thought to myself: 'It's a great pity a man can't know that you're in clean linen and could strip against queens, except by the nose. Half of them can't smell anything except their own nasty tobacco.'

But he was a very nice man and what I liked about him he was so keen about Tommy.

'You will excuse me, Mrs Jimson,' he said, 'if I am making an unfortunate mistake, but I did hear that Mr Jimson is somewhat opposed to education, as a general principle.'

'He may have said so,' I said, 'but I don't think he means it. He is an artist, you know, and talks a good deal for his own pleasure.'

'Perhaps I might speak to him.'

It wouldn't be any good, I told him, for I thought that it would be awkward if he told Gulley he had been with Mrs Jimson, meaning me. But he insisted. So I took him to the shed, to keep Lizzie out of it and when he began to say 'Your wife,' I said: 'Excuse me, I'm not Mrs *Gulley* Jimson – I thought you meant Mrs Gulley Jimson. Mrs Gulley Jimson is Tommy's mother. I'm only his aunt.' So he thought it was his mistake and apologized nicely and went on about Tommy's great chances. Gulley, of course, was in a fury. He hated government and he used to say that he could be useful to burglars because all his hairs stood up if a policeman came within fifty yards, even in a tail coat.

'No,' said he, 'you're wasting my time and I'm wasting yours. You can't expect me to co-operate in the destruction of my own son.'

The headmaster apologized politely and said that, of course, he greatly disliked compulsion, and so on. He couldn't have been more tactful. I liked him very much. But when he came out with me, he said: 'Is the mother in the same way of thinking?'

'Oh, no,' I said, 'but I'm afraid she hasn't much influence over the boy – he's too wild.'

'In fact,' he said, and he looked at me, 'what we want to do is to get him away from his parents.'

'Why "we," ' I thought, but I had been thinking what a pity it was if Tommy was so clever to leave him at home. Lizzie was no mother to him, and Gulley a worse father, with his cranks.

And if they were bad for Tommy, Tommy was a plague to them, and would be worse when the baby came.

'We want to get him into a special school,' the master said.

But it seemed to me a terrible thing that any child with gifts like Tommy's should go away among a lot of savages to learn devilry. Of course Gulley and Lizzie said the same. Gulley wanted to shoot the attendance officer, till he forgot about the whole thing, in five minutes; and Lizzie wanted to send the boy to a school where the fees were two hundred pounds a year. The end of it was, I was to see the headmaster and he recommended a school he knew of, not a special school, but a pay school where they might take a clever boy like Tommy at half fees. He said that most of these cheap small schools were bad, but this one had a very good master.

It was not three miles away, on the trams, so I went to it and made enquiries.

The school seemed a nice enough place for a town school. It had a garden and a playground. I liked the master better; he was very kind and said he would examine Tommy, and if he did well, he would take him to board, for twenty-two guineas a term, which was a third off the fees.

Gulley and Lizzie said at once that this was cheap, and they would pay. So they did pay, more than I expected; for Lizzie had a little money of her own. Between us we managed very well for the first year, even the clothes. For I had some old castaways at Bellavista, which had been Bobby's, which fitted Tommy like tailor's work. It was only in the second year, when Lizzie had another baby and the first was ill, and Gulley's shed had to be re-felted, to save the poor manny from pneumonia, that we fell a little behind. And then, as I say, I had a lucky stroke, as I thought, with the antique man.

84

Now I'll admit that I never told Mr W. about my half-days at the Gulleys', and when I got away to them as I sometimes did, of an afternoon, I would invent some excuse in case Mr W. found me out. For I knew Mr W. had no opinion of Gulley and would not want me to see him again. All the worse if he knew how I enjoyed those days. For I don't know how it was, I looked forward all the week to my Wednesdays, and in the second weeks, when I went to Nancy, I would always manage an afternoon or evening on some other day, if it was only because they could not do without me, poor things, and Lizzie would keep all her washing and hold her mending till I came. But I loved to go down to the shed and even to hear Gulley say, as in the old days: 'Give me your hand, Sally,' or 'Show me a leg.'

I had always loved, since Woodview days, to sit in the same room when Gulley was working; even to hear the poor manny whistle and hum, and to see him skip up and down his ladder, gave me pleasure. For though Gulley looked old, because he would never wear teeth, yet he was spry as a boy still, and whether it was his liveliness or the perfect content of him, or only the memory of old days or the sudden way he would cut a joke at me, I liked nothing better than to take the mending there while he worked.

And I had never known him more content. He was stuck only twice in the two years, to my knowledge, and then he only went out and got drunk. Lizzie, to be sure, was upset about that, for she feared for his health, but I thought she had got off lightly, and I thought too: God forgive me, that it might be no harm if Gulley did die in his drink, suddenly, before he finished his picture and came to himself, and saw that he had been wasting some more of his time, that his whole life was wasted. For if the Garden of Eden had been a mad kind of picture, it was nature to the Living God. As for portraits, of course, he would never do one. He refused a dozen good commissions, saying he had no time to waste on them.

Now it was made out at the trial that I was only playing with Mr W. and that my real mind was with Gulley at his shed. But this was not so. For fond as I was of Gulley, in his old peaceful age and busy gaiety, and pretty Lizzie who hung upon me like a daughter, and Tommy writing to me every week, by his father, for sweets and sixpences; yet I knew Mr W. was worth three Gulleys, a better and a deeper man, and a more tried. I knew myself honoured by him and I meant to make him a good wife. And though I loved my river dawdlings and my chit-chat in the shed, I had grown fond of Ranns Park too, as any young bride-to-be. Bare as it was, with not a tree over man-size and even the pillar-boxes as fresh as toys out of Christmas parcels, it was so new and fresh, and full of young couples.

When you went out in the evening, to the little park they had, with a little new pond, and a bandstand like a cruet, and when they played twice a week, on closing days and Sundays, and you saw a couple going along with the man's arm round the girl's waist, and head on his shoulder, or lying on a seat by the bus stop, you had not to be worried or to wonder if that was another poor young girl getting into trouble or poor young man got caught by a minx; for you knew that they were married and had their lines. Their courting was a double pleasure to you, because it was love and religion too, as they had vowed.

Even the babies were nearly all new and you should have seen the new prams. Though I don't like these new box prams as deep as graves with the babies buried so far you can't see the poor little mites and they can't see the world either as babies love to do, yet I had to allow that they were bright and gay, and brought back the lovely old carriage-work in the horse days.

The shops were all new too, with new paint and tiles, and the shopkeepers so keen and polite, to get your custom. You would hope they would get on and watch them getting on. But the shopkeepers had to be keen for so were the shoppers. There were no blowsy old things with sore feet dawdling along the arcade at Ranns Park, and no notion in their heads for dinner or anything else, and no method, drifting to a tin of salmon or a box of sardines, enough to break a shopman's heart and a husband's spirit. There was nothing but young mothers marked with the first baby wrinkle between the brows, and eyes like gimlets for the cream on the milk or the lean on a chop; or brides going out with shopping-baskets and note-books and silver pencils, fresh from the wedding presents, and a look as if to say that they must fight this fight and feed their men, or die. But though they were fierce and even the sound of their heels was fierce like soldiers rattling to war, yet they were gay too. You couldn't walk out at night without hearing young girls laughing and often they would romp too, mothers as they were. There was a couple on our other side, with two babies already, but they would chase each other about the garden like children, and laugh till they could not stand, yes, and give each other such smacks, I wondered they were not black and blue.

On a summer night with all the windows open and the chatter coming out like birds going to bed, and the new lights showing on the new little trees with leaves so bright as new-born buds, you would feel the sweet joys of being alive and having your comforts, even though you were too old for romps and babies, and used to managing a man and a house.

As my mother would say: 'The young donkey complained of his long ears, but the old horse thanked God for grass.' It was a sweet thought to lie in bed at Bellavista and think there was more happiness there, to the acre, than in whole towns; more worries too, I'll be bound, but a young worry is like a baby's cry, half for the joy of it.

85

And what a pleasure to see Mr W. so lively and joyful, as any young clerk, just married, with his new furniture and his garden. He was laying down a path now and I was mixing cement and wetting bricks all the afternoon till my hands were like nutmeg graters. But I could not be sorry seeing that Mr W. had a new hobby, for it kept him amused and out in the open air, and gave him an appetite, which was just what he needed. As I'd found out long ago, Mr W. was a very natural kind of man, who only needed something to occupy his mind, and plenty of exercise, and good regular meals, to be as happy as a boy and as sweet and easy as an angel. It was not only that he treated me kindly and never forgot his politeness and respect, as a gentleman, but he would go out of his way to show his kind thoughts of me. He never came from town without some sweet biscuits, dear as they were, or sometimes peppermints, which he knew I liked, or even flowers, and he would give them to me like any prince making his offers to royal blood.

So it was till the very day before the one fixed for our wedding. I ran down that afternoon, while Mr W. was at his lawyer's about making a settlement, and just looked in at the Gulleys' to tell him that he need not worry about his colourman's bill, which was a pest to us all, and to see if there was a note from young Tommy and to get raw fruit for supper, as Miss Clary was coming, to stay the night in proper style on the last night before the wedding, as bride's friend. And when I came back, there was Mrs Loftus and a policeman going through my box.

Now I might have turned them out, as Miss Clary always said, and had Mrs Loftus up for breaking locks, for there was nothing in that box to shame me, except some of those old rubbishy trinkets which Mr W. had given me long ago and which I had not yet sold to my antique man. Miss Clary never ceased to wonder, that same night, that I did not do so, but only went back to my kitchen to put the supper in.

Then when Mrs Loftus followed me down and accused me of robbing the master, I said only that so she said, but the truth might be different, when the master came home.

But they had found my letters from the antique dealer, and a cheque from him and my Post Office book, and some little bills too, from dress shops and sweet shops, and what was worse, a grocer where I got whiskey and brandy for my visits to the Gulleys, and presents to them.

So they sent for a cab to take me off to the station. I'll never forget Miss Clary's face when she came in and found a policeman in the kitchen and me mixing a salad, and Mrs Loftus in the hall waiting for the cab. She could not believe her eyes or her ears.

'What are you thinking of, Sara? You're not going to let them take you before Uncle comes home.' But I only showed her the pie in the oven, not to leave it too long, and the cream for the custard. For I did not want to see Mr W. then. I knew I was a guilty woman. I felt like the ghost of myself, just floating along in the draught from the stove to the sink and back again.

I was not even afraid or unhappy. I was only surprised at myself and my devastations.

For the truth was that I had been picking and stealing for years past, and especially since the Gulleys had come upon me. It was not only the old trinkets I had taken to the antique man, but a gold watch, and silver fruit knives, and an ivory statue with his head off, and two stamp albums, leaf by leaf, which I had found tied up with string under a lot of old clothes. It all came out soon enough when the policeman began his enquiries.

But what was most shocking, I was told, to Mr W., as it shocked the judge, was that I had two hundred and thirty seven pounds in the Post Office and twenty-three gold sovereigns put away. It seemed as if I had robbed Mr W. when I had money saved, and I could not explain that I had promised myself never to call the Post Office money savings, until I had neither place nor home. That was why I had never used that money for bills.

You would think that I was a mad woman to go on so, for years, and to take such risks of being found out. So it seemed to me then and I could not believe how I had done such things. But now I know, and the chaplain agrees with me, that it was a case of little by little, and that the seed of sin was in me from the time when I ran about wild in a pigtail and flirted with three boys at the same time, because I could not refuse any pleasure. I was all in the moment, like a dog or a cat, and indeed, I suppose it is nature to be so, and as the good chaplain says, there is no way for man or woman to remember his duty, from one day to another, and keep upon a steady line, but by stringing his loose days upon a course of religious observance, not just Sundays, I mean, but every day and as often as he is tempted.

86

From the time that the detective took me to the station, I never saw Mr W. again. He went back to his hotel and he sent Miss Clary to me with the name of a lawyer to take care of my case, and a hundred pounds to pay him. He said, too, that if they gave me bail I could stay in the house till the trial.

I wrote to tell him how badly I felt and to ask his forgiveness, but all I had back was a note from Mrs L. to tell me that if he died, I could consider myself responsible. It seemed that Mrs L. had carried him off to the Rectory and even Miss Clary could not get to see him or hear from him, after the first day.

Miss Clary was in despair with him. She said that he ought to stop the case and that he ought to marry me in spite of all. 'The old fool,' she said, 'his heart's broken. I never saw any man so changed. But when I tell him that it's his own fault for not marrying you long ago, he says this shows it was a mercy he didn't because you have been sending money to Jimson all the time. I believe he's just jealous.'

Miss Clary even wanted me to bring out how Mr W. had lived with me, and so it did come out in the end, but not by my fault. It was the Loftuses trying to show how I had got hold of the old man, and to frighten Mr W. too, out of ever coming back to me. It was because of the Loftuses the case made such a noise in the papers. And so too, I ought to tell the truth, for his sake as much as my own family, that he was never to blame, and I was no grabber.

As for the case, it seemed that it had to go on, for the curiosity man was to be charged with receiving and the police had wanted to catch him. Besides, Mr W. had always a great opinion of the law and he did not like to interfere with it just because it didn't suit him. So the case went to the assizes. Then, of course, it came out as well about my paying bad cheques in 1924, and I got eighteen months in the second division.

I deserved no less, as the chaplain said, for no one had better chances and more warnings. Neither had my luck left me, for just when I was fretting for our quarter-day at Gulley's and Tommy's bills on top of that, this kind gentleman came from the news agency and offered me a hundred pounds in advance for my story in the newspapers, when I came out. Paid as I like. So that will pay the school bills, at least, till I'm free, and I've no fear then. A good cook will always find work, even without a character, and can get a new character in twelve months, and better herself, which, God helping me, I shall do, and keep a more watchful eye, next time, on my flesh, now I know it better.

To Be A Pilgrim

To
my wife

1

Last month I suffered a great misfortune in the loss of my housekeeper, Mrs Jimson. She was sent to prison for pawning some old trinkets which I had long forgotten. My relatives discovered the fact and called in the police before I could intervene. They knew that I fully intended, as I still intend, to marry Sara Jimson. They were good people. They saw me as a foolish old man, who had fallen into the hands of a scheming woman. But they were quite wrong. It was I who was the unfaithful servant, and Sara, the victim. It was because I did not give Sara enough pay and because she did not like to ask me for money that she ran into debt, and was tempted to take some useless trifles from the attic.

I was very ill on account of this disaster to my peace of mind, and the family put me in charge of my niece Ann. I say in charge, because Ann is a qualified doctor, and has power over me. People boast of their liberties nowadays, but it seems to me that we have multiplied only our rulers. Ann, aged 26, could lock me up for the rest of my life, if she chose, in an asylum. This would not alarm me so much if I could make out what goes on in the girl's head.

When I asked her to be allowed to see Sara in prison, she answered only, 'We must see how you are.'

And the very next day she said: 'What you really want, uncle, is a change at the seaside.'

'What, at this season?' I was startled by such a suggestion. The girl kept silence. She had no more expression, behind her round spectacles, than a stone ink bottle.

I do not like this girl. I prefer my other niece and several of my honorary nieces. I haven't seen Ann since she was a child. She has lived much abroad, and she never troubled, during her medical training, to visit me.

She has been chosen to take care of me because she is a doctor. But she is a stranger, and I can't tell how dangerous she is, how obstinate. Old men don't like strangers. How can they? For how can strangers like old men. They know nothing of them but what they see and imagine; which in an old man, cannot be very pleasant or entertaining.

'If you take me to the seaside,' I said to Ann, 'I shall go mad. Or perhaps that is the family's plan of campaign.'

'You must have a change, uncle.'

'Do you think I am mad?'

'No.'

'It wasn't you who tried to get me shut up?'

'Cousin Blanche may have – no one else.'

'Why? Because I wear a queer hat? To me, you know, it isn't a queer hat – it's a sensible hat.'

'I think you're quite right to stick to your own fashions.'

But I could see very well that she doesn't like to go out with me.

This is a small point, of course, but it shows the peculia difficulties of my position, as an old man suspected of being insane. If I ordered tomorrow a young man's suit, with enormous trousers and a tight waist, and put on my head a little American hat like a soup plate, or one of those obscene objects called a Tyrolese hat, I should look and feel so disgusting to myself that life would not be worth living. Yet when I examine myself, as now, in a long glass, with Ann's eyes, I see that I must be a queer object to a stranger, and a young stranger.

My hatter tells me that there is only one man in England beside myself, who still wears a curly-brimmed bowler. But he agrees with me that there has never been a better hat, that hats, in fact, since the last war, have gone to the devil. And are getting more degenerate, more slack, more shapeless, every day.

'If you don't like going about with me,' I told Ann, 'you can walk behind or on the other side of the street and watch me from there.'

But this suggestion was badly received. The girl did not answer at all. The effect was quite that of a keeper in an asylum. I was upset and after a little consideration, I said that I should go to the seaside if she insisted.

2

But after all, we did not go to the sea, for suddenly Ann said that the sea might be bad for my heart; why should we not go instead to my house at Tolbrook, near Dartmoor. 'It is nice and relaxing,' the girl said.

This sudden and extraordinary change of plan seemed to me even more suspicious than the first suggestion.

Tolbrook had been let for years, and the question at the moment was whether to sell it for the price of the materials, or to find another tenant stupid enough to take a place in such bad repair.

'Tolbrook won't suit you at all,' I said to the girl, 'and the worry of it has been the curse of my life. In the autumn it is a perfect hole, damp and draughty. Far better go to some seaside town, with concerts and hospitals and libraries for you, and central-heated rooms for me.'

'I haven't seen Tolbrook since I was a small child, and I've always wanted to see it. There is a kind of staff, isn't there?'

'Yes, a caretaker and one or two maids. The gardener's wife will always help.'

'Then let's try Tolbrook.'

'I can't understand why you want to go to Tolbrook.'

'It will give you an appetite perhaps.'

'And take me further away from Mrs Jimson.'

'Yes.' The girl was not at all disconcerted. 'And perhaps you won't worry about her so much.'

'I don't worry about her, but about myself. She is happy wherever she is – she is saved. But I miss her very much. It is too easy to forget what people are in themselves when you can't be with them.'

'Sara seems to have got a hold on you, uncle.'

'She is a remarkable person.'

'She rather affected the religious, didn't she?'

'No, you are quite wrong. She never affected anything, but she is deeply religious. She is one of those people to whom faith is so natural that they don't know how they have it. She has a living faith.'

'She seems to have looted you pretty thoroughly.'

I said nothing more. I looked at the girl's uncheerful, pale face; so confident in its uncheerfulness, and thought 'I might as well talk about grace to a Choctaw Indian.'

She drove me down next day in her own car. She drives fast and dangerously. Her driving terrified me and gave me a pain in my breast. But I thought perhaps she liked to frighten me and so I said nothing. I resigned myself, I relaxed to this pain, and this old man's fear, and what was strange, when we rushed into the narrow lanes of the West, and I began to recognize a cottage here and an inn there, they seemed not only charming but new, like a foreign country recognized from photographs. I was not the exile returned for a brief sad visit, but the visitor from another world.

Tolbrook Manor house has no beauties except two good rooms by the Adams brothers. Although it stands high, it has no view. It is an irregular house; a three-storey block with one long east wing and on the west an absurd protrusion, one storey high, ending in a dilapidated greenhouse. It has a two-acre field in front of it, and a farmyard behind. A small old topiary garden, called Jacobean, has been restored by one of the tenants. The crooked drive is more like a farm lane than a drive. Elms and oaks stand along it as if planted by chance in a hedge; here, three in a row, then a gap, then a clump, then two great elms so close together that one could not squeeze between them.

They talk of the deep country. In the early evening, as we drove through the lanes, I felt these words with a new force. The tall banks and hedges, the great trees in their autumn colours, seaweed green against the clear green sky, all gave me the sense of passing beneath enormous depths of silence and loneliness.

And when we were in sight of the old house, so hated and so loved, I found myself laughing. Its very chimneys, of all shapes and sizes, seemed comical to me. And its solitude, its remoteness from all rational beings, now gave me a lively pleasure. For I thought, 'At least I'll get some peace here. I shan't have to feel every moment, as I used to "the next budget will take all this away", or "how senseless to spend all one's life in patching up these old walls".'

'It's not much of a house,' I said to Ann.

'How do you feel, uncle?' She had not even looked at the house, in which she had declared so great an interest.

'Very well.'

'You are rather breathless. Is your chest all right?'

'I had a little pain just now.'

In fact, I found myself so exhausted that Ann had to pull me out of the car. She gave me some of her bitter medicine and refused to let me go upstairs. She sent for an old carrying chair that my mother had used, and had me carried up to bed.

It would seem, therefore, that the girl did not drive at eighty miles an hour in order to kill me. Though I can't make out why she has chosen, in that case, to bring me to Tolbrook. Perhaps in order to get me away from the rest of the family. There is I know some anxiety about the future of the property. I have two nephews and a niece, all with equal claims. Perhaps Ann, having been almost unknown to me, now wishes to make up for lost time. I do not blame her. She has every right to her share of the booty.

3

I had been brought to my old room. Indeed, I had asked for it; a small room, once the sick room on the nursery floor, with two round-topped windows looking out upon a great lime tree, and to the left, the yards. And my feeling, as I was laid, already drowsy, in the iron servant's bed which had served us, as children, for measles, scarlet fever, so many illnesses, was one not of returning home, but of discovery. 'So this is what it was – this dismal little room, this lumpy mattress.' Mattresses have improved in the last ten years. Everything had improved except people, manners, dress, etc.

'Good night, uncle,' Ann said, 'and if you want me, I'm on the other side of that door,' pointing at the door of the nurse's room between nursery and sick room.

'I think Robert will want that room,' I said. 'It was his room before he went abroad.'

'When is he coming?' And in the tone of the girl's voice I seemed to hear a particular interest.

Robert is my nephew, lately returned from South America. I daresay the family sent for him to prevent my marrying Sara Jimson. But Robert is an old friend of Sara's, who mothered him in his boyhood. He quite approved my intention.

Robert and Ann had met in my town lodgings. And they had not had much to say to each other. Robert, to my surprise, had been shy of his cousin; and Ann, who can spend a whole evening with her nose in a book, had been at a loss with a young man who had read nothing more recent than Dickens or perhaps Kipling.

But now it suddenly struck me that Ann's decision to come to Tolbrook had closely followed upon a telephone message to me from Robert, asking if he might visit Tolbrook before his departure.

'You like Robert,' I said. And the girl answered me, in an indifferent voice, 'I did rather fall for his nice eyes.'

I was so startled by this news and the manner of its communication that I did not know what to say. But at last I ventured to hint that Robert was not a literary or artistic person. 'Neither does he care for classical music. Nor, if you'll excuse me, girls in spectacles.'

Ann was silent, and I saw that she did not wish to pursue the subject. To my relief. For I felt that I had discharged my responsibility.

And before I was aware of it, the girl had left the room. She is, I must admit, very quick and neat in her movements. A trait she inherits from her father, my eldest brother Edward. But one that commends her to me more, no doubt, than to a boy like Robert.

Now that I begin to get used to this girl, I see that she is like Edward in many ways, even in looks. Her plainness is merely a veil drawn over Edward's handsomeness. You can see his features beneath. Her eyes are not blue like his, but smoke grey; that is, a shaded blue. Her nose is not fine but flattened and broad, like Edward's delicate beak pressed down and coarsened. Her hair is a dark yellow, old straw to Edward's bright new straw. She has what Edward had, the look of breeding; but subdued, as breeding should be. Put one of the Velasquez infantas into round spectacles and send her to a medical school, and you would have Ann. Even to the melancholy, the look of a doomed race, lonely and burdened. But all these girls nowadays, after their first twenties, have that look. Sad and responsible.

When I see Ann, daughter of that gay, that brilliant Edward, going about as if her life were finished, I want to stick pins in her. But what can I do? No one could plant happiness in a soul that rejects all faith.

4

I slept deeply, my first good sleep for months, and when I waked, early as usual, a short inquiry revealed that I was still in good health and excellent spirits. Neither Tolbrook nor Ann had upset me. On the contrary, I was excited by the thought of exploring the old house, after so many years. I opened all doors to these memories, from which, in my late mental anxiety, I had fled, and at once my whole body like Tolbrook itself was full of strange quick sensations. My veins seemed to rustle with mice, and my brain, like Tolbrook's roof, let in daylight at a thousand crevices.

It was a breezy morning, and every knock of the blind, on the window ledge, brought something fresh and gay and austere into my spirit. A sensation from the past, which I could not place. Why so gay, and why so austere. I opened my eyes and looked towards the window. The curtains were some light cotton stuff, spotted with small flowers, and the old yellow blinds, behind them, were transparent.

As the blind flapped, the curtains bellowed into the room, and cold draughts struck my cheek. I could not resist those beckoning curtains, the fresh chill of the breeze. I got up and went to the window. With precautions, not to attract my nurse's attention, I released the spring of the blind and let it roll itself up.

A pale green sky, as brilliant and cold as sea water, in winter sunshine, stood before me, infinitely high. The top twigs of a great lime, outside the nursery windows, swayed gently, and threw off another few leaves, They were almost bare already.

I stood and wondered at myself. 'You old fool, you'll catch cold.' But my excitement increased. I seemed to be expecting something.

'Of course,' I said, 'I am simply a child again. This expectation is the feeling of getting up in the morning. I am getting well after some illness and waiting to join the others in the nursery.'

I went down the passage into the old day nursery, next beyond the nurse's room, where Ann had chosen to sleep.

The room had been used by the tenants for a maids' dormitory. There were two beds in it. But the old table, cut by knives and burnt by hot smoothing-irons, stained with ink and paint, stood uncovered between the windows; and over the mantelpiece, the old steel engraving of Raphael's Dresden madonna. I stood waiting and listening.

Ann, who must have the ears of a roe, came suddenly into the room. She never runs, but for all her smallness, she moves fast and smoothly. She said in her professional severe voice, 'What are you doing, uncle? – you'll catch your death.'

5

It was true that I was in pyjamas, but I had not meant to go out of my room. I said that I had thought to hear voices in the nursery.

182

'Voices,' she said, and blushed. She always colours when she thinks me strange or mad. She tied up my pyjamas which were falling down, and said: 'You mustn't go about like that – I don't mind, but the maids might, and you know we had trouble in town.'

Ann, whose education is like a set of boxes, all neatly arranged in a filing cabinet, has put me in a box labelled 'Exhibitionist'.

It is, I gather, one of her Viennese or German boxes, which she brought back from her medical studies abroad. Next year there will be a new set of boxes, and poor Ann's will be out of date and useless.

But Edward's daughter ought to have more sense than to put people into paper boxes, and if I like to startle her sometimes, it is for her own good.

'Now back to bed,' she said, trying to lead me out of the room. 'Or you won't be allowed up to dinner.'

'It was my own voice,' I said, 'as a child, and your father Edward's and my brother Bill's and my sister Lucy's.'

'You are dreaming, uncle.'

'No, they were here – this was our nursery, you know.'

She decided to change the subject. 'I wouldn't choose a room facing east for children.'

'We got the morning sun here. That's what I remember; and running out of bed straight into the sunlight. My dear child, you must allow me to wait here a little longer in case the others want me.'

Again she looked sharply at me to see if I were playing some trick on her. And of course my words were half joking. I thought, 'She hasn't got a box for this emergency.' I said then, downwards and sideways, as if speaking to a child at my elbow: 'Lucy, you called me – have you heard that Tolbrook is being sold, to be pulled down. I am escaping at last from my prison.'

Lucy had been my dearest friend in life; dearer than any friend. And as I pretended to listen, I was startled to find that I was holding my breath.

Now, I do not believe in ghosts. They are, I believe, uncanonical. It was, I consider, merely the name Lucy, uttered aloud in the old nursery, which had a certain effect upon my nerves, and threw me into confusion. Certainly my pulse raced, my ears drummed, and my head sang. I felt very queer indeed. And then all at once, something happened which caused me a severe shock; much more than I had bargained for. The voice of Lucy spoke to me. But not from a child's level. It was into my ear, and in a phrase that I did not invent, 'To be a pilgrim.'

The voice was not that of Lucy as a child, shrill and always full of passion, excitement; but of the young woman Lucy, at twenty or so, a girl I had forgotten. It was gay and coquettish. And the words had actually been spoken in that room, by that young woman, long vanished even in Lucy's lifetime. It was a phrase private to us two, for a private reason. Sometimes a joke and sometimes serious. I had written it, as a boy of fifteen, on the fly leaf of my confirmation prayer book, under my mother's inscription. I had read it there ten thousand times since, and sung it, from the well-known hymn, but I had not understood it for many years.

I was so taken aback that I did not know where I was until I found Ann helping me back into bed. She was reproaching me, in her patient and bored manner, and saying that if she would stand nonsense, my heart would not.

I murmured my apologies, for I did not want to lose my discovery. A real discovery is not a thought; it is an experience, which is easily interrupted and lost. 'Yes,' I thought, 'that was the clue to Lucy, to my father, to Sara Jimson, it is the clue to all that English genius which bore them and cherished them, clever and simple. Did not my father say of Tolbrook which he loved so much, "Not a bad billet", or "not a bad camp", and Sara? Was not her view of life as "places" as "situations" the very thought of the wanderer and the very strength of her soul. She put down no roots into the ground; she belonged with the spirit; her goods and possessions were all in her own heart and mind, her skill and courage.'

And is not that the clue to my own failure in life. Possessions have been my curse. I ought to have been a wanderer, too, a free soul. Yes, I was quite right to break off from this place. Although I have loved it, I can never have peace till I leave it.

As for my age, did not Caxton begin to learn Greek at sixty; in order to translate books for his Westminster press. Even doctors prescribe a change of scene for the sick body and mind. As if the very mould of man was that of the Arab, the wanderer. 'Yes, I must go,' I thought. 'I must move on – I must be free.'

6

Robert came today, as always unannounced, and as usual, at an awkward moment. I was holding a conference with the garden boy among the trees near the main gate, when Robert strolled in. He saw me before I saw him.

Now my business was private. The truth was that since my illness, I have had a mysterious difficulty in getting cash. And what is a man without cash. His self-respect, his faith oozes out at the bottom of his empty pockets. But when I have asked for a cheque book, Ann has forgotten to order it. I wrote for one and it didn't arrive. So yesterday I made up a bearer cheque, with a postal stamp, and sent it by the garden boy to Exeter. Not Queensport, which is full of family spies. I told the boy to get silver. I have always liked some silver by me. And he had brought me, to my great delight, twenty-four half-crowns, which he had barely transferred into my pockets when Robert's voice sounded at my shoulder. Between the doubt whether he had seen anything suspicious, and delight at seeing him, I was highly confused, and perhaps talked some nonsense.

As Lucy's son, Robert is very dear to my heart. That is to say, whenever I see him, my feelings are thrown into an affectionate agitation which is almost painful.

'My dear Robert,' I cried. 'At last,' and so on. I could hardly express my delight. And the weight of silver, combined with the weight of excitement, filled me with anxious foreboding.

'Ohyay, it's good to be here again – and how are you, uncle,' Robert said, shaking my hand and taking me affectionately by the forearm. 'O.K. I hope – you look just wonderful.' He is, I think, fond of me, in his way. Though probably he would like me out of his way.

Robert has come back from his ten-year exile, both better and worse. His manners have improved. He is more polite. But I feel that he is, in reality, more pig-headed than ever. Almost as pig-headed as his mother, in her worst days. You can see it in his face, even when he smiles.

I was shocked when I first saw Robert, on his return. At twenty-eight, he looks like forty. His face is like a peasant's, thin and hard, coloured like the inside of an old rein; and seamed as if by cuts.

But even when he does not smile, he has always a smiling air. He has the habitual expression that I saw once on the face of a successful young pugilist, at Paddington Station. He was going to some fight in the north, and he was surrounded by a group of admirers, who continually talked about his prowess, not to him, but across him, reminding each other of his feats, and illustrating his blows; as, I am told, the courtiers of some barbarous chief flatter him, not directly, but to each other, surrounding him with a glory which seems to him, since he contributes nothing to its production, like the natural and proper atmosphere of royalty.

Robert has the little smile of that scarred young boxer; at once melancholy and knowing; as if he said 'All the same, I do the fighting.'

An obstinate smile, which alarms me. But I am resolved not to quarrel with Robert. And when now he remarked, in his usual way, that some of the trees in the drive were pretty rotten and ought to come down, I answered only, 'They'll last my time at Tolbrook,' and changed the subject.

It has been suggested to me, by my niece Blanche, that Robert would like to get hold of Tolbrook, for his own purposes. No doubt. I understand that he has brought back nothing from his ten years farming in Canada and South America. He lost his inheritance in bad speculations, and he has not stayed long enough in any job to save a new capital sum.

'Is old Jaffery still running the place?' he asked.

Jaffery is the estate agent in Queensport, and my local manager.

'Yes, yes, more or less,' I said. 'Did you know Ann was here?'

'Well, I knew she'd be with you. But I came to see you, uncle – and the old swamps and weeds that Jaffery calls a farm.'

'Ann will be delighted to see you. She is really a good-natured girl, and clever, they say, at her doctoring.'

'Well, uncle, I certainly found Ann an interesting girl to meet, but she didn't seem to take to me – she thought me a hick.'

'Not at all – that's only her modern way,' etc., and so on.

'Now there's a tree that ought to be felled. An ash. Get a good price for an ash.'

'Yes, yes, but it's not your tree, Robert; that's my tree, or rather your Uncle Bill's tree – he planted it for the Jubilee of '87 – excuse me, I think I see Ann now,' and I hurried into the house. I had not seen Ann, but I perceived that Robert meant to worry me about the trees. A bad beginning.

Even as a boy Robert always tried to alter our arrangements at Tolbrook, which caused many disputes and much exasperation.

As soon as I had put my change in a safe place, I hastened to find Ann. 'Robert has arrived. He walked from the village and his luggage is coming by the van. You must go and entertain him. Get up some beer.'

'Whiskey is what he likes – but I was just going into Queensport for shopping.'

'You mustn't do that – you must go down to him and keep him amused – and tell him not to worry me about the trees and the farm, and so on. Tell him I can't stand it. What have you done with your face?' Ann always powdered too much. I had not meant to pester the girl about this idiosyncrasy. Girls resent such criticism. But now, seeing her with a dead white face, lips painted blood colour and a pair of enormous black-rimmed spectacles, I suddenly found myself exasperated into speech. I could not bear to see the girl, who is, after all, Edward's daughter, making a repulsive spectacle of herself before young Robert.

'My face, uncle – isn't it all right?'

'No, it is not – it looks like a chamber pot crudely daubed with raspberry jam. I cannot conceive how you can make such a fearful object of yourself. But excuse me,' for I was horrified at my rudeness and lack of tact, 'Of course I don't know anything about these modern fashions – I may be wrong,' etc. I was afraid that I had hurt the poor creature. But she answered gravely that it was very kind of me. 'I'll do what I can about the face,' and she seemed to bear me no malice.

It is true that she did not make the slightest change in her make up. Indeed, I thought at luncheon that she was powdered a little whiter and had made her lips a shade darker. But I may have been deceiving myself, because her spectacles also looked larger and blacker, and I can't believe that she went to the expense of new spectacles only to spite me, unless she had a blacker pair by her, ready for such an emergency. And I thought better of Ann after this incident. It is a merit perhaps, in these modern girls, that they are not, on the whole, so touchy as those of our generation.

Though, of course, this virtue probably has its own defect, in a general coldness of disposition, and other faults, of a graver nature.

7

When Ann came to put me to bed, take my pulse, mix me a draught, and so on, she began to ask me about Robert and his side of the family. 'I was always told that Aunt Lucy was rather fierce.'

'Fierce. At your age – no, six years younger – Lucy was one of the belles of the season – a charming girl. But she had a strong will. So has Robert. I suppose Robert has already been telling you that this place is badly run. Don't you listen to him. Robert is the kind of boy who never did, and never could, leave well alone.'

'Is it true that Aunt Lucy ran away with a butcher?'

'Not at all. Brown was at one time a small farmer who may have killed his own beasts. But afterwards he was a preacher – a very good preacher.'

'How typical of Robert to say that his father was a butcher.'

'Quite so. It is typical of Robert. Though Robert was very fond of his mother. She died when he was twelve, but it was a fearful blow to him. I'm not surprised. She was a great woman. Or, I should say, she had the quality of greatness, like Brown himself. He was perhaps a rough customer. But a touch of real greatness.'

'I don't think I should have liked him very much.'

'No, you would not have liked him. Neither did I. But perhaps we ought not to boast of that delicacy and refinement. Perhaps we don't like him because we are small people. Small people never like great people. Small people are people who follow the fashion and live like frogs in a ditch, croaking at each other. When a real man comes near, they are all silent. If baggy trousers come in, all the small people will get into baggy trousers like that old fool Jaffery, who looks like a dwarf with elephantiasis. And if painted faces and long bobs come in, then all the little girls paint their faces and wear long bobs, even if it makes them look like clowns with hunchbacks. The people of character stick to the shape and colour given them by nature – to reason, and truth.'

'Perhaps we have talked enough, uncle – if you talk too much you won't sleep.'

'I don't mean to sleep.'

But she took away the tray and I was glad. For I had been thinking of Lucy and Brown all the evening, and I wanted to be with them. I had not thought of Robert's father for years. But though I had called him great somewhat hastily, now I felt that I was right. He was a truly great man, who had failed to get worldly honours only because he did not seek them.

The proof was that only by thinking of the man, I felt the excitement of his presence when, for the first time, I stood below him.

He was preaching on Tolbrook Green, from the tail of one of our own waggons, which apparently he had commandeered from our horseman, by the right of a prophet.

His short squat figure stood black against the crimson sign of the 'Wilcher Arms', hanging behind him. Its gilt lettering, sparkling in the sun, made a kind of glory round his head and shoulders; the shoulders of a giant or a dwarf; and the face of a prize fighter, pug nose, jutting brows, thick swollen lips, roaring over all the noise of bullocks and sheep.

> No focs shall stay his might,
> Though he with giants fight;
> He will make good his right
> To be a pilgrim.

At these words I felt my heart turn over, and I drove away as fast as I could. I had meant to claim the waggon. But I was afraid of Brown; I thought he could convert me, and I was enjoying life then as never before, in my first year at Oxford. Why was I afraid of Brown. I was a clever young man who was reading Kant. Brown had no arguments that did not fill me with contempt. But when he sang these verses from Bunyan, his favourite hymn and the battle cry of his ridiculous little sect, then something swelled in my heart as if it would choke me, unless I, too, opened my own mouth and sang. I might have been a bell tuned to that note, and perhaps I was. For the Wilchers are as deep English as Bunyan himself. A Protestant people, with the revolution in their bones. Who said that? – Cromwell, Wycliffe and Stiggins. Our grandfather was a Plymouth brother; he was converted by one of the Wallops, and there are Quakers, Shakers, fifth monarchy men, even Anabaptists, on the maternal side. I did not know it then because I knew nothing and nobody real, only knowledge about things. I knew no living soul, not even Lucy, until I knew Sara, and found in her the key of my own soul. A key forged in English metal for an English lock. At that time my own English spirit, like Lucy's, was a mystery to me. I fled from Brown because I felt that if I did not run, he would get me. I remember that when I reached the stable yard, in the dark, Lucy came out and called, 'Is that you, Tommy; you're very late.' I did not answer, but waited for a strapper to take the mare's head; and got down in silence. I did not quite know what had happened to me. But when I came into the lower passage by the yard door, under a lantern which always hung there, Lucy said in a startled voice, 'What's wrong, Tommy; was Jinny too much for you.' Jinny was the mare. She took my arm and said, 'You oughtn't to take Jinny – you're much too blind. Promise me you won't be dared by the others.'

She knew I was afraid of betraying my real fear of horses.

'The Benjamites were having a meeting,' I said, 'and I had to turn back in Hog Lane. I think it must be a new preacher.'

'Oh, yes, a man like a pug dog with shoulders like a fire screen. He makes a noise just like the bullocks.'

'I don't think we can afford to laugh at the Benjamites, Lucy.'

'Of course we can't,' she said, taking off my box coat. 'But I have to laugh in case they might catch me.'

I turned to her in surprise. 'Do you feel like that?'

'What?' she said laughing. 'Have they converted you, too?'

'But you mustn't laugh. I'm not joking. I have had a very queer experience.'

'My dear Tom,' said Lucy, 'we've all had that experience.'

'You can't have felt what I've felt tonight.'

Lucy smiled at me and took my arm. I had forgotten that. But now suddenly her arm glides into mine and I perceive how I loved Lucy then; with a love belonging only to that time; when we were both amusing ourselves with life. It was a love such as can only exist between brother and sister, who, because they are brother and sister, do not suffer the exasperation of the flesh. We never wished to play the martyr. We gave each other freedom to be in love with others, and even discussed our flirtations. Yet our tie was stronger than all. There was but one cause of bitterness between us, my jealousy of Edward. But that was not recognized; I did not allow myself to be jealous, and admired Edward quite as much as Lucy herself. I only did not like to see her run to him and throw her arms round his neck; to see her so deeply concerned in him that, when he was at home, she thought of no one else.

Luckily Edward was seldom at home, and so in those days I often had Lucy to myself, as on this evening, when she received me with that charming affection of which Lucy alone had the secret. Her very gesture of putting her hand in my arm, threw a spell upon my spirit, so that I began to smile, without reason, and without any regard to the conversation.

Lucy smiled also at me, but she was not laughing at me as she did so often. 'My dear Tom, you are blinder than I thought – you never seem to know anything that goes on. I have been converted by the Benjamites – really converted – at least three times. And the last time was only last year. Didn't you realize why I was nearly not presented.'

'I thought it was because father didn't want to open No. 15.' This was our old London house, in Craven Gardens, shut up for years.

'No, it was because I didn't want to be presented or be brought out or to have a season – I wanted to go on the roads with Mr Pugface and sing "Come to Jesus" outside the pubs. Father and I had the most terrible row about it.'

These words gave me a great comfort. Not because they answered Brown, but because Lucy's voice and smile carried me back into the world which made a joke of everything except friendship and amusement. 'Yes,' I said, 'of course it's only tub-thumping.'

'Well,' Lucy said, 'we'll call it that or he'll get us. And I should hate to be a Benjamite.'

Both of us were silent for a moment. And I felt as if some internal Brown were trying to pop out of a dark hole in my own mind.

Edward used to say that the effect of a Protestant education was to make people a little mad. 'It throws upon everyone the responsibility for the whole world's sins, and it doesn't provide any escape – not even a confession box.'

Mad Englishmen. Why not? Whose Sunday bells.

Ring in raw beef and fifteen different hells.

8

Ann did not allow me to go to church on Sunday, but I had prayers in the dining-room. And Robert did not come. I told him afterwards that he was no son of his father's to stay away from a Christian service on Sunday. He answered that he had meant to come 'only I was having a look round Tenacre and forgot the time'. And then he began to urge some changes in the fields at Tenacre, which is a detached part of our home farm, and also in the byres.

'You'll get it all back, uncle. Why, you've got ten cows, and you're buying milk.'

'I really think, uncle, that some of the cows are not earning their keep,' Ann said.

'I did not know,' I said, 'that you were an expert on farm management.' For I have been astonished at her duplicity. During the last week, she has been going about the fields and the yards with Robert, in mud and rain; and at table, she talks about cows, crops, as if she had been brought up to be a farmer.

'I don't know anything,' she answered me. 'Robert is the expert.'

'Expert in what?' I asked. 'I think you are both experts in making fools of each other,' and I took occasion to say, when I found the girl alone, that a farmer's wife in the remoter parts of the world had the hardest and roughest kind of work of any woman. It was work only for a peasant brought up to it.

'I wouldn't dream of marrying Robert,' the girl said. 'That would be quite fatal.'

'I should think so indeed – but, of course, it's none of my business.'

For I perceived very clearly that if I began to worry about a silly flirtation between two young people cut off from other amusements, I should get no peace at Tolbrook – or anywhere else. It is such petty worries that have wrecked my whole life and prevented me from all achievement, all happiness; from men and from God.

'No, no, you old fool,' I said to myself. 'Let them alone – let them play. Let them make fools of themselves if they like. You can't stop them.'

But at two in the morning I am brought up sitting in bed, by a creak in the passage.

'That's not Robert going from Ann's room – he said good night at the door, two hours ago. But if it was, what does it matter to you. Go to sleep, you old fuss-pot. Or if you can't sleep, think of your death, and the judgement. Something that really matters.'

But I can't go to sleep. I cover my head with the bedclothes, but still my ears strain, my heart beats; I catch myself holding my breath.

It is the misfortune of an old man that though he can put things out of his head he can't put them out of his feelings. Now, when my eyes and ears are failing, some deeper senses become every day more acute. And so I feel in these children, even while they are not in the room with me, something which makes me as uneasy as if I were full of jumping fleas.

Some secret excitement, some cunning passion; evil and treacherous, infects the whole house.

'You mustn't worry about us, uncle – I'm twenty-six, you know, and I've been responsible for myself since I was seventeen.'

Ann said this to me today, apropos of nothing. It seems that she also has the family sensibilities. So much the worse for her.

'Responsible for yourself.' I said. 'But unfortunately you're my niece and Edward's daughter. No, it isn't a matter of sentiment. How would you feel if someone stuck a knife in your leg. I suppose you would say that the leg could look after itself. As a scientist –'

Someone began whistling in the yard, and I knew by her face that it was Robert. I said, 'Run along and play. God knows which of us is the madder.'

9

When you are old, they throw 'conservative' at you as a reproach. But I can remember very well when Robert himself, as a small child, in this very house, would not go to bed without a certain lump of wood, the remains of a toy horse, in his arms. He loved his horse, and to protect that horse he would fight with his own mother, whom he also loved.

I remember a riot in our nursery, when nurse attempted to abolish our silver bowls for earthenware, saying that the crockery was easier to clean. Dorothy, my youngest sister, who died a child, set up a yell as if she were being murdered, and Lucy flung her spoon on the floor.

I daresay Lucy was not more than six. And this is my earliest recollection of her fury in its true quality. But I knew even then that she was something more than a nursery rebel. She had the genius of a leader in revolt, full of malice as well as rage.

I saw the spoon go down, and heard it ring upon the floor, with childish delight. But it was with more than childish delight that I watched Lucy, when the nursemaid stooped to pick up the spoon, deliberately and skilfully pour the bowl of scalding bread and milk over her hair and neck; and then bonnet her with the bowl.

I felt then a devilish thrill, the thrill which, no doubt, has fixed that moment in my brain for ever.

But Lucy, the rebel, began in revolution against the new. She did not think that all change was progress. She discriminated, even at six. She knew the value of order, of a routine, even in our rebellious nursery. I daresay Nature had taught her that it is precisely the stormiest spirit, which needs, upon its rough journey, some rule of the sea and road. 'The love of routine,' a scientific friend said to me once, 'is nothing to be ashamed of. It is only the love of knowing how to do things which Nature plants in every child, kitten, and puppy.'

As I stand here at the door of the nursery staircase, collecting strength for the climb, I hear Lucy's voice screaming to me furiously, 'Tom-my, Tom-my. Aren't you ready?' She is disgusted by my irresponsible conduct. She darts round the corner, a rosy child in a white fur tippet and a blue coat. She seizes my hand, jerks it violently, and yells, 'No, he isn't ready – and his face is *still* dirty. Oh, you are a nuisance.'

The jerk still jerks me now. But apparently it did not cause me any distress, for I remember nothing else until I am walking along the drive, through red mud, with my hand firmly locked in Lucy's. I wear a long yellow coat with large buttons and a round hat. Edward in a bowler and a smart overcoat, Bill in a cape, swaggering his broad shoulders, walk in front. Edward I think is even carrying a walking-stick. My father, in a flat-topped felt hat, and my mother in a tight-waisted sealskin and little round ermine hat, are already fifty yards down the drive. My father holds himself very upright; but rolls a little on his short thick legs. He is still a soldier in his back, but his legs are growing farmerish. My mother glides in her long skirt, which seems to hide a machine designed to carry smoothly forward the moulded body in its tight jacket.

Lucy is still abusing me. She shakes my hand up and down, and I hear the words, 'stupid, naughty, a perfect nuisance to everybody'.

My attachment to Lucy was a country legend. I see myself joined to her as if by a string; a small ugly child with a round red face, a snub nose, black hair growing out of his round head in tufts, like that of an old-fashioned clown, and iron spectacles. I am always running at her heels, clasping at her hand; or anxiously hunting for her, with the anguish and despair of a lost dog. I cannot be happy without her.

But to her frequent abuse I pay no attention whatever. I am pushing my new boots into the soft bright mud, and I am full of a deep content, which is a child's happiness. This content is made up of several different parts in which Lucy's hand, the boots, the hat, the mud, the familiar ceremony of going to church, and the prospect of spotted dog for Sunday dinner, all have place. My enjoyment of the moment, impressed upon my memory only by Lucy's violence, is so profound, that even now it gives me a sense of peculiar happiness. For though I have no happiness now, except in memory, it says to me, 'Happiness is possible to man among the things he loves and knows.' And it comes apparently from the touch, from contact, from a presence in the air. I was happy with Lucy because all about was a familiar world, not especially friendly to me, but understood.

An old house like this is charged with history, which reveals to man his own soul. But I can't expect a boy like Robert to understand that.

10

'What you have to remember,' I said to Ann, 'is that Robert has a devil, an obstinate, destructive devil. Eight years ago he wanted to pull down half this house and make farm buildings of it. And when I wouldn't let him, he threw up a good job and went to Canada.'

'Robert isn't spiteful. That's his great charm.'

'I don't know what he is, but he has a devil. He wants his own way, and often it is the wrong way. He's like his mother.'

Ann seemed to reflect, but I don't suppose she is capable of reflection at this moment. She goes about the house with the face of a sleep-walker. She said to me, 'Why were you sitting here? Isn't it rather late for you?'

I had been sitting in the old high-backed nursery chair which I had discovered that morning in the back kitchen passage. It had been our nurse's chair and also our ship, our castle, our throne, and pulpit.

But I didn't want to talk to Ann about chairs private to myself. And I got up and went with her.

'Why did you leave us alone in the dining-room, uncle?'

'So that you could make eyes at each other if you liked,' and so on and so forth, etc. 'I'm not going to chaperon you. I don't believe in chaperons, whatever you may think. I'm not so hidebound. I've been a Liberal all my life, as you well know. I was one of the strongest supporters of the emancipation of women,' etc., and so on, while she was leading me up to bed. 'I believe in progress, but progress upwards.'

She was perfectly grave, but I could see that she was laughing at me, and this made my head swim. But I said to myself, 'Serve you right, you old fool, if you drop down dead. Don't you know how to mind your business yet. And what if Robert does go to her room. Does that prove that he goes to bed with her. What do you know about this new world of morals, or immorals, which has floated out of the German boxes, like the ghost dancers of the high moor, who, they say, come smoking out of the earth on midwinter night, to prance and jibber round the standing stones of phallic cults older than the human brain.'

11

And when she had put me to bed, with her usual expertness, she said in her mild and inquiring manner, 'I thought, uncle, you were fond of Aunt Lucy.'

'Of course I was fond of her. She was my sister. What's that got to do with it. That didn't prevent her from having a devil. And it won't prevent Robert from breaking your heart,' and so on. A fit of temper which cost me a sleepless night.

But Ann, of course, only looked more grave, and laughed the more inside. She is as full of laugh as any bride in the first week of her honeymoon. 'But, of course,' I said, 'you don't believe in the devil. Though, God knows, I should have thought there was plenty of his work to be seen at the present day – are you going to let that boy spend half the night in your room again?'

'Certainly not, uncle. I want to go to sleep. And you ought to sleep.' And she wished me good night and went out, quite delighted with the whole world. You could tell it by the way she moved her legs. Going to the devil as fast as she could fly. And never believing that such a thing existed, as the will to evil, to cruelty, to humiliation; to lust for the spite of lust; to treachery for the pleasure of destroying faith; to malice, for the delight of stabbing innocence in the back. A devil now gathering power every day, while he quietly undermines the walls of freedom, the order of our peace.

I never hated anyone as I could hate Lucy; and I was right to hate her. For what I loathed in her was the devil. That destroyer, when you see him face to face, is always terrifying and hateful.

My battles with Lucy were a family joke, and even I could not understand why I fought her; why once, at six years old, I tried to kill her. Indeed, I often tried to kill her. But the reason was, that she made me murderous with her devil.

'What an extraordinary boy you are, Tommy.' Her voice flies at me out of the dark like a snake out of ambush. Devil's words. For Lucy did not believe them; she meant them to stab me, to destroy my faith in myself, and to increase her own importance.

'Let me alone, Lucy,' I say.

'Well, I'm only being nice.'

We are in the nursery and Lucy is holding my hand. But already I feel from the hand a kind of electricity which secretly alarms me. I want to be at peace, and to think out something which puzzles me.

A bright fire burns and snow is banked smoothly on the window sill. There is a sense of comfortable joy which belongs to all snowy days, when one is kept indoors and there will probably be muffins. But Edward, wearing an old alpaca coat of my father's, as Geneva gown, is preaching over the leather back of the old nursery chair. And I am perplexed by something queer in his voice and manner.

'I stand here as the heir of Wycliffe and Cromwell and Stiggins.'

We were fond of preaching and funerals. Such games were probably traditional with us, like family prayers, and meetings. My father, as colonel of his regiment, had held prayer meetings for his officers during the Crimea. I was accustomed to play at church. But now I did not recognize the service. What are these Stiggins, mysterious word, pronounced in an unexpected tone. Suddenly I feel that I have lost all clue to what is happening. And now Edward, pulling a long and hideous face, lets out a nasal howl, quite senseless to me. I cry out in terror, and Lucy draws me aside, exclaims with a look of wonder, 'What's wrong with him now – really, Tommy is the most extraordinary boy.'

She pities me; or rather, she practises her pity on me. And since that, for a child of five or six, is consolation enough, I cling to her. Her rosy lovely face leans towards me, and I think she is going to kiss me and comfort me. But suddenly when her lips are within an inch of my cheek, she bursts into cries of laughter, and I see that all her front teeth are missing. Her look has changed in one second from impulsive affection to that of a little demon. She is delighting in Edward's blasphemy, with wicked joy.

My tears of fright change to yells of rage. I seize Lucy by the hair, she claws my face. The boys laugh. And my mother comes in hastily; but already with an anxious and despairing look.

My mother, gentle, witty, unable to hate, was helpless before brutality. I think she was perplexed by all her children except Edward.

'What is it?' she says to me. 'What has happened? Don't shout so much, Tommy – I can't understand what you say.'

How can I explain what Lucy has done since I have not the faintest notion of it myself. I do not know even what has happened to me, or why I am suffering from this agony of shock and rage.

'She laugh-ed,' I shrieked. 'She laugh-ed at me.'

'Did you laugh at Tommy, Lucy?' my mother asks, patiently.

'I never did,' Lucy shrieks. 'He did it for nothing. The liar, the beast. I'll kill him.'

'How can you say such things, Lucy. Let go of him at once.'

'I won't. I hate you.'

Nurse appears, a country woman, low built and broad. She tears us apart with her powerful arms and says, 'That's enough – I've had enough, thank you. The third time today, mam, and I couldn't say which was the worst. I was going to speak to the colonel as it was.'

My mother protests. 'Oh, I don't think you need do that, nurse. They're going to be good now.'

My mother could not bear us to be whipped. Especially she was made miserable by the very idea of Lucy being whipped. In her own east country family of scholars and Quakers, the idea of beating any child, but especially a girl, would have seemed an outrage. Yet at one time she had forced herself to be present when Lucy was beaten, out of loyalty to her husband.

She gave up that duty, only after Lucy herself, just about to be whipped, had screamed at her, 'Go away, go away. What are you looking at? I hate you.'

After that, my mother had thought it better to stay away from our punishments. She intervened only to prevent them, when she could.

And even for that she had no gratitude from Lucy, who would say, 'Mama leaves it all to Papa. But of course she's only a Bowyer,' meaning that she didn't belong to the family. And even I could see that my father, by his abrupt decisions, at once dissolved our deadlocks; while our mother with all her scrupulous anxiety to understand our troubles, was at a loss among the violence and confusion of nursery affairs.

But though she saved us perhaps from two-thirds of our just punishments, she could not abolish whipping altogether. Nurse and my father, and the fear of hell in combination, were too strong for her. So now she was driven from the field into her room, where, I daresay, she passed moments much worse than ours, while we were dragged still howling to my father's study. Nurse, gripping us one in each hand, would knock on the door with her elbow.

My father, as I remember him on these occasions, is sitting at his enormous flat desk, before a heap of papers. He looks across them with an expression of resigned duty; the face of an old soldier in an orderly room. All his wrinkles seem to deepen and at the same time his lips compress themselves beneath his big white moustache, causing its drooping ends to move slightly outwards.

'What is it, Nurse?'

Nurse pours out a long story about our crimes, fighting, swearing. We are brought round the desk and my father interrogates us.

'What is all this?' in a patient tone.

We begin together our incomprehensible stories. After five minutes, when everything has become still more obscure, my father says, 'That's three times this week.'

Our father never went into final causes. His idea of religion was that of Confucius, rules of conduct, carefully taught and justly administered. Prayers were at a fixed hour. And it was a crime to be late. All quarrels to be made up, and all repentances spoken, before the last prayer, at the bedside; on penalty of drum-head court martial; that is, an immediate slap on the behind, so conveniently reached at that hour. And three complaints from nurse in one week, meant a whipping.

'Three times – I shall have to whip you.'

'Oh, please Papa,' we both begin to roar. This is almost as much routine as the other. And Lucy shouts, 'I won't be whipped, I won't.'

'It's no good saying that, Lucy,' my father says with mild surprise and impatience. 'You know very well that three times means a whipping. If you don't want to be whipped, you must be a better girl. Give me the stick, Nurse.'

Nurse brings him a short piece of cane which he uses for riding; and folds her arms. She always stayed to see us whipped, and used to apologize to my father, between the blows, 'I'm sorry, really, to put you to so much trouble, sir.' She sympathized with my father's feelings in these trials; she would also exclaim at Lucy's rage, 'Tch-tch – there you are, sir, her temper is a cross to us all.'

Lucy, before a beating, would always scream, 'I won't, I won't, I hate you.' But while she was being beaten, she didn't utter a sound. Indeed, I think she gripped her teeth and held her breath from the first blow, and at the last she would fly out of the room, so that no one, especially not my father, should see her cry.

My father beat according to the merits of the case. Three or four light strokes for quarrelling or fighting; but more severely for lying, stealing or other moral offences.

I used to roar through the punishment, but only my mother pitied me. And I daresay I roared the louder to obtain that pity, and consolation in her sitting-room.

12

That room was forbidden to us by my father, who understood my mother's need of a refuge from her family. It had for this reason a powerful attraction for us. It seemed to me, with its austere neatness, its hangings in white and brown, the most delightful room in the world. It had a quality that I can only describe as blessed.

My mother asked us there only one at a time, making it our refuge. For I have no doubt she could not have allowed herself a privilege; unless she had made it also, a privilege for others. Even Lucy, tempted by sweets and a large book of Crimean battle pictures, would sometimes accept an invitation to spend an hour in its quietness. I went whenever I could contrive it, especially in winter, when I could take the armchair, in brown velvet with brass nails, before the bright grate, in polished brass; with a fender before it, of semi-circular brass walls, like the golden bib worn by certain ancient prophets. In all this brass, the fire sparkled at me, with a wonderful gaiety of intimacy. It was, for the moment, my own fire.

I, with my special book, some volume of engravings only allowed to me in that room, or on Sundays, would feel such intense delight that often I could not read. I would fidget, scratch myself, look about me, suck acid drops. I would think, 'An't I a lucky boy?' or 'I wish it was further off from tea-time.'

I would spring up to stroke my mother's cat, Grey. Grey avoided us children in the house, but in that room, she accepted us as visitors. And we would stroke her in a special manner and even with a special expression, anxious and attentive like that of rustics who finger the curtains of a palace. We felt that she was a special cat, quite different from the kitchen and yard cats, which we chased over walls, scratched with sticks, or stroked with a violence which caused them to give at the hocks, and switch their tails, unable to make up their minds whether they were enjoying a pleasure or a torture.

The presence of Grey, calm and trusting, was another sign of my privilege, and an additional pleasure. I seemed in that room to be existing within my mother's being, an essential quality, indescribable to me then, and not easy to describe now; something that was more grace than happiness, more beauty than joy, more patience than rest, a dignity without pride, a peace both withdrawn and sensitive. But for me, as a child, beauty, grace and distinction. Even young children understand and love distinction of the soul, because it speaks from mind to mind, and gives them confidence in the world.

Yet in that retired and peaceful place, for some reason, I always got into my worst mischief. I spilt the flowers, broke the vases. One Sunday afternoon I managed to set the rug on fire. And I still remember my mother's face when she came in, to see on the carpet a spreading stain of red ink from a bottle which she herself had never seen before. As if by a supernatural power of mischief, I had caused it to fall from the air. It was, in fact, from one of the servants' rooms, and I myself had no idea why, in a fit of the fidgets, I had brought it down, in order to give Garibaldi's heroes, in one of my father's books, real red shirts.

My mother's expression of wonder was mixed with resigned amusement. She translated my own feeling into speech. 'The wonderful ink,' she said, 'how did it get there?' And if it had not been my father's book I had damaged, I should probably have escaped even without a scolding.

I stand in my mother's room now. It is a small room opening out of the big state bedroom on the second floor. It is the only room in the house which remains as it was. I stipulated that it should be left untouched.

I believe my tenants showed it only as a Victorian relic. But to me it is a holy place. In this cold morning light, I look at its faded hangings, its worn carpet, with the sense which only the old can know, of a debt that was never acknowledged and can never be paid, not only to my mother, but to a whole generation. Of a stored richness which can return to the spirit only in the form of the things it touched and loved.

13

But of course small-minded people hate what is rich to the mind. They hate the past, not because it is old, but because it might give them something new, something unexpected, and disturb their complacent littleness.

Jaffery, my agent in Queensport, came to see me today. I had written to him about an alteration in my will. For I felt I ought to make some special provision for Ann. And suddenly he proposed that I should allow him to advance Robert three hundred pounds for improvements to the farm, and repairs in the house.

'Nephew Brown is a real go-getter,' he says to me in his disgusting lingo. 'And a good head, too.'

'Robert has been to you, has he? I haven't heard anything about it.'

'Just met by chance in Queensport. The two young things.' And the old fool nearly winked at me. 'Nice couple they make – and we had a chat. Very striking the way that boy has got round the place in a fortnight.'

Jaffery is older than I am, but he affects the young man, wears a light suit, and probably a body belt. I have even seen him in an open-necked shirt, without a tie, a ridiculous object, like a beadle in fancy dress. He does not understand that an old man belongs to his own age and should not ape the dress and manners of another, where he appears like a foreigner. In foreign places, a visitor who tries to seem like a native, only makes himself despised.

Jaffery has an expression of absurd self-confidence on his old red face, wrinkled like a fried tomato. He speaks to me as to an invalid, gazing with discreet but sharp curiosity, as if asking, 'Is he really as mad as they say? Did he burn his house down? Does he want to marry his cook?'

'Since we are leaving the place, it doesn't seem worth while to spend money on it,' I say to him.

'It'll pay you, pay you,' Jaffery says, with the brisk air of imitation youth. 'All the time. Get it back three times over. A little cleaning up on a place like this is like a coat of paint on an old car – puts up the price at once – yes, and cropping and stocking – nothing looks worse than empty fields full of thistles – people say they're derelict, derelict.'

'My nephew wants to make a lot of changes.'

'No, no, not at all. Put in a new bathroom. Plough up Tenacre perhaps – quite time – take down a few old trees – dangerous. Clear the ditches and drains. Get a few beasts in.'

'I'll think about it.'

'No time to waste if you're going to do anything with the farm next year – ought to be at it now, now.'

I am silent. He gives me a cunning glance and says, 'Shall I tell him to leave the house alone; and not to touch anything near the house. Then you won't see any difference, not a thing.'

Jaffery is the kind of man, who, at seventy, has never known a true attachment, a real loyalty, who would sell his dearest friend for a few pounds.

'I don't suppose,' he says, 'that you have been up to Tenacre for twenty years' – his impudent glance means – 'and you will never see it again.'

'It's a pretty part, near the moor. And always more valuable for its beauty than its crop. Poor land.' But seeing that he is thinking me merely obstinate and obstructive, I add, 'I shouldn't let that stand in the way if we had the money.'

'Then that's all right. The money will be in the bank this week.'

A trick. A plot between Jaffery, Robert and Ann. And I had given myself into the hands of the Philistines by my own dishonesty of mind. Proof again that hypocrisy, even in an old fool, is the worst of folly.

'You have been very smart, Jaffery,' I said, 'but I'm not dead yet, and Robert need not think so,' etc., etc. 'Perhaps after all, I shall decide to get rid of the place. It's always been a curse to me.'

I thought that Jaffery would not like losing the agency. But he only smiled. Whether in cunning or senile imbecility, I could not discern.

But suddenly I remarked to him, 'You know, Jaffery, I often think it would be a good thing if this place were burnt down, like the London house. It would save me from being driven distracted by all you people who keep on pestering me about a lot of damned old chairs and tables and cows, which are, after all, not very important in comparison with a mans immortal soul,' and so on. Very dangerous kind of talk from a man under suspicion of being a little cracked, to a man like Jaffery, who thinks that everyone who does not love money and property above everything in the world is certainly cracked. Highly dangerous, but extremely effective. Jaffery's smile soon faded away. He began to look queer. His cunning eyes lost their assurance, and looked like all such eyes when they encounter something a little unexpected, completely imbecile.

And when I began to shout that I knew all about his plots with Robert and Ann, to put me out of the way and get hold of my property, he was fairly beaten. He jumped up. Ann came quickly in with a look which meant, 'There; he is insane after all, what a bore.' And Jaffery retreated at full speed. But I could tell by the way that he moved his turkey's neck that he was frightened. Which gave me some satisfaction. And it might give me some more, if they lock me up. Who can tell?

14

I frightened Jaffery, but I gave myself a heart attack which kept me in bed two days. I told Ann Tolbrook would kill me, and I was right. I have never had peace or comfort in this house. I have been too fond of it. To love anything or anybody is dangerous; but especially to love things. When Lucy took my books or broke my toys, I tried to kill her. And when Edward mocked at anything I was used to, anything I loved, I hated him. All children hate and fear mockery. For it is aimed at the very soul of love, which is always a serious passion.

Ten years ago I would have told you that my childhood was peaceful and happy. At that time, a very unhappy time in my life, I often took refuge in the idea of my happy childhood. But an old man's memories, like his bones, grow sharp with age and show their true shapes. The peace of the nursery, like all my peace, dissolves like the illusions of my flesh.

Now I see our childhood like the life of little foxes, wild cats, hares, does, in their savage and enchanted world. They are surrounded by marvels and enormous terrors. Their eyes and ears, their secret senses, quiver to impulses unfelt even by the vixen and the doe. They dart into the earth at a stroke of fancy which, to their mother, is beyond even explanation, since she herself has lost the idea of it. They rush at each other with bared teeth; they sulk; they starve themselves; they accept; they embrace the fate of the outcast, all in the same unreflective dream.

> Children forget their wrongs; a happy set
> Were we; or if we weren't, children forget.

I thought this couplet in Edward's first book of epigrams, a typical piece of his cynicism; but now I see its truth. The secret of happiness, of life, is to forget the past, to look forward, to move on. The sooner I can leave Tolbrook, the better, even for an asylum.

15

I open my eyes, but it is still dark. There is silence throughout the house, but it is like a threat. It says to me, 'the plot is made – there is still time to escape.' I could get up now, dress and slip away. I know every back lane for fifteen miles, for I always preferred their quietness to the main roads. I could be at Queensport in time for the seven-ten to Paddington. But where then? My family would simply hunt me down and have me locked up in an asylum.

The only person in the world who can save me is Sara Jimson. I must wait for her, and keep myself sane for her. In less than thirteen months she will be free, and then she will set me free. Married to Sara, I can snap my fingers at the family, because she will testify for me.

No doubt they will fight. They hate and fear Sara. And nothing I could do or say would make them understand how much I owe her. All of them, including, I suppose, Ann, accept the vulgar story that I was a wicked old bachelor who lived with his cook-housekeeper. They see Sara as a fat red-faced cook of forty-six. And they believe that this cook, a cunning and insinuating country woman, who had deceived two men before, swindled me and robbed me, and so enslaved me, by her sensual arts and smooth tongue, that I promised to marry her. They flatter themselves that by employing a detective, they stopped Sara's wicked plot, found her out in her robberies, and sent her to prison for eighteen months. This is what they believe, and the facts are true; yet they believe a lie. The truth is, that when Sara came to me, I was a lost soul. I had become so overborne by petty worries, small anxieties, that I was like a man lost in a cave of bats. I wandered in despair among senseless noises and foulness, not knowing where I was or how I had got there. I loathed myself and all my actions; life itself. My faith was as dead as my heart; what is faith but the belief that in life there is something worth doing, and the feeling of it.

And it is true that I lived with Sara more than ten years; and that Sara welcomed the arrangement; perhaps encouraged me to make it.

But what is forgotten is that Sara was a living woman, with a certain character, she saved my soul alive. What I had heard of her, when Jaffery hired her, was this, 'A widow who has been living with a painter, and when he deserted her tried to pass off bad cheques. A very doubtful character, but clean, good-tempered, and a good cook. She'll take a small wage and you can always lock up your cheque book.'

And I admit that when I first saw Sara at Tolbrook, I felt some curiosity and a certain attraction. Every fallen woman attracts men. And Sara, at forty-six, was still a handsome woman, fresh, buxom, with fine eyes and beautiful teeth. Her broad nose, that mark of the sensual temperament, did not displease me. I was not then fifty, and my blood still had its fevers. I thought of Sara, 'A nice armful, and no doubt ready for anything'. Then when I saw her excellent old-fashioned manners, I thought, 'And she would know how to keep her place. I could have her without upsetting the household,' etc.

I will admit, that in that time of my darkness, Sara, at first sight, made my fingers, etc., tingle to pinch her, and so on. But I did not do so, in case, after all, Sara should misunderstand me and give notice, and leave me once more without a housekeeper, when I was almost driven mad with domestic responsibilities.

So I had time to notice how well Sara looked after both my houses, how she cleaned and polished them, and how she cherished them and loved them. Yes, she loved them. I remember still how, within a week of my coming to Tolbrook, she showed me a table in the saloon, which had been scratched by some careless maid with a gritty duster.

'It ought to be seen to, sir. It's such a lovely polish,' and she passed her hand over its surface in a caress.

'Yes, yes, Mrs Jimson,' I said, 'that's a very fine table – a very remarkable table. It's been in this room more than a century, since it was made for this very room,' and I saw again, I rejoiced in the beauty and distinction of the old table. Sara had renewed to me that joy which is the life of faith. And so in those days, while she cleaned the house and set it to rights, after many years of lazy and careless maids, I came again to feel its value, to enjoy its grace.

No doubt any connoisseur, any collector, some bored old millionaire when he shows off his treasures, is seeking in your praise, the resurrection and the life. But he could not get the kind of appreciation which Sara gave, out of her generous and lavish heart, to my old things at Tolbrook and Craven Gardens. She delighted in caring for them, as if they had been her own.

We say of such a one as Sara, 'a good servant', and think no more of it. But how strange and mysterious is that power, in one owning nothing of her own, to cherish the things belonging to another.

16

This week, next year, when Sara comes out of gaol, shall see my salvation. As I wrote to her last night, 'With you I can make a new life, and unless life be made, it is no life. For we are the children of creation, and we cannot escape our fate, which is to live in creating and re-creating. We must renew ourselves or die; we must work even at our joys or they will become burdens; we must make new worlds about us for the old does not last,' etc.

'Those who cling to this world, must be dragged backwards into the womb which is also a grave.

'We are the pilgrims who must sleep every night beneath a new sky, for either we go forward to the new camp, or the whirling earth carries us backwards to one behind. There is no choice but to move, forwards or backwards. Forward to the clean hut, or backward to the old camp, fouled every day by the passers,' etc.

Or did I write this? It is always difficult for me to remember whether I have actually written to Sara; or only composed a letter in my head. This letter has a quality, which in old days I would not have approved. I would not have cared to write in so romantic and poetical a vein; it would have seemed to me dangerously open to misconception, and perhaps a little inclined to encourage rebellious and destructive ideas.

But Sara has that quality that I can say what I like to her. Possibly she does not always listen or understand; but neither will she think evil.

17

I am now quite used to hearing Robert and Ann muttering together behind the door, at two in the morning, and I say, 'What matter – I'm off.' As for the house, my poor Tolbrook, it is infected with lies and deceit from top to bottom. The cousins are in a state of infatuation, to use a polite word for that excitement. And their every emotion is simply a new lie. Ann, who hates dirt and dirty work with her whole soul, goes with Robert to clean out the byres; and all her gestures, her way of pushing a squeegee, as if she wanted to make a hole in the floor, are imitated from Robert. Even her face is like Robert's, when she thrusts up her jaw and says, 'It's not good enough.' And in the evening Robert listens to Beethoven on Ann's gramophone with a rapt expression, and says, 'Very nice – I like that – it's quite a tune.'

'It's funny,' I say to him, 'that you've become so musical. You used not to know "Home Sweet Home" from "God Save the King". And your mother was the same.'

Then he looks at me and Ann looks at me as if I had said something quite beside the point, and Robert says, 'Well, uncle, I like this man Beethoven.'

'Music often comes out in people quite late in life,' Ann says, with a solemn face. And the same night they go to bed together. That, of course, *is* the point.

18

It is extremely dangerous for anyone to get the feeling that somebody is plotting against him, even when the plot is quite obvious; and the plotters conspire in the next room. It is a feeling that drives men mad. It leads to hallucinations. And I have always been subject to anxiety.

To Edward, Bill, and Lucy my anxiety was a joke. They laughed at my caution, at my hiding my pennies under the chest of drawers, and down the crack in this very floor, in the bell trap, where for years afterwards, and even now, I like to keep a little change in silver. They would tell how I never entered a strange house without peeping through the doors, and hesitating on the threshold. They forget how often my pennies had been borrowed by Lucy, who, like many people with small value for money, never remembered her debts; and that the tins full of peas, etc., placed by Bill on tops of doors to fall on Edward or Lucy, usually fell on me. Bill's shout of laughter which always burst out too soon, a fraction of a second before his practical jokes took effect, warned the quick Edward and Lucy, but never me.

When I awoke last night, at half past four, and found myself alone at Tolbrook, I felt that I should have to get up and knock my head against the wall.

The wind was blowing gusts so hard that the dead leaves were carried through the top of my open window and slid down the inside of the blind with a noise like a cat's claws. After each gust, doors rattled and windows murmured. And I distinctly heard Ann's voice say something about the time. 'Perhaps,' I thought, 'she is talking to herself; and in any case, I'm not going to expose myself to ridicule by any further interference with these children. They have their own ideas about things.'

But a moment later, to my own surprise, I found myself in the passage, at the door of the nurse's room. I opened it quietly and turned on the light. There were two heads on the pillows of the narrow bed, and before I had time to turn off the light and withdraw, I saw Ann start up.

I felt a great relief. 'That settles it,' I thought, as I went back to bed. 'Now I need not bother my head about the girl. I shall get some peace at last.'

But when Ann, at eight, came in to take my pulse, etc., I could not even look at her.

She undid my jacket buttons, put the thermometer under my arm, and said in a tone of amusement, 'I told Robert he was making too much noise.'

I could not answer her. I thought, 'Whether I am an old fool or not, this house has changed. It is not for me any longer. I shall gladly leave it.'

'I'm afraid you are rather shocked at me,' Ann said then in a tone like a little girl who has been stealing the jam. But she was laughing at me.

But I was determined not to be angry with her. I said, 'I suppose it is a modern custom. Do you go to bed with any man who offers?'

'No, uncle, truly, it is the first time.'

'The first – don't you think it's a pity – and that perhaps some of these old conventions about chastity and so on were designed for the happiness and protection of women.'

Stooping for the thermometer, she murmured something about science, which did really shock me. 'And what will your mechanical devices do for you if Robert walks off and leaves you?'

'We've discussed that,' Ann said. 'We're not going to be too tragic.'

'How do you know what you're going to be.' And as the girl, full of that elation which she can't hide, went out of the room, humming to herself, I thought with pity and astonishment, 'She doesn't even know she's a woman – that's something these chromium-plated schools don't put into their test-tubes.'

19

Now that I cannot bear the sight of Ann, she is beginning to run after me. She kisses me good morning and shakes up my pillows. She takes me for walks and tries to amuse what she thinks are my prejudices. She has brought up the old nursery chair from the back passage to the day nursery, and cleared out the beds, saying, 'We'll make it as it used to be, and have it for our own sitting-room.' But all this affection does not deceive me. It is one more symptom of her infatuation.

> She's true; for proof today she cuts me dead,
> And headlong throws herself at papa's head.

And when she tries to make me talk about her father and Lucy and all those relations whom she has forgotten for twenty years, and disgraced, I keep silence, unless she drives me out of all patience.

'After all,' she will say in a humble and apologetic tone, 'Daddy was not so strict.' And when I do not answer, she hints, 'And you told me yourself that Sara Jimson was as good as a wife to you. Of course, I'm not blaming you, uncle – quite the other way.'

'Then you ought to – I did wrong – a terrible sin. It is fearful to think of my responsibility.'

'But, uncle, you shouldn't let that get on your mind. You were so strictly brought up. And that always produces a reaction.'

I do not answer this folly.

'Is it true, uncle, that grandfather used to beat Aunt Lucy for not being able to repeat the sermon?'

Now of all things I find most unbearable is the injustice of one generation to another. Say that it is inevitable. Say that children cannot know what they are talking about until they have lived their lives. Meanness is still atrocious. At Ann's words, I felt such a pang in my breast as if I might die, and I shouted at her, 'You have no right to say such things even if you believe them. My father was the noblest and kindest of men, and your Aunt Lucy worshipped him.'

'But, uncle, I didn't mean –'

'And what is this fearful rubbish about natural reactions – heaven knows life is bad enough without having such imbecilities rammed down my ears.'

'Uncle, uncle, you mustn't be so excited.' The girl was alarmed. She bent over me, holding my hand. 'Please, yes, I understand exactly.'

'You understand nothing – nothing at all, and I don't think you ever will. Unless Robert gives you a baby and I hope he does. That will teach you a lesson,' etc., etc. I was rude and quite ashamed of myself. But I could not stop because the girl was so upset. Upset people always make me upset. It's catching, especially between the sexes. 'And as for our childhood, what does it matter whether we were smacked or not. So long as we knew we deserved it, and nobody thought we were martyrs or heroes or any more of your text-book rubbish. Our childhood was good for us, whatever it would have been for you ninnies in your fog of flummery, it was perfect for us – I could not wish anything better for any child. We knew where we were and what we had to do, and what was right and wrong – all the things you silly geese have muddled up till you don't know your etc. from an etc.' A very coarse comparison, such as never before, except when I was in the army, had I used to a woman, much less a niece, however disreputable. It shocked me so much that I was left speechless. Ann ran off and I thought that she was disgusted with me. But she returned at once with some medicine which she made me drink. And then sent for Robert, and had me conveyed back to bed. They appeared to be deeply concerned for me. But that is a bad sign. Young people in the first rage of animal passion are always very humane; at least, in each other's presence. All the beggars in town know that, and thrust out their hats before every bride and bridegroom, into every hansom turning out of Leicester Square.

20

It is no good talking to children like Ann because they have no education; only information. They are like waste-paper baskets full of exploded newspapers and fraudulent handbills. They don't mind going to bed with each other, or talking nonsense, or making a pigsty of the world. But they are shocked that a bad child should be punished with the rod.

It would be useless to tell Ann that I and Lucy, whom she pities for our hard upbringing, probably had greater happiness in our childhood than she and Robert, in the same nursery, twenty years afterwards.

They cannot understand the virtue of law, of discipline, which is to give that only peace which man can enjoy in this turmoil of a world; peace in his own soul.

The first time I was beaten by my father, I was surprised immediately after the punishment, and when I had barely dried my tears, to meet him in the passage and hear him say, 'Run along and fetch my hat, Tommy, there's a good boy.'

I was startled by this easy greeting after what had seemed to me a tragic and even awful episode. There was, I suppose, something of my mother in my constitution. I was even offended, and I did not run for the hat; I walked. But on the way, hearing my father call, 'Can't you find it?' I broke into a run, and bringing the hat, I shouted all the way in my natural voice, 'I've got it, papa – I've got it.'

'Thank you, my dear,' he said in his usual placid tone. 'Tell your mother I'll be a little late for luncheon.' And he went out to get on his cob and ride off somewhere across the fields. He left me in so easy a mood, that when I discovered that my bruises were still burning, and I tried to recall some appropriate bitterness, I could not do so. I found myself a little boy with several new and useless weals on his behind. I made no profit at all out of my sufferings.

Certainly my father's battles with Lucy were often terrible to them both. For though my father by sticking to the regulations erected between himself and conscience a wall of irresponsibility, yet he loved Lucy, and hated to punish her, and feared the consequences. My father and Lucy were devoted to each other. My father would boast that Lucy could climb and ride and shoot better than any of us. He delighted in her beauty and cleverness. And to Lucy he was the bravest and noblest man in the world. She loved to talk about his Crimean battles, and all the history she ever learnt was army history, and especially the Crimean campaign. And in the village she visibly delighted in saying to the villagers who complained of any misfortune, 'I'll tell the Colonel about it.' As if her father could have brought back a bad daughter from London, or cured a stroke. But to Lucy an opportunity of saying 'the Colonel' and enjoying in that word, her father's glory, was not to be missed.

Yet her rage against him when she had to be beaten was fearful to see. And under his code she had often to be beaten. She was a demon of mischief.

I'll never forget the day when she challenged him, with all the cunning of her malice, her devil, to a final battle of wills. Counting, as she always did, in all her battles, upon the very virtues of the enemy, to help her to destroy him and triumph over him. She said in effect, 'You can kill me, if you dare; or own that you don't dare, and submit to me.'

She was twelve, but already a woman in all the essentials of her craft and strategy. Lucy had not then gone to school. She had governesses, with whom she battled day and night. At this time the governess was a certain Miss C., a fair, pretty mild creature, who was some distant relation of my mother's family. She was musical and clever, and, I think, rather High Church.

Lucy despised her and made her life a misery. Miss C. would weep and complain to my father who would then punish Lucy, not very severely, I think, until Lucy performed, on the same day, two crimes which deserved the severest punishment. The first was an act combining blasphemy with indecency. One of little Miss C.'s holy pictures was found in the chamber pot. So Lucy had expressed her contempt of high church religion and Miss C., in one act, probably the impulse of a moment.

But the two offences together formed, in my father's code, a very serious crime.

My father, as I say, loved Lucy with pride as well as joy, that love which is the noblest, as well as the most demanding form of the passion. He wanted for her every virtue of body and spirit. His code for women was high; not higher than for men, but different. He looked in women, above all, for that peculiar grace which inspired all my mother's acts and moods; a grace of spirit as well as body; a charity of soul which affected even her carriage and her voice. Edward used to laugh at our mother for the way in which she would caress a handsome piece of china, a cup or a plate, with one finger, while she sat at table. But the gesture was a true expression of her character, full of a sympathy which belonged even to her senses, and extended to all things.

My father, unlike his daughter, could appreciate my mother's quality as well as Lucy's. His mind may have had an inflexible character, but his sympathies were pliant and comprehensive. He understood and valued my mother's peculiar sensibility and her gentleness of spirit, as well as Lucy's courage and passion. But coarseness and brutality in a woman was to him a sin against Nature, as well as his code. He thought of women as the guardians of a special virtue given them by God. If he had passed over Lucy's crime without the most determined punishment, he would have felt guilty before God, and even perhaps before some power more universal to his feeling; Nature. Lucy's crime was unnatural in a woman, and he beat her severely.

On the same evening Lucy did not appear at prayers, and a maid was sent to fetch her. It must have been on a Sunday when some of us had not gone to church, perhaps because my mother did not feel able to walk the two miles for a second time. For it was only on a Sunday at home that we had prayers before supper, and I remember that the sun was shining across the floor while we waited for Lucy.

I remember still my feeling of suspense at Lucy's absence from the chair beside me. I had already a warning, in my nerves, of the conflict.

Lucy returned a message that she wasn't coming to prayers; she would never again attend prayers or go to church. Miss C. went up to reason with her, and Lucy gave her reason, that she hated God, who was nothing but an old Jew.

My father then sent an ultimatum to which Lucy answered that she hoped she would go to hell. The devil was a devil, but at least he was better than God. And she did not care for anybody or for anything they said to her.

This, of course, was a direct challenge to my father and all of us understood very well that he would not care to beat her twice in the same day. That such a beating might have serious consequences for Lucy and therefore for him and for all of us. And that Lucy was counting precisely on that point to defeat him.

At that age, I could not describe Lucy's mind, or the complicated politics of our nursery, but I knew them both very well. I can't say whether I was more horrified by the crisis which Lucy had deliberately provoked, or interested, from a professional point of view, by her moves in the game. My father meanwhile continued with prayers; but I thought he was slower than usual to find them, and my mother remained on her knees for some time after the last amen. Possibly she was praying for Lucy and her husband; and also, I think, she was trying to appeal to him, by this indirect method. But he probably did not notice this manoeuvre. He had no subtlety. He was putting away his books, again, I thought, with unusual deliberation. His eyebrows, already white, were arched, so that his blue eyes seemed more prominent than usual at the bottom of their round hollows. This gave him an expression of surprise, mild alarm and resignation, as if he had just discovered a large plum stone half-way down his gullet.

He seemed to stoop a little as he went out, as if to push his way through some opposing obstacle. A minute later we heard him going upstairs to his study on the second floor. Then Lucy's voice suddenly screamed out, 'I won't, I won't,' and the door closed.

I ran out of the house – why, I did not know. I felt oppressed, and I was panting as if I wanted to cry. I flew from the house as if it might fall on me. But a moment later I was standing at the bottom of the nursery backstairs, straining my ears for the sounds of the beating, or a cry. I must have been eleven years old, but I was still attached to Lucy in the manner of a small child, almost as if I had been part of her. I could not separate myself from her; I wanted to know what was happening to her, as if it were to myself. And my sensation, while I stood, hardly breathing, was not of sympathy, but only tension and fear, as if I myself were to be beaten.

My teeth clenched together, my lips opened. Suddenly without warning, Lucy came rushing round the corner of the stairs, her hair flying, her face, usually rosy, as white as a candle, her eyes wide open and staring in front of her like a lunatic, her lips parted as if to scream and yet uttering no sound. She came at such a speed I wondered she did not fall, and what especially frightened me was the movement of her hands. They were tearing at her clothes as if to pull them off, and yet she seemed unconscious of that rapid frantic plucking. She darted straight out from the passage door, called the children's door, at the bottom of the stairs. Some inspiration or mere attractive impulse made me run after her, and I saw her rushing across the rose garden towards a coppice where we often played and where, too, we sailed our boats in a shallow branch of the lake, a muddy pond. As I came through to the coppice, I heard Lucy cry out, a high screech, such as I could not have believed could come from any child's throat, and I ran faster, now terrified, breaking through the scrub. I saw her close to me, and she was now tearing her clothes, not tearing them off her, but tearing them away from her body. She was already half-naked, and I could see the blue and red marks of the stick on her thighs. I shouted after her, 'Lucy, Lucy,' and she stopped for a moment and half turned, still tearing. I caught her arm and said, 'Did it hurt badly, darling.' But she screamed, 'No, he couldn't hurt me – never, never – he couldn't if he tried.' Then suddenly she rushed into the pond and disappeared.

Neither she nor I could swim. Only my brother Bill of our family ever learnt to swim, and that was at Woolwich for his army training. My father could not swim, and never went near the sea if he could help it. Our holidays were spent at home, or, for a treat, on visits to some big town, for the theatres and museums.

Luckily, when I screamed, a gardener was near, and he came running. He was in his Sunday clothes, a dark blue suit and a bowler hat; I suppose he had been strolling in the garden, as gardeners do on Sundays, to admire his own work. He stood for a moment on the edge of the water, glanced down at his clothes, as if asking himself what would happen to his best suit, then handed me his bowler, turned up his coat collar and waded into the muddy water up to his neck. Apparently he couldn't swim any more than I. But he ducked down his head, where I pointed, felt about till he found Lucy, and carried her out. She was not even unconscious, and as soon as she had choked up the muddy water from her mouth, she began to kick and struggle, saying, 'He can't hurt me – never – never.'

The gardener puzzled, I suppose, by this violence in a girl who had always appeared so sensible and dignified, set her down with a respectful gesture. She ran at once back into the pond, but the man caught her before she was beyond her knees.

The fact that Lucy had been beaten twice in the same day, became a family joke, which Lucy herself repeated with pride. This humorous memory was all I had kept, and in its light I had recollected the event. But now my heart contracts with pain, as it did when, as a child, I stood and watched Lucy struggling in the hands of the puzzled young gardener, and heard her scream, 'I will – I will.' That is, she would kill herself.

I stood helpless and accepting my fate. I had even then, I suppose, a lack of resource. I couldn't imagine any way of preventing Lucy from doing what she liked. I felt as if suspended in air; but in some unfamiliar empty space, empty of Lucy.

Now Edward and Bill came strolling towards us. They had been to evening church. The evening sun was slanting from the side under the branches of the trees and penetrated even the gothic arches of the hedge timber.

Edward and Bill both wore bowlers, but Bill, as usual, looked as if his clothes belonged to someone else. He grew more square and bulky every year. Edward, on the other hand, was slim and smart; even at sixteen he was already dandified.

'Hullo, hullo,' Bill shouted, staring at us with round eyes, 'what's up, I say – has Lu been getting it again – poor old Lu.' He approached with a sympathetic expression, but stopped suddenly when Lucy shrieked at him, 'Go away, you fool, or I'll kill you.'

'Well,' said Bill indignantly, 'what have *I* done – that's stupid. All right then, I *will* go away.' He was aggrieved. Bill was an affectionate friendly soul. He had all Edward's good temper and my strong affections. But he was easily hurt in his feelings. He walked backwards, rounding his eyes and saying, 'All right, all right then – if I'm not wanted.'

Edward meanwhile asked the gardener who was still, with some difficulty, holding Lucy by one arm, what had happened, and heard my hasty explanation. Lucy muttered savagely, 'And you're worse, you conceited beast – go away – what's it got to do with you. Shut up.' With another scream, 'Shut up.'

Edward, having gathered all the facts available, smiled down at Lucy with a condescending air, and said, 'You do look a comic cut.'

To my surprise Lucy stopped screaming and answered, 'I don't care what you say or papa does.'

'A very good thing,' Edward said. 'It's quite time you stopped making eyes at papa – you're getting too old.'

Then he strolled away, and to our surprise Lucy ran after him, and a moment later we saw them talking together. Edward was trying to wave Lucy away from his new suit while, dripping with mud and slime, she threatened to take his arm. He walked backwards fanning her off with his stick. At last she ran into the house, and in her way of running we could see that she was in good normal spirits.

In fact, she never showed the smallest ill-effects of this nervous crisis, and almost at once began to turn it into a joke and a kind of glory, both for herself and my father. 'When papa beat me twice in the same day.'

But none of us was encouraged to self-pity, the disease of the egotist. Religion was not our comforter. How could we be comforted by hell fire; and individual responsibility for sin? We lived in the law, that ark of freedom. A ship well founded, well braced to carry us over the most frightful rocks, and quicksands. And on those nursery decks we knew where we were, we were as careless and lively as all sailors under discipline.

21

In the morning, I lie half asleep, and the pillow frill tickles my neck. Lucy returns to me, no longer a savage with gap teeth, wriggling with mocking laughter or shrieking in rage; she is a warm presence. We are lying in the dark, in this old iron bed where I lie now, and she is saying, 'They said I mustn't see you, so I just came. How are you feeling, darling?'

I have been ill with measles or chicken pox, and isolated from the rest.

'Haven't you been awfully lonely?' Lucy asks, and I answer sleepily, 'No, but I wish I had a book. I'm not allowed to read.'

'I'll bring you a book this minute – which would you like.'

She brings a book and lights a candle to read to me. I do not remember what she reads, but only the sight of her sitting up beside me in bed, in a flannel nightdress, with her dark hair falling in two tails down her shoulders. She is absorbed in her task which she finds hard. She has to spell out all the long words. Lucy could not read so well as myself.

But now I was stirred by a feeling that I cannot describe. I lie beside Lucy with my arm round her waist and not listening to the book, but watching her and saying within myself, 'This is Lucy – isn't she nice. Isn't she being awfully kind to me. I love her awfully – I can't say how I love her.'

But suddenly my love seemed to expand and burst into a fit of laughter. I began to squeeze Lucy and punch my head into her chest, and all the time I am laughing. The shy serious little boy, making his anxious and careful way through a world full of older brothers and sisters all capable at any moment of the most unpredictable fits of violence or mockery, gives place, like a magic-lantern slide, to a stranger. I see the serious face split by an enormous demoniac grin; the tufted hair speaks no longer of disability and ugliness, but of an unruly coarseness. I am full of violence and rebellion. I don't care for anybody; and when Lucy says indignantly, 'Am I reading to you, or an't I?' I answer with another senseless laugh and another butt.

This is the very phrase and manner of our old nurse who used to protest, 'Am I dressing you, or an't I?'

Lucy is acting nurse, and because of my exuberance I am not afraid to tell her so. 'You think you're like nurse. But you're not a bit. Nurse reads like this.' I try to take the book from her, and amidst bursts of senseless laughter, cackle like a hen.

Lucy, astonished by my behaviour, lets go of the book, gazes at me, and says at last in a dreamy wondering voice, 'The boy really is quite ma-ad.'

Suddenly she throws back the bedclothes and tries to jump out of bed. Nurse's step is heard in the corridor. But I still hold on to her, laughing; and when she tries to drag herself away, I grab at her nightdress.

'Let go, you id-i-ot,' she whispers, spitting out the syllables like a furious cat. Her anger pleases me in my lawless mood, and gives me even now a shock of pleasure as if once more I come close to Lucy. She jerks at my grip.

Nurse's voice says outside, 'All right, Miss Lucy – I hear you – your papa shall know about this.'

I know that I shall not be whipped while I am ill, so I do not care. I am still grinning, full of delight, of the mysterious senseless glory which issues in my laughter and violence. I take a firmer hold, and Lucy, beside herself, beats at my face, with the book. Suddenly the flannel gives way and leaves a huge rag in my hand. Lucy, half-naked, flies to the door just as it is opened by nurse; she is carried off at once to be smacked, and I am severely lectured. But I am still full of that glory. I don't care for anybody or anything.

22

The very idea of Lucy goes to my head. 'There aren't such people nowadays,' I think. 'And what if she had a devil. She did God's work. Out of devilry. She made something good and noble of her life. As I might have done if I had not been turned into a family drudge. If I had been allowed to go upon the Lord's work.'

'And what,' I ask, 'are you doing now, you old fool, what would Lucy think of your worries' – and such is Lucy's power that twelve years after her death she can raise me up out of the darkness. For the last two days I have been a new man. I laugh at the children. 'For heaven's sake,' I say to Ann, 'what's wrong with you this morning, you look as if you had taken a horse pill. But I suppose Robert has been showing a little independence. I'm not surprised if you go about with that face.'

For I notice that Robert, as one might have expected, has suddenly grown tired of classical music. He sucks his pipe in the evenings and reads the paper. Also all day the cousins are disputing. That is, their good nature has deserted them, and they have reverted to their own natures, which are highly different. But I must not say 'I told you so'.

Robert came in yesterday morning, picked up Ann's book from the arm of her chair, and said, 'What's this you're reading?' And she answered, 'Something you wouldn't care for – it's quite good.'

'You mean it's muck.'

And then they quarrelled for the whole of lunch-time about books. For Robert, as one might expect in Lucy's son, had always a great disgust for what he called modern muck.

And Ann, in her quiet voice, which she never raised even in anger, answered that Robert, no doubt, wanted a censorship to suppress everything modern or civilized.

'I'm just a rube, I only know what stinks,' Robert said. 'I wouldn't know about this civilization.'

'How could you if you're intolerant, and you like being intolerant. Civilization is tolerance – and that's why I hate all this censorship.'

'You're telling me.'

'Oh, no, Robert, no one could tell you anything.'

'They could tell me muck wasn't muck, but my nose would still be a born fool.'

'Not only your nose.'

The cousins speak so mildly to each other that it is hard to tell when they are disputing. But I could see now that Ann was trying to hurt Robert, and that he was annoying her by his indifference. As Lucy used to enrage me.

'Don't you mind what Robert says to you,' I told her. 'Laugh at him.'

But the girl looked as if she were going to cry, an expression which enraged me in one so young. 'It's your own fault,' I said, 'if Robert has the power to make you unhappy. Robert is like your Aunt Lucy. He will be cruel if you don't stand up to him. Lucy hated weakness in anybody or anything. She was so strong herself.'

'Yes, that's what I hate in Robert.'

'Then you are very foolish. Robert has very good qualities – above all, he enjoys life. Like Lucy. And he makes other people enjoy it. Lucy had a hard life, goodness knows, but she never moaned or groaned,' etc.

But the next day it was the same. Robert disappeared to fetch some new engine that he had hired, and Ann walked about the house with a miserable face. 'Good gracious,' I said to her, when we met for our morning walk, 'no wonder Robert runs away from you – it's a sin for a girl of your age to be so wretched, even if it is your own fault.'

The day was cold and the sky broken with cloud. A sharp wind was driving from the sea and whirling the red oak leaves from the drive right over the roofs, so that, looking up, one saw them floating among the white gulls like small agitated birds. It was so strong that Ann had been in two minds whether I was to be allowed a morning walk, even so far as the lodge.

'Robert is like his mother,' I said, 'he can't bear to see people moping and mumping about nothing. Of course, I don't mean to say that what you have done is nothing – leaving out any moral question, it is a piece of disastrous folly. But, relatively speaking, when you consider the state of the world and all the misery and folly going on everywhere, it is nothing much. And as for my walk, if you won't come, I am going by myself, and I don't care if I drop dead. At least I shall die with my boots on, as Lucy did.'

Ann gave way then and put on her coat. But we had not gone ten yards before an enormous traction engine appeared in the drive and rolled towards the yard gate, where it stopped. I could see that it was making big holes in the gravel, but I thought, 'Who cares. Holes can be filled in. I'll tell the garden boy to see to it.' I could not help feeling how Lucy would have enjoyed such an engine. Its size and power made the weather seem exhilarating. And I said to Ann, 'What on earth is Robert doing with that machine?'

'I don't know what Robert is doing – he doesn't tell me.'

'Because you take no interest. Where is all your enthusiasm for farming?'

'I suppose he is going to break down something somewhere – that's what he really enjoys.'

'Robert is a regular son of his mother – he's always full of energy.' And I thought, 'He is worth six of you, you poor thing. He may be obstinate and troublesome, but he knows what he wants from girls to traction engines.'

And going up to the yard gate, I called out, 'Where did you get this new toy? Out of a circus –'

'Oh, yah, uncle,' he shouted down from the cab where he was standing with the driver and stoker, 'that's it – out of the circus at Queensport. It was laid up for the winter.'

I was astonished. For when I looked more attentively, I saw that the traction engine actually was from a circus. I could not help laughing at this surprise. 'A circus engine at Tolbrook.' Now when I stood close to it, I saw how big it was; as big as a cottage. Its wheels, covered with gilding, were eight feet in diameter. Its cab was so high above my head that Robert might have been in the howdah of an elephant. Its funnel was blowing black smoke full of smuts as big as flies into the second storey windows. But I thought, 'Who cares, curtains will wash, and they are only new curtains.'

And as this great engine throbbed and jerked and rumbled with steam, making the ground shake and the windows rattle as if in a bombardment, one felt that majesty of power which had caused the maker and architect of the creature to decorate it in every part with painted gilt work and glittering brass. The great wheels were painted scarlet and green, and the hubcaps, as big as beer barrels, were sunflowers of gilt with silver petals.

The rivets on the fender were golden roses, as big as bath buns, so bright that you could barely look at them. The pillars of the cab were twisted brass, like those of a little temple; and on the top of the funnel there was a brass crown with long spikes, such as befitted the king of the road.

And everywhere one perceived the delight of the maker in his creation, which is, precisely, the joy of the Lord; and I thought, 'How Lucy loved a fair and the roundabouts. How she would have loved to see Robert up there, with his dirty face, so calmly smoking his pipe, in command of the monster.'

'And what's this piece of nonsense,' I shouted. 'What are you going to do with this plaything.'

The engine was making such a noise that I could not hear Robert's answer, but Ann said, 'He's going to pull down some of your trees.'

This alarmed me a little. And I waved my hat and umbrella at Robert to show that I must have an answer.

Then Robert bawled out something and Ann said in my ear, 'He's going to Tenacre – shall I say he mustn't.'

'No, certainly not – I gave my word. Some of those trees at Tenacre must be rotten, and Robert is quite right to want to clear them out,' and so on. And when they started to move the engine, I took off my hat to it and waved my umbrella to show that I thoroughly approved of his plan.

'You ought to encourage Robert,' I said to Ann. 'After all, they're not your trees. It wouldn't cost you anything to show sympathy with the boy – and if you want him to marry you, you can't afford to irritate him in trifles. Obstinate silliness is the one thing that never goes unpunished in this world.'

'But he has married me, uncle, or I've married him.'

I didn't believe her till I found, from Robert himself, that the couple had actually been married at Queensport registry office, nearly a week before.

I could not understand this marriage. Robert had had what he wanted of the girl. He knew she was useless as a wife – why then did he need to marry her. Unless, of course, in pursuit of some other purpose, such as a general plot, with Jaffery, to get control of Tolbrook.

'Why on earth,' I asked him, 'did you marry a girl like Ann, who will be perfectly useless to you?'

'Well, uncle, it was just an idea we thought up. We thought we'd see how it worked.'

'And is Ann going to Brazil with you?'

'Why, uncle, we haven't talked over our plans, and we couldn't go yet awhile – she wouldn't leave her job till she's seen it through. So I've put it off for a bit – till spring, anyhow, and maybe harvest. I'd like to see my job through, too.'

'Seen it through' was the only phrase that carried illumination. It meant, I suppose, that Ann was waiting until I died, and the context seemed to show that I was not expected to last beyond the spring, or, at worst, September.

23

But even if they are waiting till I die, and even if Jaffery has promised them Tolbrook, I cannot understand why a clever girl like Ann should throw herself away on a rough boy like Robert. 'This marriage is a perfect puzzle to me,' I told her. 'Your reasons can't be moral reasons because apparently you have no moral scruples in such a case.'

'I'm surprised, too.'

'Is Robert in love with you?'

'Oh, no, I think he just lost his head.'

She was knitting and reading, at the same time, in a chair by the parlour sofa. Her whole pose and expression, with her spectacles, her middle-aged gravity, were domestic, and afforded a strange contrast with the child's paint and powder; her peculiar attitude of mind.

'You'd better pretend to be in love then, if you want to be happy.'

'Do you think we could be happy, Robert and me?'

'If not, why in heaven's name did you marry?'

'Well, uncle, Aunt Lucy wasn't happy with her butcher, but she fell for him.'

'No, she did not fall for anybody. She would not even have understood that horrible phrase. She made her own life.'

'Then why didn't she make it happy?'

'It was a happy life, though I suppose you can't imagine it – neither could I. But then I was a young fool myself at that time. I didn't know how to be happy.'

'How is it done?'

'You must have an object in life – something big enough to make you forget yourself.'

The girl went on knitting and reading her book under her knitting. She said at last, 'But suppose you can't find one.'

'There are plenty to be found – or there were plenty in my time, if you looked for them.'

'Would you let me have that photograph of Aunt Lucy from downstairs?'

'Lucy's photograph won't do you much good' – and I was going to say that what she wanted was Lucy's spirit of life and joy, and confidence. But I stopped myself. For how was I going to bring to Ann even the idea of that spirit nourished in faith.

24

I let Ann have my own photograph of Lucy, from my mantelpiece. It is better than the one downstairs. And I don't like photographs. They are dangerous. They serve only to hide the real people from me. When I look at Lucy's picture, faded and pale, she disappears behind it. But, if, when I lie in the dark, I only think of the sound of her voice, she stands before me, warm, breathing; and always in some unexpected appearance, so that often I cry out in surprise, saying, 'I had forgotten.'

We are at a picnic on the moor. I cannot remember the year, but we are both grown up, and I see Lucy's green frock and the sky behind her head full of round clouds like new-washed sheep, pink and soft. She turns to me and I notice, as she laughs, that her mouth is slightly crooked. One corner, the left, is longer. I am so interested in this discovery that I don't hear what she is saying.

We are walking in the drive, under autumn trees, when she takes my arm and then suddenly utters a coo-ee to Edward, far off at the house door. I remember a pang of indignation because I feel her woman's malice. She wants to feel my jealousy of Edward.

And on the fatal night when she ran away. It is after dinner, late in the evening. She has come suddenly to the nursery where I am pasting photographs into my album; and her smile makes me think she is up to some mischief. She has played some new trick on a neighbour or one of her lovers. And I catch that smile. It flies to my lips, out of her secret mood, before I know it is there.

She says, 'Tommy, darling, will you do something for me? Go to father's room and get the key of the stable yard.'

'What on earth for? – you don't want the trap at this time of the evening.'

'Never mind. But if he catches you, say I want my bicycle to go to the vicarage.'

'But where are you going, Lucy?'

She looks at me with that expression of an elder sister for a small boy who asks silly questions and quotes our old catchword 'to be a pilgrim'.

'Don't be silly, Lucy. If you don't tell me, I won't go for the key.'

'Oh, please, darling.' She takes me in her arms and pleads, kissing me, with the gestures and tones of a loving compliant girl, asking a favour. But on her lips the smile of the woman who knows her real power, and could command if she chose. In spite of my real terror of having to tell a lie to my father, and perhaps losing his esteem, I go for the key.

In the same way she makes me help her to harness the mare. It is while I am holding up the shafts of the gig, for her to put Jinny in, that she answers my repeated questionings. 'I'm going to be married.'

'Don't be silly, Lucy. Tell me. Is it some joke with the A's?'

'No, it isn't a joke. I'm eloping.'

'Not by yourself?'

'Yes, by myself. He said he would send for me when he wanted me, and I had a message tonight; half an hour ago, to be exact.'

'But that's nonsense – no one can be married at ten o'clock at night.'

'Oh, we shan't be married tonight, not even tomorrow.'

'When is it to be, the happy event?' I said, chaffing her.

'We must wait for the sign, the second sign – and the third sign. At the first sign we are pledged, at the second sign we shall be married.'

'And what will happen at the third?'

'You're asking too many questions, Tommy – hold up the lanterns while I hook the trace.'

'And who is it to be?'

'Brown, my dear, Puggy Brown.' She laughs in my face with a triumphant air of mischief and joy. 'Who else would want three signs before he married *me*?'

'What rubbish.' But I feel a half belief. I catch from her being, not from her words, a tremor of excitement and fear. I know she is at some crisis of her life.

I plead with her not to do anything hasty, to think before she commits herself, and so on. Using all those phrases which must be used on such an occasion because they alone express a plain meaning in plain words. But she smiles as if delighted by her plan, and answers, 'No, I won't think any more. I don't need to think, thank goodness. You see, I've promised.'

'But Lucy, you're not going on that – one of your whims. Who is it – it's not Captain Frank?'

'My dear Tommy, Captain Frank. I would rather run away with a cold mutton chop. Come now, be good and help me with Jinny.'

It should have been a romantic scene and so I have thought it since. But now I know that it was not so. A clear dark sky, no cloud or wind; a warm night. Not a dog barks, and we can hear the maids rattling their everlasting cups in the kitchen. My senses will not rise to tragedy and separation, in this quiet yard, among familiar things. And Lucy herself, standing so close that, by the light of the match with which I am about to light the gig lamps, her old tweed driving cape, with crossed bands over her breast, her smile, her look, the feather of her breath on the night air makes elopement seem like family routine. She climbs into the gig with her usual agility, which, like an acrobat's, seems always to delight in itself; and calls to me, 'Good night, Tommy. Don't look so stupid. And you'll find the gig at the Crown at Queensport. And if they ask you where I am, say that I'm off to sing for Jesus.'

'But Lucy, for God's sake, be serious. This is some of your nonsense.'

'Yes, it's some of my nonsense.'

For of course I was quite right. Even Lucy knew it was some of her nonsense. To amuse herself or to shock us, or both at once.

'Then tell me the joke. I'll not say a word.'

'I told you the joke, Tommy. Puggy Brown has called me, and I'm going to him.'

'Just for fun – that's impossible.'

'Not a bit. It's quite easy. Just look,' laughing down at me as she drove off. And I never saw that Lucy again, the pretty lively young woman with the indescribable charm of her innocence. I had not appreciated her; and I did not understand her nonsense. For Lucy's nonsense was her own nonsense, and therefore it had courage and faith. It was set off by a devil's whim, but it flew straight forward, it broke a way through walls. And now I think, 'How did Lucy know at twenty-one, even in her whims, what I don't know till now from all my books, that the way to a satisfying life, a good life, is through an act of faith and courage.'

But then, where was my faith? I was a child and my faith was a child's; it was my world and not my possession. And when my world shook in some earthquake, I, too, trembled.

I got up to steal down into Lucy's room, a great state-room on the first floor. It is refurnished, but it still has the iron basket grate before which I sat with her on so many evenings; and the view from the windows; the paddock, the green line of the haha ditch, a corner of the lake, the woods beyond, and above them, the high moor.

She delighted in that view, the best from any room in the house. As her room was the most luxurious. No one appreciated comfort and luxury like Lucy. But she left them in a moment. Why? Not for love; not for charity. Not because her conscience troubled her. Not for the sacrifice. But for the adventure. Lucy was one of those whose faith is like a sword in their hands, to cut out their own destinies. That faith has come to me now. At least, I hope so.

'Who are you talking to, uncle?' I am sitting in Lucy's arm chair looking at Ann in a blue dressing-gown. The room is filled with a blue-grey light, as pale as her eyes. She seems to be only a little more solid than the light. She looks like a ghost these mornings with her grey-green face and transparent eyes. She is certainly ill, and I tell Robert that she ought to eat porridge and cream, and plenty of red meat. But he won't interfere. He does not perceive that, clever as she is, she is a fool in marriage.

'Was it Aunt Lucy? This was her room, wasn't it?' And when I do not answer, she says, 'I suppose she felt it was a religious duty to get married and give up her life for that brute.'

Her voice is like a ghost's voice, talking from another world, fifty years away. I don't speak to her because she cannot understand me or the real solid world, where Lucy and I loved and fought.

She feels my arm and says, 'You are quite frozen. Shall I bring you a rug if you don't like bed.'

I should like to tell the girl that I am sorry to see her so unhappy; but I am afraid that if I encourage her to talk, she will chatter about Lucy and Bill and Edward and drive me mad with her incomprehensions.

25

I did not yet believe that Lucy had run away from us until she was missed, the next morning, and I told my father, as a joke, that she had spoken of joining the Benjamites.

My father turned that dark purple of an old man who has had a shock, and said, 'So that's the end of Lucy.'

He sat down in the nearest chair, and I saw his hands and knees trembling. 'I thought it was that.'

'But you don't think she could really marry Brown?'

'Why not – why not – she won't turn back.'

And instantly I saw that the marriage was possible. I said, 'But she must be stopped – it can't be allowed.'

'Nothing to be done,' my father said. 'He's caught her.'

My mother, who blamed herself for Lucy's flight, as for all our faults, tried to console us. 'We oughtn't to grieve for Lucy. She has been called to a good work, God's work.'

'God's work,' my father would say, flushing more deeply. 'Brown's work isn't God's work. It is devil's work.'

My father made many and nice decisions, not clear to me, between different sects of the Christian Church. To him the Church of England, the Presbyterian and the Wesleyan stood apart as churches of the true God. After that came other branches of the Wesleyans, the Congregationalists, the Scots Free Church, and the Baptists. The Quakers stood in a separate place as innocent eccentrics; the Unitarians as vain and foolish word spinners, harmless only because of their poor grasp of final things. The other free sects, of all kinds, belonging to the devil. They were egotist, anti-Christ, and the worst of them was that of the Benjamites. And he could not console himself, like my mother, whose sensitive nature perhaps needed that defence, by saying that 'God's will was not to be opposed, even by repining'.

His strong courage penetrated to every part of his nature. Even if he had seen God's will in Lucy's flight, he would have suffered, because he had no idea of escape from suffering. His feelings could not deceive themselves or be deceived.

'We'll be lucky if we ever see her again,' he said to me.

I felt now very angry with Lucy for inflicting so much misery on me and on her father; and also, for some other crime, which I can only describe as giving trouble. Like all young men, I detested people who gave me trouble.

'I'll go and find her,' I said. 'I'll go to the police, if necessary.'

It did not prove so hard as I had expected to trace Lucy. The Benjamites in the village promised to find out for me where Brown was, and after ten days' delay, while, I imagine, they were writing to him and getting his leave to give the information, they sent me an address near Birmingham. I set out at once, full of indignation and confidence. 'She'll be sick of them by now,' I said. 'You know Lucy's whims, they don't last long.'

But my father answered only, 'Mind they don't catch you, that's all.'

'Me?' I cried.

'Might catch anybody,' the old man muttered. 'Why not?'

'I thought you were against the Benjamites.'

He shook his head. 'They're very catching – they make it so easy.'

Brown had left Birmingham. But I was directed to his next stopping place.

I had always imagined the Benjamites as passing from village to village, squalid in their lives, but at least among the distinction and fresh beauty of country scenes. I found them now in the back street of a large industrial town; squalid beyond my imagination or experience. I saw this wretched place on a day of late autumn when, at Tolbrook, the eye was enriched, at every glance, by the beauty and majesty of oak, elm and ash in the magnificence of their age. Here the narrow pavements flowed with a mud which seemed thick with a hundred years of foulness, the house fronts ran with a dark ooze, a sky like the arch of a sewer dripped the condensation of filth upon garbage buckets.

I knew London dirt, but I had seen it as the antique crust upon classical dignity or gothic vigour. I had never before known a town in which the dirt clung to meanness even more disgusting than itself, where the larger buildings, with architectural pretensions, grew only more ugly with size, where the middle-size houses had the air of bankrupt brothels, and the back streets, like this one in which I sought Lucy, were like the corridors of a prison, a catacomb. In these fearful gullies, a pale dwarfish people moved, through the slow rain, like prisoners condemned for life. I was a small man, but among them I felt like a giant among cripples.

Here I felt for the first time the presence of that devil of which my brother Edward had spoken in a speech bitterly attacked at that time. 'If the devil is known by his work, then you can find hell all over England. Every great industrial town is a candidate for the honour, and improves its chances of election every year. The accepted plan is to place as many people as possible in the most hideous and wretched surroundings, and give them no food but adulterated rubbish and no pleasure but drink. It is highly successful.'

Edward's speeches had often startled us by their violence, but when I criticized them, he would say, 'The only question is, Tommy, do you want your throat cut neatly by a civilized reformer, or do you want to be hacked to death with rusty knives by maddened savages. I leave out the moral arguments because they are not convincing.'

When Edward spoke so, he gave out a ruling thought of that time and of our class. Then much more than now, people feared revolution; but in secret, often so deep in their soul, that their minds did not know it. For, in that time, the rich men were still boundless in wealth and arrogance; the poor were in misery, and neither saw any possibility of change without the overthrow of society. The Tories said, 'Give the least concession, and they ask for more. Concessions were the fatal weakness which opened the way to the French revolution'; and the Communists, the Socialists answered, 'Nothing from the enemy but their blood.'

I was one of those who supported Edward. 'We have a magnificent opportunity,' I said. And like other young men, I was impatient with the government for not immediately bringing in the new world. I was amazed at their blindness in not seeing the danger of revolution.

But in this midland town, I was conscious for the first time of a deep anxiety; an oppression that became almost unbearable. As I knocked on the door of Lucy's lodging, I felt not only guilt but terror, as of the wrath to come.

It was as if I, personally, had raised this hell and peopled it with savages; and that, in justice, the savages would destroy all that I valued in the world.

26

The door, after long delay, was opened by a short plump girl, with round, pale cheeks. Her eyes, too, were pale.

'Mr Wilcher,' she said to me at once.

'You come from Tolbrook?'

'I lived there for a while.' She spoke in a calm and sad voice, but her eyes gazed at me with a peculiar boldness. This glance was a mark of the Benjamites. It meant, 'You think me low and contemptible, but I know you are beneath contempt, one of the vilest of the vile, a dweller in the sties of the world.' This look usually offended me, as a young man, conceited in his youth. But in these streets, before this house, I felt humble and apologetic.

'Miss Wilcher?' I asked.

'Sister Wilcher. She is here.'

'May I see her?'

'That's for the master to say,' and she shut the door in my face.

I rang again, but the door was not opened for several minutes. Then Brown himself stood before me. He was wearing his usual dress, long black frock coat, tight black trousers, white shirt, but neither collar nor tie. He said, 'What do you want, young man?'

'I've come to see my sister, Mr Brown, if you please.'

'That depends on her. Perhaps she does not want to see you.'

'I think she would like to see me.'

'I will ask her.'

But at the same moment the young plump girl returned and said, 'She says, send him in.'

Brown threw back the door and said, 'Go in, young man, your sister is in the back kitchen.' He paid a peculiar weight on the word 'sister', as if to say, that Lucy was now a sister in another and more religious sense.

I went through another passage into a kitchen smelling of dirt and soap. There in the middle of the floor I saw Lucy scrubbing. A stretch of wet tiles lay between us.

'Stop,' she cried, sitting back on her heels. 'Don't step on my floor.'

She was laughing at my surprise. I had never seen her look more beautiful than in her apron of sacking, with the soapsuds running down her arms.

'When will you be finished, Lucy?'

'Not for a long time. I still have the passage and then all the potatoes for supper.'

'Are you a kitchen maid here?'

'Well, you know the rule.'

'What rule?'

'The Benjamite's rule – work and obedience. And I was never taught to cook or dressmake. So I wash the floors.'

Once more she began to scrub. The curls of her hair, lank with steam, clung to her forehead and cheeks. The veins of her pretty arms were swelled with hot water, and her nails were broken back to the quick. I felt pain and fear as I watched her toiling in that foul air, among mean streets and barbarous people.

'Did you run away from us to scrub floors?'

'Oh, no, Tommy, you know why I ran away –'

'Lucy, you don't really mean to marry that man.'

'That is for God to say.'

'You mean for him, Brown, to say. Do you know what he is with women, what they say about him in the village – he has a new woman every time he comes there.'

'Now Tommy, that's enough. We'll never understand each other on that subject, and I'm too busy to argue.'

But it seemed to me now that I understood very well. The idea of Lucy in the arms of Brown gave me horror, and in that horror, was my understanding. The words came into my mind, 'And she shall be offered for a sacrifice.'

Lucy suddenly began to laugh at me. She got up, put a chair for me and a newspaper under my feet to keep them from the floor.

'You must stay with us, Tommy.'

'What me – be a Benjamite.'

'I should like to see you happy.'

I began to argue very reasonably about the wrongness of the Benjamites, pointing out the danger of a religion which appealed only to the feelings and the nerves. But Lucy continued to scrub; she said, 'When shall I see you properly? I shall be busy till six getting tea, and then there is a meeting, and after that I must get supper, and then wash it up. And at ten I shall be sent to bed.'

'Sent to bed?'

'Oh, yes, Puggy is very particular about bedtime – the night prayer is at a quarter to ten, and we must be in bed by the hour.'

'When am I going to see you?'

'Come to the meeting at eight, and perhaps I shall see you for a little before supper.'

I went to the meeting and found Brown at the corner of the street. He was speaking from a box to a small crowd of silent unhappy-looking people. The Benjamite travelling party, three young men and five women, including Lucy, stood behind the box against a wall of rusty iron. While Brown was speaking they listened, and often exclaimed in their quiet voices, Hallelujah, or Amen. I saw Lucy utter such an ejaculation, and it gave me a sense of horror and disgust. When Brown knelt to pray, they all knelt down in the mud and raised their faces and their hands towards heaven, bowing up and down in the strange manner which he used. When he turned to them for a hymn, they sang without book or accompaniment, in loud but uneven voices.

After the hymn, or one verse of a hymn, Brown would speak again, usually about grace, or the hardness of heart which refuses it.

Grace was thus explained to me by an evangelist, an American, who made a fortune by conducting religious meetings. 'Grace is a feeling inside you that God is there all the time, to help. So all you've got to do is tell these poor sinners that they've got the feeling, and they always believe it. Why, if you told them they'd got a pain, they'd soon find it for you, show you the exact place. So when you tell 'em they've got a feeling, they soon find one. And then you only got to tell 'em what it's saying to them. And they're yours.'

'What do you tell them that it says?'

'That they got to stop worrying about themselves and their troubles and hearken to the voice of the Lord.'

'And do they forget their domestic anxieties and responsibilities so easily?'

'They just do. Why, the most of men are just about half mad with worrying. They're just delighted to hear there's anyone to tell 'em what to do.'

'And what does the Lord, that is, what do you, tell them to do?'

'Young man, I tell 'em to do the Lord's work in love and charity.'

'It is not always easy to know what is the Lord's work.'

'No, young man, it is not. They got to wrastle and pray for it. And they do wrastle –'

'So they're just where they were at the beginning.'

'Not so my young friend, for now they wrastle for the Lord, and so they get grace – that makes a difference, believe me.'

But like a young man I had always an answer to one who would teach me. I quoted Edward to him.

> 'Grace, Lord, I crave. Answer thy servant's question:
> Is this Thy grace I feel, or indigestion?'

Then the American evangelist looked at me and answered, 'I pity you, young man, you are like the ass who was too clever to walk upon the beaten path.'

'What happened to that ass?'

'He stuck among the thorns and no one listened to his bray. For he was a useless ass.'

27

After the meeting I did indeed see Lucy, for five minutes. Another party of the Benjamites had come from a distance, to see the master, and she had to find lodgings for them and prepare a supper.

'But have you no rest?' I asked her.

She answered me laughing, 'No, but I have the joy of the Lord.'

And this phrase had so strong an effect upon me that for a moment I scarcely knew where I stood. I seemed to enter into the meaning of Lucy's life, and to understand her happiness; that it was a real, a lasting joy.

Lucy herself felt some change in me, for she suddenly laid her hand upon my arm and said in a tone more gentle than I had ever heard from her before, 'Stay with me, Tom, and you will find the answer to everything.'

'Is there an answer to everything?' I said. But I think there is no doubt that I should have been converted, if it had not been for an incident on the next day.

Lucy persuaded me to remain that night, in order to be with her.

'If you could stay to Saturday, you would see me and you would see that I am good for something more than dishwashing. I am the forerunner.'

'The forerunner?'

'I go to the next week's camp and find lodgings for the master and his disciples. Everyone agrees that I am much the best at the job. Stay to Saturday, Tom. You can come with me and see the fun.'

I stayed, and on Saturday Lucy took me by train to a little town distant about forty miles. She was smartly dressed and wore gloves. 'I must cover my hands,' she said, 'for they mustn't see that I'm a char. I am a lady today. Rather reduced, but still a lady, who wants a quiet lodging for herself and friends – and you mustn't mention Brown, Tommy, or Benjamites, or say how many friends I have.'

'Why?'

'Landladies don't like us. We have rather a bad name among lodging-house keepers everywhere,' and she began to laugh. 'Wait and you'll see, Tommy – but not a word about Puggy or his crew. My crew.'

We got out at one of those small country towns which is growing fast, but has not yet lost its character. It had still dignity and beauty. Its church spires and towers were still to be seen over all, giving scale to the shops and warehouses, and meaning to the whole design. But already in the back parts were found long streets of brick boxes, in which the workers lived, packed like the products of a factory.

Lucy, having walked up and down in these streets, chose a terrace, six houses in a row, with bay windows and small gardens in front of them. Three of these better houses had letting cards.

'Which shall I choose, Tommy – the one with the brass step, or the one with the new-painted door, or the one with the pink bows on the curtains. The brass steps are a good sign, but new paint is better, I think, especially when only the door has been painted. For that means the tenants have done that work themselves. I votes for new paint.'

She knocked, and we found in the house a very clean buxom woman, full of house-pride, and a little husband, with a pale thin face and a long grey moustache. He was a retired clerk, shy and modest.

The goodness of this couple, the affection between them and their pride and love of home, drew me to them, and I took occasion to say how much I admired the neatness and cleanliness of their rooms.

'Oh, sir, but if you knew what a difference this new factory has made – with all the smoke. I'm afraid you've noticed the curtains in the sitting-room, but they were clean up only last week.'

'They seem spotless to me, Mrs Jones.'

'Oh, sir.' She shook her head, smiling as one would say, 'You're flattering me.' But her round face was blushing, full of pleasure, and afterwards I saw that both she and her husband, when they spoke to Lucy, kept looking at me. Indeed, I felt our common sympathies. For the house-pride of simple people, struggling to make a perfection within their small reach, has always affected me to a deep respect.

I thought, 'These people are now not far from death, and the slums are creeping up to them on every side, but the drawing-room curtains must still be spotless, the front door shining in new paint.'

'It's a great shame,' I said to the husband, 'that factories are allowed in a town like this.'

'Well, sir, they do bring a lot of smoke and noise, too. But we needed the employment. We mustn't complain.'

'You could complain of the smoke. I hope you have complained.'

The man looked at me and smiled as if to say, 'That wouldn't do much good.' He said mildly, 'Well, they do say something might be done. But they don't seem to do it.'

While he and I talked in this way, Lucy saw the rooms and asked many questions. She must have three bedrooms, at the least, and four beds.

'How many are coming, ma-am?'

'That depends,' Lucy said, 'but we'll need all your beds.'

'I don't think I could manage for more than three visitors, ma-am, or four, with a married couple in the double room.'

'Oh, no, we won't ask you. If there are more than four of course we shall give help. We could do all the cooking if you liked, and we'll make our own beds.'

'I don't allow the cooking, ma-am, in my own kitchen. But if you could help with the beds . . . Are they school mistresses, ma-am?'

'No, why do you think so?'

'I thought perhaps so many ladies together and not knowing how many might come.'

'Well then, the three bedrooms and the sitting-room, for a week from Monday, and if more than four, to give help. You wouldn't mind two ladies sleeping in a single bed, if they can't get in otherwise.'

'No, ma-am, if it's all right for them. But I hope it won't be more than five.'

I had now begun to suspect, though I hardly believed it, that Lucy meant to bring the whole party to this little house, and I said sharply, 'I hope not, indeed.' Lucy instantly turned to me and we exchanged angry glances, like those which we had not used since childhood; hers meaning, 'how dare you, what impudence,' and mine, 'you think I am a fool, but look out.'

Lucy then smiled at me and said, 'You're not joining the party are you, Tommy, or are you going back on your promise?'

This speech, cryptic to the woman, was meant to remind me that I had promised not to interfere in Lucy's negotiations. She turned her back on me at once, and said to the landlady in a cold voice, 'I can't make any promises, but we might pay a little more if it's over four to cover extra work. Say another five shillings.'

'Five shillings each, ma-am?'

'Good gracious, no. Five shillings all extras.'

'I'd rather say so much a head, ma-am.'

'Very well, half a crown a head.'

The landlady hesitated and looked from Lucy to me. But I was tied by my undertaking, and I was not even sure of Lucy's plans; and so I made no sign. Lucy then said suddenly, 'Very well, Mrs Jones, I see you think our party might be too much for you. And the place is rather small – perhaps I'd better try elsewhere.'

I had often seen Lucy make such a stroke in our private battles. Her tone, her manner were perfectly polite, but both of them had the power of throwing an opponent into confusion. They were like a pistol suddenly brought out and aimed at his head. They caused a kind of panic. As Lucy turned away, the landlady said quickly that she would agree at half a crown a head. The bargain was struck, and Lucy said again, 'Half a crown a head for extras, and I'm not promising that there will be any special number.'

'No, ma-am, but I've no more beds and there's only two will take double.'

'And the sofa, of course, for one. Now about supper –'

We stayed the night, and the next day, by the first train, a crowd of Benjamites arrived, with a cart full of luggage, sacks, great rolls of bedding, gladstone bags, cardboard boxes, Brown's box, from which he preached, now filled with his books, flags and flag-poles. The disciples came together and poured into the little house like an army, while Lucy, standing on the narrow stairs, called out directions. 'You three men, on the sitting-room floor; you can put the bedding under the sofa for now. You, Master (this to Brown), in the front single room, first floor.'

I saw the Jones' swept to the back of the hall, looking on in horror and amazement; and feeling suddenly that I was taking part in a crime, I pushed towards Lucy and called to her, 'Lucy, you're not bringing them all in here to stay – it's impossible.'

'Lots of room,' Lucy said, 'I allowed for fifteen.' And she called, 'Put that box in the place under the stairs.'

'You can't do it, Lucy – it's a mean trick. You know the Jones' never expected anything like this.'

'Go away, Tommy, I'm busy. You elder sisters, back room, double bed – it doesn't really need a mattress. Two of you put the mattress on the floor – the other two can have the bed with some extra blankets on the springs. Mr and Mrs Black – single room on the top floor, it's a three-foot bed. Ellen, Daisy and Margaret, double room top front, in bed. May and Mabel on the floor. Ella, in the top passage.'

The thick-set young girl, whom I had known before, answered from behind me, in her slow calm voice, 'I was in the top passage last time.'

'Well, you're in the top passage this time, too,' Lucy said. 'Hallelujah, praise the Lord.'

She uttered these words in Benjamite style, that is, without emphasis, as if saying, 'It's a fine day.'

'And where are you, sister?' the young woman Ella replied.

'I'm in the first floor passage.'

'But I'd rather have the first floor passage – it's warmer, and it has a carpet.'

'But I have to be ready for the master's call.'

Ella answered that all of them were ready for the master's call, she hoped, hallelujah. But at this moment, Brown himself, who had gone into his room, thrust out his big head and said sharply, 'Sister Ella, I want you.' At once he vanished again, leaving the door ajar.

'Oh, dear,' Ella said, 'Oh, dear.' And her voice was tearful. 'There I go again, upsetting the master. Oh, dear, what a turble bad heart I do have.'

It was strange to see this stout country girl faltering towards Brown's door as if she were ready to faint, and could barely carry herself upright. When she had nearly reached the door, Brown suddenly threw it back. Then she fell down on her knees, and crouched so low that I thought her face touched the threshold.

I was moved to excitement and horror. I was in pain to see a human being brought so low, and yet I could not turn my eyes from the scene, until Lucy, carrying a large bundle upstairs, said to me in a sharp voice, 'Get out of the way, Tommy, if you can't find anything to do.'

I noticed then that no one was paying the least attention to the scene upon the landing. Women and men of all ages continued to pass up and down with their bundles within a yard of the crouching, weeping girl.

All, too, young and old, with the exception of Lucy, and one of the young men, a mere boy, seemed to wear the same expression which I had seen in Ella, and which I might call placid truculence. Three older women, bent, pale as turnips, who passed up the stairs, did not even look at me, and their air as they pushed me to the wall, murmuring softly together, seemed to say, 'We are the humblest of the Lord's servants, but who are you that dares stand in His way.'

This look among the Benjamites, the humiliation of Ella, as well as Lucy's conduct, now filled me with something more than disgust. I felt afraid. I made my way to the lower passage, meaning, if possible, to escape.

But when I struggled to the door, I saw that the little front garden was choked by a thick crowd, treading upon beds, grass, flowers. A drizzle of rain was falling, but it did not seem to trouble these devotees, who, bareheaded, now struck up the hymn:

> Who would true valour see,
> Let him come hither.
> All here will constant be
> Come wind, come weather.

There's no discouragement
Shall make him once repent
His first avowed intent,
To be a pilgrim.

The swelling voices, the sight of these rough people, let out I suppose for a dinner hour, and still in their working clothes, again made tremble in me that nerve which always responded to the ancient call of the apostles, 'Leave all and follow after Christ.'

There was a silence, and I heard Brown's great voice rolling out, I supposed from the first floor window, 'Brothers and sisters in Christ –'

Some fell on their knees in the road, raising their eyes to the window, and I saw right in front, close to the door, the girl Ella, kneeling with her hands pressed together, her face stained with tears, turned up, with an expression of such humility and adoration, that my knees faltered beneath me.

I turned and hurried down the passage, meaning to fly by the back way from this dangerous contagion.

28

But when I opened the kitchen door I found Mrs Jones in tears. Mr Jones was blustering about the police. I sympathized with them. 'I am very sorry this has happened to you –'

They would not look at me. They blamed me also for the disaster that had befallen them.

'Don't take on, Polly,' the old man said, 'it's a police job. I'm off to get them now.' But the woman leant back against the table and let her tears run without an attempt to wipe them away. She shook her head.

'No, no, Willy, how can we tell if it isn't God's work they're doing. We daren't do nothing against them. And well they know it.'

'They're going to learn better then.'

'No, don't be silly, dear. Oh, my poor house. It was Mrs Frederick's last time, and they fairly ruined everything she had. Oh, but I mustn't complain, must I, it's God's work perhaps'; and she fell down in the chair and threw her apron over her head and broke into loud sobs.

I ran to find Lucy. She was still on the upper landing, busy with beds and bedding. And I told her that Mr Jones was about to call the police.

'He can't do that,' she said, 'they would laugh at him. Besides, the Inspector is one of the disciples.'

'You've done these people a great wrong, Lucy.'

'Nonsense, it's good for them. You're always so sentimental, Tommy.'

'Good for them to have their home wrecked?'

'Well, look at the way they live, like bugs in the wallpaper. They think of nothing but making themselves comfortable. What are they good for – nothing at all.'

'Is that a Christian way to speak?'

'Here you are, sister – a towel for your room. It will have to do for all of you.'

I was angered by her coolness and said, 'I suppose Edward is right – you must have a new thrill, and you were tired of hunting.'

'Poor Edward, I'm afraid he's awfully in debt again.'

'You must have your thrill, even if it kills father.'

'And here's one for the master's room,' Lucy called.

'The master, what blasphemy it is.'

'Why Tommy, he is our master, under God.'

At these words, spoken in a peculiar voice, I felt another moment of fear. It was as though a dark wave had stretched itself before me in a bright and calm night, inviting me to approach.

'Master,' I said. 'Puggy Brown, the butcher.'

Lucy started up from her heap of bedding and said, 'Come, I'll see these Jones' for you.' Her face was red, and her eyes glistened with anger. 'You are a soft fool, Tommy, and you will never be anything else.'

'And what are the poor Jones' – bugs in the wallpaper.'

'Yes, you are all bugs in the wallpaper – coming out in the dark to suck somebody else's blood.'

She was running downstairs. I ran after her in fear that she would say something spiteful or cruel to the Jones'. But when I came to the kitchen, I found Lucy holding Mrs Jones with one hand and Mr Jones with the other. They were gazing at her with round foolish eyes, like sheep at a sudden fire, and Lucy was saying, 'A great and wonderful day for us all when the master comes – when we hear the call of grace in our hearts. Do you not feel it?' She spoke to Mrs Jones. 'Ask of your heart – don't you find it there – something which says to you, "A wonderful and strange thing has happened to me" – there, I see you do feel it. You're lucky, Mrs Jones, be wise and don't fight against this great new happiness. I fought it for many days, like a foolish child that does not know what is good for it. Tommy,' she turned to me, 'put me out of your heart – put all that anger away and ask yourself if you know where you are going or what you are doing. Are you not lost and bewildered. Do you not say to yourself every day, "Who am I – what am I seeking?" and can't answer yourself. Let us all kneel down and confess we are stupid lost creatures whose lives have been nothing but self, self, self.'

'Don't you listen to her, Mrs Jones,' I said. I was quite furious, so that I hardly knew what I was saying. I felt such rage against Lucy that I could have beaten her, and yet I knew that half my rage was fear. For her words, her voice, her look filled me with the same weakness which had seized upon me before, at the sight of Ella creeping to Brown on her knees, and again at the sound of the hymn. I say filled with weakness, because it was a positive thing, a feeling as if some spirit had entered into me, cut my sinews, and dissolved my self will. While I was warning the Jones', I was defending myself 'You saw how she tricked you yesterday – don't trust her now.'

Lucy raised her voice and began to sing, joining in the middle of a verse. And now I heard the crowd in front of the house singing. They were singing so loud that the whole little house was shaken and seemed about to be torn up and carried away on the great waves of music and passion like a hut lifted off a river bank by a rising flood. Lucy and the Jones' suddenly knelt down together on the kitchen floor. Mrs Jones was weeping and singing at once. She raised her face to the ceiling in a mournful expression, like one defeated. The old man was not singing, and he looked from Lucy to his wife, with pursed lips, and raised eyebrows, surprised at what he was doing.

Lucy fixed her eyes on me and smiled as she sang. And in her smile I saw the mischievous girl who had so often, in so many ingenious ways, used me and made a fool of me. It was that smile which saved me, or damned me, I cannot tell which. I shouted at her, 'Yes, and this is another of your devil's tricks,' and rushed out of the house. I did not even wait to get my hat or my handbag, and when, seated in the train, I realized the fact, I said, 'Never mind, I couldn't have borne that place for another minute, the hypocrisy, the self-deceit, and Lucy at her worst.'

So, too, when I came home and related the story to Edward, I made it out a victory for myself, as a reasonable, a civilized person; a lover of justice and decency. But, in fact, I had not dared to wait another moment in case I, too, like the Jones', had fallen on my knees and confessed myself a miserable sinner. The dark wave was rising over me, and I had longed to drown in it; to get rid of self; to find what? A cause. Excitement. The experience of suffering, of humiliation, so attractive to my sense. Above all, an answer to everything.

But when, three months later, we heard that Lucy had married Brown, I spoke again scornfully of her, in my grief, and said, 'That's not the way to do good in the world – she had better have been a district nurse.'

'Though I suppose,' Edward said, 'it wasn't the district nurses who cut poor Charles's head off or drove James off the throne.'

'You back up the Benjamites because they vote Radical, and you think they're going to vote for you.' Edward was standing for Queensport at the next election.

'One hand washes another,' Edward said.

'Not if they're both dirty.'

Edward laughed and raised his eyebrows. He was obviously quite surprised at my wit. And I was gratified even by his surprise. Edward was then my model as well as my hero. And perhaps my refuge from Lucy's Lord.

29

The Benjamites and a dozen other strange sects did vote for Edward, in force. They seemed to like his violent speeches, his denunciations of their political sins; as much as they enjoyed the hell-fire threats of their preachers. And Edward, like his grandfather, became member for Queensport. He was twenty-eight, but already known as a first-class election fighter, especially against strong opposition.

The Liberals were broken and divided. But as Edward said to me when I visited him in town, soon after the election, 'There are two ways of making a political career. Joining a party in opposition and taking a strong line, or joining the party in power and taking the modest and useful line.'

But I did not want to talk politics with Edward. In my first year at the 'varsity, I had become a dandy, or, as we said then, a masher. At twenty, I was ambitious to be a man of the world. And I wanted Edward's advice about women.

I visited Edward three or four times in town, from Oxford, before, one night, I found the boldness to say to him, 'Do you keep a mistress, Edward?'

'No,' in a gloomy tone, 'I'm afraid my life has been a little irregular.'

'But Edward, I heard you were rather intimate with a certain lady.'

'Most of them are only too uncertain.'

We are walking down Bond Street on a winter evening, about five o'clock. I smell the sour chill of the mud and see the yellow gas flaring through misted windows. Hansoms float past on their rubber wheels faster than cars of today, and the flash of the spokes trembles on the golden fog.

'What about that divorce case which you were going to be involved in?'

'What case?' Edward has forgotten this special fear, born of some former depression. But he adds, 'I might be involved any day. But I don't think I'd mind very much.'

'What nonsense. It would ruin your career.'

'I'm rather sceptical about this career that Lucy and you have invented for me. One thing at any rate is certain, I'll never do much in politics.'

'Now why on earth should you say that when you've already had such a success.'

'Anyone can make a beginning in politics – it's the finish that kills.'

But I am thinking all the time, 'I must get Edward on to women. No one else can tell me how one sets about getting a mistress. And it's probably quite time I had one. At the very least I ought to have a woman.'

The young man who, not a year before, had nearly been on his knees to Puggy Brown, was now seriously considering adultery or seduction.

I remember very well that I discussed with several Oxford friends the question – ought one to keep a mistress? Our argument was that in all the great civilizations, in Greece, Rome, Italy, France, mistresses played an important part. It was only in the more barbarous countries that they weren't prominent.

If no one kept mistresses in England, I thought, would not something be lost? Would England not lose her place as a civilized nation? Would not literature and art decay?

And had I the right to enjoy this art and literature, this civilization, if I did not undertake the risk and burden of a mistress.

For some months I was obsessed with this question. Something within my own mind accused me night and day, 'You are a coward, a parasite – you neither denounce mistress keepers or join them. You are Mr Facing-both-ways.' And I felt both guilty and resentful in the presence of those men of the world, like Edward, who had taken a decision.

'This Mrs Tirrit whom we are meeting this evening. Is she an intimate friend?' I ask him.

'She's a clever woman, and she thinks she can make use of me to pick out a good speculation in pictures – have you seen the Academy?'

'They say at Oxford that you and Mrs Tirrit are extremely close friends and that Colonel Tirrit is making trouble about it.'

'The poor chap is at Carlsbad most of the time – he has some liver trouble. He's there now, so you needn't be anxious. I was going to do the Academy with you, but it isn't really worth while. English art died with Turner and Constable,' and he began to talk about art, in which I had small knowledge and less interest. 'Look at French art,' he says, 'what gives it such amazing vitality – among so conservative a people – with such a miserable constitution.'

'French politicians are greatly influenced by their mistresses.'

'Are they?' Edwards says drily. 'I don't know any of them personally – do you want a buttonhole?' He sees that I am bored with art.

A flower girl is offering her tray.

'Does one wear a buttonhole in an overcoat?'

'I don't, but you might like to try it. No –' and he gives the girl sixpence and we go on.

Both of us are dressed in the extreme of fashion. Our overcoats are long and tight waisted; our top hats have fall-to sides and curled brims; and we wear little curled moustaches. Mine is black and coarse; Edward's fair and fine. In our hands we carry ebony canes; mine with an ivory head; Edward's with a gold head.

At that time I copied even Edward's clothes. At college, I sought to be of that group of rich young men who were scholars and dandies at the same time; who could talk both philosophy and horses; who pursued actresses and carried a Homer in their pockets. Edward was still remembered among them, and his name gave me admittance to their company. But though I was a scholar of my college, I had no quickness of mind; and I perceived already that these brilliant young men, like Edward, found me dull and foolish. I could never hit upon the right tone with them. For either I was too serious, or too jocular.

This was the time, when Edward, visiting our club, made a speech, defending dandyism, and quoted:

> Memento mori, spite of Keats and Kants,
> God strikes and strangers see your winter pants.

There was much laughter, but many of the young men, my companions, had a thoughtful air, even while they laughed. To them, as to me, it seemed that there was a deep significance, a whole philosophy of life, in the words. And afterwards, proudly putting myself forward before the club, as Edward's brother, I said to our great man, 'That was a wonderful couplet – the best you ever did. It's so true and it goes so deep.'

Then I saw Edward smiling at me, and I was confused. I knew that smile which meant 'Poor Tommy, he is always blundering into some nonsense.'

Fortunately another young man now took up the word and agreed with me, saying, 'That's just what needed saying, sir – that the dandy has the highest standards right through, I mean, even to his underclothes, which nobody sees. That's the real point of dandyism, and where it has such importance. It's really a practical christianity – I was thinking of the sermon on the mount. Blessed are the pure in heart.'

And of the young men standing round our visitor, most were listening with those anxious faces which seem to ask of some inner being, 'Is this true? Is it what I am seeking? It may seem ridiculous but so do so many profound ideas. I must not be frightened by the absurd.' And of the rest, only one was grinning, the foolish grin of the man who sees only the surface of things.

Edward looked round at our serious faces, and I could see that he was surprised and ready to make some joke. I was afraid he would make some ribald joke. But suddenly his face changed and he said in his pleasant good-natured voice, 'I suppose there is religion in everything if we like to put it there,' and, changing the subject, he began to talk of French painting, and Whistler.

When I remember those days and my friends of the D'Orsay Club, I have called myself a worthless young fool, but I do not think now that we were worthless. Edward was right. The tight-waisted coats, the French hats, the ebony canes, which, in the old novels, make the young men of my youth seem empty fools, were often a kind of religion.

> Adultery, sport in France. In England shame
> Unless designed to glorify God's name.

This, too, was a couplet of Edward's which we took seriously. I remember discussing it for an afternoon walk through Cumnor, with a friend who maintained that love, if true, is always from God, and therefore conferred the right and duty to break all human laws.

30

We enter a gallery, where, under shaded lights there is an exhibition of French prints and pictures. Edward presents me to a small ugly woman with a snub nose and brown eyes. I notice her bad skin, pale and covered with small pits; her prominent chin and her darting glance. 'Mrs Tirrit – my brother Tom.' She raises my hand in the air with a quick pressure, and then looking sharply at me says, 'Not the soldier.'

'No, this is the one who is going into the law or perhaps the Church.'

'Into the Church,' and her voice, like her glance, conveys an intense curiosity. I no longer see an ugly little woman with prominent brown eyes, like a French bulldog, but the friendly glance, the eager expression which says, 'Tell me.' I feel that here is someone eager to be my understanding friend, and I open my mouth to explain that Edward is wrong and that I have by no means decided to be a lawyer, when I find myself looking at the lady's back. Her glance is turned to Edward, her hand on his arm, and they are going past the curtain which divides the outer gallery from the inner. I have been dropped. But I still feel an extraordinary excitement, as if a new land of discovery has been opened to me. I wait impatiently for another glimpse of the face, whose ugliness now seems to me a charm. I turn the corner of the curtain and see a tall man walk up to Edward and Mrs Tirrit from behind. He says something to them. They turn round, and I perceive that they have had an unpleasant surprise, that this new arrival must be Tirrit mysteriously returned from abroad. I am so astonished that I stand without movement, and yet full of horror, thinking, 'So Edward is lost.'

But no one raises a hand or stick. The three are talking together. I go up to them and Edward introduces me. 'Colonel Tirrit – Mr Tom Wilcher.'

'Who is going into the Church,' Mrs Tirrit says.

The Colonel shakes hands with me, pressing my hand. He is tall and heavy. His face is long and yellow, deeply folded; that of a very sick or unhappy man. Edward waves his hand towards a picture and says to Mrs Tirrit, 'That's the only kind of Corot for me – Italian period.'

The two walk over to the pictures, and I notice in Mrs Tirrit's walk a new spring, as if she is acting a part, and enjoying it. The Colonel says to me, 'You're going into the Church.'

'It isn't decided yet. I am still in my first year at Oxford.'

'It's a serious step.'

The Colonel says no more and we walk in silence after Edward and Mrs Tirrit who stops at every picture. At last they come back to the entrance door and a cab is called. Mrs Tirrit, standing among us on the pavement, makes to each, like a queen, the appropriate remark. To Edward: 'After all, you're quite right about what's his name – the splashes – I shall buy that picture.' To me: 'You must come and see me, and don't wait for Edward to bring you. I don't want to see Edward, but you. So come by yourself.' And then unexpectedly to her husband: 'My dear Johnny, you look wretchedly ill. I shall have to send you to bed.' And in each phrase she expresses a kindness, a sincerity, which is the more convincing because of her tart humorous tone. The cab arrives, her husband opens the door, and Edward hands her in. Edward stands hat in hand – the Colonel looks straight in front of him, from his corner, with his hat on. They drive away.

'I understand now why you like her so much,' I say to Edward. 'She is perfectly charming.'

'You saw what happened?' Edward is once more gloomy and depressed. 'No.'

'Tirrit came up and said he was going to knock me down.'

'Nonsense.'

'I suppose he came home just to make a row. I asked him to wait till we had looked at the pictures, and as you see, he didn't do anything after all. Lost his nerve, poor chap. Or too decent.'

'Poor Mrs Tirrit, what a scene.'

Once more we are walking down the pavement, in the golden fog. Edward says, 'Yes, I'll bet ten to one she planned the whole thing.'

'Does she want a scandal?'

'No, but she's bored and whimsical like all these women. Too rich. And no children. And a devoted jealous husband. Yes. They mean to make trouble, between them. He's a fool, and she's capable of anything to amuse herself.'

'He couldn't divorce her, could he?'

'Why not? He will if she makes him. And then I shall have to marry her. A nice prospect.'

'Then I can't understand how you let yourself be compromised, I can't understand how you can have anything to do with such worthless selfish people.'

We are back in Edward's room among his beautiful books, his first editions, his ivories and china, his French impressionist pictures which seem even to his friends still an affectation. It is not a large room, but its contents are worth some thousands of pounds. Edward is in his shirt-sleeves. He has meant to put on a smoking jacket, but he has not troubled. He sits over the fire with the poker in his hand. Now he taps a coal, seeking for the grain, in order to break it with the lightest blow, and says, 'Angela Tirrit is one of the most charming women in London.'

'How can she be charming?'

'How is anyone charming? She has the special charm of being what shall I say? Civilized is the nearest word. Yes, she has taught me a lot.'

'A woman who deceived her husband and wants to ruin you out of pure selfishness?'

But as I abuse Mrs Tirrit, I imagine her pursuing me, driving me into all kinds of scandals, causing me the greatest misery, and finally involving me in her divorce, marrying me and using me. Using me, is the idea that occurs to me. I remember very well that I did not say 'I ought to take a mistress,' but 'How I wish some clever woman, older than I, ruthless, corrupt and fascinating, would seduce me, ruin me, and carry me off to this mysterious and exciting world where Edward is so much at home.'

'A horrible woman,' I say.

'The question is, of course, whether life is worth living,' Edward says. I cannot see the connection of this remark. But I know that Edward is speaking as he has never spoken before. An hour of confidences has struck.

'What,' I say, astonished. 'You to say that; why, even if Mrs Tirrit did drag you into the court, you would still have a dozen other careers open to you.'

Edward pays no attention to me. He taps the coal again, a big coal which ought to be left alone. A bad and extravagant trick of Edward. And in my surprise and alarm at his strange mood, I say sharply, 'Don't spoil the fire – I never knew anyone waste coal as you do.' Edward pays no attention to me. He reflects a moment, letting his cigarette hang crookedly, and then gives the coal a sharp rap. 'That's it, Tommy – is life worth living? Give a man everything in the world, give everyone everything they think they want, and they might still ask that question. Judging by my experience, they might be all the more ready to ask it.'

'Do you believe in God, Edward?'

'Oh yes, I mean I believe in His existence. But how does one keep up one's interest in Him?'

I am inexpressibly shocked. 'Edward, think of what religion means.'

'And how does one go on being interested in life. That is the important question which governments will soon have to answer. How do you maintain the vital spark. It isn't a matter of health. A perfectly healthy world would probably die out like the Polynesians. And look how poor papa clings to life – I've always envied him.'

'He does really believe in God – and heaven.'

'But then you would think he would be willing to go to heaven. And look at Lucy, she doesn't believe in anything.'

'She's given up everything for God.'

'Do you think so? My impression is that Lucy hasn't any religion at all. But she has a great sense of class. She has turned herself into a char because she feels that her own class is finished. She doesn't feel grand enough as a mere lady. She has flown to the arms of Puggy to give herself the sense of nobility.'

'I think that's nonsense.'

'Yes, quite probably – like most other things.' And having tapped the coal on all sides, he gives it such an expert stroke that it flies into thin pieces. I see him still, in the glow of the blaze, smiling at his own feat, with the air of one who laughs at his own childishness.

31

I did not find out how to get a mistress. But I did learn from Edward that, according to his man, the between-maid at home was not entirely virtuous. And when I went home, I permitted myself to knock into her. With such a sense of desperation as still makes me say, 'So does the soldier of the Lord disembark on an unknown shore among cannibals.' I tremble again before that little maid whose very name has gone from me. She was a little fat creature with a face like moulded soap; and the nature of a bird in a cage, chirping with all domestic music. You heard her voice everywhere but always with some other voice, or the sound of a kettle singing, a grate being scoured. And our love passage was a short and confused interlude when all romance vanished in her giggles and her expertness.

'How did I do it?' I ask myself. 'How was it possible?'

It is not yet eight o'clock and still gloomy; a cold winter morning, but I cannot stay in bed. I get up and go along the corridor to the linen-room. The baskets ranged beneath the shelves, and the linen lying in the close warmth of the pipes, have the air of all things seen at night, of having been interrupted in their private thought and memories. 'It was on that side,' I thought, 'under the window, where there are no shelves and the baskets made a kind of couch.' But how did I dare? So wicked and foolish an act.

But at once I remember that I had not dared. It was the little maid who contrived the meeting. So suddenly and unexpectedly, that I still wonder how she divined wishes which were scarcely clear to myself. I was walking in the passage, when she started in front of me from the nursery. By an effort, I said something to her, 'Where are you going?' or 'What do you want?'

Suddenly she darts aside into the linen-room, and as I come to the door, opens it a few inches and looks up at me with an indescribable look of mischief and challenge. Then runs back into the room. And I follow as if drawn by an elastic. The young man of my memory, serious, burdened, prematurely anxious, whose very dandyism was a moral inquiry, changes into somebody quite different, a boy who at twenty-one was utterly unsure of himself. So shy, so clumsy beneath his careful manners, that he was scarcely responsible for his own vices. Moved this way and that by every voice of power, by Pug Brown, by Lucy, by Edward.

It was some impulse far deeper than physical desire; the wish to suffer some new, some profound experience, that brought me to this room and the scene of a strange humiliation, where rules were suddenly reversed and the servant became the master, commanding with authority, and the master became a shy foolish creature who could not even find words or manage his own buttons.

'Do any ee be afeared,' the girl says, smiling, but not at all in scorn. She is full of sympathy. The shy servant who could not raise her eyes above the master's waistcoat buttons, nor speak to him above a whisper, is now, in one moment, become the superior, responsible and confident. She takes charge, and is only puzzled by my increasing helplessness. In fact, it is her competence which has increased it.

She pauses suddenly in her arrangements and says as if in doubt, 'He bees and be bant.'

This was a variation from a local saying about a girl who could not make up her mind whether to give way to her lover or remain 'a maiden still.'

Her words, her shrewd smile, fall upon my trance like rain-drops and light on a curtained glasshouse; they do not move or warm a leaf within. Yet I am sharply aware of them.

A psychologist, explaining to me once the extraordinary failure of a public man, famous for his resource and courage, said to me, 'He was in two minds at once and that means he had no will, for the will is only the servant of a desire.'

It was not fear, it was a conflict of desires, a paralysis of will, which made me feel so foolish and helpless in the hands of the little maid. Fortunately, I suppose, she had the native wit to perceive my condition and to understand that the success of the enterprise must depend upon herself. I should have kissed her little red hands, swollen and glazed with washing soda, for that instinct of sympathy, like a bird's or a cat's, which perceived that I could not go back, and carried me so kindly and adroitly forward, even with compliments upon my manly powers, to the only possible solution of my deadlock. I wonder still at the goodness of that soul, so understanding, and ask how any can deny the love of God who have known, even in so trifling a passage, the unbought kindness of the poor and simple.

And the next day when I had to pass her in the corridor, she pressed herself against the wall and looked at the floor. We were alone, and there was no reason why she should have behaved so respectfully, except her own idea of what was right and proper. I felt then for her an impulse of gratitude and affection, so strong that I feel it now. It is a true and deep love; the love which is full of respect. For I perceived in that moment that there was to be no difference in our relations, no upheaval in the order of life at Tolbrook.

When Edward knew the story of the maid, though I told it as an exploit, he laughed and said, 'I thought she would seduce you – was it very alarming?'

Edward thought that I had been the timid victim. But Edward had not much penetration into character. He was too clever. He never understood the force of moral conviction in certain souls, or its variety of forms.

32

'The young people think me an old fossil,' I thought, moving along the passage wall to find the place where the girl had stood aside, in modesty and subjection. 'But what I am now I was then. Even as a child I had a passionate love of home, of peace, of that grace and order which alone can give beauty to the lives of men living together, eating, chattering, being sick, foolish and wicked, getting old and ugly. I hated a break of that order. I feared all violence.'

I found the place, just opposite the newel of the stairs, and leant against it. It was, of course, an illusion that the wall was still warm.

Passionate Lucy threw herself upon the dark wave of fate, of God's mysterious will; and in the presence of the little maid, part of me cried, 'Foolish and wicked boy, you are destroying the peace of your home and your heart.' And another part, 'Be reckless, have faith – take no thought for the morrow – cast your bread upon the waters.'

'Hullo, uncle, I was wondering where you'd got to.' Robert stood before me, but his eyes did not look at me. He did not wish to show any surprise at my position, with outstretched arms against the wall. 'It's about the power line for old Raven. The electricity people say they can do it for fifty pounds if we decide today, while the gang are working in the village. But tomorrow they'll wind up, and after that it will cost a hundred.'

'Old Raven is eighty,' I said. 'What does he want with electricity?'

'You won't see the wires from the house.'

'No, but they'd go across the meadow behind the drive – they'll spoil the view of the church.'

I was struck by the boy's rough appearance. He had not shaved for the last two days, and his open shirt was filthy. He looked like a labourer. His rubber high boots were caked with mud. I felt that for his own sake I ought to tell him that his appearance must be painful to Ann. But I was unable to do so. I felt too far away from Robert and his plots with Jaffery.

'Sorry to bother you, uncle,' he said, 'but about this power line – it seems a good chance.'

'I'm afraid we haven't the money,' I said, for I knew it was waste of money to give old Raven power. He would never use it except for a few lights. 'Were you coming to prayers – you remember that you used to like morning prayers.'

'Yes, uncle, but I just have no time at all.'

I went into the old day nursery where for the last week or so I had been reading prayers in my dressing-gown. I had not meant to start this old custom again until the housekeeper, Mrs Ramm, one day told me how she missed it. Agnes Ramm had been at Tolbrook twenty years, and I remember her when she first came, as kitchenmaid, a round, blooming young girl. Agnes had turned out a good maid, but not of the best character. She had had two illegitimate children before she was twenty, and once at least she had attempted some approach to myself. A hussy. But now at forty-six, after severe illness, a sad woman with strong religious feeling. I was glad at her suggestion, and since Ann made no objection, Agnes and a niece of hers, who was the housemaid, attended every morning in the old nursery for morning prayers. This had become a great pleasure to me and to poor Aggie, who would often say how she had missed the comfort of it in the years when Tolbrook had been let to 'those heathen from London'.

I scarcely expected Robert, who was truly a heathen, to come to prayers; but I thought I preferred his bias to Ann's indifference. For Ann, it seems, is pregnant. And it shocks me to think of any girl undertaking the great and awful responsibility of motherhood without religion of any kind.

33

I could not speak to the girl directly on the subject because it would have involved some reference to her condition, which might have embarrassed her. But on one of our afternoon walks, I took occasion to remark on the importance of religious education for young children. 'They cannot, of course,' I said, 'understand the *arguments* for the existence of God, simple and irrefragable as they are. They can be taught only to recognize the *experience* of God, of goodness in their own hearts, and in other people's acts, so that when they grow older, they are ready for those proofs upon which faith must stand, unbreakable and triumphant.'

'Do you believe in the after life, uncle?'

'Most certainly. I don't know how anyone can bear to live without such a belief.' But remembering that she might have certain fears, I changed that subject quickly and said, 'And why shouldn't it be true. You young people choose to disbelieve it just as you tie handkerchiefs over your heads to play at being peasants. It's a fashion to attack the Church.'

'Oh, but I'm not against the Church, uncle. As I tell Robert, it seems mean to attack the poor old dear, when she's so weak.'

I was just going to answer with some indignation that the Church was very well able to look after itself when the young woman went on, in a thoughtful voice, 'Today is like the picture in the back passage, isn't it – with the old squire and the little girl,' a remark which, referring apparently to a steel engraving beside the kitchen door, entirely threw me out, and scattered my ideas.

It was a January afternoon, with a sprinkle of snow, and the grey fields, the silver sky, the cottages seen at a distance through the fine lines of the branches, certainly made a scene just like the engraving. And for a moment, as often at such unexpected strokes of imagination, I did feel like the old man in the picture, whose hat and cape coat, wellingtons and stick, I had often examined as a child, climbing upon a chair to discover, with my short-sighted eyes, whether the stick made real holes in the snow, and whether the artist had put in all the footprints.

'And this girl,' I thought, 'who is holding my arm, she is rather like the little girl in the picture. She has the same short skirt, and she wears a handkerchief tied over her head. Ann is like a peasant again, going back to the soil. She is even grey-faced like the little girl, with the big eyes that old-fashioned artists gave their little girls. Her eyes seem bigger since she began to be so ill.' And for a moment, my feeling was that reality had actually disappeared out of the world, and that such an absurd appearance from the past as myself, and so flimsy a being as Ann, the peasant from Kensington, were simply figments or phantoms.

'Did it always hang in the back passage?' Ann said. 'I don't remember it there. I thought it was upstairs somewhere.'

'It was in the night nursery. But what does it matter where it was, and I don't think this afternoon is at all like a picture. It's a real winter day of the best kind – the kind you get only in England – where human beings can still go out and enjoy themselves,' and so on. For I felt indignant with the girl for her romantic stuff which was trying to deprive me of life. I thought, 'I may be old, but I don't belong to the past. It is this sad grey-faced little girl, the imitation simpleton, who has gone back into the past, the most primitive past; she lives in a perpetual winter, austere, colourless;

a cruel and bleak winter; quite different from this glorious and encouraging scene.'

'We are lucky in our dry weather,' I said.

'It is nice to look at – out of our parlour window.'

'But you must take exercise. That's doctor's orders.'

'Robert's orders.'

'Robert is becoming a good husband. He takes great care of you now.'

'Not of me, but the baby. I am only the box labelled "fragile, with care".'

'Robert is right. You carry a great responsibility.'

'I suppose so. But I don't feel like that.'

'Don't you want to have a child?'

'Yes, I think I do. I suppose Nature is at her old games.'

'God's will is not an old game.'

'I'm afraid, uncle, I can't think God had much to do with it. It seems too natural.'

'What has the love that God puts into a woman's heart for her child got to do with your ideas of Nature?'

'But do women always like their babies? I remember two cases in Paddington.' And she would no doubt have told me about these miserable cases had I not changed the subject by remarking that it was about to snow. For I did not want any more nonsense. I am too old to be bothered with it.

34

Ann talks of our parlour. Perhaps to flatter me. But, in fact, I was glad when she brought the parlour into use again. The parlour was our family room, where, for many years of my youth, I could always be sure of company.

It is a small square room with two tall windows facing west. Its carpet has always been shabby, its chairs worn; its pictures, the outcast portraits and old prints which will not do elsewhere. A large fly-blown print of the Derby finish hangs over the chimneypiece. It has wanted a glass ever since Bill, sixty years ago, put a slug from his airgun through the finishing post.

It is a darkish room, occupied always by a brown shadow which Edward once likened to the spirit of gravy. 'I always feel,' he used to say, in the parlour, 'as if the Sunday joint were going to walk in and take the best chair by the fire.'

Yet Edward, too, loved to stretch himself in the parlour, with unbuttoned waistcoat, and his feet as far as they would go up the side of the mantelpiece, while Lucy, perched on the arm of his chair, would tease him or comb his hair.

There in wet weather we used to play whist for matches; there Bill organized picnics, gathering together the luncheon baskets, the sandwiches, the rugs, the dogs, and shouting furiously, 'Where on earth is Lucy, where is Mama, where is the French mustard? No, I want to see it. Very well, the basket must be unpacked again.'

And after our father's death, it was the smoking-room, where we sat till the small hours, in that community of gossip which is the ground of family life.

Now in these winter afternoons, when Ann reads and smokes on one side of the fire and I on the other, the parlour is again the parlour. True, we converse little, but there is comfort and company in the air. For while two of us sit in the old room, it is again a family room. It gives out again, like a dried flower warmed in the hand, its essential quality, a rich ease.

And Ann, with her unexpected power of knowing my feelings, if not my thoughts, said to me one evening, 'I wonder will this baby be sitting here in another fifty years or seventy-one years.'

I was surprised by such an idea in Ann's head. But it gave me a keen pleasure. For I had wondered already if perhaps Robert and Ann would not decide to settle at Tolbrook, either as tenants or as my managers.

'Tolbrook has been a great anxiety and burden to me, and I am leaving it,' I said, 'but Robert seems to enjoy estate work, and he will not find a prettier piece of country or better land.'

'Wouldn't you like to see the house stay in the family?'

'Yes, of course I should. Though I don't know if that isn't perhaps a weakness on my part.'

'The trouble is Robert,' the girl said, 'he is too fond of the place.'

'It was his own home – the only real home he ever had.'

'Yes. But Robert is the kind of man who would always be cruel to what he loves.'

35

This idea, that Ann herself might be inclined to set up a family line at Tolbrook, occupied my mind with such force that for some days I thought of nothing else. And the girl's new domesticity, suggested, I suppose, by her condition, encouraged me to speak of a matter even closer to my heart, the religious education of her child. I pointed out that Tolbrook had always been a religious house, and that the whole value of its tradition, to a family, lay in that fact. 'And what can be more important to a child, than a religious education. It's the first years, too, that count – that give direction to his whole idea of the world – his whole *feeling* about it.'

It was just before tea, and Ann, with her spectacles falling down her nose, was reading, smoking and knitting. She looked reflectively at me and said, 'Yes, I suppose that is true,' and then asked me what a chaise was like.

'A chaise?' I think my surprise was justifiable.

'I always thought a chaise was an open carriage, but here is Julia Bertram in *Mansfield Park* talking about being boxed up in a chaise.'

'You may be surprised to hear that chaises went out thirty years before I was born. Do you feel no moral responsibility at all towards your child?'

'I expect I shall feel too much. Yes,' and she blew a cloud of cigarette smoke. 'I'm terribly afraid I'm the type that makes rather a fussy mother.'

She was wrinkling her forehead, a bad habit; but I thought it the wrong moment to warn her of it. I was gathering up my forces.

'This poor child,' I thought, 'is lost already – she is blinded by prejudice and ignorance. And if I speak to her of God, she probably imagines an old man in a grey beard and a very bad temper. It is useless to appeal to her on religious grounds. But there are others.' And drawing up my chair, I said, 'My dear, I understand your difficulty about religious instruction. But let us make a bargain. If you will allow this child to be brought up in a reasonable Christian faith, I shall settle two hundred a year on him, in your trust. Yes, and you know,' I said, 'he would have a very good claim to Tolbrook. I might even undertake to leave the place to him. I should be glad to find in Edward's and Lucy's grandchild a successor,' etc.

'But I'm not sure if I want him to be a Christian,' Ann said.

'Wait a minute,' I said, perhaps too hastily. 'Of course, you won't be forgotten. Not at all. I have already made some provision for you. But in a case like this, I should be prepared to go much further.'

'Made provision for me,' the girl said, in a most rational tone. And I, thinking I was on the right track at last, explained my recent instruction to Jaffery which would be communicated to her in the next week or two, etc. That she was to have a thousand pounds on my death, and a hundred and fifty more for every year I should live after her undertaking the care of me.

'So the longer you live, the more I shall get.'

'Yes, and I might increase that amount.'

This, of course, was a delicate point, apt to be mistaken. And I added that I believed it was a not unusual provision and only just, having regard to the time she was sacrificing, etc.

The girl seemed to meditate. But when I expected an answer, she exclaimed, 'It's time you had your tea, uncle,' and rang the bell. Neither did she refer to the matter again that day.

36

The feeling. What is this feeling that I talk about to Ann, and how can she know what I mean, when I barely know it myself. When I, with all my church-going, my prayers, lose it so easily. One would say I was a dead frog, which shows animation only at the electric spark from such as Lucy. The touch of genius; of the world's genius. And when that contact was withdrawn, I became once more a preserved mummy.

As soon as Lucy went away from me, and I lost the feeling of her, I began to mummify. I called it growing sensible, responsible, etc. At Lucy's return from the Benjamites I did not even recognize her. It seemed that we belonged to different worlds.

I was coming downstairs into the hall one winter evening, dressed for dinner, and probably much pleased with myself. I was no longer the youth who had almost fallen on his knees in the Jones' kitchen. Neither was I a dandy. I was a young man, in his last year at Oxford, serious even in dress. At home, I began to take an interest in the estate and the people. I taught in Sunday school, and helped my father with the estate work. And when I heard, from some cart-tail on market days, the peculiar hollow shouts of the open air preacher, I would think, 'Yes, it's all very well to talk about God's laws and renunciation of this world's goods, but where would you be without the magistrates. And what do you say when somebody walks off with your sheep or rifles your potato clamp in the night.'

I had not set eyes on Lucy for nearly four years. And when, in the dim-lit hall, I saw near the door a poorly dressed woman standing in silence, I took her for some beggar or gypsy, come to ask a favour. She had the look of gypsy women as soon as they cease to be girls; thin and nervous. No one can tell what age they are. At twenty they have the thin dry wrinkles which will only be deeper when they are eighty, and show already bitter experience and strong will.

This woman under the hall lamp which made deep hollows in her cheeks, looked at me, in my dinner jacket and white shirt, as gypsy women look when they beg from the gentlemen on Epsom Downs. Their hard filmy gaze puts gentlemen into a glass cage like wax figures in a museum.

'Good evening,' I said. I meant to save my father a troublesome petition. But in the same moment that secret nerve moved, I knew Lucy, and I was shocked by the voice of my good evening, which had seemed cordial and now seemed distant and cold. In one instant I ceased to be the young master, the serious man of affairs, and became Lucy's young brother. 'Lucy,' I cried, 'have you been ill?'

'You didn't know me,' Lucy said. 'I'm not surprised. And look at my hands.'

Her hands were like the little maid's, but darker and more chapped. The finger tips were cracked and grey.

'That work is killing you, Lucy,' I said.

'Yes, it was killing me. But I knew the rule. It's not because of the work that I've come home.'

And she told me that Brown had taken the girl Ella to his bed. 'Six months ago, before my baby was born.'

'I didn't know you'd had a baby.'

'It was born dead. But I didn't want it to live and be a Benjamite.'

'Poor Lucy, but you're not going back to those savages.'

'Never again. Brown has broken his own precious rule, and now I want a bath.'

My mother and myself were horrified by the change in Lucy. My mother hastened to bring comforts and new clothes, the most eager sympathy. My father, who had showed his delight in Lucy's return, by a sudden gaiety I had never seen before, took no account of her sufferings. And when I spoke to him of her lost looks, he answered only, 'She's young.' I could not understand then, as I do now, that to the old, a broken marriage is little more than a broken knee in a child. When they see a daughter worn before her time, they think only, 'She must have come to this in a few years, and she is still young. That is the great thing.'

And Lucy, even more than before, sought her father's company and avoided her mother. A situation which my mother's tact at once accepted. While Lucy was at home she effaced herself as much as possible from our family party.

37

To our pleasure, Lucy was quite ready to be distracted. She had always delighted in luxury, and like Edward she seemed to enjoy it in the idea, as well as in fact. The sense of luxury about her, of wealth, of good servants, of expensive carpets and hangings, things which after a few hours one does not notice and which add much more to one's cares and burdens than one's comfort, gave her deep pleasure. She loved sheets of the thinnest linen, and Paris clothes, with the finest sewing in inner seams never to be seen by any except herself and a maid. But though Lucy bought new clothes, though she went to parties with us and romped and danced and flirted as before, she did not lose her haggard cheeks and hollow eyes. She could not sleep, and she used to come to my room in the small hours to make me talk or read to her.

It was on these nights that she made me feel the inadequacy of my life, so respectable and proper. For Lucy carried a nervous force which charged the air about her so that when I waked to find her in my room, I was suddenly carried out of its narrow domestic comfort and security into that mysterious universe of passion and faith in which she lived.

'I can't sleep,' Lucy would say, touching my forehead, 'so I came to you.'

Nothing gave me more pleasure than such words from Lucy, which meant, 'I need you.' I sprang up eagerly. 'Shall I read to you. Get into my bed, while it's warm – and I'll find a book.'

'No, you stay in bed and I'll roll up in your counterpane – read me about Pigg and the cupboard.'

I kept all Surtees in my room, for Lucy, who, when she read at all, desired only her old hunting books. And so I read to her as she demanded, the celebrated passage in which Jorrocks and James Pigg drink healths in turn to each of the hounds; and James Pigg, being asked what sort of a night it is, puts his head out of what he supposes to be a window, and answers, 'Hellish dark and smells of cheese.'

At this point I waited for Lucy to laugh, but she remained silent and said only, 'Go on about the rain, but you can leave out the poetry.'

What went on in Lucy's head while she lay beside me, wrapped up like a white mummy in my counterpane, with her black hair, already full of grey, falling in two pigtails across her shoulders. Probably very little. She was not used to reflect upon things.

'You must hunt again,' I said.

'I don't know. It's really rather a bore. It takes such a lot of time.'

'But now you have plenty of time to enjoy yourself.'

'To bore myself, too.'

'But you will love it – don't you love your Jorrocks.'

'Yes, but I know every word of Jorrocks – read me again the bit about the hound that was as wise as a Christian.'

I read the passage and said, 'It's true – a hound does know how to live and be happy.'

I spoke from that excitement which Lucy always brought to me. But Lucy answered only, 'Oh, nonsense, Tommy – a dog's a dog. Go on with the next chapter – the day in the forest. Wasn't it Pinch-me-near?'

And when I had finished she would stretch herself and say in a dreaming voice, 'How gorgeous that is – how lovely to be Jorrocks on a day like that. Read me the bit about the morning again, with the drops like diamonds on the bushes.'

I read the piece of description, commonplace in every word; but because Lucy felt it, an experience which made me long to get up at dawn. It still delights me in my memory.

'I'll go cub hunting with you Lucy, if you will hunt.'

'And put some cobbler's wax on your saddle. You would hate it, Tommy, and so should I – to see you in agony.'

'Then go with Edward. That would be real hunting.'

'Yes, perhaps I shall go with Edward. Though I wish he wouldn't waste his time and his money on all that nonsense.'

'What, do you call hunting nonsense?'

'It is nonsense for Edward with his brains.'

Lucy adored Edward and would never allow him to be criticized, even by my mother, whose favourite he was. When my mother said, with her gentle irony, 'His majesty is coming to see us tomorrow and commands that the carriage be sent to Totnes,' Lucy would flush and answer, 'Why not, mother – it will do Wilkins good to have a little work for a change.' Wilkins was our old coachman,

38

When this same year Edward was threatened at last with the Tirrit divorce case, and Colonel Tirrit fell dead in the street, on the day after his lawyers had filed suit, Lucy said that it was the judgement of God.

'Nonsense, Lucy.' I was shocked by her superstition. 'It is just Edward's luck.'

I told her that Edward was already entangled in another affair, with a young actress called Julie Eeles. 'But perhaps you think providence arranged that, too.'

'Yes, I think it might be so.'

'What nonsense, Lucy.'

'I hear Mrs Eeles is a very nice woman and she has helped Edward a lot in his worries.'

'But surely, Lucy, you don't approve of Edward's taking her from her husband.'

'If her husband is such a ninny, he deserves what he gets.'

'I thought you were a Christian, Lucy.'

'What's that got to do with it? And if you do go into the Church, Tommy, I hope you won't be a canting humbug. I'd much rather you were the real old brandified kind like that man at Combe Barten. They say he has children all over the county. But I don't suppose you'll ever get married. You're a born old maid.'

Lucy would never talk religion with me, though often she talked of Brown, giving me strange pictures of her life with the Benjamites.

'When he took that bladder of lard, Ella, into bed with him, he made me sleep on the floor and serve Ella as a handmaiden. I washed her clothes and emptied her slops. And didn't she glory in it. She would say, "Sister Lucy, praise the lamb, could you brush out my hair now, hallelujah, and please don't pull, or I shall scream." '

'I wonder she dared.'

'She knows how I hate her. But that sort of creature enjoys being hated. If you knew what a set they are, Tommy. The mean jealousies and dirty little spites that creep about in them like worms in a dead rabbit. You think they're alive, but they're only rotten. Except Ella. She's alive, like a weasel with dropsy.'

'How could you wait on her, Lucy.'

'The master commanded, and I obeyed. It was the rule – the rule.' Lucy repeated the word in a voice of mockery.

'But you say he broke the rule. It is against the rule to take another wife.'

'Not if God commands. But God did not command him to take Ella.'

'How did you know that?'

'One day it was revealed to me and I told him. And when I pressed him, he began to doubt. I said to him, Master, will you swear that it was not the voice of the devil speaking to you in the lust of the flesh; and he would not swear. God stopped up his lips. And though he prayed all night and all of us prayed, that the truth might come to him, he could not tell whether it was God who had commanded him to put me away, or the devil, who had made him lust after Ella.'

Lucy spoke this language of the Benjamites without any change of voice, and on her lips the biblical words did not make me smile.

Lucy laughed and said, 'How would you like getting out of bed at three in the morning, Tommy, and kneeling down on the oilcloth in your nightshirt and howling to the Lord for a couple of hours, to save your soul from hell.'

'Did you get up always at three?'

'No, we got up whenever Puggy had a fit of the horrors and shouted at us to pray, pray, pray, against the devil.'

'What a queer kind of religion it is,' my mother remarked, when she heard these stories.

'Do you think so, mother,' Lucy would answer. 'But you know, it does work – it does keep the devil away. Sometimes at least.' And then she burst out laughing, 'But you ought to hear the moans and groans when we all have to get out on a cold winter night. And you ought to see fat Ella tumbling out of bed like a bagful of turnips – how she does hate it. You can see the spite boiling in her little green eyes. But she has to pray louder than anyone or Puggy might have a new revelation and take another wife – and then she'd have to sleep on the floor again and empty slops.'

'I'm glad you're not going back,' my mother would say, 'I don't think Mr Brown's religion makes anyone much better or more charitable.'

'Good Lord, no,' Lucy would answer. 'Puggy doesn't bother much about tea-table virtue.'

Lucy was strange to both of us. And yet, as I say, every word she said, however unexpected, found in me a response; some secret nerve within me was excited. To what? I was going to write, to the love of God, of religion, to some grandeur of thought. But now, as I pace restlessly through the lower rooms, I feel it as something deeper, more passionate. The life of the spirit.

39

I found myself in the dining-room, which still has its old chairs, too big and clumsy a set for a modern house, and I began to hunt for those two, at which Lucy and I, side by side, always prayed. For each of us had our own chair, and many times, when my father was waiting with his books and the servants were already filing into the room, Lucy or I would discover by the minute signs known only to ourselves that we were at the wrong chair and would get up hastily to look for the right one. Then if my father said 'Sit down children,' and we had to use a wrong chair, we would feel so restless and exasperated that as Lucy said, she felt the devil tickling her all over. Once at least she was beaten for toppling such a wrong chair right over. The crash makes me start again. I begin to laugh, and it seems to me that I am grinning that demon grin of Lucy's childhood.

Here is my chair with a mark in the mahogany like a long narrow eye, a snake's eye, and a chip on the near hind leg. I kneel at it for a moment. Suddenly I feel that somebody is present, and getting up, I see Ann at the door.

'You didn't take your medicine.' She looks embarrassed. And I am angry at being watched.

'No, I forgot.'

'You don't really think I am trying to poison you, uncle?'

In my astonishment I jumped to an unlucky conclusion. I said that she had no business to read my note-books.

'I don't read them,' she answered. 'Have you written me down as a poisoner?'

'Certainly not. I wouldn't dream of such a thing.'

'Do, if you like. You ought to write everything down. It's good for you. I kept a diary myself once, and it was so awful I had to burn it. But it did me lots of good.'

'Good for what? Is this some more of your German boxes?'

No, I meant it's natural to want to give yourself away –'

Then I was sure she had been reading my books, and I said, 'I never thought you were deliberately giving me the medicine too strong – I only thought that you might say to yourself, "It's better to keep him quiet than to prolong his life, which is a useless one." '

'And that's why you arranged that settlement to pay me for keeping you alive.'

'My dear child, you and I are sensible people – we know what the world is. And I am a useless old man. While you are young and eager for life, for travel, for lots of things, that only money can buy. I don't say that the idea occurred to you that I would be better out of the way, but if it had, I should not blame you. It would be very reasonable under the circumstances,' and so on, saying no more than the truth. But all at once the girl exclaimed that I could do what I liked with my property, she didn't want any of it. And she got up and walked out of the room.

After a moment, when I perceived that she was angered against me, I hastened to find her. But it appeared that she had gone out. Her hat and cloak were missing from the back hall. And it was a cold day, with squalls of rain, as green as ice, moving continually in from the sea. When I imagined Ann, as usual insufficiently clad, lingering about the fields in this weather, and endangering not only herself but the child, I was ready to beat my head on the walls.

I felt so ill that I lay down in the saloon, itself bitterly cold in its dismantled state. And the idea occurred to me that I might actually be in some measure possessed by an evil will, by the devil.

'If that is so,' I thought, 'and I am really an exceptionally wicked man, it would explain my fallings away from Lucy, and also my bad treatment of Sara. It would also explain why this child Ann appears to be shocked by conclusions on my part, which seem to me only logical.'

40

A heavy depression fell upon me, and I was in a most unhappy condition when I thought, 'Such unsystematic argument leads only to confusion. Let me see how I stand – let me draw up what I might call a balance sheet.'

I then took paper and noted down rapidly in pencil the opposing arguments thus.

1. My past blindness and failure of understanding with Lucy, Sara, and Ann.

   My present comprehension of these failures and desire to amend them.

2. My love of an orderly and settled life, my too great reverence for tradition, etc., and the family possessions that represent tradition in material form.

   My resolve to leave it and to leave Tolbrook.

3. My suspicion that Ann and possibly Robert would not be sorry to see me out of the way.

The truth that such a wish on their part would not be unnatural or incompatible with dutiful feelings, etc.

4. My provocation of her by hinting about the will, etc.

This is wrong, but it is difficult to find out what is going on in these children's heads without provoking some expression of feeling.

5. The possible injustice of suspecting her of interested motives.

This is a crime which I must at all cost avoid. I have too often behaved unjustly before.

Conclusion, that though I am not a good man, I need not fall into the vanity of supposing myself a monster. I have lived a futile and foolish life and done many things of which I have cause to be ashamed; but I must not allow myself the luxury of those romantic ecstasies by which an Alfred de Musset makes of his common and vulgar sins a special glory. They would be out of place in a retired English lawyer of seventy – one, suffering from a diseased heart.

Let me rather, in the way of my fathers, soberly resolve to do better. Let me reflect in Sara Jimson's own words:

> A miserable sinner is the devil's pet,
> Two sins got in one bed, a worser to beget.

41

And the very thought of Sara, as usual brings me peace. For that was Sara's quality. Not the passion of Lucy which transported the soul out of darkness; but the tranquil light, like that of an English morning, which disperses shadow out of all corners.

I remember Sara dropping a china sauceboat on the stone passage floor at Tolbrook. I was close to her. Indeed, my sudden approach had perhaps startled her into letting the china fall.

Both of us were struck dumb at this accident, for the boat was old Spode, a family heirloom. And indeed I was depressed all that evening, until going to the kitchen for some trifle and consulting with Sara about the disaster, I heard her say, 'It's bad enough, sir, indeed, but it might have been the tureen. I had that in my hand not two minutes before.'

The very idea shocked us, and I suggested that it might be better not to use the Spode tureen.

'No, indeed, I think we'd better not,' Sara said, 'except when the Bishop comes to dinner, or the baronet. And I'll have to do with one boat then. Though they say, indeed,

'Tis not so bad as judgement day,
And who can tell but that's today.'

And so, in a moment, by that country rhyme, I was brought to mind of the four last things, beside which even the tureen, unique as it was, seemed a trifle. I could smile at my fears for it. Though after all, if we feel no anxiety for a beautiful and unique treasure, we may want feelings which supply more important virtues.

Two more different women than Lucy and Sara never lived; Lucy, proud, contemptuous of the people, ignorant and strong willed; Sara, compliant and shrewd, a born intriguer. But both, born in neighbouring parishes, had the same power of bringing before one's eyes the pisgah sight of wider landscape than a provincial drawing-room or a London Square.

42

Ann suddenly appeared from the garden to ask me if I wanted tea. And as she seemed in very good spirits, I asked her if it was wise for her to be out in such a wind. 'It's not me but you,' she answered. 'How is the enemy behaving?' meaning my heart.

She then took my pulse and sent me to bed, saying that I had thoroughly upset myself. I obeyed without protest. For I still felt guilty before her. It is always dangerous to forget that in every human soul, however irreligious and irresponsible, God has planted some spark of altruism, some kind and unselfish feeling. I believe Ann to be, at bottom, a good creature, spoilt only by a bad education.

This impression seemed to acquire some support when two days later, she began to attend morning prayers. But I said nothing, and I soon discovered how wise I had been, in that prudence, when the young woman asked me if the prayer book had been changed since the days of *Mansfield Park*.

'So you come to prayers as a literary amusement?'

'No, uncle, I just wondered.'

I was about to tell her that if she wished only to amuse herself with antiquarian pursuits, I had rather she did not come at all. But I restrained myself. For I thought, 'Even if the mother only plays at the forms of religion, these very forms may save the child. As a bad priest can still be the means of grace – and dogma carry the living truth,' and I took occasion to say to her that Jane Austen had always been a favourite of mine. No writer of her time had shown so true a picture of English Christianity in its good sense and social dignity.

'I used to think *Pride and Prejudice* best,' she said, 'but now I like *Mansfield Park* better.'

'You are quite right – it has a far deeper and truer experience of life – it is a book for the adult.'

'Yes, I suppose I am growing up, or old, as well as fat and stupid.'

43

March weather like this was Lucy's delight; with all the moor streams full and roaring down the stones, and winds blowing up the clouds and the rain together, so that the clouds pour along the sky, and the rain showers sail along in mid air, like enormous cobwebs, at the same pace. The sky and Tolbrook river flow the same way, and you seem to stand between two rivers, one above and one below, whirling foam and glittering bubbles to the east; till they fall over the horizon together.

Bill came home on leave that year of Lucy's return and took us walking even in the pouring rain. Bill was now a captain of Engineers, and an expert on tropical barracks. In that time of little wars, he was seldom seen in England. And we had prepared to entertain him.

But it was Bill who entertained us from the first hour. 'Who's for the moor? I say, who's been planting daffodils along the drive, good idea, what?' Bill, who did not spend a week at home in two years, knew every corner of the house and would at once perceive the smallest change. 'Who chose the new carpet in the library – it won't stand the sun, you know. Blue is a very bad colour for the sun. I say, did the woodpeckers nest in Tenacre last year?'

He had grown almost as broad as he was tall, a square red-faced man with a ginger moustache and eyes like a retriever, pale brown and transparent, and now he had begun to show that thirst for exact knowledge which, as with many soldiers of his corps, grew all his life. Bill was always anxious to get to the bottom of things. Yet he would never read the books we recommended to him. He was suspicious of learned works. And I think he was impatient of reading. He fired a hundred questions at Lucy about the Benjamites, to which she answered but shortly.

'Scrubbing floors,' he said. 'Well, it's a new idea.' He pondered it. 'Probably a good idea.'

'You should try it, Bill.'

'Well, dammit, I'm Church of England. But if I were a Benjamite, I suppose it would do me good. Scrub for the glory of the Lord. Why not?'

'It nearly killed Lucy,' I said severely. 'Look at her.'

'I don't see much damage – blooming as ever.'

I was angry with Bill, because Lucy refused to recover weight, and still could not sleep. It had already been resolved that she must have a long change. My mother was to take her abroad.

But, Lucy, to my delight, had so contrived it, through my father, that she should go alone with me. For, as she said, 'Mother will worry about me all the time, but you will only worry about the tickets and the fleas.'

Our plans were already made, and Bill himself, as soon as he heard of them, at once forgot his sympathy with the Benjamites and strongly urged Lucy to go as soon as possible. He got out a map, sent for railway guides and organized the whole expedition. 'Pisa – I did Pisa between two trains on the way to Brindisi.'

'But I want to see a lot of Pisa,' I said.

'Every day at Pisa is a day off Rome. Take your choice – but according to the guide book, and after all, it's supposed to know what it is talking about, half a day is quite enough for Pisa.'

'We'll spend a week at Pisa if Tommy chooses,' Lucy said.

'A week – what on earth will you do for a week in Pisa?'

'Me, I don't care what I do. But Tommy wants to study the cathedral or something, or the place someone was starved to death in, and I'm not going to have you organizing him out of it.'

'All right, all right, just make up your minds, that's all.' Bill was always perfectly cheerful when his advice was rejected. He had the good temper of a modest man who does not set a high price upon his own ideas. And in twelve hours, that is, on the second day of his leave, he had already arranged our trip and written for tickets.

But on that afternoon, a very wet one, while I was recounting to my mother in the saloon how wet it had been and how wet we had got, I heard a strange man's voice from the hall. He was talking to my father. 'I'm afraid it sounds like Mister Brown,' my mother said.

'Why afraid,' I said, annoyed by her tone of resignation. 'If it's Brown, I'll kick him out.'

'Yes, but he must have come to take Lucy away.'

'He can't do that,' I said, lowering my trouser bottoms, which I had turned up to show her how muddy they were. My mother with her high-arched brows which expressed so much sadness, answered only, 'Lucy will do what she feels right.' She laid a slight emphasis on the she.

I went out into the hall and heard Brown say to my father that he had come to fetch his wife. My father stood at the bottom of the stairs. Lucy, still in her wet ulster, had retreated three or four steps upwards, but now stood half turned, looking down at the two men with a critical air.

My father did not seem to know how to answer, and remained silent, and as if mildly confused. But this appearance was habitual to my father, who had long lost all resemblance to a soldier, and was more like an old-fashioned country man, short, bow-legged, plump, with a bald head and a pink face, in which his pale blue eyes were like rain puddles, reflecting a pale spring sky, from the pink Devonshire earth. He had still a large moustache, but now snow-white and drooping over his mouth, it gave him a sheepish rather than a fierce look. After a long pause, he muttered to Brown something like, 'Er-r, yes, er-r, yes.'

Brown thought that he was not understood and said loudly, 'I said Colonel Wilcher – I've come to fetch my wife and no one has the right to keep her from me.'

Brown, as I say, was an ugly man, all body and no legs; not very short, but shaped like a dwarf. His head was extremely big, and he had the face of so many great orators and preachers, advocates and demagogues, a political face; short pugnacious nose, long upper lip, huge thin mouth, heavy but shallow chin, deeply cleft; hollow deepset eyes. He was as formidable as a gorilla, and seeing his threatening movement towards my father, I ran between them and said, 'But she has every right to stay away from you, Mr Brown.'

'Er-r,' my father said.

'No one is keeping wives from you, Mr Brown. I am the last man.' And then he turned to Lucy and said, 'If you don't want to go back, Lucy, stay here – you're free, you know. Do what you like.'

Although he spoke in his usual quiet voice, we knew by his flushed forehead that he was very angry. But I don't think this was why he had taken Lucy's side. Our father had two contradictory views about women; one, that a wife must cleave to her husband at all costs; the other, that a woman, as a living soul, should have all freedom. Many of his generation held the same contradiction; they were Christians as well as Whigs. But in practice this enabled them to use their judgement and my father plainly judged that Lucy had every reason to stay away from Brown.

To my surprise, Brown did not thunder at us, but turned to me and spoke in a reasonable and almost polite tone, 'Excuse me, young sir, but she is not free – she is under God's law like every one of us here; and by that law, she must serve Him and obey Him and humble herself before Him.'

'That does not mean before you, I suppose,' I said. I was in a great rage with Brown and wished to provoke him. My father said, 'Er-r no right to speak like that, Tom,' but then suddenly walked away into the back hall and left us.

Brown spoke to me in the same earnest way. 'No, young man, and if you know me, you would not make so blasphemous and foolish a charge. God knows I have tried to serve Him, in agony and sweat, and if I have failed, then I shall answer for it to Him. Lucy, I have come for you in His name.'

He called this upstairs, and turning, I saw that Lucy was walking away upon the upper landing. I was glad that she had escaped, because I could speak freely. I told Brown that he ought to be in gaol. He had ruined my sister's health and then betrayed her. 'Do you deny that you have taken another wife?'

'Not so,' he said 'Ella was given to me by the Lord and it was by His commandment that I took her to wife, and put Lucy away for a season. And it was His command, too, that she should serve Ella on her knees and be a servant to servants, that grace might come to her and that she might know Him at last, by His spirit.'

I answered that I took no interest in his cant and that he had better go. He would never see Lucy again.

I left him and went upstairs to Lucy. I was afraid that she would be put out. I found her on her knees, packing her box.

'What are you doing, Lucy?'

'Where is he?'

'I told him to go.'

'Run and stop him – tell him I'm coming.'

These words, so totally unexpected, threw me into confusion and anger. I felt that Lucy, as my mother said, was beyond us; an unreasonable creature. I said, 'You can't go back – what has happened to you?'

'Run along, Tommy, quickly – you'll miss him.'

'Are you afraid of him, or what?'

She looked up at me and I saw again the gypsy face, calmly impatient of the protected, the comfortable, the self-deceivers. 'You know very well he's right – I am a spoilt and selfish woman. I have always fought against God, and it's my plain duty to do His will and go back to the master.'

'And what about the rule – about God's command.'

'I don't need God's command. It's common sense.'

'And this woman Ella, are you going back to be her servant – it's revolting.'

'It depends on how you feel,' Lucy said. 'What right have I to be jealous and spiteful. I've known I was wrong the whole time. It has poisoned every day here. Silly old Doctor Mac thinks it's my innards are wrong, but it's not my bodily inside keeps me awake. It's God's anger and grief. Now, Tommy, please don't pester me with any more philosophy.'

Lucy always called my arguments with her, philosophy, and nothing made me more angry. She always had the power to enrage me, and now I raged at her and said that she was quite right about herself, she had always been spoilt and selfish.

'If you won't go for the master, I must go,' she said, and began to get up. But just then Brown himself walked in and said, 'Are you coming, Lucy?'

'I'm getting ready as fast as I can.'

'Do you not ask for forgiveness?'

I was told afterwards that Brown's disciples used to ask his forgiveness on their knees. But Lucy certainly did not do so then. She answered only,

'I shall ask when I've time.' Then she pointed at a pair of boots under the dressing table and said, 'Put those boots in the bag on the bed.'

Brown, to my surprise, obeyed her with the quick humble movement of a meek husband; and Lucy continued to order him about, in a very sharp manner. At last she got up and said, 'Now you can strap this trunk and mind you don't nip that petticoat.'

I perceived then once more how limited was my imagination, and how little I had understood either Brown or Lucy; how little Edward understood them either. And in truth, as I learnt at a later time from one who had been a Benjamite, Lucy was a terror to Brown; she treated him often with such cruel and bitter contempt that he would howl to be delivered from her. She had brought him publicly to tears on more than one occasion. It was no wonder, this observer said, that he preferred other women from the sect; such as the sheepish Ella, to whom he was a god.

'Why then,' I asked, 'did Brown take her back?'

'It was God's command,' said the ex-Benjamite, who was still, apparently, a Christian of the simplest order. 'I have been told he wrestled many days on his knees before he submitted, and I think we can see what God meant. For your sister was a great power – she gave him strength.'

However Lucy and Brown suffered by the other in their partnership, she was, at that time, sure of her duty; and the moment she had bowed herself to it, she was at peace. She went to papa and made him so affectionate and tender a farewell that the old man was in tears. And to me, when she said good-bye, she smiled once more in her old kindness, as she had never smiled during her visit, and tapped my cheek and said, 'Don't look so surprised, Tommy. It's all quite reasonable – as you will find out for yourself – or perhaps not.'

Even to Bill, she was charming. For Bill, who had been forgotten, suddenly appeared at the moment of farewell.

'Hullo, hullo,' he said, staring, 'where are you off to?'

'She's going back to her husband,' I said bitterly.

'And a good thing, too. She's quite right.'

'You know nothing about it, Bill.'

'Dammit, you don't want her to separate from her husband, do you?'

'No, of course not. Bill is all for a wife's duty, aren't you, Bill?' Lucy was laughing at him. 'Like all bachelors.'

'That's not my fault, marriage is marriage.' And he added, 'I've always meant to get married, you know.'

Lucy kissed him, avoiding his moustache, and said, 'Good-bye, Bill, bless you.'

'Good-bye, old dear. But you're doing the right thing. Sure of it.'

Brown was seen at the turn of the stairs, carrying a large trunk upon his back, like a professional porter. Lucy called out to him sharply, 'Careful – don't break the balusters.' She spoke as to a slave. But Bill, exclaiming, ran to take one handle of the trunk, and said, 'You mustn't do that, sir. Let me help you.' He was full of compliments and apologies, and when they had brought the trunk to the hall, he reproached the visitor. 'Shouldn't have done that, Mr Brown – a great effort – but you might have strained yourself.'

He laughed and straddled his legs like one talking, not perhaps to a bishop, but a dean; a reverend person who required special treatment, special protection, but not the highest kind of respect.

When the Browns had left and I understood that again Lucy had gone from me, I turned my anger upon Bill. I asked him if he had not seen the change in Lucy; if he understood how greatly she had suffered.

'Was she changed?' he asked. 'Well, we're all growing older. Poor old Lu. But she knows what she's doing all right. Trust Lu. She's always taken her own line, and she likes a stiff one.' He laughed and said, 'I'll bet she keeps him in order.'

I began to laugh at Bill, and the laugh still mixes with the memory of my bitterness when I cancelled the holiday with Lucy. I had looked forward to it with joyful hope so that even now I carry in my mind pictures of Rome and Venice, and only recollect with an effort that they were always pictures, anticipation, and never a reality. For I have never found time to go abroad. Indeed, I have never been out of England in peace-time, except once to Paris, Edinburgh, and Cardiff.

44

But I know why Lucy went back to her hard life and why Brown took her back although she was his scourge. They were both people of power; life ran in them with a primitive force and innocence. They were close to its springs as children are close, so that its experience, its loves, its wonders, its furies, its mysterious altruism, came to them as to children, like mysteries, and gave them neither peace nor time to fall into sloth and decadence.

No one can understand that private quality of life, the very spring of faith, who has not known it in himself or in some other, like Lucy or Brown or Sara, one of those whose life overflowed to all about them. I feel that energy in Robert, but not in Ann. And so I am afraid for her. She is listless and careless. Like other doctors, she will not follow a proper regimen. When she should be taking exercise she leans over the parlour fire, and when it is cold or wet, she goes out without a coat to the garden or the yards. And if she is not watched she will sit down on the stone seat.

According to Robert, it is especially dangerous for her to sit on stone, in case she should catch cold below, which would be very dangerous. But he says to me, 'It's no good me talking to her, uncle. She just naturally doesn't do anything I say. She'd die first. So if you would just take a look out of the window now and then and see that she's being reasonable.'

But when I tell Ann about the danger of sitting on cold stone, she answers: 'Robert is talking about cows. He is clever with cows, and with me, too – he has got his calf. But if I am to be a cow, he will have to give me some more legs, for I can't carry so much of myself on two.'

In fact, she has now got very big. It is astonishing that so small and thin a girl can be so big. And I feel very anxious for her. A fall, for instance, might be disastrous. I have seen so many families afflicted by a half-wit, and there is no more terrible misfortune. Yet it is risked a dozen times a day by the carelessness of young women like Ann. Or perhaps by something worse than carelessness.

'Just cussedness,' Robert tells me with his mild cheerful air. 'But women are cussed creatures, especially when they're that way. Trouble is, I've no time just now to run round her – so she's bent on going out alone and falling in some ditch.'

So I find myself with a new and heavy responsibility, which keeps me at the window nearly all day. And it is true that the girl is cussed. She dodges out when no one is looking, or hides from us in some corner. Just now I missed her, and it was ten minutes before I caught sight of her from the nursery window. She was among the little apple trees which Robert has planted in the rose garden, drifting about like a fallen leaf. And as usual without a coat. I seized a coat and hurried out to her. She looked at me with a bored, indifferent face.

'It's all right, uncle.'

'It's not all right. You're frozen – your face is blue.'

'I meant your baby is all right. I'm keeping it warm.'

'It's not my baby – it's Robert's, or you might say it is Edward's and Lucy's and Brown's. You don't realize perhaps that this baby of whom you are so careless ought to be a very remarkable man.'

'Or woman.'

'Or woman. I do not mind in the least. Another Lucy or another Brown – you couldn't have a better stock.'

'You don't mean Robert's father. I thought we both detested him.'

'What do you know about him?' I said, startled to think I had prejudiced her already against Brown. 'He was a great man, a great Englishman, in the line of Bunyan, Wesley, Booth. What a preacher.' And I began to explain to her the absolute necessity, to a living faith, of the new revelation. That such as Brown and Lucy, who can give the experience of grace, are the very founts of God's revelation, etc., and so on.

'And did he really make Aunt Lucy scrub the room for that other woman, and sleep on the floor when they were in bed together.'

'What did it matter? What is going on in your head now. Don't you see that Lucy enjoyed it.'

'Do you mean she was happy with that brute?' in a tone of mild surprise, which is as much as she has ever shown.

'Happy? Yes, of course, and you ought to be a very happy wife.'

'I'm sorry, uncle, but you know Robert and I never had many ideas in common.'

'What does that matter?' I asked her, quite horrified by her ignorance. 'Good gracious, what is going to happen to you. You didn't get married because you liked each other's ideas.'

But then Robert appeared suddenly beside us and said, 'Excuse me, uncle, but I think it's time this girl was taking her milk and malt. I don't want to spoil your walk, but the wind is a bit sharp this morning, and there's a lot of flu about.'

'Why not bring me my bucket here?' Ann said, 'the other calves get it put under their noses.'

And she began to talk about dairy bulls and milk records.

When the child speaks so, I cannot listen to her. For it seems to me that she is trying to hurt herself, as Robert takes pleasure in destroying the old trees in whose shade we used to play.

'Do you *want* to spoil your life?' I ask her. 'Of course it's none of my business. But why else do you say what you don't believe. Surely you know that you aren't a cow. Cows don't read pathology. Though I suppose it is just as well for them and for us.'

'But don't you think it will be better when marriage is arranged more on stock-breeding lines,' and so on. All very reasonable and scientific. And so, as Ann, I suspect, well knows, the more upsetting to me.

'Eugenics is the next great step forward,' she says, in her dreamy voice. 'Don't you think so, uncle?'

'A great improvement would be made, certainly,' I answer, 'for instance, in discouraging the mental defectives from marriage,' and so on. But all the time I am getting more and more upset, until at last I am finally driven from the field. I have to take refuge in my room, which is very cold this weather. Ann, to do her justice, wants me to have a fire, but I have never cared for fires in bedrooms. A needless and enervating luxury.

45

Ann would say that on the subject of marriage I am a sentimental old Victorian. But what is sentiment. It is only a feeling about life. Every age has its feelings, and if they are strong and good feelings, surely they are not disgraceful. And what Ann thinks a sentimental idea about women was only one part of a whole collection of feelings, which made up the spiritual life of a whole society.

When Bill came home in '89, and announced that he wanted to be married, he was not in love. His feeling was that he ought to be married.

Edward asked him if he had anyone in mind. But he answered, 'No, that's the problem.'

'Then why do you want to get married?'

'Well, old chap, I'm going on for thirty, and if I don't get married soon, I'll turn into a damned old bachelor. I'm a bit that way already.'

'What are the symptoms?'

'Why, getting finicky about things – and turning against the whole idea, too. In another two years I shan't be able to face matrimony at all.'

'Why should you?'

'Why should I?' Bill was surprised. 'What, not get married? Well, dash it, what would happen if no one got married.' He was indignant with us for taking the matter so lightly. 'And besides, it isn't natural to be single. But you know that as well as I do. And it's the happiest kind of life.'

'Why is it the happiest kind of life?' we asked him, for it was the rule to draw Bill out.

'Why,' said Bill, turning his indignant eyes upon us, 'because it's natural. But the trouble is, I thought I'd get six weeks to be hitched, but I only got a fortnight on account of this new fuss with the old Mahdi. So I shall only have time to look round. Are those nice girls, what's their name, still at Rose Hill?'

'You mean the Farrens. No, two married and one's dead. Good heavens, you didn't think of them, did you? There are dozens round here far better looking than the Farrens.'

'Yes, but they wouldn't have me in a fortnight, or their mothers wouldn't.'

'Of course they would,' Edward said. 'They'd marry anyone to get away from their mothers. And you're the hero of the day – the girls would draw lots for you.'

'What girls were you thinking of?'

'There's Amy Sprott for one – I saw her looking at you yesterday,' Edward said, using the first name that came into his head.

'Amy,' Bill said, 'what Amy?' frowning and trying to recollect the girl whom he had probably never seen.

'Daughter of old Sprott in the I.C.S.'

'Is she pretty?'

'Depends on your taste.'

'All the better if she isn't. The pretty ones are generally spoilt,' Bill said. 'Amy, Amy, I seem to remember an Amy, brown eyes and rather good at croquet – or was it tennis?'

'Blue eyes, but she does play croquet.'

'Oh, but she wouldn't have me – I mean not right away.'

'I wouldn't mind a bet on it.'

'It's not a thing to bet about.'

266

Bill said no more upon the matter until the next afternoon when there was a tennis party. By that time both Edward and I had forgotten the conversation of the day before. We were arranging matches and talking to the guests, especially two very pretty girls, the daughters of our neighbour Sir T. A. There was a special relation between us and these two girls, because it was known that the parents on both sides were anxious that one of us should marry one of them. Suddenly Bill drew me aside and asked which was Amy Sprott.

His gravity frightened me. For the first time I thought, 'Can he be serious. Suppose he really married that dumpling Amy Sprott, because of our stupid joke, and ruined his whole life.' 'My dear Bill,' I said, 'you don't need poor Amy. You have half a dozen of the prettiest and nicest girls in the county to flirt with.'

'Yes, but which is Amy?'

I laughed. 'But Bill, we were only joking about Amy.'

Bill looked at me with an absentminded stare which was a trick of his. It showed not anger, but obstinacy. 'Come on,' he said, 'introduce me.'

'She isn't here. I expect she stayed away because she knows she can't compete. Besides, she's fearfully shy. She's really only a schoolgirl, and gauche at that. Come.' I took his sleeve. 'I'll introduce you to a really charming girl.' Bill jerked away his sleeve. Now he was angered. He said sharply, 'I wish you'd mind your own business, Tommy. Can't I choose my own friends?'

'But you've never seen Amy in your life. Edward was pulling your leg.'

'Kindly shut up and put your silly head in a basket.' He walked off, furious. And I saw him speak to Edward, who at once sent off a note to the vicarage. Amy was staying there with her uncle, for her father was in India. Half an hour later, too late for tea, we saw her approaching, with the old gentleman, from the drive. The whole party gazed at her, in her dowdy cotton frock, like a servant's print, and a straw hat which was visibly her school hat with a new ribbon. The girl was crimson with heat and embarrassment.

'Is that Miss Sprott?' Bill asked. He jumped up, walked across the ground and presented himself. He then spoke to the uncle, who nodded several times, and came towards us with a benevolent smile. 'So you wanted to see me, Mr Wilcher,' he said to Edward.

Edward, much amused by Bill's strategy, invented a question about the political feeling in the village. For the Gladstone government, which we all supported, was then in opposition.

We were gazing at Bill. He spoke to the girl, and we saw her start and blush and stare. She came quickly towards her uncle. But Bill, following at her elbow, continued to speak.

She was now close to us, and even our visitors noticed that something strange was happening. As for me, I have never seen a more candid expression upon a girl's face, the round red face of a countrified miss which I had thought so inexpressive of anything but the crudest feelings – joy, greed, embarrassment. You could see that she was amazed and unbelieving, and yet she was saying to herself, 'But perhaps it is true, perhaps it could happen like this.'

After all, if Bill, at thirty, having lived in the service from eighteen, had an idea of a world as simple and clear as the field-service book; the girl, from the convent of an English school, was not much more wise. Bill continued to speak with energy and passion. Bill was never short of words. The girl hesitated, stopped, and for a moment stood on one foot. It was the pivot of her life. She turned suddenly and walked away from her uncle, with Bill beside her. The engagement was announced the same evening, and they were married by special licence four days later.

This was no romantic freak. To Amy and Bill, I am sure, it was the common thing. To simple-minded persons, miracles appear like nature. In the same way, they expected to be happy, to love one another, etc., and therefore they did so.

46

'A kind of faith cure,' Ann said to me, and I thought I must have been speaking aloud.

'I don't know what you would call it.' But I thought 'Not a cure for anything. It was the whole idea of an age, and how could I convey that, or its strength. For only the idea can fight against the cruelty of fate. It is in some strong well-founded idea that men and women, and whole nations, float as in a ship over the utmost violence of chance and time.'

'It was very romantic,' Ann said in her voice of a small girl who has a pain and knows that she mustn't eat cake.

'They were not a sentimental couple. Their arguments were a family joke. But they were devoted all their lives.'

'Yes, I suppose romantic people could go on being happy – it was a kind of hallucination.'

'You speak as if your uncles and aunts had been weak in the head.'

'Oh, no, but Aunt Lucy and Uncle Bill do seem a little mad – with a good kind of madness.'

'You think we're all mad. You think me mad.'

'Never, uncle. You are much too clever at getting your own way.'

I was astonished. 'So you think me cunning. Lunatics are famous for their cunning.'

'Well, look. Robert meant to go back to Brazil, but here he is tied to Tolbrook. And I meant to be a distinguished pathologist, and here I am, a silly little wife with a big tummy, also tied to Tolbrook.'

'And I did all this – why, it's perfectly ridiculous.'

'Perhaps you didn't know you were doing it. You only suggested that I should see Robert again if we came to Tolbrook. And you knew I had fallen for his nice eyes. And then you happened to catch us together. And then you gave Robert all these new toys to play with – a little at a time. Like giving cut wool to a kitten till it's quite tied up. And now you have got the baby you wanted and you have decided that it's going to be an Edward or a Lucy.'

'What nonsense, what nonsense. Though these are good English names. And I suppose, if you have a son, he will be in the eldest line, and they are all Edwards.'

For it was true that I had sometimes hoped for another Lucy or Edward. And I had perhaps shown my preference to Ann.

'But I'm not blaming you, uncle, for wanting the family to go on. The family is like you, isn't it, and of course you want to go on.'

'Loftus and Blanche are carrying the family on, with their son.'

'I'm not saying you meant to do all this, you know,' the girl said, as if I needed assurance, and she began to talk about the unconscious will, and so on; unpacking some of her German boxes. 'You know,' she said, 'I didn't think I meant to marry Robert, and yet I was mad to get him. I was quite in despair until you suggested that he might be at Tolbrook.'

For a moment she made my head turn. Everything began to dissolve out of its familiar shape into a mysterious twilight like a witch night under summer lightning.

But I knew very well the danger of such notions to an old man. It was enough to make me mad. I answered, therefore, that she was talking nonsense.

'All this hair-splitting between a man's will and his deed leads from one piece of nonsense to another. How can you tell what anyone's intentions are except by his acts.'

'I was thinking of acts. I know how I ran after Robert. It's frightful to think how scandalously I behaved. Poor Robert. I should be sorry for him if it weren't Robert. How we have taken him in, the pair of us.'

'Don't say such things. How can you tell what we did or what Robert himself wanted. Who can look into others' motives. Look at your own achievement – that is plain enough. And look at Robert's achievement.'

Ann, who was as usual dawdling over the fire, suggested that I had not yet seen all Robert's destruction.

'What has he destroyed?'

'You haven't been to Tenacre lately, have you?'

'But I am all for Robert's improvements at Tenacre. I thought his idea of the circus engine a stroke of genius.'

'Well, you kept him off the trees here, and I'm glad – I don't want him to spoil our view.'

'We mustn't get too fond of the view, as you call it – we have to move with the times. Or the time will move us. And modern agriculture shows a very valuable and interesting development. I'm all for the machine.'

'But then,' Ann said, 'you're like me – you don't like horses,' the kind of remark that always angers me. 'Why do you do the devil's work Ann – trying to make me believe that there is nothing in the world but selfishness and self-seeking.'

And the girl answered me, apparently in all sincerity, 'A world like that might be rather restful.' A remark that drove me from her, in fear as well as anger. An abominable remark that tunnels like some devil's miner, into the very ground of hope and love, to blow all up.

It kept me awake half the night, in wonder at this devil's power; and terror of his persistence, his cunning. 'But damn it all,' I say, 'you old fool, you know there is love, there is hope, there is faith. Does not everything in this house say to you "God is".'

47

The small round-topped windows of my room are the last relic, so they say, of a priory whose ruins are built into this wing. They are perhaps seven hundred years old. The initials, W.A.W., cut by Bill in the keystone on the left, are already filled with paint, but from my bed I can see the faint shades of some of the downstrokes. I cannot remember why Bill and Amy chose this room, which was no longer the children's sickroom, and not yet my bedroom. But it was a favourite room with all of us when we came home, because it had a wide view and stood next the upper closet where there was a hot-water tap. And near the only bathroom.

Amy was seventeen at the time of her marriage in '89, Bill twenty-eight. Edward said that Amy had not yet taught herself to use Bill's christian name before he was once more on the sea. She was engaged on Tuesday, married on the next Saturday, alone by Tuesday week, and a mother before she saw her husband again, three years later.

Bill was the joke of the family, but now I do not laugh at him. I think now, with surprise, that he was the best of us and that we laughed at him and at Amy, because we could not see them in truth or know them as they were. It was a fashion to make a joke of them, and I followed the fashion all my life.

Bill and Amy had the unbreakable faith of children who come home every day to a new world; and from that faith, they looked out, as monks once looked from this room, at the world as a spectacle. They did not need to think of themselves, for they knew exactly their purpose and their due. So, even on the last day of his leave, Bill spent half the night mending his mother's work-box, and Amy did not protest. She might not see him again for years, but she had undertaken the venture of Bill's wife. They were not a sentimental couple. Lucy used to say that when Bill left Amy for the first time, her last words, called after the railway carriage, through her tears, were, 'Where did you leave my bicycle pump.' And that Bill answered at the top of his voice, 'Don't forget you're punctured behind.'

We were already laughing at Amy, as well as Bill, and we took her grief very lightly. I can remember Edward remarking that her swollen eyes and pink nose made her look like a sucking pig. 'She only needs a good brown sauce and she would be quite presentable at the dinner table.'

Yet Amy became a true member of the family. When she was at Tolbrook it was always the cry, 'Where's Amy?' She was sent on all parish errands, and answered for everybody's buttons. If anything were lost, broken, torn or forgotten, Amy was called to account. The very servants would say of any loss or any omission, 'I thought it was Mrs William, mam, who was looking after it.' And this seemed reasonable and proper to Amy herself, who spent all day running up and down stairs, even when she was within a week of her time. She was used, I suppose, to the position of niece in houses where her presence was always a trouble or deprivation to others; where there were questions every day, whether she should be left out of a party to which the children of the house were invited, or if she could be asked to give up her bed for some valued visitor, and to sleep on a sofa.

Bill, when they were at home together, used to make the same demands upon her. Bill's shouts for Amy were louder than any others. On the other hand, he too was always busy with small tasks; he organized picnics, otter hunts, badger digs, rabbit shoots; he made Amy climb the local tors or bathe in the moor streams, which turned her nose so red that he would complain of it, 'Look at Amy's nose. But she won't do anything about it. I don't believe she's taken a single cold bath since I've been away. Her circulation is disgraceful.'

Amy, for her part, would try, without success, to make Bill wear mufflers and overcoats, which he detested. Both were stubborn and dogmatic. Bill was low church, Amy high church, and they scorned each other's services. Bill would say loudly that Amy's parsons in petticoats could only catch women, who were idiots about religion; and Amy would answer that the parish church always sent her to sleep and gave her a crick in her ribs.

'You can't have a crick in your ribs. Don't you know ribs don't bend,' Bill would answer,

'I'm sure mine do.'

'And you call yourself a red cross nurse.'

'Well, there's a special bandage for broken ribs.'

'But that doesn't prove that ribs have joints.'

'I haven't done the joints, but ribs must join on somewhere.'

'Listen to that,' Bill would cry. 'Well, damn it all. I give you up, Amy. You'd break the heart of a brass elephant. I'll never argue with you again – that I'll swear.' But in three minutes he was arguing with her again. Bill lost his temper with Amy twenty times a day, and gave up for ever; but they never quarrelled. They were inseparable on leave, and one was never seen without the other.

I laughed at them when they were alive, but they always brought new energy to Tolbrook. Lucy came here only to escape from her life; but Bill, arriving from China or Lagos with silk robes or spears which no one wanted, was always like a small boy coming for his holidays. He had the same projects, impossible to fulfil; the same eagerness for news; and he had a small boy's astonished and aggrieved air when he discovered that we had not been shooting or fishing or picnicking lately and had not formed any plans for shoots or picnics. He made us see what was going on under our noses. 'I say, what a gorgeous morning. What about the moor? I say, did you ever see such a sky. Quick – it's fading already.'

When, on these mornings, the window arches of the old cell frame a cold spring sky and the first buds on the great lime, I think, 'The medieval monks who looked out of these windows at sky and buds did not see them with clearer eyes than Bill's.' Both looked out from a security and faith as strong as a child's surrounded by the unseen care of its mother. Bill's cry of 'I say, look at this, look at that,' had the same medieval quality, of 'Loud sing Cuckoo', that true lyric; which is a cry of delight and welcome.

The homeless priest with no part in this world, the homeless soldier, without inheritance, had the same innocence, which did not even know its own happiness.

Bill's delighted 'I say', and the monk's song, make my heart beat. I find spring through memories and the ideas of a scholar. The life through the tradition. This morning, now that Ann has pulled my curtain, I see a sky as pale as Bill's eyes, or Ann's eyes, and three clouds like sheep in full fleece moving so slowly that they seem still to a single glance.

Ann has closed my windows. But the frames are loose and the gusts, which make the lime buds swing, blow through, as cold as the sky and quick with salt.

All about Tolbrook in this south-west country, March has always smelt of salt. Its sky has the translucency of an ocean sky where there is no dust, and all the birds are as white as foam. Gulls fly over our furrows all the year, but especially now, when the winds roll them about in the air like small boats in an offing.

When I look back again at the window the three clouds have jumped up towards the left-hand bow of the frame and the house seems to rock beneath me like a ship. I, eating breakfast in bed, and always the worst of sailors, feel as if I were at sea, as if England itself were afloat beneath me on its four waves, and making the voyage of its history through a perpetual sea spring.

> Faithful to ancient ways, the English crew
> Spread old patched sails, to seek for something new.

The monk, in his sleepy routine, who seduced my weakness just now, where is he? A new vigorous generation snatched his peace away; the generation of my ancestors, who made a farmshed of his chapel and bore their half-pagan children in his holy cell. Who once more pulled up England's anchor and set her afloat on the unmapped oceans of the West. Why do I ever forget that the glory of my land is also the secret of youth, to see at every sunrise, a new horizon. Why do I forget that every day is a new landfall in a foreign land, among strangers. For even this Ann, this Robert, are so changed in a single night, that I must learn them again in the morning. And England wakes every day to forty million strangers, to thousands of millions who beat past her, as deaf and blind as the waves. She is the true flying Dutchman. 'O Sealand, where do you travel on this voyage without a port, through countless sunfalls and day springs, with the wind in your face. And in your eyes, the blue of infinity, the changing clouds, the gull whose only home is air and ocean.

'As their feathers glitter with the crystal salt, so do your buds. The clouds light upon the rollers of your downs like Mother Carey's chickens, when they shut-to their wings on an Atlantic comber.

'Your ploughmen sight their first furrow on a lighthouse, and roll upon their sea legs like sailors. Your sailors, ploughing the sea for a crop of salted babies; born under the spray of a thousand bare-walled ports, dream of steeples like masts and church towers with fighting tops. Your bells, in this light air, sing like a ship's bell under the hand of a quartermaster, on urgent summons to duty, to watchfulness,' etc. A favourite quotation of mine, but on the other hand the proper conduct of a ship requires a certain discipline, an order.

48

'Robert thinks there's going to be a war, uncle.' Ann, having brought my breakfast, balanced herself carefully on a chair.

'Does he mean in China?'

'No, he thinks Germany means to make war. Hitler, he says, is planning a war because we are so weak.'

'Who is Hitler?'

'Don't you read your *Times*, uncle?'

'No, I haven't read the papers for a very long time. I'm too busy.'

'Robert would like to go off to Brazil before another war. He says this country is finished – it's too soft.'

'What do you say?'

'I think we may be a little too civilized for war, but perhaps that is what Robert means.'

'You couldn't go to Brazil with a young baby.'

'Robert thinks the baby a good reason to take me abroad.'

'Brazil would not suit you at all. It is very hot; and all this talk about Germany's revenge is chatter. Germany is sick of war since her defeat.'

'But Germany does rather believe in war, doesn't she?'

'So did France until eighteen-seventy; that cured her of swashbuckling.'

'The German general staff is said to be making an enormous air force.'

'When I was a young man we all expected war with France. It took us a long time to realize that France was tired of war. I remember that your Uncle Bill, before he was married, spent his leaves bicycling in France and studying the railway system and the ports. And he made your Aunt Amy learn French, so that she could come with him on his next leave. That is to say, he tried to teach her. He used to give her lessons. I can remember her walking up and down the library, with a distracted look, saying over and over again a long list of words beginning:

Wagon – railway truck.

Wagon-écurie – horse box.

Wagon-étable – cattle truck.

Wagon-frein – brake van.

'I would examine her and she always broke down. She would say to me in despair, "I'll never know it – he'll be furious." *He* was Bill; she was shy of calling him Bill to us. But it never struck her that learning military French was an odd way to spend time during a nine-day honeymoon. She was used, I suppose, to the idea of school life, and quite prepared to find in Bill a severe master.

'Yet, as I noticed, although she worshipped Bill, and seemed so submissive to him, she paid very little attention to his wrath when she failed in her French words. She would look at him with a round, anxious eye and a flushed face while he stormed at her, and say, "Your tie is crooked."'

'Have you finished breakfast, uncle?'

I thanked her and she took my tray. But on the way to the door, she perceived that her mind had wandered, and she said, 'So you think we are quite safe from Hitler.'

'I think the Germans would hate another war.'

'Which chair did you say was the nursing chair, uncle?'

'The little mahogany chair with the legs cut short, and the broken back.'

'I must put it back in the nursery.' She went out and I was glad to be alone. For I had not before remembered Amy so well, and I felt that I had done her great injustice in her life.

49

It is strange to see how men's and women's lives follow their own separate courses in the midst of happy marriages. They are like two streams of different colour, which can always be distinguished even in the same river. Perhaps at the first rushing together, they seem to be one, but it is merely a single confusion. And almost at once the two currents reappear, crossing and recrossing in a continuous change of pattern, but always distinct. Amy's own life continued from the day of her marriage. Even in those few days while Bill could stay with her, she was asking his advice about her winter coat; and deciding for herself how she would arrange her room, with Bill's books on one wall and her Indian embroidery panel on the other. When Bill went away, she wept for two days, but at the same time made herself new curtains for her room. I can see her now on the evening of Bill's departure. She is sitting in a dark corner of the little dining-room, the tears in her lashes, discussing with my mother the best colour for a bedspread.

'Blue is so cold for an east room,' my mother says.

'It always looks clean.'

'It won't match your pink curtains.' My mother hated a clash of colour.

'Blue is really almost my favourite colour. But I don't know whether he likes blue,' with a break in her voice.

'Bill; no, I don't think he does. He didn't like your blue silk, did he?'

Then there is a long pause while Amy struggles with her tears.

At last she says with a gasp like a sob, 'Yes, I think I'll have blue.'

Amy was pregnant for three months before she knew what was wrong with her. It was then discovered only because she caught influenza, and when the doctor came to see her she asked him about a lump in her inside. According to the family story, when the doctor questioned her and told her that she was pregnant, she answered, 'Oh, it can't be that – my husband is in Africa.' She had some idea that a baby could be hatched only by a continuous warmth of closeness.

Yet she showed neither surprise nor excitement. She only stopped doing her French exercises, and began to sew baby clothes.

Amy, without mother or any relation in England save the old vicar and two maiden aunts in Yorkshire, was ignorant even for a girl of those days.

But her ignorance did not oppress her. She advanced through life like an explorer through unknown country, ready for anything; not in conceit of herself, but in the belief which says, 'It's all happened before, so it can't be so terrible.' She expressed that very creed to my mother, before her lying-in. My mother wished to encourage the child, not yet eighteen, and said that she was sure everything would go well with Doctor Maccurdy.

'Oh, yes,' Amy said placidly, 'and I suppose it's all arranged for inside.'

Amy took very little interest in her inside. She left it to God, who, in her view, had constructed it. But what was strange in those first three months before she knew what was happening to her, she visibly changed from a schoolgirl, playing at various pastimes, into a woman of purpose. What Amy's purpose was, I do not know, and she did not know any more than a bird, who begins, at certain times of year, to make certain arrangements; but even her walk and her expression were different while she went about the small trifling tasks which seemed to fill her time. It was not perceived till long afterwards, that in that first year she had somehow procured savings, a bank balance, an investment in Consols, an extensive knowledge of private schools, taking sole charge of children, a steamer trunk of a new pattern from America, and a complete set of clothes suitable for the tropics. It was found also that she had almost complete control of Bill's finances, received most of his pay, and kept careful account of his liabilities.

50

Amy's son was born suddenly in May. The doctor was late, and the girl had no chloroform – she suffered extremely. But when I saw her afterwards, her first remark was, 'That went off very luckily, didn't it? I was sure it was going to be a daughter.'

'But you wanted a son.'

'Of course I did. That's why I was sure it wouldn't be. And it worked beautifully. And they're getting the blue bows this afternoon.'

'Didn't you have some of both kinds ready?'

'Oh, that wouldn't have done at all. You have to be absolutely sure, or it doesn't work. I didn't even choose a name, but, of course, it must be William.'

Amy was a devoted mother; but again, in her own way. An early question of hers to my mother was, 'How young do you smack them?' I remember her as she sat nursing her baby, and looking down upon it with an expression I haven't seen for many years; a smile of detached calm amusement, as if the baby were a joke, of good quality, but too familiar for laughter. And even as I look, her hair becomes white, her broad cheeks darken; she is an old woman, looking, with exactly the same smile, at another baby, whom I do not recognize, a small sickly creature with bluish skin and eyes so pale that one cannot call them grey or blue. This baby gazes upwards with a fixed look of grave curiosity.

Who is it? It could not be Amy's youngest, who died at three of Malta fever.

I went to look at the old screen, close stuck with family photographs, which once stood in the nursery, and now in the attic. It was not there, but as I went back along the corridor I was surprised to see it once more in the nursery. Workmen had been employed there for the last week, their trestles and buckets barred half the doorway. But their work was finished, and alone in the middle of the room stood the nurse's old chair, the old screen and the old high chair, consisting of a small armchair standing on a table, which all of us had used. I wondered where Ann had found it; and by what luck she had chanced upon a nursery wallpaper so like that of my childhood. I hunted the screen for Amy. Here was my mother in her furs, beautiful and sad; and I thought, 'She has the look of an exile who can never go back, the one who has been turned out of paradise. All exiles, whatever they were at home, have the same look of angels deprived. As if exile itself refined the soul by giving it the love that can never be gratified.' But here next her is Edward in an incredible bowler and a three-inch collar, which makes him look almost foolish. Here is Bill in uniform, with his moustache curled up at the ends. That was Amy's doing. She always admired the Kaiser, because of his blue eyes and because he was the Queen's grandson. And gradually she changed Bill's moustache from a set of bristles to something a little like the Kaiser's. And here is Edward again, old and worn, with his young second wife beside him, and in his arms the thin little baby, whom I saw just now in Amy's lap; Ann, in her christening robe. And here is Amy at last, in a corner, between Heenan, the prize fighter, and Ellen Terry. She is in a form I had utterly forgotten; very young with round, frightened eyes, and balanced on her head an enormous hat covered with ostrich feathers. Even I can tell that she is dressed in the most fashionable bad taste. Bill is beside her in a cap three sizes too small, and his eyes jumping out of his head. He glares as if to say, 'How dare you look at this lady. She's my wife.' It was taken on their three-day wedding trip at Torquay.

But Amy's look pierces me. It says, 'Why do you laugh at me?' I had forgotten that look. But I remember how, one evening after we had all been laughing at one of her unexpected remarks, at bed-time when I went to get my candle in the hall and found her there, she asked me, 'What were you laughing at?'

'Nothing,' I said. 'A family joke.' I could see that she was hurt and bewildered. And yet I went upstairs still laughing within myself, and it is not till now that I perceive our cruelty.

'Do you recognize the wallpaper, uncle?' Ann's voice asked me. She was standing at my elbow, but I did not answer her.

'We found some of the old original under the whitewash and they still had the pattern – at least they had the blocks and printed me a few lengths. Robert thought I was being extravagant, but I said it was a fancy. Fancies are often useful when I want to get my own way.'

I took care not to answer her in case Amy should disappear from my memory, and I remained silent while Ann decided that I ought to go to bed, and put me to bed. I can tell that she thinks me madder, and she is even anxious about me, perhaps in case I am about to become violent and murder her. But I can't waste time upon this hypocrisy of trying to appear rational. I leave that to younger people.

I am an old man, and I have not much longer at Tolbrook. This is April, and before next April I shall have left for ever. I want to use every moment of these last months at home with those I love, with Lucy and Amy, Bill and Edward.

51

In spite of all my precautions, when at last I was left alone in the dark, I had lost touch with Amy. I couldn't even recall the shape of her face, or the dressing of her white hair. Yet her presence was close, and all night, while I dozed or waked, I felt as if she were in the house, upon one of her long visits.

'My dear,' I thought, 'if you were here and I could see you, I should ask you to forgive me – or perhaps you would not understand such a request. It might frighten you after all these years when our relations had been established in a certain form. You knew me even longer than you knew Bill. Yes, long before.' Then to my surprise I thought I saw Amy standing before me, not as an old white-haired woman, but as the young rosy, too rosy and too plump young girl, who had once romped with me at Christmas parties, until her nose and her forehead shone like apples. She was laughing at me in a very unconstrained manner, and I remembered how once I had kissed her in a forfeit and suddenly felt an excitement, and I had thought for one moment 'I should like her very much for a wife,' and in the next, 'you might as well marry any plump milkmaid within five miles and get tired of her in a fortnight.'

'Was I a fool, Amy?' I asked, 'or would you have been the same wife to me as to Bill. For he was noble and simple, and he expected a great deal from women; and I was suspicious and divided and asked nothing from anybody. I was shy and ignorant of women, too, like all sensualists, and Bill was shy of nobody and nothing. How much did Bill make your soul, or how much did the common soul of you and Bill arise from some accidental fitting together of your natures?'

The fat young girl looked at me and put out her lips as if to invite a kiss. Her little blue eyes were full of Amy's gaiety. Old as I am, I was moved and attracted by that gesture, always charming when it is good-natured; I put out my arms. But they were held back, and as I struggled I was annoyed and also I felt confused, guilty, as if I had been caught in some shameful act. Amy was still laughing, but her face had disappeared and gradually I perceived that I was struggling with my bedclothes and that some woman, not Amy, was talking in a soft voice outside my door. Her voice had that wavering rapid beat of a woman's who feels a desire to laugh or cry.

I put my hand under my pillows and rang my father's repeater. It was half-past six. I opened my eyes and saw that the room was full of light.

The chatter of the maids outside my door made me suspect that perhaps Ann had sent already for an asylum van, and that I was locked into my room. 'She would be quite justified,' I thought, 'by my extraordinary behaviour last night when I would not speak to her or even look at her.' I got up carefully to try the door, and found it locked. This startled me so greatly that I felt extremely faint and hardly succeeded in reaching my bed.

But then immediately a terrible pressure departed from my blood. A pressure that I had not noticed before, and such peace came upon me that I was astonished. I thought, 'I can do nothing more – everything is settled.'

52

Such was my sense of peace while I waited for the asylum van to take me to that home of rest, that I was resentful when suddenly Robert came in.

'Are you all right, uncle?'

'Of course I'm all right. You are up very early.'

'No, I always get up at five. But I've been kept in this morning because Ann's pains have started and the doctor hasn't come yet. I think you'd better take your medicine. You look rather blue – what does Ann give you?'

At these words I felt that excitement which comes to me before a struggle. I knew that I should have to fight this child's battles.

'The yellow bottle. Supposing it is a son, Robert, I suppose it ought to be an Edward. As Ann is your Uncle Edward's only representative.'

Robert said nothing and left the room. I saw that he would object to the name Edward. Now the drug began to take effect and I felt strong. I could not remain still. Nothing prevented me, in Ann's absence, from doing what I liked, and I got up and dressed and hurried out to obtain news and to find Robert. But when I discovered him in the yard repairing a tractor, he received me in an indifferent manner.

'Hullo, uncle, has the doctor come yet?'

'No, he hasn't come yet, and I'm sure Ann would like to see you. Has she talked to you about names?'

'No, I must go and see her. I'll go in as soon as I've found out whether this damn thing is going to let us down in harvest when it's too late to do anything.'

But, in fact, when the baby was born, he was three miles away at a blacksmith's. I myself was the first to see Ann's son. He was a disappointment to me; red faced, with black tufts of hair. Exactly like myself as a child. But his eyes were blue, and I thought, 'Perhaps his second hair will be lighter, and babies' noses are always unpredictable.'

'Well, uncle, what do you say. I have given you an heir.'

Ann spoke as if laughing at me, but I was surprised to hear her speak. She was lying flat on the bed, so thin-cheeked and white that I was reminded of the thin baby in Amy's lap.

'Yes,' I thought, going out to find Robert, 'there is no doubt that the baby in Amy's lap is Ann. But when did Amy nurse Ann. When Ann was born, in 1910, Amy was in India. And she came to Tolbrook only in the next year. Edward and his wife had then gone away.'

The problem agitated me during my drive to the forge, where I found Robert waiting his turn until a horse could be shod.

'Ann has a son,' I told him, 'his eyes are like his grandfather's, but his hair, at present is dark.'

'And how's Ann?'

I had forgotten to ask after Ann, but I assured the boy that she seemed very well. 'Good enough,' he said, 'I'll be there in no time. I'd have been there before if it hadn't come so quick. Trouble is, this is about the busiest time for me, and I don't want anything to go wrong with the first corn harvest. It's a pity Ann couldn't have put off the baby for a month or two, till after the apples, anyhow.'

I ventured to suggest that Ann might be expecting to see him, but he answered only, 'There's one good thing about Ann – she's not so much of a sentimental girl. She'll understand I just couldn't be round the whole time. And I couldn't lose my place now when I've been waiting more than half an hour.'

So we waited till the horse was shod and then Robert gave directions to the smith about the mending of a drawbar. 'Sorry, uncle,' he said, 'but next week half the farmers round will be sending in their binders and tractors for new parts, and if I waited till then, I might as well wait till next year.'

At last he was ready and took his seat beside me in the old motor which was used for farm work. 'I remember that from the old times,' he said, 'when I used to see the road outside the smithy blocked up all harvest with these old cutters waiting repairs and horses wanting shoes. I always said if I had a farm I wouldn't stand in that row and look like a fool while the wise virgins were getting their stuff into the threshing yard.'

'You've done good work here, Robert,' and then I spoke of the need to choose a name for the boy, and to give some thought to it.

'A small point,' I said, 'but sometimes more important to a child than people may think.'

'Just what I tell Ann,' Robert said, to my surprise and pleasure. 'If I'd been called William, I might be a soldier now, like Uncle Bill.'

'Your Uncle Edward had great qualities.'

'Yay, Ann's set on Edward. But I seem to fancy my own father's name, Mathias.'

'That's not a family name.'

'Well, it's not a Wilcher name, but it's a Brown name.'

'But the boy is more Wilcher than Brown. And suppose he was to inherit Tolbrook some day – just supposing it. How would he feel with a name like Mathias?'

Robert said no more. He always had that bad habit of breaking off an argument as if he did not care what anyone might say. He had made up his own mind.

He stopped the car to shut a gate, and I asked him, 'Where are we?' For I could not recognize the fields.

'Tenacre.'

I got out of the car to look for Tenacre – but saw only a large field extending over the top of the low hills which made the horizon. I could not find a single landmark. 'Where is lover's lane where you and your mother used to walk on your way to church, and where the woodpeckers nested every year?'

'Well, uncle, all those beeches and elms were pretty rotten, and we wanted to put the fields together, so we grubbed the hedges. I thought you knew. It was done last October, this field is fifty acres now and goes right down to the main road. We put in potatoes because it was too rough for roots. Not too good for wheat either. But all it wants is a little feeding – a ley next year and more stock.'

I looked at the new broad landscape in front of me. Every landmark was gone. Not only the winding farm lane with its great trees, the beauty of this valley, but the very shape of the ground, once marked by the curve of hedge and shrub.

I saw that the boy had tricked me. But I said to myself, 'There's nothing to be done. Nothing is to be gained by anger. On the other hand, I can still save something by diplomacy, by tact.' So I said, 'It's a wonderful change – you have certainly done great things here.'

'Well, uncle, I've done only just what I could to get the place going again. I won't say it was run down a bit, I'll say it was so dead you could smell it. And from what the old chaps tell me, it hasn't been a real going concern since grandad's time. He cut some drains and built some cottages – and he made the first tenacre out of a couple of yards and a bit of moor.'

'Yes, yes,' I smiled and looked about me at the strange raw landscape. 'A fine piece of work. Edward would have liked it. He was all for modern methods,' and I was going to mention the name again, and perhaps to make a definite proposal for a legacy to any Wilcher grandchild carrying Edward's name, when I began to feel very queer. It was as though the pain of loss kept on growing all the time in my heart. I paid no attention to it. I did not allow myself to think of that loss, but it kept on growing.

It was true, of course, that I had suffered a catastrophe far beyond Robert's imagination. A country landscape is not like a piece of town, where the streets seem to say, 'We are thoroughfares, do not linger here.' And the houses, 'We are conveniences, don't stay too long. Somebody else is waiting.' Here every field and hedge was an invitation to pleasure, not only of memory but of sight, of interest. In lover's lane, now abolished, gener-ations of mothers had seen their daughters courting. For though it was a private lane, gated at both ends, the great trees made it a favourite tryst as far as the village. And all these trees, banks and paths, said to every passer, 'Wait and you shall enjoy us.' A great loss; and though I turned my mind from it, it swelled up of itself till suddenly, to my dismay and horror, I perceived that my heart was affected. I was going to faint.

I was obliged to turn to the car, but I could not find the door or climb into it, and Robert was alarmed. 'Where's that bottle Ann gives you?'

Much to my surprise, there was a little phial secured by a piece of elastic sewn to my pocket lining. Robert drew it out and put it to my lips. I swallowed the bitter contents, but they seemed to have no immediate effects. My breast was contracted by a pain like screws clamped on my heart. My eyes saw darkness and my head was full of fiery confusion. Robert helped me into the car and made me lie at full length across the back seats. He appeared greatly concerned, and said several times, 'You know, uncle, I wouldn't have anything happen to you.'

Robert was fond of me, I knew, a good-natured boy. But an obstinate one. And now it seemed that he would win this battle, by the treachery of my miserable heart.

But I thought, 'It is my own fault. Haven't I known all my life that it was folly to give my affections to sticks and stones and all that helpless hopeless tribe,' etc., etc. It was all very well to philosophize, but there was that great swelling pain in my breast which I could not get rid of. It was as though the very spirit of those murdered trees had come to revenge themselves upon me.

Not upon Robert, you notice. Because they could not enter into that alien soul. It is only our nearest and dearest who can haunt us, and spite us.

53

My fainting fit, as usual, passed very slowly, from that darkness and confusion of my whole body into a condition of tranquil weakness. I found myself lying on my bed in my own room behind the drawn blinds, in a twilight which seemed to belong to my spirit. The light from the July sky was warm, but it seemed that I lay in perpetual winter, frozen still, without hope of spring. I breathed in the air of infinite resignation, sad and clear, through which all objects appeared in their own colours; neither gilded by the sun, nor glorified by autumn mist. All appeared small, distinct, separate; and charged with several mortality. 'We die,' they said to me, 'we die alone and all our hopes die with us. Anger is foolish, struggle is useless, and self-pity is self-torture, for there is no help from anywhere.' And I remembered the verse of Edward written in his own failure and despair:

> The art of happiness? High art it is
> To walk that tight rope over the abyss.

Love is a delusion to the old, for who can love an old man. He is a nuisance, he has no place in the world. The old are surrounded by treachery for no one tells them truth. Either it is thought necessary to deceive them, for their own good, or nobody can take the trouble to give explanation or understanding to those who will carry both so soon into a grave. They must not complain of what is inevitable; they must not think evil. It is unjust to blame the rock for its hardness, the stream for its inconstancy and its flight, or the young for the strength and the jewel brightness of their passage. An old man's loneliness is nobody's fault. He is like an old-fashioned hat which seems absurd and incomprehensible to the young, who never admired and wore such a hat.

One day, soon after I came down from the 'varsity, my father exclaimed to me, 'An old man like me has no right to mind what anybody does.' I thought myself a man of the world, but I was merely surprised and embarrassed by this ejaculation. My whole idea of my father, and with it, my idea of the world seemed to waver. I did not know what to say and I can still see the look of his blue eyes fixed upon me with the appeal which I cannot understand; and their profound sadness, as he turns away.

I wonder still why he confided in me. But the beloved Lucy was gone, Bill was in Africa, and he had never been close to Edward.

I asked my mother that evening after dinner, 'Isn't papa well?' But she answered only, 'I think he may be worried about Edward's debts.' Neither of us perceived the warning of change, of crisis. It seemed to us both a time of great and unexpected happiness.

Tolbrook had never been so gay. For during an important election, some of the Liberal chiefs had chosen to hold council there. This was partly, no doubt, in compliment to my father, a devoted supporter; and my parents had gathered all the magnates of the county, with their wives, sons and daughters, to meet them. Every day there were meetings, conferences for the great men, picnics, and luncheons for their ladies. And almost every evening, dinners and dances. And what delighted us, and especially my mother, was Edward's success. We suddenly perceived that he had become a personage. We had heard, of course, that he was a rising man, but as in all families, some secret domestic acid darkened and dissolved the evidence of his triumphs, until it was before our eyes in the deference paid to his opinion by others. But perceiving it, we were carried away. And all of us, as by a change of light, showed new characters. I felt my dignity as Edward's brother, and found myself raising my voice at the dinner table. My mother was talkative, and, I must use the word, flirtatious. We remembered the tale that, at Cambridge, she had been a flirt as well as a belle, and we dimly understood the excitement of an old gentleman from the university who had described her as 'the most enchanting girl I ever met – as clever as she was kindhearted, and twice as beautiful. But, of course, we were too dull for her. We weren't really surprised when the handsome hero carried her off under our noses.'

My mother perhaps had not escaped dullness among the soldiers' wives or in a west country manor house; but now, with the house full of clever and interesting people, and, above all, with her darling Edward beside her, she was so happy that her very step, her smile, her glance, seemed different. As she said to me, with a moment's look of doubt, 'You know your father doesn't like to worry me,' Edward came smiling to her, and with a very low bow, asked her to dance. To which she replied with the radiant glance that I had seen before only in young girls at their first ball, 'Is that a command?' And her movement, as she yielded her body, still slim and beautiful, into his arms, was moving. For after all, it was not that of a young girl, but of a woman in her fifties, who had suffered already great joys and bitter long-lasting grief.

I was smiling with pleasure in my mother's beauty and gaiety, and I myself was intoxicated as with a triumph. I felt for the first time that sense which belongs only to a successful family, as if life and even the capacity of pleasure were increased to that family.

The house itself, I thought, felt that happiness with us. The big Adams' saloon seemed, like my mother, to have been waiting only for this day, and now, while the dancers turned in the old Viennese waltz, already growing faster, I felt, in the spring of its floor, a joyful pulse, as of a sleeping beauty waking to a royal destiny. The great chandeliers, out of their covers for the first time since Christmas, trembled like the jewels on the ears and breasts of the women; the smiles of the marble fauns supporting the mantelpiece, seemed to come to life under the jumping candle flames, as the bare bosoms of flushed and panting girls, whirling by, almost brushed their marble lips.

I was not a dancing man. I was both too clumsy and too shy. But to see others dance gave me a keen exciting pleasure. The music, the noise of feet rasping the ground in rhythm, the motion of the skirts swung outwards, above all the feeling, 'All this happiness, this excitement, these flirtations, these thumping hearts, are a family event. Tolbrook and Edward have created them,' went to my head. Even as I walked now and then through the passages, on a visit to the buffet, or to my own room, in order to make sure that my hair had not started up into tufts, as it was apt to do, or to clean my spectacles with a silk cloth, I felt that the back parts of the house were full of pride and excitement. They were like children, on party nights, waiting with patience but the keenest anticipation for a glimpse of some distinguished visitor in a red ribbon, some renowned young beauty in her satin and diamonds – above all, some dowager, combining importance with a splendid maturity, moving through our simple hall, and raising it, by the very movement of her body, the poise of her head, the sound of her voice, supremely confident and gracious in that confidence, to palatial dignity.

Dowagers permitted themselves to waltz at our country dances. My mother, perhaps because she herself adored dancing, always found, among the bachelors of the Hunt, some of those dancing men who, even in their sixties, will never consent to sit down while they can find a woman to hurl. My mother, at Tolbrook, gave them very distinguished partners, ladies who perhaps had not danced for years until they permitted themselves, in our remote parts, to be squeezed and tousled by farmer squires whose manners with ladies had long become adjusted to the tastes of farmers' wives. I heard one of them address a duchess as 'You gels', and the lady seemed to enjoy it.

It was my special delight to see women such as these in the rich and brilliant dress of that day, frilled and flounced from hem to bosom, moving through the dance with stately impetuosity. They brought together in one vehement impression the sense of magnificence, power and vivacity. The red coats of our bachelors which were usually the most eye-catching ornaments of our ballroom, could not stand against the frocks, above all the shoulders, of these splendid matrons. Whiteness, by mere perfection, overcame scarlet tails and the rainbows of their own silks, as in spring, the snow cap of some tor outdazzles the emerald grasses and jewelled flowers below.

And when I caught sight of my father wandering among them, like an old blind sheep lost on a familiar pasture, I felt only distress as at an impropriety. We had thought of our father as a man of the great world, the brilliant young staff captain from the Crimea, who had carried off a beauty; and I was shocked to see this confused old man, with round red face and wool-white dabs of hair, who wandered silent and embarrassed among the guests, like one of his own labourers brought in from the moor to celebrate some family anniversary.

I learnt to avoid him, for when he caught my eye, he would at once come towards me and say something incomprehensible. 'Ridiculous,' and he muttered something about Edward's support of old age pensions, put before a royal commission that year. 'Pauperizing whole country –' I knew that my father, a devoted Gladstonian, disliked all the ideas of the young radicals led by men like Lloyd George. And I answered something about moving with the times.

'Yes, moving where. Ruin. Turning good English workmen into parasites. And look at the price of corn – what's going to happen?' I shook my head and looked wise.

His shaking hand touched my sleeve, as if seeking for comprehension. But I was merely alarmed. I said, 'Let me get you something, papa, something to drink.'

He remained gazing at me for a moment like one who perceives that his language is not understood. Then he gave a long slow sigh and walked away, with his slow waddling movement. And I thought, 'Poor papa, I had never noticed how old and stupid he was getting.'

Two days later, on the evening after our greatest party, the catastrophe fell. We were relishing that hour, when, languid and sleepy, a family gathers for a last gossip before bed. When they enjoy at once, the memory of keen delights, the anticipation of long and luxurious sleep, and the present comfort of restored privacy and unity.

We were in the parlour and Edward was amusing us with an account of some sharp exchanges between two Ministers in the recent Cabinet.

Edward was at his best. He was not a man who gave one quality of entertainment to his friends and another to his family. We knew that he forgot us as soon as we were out of his sight. He never wrote to us, rarely knew anything about our family affairs. But we perceived that, when he was with us, his affection was real and quick.

And perhaps that week, which had been so happy for my mother, was also the happiest of Edward's life. For what glory is so sweet as that rare but ungrudged admiration of one's own people. He delighted in our respect; our pleasure.

While Edward chattered and we laughed, my father was walking about the room, in his new restless manner. But we did not notice him, for my father's presence had never repressed our spirits. He was too gentle, too even tempered. Above all, he had no nerves. He did not mind noise, or games, however boisterous, at his very elbow.

Suddenly my mother, with that mischievous smile, which was peculiar to her when she spoke to Edward, brought a piece of newspaper out of her corsage and handed it to him.

'Is that yours?'

'What, has it got into the papers?'

'How strange,' she said, 'that it should reach the papers. The Post Office is so careless.' Her voice had that lively tone of the coquette who is not afraid to wound, because she loves. Her stroke was a caress. Edward laughed. 'But I didn't send it in to *this* paper, mama.'

'What is it?' I said, and I was poking my face between their heads to read; when to the surprise of us all, my father's thick little red paw intervened and carried off the paper. He put on his pince-nez, which dangled from his neck on a thick ribbon. His hand shook so much that this operation took some time, during which I think we all began to feel apprehension. He read the couplet and threw the scrap of paper into the fire.

'Rubbish,' he said in a loud harsh voice which we had never heard before. 'Dangerous, foolish,' and I think he said 'lewd', though, in my incredulity, I may have misheard. 'I'm ashamed – any son of mine – bad enough to write such stuff – but to print it –'

The verse which caused this violent agitation was one of the few political verses which Edward allowed to get into print during his life-time. It was a mild joke about Gladstone and Home Rule. To Edward, and therefore to me, Gladstone was an old-fashioned Whig, and already an obstacle to progress. We condescended to him as the Grand Old Man. It was not for many years that we realized how great he had seemed to my father's generation; a prophet, a leader sent from God.

My mother blushed a soft pink, her deepest sign of feeling and said, 'But my dear, Lord Rosebery himself showed me the paper. He was laughing and he said, "I think this is something by your clever son, Mrs Wilcher." '

'No, no. All rubbish – disgusting, vulgar – but what does it matter. You'll never do any good.' My father was purple and struggled for words as if choking. He stood before us, jerking his arms and legs like an absurd marionette on wires, which can't resist their manipulation. 'Rubbish. How can anyone trust a man who swindles his own family. Nobody can trust him. He's spoilt. We've spoilt him. And look at him. Doesn't even know what I'm talking about.'

We stared in horror and astonishment. Even Edward was moved. His handsome face became a little pink. He got up and went towards the old man, saying in affectionate and contrite tone, 'But, papa, I hope I'm not so bad as that. I've been careless perhaps –'

'No, no. Too late. Spoilt. What's the good of talking. I told you twenty years ago that he was getting spoilt.' He made an angry gesture waving Edward back and suddenly shouted, 'But he's not going to ruin you – I won't allow it. Lucy and Bill. And your mother. You don't care what happens to them. But I'll stop it – I'll stop it.'

Suddenly he staggered back, put his hand to his head, and would have fallen. But Edward and my mother, who flew to his help, caught him in time. They laid him on the sofa, and in silence undid his collar, raised his legs. I was sent for the doctor. My mother came to give me some last instructions in the hall, and as I looked at her, still in her ball gown, with bare shoulders, I thought suddenly, 'How old she looks,' and I said, 'Mama, you're quite worn out – go to bed and leave papa to us. It's only a touch of heart.'

For, of course, like other young people, I could not know the intuition, which had told her already that my father, as she had known him, was finished. Nor did I know why she already blamed herself for his collapse.

She shook her head and said, 'How could I go to bed, Tommy, when your father may be dying. Now remember that if you can't get doctor so-and-so,' and repeated her careful rapid instructions.

The doctor came sooner than we had hoped. He diagnosed a slight stroke, and promised a cure. But though my father recovered his speech and movement, he was never cured in spirit. He became reclusive, and silent. He did not like strangers to see his shaky hands or to hear his faltering tongue. He still insisted upon managing the estate; but he handed over most of the outdoor work to me. And inevitably he became out of touch, and superseded. For it was often impossible to tell him all that was going on. There was no time for long detailed explanations.

54

A strange young woman, in nurse's uniform came into the room, smiling. Even her walk was like laughter. She came up to the bed and said, 'And how are we now, Mr Wilcher?'

'I am quite well, thank you.'

'Mrs Brown sent me to ask and to make sure that you take your medicine.'

'Tell Mrs Brown that I have taken my medicine and that I am feeling very well indeed.'

The young nurse was still smiling so that her plump rosy cheeks dimpled. It was obvious that she could not contain the energy and delight which throbbed in her healthy young body. 'You don't ask after your grandson, Mr Wilcher.'

'My great-nephew. How is he?'

'He is just taking his first meal. He is a very greedy boy.'

Her teeth flashed and her colour deepened. She laughed and said, 'Mrs Brown says that he is biting her as if he could eat her.'

'Please give my compliments to Mrs Brown and congratulate her on this important event.'

The young woman looked at me under her lashes and her smile said, 'What a comic old thing it is.' Then she answered, 'And if you want anything, Mrs Brown says be sure and ring your bell.'

She went out with a rustle of her stiff skirt, opening and shutting the door with a complete about turn, as if performing the figure of a dance. I heard her call out in her laughing voice:

'It's all right, Mrs Brown. He's all right.'

I could not help smiling at the tone of this assurance. 'A charming child,' I thought, 'her face too square, her cheeks too plump and rosy; but what a wife for some lucky man; what a companion and a mother. It is a pleasure to have her in the house.' And as if the young woman's gaiety had been catching, I felt a stir of pleasure 'as English as this room, this weather,' I thought. 'How I should like to have her for a daughter or niece-in-law, a piece of candour and simple woman stuff. What babies she would have. What spring in her heels. I daresay she has a temper with those thick eyebrows, but what is the harm. Real women always have tempers because they are high metalled. Some farmer's daughter, I suppose, and nothing in family. But what does that matter. All the better if she has had an old-fashioned upbringing.'

And indeed, the next morning, when, judging myself rested, I went to take the prayers which, by Ann's request, were given in the night nursery by her bedside, the little monthly nurse attended and said her amens louder than any I had heard since Sara's day. For Sara's amens had been the loudest of any housekeeper that I can remember.

The room was very warm and smelt of the baby, which was lying in a peculiar cot, made of canvas, next Ann's bed; a little thin creature with black hair and a sharp nose. He was sucking his fist and uttering now and then an impatient cry. The morning sun threw the shadows of the square window panes upon the floor, and the bath and a towel-horse opened before the fireplace. The nurse, in her blue print, knelt at a chair and thrust herself out behind in a fervent manner. Ann, wearing a lace cap which I had never seen before, and which made her resemble the portrait of my great-grandmother, propped herself on one elbow and kept putting out her hand to disentangle the child's fingers from the hem of his sheet.

From outside we could hear the hens clucking, and one of the men stumped across the yard in his long boots. A horse standing, perhaps by the gate, now and then threw his head and made a sudden loud rattle of trace chains. Now it happened that the day was that of St James, and the collect that which describes how the saint left all to follow Jesus; but as I turned to it, I came in the page before on the gospel for St John Baptist's day, and since it seemed to me appropriate to the scene, I read it. 'Elizabeth's full time came that she should be delivered and she brought forth a son.

And her neighbours and her cousins heard that the Lord had showed great mercy upon her; and they rejoiced with her. And it came to pass that on the eighth day they came to circumcise the child; and they called him Zacharias, after the name of the father. And his mother answered and said, Not so, but he shall be called John. And they said to her, There is none of thy kindred that is called by this name. And they made signs to the father, how he would have him called. And he asked for a writing table and wrote, saying his name is John. And they marvelled all. And his mouth was opened immediately and his tongue loosed, and he spake and praised God. And fear came upon all that dwelt round about them; and all these sayings were noised abroad throughout all the hill country of Judea. And all they that heard them laid them in their hearts, saying, What manner of child shall this be. And the hand of the Lord was with him.'

55

Now though I had begun to read in a spirit of formal duty, to improve the occasion, the words took hold of me and carried me into grace. They opened for me, if I may speak so, a window upon the landscape of eternity wherein I saw again the forms of things, love and birth and death; change and fall; in their eternal kinds. I was reminded that the ordinary birth of a small and ugly child, so disappointing to me who had looked for a fair Edward, was a true miracle and mystery; the birth of a soul to which, however simple, was given a divine power. So strongly was I made aware of God's presence and visible deed in the quietness of the room, broken only by the clucking of hens outside, the snuffling of the baby, the sudden clank of the horse's chains, that tears were forced to my eyes, my voice wavered, and I was obliged to break off from my reading. I resumed it, but could not finish. It was with difficulty that I uttered the last prayers.

The nurse's amens, so charged with ardour, and Ann's silence, appeared to me to show an equal emotion, and I felt it a duty and perhaps a great opportunity, to speak to the young mother, a few words such as might bring to her confused feelings a clear idea of the privilege granted to her by God and the solemn responsibility laid upon her, etc.

But before I had managed to rise from my knees, a difficult feat for my muscles, the nurse having called out the last and loudest amen, jumped up and said in her gay voice, 'Good gracious, isn't it half-past eight?' And Ann, smiling at the baby, began to unbutton her jacket.

I perceived that, far from being moved, they had probably not heard a word either of the gospel or the prayers. The nurse took me by the arm and guided me to the door. 'Now, Mr Wilcher, we're rather behind this morning.' Before I had perfectly collected myself, I found myself in the corridor. But after a moment of surprise and indignation, I reflected that the two women, in their present cares, were, in a measure, under continual inspiration. They were like those simple Indian nuns, who, unable to comprehend anything of theology or even to read, nevertheless are often closer to God than the most learned professors. They are free, I thought; they have not given their hearts; and when I am free, with Sara, I, too, shall forget myself and my cares. And I sought Robert, to praise his work at Tenacre.

'He's in the saloon,' a maid told me.

I was surprised, for the saloon, being disused, had been locked up for many months to keep out the draughts which blew through the house from its neglected windows and the cracks in its floor. I could not even find the key, and decided to go round by the garden entrance. I had not entered this part of the garden for a long time. And now, approaching the saloon from the outside, I noticed a broad, muddy path broken through the laurels, reaching to the double French windows of the great room. The doors, enlarged by the removal of a central post, were open and inside on the floor of the room, under the white pillars and gilt decorations of its cornices, stood a new reaper and binder and a two-furrow plough. Sacks had been spread on the parquet below the machines, but the iron wheels had splintered the sills of the doors, and broken the outer step.

I stepped into the room and looked about me. Rakes and hoes were leaning against the classic panelling, garden seats were planted before the inner doors, and a work-bench stood under the great central chandelier of the three, under which, as my grandmother has recorded, Jane Austen once flirted with her Irishman. Upon the one chair remaining in a corner, a yard cat was suckling two kittens. It needed nothing more to say that barbarians had taken possession. She did not even run from me, but lay watching, with up-twisted neck, and the insolent calm ferocity of some Pict or Jute encamped in a Roman villa.

British country gentlemen of the fourth century were, I suppose, often more cultivated than ourselves. Their families had lived for two or three centuries in those beautiful manors, among an art and literature already ancient. Their comforts were beyond ours. And when we look at their bath houses and see the marble steps worn hollow by the naked feet of a dozen generations, we feel so close to them that we suffer for them in their terror and destruction.

A gentle and quiet people, who loved home as no others; whose very gods were domestic. But this room breathes of a double refinement; the Roman art of life, distilled through the long spiral of English classicism.

It has been our pride for a century. Even my father would boast of the architects, who came from all over the world, to photograph its decorative plaster, and to measure its panels. Some have called it too delicate in its simplicity. But what beauty in its grace, its dignity; it is a room where no one could forget the duties as well as the privilege of gentle breeding.

But now I felt embittered against it. 'Now you are crying out for help, too – you are jumping upon my back. And all your load of beauty is another burden. "No," I said, "you can go to the devil. I have enough to do. If I can save this child's soul, if I can make his mother understand that he has a soul to be saved, then I shall have done quite as much as anyone could ask of me." ' I heard Robert's voice at my elbow. 'Hullo, uncle, I thought as we weren't using this old barn, it might do for some of our stuff. It will save a new machinery shed at least.'

'An old barn,' I said, for I thought that the boy was needlessly provocative. 'It is a masterpiece.'

'Yay,' Robert said, 'I always liked this room best of any I know. It's grand. Good for dukes. Sixteen foot high, I measured it to see if it would take a thresher. I didn't tell you I was after a second-hand thresher – we'll have to put it somewhere out of the rain. But I won't do the building any harm, uncle. It's only temporary. And if we had to make a door for the straw we could take down a panel next the fireplace and knock out a few bricks.'

'Thresh in here – you'll shake the whole house to pieces. No,' I said, 'not while I live. And you're not going to kill me either, by giving me shocks. I'm not going to die yet for a long time,' and so on. I lost my temper with the boy and told him to take his damned machinery into the yard.

And to my surprise, Robert was most agreeable. He apologized three times and we parted on very affectionate terms. True, that was a week ago, and I do not believe that he has yet removed his plough and tractor. But I do not care to look. I have laid down a rule: no threshing machine in the saloon; and I should be stupid to fight about details. I should also be stupid to find him in default, for if I took no further steps, I should lose my authority, if, indeed, I have any.

56

And as for a plough or so, temporarily deposited in my house, why should I quarrel with them. Taken in the proper spirit, they can be an inspiration. I must not forget my first visit to Sara in her room at Craven Gardens. I was astonished to see that miserable attic in which she was living. The paper coming off the walls, a leak in the roof, a torn piece of linoleum on the floor, several handles off the chest of drawers, etc. The stove in the fireplace was broken and useless.

The only comfort to be seen was in the bed, which showed three mattresses, two of hair and one of feathers, and one of my best eiderdowns.

The sheets, too, were my best linen. But even this luxurious bed had one castor missing. Its foot was propped upon two books.

Now it was true that just at that time, after the great strikes, I was obliged to use the strictest economies; my town house was in very bad repair. But I was shocked by this room. 'Why,' I said, 'these are poor quarters, Mrs Jimson. Can't you find any better?'

'Well, sir,' she said, 'I couldn't put a maid in here, or she'd go.'

'But what about you?'

'Oh, I don't mind, sir, so long as it's somewhere to myself. And quiet for sleeping.'

Then we both looked at the bed. But Sara did not blush. She said only, 'I was just dirtying out those sheets, after Master Robert went back to school.'

And when I suggested that we might find a better piece of linoleum, she urged me not to waste my money 'on fallals'. I was pleased by my housekeeper's loyalty and economy. For I saw she identified herself with the interests of the family. But now, remembering that room, I realize for the first time that Sara slept in it, little changed, for nearly twelve years. I think the roof was mended, and I gave her a rug for the floor, but certainly she never had a fire there. Yet never once had she seemed to reflect on the hardness of her life. She seemed even to rejoice in depriving herself because it helped us both to save on the bills.

'A true soldier,' I thought, 'even to making herself comfortable. Bill would have appreciated her.'

And I saw, as by a revelation, that deep sense from which Sara had drawn her strength and her happiness, the faith of the common people. That faith which is expressed in so many proverbs, 'A great inheritance; two of each and one gullet.' 'Give me hands, give me lands.' And I entered into the minds of those who for generations have known life as an enterprise for their bread. Who do not think in terms of inheritance or profession, but of a temporary shelter and a month's wages.

Sara gave me that service, but she never unpacked her box. She was ready to move on, at any moment, to some other billet, and to begin life again under whatever conditions she might find there, whatever mistress or master.

I said to Ann, 'Perhaps if you have Edward for the baby's name, Robert ought to have Mathias.'

'I don't see why. To turn away bad luck?'

'How – turn away bad luck?'

'Because we are getting our way about the other names.'

'What nonsense. No, I was thinking of Robert's father – a great fighter. Perhaps a boy, in this new world, might take some profit by his memory.'

'I shouldn't like to have a preacher in the family.'

'Why not, indeed?' I was surprised and shocked.

'There'll be nothing to preach about by the time he's grown up.'

I answered that there would always be plenty to preach about. 'And why do you suppose that the Christian faith is dying. Don't forget that Christianity has a way of reviving itself, of rising again from the very grave. It has done so a thousand times. For it springs out of the very roots of the spirit,' and so on. And I convinced myself and said 'The baby must be Mathias as well as Edward. I shall tell Robert so.'

But the girl answered with surprising warmth, 'You are not going to desert me, uncle.'

57

And, in fact, the boy was christened Edward John Wilcher. But the excitement of this victory, if it was a victory, was overcast for me by an unexpected misfortune.

Ann, as soon as she got out of bed, showed an unexpected energy. The lazy girl who had spent whole afternoons with her nose poked in a book, till I had been obliged to remind her that nothing is more disgusting in a girl than a stoop, now became busy and even a little troublesome. She was inclined to pester us all, with her spring cleaning, and her punctuality. It was as though maternity which had hollowed her cheeks and deepened her eyes and marked her body, had released in her a whole set of female instincts formerly hidden and suppressed in her soul under the heap of little boxes. She was rougher, ruder to me, and yet she seemed more affectionate, more like a daughter.

So one day when she found my bedside table full of unopened letters, she rated me, 'Look at this, uncle. What are you thinking of. Some of them are eight months old.'

Now the truth is I had not opened any letters from certain members of the family, because I knew that they would be full of complaints against Ann. My niece Blanche had written such letters; and even my dear niece Clary, her sister, who had married, much against my will, a boy half her age, and opened a shop, had sent me warning letters against Ann. It seemed that the whole family, having appointed Ann to look after me, now accused her of keeping me a prisoner.

This was probably true. But I was in no position to resent it and therefore I could not afford to be agitated by their charges. I was too busy. So I opened no more of their letters.

'I must have forgotten them,' I said.

'But, uncle, you really can't ignore people like that. Here is Cousin Blanche's writing. Yes, she has written to you almost every week – there must be twenty from her alone.'

'You read them for me.'

'I couldn't do that. Cousin Blanche wouldn't like me to. She hates me, and I can't say I like her.'

To keep the child quiet I promised to read the letters, but I did not do so. I put them into a broken ventilator and by God's mercy I forgot all about them again.

An old man is obliged to be a coward, not for his essential self, his mind and will, but for his body which may betray that will. He is like a general compelled to fight his last campaign, with weak worn out troops, badly equipped and liable to run away at the least reverse. He must use all his self-control, his ingenuity.

I had executed a skilful retreat. But I had not allowed for Ann's new coarseness of mind. Two days later she told me that Blanche was coming to see me. 'I telephoned to her and said that it wasn't my fault if you refused to have anything to do with her.'

'I do not refuse,' I said, 'a soldier does not refuse to be shot. But he doesn't desire it. No, I can't see her. It is impossible for her to understand me or for me to argue with her. She is as stupid as a horse.'

'But, uncle, it's not fair to let her think that I keep her away.'

'No, no, certainly not. But I can't see her – I have to see Mr Jaffery first.'

'I don't mind in the least what you do about your will, but you mustn't get excited. Having babies is too much for you altogether.'

'I'm not excited. But I won't see Blanche.'

'Well, I've asked her to tea with us today.'

I said nothing. But I sent a wire by the garden boy to say I could not see anyone. I was in bed.

Yet Blanche contrived to see me, for as I was walking through the village with Ann, she suddenly appeared before us, and Ann at once went into the village shop. Another of her plots.

58

Blanche Wilcher is a big and handsome woman. Her hair is still dark, and her cheeks are red. She has grown stout in late years, and it suits her big frame and upright carriage. I have always admired and respected her, though often I have found it necessary to quarrel with her. For if one is on good terms with her, she is apt to give too much advice. But she is a good Christian, a good honest soul, and now, kissing me on both cheeks, she said with emotion, 'At last, poor uncle. How are you? You are terribly thin.'

'How are you, my dear, I haven't seen you for a long time?'

'Tell me, Uncle Tom,' she took me by the arm and drew me down the road away from the shop, 'Do you get my letters?'

'Yes, my dear. It is very good of you to write so often.'

'Then did you really allow Robert to cut down the oak wood?'

'No, has he cut it down?'

'But I wrote about it long ago. Did you get the letter about what Ann was saying about you – that you ought to be shut up?'

'No.'

'Just as I thought – the girl has been intercepting my letters. That is a criminal offence. I really ought to go to the police.' Her face began to grow redder. 'Don't you see, uncle, what that couple are doing to you? It's a conspiracy. They agreed about it before that deceitful girl accepted the job of nursing you.'

'Yes, it's very likely.'

'Is it true that they lock you up in your room?'

'Sometimes at night.'

'It's incredible – terrible.'

She was greatly moved and in spite of myself, I began to shake. I thought, 'I have been foolish and unjust. I must make a new will. For Blanche ought to have the place. She is just the right person, a Christian and a parish worker, the perfect squire's wife. She has even put some backbone into that lazy fellow Loftus and made a magistrate of him.'

'Would you like me to go to the police, uncle?'

'It wouldn't do any good. You see, Ann is a doctor.'

'But she has no right to treat you as if you couldn't look after yourself. It's a scandal. It's got to be stopped.'

'Stop what?' I said. For Blanche always upset me. So sure of herself. And besides, a reactionary of the worst kind. She belonged to the feudal age. I didn't object to a reasoned conservatism. There was, goodness knows, plenty to be said for maintaining such little civilization as we had accomplished. But I had no patience with the blind worshipper of exploded systems.

'Stop treating you like this.'

'Well, you know Blanche, I'm a bit of a nuisance. I am so restless at night.'

'That's no excuse.' And she looked at me with alarm.

'I daresay they think I might set the place on fire as I did to Craven Gardens.'

Blanche becomes very red. 'But, uncle, you never did so.'

'Well, you know that the insurance company nearly didn't pay up.'

'It was the electric wiring went wrong.'

'Ah.' And I grinned at Blanche so that she fell back a step. 'But then I knew it was wrong. I even smelt that fire, and I could have stopped it. But I thought, I've never had any peace with this damned house – it's a perfect incubus, what with repairs and servants and wondering whom to leave it to. So I let it burn. I may even have assisted it to burn.'

'Uncle, you don't say this kind of thing to other people, do you?'

'Oh, no, it's just between ourselves. If Ann suspected anything like that, she would send for the asylum van tomorrow. And then I couldn't marry Mrs Jimson.'

Blanche was quite taken aback. And I could see in her face the reflection of a terrible struggle. She was wondering whether it would be better to have me certified and so to save me from Sara, but to leave Ann and Robert in possession; or to get me away from them, at the expense of seeing me married to Sara.

'Of course,' I said, 'I should not think of setting fire to Tolbrook. It hasn't even occurred to me. The place has been a great nuisance to me, but since I am leaving it as soon as Mrs Jimson is ready for me, I do not feel the burden so much as I used to.'

This suggestion, that I might set fire to the house if I wasn't allowed to marry Sara, quite overwhelmed my poor Blanche. She became as red as beetroot and gave up the struggle. But to my confusion she was still more affectionate. 'Oh, Uncle Tom, I do feel so worried about you – can't I help you in any way?'

Then I began to shake again, and I looked round for Ann. 'Where is Ann?' And I went towards the shop, calling, 'Ann, Ann.' But Blanche kept beside me imploring me to be on my guard against both Ann and Robert. 'They are simply robbing you.'

At last I fairly bolted from her into the shop. I could not bear her kindly feelings. But Ann had gone out by the back way. It was Robert who rescued me. He happened to drive past in a waggon with two of the girls who, for the last fortnight, under the name of pupils, seemed to spend most of their time wandering about the yards in white smocks, or carrying out cans of tea to the fields, where cutting had begun.

I hailed them, and Robert pulled up.

Blanche was now in tears. She kissed me, though I believe she would have liked to hit me at the same time, in exasperation; and she begged me to send for her in any trouble. Robert and one of the girls then hoisted me into the cart without much ceremony, and we drove on, leaving my poor niece in the road. But I felt such an attack of sympathy for her, so near me in my deepest feelings, in my love of Tolbrook and the old grace of life; in her Christianity, which is that of a country woman, the simple calm faith of the village church, that I knew it put me in danger of a serious attack. I therefore removed her quickly out of mind and reflected on the charm of the evening; and upon Robert beside me, dirty and smelling of sweat, and I thought, 'Now it is too late to change anything – I am committed into the hands of this rough obstinate boy – he is my fate. I have nothing to do any more with the farm. My trees are at his mercy.'

It was a hot afternoon when the air, already full of chaff dust, itself seemed thick and sleepy. The very sound of ball upon bat from the village boys playing stump cricket on the rough field near the church came through this thickened air with a drowsy note. It reminded one of afternoons spent lying in the long brittle grass, between the tents, in the last day of some county cricket week. The trees, creatures so sensitive and quick, stood now motionless to their topmost leaf, dozing on their feet like horses. The wheat was as red as a fox's back, and the barley quivered as if transparent clouds of steam were passing over its awns. The hedges were covered with pale dust so that they were almost the same colour as the hay which had been sticking among their thorns and brambles since June.

On summer days like this in harvest, the richness of the ground seems charged upon the air, so that even the blue of the sky is tainted like the water of a cow pond, enriched but no longer pure. It is as if a thousand years of cultivation have brought to all, trees, grass, crops, even the sky and the sun, a special quality belonging only to very old countries. A quality not of matter only, but of thought; as if the hand that planted the trees in their chosen places had imposed upon them the dignity of beauty appointed; but taken from them, at the same time, the innocence of natural freedom. As if the young farmer who set the hedge, to divide off his inheritance, wrote with its crooked line the history of human growth, of responsibility not belonging to the wild hawthorn, but to human love and fatherhood; as if upon the wheat lay the colour of harvests since Alfred, and its ears grew plump with the hopes and anxieties of all those generations that sowed with Beowulf and ploughed with Piers and reaped with Cobbett. Even at my own last harvest at Tolbrook, nine years ago, the gardeners' boy brought me from the field a little plait of straw. He did not know what it was or why he brought it, or that he was repeating a sacrifice to the corn god made so long ago that it was thousands of years old when Alfred was the modern man in a changing world.

The English summer weighs upon me with its richness. I know why Robert ran away from so much history to the new lands where the weather is as stupid as the trees, chance dropped, are meaningless. Where earth is only new dirt, and corn, food for animals, two and four-footed. I must go, too, for life's sake. This place is so doused in memory that only to breathe makes me dream like an opium eater. Like one who has taken a narcotic, I have lived among fantastic loves and purposes. The shape of a field, the turn of a lane, have had the power to move me as if they were my children, and I had made them. I have wished immortal life for them, though they were even more transient appearances than human beings.

59

And I thought, 'In fact, I have been ungrateful to these young people, especially to Robert. For he has at least set me free. I need worry no more about those old tottering relics in the fields. Let him respect only the house, for his own son's sake, and I shall be a fortunate man.'

And I hastened down, after supper, to congratulate him. 'You're quite right,' I said, 'about my father's changes. Revolutionary. I have been looking at the plans. And my grandfather actually pulled down the ruins of the old chapel to build a byre.'

'What a pity,' Ann said.

'But – what an act of courage, to destroy walls six or seven centuries old. A strong man. But he was the lay preacher who remembered the Wesleys. He was an Edward, too.'

'I should think the place would have gone bust a good while ago if someone hadn't kept it on the move,' Robert spoke in a sleepy voice; his face was hollow with exhaustion, and shone still as if varnished with sweat. He had not shaved that morning, and now his chin was blue. He was carrying a gramophone under his arm, and Ann had two lanterns in her hand, old and dusty. One had been patched with a piece of cracker paper pasted to the frame.

'It is as if Tolbrook itself were on a pilgrimage,' I said. 'It is like a gypsy van, carrying its people with it.'

'You promised to go to bed, uncle,' Ann said.

'Yes, I am on my way. What are you doing with the old lanterns?'

'We are going on the lake.'

'You ought to send Robert to bed. He is almost asleep.'

'It is Robert who suggested a water party – he found the lanterns in a cupboard. Are they the same lanterns that you used to have at the old water parties?'

'I don't know, but the lake has nearly dried up since the dams broke, and there are no boats.'

'Robert had the old punt mended and there is still enough lake. You call it the pond. Shall we go, Robert?'

'Where's Molly?'

'Is Molly coming?' Ann turned her sharp, haggard look towards Robert. 'I don't see that we need take Molly.'

'We can't leave her alone all the evening. After all, she's paying us.'

Molly was one of the two farm pupils. It seemed that both these girls not only worked for nothing in the yards, but paid for their teaching and keep. A stroke of genius in Robert, I thought.

But Ann had a different explanation. 'They've fallen for Robert, and fat Molly thinks she's going to get him, too.'

I thought this merely jealousy on Ann's part and warned her against this foolish vice. Molly had been known to me from a child. A tall, fair, thick-set girl with a heavy snub nose and a curled chin, daughter of a yacht chandler at Queensport. She had grown up a silent creature, who never spoke to me. But her family was highly respected, and I knew that she had been well brought up.

Robert was calling towards the back parts of the house, 'Molly,' and at last she came with downcast eyes and the sly face which means only that a girl is shy. The three went out together. Robert and Ann looked already an old disillusioned couple. It was strange to see those three young people walking soberly across the dry short grass in the twilight, on their party of pleasure; a yard apart, with bent heads, and uttering no word.

60

'When I leave Tolbrook,' I thought, 'I shall be beginning life again, where I should have begun it forty years ago, when I resolved to be a missionary, to throw myself into that dark wave which had already carried Lucy away.'

I heard the gramophone through my curtains, playing the water music. And looking out I saw that Robert had hung the lighted lanterns from sticks at each end of the punt and launched it upon the pond. He was pushing it forward with a crooked clothes pole, which still had its fork at the upper extremity. Between the stems of the alders, I could see it floating in a clear space of water like a small grey cloud on a green sky. The long broken reflections of the lanterns were like flames wavering in the air.

Punt, lanterns and music were insignificant in the great space of the evening, and the three young people seemed to be performing a rite rather than enjoying themselves. The air was growing cool, and I knew the punt was leaky and rotten. Every moment or two Robert handed his pole to one of the girls in order that he might change the Handel records and wind up the gramophone. I thought of the children who play at balls or presentations in a stable yard, and sit upon the cold iron of an upturned bucket balancing a paper crown, only for the pleasure of the idea.

But who can say that our old water parties, with their dozen boats, their band, their decorated bowers on every island, were not acts of the same kind; realized romance, living poems. In which we sought for something ideal, something beyond the fact, some abiding place.

The last, the greatest of these water festivals was for the Jubilee. And I came to it unwilling from a party of young men who, like myself, thought themselves dedicated to God.

I was the eldest of them by two years. I had spent more than two years, since my father's illness, as his helper. The other three were still undergraduates; but in mind, I think I was still the simplest.

For forty years I have looked back upon that reading party as upon my happiest hour. I see myself climbing Snowdon by the long Pig Path, a slim young man in a straw hat and a dark grey suit, carrying a long alpenstock in his hand, carved with the names of Alpine peaks, which he has never seen, and talking gravely to his friend. The friend is even shorter, but rather fat. He wears brown knickerbockers, a high collar, and a red tie, and a round cap with a glazed peak, like a yachting cap. The rest of the party follow behind in two pairs.

The alpenstock makes me smile, and yet I can enjoy my own affectation. For that young man has gone from earth even more completely than if he had died; and I can know him and value him as if he had been my intimate friend. He was grave and a little pompous; but the gravity was partly due to the knowledge that he was very plain, with an absurd ugliness. His red face, his snub nose, his stiff black hair, his round spectacles and peering startled eyes, were comic in themselves. And when he forgot them and began to chatter, to wave his hands, he became at once grotesque. Yet he often did forget them, for he was greatly liable to enthusiasms. It was a common experience with him, to burst into rhapsodies over a view, a piece of music, a face, a poem, and find himself surrounded by discreet smiles. He would then become dignified, until, in another few minutes, he would once more forget that Nature had cast him for the droll and not for the poet.

In this holiday, he was more than commonly excited by the mountains, by new friendships, by talk; by the vast and exciting ideas which, in that Jubilee year seemed to infect the air itself with an intoxicating essence. I do not mean that we were carried away by the pageant of imperial triumph. We were all young Liberals, of a religious turn. But those who think of Jubilee year as a vulgar glorification of power and wealth forget or never knew its sense of blessedness. History does not move in one current, like the wind across bare seas, but in a thousand streams and eddies, like the wind over a broken landscape, in forests and towns. At one place, through some broad gap, it makes straight forward; in another, among the trees, it creeps and eddies. It flies through the cold sky at gale force; on the ground, a breeze scarcely turns the willow leaves.

We write of an age. But there is no complete age. In Jubilee year, the old men remembered Peel and Canning and Cobbett; the old admirals had fought in sail; the old generals had been brought up under Peninsular colonels. Middle-aged men spoke of Dizzy and the New Tories; they had hunted with Trollope and Surtees; the young ones were full of Kipling and Kitchener, Lloyd George and the radical Chamberlain.

Men for whom the Empire had been a trust from God to evangelize the world, Indian veterans who had heard Lawrence pray and Havelock preach, stood beside youngsters from the Kimberley mines for whom Empire meant wealth, power, the domination of a chosen race.

On both sides it was a battle of faith. Rhodes was already looking for the reign of eternal peace and justice under the federated imperial nations, and against him, the Radicals passionately sought national freedom for all peoples. The first spoke in the name of God the law-giver, for world-wide justice and service; the second in the name of Christ the rebel, for universal love and trust; and both were filled with the sense of mission.

So in our arguments, our endless talk, we used often the words God, Christ, and value. We spoke of the crisis of the times and the duty of an imperial responsibility. We felt that our lives had fallen in an age of revolutions and heroic adventures.

The young man, that I was then, in spite or because of his absurd looks and small size, had resolved upon the boldest adventure. Or rather, he found himself in such a mind that any other life was not to be thought of. But this ideal adventure had not yet taken shape, and he wavered between the diamond mines, some tropical service under the crown, in the remotest parts, or the missionary church.

61

My friend in the strange cap, which was a bicycling cap, was training to be a minister of some free church. He was poor, his father was a labourer; and he treated us with a ferocious contempt. I think his contempt of our wits was justified, for he had better brains and was far better read. His strength was in logic, and he asked always for definitions.

'If God is immanent in the world, then He is not only in experience, but in reason,' I say, 'for if we find Him in experience as love and altruism, it is only by reason that we distinguish this love, this goodness, and resolve that it is good, not only in itself, but for the world,' etc., and so forth.

'What do you mean by immanent,' my friend demands. 'Is hydrogen immanent in water? or the kernel in the nut? If He is like hydrogen how do we know Him as Himself? Hydrogen is lost in the water molecule.'

'I suppose He must be like the kernel.'

'Take the kernel out of the shell and you still have shell and kernel. They are distinct, and therefore transcendent to each other. But perhaps you meant that?'

'You can't deny that God is in the world or how do we know Him?' I am full of enthusiasm, and for some reason, my friend's crabbedness increases it. I stop, mopping my face, 'Glorious – what a view.'

'The old ontological argument,' says the other with fearful scorn, which also proves the existence of double-headed eagles and green dragons. And how do you define 'in the world', and 'I know'?

I take off my coat and hang it from my shoulders by my handkerchief tied through my braces. This device gives me great pleasure, and I say, 'It's easy to argue, but you know you do believe in God.'

'Certainly,' he answers. 'But not from argument. No logic can prove the existence of God.'

'Then how do you know Him?'

'By revelation.'

'Do you mean in the Bible?'

'Certainly. And I know no other way. Or don't you believe in the Bible? If not, why do you call yourself a Christian?'

But I do not want to argue. I want to enjoy myself, and perhaps to be converted. I stop again and cry, 'Look at those fields. Like jewels. Beautiful.' And I say as if I had just thought of it, but in fact repeating something that I had heard, 'Beauty is perhaps the happiness that God intends for us. Because love is a duty and not necessarily a pleasure. But beauty is pure enjoyment, God's happiness.'

'What exactly do you mean by beauty?' the other asks. He has a small brown moustache and when he asks one of his sharp questions, he points it at me like a weapon. 'Is a cowpat beautiful?'

'No, of course not.'

'If I say a cowpat is beautiful, will you contradict me?'

'Yes.'

'Then who shall judge between us? Your beauty is a matter of opinion.'

'Don't you believe in beauty?'

'Certainly.'

'Then how do you know what is beautiful.'

'By revelation.'

I admire him more and more, because of his fierce scorn, his sharp voice, his ferocious logic.

'You're as bad as all the rest, Wilcher,' he says to me. 'You won't face facts. Either the Bible is true – every word of it – or it isn't. Either you accept the God of the Scriptures, or you haven't got a God at all.'

'But everyone interprets the Bible in his own way. And if every man did exactly what he thought right, there would be anarchy in the world.'

'You mean religious liberty? Quite so, liberty or authority. God or the devil. And you can't have a little bit of both. You've got to choose.'

'A world of anarchists would be full of evil.'

'That's none of my business. If I am to preach God's word, the only question is, have I faith in Him or have I not?'

His words open before me dark pits which only serve to convince my enthusiastic feelings. I stop upon the narrow path a few feet wide, between two precipices, which leads to the mountain top, and tremble at the idea of falling, falling. Such heights make my head turn. And I say, 'To believe in God is an act of faith. Yes, one must make the act.'

62

As I say this, I feel the very presence of God, not only within me, but in the whole surrounding air, as love, friendship, beauty, so that it is as if these feelings existed not only within me but in the nature of things; as if the mountains, the clear sky, the little fields below, my friends, were bound together not by my feelings about them but by a reciprocal character of delight and understanding. I think I know what it means to have perfect faith; and as I turn again to climb, I perceive that I belong to God. I must do his will, etc.

'I am converted,' I say to myself, with that keen pleasure which comes from accomplishment. My excitement has acquired a meaning, and so I can understand it and respect myself as a reasonable being. What glory, for a small undignified person, at whom others were inclined to laugh, to be a missionary.

It was with this feeling that I returned home to entertain county neighbours and the Lord Lieutenant. I moved among the crowd with that sense of separateness and importance which one perceives still in young men at that critical age, when they attend parties in their own homes. They feel that they have better things to do than to gossip and dance and be polite. And perhaps it is true, for they are deciding the whole course of their lives.

Of course I enjoyed myself at the party; I enjoyed the ices, the strawberries, and even the sense of my own aloofness. It was with pleasure that I thought, 'How ridiculous all this is – to spend two or three hundred pounds in order that we may be bored by the A's, the B's, and the C's.' For in my new secret resolve to be a missionary, I had a point of view. In the faces of the groups that passed I seemed to see the same reflectiveness, and I said to myself, 'Why do we go to all this trouble, for nothing?'

Among the islands of the lake, each with its lanterns, boats crowded with young men and girls, in the full-sleeved bright dresses of the end of the century, floated like other smaller islands, or like great tufts of flowers, drifting in the water. One heard laughter and saw among these flowers, faces that seemed to my short-sighted eyes, beautiful and gay; but when I came near in my skiff, taking some message to the band on the largest island, or announcing supper to the boats, I could recognize Mary this or Phyllis that, plain and dull, and hear the forced sound of the politeness and the laughter, and catch at a yard's range glimpses of boredom and endurance. Mary was in the wrong boat with that intolerable Archy crushing her only frock; Phyllis, a parson's simple-minded daughter, was among a set of town visitors who ignored her.

'Why do they come – what do they want,' I thought, 'they are all looking for something, some happiness; but they don't know how to get it. All this contrivance and expense is meant to give them the chance of this happiness and so they are delighted to come. But when they come, they are bored and frustrated.'

I thought of haggard, unhappy Lucy, perhaps scrubbing a floor or cooking a meal at that moment, and I thought, 'She has found out what she wants, and so she does not even consider happiness.'

Yet during these serious and important reflections, perhaps because of them, my excitement and pleasure increased. I paid compliments, looked boldly at the pretty girls and ran about making myself useful and prominent. I caught myself smiling all the time and in the same way, I saw the most anxious and depressed look on some girl's face give place to a sudden smile. Everyone, at every few moments, would glance about, even in the midst of talk, at the lanterns, the boats, the glittering water, full of coloured lights, and smile as if to say, 'How glorious to be here on such a night. How lucky I am.'

And the reflection 'this is an occasion' passed at once to the exasperated thought, 'But nothing has happened to me yet.'

I felt now that I understood those looks of desperation which I had seen already a hundred times, in young girls, at balls and parties, when they thought themselves unnoticed; a look which flashes into their youthful cheeks and mouths and eyes as it were from behind, and for a second makes them fierce and terrified. It arose, I thought, from the sense, 'I have only this hour – nothing has happened to me yet. What if nothing ever happens to me?'

But I felt no sympathy, only, in spite of my importance, an answering quiver of the nerves. And sculling to another boat, full of old couples, rowed sedately by two footmen; and seeing the calm patience of their faces, I would think, 'And I suppose they are pleased to be here because they think their children are pleased.' But when at close quarters I saw the mild appreciation of their glances among the murmur of family gossip, so worn out that they did not trouble even to listen to it, but nodded their heads and smiled at the movement only of a chin, I would forget my adventurous vocation and say with envy, 'Perhaps they are the lucky ones. They have got over their troubles, and only have to die.'

'Supper, supper. Lady A. – oh, how do you do, Mrs B.?'

The news scarcely moves them except to polite nods and smiles. To the boats of the young people it comes like a message of reprieve to condemned prisoners. Each of them thinks, 'Now is my chance to get another partner – I shall be in that other boat' or 'No more boats for me. I shall stay in the ballroom.' They row furiously to the shore, splashing frocks, shirt fronts.

And suddenly the flower beds explode like rockets and shoot into the dark fragments of blue, red, white, and gold. I, too, my errand finished, hurry to supper. I do not care for any girl there; I abhor the dull ones, and I am fearful of the brilliant. Yet I have the feeling that next minute, the minute after, some extraordinary joy must come to me.

I did not reach the supper table because Edward pounced on me in the hall. 'Just the man I want. Julie is here – she came with the Barrets. Apparently they know too little or too much. But she mustn't come to the house, and I want you to take supper to her on Lucy's island. That's where I left her. She's waiting for me. Tell her I got caught by somebody.'

'Is Julie Eeles here? But she must have been recognized. The whole county will be talking about her.'

'I daresay,' Edward says smiling.

'But it's absolute madness.'

'Run along and keep her amused till I come.'

Such a mission filled me with panic. But I could not refuse Edward at a crisis. I thought, 'It has come at last – the scandal that will destroy him.'

63

We all say of certain men, like Edward, brilliant and spoilt by fortune, by parents, that they are rushing upon destruction. Yet when their destruction comes, as it always does to the spoilt, it is both sudden and unforeseen. We say, 'Of course, that is just what was bound to happen to a man like that. It was in his character from the first.' But we have never predicted just that kind of ruin for him. So all Edward's reverses to the final disaster took us by surprise. And now, while I hurried towards the lake, with a basket of supper, I said to myself, 'Julie. But she has been so discreet and so safe. She can't seek a divorce, and she hates a scandal.' Julie was a Catholic, and we had always understood that she was very strict.

Julie had been separated from her husband, a police officer in India, within a few months of the marriage.

'But she has changed her mind or lost her head, as young girls do. Passion has carried her away,' I thought. And I felt, 'God is not mocked. Edward in his sin did not allow for all the consequences of that sin.'

Julie had been Edward's mistress for two years. She was still very young, but she was described to us as an extraordinary person, the most beautiful and talented of her generation, who had conquered London in a few months, during a short Ibsen season, and then at once married and disappeared into privacy.

All that I had heard of Julie terrified me, and nothing but Edward's danger would have persuaded me to present myself to her. It was with a sense of one engaging upon a desperate enterprise that I took my skiff to the island.

We all had our separate islands. Lucy's, chosen in the first place for its remoteness, was at the far end of the lake; so small that it barely contained its bower, a kind of tent of willow branches, set up against the stem of a weeping willow. It was lighted by three fairy lamps. And inside we had placed a rustic bench for two and hidden a box of chocolates, with a motto. I think it was, 'Love looks not with the eyes, but with the mind,' a favourite of my mother's.

Inside I found a thin pale girl, who jumped up and looked angrily at me. She seemed to me, as far as I could see in the dim light, very plain. Her pale hair was drawn smoothly back into a style quite new to me; her small round forehead projected in two shiny bumps, her eyes, very large and black, were also too prominent; and her nose was much too long. I presented myself and explained that Edward was kept for a few moments by family duties. We were to start supper without him. The girl listened in silence with her eyes fixed upon me like a tragic actress preparing for her great scene. I trembled. 'Now for it,' I thought. When I had finished, she gave only a little sigh and said, 'I was wrong to come – I shall go at once.'

'No, no, Edward will be awfully disappointed.'

She gave another sigh and said, 'I wish I could believe you. But I can see you are very good natured. Must I eat supper?'

'Of course you must eat.'

'Yes, I must, since you have been so kind. But I am only wasting your time.' We sat down on the bench which was like all rustic work, a torture to the flesh. We were sad, ashamed, formal. The girl sighed between each mouthful, and I tried to make talk. At the same time, of course, I was burning with excitement and curiosity. I thought, 'This girl is Edward's mistress – I suppose she had a dozen lovers before. She is an expert in love, a courtesan.' And this idea set me on fire. I no longer thought Julie plain, but beautiful. I pressed against her on the bench and at every moment my eyes were turning to look at her again.

'Do you think Edward means to come?' she asked.

'Oh, of course.'

'Why, of course? Why did he send you? I offered to go away. But he is longing to get rid of me.'

'That can't be so.'

'Oh, yes. I've been asked to tour with a company in America and he says it's my duty to go. So that he can break with me.'

'I can't believe it.'

'He's quite right. He's awfully in debt, and I simply don't know where money goes.' She spoke as if musing on a bodily defect. 'I wonder,' she said, 'if Edward has chosen you to succeed him.'

'To succeed him?'

'Edward often sends his friends to me with that idea. It would save him so much trouble if I fell in love with someone else.'

I was shocked by such a notion. But Julie had the power, belonging to all those who stand outside convention, of making common moral ideas seem ridiculous or artificial. So a wild tree growing through a Roman imperial pavement makes it seem faded and paltry.

'He knows he can always find someone to love him,' she mused, 'and that he will love them, too, for a time; he has an affectionate disposition.'

'Yes, he is very generous.'

'If Edward does leave me,' she said, 'I shall go into a convent. I always meant to be a nun. And when I went with Edward, I was fearfully ashamed. Though my husband treated me so badly. I hid myself in the hotel. What peace it must be in the Carmelites – only to love and to pray. Which is love, too.'

'What?' I cried. 'A convent? Oh, no. To bury your genius like that. It would be very wrong. I think it's a great pity you ever left the stage. You were famous already, and nobody else could do what you were doing,' etc., etc.

I had never seen Julie act, and I thought Ibsen revolting. I fully agreed with those who wanted to stop the production of the plays. Yet I was perfectly sincere when I urged her not to waste her genius. 'It would be a perfectly wicked thing,' I said.

'But you don't believe in God, and I do.'

'I am going to be a missionary. I am preparing for it now.'

'You Protestants are queer people – you say you believe in God, and yet you don't want to please Him.'

'I suppose Edward has told you that they all want me to be a lawyer and look after the property. I loathe the idea.'

'But if it's your duty – perhaps God meant you to be a lawyer. Perhaps it is the burden laid upon you, the test.'

She was leaning towards me, resting her palm on the back of my hand and speaking so earnestly that I was enchanted. And suddenly I interrupted her, 'I envy Edward very much.'

She stopped. 'Why?' But her expression had changed. She was not laughing at me, but even in the dim light I could see that look which means on the face of a pretty girl, 'This man is in my hands.'

Suddenly she was on her feet. 'I am so glad we met tonight. I think God must have arranged it, don't you? But it must be awfully late.' She went to the skiff. 'You must come and see me – you must promise.'

I promised. As I sculled out into the lake, whose water under the lights seemed like Indian ink splashed with quick-fire, I heard her voice say with that positive and earnest force which charmed me, 'No, no, a missionary, that's absurd. When your duty is so plain.'

From the beginning, I knew Julie's opinion of me. She saw me as a country cousin, a foolish ugly boy whom she could twist round her finger. She set to work at once to make use of me.

I saw this and I enjoyed it. How can I explain the strange feelings with which, after Julie's departure, I wandered about the grounds that night. I fancied myself Julie's slave, and my imagination went at once, without my volition, into humiliations of a peculiar kind. I wanted to suffer not only for Julie, but by Julie.

I exaggerated for this purpose Julie's strength and even her wickedness, saying, 'A woman like that would stop at nothing.'

Yet at the same time, I was full of reverence for the girl. I said to myself 'What beauty, what sincerity, what true religious faith. And her life is a tragedy, she deserves every help.'

64

Strange cries, like two or three people wailing and mocking, came from outside my window, and startled me for a moment. Somebody was playing rapidly a broken rhythm on strings, and then again the voice cried 'Wah-wah-wah.'

I looked out and remembered that the children were on the lake. The punt was on the far side of the water, but it seemed to me that only two of the party remained in it, Robert and the Panton girl in her white dress. I thought Ann had landed on the island.

The water music, no doubt, had come to an end, and Robert had put on his gramophone some modern record of what he calls jazz. I hear it often from the separator shed.

'Ann hates that music,' I thought. She has left them as if to say, 'I don't care to enter into competition with fat milkmaids.'

The music was astonishingly loud. The wah-wah-wah throbbed on the air like the cry of a giant voice. It fell upon my spirits like an extreme bitter sadness. I had never perceived before that the cries of the saxophone were like a human voice, the voice of one brought down to the lowest scale of human feeling; when human mocking passes into animal despair. Oh-oh-oh, wah wah-wah. The thing was weeping and mocking itself. The voice crying in the wilderness.

The moonlight on the grass, like a blue rime, the leaves moving suddenly and then hanging still, the slow wavering of the quicksilver water seemed to lie under the spell of this sad and trivial music like simple creatures enchanted by some complicated foreign toy. And I thought of the words:

'Nevertheless, as concerning the tokens, behold, the days shall come; that the way of truth shall be hidden, and the land shall be barren of faith.

'And blood shall drop out of wood, and the stone shall give voice and the people shall be troubled.'

65

At Tolbrook in that Jubilee year, we were singing 'Mandalay'. It brought tears to my eyes. They say now that our tunes were sentimental like our religion. That already, as my angry friend on Snowdon so rudely declared, we were degenerate and self-deceiving, etc. And if I told these melancholy youngsters who now listen to mockery like a passion of the flesh, 'On the day when I went to make love to my brother's mistress, I had in my pocket a letter to a missionary friend, promising to join him in his work,' they could well answer, 'We are not surprised. Your whole life was illusion and hypocrisy.'

But though I may have been a young fool when I darted through the sleepy dusty streets of Mayfair, to Julie's flat, I was not altogether contempt-ible. I was not ashamed of my sentiment. I sought some ideal. And if I went seeking it in a frock coat, a tall hat, not very fashionable, and a new pair of gold-rimmed spectacles, I was at least sincere. When I thought, 'Suppose I am refused the door,' I felt as if I should fall dead.

But the maid did not refuse me. And Julie received me with warm pleasure. 'My dear Tom, how good of you to call. I was so bored with my own company. Sit down while I make tea.'

She puts me in a chair and disappears. I jump up, trembling with excitement and audacity, to explore the room. It seems to me beautiful and strange. On the walls, covered with a plain brown paper, are Japanese prints in white frames, and a few drawings, signed by the artists. A Beardsley, a Beerbohm print, an impressionist sketch by Manet. The floor is covered with Persian rugs. The chairs are upholstered in flowered linen. Along one whole wall, a low white bookcase is full of books in bright bindings. I see a complete edition of the Yellow Book in its thirteen volumes, Beerbohm's works, Dowson's poems, Davidson's plays. And when I open them, I find many of them inscribed, 'To dear Julie', 'To dearest Hedda', 'To my old friend, Julie', with the signatures of the authors and artists.

I had never seen a room with plain walls, plain curtains, with no gilt frames or silver ornaments; with no decorations but the austere prints. For even Beardsley in his black and white was priest-like. I thought, 'It is like a cell, of one whose faith is in beauty and love, but a noble beauty, a proud and reserved passion.'

'You like my Beardsleys, Tom?' Julie found me gazing at a strange drawing which would, I think, have shocked me in any other room.

'Edward gave that to me.'

310

'They say he is decadent and amoral.'

'Poor Aubrey. He's dead. He died a month ago at Mentone. But he has been reconciled to the Church for a long time. He asked his friends to destroy drawings like that, and Edward said I might burn it if I liked. I had it in a drawer. But I have hung it up because I loved him and he was a great artist. Tom, I wanted to see you. I was going to write to you about Edward.'

'Can you be a great artist and have no morals? I mean, in your art.'

'Of course not. But his art is moral. It's a criticism of life. You know what Edward said about him.' And she declaimed:

'See funeral gondalas in black and white;
Bury our Venice age, with Beardsley rite.'

I saw that she wanted only to talk about Edward. And I gave way to her for the pleasure of watching her lips. During the whole of our tea-time, she discussed the need of marrying her lover to some rich woman. 'Someone like Mrs Tirrit, who could entertain for him.'

Julie was intelligent as well as beautiful, and her mind, at that time, had the same forms as her body; an austere grace, a balanced quickness. She had all the qualities of a great actress; above all, that seriousness before life which we saw again in Duse. She had all, except ambition. Or if she had ambition, the other motives were stronger, especially that gravity which made her say so often, 'But we must think.'

I heard the phrase now for the first time when she said, 'Edward won't think for himself. So we must think for him.'

'You are the most beautiful woman I ever saw, Julie.'

She turned her eyes to me with a grave earnestness; her usual manner of acknowledging a compliment. It seemed at once to thank me and to say, 'But you and I have more serious things to think about.'

She laid her hand on my arm. 'If I go away, you will have to look after Edward,' and then after a pause, 'What shall we do about his debts?'

'They were paid last year.'

'He must have a thousand pounds by next week. And he's no one to turn to, unless you help him. He's in despair.'

Her face was close to mine, and her big eyes seemed to grow bigger. They say the eyes of a mesmerist appear enormous to his victim. I echoed, 'I might try with papa.'

'Why not, Tom. You know how much influence you have with your father. Oh, dear, who is that?'

There was a knock on the door, and seeing that I must catch my chance before it was lost, I bent forward to kiss Julie. But she saw my intention, and, to my surprise, advanced her lips, and gave me a kiss, so light, indeed, that I hardly felt it. And then, springing up, retreated towards the door.

A woman came in, an actress friend, whose features had seemed beautiful to me in the photographs, but now appeared large and coarse like the carving of a figurehead. She stared at me out of her greedy, disappointed eyes, like a dog at another's bone. I was seized with panic and rage, and took up my hat. Julie came to the door, pressing my hand, and said, 'So it is a promise.'

I ran down the street as if pursued. I could not forget Julie's kiss and her smile. The very smile of Lucy when she condescended to charm the ugly little brother. And what promise did she mean? I had never promised. It was a trick.

But I was full of elation. 'How wonderful she is. How beautiful, how strong. She knows what she wants and she takes it.'

66

But as it happened, Edward got his thousand pounds very easily. For my father, when I hinted that Edward had another debt, answered at once, 'Yes, that woman wrote to me about it. Says it's all her fault, and she's leaving him. Going to America.'

'But if she's going away, Edward may be more economical.'

'No, no. It's not in him. But I'll have to pay. Or he'll go to the Jews.' And he said again with bitterness, 'Edward's got the whip hand of me. A waster with talent. Can't throw him out. Can't do anything with him.'

To pay Edward's debts, old and new, my father was selling an outlying farm at Torcomb. He was ill with depression and I could not understand why the loss of Torcomb affected him so much. 'It's a poor place,' I said, 'the land is third-rate, reclaimed moor.'

My mother answered sadly. 'Yes, your father paid too much for it. How could a soldier know about land. But it's always been a worry to him.'

'Just as well to get rid of it.'

But after the sale, my father became still more helpless and dependent upon me. And he began to speak of his death. 'Better clean up those papers, Tom. Lighten the baggage.' One day, looking about his beloved room, he said, 'Not a bad billet, but I've been here too long.'

He embarrassed me and he caused my mother great pain. I was sometimes angry with him and thought him inconsiderate. Now I understand his struggle; and know he was only being frank to those he loved. We failed him because we were shy and could not speak to him of death.

Meanwhile, I had the whole estate work on my shoulders. My training at the missionary college had again to be deferred. But I prepared myself for my vocation. I read some theology. I wrote essays for old Stott, the vicar, who was a D.D. I gave addresses to local clubs, especially on India, which was to be my own field. I read and thought so much about India, that it came to be believed, even in our own neighbourhood, that I had been there; and I was asked to give lectures in Indian costume. As there seemed no reason to disappoint the clubs, I agreed to wear costume, and sometimes I stained my face, to agree with the costume.

'Here is our Indian Sadhu,' my mother would say, smiling. For I would often return in costume, to save the trouble of changing in our draughty parish hall. And because I was pleased to be stared at by the people. In fact, I looked much handsomer as a Hindu with a dark brown face than in my proper form, with a red one.

'More like a sweeper,' my father would say, 'and boots on his feet.'

'He is a good enough Indian for Queensport. And the dress suits him,' my mother would answer. As a woman, she perfectly understood why I liked to keep my dress on, even though I might appear ridiculous.

And as I ambled through the lanes on the yard pony, I would say to myself, 'Suppose now, instead of having two visits and a dozen trivial things to do before luncheon, I were an Indian sage, sitting in the dust of some holy city with my begging bowl beside me, and nothing to do but think of God's glory. No hair to cut, no farmers to interview, no shopping to do, no letters to write; no wretched little bothers or interruptions. But only peace and contemplation.'

Then it seemed to me that I had entered into extraordinary happiness. That I was in a new world where the very air was peace and calm joy; and the ground of it was the eternal truth.

There, I thought, is the abiding place. And all I want to attain that blessedness, that everlasting security, is a single act of will. To renounce the shows of the world. And I would quote, 'He who loveth silver, shall not be satisfied with silver. This day is vanity, if I have made gold my hope.'

I would think often, To set one's heart upon the things of this world is the most plain folly. Because this world, solid as it appears, is a construction only of desire. All those cottages, those fields, and the very lanes are the deeds of desire. They are the spirit of man made visible in the flesh of his accomplishment. As he seeks, so he builds. There is the villa put up by old Stott when he retired from the parish, to grow his roses. And there is the wooden shed put up by old Brewer for his own quarters, so that he might marry his grand-daughter to a man of family. The country people laugh at him and say, 'All the striving and scraping of eighty years thrown away to catch a young fool of a clerk for an ugly girl.' But so Brewer desired, and he sleeps under his leaky shed in triumph and joy because his grand-daughter is married to a pretty man who sails a yacht and plays golf.

'Man lives by his ideas, and if his ideas be mean, then his life shall be mean. If he follows the idea of his body, then his life shall be narrow as one body's room, which is a single grave. But if he follow the idea of his soul, which is to love and to serve, then he shall join himself to the company

313

of all lovers and all the servants of life, and his idea shall apprehend a common good. And if he follow the idea of the Church, he shall embrace the idea of a universal goodness and truth, which is the form of the living spirit. And its name is wisdom. And its works are love and the joy of the Lord.'

67

'Good morning, sir.' Old Brewer is standing at his yard gate. He sings out the sir like a challenge. He has sent for me, but he does not open the gate for me. He leans upon it and stares at me out of his little blue eyes which are like triangular splinters of bottle glass. His face is as hollow as a bowl. It is like the inside of a walnut shell, crinkled, dry and yellow. His mouth is hidden in one deep pocket, his eyes glitter in two more. Every line is the track of cunning, of avarice. And yet the whole map of the man, as drawn by eighty years of calculation, is now transformed like a dusty web caught in a late ray. The whole face is illuminated by triumph and pride.

'Yess, *sir*.'

'About your parlour wall.'

' 'Taint a wall, *sir*. 'Tis a sponge.'

'It was put right before. I see by the books you had a new drain pipe Jubilee year.'

'Oh, Jubilee eighty-seven.'

'No. Diamond Jubilee. Two years ago. Why, there's no pipe here at all. You've taken it away.'

'It took itself away, *sir*. It fell down, 'twas nothing but a flake of rust.'

'A cast-iron pipe doesn't rust away in two years.'

Brewer pretends not to hear, and says loudly, 'Nothing but rust. Fifty years old and more.'

I know very well that the pipe is doing service, at this moment, somewhere about the farm; as a drain, or a feeder, unless Brewer has sold it. But I know that the old blackguard will swear he never had a pipe, or that the builders put in an old one.

I look at him, and he looks at me. I see his mean cunning, his fathomless cynicism; he sees my anger and hesitation. I don't know, in the face of such complicated impudence, what to do next.

All my fine thoughts are scattered. I am full of rage and disgust. Like other peaceful people, I hate to be swindled. I think, 'You damned old Barabbas, hell was warmed for you. And I should like to see you fry.' But I am wary. In a country place, one has to be careful of one's words. With a strong effort, I keep my temper. I say only that perhaps I had better consult with the builder. And I take my leave, with polite inquiries.

The miserable old crook goes to open the gate for me. He did not open when I came because he was preparing for a conflict. He opens when I go because he has won the first battle. He thinks of me as a poor creature, to be laughed at. His politeness is a condescension, and he laughs up into my face as he shouts, 'Fine day, *sir*. 'Member me to Colonel.'

I remain in a fury all day, imagining fantastic means of bringing just punishment upon this slippery reptile. I find tranquillity at last, only in writing to Lucy or Julie.

I write to them both every week. To Lucy, about the family, to Julie about art, beauty, etc. To both about Edward.

Neither answers except at long intervals; unless by any chance I miss a post. Then Lucy sends me an indignant note, and Julie cables. In two years I have three cables from her, and two cards with Christmas greetings. One note asking for Edward's new address, and one letter of nine foolscap pages, analysing, with a great deal of subtlety, Edward's feelings for her and hers for Edward. 'He loves me better than anyone in the world, when he loves anyone, and is not more in love with some idea, or book, or picture, or horse. He is only tired of me because he can't expect anything new from me. He soon exhausts a woman's possibilities – he charms her to put out all her leaves and flowers and fruit at once, like a tropical sun shining on an English plant. And then he goes past. I often wish that he would make up his mind to leave me. The agony is wondering when the break will come.'

Julie wrote that she loved America and she could never come back to England and to Edward. But she begged me to continue writing to her. 'For I know no one else in the world I can trust.'

When I read this, I was well rewarded for my scores of letters.

68

Lucy in one of her rages accused me of stealing from Edward both his inheritance and his mistress. It was a woman's stab, carefully poisoned with spite. No doubt I desired Julie and I was possessed by that desire, but I never said to myself, 'I shall have that woman.' And for six years she and Edward between them did their best to drive me mad. Julie suddenly returned to England, in the middle of Edward's most ferocious election. This was in 1900, during the Boer War, at Ragworth, near Liverpool. Edward had given up Queensport to M., one of his chiefs, because it was a safe seat. Ragworth was very unsafe; half rural and half urban; with many Catholic Irish dockers, nonconformist chapels, slums, a rich suburb.

No one can imagine the savagery of that election. I can still hear that terrifying noise, the yells of a mob, seeking to kill, to torture; not blindly, but deliberately; so that their howls were mixed with laughter and triumph. Nothing can make one understand, so suddenly and so well, the contempt of those who have loathed mankind, the fear of those who cling to authority; to some established church, which keeps, at best, order among savages.

And both sides were quite ready to organize violence. We encouraged the Irish to howl down the Unionist speeches. The Unionists told the women that we wanted the Boers to kill their husbands and sons in South Africa. Canvassers spent almost their whole time appealing to the worst instincts; fear, greed, hatred. The poor were told that the rich were monsters of cruelty and vice; the quiet little clerks in the suburb were told that the Radicals and the socialists were idle drunken brutes who wanted to take all they could get out of the country, and give nothing back.

At first, these tactics alarmed me. But when I hinted my doubts to Edward, he laughed and answered, 'Politics isn't church work – it's a battle of wills.'

Never had Edward seemed greater to me, or more brilliant. I saw his enormous energy, his resource, his courage, his good temper. I was moved, as never before, by his speeches. 'They call our people savages,' he said. This was after a policeman had been kicked to death. 'But if they are savages, who made them so. They did not educate themselves and build their own slums. Millionaires don't break windows. Even clerks at three pounds a week don't break windows. On the contrary, they are more civilized than millionaires.'

This was to the clerks. To the dockers, of course, he simply attacked the millionaires and the government. He told his canvassers, 'Attack, attack – that's the secret.'

And I was carried away. I was more ferocious than the dockers. I said of our opponents, 'These devils must be fought with their own weapons.' And I, too, assured working men in the back streets that all wars were started by millionaires, in order to make money, and destroy democracy.

I was shocked and disgusted when Edward, after a meeting in which his eloquence had brought tears to our eyes, passed me this scrap of paper:

> Let tyrannies all to free republics pass
> The one by coppers ruled; the others, brass.

The chairman was still on his feet, asking for a vote of thanks to our 'gallant galahad of freedom'. And after the meeting I asked Edward how he could be such a fool. 'Suppose anyone but me had got hold of that – it would have ruined you. This is not a time for cynical nonsense,' etc. And when Edward laughed, I grew still more angry with him. For it seemed to me that here was a fearful danger to his career, and to our cause; his vein of rashness and cynicism.

69

And in the midst of a violent dispute with Edward about his habit of drinking champagne, at dinner, a mad thing to do in such a constituency, I was thunderstruck to see Julie walk into the room. We were in Edward's hotel which was also his headquarters; full of his canvassers and supporters; I had passed, two minutes before, three Baptist ministers sitting on the stairs together, waiting to obtain his support for their temperance society.

I was horrified, yet I was overwhelmed. For several moments I could find nothing to say. I was as confused as a boy in his first passion, who cannot speak, because he has no adequate word.

I had never seen Julie so beautiful or so magnificently dressed. She had had a great success in America. She had a new reputation, new clothes, new jewels; even a new appearance. She was heavier, more imposing. And her face had that special look which belongs to much-flattered women like the radiance of peaches which have been warmed in sunshine. I felt astonished that I had found the audacity to make love to this splendid being. At the same time, some deeper confidence returned to me so that I was filled with joy. As if the hermit in my soul had said, 'Oh, man of little faith, see – your paradise is even more magnificent than your invention.'

Julie pressed my hand affectionately and said, 'How good to see you. It was my friends I missed. I had to come home.' And her eyes looked about the room, a private room at a mean hotel, with delight. 'No, it was everything – everything here.' She opened her palms downwards and outwards, the gesture of a woman who has just arranged some flowers in her drawing-room. 'I am longing to see my things again.'

Edward, in a cool and rather bored voice, asked her to sit down and eat something. She looked at him and said, 'I suppose I shouldn't have come – but I couldn't wait – after two years.'

'I am delighted – charmed – if you could excuse me for a moment.' He went out, no doubt to see the ministers, and suddenly to my own astonishment, I said to Julie, 'Of course, you can't stay here tonight – I'm sure you understand that.'

'But why not, Tom. Who will know? I've signed myself as Mrs Smith.'

'And your picture's in this week's paper. Don't you realize that you might lose us the election.'

Julie gazed at me with surprise. And her surprise, my agitation, made me still more indignant. 'It is really rather thoughtless of you.'

Then she laughed and said, 'How nice you are, Tom. I'd forgotten how nice –'

'But you don't seem to understand – how am I going to get you out of this place – we are surrounded by spies. All the publicans are against us.'

And, in the end, I had almost to push her, wrapped in a man's macintosh and wearing a cloth cap, down the back stairs. Yet all this time, while I bullied her and cajoled her, I was madly in love. I was seized for the first time by that kind of desire which is capable of violence. I adored her, I respected her, and yet I could not forget, 'She is not a respectable woman.' I did not think of possessing her; but her very flesh, because it was that of a mistress, gave fire to my passion.

Edward, so far from resenting my bold handling of Julie, congratulated me on getting rid of her. 'I thought she had more sense than to turn up now, but I suppose she's one of those people who haven't got a political sense. They're common enough – after all. Either that, or she wanted to revenge herself for something. I have been rather slack about answering her letters.'

'Julie is the last woman in the world to do a spiteful thing,' I said angrily. 'She's the most loyal and devoted creature in the world, as you, of all men, ought to know,' and so on. For Edward's ingratitude enraged me. And though I persuaded Julie to retreat even beyond Liverpool, and found her quiet lodgings in Chester, I made Edward write to her every day. That is to say, I typed a letter which Edward signed. And with Edward's letters, I sent my own.

70

All these letters to Julie are now in my possession. And I notice that I always wrote to her of Edward as a hero, a prophet, and of myself as a poor fool and weakling. Why, I cannot tell. Except that all lovers seem to enjoy humiliating themselves before their mistresses.

It was true, of course, that, at critical moments, I was apt to do foolish things, or the wrong thing, or nothing at all. I was, too, a bad speaker; and my voice, in moments of excitement, rose to a squeak. For this reason and because of my general appearance, I adopted usually a slow and rather pompous form of address; but forgot both my dignity and my measure, as soon as I became excited by my subject. Thus my speeches in defence of the heroic Boers were described, fairly enough, by an opposition paper, as a series of squeaks, inaudible to anyone but the reporters, and the policeman whose unhappy duty it was to protect this miserable little Englander, little in every sense, from the just anger of decent people.

And I was often glad of the policeman. Yet I was glad, too, when his absence brought me into an adventure which brought me a compliment from Julie and even from Edward. Despite myself, I obtained the name of hero which reached even Bill in South Africa.

My glory was easily obtained. I mistook the time and place of a meeting, and began to speak to the wrong audience in the wrong place, at the wrong time. That is, I attacked the Unionists before a Unionist crowd, just outside a Unionist public house, on the evening of market day, when the place, a small country town, was crowded with young farmers and labourers.

And when the crowd grew dangerous, I was first of all too blind to see that they had been reinforced by a band of hooligans, organized to attack our speakers, and then, when they began to press upon the speaker's cart, I was so paralysed by fright that I stood my ground, and even continued to squeak. My committee ran away, but I could not move. And my feeling, when the mob seized me, passed beyond both defiance and terror. It became almost a sense of welcome as if my nerves cried out 'Yes, I've been waiting for this all my life. Get it over. Let us have some peace at last.' I can't help remembering how tamely I submitted to the rude hands which took hold of my legs and arms, and what is worse, that I apologized all the time, especially to one great brute whom, by accident, I had kicked in the mouth, as I was dragged from the cart with my coat over my ears, and my trousers up to my knees. 'I'm awfully sorry,' I heard myself squeak, 'I hope I didn't hurt you.' And when I stuck between the posts of a railing, I apologized to the whole mob, 'I'm so sorry – something has caught – I think it's my trousers.' True, it was my trousers, which gave way just then and were torn almost off, whereupon the crowd, delighted, tore off the rest and most of my clothes. I was obliged to sit in the pond, for several minutes, freezing, choking and bleeding, until the rescue party of police could find a cape with which to cover my nakedness. A ridiculous and humiliating scene. But only the mob heard my apologies and no one attended to the mob. Everyone supposed that I had faced it with reckless courage and fought it like a warrior. The friendly papers made a fine story; and all my supporters regarded me as a champion.

From Julie, of course, I hid nothing. I may even have exaggerated my terror, the misfortune of my trousers, and my ridiculous appearance in the pond. But Julie agreed with Edward that I was a hero, and paid me this compliment: 'Edward is lucky to have such a good brother.'

In fact, my heroism didn't raise me very much in her estimation. She had the actress view of heroism, that it was something all men ought to possess; just as all women ought to be capable of devotion.

71

Edward won his election by forty votes. But I did not see the triumph, for two days before the poll my father had a third stroke, on a visit to Torcomb, and fell helpless. What was he doing at Torcomb, already sold? Apparently, having visited the hamlet once a week, at least, for twenty years, he could not break himself of the habit. He went to look upon the fields which were no longer his; the cottages which he had built; and climbing upon the steep moor sides on a hot day, he had burst a blood vessel. He was brought back to Tolbrook on a cart and lived only a week.

He could not speak, but he could think and feel, and write, not very legibly. So on the last evening of his life, while I sat with him, in his dressing-room, he wrote for me these words, 'Too long in same camp.' But I did not understand what he meant. I thought 'his mind is wandering back to his soldiering days. The camp bed suggests this.' For he was lying on his camp bed, which was kept in the dressing-room, for temporary use.

But when I had read the words and made no comment on them, he wrote again: 'God's work – quite right, go into church. Set heart on God's things. Other things go from you.'

I understood that he was thinking of Tolbrook, and it was hard for me to be patient with him. These slow long exchanges at his bedside took much time, and I was distracted with anxieties. Julie, for instance, had decided to take a flat in the same building with Edward, a huge mansion of flats, then not so common as now, in Westminster. I was writing, even wiring, to her daily. For I could not get Edward to be firm. And at Tolbrook one of our old tenants had gone bankrupt, owing two years' rent.

I answered my father, 'But you have pulled the property together. Tolbrook is saved for the family.'

He stared at me out of his blue eyes and made suddenly a violent effort to speak. His face turned dark, and sweat poured down his forehead. I quickly gave him pencil and paper again. But he could not write. He had too much to say to me. I thought, 'Poor papa, he is trying to tell me that his life's work has been wasted, etc., and that the only happiness open to a man is to set his heart on heavenly things,' and so on.

I tried to soothe the old man, but I could not do so. His excitement grew worse, and I had to send for the doctor, who gave him an injection. I looked upon that operation with calmness. But now, when I remember my father's eyes, as he watched the syringe brought towards his helpless body, I feel such a pang of grief that my own heart knows the pain of death. For I know what he was saying to himself, 'Now they are putting me to sleep, because I want to tell them this thing, which only I can tell. Only a dying man, upon his death bed, can know it. And because they do not know it, they don't know its importance, they don't want to hear it. And they will keep me asleep till I die.'

At the first prick of the needle my father struggled again. Or rather, not he struggled, but something within him violently strove to overcome the weight and barriers of his dead flesh. Then quickly the morphia took effect. And during the night, he died. Without knowledge of the agonies which life can bring, and of this last long agony in the presence of death, I could

320

not understand the look on his face, and in his eyes. Only the old know enough to console the old; and then all their friends are dead.

72

My father altered his will, by codicil, at the time of the Jubilee. But afterwards he had rescinded the codicil. The will stood, which left all the real estate to Edward; a life interest from £10,000 to my mother, and £3,000 apiece to the rest of us. I resolved, with this money, which gave me a small income, to join our college mission, in the East End of London, as lay warden.

Whether I was attracted to this new career by the secret wish to be near Julie, or by exasperation with the petty worries of Tolbrook and with Edward, I cannot tell. But I failed to escape because Edward could not be persuaded even to sign a new lease, or a cheque for the repairs. On the day of the funeral, he disappeared into space. That is to say, we only knew where he was from the papers or sometimes from Julie.

In fact, having won his election, among the few Liberals returned that year, Edward was in demand all over the country. He was hated by millions, and loved by thousands. He was known for the first time in every part of the nation, to those who never read the front page of a newspaper, but hear, like their ancestors, political news only at the market or the work bench.

The manner of this fame startled me. But just because I was secretly alarmed to find that a man could become powerful only by being violent and singular, I would not allow any criticism of Edward. And when my mother, reading in the local papers of Edward, as 'one of those Englishmen who have not forgotten their Liberal principles,' etc., said, 'I suppose this means notorious,' I was angry with her, and said that she did not understand democracy.

I had found out that this statement always shamed criticism. No one ever asked me if *I* understood democracy. In the same way, when in my new responsibilities to the estate I was asked any question about business to which I did not know the answer, I looked resigned like a grown-up pestered by children, and said, 'Well, it's rather complicated.'

Or I would merely keep silence and assume a preoccupied expression. For I was distracted with worry. Responsibility is an idea. For three years I had made all decisions. But because I had acted in my father's name, I felt no burden. Now when I was asked to decide this or that, I hesitated. I lay awake at night under the burden of this thought, 'Destiny, the happiness of others, depends on me.' For the first time I understood that heavy word – 'duty'.

It was no consolation for me to find, in my first search among my father's papers, that he had felt the same burden, and also that he had made great mistakes. The Torcomb purchase had nearly been a disaster. He had spent thousands on draining and improving that wretched place, to no profit. But I said to myself, 'If only luck saved my father, so careful and circumspect, what shall save me?' I felt as if the very frame of things in which I had lived so securely were falling apart, like broken screens; to show behind, darkness and chaos. Tolbrook suddenly appeared to me like a magic island, preserved in peace among the storms of the world, only by a succession of miracles. As I walked through the rooms, the very chairs and tables seemed to tremble in their silence, like dogs without a master, asking, 'What will happen to us now?'

73

And responsibility does not only weigh down the soul, as with iron chains, it divides. The man who makes decisions, stands alone. He must be obeyed, but he is criticized, attacked, belittled. When Lucy came flying home to see us, I received her with love; but her first words were a challenge, 'What are you doing about father's chair, he promised it to me? I must have something from father's Tolbrook.'

'He said nothing about a chair, and it's Edward's now.'

'It can't be Edward's. It's mine. Even Mama says I can have it.'

'If it's yours, why did you need to ask Mama.' I went to our mother, who denied any agreement with Lucy about a chair, but said, 'She ought to have it, perhaps.'

'Why? You always give in to Lucy. You spoil her.'

My mother was herself ill. My father's death, so long expected, overwhelmed her, almost as if she had caused it. She asked me once, 'Why did you not fetch me that last time.' She meant in the hour when he died. And before I could say that I had not expected his death, she answered, 'But perhaps he did not want me'; and then quickly, to ease my embarrassment, 'To see him so ill.'

For my mother, I suppose, a lack of sympathy between herself and that husband, to whom she had been so devoted a wife, had gradually become a sin to her conscience.

At that time she could not sleep, and I think, when we believed her sitting idly in some melancholy dream, she was often in prayer. But I, like Lucy and perhaps by Lucy's influence, was exasperated by her absentmindedness, her lack of decision. 'Do you want her to have the chair, Mama? What do you want?'

'Lucy was devoted to her father, and he to her.'

'But about the chair; you understand it's Edward's chair, and we're responsible for Edward's property.'

'Our statesman doesn't concern himself with chairs, except perhaps the Speaker's.'

But seeing that I could get no support from my mother, I went back to Lucy and said, 'Just what I thought. You never asked Mama for the chair – and as I'm in a position of trust –'

'Nonsense. You're in a position of grab. And you mean to hold on. Very well, then. Keep your old chair.'

And thus began the battle of the chair which divided me from Lucy for eight years. For Lucy cheated me. While awaiting a letter from Edward, I came back one day from Queensport to find not only the chair, but my father's camp bed, Indian pillow and carpet being loaded on to a cart. I began at once to take the things into the house. Lucy met me with the carpet in my hands, and there was a kind of tug-of-war in the hall. Meanwhile the cart drove away.

'Really, Lucy,' I said, 'you have no conscience. You could go to prison for this.'

'Then send me to prison, you wretched little pettifogger,' she answered coolly. 'I'm sure you're quite capable of it.' And we parted in bitterness. Indeed, when Lucy found out, on arrival, that I had removed the pillow, she wrote me a letter so abusive that for years afterwards we had no communications.

Lucy could always enrage me by calling me a pettifogger. As I could anger her by calling her a hypocrite. For both words came so close to the truth of our natures that they took its light and cast a shadow on our souls. To Lucy, fighting pride with pride, it was easy to think that humility was pretence; and for me, clinging to order and rule in the turmoil of the world, it was easy to think that the word was greater than the spirit; that I valued not my father's memory, but a piece of property.

74

I was far from sleep. I got up and went downstairs into my father's study, which had long been mine. The chair was back in its place. Lucy had brought it with her when she came home for the last time. An ugly yellow chair in varnished oak. But now I saw it again with Lucy's feeling; I entered into her world, and I felt a strange sensation; a movement of the blood, a thrill in my breast. I felt my father's presence; and Lucy's thought of him; his innocence. He was present in his own being, as if Lucy's love had re created him for me. I knew why she had wanted that relic of him, to give her faith in man's goodness.

The worn carpet had disappeared. I had expected to see it with the marks of my father's feet on it from door to desk, and I gazed with wonder at the bright new turkey which covered the floor; a carpet which Sara had made me buy, to keep my feet warm while I worked on cold winter days.

I remember that I had asked for the old carpet to be renewed, a plain grey, and here was a turkey of the most brilliant crimson. Sara had loved bright colours. I can't remember how she persuaded me to accept this atrocious vulgar object. But Sara was very persistent in getting her way; and would wait two years, three years, for an opportunity, only to change the stair rods or re-cover an arm-chair. And if she did not like a rug or a chair cover, it would soon look shabby, and even develop holes, as if the force of her dislike could destroy the material.

She had urged, I remember, 'A nice red turkey, to keep you warm, sir, for you know you feel the winter,' as if the colour would warm me as well as the pile, and put new blood into my veins.

And though I can't like its vulgar red, yet it makes me smile; it resembles Sara's rosy cheeks, her gaiety, her obstinate resolve that others should enjoy what she found good: warmth, food, affection, soft beds, a domestic sensuality about which her religion was like the iron bands nailed to a child's tuck box.

I was warmed by the very memory, and yet found myself shivering. Rain had been falling on the window for some time. But now I heard a call. I went to the window and saw that the night was clear. What I had taken for rain was pebbles striking the wall, and I looked down to see Ann standing alone under the window. From the lake I could hear, but now much fainter, as if the lid of the gramophone had been closed, a confused noise like jackals screaming and monkeys chattering.

Ann waved to me, and when I opened the window she called, 'Don't do that, uncle. Go to bed at once. Wait.' She came running upstairs and took my arm. 'What are you doing here at this time. I couldn't believe my eyes when I saw the light. Do you want to catch pneumonia.'

'It is a warm night. Did you leave the others to look after me?'

'No, I left them. I don't like jazz, and I don't much like Robert's girl. If he wants to go off with that Molly, I wish he would do it.'

'What rubbish,' I said, for I was seriously alarmed. 'Robert only feels a sense of duty to the girl because she pays a fee. He's quite right. And what do you do to please Robert, going about with that long face and wrinkles in your forehead.'

'Suppose Robert did leave me, uncle, would you let me stay on here? I should have Jan, of course. And I could pay my share. Young Doctor Mac is quite ready to take me as a partner.' They call the boy Jan, copying the local pronunciation of his name.

All this startled me so that I was confused. And perhaps I felt a temptation. But I told the girl she had no right to break her marriage. 'That at least is plain.'

'But it's failed, uncle. It's finished.'

I thought by her voice that she was going to cry. Which alarmed me greatly. For do what I would, I had come to feel with the girl and I could not bear her unhappiness so close to me. Women's unhappiness is always more persistent and hopeless than a man's, especially nowadays when the poor things have lost God and all the powers of grace. When they have cast themselves loose on the world without even rules of conduct, good or bad, to hold them up against those terrible enemies, terrible especially to women, of time and conscience. 'My dear child,' I said, 'your marriage has hardly begun – it hasn't had time to fail. And if you break it, perhaps you will break your heart, too. The only thing we can rely on in a tight corner is our duty. That's the only way out. Duty, duty, that's the salvation of poor humanity. Do your duty and then if everything goes to the devil, you won't have to blame yourself for your own misery, which is the worst misery of all. I think it is really what is meant by Hell.'

'I can't help that, uncle. I know I've deserved the worst. But I'm not going to fake anything. I can't make a pretence of marriage which isn't a marriage at all.'

'Good God, you poor silly dunderhead. What in Heaven's name do you think marriage is – a sugar plum dropped into your mouth off a gingerbread tree –? it's you modern girls are sentimental.'

But of course she did not listen to me. She thinks that because I am old I know nothing about the real world in which she lives. She kissed me suddenly and said, 'So you will let me stay. I don't bother you too much,' and went to the door. 'But you can't trust Robert to do anything that suits you. And of course we won about the name. He can't forget that.'

'Robert is not so small-minded.'

'Names are not a small thing to Robert. Not when they are family traditions.'

'Mathias is not a Wilcher name.'

'That's why he wanted it. And that's why he wants to turn the Adams' room into a machinery shed. There's a lot of Wilcher in Robert. He's a real old Protestant inside. He'd really like to make a whole new god for himself if he had the time after making me over.'

325

75

When Amy was pregnant of her second son John, in the year after the Jubilee, and near her time, she had a wire, at Tolbrook, to say that Bill's troopship was arriving in Liverpool. He had been at Omdurman.

Amy's first child, William, now eight years old, was already at boarding school; but a second had been born prematurely, at sea, and did not live. Amy was therefore under strict supervision by the local specialist, a Queensport man.

Bill's wire seemed to cause her much perplexity. At intervals during the morning she was found wandering about the house, with the wire in one hand and some garment in the other, asking each of us in turn, 'What shall I do?'

We all said that she must not dream of travelling; Bill would not expect her. The doctor had given strict orders that she was not to stir beyond the garden.

After luncheon, she appeared in a coat and hat to say good-bye. We cried, 'But what madness. And at any rate, you can't go now. It's too late. You couldn't get ready in time to catch the train.' And it turned out that she had packed, ordered the trap, and looked up her complicated train connections during the morning. She left the house and caught the train with ten minutes to spare.

We laughed at this new evidence of Amy's oddity. 'I suppose,' I said, 'she asked advice out of a kind of instinct, as a dog barks after rabbits in his sleep.'

And the baby, as the doctors had foretold, was born on the journey, actually in the train.

This story, too, was treasured as a family joke. We told how Amy, her pains beginning, had asked an old gentleman in the carriage if he were a doctor. And upon his answering 'No,' why did she think so, she had answered, 'I didn't really think so, but I wanted to bring up the subject.'

This tactful approach had had no results. The old gentleman simply returned to his paper. And Amy had been too diffident to make any further advance towards an understanding, until it was too late even to stop the train. The old gentleman, seeing Amy collapse, and suddenly realizing the position, had rushed out for the guard, who then hunted through the train for a doctor. Without success. At last he brought her a very young man in a horse-cloth waistcoat, with a gold horseshoe in his tie. He explained, with whispered apologies, that this was a student vet., 'But it's the best we can do for you, Mam.'

'Oh,' cried Amy aloud. 'Don't apologize. You couldn't have done better. I'd much rather have a vet. than a real doctor.' And then she explained to the blushing lad why she preferred him. 'I'd be ashamed to ask a real doctor to manage in a railway carriage. But, of course, you won't mind, will you? You're used to cows.'

And she took charge of him, reminding him to wash his hands, and making him spread out newspapers, to save the company's cushions. And she made him get the newspapers from the next carriage. She would not give up her own *Morning Post* which she was keeping for Bill. She held the *Post* during the whole delivery, a very painful one, in order to make sure that it would reach Bill intact.

To Bill, of course, it was an episode which he used as a weapon against Amy. He never forgave her for endangering the life and, above all, the health of his baby, by what he described as a 'piece of her usual obstinacy'. He would tell us that part about the old gentleman with extraordinary indignation even fifteen years later. 'And she had only got to pull the cord.'

To which Amy would reply, 'The notice said it cost five pounds.'

'It says, "For use without due cause". If you hadn't due cause, who has?'

'Well, I knew it might start before I started.'

'What's that got to do with it?'

'It didn't seem quite fair to put it all on the railway, and you know we were saved a lot of expense. That nice boy wouldn't take anything but two glasses of beer at Chester.'

'My God, and it didn't worry you that John might have been crippled for life.'

We laughed at them both, but now, remembering Amy's untroubled expression before Bill's anger and terrible suggestions, I ask, 'How was it that Amy always knew what she ought to do, and did it, and so calmly accepted the consequences?'

I thought her simple. No one is simple. But I can see now that Amy, in the very conflicts of her duty, as wife and mother, had strict though complex principles. Sometimes Bill came first, sometimes a child. But Amy was a woman of principle, and what strength that gives to the humblest soul, what wisdom to the most modest intelligence.

Edward used to say that Bill and Amy's conversation on any subject, but especially a political subject, explained to him the history of the Greek word 'idiot'. 'They are the most private citizens I ever met, even in a village pub.'

But it has struck me since, that what I enjoyed in Bill and Amy was this very quality of remoteness from Edward's world. Indeed, it was not long after Edward's election that I began to feel, in that world, an uneasiness which I cannot exactly describe, and which has sometimes caused in me, I am afraid, an unworthy ingratitude towards public officials of all kinds.

It was this feeling which produced my first bitter quarrel with Edward at one of his own political parties. The date must have been in 1902, because I know that one subject of our interest was the peace terms after the Boer War.

I had been trying, for some weeks, to make Edward come to a decision on various points, such as Julie's debts, the agency which remained in my hands because he would not appoint a successor; and an IOU to Bill. Edward had already borrowed five hundred pounds out of that small legacy, which was all that Bill possessed.

I had resigned the agency by wire and by letter. Edward had answered neither. I came to the party, my first chance in three weeks of seeing Edward personally, determined to free myself from my servitude.

I found his big room, on the seventh floor, with an excellent view of St James's Park, crowded, as usual at his parties, with very incongruous guests. Some, to judge by their uneasy and pompous solitude, were from the constituency; some, by their tweeds and ties and hair, from Chelsea; and some, as obviously, were ladies of the highest fashion, moving quickly here and there and darting quick glances of recognition at nobody, to hide the fact that for the moment they knew only nobody. Two young officers chatted together like polite conspirators; a famous millionaire looked at the pictures with the face of one who asks, 'Ought I to invest in these absurd things?' and two political groups, all of men, talked vigorously among themselves. All these latter, young and old, had the same kind of assured manner, which was quite different from the unassuming social confidence of the guardsman or the arrogance of the rich merchant. One could tell at once that they were all used to playing the statesman, in some circle, large or small, and to public speaking. They threw into their voices notes of geniality, indignation, and importance.

Edward's secretary, a very fair young man, with the manners of a bishop, came up to me and asked me if I knew where he was.

'No, isn't he here?'

'He isn't at Mrs Eeles?'

'No, I saw her just now.'

There was a slight pause, as if we might come to some understanding about Julie.

Julie, after all, had taken a flat in the buildings, at Edward's own request. Their only concession to public opinion was that she lived on a different floor. And I was still in daily fear of a scandal. I had not yet discovered that women were not to be Edward's ruin; that he was protected by one of those strange conventions of British public life, which prevents any reference to the personal lives of public men, however bad, unless they come into the courts. Even personal disfigurements must be respected. So that Gladstone's missing finger appeared in all caricatures, even by his enemies; and the newspapers never referred to the continuous drunkenness of Mr A., a cabinet minister, or to even more scandalous liaisons than

Edward's. He suffered more with the party, by writing epigrams and collecting French pictures, than by keeping Julie Eeles.

The secretary, though my ally in anxiety, was never equal to a private confidence with me. He was too loyal or too official. He regarded me merely as Edward's man of business. 'How is she?' he would ask, with dignified reserve, meaning, 'Is she going to behave?' And I answer it, 'Quite well. But she won't be coming to the party.'

'No,' the young man murmurs, 'I should hope not.' As if an undergraduate had peeped out of the Bishop's window.

'Exciting times,' I say, to relieve our mutual embarrassment.

'Oh, yes, this Williamson letter.'

'I meant, about the peace,' and as one of the political group turns to include the secretary, I say, 'What terms are we going to give them?'

'Terms? No terms at all.'

Another exclaims warmly, 'I'm not going to deal with people who shoot our men under a white flag.'

'Is it quite certain that the letter was meant to be private?'

The discussion breaks out again with still more energy, and gradually I perceive that it is all about a bye-election, and some action by the other side which is considered unfair. A letter has been published showing that some Liberal leader disapproves of his own candidate.

'I was speaking of the end of the war,' I explain.

'Oh, yes.' They all look at me, and their faces say plainly, 'A layman – an idiot.' Then the oldest, a tall man who was afterwards minister, makes me a little speech. 'In my view our policy should be to aim at so and so.'

'Or the Welshman will give trouble again,' another interrupts.

'But you mustn't forget the Roseberyites.'

The door opens and Edward comes in with Bill. Edward is always late for his parties. He seems as usual, both busy and unruffled. He carries a portfolio under his arm; but he is dressed as for Ascot, in a pale grey frock-coat, with an orchid in his buttonhole.

I push up to him and he greets me with an affectionate smile. 'How nice to see you, Tom. You're staying?'

But I'm not to be cajoled any longer. I answer angrily, 'Did you get my letter about the agency?'

'Just a moment.' He turns aside and at once he is surrounded by the fashionable ladies, the young politicians. All but the two soldiers, the banker and the two or three older men whom I take to be M.P.'s, hasten towards him and enclose him. I salute Bill and ask after Amy, who has just had a baby, her third boy.

Bill, invalided with a wound and enteric, is still, after a year's sick leave, very thin. His moustache is already grey, and he looks ten years older than Edward. But he is full of life. His expression, the quick turn of his head while he looks round the room, even his attitude, incautiously curious, distinguishes him from all the rest. One says at once, 'Soldier on leave from foreign service.'

'Don't like these new coats much,' he says, 'too tight.' Bill's own coat, of the cut of 1894, is like a sack. 'Who's the old bogey with the bow window?'

'Ah. He's a banker.'

'Oh, I thought he might be minister for something. I say, Edward's getting on, isn't he? Is it true, they've picked him for the next Liberal Cabinet. Or is it just another yarn?'

'They'll have to give him something.'

'If they get in. But I think they've finished themselves over this pro-Boer business. I told Edward so. But he says they had to do it. All the dissenters were against the war. Edward,' calling out, 'I was just telling Tommy that you're going to be sorry for all that treason you people talked while our chaps were getting scuppered.'

Edward turns his affectionate smile towards Bill; a dozen other faces turn the same way with different expressions. The fashionable ladies with a smile which could stand, with very slight change, for congratulation or derision, as required by public opinion. The young political men with every shade of surprise and contempt.

'The fact is, Bill,' Edward says smiling, 'My constituency is full of treason, and as the representative of traitors, I –'

'You wait till the army gets back,' Bill interrupts him.

The silence is broken at last by a young man with very black hair, and gold spectacles. He says thoughtfully, 'The army.'

'Yes, the army,' Bill says, looking round him like a bulldog. 'Doesn't that count for anything?'

'Not in a democracy, Bill – or I hope not,' I say hastily. 'The army, as an army, has no political power.' I want to save Bill from exposing himself to these experts.

'Not even if it voted the same way. Because you see,' the young man speaks as if to a child, 'there's not enough of it.'

'And besides,' one of the M.P.'s remarks, leaning back and smiling down at Bill across his big wing collar, 'the war is over – as a political issue, it's as dead as Queen Anne.'

'Feeling at the moment is rather against the army,' another says, 'I noticed that particularly at my last meeting. There were two questions about the conduct of troops in the village.'

'A good sign,' says the first. 'Getting back to sanity.'

One of the country visitors, a little man with a hatchet face of which the cheeks are almost beet colour, who, till this moment, has stood aloof, glaring at everyone, now flies at Bill and, shooting forward his head like a biting tortoise, exclaims, 'So you're a soldier!'

'That's it,' Bill answers surprised, 'Major Wilcher, at your service.'

'Then allow me to inform you, Major,' and the little man stands on his toes like a game-cock about to strike. The crowd closes in as round a cockpit. I make a plunge at Edward, and say, 'I suppose you're going to dodge out of everything again.' I am furious with him, and my fury is the expression of my uneasiness for Bill. It is the revenge of the private citizen, the humble idiot, upon what is called a public man, with his special immunity. I want to break that shield of preoccupied egotism.

'Dodge out?' Edward looks at me in surprise. 'What's wrong with Julie? Of course, something about a bill.'

'She's had a summons and she's afraid your name may come out.'

Edward's eyes wander, and his face assumes the look of a small boy on holiday, who is reminded of some duty.

'Well, can't you do something about it. But I forgot, you've chucked up the job – wait a moment – I must see so and so.' And he goes off to a new arrival. He becomes at once animated, charming, interested.

But I am suddenly so enraged against him that I forget myself. I push forward saying, 'Excuse me, sir,' and then to Edward, these words which astonish myself. 'You great public men may be very important and all that, but merely private people do have some rights. And I want to know what you're going to do about the agency, and Julie's bills,' etc., etc.

Edward takes this rebellion with perfect aplomb and good nature. 'Julie? Nothing to do, old boy, I assure you. But I'll see her, if you insist.'

'It might be a good idea,' I say severely.

'Right.' He turns and makes for the door. And at once, of course, I feel ashamed of myself. I reflect that Edward has, in fact, important responsibilities. That one must not blame him for a certain carelessness in domestic relations, since public men suffer special disabilities, etc., and so on.

'Oh, damn it,' I think. 'It's settled, at any rate.' And I look round for Bill. I long to escape from all these anxieties and confusions. 'Perhaps Bill would like a walk.'

Bill is now fairly driven to the wall. The enraged evangelist is haranguing him like a murderer. An interested semi-circle stands about them, gazing as at a cock-fight. Bill, with an air of surprise, is saying, 'Yes, yes, two sides to every question. Oh, yes, I'm not maintaining –'

And he seems astonished by the other's violence.

Suddenly Amy appears beside him, carrying her baby in her arms. The politicians gaze at her in astonishment. She is dressed in electric blue, which gives to her high complexion the brilliance of a ribstone pippin. She is almost cubical in shape, as always when she is nursing; and her hat, of the largest size, is perched upon the top of a roll of hair, so high, that it is nearly as long as her whole face.

Amy looks with surprise from Bill to his antagonist, and gradually becomes redder. Suddenly her hat trembles, and turning to the evangelist, she ejaculates 'Rubbish.'

All are taken aback; not least Bill's opponent, who gazes at Amy with visible confusion. And through his eyes, I see that Amy must now appear to strangers like a formidable person. A comical idea. At last the man collects himself, 'Excuse me, madam, that isn't exactly an argument.'

'Oh yes, it is,' Amy says with royal emphasis, 'It's my argument.' And she walks off.

Bill, apparently shocked by Amy's intervention, follows her protesting, 'But it's not rubbish at all. Lots of people have that kind of view – it's a religious view.' Classifying the view under its proper head.

Amy, in this new role of the regimental matron, amuses me so much that I can't take my eyes off her. 'I'm sorry that fellow worried you – a bit of a fanatic.'

'Bill, listening to him like that. I've no patience. After the way they've treated the army.'

Bill answers mildly, 'My dear Amy, it takes all sorts to make a world. In a democracy –'

Amy is still moving away. She is now in retreat from a field of battle in which her own boldness has proved more alarming than the enemy. 'And it's long after baby's bed-time.' As if the democrats have prevented the baby from being put to bed.

'I notice that,' Bill says. 'I suppose you were showing him off again. No wonder he can't sleep. His nerves are in rags.'

'Nerves! A baby of two months with a nervous system.'

'Have you never seen that poor child jump when you drop something, or push the pram over a kerb?'

'It may jump, but that's instinct. It's not nerves.'

'Well, I give you up. But it's not my fault if the child has fits when it grows up.'

Amy carries the baby away, but calls back in a warning voice:

'I can't wait.' She disappears into a bedroom and Bill turns to me. 'One doesn't expect them to understand politics, but babies, you'd think, would be safe with them. Not a bit, old man; not a bit of it. Women know nothing about babies. Like to see your new nephew washed?'

I go in and find Amy, in an enormous apron, sitting before a wash-basin balanced on a piano stool. A battered uniform case, strangely painted with small red crescents, stands open beside her with various toilet articles disposed in the open lid which serves as a dressing-table. Amy is undressing the baby which is uttering loud furious cries.

We draw up chairs and I say, 'I'm afraid it's very inconvenient for you here. They don't cater for babies. We could have sent you a bath from Tolbrook.'

'We don't bath him now old chap,' Bill says, warning me not to expect an important pleasure. 'This is only a wash. Head and tail, how is the bottom, old girl?'

Amy turns up the baby which, head downwards, stops crying and makes desperate attempts to reach her breast.

'Better, I think,' Bill says at last. 'But I think I'd better do the powdering today. You want to give some mind to it.' And he says to me, 'All these creases. Marvellous legs, aren't they?' He takes hold of a leg and displays it to me. I am reminded of Edward showing a first edition.

'Come, we must get on,' Amy says briskly, and plants the baby in her lap. It utters a yell of rage, then puts its thumb in its mouth and sucks loudly. Amy vigorously washes its head causing its skull to roll about on the neck as if it might be dislocated.

Bill says, 'Easy-easy –' The baby continues to suck its thumb as if its head is none of its business. It submits with the same indifference to having its nose and eyes cleaned. It screws up its face with a disgusted air, sneezes several times; one expects shouts of fury; but the moment Amy removes the towel, the small features spring back, like india-rubber, into an expression of dreamy greed, and the thumb goes back into the mouth.

'Quite good now,' Bill says, in a tone of keenest satisfaction. 'As a matter of fact, Tom, you couldn't have a better-tempered child when it gets a fair deal.'

The baby suddenly takes out the thumb, doubles itself up, closes its eyes, and utters a long shriek of fury. Amy smiles, picks it up, turns it round and drops it across her knees, to wash its back. Yells change to a modulated wail, like a slowly deflating rubber pig. But now and then, in the midst of this thin wail, it throws in a short phrase like the beginning of a song. It seems to be composing, and listening to itself.

'What a back,' Bill says, spanning out the back with his thick, short fingers. 'You won't see many better backs than that. You did a good job there, old girl. Set him up for life with a real good spine.'

'I hope he'll have my digestion,' Amy says. 'That's the important thing – digestion.'

'Nonsense. He's not a prize pig. Besides, you can't have a good digestion without a good back. No play for the stomach.'

'Then I don't know why your digestion is so bad.'

'My digestion is first class, except when I've just had enteric, or malaria.'

'Look at the fuss today about the chops.'

'Chops. You mean those raw horse collops. And that was the first time in years. I never make a fuss about anything. If I did, I should be doing nothing else.'

Amy is pulling on the baby's nightdress. The baby is now uttering a series of short loud yells and trying apparently to throw itself into the air. It bends its back, waves its clenched fists, jerks its head. Then sucks and pants, pushing out its tongue. It is a picture of frantic desperate greed. Amy says placidly, 'That isn't good for you, anyway. You know how fuss upsets your stomach.'

'Fuss,' Bill says. 'Fuss again. Good God.' He utters a short laugh. 'The joys of married life, Tommy. You don't know what you've escaped. Babies, schools, dentists, quarters, bills. And on top of it, you're told that you fuss.'

'You're not going, Tom?' Amy says, warning me that she is about to feed the baby.

Bill says, 'You're ready, are you? Come on, Tom. We'll scoot.'

I should like to stay and see the baby fed, but Amy and Bill are firm. Amy, unbuttoning her bodice, calls after me, 'But you won't go away, Tommy, will you? I haven't seen you yet.'

And after the baby, now a mere bag of milk, has been put to sleep in the uniform case, which is its travelling bed as well as its campaign luggage, we go walking in the park.

Amy and Bill look about them with delight. Bill sniffs the air and remarks on the smell of narcissus, and the number of flannel suits, now in the park. 'But I suppose this new labour party has made a difference.'

He stops opposite a flower-bed and says, 'Look at these trumpets. What's their name? I must really get up daffodils from someone who knows what's what in bulbs. Come in useful when I settle down.'

I am still full of laughter at the couple. I have several stories to send to Lucy. But when Bill begins to talk of taking Amy back to the flat because she mustn't be tired, I support Amy's protest. I want to go on walking with them in the park. I feel with them a complete peace and confidence. I do not need to apologize; to defend, to rage against Edward's smiling selfishness or Julie's infatuated devotion.

It is true that Bill and Amy were private citizens, without ambition to be admired even in our own circles; but how delightful was their company to me, after political drawing-rooms. With them I breathed an air free of self-seeking; as fresh as a spring day here at Tolbrook; where there are not even tourists to appreciate its candour.

76

Robert came to me this evening when I was sorting some of Edward's papers, and said to me, 'I don't want to be a nuisance, uncle, or ask too many questions, but I've been wondering just what your idea is in getting at Ann.'

'What do you mean, Robert?'

'Well, I mean just the whole thing, uncle. First, it was the nursery chairs and the nursery wallpaper, and then it was the names, and now it's the kind of way she should bring up the boy. You've got her kind of switched back.'

I was sitting in the little room behind the saloon which used to be Edward's study, a high narrow room panelled in dirty white, with many shelves. Our tenants had used it for a store, and empty jam pots still stood on the upper shelves. In the lower there were those remnants of Edward's library, eighteenth-century novels in calf French paper backs, which had survived because they had neither interest nor value for servants or shooting guests. An upper cupboard had been used to store Edward's papers, and now at Ann's suggestion, I was putting them in some order. She had brought down her father's old desk from the attic; and found his study chair in the library. Her plan, indeed, in which I had warmly agreed, was to restore the room, which we both found one of the prettiest in the house.

On this winter day, with a big fire, and a new carpet on the floor, reproducing, as far as I could remember, Edward's French carpet, it was already, in spite of empty shelves and dirty paint, extremely pleasant; and I was possibly enjoying myself more than usual, humming, etc., over a task at once exciting and useful, when Robert made his unexpected attack.

He had just come from market and wore a blue suit with yellow shoes which, for some reason known only to himself, he affects on market days. He looks more like a sailor on shore leave, or a commercial traveller of the humbler kind, than a farmer.

I was extremely startled by the boy's speech, and answered that he was talking great nonsense.

'How could I do such a thing?' I asked. 'Ann is the last person to be influenced by anything anyone would say,' and so on.

'Well, I don't know how it is. She's changed so much, and all the other way from me.'

'But how am I responsible? I didn't do it. Every woman changes in her first year of marriage. It is a great experience for a woman, especially if she has a baby – far greater than happens to any man.' I grew indignant at this attack. And I thought of Edward's saying, 'Marriage, to a woman, is a conservative education.'

'Of course,' I said, 'Ann has changed, grown steadier and wiser, more affectionate.'

'Well, uncle, she may be more affectionate to some people, but she doesn't show it to me.'

'Who's fault is that – you don't try to please her. You don't even shave every day. You may think that's nothing. But it's very important to a woman. If you have driven Ann away from you, it's your own fault.'

'I didn't drive her to early service.'

'Why shouldn't she go to early service – mustn't she have any religion of her own. I'm surprised at you, Robert. You young people talk about freedom, etc., and then you try and interfere with your wife's religious observance,' and so on.

'I just wonder what she's playing at, and why you keep on at her. Whether you want us to split up and me to get out and leave her to it, and you to keep the kid.'

'I never heard of such a thing.' For now I was really upset. 'Good heavens, is that the way you think about me,' and the rest. I spoke with energy for the truth was, my conscience was disturbed, I had never dreamt that Robert would resent my efforts to teach Ann some rational belief. But I remembered that only that morning I had been speaking to her, perhaps too insistently, about the necessity of religion. 'The world is senseless without faith,' I had said, 'a mere fantastic play of injustice and folly.' No doubt true and necessary to the poor child's happiness, but possibly indiscreet to Robert's wife.

'I don't want to upset you, uncle,' Robert said, having upset me extremely. 'I'm not trying to make any sort of trouble between you and Ann; not at all. I've just been wondering, that's all. Especially since Ann grew all that hair. That seems to have made a big difference.'

Ann came in with a step-ladder, and a paint pot, etc. She was about to paint the upper cupboards. She stood beside Robert during his last speech while he continued in the same voice, as if it did not matter if she heard it.

'You were pleased when I grew my hair,' Ann said, whose hair was now in a neat bun. She showed me the paint. 'Is this the colour, uncle. Georgian green they called it.'

I said that the colour, in Edward's time, had been a little paler.

'I'll thin it,' Ann said.

'I was pleased when you grew your hair,' Robert said, 'but I thought you were growing it from sense and not from some nonsense.'

Ann climbed up her ladder and began to paint. She asked from above, 'What sense and what nonsense?'

'Well, I should say it's sense for a woman to be a woman. And I should say it's getting on for nonsense for anyone to play-act at being their own grandmother.'

'Play-acting. But why do you think I'm play-acting? It's quite fashionable to do your hair in a bun and wear pork-pie hats.'

'Well, perhaps it isn't play-acting, but I don't know whether I shouldn't be just as pleased if it was.'

I was alarmed by his tone. The young people had had many of their discussions lately, and I had thought that there was more obstinacy and anger in their politeness, than in their former rudeness. I said that Ann liked to be in the fashions, and I thought it a very nice womanly fashion, etc.

But I was so frightened that I could hardly breathe. I thought, 'What is going to happen now?'

Luckily Ann, even without looking at me, seemed to understand my distress, for she suddenly came down the ladder, murmured something to

336

Robert and took him out of the room. She then returned at once and said, 'He hasn't worried you, has he? How's the enemy?'

'I feel very well'

'H'm. you've done enough for the day,' and she made me rest.

And, in fact, I did not feel at all well. I was assailed by new fears. 'Everything,' I thought, 'is going to be turned upside down. And whose fault is it, mine or Ann's or Robert's. Or the evil genius of the place?' I looked at Ann on her ladder, vigorously and skilfully painting the panels, and I thought, 'Is Tolbrook claiming another victim?'

77

Government rascals! so cries honest Hob.
True, God made rascals; each man for his job.

Forty years ago, when I complained to Edward of my lost career, he smiled and said, 'You've got what you wanted. You always meant to live at home. It's a shame the place wasn't left to you.'

I raged against him. To a man like Edward, I was one of those poor creatures, lawyers, bankers, the little clerks, who haven't the spunk to take a risk. And what is the truth? That all these quiet little men are the victims of ideals, of passions. They are the lovers, the pilgrims of the world, who carry their burdens from one disappointment to another, and know it is useless even to complain. For their own comrades will despise them.

They are the private soldiers who do the hard fighting, while the generals take the glory.

Bill used that very image to me on the evening of Edward's party. 'You and I are rankers to Edward.'

But to Bill, of course, that was a natural and proper relation. He had no envy, no grudge, in his composition, and no idea of justice either. Bill, as he grew older, became simpler, and also less consistent. Just as he surprised me by his respectful attitude to the pacifist, he now threw me into a fury by taking it for granted that I should continue in the agency.

'You can't resign, Tommy – what will happen to Edward?'

'I have resigned.'

'And what are you going to do with yourself?'

'I'm taking orders, as I always meant to do.'

'Well, that's the end of Tolbrook.'

'I'm sure Tom would make a very good clergyman,' Amy says. 'At least he is a gentleman, and doesn't drink.'

'But I never thought you would let us down.'

'Blame Edward for that – not me.'

And then Bill makes his remark about the rankers. 'Edward is exceptional. That's not just my own idea – I've made inquiries from people who know. Anything we can do for Edward is worth doing.'

I am silent in bitterness, not now against Bill, but against fate; my own weakness, what you will.

I seem to be thrust into a long tunnel from which I shall never again escape until I reach the speck of light at the far end. That light is my death. But the tunnel is not dark. On the contrary, it is lighted throughout by a kind of pale sad gleam in which everything is exceedingly clear and long familiar. I see the chairs, tables, pictures; and even my London office, with its worn carpet and ink-stained wastepaper basket, standing in dumb patience, as if waiting upon my decision. They have already that dejected look of things at a sale, where everything seems to say, 'We are betrayed – there is no faith or trust in the world.' I think angrily, 'But what nonsense this is. Sentimental nonsense, and so is all this talk about the family tradition. We may have stood for something once. We kept up the Whig tradition and put evangelists into the living,' and so on. 'But that's all out of date, exploded – even if all the country houses go the same way as the Roman villas, they won't be missed. They may have been centres of civilization once, but they did not succeed in civilizing the barbarians – that needs bigger resources.'

We have reached the flats. Bill, sighing deeply, shakes hands and says, 'Well, Tom, I suppose, if you must, you must – but I never thought you were that sort.' And Amy says cheerfully, 'Oh, well, it's not quite settled yet, is it?'

And from the lift she gives me an encouraging look, as if to say, 'You'll try to be good, won't you?'

78

And as soon as the lift is out of sight, I fly up the stairs to Julie, whose presence in the building is not supposed to be known to Amy. I need consolation and support. Raging, I rush into her apartment and tell her of the plot to nail me to Tolbrook. 'Bill's in it, too.' For I like to be unjust to Bill.

Julie is wandering from one room to another, in petticoat and corsets, among heaps of silks and underclothes. She pays no attention to my complaints, and I demand angrily, 'Has he been?' He, for us, is only Edward.

'No.'

'Then what are you dressing up for?'

'I thought he might want to go out with me.'

'Why, did he say so?'

'He often does after a party.'

'And you haven't seen him for a fortnight. How can you continue with Edward?' etc. And I tell her that if she does not leave him, she will wreck her whole life.

Julie puts down one flowing garment and takes up another, throws it into the bedroom, and comes back again. Her habit of going about half-naked before me, like a Roman princess before a slave, always pleases me; even in my anger, I am gratified by a confidence, charmed by the woman's beauty. But the more warm my love of Julie, the greater my rudeness. For she never pays any attention to me, and I am like those Indian pagans who kick their gods when they will not hear their prayers.

'I can't understand you,' I say, 'making yourself so contemptible. It's revolting. Letting Edward use you.'

'He uses you, too.'

'Not any longer.'

'Perhaps we were made to be used. I shouldn't like to feel useless. Perhaps I need Edward to use me and you need Tolbrook to use you. What will you do without Tolbrook, Tommy; and Edward to badger? Won't you feel a little bit unimportant?'

'What nonsense,' I say, but I feel a strange moment of uncertainty. I hear again Bill's shocked voice, 'I never thought you would desert the old place.'

'I suppose Edward is used, too, by somebody or something. He's getting more ambitious.'

'I've done with him.'

Julie looks at me. I am sitting on the bed among the dresses which swell up on each side of me, and my feet, of course, do not reach the floor. Probably, in my frock coat and patent leather boots, my high collar and formal tie, I appear a little absurd in this situation. Julie suddenly begins to laugh. She stoops down, red with laughter, and I see her breasts, now plump and round, within her wide-topped stays.

I do not usually mind being laughed at by Julie, but now in that uncertainty which is rising so fast in my soul, I am more touchy. I exclaim angrily, 'What are you laughing at?'

'If you could see yourself,' she says, 'the rebel.' And coming up to me she takes my face between her hands and kisses me. 'Don't be angry with me. I am suffering. I have been such a failure. Even in love. And I thought I knew how to love. I am only a burden and a nuisance to Edward.'

'Then leave him.'

'I've tried but he says he needs me.'

Suddenly Edward comes in. He is surprised to see me. 'Hullo, Tom, are you staying?'

I am already off the bed. I answer with indignation, 'Of course not. What do you mean?'

339

'I meant with me. Bill would like to see more of you,' and then to Julie, 'I was wondering, Julie, if it wouldn't be rather nice to have dinner somewhere out this evening, if you're free.'

'I should love it,' Julie says gravely. 'But have you the time – ought you to spare the time?'

Julie, I think, is always too serious with Edward. He would like a more irresponsible mistress. But he answers with a pretty speech about needing her company more than any amount of time, and we leave her to finish her dressing.

Edward, as soon as the bedroom door closes, drops into a chair and takes a book out of the nearest shelf. In one minute his expression passes through affectionate earnestness with Julie, blank indifference as the door closes, and becomes attentive as he opens the book. I ask him, 'And what about this bill of Julie's? She's been half mad with worry.'

'I'm paying it. I told you I would.'

'I thought you were broke, Edward. You told me so last week.'

'So I was, old boy.' He drawls, turning a page, 'But a kind friend came to my help.'

'It isn't Bill, I hope?'

Edward is silent.

'It was Bill then. I didn't think you would rob Bill, with three children and nothing in the world but the few hundred papa left him.'

'I'll pay him back.'

'How?'

'Oh, I must sell, of course. In fact, I've had an offer for Tolbrook already – a surprisingly good offer – they'll take the timber at once.'

'And what will happen to mother?'

'I thought she might go back to Cambridge. She's never really been happy in our wild parts. Listen to this, Tommy, I'd forgotten my Dorothy Osborne. "This is all I can say. Tell me if it is possible I can do anything for you, and tell me how to deserve your pardon for all the trouble I have given you. I would not die without it." And they talk about Madame de L'Espinasse's love letters. Give me a Dorothy – it's a thoroughbred to a neurotic poodle. Latin fire and passion! A cat on the roof. No, give me the English girl for power and breeding. And, mind you, I'll bet Dorothy beat any Pompadour at her own game, and did it with a style those puddings never dreamed of.'

I say nothing. I am dumbfounded. I can't tell whether Edward be the most selfish or the most admirable of men; so much above petty considerations of money, etc., that I can't even understand him. I stare at him in silence. I ask myself with a kind of dismay, 'Isn't he afraid? Doesn't he fear some retribution – a bad conscience at least? Can one live without any decent principles?'

340

He does not even glance at me. He continues to read, his cheeks are flushed with pleasure, his eyes sparkle.

Julie comes in, dressed with a splendour suitable to her new stately beauty. And that growing softness of her figure seems to have invaded her glance, her expression. What had been passion and fire in the young girl was now more tender, more gentle and resigned.

'I am reading your Dorothy Osborne,' Edward says to her. 'Listen to this: "I know you love me still, you promised it me, and that's all the security I can have for all the good I am ever like to have in this world. 'Tis that which makes all things seem nothing to it, so high it sets me, and so high, indeed, that should I ever fall, 'twould dash me all to pieces." '

'I'm glad you like my Dorothy,' Julie says, as if speaking of a friend. She is flushed with pleasure.

'Like her? I was in love with her from the first time we met – about seventy-eight, at Clifton, where my form master introduced me.'

'Why is she so attractive?' Julie asks, 'and how could she love that stick Sir William Temple?' And they begin to discuss the character of a woman dead for nearly two hundred years. 'And yet they say she was very happy with him.'

'A woman like that makes her own happiness. Besides, these were early times, you know – that vitality you get in her letters was everywhere. Look at Pepys.'

They have forgotten about me, and when I take my leave they turn towards me the kind faces of a grown-up brother and sister towards a small child, returning to his toys in the nursery.

And as I walk in the park on my way home, I seem to hear not only Bill and Amy, and Tolbrook, but the very park trees, humbly accepting the dirt of London poured upon them from the smoky twilight. 'You mustn't desert us, your own people. The humble and the helpless.'

I remember Edward's absentminded voice. 'They'll take the timber at once.'

The next day I wrote to Edward, proposing to accept the agency, on proper conditions of pay, etc., and a proper security for the house. I lent him a thousand pounds, secured on the timber, in order to pay off Bill; and obtained a promise, for what it was worth, that he would borrow nothing more except through me or the firm. I joined the firm at once. It was still called Wilcher and Wilcher, although the actual partners were Pamplin, Jaffery, and Jaffery. Within a week I began to read for my articles as a solicitor. And all my reward for this sacrifice was a new heap of bills from Edward's creditors, and the remark, in passing, from Julie, 'You were born to fuss, Tommy. You buzz at me like a fly. But I suppose somebody must buzz.'

'The point is this,' I say to Ann, 'somebody has to keep things up, and if Robert won't make a success of this marriage, you must.'

'Why me?'

'Because if you don't, it will be the worse for you – much worse. Oh, I know it isn't fair,' I said, for I was feeling angry against the injustice of things, 'But so it is.'

'Well, it's too late, uncle. This marriage has fallen down already. I haven't seen Robert upstairs for a fortnight. I don't even know where he sleeps.'

'Then you must get him back. And don't talk of a marriage falling down. It's not a card-house. It's a living relation – it's different every day.'

'You ought to have been married, uncle.'

'You think I know nothing about it.'

'Oh, I know you lived with women – I suppose it's the same thing.'

'Not at all the same thing – a completely different thing. You mustn't think there's any substitute for marriage – for the sacrament, the contract – the security.'

'Security,' Ann said. 'Well, I've always got my job,' and these unexpected words threw me into confusion and despair, they were like that little shake to a kaleidoscope which produces in an instant a completely new and unexpected pattern. I felt as if marriage, the home, all the most stable and valuable parts of social order had suddenly burst into fragments and formed themselves into something quite different.

In fact, this mere sentence alarmed me so much that I took occasion to say, that evening after supper, to Robert and Ann together, that I had been intending to see Jaffery about a final disposition of my property, but that certain recent events gave me pause.

The children kept silence. Robert was smoking a pipe on one side of the parlour fire; Ann cigarettes on the other. Robert had the paper, Ann a book; but neither was reading. Since their late difference, they do not seem to like reading in each other's presence.

'You understand,' I said, 'that I should prefer to leave a family house to continue as a family house – that is, to a united family,' and so on.

The children were still silent. So I spoke about the importance of having some capital for farming; and a going concern, as at Tolbrook. And, in fact, I was preparing to suggest that, if they could adjust their differences, I should leave Tolbrook to them in trust for Jan, and the heirs male, when I noticed a certain look on Robert's face; and its reflection on Ann's.

Now I had noticed this look once or twice before when I had spoken to the children of the division of the property; and though I knew it was a piece of folly, it always upset me. What, after all, could be more important than a man's will. I am ready to confess that I made my first will at the age of eight, when I left all I possessed to Lucy.

It was revoked, on the next day, I think, by a codicil leaving everything to the Zanana Mission when my mother became its local secretary. And I am proud of that precocity which showed, even so young, a sense of responsibility without which no one is fit to own even a money-box.

'I see you think I am a kind of moral idiot,' I said to the children, to all our surprise. For all at once I had lost my temper. 'An old miser who can only think and talk about money and shake his will every time that he's crossed. But it's you who are the idiots, yes, perfect idiots – not to know that money is important – extremely important. I've had to do with money all my life, and I tell you that it's not only the root of evil, but the root of good, too,' etc., and so on. 'A few pounds more or less in a legacy may change a whole life – save some poor woman's happiness or her children's future.'

But Robert continued smoking on his side of the fire until I had finished, and then took out his pipe and said that he quite agreed with me. 'I could do with a million this minute, if it hadn't too many strings on it.' And Ann lit another cigarette and said thank God for her job – it made her independent at least.

'Okay,' Robert said. 'You're independent – and I'm free.'

'What a good thing we're both satisfied.'

'Satisfied with what? With the life of animals shut up in a dark room full of your own dirt – no love, no hope, no heaven, no regard for past or future. But the truth is that I ought to leave the place to Blanche. She may be a prig, but she's a Christian at least, and knows how to value the things of the spirit, and a family property, which is one of them.'

But they were not even offended by my rudeness. So impossible it is for an old man to make any impression upon the arrogance of youth.

80

But I am right and they are wrong. Money enters into the whole fabric of society. Nobody attends to it, any more than they trouble about their own blood until it runs thin or does not run at all. And when I was condemned to be a lawyer and money-manager, I was put in the position of that heart which in a man's body does all the work and gets no attention or thanks whatever. The brain, the will, the passions, what do they care about that poor humble creature, pounding away for ever in his dark prison, on the everlasting treadmill which gives to brain, will, etc., their light, and their life.

I say I had no thanks. But the truth is, I had less than no thanks. I had condescension or scorn. For, of course, as an essential organ, I was obliged to say to brain, passions, etc., just when they were in their most furious state of exaltation, 'Take care – don't forget me – there are limits,' etc.

In 1906, that year of revolution, I spent several hours and thousands of words, by telephone and letter, trying to make Edward understand that he was bankrupt; and that his creditors wouldn't wait. But he answered me not at all, or with those good-natured smiles which meant, 'Poor Tom, he doesn't comprehend great events even when they take place in front of his eyes.' Edward was waiting for a place in the new Cabinet. He could not give his time to lawyer's letters.

And what was strange, I was held cheap, not only by Edward and Lucy and Julie, but by my own comrades in the ranks.

I was then thirty-eight, but not yet out of my articles, a lawyer's clerk. I was one of a million London clerks, who, in top hat and black coat, beat every day to and fro in the dark gullies of the streets, under a sky of smoke. The black houses overhung us like the houses of the medieval city, grown only in height and in dirt. The soles of our boots, the iron shoes of the horses, made the loud monotonous music to which, as it seemed, we marched upon a thousand errands, which were one in object, to defeat some enemy. We were like a besieged city, and the narrow faces of the passers, grey like the dust, each absorbed in its own thought, were like those of a garrison, under threat of terror and destruction. But now the trumpets were sounding for the relief. The new age was at hand, when all should be free, etc. And we believed. The gloomy or reserved air with which we received these tidings were not due, as a hundred times before, to disbelief. We knew that the time had come when prophecies should be fulfilled.

Why, I don't know. Why do the people ignore political threats, violence, the most solemn promises, until a certain moment, when they suddenly agree among themselves. 'This time something is going to happen.' It has nothing to do with the newspapers or the political prophets. A dozen times in my life, all the prophets, the men in the know, have said, 'Prepare for the worst'. The newspapers have declared, 'We are on the eve of tremendous revolutions.' And the man in the street, the farm labourer at the plough tail, have paid no more attention than the sparrows and the cows.

And at another time when the prophets are buying consols and the newspapers are declaring that the political weather is set fair, the little men say to each other, 'This time something is going to happen.' Is this the famous political sense which is supposed to belong to certain peoples? Or is it merely a judgement of circumstance closer to the people and the wage earner, than to the clever men in clubs? Does something happen, on these occasions, which hits the sense of the common people, and clerks on the buses, so that they find everywhere a unanimity of expectation?

We, the rankers, believed in those trumpets. But we looked at each other, just like rankers, as if to say, 'All right, but what then? What have you and me got to do with these splendours?'

I remember one of the clerks at the office, a middle-aged man, saying to me, 'Great times, Mr Tom.' He was a good Radical like myself; but then he added, 'Not that they'll make much difference to the gas in our office.' The bad lighting was an old grievance. And his look and voice both expressed the idea that for people like him and me, mere fusty clerks, the gas supply must seem more important than the most glorious of social revolutions.

81

And this feeling made me especially critical of Edward, and also violent in my politics. I demanded in the same breath, the destruction of all privilege, and a strict account of Edward's debts.

And Edward's financial position, at a critical moment in his fortunes, enabled me, or rather the firm, to impose terms. The first clause in our agreement, a clause not put into writing, was that he should leave Julie and marry Mrs Tirrit.

We insisted on this. For only Mrs Tirrit could satisfy the creditors, who were prepared to accept, on her verbal assurance alone, a delay of proceedings, and afterwards twelve and sixpence in the pound. They wanted fifteen shillings, but the lady refused them. Mrs Tirrit was rich, but she was also a woman of business. She did not mean to pay for Edward more than was absolutely necessary.

This agreement gave the firm and especially me, much satisfaction. Should I say that we felt a real pleasure in humiliating the glorious Edward? Lucy thought so. But I should be wrong and Lucy was wrong. We were not vindictive. We were only in revolt against the self-deception, the irresponsibility of our hero and master. We were the head and stomach, saying finally to the poetic genius in the upper storey, 'Come now, please to remember that you also are human.'

It was a shock, therefore, especially to me, to find that Edward did not break with Julie, as we had arranged; but merely kept away from her. Mrs Tirrit heard nothing from him. And what was still more disquieting, he suddenly bought an enormous motor car, for which, as we soon discovered, he had paid cash.

He was getting money from somewhere, and our whole arrangement threatened to collapse.

When I challenged him with trickery, he answered only that he had to have a car 'for business purposes'. He could not get through his work, that is, his tub thumping, without it.

None of us thought of Bill as the source of these funds, until I happened to meet Amy and she let out the secret.

Bill and Amy were just returning to India, and we had arranged to meet at Paddington, so that I could see them off. I knew at once that they had something on their minds.

'Nurse has broken her leg,' Amy said, and Bill at once closed in upon me. 'This morning at half-past seven.' Amy was carrying a six-month baby in her arms, her fourth, a daughter; Loftus, the third, aged two, was sitting among the hand luggage with an angelic expression on his round pink face.

Now, though I approve of large families, I could not help wondering how Bill and Amy proposed to bring up four children. William, at his public school, was already costing Bill more than he could afford. The very sight of Bill and Amy, therefore, surrounded by their family, always made me feel anxious, and perhaps a little impatient. I was tempted to ask how many more children they meant to have, and why. And in any conversation with them, I was apt to bring the financial aspect to their notice. 'Broken her leg. That may be a serious liability. How did she break it – in your service?'

'It isn't about nurse –'

'It had better be about nurse – who's going to pay for the hospital?'

'It's Johnny,' Bill says. But at this moment John comes running up with a large parcel. He is a thin little boy with Bill's rough hair and his mother's grey-blue eyes. Amy waggles her right-hand fingers at him in the air, under the baby's head, to show that she can still hold a parcel, takes the parcel, and says, 'Is it true about Edward, Tom?'

The abrupt change of subject startles me, and I exclaim 'What about Edward?'

'Something about a tailor who wanted to summons him.'

'Edward is very hard up,' I say.

'I told you, Bill,' Amy says mildly, and her tone gave me at once the information I am seeking. 'Good God,' I say, 'you haven't been lending Edward money again?'

Bill turns on Amy, 'There, I said you'd give it away.'

'I didn't give it away. Tommy knew already.'

'He certainly did not. Did you, Tommy?'

'Do you mean Edward actually took your money and asked you to keep it a secret?'

'It was a debt of honour,' Bill says, 'and it's none of your business, if you'll excuse me, Tom.'

'I said you'd lose your money, Bill.' Amy speaks with the patient mildness which always exasperates Bill. Her face is flushed, her hat is crooked, but her hair is neat and her expression is that of a policeman on point duty. I notice again that Amy has changed from the bride at whom we laughed, fifteen years before; but I should still laugh, from custom, if I were not so irritated.

Bill answers her, 'You said we ought to do what we could for Edward, for papa's sake.'

'I said a thousand pounds was quite enough – and more than we could afford.'

'You did not, excuse me. But what's the good of arguing. Edward had to have the money.'

'Edward is bankrupt,' I say. 'He owes at least twenty thousand that he can't pay. And you're unsecured creditors. You'll never get a farthing of your money.'

'H'm,' Bill says, obviously disbelieving me. 'I don't understand business. But Edward's career might have been ruined.'

'Edward is a great man in politics,' I say severely, 'but in finance he is simply a dangerous lunatic. And you have enabled him to dodge the only settlement that could have saved him.'

'Finance,' Bill's air seems to say that finance is not of much importance to anybody; except little lawyers.

But before I can point out his mistake, the train comes in, and the couple are summoned to see their stack of luggage weighed and put aboard. Each has a different count. 'Damn it all,' Bill is shouting, 'you've been counting the lunch basket. A lunch basket isn't luggage.'

'Luggage is luggage, whatever it is.'

'A lunch basket is gear – for the rack.'

'But it's going in the train.'

The boy John dodges round their legs. He continually puts out a hand to them, then draws it back again as if fearing to be obtrusive. They look at him every moment, glancing quickly over him as if fearing to catch his eye.

'Want a job, Johnny?' I see the boy's look of apprehension. It is plain that he dreads being away from them even for a moment.

'Go and get me a paper. Here's threepence.' The boy dashes away.

'You've probably thrown away that boy's chance for life,' I say bitterly. 'How are you going to give your children a start, without capital.'

Bill and Amy look at each other with a peculiar expression of anxiety. I think I have made an impression at last. I say, 'Every pound you give Edward, if you have any more to give, is as good as another nail in his coffin.'

'We were just wondering,' Bill says, and I perceive that I am to hear the important communication that has hung over me from our first meeting.

'It's about Johnny,' Amy says. 'He's a little young for boarding school at six, but we couldn't take him back to India for two years. It wouldn't be worth it.'

'It's getting him to Paddington,' Bill says. 'Nurse was going to do it. And then we thought of sending him with an outside porter.'

'Of course, there'll be a master to meet him there.'

All this a preface to a request which, after all, is not made. Bill and Amy, either from modesty or pride, we never decided which, are both of them extremely averse from asking any kind of favour.

'And we were just wondering –' Amy says.

'He wouldn't be a nuisance,' Bill assures me. 'He was a bit upset at first when we told him that he had to stay behind. But he's pulled up his socks in the last day or two. Poor little devil. He knows there's no getting out of it.'

I say with mild sarcasm, that if this is all that's troubling them, I should be delighted to take the boy to Paddington. They overwhelm me with thanks. Sarcasm has no more effect on them than rain on a couple of tortoises.

'If you *did* have time,' Amy says, 'you might perhaps give him a meringue. He's very fond of meringues. But really, Tom, it's a scandal to waste your time.'

'Whist,' Bill says. 'Here he is. Not a word.' And John dashes up with the paper. 'Good lad, record time.' But the boy's haste is obviously to return to them. Amy waves her left-hand fingers in the air and says, 'I'd better have that, Johnny. Your father'll want it in the train.' Johnny puts the paper into the hand, which firmly grips it under the baby.

The porter comes to report all the heavy luggage aboard. Amy and Bill turn to the hand luggage, and find that Loftus has been eating the labels.

'I said he was up to something,' Bill cries, carrying the child like a sheep, hanging down between his hands.

Amy, not yet distracted, murmurs, 'Never mind. It's flour paste.'

'But what about the luggage –'

'Put him in with it – it will keep him quiet.'

Bill thrusts Loftus into the train, who, with a filthy face, and pieces of label sticking to his mouth, chin and cheeks, looks at us still with angelic eyes, while a porter throws the hand luggage up on the rack. Amy and Bill count together, 'One – two – three – four.'

'And the lunch basket,' Bill says. While Amy counts five.

The guard is blowing his whistle. Bill says to me, 'Good-bye, old chap, and remember we mustn't let Edward down.' Amy kisses me, warmly and unexpectedly, and murmurs, 'You won't forget the meringue.'

I cannot think what she means, till I see that both she and Bill are smiling at the boy. 'Good-bye, old chap.' Bill shakes the child's hand. 'And don't forget to write to your mother.' Amy hands the baby to Bill, lifts John up and kisses him on both cheeks. She is still smiling, but her eyes and nose turn scarlet and tears suddenly appear on her cheeks. She hastily climbs into the train, and Bill hands her the baby, which at once wakes up and utters a loud cry. The train moves, and Bill dives through the door. I see Amy saying something behind the window. But I hear only the baby's screams and an affected voice beside me calling, 'Good-bye, Moms, my love to Paris.'

Probably Amy has been reminding me about the meringue. The train has gone, leaving an empty hole at which both John and I gaze. Then I take the boy's hand and lead him to the station hotel. To my relief, he does not cry. I say, imitating Bill's cheerful address, 'Well, old chap, that's over. Would you like something – a meringue?'

The boy, to my surprise, shakes his head.

'Oh, but I'm sure you'd like a meringue – a double one. They have wonderful meringues here.'

He shakes his head again. I notice that he is trembling all over, his lips, his hands, his knees, even his body. His face is extremely white, and he opens his eyes with a look of amazement, as if he perceives something incredible.

I take him to a cab and we drive to Paddington. He sits quiet; and I think, 'He's being brave, thank goodness. I'd better let him alone.'

My bitterness against Edward has been followed by discouragement. I feel that I have been beaten in the struggle. I think, 'I can't deal with Edward any more. I'll throw up the whole business. I'll go and explain it to Julie. I shan't blame Edward. I'll only say that he's too much for me, that I don't understand these politicians. I'm only a private person.'

Suddenly I remember the boy, and I say to him in an encouraging voice, 'So you're going to a boarding school. You'll like that very much. It's a very happy time.'

He shakes his head.

'I liked it. I thought I shouldn't like it, but I really enjoyed it quite well.'

I see to my horror that tears are trickling down his cheeks. He cries like his mother with a stoic face. And after a little reflection I encourage him, 'Don't cry, old chap,'

'I'm not crying,' he says in a low voice, 'It's my eyes.'

We are at Paddington. But no master accosts us. The boy, thank heaven, has stopped weeping. I say hopefully, 'Just time for something – a cream cake, or what about a cup of chocolate?'

'No thank you, uncle.'

He disengages his hand from mine, and I look down to see if I have given him offence. But he looks up at me with a face which startles me by its perfect comprehension of my course of feeling. He says, 'The master will be coming.' He means, 'Perhaps I'd better not be holding hands when this envoy from the unknown world of exile comes upon us.'

The master arrives. He is a short hook-nosed man with a friendly manner. He taps John on the head and calls him young feller – he beams at me and says loudly, 'The worst is over, I see.'

349

I can feel, rather than see, the expression on the child's face as he hears this; and I can feel the sense of loneliness and smallness intensified within him by words which mean, 'These small animals needn't be taken too seriously.' I feel for the child, but I cannot think what to do or what to say to him. The master waits a moment, looks encouragingly at us both, then at his watch. He remarks, 'We've five minutes. What about a bun, young feller.'

The boy shakes his head and says, 'Good-bye, uncle.'

'Good-bye, my dear.' I offer him half a crown. He takes it, and says nothing, not even thank you. The master, to my surprise, turns his back, and at once the child puts out his arms and reaches upwards. I understand his motive in time to stoop. He embraces me and whispers in a voice which already seems to come from a distance, 'Good-bye, uncle. Thank you most awfully for everything.' Probably a formula taught him by his mother, for use after parties.

Then he is walking away with the tactful master. I notice a half crown lying on the pavement, but I do not realize that the boy has dropped it until I am several yards away. And when I return for it, it has already disappeared. Someone of the group of porters and loungers standing opposite has picked it up, and when I look at them several of them stare back at me, with those wooden faces which say, 'Think what you like – you can't do anything.' I feel again a deep oppression of weakness, as if the whole of the civilized order about me, in which Bill and Amy walk so confidently and so rashly, and the young John carries his grief with so much dignity, is nothing but an appearance, a dream. And from the dream, our unhappy people, especially Bill, Amy, etc., are about to be awakened.

I had an appointment with Julie, on Edward's affair. But now I went to her, on my own, in the mood of the private soldier, who says, 'If they want hell, then to hell with it.'

82

Julie, in the last year, had moved into a new flat, in West Street, just off Park Lane. I think her move had been an attempt to break with Edward. She herself had been urging him to marry Mrs Tirrit. But if it was an attempt, it had failed. Edward had continued to visit her, sometimes every day, sometimes not for weeks.

I found her still in her bedroom at eleven o'clock. She kept late hours, night and morning. But to me the bedroom was open, and I sat down beside the dressing-table while the maid brushed out her hair.

We spoke trivialities, about Edward's triumphs and an Ibsen revival in which Julie had been asked to take a part. 'But I could not act Hedda Gabler

– I should feel ridiculous waving a pistol now.' Her eyes meanwhile asked me, 'Why have you come?' She said, 'I like your morning visits,' meaning, 'you have come for some special purpose.'

The maid went out, and she said 'Edward has made up his mind.'

'No, he's done nothng – except steal his brother's fortune,' and I told her the story. 'I'm leaving him. I shall go abroad. I want a holiday after all this. And you, Julie, you can't stay after this. Why couldn't you come, too – let's leave this miserable confusion once and for all.'

'If he dismisses me, I should like to come with you, but I couldn't run away.'

'You call it running away – when he has not kept a single obligation to you. It's he that runs away.'

'No, he simply puts things off. And suppose he did really need me. He does sometimes need me, you know. When he is sick of politics.'

'Yes, as a relaxation.'

'Very well, a relaxation. That's something. We chatter about books and old friends – it doesn't seem very much, but I suppose it is a change for him. No, I'm tired. I wish he would make up his mind what he is going to do. But I can't go till he sends me away. The one thing is not to get muddled.' And she spoke of some friend who had committed suicide.

'He wasn't tired of life or even unhappy, but he got in a muddle. He stopped knowing what he wanted. I remember he had some sort of quarrel about a dog which had bitten his wife; and he lost his front teeth in an accident.'

I had never felt more admiration of Julie's wisdom and courage. We spent most of that day together, at Kew, which was one of Julie's favourite gardens. I remember the peculiar pleasure I felt when she spoke of friendship. 'It is the only thing worth having, but how rare it is. People talk about their friends, but how many have any friends. Most people go through life without friends, and they don't even know what friendship is.'

'You have hundreds of friends, Julie.'

'I had one once, but she died long ago.'

I did not say, 'But we are friends,' because I feared her answer; which was bound to be sincere.

'She was a real friend. I could absolutely depend on her, and yet she was very critical of me. She used to abuse me like a pickpocket. It was she who made me act.'

We were in the great palm house and the tropical heat brought out the colour of her cheeks and made her astonishingly beautiful. At thirty-two, Julie was growing more plump. But it suited her. She seemed like some dark Creole beauty while she strolled under the arching palm leaves and pondered, with downcast eyes. Her long lashes threw a green shadow on her cheeks. Little beads of sweat stood on her round forehead. 'We had

fearful quarrels, but they were good for me. She hated me to say that I was
going to be a nun.'

'Do you still wish it?'

'No, I don't think so. I should have to forget so much that I don't want
to forget. I should feel so disloyal.'

And in the midst of my admiration I thought for the first time, 'Why
shouldn't this woman be mine?' And all my uneasiness, my sense of
insecurity, of the moral and social revolution which for the first time had
become real to my nerves, formed one urgent wave of rebellious passion.
It was the revolutionary movement, I suppose, in its private form. 'I shall
have her,' I thought, 'good and noble as she is. Why not?'

And I said in a voice carefully respectful, 'I'm glad you're not going to
leave us, Julie. We need you.'

'Only the religious are happy in a world like this. But I haven't the right
to stand aside,'

83

'It would be very nice just to let things slide,' Ann said. 'But I don't feel I
ought to let Robert walk right over me. It's bad for both of us.' And that
afternoon, as we were going out for our walk she attacked him, most
unexpectedly to me, and I think, to her. A moment before we had been
anticipating our walk, with some pleasure.

The weather was mild for February. In the morning it had rained, and
the yards were flowing with pools and rivulets between the stones. But now
the sun had come out and filled the sky with a dark blue-green radiance.
It was like sea water in an aquarium lighted from some hidden source, and
the big ragged clouds, which floated in it, seemed to be dissolving at the
edges like gouts of yellow foam, after a storm. The pools reflecting this sky
were darker still, like great table sapphires, and the noise of water running
from spouts and wall drains, had the gaiety of fountains, so that one could
not help smiling with pleasure.

But as we crossed the yard from the back door where we kept our winter
coats, we came upon Robert. He was loading muck. The cart, oozing black
filth at every crack, stood crooked, with one wheel raised upon the footway
outside the stalls; and the horse, steaming from each curl of its winter fur,
let his head and ears droop. Robert himself, in old khaki trousers, a leather
jerkin, and long rubber boots, was dirtier even than usual. His nose and
cheeks frost-burnt by the hard weather before Christmas were scarlet; and
his eyes, among their redness, were bluer than I had ever seen them. I
thought, 'How Lucy would have delighted in this son of hers.' And in the
thought, I enjoyed such a keen pleasure that I hardly noticed for the first

minute or so that Ann and he were quarrelling. As usual, they both spoke in the most casual tones.

'When are you going to make up your mind about Molly, Robert?'

'I made it up a long time ago. I like Moll. May be a bit obstinate, but a good girl.'

'Stupid people are always obstinate,' Ann replied.

'She's not so stupid. Only a bit shy. You make her shy.'

'Then take her, Robert. She's just longing to fall into your arms. And you know you're always hankering after her – she's so nice and soft, everywhere.'

'I wouldn't say – Molly is not so soft – she does a man's work here – she can carry her sack with everybody.'

'Then go along Robert, what are you waiting for?'

Robert looked at her for a moment, and then loaded another forkful into the middle of the cart. At last he said, 'There's a few little points – what about the kid.'

'Oh, Jan would stay with me, I suppose. You would have plenty more with Molly. I'm sure she'd be a good breeder.'

'Sure she would, and she wants 'em, too.'

'She told you that, did she?'

'Yah.'

'So you really have been thinking of her.'

'Well, Annie, you know how it is. A man often thinks of a girl, how she would be as a wife, not just his own wife; but a wife. Same as a girl thinks of a man; suppose he was my husband, how would that work out – taking the good and the bad and allowing for discounts. He's nothing in his face and he's small, but they say the small ones have more jump to 'em and last out better. But he's got a nice voice, and his nails are clean. Not meaning to marry him, but just running him through their fingers for a sample.'

'Molly looked a little finger-marked.'

'Now, I just wonder if that's a fair way to put it. It's smart, but it's not what I'd like to say of you. Seems to me a bit on the whisker side.'

Ann had apologized and said that she was sure Molly was as good as she was fat.

'And not so fat either. She's got a good frame.'

Ann took my arm and turned me towards the gate. 'Then why not buy it – it's going for nothing. Only don't keep me waiting too long – I get tired standing on the side lines.'

'Yah, it's tough on you.' And he threw another forkful. We went out into the drive.

This exchange threw me into some agitation. It revived my anxieties for the marriage.

'Robert is a fine fellow,' I said. 'He has great strength of character.'

'Oh, don't let's talk of Robert or even think of him.'

We walked on in embarrassed silence. My alarm and agitation increased every moment. I felt that it was I who had committed some crime.

As we walked down the path among the bare trees, I looked at the girl and thought, 'Yes, Robert is right. She has changed away from him. And not only in her dress, in her hat, her hair with its corded net, resembling the net of a chignon, her bodice and her long buttoned coats. The Victorian dress, as she said herself, was a fashion. Her bodices were not real bodices – they were fixed with a contrivance of steel teeth which slid beneath her arms. Her wide skirt was not much below her knees and her stockings were flesh colour. The dress meant little; the real change was in her thought, her speech, her ideas. Her church going, perhaps, was only play, like her imitation chignon, but her housekeeping and house furnishing was not play. Her love for this place was true and strong. She spoke of home as only those speak for whom the word has gathered meaning.' But simply because I felt more in sympathy with the child than ever before, I was afraid to speak to her, as usual, even about the old house, her father's life and work; the tragedy of his failure.

I perceived that there was some secret agitation in her soul, or at least, her interior. But I could not tell its nature.

84

I don't know if I, more than others, am shut out from understanding of my fellow creatures. But their actions have usually surprised me. I cannot describe my astonishment when on the very evening of the day, during which Julie and I talked so gravely about her duty, she attempted suicide. She was found at ten in the morning, unconscious in a roomful of gas. I had a note from the maid and hurried round in time to meet the doctor and a policeman, who had broken in the door. The policeman wrote down particulars, the doctor listened with a stony face while I swore to Julie's carelessness and pointed out that she had not closed up her keyhole or the cracks of the window frames.

'The rug was against the door and the damper of the chimney was closed,' the policeman said.

The doctor said nothing. It was obvious that he stood aloof from corruption in his professional and scientific honour. I made sure from the policeman that nothing more could take place until Julie was well enough to make a statement. And I hurried to Whitehall.

Astonishment had succeeded horror. But now anger united both in a resolution to bring Edward to his senses. If I had seen Edward immediately, I have no doubt that there would have been a violent scene.

But the ante-room at the Ministry was already full of visitors, and Edward's secretary could promise only that I should be let in at the earliest possible moment.

Edward's ante-room was always full because of his unpunctuality, and because his friends liked to see him at the Ministry, where on most mornings they could be sure of finding him. So that whereas in some great Ministry, the Foreign Office or the War Office, one might find only two or three persons waiting; in Edward's there were often a dozen and more, either without appointments, or kept half an hour beyond their time.

The secretary obviously found this arrangement quite natural. To him I suppose Edward was a person so important that his convenience came before that of all others.

And I felt the impression of power, not only in the matter of these people waiting on Edward, but even in the suspicious glance of door-keepers, and the height of the room. For the ante-room, at least twenty feet high, which seemed much higher than its breadth, reminded one of those palaces whose giant magnitudes seem to say, 'We are the habitations not of ordinary men but of ideals. Royalty, majesty, national honour, live here, and as they are greater than any single men they need a bigger house.'

I thought that I distinguished the same feeling in some of the visitors, who now and then threw a glance towards the high dirty ceiling as if to wonder if they had not underestimated the dignity of public business. Some others, obviously private visitors; a fashionable young woman, probably a comedy actress, to judge by her powdered face and her Dana Gibson figure; a well-known picture dealer from Bond Street; an old man with a farmer's complexion but a peculiar glance, colder and sharper than any I had seen, who was probably a trainer, and two young men who were certainly undergraduates, looked only at each other. A deputation from the constituency did not look at anything. They were used to the high ceilings which go with high responsibility. They had those looks of mixed ferocity and resignation, common to all such official parties from the remote country, their jaws set with resolution, their brows wrinkled already with doubt, as if the sight alone of a busy office, in the great city, had caused them to reflect, 'There may be other sides to our argument.'

Upon me, so well used to such places, it had the same effect, and before I was summoned into Edward's presence, I had had time to reflect on his peculiar situation as a public man; his special burdens, etc., unknown to my experience. And I approached him with a circumspection and reserve, of which, half an hour before, I would not have been capable.

I found him behind an enormous desk in a room not perhaps so large as that of the chief ministers, but larger than a small house. He sprang up and came to meet me at the door.

Edward was a junior minister of a young ministry, but he had already made it important in the public eye, by promises of railway reform, of tramways for farmers, of a reorganization of canals, of a new charter for dock labour. He had made himself popular and feared, and so he had increased his actual power.

Power makes most men cautious, reserved; or at least, circumspect. Men in power have a special manner, and even a special look. Their courtesy seems to say, 'Do not think ill of me,' their look, 'I carry burdens and secrets.' With Edward, power seemed to have made him more friendly with all the world, and more indiscreet. It was only now, approaching him in the office for the first time, that I saw under the genial manners the air of preoccupation and apartness, 'My dear Tom, I'm glad you've come – I'm afraid I'm awfully busy.'

'It's about Julie.'

'Oh, yes, but just a moment. Do you remember who owns the Queensport ferries? Some local farmers' committee want a light railway instead – as you can understand everyone within twenty miles of Tolbrook has been putting up schemes to me. But I've an idea that this committee is the same gang that tried to get control of the ferries last year.'

I told him that Julie had attempted suicide and might be arrested. His expression changed to a peculiar look of resolution. I did not see that look again until the moment when he finally recognized his failure. He said after a moment, 'I can't stop her being charged.'

'Come and see her. It may make all the difference to her statement.'

He shook his head. 'Wouldn't do any good.'

'You mean you can't be bothered.'

'I haven't time.' He smiled. 'Even the Transport Minister has certain small responsibilities,' and he began again to talk about the light railways and the Queensport proposal.

I listened with despair. I thought, 'This man is so completely spoilt and self-indulgent that he will not suffer a moment's discomfort to save himself from ruin. Yet he is so ambitious that he can hardly bear to be a junior minister, at forty-six.' I said, 'Why ask me about the ferries? You know they are quite adequate. A light railway would cost more and waste all the ferry equipment.'

Edward patiently brought up more arguments to show that the railway, though more expensive, would be an improvement.

'You mean a change,' I said, 'and something in the papers to make people say that you are being energetic.'

Edward smiled, and once more I saw the new statesman beneath the old irresponsible. Even his smile appeared to say, 'How can they understand us or our problems.' But it passed at once into his charming affectionate look, and he spoke, as usual, as if I had said something intelligent. 'It does look like that, doesn't it, and of course there is something in it. A government has to show energy and do something, and that means making changes – sometimes, I daresay, unnecessary changes. But do you know, one of the things I'm beginning to realize in the last few weeks is that a lot of change starts by itself simply because there happens to be a new government. There's a change of feeling and expectation which is like a change in the weather. You can feel it. Of course, political weather changes every day, but this is like jumping from mid-winter to mid-summer in five minutes. And of course, the expectation is always beyond what any government can do. People want a new heaven and a new earth before the end of next week.'

I listened with astonishment. At last I interrupted, 'I can't wait. But if you may remember we came to a certain agreement. You have broken that agreement, by borrowing from Bill, and by visiting Julie. Now you refuse to visit her when she needs you. Very well, you can't have it both ways. You must decide whether to carry out the agreement, or to stick to Julie. Or I will throw up the whole business.' I grew angry again. And I added some phrases about his shilly shally and untrustworthiness.

He answered me with affectionate earnestness, 'It's quite true, Tommy. I do put things off, and I've treated Julie disgracefully. But I'll decide today. I'll let you know before this evening. And you must let me know if it's all right about the inquest.'

'And if it isn't all right?'

'I'll hear soon enough from my friends – good-bye, old man. And don't think me too ungrateful for all you have done,' etc.

I was too angry to wish him good-bye. Yet I was confused as if perhaps I was not fit to judge a man who exerted power from such large rooms, and whose desk alone was as big as six ordinary desks. It seemed to me that what I called weakness in Edward, might be strength, in the mysterious circles of power, and that he might know his own business in the world far better than I.

85

We were saved after all by the doctor, who, it appeared, was one of those who, at sixty-nine, grey-haired and worn, expected a new heaven and a new earth. When I called upon him again he greeted me, 'I had not understood that that silly woman was a friend of Mr Edward Wilcher.'

'My brother, yes. They are very old friends. Lately there has been some little difference between them – my brother's political work gives him little time for society.'

The doctor pursed his sharp lips, 'A great work – these are great times.'

'Women do not always understand the claims of a man's work.'

'Never, never,' his precise voice abolished Julie. 'I read your brother's speech about the scientific age and a scientific government – a truly modern state.'

And he spoke for a long time on the importance of the scientific approach to politics. I do not know what he meant, and I do not think he knew himself. Under his hard dry skin, behind his sharp eyes and mouth, he was another enthusiast carried away by some secret dream, or impulse; to desire change, change; a new world at all costs. He had almost forgotten Julie when I brought him back to the subject. 'If the case does get into court, you will be called.'

'I shall say it was obviously an accident.'

'What about the rug and the damper closed in the grate.'

'Leave it to me,' the doctor said with the air of a Cabinet Minister. 'I shall go round and see the young woman.'

In fact, he waited at Julie's bedside until she came round. The policeman was also present, and made some protest against the doctor's first remark to Julie, that she mustn't be frightened. She had suffered an accident with the gas. But he took the case no further. A police officer is not advised, in such a case, to stand against the medical evidence. When I was called into the room, the constable had already withdrawn, and the doctor was giving his last instructions to Julie's maid.

'Your friend has been very careless,' he said to me, pursing his lips in a discreet smile.

'She has been well punished for it.'

'The worst is over.' He did not wink at me, but his whole expression, his lively movement as he packed his stethoscope into his inner breast pocket was like the wink of a triumphant conspirator. The old man felt, for that moment only, that he was an instrument of government, that he disposed supreme power. He drew me into the landing to talk again of Edward's speech. I had forgotten it; Edward had forgotten it as soon as it was uttered; but to this dry old man it was plainly the wisdom of the angels. I invited him to meet Edward, and he was moved as if by the offer of millions. 'I have no claim.'

'He would like to thank you.'

'What for? Nothing. Don't mention it.' He was blushing over the bones of his cheeks like a girl. 'But I should esteem it a very great honour.'

He left me astonished once more at the simplicity of good men, and Edward's prestige, achieved so easily and unjustly. 'For what has he done,' I thought, 'except talk and make the right friends. And now he is a man of power, a ruler, and people like this doctor, honest good people, look up to him and trust him.'

> God loves democracy; the proof is plain
> It cannot die; tho' hopelessly insane.

86

The sky was darkening in the east to the grey black of heather ashes, a burnt moor. A few small clouds floated in this thick darkness, like grouse feathers. The sun was going down behind the moor, and, as turning our backs towards it, we came towards the house, the trees, still bare of leaves, were shining before us like gold wire, and Tolbrook was like a gingerbread palace with gilt chimney pots.

'Hansel and Gretel ought to be living here,' Ann said.

'I never liked Hansel and Gretel so much as Alice. Too foreign. But I suppose they are both out of date nowadays.'

'I like Alice the best,' Ann said. 'Alice has more character than all the others put together.'

And I thought, 'She has certainly changed. A year ago she would not have thought so, or spoken with the same conviction.'

'But you would have thought the real Alice a terrible little prig,' I said.

'I don't think so, uncle. I rather envy Aunt Lucy and Aunt Amy. They were born at a good time.'

'All that is romantic nonsense. Lewis Carroll used to try to stop the new plays at the Oxford theatre – he didn't like anything that might shock his Alices. His world is a long way off – further than ancient Rome.'

'I expect they were just like us,' Ann said, 'only perhaps they had more sense.'

'No,' I thought, 'not at all like you. You can't even understand a world that believed in heaven and hell. It was buried thirty years ago when Church and State were overthrown. The cloth caps came to Parliament in 1906, and their cry was not for eternal life and the judgement of God, but for the world's life and justice on earth. A revolution deeper than the French. Rousseau said, "Trust human nature to do the right thing." But now they say, "By our will we shall remake the world, and humanity also." '

The blue shadows had stretched across the fields and were rising up the front of the house until nothing was left except the golden chimney pots against a sky as dark as a lawyer's blue bag. 'It is like a Christmas card,' I thought, 'except that it is real and I am seeing it, and it is far more beautiful than any picture. Because it is real, and so it must die. It is dying so fast that I can hardly bear to look at it.'

'I don't mean that they were born with more sense,' Ann said, 'but there seems to have been more sense going round. It was easier to be sensible; nowadays, you have to find out everything for yourself. And before you know anything that matters, you're old.'

I thought she was asking me a question, but I did not know what it was.

What do women seek in life as women? No man knows, because his whole body and his feeling of life is profoundly different. And because his experience is different, his mind and thoughts are different. I have always been attracted to women, as by a foreign country and a mystical religion. Once I dreamed of being an Indian sadhu, because I thought that by renouncing self and all possessions, all pride, I should enter into a final peace and joy. So I have felt of women; of Julie and Sara, but especially of Julie.

I was passionately in love with Julie, but what attracted me to her more than anything else was the sense of her nature. It seemed to me that in being Julie's lover I should enter into an experience at once noble and intense, a happiness both secure and exalted.

It is notorious that lovers have feelings of religious worship and reverence for their mistresses, and that sensual images are abolished even from their most secret thoughts.

But that was impossible for me with Julie. She had been Edward's mistress, and my passion was full of sensual images. Yet as in the visions of the mystics, these very images increased my religious sense of respect for a woman whose own instincts were as deeply religious.

Yet when Edward, not on the day of the ultimatum, but a week later, at last faced facts, accepted the terms, and broke finally with Julie, and at last she was free to be my mistress, I was seized with fear and reluctance. I no longer ventured into her bedroom. And because I thought of her with passion, I was as shy in her presence as the most foolish youth before some village girl.

I was glad of the excuse of business, to see her every day. For, as Edward's man of business, I had to make many arrangements about their joint property and about Julie's debts. So it came about very naturally that I spent part of every day with Julie.

Julie's attempt to kill herself was never spoken of between us. She did not insist to me that it had been no attempt, but an accident; she referred to it only once, 'When I was so mad and criminal.'

She did not let that moment of weakness affect her spirits. She was too proud. Or perhaps she was saved by confession and absolution from an evil despair. But I think she suffered, as by an illness or a wound, from its effects. She became more dependent on visits and company. And if I was prevented from seeing her, she showed disappointment. She turned to me in all her difficulties, more for company, perhaps, than the assistance itself. Though, as it turned out, I was soon paying most of her bills. For she had refused Edward's settlements, and her marriage settlement was barely three hundred a year.

And as I came to do work for her at the flat after office hours, I had an excuse to stay late. Now and then, saying that it was too late to find a cab, I slept on her sofa. I do not know even now how far this was a deliberate contrivance, or the automatism of a steel filing which cannot leave the magnet.

On one of these evenings, Julie said to me, 'It's nice of you, Tommy, not to make love to me. Most men would in your place.'

'It's not that I don't love you, Julie.'

'Do you really love me? I thought we were friends. We mustn't spoil our friendship.'

'I've been in love with you for years.'

And on the next evening, when I stayed till after two o'clock and then proposed to sleep in the sitting-room, she said to me while I was pretending to make my arrangements on the sofa, 'Of course, Tom, if you would care to sleep with me, please do so. It is the least I can do for you.'

I was silent in my embarrassment. Julie said gravely, 'It would give me pleasure, too – I should like to feel that there was something I could do for you –' and she opened the inner door for me, so that I had to pass through.

'It will please Edward, too. He's had it in his mind for a long time,' Julie said. She was neither amused nor tragic. She pondered on the fact. 'He told me years ago that you and I were exactly suited. He really believed it, you know, because he has no feelings for people, only for ideas – he labelled us both; type, religious, species, amorous and sentimental, and thought how nice it would be if, when he found me a nuisance, he could pass me on to you.'

'No, Julie. I can't believe that.' I was in her room, and to my own surprise, felt ready to faint with embarrassment and excitement. My head swam, my legs trembled. I was nearly forty, but still very naïf.

'But we mustn't blame him, Tommy. That is Edward's charm – his independence – you can't blame a man for his charm. It wouldn't be fair. And if we are his victims, it is our own fault. It is because we enjoyed being fascinated – what is more delightful than to make oneself nobody, nothing, as light as a needle, and submit to some powerful magnet. Even now the feeling of Edward is like a vibration – it makes you quiver. But come, Tommy, you're getting cold – you can have Edward's pyjamas. I have a drawerful of his things.'

I stayed and, what was not strange perhaps, I was disillusioned in that moment. Rousseau describes the matter of fact conduct of Mme de Warrens in offering herself as an instructor in love. Her calm good nature seems to have charmed Rousseau, but Julie's did not charm me. She was still the most attractive of women, the most graceful, but her whole action now, with its carelessness, its *sans gêne*, seemed to say, 'I do this to please you, but it is a silly business.' There was no exchange, no true intimacy of spirit.

I recognized my bitter disappointment, the next day, and swore that I should not sleep with Julie again.

But Julie sent for me the same afternoon to explain some document to her, and I could not refuse to go. I saw her nearly every day. She expected me to do so, and every few days she would say, 'Wouldn't you like to stay with me tonight,' or 'would you like to go to bed for half an hour before your train.' And if I excused myself, she would look at me with surprise and say, 'Don't you like me, Tommy, in that way.' Then I was obliged to answer that I liked her very much in that way.

And I wondered at the simplicity of women, even so intelligent as Julie, who thought that the mere physical act, without mutual excitement or passion, or adventure, could have any importance or give an abiding pleasure.

88

Ann did not repeat her question. Probably she had not asked it of me, but of herself. And when we came to the house, she turned abruptly aside into Edward's study behind the stairs; now completely refitted and restored. 'I love this room,' she said, with unusual warmth, 'How Daddy must have liked working here.'

'He used it only in the last few years of his life. I'm afraid he wasn't very happy here.'

'Robert says he was a bit too civilized – but that ought to be a good thing – at least for a man.'

Now that Ann was herself unhappy, she began often to talk of happiness, and especially of her father's life. His easy success and his sudden failure.

'Perhaps his success was not so easy as it looked – he had courage as well as energy.'

The girl pondered, sitting hunched up in the single chair before the empty fireplace, like Edward himself in his last years. 'Plenty of people have courage.'

'Courage to bear misfortunes. That's common enough. The only alternative is so unpleasant. But your father had the courage to make decisions. Even in party politics he took his own line. And that kind of courage is not very common.'

'It's awful the way people are wasted – even brilliant people like Daddy – knocking himself to pieces on those old politics.'

'But was he wasted? He helped to make a revolution.'

'A revolution – to get rid of the poor old Lords. I'm glad it didn't come off. The Lords, at least, are harmless.'

'Yes, because we made them so. But I suppose you modern young women are never taught anything about modern history, in your expensive modern schools,' etc.

It is hard for me to be patient with young creatures like Ann, who say of our struggles, 'A lot of noise about nothing.' For, in fact, there are no political battles nowadays to equal the bitterness and fury of those we fought between 1900 and 1914.

It is a marvel to me that there was, after all, no revolution, no civil war, even in Ireland. For months in the years 1909 and 1910, during the last great battle with the Lords, any loud noise at night, a banging door, a roll of thunder would bring me sitting upright in bed, with the sweat on my forehead and the thought 'The first bomb – it has come at last.'

For, to tell the truth, I was in terror of this revolution which I expected every day. Why then, you say, did I sign petitions, write ferocious letters to the Press, which, even if they were not printed, expressed the most republican principles; and why did I help Edward in his own more violent campaigns? I answer that I don't know. I am amazed at my own actions; and I think I was often surprised even then. It was as though my muscles had fallen under the control of some central power, called democracy, inhabiting the English air, and obliging me to do its will. Or perhaps I was only obeying some secret democrat planted by tradition or some evangelical country nurse, in my own brain.

> Hard-breasted Nan snubbed Socrates. With zeal
> Her harder hand moulded the Greek ideal.

I can remember one night when after one of Edward's speeches we were both accosted in the ante-room of the hall by one of the more moderate members of the party, a Quaker manufacturer.

He remonstrated with Edward on a part of his speech which threatened bloodshed if the Lords did not give way. 'I don't think, Mr Wilcher, you meant to encourage actual bloodshed – but many people must have thought so. And we don't want to inflame dangerous resentments.'

My whole soul cried out 'Yes, yes, yes,' and yet I found my mouth assuming a politely superior smile. And I heard my lips say that a democracy must not be afraid of revolutions or it would cease to be a democracy.

And Bill, that stout loyalist, in writing to me about Edward's prospects, offered to bet that he would be first President of the British Republic.

The very idea kept me awake all night, or brought me strange and ridiculous dreams. Chatham, Castlereagh, Wellington, in full robes, seemed to hover over me with reproachful faces. I would even be haunted by coronets, ermine, and woolsacks, without anything inside them at all. And all accused me of cruelty and meanness. 'Why do you attack us, the harmless dignities of old England?'

89

> Freedom at any price. So cry all those
> Who've had her once, paid through or with the nose.

When I think of these words, my heart still turns over. For I feel, not only the fearful truth of them, but I know it in my own heart. I see again the horde of savage brutes pouring out of St Antony's ward to loot Versailles, and to insult that king whose only fault was his gentleness, his hatred of violence, his civilized distrust of everything extreme, ostentatious, vulgar; from Mirabeau's style of dress to his own state bedroom. And what is worse, more terrifying, I feel that I too could have served in that mob. As I sought the joy of the Lord, so I could seek that joy of the devil. As I was drawn to Julie, not only by her gentleness and beauty but by the idea of her corruption, so I could have embraced the fury, the lust, the cruelty of Marianne. Drawn to filth by its filthiness, to villainy by its wickedness. Not to have any scruples, any responsibility, any duties. To lie for ever in a sweet unrest, etc., upon the old hag's poison-dripping breasts, and so on. In those days my tall hat, which in our firm, partners still wear, or, indeed, I hope they do; my frock coat, which was uniform among us, until the death of George the Fifth, who preferred it to the morning coat, seemed to weigh upon me like that armour which in Venice torturers clamped upon some state prisoner, to drive him mad with its constraint, its weight.

'What is this freedom?' I thought. 'This terrible power which sooner or later overthrows all its enemies, and creeps like madness in the veins of a respectable lawyer of forty.' I was terrified of this secret and stealthy power. And so I raged against the folly of those who opposed her.

And against Edward who, of course, was under Freedom's special protection, I could only express my irritation by attacking his extravagance, or his cynicism.

'Things are much too serious to be taken seriously.'

'I hope you'll keep that to yourself. You have done yourself quite enough harm with your verses.'

'But then, I should have hanged myself without my verses.'

This was the time when he wrote about his own chief:

> Haul our great rebel's flag to Ritz's top
> The statesman's art is knowing where to stop.

It was sent to a friend who at once communicated it to his enemies. For no one, at that time, not even Lloyd George, was better hated. He was turned out of several clubs, and cut in the street. Old friends wrote to him calling him a renegade who had betrayed his class; a Judas who sold his honour. A hypocrite who, enjoying wealth, attacked the rich.

Edward was, in fact, very well off. For though Mrs Tirrit had died a few months after their marriage in 1906, she left him almost her whole fortune for life, so long as he did not re-marry.

But in politics, only politicians use their sense and keep their tempers; that is, in private. Edward's friends would hear no defence of a rich man who did not defend riches.

Their chief charge against him as always in such cases, was, 'He does it to get into the limelight'. Undoubtedly Edward, in 1909, as in 1900, was more discussed than most of his colleagues. That is to say, he was talking himself into power.

Then in the first election of 1910, he lost his seat by fifteen votes. He was not offered another at once, because many seats had been lost, and the Cabinet did not wish to take risks. Also, I suppose, Edward had his political critics and rivals. The more cautious who thought him too violent; the more extreme who did not like what they called his dilettantism; that is, those tastes and pursuits, which for Edward, were the culture he was fighting to preserve.

Suddenly he went away to France for a holiday. We said, 'He is biding his time.' And, in fact, a month or two later, when a seat fell vacant, he was offered it by the local committee. He did not accept it. And we said, 'The time has not come.' For, in fact, the Lords and the Commons were still negotiating.

And then we heard that he had married a young girl. I hurried to Paris, full of foreboding.

I found Edward in the royal suite of a great new hotel, with American lifts and half a dozen bathrooms. He was already surrounded by artists and writers. New and extraordinary pictures stood against the walls.

'What are you thinking of?' I asked him. 'Surely it's madness to be out of England now. There might be a crash any day.'

'They know where to find me if they want me. Meanwhile I think I owe myself a holiday. I haven't had a real holiday for thirty years.'

90

We thought Edward would ruin himself with debts or women. We never imagined the real catastrophe, that he would retire from the battle to enjoy that civilization which he had given so much energy, so many years, to defend.

'A bit too civilized.' Robert's words. The very voice of his time in judgement on ours. I thought it nonsense, but now, as I stand in Edward's room, I feel not its truth but its meaning.

> I knew Versailles, said Talleyrand; nor since
> Such tolerant grace of life. True! traitor-prince.

What was Edward's charm; and Julie's and Mrs Tirrit's; so different in character? A universal tolerance, based on a universal enjoyment. They were faithful to friendship, to kindness, to beauty; never to faith. They could not make the final sacrifice. They took a holiday at the wrong time; or could not bother to keep up with the new arts; or, like Mrs Tirrit, did not face, in time, the doctor who would say, 'You must have an operation.' They would rather die in peace than live in pain.

I argued with Edward for an hour, but at the end he would promise to come back to England within the next weeks, only if there were an actual deadlock between Lords and Commons, or the Prime Minister sent for him. 'And now,' he said, 'what about those papers?'

For I had brought some papers to sign. Edward was raising another mortgage on Tolbrook, for which, by good luck, my firm had been able to find the money.

Edward himself appeared to be living at the rate of many thousands a year. But no one could conceive where he was finding the money. His new wife, daughter of one of those cosmopolitan families who live in hotels: by nationality half-Belgian, half-Irish, by education English and Parisian, was not rich. Her parents spent too much upon themselves to give her much dowry.

She came in, one of the most beautiful girls I had ever seen. Her hair was like the glossy rind of a chestnut; her eyes were a sea blue; her only fault was a too pale skin, and too rounded cheeks.

Edward jumped up to receive her; she showed her pleasure in a smile unexpectedly frank and unsophisticated. Her dress, her turnout, her manner were those of a woman of the world. Her smile, her glance, her speech, were naïve. She said to me, 'Tell Edward that he must go home and teach this stupid old government a lesson.'

And, in fact, to my surprise, the new Mrs Wilcher was my ardent supporter. But though I expressed my support of her views, I did so in a guarded manner. My late ardour had suddenly acquired caution. For I could not help reflecting that the influence of so young a person might be imprudent.

Edward paid no attention to either of us. He had picked up his wife's hand, which was singularly small and of a perfect shape, unusual in very small hands, and while pretending to admire her rings, was admiring its beauty. She let it lie in his palm, but continued to discuss his affairs with me. 'What I say is, he's got a duty to the people. Even if they have treated him badly.'

'Your rings need cleaning, Lottie dearest,' Edward said. 'What are diamonds without a drop of ammonia.'

'He told me there was going to be a revolution, and now it's come he's playing round here with all these fancy painters instead of taking his proper place at home.'

'Fancy painters,' Edward said laughing, 'she means some of the greatest in the history of art. Look at this, Tommy'; and he showed me an extraordinary daub of misshapen women among trees of metallic green. 'Cézanne.'

The girl did not look at it. She said in her lively voice, in which the earnestness of a young girl seemed to struggle with the secret gaiety of a bride, 'Art is very important, I know, but these are historical times when our oldest institutions are being turned right upside down. Why, there might be a republic next week, and how would Edward look then.' And she spoke of the importance, to a statesman, of being on the spot when a revolution began. She quoted Mirabeau. It was obvious that she was well educated, and yet she had kept that kind of simplicity and vigour which good education so often destroys.

Edward, standing beside her, continued to play with her hand, took off her rings and put them on again, yet with such finesse that he did not embarrass either of us with the idea of amorous folly. He seemed to be laughing at himself as well as the argument.

'Politics is not my affair, Mrs Wilcher,' I said. 'I came on business; but I quite agree that this is supposed to be a great opportunity for the more extreme wing of Edward's party.'

'Oh, no,' Edward said, 'they didn't like my speeches about abolishing the Lords. Our party is not quite so ready for the revolution as you might think.'

91

I was alarmed for Edward, but I thought, 'He knows his own political business better than I do. He understands the real workings of party politics, and perhaps he would not like to explain them even to me.'

So when Julie asked me if Edward had not injured his career in going abroad, I answered, 'Not at all. He has shown them that he has some sense of his own value. I told him that it was quite time they gave him something better than the Transport Ministry.'

'All the same, I'm glad he's not making those speeches. How I hate all that Socialist stuff.'

'My dear Julie, as Harcourt said a long time ago, we are all socialists nowadays.'

Julie was profoundly conservative and pessimistic. The porter was caught stealing her silver, but she would not prosecute. 'Nobody believes in God any more, so why shouldn't they steal. And I'm so sorry for that lad, he's so young and poor and so eager for life. You can see it in his eyes. The flats pay their people so disgracefully. I don't see that we have any right to nice things while a young man like that can't even afford to keep a woman.'

'That's what Edward thinks.'

'But they teach so much spite and envy – they're making all the world miserable and squalid, instead of only part of it.' I laughed at Julie's politics. She never understood the democratic process. But I was delighted in her flat, in her company.

The flat was not that one to which I had hurried in 1898, a young man full of amorous excitement in the thought of an actress and a mistress; but everything in it was the same. The white-panelled woodwork, the Beardsleys, the Whistler pastels, the Japanese prints, the authors' copies from the 90s. The same cloisonné cigarette box stood on the sofa table beside a book, always open and face downwards. Julie was always in the middle of a book, usually an old one. I have seen *Stories Toto Told Me*, by Corvo, lying on that little table for three months. Yet I, too, was always pleased to turn the book over and read where she had read, looking through her eyes into that world of the past, always tranquil, always beautiful, like a mime show.

These rooms had for me the quality of Julie's own character and mind, something which belongs only to a civilization in its perfected form. Its simplicity, its lack of pretension, of any strong character, even of strong colour, its good taste, which seemed unconscious, and which was, in fact, the consequence merely of Julie's integrity, had also the calm of profound reflection. The books, the prints, the small bronzes, all expressed ideas of life, which were simple only in form, like Julie's beauty, her dress, so expensive and carefully thought out; or her talk, which conveyed so many subtleties.

In Julie's flat I felt the repose of comprehension. I was known there even by the books. I was accepted like the cat, and like the cat I felt myself at home. But I was no longer fascinated. I saw too plainly Julie's weakness; her idleness, her habit of dependence.

Julie did not love me, but in a surprisingly short time she came to need me. She needed even to worry about my tastes and my pleasures. So it was that she became the pursuer and I the pursued. Yet willingly pursued for many years. Julie's flat gave me, I suppose, what husbands find at home, a private and stable world of their own.

And Eeles' death, early in 1912, of fever, seemed to remove the only possible threat to this domestic bliss. Julie grieved for him more than I had expected; but not in a manner to distress our comforts. In two months I could congratulate myself that the man was forgotten.

But one evening, Julie said to me, apropos of nothing, 'I suppose we could now get married, if we liked.'

I can't describe the effect of these words. They deprived me of the power, not only of speech, but thought. I could not even form an answer. And after some moments' embarrassed silence, I got up, made some excuse, and, though it was my night for staying, went away. But from Paddington, thank God, I had the presence of mind to send two pounds of chocolates with a card expressing my love.

If I had not been inspired to this simple act, I do not think I could have borne the recollection of that crisis in my life. For the upshot was that I did not see Julie again for more than a year. I wrote. I took care of her business, I paid her rent, etc., but I could not bring myself to meet her. In cold blood, I perceived that, after her unlucky speech, I had no alternative but to marry her or to brutalize these relations, which had become, though troublesome, civilized by a mutual accommodation.

My conduct may seem absurd and even pusillanimous. I can't explain even now why I felt so convinced that it was impossible to marry my mistress. But I have this excuse, that by this time, Tolbrook had come almost entirely into my possession. It was saved. And I felt perhaps that to bring a Julie to Tolbrook would be an impiety to my father's house, now in my care.

92

Mrs Ramm came to tell me that tea was ready. She appeared a little surprised to find us still wearing our hats and coats in the half-finished room. And we were perhaps equally surprised. Ann crouching still over the empty fireplace, straightened her back and pushed up her spectacles; I, half propped against the library ladder, asked, 'Is Master Robert in yet?'

'No, sir, he's gone.'

'Gone. Where?'

'He went out with a bag, sir. He said you would understand.'

'Oh, I see,' Ann said, 'he must have had that phone call he was expecting.'

This did not deceive either Mrs Ramm or myself who could see that the girl was astonished.

'I wonder has he gone off,' Ann said at tea.

'Gone off – impossible. He wouldn't do such a thing.' For I was naturally taken aback. 'How could he leave the farm with no one to take care of it. And what will he live on?'

'He might, all the same,' Ann said thoughtfully. 'Just to show me where I get off.'

I did not believe for one moment that Robert had taken so decisive, so violent a step, without preparation or capital. But I was distressed by the very idea. I could not eat. 'You ought to be ashamed,' I said, 'to speak so of your husband.'

'But don't you think it's true, uncle,' she asked. She seemed perfectly tranquil. 'No, perhaps he is not vindictive, but only likes to teach people a lesson.' And after reflection she continued, 'The truth is, I suppose, that he wasn't a born brute, but he thinks he ought to be a brute. He's like these Nazis and Fascists, who behave like beasts on the highest principles, as if it were a new religion to give philosophers castor oil, and knock people's teeth out for being Christians, and rub women's faces in the mud.'

'Robert – what nonsense – he would never rub anyone's face in the mud. He is all against these Nazis as you call them.'

'He put his fingers on my mouth the other day and made a face – it's the same thing. And he's very rough in other ways, too. He's always learning me to be a woman. But I suppose it's something to do with the Time spirit.'

'No, no,' I said, 'that's enough.' For I could not bear to hear any more out of the German boxes, at such a time. 'Robert is a good-natured boy, and very hard-working. And don't you think that we could do without him. He's taken all the responsibility here,' etc. For I was not only disturbed in my conscience; I felt already a thousand new problems pressing upon me. 'And if Robert has taken a holiday, I don't think you have any right to blame him.' Seeing all at once that the girl was very white, and conceiving that she must be distressed, I went to bed. But not to sleep. For the more I thought of the situation without Robert, the more I disliked it.

'Robert,' I thought, 'has changed everything – he has picked his own men – how am I going to run a modern farm with a lot of youngsters who go about in blue overalls with oil-cans in their hands.' And I felt again the tragedy of revolution, that it can't be reversed. 'No, nothing can be put back again – a man who is out of date is out of time.'

93

And early in the morning, I found myself in Robert's little orchard, on the site of the old shrubbery. The cold spring wind blowing round my legs and up my dressing-gown awoke me. I was glad that some instinct had made me put on a hat. How I had got out of the house at such an hour, I could not imagine. The place was familiar to me. But now to my startled eyes it appeared unnatural; a magic copy or original form of that reality. I seemed to have been transported into another world, of celestial beauty, but cold and unfriendly. Robert's little trees, in flower, were like standard roses of a new and extraordinary kind, the grass seemed to wear unnatural green, the sky, a blue so pale yet piercing that it alarmed me like a new sky, which is far more unexpected and terrifying than a new earth. Even the birds, which were making so much noise that they deafened my very thoughts, seemed to be of a new species; more bold, harsh and excited than earthly birds. Exalted spirits of birds, impudent and furious with passions. The very beauties of the place, the glitter of flowers, the scents, the waving branches, the colours as delicate as pastel and radiant as cut jewels, increased my panic. For I felt that I did not belong among them.

But suddenly a gust blew down a few raindrops, and at once the ground grew solid under my feet. The sky faded to the usual pale blue of a cold spring morning, whose blue is mixed with thin cloud. And I saw beyond the hedge the great trembling mountain of the lime, with its leaves like green flowers. For the imagination, apparently, it does not rain in heaven. And seeing that one of the little new apple trees was dead, among the white bouquets of the rest, I thought, 'I must tell Robert.'

And then instantly I remembered that Robert had gone, and felt the pressure of that event upon my brain. I heard again the cow mooing which had perhaps brought me from my bed. For I had certainly heard her in my sleep and been oppressed by the agonizing dream which affected me so often in the old days. That the cows had not been milked.

'Yes,' I thought. 'It was that cow brought me out of bed. I suppose she has only been separated from her calf.' But I went to find her in the shed, and afterwards I walked through the yards. All seemed in order there. A window flew up and a door opened. A boy rode into the yard on his bicycle. He was yawning to an enormous extent, but, seeing me, shut his mouth quickly and opened his eyes. I approached him and wished him good morning.

'Good morning, sir.'

'You've come to get the cows in.'

'No, sir, I've come to fetch away the drill.'

'Who is in charge of the milking?'

'I don't know, sir.'

He retreated backwards from me and I saw him looking at the windows as if for help. Probably he had been told that I was mad. Now in such a case as I know by experience, it is useless to attempt any kind of intimacy. For if you talk sense, the other says to himself, 'Madmen are all like that – they are as clever as monkeys. They pretend to be like anyone else, till they can get close to you and bite your nose off or strangle you,' and, of course, if you don't talk sensibly, they say, 'Oh, poor chap, he's getting worse every day.'

But the incident did not improve my spirits. 'How,' I thought, 'am I going to attend to all these new duties if people treat me as a lunatic. It's enough to drive a man mad.'

And when I went into the house to tell Ann that no one was in charge of the cows, I found her at the telephone, in pyjamas, with her hair strangely screwed up in curlers. Mrs Ramm stood by, and the two, between Ann's cries down the instrument, conversed in low anxious voices.

'What are you doing, uncle?'

'Nobody is looking after the cows, and it is nearly time for prayers.'

'Farley is acting as foreman.'

'Old Farley – Robert wouldn't like that.'

'He knows the place, and you said you liked him.'

'But suppose Robert comes back.' For I was still convinced that Robert would come back.

'Then he can make his own arrangements,' and she began to call down the telephone, 'Hello, hello, Queensport. Is that the Labour Exchange? Hello.'

'Does Farley understand this new kind of farming?'

'It's not really new, uncle. I always thought Robert rather old-fashioned. He doesn't keep in touch with research. Don't you think you ought to go and dress? Why are you carrying your clothes?' It was true that I had my coat and trousers over my arm. But as soon as I saw this I remembered the reason. 'I thought they might be forgotten – I was going to brush them myself.'

'Don't worry, uncle. They'll be brushed.'

Both the women wore that expression which means 'Don't fuss.' I thought that there was every reason to fuss. But it was no good saying so to Ann and Mrs Ramm, who had already made up their minds that old men are fussy.

And when I went to the nursery for prayers, there was the child Edward Wilcher, whom they call Jan, crawling about the floor, alone and unattended, with knives on the table and a bright fire in the grate.

The truth is not that old men are fussy, but that they have learnt from experience how much the young trust to luck; until some disaster falls upon them, by their own fault. And at that moment, of course, they cease to be young. They, too, become anxious and careful.

94

The flames of the lime, like burning salt, were so bright in the morning sun, that they shone even through the calico blind and made a green light on the nursery wall. I pulled up the blind to forget anxiety in admiring this beautiful tree, so long beloved. The boy began at once to haul himself up by my dressing-gown. He is now, at fourteen months, a rapid crawler; very strong in his limbs, and he likes to balance himself on his legs against chairs, etc. He has become, as I hoped, a handsome child, with his grand-mother's eyes and his father's hair; and he continually bursts out laughing with an expression which says, 'I can't help it.' He looked up at me now with that intent gaze of a small child who is beginning to distinguish human beings from other tall objects, as creatures able to move and act, to make noises and to communicate to him unexpected feelings.

The relations between this child and myself, if I may say so, are established on a footing. His mother and father, like other young mothers and fathers, have been under the illusion that I could not handle children and did not like them. This is absurdly far from the truth, which is, that children, and especially this beautiful child, so like Edward in beauty, Lucy in energy and courage, give me an intense delight, but a delight mixed always with a deep anxiety. I feel, 'I mustn't hope too much. I must be careful what I do or say. A careless word, an abrupt action may injure the delicate muscles; pervert the virgin brain.'

As a young man I have often jogged a small child on my knee; but I know a man who killed his own son at the game of ride to market.

Therefore, when Jan approached me, Ann or Robert were wont to cry, 'No, no, run away. Don't let him bother you, uncle.'

But as I say, we understand each other. The proof is, that the child always does come to me, and his glance clearly distinguishes me as a friend.

And now in his look, his clutch, I felt a pleasure, strange to me for many years. I did not forget that sense of anxiety and tension which had upset me during the night, but it became reasonable. I felt, 'But all this is justified. Tolbrook may be a great nuisance,' etc., 'but it fulfils a purpose. It is necessary. It is a complete thing. It is living history.' And the responsibility that lay upon me became at once heavy and exalted, to be a master of a house, with children; that is a high dignity.

When Ann came in, I told her that Jan had been left alone with knives and fire. But she was absent-minded. She said that perhaps we'd better have prayers quickly because a new milker was coming to see her.

'Is it wise to take milkers from a Labour Exchange? How do you know what bad characters may come about the place, and ruin your cows?'

'This milker is from the village, and we had to have one. Molly has gone.'

'She can't have gone with Robert.'

'So they say, and why not? After all, it's what we expected. Have you got your books?'

The boy gave a sharp angry cry to catch my attention, and I hastily looked again in his direction. One must be prepared with children to attend to several things at once. At the same moment Mrs Ramm and the two girls who are all her staff in these degenerate days came into prayers. He turned his head then, almost round, like a parrot, to stare at the newcomers, sat down without bending his legs, and instantly crawled towards them.

But Ann caught him, took her place, set him in her lap and turned towards me her face with the look which meant, 'Time for the next thing'.

I feel in these days the new importance of the prayers. For the girl listens with a new attention. I daresay she is suffering. I choose my reading with care, and I throw my heart into it. It is an exhausting effort, but I am sure that I ought to make it.

'Save me, oh God, for the waters are come in, even unto my soul. I stick fast in the deep mire where no ground is.

'Let not the flood drown me, neither let the deep swallow me up.

'And let not the pit shut her mouth upon me.'

When I say these words, my own heart contracts with pain and terror. I think, 'What sad old man, what broken-hearted woman, sinking into the last darkness, uttered that cry of despair? And what is to be my own fate in the next months or years?' And I prayed not only for Ann, but for myself and for all those who have walked in the shadow of that death.

'Draw nigh unto my soul and save it;

'For Thou, oh Lord, art the thing that I long for,

'Thou art my hope, even from my youth.

'I am become as it were a monster unto many; but my sure trust is in Thee.

'Oh, let my mouth be filled with Thy praise; that I may sing of Thy glory and honour all the day long.'

Then God, indeed, gave happiness, and I thought, 'Am I not indeed blessed among men, with this honest girl for a daughter and this child, to bring once more to the old house, and my old age, the revelation of God's mercy and love.'

My heart was unlocked from that fear, the darkness was drawn away as by the sun which glittered on the wet window panes; and when I rose from my knees, I went towards Ann meaning to say to her some word of encouragement. But she with the boy under her arm was giving directions to Mrs Ramm about the spring cleaning, and it was only the boy who, twisting his neck to look up at me, noticed my approach. He did not smile, but his expression was full of curiosity and intentness; his hand, stretched up towards my sleeve, was asking, 'What is this new thing?' And in the same instant, he was whirled away to be dressed. Mrs Ramm hurried one way, the servants another. Downstairs I heard the telephone ringing. And all at once Jan next door in the night nursery uttered a loud howl of rage. I felt that the top of my head would blow off. But I thought, 'This is life – I have just thanked God for it. If I am to fall dead in a fit, at least I shall have fulfilled a purpose.'

95

Children bring turmoil to a house because they are full of energy and invention. They love life and they can communicate that love, which is the body of faith.

But I don't suppose Lazarus enjoyed his resurrection, and I remember that in 1912, when Lucy came home to Tolbrook with her young son Robert, then aged two; and soon after her Amy arrived from India with her two youngest, John, twelve, and Loftus, eight; together with a friend's child, Francie, aged two, I complained bitterly that the last refuge of peace had been destroyed.

This was a time of misery for all who loved decency and reason in human affairs. The Irish threatened civil war; the suffragettes were burning letters and beating policemen; and the air was filled from all sides with the threat, 'If you do not give us what we want we shall make life impossible for everybody.' I was a strong supporter of the Nationalist and Suffragette cause. For I said, 'Freedom must be served.' But I was much disturbed. And when I came to Tolbrook for rest I found the house rocked from top to bottom because there was no Scotch oats for Robert's breakfast.

Lucy, I suppose, was suffering. Her husband had gone abroad on a world preaching tour with Ella, and left her behind. She would not admit the least criticism of Brown, but I think her nerves were in pain. Amy, for her part, had just lost her youngest child, the only daughter, and grief seemed to have the effect of making her more slow and obstinate. Lucy used to say that even to watch Amy cutting bread made her mad. 'She looks all round the bread first as if it was a field of battle. I suppose Bill would call it a reconnaissance.'

Moreover, Lucy and Amy did not agree, at any point, about the management of children. Lucy was a martinet. She would spring from some uproarious game and exclaim to young Robert, still rolling on the floor and kicking up his short fat legs in delight, 'Now then, young man. That's enough – off with you,' and if Robert did not immediately obey she would snatch him up and walk off with him to bed. If he fought her then she would at once slap him, not angrily, but with a cool determination to hurt, which shocked Amy. When Amy or I protested she would say, 'I'm not going to spoil the boy.'

'But, my dear,' Amy would say, 'Robert is so good – I wish only that Francie was half so obedient.'

'He hasn't learnt yet when it's time to stop playing,' Lucy would answer, 'and unless he learns it now he'll never learn it.'

But though Lucy was a stern mother she was far more particular on some points than Amy. I remember a savage battle because Amy and my mother, left to look after the young children, had taken them driving into Hog Lane, which was the Tolbrook slum. My mother was used to give most of her charity to these very poor people. I think she was shy of the superior cottages. And for years she had visited Hog Lane two or three times a week. Amy saw no harm in going with her and taking the children.

My mother, now over seventy, had taken great delight in the grand-children. I suppose she had lived a very lonely life at Tolbrook for the last nine years. She saw me only at week-ends, and then I was always busy and usually worried, especially by her accounts. Probably the re-opening of the nurseries had given even more pleasure to her than to me. True, she spoilt the children. 'A typical granny,' as Lucy complained. But even Lucy admitted the right of an old woman to spoil babies.

Now all her old anger against the mother with whom she had fought for so many years, that mysterious woman's war, returned in one wave, 'What!' she cried to me. 'Robert in Hog's Lane. But, of course, mother would!'

Lucy had come in from some Benjamite meeting, and I think that religious fervour always heightened her intolerance. She flew to the nursery, where my mother and Amy were taking off the children's coats and talking to them in the manner of the nursery.

I remember that this also irritated Lucy against both my mother and Amy. 'Listen to them,' she would say. 'Doting.'

And this was unfair. Amy never doted. She always seemed to amuse herself with small children, rather like a slightly older sister. And although my mother, to our surprise, had suddenly shown a new manner, a new briskness, it was not silly, but merely a little comic. Among any children, whatever they were doing, she would stoop down and utter a series of short ecstatic cries, as if enchanted by their cleverness. Though I think sometimes she did not really notice what they were doing. And so now, as she drew off her darling Robert's coat, she was crying, 'There now, that's one sleeve – isn't he a clever boy. And now the other. Oh, he can do it himself – he doesn't need Granny,' and so on.

Lucy snatched the child out of the old woman's lap and exclaimed, 'You want to kill the boy, I suppose.'

My mother looked up with astonishment and confusion.

'You know they've got diphtheria in that filthy place – and worse things than diphtheria – but of course that's just why you would take Robert there.'

My mother began to struggle to get up, and I went to help her. I thoroughly approved of Lucy's objection to Hog Lane for the children, but I was shocked by something in my mother's face. I can only describe it as guilt and terror. 'Rubbish, Lucy!' I said. 'Mama didn't think, that's all,' and I took my mother to her room.

'Why do you let Lucy speak to you like that?' I said. I was angry with her for her patience. 'It's abominable.'

'Perhaps she was right – there may be diphtheria – I should have considered.'

After that she came little to the nursery, and seemed to avoid touching the children even in Lucy's presence.

When I reproached Lucy for her violence she answered only, 'I've no patience with mama's grovelling to those guttersnipes. We've got one or two like that among the sisters, and they're the most hopeless jelly-fish of the whole zoo.'

Amy, however, continued to take Francie to Hog Lane. And when Lucy abused her, in startling language, she answered placidly, 'It's not their fault they're dirty – they're that kind of people,' as if speaking of some foreign race.

'It is their fault. They're dregs. They wouldn't stay in Hog Lane if they weren't. It's just because they're dregs that mother kow-tows to them.'

So Amy, with her eighteenth-century idea of the world set in castes labelled the Church, the Bar, the poor, etc., seemed more democratic than the evangelist Lucy, who judged rich and poor by the same iron standards.

And when I was most exasperated by Lucy's violence, or Amy's obstinacy, and their long-drawn battles of gun against fortress, I would come in and find them romping with the children on the floor, creeping about on all fours, and barking or mewing or snorting, in a ludicrous manner. And the two middle-aged women with their grey hair, their deep lines, and stiffened bodies, the one too thick, the other too gaunt, would giggle as wildly as the children, until they were crimson and helpless, and rolled over to let the children crawl over them. And this undignified spectacle gave me a strange and keen kind of happiness which was mixed with pain. As if there were something incurable in the world's suffering which was also its secret root of joy.

96

Lucy, as one might expect, had a hearty contempt for Francie. She disliked little girls and probably all women. But Amy expressed a warm admiration of Robert.

It was our joke that Amy, watching Robert one evening in the bathroom when both the smaller children were sitting on their pots, said thoughtfully, 'After all, you can always tell that Robert is a gentleman. It's his expression, I think.' The 'after all' was a reflection on Robert's paternal ancestry, which gave Lucy great pleasure for years afterwards. Robert was an energetic child, obstinate but always good tempered, and with all a small boy's power of amusing himself. Lucy had a passionate but critical attachment to him.

But the worst quarrel between Lucy and Amy came from a strange accident. Robert fell into the lake and was rescued by John. This boy liked to wander about alone. And he was lying in a field when he saw Robert running down from the house. Robert, who had just learnt to walk, loved to escape from his mother. He disappeared among the trees. But John, remembering the lake, came running across the fields, and when he could not see Robert, looked for his footprints in the muddy bank, dived in and brought the child up, not even yet unconscious.

Lucy, when she discovered the facts, said to us, 'That boy's too good for Amy. He's got more sense in his little finger than her whole family from Adam,' and she began to make much of John. She took him riding with her, and bought him an expensive camera for which he had been longing. For Lucy, whose money had been invested, by my advice, in building land near Ferry, was far richer than Bill and Amy, who were always in debt.

John had grown into a tall fair boy, more like Edward than his own parents. I had taken to him at once, and, indeed, at this time began that warm friendship which gave me so much happiness and pain for many years. I would take occasion, even then, to talk with the boy about his studies, and I was glad to find that I could help him in some points of Latin syntax, etc. And I was charmed to see his devotion to his mother. A natural and proper thing, but always delightful. One would say that John, who had not seen Amy for five years, had fallen in love with this heavy plain woman. He would colour when she glanced at him; he would lie in wait for her; he would grow suddenly talkative and lively when they were going out together; he would secretly buy her presents and surprise her with them.

Amy, for her part, was visibly delighted and a little nervous. She would speak brusquely to the boy like a shy, young woman, who does not know how to manage a love affair.

It was Amy's ambition that John should go to the varsity. I don't know how this strange idea had occurred to her, for Bill strongly opposed it. Bill wanted him to go to Woolwich and be a sapper, 'The finest job in the world, bar none. You ask anyone who knows.' But at the moment Amy was in possession of the field of battle – that is, John's mind. And she often urged him to his work.

Then Lucy would say, 'A good thing if he doesn't get a scholarship. The varsity is the ruin of boys. Don't you listen to anyone, John. This is your holiday, don't forget that. I tell you what, we'll go for a picnic on the moor, behind Torcomb, I want to see some people round there.'

John and Amy, who had planned to go sailing together at Ferry, looked alarmed. For a picnic on the moor meant that they would be left to look after Robert while Lucy visited some outlying Benjamites.

Neither Lucy nor Amy kept a nurse; Amy was too poor and Lucy would not trust any nurse with Robert.

'But John was taking me for a sail,' Amy would say.

'You can sail any day, but this is the day for the moor.'

And, in fact, Amy and John never had their sail. Either the weather was too calm or too stormy; or if there were a fair breeze, Amy had to look after my mother, or John had to look after the children.

John, like his mother, was a born family slave. He was reliable and good natured. Amy, for her part, having once been useful to my mother, found herself indispensable.

My mother was the opposite of a tyrant. But she needed a nurse, and especially after this difference with Lucy she could not bear strangers near her. She would rather endure solitude or risk a fall; much rather die in peace. But she could not be allowed to die, and so one of us always stayed with her, and it was usually Amy.

For I was busy, and Lucy, I think, could not bear to be with the mother whom she had treated with such cruelty and injustice.

97

When I intervened on Amy's behalf to point out how important it was for John to get a scholarship, Lucy answered me, 'Why shouldn't you pay with all the money you've made out of Edward?'

I knew that this was a deliberate provocation. Yet I always lost my temper. I would cry, 'That's an abominable slander,' etc., and I should have liked to kill Lucy. Her poisonous tongue made wounds that nothing could heal. No one was more quick and clever in twisting malice and truth, falsehood and injustice, into one burning dart and feathering it with a plume drawn from the victim's own breast. She had a devil's genius in striking at the very roots of the soul, and paralysing its nerve.

It would flash upon me, 'It's true. I have got Tolbrook from Edward and now the London house as well. It's true I carried out the separation between Edward and Julie. If I had not done so they would almost certainty have drifted together again. And Julie did always encourage Edward and help him in his career. She gave him a refuge; she gave him absolute loyalty. Yet, if I had not arranged the separation, Edward would have probably been ruined, and if I had not saved Tolbrook it would have been lost to the family.'

And my reward for years of heavy soul-destroying worries is to be thought and called a usurer.

The love of possessions. It is spoken for a reproach, and I feel it like shame. But what are these possessions which have so burdened my soul.

Creatures that I have loved. The most helpless of dependants. For their very soul, their meaning, is in my care.

A woman loves her baby in its weakness and dependence, but what is more dependent than a house, a chair, those old books, a tree.

In these savage family quarrels of 1913, I would clap on my hat and go out to walk under the trees. And gradually I would feel their presence. I would even stop to touch their bark, as I had seen Amy, after some quarrel with Lucy, take Francie upon her lap. She, too, was unresponsive, but Amy had consolation in her.

All the Tolbrook trees, even so far as Tenacre, now a desert, were like children to me. I knew their shapes from every side. They were present to me even when I sat at a table, and the loss of any one of them, by storm or decay, was a pain to me even while I did not recognize it. I would feel, perhaps in the midst of conversation, a sudden discomfort, 'What's wrong – what have I forgotten?' and then, 'Was it that speech this morning of Lloyd George at Limehouse, or the Germans' new battleships, or that suffragette beating the policeman with a whip, or my mother's bad cold?' and then suddenly it would come upon my mind, 'No, of course, it's that elm which was blown down last month in Pool's Paddock – what a gap.'

98

All the trees were dear to me, dearer than my own life, and perhaps my soul's god. But specially the great lime. I had always known it. Its delicate branches against the winter sky, its thin quivering leaves in summer, had stood before my bedroom window and the nursery windows on the same floor, for all my life. They were among my earliest memories. In illness, I had watched their moving shadows on the wall and seemed to breathe the scent of their flowers. On moonlight nights of summer, too hot for sleep, I had lain awake and seen the criss-cross of the outer sprays, drawn by the rising moon, gradually pass across the ceiling and down the wall, till they reached my counterpane and feathered it like a wing. Sunlight falls upon a lime as upon no other tree. It pierces the oak as with red-hot arrows; it glances aside from the elm as from a cliff; it shrinks from the yew as from a piece of darkness; it tangles itself in the willow and seems to lie there half asleep; among the crooked apple branches it hangs like fruit. But over a lime it falls like a water made of light, the topaz colour of the moor streams, and full like them of reflected rays, green and sparkling.

Only to stand beneath the lime was such a delight to me that often I turned aside to avoid that strong feeling. Especially in summer, when the tree was in flower, pouring out that sweet scent which seemed to float on the falling light like pollen dust on the moor waterfalls, and every crevice was full of sailing bees; I shrank from an excitement so overwhelming to my senses. The organ noise of bees, like vox angelica, the scent which made the blood race, the slow smooth fall of light in its thousand rills, over the living flesh of this beautiful and secret creature, enticed at once the eyes and the imagination. Within that burning tree I felt God's presence. And there I bathed in an essence of eternity. My very consciousness was dissolved in sensation, and I stood less entranced than myself the trance; the experience of that moment and that place, in the living spirit.

And though I had sworn to hate Lucy for the rest of my life, I would find myself, half an hour later, strolling arm in arm with her through the garden, in the midst of a serious discussion about my mother's health, or the gardener boy's bad morals, not in forgiveness, but simply in forgetfulness. The wound was there still in my breast, it would hurt for the rest of my life among thousands of others dealt me by Lucy, but I did not notice it any more than a rushing stream feels a new stone cutting its tide; or a growing tree suffers from last year's bullets fired into its bark. I was alive in that family weather, cordial to all living things, the good and the evil.

99

When Edward suddenly arrived in England and told us that in six months we should be at war, I was not only incredulous, but angry. I said if war broke out, it would be the fault of such as he, alarmists and warmongers. We did not quarrel because it was impossible to quarrel with Edward, but I gave him no support in his campaign for preparing the country.

I persuaded myself that he was trying to make a new position for himself and to form a political group.

'You'll divide the party,' I told him.

'What will happen to the party when the war starts.'

'Come Edward, even the stupidest soldier knows the consequences of war in modern Europe – the destruction – the ruin of all that we have built up.' I daresay Tolbrook was in my mind.

'That's the great attraction, Edward said, 'at least to certain energetic minds. The engineer, for instance, he likes to start afresh from a blue print. And the artist, he likes a clean canvas.'

'It isn't a matter of epigrams and paradoxes.' I was annoyed with Edward.

'No, it may be rather a serious matter for us. We've never allowed for the artistic temperament. The Kaiser has it – and it flourishes in Vienna.'

Lottie stood some way off examining Ann in a new dress. Like other very young mothers, Lottie treated the small fragile Ann rather like a toy, to be dressed and undressed. The baby had her own trunks, her own maid, as well as the nurse. But she was a delicate creature and spent most of her time in Amy's lap, listening to Amy's very small stock of nursery rhymes.

Lottie called to us across the room, in her voice which was still a schoolgirl's, full of life but with little inflexion, 'Got your answer yet, Edward?'

'No, I didn't.' Edward had written to some party conference, announcing his intention to speak.

'I said it was no good writing. You tell him, Tommy.' She came towards us. 'He's being too nice to them. That lot don't understand Edward's niceness. He must be really nasty before they take any notice.'

'It's not quite like that in England,' Edward said smiling. 'And as for the conference, I mayn't have time for it if the P.M. sends for me.'

'Is the Prime Minister sending for you?'

'I dropped him a hint when I arrived. I can a tale unfold, but not on paper, and not to the embassies.'

> 'The Foreign Office? All John Bull must know
> This writing on the outer door: F.O.'

Lottie quoted, startling us both.

'My dear Lottie – that's not for publication,' Edward said.

'I don't care,' said the young woman. 'It's time some of those old fogeys did get a shock. And if you don't do it, Edward, no one else will.'

Edward began to smile, charming and nonchalant, but the girl exclaimed in a peculiar tone, patient and yet implacable, like that of a keeper who sees a young spaniel shirking the gorse. 'No, no, we're going right in with both feet – that was the promise – or are you lying down on me again?'

'Certainly not. A shocking suggestion,' Edward said, checking his smile. 'No, no, I'll give 'em an ultimatum – and hang the risk of party splits.'

And, warmly encouraged by Lottie, he held meetings on his own account, wrote letters to the Press, joined the militia, and was photographed, in uniform, for the illustrated papers. He even spoke for the Navy League.

All this made me very angry. I said, 'Edward is a clever fool. See, he has suddenly got tired of his holiday and his art and wants to play at politics again. But he is a typical party politician; no sense of responsibility. He is blinded by ambition, by that secret demon which infects all politicians, whether they like it or not.'

And when Edward's meetings failed, and *The Times* refused his letters, I did not know whether to be more angry with the country for humiliating our family great man; or with Edward for stirring up, as I thought, war fever.

100

My life, which these children think so flat, might be described as three great waves of passion and agitation. The first rose in my youth, out of that inland sea, and gradually grew higher, darker, heavier, more dangerous, until, in the great war, it fell with one tremendous crash. And after that war, out of the confused choppy ocean of my middle age, arose another wave, not so high as the last, but faster, wilder and blacker, which finally dashed itself to pieces in a swamp; and became a stagnant lake, among rotting trees, and tropical serpents. From which Sara, like a mild English breeze, came to rescue me, by blowing away the vapours, and sweeping me off from that oozy gulf into a third wave, a bright Atlantic roller, smooth and fresh, which was just about to come into port, when it struck upon a sand bar and burst into foam, bubbles, spray, air, etc. But like the waves you see from all these western cliffs, never finding rest.

I believe I have been more agitated during this last week in Tolbrook than any time since before the last war. For one thing, there is a new war fever about; and this time a true fever; a disease, a distemper of the blood. I can't bear to read all this stuff about Hitler and the Nazis, as if that set of cunning rascals were likely to contrive their own ruin by provoking war. Thus I cannot look at the morning papers. And, for a second thing, it seems that Robert has actually gone off with Molly Panton, a thing I could not believe.

Ann has now all the evidence she wants from Robert himself. The couple have obtained work in a Lincolnshire farm of large acreage, where they are acting, apparently, as humble workers. The girl is in the dairy, Robert is a general farm labourer.

And when I express my wonder that Robert should leave Tolbrook for such a position, Ann says only, 'It's just like him.'

'What is like him? – he is a skilled farmer, and a very ambitious one.'

'It's this Adam and Eve idea,' Ann says, 'which is going about. When Adam delved and Eve span. Men must work, if possible, in a muck heap, and women must weep, if possible, into a new baby.'

'What fearful rubbish – what is all this. Do you mean Robert models his life on Genesis?'

'No, but Genesis came out of the ideas of people like Robert.'

'My dear Ann, you are a great donkey – to talk such stuff. It's the kind of stuff which poisons everything with its stuff. Because it sounds like sense.' I was angry with the girl. And she answered me:

'Yes, perhaps it is nonsense. After all, what do I know about Robert – I couldn't even keep the creature happy.'

'Come now, that's enough – and what is this garment you're wearing?'

For she was in a kind of cloak; at eleven in the morning.

'It's only a dressing-gown – I didn't dress properly, because I was going to work at the papers,' meaning, I suppose, Edward's papers. She has suddenly resolved to write a life of her father; a project which I encourage. For I always wanted to see Edward receive justice from posterity, and I wished, too, for Ann to have some occupation. Nothing, I felt, was worse for a girl in her situation than idleness.

'A dressing-gown,' I said, 'to write in. But that's an exploded idea. It went out even before my time. Good authors don't write in dressing-gowns. And I hope you're not going about the house in that ramshackle state – for it doesn't suit your style at all.' And I pointed out that her best point was her figure, at least from the waist upwards, and that she would be foolish to forget it.

The girl then went and dressed. And coming down again, she said to me, 'I mustn't fall down on this job, too, must I?'

'What are you talking about – your book?'

'No, I meant giving satisfaction as a niece.'

But I could see very well that she was amusing herself at my expense. Which I do not mind, so long as she does not become a sloven. Which, for a girl, is the quickest road to damnation. Quicker even than drink.

101

Edward's papers, my own memoranda among them, astonish me again by the wrongness of my ideas on every conceivable subject; and the rightness of his. But I should not be surprised. I am simply stating the fact that Edward was a man out of the common run, and I was not. And therefore, of course, I acknowledged his general superiority, as any fool must do; and yet found every single particular thing he did foolish; as fools always do.

'All this war agitation,' I told him, 'is doing you no good at all – it's only annoying the party chiefs.'

'What will happen to the party when the war breaks out.'

'Oh, if you're counting on war, you'll be mistaken.' I had so nearly said 'again' that Edward coloured slightly and I felt myself redden.

The fear of war now so possessed me, that I hardly thought of anything else. One day in town I met Julie and Edward together, near Berkeley Square, just outside the discreet little tea-shop, which at one time was a rendezvous for what Edward called the three-quarter world; women like Julie, ostensibly respectable widows, or wives with husbands abroad, and their lovers or keepers.

I had not visited Julie since that unlucky proposal after her husband's death. We had exchanged some birthday letters, but it was already becoming understood between us that we had separated for good. I had even arranged a settlement which Julie, less proud than she had been seven years previously, accepted.

I had congratulated myself on the success of this difficult negotiation; which had left behind it neither bitterness on Julie's side, nor any deep regrets on mine.

The sudden and unexpected meeting might well have startled me. Yet it was not until we had walked as far as Julie's flat and had spoken for some time about a recent speech of Lord Roberts who, of course, I looked upon as a dangerous firebrand, that I noticed the silence and embarrassment of the others.

I thought, 'What! has Edward gone back to her – he can't be such a fool.' And at the same time I was enraged that so trivial an anxiety should intrude upon this terrible crisis. I said, 'Where are we going – West Street?' – where Julie's flat was.

'No, it hadn't been suggested,' Edward said, after a moment. His caution further irritated me. I thought, 'Heavens, he doesn't think I'm jealous, does he?' And I said, 'Where then? – it's rather cold for the park.'

'If you like to come up,' Julie said, and before I remembered that I had, in fact, not intended to enter Julie's flat again, I found myself in my usual arm-chair, before the usual bright, too large fire, surrounded by the usual pale clean colours and delicate scents.

Julie, on the other hand, did not lounge in her chair, but sat upon a piano stool, at a great distance from me. Edward stood awkwardly by the fireplace, and his whole attitude, I thought, even the way the collar of his coat stood out from his neck behind, forming a little pocket, expressed a sense of defeat, and surprised humility. 'I suppose he came to Julie for consolation,' I reflected, 'because Lottie is too hard on him.' And I became more and more indignant with him. 'If only you would stand up to people like Roberts,' I said. 'That would have been the way to make yourself indispensable.'

Edward started and said, 'But Roberts is right – we aren't prepared for war.'

'War – war – why do you harp on war? Nobody wants a war.'

'Don't you think so?'

'What?' I was astonished.

'I should say a lot of people are always ready to welcome a war. Of course, they don't say so. They usually say the opposite.'

'Most people,' Julie said.

'Rubbish – what nonsense – speak for yourselves.'

'First there's the young – the sporting ones,' Edward said. 'And the young carry a lot of political weight because they are energetic and have so much time to give to politics. Papa and Mama have other things to do – like paying their bills.'

'I can feel war coming,' Julie said. 'And it's quite time.'

'Do you want war, Julie?'

'We deserve war – we think of nothing but comfort.'

'Yes,' Edward said, 'there's another group of war welcomers. I'd forgotten them – the people who feel that the world is wicked – that it deserves punishment.' He sat down and picked up the poker. But at once laid it down again and glanced at me. The gesture and the glance were that of a man who has begun to ask of his smallest action, 'Is that wrong – does it tell against me?'

It made me perceive, for the first time, the extent of Edward's failure. For one measures failure commonly by its effect upon the one who has suffered it. I felt, 'If Edward is shy of my opinion, how vast must be his fall.' And with a sick heart I said, 'Yes, the fire could do with a poke.'

'People are right,' Julie said from the back of the room. 'It is quite time the world was punished.'

'There you are,' Edward said, 'Julie thinks we ought all to be shot or ruined. The good want war because they want to suffer and the bad want it because they want the other people to suffer.' He spoke without his usual animation, but in Julie's melancholy tone, of one who accepts fate. 'Plenty of people are ready to take any risk to themselves so long as they can get the revenge on somebody else – often some purely abstract enemy, like Germany or France or England. See how the Irish nationalists delight in hatred of England – which is a pure abstraction.'

'But we know there is an evil will,' Julie said, 'and the evil will delights in all evil.'

The room was growing dark and Julie, on her piano stool, was only a white form in the twilight, with one bluish cheek and shoulder where the light from the uncurtained window fell upon her from one side. Edward and I, in the golden light of the fire, seemed to be in a different world, and I think we both felt it. Edward jumped up and said, 'Have my chair, Julie – aren't you cold there?'

'No, thank you – it's too hot.' And she said in the same voice, 'After all, we are evil ourselves – we have plenty of bad thoughts.'

'Not you, Julie. You are the best friend anyone could hope for.'

'No, no,' in a voice so passionate that both of us were silenced.

I thought, 'She wants Edward, and she is angry that she can't have him – she has always been in love with Edward,' and I became still more impatient with these triflers. I said, 'All this seems to me pretty wild stuff. The question is simply, is war inevitable? *I* say, so far from being inevitable, it isn't even natural. And if it does break out it's our own fault for not stopping it.'

'Another large group,' Edward said, touching the poker but withdrawing his hand again. 'Another large group,' he resumed, 'probably the largest of all, is the people who are dissatisfied with their lot – the failures.'

He paused and I felt that he had plumped the word out in defiance of embarrassment. I was so irritated against him that I nearly exclaimed, 'That is *your* reason for believing in this war.' But thank God I was able to control myself. I seized the poker, to rescue it from Edward's hand, and poked the fire before I recollected that I had no longer the master's right over that fire.

There was a long pause. The fire had now sunk to a red glow. It illuminated only a few square feet of the beautiful Persian rug; Julie's book, lying face downwards, *The Hound of Heaven*, in a first edition; and Edward's boots, which were not well cleaned. The rest of the room was felt rather than seen; and Julie was only a shadow among the thick uncertain shadows of furniture in the background. But the sky through the dark frame of the window had become brilliant with the strange light of a London dusk, neither blue nor green, gloomy but limpid, like a clear sheet of glass, apparently transparent and profound, but showing no star. It was like some vast shallow jewel lit by a cunning arrangement of lights hidden behind it. Its beauty gave no sense of expansion to the spirit, but only oppression. And I actually found myself on my feet with the thought in my mind, 'I could catch the last train and be at Tolbrook before midnight.'

But instead I proposed to turn up the light.

'I don't think I want the light,' Julie said.

I noticed again something strange in Julie's conduct. 'Why does she sit there away from us, and how did she come to meet Edward in the tea-room? It must have been by appointment – and probably not the first time if I caught them together. I pass that corner every day, but all the odds were against my catching them on the first occasion.' And then at once I dismissed the whole thing from my mind. 'I suppose I'm in the way, but what does it matter – let them sleep together if they like. I've no time for such nonsense while these lunatics threaten war.'

'They're pretty numerous, too,' Edward murmured.

'Who are numerous?'

'The failures – the dissatisfied. About nine-tenths of the population, I suppose.'

I laughed. 'So, according to you, nine people in ten want war.'

'Oh, not all the time, of course, only now and then. It's only when they have a majority all at once that you get trouble.'

'According to you, we ought to be at war all the time.'

'Luckily modern war is expensive and complicated and needs a lot of organization. That's its one advantage, if it is an advantage. In the Middle Ages any baron could make war any afternoon. Many did. But now war can't be run except by a special department, and so you don't get quite so much of it.'

I got up. I could bear no more. 'It's no good talking to you, you can't be serious on any subject. I've got twenty minutes for my train, so I must fly. Don't let me take you away.'

Edward got up. 'Yes, it's quite time I rid Julie of this nuisance. You're not going down home, are you?'

'Yes, I thought so.' For I had resolved to catch the train.

'I might really come with you, apparently there's nothing for me to do in town. I suppose there is a dining car on the train.'

'But perhaps Julie would rather you stayed.'

'I thought you were going to dine with me,' Julie said.

But Edward excused himself in somewhat lame terms. He seemed too dispirited even to use his social resource. And we took a taxi to the station.

We spoke no more about the war danger. I was too much annoyed by what I called Edward's cynical frivolity.

Neither did we speak of Julie. I could not be bothered, at such a time, to tread tactfully among complicated sentiments.

102

But one consequence of this meeting was unexpected. For in the next week when I was back in London I found myself, at five o'clock, at Julie's doorstep. It had been, till six months ago, the usual hour for my arrival. And in some fit of distracton I had reverted to the habit. But now, since I was there, I went up. Julie was in. She received me with a kind of calm, gentle surprise which gave her, I thought, a stupid look. Indeed, I thought, seeing her again, that she was growing plain. Her plumpness was unbecoming. Her pallor had an unhealthy look. Her eyes and forehead were full of fine wrinkles. And while we were waiting for tea I felt sorry for her. I thought, 'She is finished – she has let her life ebb away,' and I said with a roughness which surprised my own ear, 'You should take more exercise, Julie, you're getting too fat.'

'Yes,' she said, sitting with bent head, and one hand gently stroking the back of the other, an old trick. 'I am really ashamed to think how I spend my time. I don't know where it goes to.'

I could have told her that. It went in long meditation and trifling tasks. Julie was thinking all day long, even while she dressed herself, ate or wrote a letter, of some friend in the past, someone who had loved her or whom she had loved, or ought to have helped.

'You should take up some useful occupation,' I told her.

And Julie answered, as usual, with good nature, 'But what could I do that was really of use? I thought of district visiting, but you know I could never talk to poor people to do them any good. I tried once and found myself agreeing with one poor wretch that it was no good trying to keep clean.'

'No, you wouldn't be any good in doing anything unpleasant. But why not act again?'

Julie shook her head. 'No, leave me my memories of the time when there was great acting and great plays to act.'

Then we began to talk about this great period. I knew nothing of the stage. It may be true that, as Julie believed, the only time when there had been real enthusiasm for the stage, and great acting, had been in her youth. It is not probable I did not quite believe it then. But I liked to listen to Julie's chat, and to hear her quote, to see her animated, and so we passed the evening, and I stayed the night.

I do not know why or when I decided to stay. Perhaps I did not decide at all. But finding myself at peace for a moment, in that quiet familiar room, I could not take myself away from it. And idly sought that other pleasure of the past. Yet I knew even then that this act must change all my relations with Julie.

But I said to myself of Julie, as I said to Edward, 'No, I can't really give my mind to such trifles in a time like this.' And when, by her silence, however melancholy, she permitted me first to stay and then to enter her room, I affected to be carrying out the old routine. I allowed myself to believe, when I climbed at last into her bed and took hold of her and arranged her body to suit my purpose, that I was performing a trivial act which might, for a moment or two, take from our minds the weight of our anxieties. But the truth was, I was trying to fly out, by that door, from oppression and fear. And Julie's gentle acquiescence hid from me the violence of my deed.

103

And I flew from Julie at the end of the week, from her talk about Henry Harland and the rest, to the tense and balanced life of Tolbrook, where Lucy and Amy still bickered and did each other mutual service, where Edward was still waiting to be summoned into the Cabinet, and Lottie, in her sharp schoolgirl's voice, nagged him every day for submitting to neglect.

She would say to me in Edward's presence, 'The trouble with Edward is he's too proud to make a noise as if he wanted something, but I don't see he's got much to be proud about yet.'

The girl's youthful sincerity, which was so charming, could also wound, and we could see that Edward was henpecked. Yet what was pitiable and I think humiliating to himself was his need of Lottie. He received her sharp abuse with an uneasy smile, and repaid it with compliments and expensive presents; he followed her everywhere and seemed unable to let her go out of his sight.

But Lottie grew more bitter. She was enraged against Edward. for she had thought him a great and important person. And now he had turned out, as it seemed to her, defeated and patient under defeat. In a young woman, scorn is hatred.

She had a trick of quoting against him his own writings, and one day, in the presence of her mother, Lucy and myself, and several visitors, having complained that Edward would not give to the Press some private knowledge, injurious to a minister, she quoted to us in the clear elocution of the well-trained young person:

> 'Statesman and scholar, he disdains to try
> The hero's role before the scholar's eye.
> A statesman still in judgement, smiles at praise
> For trifles which amuse a scholar's days.
> Modest in triumph, silent in defeat,
> No littleness could tempt his vast conceit.'

Edward, with the perfect manners, which were all he had left to carry him through humiliaton, smiled and said, 'Oh, yes, so-and-so,' mentioning a well-known statesman, 'but I've thought once or twice since that his graceful attitudes may be due to nothing but shyness.'

'So-and-so modest – no more than you are, Edward!'

'But don't you think he might be nervous of losing what fragment of self-respect remains with him after thirty years in politics.'

'Self-respect. You really make me tired, Edward. You're just too soft.' And suddenly she jumped up and left the room. Moreover, some days later she left the house, taking Ann upon a visit for which Edward was not asked. And remained away for the next two months.

104

I did not notice the progress of Edward's despair, which advanced, like a fatal disease, imperceptibly.

I was too busy, too distracted by the daily conflicts of Tolbrook, and the political crisis, to think of Edward oftener than at a week's interval.

I was now fighting against the smallest preparations for war. I was like the man who is so frightened of cancer that he will not go to the doctor for stomach ache.

There was a new Navy Bill that year, and some of the local Radicals were protesting against it. I had already split with the local committee, but I joined eagerly with these groups of anarchists and pacifists. I even paid out of my own pocket for advertisements in the newspapers saying that the Government policy was leading us into war; that we should offer friendship to Germany and not provocation.

I was glad when Bill and Amy came to live near us, not because he was my brother, but because I hoped for his support. We were very anxious to secure army men for our platform, and I hoped that Bill, who was, after all, an old-fashioned Christian, would come out against the Navy Bill. He had also a grudge against authorities. For after a fall from his horse two years before he had been put on half pay; and lately, in spite of his protests, invalided on pension.

'I'm fit enough,' Bill said, 'but I'm sick of this nonsense. No more boards for me. Amy and I have had enough of wandering. We want a home before we die.'

And, in fact, they took on lease, with the option to buy, a small and hideous red-brick cottage on the Queensport road, beside the Longwater Estuary. They had nothing but Bill's pension, and three children dependent on it. Willie was a lieutenant, but he still needed an allowance. The other two were at school.

It seemed to me an act of madness for such paupers to buy property, when Tolbrook was open to them. I wondered if perhaps Edward had paid them his debt.

But Lucy, who knew Edward's secrets, wrote not. 'How could the poor boy pay anything when he hasn't a penny of his own.' Her explanation of Bill's rashness was simply that he had no money sense. 'He's never had any idea of what things cost. He and Amy were mad on having this place of their own, and they couldn't restrain themselves.'

'They won't have it long if Edward's war breaks out.'

And, even as I shook hands, I asked Bill if, as a soldier, he could advise any nation to plunge into a European war.

'I don't know anything about it,' Bill said, 'I'm out of touch, you know. I say, you've been a long time coming to see us. What do you think of us?' Meaning by 'us', apparently, the house. 'Not too bad in front, after all, when we've put up the porch. But, of course, it's not Chatsworth or Hatfield.'

They were full of that excited impatient hospitality of a young couple who have set up house for the first time. 'Come and see my range,' Amy said, 'it's old-fashioned, of course, but really far better than those flimsy things they make now.'

'Oh, the range,' Bill said. 'Tommy doesn't want to see ranges. Come along to the garden. Of course, it's really only a rubbish heap at present – old bottles and brick-bats.'

'According to Edward' I said bitterly, 'you won't be able to enjoy even brick-bats and bottles for more than another six months.'

'But does Edward really know. Is he in touch with anyone on the staff? Look at that lovely bit of ground. All sloping south – and real good stuff under the weeds.'

And I could not get Bill even to discuss the war danger except from a professional point of view. He had a story that the Germans wouldn't make war that year because of a new Russian gun-sight, just coming into production; and because the French army was getting too good, and because we had a wonderful new rifle just going into production. And when I lost my temper and asked him if he thought Europe was about to be ravaged because the German general staff wanted to play with its new toys, he answered, 'Not quite – but it's their job to know the best time for a war,' and then urged me to admire his jonquils.

It was a relief to me to meet John who was at home from school for the Easter holidays. John had taken his scholarship, among a famous band. I felt that he was to be an honour to the Wilchers, and I delighted now in his gentle manners and sensible looks. I thought, 'He, at least, will understand me.' And I said, 'You don't want a war, do you, John?'

'Is there going to be a war?' he asked, and in the same breath invited me to see the new landing stage, at the end of the garden; and his boat.

'Many people seem to think so,' I said, 'and by thinking so, they are creating a certain danger.'

'There always seems to be a war somewhere, doesn't there? She's got nice lines, hasn't she?' showing me a little tub of a dinghy lying below the garden, 'but, of course, she's completely rotten under the paint. You could put your finger through her. Would you like a sail?'

At once, feeling perhaps that I was not inclined for a sail, he added, 'But perhaps we had better wait for a better day, with more wind. And besides, the paint isn't really dry.'

'Yes, perhaps we had better wait,' I said, for I had already touched sticky paint with hands and umbrella.

'The wind is getting up though. There's a flaw now – and it's going the right way.' The boy pointed at a thumb mark of breeze on the smooth Longwater. 'But, of course, it's only a flaw.'

The struggle in his mind between longing to use the boat, his own first boat, and common sense, was hard. He said sadly, 'I only painted the rudder this morning. And there's no tiller.'

'That settles it,' I said. 'What a pity! I should have liked a sail with you, very much.'

'Though I could steer with an oar. Yes, uncle, why shouldn't we try after all. You could sit on a newspaper.'

'It would stick to the paint and ruin all your beautiful work.'

'Oh, I don't mind that, I can easily do it again. Just wait while I run for the gear.'

And he took me for a sail, which, just as we had expected, was a complete failure, and caused in us both the highest degree of chagrin and embarrassment. I became covered with paint; there was no wind. And while we drifted along the shore of the Longwater from one mud bank to the other, the poor boy, extraordinarily sensitive to another's feelings, frowned and said repeatedly, 'I am most awfully sorry, uncle. I'm afraid it was a bad day for a sail, after all.'

'Not at all, John. It's the wind dropping. That's just bad luck.'

'Oh, I knew there wasn't any wind. I was a perfect ass. I can't imagine why I chose such a hopeless day.'

He was almost in tears; and I, exhausted by inventing consolation, was at last silent and almost as dejected as himself. Fortunately, when we came back at last, he recollected that I had not yet seen a wornout millstone, discovered in the kitchen garden. He showed it to me with pride and said, 'We don't know what to do with it.'

'Perhaps a miller could find some use for it.'

'Oh, no, we must use it somewhere – after finding it like that,' as if he owed a duty to this foundling.

I felt ever more attracted to this sensible affectionate boy who felt a duty even to broken millstones. I was deeply touched by his attentions. And I sought his sympathy. 'You don't believe in war, John. Wars have never decided anything. They are the most useless kind of madness.'

The boy reflected thoughtfully, 'War has never decided anything,' and all the way to the house he seemed to reflect on my words. But as Amy came out to greet him, he said to her, in a heart-broken voice, 'No wind, Mum, and the sail isn't big enough yet.'

'I must sew on another strip.'

And at tea, while John and Amy discussed the plan of the new sail, Bill, who did not take tea, told us, as an illustration of the dangers of war, a long story about some patent improvement in the Maxim gun which had been offered to the British Staff and refused. 'May cost us the war,' he said gravely, 'Yes, pretty big responsibility these chaps had, whole of the empire, millions of lives, depending on 'em.'

I was defeated. I could not even argue with Bill. I could only remark, when John was listening, that perhaps if there were fewer experts on the machine gun, there would be fewer wars.

'Unless they were all on one side,' Bill said.

105

Amy had approached me privately about Bill's health. His digestion was giving trouble. Would I persuade him to see a specialist?

But I have always been doubtful of specialists, and I was not on good terms with Bill. For I could not bear his fixed intention of making John into a soldier; I advised Amy to try carbonate of soda, and I took every opportunity of conversation with the boy. But I was rarely able to be alone with him. For as soon as I was seen at the cottage, Bill would thrust a spade or fork into my hand and set me to work. During that spring of 1914, I spent nearly all my week-ends at navvy's work. Amy and I would dig, Bill, who was not allowed to dig on account of his mysterious pains, would be nailing trellis on the arbour; John would be whitewashing the back of the house in an absent-minded manner; and Loftus, sent to weed, quietly doing nothing in some corner.

And if I spoke of the dangers of militarism, for John's ears, Bill would say only, 'It's a tricky question. Damn the arbour. It's a regular swindle. They said it was ash and half of it is deal.'

'You wanted the cheapest,' Amy said.

'Excuse me, you wanted the cheapest. I wanted to go to the Army and Navy.'

'I said that it wasn't safe to buy from a firm we had never heard of. That's very nice, Johnny. Now the bit under the window.'

'You said we couldn't afford five pounds twelve for a luxury – look it that boy, look at him.' This in a tone of despair.

John, in fact, had paused in the middle of a stroke with his brush. I thought that he was reflecting still upon my theme, until I saw that he was leaning through the kitchen window to read the newspaper spread upon the kitchen table. The brush was still pressed against the brick wall, but it was motionless.

Amy's back was turned to the house, but, as if feeling a danger, she now quickly looked round, and called out, 'Mind your brush, Johnny, it's dropping.'

But Bill's shout drowned her '*John*, what the hell are you playing at.'

The boy jumped, and the brush moved. Bill grumbled loudly, 'Regular bookworm. Can't resist a bit of print. I don't know what's going to happen to him.'

But afterwards, when I asked John what he had found so interesting in the newspapers, he answered that it was an article about Captain Slocum.

'Who was Captain Slocum?'

'He sailed round the world in a twelve-ton yawl.' The boy was surprised that I had never heard of this hero. And when I remarked that the European situation appeared very dangerous, he answered only, 'I suppose it always is – at least rather.'

'Don't be so sleepy,' I said. 'A boy of your age should take an interest in things. And European politics are going to affect your whole life. Very much so.'

He reflected for a time, and then said, 'But I suppose the political people are looking after this.'

It was as though I had heard again the voice of Amy saying that no doubt her insides knew how to look after her baby. John, too, appeared to be a private person.

But now I was frightened by the privateness of such as Bill and Amy and John. I answered angrily, 'And who is looking after the political people? Did you never hear of democracy or imagine that it had duties as well as rights?' etc., etc.

'But I haven't got a vote, uncle.'

'What does that matter? Any sheep can vote. The thing you've got to do is agitate – agitate. Look at your Uncle Edward.'

And the boy with his peculiar detached tone of a sixth form boy murmured, 'A scene of agitation.'

'Of course, what do you expect with people what they are – especially political people. Besides, that's the way democracy does work – the biggest agitator wins – it's a battle of noise and impudence and egotism.' And, in fact, I found myself speaking of democracy with great bitterness. So that I stopped in some confusion.

But the boy was calm and aloof in his private world of reflections. 'The art and craft of government,' he murmured.

'But, of course,' I said, 'it's the only government for us in England – in fact, it's the only reasonable government anywhere, because people can agitate and make nuisances of themselves when they feel like it. And if you don't let them, they'll get into worse mischief in revolutions and general throat-cutting.'

106

Tyrants hate Truth, death takes them by surprise,
Hail Democrats, who love the larger lies.

When I suggested to Ann just now that this would make a good heading for her war chapter, she answered, to my surprise, 'You don't like democracy much.'

'My dear girl, I've never faltered in my belief in democracy.'

'Yes, you believed in it, so did Daddy. But you didn't like it. I used to think that democracy was rather popular in those old days.'

'Democracy in those old days, as you call them, was the creed of the whole nation.'

'So it is now. But everybody abuses it all the time – I only wondered if you did the same in the last century. I want to get the angle.'

'Oh, yes, the angle,' and I felt as if the cool refreshing breeze of exact scholarship had blown on my forehead, already growing warm with indignation and excitement.

I did not know that a woman was capable of this careful approach to an historical problem. I had almost written too careful, too balanced. Ann has spent three weeks on her war chapters, and she is busy two or three hours a day. And if I cannot praise her style which is that of a medical journal reporting a case of infantilism, I have to remember that the young of this age do not study Pater and Newman, as we did in the 'nineties. They have their own models in the *Police Gazette*, etc. Ann's curt sharpness, as of an examining prison matron, is not due to condescension towards Edward and myself and other antiques. On the contrary, if the girl has a bias, it is in Edward's favour.

'I suppose,' she said to me, 'they wouldn't have Daddy back in the Cabinet because they were afraid of his brains.'

'Or perhaps they didn't like his ferocious attacks upon them. As he used to say himself – a government is not so inhuman as people think – it hates to be abused.'

'They could have taken him back after the war started.'

'Yes, perhaps they were always doubtful of him. They may have felt he wasn't single-minded enough. They didn't like his writing, especially things like essays and criticism. Just as the Tories never liked Balfour's writing philosophy.'

We were sitting in Edward's room. It had become our favourite in the mornings, when it caught the sun. And in the evening, when the tall curtains were drawn and a clear fire burned, we often talked till long after midnight. We agreed that it was the warmest and pleasantest room in the house. For in the last seven weeks, since Robert's departure, Ann, by the aid of my memory and a good decorator, had restored to it almost all the elegance of its high day. The shelves were once more full of books. Edward's writing table stood in the window. And on the walls hung his portrait; a drawing of Lottie with Ann sitting in her lap; and a reproduction of two French impressionists which had once belonged to him. Even his inkstand, his pens, his crops and sticks were in their places. For I had put all Edward's things away at his death, labelled with his initials.

It gave me great pleasure to see this beautiful and dignified room, restored to use and life. It was a room which, unlike Julie's, spoke of courage and enterprise. The strange but brilliant pictures, which still gave me a certain discomfort, the strong colour and bold decoration, the solid funiture and noble books, both from the most manly and lively century of our history, these were an inspiration. They said, 'This is a place not for retirement but for counsel with strong minds; and meditation upon great examples.' But a keener pleasure was to see Edward's daughter, in his own arm-chair, sitting at home once more among his own possessions, so piously gathered by her energy; and his grandson playing on the floor with blocks which had been cut from a bough dropped from Wesley's oak; for Edward's great-grandfather.

Some old books and chairs, a child's blocks; are these things to give happiness in a world of miseries? No more I suppose than the features of an old friend in a world of strangers.

But with what joy does a man of my age see a friend's face; a man that is, who is exceedingly lucky to have one friend in the world.

Indeed, I am enjoying such happiness in these summer weeks that I can hardly believe myself to be Tom Wilcher, that life-battered gnome. Peace has come to me, as I suppose it always comes, by surprise, and out of the very midst of storm. And this happiness, which I have never enjoyed before, a calm gentle home-keeping happiness, is none the less precious to me because I am old.

For I have discovered that old people, even such old people as myself, with bad health and worse consciences, can enjoy life with as much appreciation as a child eats his breakfast; or Jan, here, sucks a lollipop. And this happiness is not grounded in delusion, or some deceit, put upon me by the family contrivance. For Ann herself declares the same contentment. She said to me only last evening, 'I've never felt so at home in any place before. But, of course, I never had a home. When mother married again, I went to school in Chicago. And then it was Lausanne, and as soon as I had got money of my own, I cut away and went to London. I wanted to live in one of the real cities and mother was in New York, and I couldn't do medicine in French. The first time I wrote London, England, on my notepaper, I felt as proud as if I had had a big success. In spite of the other eight million.'

I was thinking that Ann, after all, was very like Edward. No feature was the same, only the hair and the eyes. But her voice was like his in a female edition, and she spoke often with the same tone, as if secretly amused at her own follies.

'But are you sure that chair was really the one father used for the writing table?' she asked me.

'Almost sure – it was very like it.'

'We must be quite sure or the charm won't work.'

'You shouldn't talk about faith arising from chairs as if you were a savage. Faith is an act of the intelligence, as you ought to know,' etc.

For I value very much the girl's intelligent and honest mind, which, I see very clearly, has brought to me much of the relaxation of this peace, so novel and delightful to my soul. And so I find her follies the more deplorable.

'Good writing isn't a matter of chairs, but hard work,' I said to her, 'as your father knew very well.'

But she had already returned to the inquiry. There was a Lottie in the girl, the perpetual schoolgirl, as well as an Edward. 'I suppose politicians are always suspicious of an original mind, that's why governments are always behind the times. And army staffs. A real genius, like Napoleon or Marlborough, always makes them look silly. But, of course, he has to get power first, and that usually takes a revolution.'

I suggested that Edward, though a clever man, was hardly a genius; and, secondly, that geniuses might be dangerous in government. 'What you want is a steady conscientious kind of man.'

'Lawyers and bankers.'

'Quite so. I am not ashamed of my trade – not at all.'

'But I wasn't thinking of you, uncle. I don't think of you as a lawyer – you are much more a religious man.'

'And why should not a lawyer be a Christian – or try to be one?'

Ann did not answer me. It was a modern trick of hers to break off a conversation when she chose. Probably, in her modern school, just as she never learnt how to enter a room, or to keep her back flat, or to make herself charming, she was never taught how to begin, maintain and conclude a real conversation. And the pity of it was, that she was very teachable. When I saw her sitting bunched up, with her nose and spectacles poked into a book, I showed her by demonstration what a figure she cut: 'Like a monkey on a stick with a pain in its stomach.'

'Thank you, uncle, I know I'm rather stoopy,' and she did really make an attempt, once or twice, to sit up.

I was greatly touched by this response to interference which was, of course, extremely tactless.

'You are a good girl,' I told her. 'You never harbour malice.'

But she did not answer me. She was too deep in her book of political memoirs. Probably, of course, her patience is merely contempt for my opinions. Be it so. I enjoy now, because of that patience, whether from the heart or the mind; because of that efficiency, whether devoted or merely professional; because of that tolerance, whether due to charity or indifference, a happiness that I have never known before. So that often I feel guilty and ask myself, 'Can this go on? How have I deserved such peace, at Tolbrook of all places? And with this painted chit from the laboratories.'

107

Our only quarrels now were on the subject of Nazis, etc. For Ann thought that we ought to come to an arrangement with Germany in order to avoid war. 'There is no danger of a German war,' I pointed out. 'The real danger is civil war. France, Spain, and Italy are divided from top to bottom between

Catholic right and Communist left,' etc. 'Yes, we may well have more wars of religion which would indeed destroy civilization.'

'Would that matter very much?'

Now this is a question that always enrages me. And I told the young woman what I thought of her. 'You ought to have more sense. You're not a born fool, at least. Or don't you have any idea what civil war means. In Germany, during the thirty years' war, more than half the population, about fifteen million people, died of starvation or disease, or murdered each other,' etc. 'Nothing is too bad and too cruel for men who have been turned into brutes. Yes, and it's the young people like Robert and you who might bring about this awful misery simply by talking nonsense about our civilization having no value.'

She did not answer me, and I thought, 'There now, we're quarrelling. And it's your fault, you old fool. You ought to be more careful. But what is one to do? Why must these children always talk rubbish? Why must they make everything more confused and more perplexing?'

But Ann, after knitting half a round, answered only, 'And, of course, there's the Maginot Line.'

'I agree with you, my dear. History will say that Maginot, that modest little soldier, was the greatest of all. He made civilization safe, by making European war a doubtful and dangerous enterprise.'

108

My own words filled me with wonder at the survival of civilization, by trifling strokes of luck, by the narrowest escapes. For what is it, a fabric hanging in the air – a construction of ideas, sympathies, habits, something so impalpable that you cannot grasp it. You look for its friends, and you find that it has none. Nobody cares for it any more than they care for the ground under their feet or the air they breathe. And it survives in spite of this mass of ignorance, selfishness, spite, folly, greed, hatred which makes up the ordinary political life of the world. As Edward wrote:

> 'Descent from apes. Quite so. But please to crack
> This nut, professor. How long climbing back?'

We are apes and worse than apes. We know the light and turn from it. We do evil for the secret delight of it; not because it is delightful to our senses, but because it is evil. It was this terrible truth which I had grasped in the years 1913 and 1914, before that last and most savage of wars. I saw the enormous power of evil, and the weakness of good, and in my terror I ran about like a man who has just noticed that his house is in danger of collapse. I begged everybody, 'Not so loud – don't shout – don't stamp your feet – for God's sake don't quarrel – keep quiet,' and I pointed to the large cracks in the walls, the holes in the roof, the glass flying from the windows. And to my horror, some of the people began at once to shout louder and to stamp on the floors. When Edward spoke of the secret and everlasting conflicts of life, I called him a cynic, and when Julie reminded me of the evil will, I was angry with her. But now I felt that evil will. It seemed to me that millions delighted in wickedness, a little wickedness, and that when all these little spites pushed the same way, war must come and civilization must fall.

109

But what is strange, the moment war broke out all my terror and foreboding disappeared. I ran to the recruiting office. I was one of those who stood for fifteen hours in Whitehall, with thousands of my kind, men of all ages, of all classes, trying to enlist in the new armies. And I neither felt nor met despair. On the contrary, I felt an extraordinary gaiety and lightness of spirit, and round me I saw and heard the same gaiety, smiles, jokes. Everyone was friendly, talkative, and what was new and strange, too, everybody was making a joke of what he had left. One man said, laughing, 'God knows what's happening at the office – I thought I was busy today.' Another answered, 'Yes, that's it, isn't it? I was saying yesterday that I hadn't had time for a holiday since last year, and here I am for the duration.' Young City men with their hats on the backs of their heads leant against the wall, and their whole attitude seemed to say, 'To the devil with care and decorum.' Neither was this the spirit of refugees, of beings suddenly flung out of old settled routine by some catastrophe. I saw such after a mine disaster – they were as crushed in spirit as if the earth had fallen upon them; even the children were gloomy, bewildered, with the sudden wrinkles of old age. These men were lively, watchful, receptive; all their faculties and their tongues active; you would have said that they were going on a kind of holiday; or if they were, after all, too serious, too tense for summer visitors, then upon a religious holiday, a pilgrimage.

And in forgetting anxieties, in forgetting things, all these men seemed to notice people more. I, who had been walking through crowded streets for years without noticing a single person, now felt interest and sympathy towards all my neighbours. I wondered about their lives, their feelings; I wanted to talk to them, to hear them speak. So it was all round me; one heard everywhere lively, friendly conversation. Everyone was ready to talk, to confess himself. And I thought of Chaucer's –

'Sundry folk, by aventure y fall,
In fellowship, and pilgrims were they all.'

We were all sent away. The War Office was not ready for us. But I went from the queue as from a place of revelation. I thought, 'How mean and small my life had become, and I had never noticed it.'

Others felt it, too. The nation was dedicated. No one was ashamed to speak of honour, freedom, love and truth. Churches were filled and soldiers wrote of religion.

110

I was sent to France in 1916 as a stretcher bearer. I was too old for the infantry, and I refused a commission. But the last weeks of that bitter winter in the Somme trenches gave me pneumonia and left me with a damaged heart. I was invalided out of the army in September, 1917, and came home to Tolbrook after more than a year's absence. I had been happy in the army at war. I had lived among grumbling and that private soldier's wit which makes of all life, its glories, as well as its miseries, something obscene or contemptible. I, too, had spoken of a dead comrade as a stiff or a landowner, and called the cemetery the rest camp. I enjoyed being called Pinkeye, Little Tich, or Shorty, and told that I had the duck disease because of my short legs. And when I used speech which filled every sentence with obscene images, I was expressing not anger, but a secret desire:

'All women bitches, liberty a lie,
So soldiers, who for home and freedom die.'

We were like monks who have forsworn the world, who have no responsibilities in it except to save it by the devotion and sacrifice of their lives. But while we threw dirt upon that which we loved, we exaggerated its virtues. So in London I was shocked by the fat complacent faces of profiteers, by the crowded restaurants, and the imbecilities of the stage, by the swarms of young girls walking the streets, not even for money, but pleasure.

At Tolbrook, indeed, I seemed to find dignity and peace. Lucy had gone back to her husband on his return from abroad, just after the outbreak of war. The nurseries were closed and I was no longer waked in my room along the passage at six o'clock in the morning by Robert singing in his bed, or trying to shake it to pieces. The housekeeper was competent, the food very good after army food. My mother, though, at seventy-eight, bent and crippled, apparently content in her daily routine of prayer, reading, and correspondence with mission friends.

But now, for some reason, I could not find serenity in her room. When I read to her or prayed with her, I would feel its stillness like a tension of the nerves. And the silent attention of the old woman, with her white thin face, seemed to ask of me an effort that I could not give. The effort, I suppose, of a comprehension, a sympathy that she had never had from any of her children, except Edward, who rarely troubled even to write to her.

And if, removed by experience of war, from Lucy's masterful influence, I began to feel, in some dim way, that my mother, whom I loved and reverenced, had yet suffered the cruellest injustice at our hands, by the mere whim of her daughter, and her own sensitive pride of spirit, I had not the patience, at such a time, to break an old, and therefore easy, routine of formal affection.

I found myself restless and troubled. I missed not only my friends of the war, but something which had belonged to us all from the day of our enlistment – a peace of the spirit. I had left noise, dirt and servitude at the front, expecting peace, and I found that peace had stayed with the servitude. And I began to spend nearly all my time at Turner's Cottage, as if some of that peace might be found with Bill, simply because he had been a soldier.

Bill now looked very ill, with white hair and a grey face. I could not have recognized him except for his pugnacious jaw. But he refused to discuss his health or a doctor. 'Doctors! What's the good of doctors? What do they know about anything? Nothing. Come on, and I'll show you my apples. Good solid path, isn't it; fifteen inches of broken brick under it. Made it myself last year. There you are, how's that for three-year trees? Hi, Amy, there's some windfalls.'

And Amy, coming in her stately manner, would gather up the windfalls as if retrieving an empire.

I was shocked by Bill's looks and by his whole attitude towards his responsibilities. I took occasion, as soon as I could get him alone, to point out that he must consider his health. 'Suppose anything happened to you, Bill – we're all mortal – what would happen to Amy and the children.'

And Bill, after a long pause, answered in a meditative fashion which I noticed for the first time, 'Well, Tom, I look at it like this. We're all in God's hands.'

Then suddenly laying a hand on my arm, he drew me towards the end of the garden. 'Have you seen our new view?'

But I was in no mood for seeing views. I could not help asking myself who would pay for Loftus and John, still at school, if Bill died. 'I daresay I'm as good a Christian as you are, but we have to think of children's futures,' etc., etc. And then I suggested that he should make Edward pay his debts. 'Edward owes you more than two thousand, and he could pay very well – he's spent that on presents for Lottie in the last six months.'

'No, no,' Bill shook his head. 'Poor old Edward, he's worried enough.' He was still drawing me towards the end of the garden, and when I protested he said mildly, 'But you believe in providence, Tommy.'

'Of course I do, but I think it's our duty under providence to use some foresight,' and so on, and I repeated my arguments about seeing a doctor, and overhauling his financial position.

But Bill did not even attend to them. He remarked that providence had intervened on his behalf many times. For instance, 'when Amy didn't die of that miscarriage on the trooper'; and 'when we got this place so cheap.' And then suddenly pointing, 'There you are, I always said that the willow ought to go. Fine tree, but we took a chance, and look at the result. Magnificent!'

What enraged me against Bill was the suspicion that his talk of providence was only a kind of trick to avoid responsibility. I thought, 'To a man like Bill, untrained in logic or self-criticism, the doctrine of providence is simply a temptation to avoid the trouble of thought.'

'Just forget your mud pies for a minute and think of your family,' I said. But Bill looked at me with his vague meditative eye, as if I had not been there, and before I could say more John came out from the house. He had just returned from some reading party on the moors. At first sight I was disappointed in the boy. He had shot up into a tall, thin boy of seventeen, with his hair in his eyes and a stooping back. He had lost his looks. His forehead was too high, his nose too long, his eyes too small. He told me that he had been reading the Republic.

'Plato,' Bill said. 'Yes, I must look into Plato. I always meant to do some philosophy. But just now potatoes is what we want,' and he laughed, as if surprised by his own joke. 'Get a fork, Johnny, and break up that strip of grass.' And he called out to Amy, 'Now, Amy, that's not two spits – a spit and a half is about the size of it. Deep trenching is the thing – all the books are definite on that point. And we'll need our potatoes pretty badly if the war is going on another year.'

John murmured, 'The war is always with us.'

'Well,' Bill said carelessly, 'I suppose it's got to go on till we win – or they'd win.' And he said to me, 'John is a bit of a pacifist, you know; been listening to all this "Stop the war" stuff.'

'But you aren't a pacifist, John,' Amy said, contradicting Bill. I noticed that Bill and Amy now avoided argument, except by this indirect method. And they showed new affection for each other. I saw them walking arm in arm on several occasions when, no doubt, they thought themselves unobserved.

'I don't know what I am,' John said, languidly raising a very small fragment of dry earth on his fork, and looking at it with a bored air. 'But war doesn't seem to do very much good – not obviously.'

'Good,' Bill said. 'No, did anyone say it was any good. You might as well ask, what's the good of cancer?'

At these words, Bill paused. Amy became scarlet, John very white.

And I felt a terror as if something unbearable had happened. But Bill continued in the same mild tone. 'No, I don't see it's any good. No one wants a major operation, I suppose, or a war. But if you ought to have one, you've got to have one. It's not going to rain, is it?'

We all looked up and declared that it might rain. Or it might keep up. And the digging continued. It appeared after all as if nothing had happened. Bill's pause had no significance. Amy said something about the roots. Bill, who was not allowed to dig, advised a mattock. And I thought, 'It was only my nerves. Dyspeptics like Bill always look wretchedly ill and live to a good old age.'

111

Two of John's friends, from the reading party, came to tea. Both had the same slouch, the same long hair, and they talked about the Republic among themselves, in a mild and absent-minded fashion. I was infuriated against them all. I said, 'What, has this apathy, this decadence, struck even into the schools.'

And I made some sharp remarks about the men in France, suffering every horror, while, at home, skrimshankers amused themselves with summer holidays. None of them answered me. On the contrary, afterwards, while we stood watching John prepare his boat for a sail, they were polite to me, in their absent-minded fashion. They asked me about my experiences in France; they sympathized with my illness. They seemed like elder statesmen condescending with a fractious child. But suddenly I heard one of them say to John, 'My last sail, I suppose.'

And John answered, 'Have you heard?'

'Yes, I report on Monday.'

'What, are you joining up?' I asked.

'I'm called up, sir,' said the boy.

'What unit do you mean to choose?'

'I suppose they'll decide that.'

'Doesn't make much difference,' John said.

'No, I suppose not,' said another.

Then there was an unexpected silence, and, looking at the boys, I saw upon all their faces a strange expression, preoccupied, and, as it were, waiting. They reminded me of those faces one sees in railway waiting-rooms, at once resigned, impatient, bored and suffering, of harassed travellers who have missed their connection, and expect nothing but disappointment from their journey.

It occurred to me suddenly to ask, 'Has your school had many casualties yet?'

'All last year's sixth have gone,' one of them answered, speaking to the air.

'Seventeen out of nineteen,' John said from the boat. 'But they say Jimmy won't die. He'll only be blind. Anyone got a piece of string.'

I felt ashamed and I began to feel shy among these boys, condemned to death. I spoke of their magnificent services in the air force, etc. They listened politely, but without comment, and John said, 'Come on, boys, I think she'll hold now – and if not –'

They got in and sailed away, leaving me upon the bank. I had not been asked to join them, and I was glad because I should have felt like an intruder.

112

I was ashamed, and my love for John returned with a force I had not known before. I said, 'What right have I, with two thirds of life behind me, to criticize these boys, meeting their hard fate with such unassuming courage?'

I proudly accepted John's confidence when he offered it to me. I delighted in that good nature of a boy who had still the humility of childhood, without its selfishness. So free from touchiness, that when, in the midst of our talk about the Greek way of life, etc., I ventured to urge that a haircut would give much pleasure to his father and greatly improve his appearance, he answered at once, 'Do you really think it worries father?'

'Very much. And me. It gives a wrong impression. It makes you look aesthetic – one would think you are trying to seem like an artist.'

And he went to Queensport that same day to visit a barber. True, when I saw him the next morning his hair did not seem to be any shorter, except at the neck behind, but he seemed to think that it was shorter, for he asked me if he would not pass for a convict, or a soldier.

'Has it been cut?'

'Yes, I told the man to cut it short,' in a tone of mild surprise.

I gave up this problem. For I saw that hair, for some reason, meant so much to the boy that he could deceive himself about its length, and that even barbers understood his secret desires.

We were sailing in his cranky little boat, a pursuit which caused me acute misery. For wet, especially in the seat, always gave me rheumatism; the motion of a boat, even on a calm day, made me ill; the necessity of continually getting up and moving across to the other side of the boat, and ducking my head under the boom, at the risk of my hat, broke up every conversation and exasperated me extremely; and, finally, I could conceive nothing more stupid than to proceed by zigzags, from nowhere to nowhere, for the sake of wasting a fine afternoon. Neither, if I might mention such a point, though it is probably unimportant, have I ever been able to understand why there was no accommodaton provided on small yachts, for things like sticks and umbrellas; whereas land conveyances, such as gigs and even governess carts, always have a basket designed for their proper storage and protection.

Yet when John asked me to sail with him, a common accident, for it was his only idea of entertainment for guests of all ages and both sexes, I never refused. For I felt it a privilege. And I would have sacrificed more hats, umbrellas, and suffered even worse attacks of lumbago to keep the regard of so honest and candid a soul.

It was during these happy weeks of John's holidays that I resolved to make him my heir. I could not think of anyone more likely to do the family honour, and to maintain its tradition.

113

And in this perception of John's unique quality, in my deep attachment to the boy, I began to understand for the first time the anxiety of parents in wartime. I recognized in Amy's face, sometimes when she looked at John, the expression of a feeling which never ceased its steady pressure upon my own soul. A slow, perpetual fear, mixed with a kind of desperation.

It was useless for me to say, 'The war will be over long before John is old enough to fight,' nothing removed that pain.

And just as I understood Amy, I began to understand also the real motives of some of our neighbours who opposed the war, and demanded a peace of accommodation.

True, I did not agree with them. I was already a keen supporter of that great idea for a League of Nations, which has since done so much to give Europe security and confidence. I can even claim to be one of its earliest advocates. I was the first to form a League committee in our district, and to address public meetings on the subject.

It was at such meetings that I first discovered how unreasonable and bitter people can be, when they are frightened. They would not listen even to my proof, that their very fear, for sons, husbands, lovers, was the justfication of my argument. That war must be put down by force.

Perhaps in those early days I placed too much emphasis on the force needed. As it turned out, little has been required. But I was astonished at the violent opposition which I encountered.

When I asked some women if they realized that they were throwing away the lives of young men yet unborn, perhaps their own grandchildren, etc., by their pig-headed unreason, and senseless Anti-nomianism, I was actually assaulted, etc.

But I am afraid that many of my meetings ended in disorder. For I was in a highly nervous and excitable frame of mind.

So also I was led into a foolish quarrel with the curate in charge at our own parish church.

This man denounced the whole idea of a League, with sanctions, as an imperialist plot to exploit victory and humiliate Germany and Austria.

I therefore approached the fellow, a lanky tallow face from Cambridge, asked him to tea, and brought up the subject of evil. I suggested that the modern church did not lay enough emphasis on the positive nature of evil, etc. He answered that in his view the Church ought to go in for socialism.

I saw, of course, that he was trying to evade my point, and I put it to him plainly, 'Do you believe in the devil or don't you?'

To which, twisting up his mouth into a conceited knot, he answered that, even in the Fathers, the reality of the devil was not so strongly developed as laymen supposed. He was regarded rather as a negation of God, or a general name for the characteristics of man's fallen nature, and so on, a heap of heresies.

'Excuse me,' I said, 'but I heard you argue, from the pulpit, that the best proof of a personal god is the existence of the good will in man, of love, charity,' etc., and so on. 'The usual thing, and quite right, too, nothing could be better.' For I wished to do him justice and to show that I was not prejudiced against him. 'But if so, surely the evil will in man, his lust, spite and cruelty, his love of supporting a bad case by mere argument, out of pure conceit' (for I thought I might touch his conscience here) 'are proofs of the devil's real existence – and a pretty devilish existence, too, at the present moment of the world's history.'

But it proved useless to argue with the fellow. He answered, according to rule, that good will was a principle of unity, superior to individuals and pointing, therefore, to a Power superior to all individuals; whereas, spite and hatred, etc., were self-regarding vices in the individual, factors of disunity requiring no higher power beyond – all the usual sophistries – and I remembered too late that it was always useless to argue with dishonesty which would not acknowledge the plainest facts. So I said, 'This matter is too serious for logic-chopping – the point is simple, do you believe in your own professed creed or not? Do you believe in the devil and the need for fighting him and for supporting any measures, military or otherwise, to defeat his purposes?'

'The devil,' he answered in his abominable accent, 'is said to be a gentleman, and therefore probably supports the government, so that I certainly disapprove of him.'

This horrible levity upset my temper, and I said that the matter was scarcely one for raillery, and that if he were not my guest, and entitled to special consideration, I should be obliged to tell him what I thought of his hypocrisy, manners, appearance, etc.

He withdrew then at speed. For I admit that I had now lost my temper and uttered some abuse of which I was afterwards ashamed. But it was untrue, as reported in the village, probably by the wretched creature himself, that I had threatened to mutilate him. Though it has occurred to me since, that emasculation would have been the appropriate fate for one who had performed a similar operation on the doctrines of the Church.

I had silenced the Judas, but he was not to be defeated for, as I might have reflected if I had not been led away by the dispute, he was already sold to the devil's service, who had armoured him already with the impenetrable brass of intellectual conceit. He actually preached against me. I could no longer read the lessons in church, and finally was obliged to cease from attendance. For I could not take communion from the hand of a blackguard who had betrayed the creeds, and denied the devil, at such a time of crisis.

This separation from my beloved church was a great grief to me, and I blamed myself for my impatience with a wretched nincompoop who was perhaps, from education, incapable of that moral courage necessary to acknowledge the evil nature of man; as well as the good.

My excuse is that my friends were being killed and, above all, I felt that secret fear which is a much more powerful motive than the strongest principles.

John was barely seventeen. Amy and I congratulated ourselves privately that the war would be over before he was called up. But in the spring, by giving a false age, he succeeded in joining the air force. His explanation was that all his friends were fighting, or dead.

114

The fear in which those live whose sons and lovers are fighting is like deep water; it is calm as well as deep. I don't think Amy and I ever expressed to each other the least anxiety about John. It was Bill, to whom John was now a hero, who said, 'It will be a damn shame if Johnny gets killed. The country can't spare boys like Johnny.' And Amy would answer mildly, without even a change of colour, 'We really could be getting the lettuces planted – it's so mild.'

We did not talk or think of Johnny getting killed; we only lived with the fear, the feeling of it; almost the certainty of it. My mother remarked once on my habit of leaving at a moment's notice an excellent dinner and splendid fire at Tolbrook, in order to travel four miles through muddy lanes to a cold supper and freezing draughts at the cottage. 'That's three times this week, and poor Amy never has warning.' I wondered at myself. But I perceived at once the attraction; I wanted to share with Amy a feeling which she alone in the world possessed in the same force.

It was probably raining. I could not ride a bicycle and was obliged to use the trap, without a cover, and the yard pony, a sluggish beast shaped like a beer barrel, with a trot like a carpet beater. I remember still those nights, as one remembers scenes from a time of crisis; the streaming rain, blowing in my face, the clouds smoking through a sky like the last day; the hooves rattling and splashing on roads which were unseen in the black shade between their high banks. Until some green and ghastly ray, darting down between two clouds, suddenly flashed upon them, and showed them like rivers of Tophet, liquid sulphur winding through hellish rocks of darkness. And when at last I would come in sight of the Longwater, it, too, would have a diabolic aspect; unexpectedly bright, as if from an infernal and pallid fire; seeming composed not of water, but some heavier liquid, perhaps molten beer bottles. An image that should please my temperance friends. And these heavy waves, flowing all in one direction with a deliberate movement, formed, I thought, a kind of reproof, as of satanic order, to the turmoil in the sky, and the agitation of the bare trees, dashing and rattling their branches overhead and flinging down their subsidiary showers like a crowd of hysterical ghosts from some churchyard of the drowned.

Under such a storm the cottage appeared ridiculously small and flimsy. I would always feel surprised at first sight of it, and say, 'That can't be it. That's the boat shed.' And it was like that pleasure with which we look into a toy house and find it occupied by a complete family, and its furniture, that, when I had put the pony in the coalshed, and thrown Bill's old rug over it, I would knock at the door and see, as it sprang open, Amy's little maid, and Amy herself, at full size, among tables, chairs and lamps, etc., and to hear from within, Bill's call of welcome.

Such arrivals, for some reason, always animate a company, and for some minutes we would all hold out our hands to the parlour fire, laughing at nothing and congratulating each other on an encounter which happened four times a week. Then Bill would say, 'All right, old girl. I see you telegraphing – Tom doesn't want anything extra, except beer, do you Tom?'

This was because Amy was attempting, by various grimaces over his shoulder, at the maid, just inside the door, to express complicated messages about the cold meat and the remains of an apple tart.

Nothing, of course, could prevent Amy from going to the kitchen to provide a meal of which half could not be eaten, and her obstinacy would cast a first shadow upon our hospitable feelings, on both sides.

Bill would say, 'Can't do anything with Amy. Might as well try to push an elephant off a bun,' and we would sit silent, for we were always a little shy when left alone together.

Then at supper, with Amy's return, we would revive and gravely discuss the weather, the war, the rations, and John's last letter.

Although the eldest son, William, was now a staff captain in the regular army, and had greatly distinguished himself, I can't remember that we often discussed his letters, which were, I imagine, few and dry. He was, I think, a young man whose manners, by their cold polish, which belonged rather to the Rifle Brigade than the R.E., had always given his parents some uneasiness. And I have heard that in the regular army during the generation between 1902 and 1914, possibly by reaction from the scrambling ways of the Boer War, the manners of subalterns did assume a reserve, an aloofness, which was not qualified, like the arrogance of the old guard, by any ideal enthusiasm for Bible reading or imperial responsibility.

Bill or Amy would always inform me what William thought of the war, what the general had said to him, and what he had suggested to the general, with the manner of those who conceal their pride in a possession which is also a national property. But in John they delighted frankly, like those who show their own back garden with wonder that so modest a plot can produce real flowers and edible fruit.

We chattered and we laughed. Amy, whose laugh was a private convulsion, as if a silent earthquake was heaving at the rocky bondage of her stays, would make her chair creak so loudly that Bill would cry, 'Easy, old girl – take the sofa if you want to laugh. It's stronger.'

And even while Amy laughed I could feel her fear. It had grown to be part of her. It had changed the shape of her lips when she laughed, and the expression of her eyes.

It was preparing us both for the news of the disaster to the fifth army in 1918; John was reported severely wounded and a prisoner. On the evening when Amy told us this news I felt not despair but a kind of relief. I said to Amy, 'He's got a chance,' and in Amy's voice, replying that the German doctors were said to be quite good, I heard exactly the same note, like an echo. 'After all,' we thought, 'he may escape.' The darkness of our fear made that hope seem almost like a rising sun.

115

I had been reading *The Student in Arms*, the story of a young subaltern soldier who, like John, had felt it his duty to offer his life for the free spirit. I found such comfort in the book that I took it to the cottage.

I soon wished that I had been more prudent. It was a custom at the cottage for Amy to read aloud in the evenings, and now she read us *The Student*, which I knew from cover to cover.

Amy was a bad reader. And Bill had developed an extraordinary absent-mindedness, which made a severe trial of our patience. Bill at that time was a very sick man who could barely walk across the room without support. Yet he would continually get up in the middle of one of Amy's sentences to look out of the window to see if the sky were clearing, or to make sure that some sapling was still firmly tied to its stake.

And I now began to notice that the garden had become an obsession with Bill. I suspected that most of the time when he seemed to be in deep meditation he was reflecting only upon shrubs, bulbs, or a new layout for his roses.

Amy would read: 'Here are two contemptible fellows, a philosopher without courage and a Christian without faith.' And Bill would take his pipe out of his mouth and say, 'It's stopped.'

'What's stopped?'

'The rain — no, it hasn't,' and then, 'Johnny might have said that — it's true, too.'

'Do you think so?' I would ask. 'Is John a convinced supporter of the Church?'

'But he's very philosophic — takes the rough with the smooth. Poor chap, he's had to.'

'Good heavens, Bill, but that's not what the book means. It means that a philosopher must be honest even if his conclusions expose him to ridicule or lead him into pessimism.'

'Yes, the rough with the smooth. What a gust. Thank God the leaves aren't out.'

'But Bill, it refers to a duty, not a way of life,' etc.

'Isn't duty a way of life — probably the best way?'

'Yes, yes, but let's stick to the point,' etc., and it would end by my telling Bill that he didn't know the meaning of words, and so on. Amy would then complete my exasperation by saying, 'I think Tom's right. John was not really so philosophic. Too particular about his food. But he was always quite fearless.' And she would take off her spectacles and look at them thoughtfully. Amy had lately been obliged to use spectacles for reading.

411

But she did not like them, and complained that she could not see through them. To which Bill would reply, 'Then try without them.'

Amy would then put on her spectacles again, screw up her eyes, make some extraordinary grimaces, and begin to read like a child, one syllable at a time, until she forgot herself in the interest of the work. 'Death is a great teacher – from him men learn what are the things they value.'

'Something in that,' Bill would say. 'Yes, it must be a bit of a surprise to get to the other side. I daresay it will be considerably different from what we imagine.'

'But what he means, Bill, is that in the face of death a man gets a new scale of values.'

'I don't see that. Besides, it isn't true. When you're up against it you get the same kind of values, only more so. My God, I remember when I stopped that potleg in Ashantee, how I longed for a pipe. I thought I was a goner that time. But all that's old stuff now. Know anything about root-pruning, Tommy?'

'No, but I daresay they do it at Tolbrook.'

'We dug up John's plum tree and cut off its roots,' Amy said, 'but it's dead.'

'My idea,' Bill said, 'my funeral entirely.' He seemed to make this admission not as a duty but because he wanted to dwell on the misfortune. 'But it was all in the book.'

Hoping to divert him from the reading to the garden, I tried to continue the subject, 'Which book was that?'

'Let's finish the chapter, old man. Carry on, old girl.'

'In the time of danger all true men are believers – they choose the spiritual and reject the material.'

'I think myself it was a bad tree.'

I burst out laughing, then, and Bill, taking his pipe out of his mouth, asked me in surprise, 'What are you laughing at?'

'You.'

And I was alarmed at the same moment that he might be hurt. But he answered only, 'Is that all,' put back his pipe, and said 'Carry on, old girl, you stopped at the word material.'

116

And remembering those nights, so wearing to patience, so sweet to memory, I took down the *Student* from my private shelf. 'It was a great book at that time,' I thought, 'for it expressed the best feeling of the time – the sense of duty, of sacrifice; the desire for a better world,' and when I opened it that hope, that desire rose again from its pages with all the sadness and the power of the young man who knew he was to die. It moved me again, and I thought, 'If only I could get Ann to read it, would it not enlighten her spirit?'

For I was worried about Ann. She looked ill and anxious, and yet she would never rest. She would sit down to read, jump up to telephone to some dealer, run out of the room to see that Jan was asleep, and then begin checking the day's accounts, all in the same five minutes. She was always tired, always busy, and yet I never saw a smile. A new line was growing between her brows, and when I said to her, 'Don't frown, you're making yourself ugly,' she did not even hear me. 'And you ought to rest more – you give yourself no peace.'

'Peace,' she said, as if the word had become old-fashioned, and even sentimental. 'When there's time, uncle,' and she would run off again.

I laid the book open on her work-basket as if I had put it down in a fit of absentmindedness. But she threw it on the floor to reach my socks.

'My book,' I said.

'Did you want me to read it?' She picked it up. 'Who is Hankey?'

'He was a young officer killed in the last war. Some people think he was one of the greatest losses we had. His books gave new faith and happiness to thousands.'

'In the last war?' She was still at her war chapters. 'I must read that.'

Ann kept the book for a week. Each evening she sat still in front of the fire, reading with such concentrated attention that I had great hopes of her salvation. But one morning after prayers she gave it to me and said, 'Your book, uncle. I'm afraid I've kept it rather a long time. But I've so little time now for reading.'

'What did you think of it?'

'It does give a new angle on the period.'

'I didn't recommend it to you as a historical document, but to do you good, if possible. To make you understand something that you don't seem to understand, that the only door to happiness is faith.'

'I suppose that's why it does seem a little dated – the bits about faith.'

'Don't you want to believe in anything, you foolish girl?'

'Well, uncle, I'm rather busy just now.'

'Hankey says that if you're doing what is worth doing you ought to enjoy it.'

'Well, I don't. I hate this farming job. It's never done, and it's getting worse.'

'Because you fuss. You try to do everyone's work. Where are you off to now?'

It was time for our walk, but she was dressed in an old pair of dungarees.

'To look at the byres. I can't leave them to Farley.'

She went into the byres and afterwards to the fields. I saw her riding away on the yard pony. We had no walk, and she forgot even that I had missed my walk. She sat at luncheon still in her blue dungarees, and after a long troubled reflection she said, 'I don't trust Farley one inch. I knew he was always against what Robert was doing, and now he's trying to undo it all.'

'Perhaps Robert went a little too far.'

'Robert did a good job here. I'm not going to have it spoilt by an old fool like Farley, who doesn't even know that he's a mass of stupid jealousy.'

'You're very hard on people, Ann, as well as yourself.'

'Am I?' She was naïvely surprised. 'No, I don't think so. I don't think I'm hard.'

She continued to reflect upon my remark, for half a dozen times in the midst of those anxieties which troubled her all day she would say, 'No, I don't think I'm hard. I know I spoil Jan.' And again I saw the look of anxiety and doubt as of one struggling with abstruse and complex problems. 'I may be a fusspot, but that's not the trouble. I just don't know things thoroughly.'

117

In 1919, immediately after the armistice, the child Ann returned to Tolbrook, where she was alone with her nurse and my mother. But my mother's memory was failing. She did not recognize people, and often called them by the names of the dead. Edward was in Constantinople with the staff; his wife was in France with an American canteen.

The house was very quiet, for Ann was a silent and reserved little girl. A woman came every day to give her lessons, which she learned very easily, and yet with anxiety. For she would always make me hear her.

She would appear before me silently, in the evening, and wait till I spoke to her. Then she would say, 'Please, uncle,' and hand me a lesson book. And I would ask, 'What are the chief rivers of England?' or 'What are the chief events of the reign of Alfred the Great?'

At once the child seemed to grow even paler, wrinkles appeared between her eyebrows, she fixed her grey eyes on the sky through the top of the window, and began, carefully, to repeat her lesson. She was always right, yet she hesitated often. Seeing the child's anxiety and self-doubt, I sometimes ventured to prompt her. But I found this was a bad policy. For she would flush and cry, 'Oh, no, uncle, you mustn't tell me.'

'But, dearest child, I wanted to help you.'

'But you mustn't, you mustn't,' stamping her foot. 'How can I know if I really know it? Now I shall have to start again.'

Once or twice, at a prompting, she broke into tears. And I gave up the practice.

Yet I believe we were great friends. It is hard to tell if children truly care for one, unless one is clever at pleasing them. I am not clever with children; I can't tell stories, and I am shy of intrusion. Yet Ann would greet me always with warm affection, and though she was independent and liked to go walking by herself, she would often accept an invitation to come with me. Then she would take my hand and seemed to feel a kindness.

Our walks were largely silent. She was not communicative. And on those evenings when I sat reading to my mother I had often to remind her that the child was in the room.

She would sit on the floor cutting out war pictures for a scrapbook; or drawing, with so little sound that it was easy to forget her presence.

Yet if I or my mother happened to say, 'Where is this or that, my mother's spectacles, my book, the newspaper, the blotter?' the child would at once rise up, find the object, and silently bring it to us.

'Dear me!' my mother would say. 'Dorothy is like a little imp the way she pops up.'

And just as Ann knew where everything in the house was to be found at any moment, she had always the latest news of her father and mother. She remembered their letters to the last word, and with the aid of the governess, followed their movements on a map.

She would say, 'Daddy is at Cairo now. It's fearfully hot there.' And ask, 'How do you get fever? Is it a microbe?'

'I don't know, my dear. But there won't be any in Cairo. It is very civilized in Cairo.'

'They have lepers there – and plague. The French soldiers had plague in 1796. What is plague like?'

'Your father is quite safe from plagues.'

'Yes, of course,' she would say with her usual politeness.

'An old-fashioned little thing,' my mother once called her, in her own hearing. But a week passed before Ann asked me one day what it meant to call a person 'old-fashioned'.

'Quiet,' I said.

'Nurse says it means prim. What is "prim" exactly?'

'Nurse is talking nonsense. It is a very good thing to be old-fashioned. It means serious and thoughtful.'

'Well, I should like to play with somebody, but Francie only shouts.' For Francie was visiting at the cottage.

It was true that Francie was a noisy child. When Amy brought her to Tolbrook she would rush at Ann and shout, 'Come on, Ann, let's play at something.'

'Yes. What shall we play?'

'Oh, anything – come on.'

'Let's play tig.'

For answer Francie would hold up her skirts, put her head between her legs and stick out her tongue. Francie was an accomplished buffoon. But Ann did not laugh. She was always surprised by Francie's jokes, and she would say, 'Is that a game?'

Francie would then pull Ann's hair and rush away. Ann would run after her, catch her, and retaliate. The delicate, slender Ann was extremely strong and courageous. She would chase the biggest village boys if they dared to abuse her. Thus the stout Francie would soon be in tears. She would run for protection, and the embarrassed Amy had to console her.

When I reproached Ann on one occasion for making Francie's nose bleed, she answered with the same anxious look, 'What ought I to do?'

'She's your guest. You oughtn't to hit her.'

'But she was chasing the yard cats.'

The yard cats were Ann's special friends. Half savage like all farm cats, living a wild life among the barns and stock, they would come running to Ann as to an envoy with a flag of truce.

'You should tell her not to.'

'I did, but she didn't care.' And, after a pause, she remarked with a sigh, 'Francie is a difficult child. I would rather go to see her and she can entertain me.'

Amy, however, did not ask Ann to the cottage. For she had taken a strong dislike to her on Francie's account. Amy was capable of unreasoning feuds, and they were deep and strong. I daresay she hated Ann when Francie, once more defeated in battle, came weeping with the puzzled Ann hovering behind, not sure whether she had done right or wrong.

118

William, now acting Major, with a D.S.O. and M.C., was killed a few hours after the armistice in one of the last actions of the war. And there was no news of John. I was afraid to go to the cottage. I stayed away, on various excuses, for a fortnight. I can bear my own grief, but I can't bear that of other people and I dared not meet Bill and Amy. I knew that they would talk about their sons.

This was a time of great dejection. I had not cared for William, but I could not help feeling that his death, at the beginning of a distinguished career, was a fearful waste to the family.

Even the disappearance of the curate at Tolbrook, on promotion to a very good living, could not raise my spirits. I seemed to see all round me, what no one had expected after the great heart searchings of the war, general apathy and disintegration.

In church, where once more I was enabled to read the lessons, I found suddenly a small and apathetic congregation; smaller than I could remember. The young did not come any more. The young wives whose husbands had been at the front, the boys and girls whose fathers and brothers had been in some Navy ship, now stayed at home or amused themselves. Many of the old faithful, who, before the war, had never missed a Sunday, were dead, and no one came to fill their places. And suddenly a great many voices were heard accusing and demanding, or jeering. For the first time I met young men and girls, the generation of John, which had been too young to fight, and found in them that cynicism, which I did not know how to answer. For they said 'The war was a bad joke played on us by a lot of old fools' and when one answered 'The war is over and you have your lives before you' they said 'Life, oh, yes,' as if they were making another joke.

It was the cynicism of the young which shocked and frightened me. It was as though the spring leaves, deliberately, for some secret and devilish purpose, distilled poison in their own sap and withered on the twigs.

We heard by wire that John was coming home from a German hospital and Amy and I hurried to London to meet him. But in all my excited joy, I still felt a private terror that he too might have caught this disease of the will.

We scarcely recognized the young man, who, laughing, limped up to us on the platform, and embraced us both. We had last seen John a schoolboy, clever, affectionate; but still a boy. We walked now, rather shyly, beside a man of the world. Even his conversation had changed. He no longer seemed, like a boy, to carry about secrets, from which, at unexpected moments, some cryptic speech unwound like a strange plant out of a wall. He spoke in lively tones, easy and self forgetful.

'And how are you, John?' Amy exclaimed, as we made our way through the crowds.

'Oh, very well. And they say I won't even limp – I only need some massage.'

And two minutes later, Amy, not being able to think of anything else to say, asked 'And how are you really?'

'Never better, Mums.'

He looked round at the station, that place where one never sees a cheerful face, and said, 'I never thought I'd see this again. Very nice. Very nice, indeed. It's a gift.'

'And how are you really, Johnny. Really and truly?' Amy's voice and look expressed her wonder at this son become so suddenly a man. Her question seemed to say, 'Shall I understand the words of this delightful stranger?'

'Very hungry, Mums darling, and fearfully greedy. I want a really expensive lunch. And it's on me. I'm rich, you know. Or I shall be when the army pays up what it owes me.'

And when I spoke to him at lunch about the cynicism, the moral defeat of the new generation, he answered 'Our lot aren't worrying – life is too nice.'

'What do you think about this talk of a social revolution.'

'I don't know anything about anything. But I've a sort of feeling of earthquakes about. I think we ought to have oysters, don't you? Don't be alarmed, Mums, I know you don't like oysters, but my plan is that you shall ask me to eat your share for you, and after a time, out of pure filial feeling, I shall give way.'

And at the cottage, so far from being bored, cynical, he amused himself all day with the gramophone, his books and country walks.

And I said to my friends in town, my partners in the London office, 'All this talk of the revolt of the young is largely a newspaper sensation, got up to hide the flatness of the news. The best of the young, the ones with some intelligence and force of character, are extremely sensible people and most delightful to know. For instance, I have a nephew,' etc., etc. And I daresay I bored them all with my talk about John.

119

The only shadow upon this very happy time was a sudden worsening of Bill's illness. In a few weeks he became a skeleton. His face was clay colour. He was so weak he had to be wheeled about in a chair. He could not even smoke; his pipe made him vomit.

And now, when I delivered an ultimatum that a specialist must be obtained, he told me that he had seen a specialist years before. 'They had an op. you know, that time my horse rolled on me, and found it wasn't ribs at all. Hopeless. Sewed me up again. Gave me six months, and that was five years ago. Good work, old boy. Five years.'

'And does Amy know?'

'She found out pretty soon. She's smart, Amy. You can't keep her in the dark very long.'

What astonished me was that Bill had known of his condition when he took the cottage. I asked myself, 'How could a sensible man be so imprudent; or is he, like Edward, simply depending upon me.' My anger revived. And that I could not reproach a dying man increased my resentment.

But so it was, that in a few days, I seemed to become accustomed to Bill's dying. I daresay the reason was partly that neither Bill nor Amy seemed to pay any attention to it. And so I found myself arguing, and joking as before. And I pointed out to Bill how irresponsible he had been, in lending his money; and in case he might be thinking of me when he spoke of providence, I mentioned that war taxes had practically ruined me.

But Bill anwered only that these were funny times and the devil only knew what was going to happen to anyone or anything. 'Mama says she will pay for Loftus' schooling, and Lucy thinks she can get John a job through one of her Benjamite friends.'

'What sort of job — Lucy is probably thinking of a grocery shop. And I could take John into the firm.'

'A good idea,' Bill said, in his absentminded manner. He was sitting in his chair outside the house on a March afternoon, cold and grey. His excuse for being out was a few small breaks in the clouds through which the sun sent down narrow pencils of light. Half a dozen of them were always travelling slowly across the fields like the rays of some explorer's apparatus. The groups of bare trees, fields or cottages, suddenly illuminated by this magic lantern, had the air of creatures suddenly awaked from hibernation. They seemed to say, 'Let us alone, we may have been cold; but we were at peace.'

'The prettiest spot in the country,' Bill said, suddenly, pushing out his putty-coloured face from his rugs, and turning his yellow eyes about. I was startled by the contrast between his easy acceptance of my offer and his enthusiasm for the place. I said, 'And I won't charge any premium.'

'Thanks, old man. Just wheel me down the path, will you? I want to show you something.'

I wheeled him down the path. I thought: 'Is he really so selfish or can't he think of anything but his gardening and his views.'

'Our premium as you know is usually pretty high,' I said.

'Yes, old man, it's good of you. But John would make his way anyhow — there you are.' Showing a gap through the trees which revealed almost a mile of cold, troubled water, olive coloured, laced with yellow foam; and various low hills, squared out between black hedges into fields of dark purple or dark blue-green. The few willows opposite were tossing their long branches in the wind as if trying to warm themselves. 'Pretty good,' said Bill, 'but just wait till the sun comes out.'

'And what's going to happen to Amy if you go. But I don't see why you shouldn't have another five years.'

'The M.O. says three weeks. Excuse me, old chap, but your foot is rather near that sapling. Don't do to knock the bark off. That's a weeping willow. In ten years this will be the prettiest spot in the garden, or Queensport for that matter.'

And I found myself promising Bill that I should secure the cottage for Amy. 'If necessary I'll advance her enough to buy the freehold.'

My own words surprised me. And I still do not know what had suddenly made me feel small and mean beside the improvident Bill with his absurd passion for a small garden. My wonder at the improvidence remained, but it was thrust aside by the sense that to Bill dying, a few trees, flowers, etc., planted and established by himself; a view opened, might have a special value and importance.

Bill himself showed no change of mood. He said in the same detached tone: 'It would be a good spec.' And then, as if asking for my approval: 'The idea is, you come down here on a hot day and have tea under the new willow and you'll have the view in front of you all the time. My idea is that you need two or three different tea places in a garden.'

'A very good idea. A splendid idea.'

'And look at the view – right across the estuary. Bold Head and even a bit of the sea outside. Just right incline three paces. There you are, with the sun on it. A spot of real true blue, or is it green today. Here, move me over, will you. Ha, I knew you could see the coastguard station. Amy said you couldn't. I call you to witness, Tommy.' And then he remarked with strong and deep satisfaction: 'I always said this place had never had a chance. I think we've done it pretty well, on the whole.'

'Very well, Bill. I hope it will be a home for Amy and the boys for the rest of her life.'

'It might and it mightn't.' Bill reflected a moment and sucked his lips as if smoking. 'Of course, old boy, I should like that a lot but I haven't counted on it. And if you try anything, go carefully, very carefully. Fact is Amy doesn't generally want to do what I want to do. She's been the finest wife a chap could hope for, as you know, I couldn't have done without her. But there it is. We all have our little ways, and that's hers. She reacts. So I haven't set my heart on anything like a permanency here. In fact, I don't expect it.' He spoke as if he might have expected to live, in spirit, at the cottage for eternity. 'But I think you'll agree it's not a bad job. It was worth doing.'

'It's one of the most beautiful gardens I ever saw.'

'Oh, well, I'm not a gardener. Not a real expert. I just had an idea about the place.'

120

Bill died suddenly three weeks later. But Amy would not accept the money, even on the most business-like terms. She said in effect: 'If I borrowed all this money from you I'd never know how I was going to pay it back.'

I accused her of being too particular, and we had a little argument. For Amy was an obstinate woman. 'A sister,' I said, 'should not object to being under a small obligation to a brother.'

'A debt is not an obligation,' Amy said. 'It's money.'

'Legally, my dear Amy, it is an obligation.'

'That makes it all the worse.'

'You haven't answered my argument.'

'But we're not arguing, Tommy. You can't deny that it's about money. And there's no arguing about money. Money's money.'

I tried another line of approach. 'All the same, Amy, Bill would be very upset if you sold. He loved this place.'

Amy turned scarlet. I saw that she was getting upset. She said: 'Do you think they mind what we do?'

Amy's picture of Bill leaning out from some material heaven to watch her doings startled me, and I answered: 'I meant only that he wanted you to carry it on.'

'He would never want me to do what was wrong,' Amy said.

'But he himself suggested an advance.'

'Bill was always rather careless about money. He said I ought to trust God more, but I said that wasn't the same thing as getting into debt. Not when you've got children. No, Tommy, I'm sorry.' Amy was growing calmer as she perceived her own conviction. 'I know I should never be comfortable about it. Even if Bill doesn't understand.'

So the lease was sold, and I saw the strange spectacle of Amy, whenever she came to Tolbrook, going down to Queensport, to look over the hedge at Bill's apple trees, to see how they were growing. She was very pleased with the new owners for their care of the place.

121

I took John into the firm as I had promised. And he did extremely well. He had a scholar's memory for detail, and a scholar's conscience for exactness. He was apt to be unpunctual, but even in that fault he improved after I gave him, for his Easter present, a good alarum clock.

Loftus had entered Woolwich that year. He had always meant to be a soldier. Amy therefore came to make the family home with John. She took a small flat for him in Bloomsbury; and he appeared well content with her very limited ideas of entertainment. Amy, of course, was extremely happy. Her expression while she presided at John's table was ridiculously like that of a middle aged bride.

I had planned that John should live with me. But I saw more of him than Amy, both at the office and on our daily walks. Almost every fine day we walked together in the park after office hours; and I believed that John enjoyed our conversaton as much, or almost as much, as I did.

Of course when I say that, I allow for that grace of temperament in the boy, who was never, to my knowledge, rude to anyone in his life. It is possible, therefore, that I bored him with some of my middle-aged chatter, about old times, and the political situation, or even about theology. But it was John who urged me to publish my book on the need for a new statement of the Christian belief, with special regard to the positive power of evil; and the real existence of the devil. And our discussions on the subject gave me the happiest evenings of my life. I write advisedly. I enjoyed with Lucy a keener delight; but never that serene mood of happiness with which I strolled beside the beloved boy in the evening of a London day and spoke with him on the common ground of great subjects.

We would wander sometimes far from our course on the rough grass. The noise of the city, ceasing to be an interruption, became a friendly ground bass to the chirp of the sparrows, the obbligato of London sheep. It seemed to say: 'You are at home in a world which is all domesticated, where even nature serves only for the walks of friends and lovers.' The London evening sky filled with sober radiance was like a Dutch picture, by that most home-loving of people, whose very sketches seem to distil the peace of family hearths into dumpling bushes and meditating cows.

The very blackness of the trees on which the spring buds glittered like emeralds was familiar, like the thick domestic smoke upon an old fireback. I had pitied the London trees, like wild birds in a cage, but now love was mixed with pity, and I would say to John: 'Shall we go on the grass' in order to pass beneath the trees. And he always agreed.

'We've plenty of time,' he would say.

'Yes, you're young – you have all your life before you,' etc. And I would say something about his gifts and the great openings afforded by the modern world. For I always liked to nurse John's ambition. And I remember he answered once in a phrase that might have been Edward's, 'Yes, I suppose you always get a good many openings after a bombardment, very large ones, but rather muddy at the bottom.'

'My dear boy, the career is always open to talent, and work.'

'Oh, of course, I was only joking.'

It would begin to grow dark. The lights of Piccadilly became visible through the trees and in the old bow windows of Park Lane, filling for the season, blinds were drawn. John would take my arm, perhaps to guide me, for I was apt to walk into trees or railings in the twilight. But the gesture, even if its motive was partly utilitarian, to save trouble, was also that of a true affection. John was interested in my preservation from accident. It gave me such pleasure as I could not express. 'My dear John,' I would say, 'I mustn't keep you. I am sure you have a party somewhere, with charming young ladies only too anxious for your attendance.'

'No hurry, uncle. Mind that tree. Yes, I think you're right about openings. There will be plenty of chances when the smoke clears away a bit. Of course, just now everything is a bit unsettled. And the big noises seem to be chiefly big noises.'

For John, as much as I did, disliked the superficiality and pretension infecting not only politics and literature, art and manners, but even the Church, in those disturbed times.

122

My remark about the charming young ladies pursuing John was not without a purpose. For once or twice a young woman had called for him at the office, a creature whom, at a first meeting, I took for a young prostitute from the cheaper streets. Her figure was slim and flat; her face disproportionately large and round. In repose, with its small features, large blue eyes and brassy hair, it reminded one of those dummies put in hairdressers' windows. But it was seldom in repose. Gladys was always jerking her head, twitching her little mouth, rolling her eyes and humping her shoulders. In conversation she would wriggle her behind as if it itched; and frequently she plunged her hand into her breast or down her back in order to scratch herself. Her voice was the chatter of a colobus monkey; her laugh the shriek of a cockatoo. She was daubed like one of Edward's pictures; and her nails were always dirty.

I did not care for Gladys, but when I suggested to John that she was scarcely the kind of girl to be brought into an office of our standing, he answered with amusement and surprise, 'But Gladys is not that sort, uncle – her people think no end of themselves, I can tell you, and she went to school at —' – a famous school of which I cancel the name, in justice. 'What don't you like about her? Of course she's got up a bit and she runs on a bit – but that's only the fashion. She's really rather a good soul, and she has a lot of guts, too.'

'I see them only too plainly,' I said. 'But I suppose stays are out of date, like my prejudices.'

John smiled and answered that Gladys did not need stays; her figure was so good. 'She's always in first-class condition, as I daresay you've noticed. She does her exercises three times a day.'

I met him everywhere with Gladys, even at Julie's. I had not wished John to know Julie. He met her only by accident one day when I had taken her to the theatre. And I did not introduce them. But he asked me about her, and insisted on calling. And then it appeared that he knew very well in what relation she stood to me; that all the family were aware of it. He charmed Julie and he was charmed by her.

'You can see,' he said, 'that she was magnificent in her great days,' and I could not tell him that Julie had had no great days, and that she seemed to me much deteriorated from her little days.

Julie, during the war, had worked with enthusiasm at a soldiers' club, serving in the canteen, and also giving little recitations, etc. And she was still frequented by the many friends, among all ranks, whom she had made. She kept open house, and she was drinking too much. And when she found herself misunderstood, or even robbed, she would say, 'Anything I can do for these boys is not too much. How could it be?'

And in these words so calmly spoken one felt something mysterious and false. Falseness now seemed to be taking possession of Julie. It peeped from the most unexpected corners, as bats and rats suddenly show their whiskers in the crannies of palaces too long unused.

The rich material was there, the dignity, the sincerity, but all began to seem meaningless and therefore tawdry; as palace velvets, when the palace becomes a show for trippers, begin at once to look like plush. The slender tragic actress had changed into a theatrical poser, who was apt to give a little performance, at certain cues, such as the words friendship, courage, loyalty. And like all such performers on the carpet, without her limelights, she seemed amateurish. What John took for the grand manner of a former age was simply the flummery of any age.

And she made such a fuss about John, that I was ashamed for her.

Now, to my astonishment, I saw her offering the same attentions to Gladys, who, for her part, lay on Julie's sofa most of the evening, her feet in the air, her skirt to her thighs, smoking thirty cigarettes, drinking half a dozen whiskies, and telling us about her boys, how often they had tried to rape her, how nearly they had succeeded, how she had got rid of some of the others, who were too dull, or ugly, or poor, or who didn't know enough to attempt a rape.

All this time John sat by, looking from Gladys to us with the expression of one who says, 'Admire this wonder –'

I did not know whether to be more amazed that John should bring a girl whom he at least thought respectable, to visit a kept woman, or outraged by her manner to Julie.

I could barely keep my temper until the pair had left, before I asked Julie how she could endure such conduct. 'What are you thinking of – allowing John to bring that nasty little beast here and encouraging her to behave like that.'

'She is indeed a horrible little creature,' Julie answered. 'But, she is a friend of John's, and I owe it to him to make his friends welcome.'

'Nonsense; we owe it to him to open his eyes about Gladys.'

'I hope you won't be so foolish as to interfere between John and one of his girls,' Julie said. 'They'll only laugh at you – or perhaps stop coming here. And I don't want to lose John's friendship.'

'Laugh at me,' I said, 'let them.' But I was angry with Julie, and I exclaimed, 'Really, Julie, you are getting flabby. What is the good of us if we don't stand by what we believe? Do you think it is a good thing for girls to paint their faces like the lowest strumpets and go about in short skirts or even short trousers and drink and swear like bargees?' etc., etc. 'We may be old fogeys,' I said, 'but we have some standards and I am not going to desert them simply because they happen to excite amusement among a few ill-taught children.'

And I spoke to John, who, as I had expected, took it very well and apologized for the girl. 'She was a little tight, of course – but she had no idea of being rude to Aunt Julie – she admires her tremendously,' and so on.

The idea that this sensible boy might be so stupid as to marry Gladys had never entered my head until Amy came to me one afternoon at the office. 'Have you seen this girl that John is in love with?'

'In love? He didn't tell you that he was in love.'

'No, but he is,' Amy said. She looked so solid, so stupefied that I perceived her desperation.

'Rubbish. Have you seen the creature?'

'Yes, I met them at luncheon. John invited her to the flat. He's bringing her to Tolbrook on Monday, to see Edward.'

'All that means nothing, Amy. You don't understand these young people nowadays – they form all kinds of friendships, without the least intention of marriage.'

'I don't think she likes me, either,' meaning apparently that the luncheon party had not been a success.

'You needn't be worried,' I said. 'John has had plenty of girls. But I'll give him a hint, if you like?'

Amy was persuaded at last to go home. But she had made me nervous. I began to reflect on the imbecility of young men with girls. And by the next day, I was in a panic. I went down early to Tolbrook to obtain Edward's help in this dangerous crisis. 'Of course,' I said, 'there's no question of an entanglement, but the girl is a bad friend for the boy. She encourages him to be casual. And you might let John see what you think of her. You have a lot of influence in that quarter.'

123

Edward had remained in uniform for a long time after the war. He had some post in the local demobilization office. Perhaps he had liked to feel that he belonged, even in so small a way, to administration. But now for some months he had been retired; and he had already fitted up his study behind the stairs, where I now write. He had decided to give himself to literary work, an autobiography, a political history of the last thirty years. All of us, especially my mother, encouraged him in his ambition, saying that it was exactly suited to his capacity. But Lottie had refused to come back to him, and what was unexpected, he seemed astonished by this blow. He would not even speak of it and when my mother, with that humour which still flashed amid the ruin of her mind, like a jewel among debris, would say, 'Our princess is still looking for her red carpet, I suppose,' he was visibly wounded.

My mother had looked forward with delight to Edward's return. The little old woman, now so bent with rheumatism, and so diminutive that, even among us who were not tall, she seemed like a dwarf, once more showed a kind of coquettish gaiety. She seemed to flirt with Edward, and uttered those little ecstatic cries which we had not heard for many years. But this excited happiness made me nervous and alarmed Edward. I was used to think of my mother as a saint, troublesome in her unworldliness, but always to be respected. I did not like to see her behaving without dignity. And Edward was wounded by her jokes.

She herself soon realized that he was uneasy in her company. She said to me one evening, when I read for her those last prayers without which she would not face the night, 'Edward has grown very touchy these days. Have I said anything to hurt his lordship's feelings?'

'Perhaps, Mama, he wouldn't like to hear you say that.'

She answered with wonder, 'But does he really mind what I say?'

'Yes, I think he does. You see, he feels that he has disappointed us all.'

'But I'm not disappointed in him. I think he is much nicer since he left politics. I could never bear that Chamberlain man.' My mother was speaking of the radical Chamberlain of forty years ago.

'He thinks you laugh at him.'

'So I do, but surely a mother may laugh at her own baby – her eldest.' She thought for a moment and said, 'But I must be more careful. I shouldn't like to hurt the poor darling.' And within five minutes, when Edward came to say good night, I heard her say to him, 'And so our Prime Minister has torn himself away from the Cabinet.' She called Edward's new room, the Cabinet.

Edward paid only duty visits to his mother's room. And after a few protests to me, a few exclamations of surprise and pain, she accepted this new deprivation. She said only once, 'It is strange for us both to be lonely in the same house.' And looking at her then, with the great bony orbits of her eyes, like those of a skull, I thought I had never seen a face more sad and more resigned.

And even then I thought only, 'It is sad to be old and weak and troublesome.' I did not perceive for many years the long slow tragedy of a woman, obliged to accept the niche that her children, thoughtless enough, had made for her; and to live in it, as life prisoners live in a cell. But that, I daresay, is the common fate of women like my mother, whose very love makes them feel guilty, because they could never satisfy its demands, whose

426

pride of soul prevents them from complaint or self-pity. They are, I daresay, the proudest and the humblest of creatures; the most lonely and the most self-reliant. To her dying day, my mother discharged those duties which she had laid upon herself; visits, a correspondence which often kept her up half the night; personal charities, the accounts which were always wrongly added. I do not suppose she thought of herself as an unlucky woman, who had married the wrong man, and had a family as strange to her breeding, as young wild cats to a Persian.

124

My mother never became an eccentric. If she could not sleep she lay patiently in her bed, or read a book. She was too considerate of others, too proud, to give way to singularity. But Edward, in his loneliness, soon fell into strange habits. He would spend half the night walking, or even driving, across the lanes and over the moor roads. Shepherds and the cowmen going out to first milking, were startled by the sudden appearance of a horse and trap coming down from the moor, with reins dragging, and the driver sound asleep in his seat; held from falling only by his driver's apron.

When they waked him and warned him of his danger he would always deny that he had been asleep, and then, addressing them by name, ask after their families and speak of the beauties of the moor, at this time of the morning.

Edward had that art, so necessary to a politician, of remembering faces and names, even for twenty years, after a single meeting.

'But you do go to sleep,' I told him. 'And it's very dangerous.'

'Of course, I do, but it's the only sleep I get,' and he changed the subject. He could not endure any talk about himself.

'My health is excellent,' he would say. 'This is just the life that suits me. I can get on at last with some real work.'

'Your history?'

'That and perhaps a novel or so. No one has written a real political novel – giving the real feel of politics. The French try to be funny or clever, and the English are too moral and abstract. You don't get the sense of real politics, of people feeling their way; of moles digging frantically about to dodge some unknown noise overhead; of worms all driving down simultaneously because of some change in the weather; or rising gaily up again because some scientific gardener has spread the right poison mixture; you don't get the sense of limitation and confusion, of walking on a slack wire over an unseen gulf by a succession of lightning flashes. Then the ambitious side is always done so badly. Plenty of men in politics have no political ambition; they want to defend something, to get some reform –

427

it's as simple as that. But then they are simple people, too, and it is the simple men who complicate the situation. Yes, a real political novel would be worth doing. I should like to do for politics what Tolstoy has done for war – show what a muddle and confusion it is, and that it must always be a muddle and confusion where good men are wasted and destroyed simply by luck as by a chance bullet.' And then he said to me, 'I'm not referring to myself.' Edward was extremely quick to know another's mind and I had been thinking, 'Poor Edward, he was knocked down by such a bullet.'

He smiled and said, 'My case was rather different. I retired from the stage too soon, or too late, as you prefer. Like most circus performers and *prima donnas*. Like most people, in fact.'

But during the daytime, at least, he seemed to work with purpose, and affected a strict routine.

Breakfast at nine, correspondence till eleven, with a secretary from Queensport, work afterwards. At half-past four Ann, dressed in her smartest frock, was brought down to his room for tea. And he would receive her with that affectionate grace which he always showed to women until he knew them too well. He placed a chair for her, stood till she was seated, and adjusted her cushions.

It was her duty to preside, to pour out the tea. When I was of the party, I could not bear to see the child's nervous anxiety, both at her entry and during the meal. Her fingers trembled so much that the cups rattled while she lifted them; and sometimes the milk flew in drops out of the jug. But Edward would say, 'Why do they always fill milk jugs too full.'

The child would answer, 'It wasn't too full; it was my fault' – with indignation against herself.

Edward would make conversation suitable to the occasion, about her walks, her lessons. But soon forgetting himself he would depart from lesson-book history.

'Yes, but we don't really know anything about Alfred's politics. The fact is, all made up history is nonsense. You want to go to sources, especially letters and memoirs. What a tragedy that so much of them are lost. Why do men like Creevey leave their papers to their women – wives or mistresses, it seems to come to the same thing. A woman who has lived with a man always sees him under the same species, Homo, uxorious, carnivorous. She can never conceive that in the world's eyes he may have a different value.'

All this would embarrass me for the child's sake and I would try to remind Edward of her presence. 'All this is not very interesting for Ann.'

'Of course it is,' Edward would say. 'Ann understands these things as well as anybody. Don't you, sweetheart?' with a smile which made the child colour. And she would answer, 'Yes, please, Daddy, do go on,' and turn paler than before, in terror of some question which would reveal her ignorance. Yet once when Edward forgot an appointed teatime, and had gone out walking in the fields, I found Ann at six o'clock, in her best frock, with the table still spread and nothing touched, in such a passion of tears that I thought she would do herself an injury.

I tried to comfort her. 'My dear child, I expect your father will be in soon now. Let me ring for some fresh tea.'

'No, it's too late. He won't want it now.'

'Then let us have some.'

'But you've had yours in Queensport.'

'You must have some then.'

'No, I couldn't.' And then, controlling herself, she got up and said sedately, 'It was my mistake. I got the day wrong. I must go and do my prep, if you'll excuse me, uncle.'

She never allowed the least reflection on Edward. And when sometimes he remembered to say good night to her, she would for once forget that strong anxiety which weighed upon her whole life. Then I saw her face smoothed of all its unchildish lines. Nothing showed then but an abounding, eager love and she would throw her arms round his neck with abandon.

125

Edward agreed with me that no other single cause was more influential in a man's life than his marriage. Nothing more disastrous than a bad one. And he promised to support me against Gladys.

And when Gladys and John arrived, and I presented the girl, he made occasion to remark that politics was like marriage, those who were out wanted to get in, and those who were in complained bitterly of its slavery. 'But we do not take them too seriously.'

'But surely,' John said, 'you are glad to get out of that gang?'

'I like to pretend so. I assume the graceful attitude of the man who has just been thrown out of the window.'

Edward and John were old friends with tastes in common. And while they were quoting Horace and Catullus, I saw Gladys's greedy, cunning eyes, looking from one to the other with that expression which, in a woman's face, means 'what fools, what bores – when are they going to look at me?'

And she broke in loudly, 'Poor little me, my education stopped at English.'

Edward smiled and bowed. 'Who said that the world is women's book. I always thought it would be better to say, a charming woman's book. For the world opens itself to charm, but it's apt to close up before a red nose or a fish mouth.' Edward, in paying a compliment, had the fashion of the earlier time. He embedded it in a little speech which gave it general value and prevented it from embarrassment to the receiver. My father had used to say bluntly, 'You're looking well today, never saw you prettier.'

I had heard John say to Gladys, 'Hullo, piece, you look like a virgin in the desert – meaning the cocktail.'

Apparently the young woman preferred the new style for she said to Edward in her loud, raucous voice, 'Is that a short way to tell me I'm a mess?'

'Not at all. Quite the reverse.' And Edward, instantly adapting himself to her outlook, took the young lady by the forearm and said, 'You are far from a mess, as you know very well. I really think I must cut John out.'

'That wouldn't be hard,' said she, grinning and becoming all at once soft and flexible; so that she seemed about to fall into Edward's arms. 'But what a naughty man it is. You've had some, I can see that – thousands, I suppose.'

'Not at all – I have been only too lucky at cards.'

And he began to flirt outrageously with the girl, who ended by sitting on his knee and ruffling his hair, etc. 'Here's to Ted and to hell with John – too bloody pleased with himself, anyhow. All right, John, you think it's funny to see me get off. But you wait.'

John in fact was laughing at the scene. Every moment he turned his eyes towards me as if to say, 'What a child it is – how charming.' And on Edward's face, I saw the same smile, forty years older.

But what was strange, neither was cynical. In both, so like each other except that Edward had the more regular features, one saw the same good-natured indulgence. And again in the midst of my impatience with Edward, I felt that sense of a disease, creeping through all veins, of every age and sex. And I brought up the subject of the corruption of the time. 'These night clubs – did you see that last prosecution – and they say Berlin is worse.'

I had hoped that Gladys would now show her true colours, and I was successful. She laughed and said 'Nunky is shocked at us.'

'Yes,' Edward said, 'unless he is envious of us.'

'But why must this corruption overwhelm the whole of Europe at once?'

'It is always so after a war – people want a holiday or perhaps I should say an unholy day.'

'But is that true. This gloomy corruption, this moral defeatism, the exaltation of selfishness can't give much pleasure,' etc. I saw them smiling at me, but I was all the more determined to make my point. Gladys jumped off Edward's knee, put an arm round my neck, kissed me and said 'You're just right, old dear. We're a bad naughty lot – but we do get some fun. And if we didn't, someone else would.'

'True,' Edward said. 'One doesn't like to miss one's share, even of headaches.'

Tea was brought in and Ann entered the room in her stiff old-fashioned frock. I saw her look at Gladys with a kind of horror. She had never before seen a painted face. They were still unknown in our neighbourhood.

Gladys, for her part, showed that contemptuous indifference towards Ann which I had noticed in girls of her age and time. She had in her own words, 'no use for children'.

Edward made Gladys a bow and said, 'The bride will pour out for us.'

'The bride – here, what are you getting at? Do I look so bedded? Well, I warned John.'

Gladys, who seldom laughed, but often smiled, with much good humour, now smiled upon us all as if to say, 'We're all friends here, aren't we?' Then she sat down at the tea table and Ann retreated to the farthest corner of the room.

I asked Ann afterwards what she thought of Gladys, meaning to warn the child against so bad an example. But Ann said only, 'She's from London, isn't she?' She seemed, as usual, to be storing knowledge for use.

'I hope you will never paint yourself like that.'

'I wonder where she gets it?'

And I dared say no more. For, I asked myself, 'Is there any door by which this corruption cannot enter, even into a child's mind, by way of her serious and candid respect for knowledge.'

126

It was useless being angry with Edward, as irresponsible as John himself. And in my alarm I saw nothing for it but a direct attack. I wrote and told John that Gladys would be the worst possible wife for a lawyer, and happening, on the next day, to meet Gladys herself, in the vestibule of the office, when she was waiting for John, I asked her if she did not think John was staying too late and drinking too much. 'You mean no harm,' I said, 'but you are doing harm. The boy is not giving his mind to his work.'

She merely gazed at me with a blank face and half-open mouth; an arrogant pose which means in such persons 'What is this freak?'

'I suppose you think I have no business to interfere,' I said, 'but John is my godson, and I don't want to see him ruin his life before it's well started.'

Then suddenly she became animated, jerked her shoulders one way, her behind the other, laughed in my face and said, 'That's all right Uncle Lucifer. You needn't be afraid for your precious infant – it's not John would be ruined if we clicked,' and she told me she wouldn't dream of marrying a man who couldn't afford even to keep a car.

The strange appellation, Lucifer, startled me so much that I did not know how to answer. It was only afterwards, from Julie, that I discovered it to be a reference to my legs, or rather trousers. My good city tailor quite agreed with my dislike of seeing men drape their legs in two skirts, and my trousers were cut on the old manly basis, to show the limb. The infantile mind of Gladys had found this reasonable fashion, or rather, principle, amusing; and she was accustomed to refer to me as Lucifer legs, or more formally, as Uncle Lucifer.

And before I thought of some suitable comment on her statement, that marriage, in her view, was simply a question of cheap motoring, John came downstairs, she blew me a kiss, and said, 'Take care of them, Nunky, London wouldn't be London without them,' and walked off on John's arm.

127

I hear people talk of the modern girl, the new generation and so forth, but two women more different than Gladys and Ann can't be imagined. Is it wrong to suppose that young people like John and Gladys, brought up among the slogans, etc., of war, grew up different from those like Ann and Robert, in the next generation, who began to think for themselves, among the confused problems which started up on every side, with the peace?

When Lottie sent for Ann in 1920, to go on a visit, I remember the child's pale set face as Edward and I saw her off, with her nurse, at the station. She had not seen her mother for three years and knew nothing of her. She was leaving the father whom she worshipped. But she did not cry. I suppose she had already learnt, in that time so hard for children, that tears were unpopular. Grown-ups had no time for consolation. She seemed only to shrink, to grow thinner and more fragile, more plain, as she stood holding Edward's hand; and when she had kissed him, for the last time in her life, she turned away quickly and climbed into the carriage as if in flight.

But even then she did not cry. As the train moved, I saw the narrow, pale oval face, as white as paper, behind the window glass, and the peculiar intensity of her look at Edward. She was frowning as if to concentrate on something that she could not grasp. She was not sure, even then, that she had enough of him to remember. I suppose for all her love of Edward, she had never come very near to comprehending him. And now I see that concentrated frown again when the woman stands before some new task, some new problem. Yesterday it was the question of breaking up some fallow; or rather, the question whether Farley's advice was to be trusted. Today, at luncheon, she said to me abruptly, 'Molly's going to have a baby.'

'What Molly?'

'Robert's Molly. Robert wrote this morning.'

I was shocked. For I had always hoped for a reconciliation between the young couple. 'Then I suppose you will have to divorce him.'

'Yes, but this baby must have started here – three months before Robert went off with the girl.'

'I'm not surprised – you practically invited him to go off with her.' For I was much upset by the idea of this divorce.

'I never thought Robert could do such a thing – I wonder where they did it.'

'Robert has behaved badly, but so have you – I can't think how you could be so stupid – throwing away a good husband like that.'

'A good husband?'

'He might have been a very good husband. He had a sense of duty – that's the main thing. But of course you don't believe in nonsense like a sense of duty. You never found it in your test tubes,' etc. An unfortunate speech which I have regretted.

But Ann answered only, 'Yes, I suppose I wouldn't take high marks on men.'

'The only thing you seem to understand are text books which are always stuffed with nonsense,' but seeing then her look of anxious perplexity, her pinched cheeks and troubled eyes, I felt sorry for the child, and told her that on the whole I blamed Robert more severely, etc. Which was not true, but perhaps justifiable in the circumstances.

But she is still, three days later, pondering day and night. You can see the questions passing round and round her brain, like coloured chemicals in an apparatus. 'How did Robert do such a thing – whose fault was it? Shall I never get to the bottom of all this?'

And so her predecessor, the little girl of ten, looked at her father eighteen years ago. Edward, as I noticed as we came home, had a look merely of surprise and resignation. He had not expected this blow to hurt so much. He did not ask why he had suffered it. But, in fact, one can say that the loss of wife and child killed the man. He had not seen Lottie for four years, and he had paid little attention to Ann at Tolbrook; but when Lottie now asked for her divorce, and for Ann, he gave up all pretence of a desire to live and to work. I urged him to fight at least for Ann, but he answered, 'What sort of a father have I made? No, it isn't my role.'

He ceased even to read, and spent whole days strolling about the grounds, or sitting, almost motionless, in his chair. When I told him that he ought to be finishing his book, he would answer, 'It's not worth finishing. Amateur stuff. I know enough to know that I don't know enough. Even the foundations have shifted. And I'm too old to begin a new education.'

'You're not old at sixty three, Edward.'

'We don't make old bones, as a family – we live too much on our nerves and sense. And there's nothing so ageing as failure. Why, I can hardly get round the lake; and look at my fingers, stiff and swelling in every joint. *Degommé*. To come unstuck. The perfect word.'

He was sitting in his room, and though it was September, he had a fire in the grate. His thin body had always felt the cold.

'But Edward, don't you think it is a pity for people to talk so much about earthquakes and avalanches and so on – it's only the sensational newspapers and the politicians, translated into schoolboy Byronism? It's just something to say –'

I spoke with warmth because I had just been discussing this subject with John, during the week in London. And I had been struck as well as pleased to find that John had agreed with me.

Indeed, I was enjoying at that time, in my renewed friendship with John, a resurrection of hope and enterprise. I had instituted in the office, the new reform of wearing short coats; and also of typing, instead of engraving our wills, bringing us up to date in both respects. And with John, I was on the closest terms of intimacy. We would even discuss Gladys and agree that, in spite of certain good qualities, she was not a suitable wife for a lawyer, in a firm of our standing. And what had surprised me, Gladys bore me no malice for my intervention. She seemed to treat the whole affair as a joke, comparable with my trousers, collar, waistcoat, etc., in which she never ceased to find amusement. She would greet me as 'Uncle Spider', and ask me how I got my feet through 'them'. 'Or perhaps you start at the bottom and go to the top instead of from the bottom to the bottom,' and I would smile at these mild but rather vulgar jokes in order to preserve the harmony of our band.

'I don't think,' I said to Edward, 'that young men of sense (meaning, of course, John) are fairly represented in the newspapers – they're not so silly. It's only the half educated – the class that does swallow print, who talk about a futile world,' etc.

'A large class,' Edward said, 'perhaps the majority. Yes, it's interesting to see how revolutions actually come about – how they cast their shadow before them – no, not a shadow' – Edward visibly elaborated the material for a couplet – 'a bar of heat. It's as if a furnace door has been opened – the furnace where new societies are forged, and the heat at once begins to melt everything, even a long way from it, things which will not be ready for the crucibles for a long time – ideas, institutions, laws, political parties, they all begin to lose their firmness.'

I had often heard Edward on this subject. He had thought to see the same process twenty years before, and I was about to remind him of the fact. But I remembered suddenly an old couplet of his:–

> Men, women, laws relax. When Angelo doffed
> His coat, they say, the waiting stone turned soft.

And suddenly the idea came home to me and I was frightened. It seemed that the very ground grew thin beneath me, and everything about me began to change form, to dissolve. As if there were an infection of change in the very walls, books and Edward's bent figure, white hair and hollow cheeks.

Edward tapped the bars with his poker; outside it was growing dusk, but his curtains were not drawn, and a warm breeze languidly moved their folds, and made a tassel swing against the pane. They were still cutting in some field across the paddock, and the reaper as it circled, made a regular crescendo, from the sound of a distant bee, to the noise of a stick rattled on a fence. The voices of the boys and young women who were putting up the stooks, or stitches as we call them, came through on the lazy wind like the last social chirping of birds at twilight when they have stopped feeding and think of finding their roosts.

It was the kind of evening when, at one time, I had loved to be at home. But already I was assailed by a thousand anxieties, the fear of rain which might damage my harvest, the wretched prices for corn. And the voices of the boys reminded me only of a most impudent robbery, in the last week, of all the pears, still green, on one of my best trees. I thought at the same moment, 'That binder hasn't been paid for; those boys are getting worse every year, regular young criminals; this breeze smells of thunder; has Farley yet had the thatcher on the wheat stacks'; and at the same time, curtain, binder, boys, stacks, even the wind seemed to fade, by Edward's talk, into the mere colours and sounds of some mysterious historical play.

'All that is very pretty,' I said suddenly, in a voice so loud that I startled myself. 'But it is only simile,' and so on. 'What exactly is this mysterious process of what-do-you-call-it, melting, softening?'

'I suppose it is simply expectaton of a new order,' Edward said. And I thought he was enjoying himself, as always in an abstract inquiry. 'It is an intelligent anticipation of the wrath to come. But, of course, it affects people differently – Julie sentimentalizes, and John, it appears, marks time, or perhaps he has simply withdrawn gracefully. Every revolution has that handicap – that as soon as it starts a lot of the best brains in the country go out of commission – I mean those with independent judgement, the really scholarly and scientific brains, the ones that a revolution needs above every other.'

'John has been slow to settle down – it's only natural after all the excitement of a war.'

'No, he is standing aside. People like John feel that they aren't wanted – that there's no place for them among the turmoil, the chatter, the spite and the nonsense of all sorts – he was born to serve some independent truth – he could have made a first-class researcher or scientist,' and so on. I listened, but I could not attend because the binder had stopped and the voices out there in the field were all talking at once. 'It's broken down again,' I thought, 'that means that the barley won't be finished tonight –' and I kept on saying to Edward, 'There's something in that perhaps,' or 'All this is based on a premiss that I don't accept,' but I was actually distracted. And the end of it was that I could bear suspense no longer. I jumped up, took my hat and umbrella and hurried down the field. Great rain drops were already falling. The sky over my head was dark blue. The sulphur coloured clouds that I had seen from the window rushing eastwards occupied only half the sky, on the east. I walked, therefore, in the bright evening sun, and the tumult of the clouds, which looked like a mass of troops and people in headlong retreat, through huge rollers of dust and smoke, resembled a moving picture. The wind had dropped, the leaves stood motionless; I was surrounded by an immediate silence so deep that the falling drops sounded as loud and startling as bullets, and their drops fell from no visible cloud; out of the blue sky. But when I looked closely at this sky, it seemed unnaturally dark and thick, the blue of wood smoke.

I thought every moment, 'Now it is going to break.' And as I do not like thunder and was fearful that the lightning might strike the steel point of my umbrella, I hesitated whether to go back to shelter or forward to the binder. But my feet decided for me. They carried me forward at a round pace, and on consideration, I approved their resolution. It was no time to avoid a plain duty.

The thunder did not break. Instead, the drops increased in number and suddenly became a flood. The trees, the hedges and the fields, the sky itself and all its gesticulating silent mobs wavered like reflections in a stream, suddenly touched by a breeze, and then dissolved into an air which was largely water. I found myself alone among warm cataracts, with no distinction of material for the senses, except the variety of noise; the dashing of leaves, the roar of boughs, the hissing of a copse, the rustle of hedges, the tinkle of drains. Which proved so delusive that in the thickened twilight I lost my way and found myself walking in the stubble, mixed with new clover, of a field already cut; an accident not surprising on such an evening. But now of such bewildering effect that, as I stood, with every clover leaf pouring its waterfall into my boots, I felt as if the very earth were liquifying under my feet, as if the familiar trees, fields and sky had actually melted into some primitive elementary form, and that the world of German philosophy, in which everything can be anything else, as the philosopher pleases, had actually realized itself in a universal nothingness, whose very colour was uncertain. And I, the very last individual being of the old creation, though still solid in appearance, and capable of supporting a hat; as I ascertained by touch; trousers, umbrella, etc., as I perceived by sight, was yet already wavering in essence, beginning to lose the shape of my ideas, memory, etc., preparatory to the final and rapid solution of my whole identity.

I do not mean, of course, that I continued in such a delusion. It was the weakness of a passing second. Yet it caused me to feel again how insecure are those chains of assumption by which we conduct our lives; how easily broken; how necessary to be anchored to a faith which, being of the mind and the spirit and so forth, can defy the corruption of sense and the whims of fashion.

As the rain thinned to the consistency of a shower bath, I recognized the field and in the same instant saw a corn stack in front of me. The oats. Only half covered with a worn-out rick cloth.

'That will cost me fifty pounds at least!' I thought and went to find my manager. But he, as usual, had a dozen good excuses, of which the chief was the invariable one, that I didn't provide enough rick cloths.

'Why, then, didn't you thatch?'

'Well, sir, it didn't seem worth while when we were threshing next week.' A nice young man, whose very politeness and genteel accent, seemed to say to me, 'Why worry – especially about the oats?'

128

My mother died in her sleep, and it turned out that she had left everything to Bill's children; nothing to Amy. Apparently she thought of Amy as provided for by Bill, and her pension. John, therefore, received three thousand pounds.

Gladys at once proposed to marry him. John, I thought, had been cured of Gladys, and his reception of her proposal assured me of it. He told me that he didn't think it would work.

'Of course it wouldn't work – she would drive you mad with her noisy silliness.'

'It's not that – but she's used to a lot of attention and a good deal of society. And I've got my exams. I can't really spare the time for honeymooning.'

A month later he married Gladys in a registry office and invested his legacy in a small motor repair works belonging to one of her friends. She obtained the use of half a dozen cars by this master stroke. The works were in a small and dismal village near Birmingham.

John, since Gladys did not like housekeeping, took the upper part of a house there, and Amy went with the couple as housekeeper.

I found John dawdling through a few hours' work a week, in which he had no interest whatever. Gladys was out motoring all day with her young men. Amy alone seemed completely happy and useful, cooking, shopping, and even scrubbing for the household. She was obviously puzzled by Gladys, but gave her warm praise. 'She's not a bit jealous – I see John as much as I like.'

I asked the boy how on earth he had come to marry Gladys. And he answered vaguely, 'I'd gone about with her a lot and she seemed to want it.'

'Good heavens! Is that a good reason for throwing away your life; and I thought you were taking so much interest in the law.'

'Well, uncle, I suppose it's not very certain that the law will go on much longer, I mean, in its present form. Or the estates we look after.'

And having, in this one phrase, demolished the ancient and majestic structure of English law and English property rights, he added, 'But, of course, everything is a bit shaky just now.'

Of John's two partners, one, Gladys's friend, a middle-aged man who had already made a war fortune, did not appear at the works more than once a week, for a few hours. The other, a young man, like John, lately demobilized, was working twelve hours a day, but drinking all night. He was a great red-faced boy, his eyes already bloodshot with drink.

'Five years of this,' he said, 'and I'll be able to do something worth while.'

'What do you want to do?'

'Copra. In the south seas. Get away from all this. Have my own schooner. But I wish you'd get that fella John to pull his weight. He always gets his nose in a book. Too much bed-work, too. That bitch Gladys gives me a bad pain.'

Two months later the slump ruined the firm and both the partners. The red-faced boy shot himself. John became a motor salesman, in a London firm; and Gladys took work in a fashionable flower shop. She was said to be popular with young men, and out of hours she always had the use of some young man's pocket and car. On one occasion she and two young men were arrested for insulting behaviour, in a small country village, and it was shown that all three had been sharing a room at the inn. John went down to bail them out. But when I expressed to John my horror at this wretched life, without sense or order, he answered with his usual cheerful nonchalance, 'But have we done so badly, considering.'

'Considering what?'

'Oh, everything. We've never been actually on the rocks and, of course, Gladys is a trump – when we're stuck, she just turns to –'

'Are you going on all your life like this, living from hand to mouth, in a flat; don't you want some family life, children?'

'Well, things are a bit uncertain, aren't they, and I don't think Gladys is particularly keen on children. She'd rather keep her job.'

And sometimes I grew angry with him. 'You're a drifter, John. You're getting nowhere. And you could have made a career for yourself, you could have been somebody.'

'Well, I suppose they also serve who only stand and sell – though of course dustmen take a higher place. I often feel I ought to be a dustman and do a really civic job.'

The country flat had consisted of three rooms. But in town they had only two. I entered one day upon a ludicrous scene. Amy was lying in the sitting room upon a couch much too short even for her short figure. She resembled a very large blue skittle with a red knob, balanced miraculously on the top of pink sausage. Gladys and John were looking at her, the first with the expression of one who examines a doubtful cod in a fishmonger's; the second with embarrassment. Amy turned her head from one to the other. 'It would do very well – I'm perfectly comfortable.'

'You don't look comfortable.'

The question was, could Amy sleep in the sitting room. I said at once that it was impossible for Amy to sleep on that couch. I was outraged by such a suggestion. Amy, after all, was Bill's widow.

'That's what I say, Nunky,' Gladys said. 'She'd stick out both ends and get double pneumonia in her feet.'

But Amy was indignant. 'I used to sleep on much smaller beds in India. I'm *quite* comfortable.' And thinking perhaps that her appearance lying down was not a good argument for the couch, she put her feet to the ground, sat up and looked at us. I was struck by her intense anxiety, which seemed rather comical, in the circumstances. With her round face, her little round forehead deeply marked with orderly wrinkles, her fixed gazing eyes, she might have been a portrait of desperation, carved by a Dutch doll maker.

And yet, as I observed with surprise, Amy had somewhere found a real dignity which, at this unfavourable moment, or because of it, was somehow revealed to me. It consisted perhaps only in resignation to the blows of fate, and a flat back.

Her desperation, so comical to me, suddenly acquired some excuse. For now to my surprise, Gladys said, 'Then that settles it – we couldn't fit a bigger couch into this dog kennel.'

John and I protested with force. I at once measured the floor with my umbrella, which was exactly one yard in length, with inches nicked on the handle. I have all my umbrellas made to this pattern, which has shown its worth in many a family discussion.

So I proved now that there was room for a six-foot couch in the window. 'We'll get a box couch,' John said.

'And where shall I keep anything without the cupboard?' Gladys asked.

'We can have a couch with a drawer and put the pillows there.'

'Then we'll all be living in our drawers, unless I park my frocks in the car and sleep with Doggie.' Doggie was one of her friends.

Amy said that she couldn't put Gladys out, to which Gladys answered that, on the whole, she would quite enjoy a change of husband.

John now proposed to look for a three-room flat. 'If you can find the rent,' Gladys said. And, of course, the end of it was Amy's expulsion. The wife in such a case has the last word. And Gladys had long resolved to get rid of Amy. She was tired, so she confided to Julie, of hearing her think about John.

I do not know if I understood the nature of Amy's disaster. I remember that I was desperately worried just then, by the financial situation, the bills, the taxes, the cost of repairs at Tolbrook, and the whims of a new house-keeper. I could not ask Amy to Tolbrook, because of this housekeeper's strange condition of temper. But I had the grace to take her to the station.

Her belongings seemed to be reduced to one trunk and a string bag, and when I asked her if she had no more, she answered, 'I had to cut down a bit. There wasn't room in John's flat. It's rather a blessing when one's on the move.'

'Where are you going?'

'I thought of Broadstairs.'

'You know someone at Broadstairs?'

'No; I've never been there – but Mrs Johnson, she's the widow of Bill's first colonel, has given me the address of a boarding house; she says it gives the best value on the coast.'

'A rash statement,' I suggested.

'Well,' Amy said, 'she's been a widow for twenty years – you'll write to me sometimes, won't you, Tom – about Johnny? He's never been a very good writer himself.'

129

Edward caught a mild influenza that winter which quickly developed into pneumonia. He seemed to have made up his mind that he was to die. Yet he was more cheerful than he had been for years; he chaffed his doctors when they told him he was in no danger; he flirted with his nurses. And on the last morning of his life he congratulated me. 'You knew what you wanted, Tommy, and you made for it, from the beginning. It's the only way. The new age can only use specialists.'

'But, Edward, you can't compare my work with yours. You have made history. I have been a small cog in the machine.'

'You gripped something. I hit the air.'

He died unconscious the same night. And when I was sorting and bundling his papers, among a mass of unfinished work, I found these verses:

> Life tragic to the soul; to mind a joke
> Now tragi-comic, gives its cruellest stroke.
> Grief for the dead, tho' sharper it returns;
> That grief which only grief, by grief relearns,
> Tempers the heart in which it beats and burns.
> But that comedian who sold comic truth
> For laughs, and missed the laugh; age playing youth
> To seem a doting fool; those heroes' scars
> Who shot themselves in aiming at the stars
> Of glass, third class, can find no anodyne

Hurt pride in its own pride still seeks to pine;
Self ridicule puts poison on the knife
And leaves a wound that festers all your life.
Now dead ambition which no rot can sink
Bloats on the soul corrupting in its stink;
Not time destroys the old but creeping spite
For all they fought for, in a bungled fight.
For fame along the street, June's summer gush
Choking the sun with gilt, the leaves with plush,
For triumphs lost which won would still be mean –
They die of laughing at their might have been.

I had read them again in the last month when I handed to Ann for her father's biography all that material which I had kept against the day when posterity might do him justice. Today when I went to Edward's writing table, so neatly arranged, I found them in the rejected basket under the samples of oil cake, twine and seed which have now begun to appear among Ann's correspondence.

'Why don't you like those verses?' I asked her, when she came in to see if tea had been brought to me; and to make up my fire.

She took the paper by the tip of one finger and thumb in her hand which was her chief beauty. Not so small as her mother's, but with those tapered fingers and smooth joints, which very small hands rarely possess. I saw now that the hand was not only dirty from some farmyard work but that the skin of the finger tips was cracked, and the finger nails broken.

Ann put the paper close to her short-sighted eyes, read, frowned, and said, 'A little too fussy, don't you think; it sounds as if he took it all too seriously. I don't want people to think that about him.'

'Ah, of course, our times were not very serious.' I spoke with irony.

'Yes, it will have to be a period piece – to get the proportions right.'

'A period piece, for Edward –'

'All that old politics looks so small from this end of the telescope – and when politics gets to look small, it looks mean, too. But poor Daddy wasn't mean – no, it's rather tricky.'

'My dear child, your father was a century before his time. That was his tragedy. Even his supporters thought him extreme – he used to talk about abolishing marriage.'

'Yes, that's what I mean. That's how they used to think. I shall have to look up the early communists, too.'

She put down the paper and called through the window, 'Farley, Mister Brown says I'm quite right about those milk records and I want them tonight.' She went out, saying angrily that if Farley pretended to be deaf, it would be a good excuse to get rid of him.

Ann does not seem to find it odd that her correspondence about the divorce should include bulletins about the farming at Tolbrook and almost continuous advice from Robert.

Edward's verses were still lying where she had left them weighted down with a sample packet of a new sheep dip; and I felt that not only Edward but I too was receding into a past which was irrecoverable. I looked round at the little room and before my eyes it seemed to change from Edward's familiar study into a museum piece, detached even from Tolbrook, by its new paint and its old books, so carefully revarnished.

To Ann, I am a museum piece. I can't tell whether she guards me from Blanche and from Sara, from all those agitations of the outer world, because she sets some value on my life, or because she has a sense of duty. Probably her motives are not only unknown to me but beyond my comprehension.

We can understand new ideas in the world, but we cannot share new feelings. In the last terrible years of Julie's degeneration, I found myself still climbing her stairs, like a convict who, in a world changed out of recognition, turns back to the gaol which he knows.

The feeling in that room was known to me and though Julie and I disliked each other, we understood each other's words. But when Gladys or even John spoke to me in those years, I was not sure that I understood. I was not deaf, but I felt the uneasiness of the deaf, who strain to comprehend something which eludes them.

One day, John, in a moment of confidence, said to me, 'Of course, Gladys has her own morals – she is almost systematic.'

The word systematic seemed to offer me a chance I sought, to tell him that Gladys was consistently unfaithful. But John's next words, in a dreamy voice, were 'Yes, she's rather strict, in her own way.'

'She seems to make it a rule,' I said, 'to get drunk three times a week, at Julie's – you are all drinking too much.' For I was greatly troubled by these drink parties at Julie's flat. Two or even three times a week they would meet and drink together till late at night. Yet they did not meet for drink, and certainly not for conversation. They seemed to be driven together by a force outside themselves, like the gravity which makes loose balls roll together at the bottom of a bowl. It was, I think, because they had nothing to give each other, except bare company, that they drank.

And when I reproached Julie for these beastly habits, she would answer with dignity 'I've never been drunk and I've never seen John drunk. Gladys is drunk every night but that's not my fault and at least I keep her off the streets.'

And, in fact, Julie did not get drunk. She became only blowsy and red. Yet I can't remember a more horrible sight than to see her, still a dignified façade, and Gladys, with her sparrow's character of lechery and impudent courage; and John, scholar in the very spirit, sitting in that room which still seemed beautiful and civilized, drinking and talking together the endless nonsense of the half drunk.

Each became a parody of his own nature. Julie's dignity was turned into pompous hypocrisy; Gladys's frankness became obscene, imbecile; John's good nature and unselfishness became sloth and boredom. He would lie across a sofa, unbuttoned, his long hair falling down his perspiring face, and throw out, with lazy grin, some classical allusion, which the others neither understood nor heard. Unless Gladys catching it up could turn the sound of it into an obscenity.

Julie, in the morning, when her head ached and her whole flabby body seemed to be dissolving in self pity, would say to me 'I could kill that little fool Gladys, but John is so weak. She kept him away all last week because I told her that in my time only harlots painted their finger nails.'

130

Yet when we had absolute proof of Gladys's infidelity, in Julie's flat, she refused to let me speak to John. 'You will simply drive him away.'

'It is a duty,' I said, 'perhaps the best chance to save the boy from that Delilah.' And I wrote to him.

The proof was clear. Julie's maid had surprised Gladys and the middle-aged dealer, whom she called Doggie, on the sofa together. I told John that he could divorce his wife at once.

I received no answer to my letter. But a few days later Gladys came to Julie and me, just after luncheon, and told us coolly not to interfere in her affairs. 'Why, you silly old sods, when were you born? If it wasn't for me and my friends, like Doggie, John would be in the workhouse. And let me tell you I've been a bloody good wife to him, as well he knows. Good-bye and sleep well, that's for John, too.' And she went out.

'You see what you've done,' Julie cried. 'Can you never stop meddling?'

'Is that what you call meddling?' I said, quite furious with the woman, 'to try and rescue John from that vampire.' And in my rage and alarm, I put on my hat and took a taxi to John's place of business. It was one of the smaller shops, of the highest distinction. Its showroom was furnished luxuriously with fine rugs, cut chandeliers, palms, and so forth. John was engaged with a client, a woman. But his fellow salesman knew me and did not trouble me. I pretended to examine the cars. John affected to enjoy his work, but it always made me uneasy to see him humouring his clients, whether they were of his own class, who were excessively polite and smiling, as with their servants, or some rich woman, of a lower class, insolent and mannerless. At the moment, he was dealing with two such women; mother and daughter; a fat beast with the bulging jowls of a

French pug, and a skin like a leper, whose expression, as she looked round, was so ridiculous in its arrogance, that one would have laughed at her, if it had not been for the cruelty of her stare, her crooked mouth; the young girl had the smooth mask of profound stupidity, ignorance and conceit, painted to give the idea of luxurious perversity. But it was marked already with the peevish ill-temper which goes with small minds and petty selfishness. Both women wore furs and jewels of great value.

'How much is the landaulette?' the old one snapped at John, throwing back her head in order to droop her thickened eyelids at him. The boy answered her with smiling courtesy; the grace of an ambassador which, no doubt, she took for servility. And the young woman meanwhile stared at him with unblinking eyes. You could see the idea passing in her infantile brain, 'What sort of animal is this – I suppose he is a man of a sort.'

The old woman was poking her leper's finger with its soft bleached skin into the upholstery.

'Special process. I've heard that tale before.'

'We use nothing but the finest hides – if you would like to see –'

'Are you telling me that I am a fool.'

And the young one drawled 'It's not his fault, mother – he's only doing his job.' All this in tones which reached and were meant to reach the whole shop, including myself and three new visitors, of the better kind, now surrounding the other salesman, and chirping to him their gay inquiries and little jokes, like old friends from the country, or canvassers seeking a vote.

New arrogance, for some reason, always wishes to display itself to the greatest possible number of people, and to disgust them.

Or perhaps only to take revenge, like this old creature, for some secret meanness, eating out the soul.

'But I knew your cars were rotten' she screeched. 'Everybody knows they're rotten.' A statement which caused the other party, carefully not looking in her direction, to redouble its bonhomie with the second salesman.

At last the hag went out, and the daughter stayed only to drawl again at John 'Thank you, but I'm afraid we want something rather better.'

I hurried to his side and he received me with the usual affectionate smile. 'Hullo, uncle.'

'Can I see you at tea?'

'Why not now –?'

'I thought it was against your rules.'

'The manager's out. Let's get in here.' He opened the door of a large limousine, and we reclined on the wide seats, as soft as a bed. It was impossible to sit upright upon them.

'What abominable people,' I said to John. 'How do you bear them?'

'Did you think so – the girl was rather pathetic, poor dear. Did you notice her bad teeth – she probably affects that poker face to hide them.'

444

'No, I didn't. I could not bear to look at such a creature. How can you stay in such a job?'

'Perhaps it's all I'm fit for, uncle – at least nowadays.' I knew the boy had deteriorated at a terrifying pace. In his yellow dry face and pouched eyes, I saw already the corruption of weariness. But his acceptance shocked me. I said 'Rubbish, you only have to pull yourself together, and find an object in life.'

He was silent; idly swinging the tassel of the car. Silence and gesture meant that I was talking nonsense. We both knew that he had failed to find any object in life big enough to engage his interest. And taking new resolution for my desperate enterprise, I said 'Gladys came to see us this afternoon.'

'Yes, she told me she was going.'

I was startled by the boy's careless tone and his glance at me. It was a glance full of cold boredom which seemed to put between us an immense distance.

'Did she tell you why?' I asked.

'Something about her friend Doggie, and a scene at poor Aunt Julie's.'

'D'you approve of this man?'

'He's a friend of Gladys – he doesn't bother me much.'

'But, John, as a husband –'

He interrupted me. 'I don't worry about him. Gladys's affairs are too complicated. And, as you know, we get on pretty well, very well – she's not had such an easy time.'

I did not feel horror at a speech which meant that John was indifferent to his wife's unfaithfulness; I felt only confused, and, as it were, out of my element. The car which enclosed us, like a drawing room on wheels, terrifying in its elaborate luxury; the seduction of the cushions, which seemed to draw me down into an attitude of defenceless acquiescence; the heavy air, scented with some perfume which also seemed to impregnate the leather, silk, carpets; their very dust which revolved in the pale sunshine, filtered to us through four layers of plate glass, all seemed to belong to a civilization, which, like John, found me superfluous.

I said, 'I don't want to make trouble.'

'No, no,' he said 'of course not – all for the best.'

But I was glad when the manager returned and we were obliged to get quickly out of the car and break off our interview. I felt as I went away that harm had been done, though I could not tell what it was. And in fact, my friendship with John came to an end. Neither he nor Gladys visited the flat again, and when I went to find him, though he was as charming as before, he was plainly embarrassed by my persistence. No doubt he had to choose between me and his wife.

Strangely, it was with Gladys that I regained acquaintance; on our old terms of mutual forbearance. For when a few months later John lost his job, I helped her to support the household. And when in the next year, he was run over by a car in Bond Street, we made arrangement together for his removal to a private ward of the hospital and for special treatment.

In those days, I grew almost fond of Gladys. She seemed devoted to John. One would have said that his death would break her heart. He died, and she went at once to live with the man she called Doggie. She laughed at my disgust; 'I know how to manage Doggie. He's such a dirty dog, I don't mind what he does. And I think I owe myself a good time.'

'Can you have a good time with that man?'

'My god, yes. He's got about five thousand a year and he'll spend it, too, if you give him a fair deal, or he'd better,' and she said to me with a contempt which I could not reproduce, 'You've got me wrong, Nunky – I'm not going to the devil. I've got a good grip on things. I'm not like that old soak, Julie – I'd be ashamed.'

131

A rock, his faith, defying all the shocks
Of time and tide; and dead like other rocks.

When I think of John, I am still frightened. How does faith fail? Why does its sap cease to run? Not by age or disease. John was young and strong. When I said prayers this morning, I said to myself 'I must love these words, I must rejoice in truth.' But in that act, I felt my spirit withdraw from them like leaves touched by frost, some devil's breath from the perverseness of my will.

I looked at Jan kneeling in his mother's lap. For though he can't speak, he has learnt to pray. He imitates me. At first he used to clap his hands together, not being able to distinguish between clapping and praying. But now, having looked closely at his hands, he puts them carefully together, and when he has done so, takes them apart again several times, to look at them again, as if he might find something in them.

I said to Ann this morning, 'He will thank you some day, for an experience that is already becoming part of his very nature.'

Ann looked doubtful and her doubt at once infected me so that I asked myself, 'Do I mean anything by those words?'

'I don't suppose it can do him much harm. Robert won't approve, but we needn't mind about that.'

'Robert won't approve?' I asked.

'He wants me to go and meet him about the divorce, and I shall have to take Jan.'

'My dear, you can't meet that woman.'

'I don't intend to – could you manage for a week-end. Mrs Ramm knows your routine.'

'I suppose I shall have to.'

Both of us, no doubt, were feeling a certain depression. Ann said 'What a life.' Her anxious glance was fixed on the boy. He was running silently about the room in his combinations, turning and twisting unexpectedly, like a gnat dancing on the air.

'At least, you will get the thing over,' I said.

'Perhaps, but it's getting rather complicated.'

The boy stood on one leg opposite the fireplace, and raised the other as if trying to perform a figure of ballet. His face was absurdly affected. Then suddenly he stood still, bent his knees and his neck and looked at the floor. A pool formed on the rug; Ann darted at him 'You naughty boy, what on earth made you do that.'

She whisked him away to the night nursery. His glance backward over her shoulder was at the pool, with an air of tranquil curiosity. But though urine was the worst thing possible for the blue drugget of my new rug, I could not help laughing.

Why does a child make gaiety spring in the heart, even with its mischief? Because he cares for nothing. He does not know the complication of the world. And Lucy, a hard and obstinate woman, could always throw power into my soul by the same innocence. She did what she chose. I remember the day, soon after John's death, that I met her for the first time in years at Queensport station.

She was white-haired, shrunken, with cheeks so thin that one saw through them the shape of her gums, and the dry corded muscles of her jaw. Her nose was like a finch's beak, hooked, yellow and shining. The blackened skin round her eyes gave them the piercing brightness of lights behind a dingy curtain.

'But you're ill,' I cried.

'Rubbish.' She kissed me with that passionate eagerness which she showed always when we met after a long separation, and leaning back from me, exclaimed 'You're just the same,' smiling as if to say 'and just as ridiculous.'

'What's happened?' I asked her. 'Is Brown off again abroad?' For I always hoped that Brown would once more go to India and leave her to me for three or four years.

'Nothing's happened,' she said sharply, 'I've just come home for a little.' Her sharpness showed that she did not want to give me her reason for so sudden a return. And in fact I never heard it. Whether she knew that she was gravely ill; or whether, as was likely, she acted upon an impulse deeper than reason; the instinct which makes a wild animal struggle towards its hole, even in the blindness of its death agony, Amy and I agreed that she came home to die.

447

'Then you must have been ill' I said to her, 'I never saw you so thin.'

Lucy gave an impatient jerk of her chin and looked about her. 'But what have they been doing here – where's the station master's garden?'

'They've cleared it out to make a place for motor buses.'

'They would – the fools.'

'The buses had to go somewhere.'

'I don't see why – who wants the buses?'

'Brown doesn't believe in modern progress?'

'Progress downwards, through the stink of oil and tar. Hell is fired with petroleum,' and, seeing me laugh, she said with her cool fierce glare, 'What are you laughing at? – that's Biblical – and all this nonsense is Biblical, too. These are the days of trial – when the devil has a free hand. But I suppose you're too blind to see what's going on under your nose – or you don't want to see it.'

'There are some things I don't like, certainly.'

'Only some things,' said Lucy coolly. 'What has old Nanny Pinkham done to her cottage? – she's ruined it, the fool – it looks like a cheap tea house.'

'Mrs Pinkham is dead. Someone from town uses it for week-ends. Are you getting any converts, Lucy?'

'Not many. How glorious it is today – just right to come home on.'

It did not seem to me a glorious day. It was November, with a sharp north-east wind and a mackerel sky, as cold as sea water, sprinkled with foam. The cows stood with their backs to the wind, and their red coats darkened when the hair was blown the wrong way. The banks were full of dead weeds, black and red; tangled in grey bennets. The muddy road was full of shallow pools like tomato soup, which threw up drops as high as our heads. And the trap, dipping and rolling in old ruts and new holes, nearly jerked us out of our seats.

'Thank God,' Lucy said. 'They haven't put down this beastly tar in *our* lanes – in the north every road is black – devil's roads.'

'I heard that your Tolbrook congregation was less than it used to be.'

'It's finished. Old Mother Brown was the last.'

'So the Benjamites also feel the religious slump.'

'Each week brothers have fallen away. There's the moor now – did you ever see such a colour – blue-black fire – I try to remember it but I never can.'

'Why does a religion die, Lucy? It's very strange when you think of it. Why do people cease to take any interest in God. Even the simple people who know nothing about theological quarrels.'

'The people only want something for nothing,' Lucy said. 'We are well rid of them, as I tell the master.'

'Then your sect will die.'

'I believe. And the master, bless the lamb.'

'You aren't a religion.'

'Drive, Tommy, drive. Get her head up – make her go.'

'It's very rough here.' But I touched the mare, and in her surprise she cantered a few paces, rocking the trap like a small boat in a rough sea.

Lucy burst out laughing. 'Make her go, Tommy. Oh, how I love that rattle of real iron tires on a real road – I haven't heard it for years.'

'Your Benjamites will die out, Lucy.'

'Well, what does that matter. Besides, there are still two or three hundred of the true believers.'

'Not very many if you are the only ones to be saved out of the whole world.'

'I think it is a good many, considering what the world is. How many ought to be saved out of a thousand million lice and bugs?'

'You shouldn't talk like that, Lucy.'

'What are you afraid of, Tommy?' Lucy turned her laughing face towards me. 'Your people can't hear me. You're like an old maid, when consols go down to fifty. A pity you never married. But I suppose you were afraid of a wife.'

Lucy brought me no consolation, no encouragement. Yet already it seemed that the heavy weight which had oppressed me was lifted. And her glance round the hall as she entered Tolbrook, her peculiar shiver of delight, as she grasped herself by the forearms, and turned up her sharp chin to look, her cry, 'So here I am again' made me laugh and gave me a sudden exhilaration.

I also found myself looking round at walls so familiar that I had not looked at them perhaps for years, except to ask if they needed repairs; and I had suddenly the indescribable sense of life rising in my soul; of power.

There is a drawing of the raising of Lazarus, by Rembrandt, which expresses, as no words could do, that sense. He looks at the people standing round his grave with a face of haggard amazement, as if he is saying, 'This is what it is to be alive, and when I was alive, I did not know it.'

Once more I walked with Lucy through the rooms, through the yard and the familiar fields, and at every step, we recalled some childish event.

And through Lucy's eyes, I saw again the richness which had been given to us; the fortune of those who have had a lively childhood and who have never lost their homes.

Lucy made it for me by the power of her spirit, which created again that beauty. For I did not see then that beauty must be made again and that when love dies, the form that expressed it is also dead.

132

Ann left this morning, in snow, a quick heavy fall which has given us a blue sky. All the rooms in the house are filled with its reflection. It is as if the sky itself had entered into them, bringing an air more pure; a stillness more serene than any known on the earth's surface. Here in my mother's bedroom, long dismantled, I seem to float in another world, far detached from the turmoil of history; and full of another brightness, another tension, than the fire and conflict of human life. I could believe that my mother's spirit has returned to this place in which her heart suffered, in private, so long and uncomplaining a martyrdom; in which her spirit created for itself, so strong a fortress, transparent to our eyes, and therefore indestructible even by Lucy's fury. The heavy mahogany furniture, the four poster have gone. My tenants preferred twin bedsteads from the Tottenham Court Road. The great bed was too stately for their modesty. It asked too much. It imposed a grandeur which was insupportable, and therefore laughable to nice people whose modest ideal was that unassuming comfort in which every luxury and indulgence can be enjoyed without even the sense of privilege; with the warm security of maggots in a dustbin, under yesterday's ashes. My young millionaire from London plumed himself on his lack of ceremony, on not even possessing a dress coat.

Only the plaster work remains from the magnificence of the past; some absurd cherubic angels blowing trumpets and playing dulcimers and zithers on the ceiling. Who, in this borrowed light of the sky, seem to give out from their bulging cheeks and dinner plate halos, a faint radiance of pale blue light, as if some angelic essence, transmitted from above, made them recall their birth, in an age of romantic faith.

'Excuse me, sir.' Mrs Ramm is peeping round the door.

'Yes, yes, yes.' I jump off the bed.

'It's Mr Farley about the dairy boiler – he says it's leaking.'

'Go and ask the mistress – let him write to her.'

'When is the mistress coming back, sir?'

'I don't expect she's ever coming back' I say, to my own surprise. And I walk past the woman and go down the corridor, as if I am busy. I am not going to be troubled any more about burnt boilers or sick cows, or stopped drain pipes or damp walls. I am too old. I have my soul to make which ought to have been made long ago.

And perhaps it is a good thing that Ann has gone. I was getting spoilt with company. I had got used to chattering with my nurse. So that now I miss her and wander from room to room, as restless as a hungry man who keeps walking, because he is afraid to sit down and accept starvation.

It is easy to lose the art of being lonely, and fatal to an old man, the last of his generation, who, if he wants any warmth in his heart, must feed his own fire. For whom loneliness must be a natural condition. A thousand times in my life, I have called myself a lonely man. Even while Lucy was alive, but estranged from me, I pitied myself for a lonely and worried old bachelor. But in fact, I did not know what real loneliness meant, for even when I was not thinking of Lucy, or thought of her with anger, my soul knew her presence and her life. Even when I hated Lucy, she was my sister, dear to my very bones.

And perhaps it was a premonition, in my secret feeling, of her loss, that made me more furious against her in the last month of her life than ever before. Within a day of her arrival we were quarrelling because she would not see a doctor. And I remember my rage while I stood in the hall and shouted to her on the stairs, 'Die, then, if you like, but I'm damned if I bury you here.' A scene that now, while I stand in this silent hall, filled with the pale snow light, as of a house long dead and changed into a ghost, can still move my flesh with horror, and with bitterness.

Lucy, in return, threatened to leave Tolbrook. 'You won't need to bury me anywhere. I'll bury you first.'

Yet both of us were equally furious with Amy for breaking in upon our family reunion. She wrote to Lucy: 'If you won't have a professional nurse, let me nurse you. I have had a good deal of experience, you know, especially of fevers.'

I was especially angry, because my only hope of seeing proper treatment for Lucy was a trained nurse; and now, of course, she said that such a nurse would be waste of money, since Amy was available.

I daresay her real motive was contempt and disgust for the body which thwarted her will, and irritation with Amy. She said in effect: 'If Amy thinks she can nurse me, let her try the experiment on me and we shall see how it turns out.'

I had not met Amy since her expulsion by Gladys. And I think she rarely saw John himself in his last years. We exchanged letters at Easter and Christmas, but between while I sometimes did not know her address; years had passed without my counting them, and now when Amy came to Tolbrook, from some south coast boarding house, I was surprised to find her changed. She did not seem to stoop, but she had a rounded back, broad and soft, and she complained of breathlessness. Her hair was the silver white of an old woman; and she had an old woman's deliberate cautious movements, exasperating to the older Lucy. But she would never sit down if there was anyone to be waited on. At Tolbrook she was once more the servant.

'She's stupider than ever,' Lucy would say. 'It's really a wonder what she thinks about.'

And in fact Amy never read a book or a newspaper, beyond the morning's births and deaths. Only sometimes, when she was forced to be at rest, on a journey, or in the evening, before the lamps were brought in, when it was too dark to sew, one saw a look of confusion and wonder on her face. Her eyebrows would go up, her lips purse, her hand would go to her cheek; she would gaze at the fire with the expression of one who asks, 'What am I doing here – how have I passed through such things?'

It was at such times that Lucy would utter her sharpest speeches to Amy, saying 'Is that shirt meant for Tommy or Loftus?'

Amy would then start and take the offending shirt out of her basket. 'For Loftus, dear.'

'Loftus in a pink shirt – he would sooner die.'

Loftus in fact was an extremely smart and correct young soldier, who on his rare visits had charmed us all and especially Lucy. I think Lucy, as well as Amy, had paid his debts. And she seemed always to be defending him against some imaginary critic.

Amy, having adjusted her spectacles three times and looked with mild indignation at the fading light, would say, 'Do you call it pink?'

'I wonder are you colour blind, Amy – that would explain a lot.'

Amy, understanding that this was a criticism of her taste in dress, would answer mildly, 'Bill always liked me in blue and I always think it looks nice in itself.'

'Bill hated you in blue. And he was quite right – it makes you look like a beetroot in sugar paper.'

'Queen Alexandra was fond of blue and she had very good taste,' Amy said. 'Of course she wasn't my colouring.'

'You don't think that matters,' Lucy said, angrily twisting her shrunken yellow face.

'Yes, but people can't very well object to blue,' Amy said, meaning perhaps that the Queen had justified blue and so she was entitled to please herself, by wearing blue frocks, even if they did not suit her. Amy's peculiar logic, her dress, her deliberate manner, her cheerful ignorance, all irritated my poor sister to extremity; I think, above all, she was irritated by Amy's silent uncomplaining grief. She herself had never hidden her feelings. She liked to talk about her dead, to express her bitterness or her pleasure. Dying, she could still make jokes, talk nonsense and laugh; quarrel with me about trifles, or fly out against some old enemy.

With Amy she quarrelled a dozen times a day. She was the worst possible patient and neither obeyed Amy's rules, nor took any remedies. Yet if Amy was out of sight she would ask for her. The two women were inseparable and deeply concerned in each other.

'I can't understand how Lucy could bring herself to live with a man like Brown,' Amy would say. 'So coarse and common and not even faithful to her. She is so fine. She does not really care twopence for anybody. If only there were more like her.' And Lucy would say of Amy, 'It makes me rage to see her so lonely. Bill had no business to die like that. But, of course, she killed John by letting him marry that filthy creature. And, after all, she doesn't know how to appreciate life. Too slow.'

These words of Lucy, even then, gave me a shock of pity, and I asked her, 'Have you been so happy, Lucy?'

'Happy?' she answered briskly. 'Yes, I am so happy to be at home again that I could dance –'

'Yes, at home.'

'And with the master, too, praise the lamb – I've been happier still with the poor master. Yes, it's been glorious sometimes – to hear him speak, and feel how he moved those savages, it threw a glory on the whole world. I'll never forget one meeting – it was last winter – he carried us all away, even that pig-woman Ella was sobbing, and I was flying in the air. And afterwards we walked through the frosty lanes and the dumps like mountains, it was a Welsh mining place – the finest mutton you ever tasted. I only wanted some home-made jelly.' And, laughing, she said, 'How I love being alive – I can't imagine myself dead and the world going on without me. I should like to be the wandering Jew, and go on for ever.'

We were walking through the lower floor, which was now the farthest extent of Lucy's exercise. She could now barely drag herself with the help of my arm or Amy's, through the four rooms and back again. We were economizing in fires for lack of servants and the house was very cold, especially in the winter. Often we both wore overcoats, as if for a journey into the fields, and I remember that Lucy would stop in the big room and look out of the windows at the sleet falling on the grass blackened by rotting leaves, the streaming trees, and the clouds hanging down in long grey rags like torn sails, and say, 'Isn't it grand to be out,' as if the carpet were grass, and the pictures, the chairs and sofas about us were natural objects.

She loved especially the rattle of sleet or hail on the big windows, and when I reminded her that she had always hated cold and, above all, wet weather, she answered sharply: 'What nonsense, Tommy. I never hated any weather at Tolbrook.'

'I wish you hadn't gone away from us.'

'So do I, but I had to, and I must go back next month. The master wrote yesterday.'

'But that's impossible and wrong. You can't go back. It will kill you. Why should you go back? Robert will be coming next week – back from school.'

'My dear Tommy, you don't propose to lock me up here.'

'You'll have Robert here. You know you can't go back. You only suggest it out of perversity.'

'Rubbish, Tommy. I must go back because I'm needed.' And the old dispute broke out with more than its old ferocity. For as we grew older we grew more rough. We did not mind hurting each other. And this was not because we were hardened to blows, but because we were more desperate.

I wanted to say to Lucy now all those bitter things which I had kept silent and hidden. 'You are the complete egotist, you live only for yourself.'

And Lucy answered, as usual, that I was a mean small-minded creature, who had crept away from life into a woman's pocket. 'You hung upon me, and then it was that poor creature Julie. I'm not surprised you drove her to drink.'

She was too weak to let go of my arm, and while we disputed we still walked slowly through the rooms.

'I may be disgusting,' I said, 'but you are a spoilt obstinate vain woman who has made a god out of herself. Yes, you think you are a martyr to religion, but you are only worshipping yourself and sacrificing to your fearful pride.'

'Yes, a coward – a mean stupid coward!' Lucy gasped, hanging on my arm to keep herself from falling.

When I recall that quarrel my muscles contract. I jump up from my chair and exclaim aloud. I shiver as at the recollection of a crime. Why did I lose my temper with a sister who was more dear to me than anyone in the world? Why did I hate her so that even to her death I was furious against her and continually tried to hurt her?

Our quarrels were not easily made up. We knew how to hurt each other. We should have fought for days if it had not been for that old rule of my father's that all family quarrels must be made up before the last bedside prayer.

That rule had not applied in the time of our separation. Some of our fights had continued for months, and even years; like the battle of the chair. But strangely, when we were in a house together, we obeyed it. I can remember sitting in my room feeling against Lucy the savage anger which she alone could rouse in me. Yet I did not go to bed. It was as though I could not go. I did not think 'I must not pray until I have made it up with Lucy.' But the compulsion lay upon me as if the very air of the old house had within it an order of tradition, a platonic form, shaping my conduct.

So at last I said to myself: 'I suppose I'd better say good night to the woman – she's really not responsible.' And I got up and went to her room. But before I had opened the door it sprang open before me and Lucy stood there laughing and holding up her arms. It was strange to see in the little old woman, dried as a mummy, with her witch's nose and chin, her fierce eyes, the gestures of the beautiful young girl, frank and coquettish. 'I heard you coming, Tommy. I knew you would have to come – because of Papa.'

Even then that malicious delight in my defeat might have driven me away. But Lucy, seeing me hesitate, grasped at my arms to pull me into the room, crying: 'No, no. You must stay and talk to me. Do you remember –' And we talked half the night, like children, with our arms round each other's waists; so bound together by love that we seemed to have but one heart and one delight between us.

What was that heart, that delight, in two creatures so different. It was something deeper than the love of man and woman, brother and sister. It was the very soul of the home, of the family, it was living history. My father lived there still, not in himself, but in what he had given to our memories, and to our minds which seized upon them. When we laughed at some old trifling joke it was with a laughter which carried us away, out of ourselves. And when we spoke of Edward, of Bill, of our father and mother, it was with a love quite different from what we had felt for them alive. It was something that we had never known before, greater and deeper than ourselves. We were enchanted and we cried together: 'Why did we never appreciate our father enough? Why did we never see the staunchness of Bill?'

And when at last we separated we kissed each other with warmth which said, 'We are the last; we mustn't lose each other.'

Yet our quarrels broke out again on that same day. We were obliged to quarrel, by that very sincerity which belonged to our family feeling. And Lucy, when she gave me power, gave me anger.

We were quarrelling bitterly within half an hour of her death. Lucy, for the last time in her life, lost her temper with me and cried: 'What have I got to do with Bill? He was really ill, and I am not. I certainly won't let any of your doctors poke me about. And I won't drink any of Amy's poison. If she hasn't enough sense to let me alone, she certainly hasn't enough to cure me.'

A few minutes later we found her lying on the floor in a faint. We lifted her into a chair, and Amy ran to send for a doctor. 'This is our chance,' she said. 'She can't stop us now.'

Lucy opened her eyes suddenly and said: 'I wasn't really fainting,' like one who denies that he has been asleep.

'You're very ill, Lucy. You mustn't move.'

'I don't want to move.' And then she said in a surprised voice: 'I suppose I'm not going to die.'

'No, of course not, Lucy.'

'I feel very queer . . . I can't see properly.' And her voice was full of indignation and surprise. 'I do believe I'm dying.'

Her agitation was so great that I had to keep her from struggling out of the chair.

'I won't, I won't,' she said. 'Why, I'm not sixty yet. And Robert coming home. Let me up, Tom. You fool, let me up.' She was trying to shout at me, but her voice was failing.

'But you must keep still, my darling,' I begged her. 'Don't exhaust yourself. You'll be all right soon. Amy has gone to call the doctor.'

'Nonsense. I tell you I'm dying. Don't let her come in. We don't want any strangers.' She was pushing out her hands as if to thrust someone away, trying to force her voice which was not louder than a raucous whisper. 'Tommy, promise me, keep Robert away from them . . . they don't understand children . . . and make a gentleman of him. He can do what he likes afterwards, but first, a gentleman . . . keep him at school . . . Latin . . . with a proper education . . . you'll find I've left enough money.' And then putting up her arms, 'Promise me, Tom, quickly. There's no time – quickly, Tom.'

She fell into unconsciousness again and never recovered from it. She had a kidney disease which might easily have been cured by treatment. Fortunately, the doctor arrived before her death, and gave us a certificate without a *post mortem.*

133

I did not only miss Lucy; I was deprived of her as one is deprived of some essential organ. Virtue had gone from me and from the house. It was now that Tolbrook began to frighten me by something more than loneliness. I felt for the first time in its quiet corridors, what I feel now, the weight of a deserted and childless home. As if some old unhappy creature hung upon my shoulder, with the crushing force of masonry.

Ann has written me two letters. It appears that this girl is one of those who do not know how to show affection, save with a pen. But this very kindness convinces me that she will not come back. My happiness with her was illusion. 'She got tired of Tolbrook and of me,' I said. 'And why not? A clever girl buried in this hole with a dull old man.' I thought that she had come to love Tolbrook, but her sentiment for the place was only a passing interest. She came to family prayers to see how Jane Austen's characters felt, and she set the old rooms in order to know her father better. And she knows neither him nor me. She belongs wholly to the young world, curious, scientific.

> 'Professor B, profound in his acumen,
> Knows everything, as eunuchs know their women.'

I miss the boy's voice, his bare feet running in the passage, from the bathroom to the nursery.

When living and dead inhabit the same house, then the dead live, and life is increased to that house. In Ann's eyes I saw her father, and sometimes in her voice there was the tone of Lucy's courage. In the child's step, how many children ran along the upper corridor. But when the living go from a house, then the dead are cut off in their death. And death stands in every room, silent and unmeaning.

The servants are watching me. When at night I can't sleep and go to Lucy's room, or to my mother's, now entirely empty, I hear boards creak and voices whispering. No doubt Mrs Ramm has orders to wire or call the police, if I should try to escape.

And at dawn, when I fall down upon a chair and sleep, I have such terrifying dreams that I would rather not sleep at all. This morning I dreamed that Tolbrook itself was growing smaller and smaller. The walls closed in; the roof came down upon me. The house became a coffin and it seemed that I had been shut up in it alive. The undertakers were screwing down the lid. I heard even the grating of the screw in the hard wood and tried to cry out that I was not dead yet; to strike up against the coffin lid. But my arms were pinioned and my jaw was tied. I could neither speak nor move.

And what was most terrible; all my body, quite apart from me, seemed full of bitterness against me. As if every cell were complaining, 'What has he done with us? We are betrayed.'

154

I waked up, streaming with cold sweat, in the saloon. I had been lying in a broken-down arm-chair, opposite a binder, whose arms seemed to quiver at me, like the whiskers of some devilish insect, asking 'What is this intrusive creature?' It moved and stretched out a monstrous eye upon a thick stalk. I jumped up and saw that this eye was Mrs Ramm's head. She had been hiding behind the machine. She said to me in a trembling voice, 'You ought to be in bed, sir – you're not well.'

'Agnes Ramm,' I said, 'if you go on watching me, I shall push you downstairs.'

I could see that this frightened the fool. She went off at once to send a report to her mistress. I went upstairs, dressed in my town clothes and packed a bag with my notebooks and a clean shirt.

Then I turned back the carpet and opened the bell trap. And again I was able to congratulate myself on my foresight in keeping always a store of change. There was in the trap over forty half-crowns and a dozen florins, dropped down the crack, no doubt in mistake for the nobler coin, on a dark evening, or when there was danger of surprise. There were also twenty-seven letters to Sara, written since her silence and kept for the address, which had, by some means, been withheld from me. These letters I also packed; they contained much private matter; and divided the silver between my pockets and the toes of my pumps, which, stuffed with socks, form an excellent travelling cash box.

I then went down the nursery stairs and out of the nursery door, into the rose garden. It was not yet seven. No one even imagined an escape, carried out with such speed and resolution.

And since I did not need to go for cash to Queensport, where I should certainly have been recognized, I was able to take a bus direct to Plymouth where I safely joined the main line express.

I can't describe my astonishment and delight in this escape, in the rapid motion, so long forgotten, of the train. The telegraph wires hopping by like frogs; and the great trees, still bare, sailing down the wind like the rigged ships, I used to see towed into Queensport.

'After all,' I thought, 'I am a Wilcher – I am like Bill and Lucy; like my father who spent half his life in camps and lodgings. It is in my blood, which is all English. The Latin, the Celt strike root; they want only to make a home somewhere; and if they must wander they take with them always a dream or legend of home. But the English soul is a wanderer, a seeker. You find it in every corner of the world, dressed in some local imagination; studying Chinese antiquities, or ready to assure you that salvation is in the Hindu yoga. The English have taught every nation to admire its own culture – they go to the Pacific, and say "Glorious people, keep your nakedness and your sacrifices, they are far preferable to our own miserable governments and ideas"; they go to Africa and become Mahomedan; they sail among the South Sea Islands and say, "This is paradise and here only I have found civilized people, beautiful and kind, wise and holy"; they are enraged when they see some barbarous race put off its beads and its wildness, and study English and wear trousers. Then they cry, "What are you doing in trousers, you poor wretch? Why do you put on that hideous dress of degenerate Europe?" and so on. No,' I think, gazing from the window at a flying village on its green carpet, 'when I wanted to be a missionary, when I dressed up like a Hindu to talk about the Indian wisdom, I was fulfilling my destiny. And that house which I loved and hated so much has been my treacherous Delilah. It brought me back from God, from India, from Sara. But not again.'

In fact, I was in London before two o'clock, and no one stopped me at the station barriers. I had escaped.

My plan was to go to Holloway and obtain Sara's address from the chaplain. And within two hours I had the address in my hand. Owen's Lane, Lewisham, an easy journey. I took a room for that night in a central hotel, a great barrack with many hundred rooms; for I knew that if the family pursued me, they would seek me in one of my usual stopping places in Kensington.

135

I was again in London; but, as never before, a stranger, a man without a home. I have said that it was the art of a woman like Sara, a servant bred, to make herself a home everywhere. But now I saw that to the wanderer all his world is home. He is the least homeless of men because he possesses all, the earth and the sky, the houses and the trees, with the eyes of a homekeeper, and all men and women are his familiars.

This was the secret I had discovered when, at the outbreak of war, I stood in a row with the other volunteers and found that we were friends. We had left our homes to be at one in the family of those who have thrown themselves naked upon fortune.

In London I found cold and bright weather. The sky was as pale as glass and the few small clouds seemed like snow flocks or the tops of hidden Alps whose lower slopes were hidden in a blue-green mist. The pavements rang in this cold air like bells and on every side one saw pink cheeks, pink noses and sparkling eyes and teeth. I could not help laughing as I walked through the streets, for I thought, 'It is said that war hangs over this unhappy world, that the people are full of foreboding and uncertainty. But see these young men in their spring overcoats, these girls laughing among their furs and chattering like pies, what is politics to them but nonsense in the papers. They think not of danger or death, but life.'

And I felt one with them. I was young again, without a care. For that is what it is to be young; to be careless. The young are born pilgrims. Babies, as soon as they can walk, begin to explore the world. As every nurse knows, their first idea is to escape from their keepers. They are free born and look upon the whole earth as their possession. To be free is to be young.

And as I walked through Trafalgar Square, under the glittering mountains of the sky, I kept smiling at the people, who seemed, as far as I could tell through my spectacles, to smile at me, I even felt an inclination to say to them, 'I have come to town to get married. Yes, I am starting a new life, with the woman I love; or, more strictly speaking, a woman I sometimes love and always esteem,' and so forth. Just as formerly, when I had stood among the queue of war recruits, in 1914, I had wanted to tell the story of my life to anyone who would listen to me; and I myself had heard with pleasure a great many rather long and somewhat dull confessions.

And at last my confidence did overflow into speech. I found myself talking to a gentleman in a brown bowler at the corner of Pall Mall, opposite the Athenaeum. Possibly I had been attracted by the hat whose peculiar colour revealed an expansive nature. I was saying to him that it was a fine evening for so early in the year; that London was looking its best. And then I told him that in fact I'd come to town on a very pleasant errand, etc., not unconnected with matrimony, and so on. The old gentleman, who was obviously an important person, answered very reasonably that it was a fine evening, and a good idea. He wished me luck, etc. But his eyes, which were very round and prominent, said that I was either drunk or foolish.

This warned me that I was in no position to be unconventional. But so it was that ten minutes later I found myself again in conversation with a newspaper seller outside the National Gallery.

To him, adapting my words and manner, I said that it was tip-top weather for a holiday. 'And, in fact,' I said, 'I'm on the loose – I'm taking to the roads from now on.' And since the man remained silent and serious, I added, to show that I had spoken in joke, 'I speak figuratively, of course.'

Almost at the same moment I seemed to remember the man's face; that he knew me; and that he was planning some means of detaining me. 'Ridiculous,' I said to myself; and smiling, I made a further remark about the gypsy in every human soul, etc. But the man, who had a peculiarly white face, continued to stare. And suddenly I began to feel alarm. But I was walking away with dignity, when I almost ran into a policeman.

Now since that unhappy time, from which Sara rescued me, when I actually came into the hands of the police, I have always had peculiar feelings in their presence. When a policeman looks at me, I never know quite what I am going to do. And this time, I jumped, and then, gazing at the man, said in a loud voice, 'I can see you know who *I* am.'

The man, who was, I suppose, coming off duty, and had, like so many policemen, a very short nose, looked at me attentively, but with that careful lack of interest which policemen show on such occasions. He answered at last, in an unexpectedly brisk lively tone, 'No, sir, I'm afraid not.'

'My name is Wilcher,' I said. 'Thomas Loftus Wilcher, and I've just made a remarkable smart get-away from my family who thought they were going to shut me up in a – But never mind. Good afternoon' – and I walked off with even more dignity, though I was almost fainting with indignation. I was furious with the police, with everybody. And when I got to my hotel I went and locked myself in my room. I did not come out even for dinner. And I thought, 'Nobody in this world understands anybody – nobody except Sara. For Sara has charity in her soul.'

136

It was that misunderstanding which made me a criminal. For one day, just after Lucy's death, I happened to be walking in the park; and such a weight of desperation fell upon me that I wanted to cry out or kick the railings.

It was a Friday. Always the worst day in the week. For first, it was that day, before I went to Tolbrook, when I realized that once more I had not been able to get to the end of anything. Unfinished work was piled upon my table; and more problems awaited me at home.

And all this work was like draining water in a sieve. For the whole social fabric was obviously dissolving. The European currencies had already collapsed; and we, in England, were asking ourselves how long we should be an exception.

Secondly, Friday was the day of my visit to Julie. And there was no doubt, since John's death, that Julie and I hated each other.

Yet, because of this hate, this tension, I must be particularly careful not to give her cause of offence. And all our intercourse must be guided by a fixed routine; as, during the war, in some dangerous areas of the front line, we had been guided by cords stretched from one piece of cover to another.

So I had always to enter with an air of gaiety and to cry, 'How are you, my dear?'

Often Julie would not answer me. Sometimes I could not even see her. For she would sit for hours silent and motionless, doing nothing, in a half-dark room. It was only after a moment, while I looked round, possibly with relief, that I could distinguish her in some corner; a pale bloated mass which I had taken for a heap of cushions.

The room was still kept neat and clean by Julie's devoted maid, but it had become revolting to me. I would say to Julie, 'What, sitting in the dark, my dear – let me turn up the light. Oh, I see, you've been reading some Moore, *A Drama in Muslin*.'

'No, I wasn't reading it – I know it by heart.'

'Nothing new from the library.'

'Nothing good – everything is so dull.'

But often she would not answer me at all. If she had been drinking she was always in an angry mood and could not bear to speak to me. I knew that she brought men in, not the young soldiers, who like the poets of thirty years before, had found wives and jobs and settled in life, but various dependants or failures. One was a broken actor older than myself; another was an ex-stock jobber, who had been in prison. But even when these hangers-on were present, Julie showed no animation or pleasure. I would find her drinking with one or another in silence; and they would look at me with contempt and irritation; as if to ask, 'What do you come here for, to interrupt us in our contemplation?'

Sometimes Julie did not speak to me for weeks; yet every Friday or Saturday, I would stay the night with her. Why did I perform an act become so hateful to me. You say it was habit. But habit is not whim. My habit of going to Julie once a week, was also her habit. If I broke mine, I broke also something of hers. And I could not know how that break would affect her. I said to her once, 'If you would rather I didn't come in, you have only to bolt your bedroom door.'

But she did not bolt the door. And I continued to go to her bed, for fear of some worse catastrophe to us both. For I felt in Julie already that sullen rage against the world, which in the end brought her to an asylum.

I used to urge her to go to church. 'You are a believer, Julie,' I would say, 'You have faith – how long is it since you went to mass?'

And she answered me in her slow voice, which had still the dignity of its elocution, 'I don't go because I don't choose to go.'

'But isn't that a mortal sin in your church?'

And suddenly furious, she would cry, 'Why can't you leave me in peace?' These fits of rage were terrifying in the gentle, calm Julie. I would swear, after each outburst, that I should never see her again.

But the time had not come when Sara, by bringing back to me some joy in life, gave me power of faith to take that fearful risk of a breach with Julie, which confronts me still with the question, 'Did I murder Julie's soul?' A responsibility to be borne only by the living faith which knows in the heart 'I have done evil but I may yet do good.'

I dared not leave Julie then and so, as surely as the week-end returned, I would go back to her.

But on this Friday, to my great relief, I found myself twenty minutes early for Julie. I sat down on a free seat. But such was the pressure of my agitation in these days, that I could not sit still for a moment, I jumped up at once.

It was a fine evening in late spring. The tulips were open and there were many strollers gazing at those unflowerlike objects; civil servants, typists, etc. Now, I did not usually notice people at all in those days. I was enclosed in fears, I had sunk into the darkness of anxiety, and there was no Lucy to light within my cell the flame of rage or love. But as I jumped up, I collided with a group of passing girls. I apologized and one of them smiled. And now as I walked up and down, I could not help noticing all these girls who crowded the path. I noticed their ugly hats, their short unbecoming frocks, which revealed so many ill-shaped legs, and especially their faces, which seemed so bored or merely blank. 'In my young days,' I thought, 'no girl permitted herself to look like that in public; arrogant, or blank. If she had not the sense to seem attractive, then her mother instructed her.'

Especially there was one young girl, in a scarlet hat, who passed me three times in ten minutes, with a face so blank and stupid, that I could not bear it. She had no more expression, as Lucy would have said, than a new potato. Only her eyes showed some mild intelligence as they examined the dresses, the shoes, stockings, hats and, finally, the faces of other girls. Yet she was not ill-favoured; her features were neat, her complexion healthy.

'Good gracious,' I thought, in my exasperation, when I passed her for the third time. 'Look at you, young and passably good looking, and nothing to trouble about, and all you can do is to gaze about you like a Dutch cheese. Wake up, for heaven's sake.' And then I thought, 'But, of course, she doesn't know how to wake up. She is some quiet little typist, who passes her time between a dull office and a prim little suburb. And she has come to the park with some vague notion of seeing the dresses and the flowers, and perhaps having some adventure. Or, if she doesn't think so, the little donkey, that is her real motive. She is secretly hoping for an adventure.'

And then at once I thought, 'Suppose next time we passed, I said something to her – some little compliment, or perhaps something more particular, even a little startling.'

'Pooh,' I said to myself, 'you old fool – she would just think you a nasty old man or she would call for a policeman. And, besides,' I said to myself, 'I shan't see her again. That's four times. Even a goose like that can't walk up the path for a fifth time, with a face like an unaddressed envelope. No, no,' I said to myself, 'You won't see her again.'

I turned round and looked sharp about me. But I could not see her until I had nearly reached Hyde Park Corner. And then, suddenly, I caught sight of her absurd red hat and pink nose. She was sitting on a free seat beside the path and looking at the passers. And the next moment I found myself on the same seat, almost touching her. My heart was beating so that I could scarcely breathe. But my jaws grinned, and I muttered something. I saw the girl's eyes fixed on me with the same mild curiosity. She said, 'I beg your pardon.' And I began to pay her compliments, and also to tell her how nice it was for her to be young; and to have all her life before her, and so forth. In fact, I was simply amazed at myself, especially when I went on to say that no doubt she would find a nice young man soon, who would teach her how to make better use of her time – and so on.

All this time she was looking at me with the same blank expression. Only her face grew gradually redder. All at once, she raised her hand and knocked my hat into a flower bed. Then she got up, faced me, and still with the same wooden face, took her dress by back and front, gave a little jerk and wriggle, to get it down. And she walked off.

I picked up my hat and ran after her. 'And now, I suppose you will call the police.'

But she only looked at me severely and answered, 'I should think you'd better have someone to look after you.' A nice sensible good natured child, with good principles. Probably a member of the church. I felt such esteem for her, mixed with my exasperation, that I didn't know whether to pinch her behind or kiss her hands. However, she jumped suddenly on a bus, and I found myself alone on the pavement.

The surprising episode left me so confused and excited that I had walked almost to Apsley House before I perceived that I was wasting time. I then looked at my notebook to discover my next engagement, and I saw, of course, in the correct day, among a mass of pencil memoranda, a J in ink underlined twice in red. And I recollected that this was Friday, my day for Julie. I can't describe the sense of disgust and futility, with which I then hastened to West Street; and entering with an air necessarily more brisk and friendly, because of my lateness, cried, 'Good evening, my dear – I'm afraid I'm a little late.'

Lucy used to call me a hypocrite. But this was a typical piece of incomprehension. Any man who was not a brute must have pretended some kind feeling to Julie; and since she was still a sensitive and understanding creature, the imitation had to be good. And so it was the more troublesome to me.

137

I was not only astonished at my conduct with the young girl in the park; I was horrified at myself. For I had used some phrases to her which were calculated to shock her modesty, and which, it seemed to me, I had chosen for the purpose. To wake her up. To excite her. To make something happen, for myself as well as for her. I could not believe how such words had passed my lips. But two nights later I was talking in the same manner to a woman who might have been one of my own servants. For it was twilight and the place was my own street.

How I began this conversation I do not know. I found myself as before, beside the young woman and in full speech, before I knew what I was doing. And again my last words to her were, as she escaped into a house, 'I suppose you will tell the police.'

For I have no doubt that part of the fascination, the spell which this new life of adventure cast upon me, was the danger of ruin and disgrace. They say that if a service be only dangerous enough, it will always find volunteers. I must not say that I wanted to be arrested. Many times in the next weeks, after one of these enterprises, I would lie awake all night shaking in terror at every sound and saying to myself, 'That's the police.' And next day, mixed with my self-loathing, there was triumph, as if I had won a great success against the laws of the country, and decency, and of everything that I respected. And as my adventures became more bold and more scandalous, so the loathing and the triumph increased.

Part of that triumph, which proved it to be the devil's, was in its distortion of the whole moral world. Having abandoned the pure light of Heaven, I saw not merely my own bad deeds, but the whole world of my action, illuminated by the fantastic glare of putrefaction. So now I delighted in opposing a suggestion in the firm, that soft collars should be permitted in office hours; not, as formerly, out of loyalty to the old Westminster collar, which I wore myself, but because the senior partner, old Pamplin, was inclined to give way on the point. I enjoyed telling Pamplin that he was growing slack in his ideas. For he was a great upholder of duty; Church and State. And the times appalled him. Every week, with his beaked nose and round blank eyes surrounded by wrinkles, he seemed to grow more like an owl; startled by the collapse of its barn and the intrusion of daylight.

The old man, in his gloomy slow voice, would say to me 'England is finished – no sense of duty anywhere – no honesty – the only question anyone asks, what can I get out of it?' And I would answer, that on the contrary, I thought the country was doing very well. 'All these new houses, new schools – it's astonishing. Democracy may be bad at war, but it is good at peace,' etc.

'I don't like your new houses, and what do they learn in the new schools, egotism, materialism; to grab, and to do the least work for the most money.' Pamplin was the kind of Tory of whom Edward wrote:

> Leave politics to us, the tories cry,
> For politicians cheat and rob and lie.

Now the truth was, that I myself felt such uneasiness about the state of the country that I was ready to jump into the Thames; but now, out of mere perversity, I would purse up my mouth into a devil's grin, and say, 'It seems to me that, as a democracy, we ought to be carrying out even bigger changes. For instance, in the law,' an idea, which, of course, made the old man turn quite green with fright and anger. For he loved the old law almost as much as I did.

In the same way, I enjoyed arguing with the vicar, that what we wanted at Tolbrook was the real old country sermon on hell fire; nothing but hell could do the farmers good. And then I would go out and look about in our own country lanes, to catch some factory girl coming home from Queensport on her bicycle.

I find in my commonplace book this quotation, which I must have written down at the very time when I was pursuing this strange and horrible life.

'The soul which is deprived of its essential activity, in works of faith and imagination, quickly corrupts. Like all spiritual things, enclosed within the prison walls of fear and doubt, it grows quickly monstrous and evil. It is like a plant shut away in darkness, which, still living and striving, throws out, instead of green leaves and bright flowers, pallid tentacles, and fruit so strange, so horrible that it is like a phantasm seen in a dream; something at once comic and terrifying. The dumb stupid creature appears suddenly to be possessed of a devil's imagination.'

The devil loves to look upon his own corruption. Despair is his secret joy.

I had my narrow escapes. I was assaulted and threatened. A young man who intervened on one occasion when a young woman showed offence, attacked me with a stick; but I nearly ran him through with my steel umbrella. I remembered Edward's old advice, founded on history, that, with the white arm, the thrust has always defeated the cut. So in this little battle, the force of evil, better instructed, utterly defeated that of virtue, which was left breathless on the ground.

At last, of course, I was caught. Somebody followed me home, and the police came to warn me. They also warned my family. I received a shock. I swore to reform and for some months I did not offend. And then one evening I found myself in a situation more disgraceful than any before. What astonishes me now is that I was not locked up in these years before Sara came to save my soul alive. For I took ever greater risks. The demon, that possessed me, could find pleasure only in defiance.

My family, and especially my niece Blanche, formed the plan of shutting me up. Sara, at a later date, warned me of it; but so far from making me more cautious, I think the warning increased my rashness. I actually welcomed the visits of Blanche's specialists, villains hired to sign away my freedom. I did not know, and I do not know now what qualifications these creatures possessed. They are a special class. I suppose that in the queer monstrous growth of a modern state, they have been developed in one of the darker corners, to fulfil the functions of getting rid, in an easy and respectable manner, of old people who have become troublesome to their families.

Blanche's favourite was a little young old man with a face like a Manchester terrier. His hair was flaxen, his huge eyes were water coloured; his sharp nose was as pale as if powdered; his hollow cheeks were pale green. He was dressed also in a suit of pale yellow tweed; with pale lemon-coloured boots; and he talked to me about his farm in Surrey, his Guernseys, his Punches. But all in a little pale voice; and looking all the time into the air as if he were thinking of something else; a sad memory.

Of course, I told him that I had been the victim of coincidence and that the girl had made advances. That is common form in these cases. Neither of us believed it. But it served to break the ice. Every situation has its polite routine, imposed by its own forms, and the form for a patient of my type is to say, 'I have been the victim of a miscarriage of justice.'

'Yes, essackly. Of course.' The poor little creature sighed. 'Quite so,' and then he proceeded of course to the next step. 'It's very natural, of course, to feel a certain attraction – at any age. A pretty girl, yes,' he sighed again and his eyes wandered over the ceiling. Then he murmured, 'I used to like breaking things myself. Yes, a good smash – I saw an old lady yesterday who had broken all her china and torn all her clothes off and walked down a crowded street, in the rain.'

'And I suppose you're going to lock her up,' I said, getting angry. I knew it was dangerous to support the old lady. But I was tempted by the danger, by the pale eyes of the little terrier, which now turned upon me their cold pale surface. 'What nonsense,' I said, 'I know exactly how she felt. She thought, "Here am I, a nice respectable old lady in a black silk dress, and two petticoats, and stays and drawers, with lace edges, and chemises and all the rest." ' The terrier, while I went through this list of feminine apparel, kept on gazing at me and his eyes seemed to grow more and more like the gelatine, which my clerk used to take a copy of circular letters.

' "Here I am," ' I said, ' "a respectable old lady, and all my brothers and sisters, and nephews and nieces, think that they have me safe, stuck down in this parlour, and tied up with strings and buttons and busks, so that I can't be anything else but be a respectable old relative, until I die and leave them my money. Yes, they think they have got me boxed up for life, and almost as good as in my coffin. But they're wrong, I'm not dead yet. I've got legs and arms, I've got a body. I'm a human being after all. See." And off came the silk dress, the stays and the petticoats and the buttons and the strings, and there she is walking down the street as naked as Eve. I wish I had been there to see.' And I burst out laughing. All this was so dangerous that it made my blood tingle. I trembled with excitement. I thought 'Shall I pull his nose. That would do it.' But all at once he said to me, 'Yes, exactly. I know the feeling. It's quite natural. Quite a lot of people get into prison for no other reason. They even confess to murders they haven't done, you know.'

'Oh, I've heard of that.'

'Anything to break the pattern,' he said. 'personally, I go in for rock climbing.'

'Rock climbing?'

'Yes, it keeps the nerves on the stretch. It acts as a safety valve for all that superfluous energy – and it breaks the pattern. Asylums, you know, have plain walls.'

He sighed and said, 'Of course, there are graffiti – errand boy type. The walls have to be washed down fairly often.'

I hate men who use foreign words, and I grinned angrily at him.

'Why not? Mad people all go that way – it is too much sex that inclines to insanity.' Another very dangerous suggestion.

'No,' he sighed. 'I think they only draw their diagrams to break the proprieties – having nothing else to break.'

We then had a very reasonable and pleasant little talk, about various forms of insanity, perversion, religious mania, etc. I suggested that according to his views the ideal religion would be something quakerish or perhaps anabapists, without any forms at all.

'Not altogether. The free religions produce some of the most violent cases – the older church tends more to private perversions or melancholia. Protestants go in for homicidal mania, and Catholics for hysteria.'

'So the ideal religion would be free church one week and catholicism the next.'

'Possibly.' This was the highest extent of his agreement to anything, 'or perhaps, a judicious mixture of routine and stimulation.'

'Your conclusion points to my own religion, the Church of England. So that even pathology defines it as the best religion.'

'Perhaps. But the question is slightly out of my depth. I am a pathologist, you understand.'

'Yes, that is also a religion – but if you'll permit me, a bad one – a mere polydiabolism or perhaps I should say, a parapolydiabolism, since even your devils are figments, roughly adumbrated in bad grammar and worse logic.'

'There is much in what you say.' In fact, we parted with mutual esteem; or, at least, toleration and suspended judgement.

If the terrier had been paid to drive me mad and then certify me, he was either very stupid or a great fraud. For I was certainly on the very edge of pulling his nose and shouting 'Boo', when he began that sensible and reasonable conversation.

To change the pattern. To get into prison, into an asylum. You would say whole nations grow suddenly bored at the same moment; and tear off their clothes to dive into vice; or fascinated by some dark unknown sea, draw nearer and nearer to it, walking on the very edge of war and destruction.

> All breaks, all passes save God's cry to men.
> Break all, die all, that ye be born again.

139

24, Owen's Lane, was in a terrace of small single fronted houses in worn yellow brick. It was an old street, but in good repair. Doors were painted, bells had been polished. As a judge of property, I could see that it belonged to a good estate, probably a large one; and let to good tenants.

I will admit that I felt strangely confused as I rang the bell. My heart was beating violently and the effort was painful and alarming. No doubt any man's heart may beat at such a crisis in his affairs, but it does not remind him that all his affairs may end at any moment.

The door was opened by a fair young man, wearing dark green trousers, and a tweed coat. He looked at me with suspicion and said, 'And who may you be?'

'Does Mrs Jimson live here?'

'She does. What about it?'

'I should like to see her, if you don't mind. My name is Wilcher.'

'I thought so. Well, you can't see her. I know all about you, Mr Wilcher, and you're not going to come near Mrs Jimson again, if I can help it.'

'But she's expecting me. It's all arranged.'

'Who arranged it? You wrote. That's not arranging. It takes two to make an arrangement. You take my advice, Mr Wilcher, and go away before worse occurs.'

'Excuse me,' I said, 'I came to see Mrs Jimson, and I mean to see her.'

'Don't you come in this house or I'll throw you down the steps.'

I now began to feel myself growing angry. At the same time I reflected that anger was very dangerous to me and my cause. A heart attack would render me quite helpless and defeat me.

'Young man,' I said, 'I don't know who you are, but I must beg you to mind your own business and let me take care of mine.'

'Mrs Jimson is my business, like any decent chap's. That's enough for you.' Then he quickly closed the door. Luckily I had already placed my foot in it.

'I won't get off,' I said, for I was now quite infuriated, 'until Mrs Jimson tells me to go.'

There was then a moment's silence, and it suddenly occurred to me that Sara was also behind the door. I heard something like a whisper. And I said, 'Are you there, Sara, if so, let me in at once.'

There was another silence, and I thought I heard a board creak, as if Sara's heavy body had retreated down the passage. Then the door was flung back and the young man waved his hand in my face. 'Get off, I tell you, or I'll call an officer.'

This mention of the police, of course, enraged me greatly. And I shouted, 'I won't get off. I'm coming in.' And I jumped into the hall. The young man was taken by surprise. I had pushed him a yard or more before he began to push. I had now lost my temper and I was pushing so hard that I might have pushed him right down the passage. But at this moment, my head began to swim, a frightful pain constricted my heart, and I was obliged to stoop down into a very ignominious position.

I then found myself sitting on the doorstep. The door itself had closed behind me, and I perceived that I had been pressed back. Luckily I did not faint. Having taken a dose of Ann's medicine which was always in my pocket, I went to the inn at the corner of the street and wrote from there a note to Sara, explaining that I had come to fetch her, enclosing a cheque for five pounds, and asking her to join me at the hotel that afternoon or the next morning. I delivered this note into the letter box of No. 24, and returned to my hotel, where, I am bound to admit, I passed the rest of the day in much agitation.

I dared not believe that Sara had betrayed me; that she had really allowed me to be driven from the door. On the other hand, why had she not answered my letters or sent her address? I fell into much dejection. The hotel, the streets, which had seemed so encouraging on the day before, in their life and bustle, had now a stupid look, as if, after all, they meant nothing.

The evening papers were full of some new threats from the man Hitler, and new dangers to peace. But I could not make head or tail of them. One said that Germany had great grievances which ought to be satisfied; another that Hitler could never be satisfied; a third showed an American caricature of the British lion having its tail cut off by Germany and Japan.

I sat in my room all the afternoon waiting for Sara. She did not come, and I could not rest. I lost myself in corridors. I wandered through enormous halls with roofs of coloured glass, where thousands of people in dark gloomy clothes and black hats sat drinking at little tables. And all their faces seemed to wear the same expression, 'I am I, that's all I know about it.'

I came into a great drawing room with a bright fire, but nobody in it. One evening paper lay on the carpet. There were no pictures in the room. It seemed like a waiting room without a purpose; with no journey beyond it. I was tired. My legs would scarcely move. But I dared not sit down in one of the great chairs, for fear that my heart would stop. I could not die in a waiting room.

Where am I going, I wondered as I faced again that huge field of dark coats and white faces, corn high, silently drinking from cups and glasses, each as solitary as a stone on a beach.

'And where are they going,' I thought, 'Do they know? When Chaucer wrote of pilgrimage, in England, then every man knew where he was, and where he could go. But now all is confusion and no one has anywhere to go. They leave home only to sit under glass roofs, in black overcoats and black hats, with faces so private and cunning that you are afraid of them.'

A pilgrim is not a lost soul, I thought, nor a wanderer. He is not a tramp. But these are lost souls who don't even know that they are lost. They read three newspapers a day saying different things, and then they put on their black overcoats and hats and come to some place like this, to look at each other's hats and coats and to feel nothing, to say nothing, to think nothing, only to wait. And all the time, something called history is rushing to and fro and changing the very shape of hats and coats and trousers and collars.

I did not go to bed. Motors roared in the streets. And from the court there was the hum of some engine, discreet but relentless. I seemed to be bound in the midst of complicated enormous machinery. And I felt that at any moment, the room itself would be called upon to play its allotted part, it would begin to revolve; its walls would close and crush me to death; or it would sink slowly down, into the earth, to be passed again through the fire.

140

In the morning, a note came from Sara, apologizing for my treatment on the day before, and asking me to come and see her at ten o'clock. It was for me like a resurrection. I took a strong dose of Ann's medicine and went again to Lewisham. The medicine had the effect of making my heart beat too fast, so that I was extremely giddy and once or twice I fell down. But I kept on smiling and laughing at the people so that they helped me up and did not think that anything unusual was taking place. In any case, I perceived that they could not tell, merely by seeing me fall down, that I had run away from home.

The young man, Fred, again opened the door, and this time he began at once to shout at me. But before he could attempt to push me down the step, I heard Sara's own voice. She came down stairs as fast as she could, calling out, 'Now Fred, now Fred, don't be so silly.'

And pushing past the young man, she said to me 'Oh, sir, I am so sorry. Never mind what Fred was saying. You know you're always welcome. If you would come into the parlour.'

She was older than I remembered her. Her hair was grey and she seemed broader and redder. Her arms, which were bare to the elbow, were of surprising thickness and weight. But her eyes still expressed that lively good nature; her voice, that delight in a friend, which had long ago endeared her to me.

'Come in, sir. If I may say so, you don't look quite yourself. But who does this weather? All these colds about. A green Christmas and a full churchyard, I said so to Fred and we've had three funerals in the street this month alone.'

Speaking so, she had hustled the young man to one side. He for his part, seemed ready to oppose her and said, 'Now, Sara, you know what I said.'

'Why, yes, Fred,' in that caressing voice which I had heard so often, 'I know – I won't forget. Now if you'll just go off and see that nothing boils over,' and she guided me into the parlour and shut the door on the furious young man.

'He's on the railway,' she explained to me, 'Night work, and he ought to be in bed by this time. But I can never get him into bed. You know what these young ones are – never want to go to bed and never want to get up. But such a nice fellow. And so good to me, too. Well, you see –' and she laughed, while she dusted down a chair for me with her apron. When she laughed, she shook all over. 'You would think he wanted to eat any other man that came near the house. Why,' she said, sitting down, 'You wouldn't believe it, sir, but he wants to marry me. Of course he's not so young as he looks. These fair ones cheat the wrinkles – forty-two and two little boys. They're at school now or I'd like you to see them, sir. Like little angels to look at, but as Fred says, the other thing for mischief.'

'But, Sara,' I said. 'What about our arrangement? You know that I was going to take you away. What's all this about Fred?'

'Oh, you needn't mind him, sir,' Sara cried, laughing. 'He's easy. And as for your kind offer to me, sir, I can hardly believe it yet. But you always were the very best of men to me, whatever Fred may say, and indeed I don't deserve half what you did for me or would do –' and she ran on, speaking of me in so affectionate and grateful a manner that I could not help laughing. 'Come, Sara,' I said, ' we all know that you're a great flatterer.'

'No, indeed,' she said, very seriously. 'I couldn't flatter a good heart, for we all know that good hearts like honest tongues are few and neither gets its proper due. And indeed, sir, you've been an angel to me and the only thing is whether you haven't thought too much of me, and might be disappointed.'

So then I forgot all her fatness and her coarse cheeks and her new habit of saying sir at every other word, and I sat down beside her on the sofa and told her that I could never be disappointed in one so truly good. And so on. Indeed, I grew romantic and said much that would look ridiculous in print. And Sara said that, in that case, she would have me; only she must have a week to pack. 'A week,' I said. 'How can I wait a week?' For I thought that long before that, the family would discover where I was.

But Sara was all compliance. And the end of it was, she would go and pack that minute, and send Fred out to get rid of him.

Then she brought me a tray with tea and cake, and a glass of brandy; and told me to rest quietly until she came again to tell me that the coast was clear.

141

And now I was too inspirited and too impatient to rest. As I moved about in Sara's room, I was amused by my passing jealousy of Fred. 'What right have I,' I thought, 'to be jealous of anyone. And is it not just like Sara to make this new nest for herself, and adopt this new dependant.'

I recognized on the mantelpiece two little figures, in white Sèvres, one without a hand and the other mended in the neck, which had certainly come from Tolbrook. And this also made me laugh. 'How that would shock

Blanche. But with Sara, how natural. We were letting the house. Why leave to tenants these charming figures which they would not miss?'

And as I turned from the figures, I seemed to recognize a chair. Surely it had been in the attic at Craven Gardens. A hideous object of carved oak, with rows of little spindles in the back. And I was astonished. How on earth, I thought, did that chair come to be transported from Craven Gardens, which was, in any case, burnt out, four years ago, to a cottage in Lewisham.

Four years ago I was shocked to find that some of my trifles had passed into Sara's keeping. But now I was not only amused; I felt a secret exultation in Sara's impudence, and more than impudence. Something far deeper. Something that had come to me also from Lucy. A freedom. An enterprise. And looking round, I saw a dozen more objects from forgotten corners of Tolbrook and Craven Gardens; an engraving of Wellington at Waterloo; a glass picture, cracked in four places, of Cherry Ripe; a little tripod table with one foot broken short. Apparently Sara had permitted herself to take nothing that was in use, or in good order. Everything was cracked or chipped. A woman of principle. And by this strange route, I pierced again into the living Sara, with her peculiar attitude to life. As of one who faces a powerful but stupid enemy with the ready invention of a free lance, and the subtlety of a diplomat.

I remembered the first time I came to know Sara's quality, as a life manager. It was during Robert's school holidays. My nephew, from the beginning, struck up with Sara a friendship which alarmed me. For at that time, I knew nothing of the woman except what I had heard. Young Jaffery, as we called him, though he was my own age, had engaged her for me, and he had described her in his own detestable language, as a 'bit fly blown'.

'She's been before the Bench for cashing bad cheques, and before that she was living in sin with a so-called artist, who also has a police record. But they say she can cook and she's the only one who is willing to go to a place like Tolbrook at the wage you suggested. On the other hand, she can't afford to be particular about conditions.' All this meant, of course, that I myself had not too good a character, after recent scandals; and that I was also a skinflint. For Jaffery was the kind of fool who, in order to be smart, could not resist being offensive.

But having only Jaffery's description to guide me, I had always thought of Sara as a bad lot. Though I soon found that she was a good though extravagant cook, and a sensible housekeeper; I did not care for Robert to be too intimate with her. And when I caught him running to the kitchen, I would say, 'Mrs Jimson is busy. You mustn't order her about like that. It's not her place to wait upon small boys.'

'Oh, Sara doesn't mind,' he would answer, 'she likes it, the old trout.' And this very roughness of manner and speech seemed proof of the contagion I feared. I said to him severely, 'She's not an old trout. She's a

473

responsible person. You ought to know by now that servants have a right to proper respect.'

'I like old Sara,' he said. 'I can do what I like with the old nose.'

'What do you mean, old nose?'

'She's rather ashamed of her nose. So I call her old nose,' and he burst out laughing.

Robert had been a great anxiety to me. For I was responsible for him to Lucy, and yet I had never succeeded in getting close to the boy. I had not seen him for some years before Lucy died. He had been at school, and in the holidays, Lucy had either sent him to the seaside with Amy, or gone visiting with him. She never let him come near the Benjamites, if she could help it.

After Lucy's death, I went to see his schoolmaster, and the boy was brought in to me; short, thick set, small for thirteen, with his father's build and his mother's look. He was said to be lazy at his books but good at English. His English verses were the best in the school.

I explained to him that he would live with me at Tolbrook. That his father, who had but lately set out on his world mission, had approved this arrangement.

He listened to me with his peculiar intenseness and said nothing.

I had seen him at his mother's funeral standing beside his father among a group of Benjamites. He had shown then an unexpected violence of grief which drew me to him, as to one who had loved Lucy. And so I spoke now of Lucy's wish that he would work hard and complete his education at one of the great schools.

He listened and said suddenly, 'I want to go to so-and-so – it does engineering,' mentioning a school I had never heard of.

'But your name is down for so-and-so,' I said.

'Yes, but I want to be an engineer.'

'You can be what you like, but first you must have a good education. The school you mention may be good, but I know the one I've chosen is good and I can't take risks in such an important matter.'

He said no more, but he looked at me with Lucy's obstinate expression. And his report was bad.

But when at Tolbrook I told him that it was a disgrace, he answered cheerfully, 'I thought it might be pretty rotten.'

It was impossible to tell if the boy were irresponsible or only careless. He was noisy and dirty in the house, he never opened a book and if he were reproached for any fault, he showed a face like wood and said nothing. But it was difficult not to like his gaiety, his spirits, his friendly air. He would come to table with filthy hands and begin at once a friendly conversation about the weather, the crops, or the local gossip. An eagle had been reported over the tors and so-and-so had missed a lamb. Such-and-such a farmer had bought a reaper and binder, but it had stuck in his gate.

And I could never tell that his lively talk was not merely a device for preventing some remark upon his hands. For if I should say, 'Robert, your hands are dirty,' he would not answer. You would suppose that he had not heard me. And such cool obstinacy alarmed me, for I thought, 'What will become of one so confident and unteachable.'

142

It was Sara who prevented what might have been a disastrous quarrel with the boy. Robert asked me one day if he might mend the clock in the back hall, an old thirty-hour grandfather clock of the Stuart times. Its single hand had not moved in my life-time. I answered that the relic was too fragile; it should be left alone. A few days later, on examining the clock, I found that the works had been removed; only the face was left. The hand had been pegged to a board.

I taxed Robert with taking out the works and he admitted the deed.

'But didn't I tell you not to touch the works?'

'Well, uncle, they weren't any good, were they?'

'That depends on what you mean by good – they were a valuable movement by a famous clockmaker – now I suppose they are ruined' and so on. And I told him to put them back at once.

But he did not do so. At this open rebellion, I was at my wit's end. If I gave way, I perceived that the boy's character, already headstrong, would be entirely wrecked. And how could I enforce a decision? I could not use violence for, even if I had been able to contemplate an act of cruelty, it was against my principles. I therefore pointed out to him that without mutual trust, we should both be unhappy; and in this case at least, he was in the wrong. For the clock was mine and so forth. The boy answered that I need not worry about the clock, because he would make it go. And there was a sharp dispute, in which I spoke severely of his obstinacy and lack of good will.

The boy then disappeared. Imagine my alarm when he did not come to luncheon or tea or supper. I sent out the men to look for him. And finally, in despair, I consulted Sara.

'Don't you worry about young Master Robert, sir,' she said. 'He'll come back for supper. And I've got the bits of the clock all safe.'

'The bits of the clock?'

'Why, yes, sir – the poor little man took it all apart and he can't find how to get it together again. He's been terribly upset about it.'

'And where are these bits of my clock?'

'Well, sir,' and the woman looked at me as if to say, I suppose you must know. 'The truth is, that they're in my room.'

'In your room? Your bedroom?'

'You see, sir – I thought if I gave him a tray for the wheels and things, they'd be under my eye, and I'd know he wasn't losing any of them.'

'And also, I suppose, your bedroom was a place where I wouldn't be likely to catch Master Robert doing what I told him not to do.'

Sara then turned very red and assured me that she had no idea of such a plot. But I told her that she was spoiling the boy and that her bedroom was no place for him. In fact, I had almost decided to send her away on the spot.

'Show me the clock,' I said, 'or what's left of it.' She took me to her room, and I saw on her chest of drawers, which was also her dressing table, the lid of a cardboard box filled with the remnants of the clock. Tools lay on the only chair, on the window sill, and on the floor, which was strewn with chips of wood and metal. A vice was fixed to the washstand, and in the chamber pot, standing in the basin, spindles and wheels were soaking in dirty paraffin. For a moment, I was too much disturbed by this last familiarity between the couple, that Robert should make free of such a utensil in a servant's room, and that Sara should permit it, so to speak. And Sara's own conduct increased my embarrassment; which may have been absurd, but was I think justified. For, instead of ignoring the object, she held it out to me to show me that the wheels were in safe keeping. 'They're all there, sir – I thought I'd better leave them in the oil because of the damp. I'll see they don't get lost and when Master Robert goes back to school, any clockmaker can put them together again. And I'm sure, sir, he never meant any harm – it's only that he couldn't bear to see any clockwork about, and not make it go. You know what clockwork is to boys, sir – it just goes to their heads and there's no stopping them. So I thought I'd see he came to no harm. It's what they say "One way in by the door, and ten by the windows"; and Master Robert's so easy and good-hearted you can turn him which way you like.'

And, in fact, it now began to strike me that Sara had managed a difficult problem with some skill. She had saved the clock.

'And do you know where Master Robert is now?' I asked.

'Why, no, sir, not just now. But he'll come back, never fear. Only of course he's a bit upset and perhaps if no one said anything about the clock.'

'You spoil Master Robert, Mrs Jimson.'

'I hope not, sir. But as they say "Yesterday is neither a maid wed or a man fed." And I was just wondering – if nobody should say anything. It's not that Master Robert wouldn't understand that nobody was saying anything – on purpose. He's sharp enough.' Sara's grammar became confused, but as I found out at a later day, the confusion of her grammar was always the mark of a clear intention. I understood her very well, and gave her to understand, discreetly, that if the clock could be restored, I should not be severe on Robert. And it turned out that all this time the boy was eating a large supper in the back kitchen. What's more, he returned next day to our usual routine, without offering either explanation or apology. Yet I could not help feeling that a serious crisis had been avoided, by Sara's tactful management. The clock was duly replaced. And several years passed before I discovered, or rather, one of my tenants discovered, that a great part of the works was missing.

143

And long before that time, Sara had become indispensable to me. I had learned to appreciate the quality of a woman who could devote herself not only to a wilful small boy, but to chairs, tables, carpets, and even vegetables. I have heard her object to a kitchen maid that she did not know how to treat a potato.

One forgot the thick, coarse figure, the rough features, in the light of a spirit which gave always encouragement. From the beginning, I had noticed one good quality in Sara, her regularity at prayers and church. But I knew she had been well brought up by a god-fearing mother and thought her piety merely habitual. I came to discover how strong and rich a fountain of grace played not only in the energy of her religious observance, but in everything she did, and in her most casual remark. All was coloured by these country maxims, so often in her mouth, which rise from a wisdom so deep in tradition that it is like the spirit of a race. Never sigh but send. Hot needle and a burnt thread. Give me today and I'll sell you tomorrow.

And yet Sara had her faults. She had her obstinacy, I remember that she made up her mind that the pictures wanted washing; and though I forbade her to touch them, she washed them all, with soap and water, in my absence, and afterwards excused herself on the ground that she had misunderstood me.

Then we looked at each other and I said, 'I told you not to wash them.'

'I think they look brighter, sir. I polished them off with new potato. Now if you could get someone to put a touch of varnish on them, they would be twice so gay.'

She had her own mind. She kept her own counsel. She was devoted but she was never servile. And I rejoiced in her quality which belonged to my own people, whose nature was rather affection than passion, whose gaiety was rather humour than wit; whose judgement did not spring from logic but from sense, the feeling of the world. Only to hear Sara's step in the passage was a reminder of the truth, which was the tap-root of her own faith, that we were travellers in the world, enjoined to live 'like men upon a journey'.

144

Now, whether it was the tea, the brandy, Sara's good fire, or happiness and peace of soul; or all together, but I went to sleep on the sofa. I had not slept for two nights and I slept well. When I awoke it was nearly one o'clock, and I was extremely startled to find myself in the strange room, dark and quiet; with a pain in my legs and the fire going out. And what was still more bewildering, as I looked about, I seemed to be carried all at once to a hundred different situations of my past; I seemed to fly into pieces. I looked at the rug and I seemed to see a baby crawling over its Turkish reds; I looked at the table cloth which was however only half a table cloth, and I was playing beggar-my-neighbour with Lucy, amid cries of rage; a brass oil lamp on a tall stem, started from the corner to remind me that, under its discreet shade, I had flirted with a fat schoolgirl in pigtails, Amy. And at sight of the mirror my moustache, shaved off forty years ago, grew again. I stroked it and said to Edward, with Bill's moustache manner, 'My dear boy, if you must poke the fire, do it properly. Give some thought to it.'

And at the same time, I was listening to a murmur of voices in which I seemed to recognize first Lucy and then Edward; but mysteriously changed. 'No,' I said, becoming more wakeful and putting down my legs. 'It is Robert and Ann.'

I jumped up, now very wide awake, and rushed to open the door. But as I opened it, Sara bustled in, in fact, walked straight into me and nearly knocked me down.

'What are you doing, Sara?' I asked her. 'Who have you got there?'

'It was only Fred, sir, I was just trying to make him have some sense; gracious, look at the fire. And you'll need it for your dinner. I mean your luncheon. There, I'll pull up this chair, and the little table. Don't worry about Fred, sir. If you stay quiet in here just another five minutes. He's got to go on duty; and, oh dear, what a trouble he's been. Why, would you believe it, a boy like that, for so he is a boy to an old woman like me – I hardly dare to go out of the house, even to do my shopping or to fetch the beer. They say widowers don't make jealous flesh, but Fred is so touchy as a hedgehog.'

So she ran on, talking of Fred and Fred's children, and his delicate chest, and his colds, and even his favourite dishes.

I had heard Sara chatter but I knew that she was not a foolish woman. She could hold her tongue when she chose. So I looked at her and listened to all this talk of Fred, with surprise; until meeting her bright brown eyes fixed upon me with so much candour and affection, I saw, as through the brightness of a clear window, both obstinacy and cunning gazing out at me.

I had long recognized in Sara, among her great virtues, very great faults, of which the chief was a resolution to have her own way. Indeed, you can hardly call it resolution any more than you can say of a tree that it has a resolution to grow; or of streams that they are determined to run into the sea. She was as persistent as a natural force. And to that persistence all her virtues as well as her vices were made to contribute. She could use her kindness, her affection, as well as her talkativeness, for her own purpose, whatever it was.

'What are you doing, Sara?' I said. 'What are you plotting. I know all your tricks – you thought I didn't see them before, but I knew all the time that you were as cunning as an old monkey.'

Sara turned very red and opened her eyes as if in alarm, but she continued in the same voice of cajolery, 'Oh, sir, I know I did deceive you, indeed, I behaved very badly to you.'

'Yes, yes, but our arrangement, woman – what are we going to do?'

'Yes, of course, sir, our arrangements –' Sara stopped with such a peculiar glance at the door, that I too glanced towards it. I had expected to see someone come in. 'Yes, sir,' Sara said, 'of course we shall have to arrange things, won't we, and you needn't be afraid of Fred. He's a little bit sudden sometimes, as they say, but you couldn't find a better boy anywhere, no trouble at all – for goodness knows it's not his fault if he has a delicate stomach.'

At these words, my head turned round. I shouted out, 'You are deceiving me, Sara. I thought you so good and religious, and wise, but you are nothing but a cunning greedy creature, a regular peasant. I suppose you have caught this boy Fred just now, as you caught me, and catch everyone – yes, that's what you do. You pretend to be so religious and modest and respectable, and all the time you're leading a man on, and heading him off.'

And I rushed at her. I had never hit anyone in my life, much less a woman; but at that moment, so had Sara maddened me with her talk and her honest look, that I believe I should have hit her. I meant to hit her on the nose.

But my head continued to turn round, the darkness came in front of my eyes, and instead of hitting Sara, I tumbled over a chair and she caught me from falling.

'There, there,' she said, carrying me across the room like a child and putting me on the sofa. 'You shouldn't, sir – it always was bad for you. Yes, it's just what you say. I've been a bad woman. Well I know it. Though I hope they taught me better at Holloway. There, sir – don't get up. You're really not fit to be going about, and if you wait a moment, I'll – but there they are. Here's Master Robert, sir, at last, and his nice little wife.'

Robert and Ann came into the room and I saw Robert kissing Sara and apologizing for their lateness. And it turned out that Sara had wired for them on the day before, and her message to me had been a trap. I did not forgive her and I told her so. Yet she showed not the least remorse but continued to chatter about Fred, and dear Master Robert and his nice little wife. 'I'm so glad he got a clever little wife like that for I always thought that he would go marrying some great lump.'

Ann and Robert had brought a taxi with them and I was glad when they had carried me into it, and taken me away.

But when I spoke of Sara's treachery, Ann answered that Sara had behaved with great good sense. 'I never much liked the idea of your Sara,' she said, 'and I don't see the attraction now, but she's certainly got a head on her shoulders.'

'How long has she been living in this place?'

'I don't know. I gather she went as housekeeper to a widower.'

'I don't think he'll be a widower very long.'

'I don't know about that,' Robert said. 'Sara's refused him several times.'

'How much has she refused him?'

'Well, what does it matter at her age. Poor old Sara, I should think she might be allowed a little fun. And I'll bet she makes Fred happy.'

'Yes,' I said. 'I'm sure she will. And there is no doubt that she has acted with good sense. I shall write to her and tell her so. And if she would accept a wedding present, I shall ask her to choose a piece of furniture from Tolbrook. A sofa, perhaps. Her sofa was a poor thing. I suppose it belonged to Fred.'

Ann and Robert looked at each other as much as to say, 'He's wandering.' And I began to laugh. I thought, 'All the same, this is the end of me.'

'Where are we going?' I asked the young ones.

'Home,' said Ann, 'as soon as we can. But I don't think you had better go much further today, uncle.'

They did not ask me any longer about my own wishes. And I did not protest. It was somehow understood among us that I had no right to protest. I had become a dependent member of the family, like Jan, for whom these responsible persons, Ann and Robert, would make all necessary arrangements.

So I was carried to a nursing home, where I spent the next six weeks. And then back to Tolbrook, where I was again under strictest orders.

145

It is September. I have been out of bed for a fortnight, but it seems that I have enjoyed a family life for a long time. To an old man who has admitted that he is finished, the years fly, but each day is a gift of heaven. To streaming windows, he says, 'Once more I see the beauty of your melting lights and hear an English shower.' He greets each spring and harvest as a piece of good luck.

Robert is threshing in the great saloon. He did not ask me if he could bring a threshing machine into the house, but I was waked yesterday morning by what seemed to be an earthquake. The floor shook under me, the windows rattled, the plaster fell from the ceiling, and the air was filled with a loud, roaring sound, with explosions and cracks like rifle shots. But before I could get out of bed, Ann opened the communicating door between our rooms and said, 'It's only the threshing – Robert said he was beginning after breakfast. But I suppose he couldn't wait.'

'Is he coming to prayers?'

'I'll send out and tell him.'

And in a few minutes, Robert, still in his blue overalls, comes into the nursery. For since we have returned home again, he has been as regular at prayers as Ann. I even think he is more serious than Ann, for I can feel his attention. I do not ask why this miracle has happened, or how Robert and Ann were reconciled. When on my first day out of bed, I saw the girl, Molly Panton, forking the new straw into the bull pen, I exclaimed to Ann, 'What, is she here? And what about the baby?'

'The daughter's here, too.'

'Good God, what are you thinking of? What will the people say?'

'Robert doesn't seem to mind. And I suppose she's too stupid to mind anything.'

'You had no business to allow such an arrangement – it's perfect madness.'

'I had no choice. It was one of Robert's conditions.'

'So Robert made conditions?'

'Trust Robert.'

'No apology, no explanations?'

'He said he wanted to keep an eye on the daughter, and he'd never get anyone better than Molly with cows.'

'And what were your conditions?' I asked, feeling ready to shake the girl.

'I didn't make any. I saw it wouldn't do.'

'Why, it's incredible. What are you made of – are you Robert's doormat – have you no pride at all?' etc. For I was disgusted. 'And have you reflected that you've wrecked your life – and probably Robert's. It's ruin for a boy like that to get his own way.'

'Well, he has got a way and I wasn't sure I had, and you know, uncle, it's not a final arrangement. We're just going to try how it works – there's no promises on either side.'

481

'I see, everything left to chance and luck, and you expect it's going to work, as you put it. The work will be yours.'

'Yes, it's going to be rather a job, but up to now, everyone has been a model of discretion – even Robert.'

'Discretion,' I said, and then I could not help laughing. 'Very well,' I said. 'I'm an old fool – I don't understand anything, but I thought you modern girls had some pride.'

'Well,' Ann said, 'I am rather inclined to be proud of this arrangement – even Robert can't say I've been prejudiced. And as for Molly, you know, uncle, I feel rather sorry for her. I still don't know why she wants to hang about.' A touch of feminine spite which gave me a little solace, for I felt that, after all, the girl was not completely incomprehensible to me.

'I daresay,' I said, 'she hopes for another baby.'

'I daresay,' Ann said, in a mild tone. 'But it's not going to happen yet. Robert did promise me that – only one at a time,' and she added, 'otherwise Robert himself would look ridiculous. Not that he cares. But I do. Or, I think I do.'

The scientific inquirer peeped out again, and indeed every time I think I have come close to this girl's nature, she recedes from me again into a distance that I can't penetrate.

She is again pregnant. I gather she is already in her fifth month, so that she lost no time in what she describes as the Lincoln negotiations. But if perhaps she has a Delilah of the more scientific kind, in her composition, she does not betray her to me. She appears, more than ever before, preoccupied with some problem, and as before, in her pregnancy, she is careless and troublesome to us. She will not take her emulsion, etc., and insists on going out alone, unless Robert or I can catch her.

She worries us both. Her face is yellow and appears shrunken. New wrinkles mark her eyes and forehead. She labours through the fields, she throws back her head and hollows her back to carry her burden, and fixes her eyes on the horizon. She does not notice the apple-scented lanes, the bright crops, the trees heavy with leaf, trembling under the warm breeze. When, to distract her mind, I invite her to admire the season, she answers vaguely, 'You aren't tired, are you? You mustn't get tired.' And when I speak of her writing, of her father's papers, she says, 'I suppose they will have to wait.'

In the news she takes no interest whatever, much to Robert's indignation, who declares that there is going to be a war. 'And serve you all right if you won't take the trouble to look facts in the face.'

'But if you look them in the face,' Ann says, 'they get nervous and pull another face. I see the glass has gone back – it's just as well you're threshing under cover.'

'It is lucky,' I ventured to remark, with some irony, 'that the Adams brothers used the classical proportions of the double cube, there's no other drawing room in the county would take a threshing machine.'

And both of them turned to me with the politeness of those who have forgotten a guest.

'Well, yes, uncle, it's just the place – might have been made for the job – and if one or two ceilings shake a bit loose it was quite time for 'em.'

'You really are better today, uncle. We must go for a real walk.'

146

But Ann, though she walks with me, prefers, I think, to be with Robert. And since I like to be with her, I spent all this afternoon in the saloon. The huge machine, like a species of Roman siege engine, towers in the middle of the floor, driven by a tractor among the broken laurels. The driving band passes through one of the beautiful windows from which the panes have been knocked out of the sashes. The carts are backed in turn along the west side, brushing the painted walls. And behind Farley, who is feeding to Robert on the top of the machine, I see over the middle window a rural trophy in plaster of delicate scythes and sickles, sheaves and hayforks, tied up in pale blue ribbon. But the thick chaff dust, which lies along every panel moulding like yellow snow, is already hiding their beautiful detail, characteristic of Adams' refinement.

Farley's head, when he takes his stand upon a new load, almost brushes the cupids on the ceiling, painted among Adams' fine plaster by Angelica Kaufmann. They seem to be flying round the old man's bald brown skull like cherubim round one of El Greco's saints. He feeds with deliberation, throwing each sheaf where it is wanted, and the expression on his dried-up face, wrinkled as an old fence post, is that of an eternal patience.

The girl Molly lifts off the filled sacks and twisting up their loose necks drags them across the floor with her huge arm to the side door, where Robert, by taking out a panel and knocking down the bricks, has made a loading platform. The grinning and horned Pan, who, in white marble, plays upon his syrinx, under one end of the magnificent mantelshelf, famous among the scholars of architecture, carries on one horn some labourer's luncheon, tied up in a red handkerchief; and round his waist, mixed with the marble flowers and grasses, hangs a bunch of real onions on a string. His grin reminds me of Robert's smile.

The whole building, floor, walls, and roof, shakes and thunders, and through the mist of fine dust rising and falling in the air on every draught, long bars of yellow sunlight decline, hiding the far end of the room in a blue shadow.

Ann has placed herself on a pile of sacks, between two windows. She has a book open on her lap but does not read. She knits and looks occasionally out of the window, or at Jan running about among the mountains of chaff which rise below the thresher, or at Robert high up on the machine; but always with her preoccupied air, like one who looks at a passing landscape, a strange child, a figure on some distant mountain.

In a pause of the roar, while the tractor is stopped to tighten the driving band, she says, 'That child is full of fleas from the draff.' And Robert's voice answers from among the gods and goddesses on the ceiling, 'He may as well get used to 'em now.'

The two old men, who are shovelling this draff away to keep it from swallowing up the machine, look at the child with mild speculative faces. They are those old labourers, twisted and knotted almost out of human shape, lame, stooped, with distorted arms and crooked, swollen fingers, who are seen only in harvest time, when they creep out again into the sun, to do some humble task which does not need much strength.

Jan runs up to one of them, seizes his broad draff fork by the shaft; and, trying to shake it, looks up, laughing. The old man looks down without a smile. His face, like Ann's, seems to express a deep preoccupation, neither sad nor cheerful; but questioning.

Ann calls, 'Come here, Jan, you mustn't be a nuisance.'

The boy looks round and then rushes away to the other side of the thresher to hide from her, and to do what he likes.

Ann continues to knit. It is Robert who comes down from the thresher, takes the child from under the wheels of the cart and carries him back to his mother. 'Keep him here, will you? That band would cut him in two.'

'He won't stay, you know.'

'Make him stay – you don't want him killed, do you?'

'Stay here, Jan.'

Robert climbs the thresher by the wheel and gives the signal. The machine once more shakes the room, and the grain pours out of its filters into the sacks. Jan runs off looking back at his mother with a broad smile of delight, which says very plainly 'I don't mind *you*.' Ann gazes at him with her absent expression and says nothing. A moment later he is creeping under the cart wheels.

Is it in the armchair, a tattered *bergère*, in white and gilt, last of the drawing room furniture; and the very ruin of this beautiful room is become a part of my happiness. I say no longer 'Change must come, and this change, so bitter to me, is a necessary ransom for what I keep.' I have surrendered because I cannot fight and now it seems to me that not change but life has lifted me and carried me forward on the stream. It is but a new life which flows through the old house; and like all life, part of that sustaining power which is the oldest thing in the world.

Tolbrook, so Jaffery says, is losing value – it is already not much better than a farm house. But is it not a fall back from death to life.

Robert, I suspect, is more Brown than Wilcher, a peasant in grain. But he does not destroy Tolbrook, he takes it back into history, which changed it once before from priory into farm, from farm into manor, from manor, the workshop and court of a feudal dictator, into a country house where young ladies danced and hunting men played billiards; where at last, a new rich gentleman spent his week-ends from his office. And after that, I suppose it was to have been a country hotel, where typists on holiday gaze at the trees, the crops, and the farmer's men, with mutual astonishment and dislike. Robert has brought it back into the English stream and he himself has come with it; to the soft corn, good for home-made bread; the mixed farm, so good for men, to the old church religion which is so twined with English life, that the very prayers seem to breathe of fields after rain and skies whose light is falling between clouds.

That was Sara's religion which served her like her pans, her rolling pins, her private recipes for clearing soup and saving a burnt stew; a wisdom and a faith so close to death and life that we could not tell what part of it was God's and what was man's sense; the sense of the common English, in a thousand generations.

I need not strive to send into Robert's heart and Ann's mind some arrow of conviction. For when I read to them in the mornings, the old prayers, and they kneel at their familiar seats, they are already in the way of the country faith. For that is not an argument. It is an act and a feeling.

147

When therefore Jaffery and my niece Blanche protested against the change in the house, I told them that Robert had my support.

Jaffery laid this trap for me. He wrote to me reminding me that I had given instructions for a new will some months before, but never signed it. He asked me if I should like to sign it in private. So I sent him a message by the gardener's boy. He was our agreed messenger when I did not want to excite curiosity in Ann or Robert or the servants.

Jaffery arrived suddenly at a corner of the drive and took me to his Queensport office. I left a note to tell Ann that I had to see an old friend. This was true, for Jaffery was officially an old friend.

I found on Jaffery's table a long row of papers tied in pink tape and many bundles of letters.

'What's all this?' I asked.

'Your wills and instructions. From your own boxes; seventeen completed wills from the London office, five at Lloyds Bank, seven at the Westminster Bank and three here.'

'Yes, I kept them in case of any legal questions. As you know, a destroyed will may be proved. I don't like destroyed wills. Better to cancel them.'

But I was annoyed with Jaffery. I could see he was playing some trick. He is a smart man and smart men are always doing foolish things, especially at some serious moment.

'I only want to see the last, to cancel it, and the new one,' I said severely. 'You can pack up all the rest.'

'There you are,' and he unfolded certain packets.

These in fact were my last three wills and the new one, not yet signed. The first left everything to Loftus and Blanche, the second left £2,000 to Robert and £500 a year to Ann and another £100 for every year that I should live after she took charge of me. In a codicil I increased this sum to £200. Then there was a will, made after Robert's flight, leaving Tolbrook to Ann as trustee for my great-nephew Edward John Wilcher Brown.

Now, by my last instructions, I was leaving the landed property to Robert absolutely, and £5,000 to my niece Blanche.

Frankly, will making has been a responsibility from which I have too often recoiled. The burden was too heavy. To do justice between so many conflicting rights and needs.

Neither was I in good fettle for such a task. For, first, I was upset by Jaffery's folly. And no sooner had I sat down to read the draft than Blanche came running in. The woman was breathless and crimson from running, and yet she cried, 'What luck to find you here, uncle. I just looked in.' Plainly Jaffery had sent for her.

I was angry at this plot and told them that if Robert wished to use Tolbrook for a farm house, he might do so.

'But, Uncle Tom, you don't realize –' The big woman, still panting with haste and with anxiety to use this lucky and important moment. 'He doesn't care one farthing for Tolbrook or you, and neither does that creature Ann. They only came back –'

'Excuse me, Mrs Wilcher,' Jaffery interrupted. 'We hardly know the full reasons.' And I think he made some warning signal to the woman, for she went on, 'No, Mr Jaffery, I will speak. For my uncle's own sake. And you know very well they wrote to you about a nursing home. Yes, uncle, they were going away together, to South America I believe it was, and they were going to put you into a home –'

'That's very likely,' I said, looking with surprise at the woman. For I saw that she wanted to please me, to ingratiate herself; and yet she was already eager to hurt me.

Blanche's chief fault in life is too great love of justice. She resents too much injustice to herself. And hating injustice, she seeks always to punish

486

those who do injustice. So that now she wanted to please me and to punish me at the same time. 'They were going to shut you up,' she said, 'and the only reason why they didn't do so –'

'Really, Mrs Wilcher.' Poor little Jaffery, for all his airs of the dashing country bachelor, is a creeping little man in his soul. 'You shouldn't impute motives.'

'Impute, what nonsense, Mr Jaffery,' cried Blanche, who fears nobody. 'You showed me the letter yourself. Saying that uncle was so ill they'd changed their minds and would come back and see him out. The very words, uncle, see you out. They're just waiting for you to die and Master Robert goes to church to keep you in a good mood.'

'Well, Blanche, it's certain that I must die, and I suppose I can't last very long now. My heart plays very queer tricks and my feet are too big for all my old shoes. And, as Sara used to say:

> "When your head begins to swell
> Jack Ketch will pull your passing bell.
> But Christian feet when they grow long
> Seek to reach the churchyard throng."

And now I see it is getting late, I'm afraid I must go home.'

'But, uncle, you don't mean to let them do what they like? You don't want to see Tolbrook sold just to anybody?'

Blanche made a rush as if to seize hold of me and prevent me escaping from her, but stopped half way on the recollection that I was ill or mad or both; and might therefore cheat her by falling dead or uttering some violent nonsense.

'Good-bye, my dear Blanche,' I said. 'You have done quite right in telling me plainly that I can't live much longer. I suppose you couldn't state a month for my death?'

'But, uncle, I hope you will live for years, and if you could only turn that couple of harpies out, I am sure something could be done. There are wonderful treatments now. Loftus is completely cured of his rheumatism by a bone setter who broke his neck.'

'If I want you, you can be sure I'll send for you,' and I went away as quickly as I could, because I felt so much ashamed of cheating her of Tolbrook.

Jaffery, as he drove me home, kept saying that we had done nothing, after all, about the will.

'It doesn't do to let these things slide,' he said.

'Yes, I'll let you know. But it needs some thought.'

For I began to feel very strange. And, in fact, before I reached the Manor, I went to sleep and didn't know how I had got rid of Jaffery, or reached my bed, until the next afternoon.

148

I waked up to see Ann's shrunken anxious little face, and swollen body, perched on a bedroom chair beside my pillow. She was sewing and frowning through her spectacles at her work. She is a slow but careful needlewoman, having learnt to sew, I imagine, only in the last year. Seeing that I was awake, she said, 'What did you do that for, uncle? Mr Jaffery could have come here if it was so important.'

I could see she was longing to know what I had been up to; and indeed, I suppose it is a pretty serious matter for these children what I do with my property.

I said to her, 'Robert has no capital and I suppose you haven't saved much.'

'Nothing,' she frowned at me as if to say, 'What's going on now in the old lunatic's head.'

'Do you want to go to Brazil?'

'No.'

'Are you going?'

'If Robert goes, I suppose I shall have to. That was the bargain. Brazil or Lincolnshire.'

'Lincolnshire. Why on earth Lincolnshire?'

'Robert rather fancied the farming there.'

'Are you so happy with Robert?'

'I wasn't happy without him. And I had the children to think of.'

'Only one then.'

'Robert says there's going to be five, at least.'

'Robert, Robert, Robert – isn't there any Ann left?'

'Well, uncle, I rather agree with him there – if you have a family, I think it ought to be a family, for the family's own sake.'

'I see, so you've arranged everything. And as soon as I'm out of the way, off you'll go. How long have I got, do you think?'

'You'll have to be very careful. You very nearly didn't come round yesterday, after Mr Jaffery brought you back.'

'Well, am I going to get up again?'

'Not just yet, at any rate.'

I was angry with the child, and I was going to say 'You are very cool about it.' But when I looked at her I thought 'She is unhappy, and perhaps she is lonely. Or why does she want to sit with an old nuisance like me? The young may be younger than they were in my day, but they grow old more quickly. In a world without manners or reserve, they find too soon that loneliness of spirit which I found only in my old age.' And I said to her, 'If you didn't dip your face in a flour bag and put that raspberry jam on your lips, I should like you much better.'

But she did not seem to hear me. She is as obstinate as a mule, as Lucy, as Sara, as Amy; she wouldn't wash her face to get Tolbrook. I lost my temper and said to her, 'It's no good waiting. I'm not going to tell you what I did at Jaffery's. So go away, for goodness sake. And give me some peace from all of you.'

Then she went out so quietly that I was perfectly enraged against the whole race of nurses who oppress us with their patience.

149

Of course, I am very unfairly prejudiced against Ann. It is absurd to be angry with the girl for painting her face. She is really a good girl of whom I am quite fond. There is certainly a good deal of the conservative in my composition. I never read of an old house pulled down, but with a pain in my very heart. The loss of Devonshire House gave me my first touch of angina. And still that long wall of dirty yellow brick in Piccadilly, with its two gates, the low plain house behind them, seem to my memory more beautiful than all your European glass, steel and concrete.

I walk once more before them, in a new frock coat. The gates open, and I see the old Duke, with his sleepy eyes, his heavy beard, his huge hat. The Duke is my enemy, for he has deserted Gladstone, and I am then a violent young Liberal. But I am taken by surprise, my hand springs up of itself, and I take off my hat.

The Duke is equally startled. He slightly moves his eyelids and takes off his own hat, with an awkward hasty movement, of the shy man, who hasn't prepared himself. We pass with mutual astonishment. And then I recollect myself, and begin to abuse the Duke to myself, saying, 'If Home Rule is lost, then the Lords will be responsible for all that happens in Ireland.'

But I feel strongly as if the Duke and I are joined together in some private relation. I am laughing at our confusion, our bows. I tell the story to my friends at Oxford and make fun of the Duke. But I am still enjoying him, as a piece of history, of England.

For the truth is, I have always been a lover rather than a doer; I have lived in dreams rather than acts; and like all lovers, I have lived in terror of change to what I love. Time itself has haunted my marriage bed like a ghost of despair. And on the day when I possessed Tolbrook, my keenest fears began. It was not till I was a pillar of the old order, that I felt how the ground trembled under my feet; how close beneath the solid-looking stone was the primitive bog.

When I was small, we children often played in the linen-room. We used the big square baskets, with their leather corners, for galleons; and fought out the Armada under the shelves. But one day, at the end of a game, someone, probably Lucy, tipped me, heels over head, into a half-filled basket and shut down the lid. I remember still my first surprise, my laugh, my expectation of something delightful; a new game; and then, when nothing happened, and nobody answered my cries, and I found that I could not open the lid, my panic.

I knew that this was a joke and yet I felt that I was going to be murdered. That my brothers and sisters had planned to get rid of me and leave me to choke and starve. When I screamed for my mother and she did not come, I believed at once that she, too, was in the plot. She was tired of me.

People think that a child's faith is absolute, because instinctive; therefore very strong. It is not so. Because it is unreasoning it is easily upset. A child does not live by faith, but by forgetfulness. It forgets itself so quickly that it forgets its terrors. But those terrors are more terrible, more far-reaching, than any grown-up's; because of that childish ignorance of security. For me the very earth was not solid; it might swallow me; the water was not bound by the nature of a liquid, it might rise in one wave and chase me up the steepest mountain; the sky was not emptiness, it was full of demons; the night was not an absence of light, it was the presence of a thing, a creature, which shut me off from all who loved me, and hid me from all help, in order that it might jump upon me and strangle me. As I say, even my brothers and sisters, who seemed to love me, my mother who spent her life in caring for me, were capable, to my faithless mind, of turning upon me and murdering me.

In one of these baskets, yes, I know even the basket, because it was the only one with a lock, and it is there still, as good as new, or rather, made better than new, cleaned and polished and oiled by the faithful, busy hands of Sara, whom my faithlessness attempted to murder; in that basket more than sixty years ago I suffered a torture so extreme, so fearful that it twists my heart now. Even this moment I feel a pain that might kill me, but I do not care if I die; I do not value life. Let me not fly from this real sense of life, too; this pain, for childish suffering and for the child itself so far from me, that he is no longer myself but a different being. And through the child, it is a pain for all childhood, so easily hurt, so helpless. For no power can protect a child from his own ignorance. No kindest nurse, no far-sighted anxious mother, assuring it every day of love and sympathy, can give its weak half-formed brain the power to judge of truth and falsehood, of the real nature of things. The strongest assurance from the most loving familiar lips will be abolished in one instant by a smile from another child, the bark of a strange dog. What surprises me is not that I screamed in the basket, but that I did not die there, that my childish heart and brain could stand such shocks of agony without bursting. I do remember that I did not recover from it for some hours or perhaps days. I could neither eat nor sleep, and I had one night, I daresay, the same night, a kind of fit which caused my mother to fear that I should be an epileptic. The doctor was sent for, and, wise man, listened to a plea which my father had refused, that I should be allowed to sleep in my mother's bed. My father did not believe in coddling children and he had, in this special case, another reason to stand in my way. He did not want my mother to be troubled by a restless child, during her own light sleep.

But now he gave way, and for two or three nights, so blissful that they remain ineffaceable in my memory, I took my father's place in the big bed. I still see, with a child's magnifying eye, its posts diminishing towards the immense height of the ceiling, with its plaster cherubs, or as I thought of them, fellow babies, playing their Christmas trumpets. I remember my fascinated delight in the glossy red satin lining of the curtains, and the tall mountains of pillows, like a tor under fresh snow, which stood over me when, having slipped to their foot, I waked in the morning. I was in paradise. And yet I knew, even then, that kind as she was, my mother suffered me with difficulty in her bed; and that she had never cared greatly for my plain face, my awkward ways, my spectacled eyes. I got on her nerves, as they say.

It was by mere contact, I suppose, that I regained, on my mother's breast, the power to live, to believe, taking it directly from that warmth, that life, which had given me life already. As I took from Lucy, from Amy, and from that little maid whose name I can't remember, from Bill, from Sara, some direct communication of their energy, their confidence.

150

It is almost comic to see Ann's anxiety, while she goes in and out. It has made her so restless that she can't even read. No doubt some rumour has come to the house. She knows that Blanche was at that mysterious conference. And Mr Jaffery is always appearing in her conversation.

No doubt she thinks I am spiteful to keep her in suspense, with the spite of the old. But I feel no spite. I simply find myself prevented from discussing with her this matter, which is the last fragment of my privateness. And what a flatness afterwards.

> One flesh, one mind, in wishing to be two,
> For two can love again, as strangers do.

Today, after fiddling about for ten minutes with my pulse, temperature, pillows, etc., she plumped out, 'I suppose Mr Jaffery wanted to see you about your will.' Then she turned red; or rather, two patches as big as pennies, appeared on her cheeks under the powder. I wish every girl who powders could see herself blush magenta. Nothing is more ugly.

I almost burst out laughing at the girl's naïvety. But I answered after a moment: 'No, I cancelled it. If I die now, there won't be a will. Everything will be sold, the house, farms, furniture, pictures.'

'But, uncle –'

Ann was now redder still. The mauve patches were as big as pen-wipers. She looked at me with eyes full of dismay. 'Did you want the place to go – isn't it a fearful pity?'

I saw that she was really fond of the place, that she was going to suffer at its loss; and so to upset my mind again. And I thought that I was entitled to some peace on my death bed. So I answered rather more sharply than I intended, 'Whose fault is that – if you let Robert take you away and Jan away to the ends of the world – in Brazil or Lincolnshire?'

She stood silent, shaking her thermometer, but not looking at it.

And I thought, 'She is really a good-natured girl. And we all treat her rather badly, I am treatng her badly. But she is strong, and strong people always have troubles piled upon them. Weak people even like to worry them and throw new burdens on them. When you say to children, "This toy is made so that you can't break it," then they are sure to treat that toy as badly as possible.'

So, when we used to send Amy to buy something for us in Queensport, we always gave her the most careless instructions, and said 'You'll get it easily – plenty of the shops have it.' Even though we ourselves had failed everywhere. But to any of the maids or to my mother, we gave the most exact and careful particulars.

151

When I heard that Amy was dying, I couldn't believe it. It was the year of the great strike, and I was oppressed with terror. I thought that at last civil war had come to destroy the very soul of England; its kindness. I found her in a dismal little boarding house on the south coast. I had never visited her there before, I thought I had no time. Neither had I reflected that Amy was now a poor woman. Her son, Loftus, was indeed already well off for he had not only his share of my mother's estate, but he had inherited a large sum from her sister, his godmother. But he, no more than I, perceived that his mother was almost in poverty. She did not mention it. And both of us, I suppose, were preoccupied, Loftus with his polo in India and myself with the state of the country and the decline of religion.

'My dear Amy,' I said, when I saw her bare room, looking out on a coal yard, 'I'd no idea you lived in such a place.'

'The people are very nice,' Amy said. She was propped up in bed with pillows and barely able to turn her head. 'And there's a good attic.' She had had rheumatic fever, and now her heart was failing. A nurse sat beside the bed, a red round-faced woman in gold spectacles. She had been giving oxygen at intervals during the night and I remember the first thought which occurred to me, 'How strange to take so much trouble and to go to so much expense only to keep poor Amy alive.'

The thought came to me, but I did not accept it, because I knew now that Amy was dear to me. Yet so strong was custom that I could not help feeling ready to laugh at the old woman.

'A good attic,' I said. 'Have you another room upstairs?'

'No, the boxes,' she whispered. 'Such a nuisance in lodgings.'

I remembered that Amy had spent almost her whole life in trains, in lodgings or in other people's houses. She had come to see everything from the traveller's point of view. 'Yes, I can see that an attic is useful,' I said.

'And water in the room,' she whispered.

'Oh, they all have that now.'

'All the difference.'

'Yes, water in the room,' I wanted to laugh at this extraordinary conversation. 'Saves servants, it probably pays.'

'Wash things – in your room,' Amy whispered. 'Landladies don't like bringing hot water,' and she added after a moment 'naturally.'

'Naturally, of course.'

'And washing – such a difficulty – when you have to move quarters.'

'Yes, I can see that.'

'Very lucky find this place – gas ring, in corner. Make my own tea.'

'Yes, that's a great advantage.'

'Bill – great fuss about his tea – liked to see the water boil.'

'Was he – did he? I've missed Bill. We've all missed him.'

'All nonsense – that women can't make tea.'

'Did he say that? But Bill was very fond of you, Amy. He used to tell me what a good wife you were.'

Amy was silent for a moment and the nurse got up to feel her pulse. Amy looked calmly at her and shook her head as if to say 'Don't bother me.'

'Have you a good vicar here?' I said, seeking for an appropriate subject.

Amy shook her head. 'Very high.'

'I thought you liked the High Church.'

'Not with bells. Too foreign.' Her voice began to fail and she turned her blue eyes towards me with that look of shy good nature which I had not seen for forty years. 'What a nuisance for you – to come down.'

Suddenly I felt that I couldn't bear to lose Amy. My throat choked; my eyes smarted. 'You're not going to leave us, Amy. All you want is a good long rest. It's wonderful how hearts respond to a good rest. You must come away with me somewhere.'

Amy shook her head. 'Got to die sometime,' she whispered. 'I've been lucky – thirty years with Bill – and the boys, so much happiness.' She waved her hand and made a pluck at the air.

The nurse quickly put the mask over her face. She murmured to me, 'Very weak.'

But when the mask was taken away again, Amy spoke quite briskly and strongly, 'Yes, the curate came, but I sent him away again. He's a pacifist, like that man at Tolbrook. I wouldn't have him – I said, what about his oath.' Amy, I imagine, thought that clergymen took an oath of allegiance.

'You sent him away?'

'I couldn't stand him – talking about Bill.'

'What did he say about Bill?'

'About me seeing him soon.'

'I hope we'll all be together again soon, Amy. And Bill has been waiting for you.'

I said this for comfort to the poor woman, but her expression did not change. Like Bill himself, she seemed to take little concern in what happened after her death.

She reflected a moment and said, 'I never could understand how Bill stood them.'

'All sorts to make a world,' I quoted Bill.

'What we want – Christian soldiers.'

'Bill took after his father – he was always rather evangelical. Now Amy, if there's anything you want done – here I am.'

Amy reflected. 'Thank you, Tom. I think I've done everything – I wrote to Loftus yesterday and I told the undertakers.'

This information took me so much by surprise that I could not answer. Amy continued, 'But you might see they don't put in any extras. The estimate – in my blotter. You know what undertakers are.'

Her voice was now failing again and the nurse started forward. But Amy made an impatient gesture. 'All right, nurse,' and to me she said, 'You'll stay to lunch.'

'Well, Amy –' I hesitated. 'I left my bag at the hotel.'

'But I've arranged for lunch. Veal. Your favourite.'

'My dear Amy – it's very kind of you.'

'I really wouldn't like to disappoint Mrs Biglow – a special favour – to me – and she's so busy, this time of year.'

I thanked Amy and promised to stay to lunch. She lay still for a moment and then she said, 'I'm going now, Tom.'

In my distress, I did not know what I ought to do. Amy and I had rarely embraced and now we seemed too old to begin. But Amy had her usual expression of calm reflection. She murmured thoughtfully, 'Yes, I think that's all – except, oh, yes – my summer stays at the cleaners.'

'My dear Amy,' for I was shocked that she should waste her last moments in this way.

'Yes, but they're C.O.D. I don't want Mrs Biglow to be bothered – she's rather excitable – May – the new season.'

As Amy said this her face changed and the nurse brushed me aside and put the mask over her face. But she was too late. Although Amy was kept alive, by injections, for another hour, she did not again speak.

I found that I had very little to do for Amy after her death. She had arranged for her own funeral; to Tolbrook; and even for the inscription on the stone which marked Bill's grave. 'And his wife, Amelia Alice, born Madras, India, April 14th, 1871. Died . . .'

'And when the trumpets blew, the walls fell down flat.'

152

When Lucy died I had felt the pressure of confusion, as if I had lost with her a guiding force of revelation; and now, when I thought, 'Amy is gone,' I felt afraid. For when we had said at Bill's death and John's death, that Amy was saved by her faith in the resurrection, we had been wrong. I don't know what Amy believed, but her faith did not need theology. Its strong roots were in a character which nothing could shake.

When we laughed at Amy as a young bride, left alone in our household of clever young people, she withdrew into her pride. But she was brave by nature, she did not sulk in it. She used it only for her home and her refuge. For her pride was not vain; it was nothing more than the ordinary self-respect which all brave people have by nature. She set no great value on herself and so she had no self pity.

And now lying here, I miss Amy more than all those whom I have known. I know why Amy sent away that curate and why she would not let me talk to her about the consolations of religion. She did not want them; perhaps she did not altogether like them. Perhaps in her shrewd mind, as simple and strong as Sara's, she was sceptical of Heaven.

Amy and Sara, countrywomen both. They didn't submit themselves to any belief. They used it. They made it. They had the courage of the simple, which is not to be surprised. They had the penetration of innocence which can see the force of a platitude. Amy's 'got to die sometime' has been on the lips of every private soldier since the first army went into battle. For her it was still profound.

To Amy, death in this true shape, was a familiar, and she received him like an afternoon caller. But to me here death is a wonder. When I look now at the last horizon, I see him rise into the sky, more illuminating than the brightest sun, colder than the arctic moon; and all the landscape is suddenly altered. The solid hills melt into cloud; and clouds affirm a reality.

Familiar shapes are changed before my eyes. And seeing these strange patterns, these immense shadows reaching to my feet, I say, 'I never knew this place before. I have lived like a mole in a run; like a cat in a kitchen.'

153

There is nightshade in my medicine, and I think Ann gives me too much. It makes me feel as if I were turned into an aeroplane; throbbing and floating on the air. It gives me so many ideas at once that I feel confused. Just now I saw Ann looking at me with a startled face and I knew that I had been talking and laughing. But her sad expression made me angry and I said, 'Why are you so closed up? It's pure obstinacy at your age.'

I could see Ann thought I was quite mad. She smiled in a hesitating way and shook her head. 'Yes, you're just determined not to feel any kind of pleasure. It's the nonsense of the age. Every age had its nonsense and this age likes to be hard and careworn. But I've no patience with a girl like you – you have plenty of faith – but you refuse the happiness.'

'I'm afraid I'm not much of a Christian, uncle. They didn't catch me young enough.'

'What does that matter whether you're a Christian or not?' I said. And I was so much surprised by my own words that I suddenly began to smile, like someone who has made an epigram by accident. Ann began knitting again so that she needed not to look at me. She was disturbed by this smile. Once people think you're mad, your most ordinary actions seem mad; like picking up a pin in the street, or smiling at your own thoughts and discoveries.

'Yes, what does that matter – faith is nothing to do with Christianity. Look at Sara and look at your Aunt Amy. Yes, look at Amy. She had a happy life, she said, and she was quite right. I envy her. But her religion was nothing to her happiness – it was simply regimental. She was happy because she had strength. She became a woman of power. She didn't need anybody or anything – in fact they needed her.'

'You oughtn't to talk too much.'

'That's impossible now – to talk too much. Why shouldn't I talk?' and I began to laugh at Ann's face. I could see she was even frightened. The first time I had frightened her. 'But you think I'm talking nonsense.'

'I'm sure faith is a very nice thing to have,' she said.

I wanted to shake her. But instead I said in a soft voice, 'But you have it, my dear – you have it. How could you go back to Robert without faith.

Yes, you are very strong – I daresay stronger than Robert. But he is for happiness – why, you can hear him whistling now in the yard. He lets himself be happy when he feels like it. But you keep up this play of carrying a world on your shoulders. The world is at your service – you have only to enjoy it.'

I stopped to see what I was saying. Ann got up and left the room so skilfully that I did not notice that she had gone till I turned to her again. She has the idea, I think, that she upsets me; and that if she tactfully keeps out of sight, I shall be more likely to make a fair will and give Robert some capital for a new start.

154

I admired Bill for taking death with such excellent manners. But now I see that he was doing something quite natural and inevitable. When death rises high above the horizon, the landscape draws in its shadows. It becomes flat and ordinary. Its details are even insignificant. But there is room for more of them and like small copies of the real, like miniatures, they become more dear. As I lie with nothing to do but feel the world agitating round my bed, not only the fields about this house are present to my mind's eye but the moor, the Longwater, Queensport, and beyond them, all the villages and towns of my country, with their spires and towers and chimneys standing under this broad day-time of eternity, their streams reflecting its face, in the innocence of creatures dependent on the whims of the spirit. And the dirty back lanes where I found Lucy, the pond into which those Tory rascals threw me, in the war election, the squares and streets and parks of London, become as familiar to me as the rooms of this house.

I walk upon the fields of the whole island, as upon my own carpet, and feel the same exasperation against them, for being a perpetual burden on my regard; I love the noble buildings as I loved these old chairs and tables, with anxiety and irritation. For I know very well that they are not being properly looked after. I love this island as I loved Tolbrook; and tremble for it; and perhaps I shall be happy to get some peace from both of them. They have broken my heart between them.

What does it matter who gets Tolbrook, it is only one room of my house. I really have no time to make a will. I shall probably die without one. Then Blanche, Robert and Ann would get each an equal share, which is probably a fair division. For Blanche has the best claim; Ann has the most need, and Robert is Lucy's son.

155

A small boy is whistling in the yards, on three notes. He is pretending to whistle a tune known only to himself, and he thinks that everyone is deceived; whereas it is perfectly obvious that he has only just learnt to whistle and doesn't know any tune. I have heard him often during the last fortnight and he has enraged me. But now he makes me laugh so that I shake the bed and get a pain in my chest. What do I care about the other world? One dies and learns. Probably these young people who don't believe in Heaven are right. Perhaps I have been talking nonsense to Ann, and pestering her to no good. If so, I shall not tell her.

What did Amy care for Heaven? What do I care, so long as I lie in Tolbrook churchyard? I shall ask them to bury me without a coffin.

The truth must be confessed, that I am an old fossil, and that I have deceived myself about my abilities. I thought I could be an adventurer like Lucy and Edward; a missionary. I shouted the pilgrim's cry, democracy, liberty, and so forth, but I was a pilgrim only by race. England took me with her on a few stages of her journey. Because she could not help it. She, poor thing, was born upon the road, and lives in such a dust of travel that she never knows where she is.

> Where away England, steersman answer me?
> We cannot tell. For we are all at sea.

She is the wandering Dutchman, the pilgrim and scapegoat of the world. Which flings its sins upon her as the old world heaped its sins upon the friars. Her lot is that of all courage, all enterprise; to be hated and abused by the parasite. But, and this has been one of the exasperating things in my life, she isn't even aware of this hatred and jealousy which surrounds her and, in the same moment, seeks and dreads her ruin. She doesn't notice it because she looks forward to the road. Because she is free. She stands always before all possibility, and that is the youth of the spirit. It is the life of the faithful who say, 'I am ready. Anywhere at any time.'

Or perhaps, to be honest, I should say that she is a bit of a Protestant and therefore a bit of an anarchist, and so forth. Which characteristics may be discovered in one or two other peoples of similar stock, history, etc., who are also apt to find themselves in new lodgings at short notice; with new aspects from the windows of their spirit, and new bugs, fleas, etc., in the mattress, to keep their bodies on the jump.

I never liked lodgings. I was too fond of my dear ones at home. And what if they were trees and chairs and furniture and books and stones?

Material love. What is material? What is the body? Is not this house the house of spirits, made by generations of lovers? I touched in my mother the warmth of a love that did not belong to either of us. Why should I not feel, when I lie in English ground, the passion of a spirit that beats in all English souls.

Ann came in to put me to bed for the night. She found my notebook on the bed and silently removed it. She did not reprove me for breaking her order to lie flat and do nothing, and in her silence, it was understood between us that whether I die today or tomorrow, does not matter to anybody. But for her that is a defeat; for me it is a triumph.

'You look as if you'd swallowed a safety pin,' I said to her, making her look at me with Edward's eyes, which should be gay. 'You take life too seriously.'

'Don't you think it is rather serious?'

'My dear child, you're not thirty yet. You have forty, forty-five years in front of you.'

'Yes.'

The Horse's Mouth

To
Heneage Ogilvie

1

I was walking by the Thames. Half-past morning on an autumn day. Sun in a mist. Like an orange in a fried fish shop. All bright below. Low tide, dusty water and a crooked bar of straw, chicken-boxes, dirt and oil from mud to mud. Like a viper swimming in skim milk. The old serpent, symbol of nature and love.

> Five windows light the caverned man; through one he breathes the air
> Through one hears music of the spheres; through one can look
> And see small portions of the eternal world.

Such as Thames mud turned into a bank of nine carat gold rough from the fire. They say a chap just out of prison runs into the nearest cover; into some dark little room, like a rabbit put up by a stoat. The sky feels too big for him. But I liked it. I swam in it. I couldn't take my eyes off the clouds, the water, the mud. And I must have been hopping up and down Greenbank Hard for half an hour grinning like a gargoyle, until the wind began to get up my trousers and down my back, and to bring me to myself, as they say. Meaning my liver and lights.

And I perceived that I hadn't time to waste on pleasure. A man of my age has to get on with the job.

I had two and six left from my prison money. I reckoned that five pounds would set me up with bed, board and working capital. That left four pounds seventeen and six to be won. From friends. But when I went over my friends, I seemed to owe them more than that; more than they could afford.

The sun had crackled into flames at the top; the mist was getting thin in places, you could see crooked lines of grey, like old cracks under spring ice. Tide on the turn. Snake broken up. Emeralds and sapphires. Water like varnish with bits of gold leaf floating thick and heavy. Gold is the metal of intellect. And all at once the sun burned through in a new place, at the side, and shot out a ray that hit the Eagle and Child, next the motor boat factory, right on the new signboard.

A sign, I thought. I'll try my old friend Coker. Must start somewhere. Coker, so I heard, was in trouble. But I was in trouble and people in trouble, they say, are more likely to give help to each other than those who aren't. After all it's not surprising, for people who help other people in trouble are likely soon to be in trouble themselves. And then, they are generally people too who enjoy the consolation of each other's troubles. Sympathetic people. Who'd rather see each other's tears, boo-hoo, than the smile of a millionaire, painted in butter on a barber's shave.

Coker kept the public bar at the Eagle. About five foot high and three foot broad. Face like a mule, except the eyes, which are small and blue. Methylated. The Eagle is down on Thames-side and gets some rough ones. But see little Coker run a six-foot pug through the door, by the scruff and the seat, his ears throwing off sparks like new horseshoes. Coker has a small hand, but it feels like hot marbles. Coker has had a hard life. Long-bodied and short-tempered.

There were three chaps hanging round the door for the bar to open, and I asked 'em, 'Is it true about Coker?' But they were strangers. Come up on an empty gravel barge. They didn't know Coker. Just then I saw her coming along with a string-bag full of knitting and her slippers. Snugs for the snug. I smiled and raised my hat, took it right off.

'Hullo, Coker. So here we are again.'

'So you're out, are you? Thought it was tomorrow.'

'I'm out, Coker. And glad to see you. I suppose there aren't any letters for me?'

'Have you come to pay me my money?' said Coker, with a look that made me step back a pace. 'That's all right,' I said quickly, 'I'll pay you, Coker, I couldn't do anything about it while I was inside, could I?'

'As if you ever did. But you won't get any more.'

'I wouldn't think of it, Coker.'

But Coker was getting fiercer and fiercer. Working herself up. She squared at me as if she meant to give me a knock. And I took another step back.

'What about that lawyer of yours who was bringing a case? You told a lot of people. I should think they'll all want their money back now you're out again.'

'You'll get your money back, Coker, with interest.'

'Yes, I'm going to,' and she put the key in the door. 'Four pounds fourteen. I'm going to see about it Wednesday. And you're coming with me; to see that woman who's giving the evidence. And if you're having us on, it looks like another police job.'

The three chaps were looking, but what did Coker care. I like Coker. She doesn't give a curse.

'Why, Coker, I'll come with you. Yes, it's quite true we got the evidence. And the money.'

Coker opened the door and went through. When I tried to follow she shut it quick to about six inches and said, 'We're not open.'

'I'll sit in the passage.'

'Haven't you got any socks?'

'No, I don't need 'em.'

'I'm not going to get you any. So you can take 'em out of your pocket.'

'Search me, Coker.'

Coker thought a bit with her nose out of the door. Like a tit looking through a fence. Then she said, 'You made a nice fool of yourself. What did you go and utter menaces for?'

'I got in a state, Coker. I got thinking how I'd been done. And that always makes me mad.'

'You were lucky to get off with a month.'

'Yes, it did me good. It cooled me down. Come on, Coker, I'll sit in the passage. I don't want any tea.'

'And what about our licence? Wednesday morning at nine. Don't you forget, and keep off that telephone.' She shut the door. She was gone. I was surprised. I was surprised, too, that Coker was so keen on the money all at once. Bad sign. The three chaps were now about seven. Getting near opening time. I said to one, 'It looks like it's true about Coker. She's different.' 'I bubbeg your pardon.' 'Nunnever mind,' I said, catching it. I recognized him. Green eyes. Hay hair. Big flat nose like a calf. Schoolboy. One of the lot that went to the bun-shop just opposite where I used to live. Scholarship class. Talk about Ruskin and Marx. He had his satchel and I wondered what he was doing outside the pub when his nose turned pink and he said, 'Mr Jijimson.'

'Yes', I said, 'Mr Jijimson, that's me.' 'I sspoke to you once last Christmas.' 'Oh yes, of course,' though I didn't remember. 'Yes, of course, very interesting. How's school?' and I moved off. 'You said that William Bubblake was the greatest artist who ever lived.' 'Did I?' For I didn't want to talk to the boy. He wouldn't know anything about anything except a lot of words. Ask you a lot of questions, and when you answer, it's like shooting peas into a can.

'Sorry I can't stay,' I said. 'Busy.' And I made off. Sun all in a blaze. Lost its shape. Tide pouring up from London as bright as bottled ale. Full of bubbles and every bubble flashing its own electric torch. Mist breaking into round fat shapes, china white on Dresden blue. Dutch angels by Rubens della Robbia. Big one on top curled up with her knees to her nose like the little marble woman Dobson did for Courtauld. A beauty. Made me jump to think of it. You could have turned it round in your hand. Smooth and neat as a cricket ball. A Classic Event.

2

I could see my studio from where I stood, an old boathouse down by the water wall. A bit rotten in places, but I had been glad to get it. My trouble is I get big ideas. My last one was the Fall, twelve by fifteen, and you can't get room for an idea like that in a brick studio under two hundred pounds a year. So I was glad to get the boathouse. It had a loft. I took the planks off the beams at one end and got a very nice wall, seventeen foot high. When I had my canvas up, it was two foot off the floor, which just suited me. I like to keep my pictures above dog level.

Well, I thought, the walls and roof are there still. They haven't got blown away yet. No one has leant up against 'em. I was pleased. But I didn't go along in a hurry. One thing at a time. Last time I was locked up, in 'thirty-seven, I left a regular establishment behind. Nice little wife, two kids, flat and a studio with a tin roof. Watertight all round. North light. Half-finished picture, eight by twelve. The Living God. Cartoons, drawings, studies, two painters' ladders, two chairs, kettle, frypan and an oil stove. All you could want.

When I came back, there was nothing. Wife and kids had gone back to her mama. Flat let to people who didn't even know my name. And the studio was a coal store. As for the Living God, my drawings, cartoons, ladders, they'd just melted. I hadn't expected to see the frypan and kettle again. You can't leave things like that about for a month in any friendly neighbourhood and expect to find them in the same place. But the Living God with his stretchers and stiffeners weighed a couple of hundredweight. When I came back from gaol even the smell had gone. Coker said that someone said the landlord took it for the rent. The landlord swore he had never seen it. I daresay he had hidden it somewhere in an attic, telling himself that it might be worth thousands as soon as I was dead, and the more I was worried, the sooner that would be.

The top of my boathouse suddenly nodded its head at me, as if saying, 'That's it, old man.' Then I saw that a couple of kids were taking a plank off the roof. More patrons, I thought. When they saw me coming, they slid off the roof and ran. But not far. Crouching round like a couple of wolves waiting for the old horse to drop. I didn't need to unlock the door. Somebody had done it for me by knocking off the hasp of the padlock. And when I opened it, two more kids got out of the window on their heads 'Don't hurry,' I said 'there's plenty of time before dinner.'

There was nothing inside except a lot of pools on the floor from last night's rain. And the picture. I got another surprise. A big one. It was still there. Why, I thought, it's not bad in places. It might be a good thing. The serpent wants to be a bit thicker, and I could bring his tail round to make a nice curl over the tree. Adam is a bit too blue, and Eve could be redder – to bring up the blues. Yes, yes, I thought, getting a bit excited, as I always do when I come back to work after a holiday, I've got something there. Adam's right leg is a gift, whatever you may say. Nobody has done that before with a leg. What a shape. I must have been tight or walking in my sleep when I knocked that off. And yet it's leggy all right. If that limb could speak, it would say, 'I walk for you, I run for you, I kneel for you. But I have my self-respect.'

Just then a stone came and knocked out the last window-pane that wasn't broken already. And I heard a voice, 'Ya, mister, how did you like chokey?' Those kids had had a fright and they were getting their own back.

Next minute I heard a different kind of yell, and when I went to the window I saw them making for the street with young Nosy on their tails.

He came in two minutes later, blowing, with the sweat on his nose and his cap falling off the back of the head. 'It's a shushame, Mr Jimson. I hope they haven't done any damage.'

'Not to speak of. There's quite a lot left. And it's an expensive canvas. Make a good floorcloth for any scullery.' 'Why, it's all f-full of holes, and they've cut a piece out.'

For somebody had been shooting at the birds with an air-gun and there was a piece about a foot square cut out of Adam's middle with a blunt knife. 'What a shushame,' said Nosy, and his nose turned pink. 'You ought to tell the po-police.' 'Well,' I said, 'Adam hadn't got a bathing-dress.' 'It's disgusting.' 'So he was, and somebody has made him respectable. Some mother, I expect. Anxious about her children. There's a lot of very good mothers in this district. You'd be surprised.' 'But the p-picture's ruined.' 'Oh no, I can easily put in a patch. It's the little holes are the nuisance. Are you going to school yet?' for I wanted to get rid of him. I wanted to get on with my work. 'Nunno,' he said, 'it's dinner-time.' 'Don't you do any work in your dinner-time?' 'S-s-sometimes.' 'If you want to get that scholarship and go to Oxford and get into the Civil Service and be a great man and have two thousand pounds a year and a nice clean wife with hot and cold and a kid with real eyes that open and close and a garage for two cars and a savings book, you'll have to work in your dinner-time. All the good boys round here work in their dinner-time.'

'They've been writing names all over Eve, Mr Jijimson. It's b'beastly, b'beastly.' 'Yes, they seem to have appreciated my picture a whole lot.' 'I wonder you can go on pa-painting, Mr Jijimson, for such people.' 'I like painting. That's been my trouble all my life.' 'I wuwish I could paint.' 'Now, young chap, you go home quick; before you catch anything.' And I chased him out.

3

Yes, I thought, but the trouble about a leg like that, it sticks out.

It's like a trumpet in the violins and a trumpet doesn't mean anything by itself. Any more than a sneeze under the stage. And if I work any brass into the top left-hand corner, it will have to go into the right bottom corner as well, into Eve, in fact, and she'll come right out of the canvas into the stalls. Only way to hold her down would be to make the serpent's head scarlet.

Carbuncle. Blood colour. And about twice the size. But that's all wrong. The serpent has got to have a white head and sky-blue eyes. That's the feeling, anyhow. That's how I feel it. Let's see. And I went to open the locker where I kept my tubes and brushes. The padlock was all right. But when I opened the lid I got another surprise. Somebody had taken out a bit of plank from the outside and cleared the lot. There was nothing there but a cigarette tin. Well, I thought, it's natural. You can't leave brushes and paint around where kids can get them. They all love art. Born to it.

All the same, the situation had its comic side. Here am I, I said, Gulley Jimson, whose pictures have been bought by the nation, or sold at Christie's by millionaires for hundreds of pounds, pictures which were practically stolen from me, and I haven't a brush or a tube of colour. Not to speak of a meal or a pair of good boots. I am simply forbidden to work. It's enough to make an undertaker smile.

But then, I said again, as I walked up and down Ellam Street, to keep warm, I mustn't get up a grievance. Plays the deuce. I must keep calm. For the fact is, IT'S WISE TO BE WISE, especially for a born fool. I mustn't exaggerate. The nation has only got one of my pictures which was left it by will and which quite likely it didn't want; and only one millionaire has ever bought my stuff. Also he took a big risk of losing his money. Also he is probably far from being a millionaire. So I have no reason to feel aggrieved and ought in fact to thank God I haven't got corns and bunions.

Just then I found myself in a telephone box. Habit, I suppose. I never pass an empty telephone box without going in to press button B. Button B has often been kind to me. It didn't give out anything this time, except an idea. I had some coppers, so I rang up Portland Place. Put a pencil between my teeth, and asked for Mr Hickson. The young butler answered in his voice like a capon's crow, 'Who shall I say?' 'The President of the Royal Academy.' 'Certainly, sir, please hold the line.' Then Hickson droned at me like a bankrupt dentist with toothache, 'Mr Hickson speaking.' I kept the pencil well in front and gobbled, 'Mr Hickson, I understand you possess nineteen canvasses and about three hundred drawings by the celebrated Gulley Jimson.'

'I have a collection of early Jimsons.'

'Of which one small canvas was sold last year at Christie's for two hundred and seventy guineas.'

'Seventy guineas, and it wasn't mine. It belonged to a Bond Street dealer.'

'Even at that rate your nineteen canvasses are worth at least two thousand pounds, while the drawings and sketches would amount to about two thousand more.'

'Excuse me, but what name did you mention?'

'I am the President of the Academy. I understand that Mr Jimson is now destitute. And I was informed on the best legal advice that you have no right to his pictures. I understand that you conspired with a drunken model to rob him of this valuable property.'

'Is that you, Jimson?'

'Certainly not,' I said, 'I wouldn't touch the bastard with a dung fork. But I have to inform you that he means trouble, and he's a dangerous man when he thinks he's got a grievance. He is in touch with your accomplice Sara Monday, and he has powerful friends who mean to bring the case to law.'

'Then they will lose their money, as they have no case.'

'No doubt, Mr Hickson, you've got tip-top lawyers who could do down Magna Charta and George Washington. And you have my full sympathy. Such dangerous blackguards as Jimson oughtn't to be allowed to live. But I'm speaking as a friend. If Jimson doesn't get his rightful due in the next week, he fully intends to burn your house down, and cut your tripes out afterwards. He means it too. I have it from a mutual acquaintance. So I thought I'd better give you a straight tip.'

'If you're a friend of Jimson's, perhaps you'd better make him understand that he won't do himself any good by this sort of behaviour. He will only get himself another spell of prison, a very much longer one. As for his being destitute, if he is so, it is entirely his own fault. Good evening.' And he hung up. But he took the receiver off again. Because when I rang him again five minutes later, in a female voice, as the Duchess of Middlesex, the number was engaged. And it went on being engaged for half an hour.

This made me a bit impatient, and I began to be rough with the instrument. Till I saw a copper looking in at me. Then I pretended to take a call. And made my getaway.

In fact, I realized that I had been getting upset. I hadn't meant to say anything about burning Hickson's house down. Now, when I say anything like that, about shooting a man or cutting his tripes out, even in joke, I often get angry with him. And anything like bad temper is bad for me. It spoils my equanimity. It blocks up my imagination. It makes me stupid so that I can't see straight. But luckily, I noticed it in time. Cool off, I said to myself. Don't get rattled off your centre. Remember that Hickson is an old man. He's nervous and tired of worry. That's his trouble, worry. Poor old chap, it's ruining any happiness he's got left. He simply don't know what to do. He sends you to jug and it makes him miserable, and as soon as you come out you start on him again. And he's afraid that if he gives you any money, you'll come after him more than ever and fairly worry him to death. Simply daren't trust you. He's wrong, but there it is. That's his point of view. He daren't do the right thing and the wrong thing gives him no peace. Poor old chap. It's an awful problem for a poor old bastard that let down his guts about forty years ago, and has rolled in comfort all his life.

And I was so calm, that when I felt my pulse, it barely touched seventy-eight. Pretty good for a man of sixty-seven.

4

All at once I remembered the oilman. I owed too much at my colour-shop to get anything on tick, but I had often seen paint and brushes at the oilshop. So I went along and asked, 'How much for those little sample tins, interior decorator's stuff?' The oilman was a nice old chap. Bald head. Pince-nez. Looked at me and said, 'Mr Gulley Jimson.' 'The same,' I said. 'The penalty of fame, so far as it goes.' 'Excuse me, Mr Jimson,' he said, 'I think we've got something of yours.' And he went into a glass dock where he kept his desk. 'I'd be glad of that,' I said, 'whatever it is.' 'Yes,' he said, 'I thought so,' looking in the desk. 'A little account.' 'Thank you very much,' I said, 'I'll send you a cheque.' And I went off quickly. But he came on nearly as quick. He was at the door sooner than I had expected.

Lucky thing there was a coal-cart at the kerb. I nipped under the horse and round the back of the cart. Stood there with my legs by the front wheel. Got a nice view of the oilman in the shop window opposite. He was a bit surprised. Looked up and down. Came out at last to have a look under the cart. So did I, the opposite way, and when he came back to the horse's head, I was round by the tail-board. He went in then and I went home top speed. I'd got an idea. That red cloud ought to be scarlet. Have a clash in the reds – pillar box and crimson lake. Get them moving. I'd only had time to borrow four pots from the oilman. He kept his books too well; didn't give me time to choose. But I had two reds, as well as a blue and a white. No brushes. All wired to cards. It's five years since I borrowed a brush from one of these shops round here. Too many young Raphaels on the grab.

But I made a pretty good stump brush out of a bit of rope and knocked out the idea for the two reds on the wall. Touch of scarlet in the clouds. Crimson apples. Eve terracotta with a scarlet reflection. Pretty good idea it seemed to me and kept that leg quiet. But I didn't look at it long. It had come up too quick. Ideas that shoot up like that won't bear the sun. They need time to make a root. I cut for the Eagle. To see if Coker was in a better temper. And know if anyone could lend me a bed, a kettle, and a frypan. Or at least a frypan.

5

No one in the bar but Coker. 'Is it Willy again?' I asked her.

Willy was Coker's young man. A warehouse clerk shaped like a soda-water bottle. Face like a bird. All eyes and beak. Bass in the choir. Glider club. Sporty boy. A sparrowhawk. Terror to the girls. Coker was church, teetotal and no smoke. Willy her only weakness.

Coker drew me a can and waited till I'd paid for it. My last bob. But she threw me a pair of socks across the altar. 'And they aren't Woolworth's,' she said. 'Don't you pop them or I'll cut your liver out.'

'Thank you, miss, I was wondering where I was going to put up. They've knocked out all my windows at home.'

'You're not going to stop with me again. I've no room. You'd better try a Rowton.' 'Rowton's all full,' I said.

Coker said nothing. But she was absentminded. When she's got that look, as if she isn't sure if a suspender hasn't given way somewhere, she's usually friendly. I was just going to ask her for an advance of five bob on the fortune that was coming to me, when she said, 'I got them socks for Willy.'

'Not had an accident, has he?'

Coker thought a bit and her face was as blank as a sanitary brick. Then she said, 'He's gone off with a Blondie.'

'He'll come back if you want him.'

'Not him. She's a widow too. Five years older.'

'You'll soon get a better than Willy. The dogs leave sweeter bones on any doorstep.'

'Not me,' she said. 'Willy was a piece of luck. Due to the carols last Christmas – in the bad light.'

'You're still in the choir.'

'Never again, Mr Jimson. No more religion for me. I hate God. It isn't fair to make a girl and give her a face like mine.'

'Don't let it get you down, Coke. Don't get in a state. That was my trouble, getting in a state.'

'I shall if I like,' said Coker. 'That's the only advantage I've got. I don't give a damn for myself. Why, even when I was a kid, and I got my earache, I used to say, go on, ache; go on, you bloody flap. Give me hell. That's what I'm for.'

'Don't you believe it, Coker,' I said. 'You're young. You don't know. Things are never so bad they can't be worse. Don't you let anything get hold of you. You got to keep your independence. When I was a kid my father died and I went to live with an uncle who used to try which was harder, his boot or my bottom. And when my poor mother saw me cry, she would take me in her arms and say, "Don't hate him, Gull, or it will poison your life. You don't want that man to spoil your life." "No, mums," I would say, "I'd rather die." "So you won't hate him, my darling, you'll put all that bad feeling out of your heart." "Yes, mums, boo-hoo, tomorrow." "No, today, this minute." "Not this minute, mums, it's too soon." "Yes, this minute, you mustn't let that feeling stay one minute. It's a very bad poison." "Boo-hoo," I would cry, "but I can't help it, mums." "No, my dearest darling dear, my poor lamb, you can't help it, but God will help you. We'll ask Him now," and she would make me kneel down and pray for forgiveness.'

'Well, what had *you* done?' Coker said.

'She didn't mean I was to be forgiven – she meant that God was to put forgiveness into me.'

'He couldn't do that to me,' Coker said. 'Let Him try, that's all. Yes, Captain Jones?'

A little old chap with bandy legs had come in. He put a shilling on the edge of the mahogany and gave it a slap with the flat of his hand so that it slid across to the other edge. Coker drew him a pint and gave him the change.

'Good shot, miss,' he said.

'He couldn't do that to me,' said Coker.

'Nor me,' said I, 'but my mother was a female-mother. Practical. She didn't rely too much on God. And when she got out a picture book and told me stories, I forgot my Uncle Bob and even my bottom. Yes, I would sit on my mother's knee and wonder why I felt sore.'

'Nice evening,' said the old man.

'No mother could make me forgive that Blondie,' Coker said. 'It would be a bloody crime not to hate her guts.'

'But wind's changing round,' said the old man. 'Look at the smoke of that tug – easterly – we'll have blue sky and red noses tomorrow.'

' "Don't let him get inside you," my mother said. "Don't let uncle reign in your heart – you want only happiness there. You want only joy and love and peace that passeth understanding." '

'So it does,' said Coker. 'It passed mine long ago.'

'Head wind for me if the old barge is ready,' said the little man, 'but the missus won't mind. She'll be able to keep me another day.'

'They tried religion on me,' Coker said. 'As soon as they saw I was growing out all the wrong way. They always try it on the flat-foot squaws. But it never would stick on this one, I had my pride. I said, "God has done the dirty on me and I'm not going to lick his hand for sugar left over from the horses." '

'Grace Darling, Florence Nightingale and the Rose,' said the old man. 'That's the fleet. Down on the tide with a fair wind to Gravesend or Burnham, and back by the train.'

'I thought you were Sunday school, Coker.'

'Mum sent me to Sunday school and I was Church till week before last. But I wasn't giving anything away. I kept myself to myself, thank you very much.'

'I'm a Primitive,' said the old man. 'But I'm not one of the strict ones. My missus' Peculiar. She *is* strict. But she was born happy, thank God. She can't take anything too serious.'

'Mrs Jones is one of the lucky ones,' Coker said. 'Not a grey hair at sixty, and you'd take her for thirty from the back.'

'It was in the family,' said the old man, 'with deafness. Like bull terriers. She was stone deaf before she was forty. But she took it well. She's never got suspicious. Because it runs in the family.'

'I'd rather love a dog,' said Coker. 'He loves you back again. I saw such a nice pup yesterday. Think of all that love for ten and six – that's what they asked. And beat him all you like, he'd still think the world of you. It's nature.'

'The girls get it and not the boys. My boys have ears like a water-rat's, but the girl is a bit hard of hearing already – at twenty. Of course, you couldn't tell just at first go off. She's got her tricks to hide it. Smiles and looks nice when she hasn't heard what you said. But it's hard on a girl. She knows what's coming to her.'

And I saw all the deaf, blind, ugly, cross-eyed, limp-legged, bulge-headed, bald and crooked girls in the world, sitting on little white mountains and weeping tears like sleet. There was a great clock ticking, and every time it ticked the tears all fell together with a noise like broken glass tinkling in a plate. And the ground trembled like a sleeping dog in front of the parlour fire when the bell tolls for a funeral. 'Trouble is, you can always tell there's nothing in it,' said the old man, 'I mean the smile. It looks a bit empty when she hasn't heard.'

That's all very well, I thought, I could do the girls – their legs would look like the fringe on the mantelpiece, but how would you join up the mountains? There'd just be a lot of ground stuck on. Unless you had flowers. Yes, everlastings. Yes, and a lot of nuns pushing perambulators, with a holy babe in each. Yes, and every nun with a golden crown. Yes, and the nuns would be like great black tear drops. They could be the tear drops. And they wouldn't have feet. They would go on little wheels.

'I'd rather be blind than deaf,' Coker said.

'Not me,' said the old man, 'I likes to see the world. You can do without the talk.'

Yes, I thought, You've got the girls at the top red and blue and green, like a lot of little flowers burning and then the mountains blue-white and blue-green, and then the everlastings – they ought to be bigger than the girls, and then the little black nuns under them, black or green.

'Well, you can smell,' said Coker, 'and there's eau de Cologne and rum. And you wouldn't see yourself in the glass.'

Coker began to rub her tumblers, the old man took out a penny, polished smooth on both sides, breathed on it, rubbed it on his sleeve, and put it back in his pocket. Didn't feel he ought to play. Solemn occasion. I thought of the deaf girl and wondered if she was pretty. I wondered if she knew how to be happy. Why, I thought, if I were a pretty girl and going deaf, I'd be an artist's model. I'd be an artist. Concentrate on my work. Like Edison. But she wouldn't know. Who would tell her? And if you did tell her, she wouldn't believe you.

The wind was blowing the curtains at the little windows behind the bar. I always like to see curtains blow, and feel the breeze from outside. The tide was flowing. A tug and four barges were going up like circus cars on a chain. The water was like frosted glass on the smooth side, not too bright. Over by the Surrey bank there was another flaw; as if somebody had breathed on the glass. But it didn't seem to be moving.

'Good night, miss,' the old man went out. But I caught him at the door. 'Excuse me, Captain?' 'Yes.' And I told him about the William Blake Memorial Association. I had been secretary of this Association for six months. Objects: to buy Blake's house in London. Hang originals on the walls. And have a caretaker to show the stuff and explain all about it. The idea was to charge sixpence a visitor. A hundred visitors a day would make two thousand a year.

'Blake,' said the captain, 'is that Admiral Blake?' 'No, William Blake, the great Blake.' 'Never heard of him.' 'Greatest Englishman who ever lived.' 'Was he? What did he do?' 'Poet and painter, but never had a chance. Didn't know how to boost himself.' 'Don't like all this boost.' 'Quite right. Blake didn't either. This memorial is for justice, that's all. We're selling five thousand founder's shares at half a crown down with three instalments at six months. It will pay a hundred per cent. certain. And every receipt has the secretary's signature. In ink.' 'I don't mind all that, but I'll give you half a crown for your club if it's against boost.' 'Make it five bob and I'll elect you vice-president.' 'No, half a crown's enough,' and he put his hand in his pocket. But just then Coker put her tit's beak out of the door and said, 'Don't you give him anything, Captain Jones.' 'I thought it might be a swindle.' 'You'll never see your money back.' 'I knew that before, but what is this Blake?' 'Oh that Blake, that's just the tale.' 'I see, thank you, miss,' and he walked off.

I was angry with Coker. But she only said, 'I told you none of that in my bar.' 'It wasn't in your bar.' 'You old fool, and only out today.' 'It's all legal. And where am I going to sleep? If you won't let me make an honest bed ticket.' But Coker was in a bad temper again. She said only 'Wednesday morning at nine. Don't you forget it. And keep away from the telephone.'

6

It was half-past six, too dark to paint, turning very cold. Clouds all streaming away like ghost fish under the ice. Evening sun turning reddish. Trees along the hard like old copper. Old willow leaves shaking up and down in the breeze, making shadows on the ones below, reflections on the ones above. Need a tricky brush to give the effect and what would be the good. Pisarro's job, not mine. Not nowadays. Lyric, not epic.

Stopped at the corner and put on Coker's socks. Silk and wool; must have cost seven and six. But the trouble was, I had holes in my bootsoles and the pavement struck through. Went to a rubbish basket and got some evening newspapers. Shoved 'em in my boots. Shoved 'em up my trousers, stuffed 'em down my waistcoat. As good as leather against an east wind. Thank God for the Press, the friend of the poor. Then I went in and lit a match to have a look at the picture. I had a feeling it mightn't be there. And it wasn't there, only a piece of dirty yellow paint. It gave me a shock. There, I said to myself, I've spoilt my night's rest. Why couldn't I take it on trust? Act of faith. That's all it is really.

'Mr J-Jimson.'

'No, he's not at home.'

'I w-wondered if you'd like some coffee from the s-stall.'

'No,' I said, 'he wouldn't. He's gone to bed.'

The boy moved off. I went up to the picture on tiptoe and lit another match. This time it showed me a lot of dirty red paint. Like the skin on a pot of rust proofing. My God, I said, how and why did I do that? I must have lost the trick of painting. I'm done for. I'll have to cut my throat after all.

'Your c-coffee, Mr Jimson.'

'Mr Jimson has just gone out. He must have seen you coming.'

But the boy switched on his bicycle lamp, and came right in and put the coffee in my hand.

'Mr Jimson won't be back for some time,' I said. 'But he asked me to tell you that you haven't got a chance. He isn't going to talk to you about art. He's committed arson, adultery, murder, libel, malfeasance of club moneys, and assault with battery; but he doesn't want to have any serious crime on his conscience.'

'B-but, Mr Jimson, I w-want to be an artist.'

'Of course you do,' I said, 'everybody does once. But they get over it, thank God, like the measles and the chicken-pox. Go home and go to bed and take some hot lemonade and put on three blankets and sweat it out.'

'But Mr J-Jimson, there must be artists.'

'Yes, and lunatics and lepers, but why go and live in an asylum before you're sent for? If you find life a bit dull at home,' I said, 'and want to amuse yourself, put a stick of dynamite in the kitchen fire, or shoot a policeman. Volunteer for a test pilot, or dive off Tower Bridge with five bobs' worth of roman candles in each pocket. You'd get twice the fun at about one-tenth of the risk.'

I could see the boy's eyes bulging in the reflected light off the boards, the colour of dirty water. And I thought, I've made an effect. 'Now go away,' I said, 'it's bedtime. Shoo.'

He took my cup and went away. And I struck another match to look at Eve's face. Oh my God, I thought, it's as flat as a tray. It's all made up. What a colour. Tinned salmon. Why did I do that? What a piece of affectation. What was I feeling about? And I felt all locked up. I wanted to knock my head on the walls.

The boy came in with another cup of coffee.

'For God's sake,' I said, 'Mr Jimson is not at home, and he doesn't like to be interrupted by impudent young bastards walking into his house as if it was their own.'

'Oh, Mr Jimson, but I saw they'd g-got buns.' And he gave me a bun with the coffee. 'I'm s-sorry, Mr J-Jimson,' he said, 'but I don't know any other real artists.'

'Who told you Mr Jimson was an artist?' I said. And in my agony I took a bite of bun. It was a good bun and my impression was that the boy had given me the biggest, though in the dim light he might easily have juggled himself the big one. And I was touched. I oughtn't to have been touched because obviously the young blackguard was trying to get round me for his own purposes. With coffee and buns out of his week's pocket money. But I've always had a weakness for boys like Nosy; ugly boys who aspire to martyrdom or fame.

'Look here,' I said, 'I'll tell you a secret. Jimson never was an artist. He's only one of the poor beggars who thought he was clever. Why, you know what the critics said about his pictures in 1908 – that's thirty years ago. They said he was a nasty young man who didn't even know what art was, but thought he could advertise himself by painting and drawing, worse than a child of six – and since then he's gone off a lot. As he's got older, he's got younger.'

'Oh, Mr Jimson, but they always say that.'

'Sometimes they're right, my lad. And my impression is that they were right about Jimson. He's a fraud. Don't you have anything to do with him. Let dirty dogs lie, and swindle, and so on.'

'But there are artists, Mr Jimson.'

'Yes, Jimson's papa was an artist, a real artist. He got in the Academy. He painted people with their noses right between their eyes. He started measuring up the human clock at ten years old, and he worked sixteen hours a day for fifty years. And died a pauper in quite considerable misery. Personally, I'd rather be eaten alive by slow worms.'

'What d-did he p-paint?'

'Pictures,' I said severely. I saw the way the boy's mind was going. 'Art. Jimson's papa may have been in the Academy and painted nicely, but his pictures were definitely art. A lot of artists have painted nicely. But I suppose you never heard of Raphael or Poussin or Vermeer.'

'Oh yes, they were f-famous artists – and there are s-still f-famous artists.'

'Jimson's papa was like that. Of course, when he started, he wasn't popular – rather too modern. He took after Constable and the critics said he was slapdash. But about 1848 he became fuf-famous, for about five years. His stuff was landscape with figures. Girls in gardens. With poetry in the catalogues. He used to get about two hundred guineas for a really nice girl in a nice cottage garden – hollyhocks and pink roses. He made two thousand a year at one time and entertained in style. His wife had three big receptions and a baby every year. But about 1858 a new lot of modern art broke out. The pre-Raphaelites. Old Mr Jimson hated it, of course. And all decent people agreed with him. When Millais showed his Christ in the Carpenter's shop, Charles Dickens wrote that the pre-Raphaelites were worse than the bubonic plague. And Mr Jimson wrote to *The Times* and warned the nation, in the name of art, that the pre-Raphaelites were in a plot to destroy painting altogether. This made him very popular. All really responsible people saw the danger of modern art.'

'The d-danger. But that's quite s-silly.'

'No, it's not silly. And it's time you went home to your mammy. By Gee and Jay, I'd like to see Mr Jimson hear you say that his remarks were silly. Thank God he's absent tonight. Get out quick before he comes back and wrings your neck.'

The boy went out and I lit another match. As every painter knows the fourth look is often lucky. It is always a good plan, during an attack of the jimjams, to try at least four matches. A picture left about in the dark will often disappear for three matches, and come back again, at the fourth, a regular masterpiece. Something quite remarkable. But the match went out before I could see whether I was looking at genuine intuition of fundamental and universal experience in plastic forms of classical purity and simplicity, or a piece of barefaced pornography that ought to be dealt with by the police.

'Excuse me, Mr J-Jimson, I thought you might like a s-s-s-s,' and he gave me a sausage roll. 'It's so cold tonight.'

'You are a good boy,' I said, in spite of myself. 'And so I'm telling you something for your good. All art is bad, but modern art is the worst. Just like the influenza. The newer it is, the more dangerous. And modern art is not only a public danger – it's insidious. You never know what may happen when it's got loose. Dickens and all the other noble and wise men who backed him up, parsons and magistrates and judges, were quite right. So were the brave lads who fought against the Impressionists in 1870, and the Post-Impressionists in 1910, and that rat Jimson in 1920. They were all quite right. They knew what modern art can do. Creeping about everywhere, undermining the Church and the State and the Academy and the Law and marriage and the Government – smashing up civilization, degenerating the Empire.

'Look at the awful disgusting pictures Jimson paints – look at that Adam and Eve – worse than Epstein or Spencer. Absolutely repulsive and revolting, as Dickens said about Millais. A shocking thing. Thank God Jimson's papa never saw it. It would have broken his heart if it hadn't been broken pretty thoroughly already, when the pre-Raphaelites got into the Academy, and he was thrown out.'

'How could they do that?'

'Yes, they could, because he wasn't an associate. He was just going to be when something happened and they threw him out instead. Bang. Three girls in three gardens. Lovely girls. Lovely pictures. But somehow nobody wanted any more nice girls in gardens. Not Jimson girls. Only Burne-Jones girls and Rossetti girls. So papa and mama and their numerous family had nothing to eat.' I swallowed the bun to hide my emotion. I didn't know whether I'd be able to live through the night without my picture. I'm never really comfortable without a picture; and when I've got one on hand, life isn't worth living.

'Mr J-Jimson, do you think it's a good thing to s-start in an art school?'

'Who's going to stutart in an art school?'

'Me.'

'Oh go away, go away. Go home.' And I chased him out. I wanted to be unhappy by myself. I wanted to grieve for Papa. That man suffered a lot. Even more than my poor mother who had to watch him suffer. For she had seven children to worry about as well, and children are a duty. Whereas a broken-hearted man with a grievance is only a liability, a nuisance. And he knows it too.

7

Cold morning. My legs a bit stiff. Didn't look at Adam and Eve in case it hadn't come back. But went straight out.

Frost on the grass like condensed moonlight. Moon high up, transparent. Like snow mark in ice. Birds very lively. Sparrows fluffed out like feather dusters. Met friend Ollier delivering first post. Drop on his nose, a pearl, and two more on his moustache, diamonds. 'Hullo, Mr Ollier, know where I could get some coffee?' 'Good morning, Mr Jimson, if you would care to have one with me in about five minutes.' 'Thank you, Mr Ollier.' 'It's a pleasure, Mr Jimson, to be sure.'

Took a walk up and down to crack the joints. Sun coming up along a cloud bank like clinkers. All sparks. Couldn't do it in paint. Limits of the art. Limits of everything. Limits of my fingers which are all swole up at the joints. No fingers, no swell, no swell, no art. Old Renoir painting his red girls with the brushes strapped to his wrists. Best things he ever did. Monuments.

> The pride of the peacock is the glory of God
> The lust of the goat is the bounty of God
> The wrath of the lion is the wisdom of God
> The nakedness of women is the work of God.

And the nakedness of these trees, pavements, houses, old Postie's red nose and white moustache. 'Nice day, Mr Ollier.' 'A bit chilly for October. Bringing the leaves down.' 'You're right, Mr Ollier.'

'Coming to the meeting, Mr Jimson?' 'Another meeting?' 'Mr Plant's got a meeting on the tenth.'

Mr Plant was an old friend of ours. Plant and Ollier and three or four more had a society and held meetings. They got some schoolmaster or preacher or lecturer from the Workers' Educational Association to give a lecture and smoked over him for a couple of hours. Chief idea for the married, to get away from the home for one evening; for bachelors, to find a home for an evening. There are a lot of these clubs in London. Some of them are simply habits, a few friends who meet regularly in a pub to discuss the dogs, religion, the government, and the state of Europe. I liked Plant's club because Plant had beer for his friends.

'Thank you, Walter,' I said. 'What's the subject?' 'I don't know,' said Ollier. 'But the last one was on Ruskin,' I said. 'How did you know?' said Walter surprised, as we went into the Korner Koffee Shop. 'Because it's generally on Ruskin, or Plato or Owen or Marx. But Ruskin comes first. I should think there must be about fifty meetings every night somewhere in London, on Ruskin.'

'He seems to have been a good writer,' said Postie, who is a modest man and never gives a definite opinion, out of politeness. 'Two coffees, my dear, and four bread and marg and marmalade.'

'So he was, a real artist at it.' 'And they say he knew a lot about art.' 'He was a real writer at it.' There was some coffee on the blue cloth and I pushed it about till it surrounded an interesting kind of shape. But I couldn't see what I could do with it.

'I thought Ruskin seemed to take a high view of art,' said Postie. 'So he did,' I said. 'He had private means. He needed something.' 'And Mr Plant takes a high view too.' 'Mr Plant's had a lot of bad luck in his life. Some take the high road and some take the low road.' I saw that the blue shape could be made into a kind of man, kneeling down like my Adam. But without any right shoulder. One line from the nape to the croup. A sweet line. I fell for that line. Here, I thought, why not. Bring the shoulder forward. Yes, bring his arm right out and have Eve pushing it away. Yes, have her doing the modest. Fending off the first pass. And that nice line will lie right up against the serpent – the serpent will have to come a little behind Adam to avoid two cylinders meeting at the vertical. All right, make the serpent fatter – fatter than Adam. Fat and stiff – erect. And all those red scales against Adam's blue-white flesh.

'Why, Mr Jimson, you're not going,' said Postie. I hadn't noticed it, but I was certainly going. 'I've got an engagement,' I said. 'Have another cup first.' Postie looked quite sad to see me go. He has a strong social sense. It goes with the moustache. Born for a dukedom. Perfect manners and no hurry. 'I'm sorry, Walter,' I said, 'but it's an important engagement – rather urgent.'

8

And I hurried round to the shed. Well, what, I said. It might be something. Probably not. But the fact was, I had got the feeling it was straight from the horse. And when I'd brushed out Adam's damned old knob of a shoulder and got him a new shape down the back, I had that feeling so strong that I sat on myself. Careful, I said, don't get too gay. Perhaps this damned old canvas is going to turn into something or other, perhaps not. Probably not.

Suddenly I got a pull from behind that nearly knocked me down. There was Coker in her best. Nice tweed suit, man's shoes, little rat fur round her bull neck. No jewellery. Coker in her best, dresses county. Having no figure and no looks. 'What the hell you doing, Mr Jimson?' 'Nothing.' 'What's that blue thing? If it's a man it's more like a horse. Without any shoulder on one side.' 'It's just a picture. Cokey.' 'Well, I suppose I don't know anything about it.' 'I suppose so.' 'I suppose it's what you call art.' 'I suppose so.' 'And who was going to meet me at the bus-stop.' 'That was for Wednesday next.' 'This is Wednesday. I got the morning off on purpose.' 'You don't say so. What a pity. I've just arranged to meet a man about a picture. May mean a nice commission,' and so on. Pitching a tale. For the truth was, I wanted to get on with my work. And I knew very well what this new game of Coker's meant – trouble. Arguments. And very likely a lot of bad feeling. It was three years since I'd seen Sara Monday, and I didn't want to see her again. I hadn't the time.

'I'm sorry Coker but this is a real chance for me. I might get a couple of hundred out of it, pay you off.' 'Is this true?' 'On my honour.' 'You're such a liar, Mr Jimson.' 'Swear to God.' 'What time did you say?' 'Half-past nine at the Korner Koffee.' 'I'll wait.' 'You'll be late for opening time.' 'It's worth it if you're going to pay me my money.' And she stayed. I couldn't do any more work. Only pretending. Went round to the Koffee at half past nine and put up a fuss because the chap hadn't turned up. Coker very suspicious. Wouldn't even stand me a coffee. And so to the bus.

All that idea had gone cold. It seemed to me I'd finally wrecked the picture. Adam looked like a frog and why not. I wanted to give Coker one on the nose. But only time I ever tried to give Coker a slap – and that was under provocation – she got in first with a clump which blacked my eye and nearly broke my jaw. And then kicked me downstairs. In the proper style. It's not really a kick when done by an expert. It's a punch with the foot. And the foot applied rather high on the crack. Coker shot me off the top step like a rocket, and I had so many bruises on me I couldn't take my trousers off or put my boots on or scratch the back of my neck, for a fortnight. It makes me laugh to think of it. I like Coker. She's a woman of character. There's something there that will stand the rain. But next time I have to deal with Coker on the level, I thought, I'll take a hammer with me.

'I don't know why you're so keen on this visit,' I said. 'You won't get much out of old Sara.'

'We'll wait and see,' said Coker. 'She wouldn't like to let it come into court, I should think – living with a chap who's not her husband and about ten years younger. And she's been in jug herself too.'

'And all this trouble for four pounds fourteen,' I said.

'I'm not letting them get away with it ' said Coker. 'Monday and Hickson, a nice pair. Why, they simply made a fool of you.'

Coker was getting hot, and I said no more. Coker had been working up the case for a long time, and when a woman gets the idea of justice, there's no teaching her any sense. That's why we don't have women judges. They'd be too strong for justice.

And, in fact, she went on getting fiercer and fiercer all the way. Working herself up.

'This Sara Monday,' she said, 'where did you pick her up? Is there a place for models or did you take her off the street?' 'She wasn't a model and I didn't pick her up. She was a married woman, and she picked me up.' 'What, you don't mean to say she went on the street.' 'Of course not, she didn't need to. It was in her own house when I went to paint her husband.' 'What, you don't mean to say she gave you the eye in her own house.' 'Two eyes and the aye-aye. Threw herself at me from the kick.' 'A married woman.' 'Married seven years, five kids.' 'Five kids,' said Coker. 'A woman like that ought to be hung on hooks.' 'You'd be surprised,' I said, 'the women that go for artists, especially artists that paint the nude. Makes 'em feel themselves in themselves, I suppose.' 'Don't you call them women,' said Coker, still working up her drill. 'A lot of whores, I say. And worse if they're ladies and haven't any call.' 'Sara had the call,' I said. 'Just getting up in the thirties and full blast on all cylinders. Regular man-killer. "Oh, Mr Jimson, I do love art," and she didn't know a picture from a bath bun. Never did "Oh, Mr Jimson, how wonderful to be able to paint like that." Bending her neck, too, and spooning her eyes at me. She believed in butter, Sara did. Greasing the slides. I've known some liars and crooks, but Sara was the queen. Why, she couldn't ask you to have some more cream without putting the comether in her voice and shooting off her eyes and jerking up her front.'

'Oh – it turns my liver.'

'And, what made me laugh, to see her at a tea party in her frills. Some more tea, Lady Pye; another slice, Mrs Paddle. Oh, do try. Just a little bit of the angel cake. They all loved her. Sweet young British matron – guardian of the home.'

'Don't tell me about her,' said Coker, 'I can see her.'

'Family prayers. Down on her knees every night and morning. The Scripture moveth us in sundry places. And then hop-skip round to my studio. Would you like me to sit? Not today, thank you, ma'am. But you're drawing that figure out of your head. Yes, ma'am. Wouldn't it be better from a model? Depends on the model, ma'am. Anything I can do to help? And in two two's there she is in her skin.'

'I'd skin her.'

'Church on Sunday. Bible and prayer book in red morocco with gilt edges. Cold supper in the evening. Salmon, salad, lobsters, tongue, brawn, cold beef, stout, burgundy. Trifle with a pound of Devonshire cream and a couple of pints of old brown sherry. Evening hymns in the twilight. Oh, Mr Jimson, what a lovely tune – it always makes me cry. What a sweet moon, shall we take a turn in the garden, to see if the tobacco has got another flower. Oh, Mr Jimson, isn't it a sweet scent – it goes to your head. Head was the word. And then the summerhouse and somebody had left the cushions in the deck chair.'

'Oh, the bitch,' said Coker. 'The whip is too good for them.'

'And afterwards, you know, Coker, she used to shed tears – real tears – and it was: Oh, Mr Jimson, how did it all happen, I can't believe it, it all seems like a dream, doesn't it. Just a bad dream. And I'm so fond of my husband. He's such a true good man. Oh dear, I feel so awful —'

'And you swallowed it all,' said Coker. 'Just like a man, encouraging the bitch.'

'Sara. Not on your life. I used to laugh at her tricks.'

'Yes, and let her grab you as soon as she'd murdered her husband.'

'Sara never grabbed me. Poor old Sara, she didn't have much of a success there, when she got too much of a nuisance I threw her out on her neck.'

'I believe you,' said Coker. 'Backwards. Look at you now. Hopping along with your nose stuck out in front like an old dog in the May moon – she'll grab you again if you aren't careful.'

'Never,' I said, pulling in my nose a bit and pushing out my stomach. For the truth was I had been getting up the pace. And yet I'll swear I never thought of Sara, except as a damned old nuisance. Spoiling a good day's work.

'Grab me, Sara! After all I know of her.' I said, 'Poor Sall, not likely. Why, talk of not letting your right hand know what your left hand was doing. Sara could commit adultery at one end and weep for her sins at the other, and enjoy both operations at once. She wasn't a woman – she was a bag full of women, and every one worse than all the others.'

'I've half a mind to go back,' said Coker. 'I never knew she was as bad as that.' And she stuck out her front and made her heels rattle. Coker hasn't much chest. She's all of a piece like a ship's funnel. 'All right, Coker,' I said. 'That suits me. I don't want any trouble with the old devil'. 'Not on your life,' said Coker. 'You're not going to dodge out of it. Only thing is – I hope I'll be able to speak to the creature without showing what I think of her.' 'Say what you like,' I said, 'Sara won't mind – she's solid brass to the Adam's rib. Only way to touch Sara's feelings is to hit her with something harder. On the nose. Toko on the Boko. That's her only tender spot.'

'I couldn't do it,' said Coker. 'I couldn't touch her with a bottle-brush. It's psychology with me. A woman who could show herself off like that.'

9

But when we came to Sara's door it was new painted, and the door knob shining like rolled gold. Sara all over, I thought, you can see she's adopted that door knob – loves it like herself. Rub the little darling up and give it a chance to look its best. Sara for cleaning and washing. Loved slapping things about. Getting off her steam. See Sara in her bath washing herself. Like a cat. Almost hear her purr. I didn't know whether to draw her or to bite her. And I did give her one with the back brush which made her jump. Oh, Gulley, what was that for? Just to let you know there's somebody else in the world. Good sketch I did of her – with the same back brush. Right arm in the air. Elbow cutting up against the window. Hair over left shoulder catching the light. Lime green outside. Head bent over to the left – line of the cheek against the hair. Lips pushed out. Eyes dropped. Looking at her breasts. Serious expression. Worship.

And all the same, she was a fine woman. She made me mad every way. Regular born man-eater. Coker gave me a nudge like a kick and the door came open. There was a fat old char with grey hair and a red face, breathing beer and suds. 'Why,' she said, 'it's not you, Gulley.' 'No,' I said, 'I'm Mr Gloster of Foster.' 'Well, isn't that nice,' she said.

She didn't smile. She only looked confused, like an old char when something happens out of her routine. 'You didn't see a little boy with white hair and blue stockings coming along the street? You might have heard him cough.'

'No,' I said, 'and how are you, Sara?' For I knew her well enough at a second look. She still had the build and the voice.

'Excuse me, Mrs Monday,' Coker said, 'I think you heard from me. Miss D. Coker.'

'Yes, Miss Coker, of course. I was meaning to write to you only I've been so busy.'

All said like a duchess, so sweet you couldn't tell how it was meant, if you hadn't known that Coker was an enemy. 'Excuse me a moment,' and she came bulging out of the door and went waddling down the street, calling, 'Dicky, Dicky.'

'A nice game,' said Coker. 'No, you don't, Madame. We've come and we stay' and she pushed me through the door and into the parlour. Big armchairs. A lot of knick-knacks. Souvenirs of Brighton and Blackpool. Sara all over. Photographs of Mr Monday in a jampot collar. Photograph of Sara in her wedding dress. Silver frame that she gave me once for a birthday present to fit my favourite picture of herself in a tight bodice. A bun bursting out of the bag. A Rubens Venus in a parcel. You could never get Sara into a fitted dress. You had to hang frills on her.

Sara came back, panting. 'Excuse me being so rude. I'm so worried about my little boy. My husband's little boy, I should say. Do sit down.'

'We came on business,' Coker said, standing up as stiff as a pillar box. 'As I wrote you, Mr Jimson is bringing a legal action against Mr Hickson for getting justice about nineteen paintings and over five hundred drawings. What we understand is you gave over this property to Mr Hickson for value which you had no right to receive.'

'That's right,' said Sara, 'but if you would just sit down a moment till I get the kettle on,' and off she went again. I sat down, but Coker gave me a look and said, 'Don't do that, Mr Jimson – that's just what she wants. If you sit down in her house it will all come out against you in the court.'

'Why,' I said. 'You don't know Sara. She's no idea of taking that kind of advantage. Don't need to. She's got better tricks than that.'

Sara came in again blowing like an engine, and said, 'Oh dear, I get so short of breath since I had the 'flu. Excuse me leaving you, Miss Coker. The kettle is just on. You'll have some tea, won't you? Yes, of course, I meant to write a long time ago, but the children got away with my pen. You know what they are.'

'We came about these pictures, Mrs Monday. Which you sold to Mr Hickson, having no right to them.'

524

'That's right, Miss Coker.'

'I don't call it right. I call it a robbery.'

'That's right. Won't you sit down, Miss Coker. Why, Gulley, it's a real pleasure. Of course, Mr Hickson said the pictures weren't properly finished and we owed a lot of money all round, and Mr Jimson had gone away and I didn't know when he was coming back, so when Mr Hickson said he'd pay all the debts and give me a bit to carry on, just for some of the pictures lying about, I was in such a whirl I didn't know how to say no.'

'And you didn't think any of my pictures were worth twopence, anyway.'

'Oh yes, Gulley. I always thought you were a lovely artist.'

'Go on, Sall. What's the good of keeping it up. We're both tottering into the grave.'

And I had the old feeling all over again. I wanted to give her a tap. Just to knock the crookedness out of her. Not a hard one. She wasn't my wife any more. But just a tap, platonic.

I daresay I had it in my face for all at once the old rascal bent her great neck over to one side and said, 'You may well say that of me, Gulley. But you don't look a day older. Well, what a pity my husband is on duty this morning. He'd have liked to see you.'

'I came on Wednesday because Mr Robins told me he was on duty that day. And I thought you'd like to see an old friend without him being about,' said Coker.

This was from one woman to another. Telling Sara in one sentence that her husband wasn't a husband and that she didn't want him to meet anyone who knew too much about her. But it didn't shake Sara. She'd got used to the situation. No Duchess ever beat Sara in behaving like Nature when she chose.

'That's right,' Sara said. 'He's always away Tuesday night and Wednesday morning. It's a shame.' But she kept looking at me out of one eye as if to ask, 'How much has he changed?' an old woman's look. It surprised me. I'd never thought Sara could get so old.

'And how are you, Gulley? How's Tommy?' meaning my son, Thomas William.

'Tommy is a scholar and a gentleman, and he's gone to China in a bank, so he needn't know me any more.'

'Oh, what a shame,' said Sara, looking out of the window and bending her ear that way for Dicky's cough. 'I never would have believed it of Tom.'

'Except that you put him up to it, and a good thing too,' I said, 'and I'll bet he writes to you every month.'

'And Liz and the babies?' said Sara, meaning my last wife and the two youngest.

'Gone off,' I said. 'Back to mama – when they put me away.'

'And when he'd spent all her money,' said Coker, 'and she hadn't got anything to eat.'

'I'm sure you never did so, Gulley,' said Sara, 'you were so fond of her.'

'You don't believe a word you say, do you, Sall?' I said.

'It's quite like old times,' Sara said, looking at me with both eyes and smiling for the first time. 'And how well you look,' meaning I looked so old and ugly she was sorry for me and wanted to stuff me up.

'So do you, Sall. No one would take you for thirty-five.'

'Oh yes,' said Sara. 'Oh dear yes,' giving a great sigh that shook her cheeks and chin and neck and bosom. 'You're being nice to me. But I know. I'm getting an old woman, Gulley. Well, I suppose it's only to be expected.' And she looked so broken down that I thought she was going to cry. 'Yes,' she said. 'when you really think, it's got a sad side, life,' and all at once she put her two hands on her thighs, elbows out, tossed up her head and straightened her back. And I knew that back. I saw it again, the big flat muscles under the skin, the lift of the shoulder blades and the dimples moving like little whirlpools over their spines; the lovely flexible turn of the flanks over the solid hips. Sara was smiling at me. 'What it was to be young,' she said. 'But there, those that don't know, no one can tell them.' Just as she might have looked and spoken thirty years before. It made me stare. As if that woman I'd known, all cream and gold and roses, had resurrected under that old skin. And then, before I could speak, she said, 'There's the kettle boiling. Don't come,' and heaved herself up with a groan, and waddled out, flat foot, with her crinkly old hand on her buttock, palm out. An old stump again. She left me staring. I daresay my mouth was open.

'You old fool,' Coker said. 'Why don't you stand up to her. She's turning you right round her finger.'

'Not me,' I said, 'and not Sara. I know her games.'

But the fact was, I was seeing Sara in her bath with the brush. And drying her feet, leaning down all back and arms with her hair falling over her knees, and a bluish light on the shiny flats round the spine – sky reflection – a sweet bit of brushwork.

And there was something else about the old boa constrictor that I'd forgotten. Till that moment when she squared up to me and threw me her old smile. Herself Sara. The individual female. The real old original fireship. Yes. The old hulk had it. Still. A spark in the ashes.

'Not but what you can't get right down in the dirt if you want,' said Coker. 'And splash yourself. So long as I get her evidence that she stole the pictures. And I will, too, if I stop here all day and the guvnor has to open his own bar by his own graft and gives me the sack for it.'

'Don't worry,' I said, 'Sara won't give any trouble. That's not her method.'

Sara came panting in with the tea and a cake with a big slice out of it. 'I must apologize, Miss Coker,' she said, 'offering you a cake with a slice out. Any other day this week you'd have had a proper cake. But the truth was, Dicky kept on asking me and he has such a cough, poor lamb. And then you came. But it always happens like that, doesn't it. You'd think there was a special providence just looking out to catch any woman that tries to have things nice. I'm sure you've noticed it, Miss Coker.'

'I've noticed you keep off the subject of Mr Jimson's pictures.'

'That's right,' said Sara, 'I've been so worried about little Dicky's cough and his going to school, I couldn't think.'

'And you admit,' said Coker, 'you had no right to dispose of these pictures.'

'That's right,' said Sara. 'Well, Gulley, I can't get over it seeing you again. And how's dear little Liz and the new baby? But, oh dear, you told me, didn't you. Let me fill your cup, Miss Coker.'

'And will you sign a paper to say you didn't ought to have agreed to Mr Hickson's swindling Mr Jimson out of his legal property.'

'That's right,' said Sara, getting up and looking down the street. 'Well, I could have sworn that was Dicky's cough.' And she sat down again in the old way; looking at the chair first like a cat at the rug, and then giving it a pat, and then pulling up her skirts and then taking her seat. Taking her seat is the word. And then disposing her skirts, and pushing out her front and arranging her arms, and throwing up her top chin, and assuming a handsome expression. She hadn't got the face, but she still put on the expression. I'd seen her do the whole act a thousand times and wanted to give her a rap. Just to bring to her attention the existence of the forgotten man. A slap on the nap. And I pulled my chair up nearer. Took up a strategic position on the left flank.

'Why, Gulley,' Sara said, 'you never told me about your painting. Is it going on nicely?' And again she looked at me with all her eyes and ears. Sara never asked me about my painting unless she was feeling tender. It was in the nature of a pass. And as Coker had her nose in her bag, I gave her a pinch – not a hard one. And Sara gave a little jump and a squeak and said, 'Oh, Gulley, you mustn't.' But then she turned quite pink and went on smiling at me with all her eyes. Like a girl of fifteen. Round eyes with a light inside. Light of youth, curiosity and devilry.

Well, I thought, here's another of the Jills in the box. But no woman really gets old inside until she's dead or takes to bridge. Scratch the grandmother and you find the grandbaby giggling behind the nursery door at nothing at all. Nothing a man would understand.

'And how are you really, Gulley?' she said. 'Tell me true. I want to know. How are your poor legs?'

'Still going on,' I said. And there we were smiling at each other. Just as if we'd never been man and wife. Just in pure original sympathy. The old Adam and the old Eve.

'And how are you really, Sall?' I said, patting her gently on the behind. 'But I can see Mr What's-his-Name- Robins, the present owner – I mean – takes good care of a valuable property.'

'Oh dear, he does. Oh yes. Too well,' said Sara bursting out as honest as she always did when she was touched in the right place. 'I can't have a little cold or a little pain but he wants to send me to the doctor. Why only yesterday —' But all at once she noticed that Coker had taken her nose out of her bag and was making a point at us. Frozen. And Sara became at once the duchess again, easy and false as an old madame. 'But you know what it is, Miss Coker, ladies often have a little pain, but they keep it to themselves. And I shouldn't complain of being too well looked after, should I? It's only that I never could stand doctors. Well, they've got to find something wrong. Haven't they? It's only professional. But there was my friend Mrs Blonberg, just opposite – she used to have a little pain – I'm sure it was no more than I've had myself and thought nothing of, and she went to the doctor, and the next thing she was in hospital and they cut her up on Monday and we buried her yesterday.'

'As we came on business,' said Coker, 'perhaps we'd better get on with it.'

'Oh yes' said Sara, and she gave another of her big sighs, like a burst tyre. 'But won't you have some more tea first – it's such a pity to waste a whole new pot.'

But Coker was not going to unbend towards us. 'Excuse me,' she said, 'but we haven't too much time. Here's a paper which, if you will sign, Mrs Monday, we will know where we are.' And she opened her bag and brought out a piece of paper folded up in a notebook. 'I left blanks for the numbers.'

'There were nineteen canvasses,' I said, 'and about five hundred drawings.'

'Mr Hickson says seventeen.'

'That's right,' said Sara, looking at me all the time and trying to stop giggling.

'It isn't right,' said Coker. 'Where's the rest?'

'Well,' said Sara, 'one was the blacksmith's little girl and he kept on asking me for it till I had to let him take it, though I never liked him, Gulley, whatever you say. The way he looked at me from behind – every time I passed. But there, you wouldn't believe he meant anything.'

'And what about the other one?'

'I don't know,' said Sara. 'I never could find it – it must have got lost somewhere unless that blacksmith got hold of it.'

'It wasn't that one you liked so much,' I said, 'of yourself in the bath?'

'Oh, Gulley, I never liked it, you know. I never liked the way you painted me.'

'Always taking a peep at it,' I said. 'Admiring yourself in your skin.'

528

'Well,' said Sara, 'I must say I never had any trouble with my skin, like some people,' and she looked so pleased with herself and so hypocritical that I gave her another pinch. And Sara let out a squawk and said, 'Oh, I thought it was something biting. Excuse me, Miss Coker, if you knew what trouble you have in these nasty little houses to keep them out of the furniture.'

'Well, if you'll sign,' said Coker, turning rhubarb colour, 'I suppose we must be satisfied.' And she pushed the paper and a fountain pen under Sara's nose.

'Oh, you've brought a pen,' said Sara. 'Well, that is thoughtful. I was so worried about not having a proper pen.' And she signed.

'Why,' I said, 'you've signed for nineteen pictures.'

'That's right,' said Sara, looking at me with all her feelings at once, and taking me in all over again.

'And you only gave Hickson seventeen.'

'That's right,' said Sara, cocking her head a little further over to see if it improved my appearance.

'You don't care what you sign,' I said. 'You've always got something up your sleeve.'

'That's right,' said Sara. She wasn't even listening to me. Following out her own schemes as usual. 'Well, Gulley, I can't get over it. Seeing you like this. Such a lovely surprise. And you so young and gay.'

Coker was putting up the paper. 'Thank you, Mrs Monday,' she said. 'That's all we require. Now, Mr Jimson, if you've come to stay, it's all one to me. But I got to be in my bar some time this week.'

I got up. For I could see Coker was in a temper by the way she looked. Like a wooden figure on a ship that's had its bottom knocked out.

'Young,' I said, 'go on, you old treacle pot. You know very well I look a hundred without my teeth – nearly as old as you do,' and I gave her another pinch, a good one.

Sara gave a shriek and rushed out of the door, calling out, 'Dicky, Dicky, you bad boy.' You couldn't tell whether the shriek was for me or Dicky. Probably both. The old kangaroo could always shriek in two places at once.

'Well,' said Coker, 'if I said I was surprised at you, Mr Jimson, it wouldn't be true. I seen too many nasty old men and some of them didn't know any better.'

'Never mind, Cokey,' I said. 'It's only a how-d'you-do with an old acquaintance. You're my steady.'

'Not me, thank you. I'm nobody's steady except my own.' And she went out. But not flouncing. Coker was always county in her county clothes.

Sara came bustling in pushing a kid in front of her. Skinny little chip with a blue face and red hair. Knobbly knees and no meat anywhere. Staring at us with pop eyes and sucking something in his left cheek. He wasn't walking. He was leaning back against Sara with his feet together; and Sara was pushing him along like a dirt shovel.

'This is Dicky,' said Sara. 'Oh, you bad boy. Where have you been – with that cough? Say how do you do to the gentleman. This is Mr Jimson. He's an artist. A real Academy artist.'

'Academy?' I said. 'Since when? I may be dead, but I haven't admitted it.'

'Well, you were just as good, Gulley, in your day. You know you were. Now Dicky, where's your manners? You never seen a real artist before, have you? Mr Jimson paints real pictures, big ones in oil colours. Now Dicky, shake hands with the gentleman.'

Dicky put out his tongue. Only a little way. Because you could see he hadn't quite made up his mind what to do. Taken by surprise.

'Oh, Dicky,' said Sara.

'Leave the kid alone, Sally,' I said. 'What's he done to you. Good-bye, and lay off the beer before you blow up.'

'Oh dear,' Sara said, 'but you'll think so badly of him, and he can behave so nicely when he tries. Say good-bye to the gentleman, Dicky darling. For mother's sake. And perhaps I could find a peppermint ball.'

Dicky put out his tongue a little further. But he was still a bit confused. And I gave him a pull on the ear. 'Go on, kid,' I said. 'You got the right idea. Why don't you bite me? That's the way to treat strangers.'

'Oh, Gulley, you mustn't,' said Sara.

'Never mind what mother says, you bite everybody and throw things at 'em. Make 'em respect you.'

'Don't you listen to the gentleman, Dicky,' Sara said. She was quite in a fluster. 'He's only joking.' And she said to me, 'You oughtn't, Gulley. It's a shame with a child. Here, run along and get yourself a piece of sugar,' and she pushed him out. 'You shouldn't, Gulley.'

I gave her a buss on her cheek and said, 'A nice tender chop,' and Sara took me by the arm, quite sentimental.

'Oh, Gulley, I do hope she looks after you properly —'

'She? She doesn't look after me. I'm my own man, Sall, at last. Yes, I've learnt something.'

'What, all by yourself?'

'Bachelor's castle, with barbed wire and spring guns.'

'Where is it exactly, just in case any of your old friends wanted to know?'

'Nowhere,' I said, 'just in case some of my old friends wanted to know.'

'Oh, go away,' said Sara, quite angry. 'As if I should take all that trouble – after all the trouble I'd had with you before.' And she went out calling for the boy. 'Dicky, Dicky, what are you doing with that sugar?' And just then Coker put her head in the door and said, 'Are you coming or am I going?' So I popped my silver frame off the mantelpiece in my pocket, and went out.

10

'Giving your picture to the blacksmith,' said Coker. 'Why, I suppose it might be worth ten thousand pounds.' Coker thinks all good pictures are worth ten thousand pounds. 'And I bet she did away with that other one. She's got thief written all over her.'

'So she has,' I said, 'and there's plenty of room.'

'What you laughing at? Anyone would think you were sozzled,' said Coker. 'Pull yourself together, do.'

For the truth was I was a bit excited. I'd forgotten what Sara was like. The real Sara. The old individual geyser. And she'd gone a bit to my head.

'She looked like she's been on the street,' said Coker.

Wouldn't do Sara any harm if she had, I thought, she'd always be game for a laugh, and keep her floors clean.

> Because the soul of sweet delight can never be defiled.
> Fires surround the earthly globe, yet man is not consumed.
> Amidst the lustful fires he walks, and polishes his door knob.

'Come up,' said Coker, for the truth is, I walked over the kerb at the end of the street, not noticing. And gave myself a shock. 'You aren't fit to be out by yourself.' And she took me by the arm and gave me a jerk that nearly dislocated my neck. 'Go on. You ought to be shut up. That's the fact.'

'That's right,' I said, just like Sara, to keep the woman quiet. 'For everything that lives is holy.'

'What are you talking about now. I declare you're off your loop.'

Amidst the lustful fire he walks; his feet become like brass. His knees and thighs like silver, and his breast and head like gold. Old Raudlpole Billy on the ramp Embracing the truth. Through generation to generation. The door of paradise. This way to the Holy land. Fall to rise again.

For everything that lives is holy. Life delights in life.

'Up with you,' said Coker, pushing me on the bus, and planting me between a navvy smelling like an old stable and an old woman with a sore nose and a basket full of pig's food.

> For every generated body in its inward form
> Is a garden of delight and a building of magnificence
> Built by the sons of Los
> And the herbs and flowers and furniture and beds and chambers
> Continually woven in the looms of Enitharmon's daughters.
> In bright cathedrons golden domes with care and love and tears.

That is to say, old Billy dreamed dreams while Mrs Blake emptied the pot.

'A woman,' said Coker. 'That's what your Mrs Monday is. And in another minute I'd have said so.'

'That's so, Cokey. Female.' But I was thinking that Sara at about forty had been just what I wanted for my Eve. That falls every night to rise in the morning. And wonder at herself. Knowing everything and still surprised. Living in innocence. With Sara's eyes, young eyes. But not flappers' eyes.

'Wake up, old bones,' Coker said. 'It's a fourpenny fare to the junction.' 'I haven't got it, Cokey.' 'Then you'd better get out and walk. Think I'm going to stake you.' 'All right, Cokey,' and I got up. Seemed a good chance to get away and think.

Coker looked at me like corkscrews. Extracting. 'Where are you off to now? Back to your Monday.' 'Not much,' I said. 'I've had all I want from her.' The last person I wanted to see was old Sara, wasting my time with chatter. I wanted to think. I had a lot of ideas coming. Always like that after a party. Especially a party with somebody like Sara; all alive-oh. 'Cheer up, Cokey,' I said. But she grabbed hold of my coat-tails and told me to sit down again. She didn't like to see me so pleased to get away from her. There's a lot of girl in Cokey. 'Want to get yourself run over, I suppose. Just before the case comes on.' 'I don't want to be run over. I'm too busy.' 'But don't you forget, it's another one and six you owe me – and fourpence for the other bus.' 'I won't forget.' 'You will, but I won't.'

Yes, I thought, all alive-oh. Eve should be a woman of forty with five children and grey hairs coming, trying on a new velvet. Looking at herself in the glass, as if she'd never seen herself before. And the children fighting round the dustbin in the yard. And Adam smoking his pipe in the local. And telling lies about his spring onions. Works of passion and imagination.

There was a street market on the kerb. Swarms of old women in black cloaks jostling along like bugs in a crack. Stalls covered with blue-silver shining pots, ice-white jugs, heaps of fish, white-silver, white-green, and kipper gold; forests of cabbage; green as the Atlantic, and rucked all over in permanent waves. Works of passion and imagination. Somebody's dream girls. Somebody's dream pots, jugs, fish. Somebody's love supper. Somebody's old girl chasing up a titbit for the old china. The world of imagination is the world of eternity. Old Sara looking at a door knob. Looking at my old ruins. The spiritual life.

'Now where are you,' said Coker. And we got down at the bridge. White cloudy sky, with mother-of-pearl veins. Pearl rays shooting through, green and blue-white. River roughed by a breeze. White as a new file in the distance. Fish-white streak on the smooth pin-silver upstream. Shooting new pins.

'Well,' said Coker. 'Do you know where you are?'

'Make it five bob, Cokey,' I said. 'It's easier to remember. That's three and threepence, say three and six in round figures.'

'My God,' said Coker. 'You have got a nerve. Not one farthing – I need it too bad. One and tenpence for today is enough, with the bus, and all on top of the four pound fourteen.'

'Make it a fiver, Cokey. Four pounds fourteen and one and tenpence. That's four and twopence you still owe me.'

'You get off before I call a copper. What do you want it for? And don't forget Tuesday. Nine o'clock sharp. At the bus-stop,' said Coker, 'or I'll know why and how.'

'Tuesday. What for!'

'Hickson.'

'I couldn't do it, Cokey. I can't afford it. I might shoot him or strangle him, and I haven't got the time to be hanged.'

'You be there or I'll be here. I'm not taking any more from any old tarts. I mean business, and that's Hickson.' But she gave me half a crown. Coker always barks loudest when she sees a bite coming. Because she knows she's going to get bitten. She can't resist a friend after she's bawled him out.

And I hopped into a pawnshop and took fifteen shillings on the silver frame. More than I expected. But Sara always gave good presents when she had the credit. I got some real colours and a couple of brushes at last, and made for the studio. I felt I could paint. As always after a party. Life delights in life. Especially with Sara.

11

Next morning, of course, the canvas looked a bit flat. As always after a party. But when I got back my picture eye, I saw that Adam's new shape was right. Final. Eve was the trouble. She was a bit too clever, too artistic, too flat, more like a composition in line and colour than a real piece of stuff. But I didn't know why. I didn't know if it was the temporary effect of meeting Sara or the permanent result of losing touch with the real Mackay. Losing the essential woman in the paint. I'll sleep on that one, I said. But I can do something to the foreground now, it's as empty as a beer jug with the bottom knocked out. All those nicely fitted receding planes amount to damn all but an art-school dodge. And it struck me all at once, that what I wanted there was a pattern, not in the flat, but coming and going. Leaves, waves. Tufts of grass bending in the breeze. Flowers. I began the flowers, but they felt wrong. And all at once I made a thing like a white Indian club. I like it, I said, but it's not a flower, is it? What the hell could it be? A fish? And I felt a kick inside as if I was having a foal. Fish. Fish. Silver-white, green-white. And shapes that you could stroke with your eyebrows.

'Oh Mister J-Jimson.' Oh God, there was young pink-nose looking in the window. Just going to school. Satchel on his back. 'Good morning, Mr J-Jimson.' 'Good morning, Mister poke-nose. Good-bye.'

I had no time to play and my temper was bad. I was a bit impatient.

For those fish were catching my fancy. School of herrings. In a shape something like a map of Ireland laid sideways. Cold green. Under the moon.

Ethinthus, queen of waters. How thou shinest in the sky.
My daughter, how I rejoice. For thy children flock around.
Like the gay fishes in the wave when the cold moon drinks the dew.

All the green silver noses in a row on the top of the water. But in the round. Knobs sticking out of the flat. Like worn boot nails in one of those green leather soles. And real fish eyes, glaring, bulging, astonished. I squeezed out some raw sienna on a plank and drew the rings on them.

'I've g-got a piece of canvas,' said Barbon. 'You there still.'

And there he was, inside the door. He'd just walked in. Nothing to beat the cheek of the shy, when desperate. Look out for cripples, stammerers, lame boys and ugly girls. The army of the frontier. Frontier of hell and death. Do or die. Battlers from the cradle. Saints or snakes. Pink-nose gave me a fright. 'Here,' I said, 'what you mean, coming into my house.'

Pink-nose turned red and green in patches like a bad ham and said, 'Oh, Mr J-Jimson, I knocked—' 'Well, knock off.' 'But es-s-s-s,' and he began to sizzle like a steam engine. He opened his satchel and took out a piece of new canvas. He was looking at me with eyes like a sheep just before you knock it on the head. 'Ss-s—'

'Excuse you,' I said. 'No I don't.' For I was getting in a state. 'What the devil do you mean?'

'To m-mend the hole, Mr J-Jimson – you s-said it could be glued.'

No good getting angry with the lopear. Only upset me all the morning. 'What the hell you think you're doing? Why aren't you working?'

'I'm just going to school.'

'But you're not working. You're thinking about art. Now look here, Nosy, you're on the road to ruin. Do you want to break your mother's heart, and your wife's heart, and your children's hearts, unless they're all bastards and stand on their own feet. I know what I'm talking about. My son Tommy was a scholarship boy – went to Oxford, and now he's a gentleman. A real gentleman with Christian feelings and a sense of responsibility and hand-made shoes. And born in the Institution. And how did he do it? From sticking to the books. And what you think would have happened to Tommy if he'd begun to play around with all this art nonsense. I told him. I said, "If I catch you drawing or painting, Tommy, I'll skin you with a blunt rake. Art and religion and drink. All of them ruin to a poor lad. Leave 'em to the millionaires that can afford to go to the devil first-class all the way. You've got to work for your living."

' "You needn't be afraid, Daddy," said Tom, "I haven't any taste for art." And, thank God, he did really hate the whole racket. Too polite to say so, but he thought me a dirty old faker, and his step-mother a slummock who would rather flop about in a wrapper listening to Wag-ner or Bee-thoven than wash her face or darn his socks. Tom went to a good school and it cured him of art before he was fifteen. And see where he is now. A gentleman and a scholar. Who doesn't know an illustration from a picture. And can't tell "God Save the King" from "Sleepers Awake." But here – that's enough.' For I saw that I was talking too much. Dangerous thing to tell people about yourself. They try to put you in their box. Keep you for the drawing-room cabinet. 'That's enough,' I said to Nosy. 'You get off quick. I've had enough of this.'

'But, Mr J-Jimson, I could come this afternoon at tea-time. When you're at tea. And it would only take a m-minute. I wouldn't be in the way a bit, I promise.'

'You promise. Not to be in the way. That's a good one, Why, you're always in the way. Everyone is. But you know you are, and what do you care. Git.' And I shoved him out and banged the door. And got back to the fishes for an hour or six.

Then I had a disinterested look at them and they were not at all what I expected. Nothing ever is. But after a little reflection, I waked up about half-past two in the morning and perceived that their noses were not big enough and too near together. Water too bright. And soft. Had to be harder to get the plane flat.

The middle of the night is a good time for a man to study his picture because he can't see it then; and the new scheme worked out well. On Saturday morning it looked so good that I began to like it. I promised myself a bottle of whisky, if I could borrow the price. Whisky is bad for me. I hate the stuff. And so I only take it for the consequences, as a special reward for a lucky day's work. Yes, I said admiring the fishes and already getting a little whiskified, by sympathetic magic; the fish are good; I am good; life is good; whisky, though bad, is good; when all at once I had visitors. Mr Plant and two other preachers. And you could see even by the way they walked and held up their chins that they were coming to encourage the fine arts. Out of a sense of duty, I hadn't time to run away, I could only pretend not to notice.

The first preacher was six feet high and had a nose like an overripe fig. I took him for a gospeller with Greek, learned, low and broad. The second was about five foot three inches high and had a face like a Landseer lion. Real orator's mouth, pug's nose, forehead reflecting the heavenly light. I knew him. He kept the tin chapel in Greenbank and his sermons made even leading-seamen cry. A real foghorn of salvation. As for Mr Plant, he's a bantam, half an inch shorter than Coker, and a great deal lighter built. He has a face like what Cardinal Newman's would have been if he had gone into the army instead of the Church, grown an Old Bill moustache, lost most of his teeth, and only shaved on Saturdays, before preaching.

Plantie keeps a cobbler's shop in an Ellam Street basement off Greenbank. They say he's the worst cobbler in four parishes, because his mind is so much on Plato and Owen, and Kropotkin and Spinoza, and Sacco and Vanzett, that he never hits the right nail on the right spot. But people go on bringing their boots to be murdered by him because he is offended if they don't. He can't bear disloyalty and unkindness. He's had so much of it.

Plantie is a very strong Protestant, that is to say, he's against all churches, especially the Protestant; and he thinks a lot of Buddha, Karma and Confucius. He is also a bit of an anarchist and three or four years ago he took up Einstein and vitamins.

There's a lot of religion about Greenbank; I mean real old English religion, which you don't notice any more than a badger unless you try to poke it. Then, of course, it will come up a little way towards the surface of civilization and bite you in half. It keeps itself to itself, and if you hear hymns coming out of a mews, or a terrace house down Blackboy's Yard, it may be Bunyan's great-great-great-grand-daughter teaching a class of young walruses to sing the International, or a dustman starting a revival among the Unitarian Prebaptists branch of the Rechabite nudists.

All the London prophets have strong followings round Greenbank; that is Bunyan, Wesley, Richard Owen, Proudhon, Herbert Spencer, W. G. Grace, W. E. Gladstone, Marx and Ruskin. The last two are a bit revolutionary and attract chiefly the sprouts like Nosy. A lot of the Ellam Street boys read Ruskin and catch ideas about beauty which cause a lot of trouble till the girls get hold of them and marry them and turn them into respectable Boorjoys. Ellam Street wives hate art worse than politics, and politics worse than other girls.

But preachers, being a class proof against domestic influence, often go on believing in truth, beauty and goodness, all their lives. Plantie was a very strong believer in all three, and whenever he could persuade anybody to see my pictures, especially another preacher, he would bring him in. As a public duty to art and God and the English nation.

The trouble is that though all good Protestant preachers round Greenbank including anarchists and anti-God Black-boys love beauty, they all hate pictures, real pictures. Each time Plantie sees one of my pictures, he gets a worse shock. This, of course, excites him to great enthusiasm, and makes me feel depressed. I don't care for people to admire my pictures unless they like them. So when Plantie began to cry out to the two other preachers, 'Look at that – beautiful, isn't it? Why, Mr Jimson, I think those fish are wonderful – a wonderful bit of work. You could almost eat them.' I felt a kind of gloom rise from my belly and darken my windows.

'Mr Jimson has a picture in the National Gallery,' said Plantie, blowing the trumpets of the Lord and art, with all his might. 'He used to paint from the life, but now he prefers Bible subjects.' Trying to tickle them with their own breast feathers.

The preacher with the blue nose, who had been staring at Eve like a bull at a picnic, now gave a loud sniff, and Plantie, seeing that his picture was going to be more unpopular with art lovers even than the last, made a great effort. 'This one represents the Fall. Adam is on the left. He is not quite finished down the back. Eve on the right is kneeling down. The serpent on the left is speaking in Adam's ear. The flowers at the side are daisies and marigolds. Really, Mr Jimson, I've got to congratulate you on those flowers. Don't you agree with me?' turning towards the bloodhound. 'Don't you think daisies are just right for the Garden of Eden Mr Dogsbody?' or some name like that.

But the more he tried, the worse I felt. As if I had been a happy worm, creeping all soft and oily through the grass, imagining the blades to be great forest trees, and every little pebble a mountain overcome; and taking the glow of self-satisfaction from his own tail for the glory of the Lord shining on his path; when all at once a herd of bullocks comes trampling along, snorting tropical epochs and shitting continents; succeeded by a million hairy gorillas, as big as skyscrapers, beating on their chests with elephant drumsticks and screaming 'Give us meat; give us mates,' followed modestly by ten thousand walruses a thousand feet high, wearing battle-ships for boots, and the Dome of St Paul's for a cod-piece; armed in the one hand with shield-shaped Bibles fortified with brass spikes and in the other with cross-headed clubs of blood-rusty iron, hung with the bleeding heads of infants, artists, etc., with which they beat up what is left of the grass, crying, 'Come to mother, little worm, and let her pat your dear head and comb your sweet hair for you.'

The bloodhound then opened his mouth and bayed, 'Most interesting, Mr-ah-Mister Johnson. Of course, I know nothing about art, but I wonder could you tell me if – ah – the human form – anatomically speaking, could – ah – assume the position of the male figure. Of course, I know – ah – a certain distortion is – ah – permissible.'

I had to pretend to see a spot on Eve's nose and to rub it off with my finger. And I couldn't get out a word. It was most embarrassing. There was the poor chap doing his best, and I had to pretend to be stone deaf. Come, I said to myself, say something, anything. Something they can understand. That's all they want. Something about the weather. Something to knock a hole in this awful situation and let down the pressure. Come, I said, you're not one of those asses who takes himself seriously. You're not like poor Billy, crying out:

> I've travelled through a land of men
> A land of men and women too
> And heard and saw such dreadful things
> As cold earth wanderers never knew.

Which probably means only that when Billy had a good idea, a real tip, a babe, some blue-nose came in and asked him why he drew his females in nightgowns.

And making a strong manly effort, I opened my mouth. smiled my charming smile from ear to ear, and was just about to say that the weather was colder but on the whole the rain might be expected to keep off, or not, perhaps.

When Blue-nose gave another sniff and said, 'I notice that it is the fashion for modern artists to paint the female limbs very large. I must not say that there appears to be a cult of ugliness – I merely stand to be instructed.'

Luckily I noticed that the edge of Adam's big toe had become smudged I rubbed a little white into the burnt sienna and touched it up. While old Billy cried:

> And if the babe is born a boy, that is to say, a real vision
>   It's given to a woman old
> Who nails him down upon a rock
>   Catches his shrieks in cups of gold.

Which means that some old woman of a blue-nose nails your work of imagination to the rock of law, and why and what; and submits him to a logical analysis.

Having completed Adam's big toe, I touched up some of his other members, and the bloodhound suddenly barked. 'Moost interasting, yaas. But I fearr that we are already la-ate for our engagement. Mr Fignose (or some name like that), I think we are expected at half-past five.'

Then they went out suddenly but without any loss of dignity; one of the first things a Daniel learns when he gets in the wrong den.

And little Plantie only stayed long enough to give me one subscription to the Blake Society, partly paid, to the amount of one shilling and sixpence, and to assure me that he would be back presently. 'Those gentlemen,' he said, 'were greatly impressed, and they're both on a lot of committees. They have a lot of influence.' He then hurried off to join the other preachers at the meeting.

And I took up a palette knife and asked myself if I should scrape out the picture or murder Blue-nose or only cut my throat.

But just then I noticed young Nosy dodging about in the background, and staring at the picture with eyes like another fish.

'How did you get in? Get out,' I said. 'The door was open.' 'Let it open again, whiz.' 'But it's S-Saturday.'

The universal excuse of every schoolboy, It's Saturday. They break your windows. It's Saturday. They break your heart. It's Saturday. They break their necks and run you in for a funeral. It's Saturday.

'Never mind if it's Monday,' I said with great indignation. 'You've no business to walk in like that.'

Nosy reflected a moment, and then he said, 'Who were those people who didn't like your picture?' 'Preachers.' 'I w-wanted to kick them.'

I didn't want to encourage the boy, so I didn't answer, until I said coldly and deliberately, 'Don't you talk like that about my friends.' 'Your friends.' 'They came here out of love for art, and don't you forget it.'

'But they didn't like your picture.' 'Of course not. How could they? They haven't time. A preacher hasn't time to like anything or even to know anything, and you wouldn't have time either if you'd just been bitten in the backside by a mad dog.' 'B-but that man T-Thompson with the b-blue nose isn't mad, he's m-married a grocer's widow with m-money.' 'Of course he's mad. What is a preacher? An artist. Who rattles a lot of words against his ear to make his babies laugh. And the babies cry boo-hoo, boo-hoo, God help us. So God sends a lot more mad dogs to bite them. You ought to weep for Blue-nose,' I said, beginning to scrape out the fish. 'Think of his agony when the grocer's late wife wakes in the middle of the night to give her some consolation for being alive and he hears the mad dogs, singing round the dustbins by the light of the moon. "Speech. Speech." "What's wrong, darling?" says the late grocer's wife, getting a bit impatient. "I was thinking of next Sunday – it's a great opportunity." "But you've got your sermon all ready." "Oh yes," says Blue-nose, "but I was wondering." "Now, you know it's a beautiful sermon, don't touch it, whatever you do. You'll only spoil it."

'Blue-nose doesn't say any more. Because he doesn't know whether it's a beautiful sermon or a lot of wind, wambling and wallowing among the ruined caves of the British Museum. But the mad dogs keep on singing, "Speech, speech. More wonderful speech." And Blue-nose keeps on trying to catch one of them by the tail, but they're always just round the corner. And when he sighs on the grocer's widow by accident, she bursts into tears and says he doesn't love her as he used to do last week.'

I was still scraping at the fish and Nosy was looking at me with eyes like another fish. 'What are you doing, Mr J-Jimson, you're s-spoiling it.' 'These fish stink. And what are you doing here, young man? How long have you been interrupting me?' 'I didn't interrupt you, Mr Jimson', 'How do I know?' 'But you didn't know I was there!' 'How do I know?' 'But Mr J-Jimson, you're not going to take them all out?' 'All of 'em.' 'Why?' 'They're dead. They don't swim – they don't speak, they don't click, they don't work, they don't do anything at all.' 'But why don't they?' 'God knows. But he won't go into details. The truth is, THE OLD HORSE DOESN'T SPEAK ONLY HORSE. And I can't speak only Greenbank.' 'Horse,' said Nosy, with his eye revolving in different directions. 'Here,' I said, 'what are you talking about? You're doing it on purpose. Go away.' And I made a dart at him. But he didn't move. He was as obstinate as a three-legged donkey that means to get thistles if it costs him his life. 'But I like the f-fish, Mr Jimson. Are you s-sure they're wrong?' 'No, I'm not shushure of anything except that if you don't go away and shut up I'll have the stroke.' 'What stroke, Mr J-Jimson?' 'THE STROKE! Nosy, the finisher, the cut-off. What you'll get some day with a hatchet.'

Nosy put this down as a piece of light conversation. And he didn't approve. His disposition was serious, noble and interfering. He held up a piece of new canvas and a glue-pot. 'Then, Mr Jimson, if you've finished painting, perhaps I could mend the hole. It will only take a minute.' Saying his little prayer. And just when I was going to kill him, I felt my head turn round. And I thought, 'Blood pressure, my boy – be good, be magnanimous.'

And I remembered that after all, it was always difficult to borrow a glue-pot. A wasting asset. So I said, 'All right, if you want to play. But I'll probably burn the whole bloody mess tomorrow.' More in sadness than in anger. Because of the bell ringing in my head.

12

And I went out to get room for my grief. Thank God, it was a high sky on Greenbank. Darker than I expected. But the edge of the world was still a long way off. At least as far as Surrey. Under the cloud-bank. Sun was in the bank. Streak of salmon below. Salmon trout above soaking into wash blue. River whirling along so fast that its skin was pulled into wrinkles like silk dragged over the floor. Shot silk. Fresh breeze off the eyot. Sharp as spring frost. Ruffling under the silk-like muscles in a nervous horse. Ruffling under my grief like ice and hot daggers. I should have liked to take myself in both hands and pull myself apart. To spite my guts for being Gulley Jimson, who, at sixty-seven years of age, after forty-five years of experience, could be put off his intentions, thoroughly bamboozled and floored, by a sprout of dogma, a blind shepherd, a vegetated eye, a puffed-up adder of moralities.

Girl going past clinging to a young man's arm. Putting up her face like a duck to the moon. Drinking joy. Green in her eyes. Spinal curvature. No chin, mouth like a frog. Young man like a pug. Gazing down at his sweetie with the face of a saint reading the works of God. Hold on, maiden, you've got him. He's your boy. Look out, Puggy, that isn't a maiden you see before you, it's a work of imagination. Nail him, girlie. Nail him to the contract. Fly laddie, fly off with your darling vision before she turns into a frow, who spends all her life thinking of what the neighbours think.

And if the babe is born a boy
He's given to a woman old
Who nails him down upon a rock
Catches his shrieks in cups of gold.

The fog-bank was turning pink on top like the fluff trimmings on a baby's quilt. Sky angelica green to mould blue. A few small clouds dawdling up, beige pink, like Sara's old powder puffs full of her favourite powder. Air was dusty with it.

And I thought how I used to powder her after her bath. I wonder she didn't kill me, the old Aphrodisiac. Fancy how once I was mad for that ancient hair-trunk. I ran after her skirts like a little dog, when she wouldn't have me. I wanted to cut my throat – or I thought so. And even when I got her at last, how I hung upon her. How I washed and dressed for her, and let her trot me about like a puggy on a ribbon. It was, 'Poor Gulley, don't forget your cough medicine. Now darling, what about your socks. I'm sure they're wet.' And when I was mad to paint, she was for putting me to bed and getting in after me. Stirring all that fire only to cook her own pot. Growing wings on my fancy only to stuff a feather bed.

She binds iron thorns around his head
She pierces both his hands and feet
She cuts his heart out at his side
To make it feel both cold and heat
Her fingers number every nerve
Just as a miser counts his gold
She lives upon his shrieks and cries
And she grows young as he grows old.

The powder-puff clouds were getting harder and rounder. The sky was turning green as a starboard light. And I could see it. It came right in and made a considerable impression. It made me want to sing and hit the lamp-posts.

Poor old Sall's face the first time I hit her. She couldn't believe it. Dear little Gulley to punch a lady on the neb. A flap on the tap. And when she'd done so much for him. Given up everything for him. What unkindness, What ingratitude. All those tactful arrangements and nice comfortable little formulas just thrown away.

How miffed she was. And how proud and stand-offish and self-righteous when she made it up again. Her face was saying, 'I'm ashamed of you', and the rest of her calling out, 'Help, help!'

Not that I wasn't glad to have her back. That was when I did the first sketch of the bath picture, all the bath pictures. I suddenly got hold of the idea. Mastered it. Yes, I can remember the feeling; your brushes like a carpenter's tools. Yes, I found out how to get Sara on the canvas. Some of her, anyhow. And I was always at her, one way or another. The flesh was

541

made word; every day. Till he, that is Gulley Jimson, became a bleeding youth. And she, that is, Sara, becomes a virgin bright.

> And he rends up his manacles
> And binds her down for his delight
> He plants himself in all her nerves
> Just like a husbandman his mould
> And she becomes his dwelling-place
> And garden fruitful seventy fold.

As Billy would say, through generation into regeneration. Materiality, that is, Sara, the old female nature, having attempted to button up the prophetic spirit, that is to say, Gulley Jimson, in her placket-hole, got a bonk on the conk, and was reduced to her proper status, as spiritual fodder. But what fodder. What a time that was. Not that I noticed it then. I was too busy to enjoy myself – even when I was having the old girl, I was getting after some ideal composition in my head. Taking advantage of the general speed up in the clockwork. It's not really surprising that she was a bit jealous of the paint.

I was laughing at Sara's expression when she used to look at one of my pictures and try to find out why I'd taken such a lot of trouble to make that nasty mess. When three flat-face cads under the dog's lamp-post at Ellam Street corner turned their dead cod-eyes and packet cigarettes towards me. Their faces said, 'Look at the old fool, he's drunk. Shall we push him down the gutter or isn't he worth it?'

I put out my tongue at them and dodged round the corner. I was still laughing but it was a different laugh. And I said, I mustn't want to cut out the tripes of such as the Ellam Street corner boys; it's not their fault that they lack the spirit of prophecy and art. I am upset, in fact; only because I can't hit them all on the neddy.

Just then I saw the telephone box and went in to try button B. And I thought: what a game to ring up old Hickson again. I rang him up, and he answered before I'd finished speaking his name. A big surprise. So I told him I was the Home Secretary. Put a ball of paper in my mouth. To give the official tone. Told him I had instructed Scotland Yard to set inquiries in motion relative to certain dealings in the matter of the artistic productions of the late Gulley Jimson. The late was a good idea. After all, you wouldn't expect one of these high officials to know anything about art or artists. He would be acting on a report.

'I beg your pardon,' said Hickson, and I did the piece again.

'Excuse me, sir,' said Hickson, 'are you referring to works which I bought after the Exhibition of 1921, or the small unfinished canvasses acquired from Mrs Monday in 1926,' and spoke so humbly and politely he might have been a contractor with a battleship to sell. And I thought, 'Could he really be taken in? For, of course, all this telephoning to old Hickson was a bit of a game. He nearly always spotted me, even if he pretended not to. And then he would try to get in a nasty one, on the side. Like telling me to warn myself against being a nuisance. And I would try to give the old man a prod or two, to keep him thinking. After all, he had got those pictures pretty cheap.

But this time he really seemed to be taken in. And I thought it must be the newspaper. Perhaps the Home Secretary really has adenoids; and these big bugs are always on the telephone to someone or other, especially millionaires. So I went on to say that the whole of his transactions *re* Mr Gulley Jimson's artistic output was under the gravest consideration by my technical advisers who took the most serious view of the legal anomalies involved by and for the same. I was prepared, I said, to allow for the time-factor, but I was led to think that according to my legal department, and the appropriate acts, there was at least a prima facie case—

'I beg your pardon, sir,' said Hickson. The paper was too big and made me so heehaw that the old man couldn't catch my words, and said, 'I beg your pardon,' every minute.

So we went on for some time. And Hickson even asked me to hold the line while he found a letter from Sara which he wanted to read to me.

And I was just putting my hand over the receiver in case he came back too soon and heard me laughing, when there was a tap on the glass. Made me jump a foot. And when I opened, a young chap I didn't know pulled me out by the arm and said, 'They're after you. Plain-clothes cop. Been asking down at the Feathers if you had been using their box. Alfred sent me to look for you.'

I didn't stop to argue. I got out and ran for it. I saw now why Hickson had been so sweet and reasonable and deaf for the last half hour. Been on to the local police station to look round the telephones. Probably sent out the butler to the street 'phone.

What surprised me, my legs were so shaky. Kept on trembling so I could hardly run. And my head was buzzing round. Why, I said, I'm not upset or anything. I'm not angry with Hickson. Or am I. Funny thing if a chap can get in a state without knowing it. And I was half-way along Greenbank, puffing like a steam car, when I thought: Why you damned old fool, you're running right into jug. That's just where they'll come for you.

And when I stopped I felt so queer I had to lean against the wall. Heart doing a hanged man's jig. Knees shaking like an old horse at the knacker's. Cheeks jumping up and down all by themselves.

Anybody would have thought I was frightened to death. Funny, I thought, if a chap's body can be frightened and he not able to stop it. I don't care a blast for anybody. Let 'em jug me if they like. Let 'em put me away for five years – that will about finish me. It's only what I've got to expect. I'm ready for anything. But my face isn't. It'll give me away to the first copper.

He'll take me up even if he doesn't know who I am. Loitering with a face. And I sat down on a garden wall to give my insides a rest.

Surrey all in one blaze like a forest fire. Great clouds of dirty yellow smoke rolling up. Nine carat gold. Sky water-green to lettuce-green. A few top clouds, yellow and solid as lemons. River disappeared out of its hole. Just a gap full of the same fire, the same smoky gold, the same green. Far bank like a magic island floating in the green. Rheumatic old willows trembling and wheezing together like lot of old men, much alarmed at the turn things were taking, but afraid to say so out loud.

I could do that, I thought. Those round clouds and the island in the sky, heavy as new melted lead. But what's the good of thinking about it. They've got me. For I saw that they had got me. And I began to feel better. That's that, I thought. They've got me. Here, I said to myself, that's all about it. Who are you to make all this fuss about yourself? Things are moving, that's all.

'Hullo,' young Franklin who drives the grocery van, still in his apron.

'Hello, Frank.'

'What's up? You look bad.'

'The police are after me.'

'What have you been doing?'

'Telephoning.'

'I should think you'll get about two years. And serve you about right,' said young Franklin, getting angry as if he were fighting somebody. 'You've asked for it.'

'That's it, Frank. How's the neck?'

Frank was having trouble with boils. He had a plaster on his neck and was carrying his head all on one side. I like Franklin. He's about nineteen, and is just getting his first real worries. The girls he fancies don't fancy him; the ones he fancied last year and doesn't fancy any more are lying in wait for him with kisses and hatchets. Made a bit on the pools and lost a lot on the dogs. And his best friend did him out of a good job, because he wanted to get married. Three years ago he was a happy corner boy, living like a hog in his dirty little mind. Now he's been stabbed alive. He's seeing things. The old woman of the world has got him. Old mother necessity.

> Who cuts his heart out at his side
> To make it feel both cold and heat.

He has a long old pale face like most boys of his age round Greenbank until they grow up and fatten up and give up.

'Neck,' he said, 'what's wrong with it.' Getting up another little fight with somebody invisible. 'It isn't necks.'

'Well, how's the revolution?'

'Revolution.' He spat on the kerb. 'That chestnut. Are you trying to be funny, or is it a joke?'

'Seen Walter?'

'I suppose he's at home.'

'If he's at home, it's no good asking for him. Is it?'

'Not much.'

A small boy came running along crying so hard that you expected him to turn himself inside out every sob. And when he came into the lamplight you could see he'd cried himself silly; his face was so blackened and swollen that you couldn't recognize it for a face.

'Beh-weh-heh,' he said.

Then he saw us and we looked at him; and he was surprised to find himself under observation. He pulled his face into a face shape, as quick as lightning, and went off without letting out another sound, so quietly and quickly I didn't know which way he'd gone.

'Young Dobson,' said Franklin, 'been catching it from his ma.'

'What for?'

'She married again. Got another kid and it's a bit queer in the head. So she wallops young Johnny. She'll murder him some day.'

'Why doesn't somebody do something about it?'

'Why don't they do something about anything – about Hitler?' said young Franklin.

The clouds had turned into old mahogany, heavy and solid. The fire underneath had burnt out – nothing left but a yellowy streak like a gas flame seen through a kitchen blind. Cabbage-green sky with one star coming through like tinsel behind gauze. And over on the East the blue rising as thick as a forest.

'Coming?' said Franklin, who doesn't like to be alone. And we went along by Greenbank, into Peartree Lane, where Walter Ollier lives. Frank rattled the gate to give him the sign. The door opened, and we heard Mrs Walter screaming at him that if he went out, he needn't come back. She didn't want to see him again, so long as she lived. As Walter came down the path, she put her face out of the door and said it all again, so that we could hear.

But we'd heard it all before. Mrs Ollier was a woman who didn't like Ollier to go out in the evening, or come back in the morning, or read a newspaper; or to do anything at all. She herself didn't do anything at all except open tins and smoke cigarettes, and she didn't like anybody else to do more. She wasn't on speaking terms with anyone in the world except Walter, and she always abused him. But then, young Franklin said, 'What would you do if you were a woman of that age without no ideas about nothing, no children, and nothing to do but open tins and smoke cigarettes. But what's the good of talking, nobody's going to do anything about it, or anything else either.'

'A bit nervous tonight,' said Ollier, apologizing for giving us some embarrassment.

'Ya,' said Frank.

'How's the boil, Frank?'

'Boil. What boil?'

'I thought it was a boil you had.'

'Had. Have. What of it? It's not the first, is it, I've always got one, if I haven't two.'

'Been to the doctor?'

'Doctor? You can have doctors. What do they know? What did they do for your rupture?'

'Well, they say I'm an exceptional case.'

'So am I. That's what they always say. That's what you'll die of when your guts get another crick in them. That's what my ma died of. She was an exceptional case. Nobody's never seen anything like it before. Ya. Doctors.'

'It's a nice evening,' said Walter.

'You can have it, Walter. And keep it for keeps.'

But I felt so old I wondered how my legs kept hanging on to my body. And I couldn't even think of what to do with the blank canvas. My eyes were dead as cods and my ears only heard noises.

> An aged shadow, soon he fades
> Wandering round an earthly cot
> Full filled all with gems and gold
> Which he by industry hath got.
> And these are the gems of the human soul
> The rubies and pearls of a lovesick eye,
> The countless folds of the aching heart
> The martyr's groans and the lover's sigh.

Well, I thought, I've filled a lot of canvasses in my time. Quite enough for any man. It's time I was done for.

And I remembered my father in the little Normandy farm where we went to live, or starve, because starving was cheaper in the Pas de Calais. Painting still more girls in gardens. And a whole room full of them inside. He wasn't going to be beaten by the wicked world and modern art. How my mother kept him in paint and canvas I don't know. But she did it even when we hadn't got shoes to wear. Art came first. Even before the children. But then, it was the art she'd been brought up to. It wasn't modern art. It was real art, beautiful and moral art, which is the same thing as what you've been brought up to. And papa was part of her religion.

The proof was that she gave up all for him. She was a belle of the season when she fell in love with papa's blue eyes and little golden beard, and velvet coat; with a real artist, who not only loved the good and the beautiful, but painted them. Her family was shocked. But she had all the will of a beauty. And besides, papa was making a lot of money in the 'fifties. She was allowed to marry him, and it was a great success. She set herself to serve art. But nobody was shocked at that. That was the right thing in those days. If mama had been a deb of these times, she would have set out to have a good time; but in the 'sixties, her idea was duty and devotion. Her vision was perfect service. And when papa stopped selling pictures and she found herself with five children to feed and no money, and a husband who was already brokenhearted; when, that is, the old woman nailed her down on the rock of necessity and cut her heart open she carried on with duty and devotion. She went on worshipping real art, papa's art, and she even went on having children, or where should I be now. She went on conducting her life in the grand classical style. Yes, that's what it was. And what a technique when you come to think of it. Nothing like the classical. A sense of form. None of your surface tricks; but solid construction.

If I was only fifty or so, I declare I'd go back to school again, to the life class, like Renoir in his forties, and study nothing but form, form in the black and white, for two years. Just charcoal. See what my mother became in the years of misery; a great woman; a person in the grand style. Yes, by God, you need technique to make a good job of life. All you can get. You need to take necessity and make her do what you want; get your feet on her old bones and build your mansions out of her rock.

> And she becomes his dwelling-place
> And garden fruitful seventy-fold.

Look at what Mick Angelo did in black and white or a chunk of rock.

'I hear you've been on the telephone,' said Walter.

'Yes, and the police are after me already. Smart work. They know their job, those coppers.'

'Does Mr Plant know?' said Walter. 'We ought to be making out what you ought to say. You'll have to have a story.'

'Story,' said young Franklin, quite losing his temper. 'Bloody lot of good that would be. He's done for himself, that's all. He'll get two years.'

'That's about it,' I said. 'I was warned. Serve me right. Playing the fool. I ought to get seven years.'

'They can't give you all that, Mr Jimson,' said Walter, who was upset. 'It wouldn't be right. What would they give you seven years for?'

'Being Gulley Jimson,' I said, 'and getting away with it.'

'It doesn't matter,' said young Franklin. 'Not if you look at what's happening to the Jews in Germany. Nor anybody anywhere.' And all at once he shouted out, 'Ahsitfeelintodye, Chawly.'

All the Greenbank boys talk Greenbank as well as English. Frank's friend called back out of the dark, 'Cheeroarry, ah'llbeseeinyer.'

On the Surrey side the fire was dead. Clouds all in blue and blue-and-soot. Blue-black smoke drifting up like smoky candles, and a blue sky as blue as blue spectacles with long pieces of sooty cobweb floating high up.

Stars coming through like needle-points; green-blue, and neon blue; and the river pouring quietly along, as bright as ink out of a bottle. All below as flat as melted iron, on three levels; first Greenbank hard; then a step down to the river, and a step up to the towpath; then away to the edge of the plate. A flat earth. A few knobs of trees and houses popping up to make it flatter. And all above on one curve about ten thousand feet high. Sweet as the inside of a dish-cover. The cobwebs hung on nothing in the middle, to make it hollower.

As simple as Euclid. Grand as the field of glory. Almost a picture ready-made, I said. There's more than a sketch there – it's got some composition. And my fingers ached to do it. But I said to myself, time's up. You've had fifty years to play with. So what are you groaning about?

We'd got to the railing next the motor factory and Barberry Creek. It was half-tide, and there were three barges cockeye on the serge-blue mud. So that they tilted on the ramp. Like stranded whales with their waists in the water. And a brazier full of orange hot coke making a hay-green high light on their snouts. Two men and a boy moving about throwing shadows fifty yards long, right to our feet. Carrying long tar brushes, like brooms.

It made my mouth water. I could have eaten those personal chunks of barges and that sweet individual flank of mud. But I thought, only another sketch and there's a million every day. Self-indulgence. You damned old sorcerer.

Frankie and Walter were moving down the planks, and I went after them. The river came up to us and its surface dissolved away into blue-glass sky. But the stars were floating on the water you couldn't see. Gave the plane in the middle of nothing. Barges like cliffs hanging over our heads. Little Harry the watchman smoking his pipe by the brazier. Chin in right hand, right elbow in left hand. Eyes on the air. Didn't even nod to us. Pursuing the meditations of Harry.

Franklin called out 'Bert,' and one of the men gave us a shout. Came up with a little tar-brush in his hand, like a whitewash brush. Bert Swope. Seventy-five or so. With his neck bent forward like a lizard. Long flat nose. White moustache, smoked like a kipper. Green eyes. A Greenbank walrus. Wears a jersey to show he's on the boats, and moleskins to show he's on the hard. Not to presume. Too proud and particular.

'In a minute – in a minute. Half a mo. Sno hurry.'

Bert had just put a patch on the bottom of a dinghy. He tarred it over and stood back to have a look at it. But when he stood back he couldn't see the whole effect. So he went to have a close look.

'Mr Jimson here is expecting trouble with the police,' said Ollier.

'Go on,' said Bert. Bert is an old bachelor, and doesn't believe anything he hears. 'What is it this time?'

'I've been telephoning again,' I said.

Bert went back to the brazier to take a dip of tar and gave the patch another brush over.

'What did you do that for?' said Bert.

'Just for the laugh. To make old Hickson jump.'

'Laugh,' said Franklin. 'Not much of a laugh when they put you away for two years.'

'It'll be a laugh for Hickson if they finish me off. He'll have killed me. And all legal. And he's got a lot of my pictures which will go up in value, too.'

'Here,' said Bert, bending down to admire his brush strokes from another angle. 'What's the joke? What's happened, really? Anything?'

'We must think up something,' said Ollier. 'Mr Plant will know. You can't go in again – not if it's only the same as last time.'

'It ought to be death without the option.' I said.

'What for?'

'For being an artist,' I said. 'For upsetting everybody. For thinking I'd get away with everything at once. And a medal for a good boy.'

'It's not what you'd call work,' said Bert. 'But what do I know?'

'It's more of a gift,' said Ollier.

'Like Frankie's boils,' I said. 'To keep him interested.'

'How do you start on that game, Mr Jimson?' said Bert. 'Just start?'

'No,' I said. 'It starts on you. Why I had a real job once, a job of work. But art got me and look at me now.'

No one said anything to this. Bert wasn't listening, and Franklin was angry, and Ollier was too polite and Harry was thinking as usual. Harry is a dwarf. A good-looking chap to the waist, but then two little twisted stumps. He got a wife once and gave her a baby; but she left him and took the baby with her, not because she didn't like Harry, but because the neighbours laughed when they went out together. Sensitive. A nice girl. She liked things nice.

13

If, while I am dictating this memoir, to my honorary secretary, who has got the afternoon off from the cheese counter, I may make a personal explanation, which won't be published anyhow; I never meant to be an artist. You say, who does. But I even meant not to be an artist because I'd lived with one and I couldn't forget seeing my father, a little grey-bearded old man, crying one day in the garden. I don't know why he was crying. He had a letter in his hand; perhaps it was to tell him that the Academy had thrown out three more Jimson girls in three more Jimson gardens. I hated art when I was young, and I was very glad to get the chance of going into an office. My mother's cousin, down at Annbridge, near Exmoor, had pity on us, and took me into his country office. He had an engineering business. When I came to London in '99, I was a regular clerk. I had a bowler, a home, a nice little wife, a nice little baby, and a bank account. I sent money to my mother every week, and helped my sister. A nice happy respectable young man. I enjoyed life in those days.

But one day when I was sitting in our London office on Bankside, I dropped a blot on an envelope; and having nothing to do just then I pushed it about with my pen to try and make it look more like a face. And the next thing was I was drawing figures in red and black, on the same envelope. And from that moment I was done for. Everyone was very sympathetic. The boss sent for me at the end of the month and said, 'I'm sorry, Jimson, but I've had another complaint about your work. I warned you last week that this was your last chance. But I don't want to sack you. You might never get another job, and what is going to happen then to your poor young wife and her baby. Look here, Jimson, I like you, everyone likes you. You can trust me, I hope. Tell me what's gone wrong. Never mind what it is. I'm not going to be stupid about it. Is it debts? You haven't been gambling, I suppose? Is your petty cash all right? Take a couple of days off and think it over.'

But of course I couldn't think of anything except how to get my figures right. I started as a Classic. About 1800 was my period. And I was having a hell of a time with my anatomy and the laws of perspective.

> Her fingers numbered every nerve
> Just as a miser counts his gold.

I spent my holiday at a life class, and when I went back to the firm, I didn't last two days. Of course, I was a bad case. I had a bad infection, galloping art. I was at it about twelve hours a day and I had a picture in the old Water Colour Society that year. Very classical. Early Turner. Almost Sandby.

My wife was nearly starving, and we had pawned most of the furniture, but what did I care. Well, of course, I worried a bit. But I felt like an old master. So I was, very old. I was at about the period when my poor old father was knocked out. I'd gone through a lot to get my experience, my technique, and I was going to paint like that all my life. It was the only way to paint. I knew all the rules. I could turn you off a picture, all correct, in an afternoon. Not that it was what you call a work of imagination. It was just a piece of stuff. Like a nice sausage. Lovely forms. But I wasn't looking any more than a sausage machine. I was the old school, the old Classic, the old church.

> An aged shadow soon he fades
> Wandering round an earthly cot

Full filled all with gems and gold
Which he by industry has got.

I even sold some pictures, nice water-colours of London churches. But one day I happened to see a Manet. Because some chaps were laughing at it. And it gave me the shock of my life. Like a flash of lightning. It skinned my eyes for me and when I came out I was a different man. And I saw the world again, the world of colour. By Gee and Jay, I said, I was dead, and I didn't know it.

From the fire on the hearth
A little female babe did spring.

I felt her jump. But, of course, the old classic put up a fight. It was the Church against Darwin, the old Lords against the Radicals. And I was the battleground. I had a bad time of it that year. I couldn't paint at all. I botched my nice architectural water-colours with impressionist smudges. And I made such a mess of my impressionist landscapes that I couldn't bear to look at them myself. Of course, I lost all my kind patrons. The first time, but not the last. But that didn't upset me. What gave me the horrors was that I couldn't paint. I was so wretched that I hardly noticed when we were sold up and my wife went off, or even when my mother died. It was a good thing she did die, or she would have had to go to the workhouse. And really, I suppose she died of a broken heart at seeing her youngest go down the drain.

Of course, I was a bit upset about it. I thought my heart was broken. But even at the funeral I couldn't tell whether I was in agony about my poor mother's death, or about my awful pictures. For I didn't know what to do with myself. My old stuff made me sick. In the living world that I'd suddenly discovered, it looked like a rotten corpse that somebody had forgotten to bury. But the new world wouldn't come to my hand. I couldn't catch it, that lovely vibrating light, that floating tissue of colour. Not local colour but aerial colour, a sensation of the mind; that maiden vision.

And she was all of solid fire
And gems and gold, that none his hand
Dares stretch to touch her baby form
Or wrap her in her swaddling band
But she comes to the man she loves
If young or old, or rich or poor,
They soon drive out the aged host
A beggar at another's door.

I got her after about four years. At least I got rid of every bit of the grand style, the old church. I came to the pure sensation without a thought in my head. Just a harp in the wind. And a lot of my stuff was good. Purest go-as-you-please.

And I sold it too. I made more money then than I ever did again. People like impressionism. Still do, because it hasn't any idea in it. Because it doesn't ask anything from them – because it's just a nice sensation, a little song. Good for the drawing-room. Tea-cakes.

But I got tired of sugar. I grew up.

And when they showed me a room full of my own confections, I felt quite sick. Like grandpa brought to a nursery tea. As for icing any more eclairs, I couldn't bring myself to it. I gradually stopped painting and took to arguing instead. Arguing and reading and drinking; politics, philosophy and pub-crawling; all the things chaps do who can't do anything else. Who've run up against the buffers. And I got in such a low state that I was frightened of the dark. Yes, as every night approached, I fairly trembled. I knew what it would be like. A vacuum sucking one's skull into a black glass bottle; all in silence. I used to go out and get drunk, to keep some kind of illumination going in my dome.

> He wanders weeping far away
> Until some other take him in
> Oft blind and age bent, sore distrest
> Until he can a maiden win.

And then I began to make a few little pencil sketches, studies, and I took Blake's job drawings out of somebody's bookshelf and peeped into them and shut them up again. Like a chap who's fallen down the cellar steps and knocked his skull in and opens a window too quick, on something too big. I did a little modelling and tried my hand at composition. I found myself wandering round the marbles at the British Museum and brooding over the torso of some battered old Venus without any head, arms or legs, and a kind of smallpox all over the rest of her. Trying to find out why her lumps seemed so much more important than any bar-lady with a gold fringe; or a water-lily pool.

> And to allay his freezing eye
> The poor man took her in his arms
> The cottage fades before his sight
> The garden and its lovely charms.

Good-bye impressionism, anarchism, nihilism, Darwinism and the giddy goat, now staggering with rheumatism. Hail, the new Classic. But you might say it was in the air about then, at the turn of the century when the young Liberals were beginning to bend away from *laissez-faire* and to look for their Marx, and science took a mathematical twist, and the old biologists found themselves high and dry among the has-beens, blowing their own trumpets because no one else would do it for them. And I studied Blake and Persian carpets and Raphael's cartoons and took to painting walls.

But I rubbed most of them out again. They looked like bad imitations of the old master; or made-up, pompous stuff. They didn't belong to the world I lived in. A new world with a newnormal character.

I had a worse time than the last time. I drank more than ever. To keep up my self-respect. But it didn't have the same effect. I was gloomy even in drink. I didn't seem to be getting anywhere very much. If there was anywhere to get to.

> The stars, sun, moon all shrink away,
> A desert vast without a bound,
> And nothing left to eat or drink
> And a dark desert all around.

And, of course, no one would buy anything. They didn't know what I was driving at. I probably didn't know myself. I was like a chap under witchcraft. I didn't know if I was after a real girl or a succubus in the shape of a fairy.

> The honey of her infant lips
> The bread and wine of her sweet smile
> The wild game of her roving eye
> Does him to infancy beguile.
> Like the wild stag she flees away
> Her fear plants many a thicket wild
> While he pursues her night and day
> By various wiles of love beguiled.

The job is always to get hold of the form you need. And nothing is so coy. Cézanne and the cubists, when they chucked up old doddering impressionism, caught their maidens. But the cubists did it too easily. They knocked them down with hammers and tied up the fragments with wire. Most of 'em died and the rest look more like bird-cages than forms of intuition and delight. Cézanne was the real classic. The full band. Well, I suppose poor old Cézanne did more wandering in the desert even than me – he wandered all his life. The maiden fled away so fast that he hardly caught her once a year. And then she soon dodged off again.

> By various arts of love and hate
> Till the wide desert planted o'er
> With labyrinths of wayward love
> Where roams the lion, the wolf, the boar.

I painted some cubists myself and thought I'd got my maiden under padlock at last. No more chase, no more trouble. The formula of a new classical art. And, of course, a lot of other people thought so too. A lot of 'em are painting cubistry even now; and making a steady income and sleeping quiet in their beds and keeping their wives in fancy frocks and their children at school.

> The trees bring forth sweet ecstasy
> To all who in the desert roam
> Till many a city there is built
> And many a pleasant shepherd's home.

Cubiston. On the gravel. All services. Modern democracy. Organized comforts. The Socialist state. Bureaucratic liberalism. Scientific management. A new security. But I didn't live there long myself. I got indigestion. I got a nice girl in my eye, or perhaps she got after me. After 1930, even Hickson stopped buying me. And tonight it seems that I can't paint at all. I've lost sight of the maiden altogether. I wander weeping far away, until some other take me in. The police. It's quite time. I'm getting too old for this rackety life.

14

The chaps, except Harry, were all watching Bert while he gave a last coat of tar to his pet patch. Harry kept his eye on the air. Looking after his own affairs.

'Here,' said Frankie, working up a rage as if he'd been diddled. 'What are we stopping for? We haven't got all night, have we? Are we going to get on with it, or aren't we?'

Bert, still keeping his eyes on the patch, put on his coat, a real old Greenbank walrus coat, with a yoke, double-whipped seams, and two cuts behind. Built about the same year as the Crystal Palace.

'All right, son,' he said, 'all right, all right, all right.' He struck a match and held it over his job to see what it looked like by match-light. 'All right, all right, I'm coming,' and he walked backwards till the boat was out of sight. Then he turned and marched off, poking out his head like an old dog smelling for corners.

'When we see Mr Plant, he'll know what we ought to tell them,' said Ollier, who was worrying about me all the time. But I don't mind Ollier worrying about me because he never intrudes. He's got a lot of self-control on account of his manners.

'You needn't mind about all that,' said Franklin. 'He's finished, anyhow. Done for himself, and why not?'

Young Franklin is a nice chap. He takes things hard. That's why he likes to see the worst occur.

'That's it,' I said. 'And I'd rather go quietly.'

It was Mr Plant who had helped me in my last trouble. Came running straight from work with his spectacles falling off his nose and his hands as black as wellingtons. 'What's this, Mr Jimson?' 'I've been had up, uttering menaces.' 'It's a scandal. If ever there was an innocent man, it's you, Mr Jimson.' 'Oh no,' I said, 'it's all right, I did it.' 'But look at the provocation – we must have a lawyer.'

This didn't suit me at all. In all my life I'd always tried to keep out of court. 'We don't want too much publicity, Mr Plant, something else might come out.' 'So that's what they're counting on,' said Plantie, turning pale with indignation. 'It's persecution. But I know the man who'll settle 'em.' 'We don't want any lawyers in it, Plantie.' 'But it's a duty, Mr Jimson. And if we don't get justice in the court, we'll go to Parliament.

'I know the man we want – he acted for that poor lad, Rockway.' 'Who strangled girls?' 'That's it, poor lad, poor lad.' 'He got off, didn't he?' 'Yes, we got him off. But he was never the same again – a scandalous case.' 'I remember the papers liked it.' 'That's it, scavenging. If only we could have kept the whole thing quiet, the poor chap might have had a chance. Only eighteen. But the publicity went to his head. And, of course, he got into trouble again.' 'They shut him up?' 'Shut him up – that was ten years ago. Awful to think off.' 'And the girls?' 'The girls?' said Plantie, and he looked at me with his mouth open, and his forehead crumpled right over the top. Quite confused. He had overlooked the girls and he didn't know quite how to deal with them. He hadn't got the right tools. He wasn't using Spinoza then, but some kind of old bible cement mixer. 'The girls,' he said at last. 'Poor things. Awful, terrible.' And he shook his head like a old dog bothered by a horsefly. 'It's a mystery.' And he cheered up a little. 'Yes,' he said, 'if we only knew, there's a meaning in it.' 'That's it,' I said, 'it means that girls are liable to be strangled by young devils like Rockway. Always were and always will be.' 'No, no,' said Plantie, 'there's a meaning in it. And anyhow,' he said, cheering up still more, 'we did get the poor young lad off, and we'll get you off.' 'No justice for me.' I said. 'What I need is special consideration on account of age and rheumatism and my services to the British nation in the future – about the year 2500. When they'll probably need a few good artists in their history or they won't be in history at all.'

But, of course, Plantie wouldn't listen to me. He has a lot of old English feelings under all his foreign philosophies, just as he has a lot of the real English religion under all his fandangos. He loves to fight the law. 'No, no,' he said, 'no compromise with those rascals.' And he got up meetings and took subscriptions till my name stank for miles round. And he hired that lawyer G —, who looked like a crystallized choirboy, only his head was quite bald. He came to see me in my old studio and when I had told him all about myself and my little jokes, he said, 'I see, Mr Jimson, we'll have to concentrate on character.' 'No you haven't,' I said. 'Remember I'm an artist. And you know what that means in a court of law. Next worst to an actress.' 'That's what I mean,' he said. 'And I believe you're a modern artist.' 'Very nearly,' I said. 'Yes,' he said, 'it's a difficult case. We can only stick to character and hope for the best.' And when he got into court he began at once to throw dirt on Hickson. It was wonderful. That man was a poet. The way he made it seem that poor old Hickie had been a bloodsucker in buying my pictures cheap, and that he'd been exploiting poor devils like me all his life.

No, I nearly got in a state in that case, because of all the nonsense they talked, and all the lies they told about poor old Hickie. Not knowing anything about art or pictures or Hickie or me, and what was worse, not caring. I was just going to start on to tell that chap what I thought of him, and twice I tried to put some sense into the court, and make it understand that a picture wasn't a bag of flour that goes up and down in the market; that it was a highly complicated question which had to be handled by experts and not too many of them all at once. Hickie and me would be enough for one afternoon.

But when I saw them all so serious and reverent, and even the police with their hats off as if ready for prayer, I said to myself: Don't be a fool, Gulley, they're doing their best and they couldn't do any better. They know it isn't justice and they know there can't be any such thing in this world, but they've got to do their job which is to keep the handles turning on the old sausage machine, and where would the world be without sausages?

So I said nothing. And in the end I got a month, instead of seven days, which was the usual equivalent. But it was a great victory for Plantie. It made him happy for weeks and gave him a big reputation round Greenbank. The real British hero. The man that whopped old women in law and frightened the magistrates.

We had turned east along Greenbank. The moon was coming up, as if somebody had flashed a torch under the far edge of the dish-cover. A fog of white light seeping up into the blue air. Overhead the sky was as black as Prussian blue. The stars were sparkling like electric cars. And the river crawling along, the colour of pig iron, like a stream of lava just going solid.

I could use the dome, I said, with that bite out of it, where the moon is rising. Like a dark cathedral with one chapel in the apse lighted up. I should like a sharper edge at the junction. Probably get it when the moon actually sticks up her nozzle. She'll throw a halo. A vault, and the vault will give the measure and the architecture of the dome. Yes, I said, by Gee and Jay, I should like to do that dome, the heavenly height, the eternal roof, the everlasting muffin-dish, heavy as the hand of fate, solid as the Bank of England, and glorious as the first of things. The Primary. Rap your knuckles on it and it makes a noise like a turnip.

'Hullo, hullo, hullo, hullo,' said Bert, 'where you coming to?' For the fact is, having my nose in the air, I didn't see the kerb. And when Bert had put me on my legs again, there was little Plantie standing waiting for us, under a lamp, under the dome, looking so neat and small that it made you smile. Like a fly in black amber.

Plantie in his best blue suit, with a clean collar, barmaid's, three sizes too large. With an electric-blue lightning bow tie hooked on to the stud. Bowler, eyebrows and moustache all brushed different ways.

'Good evening, Mr Jimson. Good evening, all.' His eyes were running out of their holes and then running back again, like children at the nursery door, just before the party.

'Going to a meeting?' I said.

'I've got a meeting,' said Plantie, and he tried to stick out his chest. 'Professor Ponting is speaking at my place. Professor Ponting from America.'

'What – the professor of plumbing,' said Bert.

'He's a great authority,' said Plantie, putting one finger down the back of his collar to see if the stud was holding.

'What's he authority of?'

'He's known all over Germany,' said Plantie, giving his tie a poke to see if it was still there. Plantie was obviously in a state. This was his great day. He'd got a professor to talk to his meeting.

'Nice evening, Mr Jimson,' and he looked round quickly to see if it was a nice evening.

'Very nice,' said Bert. 'Bit of all right, all right. What about that wet.'

Plantie let out a sigh, but in the middle of the sigh he snatched off his bowler and gave it a fierce look to teach it not to come unbrushed until after the meeting. Then he put it back again, and said, 'Beautiful, beautiful. Never saw such stars.' And he looked quickly up to make sure that there were such things still to be seen.

'Hitler would laugh,' said Franklin.

'Come on, son,' said Bert, taking his arm. 'Come on, come on, come on.'

'But it strikes a bit cold through the pavement,' said Plantie, slapping down his feet to see if it was a pavement that struck cold.

'Come on,' said Bert, taking his other arm. 'Come on, come on.'

'I've got to go and get things ready for the meeting,' said Plantie.

'No, you haven't. Not for another half-hour.'

'No,' said Plantie, 'or say twenty minutes.' And we all went into the Feathers.

'Have one with me, Mr Jimson,' said Plantie. 'It's my turn.'

I said, 'Since last Christmas,' but he didn't answer. Put up his hands and ordered cans round. Napoleon on the field of battle. A glorious day. Mine not to reason why.

I like little Plant. A regular old King Walrus. Genus, Chapellius. Species. Blu-suitius, Bandy-leggus. Steady as a burst barometer. Putting one foot in front of the other. On account of the curl in his legs.

Plant's father was a plumber. Old family trade. Good business and plenty of money. Plantie was going to be a plumber. But he joined up for the South Africa. Mother died and papa married a widow with kids. No room for Plantie at home after the war. He went into the boot trade, built up a nice little business, married a nice little wife. Then the Great War. Democracy in danger. Joined up again under the Derby scheme. Nice little wife hooked up with a conchie, sold the business and got clear away with everything. Plant got one bullet in the knee and one in the stomach and had fourteen operations. Every time he found a job his leg gave out, and he had to go to the hospital. Took to drink and broke the other leg. Then pulled up his socks, quarrelled with his minister, and took to cobblery and anarchism. Religion had always been in the family. His father had been a lay preacher.

'That's a fine picture of yours,' he said, putting down his can like a law of Moses. 'Great subject, the Fall.'

'I'm giving up art,' I said. 'It's a bit late, but I may still learn to respect myself before I die.'

Plantie shook his head and felt for his tie. He was wounded in his fundamentals and it made him feel that he couldn't trust even elastic to hold.

'You saw Jim, Mr Jimson,' said Alfred from behind the bar.

'Yes, thank you, Alfred.'

'Thought you'd better know.'

Alfred isn't a gossip. But he would like to be. He looks like a white rabbit powdered pink in front. His eyes are as blue as skim milk. He was born to be a village baker's wife and tell the news warm, with the new loaves.

The door banged and my hand did a jump, all by itself, slopped the beer over my nose.

'It's all right, Mr Jimson,' said Alf. 'They won't come here, and Jim wouldn't breathe a word.'

'Both of you are good at keeping secrets – like onions on the breath,' I said. 'Got to be in my job,' said Alf, wiping a glass out with his forefinger. 'See nothing, hear nothing, say nothing. That's the golden rule for the bar. You needn't be nervous.' 'I'm not nervous,' I said, 'it's my legs. But if the coppers don't come for me pretty soon, I'll knock your windows out.' 'I know what you mean,' said Alfred, 'It's the suspense working on the imagination. A lot of chaps get in wrong due to the suspense.' 'What's this?' said Bert, 'Who's in suspense?' 'The Lincoln murderer,' I said, 'this morning.' 'Mr Jimson is joking,' said Plantie, 'he knows better than that. He's an artist and an artist knows the value of life.' 'Buyers or sellers?' I said. 'What offers for the celebrated Gulley Jimson? Sound in wind and limb except for arthritis, conjunctivitis, rheumatitis, sinovitis, bug bitis, colitis, bronchitis, dermatitis, phlebitis and intermittent retention of the pee.'

Plant shook his moustache at the air. He was being grieved. I like grieving Plant. Always trying to rescue me from myself. To convert me to a wiser view of life. I don't like converters. You never feel safe with them. They've always got some knuckleduster up their sleeve. Always working round the flank for a dash at the scullery window. Got to lock up everything; and even then they keep on squinting through the keyhole.

'Mr Jimson doesn't mean it,' said Plantie, turning red. There was still a bit of the old Flanders sergeant in Plantie. 'For what is an artist for, but to make us see the beauty of the world.'

'Well,' I said severely, 'What is art? Just self-indulgence. You give way to it. It's a vice. Prison is too good for artists – they ought to be rolled down Primrose Hill in a barrel full of broken bottles once a week and twice on public holidays, to teach them where they get off.'

The moon was coming up somewhere, round the corner from the side bow window, making the trees like fossils in a coalfield, and the houses look like fresh-cut blocks of coal, glittering green and blue; and the river banks like two great solid veins of coal left bare, and the river sliding along like heavy oil. It was like a working model of the earth before somebody thought of dirt, and colours and birds and humans. I liked it even better than the dome of glory. I liked it so much that I wanted to go out and walk about in it. But, of course, I knew it wouldn't be there. You never get the real world as solid as that. It was a trick of the light. Alfred's old white cat, jumping on the wall, spoilt the weight of it. I had to put up my can to blot her out.

'I respect artists,' said Plantie. 'they give their lives to it.'

'And other people's lives,' I said. 'Like Hitler.'

'Hitler,' said Frankie, not angry but sad; as if he couldn't bear much more. 'Who said Hitler? Is he on the wireless or isn't he? Why do they all go on talking *all* the time?'

'Do you think there'll be a war, Mr Moseley,' said Alfred. Mr Moseley had just come in. A smart young man of fifty with a face like a raspberry, and suits and shoes so beautiful that they make you look again. Visions that reveal clothes to you. Mr Moseley is a prophet. He sells racing tips and takes bets. 'Yes,' said Mr Moseley, 'of course there'll be a war.' 'I believe you're right, Mr Moseley,' said Alfred. 'You bet I'm right. Double and split.' 'But do the Germans want a war?' 'Don't know what they want till they get it,' said Mr Moseley, 'and then they want the other thing.' 'I believe you've said it, Mr Moseley.' 'Everyone likes a change,' said Mr Moseley, 'to keep up the circulation.'

'But what I can't understand is, what Hitler really wants,' said Walter. 'Doesn't want anything,' said Mr Moseley. 'He's got ideas. That's the trouble. When a chap gets ideas, you look out —' 'I believe you're right, Mr Moseley,' I said. 'He's got ideas that chap. And he wants to see them on the wall.'

Mr Moseley gave me a look but didn't say anything. I didn't blame him. I couldn't expect a suit like that to talk to my overcoat. And I was thinking of Artist Hitler.

But when they find the frowning Babe
Terror strikes through the region wide
They cry the Babe, the Babe is born
And flee away on every side.
And none can touch that frowning form
Unless it be a woman old
She nails him down upon a rock
And all is done as I have told.

'Since you've said it,' said Franklin, 'what is it all for – what's the good of art. You can have it. It's just another racket, it's a put-up job from start to closing time.' 'That's it, Frankie,' I said, 'a put-up job.' 'And they know it, too,' said Frankie, turning quite white and breaking into a sweat with indignation against the enemy. 'The buggers know it – just like the bloody parsons know it. And the bloody government. Putting it over. Taking advantage.' 'That's it,' I said, 'they're all at it, like ticks on a mad dog. When he's too busy charming the moonshine to scratch himself in detail.'

Plantie looked at his watch and looked at us all round. Then he moved his moustache and eyebrows and spectacles in an earnest way, and said that he'd have to be going. But no one said they'd go with him. Not even Ollier. Plantie always makes the same mistake. Asks people to go to his meetings. Even Ollier, who thinks as little of himself as any hero of the war before last, would never go to Plant's meeting when Plantie asked him. He was always there. But he went under his own steam.

Plantie looked at me again; then pulled up his trousers and trundled out. You could see he was afraid that nobody would come to his meeting.

'Poor old Plantie,' said Bert. 'Gone to put on his braces for his uplift.' 'Meetings,' said Franklin. 'What's the idea? That's all I ask. What's the real idea? What are they getting at?'

'They aren't getting it, they're giving it,' I said. 'A chap has to get rid of his ideas somewhere, or they'll turn sour and give him a pain.'

All at once Alfred gave me a wink and I saw a nice young man standing beside me in a tweed coat. Student you would have said. Except for the way his shoulders filled the sleeves. And the look in his eye. Like a filing clip. He touched my arm and stepped back from the bar. 'Hello,' I said, 'it's Bill Smith.' But my legs were going from me. Seemed to be nothing in my trousers but the draught. I just floated after the smell of tweed. 'My old friend, Bill,' I said, 'how are things at Botany Bay?' 'Mr Jimson,' he said, confidentially, as if speaking through a ventilator to the prisoner next door. 'No,' I said, 'that's my first cousin once removed. He moved out just now. He's an artist who's always getting into trouble with the police. Shall I go and call him back?' And I went out. But the copper came along. And outside he took my arm. 'Excuse me a moment, Mr Jimson.'

'Which Mr Jimson?' 'Did you at six thirty this afternoon send a telephone message of a threatening character to Mr Hickson, 98, Portland Place.' 'I only said I'd burn his house down and cut his liver out.' 'You know what will happen to you if you go on at that game.' 'Yes, but what will happen if I don't? What will I do in the long evenings?' 'Mr Hickson doesn't want to prosecute. But if you go on making a nuisance of yourself, he'll have to take steps.' 'Would he rather I cut his liver out without telephoning?' 'Put yourself in his place, Mr Jimson.' 'I wish I could, it's a very nice place.' 'Well, you heard what I said. Do it again and you're for it.' 'That's a good idea. I'll call him up at once.' A hop, step and jump for the Feathers. But there they were in a row, Ollier, Swope and Franklin, looking at me.

'What's up,' said Bert. 'Who was the chap?' 'C.I.D.' 'Well, I wondered.' 'And you could see he was changing his mind just because I'd told the truth.' 'What did he want with you?' said Franklin. 'It's a painful subject, Frankie, super-tax.' 'I knew I'd seen him before,' said Bert. 'Schoolmaster, ain't he, Jimmy, got run in last year for drunk and —' 'It's seven struck,' said Ollier, changing the subject. 'I'm off for the meeting.' 'What's it about?' said Bert. 'Religion and humanity.' 'That's a good one, son. That's all right,' said Bert. 'For those it's all right for.' And young Franklin turned round and walked off very fast. But he went round the lamp-post and walked back again. They come to most of the meetings. Both being on the loose. I've seen Bert, in his white coat with the yoke, and four other old walruses from Greenbank, at a meeting on the Gold Standard. But it was an open-air meeting. Bert couldn't go to the Gold Standard indoors. He likes something to bite on; religion or the white slave traffic. All alive at seventy-five. But he's a bachelor. Driven in on himself. Banked down and still burning, the fire in the hearth.

15

Plant has two rooms down an area in Ellam Street. Shop in front, sitting-room behind. We went in through the shop. Smell of boot polish like a lion cage. Back room with an old kitchen range. Good mahogany table. Horse-hair chairs. Bed in corner made up like a sofa. Glass-front bookcase full of nice books. Chambers's Encyclopaedia. Bible dictionary. Sixpenny Philosophers.

I made off to the dark corner by the back window looking out on the dustbin. There was a nice old comfortable sofa for a snooze. Or to flirt if I felt flirty and anything came in to flirt with. Dirty in the cover, but good springs in the seat. But I hadn't got settled before Plantie came running up to me. 'Are you all right, Mr Jimson?' 'I'm all right.' 'You know your way to the —' 'Yes, I know my way to the —' And then he was off again to shake hands with the Rev. Such or the Mr So. He had four dog collars there, including Cabbage-nose. A great day. He was in such a fizz that he couldn't contain himself. I saw him twice make his way to the —. And then up he comes again. 'You all right, Mr Jimson?' 'I'm all right, Mr Plant.' 'That's all right, Mr Jimson.' 'I know, Mr Plant. Down the yard.' 'Good meeting, Mr Jimson.' 'There's a lot of it.' 'Yes, there's twenty-two, not including Walter or myself.' 'What does that old woman come for?' 'Why not?' 'Women generally have something better to do.' But Plantie was away again. He always goes off his head at a meeting, charges up and down like a sergeant on a field day, and gets his collar up at the back.

The people kept floating in. Like fish in an aquarium full of dirty brown water, three dimensions of fish faces, every one on top of the other. Bobbing slowly to and fro, and up and down. Goggle eyes, cod mouths. Hanging in the middle of the brown. Waiting for a worm or just suspended. Old octopus in corner with a green dome and a blue beak, working his arms. Trying to take off his overcoat without losing his chair. Old female in black with a red nose creeping about in the dark corners like a crawfish, shaking her bonnet feathers and prodding her old brown umbrella at the chairs. Young skate stuck up the wall with bulgy white eyelids and a little white mouth. Never moving. You'd think he was glued to the side of the tank. People kept falling over and sitting on me. I took a chair into the scullery to be out of the way, and shut the door to be at peace. For I knew where Plantie kept bottled beer, under the scullery draining-board.

But pretty soon the chairs came knocking up against the door. just as I was opening the first bottle they knocked it ajar. As the people in front made themselves comfortable and stretched their legs and pushed backwards to snatch a little floor from the people behind. As happens at all meetings, except in a church with good Christian traditions, where they screw the pews to the floor. In the end they pushed one chair backwards right through my door, and when I tried to push it back again, Plantie got up and began to shake his moustache and introduce Professor Ponting, who turned out to be the moon-coloured young gentleman against the wall; the skate.

'Ladies and gentlemen,' said Plantie, 'we have tonight the great privilege —'

I pushed the chair forwards and the Christians pushed it back; ten to one. But still I might have got the door shut if just then the old crawfish hadn't come working sideways along the row, apologizing and groaning, and sticking her umbrella into everybody's eyes; until she got her backside wedged up against the scullery door. Then everybody began to hiss at her and she got her umbrella jammed between a chair and an old man's waistcoat, and some good Christian, looking carefully the other way, gave her a hard shove with his shoulder and she tumbled into the scullery. She fell on the empty chair, panting like a steamboat, and then began to push her dress about and pull her bonnet and jerk her legs and elbows, as old women do when they're flustered. But all at once she felt me just behind her and gave a jump and turned half round. And I said, 'Sara.'

'Oh, Gulley,' she said. 'You did give me a start.' And she went on panting and heaving and pushing herself about. 'Oh dear, I do get so breathless.'

'And what are you doing here, Sall? In a bonnet, too.'

'Well, didn't you get my card, or my letter.'

I remembered then that I had had a card from Sara, care of the Eagle, saying that she had to visit an old friend's grave on the Saturday in my part of town, and not to trouble about being in, as very likely she wouldn't have time to call. A real Sara card, meaning just the opposite. And then there had been a letter. But I had forgotten to open it.

'There was a card.' I said. 'But it said not to expect you. So I didn't tell my staff to prepare dinner.'

'The Eagle said you were here. But I didn't know about the meeting. And then I couldn't find you. Oh, Gulley, aren't you glad to see me, when I've come all this way.' Now I looked at Sara, I could see she was in more than a fluster. It wasn't only that her nose was redder than before, but her eye was wet. And her panting wasn't all due to exercise.

'Have another one with me,' I said holding up the bottle.

'Oh no, Gulley, I couldn't. I've had enough already. Well, you can see I have – what with the worry and the cold wind. And how are you, Gulley?' she said, looking at me as if I were a landscape about twenty miles away. 'How are you? In that awful shed all alone with no one to look after you.'

'I'm all right, Sara,' I said. 'Don't you worry about me. 'It's how are you?'

'Oh, I don't know why I came. And look how late it is. But being only a mile off, at the graveyard, and wondering how you were managing —'

I poured out the bottle into two glasses and held out one to Sara. Her hand closed round it, without noticing. The sensitive plant. 'And it being Fred's day on. Oh dear, what's the time?'

'Eight, just gone. What time is Fred coming home?'

'Ten, but I'm getting back by half-past nine. Not a minute after. Not while the poor boy's so upset.'

'And what's wrong with Fred?'

'Oh everything – but it's really his stomach, poor mannie. And his married sister that lives opposite. She never liked me doing for him. Though how he would do for himself, I don't know. As nervous as a maiden. It's those engines in the yard. Running backwards when you're not looking. Oh dear, I shouldn't have come, should I?' But she kept looking at me like a young lass when she first feels her front and wonders what she wants.

'He's a bit jealous is he, your Fred? Well, I'm not surprised. I should think he'd better.'

'I've been good to him, Gulley, truly I have. But you oughtn't to have come like that – not to the house, I mean.'

'How did he know?'

'There's plenty to tell him down our street – not forgetting the sister. And, of course, he likes to know who comes to the house – it's natural for a man. And where I am.'

'And where he is.'

'Oh dear,' said Sara, taking a pull at the porter, as if by accident. And wiping her mouth with the back of her hand. Reflex action. 'I oughtn't to have come, really. It does make you feel old, acting silly. But it seemed such a chance. Don't you hate to feel old, Gulley?'

'No, what I hate is to feel young, and then my arms and legs go back on me.'

'Oh, it's different for a man, But I feel so old, I could cry. And I feel it all the time. Everything seems to say to me: You're an old woman, Sara Monday. No more fun for you in this life. You'd better go and bury yourself.' And there were tears in her eyes.

'We're not so old, Sara.'

She shook her cheeks at me. 'An old apple and an old wife have but a creaking life.'

'Why, Sara, what's wrong with you? Tough as an old saddle.'

'I don't know,' said Sara. 'But I'm so breathless Fred keeps on saying I ought to go to hospital.'

'What for?'

'Well, I had a little pain – in my inside.'

'Growing pains. Was it your stomach?'

'That isn't it – it's one of those pains you can't quite tell where it is.'

'I know them. Forget them, Sall.'

'So I should if only Fred would forget them. But he'll drive me into hospital at last and then they'll find something. Trust them. Oh, those hospitals. They gave little Morris Hagberg the wrong anaesthetic only last week – burnt his throat to cinders – that's two in a month.' And she looked so sadly at me I was quite surprised. 'Come, Sara,' I said. 'You never used to talk like this.'

'And there was Rozzie – I'll never forget Rozzie lying there in the infirmary without her leg.'

Rozzie was an old friend of Sara's and of mine, who had died in the workhouse infirmary after an accident.

'Well,' I said. 'Don't go and get run over by a bus on the way to the local, like Rozzie.'

'Rozzie crying because they wouldn't even let her have her stays or put a little powder on her poor face. Oh, Gulley, if I could trust you to keep me out of those hospitals and infirmaries. I believe I'd go off with you.'

So that's it, I thought. She wants a change. The last flutter of the old candle. But no, I'm too busy.

'I should think he's fond of you, Fred,' I said.

'But he's so set on those places. He's so scientific. And what does he know about how a woman feels to be dragged about on a slab like butcher's meat, and left to die among strange walls, in sheets that never belonged to any human soul, much less her own self. I'd rather be drowned or poisoned.'

I put my arm round the old thing. 'Come, Sall, you're not dead yet.'

'It's not the being dead – it's the dying. And being so helpless. Look at poor Rozzie, she was so big and gay. She was bigger than I was, and never cared for anything till she lost her leg and her money.'

'Rozzie wasn't so tough as you are, Sall. She may have been bigger and noisier, but she was softer.'

'All the same, Gulley, you'd have picked Rozzie first if you could have got her.'

'Never,' I said. Though, in fact, I had been on pretty close terms with Rozzie and there were times when I did prefer her to Sara. Her hips and legs were better, and her temperament more placid. You always found Rozzie where you left her, and she didn't intrude on your private character, like Sara. She stayed on the outside.

'You proposed to Rozzie once?' said Sara.

'Never,' I said, which was true. I hadn't proposed because it hadn't been necessary. 'Do you ever go back to the grave?' said Sara, and I knew she had found out something. 'I have been,' I said. For in the last two years I had had a kind of understanding with my son Tom, who was also Rozzie's only son, to keep her grave decent. 'That is,' I said, 'I've passed that way. It's a short cut to the Red Lion.'

'It wasn't you left all the flowers last year on her funeral day. The sexton said it was a gentleman in a blue overcoat.'

'A gentleman – come, Sall. I haven't been a gentleman for forty years.'

Sara shook her head at me. But she was a little more cheerful. 'Poor Rozzie, she had a terrible skin. It was a cross to her.' 'Oh terrible.' 'And her face was all crooked.' 'I remember.' 'Her mouth was on one side.' 'Poor Rozzie.' 'She was a dear,' said Sara, 'and I wish I'd gone to see her oftener in the Infirmary.' 'Don't blame yourself Sall, it's all over long ago.' 'That doesn't make it any better. Oh dear, I wish poor Rozzie was back again. I'd be a better friend to her.' 'No, you wouldn't, because you wouldn't know she was going to fall under a bus and die in the infirmary.'

'That's true, I wouldn't,' said Sara, and she gave a great sigh. 'Oh dear, why can't we know before.'

'And there's another thing,' I said. 'Rozzie would never have lasted as you have done. She was too soft and too lazy. She would have been an old woman by now.'

'And so am I an old woman.'

'Come on, Sall,' I said, squeezing my arm round her. 'Drink up, and you'll feel better.'

'Drinking up won't do any good to thoughts. They're too deep.'

'No, but it'll do good to your feelings, and then your feelings will do good to your thoughts.'

'Oh, Gulley,' said Sara, taking off the rest of her glass. She was crying and smiling all at once. 'You'll be the ruin of me all over again. Why, look at me, coming all this way, and upsetting Fred and everything. I ought to be pole-axed.'

'I hope you haven't been imprudent, Sara,' I said.

'A lot you care,' she said, 'but there, if you were a woman, you'd know what it feels like to get older and older, and to know that nothing will ever happen to you any more. Nothing nice, that is.'

'Go on, Sall,' I said. 'You're not so old as all that or you wouldn't be here today.'

'Oh no, Gulley, it's because I'm old I'm acting so silly; yes, and it's worse than just coming out of my way. Well, you didn't get my letter, and a good thing too. I kept on thinking of the good times we had. Oh dear, you were a bad husband to me, Gulley, but you did know how to enjoy yourself, and I do like people that know how to enjoy themselves, man or boy. And, oh dear, look at your boots and your socks. Well, I meant to bring you some socks, but then I wasn't sure if you wouldn't think I was being a nuisance and trying to make up to you after the last time.'

'Bring me all the socks you like, Sall. I've no meanness about me. I'll never refuse a gift from a friend. I'd take 'em even from my enemies, if they offered. So thank you, my dear, and drink up.' And I filled her glass.

'No. No, Gulley, it's bad for me. Though why I should want to do good to myself I don't know. Oh dear, that time at Bournemouth. With that sweet sunset the first day. Roses and violets. And the waves just whisking the pebbles. Oh dear, and the policeman nearly caught us —'

She dipped her nose again, and then gave a sigh like a grampus when he breaks surface. I gave her old stays another tender pressure. I doubt if she felt it through the armour. And the voice of the skate came through the yard window.

'The boundless possibilities of human happiness when guided by those natural loves and fraternal sympathies planted in the soul.'

'Oh well,' said Sara, 'I suppose I'll get used to it in time. Time slow but sure will all your troubles cure.'

'The nature of man is love. Look at the little helpless child, born so utterly dependent. Dependent only on love.'

'He speaks nicely, the young man,' said Sara. 'I shouldn't think he'd been married, do you? I'm glad it's about religion. I haven't been to church for a long time, I've been so busy.'

'And so it is to love alone that Nature entrusts her most important task. Love, the source and guarantee of all our hopes.'

'That's right,' said Sara. 'Though goodness knows, children are a work, too. But it would be better in church. Church is more homely. Well, after all, it is the house of God. Yes, I always liked church, even on a weekday, and it saves time without a sermon. Oh dear, that awful service when Rozzie died – in that cemetery chapel. I'd rather drown myself than a pauper funeral.'

'Come Sara, you've had a good innings – you've squeezed the lemon. Three husbands and five children – not counting the stand-ins, the Freds and the Dickies – it's a lot of happiness for one woman.'

'Don't talk of happiness like that, Gulley, as if it was all over. I never was happy unless I was with you, and you gave me a chance I always say there was no one like you for gaiety. Oh dear, when I saw you on that Wednesday, it did bring back the old times, and what times they were.' And there she was looking at me as if she could eat me without sauce, the old crocodile. I've set the tow alight in the old cask. I thought, It's the last flare of the old bonfire; and there may be a lot of combustible there still. You can't tell by the bung. I'll get my face singed unless I'm careful.

'And you couldn't have done better than Fred for a quiet billet,' I said.

'Yes, indeed Fred is a good home. Only for the worry about the bills. Well, what if there are a few little set-offs, after four years. Why, I always give him the best of everything. And if we had to get rid of the lodger, that wasn't my fault. There! jealousy, as they say, is the mustard to a good meat. But I wish I'd met you first, Gulley, in my maiden time.'

'You made a very good match with old Monday – plenty of money, and he doted on you.'

'I'll never say a word against him. And, indeed, I blessed myself, Gulley. I thought I was well enough. But now I know better. You know what it is with a man like that – so nervous and weak in his spirits. You have to be keeping it up all the time and working at yourself lest you fall away – and then with the children coming as fast as mine did, it was work, work, work, and no end till they got married and my dear Edith went to China, and so it was good-bye. But there, I knew it was ordained. And if I didn't know what was due to my teens and had to learn artfulness and contrivance in my bridal moon when even the plainest pug may give herself the right to put off her brains with her suspenders. What did I know but it went with the service. Like the second housemaid to clean the upstairs door handles, and thank God and my dear good mother if I was foolish I was dutiful and took my gaiety as the tinker's donkey takes grass, between the kicks and the hard pull-ups.'

'In that kingdom of love which is the home, does any father ask for laws to assist his authority? Does the mother send for the police?'

'I like the young man, he ought to be a preacher,' said Sara, stopping. 'Yes, indeed,' she said, giving another gentle sigh that made her stays creak like an old shutter. 'I ought to go to church – it always did me good. But then the people will look at you if you're keeping house for a widower, or perhaps I only think they do.'

'And Fred didn't like the lodger.'

'Now, Gulley, you mustn't think anything against the poor man – he was old enough to be my father almost – and a great wen on his neck. And if he was with the Cleansing Department, I always think it's a shame the hard dirty work they have which somebody has to do. I'm sure Fred would make enough fuss if the dustbin wasn't emptied. But there, I'm not going to say anything against Fred, being particular. I'd always rather Sir Whimsy in a clean shirt, than Master Easy to lie in dirt.'

'Meaning me,' I said, for I remembered how Sara had made me set up a night-shirt instead of sleeping in my winter drawers.

'Oh no, Gulley, for you know how I took you; you hadn't got a whole pair of trousers. Well, I've never been sorry, for if I hadn't gone to you, I would never have known the true sweet joys of life. But there, you're laughing at me. I know I'm acting silly. It's being old and seeing Rozzie's grave and thinking of the hospital and perhaps, I've had a drop. Well, I know I've let myself go, Gulley. You may well look at me, a regular old jelly. Sliding round like aspic on a hot plate. Yes, I always needed a man to peg me down, a real man. And I only found one. But, I mustn't say that, must I. And now it's all over, I'm only fit for a warning.'

'Don't say that, Sara,' I said, giving her another squeeze. And meaning it. For you couldn't help liking the old trout. The very way she was speaking; easy from her soul as a jug runs when you tilt it to a wet lip; it made me tingle all over; it made me laugh and sing in the calves of my legs. It made my toes curl and my fingers itch at the tops. It made me want to go bozo with the old rascal. What a woman. The old original. Clear as a glass-eye and straight as her own front. The very way she worked her great cook's hand, jointed like a lobster, round her glass; and lolled her head on one side, and turned up her eyes and heaved up her bosom when she sighed, enjoying the feel of herself inside her stays; it made me want to squeeze her till she squealed.

'Don't believe it,' I told her. 'You'd still walk away from any hop-pole girl, in a light breeze. You've got the genius, Sall, if that's what it is.'

'Oh dear, but they were good times, weren't they – sweet, lovely times.'

'And not so bad now – does Fred go out every Tuesday and Saturday night?'

'But, Gulley. You wouldn't have to come to the house again. It's the sister – she watches all the time, and it does upset Fred so much when anyone comes, it's not fair to a man with his delicate stomach —'

'No, and you don't want to lose a good home, do you – and I don't blame you. Why should you with your mornings off and every Saturday.'

'Oh, Gulley, you make me feel like twenty-five again, in my first ripening. I never knew a man like you to hold a woman. You used to make me feel quite queer,' and she drank her drink quickly so as not to spill it and tried to put her head on my shoulder. But her neck wouldn't bend so far, and she only managed to hook on to my coat seam by one eyebrow.

'Nature, that supreme creator, intended man for happiness and peace, in the enjoyment of all her beauties —' the skate was saying.

'It all helps,' said Sara, 'but not unless there's some kindness on both sides – and perhaps when Nature goes out, the kindness comes in. I think we're both kinder sort of mankind than we used to be, Gulley. When we had our nature more fidgety, and, indeed, it may be intended for peace in our old age —'

'Damn old age,' I said, 'I'm not old, and if I wasn't so busy and had the money, I'd take you to Brighton tomorrow.'

'Too busy,' said Sara. 'Oh well, I suppose that's a good thing. But, oh dear, how I used to hate that word. Why, even on our honeymoon at Bournemouth, it was always: Just keep like that a minute, Sara, while I catch the slant of the left shoulder.'

'Well, Sara, and I wouldn't mind drawing that shoulder again – when you come to me next week. I shouldn't be surprised if your back and thighs weren't as good as ever they were.'

'Oh dear, I could never make out whether it was me or my flesh that you wanted – that was the beginning of all our trouble.'

'Who made the trouble? It was nag, nag, nag —'

'I never nagged you, Gulley. I would never do such a thing to a male body. I've more contrivance than that, I hope. And who hit me on the nose. Well, look at it even now.'

'It was the only way to teach you to keep it out of my business.'

'Well, perhaps I made too much of the nose, Gulley, but you know a woman has her feelings, especially a young woman, before she learns sense.'

'You were forty when you hooked me.'

'Ah, but that is the youngest time – I mean in your feelings – that's when a woman acts her youngest and silliest. Well, I was a silly girl I know, but I couldn't bear for you to hit me on the nose – it wasn't the pain, it was making it so red and ugly. Well, I always knew my nose was my weak point —'

'Point —'

'There you go', and Sara began to laugh and cry at the same time. 'Oh, isn't that you all over. Oh, it's cruel. Well, I know it always was too soft and spready, and you know you did make it worse. I'm sure you broke the gristle – yes, if I've got to carry about this awful sponge now, it's because of you.'

'And a few score hogsheads. Come, Sara, fill up and don't let it stick to the glass. You and I were a pair of fools, but that's no reason why we should go on being foolish – you come along next Saturday and bring some beer, and I'll do a nice sketch or two and give you a copy. You always liked to keep a drawing of yourself. I daresay you have some now.'

'You only want me for a cheap model, Gulley, I know.'

'The best model I ever had. Why Sara, they're giving thousands for those old sketches of you in the yellow bath. And you've got it about you still,' and, in fact, I could have painted the old trollop that minute if I could have got her clothes off. There was always something about Sara that made me want to hit her or love her or get her down on canvas. She provoked you, and half of it was on purpose.

The skate was working himself up. 'On the one hand the home; a little sketch or picture of that paradise which Nature meant for the whole world.'

'Yes,' said Sara, sighing again, and a tear or perhaps a drop of porter sweat rolled off her nose into the glass. 'That's what I always felt – if only people could be sensible and not so jealous and spiteful – there's such a lot of happiness that God meant for us.'

'And what do we see about us,' cried the skate, working himself up and answering his own questions like the end man at the nigger minstrels. 'Nothing but crime and hatred and wars —'

'And just when you get some sense,' said Sara, 'and know that you can't have happiness brought up on a hot plate, you're old and it's too late —'

'And why, because of property,' said the skate, 'that institution of the devil. The love of things, which is the enemy of God's love —'

And I heard old Plantie calling out 'Hear, hear,' and clapping his great walrus flippers together.

'I daresay you've got something put by, Sara,' I said, 'so that even if Fred does turn nasty —'

'Oh dear, what's the time?' and she got quite agitated.

'That's all right, Sara, drink up and we'll catch the bus – but first you can come round to my place and I'll show you where I hide the key.'

'You really think I'd better come,' said Sara, quite shaky.

'Not if you're afraid for your virtue.'

'Oh dear,' and she was giggling like any dairymaid in the strawhouse. 'Don't talk so. It's not nice at our age, I'm too old.'

'You wait and see who's too old – and we'll have a bit of supper somewhere.'

'Well, of course, Gulley – you must let me give you supper, and I'd have brought something over today only I had to get away quick when that sister was out at her shopping, and there's some shirts too that Fred thinks are tight in the neck. I'm sure you could do with some winter shirts.'

'Property, that devilish invention to which we owe every evil, envy, hatred, thievery, the police, and all the cruelty of law, armies, navies, war —'

There was more clapping, and Sara drank up her glass in order to clap for herself. The old blancmange was dissolving in sentiment and drink; her nose was on fire and her little grey eyes were swimming, and while she slapped her fat hands together, all her chins and her neck and her front shook up and down and even her backside quivered in the tight black bombazine, or whatever it was.

But all at once she saw me looking at her, and just like the old Sara she knew at once what was in my mind and said, 'Well, aren't I a picture of fun. But there, when you're old, what can you do. If you don't feel anything about anything, you might as well be dead.'

And I gave her another hug. For she had got round me so far that I was all on the jump, and ready to carry her off that minute. Though I ought to have known I was much too busy for females, except in the way of work. 'Don't you mind, Sara. Go on being Sara. Let yourself go. Act how you feel, and if they laugh, who cares. Why, they laugh at me. And I laugh back. That's one advantage of turning into a damned old scarecrow. Drink up, old girl, and we'll laugh at 'em together.'

Just then there was a scruffling next door, like the beginning of a dog-fight, and next moment the whole meeting got up and began to sing Jerusalem. So Sara jumped up, too, and began to sing as loud as she could, stretching up her neck and shutting her eyes, like a prize tenor.

> Till we have built Jerusalem
> In England's green and pleasant land.

'Well, I always did love that song,' she said. 'It's the tune, I suppose, and whatever you say about Jews, they're good family people.'

'Come on, Sara, there's only one bottle left.' And I poured out.

'Oh, Gulley, I couldn't – I'm quite swimming, well, I suppose we can't get out till the people have moved.'

'And very comfortable here, too,' I said, getting a firmer grip. For the truth was that, what with memories and beer, and Sara herself, we were both a bit glorious and we seemed like young things again, in our forties. And we fell to kissing, and so on. And Sara was half laughing and half crying. And our chairs fell over against the wall.

However, after a time, I found that I had my head jammed under the scullery shelf and I was nearly smothered with Sara, who seemed to spread her bombazine all over me and I had a stabbing in my thigh that I thought must be my sciatica, till I realized it was Sara's umbrella jammed in between the legs of our chairs. So I began to wriggle out of the clinch, and Sara said, 'Oh, oh, mind my hat – oh dear, oh dear, I've got the cramps,' and then when we saw each other, she was more crying than laughing. 'Oh dear,' she said, 'I'm ashamed, Gulley, you can laugh, but we're too old. And dressed in my Sunday blacks for poor Rozzie. No, it's not right – it's so uncomely. No, you can't get over it, Gulley, being old. Well, if I had a beauty cure perhaps, and a tea-gown like some old actress and was in a nice room with silk sofas and flowers, but there, I'm talking silly. I'm too old, and look at my stockings, I know half my suspenders are pulled right out. I feel all to pieces, and what's the time – you don't say it's half-past ten' – and the old lady began to get in such a fluster that I was afraid she'd have hysterics.

She grabbed up her umbrella and made for the back steps. I ran along with her and tried to soothe her down. 'Come, Sara, you needn't run – you'll blow up.'

'Run, why I'm lucky if I catch the last bus, and Fred home any minute now, and perhaps that sister with him. Oh, you don't know, or you wouldn't have come to the house, Gulley. They ferreted it all out – what with that girl Coker and Hickson, yes, even about the pictures.'

'Well, Sall, if Fred does turn you out, you come along – come back to me.'

'Oh, he wouldn't do that. Not Fred. He couldn't be so stupid. Why, what would happen to Dicky, yes, or Fred himself. With that nasty herring gut of a creature. Is that my bus? Well, it can't be helped, I can't run any more. Oh, I've got such a pain, whatever did I drink all that beer for?'

But I got her to the bus-stop at last and while her bus was driving up, she came to her senses for a minute, as Sara always could, in the most exciting situations, and she took me by the coat and turned up her eyes and said, 'I shouldn't have come, Gulley, should I. Just upsetting us both. But we were happy, weren't we, and I'll bring those socks and shirts, and there's an old overcoat, too, or if I don't dare to come out so far again, I'll post them to you. Only don't come to the house or write. It's not safe, truly it isn't. And look after your chest. You ought to have more woollies for winter, you know you ought. I'll put some in, chest thirty-two, it used to be. Well, if they're too big now, they'll shrink. And if I can't come again, we were happy, Gulley, weren't we. I mean in the good times – we were the happiest couple. Oh dear, here's the bus – you'll never say we weren't the happiest couple. Even if you did spoil my nose. Oh, I thank God for that time, and you were a sweet husband when you liked.'

'Come on, Sall,' I said. 'Get up, old lady.' For I thought she would dissolve away on the pavement.

'Yes, I thank God for it. We've got something better than noses, haven't we. We've got our memories and they last better than any nasty flesh.'

And she had me nearly flustered as she was. As the bus moved off I was in two minds about jumping on the platform and running off with her. And after the bus had gone, I walked down to Greenbank in a high state of enjoyment. What an evening. And I couldn't get the old girl out of my eye or my feelings. I kept on seeing her hand tilting the glass, and the turn of her body from the waist; stiff enough, but I could see the woman inside; the real old Sara that had made me mad and especially with the brush.

Yes, I thought, and that's what I've been missing in my Eve, something female, something that old Cranach had, yes, something from Sara. And not just the hips either, and the high waist; it's something in the movement; and as soon as I got back to Plantie's I opened one of his old encyclopaedias and began to draw what I wanted on the end-papers; the everlasting Eve, but all alive-oh. She came out strong like Sara, the Sara of twenty years ago.

16

When Plantie came down the steps from seeing his Prof to the Tube, I put Sara in my pocket and the Encyclopaedia on the shelf. Then I helped Plantie to pour all the odd bottles together into a jug and we sat down in front of the fire to try the mixture. While Plantie talked of Ponting and Proudhon and Comte and Spinoza.

The trouble of staying with Plantie is the talk. These old blue-suit walruses are great ones to talk. I knew a dustman down Brocket Yard who would talk all night about the number of the beast. But he was one of the old school, with a bowler hat like a paddle steamer. Plantie's great hobbyhorse is Spinoza. The reason I suppose is that Spinoza was all for making the best of a bad job. And Plantie, having had a hard life, is the same way of thinking. Motto:

> KEEP YOUR PECKER UP, OLD COCK.
> HERE'S THE CHOPPER COMING.

'To contemplate the glory of creation,' said Plantie, blowing clouds of smoke like a chimney on fire. He'd taken off his collar and tie and boots, and was prepared to be happy. I said nothing for fear of provoking provocation. But I drank the more. A good mixture. There was some gin in it as well as lime-juice and lager, black-strap and wallop.

Plantie put one foot on the fender and wagged his big toe, and said, 'Yes, Mr Jimson, the greatest of philosophers.'

This was provocation. Because Plantie knew I didn't like Spinoza. I used to, of course. In the year when I couldn't paint and went to the devil, and philosophy, science and the newspapers, I fell for old Ben Spinoza myself. Like everyone at first sight. The old Eye got me. And I, too, went round offering provocation. I once bit a man who didn't like Spinoza; or perhaps he'd never heard of him, and didn't want to hear. I remember he was trying to grind out my guts with his knees. He was some kind of idealist; took a real interest in fundamental things. But just after that I began to read Blake. And Blake led me back to Plato, because he didn't like him, and the pair of them took me forward to black and white drawing and formal composition. And soon after that I got too busy for amusement; and stopped reading anything but judgement summonses.

Spinoza is one of the most popular London philosophers, especially in the East End, and round the Isle of Dogs, but he is not so strong in Greenbank, which belongs more to the upper river cultural sphere. In Greenbank they drink in Plato and Ruskin with the Oxford bath water. Postie has always been a Platonist and a Dark Blue. Bert Swope was a passionate Dark Blue. On the Boat Race day of 1930, Swope tore the favours off two Cambridge men from Poplar and threw them into the river. He would have been a leading Platonist if he had ever heard of Plato. But about 1933 or 1936, Plantie, who had read all the philosophers, began to take a special interest in Spinoza. Anarchists who love God always fall for Spinoza because he tells them that God doesn't love them. This is just what they need. A poke in the eye. To a real anarchist, a poke in the eye is better than a bunch of flowers. It makes him see stars.

Plantie has had a hard time and so he likes to be told that in God's sight he is dirt. Plantie has been kicked about the world like a football, and so he likes to be told that he isn't any better than a football, except to kiss the foot that kicks him. It makes him feel more brisk and independent. It gives him confidence in himself. To say, 'I can take the worst they've got.'

When you tell a man like Plantie that he isn't free except to take it as it comes, he feels free. He says, 'All right, let 'em all come.'

But I didn't like Spinoza. I haven't got any self-respect, and besides, I'm an optimist. I get a lot of fun out of fun, as well as the miseries. And so when Plantie tried to convert me to dignified independence I quarrelled with him. We didn't speak for some weeks or months. And since Plantie is a good man and, therefore, a bit of a nagger, he's tried at least three times a year since to provoke me on Spinoza. But now that I'm broke I can't afford to quarrel with my friends, and I've worked up a technique to avoid arguing about Spinoza. I don't say anything at the time, but afterwards, and only to myself.

'He kept free,' said Plantie. 'Yes, one of the greatest and noblest men who ever lived. Because with it all, with the glass dust, and all the people who wanted to burn him alive for a heretic, he kept his happiness.' Plantie wagged both his toes, and blew out such a cloud of smoke that I wondered we didn't have the fire brigade. He was working up his happiness. 'What he said was, "Life is a gift, and what right have we to complain that we weren't given it different." No, he never complained against good or bad luck or any nonsense like that. Any more than you do, Mr Jimson.'

This was a pass at the scullery window. But I only took another pull at the jug. For the truth was I wasn't hearing Plantie, only his words. So I listened like an angel. Grinning like Essex clay in a June sun. Plantie's voice stroked me down like a warm breeze; while I swam in mixed lager, and contemplated the new Sara-Eve like another golden fish in the same pond.

I said nothing and thought nothing and never felt any of the injuries the old blowhard was aiming at me, under cover of his hospitality. And all I remember after half-past eleven is Plantie's toes going like a sewing machine, and Plantie's moustache shaking up and down in a cloud of blue smoke like the burning bush, and his bald head shining pink, while he talked about the evils of property and the police, and the joys of Nature and the contemplation of its beauties.

Then I woke up in Plantie's bed with a rug over me and breakfast ready on the stove. Plantie was tap-tapping away in the front shop. He always works on Sunday. Being a man of strict principles.

But I had a head like a dog-fight and a mouth like a vacuum cleaner, and, worst of all, the feeling of too much society.

A nice way to spend my life, I thought, at parties. And I felt so damned ill that I only wanted to get to work.

When I wished Plantie good morning, he looked at me over the top of his iron spectacles that he wears in the shop and said, 'Coming back?' gruff and short as always in the workshop.

'Thank you, Mr Plant,' I said. 'But I shall be pretty busy from now on, and I think I'll sleep on the job. Get the early light.'

Plantie knocked in another clag, and said, 'You can't sleep in that place of yours.'

'Yes, thanks, not badly.'

Plantie knocked in two clags. And I was fretting to be off. I'd had enough of talk and people for a week. Talk is not my line. It gives me a stomach ache. When I've talked a lot, I know I've told a lot of lies, and what makes it worse, not even meaning to. When you're talking a lot you haven't time to get the words right. Talk is lies. The only satisfactory form of communication is a good picture. Neither true nor false. But created. Yet I couldn't go until Plantie was ready for me to go because I'd slept in his bed and eaten his breakfast. And he wasn't ready yet. I knew that by the stiff way he worked his hammer and stuck out his moustache.

'What about supper?' he said at last.

'I'm afraid I'm engaged for supper.'

Plantie knocked in another clag, but I could tell he'd given me up, by his free style. 'So long, and thanks,' I said. 'Good-bye, Mr Jimson,' said Plantie. 'It's a pleasure.'

And so we parted friends. But I had wasted the day. I sat and looked at the canvas most of the morning. And what I did that afternoon I took out next morning. I could see there was something there, but it kept on fleeing away from me. I began to think I'd never paint anything again. I'd lost the artfulness. And even in the dark, I couldn't see my way. I only got a headache in my feet, and corns on my brain. Going round and round.

What I say to an artist is, WHEN YOU CAN'T PAINT – PAINT. But something else. So I knocked up a little sketch of Sara on a piece of plank. Sara as she was, broad as a door. And it went very well. It went so well that I forgot my feet, I forgot my head. And just as always happens, this other job of

Sara, which had nothing to do with my picture in hand, began to bend round and give me ideas on that picture, too. I began to get so many ideas about it that I should have started all over again if the light hadn't failed. Then I noticed my rheumatism, and my backache, and my poor feet. But I was lucky enough to meet Postie Ollier outside the Eagle, and he stood me a pint and a stand-up supper. He also tried to take me home to Plant's. Postie is one of the vice-presidents of the save Jimson from himself society. But he can't ask me to his own place, because he married beneath him, and his friends have to be his wife's friends, too.

'Mr Plant is expecting you,' he said. But I knew I couldn't do with any more talk.

'Thank you, Mr Ollier,' I said. 'But I shall be very comfortable in my own quarters.' And I ran away from him in case he pressed me.

Constable night. Broken lumps of cloud whirling across a knife-coloured sky like wreckage on a Thames flood. Moon running over the house fronts like a spotlight. When it fell on the willows, they trembled like girls caught in dark corners waiting for their young men.

These lovely females form sweet night and silence and secret obscurities. To hide from Satan's watch-fiends human loves.

The rain came down like glass bead curtains, glittering across the black arches. It swayed in the wind and rattled against the stones.

Shed pouring through the roof. Pools on the floor. No oil in the lamp, no matches. And a couple of cold sausages. Got into my nightdress of newspapers. Knock on the window and Coker shouted over the noise of the rain, 'Who's there, is that you, Jimson?'

'No.' 'What are you doing there?' and she poked her head through the window. 'Going to bed.' 'You can't sleep there, you old fool, in a pool of water. I heard you coughing from Greenbank Hard.' 'I've been coughing for thirty years.' 'You're a bloody nuisance, that's what you are. Where am I going to put you this time of night?' 'I'm all right, Coker.' 'You ought to be in the Union, that's the truth of it.' 'You can't put me in the Union. I'm a householder.' 'Oh come on, and don't talk so much. But you'll have to sleep on the floor, and I've only one blanket.'

'I've got my coat.' 'Sopping wet, I should think. Oh dear, what I ought to do is to leave you to go to the Union.' 'If I go to the Union, I shan't be able to paint, and you won't get your money.' 'I won't get my money out of your painting, I'm getting it from Mr Hickson.'

Coker lived on the top floor in Dahlia Road. Nice respectable villas come down to social life, and bare wood stairs. Top landing full of buckets, chests of drawers,jugs and pots. Coker pushed me into the room and stopped to tell some neighbour what she thought about a bucket. 'Nobody's going to slip their buckets on me. It's been four buckets for six months. It was three before that, and then there was the agreement. And now there's five. All right, but if it's five tomorrow night, somebody's bucket is going out of the window.'

Slice of a room, all furniture. Big bed. Four dining-room chairs piled up. Dining table on its side against the wall. Coker's summer coat hanging on one leg. Bird cage on the other. Radiogram as big as a chicken-house. Roll of stair carpet. New carpet brown, tins of cleaning stuffs, furniture polish, on the mantelshelf.

'Who's furniture, Coker? Yours or Willies'?' 'Mine,' said Coker. 'Catch Willie spending his money on anyone but himself.' 'Heard anything about him lately?' 'Dancing at the Palace with his Blondie every night.' 'I should say good riddance. Nothing but trouble to you all the time.' 'Don't you comfort me. Willie was worth trouble. He's a dead loss. And forty pounds' worth of furniture, all my blankets, two pairs of double sheets, six face towels with initials. It's enough to make a girl put herself in the water.'

'Don't you be a fool, Coker. Think of all the cups of tea and buttered scones you'd miss.' 'Don't you be afraid, I'm not drowning myself. Not while the Blondie's alive. Somebody ought to hate that bitch, and who'll do it if I don't.' 'It's a mug's game, Coker, especially for a woman. You can't get your own back. And I'll tell you why. It isn't your own when you get it. It's moved on.' 'I don't want my own back. I want to be like I am, hating that dirty tart. Why, look at all my poor chairs with their legs in the air. Like a lot of dead dogs, poisoned off. Don't you talk to me about forgiveness or I might get cross and give you a smack.' 'It's not forgiving. It's forgetting.' 'That's enough, or I'll get my mother up. Look at the floor, you old bone. You're wet to the skin. It's coming out of your boots.' 'Only my overcoat.' 'Take it off then. Don't stand goggling like a last week's bloater.' 'I did a good job today, Coker, one of those lucky days.' 'Lucky if you don't get pneumonia. Nice fool I'd look with you dead on my hands.' 'That job is going to be good – as good as anything I ever did. And better.' 'There, I knew, it's right through to your shirt.' 'The fact is, Coker, I'm first-class.' I was surprised when this popped out. But as it had come out I thought I might as well let myself go. 'Don't you tell anybody else, Cokey, but I'm one of the big fish. In a hundred years, fifty perhaps, the National Galleries will be paying fifty thousand pounds for a Jimson. And they'll be right. Because my stuff's the real stuff.' 'And nothing but rags under your shirt – you'll freeze one of these days.' 'The fact is, Coker, I'm a genius.' 'I shouldn't wonder if you hadn't a temperature this minute.' 'You think I'm talking nonsense.'

Coker was pulling me about like a rag doll and swearing at me. 'You're a nuisance, that's what you are – I suppose you'll have to come into the bed. Nice tale for the neighbours. But they'll talk, anyhow. Here, take your trousers off and turn 'em the other way round, they're dry anyhow. Back-before I mean.' And she pushed me down on the bed and began to pull my trousers off. Coker never had much patience.

'You don't believe a word I say, Coker.' 'Lift up your bottom – how can I get 'em off when you keep on sitting down.' 'You wonder how I know that I'm one of the greatest artists that ever lived – of course, there are a few hundred of 'em – but that's not so many among thousands of millions.' 'Yes, yes, you're a wonderful man.' 'All right, you can laugh.' 'I'm not laughing. Why, Mr Plant told me two years ago.' 'What did he tell you'. 'That you were a real genius. Don't you worry, everybody knows it round here. Even the kids say, there's the professor.'

'What do they say that for?' 'Well, they think you're cracked, who wouldn't. Get in now and over against the wall and keep over. I'll put a bolster down the middle to make sure.' 'What do you mean by a genius.' 'I'm not going to wait all night. And turn your face to the wall while I get ready.'

Coker undressed and knelt down to say her prayers. I took a peep to make sure, and when she got up I said, 'I thought you hated God, Coker.' 'So I do.' 'What do you pray for?' 'He's our Father, isn't he?' 'That's a funny reason.' 'Not so funny as you're a nuisance. Here, let me feel your head. I bet you got a fever. Nice bit in the papers if you croak in my bed. Oh well, it would happen to me. It's a wonder I got my legs the same length, and don't squint. Now you go to sleep.'

Coker put a loop of string on the switch; laid a bolster down the middle of the bed, and got in on the other side. Then she pulled the string and the light went out. Light went out and the moon came in through the curtain making a pattern on the blanket like water. And I felt as gay as Garrick. It's a joke, I thought, that I should have such happiness in my life and this poor kid should be damned from the kick. It makes you laugh. 'What did you pray for, Coker?' 'Mind your own business.'

'You ought to look for a nice widower of fifty with a wooden leg. Make allowances on both sides.' 'If you're being funny, I'll give you a smack.' 'You got the furniture, all you need is a husband.' 'Who wants a husband? I wouldn't mind if I never saw a man again. A dirty lot of crooks.' 'You were going to marry Willie, weren't you?' 'Willie was different. He was a gentleman.' 'Who walked off and left you in the mud.' 'He didn't know what he was doing, poor boy, when that Blondie got him. She's well known.' 'Did you pray for Blondie to get trouble?' Coker didn't answer, 'If Blondie knew how she'd got on your mind, she'd laugh.' 'Let her; she won't laugh if I get her where I want her.' 'Where does she live?' 'I'm trying to find out. What she wants is a splash of acid.' 'You'd get seven years for that.' 'It would be worth it.' 'Don't you believe it – she'd be burning on your brain the rest of your life. She's come back, in the acid.' 'I shouldn't mind if I'd got justice.' 'You can't get justice in this world. It doesn't grow in these parts.' 'You're telling me.' 'It makes you laugh.' 'What does?' 'The damned unfairness of things.' 'It doesn't make me laugh. More like crying.' 'Or cry, just as you like.' 'Suppose you let me go to sleep.'

And in five minutes she was as deep as a diver. I sat up to take a look at her. Face like a child. Breathing like a baby. She turned over like a child. Sudden earthquake. Gave a sigh, threw one arm over the blanket. Deep all the time. And what a forearm. Marble in the moon. Muscled like an Angelo, but still a woman's. Nothing obvious. Modelling like a violin solo. The sweetest elbow I ever saw, and that's a difficult joint. Not fat above the wrist but a smooth fall into the metacarpals. Just enough structure to give the life and the power. Bless the girl, I thought, she's a beauty, and she doesn't know it. I could have kissed Coker for that elbow. But what would be the good of that? She wouldn't believe me if I told her an elbow like that was a stroke of genius.

And I thought, that's the forearm I want for Eve, with Sara's body. Sara as she was about thirty years ago. Sara's forearms were always too soft. Cook's arms. Mottled brown. Greedy and sentimental arms. Lustful wrists crested like stallions, with Venus rings. But Eve was a worker. The woman was for hard graft. Adam the gardener, the poet, the hunter. All wires like a stringed instrument. Nervous fibre. Eve smooth and thick as a column, strong as a tree. Brown as earth. Or red like Devon ground. Red would be better. Iron ground. Iron for the magnetic of love. English Eve.

> And this is the manner of the daughters of Albion in their beauty,
> Everyone is Threefold in Head and Heart and loins, and everyone
> Has three gates into the three Heavens of Beulah which shine
> Translucent in their Foreheads and their Bosoms and their Loins
> Surrounded with fire unapproachable. But whom they please
> They take up into their heavens in intoxicating delight.

When we got up I tried to do Coker's arm from memory on the back leaf out of her prayer book. But it didn't have the feeling. It wanted to be in the round. 'I wish you'd let me paint you, Coker,' I said. 'It's your arm I want.'

But Coker didn't even answer. 'Hurry up and finish your tea.'

'What's the hurry for me?' 'We've got a visit to pay.' Then I noticed that Coker was putting on her country suit. 'You're not going to take me to Sara's again.' For I didn't want to see Sara again, especially after the night at Plant's. I hadn't the time at my age. 'No,' said Coker, 'we've finished with that one. Now it's Hickson's.' 'A bit quick, isn't it?' 'That's the idea, to get there before she can tip him off.' 'Sara wouldn't do that – she gave us all the evidence we wanted.' 'A double cross in each eye and a plant in her smile.' 'I couldn't go today, Coker, I've got work to do that can't wait.' 'What do you mean, can't wait? You haven't got an opening time. Nobody's going without his beer because you're on the outabout.' 'I got an idea and I got to get it down.' 'Ideas will keep without ice.' 'Not unless you turn 'em into paint – they go soft at the edges, or melt into grease and water.' 'You can always get new ones.' 'I don't want new ones, I want this one.

And I'll never get it again.' 'Then you'll get better. Here, give your boots a rub with the newspaper. I never saw such boots.' 'They're on the big side for warmth.' 'And what are the cracks for?' 'Ventilation.' 'It's not a joke. What do you think people think of you going about like an old tramp out of the Union?' 'They think nothing of me, and that's a comfort.' 'Don't talk silly.' 'Do you like to see people thinking about you? I didn't think you had so much vanity, Coker.' 'Put on your hat and don't fall over the apples like last time.' And she had me in the street before I could think of another excuse. 'It's bad when they think well of you, Cokey, because you get to think too much of yourself. And it's bad when they think badly of you because you may get to think badly of them. Take you mind off your work.' 'Where are you going to?' 'Gentlemen.' 'Be quick then – we got to catch Hickson before ten.'

I went down the steps, walked through the passage and came out at the other end. But Coker was waiting for me at the top of the steps. She jumped on me like a lion. 'I thought so – now why shouldn't I give you a smack.' 'Didn't I come up the same way?' 'No, you didn't, and you didn't do anything down there either. There wasn't time. Why, you old fool, I knew you wanted to make a getaway as soon as you spoke. A monkey at the Zoo could look more innocent.' 'I can't come to Hickson's today, Coker.' 'Don't you talk to me about your ideas, I'm not Mr Plant. You may be a genius, but you need boots and a new overcoat or you'll be dead before next winter. And a dead genius stinks as high as any other flat fish.' 'It's like this, Coker. I've had trouble with Hickson. I like Hickson, but he upsets me. And I'm at rather a tricky place in my work. Suppose we go and see Hickson and he begins to talk his nonsense, and we have a row. It might put me off the work. I don't say it would but it might. And then I might have to scrap the whole job and where would we be then?' 'You needn't speak to Hickson. Good thing if you don't after the way you talked to that Monday woman.' 'Then why do you want me along?' 'Because you're my only bona fides.'

I took a step backwards down the stairs. I knew Cokey was too much of a lady to chase a man into the gentlemen. Cokey saw the idea and she said, 'Come this once and I'll stand you a couple of quarts at a gill a time.' 'I don't want quarts.' And I took another step down. 'What do you want then?' 'I could do with a bladder of flake white, a viridian, a cobalt and chrome yellow. Also a No. 12 brush.' 'How much does it come to?' 'A few bob.' 'All right.' 'There's a colour shop just off High Street – not fifty yards off.' 'Can't you wait till we come back?' 'Something in my pockets would keep me from going through the ceiling at Hickson's.' 'All right, come on. You're a winner, you are.' 'That's a bargain.' 'Cross my heart. I shan't strangle you, though that's just about what you deserve.'

I came up then and we went along and got the colours. Twenty-three bob surprised Coker. But she surprised me. She paid down on the nail and said only, 'Caught again. But you're not going to say I went back on you.' 'No, I shan't, Coker. I think a lot of your character, especially your arms, and I wish you would sit for your arm. The left one. We could do it now in less than half an hour. I want it for my picture.' 'What about Hickson?' said Coker, and she stopped in the street and looked at me. 'All right, Coker, but you're taking a big chance. Why not telephone? Let me telephone.' 'I've telephoned already. He's expecting us. Are you coming on or are you going back on me after skinning me of twenty-three bob?' 'All right, Cokey. It will probably finish me off. But what's it matter after all? I mightn't have been born.' 'You might have been born with more sense.'

We took a bus to Oxford Circus. And I kept on moving till we got the front seats on top. Coker didn't want to move, but when I moved she had to move. 'I like the front window,' I said, 'for the view. As good as a Rolls. Better; higher and not the same responsibility not to run over the poor.' 'Yes,' said Coker, 'and when you've made me come with you and push in and push out, somebody's stuck his umbrella in my stockings. It's a wonder if I haven't two ladders this minute.' 'I wouldn't be a girl for a million pounds.' 'I wouldn't be a man if I was Clark Gable with twenty-five suits and forty pairs of shoes. I'd rather be the lowest woman in the world than the top man.' 'That's loyalty to the sex.' 'No, it's feelings. If you men were women for five minutes you'd know and you wouldn't want to change.' 'I thought you didn't like to be a woman.' 'I don't like being myself. But I'm not going to let up on it. I got my pride.' 'Yes, you've got your pride – it makes you a doormat for a sot like Willie.' 'Willie's not my pride. He was my chap, and he was good to me. You leave Willie out of it, you hear.'

It was a grey morning. Air skim milky. Grey sky, grey street, and the houses dodging by like a grey paling. Green-grey face just over the chimney pots, where the sun was hiding. Fat sulky face with one fat eye, three quarters closed. Gave it a look as if it had something on its mind. Old black rooks flapping along the sky and old black taxi-cabs flapping down the street.

'That's all right, Cokey,' I said. 'Well, you can't help it, can you? You're as God made you, more or less, with some interference from Daddy.'

Coker thought a moment and moved her little beak up and down. Then she said, 'I'm not expecting anything from anybody.' 'I'm glad of that,' I said, 'I was afraid you might be.' 'Might be what?' 'Expecting.' 'Mind your own business.' And I could feel she was trying to think of something cruel, something that would stab me to the heart, so I said, 'Never mind, Cokey. Say what you like. If it lets the pressure down, I can take it.'

Cokey thought again. But her temper had changed. And she said at last, in her bar voice, 'No one expects anything of a man, except mess and talk.' 'What do you expect of a woman?' 'Everything she can give and a smile.' 'Don't you give it, Coker, not everything.'

And Coker turned fierce again. But just when she was going to cut me to the soul, she changed her mind again and said, 'I might —'I got my pride.'

I gave it a minute to cast its warmth upon the conversation and then I said, 'I hope you didn't give anything to Willie you couldn't spare.'

Cokey didn't answer, but her mood was still lofty and calm. 'If Willie had wanted to chop off your legs with the meat hatchet, I suppose you'd have lain down on the scullery floor and lent him an apron to keep his trousers clean.' 'I'd rather my neck than my legs. And I'd rather he stuck a skewer in my heart than either. I don't like mess. But why not? Even my legs. I've got a lot of pride.' 'So you have, Coker. And it makes me anxious. Might get you into a lot of trouble.' 'I'll take it on.' 'Pride is a good chest protector but a bad bicycle,' I said. 'Its wheels only go 'round. And you want to get right away from that dirty lot of ordures, Cokey. You want to forget Willie and Blondie; and go on to the next thing. There's plenty of it, waiting to say how do you do, and it smells nicer.'

Cokey said nothing to this. She was feeling her wings; touching up her county scarf.

'I like you, Cokey,' I said. 'But the reason I tell you is that a friend's troubles are one's own troubles, and I don't like trouble. I could fall for you, Cokey, if I had time. And I don't like to see that Blondie getting on your mind, poisoning your springs. The worse she is, the worse for you. Well, I tell you, there's some fellows I daren't even remember their names, or I'd get ulcers on the brain. You take a straight tip from the stable, Cokey: if you must hate, hate the government or the people or the sea or men, but don't hate an individual person. Who's done you a real injury. Next thing you know he'll be getting into your beer like prussic acid; and blotting out your eyes like a cataract and screaming in your ears like a brain tumour and boiling round your heart like melted lead and ramping through your guts like a cancer. And a nice fool you'd look if he knew. It would make him laugh till his teeth dropped out; from old age.'

But Cokey only heard the first bit and she didn't listen to that. She only felt it, and it caused her to lean her right shoulder about a quarter of an inch in my direction. Approach to confidence. 'I tell you, Mr Jimson,' she said, 'a girl needs it with a face like mine. She needs a lot of pride. Every time I see it in the glass or shop window it gives me a smack where it hurts most, and every time I see it in another girl's face, it sticks a knife into me. Yes, even girls that I could pity, they shoot me full of hot needles.' 'And you shoot them?' 'Yes, I shoot them. It isn't what you mean to do, it's the flash-back. First time it hit me was about when I left school. At fourteen. Like a kick, and the kicks went on coming so quick I didn't have time to put up a guard. Makes a kid think.'

We were passing the gardens and the trees were lifting up their skinny black arms to the dirty sky like a lot of untouchables asking for a blessing from heaven. Which they knew they wouldn't get.

'I mean a girl, of course,' said Cokey. 'Nothing makes a boy think.' 'Only about what he can get or eat. Not about himself.' 'I wasn't thinking about myself. I was wondering who gave all the flowers to a totty like I won't say who and all the kicks to me, just because my features weren't out of the matchbox.' 'The delight of the eye beats home comforts any day. Even a chap like Willie has his poetical side. He forgets himself when he sees a real peach. That's what you're up against.' 'Don't I know it. Men are a lot of fools.' 'Or artists.' 'If Willie marries that Blondie she'll make him wish he was dead.' 'He won't want to change his poison, if she keeps her looks.' 'She's a bad heart.' 'Good hearts are sixpence a packet, but peaches are rare.' 'What do they make us for?' 'Quantity production and take the pick goodness is a throw away.' 'I got my pride, thank God.' 'It gives you a centre, but I find it cold for the guts.' 'Who said I wanted the heat?'

Hickson lives in Portland Place, top end, near the Park. Coker rang and I said, 'It's your responsibility, Coker. I didn't ask for it.' 'All right, it's my responsibility.' Man in a blue suit opened the door and showed us into a little room full of whatnots. Hickson has collected everything. I suppose it was that or drink. Man went off. 'Who was that?' Coker said. 'Hickson's man. Always in a blue suit.' 'How could I tell he wasn't a gentleman?' 'You're not meant to, first time. Look at this.' And I showed her the Japanese netsukes on the mantelpiece, real old ones. Carved all over with the wrinkles on the soles of their feet. 'Magnify them fifty times and they'd be monuments. It's chunky work. And yet look at the detail.' 'Too foreign-looking for me.' 'That's why Hickson likes 'em. He hasn't got any imagination either.' 'Well, what are they for?' 'Imagination.' 'I pity the girl who has to dust this room.' 'So do I if she hasn't got any more imagination than you have.' Coker said nothing. She was preening herself for Hickson, pulling down her coat, looking down the backs of her stockings, to see if the seams were straight. Admiring them. Real silk. Coker was very particular about her stockings.

For Eternity is in love with the productions of Time.

'What are you doing?' Coker said, turning round. She'd been looking at herself in a picture-glass. 'Nothing.' 'Take those things out of your pocket. You old fool. Do you want to do five years?' I took out some of the netsukes and put them back on the mantelpiece. All but the best, which Hickie couldn't have appreciated anyhow.

17

Just then Hickson's man opened the double door and asked us to come into the next room. The big drawing-room. And right in the middle of the wall my picture of Sara standing in the sun beside a flat bath. Right foot on a chair. Drying her ankle with a green towel. Sunlight throwing the window squares on her back and thighs. Giving the section. Solid as stone, but all in light without shadow and all direct painting. Eight by five. I hadn't seen it for fifteen years and it nearly knocked me down. 'Look at that,' I said to Coker. 'Where's your Rubens now or Renoir either?' 'Who did it?' 'I did.' 'Who is it, not that Sara?' 'What's it matter who it is?' 'How she could show herself – and such a lump, too. It's disgusting.' 'It's a work of genius. It's worth fifty thousand pounds. It's worth anything you like because it's unique; and Hickson knows it, too. Or somebody's told him. He's put it in the place of honour. Middle of the wall between Goya and Tiepolo. Best light in the room. And the frame. Take a look at the frame, Cokey. That's old Spanish, or I'm a Dutch doll with my eyes painted on the outside. What'll you bet?' 'What do I know?' says Coker.

She was pinching the curtains and running her hands over the chair coverings. Like all those visitors who are requested not to touch. Might as well ask a woman not to look. Women have three sets of eyes. In their fingers for curtains and stuffs. In the backs of their heads for their back hair. And all over them for any other woman. The eyes in the front of their face are not used for seeing with, but for improving the appearance. Hang the thickest veil in front of them and a girl of seventeen will still see the other woman, through two doors and a brick wall, with the various organs of perception existing in her skin, which changes colour, her breasts which tingle, and her brain which performs evolutions of incalculable direction and speed.

'Have you seen this picture, Cokey?'

'I see it,' said Coker, poking her finger into a Gobelins chair. 'This old stuff, it's worn to shreds.'

'And this frame. Look here.' I went up and took out my penknife and gave a prod. 'There you are, look at that.' For my knife had gone right in. 'None of your composition there. It's just what I said. Carved wood. Every bit of it. And he got it to fit. No, look there. That's a new bit specially carved to match and fitted in. Hickson took a lot of trouble for my picture, didn't he?'

Coker was turning up a corner of the carpet. 'It's a handmade carpet. I'll say that for it.' I gave her a push on the behind with my foot and made her jump round. But she saw it was a friendly act. 'Here, what are you doing?' 'Look at my picture, Cokey. That's all my own work.'

'I saw it before.'

'No, you didn't. You didn't even think about it.'

'What I think is fifty thousand pounds for a fat totty in her kinsay is a crime. And I wish I had Mr Hickson in the back kitchen for five minutes with one or two of the girls. Like Nelly Mathers that's got five under seven and her man run off with a girl in the Pools. Thinks he'll get a prize.' 'That's not a fat totty. It's a picture. It's a work of genius.' 'Yes, a dirty picture, if you ask me. If it was a postcard and some poor chap tried to sell it he'd get fourteen days.' 'It's you've got the dirty mind, Cokey.' 'You tell me it would be all the same if that was a chair or a bunch of flowers.' 'No, it's bigger. It's got a woman's quality as well as its own.' 'A totty's.' 'Every woman's that ever was.' 'You can count this one out.' 'You don't know what a picture is, Cokey.' 'I know what this is. A virility pill for millionaires. At fifty thousand saucepans –'

But my head was blowing off like a champagne cork. I forgot myself. I gave myself a smack on the top and I took Coker by the arm. 'You're a friend of mine, Cokey, and I'll tell you what I never told anyone before.' 'Yes, that you're a genius, I know that one.' 'No, that's a secret. I don't tell secrets because they come round again like crooked arrows and shoot you in the back. But this is the truth.' 'Did you never tell the truth before?' 'Not since I was a kid.' 'Why not?' 'Because when you tell the truth, you kill it. And it changes into something else. Into a corp. I once shot a kingfisher with a catapult. Knocked him off a twig into a bunch of reeds. And he looked like a piece of cheap satin.' 'You look like you're tight, old man. Take a hold of yourself before Hickson comes.' 'No, I won't. I'm a genius.' 'So you said yesterday.' 'That was because I didn't really believe it. Now I know. And I'm not only a genius, I'm an artist. A son of Los.'

'Los?'

'Los was the Prophet of the Lord
And the sons of Los build moments and minutes and hours
And days and months and years and ages and periods, wondrous buildings
And every moment has a couch of gold for soft repose
And between every two moments stands a daughter of Beaulah
To feed the sleepers on their couches with maternal cares
And every minute has an azure tent with silken veils –
Every time less than the pulsation of an artery
Is equal in its period and value to six thousand years
For in this period the poet's work is done.'

'You haven't got six thousand years this afternoon.' 'Half a minute of revelation is worth a million years of know nothing.' 'Who lives a million years?' 'A million people every twelve months. I'll show you how to look at a picture, Cokey. Don't look at it. Feel it with your eye.' 'I'm not a snail, am I?' 'And first you feel the shapes in the flat – the patterns, like a carpet.' 'You told me that one before.' 'And then you feel it in the round.' 'All that fat.' 'Not as if it were a picture of anyone, but a coloured and raised map. You feel all the rounds, the smooths, the sharp edges, the flats and the hollows, the lights and shades, the cools and warms. The colours and textures. There's hundreds of little differences all fitting in together.' 'The bath towel isn't too bad, I can see that – it's got the look of huckaback.' 'And then you feel the bath, the chair, the towel, the carpet, the bed, the jug, the window, the fields and the woman as themselves. But not as any old jug and woman. But the jug of jugs and the woman of women. You feel jugs are like that and you never knew it before. Jugs and chairs can be very expressive.

> And every space smaller than a globule of man's blood opens
> Into eternity of which this vegetable is but a shadow.'

'Say it again.' 'No, I can't stop. It means a jug can be a door if you open it. And a work of imagination opens it for you. And then you feel with all the women that ever lived and all the women that are ever going to live, and you feel their feeling while they are alone with themselves – in some chosen private place, bathing, drying, dressing, criticizing, touching, admiring themselves safe behind locked doors. Nothing there but women's feeling and woman's beauty and critical eye.'

'I'll admit she might think twice about those legs.'

'Those are beautiful legs.' 'Then they ought to have an elephant for Puss in Boots.' 'Not in a principal boy, you silly, in a picture. Those legs are divine legs, they're ideal legs.' 'So long as you're pleased with them, old man.' 'I'd like to give you one, Cokey. You'd drive a lamp-post mad.' 'What have I done? I never said it wasn't a nice bit of work. I always said you were clever, do you think I'd have any patience with you if you weren't? I'd shove you in the first dustbin.' 'You can't teach a woman.' 'Why do you want to teach me?' 'I'm trying to teach you a big happiness.' 'To look at a fat totty in her bath. I'm not a man.' 'No, you're an obstinate bloody fool.' 'That's enough before you get rude.'

I made a run at her, but she lifted her fist. So I thought better of it and took a walk across the room. And I forgot my wrath. That's the advantage of Cokey. She's dangerous. If you hit at her, she'll hit you first and harder. So that you don't lose your temper with her. It isn't safe. The best friend I ever had.

Sara looked different from the other end of the room. The formal composition appeared. Rather better than I had expected. But nothing to my real pictures. No, I thought, it's a masterpiece in its own kind. But it's not the kind I like. It's the real stuff. But in a small way. Lyrical. Impressionist. And say what you like, the epic is bigger than the lyric. Goes deeper and further. Any of my wall pictures is bigger stuff than that.

Hickson came in. Hickson had got older since I saw him last. Small and dry, black suit hanging off his back like a sack. Looked like a little beetle on its crooked hind legs. Poking out his head as if too heavy for his neck. Long white face, all folded with misery-wrinkles like a sick albino bloodhound. Big bald head and a couple of tufts of white wool. Eyes like a pair of half-sucked acid drops. Rolled them from me to Coker and back again. Then lifted up his hand half-way and let me shake it. Like shaking a piece of cold bacon fat. 'Miss Coker,' he said, in a kind of thin flat voice, like some chemical squeezed out of him by the weight of woe. 'Jimson. Glad to see you.'

'How are you, Mr Hickson?'

'You came about those Jimsons I bought in '26.' He sighed so much you could hardly understand him.

'That's it, Mr Hickson,' said Coker, 'and if you don't mind, I'll sit down.'

'Oh yes,' he sighed. 'Sit down. We'll all sit down.'

'We saw Mrs Monday on Wednesday last and she signed a paper to say she had no right to dispose of the pictures.'

'Oh yes, she told me.'

'When was that? She's been quick.'

'On Wednesday. She telephoned. Mrs Monday and I are old friends.'

'I thought she was a double-crosser. But we've got the paper, Mr Hickson. Of course we don't want to make trouble. We'd rather have a settlement without any lawyers coming in, wouldn't we, Mr Jimson?' But I saw there was a row coming, and I pretended not to hear. I got up and had another look at Sara.

'A fine thing, Jimson. Finest you ever did,' he said. But I pretended not to hear. I was staying outside this. And I wanted to look at the picture. It surprised me. Especially the shoulders and back. Sara in that picture is reaching her arms forward. You don't see the torso. Mostly left shoulder and upper arm, a bit of back and the supporting flank. Coker was talking about the paper again, asking Hickson how much he paid for the pictures at the sale.

'There were several sales, you understand. Mrs Monday left some canvases with a friend.'

'I'm sure she did. But for the lot —'

'Seventy for the first two – then forty-five, about three hundred pounds – the whole of Jimson's debts came to considerably more than four hundred.'

'And how much is that worth?' pointing at Sara with her umbrella.

Hickson put up his shoulders and made a face like a man who's had a piece of ice dropped down his neck. 'Who can say?'

'Fifty thousand pounds,' said Coker.

'Hardly. It may be worth that some day. All I can say now is I wouldn't take five thousand for it.'

'And what did it really cost you? Five quid?'

'Sixteen pictures for three hundred pounds. Say about nineteen pounds each.'

'Mrs Monday said seventeen.'

'There were about twenty but Mrs Monday wanted to keep a few canvases and I agreed to let her have them.'

'You hear that, Mr Jimson.' But I kept my eye on Sara.

'Nineteen pounds each,' said Coker. 'Nineteen pounds for that big picture,' pointing at the bath picture. 'Why, this frame cost more.'

'That is a very fine frame. It cost me a hundred and fifty pounds, and it was very cheap at the price.'

'Mr Jimson was cheaper, and he hasn't got boots on his feet. What a hobo would call boots.'

Hickson screwed himself up again. Like a white parrot in its death agony.

'Well, what about it?' Coker said. And she turned to me again. But I dodged round and took another walk down the room. 'Don't go walking like that, Mr Jimson,' she said to me, 'come here and show your boots.' But I was taking a long eye at Sara's left shoulder. The one holding the towel. It got the right light from the top corner of the room. Showed the modelling. More subtle than I had believed possible for myself fifteen years before. The insertion of the deltoid between triceps and biceps was a beautiful job. It almost did justice to the arm. A lovely place in any arm and enough to make you laugh or cry in Sara's. To wonder at the glories and the mercies of God. As Mr Plant would say.

Coker and Hickson were getting confidential. And Hickson was saying, 'I don't think you understand the whole position, Miss Coker.'

I moved off to the other side of the room. And took Sara from the new angle. And called up Coker's arm for comparison. Yes, I thought, the Coker forearm is a marvel. But the upper arm's much too tight. Too anatomical. A man's arm. And a vaccination mark right on the join. Like the pivot of a machine. As if on purpose. Like a piece of silly smartness daubed on a piece of real understanding. Amateurish. Sara had too fine an instinct to be vaccinated on the arm. On any junction of muscle. She had the vision of an artist, even if it was only fixed on herself. Her upper arm is as clean as a baby's, and that valley under the deltoid as sweet as a snow valley on the Downs. Yes, Mr Plant, I said, Mr Spinoza might look there and thank God to be alive, even if he had his lungs full of glass dust.

'Mr Jimson,' said Coker, quite loud, too loud for her manners. But I was reflecting deeply on matters of real importance. Anyone but Coker could have told that by the vacant gaze of my eye. And the way I held my head on one side. I was deaf to the world. Yes, I said to myself, when you see a piece of stuff like that, spontaneous, it brings you bang up against the facts of life. Which are beauty, and so on. So, I said, Plantie's Spinoza had the right stuff in him when he said that it was all my eye to talk about justice. Being alive was enough – to contemplate God's magnificence and eternity. That was happiness. That was joy. On Sara's top arm I blow an angel's trumpet. Oh certainly, Mr Plant, old Ben had some good tricks – aces up both sleeves.

But my point is this, I said. Contemplation is not the doings. It doesn't get *there*, in fact.

And Hickson was saying to Coker, 'But leaving the question of value on one side, these pictures didn't belong to Mr Jimson or to Mrs Monday. They were seized for debt. If you will wait a minute, I can show you the papers —'

I went a little further off. For I didn't want any interruptions. Things were too critical. Yes, I said to myself, I've got something. Contemplation, in fact, is ON THE OUTSIDE. It's not on the spot. And the truth is that Spinoza was always on the outside. He didn't understand freedom, and so he didn't understand anything. Because after all, I said to myself, with some excitement, for I saw where all this was leading to. Freedom, to be plain, is nothing but THE INSIDE OF THE OUTSIDE. And even a philosopher like old Ben can't judge the XXX by eating pint pots. It's the wrong approach.

Whereas Old Bill, that damned Englishman, didn't understand anything else but freedom, and so all his nonsense is full of truth; and even though he may be a bit of an outsider, HIS OUTSIDE IS ON THE INSIDE; and if you want to catch the old mole where he digs, you have to start at the bottom.

Hickson was telling Coker all about the sale or sell or whatever it was. 'Of course, a sale of Jimson's pictures in a remote West Country hamlet would have yielded only a few shillings, so when Mrs Monday appealed to me —'

I took a turn down the room. It was a long room. I got away among a lot of little tables covered with gold and enamel snuff boxes. Set with diamonds and rubies and painted by Boucher, and so on. Knick-knacks.

But what you get on the inside, I said to myself, is the works – it's SOMETHING THAT GOES ON GOING ON. Hold on to that, old boy, I said, for it's the facts of life. It's the ginger in the gingerbread. It's the apple in the dumpling. It's the jump in the OLD MOSQUITO. It's the kick in the old horse. It's the creation. And that's where it's leading me. Right up to that blasted picture of mine.

And I kept looking at the snuff boxes, so as not to see Coker glaring after me and beckoning with her county umbrella. The Fall is a frost, I said. It's iced all over. It's something contemplated from the outside. It doesn't get under your skin. No, not so much as Sara's back over there. It's not an event; it's a tea-party.

For what happened, I asked myself, turning my back on Coker, and putting my left and best eye to a nice little Leda by Nattier, what happens to any girl when she falls for the first time; what happens to a thousand Eves and Adams every night of the week somewhere under the willows or the palm tree shade – it's a long way from a tea party. It's not pleasure, or peace, or contemplation, or comfort, or happiness – it's a Fall. Into the pit.

The ground gives way, and down you go, head over heels. Unless, of course, you know how to fly. To rise again on your wings.

There was a visitors' book, nicely bound in morocco, lying on a buhl desk with pens and inks. I took a few blank pages out of the end and carried them over to one of the little tables where the light was good. And began to scrawl some figures that had come into my head. Eve under the willows. And the everlasting maiden, Oothoon. The eternal innocence that thinks no evil. Yes, I thought, there's Billy again. Handing me the truth. Even when I wouldn't take it. That's what he was saying all his life. A tear is an intellectual thing. And a joy. It's wisdom in vision. It's the prophetic eye in the loins. The passion of intelligence. Yes, by Gee and Jay, I thought. The everlasting creation of delight. The joy that is always new and fresh because it is created. The revelation ever renewed, in every fall.

> Oothoon wandered in woe
> Along the vales of Leutha seeking flowers to comfort her
> And thus she spake to the bright Marigold of Leutha's vale
> Art thou a flower, art thou a nymph? I see thee now a flower
> Now a nymph. I dare not pluck thee from thy dewy bed.

Leutha's vale being the valley of desire; and the marigold her own virginity.

I took another sheet and let my hand run over it. But I couldn't make out why I gave poor Eve-Oothoon a head as big as her body, and little fat legs, and why she had her hands over her ears. Unless she was trying not to hear Hickson and Coker who were getting quite excited over the papers.

And now, I said to myself, we have the marigold. The golden nymph replied, Pluck thou, my flower, Oothoon the mild.

Another flower shall spring, because the soul of sweet delight can never pass away.

And this, you see, I said to myself, was before the Fall, before innocence gave herself to passion and the knowledge of herself. For in the next verse Oothoon-Eve, who is all womankind, plucked the flower, saying:

> I pluck thee from thy bed, sweet flower
> And put thee here to glow between my breasts
> And thus I turn my face to where my whole soul seeks.

That is, to the passionate Bromion, to her lover, who is passion in the spirit.

> Bromion rent her with his thunders, on his stormy bed
> Lay the faint maid and soon her woes appalled his thunders hoarse.

I drew Bromion for some reason as something like a gorilla, but with eyes like a lemur, and tortoiseshell spectacles. I did him in blue ink. But he looked like a comic, so I had to start again on a new sheet.

Hickson and Coker were adding up accounts. 'Yes,' said Hickson, 'I should think Jimson has had about three thousand pounds from me altogether. I used to pay him two pounds a week, under no obligation whatever —'

So you said, old boy, I thought, and it ought to have been five. But I was not going to be drawn into a foolish argument. I'd other and bigger fish to fry, and I cleared off some more of the snuff boxes and spread out my papers.

Now the idea is this, I said to myself, making a blot and spitting in it, in order to draw Bromion's face the right shade of blue. That the soul of innocence, maidenhood, could never be destroyed so long as it lived in the free spirit. For it would always be new created in real virginity. The virginity of the soul which never allows experience to grow stale. Which never allows custom to hide the wonders of love.

So that the virgin Oothoon cannot understand the jealousy of Theotormon, which is chastity, her own as well as everybody else's. 'Who folded his black jealous waters round the adulterate pair.'

Theotormon is Oothoon's jealous touch-me-not which hates her own passion, or Bromion.

> Oothoon weeps not, she cannot weep. Her tears are locked up.
> I call with holy voice. Kings of the sounding air
> Rend away the defiled bosom that I may reflect
> The image of Theotormon on my pure transparent heart.
> The Eagles at her call descend and rend their bleeding prey
> Theotormon severely smiles; her soul reflects the smile
> As the clear spring muddied with feet of beasts grows pure and smiles.

And then Oothoon again:

> Why does my Theotormon sit weeping upon the threshold
> I cry, arise O Theotormon, for the village dog
> Barks at the breaking day, the nightingale has done lamenting
> The lark does rustle in the ripe corn, and the Eagle returns
> From nightly prey and lifts his golden beak to the pure east
> Arise my Theotormon I am pure.
> Because the night has gone that closed me in its deadly black.

And the night took a shape in my eye like a map of Australia. Inside this dark shape Oothoon and her gorilla, that is Eve and Adam, were fitted together in a nice compact mass while the tree of knowledge, in red ink with blue leaves, was throwing down a shower of tears and little red apples over them. I didn't know why I wanted the tears till I remembered the fish. I suppose, I said to myself, I need a small regular pattern somewhere to give mass to the big forms.

I did most of this cartoon in finger painting with two inks and spit. The red ink did not thin so well as the blue. But it gave a lovely pink, transparent as a sunrise.

All at once Coker began to call out, 'Mr Jimson, Mr Jimson.'

I didn't hear. I was busy blackening the night; the dark shape round the pair. That needed a lot of ink. But the effect was astonishing. 'Mr Jimson, will you come here – or must I come and fetch you?'

'Yes, Miss Coker.' For I could feel Coker was exasperated. I stuffed Oothoon into my pocket and went down the room. 'Mr Hickson tells me you've had about three thousand pounds from him. In loans and by the week.'

'I shouldn't wonder,' I said. 'Mr Hickson has been a good friend.'

'What I say is he's had pictures from you worth about twenty times as much, and you say the same.'

'It's a difficult question,' I said. 'Very.'

'You didn't say that when you got us to subscribe for the case,' said Coker, turning pink, 'you said you'd been robbed, you said he's got away with a hundred thousand pounds of your pictures. Yes, and now he says himself he wouldn't take five thousand for that totty over there he gave nineteen for.'

Hickson gave a kind of groan and I felt like groaning myself. I don't know anything more exasperating than talking about pictures or picture values to people like Coker, people who don't even know the language.

'It's not so easy as all that,' I said severely. 'What do you mean, for instance, when you say a picture is worth five thousand pounds or five hundred or five bob? A picture isn't like chocolate, you can't eat it. Value in a picture isn't the same thing as the value in a pork chop.'

'No, no,' Hickie moaned with enthusiasm and grief. 'Not at all. It's not the same thing.'

'Here, what do you mean?' said Coker, as red as a brick. Friction always made Coker warm, and I was sorry for her. After all, how could she know about art?

'You don't understand these things, Coker,' I said, in a kindly way. 'For instance, one might say that pictures haven't got any value at all in cash. They're a spiritual value, a liability. Or you might say that they hadn't got any real value till they're sold. And then the value keeps on going up and down. I should think Mr Hickson must have spent a lot of money on pictures that he'll never get back again.'

'About half a million pounds,' Hickson groaned. 'Including commissions to artists who never delivered any pictures at all.'

'Yes, and you've made about double,' said Coker.

'Oh no, Cokey,' I said. 'Mr Hickson has been a great patron of art, and real patrons never get their money back. Not in their own life-time, anyhow.'

'Why, anyone would think you were standing up for him,' Coker said.

'I think he's been a good friend to English art.'

'And is it true all those pictures you left behind were seized on a judgement summons?'

'Very likely, Cokey. I certainly owed money.'

'So you've been telling me a lot of lies and borrowing money from me and Mr Plant and a lot more, on false pretences.'

'Well, Cokey,' I said, 'what I said was that Hickson had got my pictures cheap.'

'No, you didn't, you old crook. I tell you what, Mr Jimson, you deserve that I should send for a copper and give you in charge.'

'But excuse me, Miss Coker,' Hickson said, 'we had a suggestion to make.'

'Yes, I'm coming to that. But I feel so cross I could bite myself.'

'I was explaining to Miss Coker,' Hickson said, 'that I had to stop your weekly allowance because you kept on telephoning threats against myself and my servants.'

'Yes, yes,' I said. For I was in a hurry to get home and see how the Fall looked in the light of my new ideas. 'And I did time for it, didn't I?'

'I am an old man,' Hickson said, 'and a sick man. I don't mind much if you do murder me, and you can write as many threats as you like. But I can't bear all this telephoning. It disturbs the servants. One man has given notice already.'

'I hadn't thought of that,' I said. 'It's a point.'

'I must have servants,' said Hickson, 'or my life wouldn't be worth living.'

I felt deeply for the old boy. What a position. 'I quite see that, Mr Hickson,' I said. 'It's a perfect nuisance. It's intolerable.'

'And if you could undertake not to telephone or to damage my property, I should be prepared to continue the allowance.'

'At two pounds a week.'

'Yes.'

'Make it three,' I said. 'I shan't live more than another two years, not with my chest and blood pressure. And look here, I'll sign a paper giving you the right to these pictures.'

'They are mine.'

'I meant, the moral right. To eighty thousand pounds' worth of masterpieces.'

'I don't want any such paper, but I will make it three and also pay any outstanding debts up to fifty pounds.'

'And give me ten pounds down.'

'Yes, out of the fifty.'

'Very well, Mr Hickson. Split the difference and it's a bargain – ten pounds down, fifty-five to come and three pounds a week, shake hands on it.'

Just then the man servant came in and said something in Hickson's ear. Hickson excused himself and went out. Then he shut the door. And Coker flew out. 'My God, you old crook, you. I've a good mind to do it to you – and I will, too.' She came towards me, and I thought it wise to withdraw. 'Don't be so hasty, Coker,' I said. 'Look at what we've got. By behaving like gentlemen. Kept our self-respect and avoided all bad feelings – and raised him a pound a week on my old allowance.' Cokey kept on after me. She was hurt in her feelings, her pride.

All at once she stopped and said, 'What did he go off for, what's up?' She ran to the door, and put her head out. 'He's telephoning.' And she turned on me again. 'Here, have you been up to anything? What have you got in your pockets? I thought you seemed a bit bulgy.'

She made for me again, and then ran to a side window and stuck out her head.

'Don't be so suspicious, Cokey,' I said, 'I didn't think you could be so mean. After the nice way Mr Hickson has behaved.'

'A copper's car's just turning the corner,' she said, pulling in her head again. And if she had had whiskers they would have been quivering like radio wires.

'Nonsense, Cokey. Mr Hickson would never treat me like that. You're imagining things.'

'Come on,' Coker said, and she grabbed me by the arm. 'Come here, you old fool.' She ran me down to a side door and out on to a landing. Then we went down a service stair into a basement and opened an area door.

'There you are,' she said, 'what did I tell you? A copper's car at the area railings.'

'I don't believe it,' I said. For I couldn't believe that Hickson would play me such a trick.

'Soon as he goes in, we'll make a run for it.'

'It's all nonsense,' I said. 'That's not a copper's car,' and I went up to look. But Coker was right. A copper got out of the car and went up the steps. When I saw that I lost my temper and went out in the road and threw a snuff box through a front window. Coker caught my arm. 'Stop, stop, don't do that.'

'It's an insult,' I said, for I was in a great rage. 'And after the way I've backed him up and sympathized with him.'

'You took his things.'

'Only a few dirty little Netsukes, so far as he knew. He didn't know about the snuff boxes.' And I sent another through the big window of the drawing-room. Coker ran off. I went on throwing things so quick there were three boxes in the air at the same minute and the windows were exploding like fireworks. Then the door opened and I saw the copper and the man coming out; and old Hickson waving his fins like a penguin in despair. So I sent the last box, a heavy diamond one, at his head, and ran for it.

I'm sixty-seven, but I'm light and I can still run. I might have beaten that copper if he hadn't blown his whistle. But then coppers started up all round me. They seemed to come out of the street gratings, and drop from the sky. And they all took hold of me at once and nearly pulled my arms off.

'That's enough,' I said. 'Be careful what you're doing. I'm Mister Gulley Jimson, and I shall put this matter into my lawyer's hands. First-class lawyers. For false imprisonment and assault. Obviously you don't know who I am. Call a taxi.'

I got six months for this piece of carelessness. I knew I was making a mistake when I put those snuff boxes in my pocket, just to get them off the table. And foolishness when I lost my temper. Blood pressure is one of my worst enemies. A traitor in the camp. It would be too good a joke to let him blow my brains out from the inside.

18

Those six months in gaol turned out well. Carried me over the spring and cured my winter cough. Gave me time to get Hickson off my mind. Time to think, and read. Learnt the good bits of Jerusalem by heart. Nothing like poetry when you lie awake at night. It keeps the old brain limber. It washes away the mud and sand that keeps on blocking up the bends.

Like waves to make the pebbles dance on my old floors. And turn them into rubies and jacinths; or at any rate, good imitations.

> Albion gave me the whole earth to walk up and down, to pour
> Joy upon every mountain, to teach songs to the ploughman
> I taught the ships of the sea to sing the songs of Zion.

A good verse carries you off to sleep. Like a ship in full sail. Why, you can hear the water under the side as it sings, and as you drop off, you can smell the spices of the cargo. Sleep in the land of Beulah. And when I got my first mail, three old bills and a demand for the rates, there was among them a letter forwarded from the Eagle, in what looked like Coker's hand. I had never seen her hand, but the writing was like a child's, very big and clear; written with the blunt end of a poker.

19 Capel Mans.,
Kensington.
9/2/39.

Dear Mr Gulley Jimson,

You will excuse, I hope, my temerity in writing to you without a proper introduction. Mr Hickson, who is so happy in the possession of so many of your finest works, was

good enough to let me have your address. I have called twice, but understand that
you are away in the country.

So I venture to write.

I do not suppose that my name is known to you, especially as I have been abroad
for some years on account of ill health. But it is known, favourably known I hope,
to serious students of British Art. Among my publications are The Early Work of John
Varley and many articles in the Press. I also carried out for Messrs Robson and Hicks
the descriptive catalogue of the pictures at Wimley Hall before the sale.

I have long been among your most ardent admirers. And Mr Hickson agrees with
me that the time is long overdue for a considered appreciation of your magnificent
contribution to British Art. What I should venture to propose is a biographical and
critical study of your whole artistic development. The title that occurs to me, subject
of course to your approbation, is The Life and Works of Gulley Jimson. This seems to
me preferable to Gulley Jimson, Master-Painter. The latter no doubt would have a
greater appeal to modern tastes, but it does not seem to me sufficiently dignified for
the kind of work which I have in mind; and which, I venture to suggest, would alone
be suitable to one whose name and genius have in his lifetime obtained so distinguished
a fame among connoisseurs of contemporary European art.

> I have the honour to be, Sir,
> Yours ever respectfully,
> A. W. Alabaster.

When I read this letter I thought that it was a bad joke. Several of the
young bastards at the Ellam Street school were quite up to it, especially the
bit about the early work of John Varley and the last paragraph. But then I
thought, All the same, people must write such letters, and artists must get
them, too. How do I know that it isn't the proper thing, even to the words?
Temerity and ardent, words like that. They may be just like please and
thank you in those circles. And as for fame, a lot of people have heard of
me by now. Hickson's always showing off his collection to all sorts of people,
from all over the world. After all, I said, it's happened before. And it's
happened to men who were less than nobody at all. Just the imitation of a
bad smell. So even if I were nobody and a good for nothing, it might happen
to me. Just like this. Fame! And then I couldn't believe it again. No, I said.
It's one of those young imps down Ellam Street, Nosy has been talking
about me. The Life and Works of Gulley Jimson. Why, nobody could believe
it. It even sounds like a joke; or a takeoff.

And then one night I waked up and thought, after all, I am a genius.
God damn it, of course I am. And why shouldn't a genius be discovered
like this? Even if Alabaster is a crackpot or a ninny. We all know what the
world is. Free for all. And the winner is the chap who gets knocked out
first and comes to while the others are still asleep. Yes, I said, this old
cabbage stalk has come out on top of the heap, and Mr Alabaster, M.A.,
who has just been let out of Colney Hatch, has crowned it with a wreath
borrowed from a dog's funeral. Mr Gulley Jimson, his life and work. Old

horse, you are now famous. The dealers will be running after you with cheques in one hand and smiles in the other. You will have commissions to pick. And the walls will come waltzing to your big front door. As many as you like.

As I was an artist, I had been put on to painter's work, whitewashing. Latrines, etc. A nice job. Though I had had some trouble to get the mixture to my liking. I like whitewash on the blue side to bring out the brilliance of the colour. And while I was putting on a second coat, I kept on thinking: Well, you're famous now. The celebrated Gulley Jimson. But I never got quite used to it. My belief is that nobody does. It never seems quite true. Or if it seems true, then it doesn't seem just what you had been led to expect.

Fame isn't a thing. It's a feeling. Like what you get after a pill. What's happening now, you think. Or is it too soon? Nothing's happened at all. Yes, there's something now – a sort of crick in the upper guts. No, that's the old dent, which the pretty barmaid made, at the Bricklayer's Arms, when you overheard her ask who was the dirty little old runt in somebody else's overcoat. Yes, you say, I suppose you're right. You were getting talked about then, too, and that's how you mistook the sensation. But ha, what about this – a sort of emptiness round the liver and confused noises in the cerebellum. Not a bit of it, old boy, that happened to you when you saw your name in the newspaper and underneath were the words, 'Mr G. Jimson's work shows a progressive disintegration and is now quite incomprehensible.' Well then, old chap, you'd better give it up. Wait a minute, what about that creeping twitch in the diaphragm? That might be fame, or it might be a touch of suppressed heartburn.

And mounting a seat to which so many bold heroes had retired for private meditation and the planning of new campaigns, I slopped another bucket of whitewash on the bricks.

The famous Gulley Jimson. Why not? Fame is a grass that grows in any dirt, when no one's looking. And a man can be famous without knowing it, like all of them in the beginning. And fame, I thought, if it's true, has its advantages. It will bring in cash. And I remembered a canvas I had seen in Ikey's junk shop, just off High Street, a big one. Fifteen by twenty. Birth of Moses, by Antonio Something, 1710, Italian style, turnips and gravy; standing in a sort of shed he had in the yard, with some other big canvases and a lot of old frames.

I've bought a lot of small canvases in Ikey's, cheap. Ikey's is a shop that never has any luck. It changes hands about every six months. It has murdered more people than even the haberdashers opposite, between the Co-operative and the Bank. One time there was a dog that would rush at people's legs whenever they tried to get into Ikey's. Ikey was then a smart young man with long yellow hair and knotty fingers; a connoisseur of real Chinese china. Every time the dog barked he used to rush out and have hysterics. I put a *Times* down each leg, and when the dog nipped me, he got such a surprise that he couldn't believe his teeth. He staggered away in silence. He must have felt like a gourmet who bites on a stick of asparagus and finds it solid drainpipe. And I walked in and bought a fine junk shop Romney with a few holes, etc., and some boot-marks on the lady's face, for two and sixpence. Of which the two was not perhaps altogether British mint silver. But the young gentleman was in such an excited state about the dog and about the bad condition of business that you could have paid him in a Bank of Engraving note and taken change. I often wished I had, for a week afterwards he hanged himself over the stairs.

But the place wasn't empty long. When I called again only a week later, Ikey's was a widow like a cottage loaf, with a face like Julius Caesar and pale green hair. Due to some bleaching powder guaranteed to make grey hair into a veritable crown of snow. She was very high and mighty. She'd put capital into Ikey's and had a family to support. She felt deserving, and she didn't like the rest of the world which was probably not half so deserving. She asked me twenty pounds for a Constable, two trees, four clouds, and a little piece of dog-shit in the foreground. The usual junk shop Constable, value four-and-six. Or with two bits of dog-shit, and a spot of genuine synthetic cobalt blue between the two bottom clouds, five-and-six. With fame, string, and patent hook ready to hang, five-and-ninepence.

Twenty pounds didn't shock me from a widow. Widows always ask too much, especially if they've got all their capital in the business. The unwidowed asking price for a small back street Constable is fifteen guineas. I offered her half a crown, meaning to meet her half-way, at three-and-ninepence, when she walked off to another customer. And she wouldn't even listen to offers. I had to take another canvas, of the same size, while she wasn't looking, and it wasn't worth the expense. For it turned out to be rotten, and I couldn't go back again to Ikey's until the widow was sold up. Which was nearly a year. And meanwhile I had to paint on old sacks, which are expensive to prime and difficult to stretch.

If Ikey's is still there, I said, when I come out, I'll buy that big canvas. No more walls for me that fall down or get knocked full of holes by charwomen's brooms. Give me canvas now I can afford it. The works of Gulley Jimson. Canvas is more portable. All the National Galleries like you to paint on canvas. They can't hang walls. And I began to think what I'd do with that canvas. Supposing of course that Ikey's hadn't sold it or been blown up or burnt down or turned into a shoe-shop. Which was almost certain. Yes, you could bet on the shoe-shop. Fifteen by twenty gave a chap some scope. I used to wake myself up at night, painting in my sleep. The movements, on a canvas, threw my blanket right off on the floor. I thought, I could do something good on fifteen by twenty. Masterpiece by the famous Gulley Jimson as reproduced in the art publication, Gulley Jimson, His Life and Works, by Professor A. W. Alabaster, M.A.

I used to lie awake on the plank, all smiles. And when I said to myself, what's the joke, Gulley, I thought, the Life and Works, etc. And the real joke, I said, will be if somebody is pulling your leg. In any case, I thought, there's a big catch somewhere, or why would it happen to me.

When I came out, and as I was passing along High Street on my way home, I just threw a glance out of the corner of my eye down Gas Lane, and there it was, the sign brighter than ever, Isaacson and Waller, Antiques. I got a shock. Well, I thought, if Ikey's is true, Alabaster must be a particularly nasty trick. I'm going to get a kick in the stomach that would paralyse an elephant. Not that it would worry me. No, I've had some. I'm not a wild ass of the desert. I'm an old hoss. I know something. I've been ridden by the nobility and gentry. Millionaires have cut an important figure on my back. Hickson kept me in the stable for years and trotted me out for his visitors. His Gulley Jimsons, his pride and his joy. My stomach has had two kicks a day for sixty years, one to put the saddle on and one to take it off. It can take anything. And eat its own hay. And organize its own kicks. And save up a bite that will take the bloody pants off the seat of government. If it likes.

And all that gilt, I thought, walking past. I'll bet some smart West End firm has bought up Ikey's and cleared out all the old junk. They'll be selling antique furniture direct from the factory and old Masters of the highest class as painted in Paris for the American market and varnished with real mastic.

But when I went into the shop I saw at once that all was well. Ikey was now a little man shaped like a flower-stand. With bandy legs and bottle shoulders. Draped in a black coat, two sizes too large. Cobwebs on his knees. Face like a cod on the fishmonger's slab. Colour like a new potato. No hair except on the backs of his hands. Gentle, cultivated voice. He's half dead already, I thought, Ikeys' have him by the throat. And I said, 'Afternoon, Mr Isaacson. Very glad to see you again, as an old customer.'

He looked at me for a moment and said in a mournful voice, 'Yes, sir, of course. I knew you at once.' 'And how are you?' I said. 'You look fine. Business good. Tell me, Mr Isaacson, have you got a good Morland? A genuine one. I mean the real thing.'

Ikey looked at my boots, and I said quickly, 'Not for myself I don't buy pictures, I paint 'em. In fact,' I said, trying it on the dog to see if it was real meat, 'I'm Gulley Jimson.' 'Oh yes,' said Ikey. 'Yes, I knew you at once, sir,' and he moved his mouth just like a smile. 'I expect you've seen my portrait in the book,' I said, anticipating things a bit, Gulley Jimson, His Life and Works. 'Yes, of course,' said Ikey, still stretching his mouth. 'By Professor Alabaster, M.A.' 'Yes, no,' said Ikey, suddenly taking away the smile again. 'I don't know – I didn't see any name on it.' And he closed his eyes as if he had such a pain that he couldn't bear it another minute.

'Professor Alabaster is the great collector,' I said, 'and he's looking for some good genuine stuff, oils.' If you want to buy something in a junk shop, ask for something else. As laid down by old Clotheswitz. It causes the enemy to concentrate on the wrong flank and upsets his communications. Often he can't say anything at all.

'Oh yes,' said Ikey, opening his eyes again very slowly.

'And he's very keen on Morland,' I said. 'You haven't got a little Morland.' It was safe to ask for Morland. Every junk shop in England has two or three Morlands from one-and-sixpence, with horse and stable in a real wood frame, to seven-and-sixpence with added straw, figure, one tree and label of the Duke of Devonshire's collection at Chatsworth.

Ikey had two. Nice brown ones. The first had a horse, stable, dog, man and tree. The second was more important. It had a stable, a dog, a horse, a peasant, a tree and a gate.

'That's not bad,' I said to Ikey, 'I like the gate. It's real. I like the way it opens. How much is that one?' 'Thirty guineas, sir.'

That didn't shake me. Thirty guineas is the usual price of a seven-and-sixpenny Morland, with gate.

'That's cheap for a genuine Morland,' I said. 'Can you give a guarantee? I couldn't advise Professor Alabaster to spend thirty guineas on a genuine Morland without a guarantee.'

'Oh yes,' Ikey breathed, in a faint voice. 'Of course. It comes out of the Wallace Collection.'

'Well, even if they did throw it out, I might bring the Professor to see it. The horse's knees are very genuine. How much did you say?'

'Thirty-five guineas, sir,' said Ikey. 'The frame is original.'

'Make it pounds.'

'Couldn't take anything less than guineas, sir. It would fetch a hundred and fifty guineas at Christie's. Only needs a little cleaning and restoration.'

This was fair enough. A hundred and fifty guineas at Christie's is a reasonable junk-shop valuation for a hand-painted Morland with real hair on the horse's belly, done with a dead match. 'Well,' I said, 'I daresay the Professor might meet you. What's that old brown thing there in the rubbish shed?'

'An old Master, sir. Splendid piece of work. Antonio Ruffiano (or some such name) Moses in the Bulrushes. Out of the Shillingford Castle collection.'

'I'll give you fifteen bob. I want a piece of old canvas to cover a toolshed.'

'That picture is worth five hundred guineas, without the frame,' said Ikey. He was indignant. He still had some kick in him, in spite of two months at Ikey's. 'And with the frame I wouldn't take five hundred and fifty.'

I turned away and put my nose up against the Morland. 'Here,' I said, 'do you guarantee that this is a genuine Morland? I mean a genuine

600

genuine Morland. The Professor is an expert, you know. You can't fool him with fakes.'

'Absolutely genuine, sir.'

'Well, look at that rustic – he's been repainted. And he's not wearing a Morland hat either.'

'That's a genuine real Morland, sir,' said Ikey. But he spoke as from the grave. He was near his end. 'The hat is one of the most genuine passages in the work.'

'Well,' I said, 'I don't like it.' And I was just going out of the shop when I stopped and pointed at the Ruffiano. 'I'll tell you what, I'll give you sixty guineas – and take it away tonight. Providing it's sound, of course, and a genuine Ruffiano.'

'Couldn't do it under a hundred, sir.'

'Split the difference and say seventy-five. Or look here, you're right about the frame. It's a good frame.'

'Hand-carved pear, sir. You couldn't get such a frame for seventy-five guineas by itself.'

'That's what I say. Fifty guineas is much too little. Split the difference and say sixty pounds for the frame alone. At least I'll let you have it for that. And that leaves two guineas for the canvas. Forty-two bob.'

'Im-possible, sir.'

'Well, say fifty bob for both of 'em.'

'Both of them?'

'Yes, the Ruffiano and the Morland.'

Ikey closed his eyes as if he was about to pass away again. Then he said, 'Five guineas.'

'Make it pounds,' I said.

'All right, sir, pounds.' We were getting to business at last.

'Split it and call it two quid and look here, I'll give you back the Morland frame. It doesn't fit anyhow. Thirty-nine and sixpence.'

In all such negotiations the proper financial course is the double entry. You get out and then you get in again. So that the enemy doesn't know whether you're advancing backwards or he's retreating forwards, or you're retreating forwards while he's advancing to fresh positions in the rear. This confuses him, as he hasn't time to look up the rules of war; or if he does remember them he can't quite see how they apply to the situation.

Ikey was trying to find out how we stood when I said quickly, 'Well, perhaps that is a bit too cheap for the Morland frame. Put it at a shilling. That's giving you more than it was worth when it was new. So I'll owe you thirty-nine bob.'

'No,' said Ikey, making a strong recovery. 'Well, I tell you what. I'll give you the Morland back. Thirty-four bob. And I'll guarantee that Mr Alabaster will pay twenty-five guineas for it certain, and very likely fifty. He doesn't care what he pays. He's an expert. He'll get it all back twice over.'

'Thirty-nine for the Ruffiano. That's the lowest price,' said Ikey.

'We'll make it guineas, Mr Isaacson. I always deal in guineas. Thirty-one and sixpence. And I'll do the insurance and packing at my own expense. Twenty-eight bob cash on the nail.'

'All right, sir,' said the old rascal suddenly. He would probably have paid me to take the Ruffiano away. 'Cash on the nail.' I felt I'd been done. I hadn't expected him to take twenty-eight.

'Very well,' I said. 'Done. And the two-and-sixpence for carriage makes it twenty-four-and-six. Cash on the nail. Tomorrow. But I'll tell you what, I'll take Antonio off your hands now.' I knew a coalman, friend of Swope, who would fetch me the canvas in his empty cart for one-and-six. And I still had nine-and-six of my prison money.

But Ikey suddenly turned obstinate. He wouldn't let the picture go without the cash.

'Very well,' I said, 'I've done my best, and I can't do more. Not if you go back on your bargain. But I must say I'm not used to this kind of treatment.'

'You said cash,' said Ikey, 'and two-and-sixpence from twenty-eight bob is twenty-five-and-sixpence.'

'We'll split it,' I said. 'If that's your trouble. Nobody can say I'm not ready to meet you. Call it twenty-four-and-ninepence.'

'All right,' said Ikey. 'But cash.'

'On the nail,' I said, 'tomorrow.'

But he wouldn't trust me. And it wasn't because he meant it. It was because he'd turned sour. And I hate a man who can't do better for himself than to turn sour. I appealed to him, 'I'm only an artist,' I said. 'I don't understand business. I get swindled all the time. There's two Bond Street dealers at this moment who've made thousands out of me. And look at my boots. But I do understand that business is built on confidence between man and man. If you don't know how to trust, Mr Isaacson, you'll never be in Bond Street.'

'No, I won't,' said Ikey. And he closed his eyes and died again.

'More likely the workhouse,' I said.

'I think so, too,' said Ikey.

'Throwing away the substance for the shadow,' I said. For I was upset. I'd wanted that canvas. If I'd had only a pound, I'd have given it to the barnacle. 'No faith, no pluck to take a chance,' I said. 'The mistake of all the men who fail in life.'

'That's it,' said Ikey, opening his eyes just enough to see my way to the door. He looked very ill. He might fall dead any minute. 'All right,' I said, 'I'll be in tomorrow to take the thing away.' 'And bring the money,' said Ikey. I saw the old boy never expected to see me again. And I thought: If the old chap holds on for another fortnight, I'll get that canvas for ten bob. But probably he won't – he'll hang himself or fall down dead. Because I never had a better chance of a big canvas. It was the finest I ever saw. Smooth painted all over in the best classical period before the bitumen came in. Not a crack anywhere. There's nothing like a real old Master for an undercoating.

The very touch of that canvas was enough to make my hand sing. I felt the colour flowing on to it as sweet as cream. My God, I said, I'll put the Fall on to it. Trouble with the Fall – it's not big enough. All at once I had the feel of the Fall. A real fall. Fire and brimstone. Blues and reds. And I saw green fire in the top left next the red tower. And the red tower opened to show a lot of squares full of blue and green flames. Symbols of something. Generation would do. Or a lot of little flames like men and women rushing together, burning each other up like coals. And then to carry the pattern upwards you could have white flowers, no, very pale green, moving among the stars, imagination born of love. Through generation to regeneration. Old antic propriety falling down on his nose and seeing constellations. Yes, the destruction of old fly button, the law by the force of nature and the unexpected entry of the devil as a lyrical poet singing new worlds for old. The old Adam rising to chase the blue-faced angels of Jehovah. And beget a lot of young devils on them.

> A mighty spirit leaped from the land of Albion
> Named Newton; he seized the trump and blew the enormous blast
> Yellow as leaves of autumn, the myriads of angel hosts
> Fell through the wintry skies, seeking their graves
> Rattling their hollow bones in howling and lamentation.
> Then Enitharmon woke, nor knew that she had slept
> And eighteen hundred years were fled
> As if they had not been
> She called her sons and daughters
> To the sports of night.

Science destroying the law of the old Panjandrum. The fall into manhood, into responsibility, into sin. Into freedom. Into wisdom. Into the light and the fire. Every man his own candle. He sees by his own flame, burning up his own guts. Oh to hell, I said, with the meaning. What I want is those green flames on a pink sky. Like copper on a dying fire.

Thundery day along Greenbank. All the willows standing still with their leaves pricked. Dusty green. Pale-lilac shadows. Tarred road reflecting the sky. Blue to make you jump. A great cloud over on the Surrey shore. Yellow as soap and solid as a cushion. Shaped like a tower about a mile high and half a mile thick, with a little Scotch pepper pot in front. Dresden blue behind full of sunlight floating like gold dust. River roughed up with little waves like the flat side of a cheese grater. Dark copper under the cloud, dark lead under the blue. I could use that cloud in the Fall, I thought. It's a solid square. To give weight in the top left-hand corner, opposite the Tower. Salmon on pink. It's an idea worth trying.

The people kept looking at me, but I didn't notice I was noticing them till a kid turned round and said 'Ya,' as if I'd insulted him. Then I realized that I was laughing. Enjoying myself, I suppose. Yes, I thought, I'm enjoying myself. The famous Gulley Jimson, whom nobody knows, is perceived laughing like an old goat and skipping like a young ram. Who cares, I said. The advantage of being old and ugly is that you needn't care a damn for anybody. Or even somebody. You can grin when you feel like grinning. And skip when you feel skippy. So long as your boots don't fall off. Second childhood. People make allowances, including yourself. Which is you in particular. Anonymous you.

> I have no name
> I am but two days old.
> What shall I call thee
> I happy am
> Joy is my name
> Sweet Joy befall thee.

The next kid that came along, I smiled upon him. Out of pure benevolence. 'Hullo, Tommy,' I said. But he turned pale and burst into tears. Must have been too young for social occasions. About six or ten. Necessary limits to fellow feeling and universal brotherhood.

The pepper pot had floated off the Tower and turned into a grey monk in a rugged gown, creeping across the sky with his hands on his breast. Blue-grey on a sandy desert with a lot of rusty bones along the edge. Nice, but no good to me. No, but I had the cushion in my mind. And I thought, I'll be painting in half an hour. Say an hour at the longest. And the Eagle this evening. And I might mention Alabaster to Cokey to see if she really did send that letter on, and if she saw him again.

19

The boat-shed came in sight. New tin chimney sticking through the roof and quite a lot of smoke coming out. Glass in all the windows. Green curtains. Gave me a surprise. Knocked on the door and Coker let me in.

'Hullo, Cokey.'

'Oh, Mr Jimson, where you dropped from?'

'Chokey, Cokey.' And I looked at her. About the eighth month at a first guess, and her face shrunk up to a peeled walnut. White as wax except her little nose which was as pink as blotting paper. Seeing how it was with Coker, I couldn't bring up Alabaster. You don't talk money and medals at a funeral.

'How are you, Cokey?' I said.

'Just how you see,' she said.

'How's that?'

'Can't you guess?'

'I always said Willie was a hound.'

'You let Willie alone.'

'Who got round you then – the roundabout?'

'Nobody got round me. I'd like to see them. Willie never did anything to me, poor boy, that I didn't let him.'

'I'm surprised at you, Cokey,' I said. And this was true.

'Oh, what's the good of talking to a man. We had the ring two months. And Willie so he couldn't sit still for two minutes. And all the competition there is. I took a chance, that's all. And a fair chance, too, for a girl like I am with a real catch like Willie was.'

'You never wrote me.'

And I thought, now she'll remember that letter, and Alabaster. But she answered that she didn't want to bother me. 'I knew you couldn't pay my money back.'

'And what are you going to do about it, Cokey?'

'What can a girl do? She can't creep up a drainpipe till she's human size again, can she? God didn't make her a spider. His idea was to make a girl and give her socks all the time and then some. First thing is, I lost my job. You can't blame the Guv'nor. The Eagle is a respectable house. Then I got remarks passed, so I couldn't bear hardly to walk down the street. Then I had to leave my lodgings because I couldn't pay the landlord. And then my mother came and gave me such a doing on both ears that I had to sleep on my back.'

'I heard she was a cruel woman.'

'Of course, she's cruel. After the life she's had. I wish some pot would fall off a chimney and knock my napper in.'

It frightened me to hear Coker speak like that. She's an honest girl. She always says what she means and means what she says. But I could see she was just about as miserable as a girl can be. 'Come now, Coker,' I said. 'You'd never do anything silly. Things will come out all the same in the end.'

'Listen to you. I wish you were like me for two minutes. And you'd know whether anything can come out the same again or anything like it. Come, if you want to be a friend, why don't you tie a brick round my neck and push me in the river?'

'I'm surprised at you, Cokey.'

'So am I. I'm surprised at myself. What I been through without doing murder on someone.'

'Well, don't do it on yourself.'

'Who said I would? I only said what a nice birthday present it would be if someone would stick me in the gizzard with a pig knife. But it won't happen. No such luck. And you needn't pull a long face at me. I asked for it, didn't I?'

'You didn't ask for Willie.'

'I mean, being born a girl. That's what I say. Here I am, another bloody girl. Come on, knock my teeth out. Turn my hair grey. Make me look like something that the dog got out of the dustbin. I can take it. Ain't I a woman?'

'Well,' I said, 'I'm glad you did come here. We'll be very comfortable, won't we?' For when I looked round I saw how the place was changed. All cleaned up. Coker's furniture piled in a corner. New linoleum on the floor. Old sheet hung in front of the picture to keep it out of sight. Two little tables, a horsehair sofa and a couple of straw armchairs. New coke stove with a japan chimney. 'You made it very nice here, Cokey,' I said. 'And I can sleep in the loft.'

'You can't sleep anywhere here. Mother'll be back from shopping in about ten minutes, and you'd better not let her catch you. She won't have a man in the place. And she doesn't like artists either.'

'Can't sleep here? Whose house is this?'

'Mother's. She paid all the back rent and she's paying the rent now. She couldn't take me home in this state, to get herself pitied, could she?'

'But Coker, where am I going?'

'Couldn't you go to Mr Plant's till you find somewhere.'

'No, I couldn't. I can't paint in a basement, can I? I got my work to do. No, I'm stopping here. It's my home. I don't mind you staying, Cokey, but this is my home.'

Just then a little woman about three inches smaller and five stone lighter than Coker came into the room. Very respectable in a black satin cloak and a bonnet. Old style. A little thin white face like a child that's been starved. And big blue eyes with pink rims.

She was muttering to herself so that I couldn't understand her. 'Good afternoon, Mrs Coker,' I said. 'I'm Mr Jimson.'

'No, this is too much,' said Mrs Coker as if talking to herself 'No, I don't see why I should,' and all at once she turned on Cokey and gave her a whack on the side of her head with her shut fist. It sounded like two croquet balls knocked together.

'Oh, Mum,' Coker said. 'I only just got up.'

Mrs Coker gave her another whack on the other ear and muttered something. Coker lay down on the sofa and put her hands over her ears. She was trembling like a horse when you beat it and it can't go on. Mrs Coker came after me and murmured under her breath, 'Out you go – you hear – I'm not standing any more.' She was shaking all over. 'I can't stand any more. Dirty wasters coming in here. It's more than flesh can bear. Go on, you hear.' And all at once I got a knock on the ear that nearly made my eyes fall out. 'Go on,' said Mrs Coker. 'Quick, too, I'm a respectable woman, and I can't be expected to stand everything. Out with you.' And I got a right and left. Next minute I was outside, and the door banged behind me so loud that the whole shed went out of shape.

It made me laugh. Then I took a bottle out of the dustbin to operate on the windows. But before I could do anything I saw I was going to be angry. No, old man, I said, you can't afford luxuries. You're too old. It's fun to play the fool, but an old chap has got to hold on to wisdom. Yes.

IT'S WISE TO BE WISE.

It pays all the time. Don't let 'em rattle you or you might as well take a dive into your coffin. So I walked away a little, with the bottle in my hand, and I thought: as for Alabaster, I expect he's dead. Or gone away and Coker didn't want to tell me. Yes, that's the way it would happen. Life and Works of Gulley Jimson. In one volume. Unpublished, without illustrations. Delivered gratis at the dead letter office, to Mister Nobody.

All the same, I thought, why should Mother Coker get away with it. I might throw the bottle through the window and move off quick before I heard the crash. Nothing to stick in the mind. And I took aim. I'm a good shot with a bottle. Trick is, don't swing it by the neck. Take it by the body and throw it like a dart.

But then I thought, I've got to get my picture out safely. I've got to paint somewhere. Better not smash up my own property. And I noticed the sky on the windows. Surprising effect. And when I turned round I saw my tower had broken up into a lot of copper bars, like puffs of sulphur smoke. And the sky behind was like the middle of a gas flame, blue fire. That's more like it, I thought, I could do something with a sky like that. And the water underneath was like melted golden syrup. All smooth waves, with the light inside as well as outside, except under the sky where it was white fire. You couldn't see it for the sparks. Giorgione might have made that sky, I thought. And probably he did. He made me see it. But he didn't make the water. I should like to do it – you'd have to use a glaze to get the double lights. And so I was thinking about the water and how I should do it without any impressionist tricks, when I came to Ellam Street. But I wasn't sorry to catch sight of old Plant's signboard fixed to the area railings. It was an interruption, but I wanted to know how to get old Mrs Coker out of my studio; or at least, how to take my picture from her. Old Plant might be an old nuisance, but he was a good friend, and he knew the Law. He would talk all night about his Spinoza and his Swedenborg and his Comte and his Robert Owen and revelations and revolutions; but I didn't need to listen. I could carry on with the Fall.

So I hopped down the area steps. But it was getting dark in the area, the blind was half down in the window; and when I opened the door I came plump upon a great fat woman in a vest and knickers brushing out a little girl's hair; and about six other children were rolling on the floor, and all of them were screaming as if they were being murdered.

I couldn't believe my eyes. Till the woman made a run at me with the hair-brush and screamed louder than all the kids together. 'Nothing today. We don't take nothing at the door.' And she banged the door in my face.

I had a look to make sure I'd come to the right house. But there was Plant's board still fixed to the railings. So I opened the door again and asked, 'Where is Mr Plant?' But the woman and all the children set up such a scream that it was like engine whistles. Then the woman rushed at me with the brush and said, 'I get the police.' 'Where is Mr Plant?' I said. 'He was here twenty years.'

'Nobody called Mr Plant. We took it from a lady called Johnson.'

'I want Mr Plant.'

'Go away. I tell you nobody hear of Mr Plant.' So I went up the steps again, and when I looked at the board it said: 'Mrs Slumberger. Wardrobes bought for cash.'

I couldn't believe it. I rang at the ground floor and a man came out. I asked him what had happened to Mr Plant, the shoemaker.

'Plant,' he said. 'Oh yes, I remember him. Old cobbler in the basement. Nice nuisance he was with his tapping and his shoe polish stink. Why, isn't he there?' 'No,' I said, 'even the board's changed.' The man came down and looked at the board and said, 'Funny, so it is. Never noticed it before.' Then he looked again, and he said, 'Here, did he ever have his name on the board?'

'It's been there for about twenty years.'

'I been here fifteen, and I bet you he never had his name on the board.'

'Of course he had his name on the board – C. Plant. Bespoke bootmaker. Repairs a speciality.'

'Well, all I say is, funny thing I should forget it so quick.'

'Yes,' I said, 'I don't know.'

I went along the streets to see if I could catch Mr Ollier on his round. Till I was beginning to think that Ollier had gone, too. I was beginning to feel as if I'd been away seven years and everybody and all the houses had been changed. When just after six, I came on Ollier emptying a pillar box.

'Hullo, Mr Ollier.'

'Well, Mr Jimson. This is a pleasure.'

'What's happened to Plant? He hasn't come into a fortune.'

'No, he ran a needle into his hand and it got poisoned. It's a bad business, Mr Jimson. You know what Mr Plant is. No doles for him. No insurance. No unions. Never would take anything from the government. And even with his friends, he always liked to give more than he got. Never kept anything back and never saved.'

'Plant was one of the old sort.'

'It's a rare old London family, the Plants. Goes back three hundred years, father to son. Craftsmen every one of them. It was a Plant made some of the clocks for Nelson's fleet.'

608

'But what's happened to the old man? Hospital?'

'Hospital and more. They took his hand off.'

That surprised me for a minute. Then I saw the idea. 'Yes,' I said, 'that was what would happen to Plant. No other way to get him except knocking him on the head with an obelisk. Take off both his legs and he'd be whistling. But his right hand. They knew his weak place.'

'Of course he didn't look after it properly,' Ollier said. 'He didn't go to the hospital till his thumb was like a saveloy. He said he was too busy.'

'That's very neat, yes. That's the way it would happen to Plant. Just a prick like what he's had a thousand times before. They'd studied him. They knew he wasn't one to fuss about himself or break his promises to the customers. How does he take it, Ollier?'

'Badly. I haven't seen him since the sale. I think he keeps dodging me so that I shan't try to do anything for him. It's hard for a man like Plant.'

'Where does he sleep?'

'I did see him coming out of that sixpenny doss back of Ellam Street. But it mightn't have been Plant. I looked the other way in case.'

'You were quite right, Mr Ollier. It wouldn't do for you to see him. Not until you lose your legs under a bus or get a stroke.'

'That's true, Mr Jimson. But if you would take him in my respects and tell him that I'm missing the club, I'd be obliged. It's made a big hole in my life, that club stopping. It's like a door shutting over me. The last door.'

'I'll tell him.' Then I made for the sixpenny doss in Ellam Street. I had two-and-sixpence left of my prison money.

20

The sixpenny doss is a double-fronted villa called Elsinore standing back from the road. Front garden had been laid down in cinders and the back garden is a builder's yard. The owner is a retired army man, a bony man with a long face like a sheep and a little black moustache. His head is bald and shaped like a tea cup. He has big round blue eyes which are always watering, and he looks as silly as a sheep. But he keeps good order. No lights and no noise after twelve, and if you don't like it you must go.

Bunk beds are sixpence. They aren't exactly spring, but they are better than sacks. More like wire hammocks made of chicken wire. And there is always a kettle boiling in the kitchen. Frypans and teapots and tin cups free up to nine o'clock in the morning and after six at night. Between tea and six the house is closed to the sixpennies. But there are cubicles for residents at a shilling a day, with slot meters for light and heat.

Room for twenty-five sixpennies and ten residents, and he's nearly always full because of the lights and because he'll take letters and let you write a letter from the address. Of course, he has a lot of letters that aren't called for. He keeps the old ones in a sack and I think he burns them after about six months. Residents, who are half of them beggars in the letter-writing way, say he knows postal orders through an envelope by the smell, and takes his share. But I don't believe it. I think the man might burn postal orders in letters but he wouldn't take them. He wouldn't bother. Not the kind that cares about money or anything else. He bought the business because it was cheap, and he keeps it going because it is going.

Time to go to Elsinore is early, at six when the doors open. I got there after seven and the kitchen was full already – about nineteen people fighting for the three frypans. They always fight for the pans, between six and eight. If you miss your chance at six, the only thing to do is to wait till nine when the rush is over. But the sixpenny customers at the doss are mostly young fellows passing through, going for jobs along the waterfront or doing a wander. Quite well-off tradesmen who would rather spend their money on clothes and girls and cinemas and fags than a bed. There was one used to come regularly in a car. Left it in the yard outside. The residents said he was a burglar who robbed villas out by Richmond, but no burglar would sleep at a doss. Too much police supervision and too much notice by the other customers. And these young fellows had no time to learn the way to do things. So there was always a riot at seven.

I edged round them till I came to the far corner next the larder, and there was an old man sitting on a box, with an old green bowler hat, and a face like a French cheese, chalk and green, hollowed out and folded up like a mummy. And a long greenish moustache hanging down over his collar. Hump on his back as if it were broken.

I knew it was Plant because it had one arm stumped off at the wrist in a stocking. But I didn't recognize him.

'Hullo, Mr Plant,' I said. But he didn't hear me. He got up and dived into the crowd, pushing and butting till he got near the range. Somebody had just put down a frying pan there. Old Plant and a young man in a blue jumper with his braces outside got to the pan at the same moment. They argued. Then Plant gave it up and came back to the corner.

'Hullo, Mr Plant,' I said

'I was there first,' Plant said. 'That's the second time I missed it.'

'A bad time for frying pans at Elsinore,' I said. 'Now at Myrtle View this is a good time. Because Myrtle View is nearly all residents at a shilling a day and they have their own pans.'

'But I'm next,' said Plant. 'He said so.'

'That's all right, Mr Plant,' I said. 'You're next or the one after. What's it matter? Plenty of time before tomorrow morning.'

Plant thought a bit, then he gave a start and looked at me. 'Mr Jimson,' he said, 'so you're back – but why aren't you at your own place?'

'Mrs Coker has taken it over for Miss Coker's lying-in.'

'She can't do that, can she?'

'She has done it. It's funny, isn't it?'

'I don't call it funny. What, taken the roof from over your head and your working place?'

'Yes, a funny turn. I didn't expect it. Not that one. And the old lady gave me two bonks on the ear that nearly burst the drums.'

'What for?'

'That's it, what for? It's all part of the idea.'

'It's a scandal,' said Plant. 'You ought to go to the magistrate.'

'And how are you, Mr Plant?'

Plant gave a start and lifted up his stump to rub his nose. And to let me see it. But I didn't look. I didn't want to pity a man like Plant. Hurt his pride. Or make him feel sad. I wouldn't have liked it myself from anybody. Pity is a whore. It gets inside you and sucks your blood.

'Ollier told me he'd been looking for you. Wants a club meeting.'

Plant waved his stump in front of my nose. 'This is a funny business, if you like.'

'That's what I said when I heard. A real surprise. It makes you laugh.'

'Didn't make me laugh. It made me think.'

'You ought to get a job, Mr Plant. Why not a watchman? Nice job in the summer.'

'No, I don't want a job. I want to think. What I feel is it can't be wasted – a thing like this. It means something.'

'Why should it mean anything? Does a kick in the stomach from a blind horse mean anything?'

Old Plant shook his head. 'It can't be wasted. It's a revelation. It makes me feel like I never knew anything before.'

'What do you know now, Mr Plant?'

He shook his head. 'That's where the thinking comes in.'

'You don't think that needle was sent from God to poison your hand?'

'No, Mr Jimson. But it might have taught me something. It might have been a revelation to me.'

'I understand that, Mr Plant. It was the same with me when I got my nose broken. When I was eighteen, my sister, Jenny, came home from school. I liked that very much. Jenny and I were the two youngest and we were great friends. We enjoyed each other more than anyone else in the world. And when my mother had to go into hospital for an operation she said, "You look after Jenny – I can trust you." "Jenny doesn't need looking after," I said. "Oh no," said my mother cheerfully, "but she's very attractive – look after her." And I said I would look after Jenny. And I went on as before enjoying myself with the girl. I was pretty good at enjoying myself. As good as any baby. But Jenny was even better. She had enjoyment to give away; so that you felt it all round her, even while she was walking down the road, and breathing the air.'

But old Plant wasn't listening. He had his eye on the nearest frypan.

'I've been thinking about your Spinoza,' I said. 'It's this question of rejoicing in the glory of God.' I said.

Plant gave a kind of sob and lifted up his stump as if he wanted to hit someone with it.

'That's all right,' I said. 'Give it another month or two and put a hook on it, and you'll be able to give a chap like that something to remember. Hook his tripes out. You'll always find him when you want him. He comes home every week or two to meet the girl down the High Road. Tells her he stops at an hotel.'

'I wouldn't mind if they didn't know it was my turn.'

'What I wonder is, Mr Plant, your Spinoza didn't go blind. He only died at forty from breathing glass dust. Not a healthy job grinding lenses.'

'He died independent,' Plant said. 'Never owed anything to anybody. And not a surly chap. No, he was the happiest man that ever lived, the God-drunk man.'

'Well, why didn't he go blind?'

'Why should he?'

'That would have been the kind of thing to happen to your Spinoza, Old Diamond Death.'

'What do you mean, Old Diamond Death?'

I didn't know what I meant till Plant asked me. But then I saw the diamond flashing different colours off every facet, and never moving from its place. The cold eye. Now if he had been set in the top of a drill, I thought, to bore the rock – he would have got hot – the sparks would have flown —

'Spinoza was the most independent man that ever lived,' said Plant, 'never asked for anything of anybody. He'd rather have died, and he did die. And mind you,' said Plant, getting fierce all at once, 'a happy man. In the contemplation of the majesty and glory of God's being.'

'Old Million Eye.'

'What do you mean Old Millon Eye?'

'I don't know.'

But I once saw a photograph of a fly looking at an electric bulb. It didn't move, and neither did the bulb.

'Didn't need anything,' said Plant. 'Why, anyone can contemplate. You haven't got to ask anyone to learn to enjoy the wonder of the world.'

'But why didn't he go blind?'

'It wouldn't have made any difference. His vision was inward. No, he could snap his fingers at the lot of 'em.'

'He couldn't have gone on making his lenses. Interesting job.'

But Plant wasn't listening. He'd got his eye on the frypan and suddenly he made another rush; just as the young man in the blue jumper took his fried bread and rasher out of it and put them in a tin plate. Plant snatched the frypan and shouted, 'Thank you,' and he made a push at the fire. But another young chap in a dust-cloth shirt said, 'Thank you,' and snatched it out of Plant's hand, so neatly, that it was gone before he saw where. Then the first young chap knocked his hat over his eyes, gave him a push that sent him flying back into the corner and said, 'Go and scrape yourself, you bum.'

Plant hit the wall so hard that he didn't know where he was. When I picked him up, I saw that his nose and mouth were bleeding. I propped him on the box and said, 'Yes, no doubt about it, Jenny had an angel's blessing.'

> The angel that presided at her birth
> Said, little creature, born of joy and mirth
> Go love without the help of anything on earth.

Plant went on moving his lips, and then I saw they were moving by themselves. The old man was crying. It surprised me. And then I thought, But it's natural. He's got a sense of justice. Poor old chap. And he can't get over it – not at his age.

'But of course she was a popular girl,' I said. 'The boys liked her. Because she was happy. And one of them, not exactly a boy, but a man of about thirty-five, with a wife and four children, made a nuisance of himself. He used to lie in wait for her and walk beside her through the town, telling her that she made all the difference to him, and so on. The usual story from a married man of thirty-five to young girls. And usually the truth. He was a thin chap in spectacles with a long bald head, and no chest to speak of. Looked like a consumptive lay preacher. But he was one of our engineering staff. Draughtsman. Name of Ranken.'

Plant wiped his nose on his stump and gave a sigh. He was getting over his bereavement.

'And one night when Ranken was a bit too pressing in the back lane, Jenny gave him a slap. She had plenty of spirit. And when she came in, she told me she was tired of Ranken. "He's always waiting for me," she said, "and it's a nuisance." So next evening I went out and there was the chap in the lane, waiting. And I told him to clear off. I remembered my responsibilities and I swelled up my chest, which wasn't very much, but at least it was bigger than his, and I said, "You leave my sister alone, you blankety blank."

'He was a head shorter than I was and I made myself plain.

' "Why?" ' said he.

' "Because you frighten her and because you're not fit to have anything to do with a decent girl." "It's a free country," he said. "I'll do what I like." "No, you won't," I said. "Why not?" said he. "Because if you do I'll break your neck" I said. "Just you try it," said he. And the next day he came after Jenny again, and pulled her about in the back lane. So she called for me and I ran out and said, "All right, you've asked for it," and I made to hit him. But before I could hit him he hit me three or four times; he broke my nose and knocked out my front teeth. You see, Mr Plant, he'd learnt how to do it. He'd done a bit of boxing. And then he knocked me out and fractured my skull on the pavement. I was three months in hospital. And when I came out, he'd run off with Jenny to London. She had a bit of money, you know, in the Post Office. She thought him the finest man in the world. She thought I'd been unkind to him; that everybody had been unkind to him. Well, of course, Ranken had had his let downs. Who hasn't at thirty-five. Especially fitters and draughtsmen, and scientists, and garage mechanics. All of them have got ideas that ought to have made their fortunes and fame, if only some firm had taken them up. But it wasn't any good telling Jenny that England was full of Rankens and all their boxes were full of neglected genius. She didn't believe it. There was only one Ranken in the world for her. And she'd hardly speak to me for having been so nasty to him and provoking him to crack my skull.'

Mr Plant had stopped crying. But he wasn't listening to me. He shook his head. 'They talk about accidents happening, Mr Jimson. But it isn't all accident. When it's one that finishes you off. It's too big.'

'Big enough. You should have seen Jenny after the first year with her darling Robin – skin and bone and her eyes coming out of her head. But, of course, not admitting anything. "How goes it, Jenny, you look a bit low?" "Me, I'm all right. It's only that poor Robin does have such awful luck!"

'It made me swear, Mr Plant. But I was young then. Young and innocent. I didn't make allowances for other people doing what they liked, as well as myself.'

'We ought to be grateful, if we only knew,' said Mr Plant.

'That's it. Go love without the help, etc. – a first-class tip for the six o'clock. Last race.'

Just then I noticed that the young chap in the dust-cloth shirt had put his coat down on the back of a chair. Near the stove. And he was engaged in tearing a teapot from another young chap, a smaller one. So I went over and poked the fire and played with the shovel. And a coal flew out. Then I went over to Plant and said, 'Come along, Mr Plant. I've got half a dollar. Let's go to the good pull-up and get a cut off the joint with two veg.'

Old Plant shook his head. 'I owe you ten bob,' I said.

'Do you?' said Plant, a bit suspicious. But he got up. As we were going out of the kitchen, we heard a lot of shouts and awful curses. 'Why, what's up,' said Plant.

'Somebody's coat on fire. Burning nicely. Might have had a live coal in each pocket.'

'In each pocket. How could that happen?'

'I don't know,' I said. 'But it's a pity. Poor young fella. Going to see his girl. What a shame.' And I was sorry for that young chap. So as not to be too excited. Taking a chance like that. Might have got something on my mind. Vengeance is mine, saith the Lord. Safer to leave it to Him. He won't do anything about it. It's not His game. He's too busy getting on with the next thing. But why should you know?

21

I didn't tell anyone about Alabaster because I didn't believe in him any more. Effect of daylight. Anyone can believe anything in chokey, or at night time, but daylight makes even generals look like fairy tales.

I wasn't surprised therefore, when, just for the joke, I telephoned 19, Capel Mansions, and was told that Professor Alabaster didn't live there. The porter had never heard of him. Nor even of Mr Alabaster. Unless his name was Bastard. No, I said, it wasn't Bastard. That was a pity, the porter said, because a Miss Bastard had once lived next door about seven or eight years ago. Yes, I said, it was most unfortunate. And I hung up.

And when I came out of the box, I was relieved. No doubt about it. I examined my diaphragm and its sensations were undoubtedly those of relief and repose. The fact is, I said to myself, as I turned towards the studio, I have escaped a lot of trouble – and perhaps a great misfortune. Suppose this Professor had come true, suppose he'd made me famous, what then. Every time I wanted to get on with my work, ting-aling, somebody at the door, wanting their portraits painted; or whong, whong, somebody on the telephone, wanting me to go to a party. And what would I get out of it. Nothing but worry and kicks. For the benefit of Prof. Alabaster. No, I said. I'm well out of that racket. My job is to get that old woman out of my house, and the new canvas in.

My plan to get Mrs Coker out was to make her think the place was unlucky. Women are very superstitious. I had already written her a letter in large print.

MRS COKER. A WARNING. DON'T LET THAT BLACKGUARD JIMSON PERSUADE YOU INTO TAKING HIS ROTTEN OLD SHED. IT IS HAUNTED BY THE SPIRITS OF THE BOGG FAMILY, WHICH DIED OF FEVER THERE AND WAS EATEN BY THE RATS.

And in the evening I went along that way and scratched on the walls with a long stick. Mrs Coker ran out with a poker in her hand. But I was well away by then. It was important that I shouldn't be seen.

On the next night I put a lot of dry brown paper through the scullery window and dropped a match on it. There was such a smoke that you would have thought the place was on fire. Mrs Coker came out again coughing and sneezing and shouted for the police. She didn't expect the police to hear. She wanted to frighten me. The silly old woman didn't consider that the fire might well have been caused by rats. Rats have caused a lot of fires by gnawing matches, or if they haven't, every old woman believes they have. I should have liked to tell her so. But it was difficult to compose a letter which wouldn't give me away. Finally I sent this.

I SEE YOU HAD A FIRE LAST NIGHT. THIS IS DUE TO THOSE PLAGUE RATS. THEY MADE A FIRE BEFORE GNAWING MATCHES WHEN THAT SCOUNDREL JIMSON LIVED THERE. BUT, OF COURSE, HE KEPT IT DARK MEANING TO GET SOME MUG TO RENT THE PLACE.

Next night the old woman was popping out every minute with her poker and walking round the shed. On guard. The plan was working well. But what worried me was the state of Ikey's health. For, I thought, it would be just my luck if old Ikey dropped dead and that canvas was sold or cut up for floor-cloth.

I had been several times to take a look at it. You could see the top corner of it through a crack in the yard door, which gave a view of the shed. And every time I saw it, I liked it better. But every time I saw Ikey, I liked him worse. He was going to pieces at a fearful rate. As sure as I'm Gulley, I thought, the very day that old Mrs Coker throws in the towel and goes, Ikey will take spirits of salts or simply fall dead in his dust of ingrowing despair. Which, statistics show, kills more people every year than all the other kinds of heart disease put together.

I thought of going in and telling the old jellyfish that if Ikey's was killing him, he'd only got to go bankrupt and he'd soon find that bankruptcy itself can be a pleasure. I'd been bankrupt four times. There's nothing like a good smash for getting rid of small worries, the things that don't matter, but peck a man to death.

I thought of it, I say. Or I think I was thinking of it, on the Wednesday morning. But when I was peeping through the front window to see if he was alone, all at once his face came floating up quite close to me. And it was as blank as a whitewashed wall, as stupid as a corpse that's been a week in the water; more wretched than an old clubman at an empty bar with nothing to talk to but the whisky advertisements. And you see him looking at them as if he had forgotten how to read and they might hold the secret of the universe.

No, I said, it's no good. It's no good telling the poor old bladder that life is sweet, brother. Because he doesn't want it to be sweet. He's tired of enjoying anything by himself. He hasn't got the jump to laugh by accident. The grace of God can't reach him even through a Nellie Wallace. No, he can't go on. Why should he? He doesn't even get paid for it. He'll take prussic acid and there'll be another crash, and this time the landlord will put a match to the whole thing and take the insurance money. And it would be a moral act. Ikey's is a death trap.

So I was walking along in a dejected spirit, for I couldn't work, when, just as I was turning into Greenbank, to take a long view of the studio and see if the enemy's flag was still flying, I mean, smoke still rising out of the chimney, a nice young gentleman came walking along. And he was watching me all the time. Not with his eyes. He was too polite. But with his left ear and left elbow.

He wasn't a detective. Though he wore a neat brown suit and a brown hat. He had too long a neck and he turned out his toes. He was walking like the front legs of a French pug. He had round shell spectacles and his expression was intellectual as well as watchful. That is to say, he looked so that any good vet. would have said, at a first glance, that poor dog has worms.

What does that poor animal want with me, I wondered. Can he be a brother artist. He looks as if he might be capable of a wash-drawing in sepia; or decorating book-ends with transfers.

Suddenly the young man gave his neck a twist, as if to shake a fly out of his ear; his large brown eyes, melting like jelly on a warm afternoon, filled with respectful delight, and off came his chappo. 'Excuse me, sir, but are you, by any chance, Mr Gulley Jimson. I called at your studio twice last week.'

Alabaster, I thought, and I nearly laughed in my own face. Here was my professor, a kid just out of school. One of the up and at 'em boys, looking for a stepping-stone to higher things. 'No,' I said, 'my name is Henry Ford, incognito.'

But he had outside information. He knew me. 'My name is Alabaster. I don't know if you received a note of mine. I'm afraid it was never forwarded. But I am a student of art, I have written much on the British School, and I have long been a fervent admirer of your magnificent works.' 'How do you do?' I said. 'How are you? Quite well, I hope.' 'Yes, thank you. It was a great pleasure to me to see Mr Hickson's wonderful collection.' 'Yes, Mr Hickson has been a collector all his life. What he hasn't collected isn't worth the investment.' 'And he and I agreed that it was a crying scandal that your splendid art is still so little known outside a limited number of connoisseurs.'

'Mr Hickson wants to bull the market, does he?'

'He thinks it is quite time there was a proper appraisement of your contribution to art.' 'He'll have to be careful. He may do a lot of harm. He tried to get up a Jimson boom once before in '25. But first of all the General Strike broke out and then his publicity agent had an attack of delirium tremens and got converted and wrote that in his real opinion I was anti-Christ, and one of the chief causes of the decadence of British youth.'

'I think I remember something of that disgraceful agitation.'

'It did me a lot of good. I got several offers from dealers. I made money that year.'

The Professor smiled quickly like one who says, 'the eccentricities of genius. But really it's a pity.' Then he became very serious again, and in fact almost blue, and said, 'Mr Jimson, I have been planning for some time, subject to your approval, of course, and I hope, assistance, a definitive biography, and a descriptive and appreciative catalogue of your art, with reproductions of principal works.'

Reproductions of principal works was a good one. If I hadn't been in company, I should have lain down on the pavement and kicked my legs in the air. Was he real? I couldn't make up my mind. I was pretty sure he wasn't really real, by something in his left eye. It seemed to say, I call myself Alabaster, but God knows what I am really. Probably an optical delusion due to public indigestion.

'That's a nice idea, Professor,' I said. 'Are you an experienced biografter?' 'I wrote a short life of old Crome for my book on his early work.' 'How long?' 'About forty pages.' 'I didn't know old Crome lived as much as that. I should want about four hundred at that rate.' 'A full life might occupy a second volume.' 'Did old Crome have any reproductions?' 'No, there was only a frontispiece.' I stopped at the corner of Ellam Street and drew myself up. 'I shall want reproductions.'

The Professor at once realized the decisive nature of the occasion. Or rather, he was as nearly sure of it, as he could be of anything. He said firmly, 'Most certainly.' 'Coloured ones,' I said. 'That was what I planned,' said the Professor. But his left eye was wandering again, as if the whole thing was a bit of nonsense.

'With lace edges,' I said. 'Lace edges?' said the Professor, and I think a button fell off his trousers. 'Like tarts,' I said, 'and hams. The best quality. If we're going to do the thing at all, we ought to do it well. We don't want to make any mistakes. I know a chap, a friend of mine, who used to paint girls for magazine covers. The best class of girls, eleven feet high with eyes as big as eggs. Well, one morning he put on his best suit, called a taxi and drove to the Tower Bridge, where he took a pint of poison, put ten pounds of lead in each pocket, tied his legs together, cut his throat, shot himself through the head and jumped over the parapet.' 'Poor fellow,' said Alabaster. 'Yes, indeed. He was always a drifter. Never worked things out. Never had a real plan. They saw through this job at once, picked him up, pumped him up, sewed him up, plugged him up and got him back to work in six weeks.' 'I suppose he just went and did it again.' 'No, he'd lost his nerve. One of the nurses married him soon after. He made no resistance and we thought that after all he was dead. But his wife was a nice girl. She brought him alive, and now he's doing those girls again to support his beloved family and he looks just like St Lawrence frying over a slow fire. He'd like to scream all the time, but he knows the agony is going on too long.' 'I'm afraid there are many like that among the commercial artists.' 'Yes, and if I am going to be a commercial artist, I shall want my gridiron upholstered in the best brass nails.' 'Nobody could call you a commercial artist, Mr Jimson.' 'Blow the trumpets, sound the drum, Tantara, Boom. Twelve reproductions in colour. Why not twenty-four?' 'The only question is one of expense.' 'That doesn't matter in a case like this.' 'Certainly not.' 'We're aiming at the highest class of publication.' 'Of course, an edition de luxe.' 'And neither of us is paying for it.' 'Exactly, but of course the publishers,' the Professor hesitated to wound my ears with the facts of life. But he took a deep breath and threw his heart across the ha ha, 'Publishers are sometimes apt to take a business view.' 'Reproduce some of Hickson's Jimsons and make him pay for the whole edition.' 'Mr Hickson has already given me his support.' 'Have you got it in your pocket?' 'No, it is to be paid over only on the completion of the publisher's contract.' 'Got a contract?' 'Not yet.' 'Got a publisher?' 'I have approached three.' 'How far did they run?'

Mr Alabaster smiled as if to say, 'The unbending of greatness. How delightful.' He said that he expected an answer from Muster and Milligan. 'Never heard of them.' 'A new firm, but very enterprising.' 'Will they pay?' 'It would not be usual to pay an advance.' 'I meant me.' 'I don't think, Mr Jimson, the artist usually receives any direct financial benefit.' 'Then I don't mind.' 'You will receive a great deal of publicity.' 'Favourable publicity this time.' 'Most certainly.' 'That means paying for drinks instead of selling pictures. In my experience, Professor, fame is not only the ruin of artists, it busts them.'

Mr Alabaster shook his head as if to say, How true. Meanwhile we were walking along Greenbank towards the Eagle. And I began to draw in my steps in case we should pass the door before Alabaster noticed the sign and remembered that the bar was open. 'I like your idea, Professor,' I said 'The Life and Work of Professor Alabaster, by Gulley Jimson.' 'You mean the Life and Works of Gulley Jimson.' 'It's the same thing, I give you a job and you give me a job. Let's talk it over. What we want is a quiet spot.' And having reached the Eagle, I lingered so much that the Professor shot two yards ahead before he found himself alone. He noticed this and said, 'I should like that very much. Where shall we go?'

I reflected a moment and answered, 'I hardly like to suggest a public bar, but I notice the Eagle is close by, and though it is but a primitive place with a small bar and very hard chairs, it is a free house. The beer is said to be drinkable.'

'The only difficulty is that I am forbidden by my doctor to drink beer.'

'I understand that the Eagle frequently has whisky, rum, and gin, as well as beer.'

'I was hoping that we might find more congenial surroundings at your studio.'

'I'm afraid my studio is in process of cleaning. We should not be comfortable there. Why not come and try the lemonade at the Eagle?'

Mr Alabaster opened his mouth and looked like a fish that is gasping for air on the bank. His eyes had a dusty expression, like a London pool. I thought, I've seen that look before. What does it mean?

'Perhaps in your lodging, Mr Jimson. Even in a temporary lodging.'

'No chairs at all,' I said. 'The Eagle has chairs, though they are upholstered in oak.'

'It is very awkward,' Mr Alabaster said, and then suddenly I knew his look. It was the look of a man who can't pay for a drink. 'By Gad,' I thought, 'I believe the Professor is broke.'

So I took an inventory of the smart young gentleman and there was a piece of his shirt sticking out of his trousers, a little piece no bigger than a sixpence but blue as the North star. Indication to mariners. And when I looked longer I saw that his shiny brown boots were down on one side like torpedoed ships. There was a fringe on the back of his trousers like old flags after the battle and the breeze, and his collar had an edge like a splintered mast.

'Why should we not adjourn to your flat in Kensington, Professor,' I said. 'I am afraid I have given up my tenancy,' said the Professor. 'Yes,' I said, 'I phoned and the porter was sure your name was something else and you'd been living somewhere else.' 'I wasn't exactly a resident,' said Alabaster. 'I was staying with a friend.' 'That's much the best plan,' I said. 'I prefer it myself. Let us visit your friend. He may be out.' 'I'm afraid he is away. But I should be delighted with any accommodation, Mr Jimson. Your lodgings, even if there aren't any chairs.'

We walked on. And I thought, the Professor is broke, but I like him. There's a kind of little lamb who made thee about him, which is very attractive. And though he is probably a blackguard who would sell his own mother to the bone factory for half a crown and cut a blind man's throat for glory, he is such an unsuccessful blackguard that you can't help mothering him, poor snake.

'My address for the moment,' I said, 'is Elsinore, Ellam Lane.' 'Is it close?' 'You can see the chimney-pots from here, that large villa with the fire escape.' 'A very wise precaution.' 'Yes, I never take a house of that size unless it has a fire escape. Right turn. There you are, Professor. My bedroom is on the top floor – the window with the gent's pants drying on the sill. I prefer a top bedroom for the airing,' 'So do I.'

It was about half-past seven and I said to the Professor, 'Just about my dinner time.' 'Don't let me intrude on your arrangements.' 'Certainly not, I hope you'll stay.' 'It's very good of you. But it's really too late,' said the Professor, and I thought, where have I heard that voice before, like wind blowing through the cracks of an empty church. 'Oh, not at all,' I said. 'The dining-room is downstairs. For convenience. The staff nowadays so dislike stairs.' 'Yes, of course, quite so. You are too good. If I might wash my hands.' 'The arrangements are downstairs, next the dining-room.'

'Thank you so much, I really feel that I am imposing on you.' 'The imposition is a pleasure all round.' And I thought: Yes, of course, I know that voice, the chap is hungry and doesn't know what to do about it. 'This way, Professor.' 'I can't say how much I appreciate this hospitality.'

And we came into the kitchen where about fifteen chaps were eating, each trying to turn his back on all the others at once; and to cover his plate. For to have anyone look on your food in a common lodging-house kitchen is a misfortune. The envious eye makes you forget the taste even of Wiltshire ham. And the critical eye which is the evil eye turns a cheap kipper into sulphuric acid and old leather.

I had a quick look round and there was old Plant in his corner, arms crossed, hat over his nose like a Roman helmet. Looking as if to say, Let 'em all come. On guard. The sentry of Pompeii. With pepper and salt in his pockets and the cup on a string under his coat; and a kettle between him and the wall behind. A kettle with only two small holes we got off a dump.

'All safe, Mr Plant,' though he was safe enough in his back corner. 'All safe, Mr Jimson,' with the look of the Pompeian when they dug him out of the ashes. Making quite a thing of it.

'Mister Plant,' I said, 'Professor Alabaster. He's coming to dinner.'

'With pleasure,' said Plant, taking a side glance at my pocket.

'The Professor is my biograbber,' I said 'He said snap and my fame is his bed and board.'

'I hope you will get some recognition at last,' said old Plant. 'I shall be recognized by the starry wheels,' I said, forgetting myself. 'You are an art critic in the papers, sir,' said old Plant, who thinks a lot of papers though he thinks he doesn't. 'Yes,' I said, 'the Professor is an art-cricket. He knows the game backwards, from Zuloaga to Alfred the Great.' 'You don't believe in art criticism,' said Alabaster. 'Yes,' I said, 'it exists. I even knew a critic once. A chap who could criticize pictures. Yes, he even knew what a picture was.' 'What is a picture?' 'A picture, that's the trouble really.' 'What papers did he write for?' 'He didn't write. He swore. His language was so bad that his wife and family deserted him. They were also starving.' 'What did he do then?' 'He decided to live for his mission as critic, so to support himself, he took up cricketism. Balls and bats. His special branch was the googly. The slowness of the hand deceives the sly.'

The Professor reflected a moment. He was thinking of his dinner. As one in a dream, which might still turn out not to be a dream, he said, 'The googly.'

Poor chap, I thought, he's such an inefficient scoundrel that he doesn't know the simplest motions of his craft. 'I'm surprised,' I said 'that as a cricket you don't know the googly. Slow balls right off the wicket with a break from the blind side. You start, let us say, on the modern spirit with a touch of surrealism, come in sharp on the superb Sargents in the collection of Sir Burrows Mouldiwarp. Then you mention that great offers have been made for the Mouldiwarp pictures. But Sir Burrows has up to now, in the interests of the nation, rejected all temptation to part with his unique gallery, and down goes the wicket, middle stump. Next day all the papers reveal that the Mouldiwarp collection is to be dispersed, on account of the death duties.'

The Professor fired up. The smell of kippers was biting him in a new place. 'Mr Jimson,' he said, 'if you think that I have any motive in this project which I have suggested to you except the desire to make your superb work better known to the public —'

'Hickson's work,' I said. 'And why not. It's all in the game. Hickson is a business man. And I'm a painting man. He makes money for fun and needs art to keep him alive. I paint pictures for fun, and need money to keep me alive. He wants to boost his pictures and get fun out of them, and I want to get some money and paint new pictures. And you want a job.'

'I see you have the lowest opinion of my motives,' said the Professor. 'Not at all,' I said. 'Not the lowest. I've known a lot of real artists in my time and some of them were geniuses in their way.'

Somebody was frying a chop and the smell began oozing through the kippers. It reached us like music from the never-never land. I hadn't eaten a chop for two years. Too much fat and bone for true economy. But to the Professor, brought up probably in luxury, it came like the wind of the desert to a wild barb. You could see his nostrils expand and drink it in, especially the lean. It went to his head. He became excited. 'Mr Jimson,' he said. 'Since you have mentioned it yourself, I might perhaps be allowed to suggest that you are suffering, no doubt temporarily, from some financial embarrassment.' 'Not at all,' I said, 'I'm used to it.' 'But do you realize that the art dealers would give very good prices for your work. I know one who would pay any sum for a fine example.' 'I've had any sum before and it worked out at nothing less expenses.' 'You don't know your value.' 'How much is it? Mention some sum.' 'That would depend, of course, on the work. If the gentleman I mention could see a specific picture.' 'Certainly, Prof. If your friend would run down to Ancombe in Devonshire, he'd find the finest thing I ever did, and they'd give it to him.' Alabaster took out his note-book. 'At Ancombe, Mr Jimson?' 'Yes. In the village hall. On the end wall under four coats of whitewash.' 'Oh, a wall painting.' 'Yes, but I used oil paint on a special plaster. Very durable.' 'I'm afraid my friend couldn't remove the wall.' 'Well, then there's another one, nearly as good, in Bradbury, near Leeds. I should think you could have it for seven-and-sixpence.' 'Is that on a wall?' 'No, on canvas.' 'Perhaps I could have particulars.' And out came the note-book again. 'Jacob and his wives stealing away with Laban's flocks.' 'A very interesting subject.' 'It came out well. And you say the canvas is in Bradbury.' 'Last I saw of it, it was covering a screen in a barber's shop – they'd cut it down a bit and given it a coat of black Japan, but you could still see Leah's eyes and a bit of Rachel's left leg coming through.' 'What vandalism.' 'Of course, my biggest work is the Holy Innocents, but I'm afraid your friend couldn't have that. It's in the hall of the Therapeutic Society, near Cheapside. But one of the Colonial governments took over the building and it didn't like the babies because they hadn't any trousers on. So it said the plaster was dangerous and knocked it about a bit with a hammer. And most of it fell down.' 'I think I heard of that scandal.' 'Well, why not. After all, they'd bought the house, so why shouldn't they do what they liked with the decorations.' 'Works of art ought to be sacred to civilized people.' 'These people were civilized. They all wore trousers and they never spat on the floor. They used the fireplace.'

'I can't treat that sort of thing lightly, Mr Jimson. It makes me furious.' 'It doesn't worry me, Mr Alabaster. What I say is, anyone who goes in for art deserves what he gets. If he ends up in the Academy, then he ought to thank God that he escaped worse. He might have been sweeping out a lavatory in Leicester Square. And if he ends in the workhouse he ought to say to himself: After all, I've been out for a good time. And I've had a damn good time, too. And if I'm not in a lunatic asylum or jug, it's only because no one took the trouble to set the police on me. I wasn't good enough.'

'You are too modest, Mr Jimson – your work hasn't the reputation it deserves. What you need is a business manager.'

'Bring in the business, Prof, and I'll pay you your whack.'

'Excuse me, but I am not in the art business. I am a critic. But it is precisely as a critic that I happen to know how dealers regard your work.'

'Bring along your friend and we'll sting him both sides at once.'

'I know he offered Mr Hickson two hundred guineas for the Lady in her Bath.'

'Sara in her skin. That wasn't a picture. It was a piece of stuff. But I have a real picture to sell.'

'He would give two hundred for any important work.'

'Make it three hundred, and I'll give you half.'

'I really had no idea of such a thing, Mr Jimson – but in the circumstances —'

'We're both broke, Professor. So why worry about a few hundred here or there.' 'Half is too much.' 'Not if I get the other.' 'Say the usual agent's fees.' 'Thirty-three-and-a-third per cent with a cut for the frame.' 'It's really too much, I feel ashamed.' 'Don't do that, Professor. Buy yourself a new suit and be a new man. We're in this together. You tell the tale and I make the hokey pokey, works by the celebrated Gulley Jimson.' 'I resent very much the suggestion that there is any ulterior motive in my action.' 'You're quite right, Professor. To resent. Stick to the rules. Crickets ought to resent suggestions. All they have to sell is somebody's good name. Quick, Mr Plant, there's a gap in the stove.'

Plant got up and took my frypan from under him. I found it hanging outside a shop in High Street market. Fell into my hand. Cheap tin. Regular swindle. But good enough for rough work. Old Plant always sat on it. 'You'll bust it in, Mr Plant,' I said, 'if you lean your weight on it.'

'But I don't lean my weight. Trust me. The trick is, to sit a bit sideways and forward. I could show you, but it's not so easy as it looks. I hit on it myself, by accident.'

Well, I thought, Old Plant is a bit of an artist after all. Life and Work of Godfrey Plant. Creation of dignities and responsibilities.

> Some sons of Los surrounded the passions with porches of iron and silver
> Creating form and beauty around the dark regions of sorrow.
> Giving to airy nothing a name and a habitation
> Delightful with bounds to the infinite.

'I'll leave it to you, Mr Plant,' I said. 'Couldn't leave a pan in better hands.' And I took out of my pocket four portions of fried fish with chips done up in a paper bag. They give you a bag with anything more than two portions. And a packet of lard.

Then I made for the fire. All the frypans were pushing at each other over the red, joggling together, and the owners swearing and glaring hotter than the fire. I had to put my pan on the black of the stove. But it was hot enough on the draught side to melt the fat. Then I took a little cocoa tin with a nail hole in the lid, as if for salt and pepper, and gave the fat a sprinkle. But I had some wet rags in that tin, and when I shook it, drops of water flew into the fat. And it began to splutter and shoot like a British square attacked by wild Zulus. So the boys on the red gave a jump.

'Ow,' said one. 'What you playing at, you old bastard? That was my eye.'

'I don't know how it is,' I said, 'but this fat always shoots. Because of the adulteration. But what does the government do for the poor, nothing.'

'Wow,' said another. 'Here, you swine. Your bloody pan has burnt my nose.'

'I'm sorry, gentlemen. It's this here fat. But if I get it on the red a moment, I'd soon have it done.'

'It bleeding well better, or I'll shove it down your neck and all. Hi, ow wow, what you doing?'

'Well really, gentlemen, you see how it is – it's worse than ever.'

'Get it on the red, for Christ's sake, and finish with it before you burn our bloody eyes out.'

'Thank you, gentlemen, you are very kind.'

So I got my billy on the red and in two minutes that fish began to curl and smoke blue, and the chips shone like bars of gold in champagne.

'Come on, Mr Plant,' I shouted. 'Where's that bread?'

'Here,' they said. 'You clear out. Scram, you old stinker, you smell.'

'What I want to know,' I said, in a soft voice, 'who's that stranger with the thick chin over by the window?'

And they all looked round. 'Thick chin?'

'Looks to me like an inspector.'

So they looked again. And Plant came up panting with two rounds of bread. And the castor. Which was in his charge. In went the bread. And the salt and pepper to taste.

Then one of the boys gave me the shoulder and said, 'That's enough,' and he looked me in the eye. 'None of that, you Union crab, or I'll smash your face in.'

'I beg your pardon, Mister,' I said, 'but suppose I got a jog and this pan should slip out of my hand, fat might go anywhere – why I knew some hot fat once, burnt a chap's eyes out. Nice young chap, just like you.' Looking him in the eye. 'And he didn't smash my face in. He only gave me another little push and said, "Yes, I'd like to see you." '

'If you could,' I said. 'That other poor young chap didn't have any eyes – not much face either.'

Then he pushed me off the fire. But I thought: No good giving him a poke. Lose my dinner. And it's time enough. The fish are nicely hotted. Another minute and they'd have gone dry.

'Here you are,' I said, carrying the pan to the corner. And Plant brought out the cutlery. Two forks, a knife and a skewer. Fork for the Professor. Knife and fork for Plant. Skewer and fingers for me. Fingers before forks. Especially with chip potatoes.

I divided up the odd fish and odd toast so quickly that no one saw which was which. Passing the brown. Someone had two pieces of toast. 'How do you like it, Professor?'

'Excellent. Marvellous. Tell me, Mr Jimson, can one sleep here?'

'Sometimes. After dinner. Fleas' dinner. Sixpence a night.'

'I really think I might try it. Just for the night.'

'That's all you'll get,' I said. 'For sixpence.'

'I had an invitation, but there was a mistake about the dates. So I found myself free. And I can't say I'm sorry.'

'Social engagements are a terrible bore,' I said, 'but they'll want their sixpence in advance at this Ritz.'

'I suppose it wouldn't be possible for you to add to your kindness and lend me fourpence.'

'Of course I can. Out of that three hundred pounds you are getting me for the Fall.'

We lent him fourpence between us. And stood him a breakfast. And he vanished with the fourpence. 'Well,' I said, after a week, 'I'm surprised. I knew the Professor wasn't quite real, but I thought he was a stronger dream than that. I expected that he was going to hang around my pillow long enough to distinguish him from asthma.' .

22

Then one morning I had a letter dated from Capel Mansions. On a good solid paper without deckle edges or rough grain; a lordly paper.

Dear Mr Gulley Jimson,

I am staying here for a few days with my friends Sir William and Lady Beeder, who are both distinguished lovers of art and great admirers of your work, which they have seen at Mr Hickson's.

I don't know if you have a picture available at the moment, but I feel that Sir William would very much like to see some of your latest work. He is, I may say, rather more advanced in taste than Mr Hickson, and possesses examples of all the modern schools, including some symbolist work in which I believe your murals were pioneers. Sir William is a wealthy man and a generous patron of all the arts.

Perhaps you would let me know if you have any recent work to show and we could then arrange a suitable date and place for a private exhibition.

Yours most sincerely,
A. W. Alabaster.

And he enclosed four penny stamps.

'Look at this, Mr Plant,' I said. 'What do you think of it?'

'It's just what he said. That he was waiting to go to a friend.'

'That's what I can't make out. It looks almost as if he had been telling the truth.'

'I liked that young man,' said Plantie, who was getting more like himself every day. 'I felt all the time that he was a sincere lover of art.'

'So did I. That's what made me careful. But Capel Mansions, it's a big modern place, isn't it? High rents.'

'Go and see him at his friends'.'

'Yes,' I said. 'But suppose the Professor is straight and his friends are really the sort of people who would give me money, real money for a picture, a real picture. That's to say, a real Jimson.'

'Why not?' said Plantie, folding his arms and looking fiercely at a little old man about ten yards away, who had no more idea of stealing a frypan than washing his face. 'Why shouldn't they buy one of your pictures? I agree with the young gentleman. You don't think nearly enough of yourself, Mr Jimson.'

'It's not what I think of myself,' I said. 'It's what this Beeder thinks of himself. Does he think himself cleverer than all the other millionaires who never buy a picture till the dealers tell 'em that the price will be more next week? And if so, what sort of a fool is he?' And I went away. I liked old

Plantie, but he was always too encouraging. As if he thought I was just going to hang myself, or jump into the river.

I wanted to think. I saw that this was a turning point in my life. Or probably not. A thousand pounds, I thought, or let's say fifty pounds, it would set me up for life. I could get a new studio, a good one with a roof as well as a wall. Even twenty pounds would give me a fresh start. Of course, I thought, it's not a likely tale. I haven't sold a picture for fifteen years, and my last big commission was from that old woman in Ancomb, who was more or less mad. Or she wouldn't have given me the job. And as for the Professor, he may be straight in places, but that's all to the bad. You know where you are with a complete liar, but when a chap mixes some truth with his yarns, you can't trust a word he says. All the same, I thought, even ten pounds, I'd be painting again.

So I took Plantie's advice and cleaned the top of my boots with a newspaper and went to call at Capel Mansions. Fine large new buildings in the play brick design. Fine large old porter in the Victoria R.I. style. Everything right. He pushed me down the steps without any hesitation. Quite right. And it took me some time to persuade him that I had been asked to call. Then he phoned the flat. The Professor himself came down to receive me and to apologize. Quite right, too. So did the porter when he heard I was a distinguished artist.

'Don't mention it,' I said. 'You did the right thing. I'll tell Sir William that he can have every confidence in you. After all, if a man can't get his money's worth in fidelity, what would the world be coming to. What is your pub?' 'Well, sir, I sometimes go to the Red Lion, just round the next corner.' 'I'll come and have something with you.' 'I don't get off till twelve.' 'I'll wait. That's a bargain.'

The Professor was nervous and I thought probably he had lost some more buttons off his trousers. He looked as if he could no longer rely on them. On the other hand, he was cleaner than ever and had more oil on his hair. 'You wrote to me just in time,' I said. 'I have just completed the finest thing I ever did. It only wants a touch. An important work. Nine by twelve. Of course a lot of people are after it, and the Chantrey trustees would jump at it for the nation. But what I always say is that private patrons, really generous and beneficent men like Sir William, ought to be encouraged. Especially if they are millionaires. Artists owe a debt to millionaires that can never be repaid, except in cash. For, of course, Sir William will get it all back as soon as I croak, even before.' 'What is the subject of the picture? Oh, of course, I oughtn't to ask that. But I want the general nature of the work.' 'Meat,' I said, knowing that the Professor wouldn't like the idea of the Fall. 'Human meat, in appropriate attitudes, with surrounding vegetables. A thousand is the price – guineas – that's unframed. But I could supply a fine carved frame for another hundred.

That, of course, would also be guineas, or say a hundred and ten pounds with a guarantee of genuineness.'

'It isn't the picture called The Fall?' said the Professor.

'Certainly not.'

'What Sir William wants, I think, is one of those magnificent nudes.'

'I'm talking about nudes.'

'But ah, if I'm right, this picture you speak of is one of the more recent works – more in the style of Gauguin.'

'Gauguin, who is Gauguin? You don't mean that French painter who did dead dolls with green eyes in a tin landscape. I couldn't paint in his style unless I became a Plymouth Brother with the itch, and practised on public-house signs for fifteen years. Hullo, how much higher are we going?'

'Beeder lives in the attics. The best flats are at the top, for the view.'

But I wasn't quite reassured until I saw the flat. Luckily the Beeders were out to tea and I was able to look round. A real hall, a big studio with gallery, a little dining-room off the studio, two bedrooms and chromium bathroom. Usual Persian rugs and antiques, vases, marbles, African gods, American mobiles, Tanagra, and rock crystal ash-trays. Old portraits in the dining-room, modern oils in the studio, drawings in the bedroom, water-colours in the hall. Usual modern collection. Wilson Steer, water in watercolour, Matthew Smith, victim of the crime in slaughtercolour; Utrillo, white-washed wall in mortarcolour; Matisse, odalisque in scortacolour; Picasso, spatchcock horse in tortacolour; Gilbert Spencer, cocks and pigs in though-tacolour; Stanley Spencer, cottage garden in hortacolour; Braque, half a bottle of half and half in portercolour; William Roberts, pipe dream in snortercolour; Wadsworth, rockses, blockses, and fishy boxes all done by self in nautacolour; Duncan Grant, landscape in strawtacolour; Frances Hodgkins, cows and wows and frows and sows in chortacolour; Rouault, perishing Saint in fortacolour; Epstein, Leah waiting for Jacob in squawta-colour. All the most high-toned and expensive. 'I can see your friends are rich people,' I said, 'that is, really nice and charming. I like them very much already.' And I had a look round the bedrooms. Silk under-drawers in Sir William's wardrobe. And nothing but silk. Piles of fine white handker-chiefs. 'I suppose he is the sort of man who has a clean handkerchief every day,' I said. 'He dresses very simply,' said the Professor, who was hovering over me like a guardian angel in case any small savage article might rush into my pockets and bite me in the dark. 'Perhaps we'd better go now,' he said. 'Where?' I said. 'To see the picture.' 'On no,' I said, 'there's plenty of time. And besides, I want to meet Sir William.' 'Oh, I'm afraid he won't be back for a long time.' 'When do you expect him back?' 'Not till dinner time at least.' 'That will suit me perfectly. I haven't got an engagement to dinner.' 'Oh, but it's quite likely he won't be back till much later.' 'How much later?' 'Midnight.' 'It's a nuisance, as I had a kind of understanding with the Archbishop of Canterbury to be in about dinner time if he called.

But Sir William comes first. I never disappoint a millionaire if I can help it. Not if I have to sleep on the sofa.'

The Professor looked as if not only his trousers but his pants were coming down. I led him back to the studio, made him sit down, I offered him one of Sir William's cigarettes. 'All this,' I said, 'gives me a lot of confidence in the Beeders. Living in a studio and buying pictures. I suppose they love artists.' 'They are very interested in art.' 'I said artists. Clean ones, of course.' 'They do entertain artists.' 'More than once.' 'Lady Beeder is herself an artist.' 'That's not so good.' 'She is not at all bad. She is an amateur, of course'. And both of us paused for reflection.

'Of course,' I said, 'with all this money.'

'But some of her watercolours are quite excellent, in the traditional style.'

'Of course, with all this money. The best advice. The best of everything, in fact.'

The Professor made an appeal with his eyes. 'The Beeders are two of my oldest friends. Especially Flora, that is, Lady Beeder.'

'So they ought to be,' I said. 'With all that money. You stick to them, old man. Clasp them to your soul with bands of steel – say steal. But I suppose they find you useful, too. The lady asks your advice about her painting.'

'She is really very keen.'

'Look here, Professor,' I said. 'What we want to do is to get up a Life and Works of Lady Flora Beeder and sell her the first refusal for five hundred pounds down. That's two-fifty each.'

'Not Lady Flora Beeder, Lady Beeder.'

'That's all right. You can put in the stops. I'll do the works. But cash on the nail.'

'Are you serious?' The Professor was surprised.

'Of course I'm serious. It's a question of cash. And look at my boots.'

'But, Mr Jimson, it would be quite impossible to bring out a Life and Works of Lady Beeder. No publisher, no reputable publisher, would touch it.'

'Then we'll get one of the other kind. Come on, Professor. You've no imagination. Business is business. I'm in this with you. What about the Life and Works of Gulley Jimson?'

'Do you compare yourself with Lady Beeder? Gifted as she is, she is hardly —'

'Nobody would know the difference. Not if it was done properly. Of course, we want the best paper, and a lot of coloured reproductions, and gilt edges and an introduction by the President of Something, or a Professor of the Fine Arts. But expense is no object. She's got the beans. Damn it, Professor, for five hundred down and expenses we'll put her on the Roll of Fame. We'll roll her on the floors of eternity for a year or two. Of course, when people try to hang their hats and umbrellas on a Beeder, they may find a sort of an absence. But by that time it will be too late. She'll be in all the public galleries, and the only thing the directors can do is to put her in the sun, over a ventilator, where the rain comes though the bricks, or store her with the Turners in the Tate basement until the Thames comes up again and gives her a wash of dead dog and sludge. She'll still be in the best company.'

'My dear Mr Jimson, it can't be done.'

'I see, it isn't cricketism. Well then, why not give an exhibition for her, and let her buy in about half and stick red tabs on them – and put some paragraphs in the paper about the finest type of English traditional art, solid achievement rather than flashy cleverness, a reverent approach to Nature – and so on? If that isn't cricketism, what is?'

But the Professor thought I was joking. No imagination, nothing of the artist. And the thought struck me perhaps after all he was an honest cricket. A straight bat. The noblest work of Gog.

'I thought you and I were going into business together,' said I, 'to coin me cash.'

'Is it possible,' said the Professor, 'to serve Mammon and Art at the same time?'

'It is,' I said, 'or there wouldn't be any art. Through cash to culture. That's the usual road. What's the difference between little Bob who likes pictures to chuck stones at and Nosy Barbon who would walk ten miles to meet a bad painter – about two hundred pounds in school fees, paid by the state monthly with war bonus. The history of civilization is written in a ledger. Who are the most enlightened people in the world – the rich. What is the most Christian nation: the one with most of the money?'

The Professor was shocked. 'You are joking, Mr Jimson. You would not like me to put such things in your biography as considered statements.'

'I hope you will,' I said. 'If you don't, I'll do it myself. The best of everything for everybody is what I want and it costs millions. Hell is paved with good intentions, but heaven goes in for something more dependable. Solid gold. With walls of jasper, etc. We got to build Jerusalem, and that needs a lot of finance. Pure hearts are more than coronets. I should think so. It takes about a thousand years of good education to turn them out and even then the process is not yet foolproof. We haven't got the money for the necessary research, let alone repairs to the laboratory. And the most expensive thing in the world is a work of genius.'

'Most of the French impressionists were poor men, poorly rewarded. And of the expressionist school, many were almost starving.'

'All the French impressionists lived in a country where the government paid millions a year for training artists and buying pictures. True, when it got any real artists, it spat on them and starved two or three of them to death. But you can't expect a government to know what original art is. The nature of Bats is to comprehend Balls, and nothing else. But what a

630

government can do is to encourage art schools and bad artists, and when you get a lot of art schools and bad artists, you get a lot of people trying to steal an idea from somebody else and the people they steal from are the original artists. So you get an encouraging atmosphere for original art.'

'I'm afraid the post-impressionist school was received with contempt and derision, even in France.'

'I didn't say the original artists get encouragement in their own lifetime – that's impossible. What I said was you got an encouraging atmosphere for original art, after the artists are dead. When Van Gogh was painting his masterpieces, the clever ones were beginning to admire Manet – that was very encouraging to Van Gogh, and if it wasn't, what did he care?

'And when Van Gogh was dead and rotten, and his pictures were being bought at thousands apiece for public galleries so that students could get ideas for them, Matisse and Picasso and Braque were bad jokes, but how encouraging for them to hear Van Gogh, who was nearly as mad as they were, appreciated in all the best drawing-rooms. That's what I say' (I said) 'if a government wants original art, great art, it only has to pay a lot of crickets and professors and brokendown screevers to talk Balls about art to a lot of innocent children, and teach them how to draw and paint so badly that their own mothers are ashamed of them and beg them to go in for something more respectable like selling gold bricks or white slaves. Because they won't leave off. And half of them become like Herod, devoured by worms, and the other half like Job, so rotten in their limbs that they can't find rest anywhere. And the first half go prowling round looking for something to stop up their bellies, and the second half go creeping about on all fours looking for somewhere to rest their miserable carcases. And so they gather at last in the graveyard and dig up some poor pauper with their teeth and claws and say, "Lo, he was a genius, starved to death by the government." And so he may have been. Or perhaps not. Everybody makes mistakes. Even a generation devoured by worms at government expense. But unless you spend millions you don't even get mistakes – you have nothing at all. Just a lot of social economics lying about like army disposal after the war before last or the war after next.'

Just then the Beeders came in, Sir William and Lady. Big man with a bald head and monkey fur on the back of his hands. Voice like a Liverpool dray on a rumbling bridge. Charming manners. Little bow. Beaming smile. Lady tall, slender, Spanish eyes, brown skin, thin nose, Greco hands. Collector's piece. I must have those hands, I thought, arms probably too skinny but the head and torso are one piece, I should need them together.

Lady Beeder was even more charming than her husband, 'I'm so delighted, Mr Gulley Jimson – I know you hardly ever pay visits. I did not dare to ask you – but I hoped,' and she asked me to tea. People like that can afford it. Nothing to them to send their cushions to the cleaners.

What I like about the rich is the freedom, and the friendliness. Christian atmosphere. Liberty Hall. Everything shared because there is too much. All forgiveness because it's no trouble. Drop their Dresden cups on the fireplace and they smile. They are anxious only that you should not be embarrassed, and spoil the party. That's their aim. Comfort and joy. Peace on earth. Goodwill all round.

When I first met Hickson, I could have kissed his beautiful boots. I loved them for themselves, works of art, and he was so full of goodwill that it came off him like the smell of his soap, linen, hair cream, tooth wash, shaving lotion, eyewash and digestive mixture. Like the glow of a firefly. Calling for something. Until he got burnt up, poor chap. A flash in the dark. For, or course, the rich do find it hard to get through the needle's eye, out of heaven. And to spend all your life in paradise is a bit flat. Millionaires deserve not only our love but our pity. It is a Christian act to be nice to them.

When Lady Beeder asked me if my tea was all right, I said 'Yes, your ladyship. Everything is all right. I am enjoying myself so much that you will have to throw me downstairs to get rid of me. I think you and Sir William are two of the nicest people I've ever met. You have lovely manners and lovely things, a lovely home, and very good tea. I suppose this tea costs four and sixpence a pound, it is worth it. Genius is priceless.'

The Professor kept coughing and making faces at me, but I wasn't afraid of embarrassing nice people. I knew they would be used to unfortunate remarks. Rich people are like royalty, They can't afford to be touchy. Richesse oblige. And, in fact, they kept on putting me at my ease; and paying me compliments all the time. And when I told them how I had been turned out of my studio by the Cokers, they said they hoped that I would come and stay over the week-end, to keep the Professor company while they were away.

'I'm sorry we can't offer you a bed beyond Monday, but we have only two bedrooms.'

'I could sleep on the sofa,' I said.

'Oh, Mr Jimson, but we couldn't allow you to be so uncomfortable.'

'Then why shouldn't Sir William sleep with the Professor and I'll sleep with her ladyship. You can count me as a lady – at sixty-seven.'

Alabaster turned green and coughed as if he was going into consumption. But I knew I couldn't shock cultured people like the Beeders. They get past being shocked before they are out of school, just as they get over religion and other unexpected feelings.

'A very good idea ' said Sir William, laughing. 'I am greatly complimented,' said the lady, 'but I'm afraid I should keep you awake. I'm such a bad sleeper.'

'Perhaps,' said Sir William, getting up, 'Mr Jimson would like to see some of your work, my dear.'

'Oh no, Bill, please.'

'But Flora, that last thing of yours was really remarkable – I'm not suggesting that it was up to professional standards. But as a quick impression —'

'Oh no,' said her ladyship, 'Mr Jimson would laugh at my poor efforts.'

But of course they both wanted me to see her work and say that it was wonderful. And why not? They were so kind, so good.

'Why,' I said, 'amateurs do much the most interesting work.'

The Professor began to hop about like a dry pea on the stove. He coughed and made faces at me, meaning 'Be careful, be tactful, remember these people are used to luxury of all kinds.'

But I laughed and said, 'Don't you worry, Professor, I'm not pulling her ladyship's leg. I wouldn't do such a thing. I have too much respect for that charming limb.'

Sir Willam got out an easel and a big portfolio, in red morocco with a monogram in gold. And he took out a big double mount, of the best Bristol board, cut by a real expert, with a dear little picture in the middle. Sky with clouds, grass with trees, water with reflection, cows with horns, cottage with smoke and passing labourer with fork, blue shirt, old hat.

'Lovely,' I said, puffing my cigar. 'Only wants a title – what will you call it? Supper time. You can see that chap is hungry.'

'I think the sky is not too bad,' said she. 'I just laid it down and left it.'

'That's the way,' I said. 'Keep it fresh. Get the best colours and let 'em do the rest. Charming.'

'I'm so glad you like it,' said she. And she was so nice that I thought I should tell her something. 'Of course,' I said, 'the sky is just a leetle bit chancy, looks a bit accidental, like when the cat spills its breakfast.'

'I *think* I see,' said her ladyship, and Sir William said, 'Of course, Mr Jimson, you do get skies like that in Dorset. It's really a typical Dorset sky.'

I saw the Professor winking at me so hard that his face was like a concertina with a hole in it. But I didn't care. For I knew that I could say what I liked to real amateurs and they wouldn't care a damn. They'd only think, 'These artists are a lot of jealous stick-in-the-muds. They can't admire any art but their own. Which is simply dry made-up stuff, without any truth or real feeling for Nature.'

'Yes,' I said, 'that is a typical sky. Just an accident. That's what I mean. What you've got there is just a bit of nothing at all – nicely splashed on to the best Whatman with an expensive camel-hair —'

'I *think* I see what you mean,' said her ladyship. 'Yes, I *do* see – it's most interesting.'

And she said something to Sir William with her left eyelash, which caused him to shut his mouth and remove the picture so suddenly that it was like the movies. And to pop on the next. A nice little thing of clouds with sky, willows with grass, river with wet water, barge with mast and two ropes, horse with tail, man with back.

'Now that's lovely,' I said. 'Perfect. After de Windt. Look at the wiggle of the mast in the water. What technique.'

'My wife has made a special study of watercolour technique,' said Sir William. 'A very difficult medium.'

'Terrible,' I said, 'But her ladyship has mastered it. She's only got to forget it.'

'I *think* I see what Mr Jimson means,' says she. 'Yes, cleverness is a danger . . .'

And she looked at me so sweetly that I could have hugged her. A perfect lady. Full of forbearance towards this nasty dirty old man with his ignorant prejudices.

'That's it, I said. 'It's the jaws of death. Look at me. One of the cleverest painters who ever lived. Nobody ever had anything like my dexterity, except Rubens on a good day. I could show you an eye – a woman's eye, from my brush, that beats anything I've ever seen by Rubens. A little miracle of brushwork. And if I hadn't been lucky I might have spent the rest of my life doing conjuring tricks to please the millionaires, and the professors. But I escaped. God knows how. I fell off the tram. I lost my ticket and my virtue. Why, your ladyship, a lot of my recent stuff is not much better, technically, than any young lady can do after six lessons at a good school. Heavy-handed, stupid-looking daubery. Only difference is that it's about something – it's an experience, and all this amateur stuff is like farting Annie Laurie through a keyhole. It may be clever but is it worth the trouble? What I say is, why not do some real work, your ladyship? Use your loaf, I mean your brain. Do some thinking. Sit down and ask yourself what's it all about.'

And both of them, looking at me with such Christian benevolence that I felt ready to tell them almost the truth, went off together.

'But, Mr Jimson, don't you think – of course, I'm not a professional – that the intellectual approach to art is the great danger.'

'Destructive of true artistic feeling,' Sir William rumbled. 'Don't you think, Mr Jimson, that the greatness of the French impressionists like Manet and Monet was perhaps founded on their rejection of the classical rules?'

'Oh Lord,' I said. 'Listen to them. Oh God, these poor dears – and didn't Manet and Monet talk about their theories of art until the sky rained pink tears and the grass turned purple – didn't Pissarro chop the trees into little bits of glass? And Seurat put his poor old mother through the sausage machine and roll her into linoleum. What do you think Cézanne was playing at, noughts and crosses, like a Royal Academy portrait merchant, fourteen noble pans in exchange for a K.B.E.? Jee-sus,' I said; for they were so nice and polite, the lambs, that they didn't care a damn what I said. It passed right over them like the brass of a Salvation band hitting the dome of St Paul's. They were so rich and Christian that they forgave everybody before he spoke and everything before it happened, so long as it didn't happen to them. 'Jee-minny Christy,' I said. 'What you think I been doing all my life – playing tiddly winks with little Willie's first colour-box? Why friends,' I appealed to their better halves, 'what do you see before you, a lunatic with lice in his shirt and bats in his clock' (this was for her ladyship on the maternal side), 'a poodle-faking crook that's spent fifty years getting nothing for nothing and a kick up below for interest on the investment' (this was for Sir William on the side of business common sense), 'or somebody that knows something about his job.'

Her ladyship and Sir William both smiled and laid their hands on my arm.

'Dear Mr Jimson,' said she, 'don't think I don't agree with every word. I can't say how grateful I am —'

'A great privilege,' Sir William rumbled, 'and believe me, we know how to appreciate it. Yes, most valuable and illuminating.'

'But dear me,' said her ladyship, 'it's nearly half-past eight.'

'Good God,' I said, 'I haven't got in the way of your dinner.'

'Not at all', said Sir Willlam. 'We dine at any time.'

'Perhaps Mr Jimson will stay to dinner,' said she.

And I stayed to dinner. I knew it would be good. The rich, God bless them, are supporters of all the arts, bootmaking, dressmaking, cookery, bridge, passing the time of day. We had seven courses and six bottles. But Sir William, poor chap, was a teetotaller and his wife drank only hock for the figure. A half bottle for half a figure. So the Professor and I shared the rest. He had a glass of claret and a suck of port, I had wine.

23

And after the fish, I began to swim. My eyes were opened and I saw the light. The candles kept growing into silver porches, and the flowers walked under them like green girls with chorus hats. Their flames looked at me like the eyes of tigers just waking from sleep. Lying on their sides and opening one eye at a time. Tiger, tiger, burning bright. A ravening brute with a breath like a rotten corpse and septic claws. This beauty grows with cruelty.

'You've got a nice wall there, Sir William,' I said. 'I should like to paint tigers on it. With orchids. Flycatchers and flesh eaters. Flowers of evil. Millionaire eats a poor baby for breakfast and contemplates the beauties of creation. Art lives on babies. It would cost millions to save a few thousand babies a year. Got to teach the mothers first. Then the grandmothers. Then the grand professors. How much will you give me for the tigers? A hundred guineas. All right, I start tomorrow. Through roast grouse to spiritual joy.

Joy is goodness. Do you believe in Spinoza, Sir William? To accept all the works of creation with humble delight.'

Sir William began to move his mouth which made him look so like a sheep chewing gum that I burst out laughing.

I could see old Spinoza with round spectacles and a white apron polishing a lens and looking at my tigers. On a ground of tall brown tree trunks as close together as a chestnut fence – a few tufts of green at the top. No sky. No blue, no vision. Orchids sticking out of the ground with thick stamens like lingams modelled in raw meat. Beauty, majesty and glory.

'I think she's got the toast better tonight, Bill,' said her ladyship in a little mild soft voice. 'It's not right, of course, but it's edible.'

'Much better,' said Sir William. He took a piece of toast and reflected deeply. 'Yes, distinctly better.'

The green girls began to dance under the silver porches and shake their silver hips. A lot of impudent hussies. And I swallowed down two glasses of nice burgundy.

> Oh land of Beulah
> Where every female delights to give her maiden to her husband
> The Female searches land and sea for gratifications to the
> Male genius, who in return clothes her in gems and gold
> And feeds her with the food of Eden; hence all her beauty beams.

'Won't you have some more wine, Mr Jimson?'

And I saw a face close to mine more beautiful than true. What eyes. Grey like a night sky full of moonlight and pencilled all about with radiating strokes of blue-grey like the shading of petals. Darkening to the outer edges of the iris as if the colour had run there and set. A white as bright as a cloud; lashes, two pen strokes of new bronze, dark as sunrise before a single ray reaches the ground. And what a nose, what lips. Eve. Fearful symmetry.

A voice so sweet that I could not hear the words began to speak. Too full of woman. Too enchanting. I sat with my mouth open, grinning like Circe's pig. Her eyebrows were not plucked. Only brushed and oiled. Feathers of an angel's wing.

'Have you any family, your ladyship, I mean kids?' 'No, I'm afraid not.' 'Of course not.' For children were not born in the land of Beulah. 'You think I haven't done my duty.'

'Yes, of course, your duty is to be rich and happy.' 'But we're not really rich, you know.' Looking at me as if to say, Friend, I give you my confidence. Beautifully done. 'My husband suffered terribly in the slump.' 'Poor chap.' 'Yes, terrible.' 'And yet I suppose it did some good. It made people think about the poor. Round and about.' 'I don't think any government will allow all the unemployment again.' With a serious look full of sympathy and political wisdom. Burnt sugar on the caramel pudding. 'The slump,' said Sir William, 'certainly did much to gush forward social legislation.'

'Like the Great War,' said the Professor.

'Oh, don't speak of that terrible time,' said her leddyship. 'I was only a child, but I still remember the Zeppelins.'

'Yes, the war was perhaps not an unmixed evil,' said Sir William. 'It gave us the League. It taught us to be prepared.'

They made me laugh so I choked and nearly lost half a glass full. It was all so rich. Sir William patted me on the back. 'I should like to do some sunflowers among the tigers,' I said, 'turning towards the tiger's eyes.' 'Yes, yes,' said Sir William. He thought I was drunk. 'A hundred guineas,' I said, 'that's the bargain.' 'Good out of evil,' said her ladyship, in a thoughtful mood. Italian school. Touch of Giorgione. 'How true that is.'

'Yes,' I said, 'like winkles out of the shell. We give you the pin, and the winkle likes it.'

'Oh, but Mr Jimson, speaking seriously, don't you think – in a deeper sense.' And she turned her lovely eyes on me. Spanish school. Religious touch. Spot of Greco.

'You're quite right, M'dam,' I said. 'An expert can do a nice job, even in the worst case. A girl of thirteen in our village, a deaf mute, had a kid, drowned it and swallowed about a pint of spirits of salts. But they cured her and shut her up. She was a bit off, of course, and rather violent.'

'But do you think mad people really suffer?' With a note like a dove that has laid a double egg. Oh the darling, I thought. Oh daughter of Beulah.

> She creates at her will a little moony night and silence
> With spaces of sweet gardens and a tent of elegant beauty
> Closed in by a sandy desert and a night of stars shining,
> And a little tender moon and hovering angels on the wing.

'Do try some more of the sweet, Mr Jimson.' Sweet, sweet, I can cut up a sweet with anybody. 'And some more burnt sugar.' Wonderful land of Beulah. 'You're quite right, your ladyship. The doctors had a wonderful chance with that little girl. Good out of evil.'

'That's another advance we owe to the Great War,' said Sir William. 'Medicine. Especially in mental cases, and plastic surgery.'

'Yes, a time of progress. That kid's mother had been a bit slow too, and a bit deaf and she married a chap who was a bit slower and a bit tubercular. Well, no one else would take her. And they had fourteen children who were all rather more than a bit slow or deaf or crippled or all three, a regular museum. It was a miracle that they grew up at all. Scientific miracle. It's a marvel the babies that doctors manage to save nowadays.'

'A terrible story. But science is advancing all the time, isn't it?'

'Yes, of course, and it will get on quicker still when we have more idiots in the population.'

'Don't you believe in science, Mr Jimson?'

I began to laugh. 'This place is called Beulah. It is a pleasant lovely shadow, where no dispute can come because of those who sleep.'

'I'm afraid you are a cynic, Mr Jimson.'

'No, but I'm not a millionaire. Don't you ever stop being a millionaire, your ladyship. It would spoil your art.'

'But we are poor. Really quite poor. Or we wouldn't live in a flat like this, would we, William? With only one bathroom?'

'Talking of bathrooms, I have something to ask your ladyship. I should like to paint you.' 'Not in my bath.' 'No, in the nude.' 'But I am fearfully thin, Mr Jimson.' 'I want the bony structure to go with the face.' 'I'm afraid my husband wouldn't approve.' 'He needn't look.'

'Goya,' said the Professor, 'painted the Duchess of Alva in the nude and also clothed.'

'I know the pictures,' said Sir William. 'Wonderful work – what brio —'

'Wonderful,' I said. 'The girl has no neck in the nude and no hips in her chemmy. Yet there they are, distinctly something.'

'Don't you like Goya, Mr Jimson?'

'A great man who painted some great stuff – too big for a dinner party. The Queen's nose in the court picture is alone a very serious matter.'

'A lyric artist,' said the Professor,

'On the brass.'

But Goya was making too much noise. The Queen's nose in the court picture began to trumpet at me and the walls of Beulah trembled. 'Don't talk about him,' I said. 'Let me look at your missus and give me some more port. When shall I paint you, M'dam, I'm free tomorrow afternoon.'

'I'm afraid I have an engagement.'

'No, not one you can't put off. And this is a great chance, you understand. Wouldn't you like to be immortal, like Goya's Duchess?'

'Have some more port, Mr Jimson,' said Sir William.

'With pleasure.' But I couldn't help laughing. For I could see he was put out. He was pipped. And he was only a dream in Beulah.

'We must think of your wonderful offer,' said her ladyship.

'Yes,' said Sir William, warming his brandy glass, and his voice was warm again, his voice sleepy. 'It is an honour.'

> And every moment has a couch of gold for soft repose
> And between every two minutes stands a daughter of Beulah
> To feed the sleepers on their couches with maternal care.
> And every minute has an azure tent with silken veils —

I did not feel sleepy. Far from it. Dreams were moving in front of my eyes like festivals of Eden. Land of the rich where the tree of knowledge of good and evil is surrounded with golden rabbit wire.

'Yes,' I said. 'I shall paint you in Beulah, ma'am, and your loom and your tent, it will only cost you a hundred guineas; and fifty for the Professor – cheap for immortality,'

24

When I left for home after dinner, some time after, the Professor was holding one arm and Sir William the other.

But I could not tell whether they were throwing me downstairs or protecting an honoured guest from a dangerous fall. We went home to Elsinore by car, perhaps by taxi, and somewhere on the way we were joined by Nosy Barbon. I think the Professor called for him. They seemed to know each other. And Nosy took me up to bed.

In fact, finding that I had difficulty in staying in the bed which was narrow, and that some of the other guests were irritated against me on account of my being happy while they were in low spirits, he stayed all night.

I was grateful to the boy, but I wished he had let me wallow, especially when, in the morning, I found him much depressed; at a time when I was also depressed.

'What are you worrying about now?' I asked him.

'About m-mother,' he said. 'I expect she sat up all night for me. She's such a worrier.'

'So are you,' I said. 'So it's her own fault.'

'Oh, but m-mother is a t-terrible worrier.'

'I expect she's fond of you,' I said 'Some mothers are fond of their children. It's natural.'

'She's fond of me, but I don't think she likes me very much.'

'A lot of mothers don't like their children much. It's natural. Women are so critical. The personal point of view.'

'She hates me to do any drawing and painting. I was wondering.' And he stopped. I knew that he wanted me to go home with him and speak to his people for him. Tell them he wanted to be an artist. But my head was bursting, my eyes were burning, my legs and arms were shooting like sore teeth, my mouth was like a dirty shoe, and I wanted to get back to work. 'That's enough nonsense,' I said. 'I've wasted enough time and energy on doing the polite – the sooner I can get hold of the Fall and finish it, the better. Especially if I can sell it to Beeder.'

'Perhaps if you could come round with me,' said Nosy.

'Why?' I said severely. 'Why didn't you go home last night?'

'You seemed so ill I was afraid you would fall out of bed and hurt yourself.'

This made me feel more severe still. For I saw that Nosy was inclined to make heroes and sacrifice himself to them. Like my sister Jenny, who nearly killed me a hundred times with exasperation. When I saved up fifteen pounds, out of my lunches, to buy her a set of teeth, since her own had dropped out for want of looking after, she gave the money straight to her husband to be wasted on some new working model. And when I saw her still without teeth and found out what she had done with the money, she said only, 'But I thought you wanted to please me.'

'Of course I did. I didn't starve myself for six months to amuse Robert.'

'But, darling, you did please me; you gave me great happiness – that fifteen pounds was like a gift from God. It was a gift from God since it was your goodness and love that gave it to me and saved poor Robert from despair. He was absolutely desperate when your letter came.'

'He's always desperate. All inventors are desperate unless they have a million in the bank and a tight hold on some managing director. Robert has no more hope of selling his invention than a cockroach of getting into Simpson's cheese.'

'But, darling, only last week he showed the new model to Rackstraws who are one of the biggest firms in the country, and they were delighted with it. It was the most sensitive governor they'd ever seen. And it only wanted a little simplification to be a commercial proposition.'

But I was too disgusted to argue with her. I wanted to cry. And then, of course, she wanted money. She had been too proud to beg from me at first, but love soon changed all that. Mother and I clubbed together and we raised a few pounds. All my savings went in those three years. Before I was married and had a natural protector of my bank book. And it made no difference that the new model of Ranken's Regulator was a great success. Not to their happiness. Because it simply proved to Ranken that he ought to get ten thousand a year and a factory for himself. And Jenny, of course, began to see that he'd never be satisfied. She began to feel what life was like when you live it with a man with a grievance. Like being swallowed by a very big lazy shark, who can't stop if he wants to, because his teeth all point one way, towards the dark.

And, of course, mother and I never got our money back. Even when Ranken began to draw an income. He didn't pay debts. He thought the whole world couldn't pay him enough to make up for its injustice to him. He went on spending everything he could raise on new models. But we went on lending money to Jenny. Because she was devoted. All of us danced on Ranken's string because Jenny was devoted. It made me so hot even to remember it that my head began to fry. And I shouted at Nosy, 'Here, what do you think you're after? Didn't I tell you to go home?'

'Oh ye-yes,' said Nosy, alarmed. 'It was all my own f-fault.'

'And haven't I told you a hundred times not to come chasing after me – let me alone, and get on with your job.'

'Oh ye-yes,' said Nosy, looking as if he was longing for a rabbit hole into which to dive.

'And haven't I told you that if you don't win that scholarship next month, you deserve to be pushed down the nearest drain?'

'Oh ye-yes,' said Nosy, so terrified that he had shrunk down about half size, except the nose, which was double, being full of anxiety.

'Then git-go,' I roared, 'and never let me see you again till next year.'

'B-but you will come and say something to mother,' said Nosy. And, in fact I saw that I had made a little mistake. Nosy was frightened all right, out of his wits, but not out of his character. Which was just the same, only more so. Devoted and pig-headed. As if hammering made it tougher.

'You see,' said he, greatly excited, 'it would make such a lot of difference if you spoke for me. Because mother knows you're a famous artist.'

'Then she knows wrong. How does she know?'

'I told her.'

'How do you know?'

'Mr Plant told me first.'

'If you don't get that scholarship your parents ought to throw you out. After all they've done for you. And you ought to be shot for a fool, which is worse than murder. Only four more years scratching at the books and a nice government job for the rest of your life. Four years half work in exchange for fifty or sixty of no work on a regular income and a pension after. Made for life. Not another worry in the world.'

'But I *can't* be a government official – I want to be an artist.'

'Do what you like when you get that job. But make sure of it first. How can you be an artist without money? Why, look at me. I've been painting for fifty years, and at this moment I don't even possess brushes or paint. No, you can't go in for art without money from somewhere. Art is like roses – it's a rich feeder.' I talked quite brilliantly for a long time. But at the end of it, there was Nosy, with his red watery eyes, and his ugly face looking so ugly, and worried and miserable and obstinate and devoted, that I couldn't resist him, and I let him take me back to his home.

Neat little terrace house with a little front garden. Fifteen feet by ten. With four beds about the size of frypans and a piece of crazy paving just big enough to stand on.

Nosy had a key and took me in. Parlour in chintz with a good mahogany table. Bookcase of Dickens and Thackeray. Couple of French bronzes on the mantelpiece. Gilt clock. Brass grate. Pictures – family enlargements. Death of Nelson. Trade union card with religious and royal emblems. Mr Barbon came in. Middle-sized walrus with a squeezed-up face and a head like a wedge of cheddar. Forget-me-not-eye in a couple of tit nests. A bit stooped. Blue suit with tight sleeves. About 1912. Hands like coal grabs. 'How do you do, sir? It is very kind of you to come.' 'Not at all.' 'I know your time is valuable.' 'Not a bit.' 'A famous gentleman like you, sir.' 'Not just yet.'

'But it's about my boy, Harry. My Minnie is a bit worried. You know how it is with mothers, and Harry's the youngest.' 'I know, I've had two boys myself' 'Oh yes,' he said, not noticing what I'd said. 'Oh yes, it's hard on the mother. Our eldest went into the Air Force – got killed in an accident.' 'A lot of accidents everywhere. Babies drinking out of kettles, children going under lorries.' 'Yes sir, we're not the only ones. We oughtn't to complain, really. But of course you know what mothers are.' 'I know, I've had two.' 'Oh yes, of course,' he said, not hearing a word I said. 'Yes, of course, but Harry being the youngest, and he's been such a good son. Clever, too. All his teachers thought no end of Harry. They said he was sure of a scholarship. This next September. An Oxford one. It would make the boy's fortune, you might say.'

And he went on telling me what a nice, clever, good boy Harry was. And how he had always been his mother's comfort. But now she was worrying. I knew what women were.

Somebody came in at the front door, and Mr Barbon turned himself out of his chair and turned himself out of the door. Like a crane on a turntable. His arms were long enough. Going up and down. And the hands closing from all round like iron grabs. The door handle disappeared quite slowly, but you expected to see it come right off. Soft muttering outside like an old-fashioned donkey engine. And a woman's voice saying that she wouldn't, and she didn't. Mrs Barbon came in. Small and soft, neat nose and smooth white hair. Pretty face once but too short in the neck. She gave me a look as if she would like to poison me, and Mr Barbon said, 'This is Mr Jimson, mother,' gave her a little push to make her do the polite. But she went back a bit and said, 'So you said,' keeping her eyes on me. Barbon swung round one of his grabs and pulled her sleeve. 'Mr Jimson is a friend of Harry's, mother. He's the famous artist.' 'So you say, Tom. Do leave me alone.' 'Perhaps we'd better sit down,' said Mr Barbon. 'I don't want to sit down,' said Mrs Barbon; and then she said to me, 'I think you might have let the boy alone, Mr Johnson. Instead of spoiling his chances.' 'I beg your pardon, Mrs Barbon.' 'No, you don't care. Now you've got hold of him. You just turn him round your finger how you like. Ruining his whole life and breaking his father's heart.' 'Well, Mrs Barbon, I didn't —' 'And I may as well tell you I think a lot of artists ought to be stopped. The government ought to do something about it.' Well, I was sorry for the poor girl. It was a terrible thing for her to see her only darling suddenly fly off to the devil, just when he was going to make her proud and happy for her old age. Who would be a mother? 'I quite agree, Mrs Barbon,' I said, 'it's a bad business.' 'Then why do you go on at it for?'

'But, mother,' said old Barbon.

'Please let me say one word, Tom. Without interrupting all the time. I think it's a shame, Mr Johnson, or whatever your name is. I think that a decent man ought to be ashamed to get hold of a boy like Harry who anybody can see is not fit to look after himself and young for his age and keep him running about on his errands when he might be doing his work and working up an honest Christian job and a proper life.'

'Quite right, Mrs Barbon. I —'

'Because you'd better know I don't call this a proper job for anyone that respects himself or wants to respect himself.'

'Quite true, Mrs Barbon. I've advised Harry several times to —'

'It isn't a job at all. It's a mean swindle by lazy good-for-nothings and won't works.'

'I told Harry several times,' I said, 'that he ought to be working for his scholarship.'

'And what sort of living will he make as an artist?'

'None at all,' I said. 'I don't suppose he has any talent whatever.'

'That's all you know about it,' said Mrs Barbon. 'He took the art prize only last year and he got two bronze medals from the Art Society,' crushing me for my blindness to Nosy's genius.

'Even then, Mrs Barbon, an artist's life is very uncertain. It would be far better for the boy to get his scholarship first.'

'Then why have you stopped him working all these weeks – his masters say he spends half his time dodging round your studio or going to galleries and looking at pictures.'

'I didn't know —'

'And then last night – never coming home at all.'

'I was taken ill and he very kindly —'

'All I can say is that if you want him, you'd better take him,' said Mrs Barbon, trembling all over. 'I don't want any more to do with a son of mine that goes about with such people and breaks his father's heart.'

'But, mother,' said old Barbon.

'Will you be quiet, Tom? I know you want to smooth everything down and smooth it up as if it didn't matter. But I say, it does matter if the boy ruins his whole life and turns into a nasty dirty swindler and good-for-nothing and breaks your heart after all you've done for him.'

'But, m-mother,' said Nosy, going over to her, 'it's not t-true that artists are s-s-swindlers.'

'Do let me alone, Harry,' said the woman, closing her eyes as if exhausted by unreasonable interruptions. 'What do you know about it? Of course, nothing I say will make any difference – I know that already. You'll just go your own way. And treat your poor father like dirt. I don't mind. So if you don't choose to give any kind of explanation, Mr Johnson, or even say you're sorry for what you've done, perhaps you would go and leave us alone. As for Harry, he can go with you if he likes. But if he does, I don't want him back again.'

'But, mother —' said old Barbon. Mrs Barbon then left the room, shutting the door behind her very carefully, and Mr Barbon apologized for her. 'She's a bit upset, Mr Jimson. Harry being the only one left. And, of course, we don't really feel like that about artists. It's an honourable trade. Only we were wondering if Harry would do any good at it.'

'Probably not, Mr Barbon. Very few people do any good at any of the arts. And I haven't seen any sign of genius in Harry. What he wants to do is to get his scholarship. That's safe.'

'S-s-safe,' said Nosy, hissing like a snake.

Mr Barbon then thanked me very politely for my visit and I came away. And Nosy came with me. But I gave him a lecture about the way he was treating his mother. 'She's right,' I said. 'If you go on like this, you'll ruin your own life and hers. You're breaking her heart as it is.'

But Nosy only looked more obstinate. What did he care about breaking his mother's heart. Not much more than a runaway horse cares for a shop window. Which he doesn't see, anyhow.

'B-but she's so unreasonable,' he said. 'If nobody is allowed to be an artist, art would stop.'

'Not a bit of it,' I said. 'You can't stop art. You just try, that's all. You'll always have amateurs. That is, everybody.'

'But are they any g-good?'

'Yes, the professional ones are good, the others are awful.'

'How do you become a professional amateur?'

'You give all your time to the job, and even then it's not enough.'

'Then what's the d-difference?'

'A big difference. The amateur has cash in the bank and goes on having it when he's a professional. That's what I tell you. Get some cash in the bank and then you can go in for art and be as bad as you like. You'll still be happy. Because the worse you are, the better pleased you'll be with yourself, and you'll be able to afford a nice little wife and nice little babies and nice little parties and nice little friends, and you'll get into some nice little society and get a whole lot of nice little compliments from all the other nice people.'

'But I don't want to be s-s-safe,' said Nosy.

'That's because you've had too much of safety. But it's not so safe as you think – safety. And when you've lost it. you can't get it back. Run along now and get down those books. And I tell you what, I'll teach you all about art.'

'What?' said Nosy.

'Yes,' I said. 'You get that scholarship and I'll teach you all about art. That is, all that one person can teach another, which isn't much.'

'You really mean it, Mr Jimson?'

'On my honour. Or I'd better say, on your honour.'

The boy seized me by both hands. 'Oh, Mr Jimson, how c-can I thank you?'

'We'll see about that when you've had your instruction. Now, off you go, and tell your ma I sent you.'

He turned away and actually ran towards home.

25

I turned up at Ellam Street and made for Elsinore. My job, I thought, is to get that picture out of Mrs Coker's grip – to get her out of the studio. Sir William must see the thing soon or he'll forget all about it.

And I was worried about the picture itself. Of course, a picture is always a worry. It's worse than a child for getting itself into trouble, and breaking your heart. But my recollection of the Fall was that Eve's legs were all wrong. You don't want a lot of agitation in the rising lines when the horizontal planes are so active. As far as I remember, I thought, those legs are too rococo for a landscape which ought to be as massive as rocks. Original forms. Solid ideas.

On the other hand, it seemed to me that the general organization was not bad. I had a feeling at the back of my notions that it would be better than I expected. I must have a look at the thing, I thought, if it costs me a black eye.

Now the truth was that, though I had sent letters to Mrs Coker every day, and even managed, on one dark evening, to put three rats through a side window, I hadn't yet taken the last decisive step. My idea was, if she wouldn't go by persuasion, to remove my picture and then take the windows and door off, and possibly some of the roof. Make a ruin of the place. And when she had been blown out, and rained out, I would go back again. I'd often lived in ruins before.

And I had formed, by careful observation, a pretty good idea of Mrs Coker's habits. She went shopping at any time she fancied, and she was usually away for an hour. So I only had to watch her off the premises, and then get to work with a screwdriver. And it had better be today, I thought, if I'm going to sell the Fall. I have no time to waste. I must close with the Professor at once before he gets thrown out again, or his Sir William has a fit. And the Fall will certainly need touching up, even if I pass those legs.

But I had bad luck. I waited there all that afternoon by the Eagle, and still Mrs Coker remained in garrison. I saw her now and then empty a bucket into the dustbin or throw a piece of coal at a cat, but she did not go shopping. Then it began to rain chandeliers in the afternoon sun; big drops which went through the thin spots in my overcoat like shot through blotting paper. And when I was trying to take cover against the side wall, down came young Barbon, fizzing like a ginger-beer bottle. He annoyed me. 'What the hell,' I said. 'Didn't you swear to go home and leave art alone and do some real work?'

'Oh, but Mr Jimson, I did work. And you know it's my holidays now. Since last week.'

'Holidays. The only chance you'll ever get to do your own job. As it ought to be done. My boy Tom always worked in the summer holidays. It's the best time to work because there's no masters to waste your time.'

'I d-did work, Mr Jimson. But I saw you going down Greenbank, and I thought you were going to paint on the Fall.'

'I wish I could paint on the Fall,' I said 'But I have to wait till my lady guest goes out before I can even see the damn thing.' And like a fool, I told him all about the Cokers. I am always inclined to talk too much to ugly boys, because they are so modest and so keen on everything and because they ask such a lot of questions. Of course, as soon as I explained the case to young Barbon, he got so excited that he could hardly speak. He was so sympathetic that I wanted to jump into the river. I like a little sympathy in the right place, but a lot of sympathy always makes me feel as if I had lost my clothes and didn't know where to hide. And when I had explained my plan for removing the doors and windows, he rushed off to borrow a hatchet and screwdrivers and wanted to start at once. I had to tell him that this matter was more serious than that. 'There mustn't be any violence,' I said, 'or the thing wouldn't be legal. First we have to take formal possession, and then we can remove the doors and windows. That is the way bailiffs do it. But we must establish possession first so that if Mrs Coker calls in the police, we shall be able to make them think we thought we were on the right side of the law. We've got to have a case.'

But Nosy went on getting so excited and stammered so much that I could hardly speak. And so I began to get in a state and I should have ended in committing some foolish crime if Mrs Coker, about five o'clock, hadn't come out in her bonnet, with a string bag and Cokey's umbrella, and hurried away to the shops.

Nosy and I were at work in less than a minute. Nosy started on the windows outside with the screwdriver. But I went in to get the picture down. And there was Cokey in a blue pinafore like a landslide, perched on the side of a chair and knitting a pair of baby's drawers. 'Hullo, Cokey,' I said. 'How are you now?'

'I wish I wasn't anything or anywhere either. You better look out, Mr Jimson.'

'Your mother's off to the shops, I saw her this minute.'

'Yes, but she might come back. She's got a way of coming back. Especially since last week. What did you go and write those letters for?'

'Why does she think that I wrote them?' I said. For I was annoyed. Women are so unreasonable. They're always jumping to conclusions.

'Well, you did. Didn't you?'

'Your mother had better be careful making statements like that. Which she couldn't prove. They're slander.'

'Well, don't write any more,' said Cokey. 'They only put her in a temper, and then she takes it out of me. And I've got enough on my plate as it is. The time you put the rats in, she broke her umbrella over me.'

'Your mother is going to get a lesson,' I said. For I could see Nosy at work on the window hinges from the outside where Cokey couldn't see him. 'And I've come to claim my property.'

I began to take down the dining-room chairs piled against the sheet at the end of the room.

'If you're looking for your picture,' said Cokey, 'it isn't there.'

'Where is it then?' I gave a dive and pulled the sheet on one side. There was nothing behind but the boards. I was so surprised that I felt quite queer. As if someone had kicked me in the stomach.

'Where is it then?' I said. 'If the landlord took it, I'll go to law. I'll have damages off him. It's work in hand. Even a bailiff can't touch work in hand.'

'It wasn't the landlord. It was mother.'

'Then it's robbery. What's she done with it?'

'She cut it up and mended the roof with it. Why, didn't you notice . . .'

I looked up to listen. And you could hear the rain rattling on the canvas like shot on a drum.

'You know how the boards used to leak,' said Cokey, 'but of course she had to have the canvas tarred over – it's made a lovely job.'

I felt as if the top of my skull was floating off, I was quite feeble. To lose the Fall like this, suddenly; it was like being told your home and family had fallen down a hole in the ground.

I looked at Cokey. There she was like a blue bag tied round the neck with string, with a white wood knob for a face. Calm as you please. I took my breath and said, 'You thought I'd done two years' work on that picture to get it ready for the roof?'

'No,' said Cokey. 'But I didn't care. Not after mother had talked to me for a bit. If mother wanted to cut me into slices with a saw knife, she'd only have to talk to me for a bit and I'd go down on my knees and ask her to get on with the job. You don't know mother's talk. It's chronic.'

'That picture was worth thousands of pounds, and I had a buyer for it. I'll run your mother in for five thousand pounds. The spiteful old devil.'

'Don't you call mother names. She's had a hard time and don't you forget it.'

'What's that got to do with my picture?'

'What's the good of pictures to poor mum? Pictures never did anything for her. Pictures never gave her what she'd a right to expect, did they?'

'What about my rights, Coker?'

'You don't need any rights. You're a man. But you won't be, if mother catches you here again.'

'You've changed, Cokey, you used to think a lot of my pictures.' For I was still feeble. I really thought I should cry. I didn't know how I could live without the Fall.

'Changed,' said Cokey. 'Well, you've only got to look at me.'

'I mean in your feelings.' My legs were so weak that I was sentimental. Cokey's bosom would probably have felt like old tins and door knobs, but I was ready to fall on it.

'My feelings,' said Cokey. 'I feel like I want to do murder or something, and so would you if you'd taken about a barrel full of pink pills and pints of oil and jumped off tables and run around carrying trunks on your head and fallen downstairs and all for nothing. Well, I should have known. God had something up his sleeve, ever since Willie made his first pass at me behind the church. It was too good to be permanent. I'm not complaining. But if I should have an accident with a bus or a traction engine, don't let anybody send flowers. Send along a pickaxe to bash my head in and make a good job of it. Put me in a sausage machine and can me into cat's meat and write Bitch, second quality, on the lid.' 'Why, whoever called you a bitch, Cokey?' For I was still feeling soft. 'They'd better not, but they think it. And the one that don't think it, laugh.' 'After all, Cokey old girl, this little development of yours isn't so very uncommon in the neighbourhood. I should think there must be half a dozen young ladies in the same temporary difficulty down Ellam Street alone, on any day of the month.' 'And you think that makes it any better – to get mixed up with that lot of dirty sluts.' 'They can't say anything.' 'Oh, can't they, the worse, the more. And think! You can hear them from here.' 'Well, I don't see you need mind what a lot of nasty-natured women say or think about you.' 'Oh go away, do, Mr Jimson. You men make my guts wind. And there isn't room.'

26

And just then Nosy came in by the back door to tell me that Mrs Coker was coming in by the front one. So I went away by the middle window. Nosy followed half a minute later with an ear like scarlet fever. But he didn't seem to notice it. 'I g-got f-four windows off,' he said. 'and hid them in the ditch. D-did you get the picture?'

'No,' I said, 'the picture is kaput. The Fall is finished.' And I told him what Mrs Coker had done to my picture. And the boy was so astonished that I thought he would have a fit. 'I can't b-believe it,' he said. 'N-no, I can't believe it,' and his grief was real. It seemed that he had given his heart to that picture. 'It's awful,' he said. 'How did she d-dare? The h-horrible old b-brute.' And he began to get angry. For he was truly suffering. He had lost his first love. His nose was as red as beetroot, and his voice sounded like a little dog shut into a cellar. 'It's a c-crime,' he said. 'It's t-terrible to think of.' He was young for a real grief. Irreparable loss.

It was raining warm dishwater out of dirty rags, and when I took off my hat because it was dripping down my neck, a quart fell into my waistcoat.

'B-but what can you expect of p-people like that,' said Nosy, getting angrier and barking at the stones. 'They don't d-deserve to have artists. We B-british are a l-lot of b-bloody fffphilistines, we aren't f-fit to h-have g-great artists born among us.'

'Go on, Nosy,' I said. 'Blow up the British like a true Briton. Blackguard them as much as you like. They're old. They don't expect anything better. They're used to it.'

'It's true,' said Nosy. 'They d-don't d-deserve to have great artists.'

'Nobody does,' I said, 'but they go on getting them whether they like them or not.'

For the fact is I was beginning to feel very lively. You might say, gay. I couldn't believe it at first. And so I went on being dejected.

'A wonderful picture like that,' said Nosy. 'P-put on the r-roof.'

'A serious thing for me,' I said. But I almost burst out laughing at Nosy's indignation, and I decided to give way to my gaiety. It's not an easy thing to do when you have a real grievance, and if I had been fifty years younger I shouldn't have done it. But for some time now I had been noticing that on the whole, a man is wise to give way to gaiety, even at the expense of a grievance. A good grievance is highly enjoyable, but like a lot of other pleasures, it is bad for the liver. It affects the digestion and injures the sweetbread. So I gave way and laughed.

'W-what is it?' said Nosy, quite terrified. He thought I was going mad with grief.

'I was laughing,' I said.

'You are too g-good, Mr Jimson, too n-noble. You oughtn't to f-forgive a crime like that – a crime against s-s-civilization. I'd like to cut that old woman's throat. I'd like to cut the whole B-british throat. The d-dirty fffphilistines.'

'Not exactly noble, Nosy,' I said. 'For it's dangerous to be thought noble, when you're only being sensible. It causes fatty degeneration of the judgement. The fact is, I was sick of that god-damned picture.'

'It was the f-finest picture I ever saw,' said Nosy, getting angry with me. 'You m-mustn't s-say such things.'

'I never knew how I hated it,' I said, 'till now. I've disliked all my pictures, but I never hated one so much as the Fall.'

'Mr J-jimson,' said Nosy. 'No p-please – it's not a j-joke.' The poor boy was in agony. I was blaspheming against his faith.

'But what I do like,' I said, 'is starting new ones.' And the very notion made me feel full of smiles. The vision of the nice smooth canvas in front of me, say the Ruffiano, newly primed in white, and then the first strokes of the brush. How lovely the stuff is when you've just put it down. While it's still all alive and before it digs and sinks and fades. Paint. Lovely paint. Why, I could rub my nose in it or lick it up for breakfast. I mean, of course, paint that doesn't mean anything except itself. The spiritual substance. The pure innocent song of some damn fool angel that doesn't know even the name of God.

'I love starting, Nosy,' I said, 'but I don't like going on. The trouble with me is that I hate work, that's why I'm an artist. I never could stand work. But you can't get away from it in this fallen world. The curse of Adam.'

'N-no, p-please, Mr J-jimson. You know you have s-sacrificed your whole life to art, and no one works harder. I've seen you myself working all day and never even s-stopping to eat.'

'I was probably altering something or taking something out, that's a way of starting new. But not a good way. It only leads to more trouble. More problems, more work. No, you want to start clear, with a clean canvas, and a bright new shining idea of vision or whatever you call the thing. A sort of coloured music in the mind.'

And the very words made me grin all down my back. Certainly an artist has no right to complain of his fate. For he has great pleasures. To start new pictures. Even the worst artist that ever was, even a one-eyed mental deficient with the shakes in both hands who sets out to paint the chicken-house, can enjoy the first stroke. Can think, By God, look what I've done. A miracle. I have transformed a chunk of wood, canvas, etc., into a spiritual fact, an eternal beauty. I am God. Yes, the beginning, the first stroke of a picture, or a back fence, must be one of the keenest pleasures open to mankind. It's certainly the greatest that an artist can have. It's also the only one. And it doesn't last long – usually about five minutes. Before the first problem shows its devil face. And then he's in hell for the next month or six months or whatever it may be. But I didn't tell Nosy why I felt so cheerful. He wouldn't have understood. He would have been shocked. And it is easy to offend the faith of the little ones. It also does a lot of harm.

'A m-m-masterpiece,' said Nosy, flipping a pear-drop off his cut-water. He was getting hysterical. Everything at once was too much.

'Talk sense, Nosy,' I said. 'It wasn't even finished.'

'A m-m-m-masterpiece,' said Nosy. As if I had been trying to strangle his first-born. Which was just what I was doing. 'Go on, Nosy,' I said. 'It couldn't be. Nothing is a masterpiece – a real masterpiece – till it's about two hundred years old. A picture is like a tree or a church, you've got to let it grow into a masterpiece. Same with a poem or a new religion. They begin as a lot of funny words. Nobody knows whether they're all nonsense or a gift from heaven. And the only people who think anything of 'em are a lot of cranks or crackpots, or poor devils who don't know enough to know anything. Look at Christianity. Just a lot of floating seeds to start with, all sorts of seeds. It was a long time before one of them grew into a tree big enough to kill the rest and keep the rain off. And it's only when the tree has been cut into planks and built into a house and the house has got pretty old and about fifty generations of ordinary lumpheads who don't know a work of art from a public convenience, have been knocking nails in the kitchen beams to hang hams on, and screwing hooks in the walls for whips and guns and photographs and calendars and measuring the children on the window frames and chopping out a new cupboard under the stairs to keep the cheese and murdering their wives in the back room and burying them under the cellar flags, that it begins even to feel like a real religion. And when the whole place is full of dry rot and ghosts and old bones and the shelves are breaking down with old wormy books that no one could read if they tried, and the attic floors are bulging through the servants' ceilings with old trunks and top-boots and gasoliers and dressmaker's dummies and ball frocks and doll's-houses and pony saddles and blunderbusses and parrot cages and uniforms and love letters and jugs without handles and bridal pots decorated with forget-me-nots and a piece out at the bottom, that it grows into a real old faith, a masterpiece which people can really get something out of, each for himself. And then, of course, everybody keeps on saying that it ought to be pulled down at once, because it's an insanitary nuisance.'

'I d-don't care w-what anyone says,' said Nosy, still angry with me. 'It's a s-shame. It's a wicked s-shame.' He was shivering and steaming like a sheep just out of the dip. It was his first great sorrow. Without remedy. And the rain was coming down like soda-water bubbles out of a new cottonwool in tufts. It fell slowly in a neat pattern and didn't make a sound. We came to the end of Greenbank and stopped. Nosy looked round as if to say, 'Where shall we go?' But I hadn't the price of a beer, and so there was nowhere to go.

'The f-finest picture,' said Nosy. And he looked as if he might cry at any moment. He hadn't got used to the nevermore feeling.

'The rain's over,' I said, and we turned back. 'No,' I said, 'it's a providence,' and I pulled out the top of my trousers in front to let the water run off my belly. 'That picture has had me by the throat for the last two years. Choking my life out – the worst enemy I ever had.' And as we came to the end of Greenbank we turned back again. The little rain-drops were smaller and closer. They were falling like a cold stream; slow and white which was wetter than water. It was as if the air had turned into soda bubbles. The sun came through like through a frosted window, and the sky was like the top of the sea to a fish's eye; Roman candles and blue fire. There was more water in my boots than outside.

'B-but why should everything and everybody be always against real g-greatness,' said Nosy, 'real j-j-genius?'

'Well,' I said, 'suppose you were just sitting down in a quiet corner behind the dustbin with a jug of beer and a wasp came and stung you on the bottom, how would you like the wasp?'

'Look at Keats and S-shelley, and Hopkins and S-s-cézanne and Van H-h-gogh and you.'

'And me,' I said. 'What about me?' I was upset. To get a smack like that just when I was feeling gay.

'L-look at the way they t-treat you – it's awful,' said Nosy. 'You haven't even anywhere to live – it's aw-awful – it's t-terrible.' And Nosy really was in tears, or perhaps it was only the rain down his beak which made him make such comic faces.

And I felt almost like crying myself just because he was crying. Over my own woes. And yet, as I say, I was in particularly good spirits. There, you see, I said to myself, talk to anybody in a friendly way and in a half a minute he'll be pitying you and then you'll be pitying yourself and damning the world and all the rest of the nonsense. Getting in the worst possible state. And you can say good-bye to work for another week. And I flew out at Nosy. 'What the devil do you mean, young man? Who's treated me how? What's terrible? If you had a little more sense and decent feeling,' I said, 'you'd realize that I've been very well treated. Quite as well as I deserve. Why, I haven't an enemy in the world, except, of course, that blasted picture. But a special providence in the shape of Ma Coker has now delivered me of that. At least I hope so. I daresay the snake will need another knock or two. Cut it in four pieces and it will try to bite and spit poison in your eye at one end and tie itself round you at the other. That picture was a curse to me. It left me no freedom to paint. To paint,' I said, and my fingers closed on a brush and executed a sweet stroke, from left to right, my favourite movement.

And all at once I knew why I was sick of the Fall. And I knew what I wanted to do. That blue-grey shape on the pink, The tower. The whatever it was, very round and heavy. Something like a gasometer, at full stretch without its muzzle. Or possibly an enamel coffee-pot. And chrome-yellow things like Egyptian columns or leeks or dumb-bells or willows or brass candlesticks, in front; and to the left, also round but much smoother, a fat pillar or glass rolling-pin coming out of green waves or mountains or crumpled baize – very dark green with a broken surface. And a strong recession. A dark red below, curving up towards the right, a beach or range of mountains or German sausage. The pink, rather misty, volcanic eruption or cottage wallpaper. And a swag or red across the top left, clouds of volcanic smoke, or a plush curtain. All very solid. But not hard. Three-dimensional. With great attention to texture. 'And besides,' I said to Nosy,

'I've got a far better thing all ready.' It wasn't all ready, but I felt that it was going to be ready in five minutes. 'All ready in my eye.'

'A b-better thing,' said Nosy, in a doubtful voice. Like a child whose oldest boat has just gone down the drain, when you tell him that you've got something much nicer in the cupboard. 'But it wouldn't be the F-fall.'

'Yes,' I said, for why shouldn't I call it the Fall. 'It might as well be that as anything else. The blue tower could be Adam and the red wave Eve, and the yellow things the serpents.' 'Yes,' I said, 'it's going to be the Fall, only much better. Much solider. I've learnt a lot since I started that last Fall. And I know what was wrong with it. It wasn't immediate enough. It didn't hit you hard enough. It wasn't solid enough.'

'S-solid enough?' said Nosy. 'No,' I said, 'what was the Fall after all. The discovery of the solid hard world, good and evil. Hard as rocks and sharp as poisoned thorns. And also the way to make gardens.'

'G-gardens?'

'Gardens. Adam's work. You have to make the bloody things and pile up the rocks and keep the roses in beds. But you don't get the thorns in your tender parts, by accident – you get them in your fingers, on purpose, and like it, because a garden, as old Randypole Blake would say, is a spiritual being. Why,' I said, quite surprised by my own eloquence in inventing all this stuff, 'it happens every day. It's the old old story. Boys and girls fall in love, that is, they are driven mad and go blind and deaf and see each other not as human animals with comic noses and bandy legs and voices like frogs, but as angels so full of shining goodness that like hollow turnips with candles put into them, they seem miracles of beauty. And the next minute the candles shoot out sparks and burn their eyes. And they seem to each other like devils, full of spite and cruelty. And they will drive each other mad unless they have grown some imagination. Even enough to laugh.'

'I-m-m-m,' said Nosy.

'Imagination, understanding. To see behind the turnips, to enter into each other's minds. My first girl had a face like a pig, and only one eye. She was a trifle soft too, and about twenty years older than I was at fifteen. She used to clean out the pigsty and byres, and she never washed. When we had our first quarrel, I called her bitch and bastard, which was all quite true. But she chased me half a mile with a fork. And I thought I should never forgive her. At fifteen I had a lot of dignity. But when I needed her again, I thought things over and I understood that the woman, though a pig to look at, and worse to smell, had some feelings of her own. Even some self-respect. So I went and apologized and gave her a present of some of my mother's flowers. And she burst into tears and said I was an angel. The Fall had given her imagination, too, and we made it up and were very happy several times and had some more fork fights and made it up again till my uncle caught us and had her sent to an institution where she pretty soon died. She was used to sleeping in ditches and middens, and she couldn't bear comfort. But she gave me my first taste of real knowledge, the knowledge of good and evil, heaven and hell, and she taught me that love doesn't grow on the trees like apples in Eden – it's something you have to make. And you must use your imagination to make it, too, just like anything else. It's all work, work. The curse of Adam. But if he doesn't work, he doesn't get anything, even love. He just tumbles about in hell and bashes himself and burns himself and stabs himself. The fallen man – nobody's going to look after him. The poor bastard is free – a free and responsible citizen. The Fall into freedom. Yes, I might call it the Fall into Freedom,'

'F-f-free,' said Nosy, with his eyes starting out of his head. For he didn't know what I was talking about.

'Yes,' I said. 'Free to cut his bloody throat, if he likes, or understand the bloody world, if he likes, and cook his breakfast with hell-fire, if he likes, and construct for himself a little heaven of his own, if he likes, all complete with a pig-faced angel and every spiritual pleasure, including the joys of love; or also, of course, he can build himself a little hell full of pig-faced devils and all material miseries including the joys of love and enjoy in it such tortures of the damned that he will want to burn himself alive a hundred times a day, but won't be able to do it because he knows it will give such extreme pleasure to all his friends. He's in hell, that is, real hell – material hell, nailed to the everlasting fire with a red-hot clag; and his kicks and wriggles are enough to make a cat laugh. In fact, they are the chief amusement of all the other citizens in the same position.'

'The f-f-fall into f-f-f,' said Nosy, trembling all over and twitching his nose like a rabbit in front of a doubtful lettuce.

I threw the water out of my hat and once more it fell down the opening of my waistcoat. This was due to carelessness. But I was so pleased with the enjoyments of genius which to angels look like torment and insanity, that I said to myself, gurgle, oh navel; freeze, you belly; trickle and shiver, old spout, I haven't time to worry about your troubles. Down, slaves, and weep. For I am the king of the castle. 'Yes,' I said, 'the Fall into freedom, into the real world, among the everlasting forms, the solid. Solid as the visions of the ancient man. And that's what I'm going to do in this new Fall. Adam like a rock walking, and Eve like a mountain bringing forth, with sweat like fiery lava, and the trees shall stand like souls pent up in metal; cut bronze and silver and gold. With leaves like emerald and jade, cut and engraved with everlasting patterns sharp as jewels, as crystals, and the sun like a ball of solid fire, turned on a lathe.'

'Yes, yes,' said Nosy. 'I s-see, a kind of dream.'

'Dream be damned,' I said. 'It's got to be real.'

'But will it l-look real?'

'To hell with looks,' I said. 'Nobody ever saw the real – but you can feel it – By God, I feel it now. For the first time in about two years since that bloody picture first got hold of me. Yes, I feel it – the solid forms of the imagination.'

'Solid,' cried Nosy. 'Imaginmation.'

We had come to the other end of Greenbank. And it was raining scullery taps. Out of a sky like a battle. Great jagged lumps and balloons of water, with oyster domes and a green splash. We stood among fountains, under waterfalls. And Nosy looked round thinking, 'Where are we going to?' 'You'd better go home, Nosy,' I said. 'You're wet.'

But he knew I couldn't go anywhere. So we turned back.

'Solid imagination,' said Nosy. 'Yes, I s-s-s-see.'

'What do you sus-see,' I said. For I felt I had been talking too much. Dangerous to talk too much about your work. It fixes it. It nails it down. And then it bleeds. It begins to die. 'What I'd like to sus-see is a studio – and paints and brushes – in fact, some cash.'

'I s-see the idea,' said Nosy, giving a loud sneeze.

'How can you see an idea?' I said. 'You must be a clever chap. Can you see the price of a pint in my pocket?'

'I sus-see what you mean.'

'You must be a bloody conjurer. I didn't mean anything —'

'But Mr J-jimson, you s-said you see —'

'I see my picture. In fact, I don't sus-see it. I only imagine it, and probably I'm imagining all wrong. But what the devil, you're wet through. You'll catch cold. And then what about that scholarship – time you went home. Good-bye, Nosy.'

'B-but, Mr J-jimson,' and I thought he would grab me by the coat. 'You *did* mean something else – you were talking about the truth – the real —'

Yes, I thought, I knew I was talking too much. And I said 'That's enough, Nosy, or too much. You cut along home to your mother and change your socks. It's opening time, and I rather think I see Mr Ollier going into the Eagle.'

'And you said about religion,' said Nosy, making eyes at me as if I was a slot machine with the wisdom of the world at a penny a shot. 'You go home to your mammy where you belong,' I said, 'and get on with the books. Or you'll come to a bad end.' And I gave him a push and made a dart for it into the Eagle.

It wasn't Ollier. But Bert Swope was there and he stood me a pint in exchange for rude remarks about the state of my boots, trousers, coat, etc., and the way I smelt. I like Bert. He's always a tonic when one has been talking too much.

27

When I went back to Elsinore that evening, there was the Professor waiting for me. Sir William had made an offer – one hundred to three hundred guineas. I told him at once that all I wanted was an advance of a hundred pounds. For a new studio and materials. 'I have the best thing I ever did all ready. It only needs putting down.'

The Professor looked like a judge; judicious. This meant that he didn't know what to say.

'I'd even got an option on the canvas. Twelve by fifteen.'

The Professor looked like an angel. Illuminated. This meant that he saw how to wriggle out of a difficulty. 'It's a big thing,' he said.

'Big in every way,' I said. 'The very biggest.'

'I'm afraid Sir William wouldn't have room for it. What he really had in his mind was something of the same nature as that magnificent thing at Mr Hickson's.'

'What, the bath?'

'He would give three hundred guineas for anything of that quality.'

'I haven't painted stuff like that for fifteen years.'

'You don't know perhaps where one might be found. Perhaps one of your early patrons might care to sell.'

'I hadn't any early patrons – except Hickson and one or two speculating dealers, who cashed in long ago. But if Sir William wants to make an investment, I'd let him have the new Fall for a thousand – that's guineas, of course. And what's more, I'll give him a frame, a real carved one, for another hundred – guineas again.'

But the Professor looked like a maiden lady, about to retire after the picnic, behind a bush. 'I'm very much afraid,' he said, 'that Sir William will say he hasn't room. He specially mentioned one of the Sara Monday period. Not necessarily a large one. Sir William's object is always quality.'

'The best English meat,' I said. And I was going to tell the Professor that his job as cricket and my partner was not to act as pimp to Sir William, but as salesman to me. To sell my work while I was doing it.

But suddenly I had an idea. And I said to the Professor, 'I don't think much of Sir William's taste, if he'd rather have a study from the nude than a real picture. But I believe I might be able to get him what you call one of the Sara Monday period, and a good one, too. One of the best I ever did of the old skin.'

The Professor looked like a choir-boy when the paid tenor comes in wrong. Bursting out of his collar with joy. 'Splendid. Good news, indeed. And if it's anything like as good as Mr Hickson's Bath I think I could suggest to Sir William that three hundred and fifty wouldn't be too much.'

'Guineas.'

'Guineas, of course.'

'And how do we split?'

The Professor looked like a Protestant saint when the cannibal offered him the choice of taking six wives or being boiled alive. He wanted to mortify some flesh, but he didn't know which. 'Really, Mr Jimson,' he said, 'I had no idea —'

'What about the other fifty, if you get it?'

'No, no, I couldn't take a commission.'

'No, of course not. But I tell you what, I'll form a committee and give you a token of esteem. That's either a marble clock or a cheque. Or both. Think it over and let me know. And a handbag for your wife.'

The Professor looked like a horse about to receive the nosebag. Smiling but thoughtful. 'I haven't yet committed that rash act.' 'There you're wrong,' I said. 'A good wife would make a man of you, provided that all the raw materials are available.' 'I fear I couldn't support a wife.' 'Then let her support you. All my wives supported me. It's a very good plan. It gives them a serious interest in life, and it leaves you free to get on with your work.'

But the Professor shook his head and smiled; and went round the corner and wrote it all down in his note-book. Epigrams of the late Mr Gulley Jimson. 'With reference to this flash of the typical Jimson wit, it might be added that Mr Jimson was exceptionally fortunate in his matrimonial ventures, if we can venture such a description.'

But I couldn't wait till next morning. I was in such a fret. For my idea was that if Sara still had any of the canvasses which Hickson had left with her, she wouldn't have them long. Some dealer would hear about them and jump in with an offer.

I borrowed a shilling from Plant, and I was on the bus next morning by half-past nine. By good luck it was a Tuesday, so I could hope to find the old contriver alone. I didn't want to have any difficulties with the husband.

But when I rang Sara's bell the door hopped open about six inches and a yellow woman put her face in the crack. A face like the breast bone of a chicken, all nose and hard cheek.

'No brushes, no cleaning stuffs, no buttons and nothing to give away,' she said, and began to shut again.

I put my foot in the crack. 'Excuse me, madam, does Mrs Monday live here?'

The door hopped open again rather wider than before and the yellow bird snapped her beak at me. 'No, she doesn't. She's gone, and if it's one of her bills, it's nothing to do with us. She hadn't any right to order on credit.'

'You don't know where she's gone, do you?'

'122, Chatfield Buildings, down the allotments. Mr Byles. Ask for Mrs Byles, I should think. Not that she's any right to that name,' but she shut the door so quickly that I couldn't use my foot.

Chatfield Buildings were a long way off, getting towards the river. Six sets of yellow tenements – standing up among a lot of little houses like six rusty corned beef cans bogged in a muddy pool, full of blue ripples. Half a mile of concrete road led up to them across a brickfield; and about twenty acres of allotments, straight as a drainpipe. Rows of little trees had been planted on each side, but half of them were dead, kicked to pieces by kids or scratched to death by cats. And the allotments were in their April state, a bit bare except for regiments of bean sticks and rows of tool-houses like drunken paupers staggering about in the mud; some on their noses, some on their knees, some with felt hats, some with whitewash hats, some in rusty tin.

When I had travelled across this land of Ulro, I found the buildings on the other side of a road, behind a lot of high railings, like an isolation hospital. They stood in a little desert of asphalt, where some kids were running about making a noise like a battle in a railway tunnel.

122 was on the ground floor in the fourth house on the left. When I had gone down a long dark passage, I came to a smell like washing day, though it was a Tuesday, and a pool of steaming water across the bricks. Then I knocked and out came a man about seven foot high and four foot wide in a blue flannel shirt without a collar, red braces and cream corduroys. His bald head was as white as a peeled almond, but his face was the colour of prune juice; and he had a large waterfall moustache like a spray of nicotine mixture. His nose was like a pear with a dent across the small end as if someone had chopped it with a hatchet; and his eyes were as green as bottle-stoppers. He had a black leather strap about three inches wide on his right wrist. Genus, Walrus Londonius; species, Longus Bottomus. A fine old bull from the Isle of Dogs.

'Ullo,' he barked at me. Then he thought a minute, opened his mouth and barked, a good deal louder, 'ULLO.'

I knew what he meant, and I was just going to explain that I hadn't come to murder Sara or steal the silver, when I saw, in the little triangle between the crook of his elbow and his shirt, Sara waving her head at me and making a face as if to say, 'Not a word.' So I answered, 'Excuse me, but is this 123?'

He thought a bit and answered in a bellow, 'NO.'

After another half minute's pondering he came to a further decision, and shouted, 'NO, IT AIN'T.'

'What a pity,' I said. 'Thank you very much,' and I went out again. But Mr Byles followed me to the top of the steps and when I reached the asphalt he spat on my head. But it may have been an accident due to bad aim. I don't want to think evil of a man like that.

When I got to the ground, I went round the corner into the next staircase, as if looking for somebody, and walked slowly up. You could see the railings out of the windows. I stopped at the top window for twenty minutes before some woman began to take an interest, and put her head out every few seconds to see that I wasn't stealing the bricks. So then I went down to the next window. And after about forty minutes, I saw Mr Byles come out of his door below with a spade and a fork on his shoulder, and make for the allotments. So I nipped down again and nipped into Sara's.

It was a long time before she opened to me, and then she was in her petticoat with a sack tied over it, and bare ankles. Hair all coming down in grey streaks, and face streaming. I thought her face had shut up a good deal since I'd seen her last, shorter in the chin and bigger in the nose. And when she turned round she had a regular charwoman's back, the high hump.

'Well, so there you are, Gulley,' she said. 'Fancy. You did give me a surprise. And I was just in a twitter lest you might say something to Byles. Not that he would mind you coming in, except perhaps just when he was going out to his allotment. Well, I've often wondered what had happened to you.' So she fussed off into the kitchen, chirping away, but not in the old style or even the old voice. Never looking at me or talking to me, but sometimes at the wall and sometimes with her back turned, here, there and all round, as if it didn't matter very much what she said or whether I heard her or not. Hullo, I thought, this is new. Sara's really getting an old lady, running like a mill-stream late in winter, when there's no mill to turn.

'Oh dear,' she simmered, bobbing at the corners. 'What a mess – I was just having a turnout.'

And, in fact, the kitchen was all upsides. Chairs standing on the table, a pail in the middle of the floor, mops and brooms. Rows of beer bottles against the wall behind the door. Smashed chair propped up by the window. Two other chairs standing on the table and everything steaming wet.

'Yes, just when you're having a real turnout, somebody's sure to come,' said Sara in her old woman's way; a gay voice and a sad forehead; wrinkling up her eyebrows and champing her jaws. 'Not but what I'm real glad to see you, Gulley – well, of course,' giving me sometimes her back and sometimes her shoulder.

Yes, I thought. Sara's going away from this life, she's going from me, growing old. She's applied for the Chilledstern hundreds. She's climbing on the shelf.

I put my arm round her apron string. 'I hope you are glad to see me, Sall,' I said. 'And what sort of a mess. What's happened to you – what's happened to the life policy, I mean Fred?'

'Well,' said Sara, pulling down a chair and wiping the seat. 'It was the bills. They came out before I'd expected.'

'Bills always do – haven't you learnt that yet? – how much did you owe this time?'

'I don't know,' said Sara. 'It wasn't Fred, it was that sister, Doris – she got hold of him. Well, his weak side was always petty cash. No, I don't know how much it came to – but they took all my things – there's a dry chair for you. Wait, I'll put this mat on it. You don't want to get lumbago.'

'Took all your things, Sara,' for I was surprised. And I thought, so that's the end of the pictures if she had 'em. I might have expected that. You never know where it's coming from, but you always get it.

'All my things,' said Sara. 'Two Armchairs, two tables, the carpet that Monday gave me for my drawing-room, seven silver teaspoons and the tea caddy, four damask table-cloths and nine napkins, three silk cushions —'

'They can't do that, Sara. You must get a lawyer.'

'They said there wouldn't be enough to pay and I didn't want an argument. Well, that Doris said she'd go to the police, and I didn't want any more trouble. I suppose it was my own fault. You'll have some tea, Gulley? I wish I could give you something better, but there isn't anything in the house.'

And as she turned round to fill the kettle at the sink I saw that she had a black eye. A real damson. Blue with a bloom. And shut right up. A blinder. 'Hullo,' I said. 'What's wrong with your glim, Sall?'

'A wasp stung it. I haven't got any cake. But wouldn't you like a piece of bread and jam, or bread and bacon?'

'A wasp in April,' I said. 'More like a friend. What is Mr Byles like as a master – is he particular about drinking level?'

'Mr Byles has always stood by me,' said Sara, 'and he took me in at short notice when I'd nowhere to go and didn't know where to turn.'

'Why didn't you come to me, Sara?'

'What would you want with me when you hadn't enough to feed yourself much less a useless old woman that's only fit for a coffin. No, even when Mr Byles was lodging with us he always stood up for me against that Doris, and he said that if ever I was in trouble I'd only got to come to him, and so I did, and he took me in. He may be a bit rough, but he's a Christian in his inside, Gulley, and I won't hear a word against him.'

The old lady was getting warmed up and forgetting the weight of her grey hairs. 'No, Gulley, I honour a man like Byles that stands by his word to a woman when he might fairly take it back, for the truth is that when he gave it to me, I still had a young bone or two in my flesh, but when I came round to his door and asked for a bed, I was a poor old castaway and a sight to boot, for I'd been crying my eyes away over poor little Dicky and my things and it all happening so sudden. Well, it makes me cold still to think what I must have looked like – I wasn't fit for the gypsies much less human company. And Mr Byles just threw open the door and said, "Mrs Monday, I said I'd make you welcome, and so you are, so come in and say no more about it. Least said," he said, "soonest mended." And here I've been ever since.'

'A man of few words, Mr Byles,' I said, 'his fist is quicker than his tongue. But I'd sooner he tried it on Fred than you. And I've half a mind to tell him so. I know you sometimes have a provoking way with you, one way or another, but I don't like to see you with that eye, Sara. Even if you aren't my property any longer I've got a kind of husband's feeling about your amenities.'

'I never said Mr Byles hit me in the eye, for I'm sure he never meant to, and even if he had I'm sure he had excuse with the amount of trouble they give in the department. The young ones putting all the heavy work on him just out of spite because he won't admit he's getting a bit stiff and short of breath. I shouldn't wonder if they didn't kill him one of these days, with his heart. He's often as blue as this apron after only climbing the steps, but it's no good telling him he ought to see a doctor. He can't bear doctors, and though I tell him doctors aren't hospitals, you can't expect him to change his ways at his time of life. I can only thank God he'll never make me go to hospital, and if my time is due it will come on me in my own home. I have to thank Byles for that, even if he does go and kill himself out of obstinacy.'

'Come on, Sall,' I said. 'We're not dead yet, unless we like to think so. And I daresay you had a few pounds put away in your box – they didn't get your box, I suppose.'

'They didn't leave me a shilling, Gulley. Even to bury me. Well, would you believe it, they came upon me in my bed, and that woman, God forgive her, she even went through my stays. Yes, she took seventeen golden sovereigns out of my stays, my funeral money that had been saving up for eleven years, ever since poor Rozzie died. Why, they even took up the floor, and they'd have broken in my box, but Fred thought it might be against the law. Not but what they didn't keep my box – yes, with all my things, even my mother's bible. They kept the whole box, and if it hadn't been that Mr Byles went to fetch it for me and threatened to break the door in, and wring that Doris's neck —'

'So you got your box.'

'Byles brought it away, thank God, or I really don't know how I should have got over it. Well, Gulley, you may say it's a sign of being old, perhaps it is, and I know I'm an old woman, but I don't think I could have borne it, to lose my box. Why, I got that box when I first went out to service in the year before the old Queen's jubilee and it's been with me ever since. In my grand days when indeed poor Monday wouldn't let it out of the attic for shame of its being such a poor servanty kind of thing, and in all my coming down days since.'

'I seem to remember, Sara, that you used to keep some of my old drawings and sketches in your box – sketches of yourself —'

Sara began to shake her head, so I held up my hand and went on talking fast. I knew my Sara. Never to let her tell any lies until she understood the position. Because afterwards she might feel obliged to stick to them, even when she didn't want to. Sara was a woman all through. She had a sense of honour even in drink, and she was always particular not to change her mind or admit to a lie, on the same day. 'Wait a minute, Sara,' I said. 'There's money in this – Do you want to make twenty pounds?'

Sara's face changed and she turned her good eye on me with quite a sharp look. 'I should, indeed,' she said, 'if I could do it honestly and without upsetting Byles. For 'tis the least I can do for him, not to put him out. But how can you get twenty pounds, Gulley? I'm sure you yourself could do with a new fit out from top to toe —'

'It's an offer, Sall. For one of those canvasses which don't belong to you, anyhow. But Hickson seems to have said that you could keep my property, and you and I are old friends.'

'Canvasses. What canvasses?'

'The ones in your box.'

Sara looked me in the eyes. She was trying to make out if I knew anything, or was only guessing. But, of course, by the way she looked, I knew that she had something in her box. Sara was never a good deceiver because she never took enough trouble. She had the natural art; but she never improved on it. Relied too much on her charm and the inspiration of the moment.

'There's nothing in my box,' said Sara.

'No? Hickson seemed to think there might be. And there certainly was when you first went off from me and took up with old Mr W. Drawings at least. You admitted it.'

'Oh no, Gulley. I couldn't have. I never went off from you. It was you went off from me. And as for poor Mr Wilcher, I never thought but to be his housekeeper only. Oh dear. But there's the gas going down, and goodness knows if I've got a shilling.' And she went bobbing about again. She was in such a fluster what with the pictures and Byles in the background, and my talk of Mr W., that I could have laughed. She never could bear me to talk of Mr W., because she would always swear she had never been anything but a housekeeper to him. But she knew that I knew differently.

'It's funny you should forget about the drawings, Sara,' I said. 'Because it was the day I had that explanation with Mr W. about you.'

'Oh dear, oh dear, I'll never get done.' And she went clump, clump down the cellar steps with two brooms clattering on the walls and a pail creaking in her hand. Strategic retreat, with equipment intact.

But it was ten minutes to eleven and I knew she would be back to her tea. Not the devil himself could keep her from her morning tea.

28

Wilcher was a rich lawyer, with a face like a bad orange. Yellow and blue. A little grasshopper of a man. Five feet of shiny broadcloth and three inches of collar. Always on the jump. Inside or out. In his fifties. The hopping fifties. And fierce as a mad mouse. Genus, Boorjwar; species, Blackcoatiuis Begoggledus Ferocissimouse. All eaten up with lawfulness and rage; ready to bite himself for being so respectable. He popped in one day when I'd called on Sara, and I thought he was going to run me through with his umbrella. His little hornet's eyes were shooting fiery murder. But I rushed up to him on the front door mat and seized him by the hand. 'How de do, sir? My name's Gulley Jimson. I hope you're quite well – quite.'

Sara had slipped away and he brought his umbrella to the order. Armistice. 'How de do, sir? I know your name. As an artist. I am honoured,' with a little clockwork bow, as if to say, 'You are ticked off.'

'Not at all,' I said, 'I called to see Mrs Jimson about some drawings.' This had a good effect. The little black devil put his umbrella in the stand and you could see that he was surveying his ground. Like a lawyer. His insect face became as blank as an insect's. Which meant that he was planning something – a lawyer's face always gives warning of an ambush. Like a blockhouse. Used to conceal the artillery.

'Mrs Jimson,' he said. 'Or Mrs Monday,' I said. 'I don't know what flag she's sailing under now.' 'She came to me as Mrs Jimson, but the registry office gave the name as Monday.' 'Both flags, in fact.' 'She was a widow, I believe.' 'Not mine, not yet.' 'Ahem. Then I understand that her name legally is Mrs Jimson.' 'No sir, legally her name is Mrs Monday. Though, of course, she lived with me as Mrs Jimson.'

There was a short pause while this news filtered through the loopholes of the blockhouse to Mr W. within. Who then stood on one leg, put his finger in his ear and gave a loud halloo, followed by uproarious and uncontrollable laughter; that is to say, he wanted to do so; but being a respectable blackcoat, he could only place his hands together, press them so hard that they cracked, and remark, 'In-deed. Ahem. In deed. As Mrs Jimson. Ahem. As Mrs Jimson.'

And I nearly burst out laughing in his face. It's easy to see, I thought, your kind. A housekeeper-keeper every inch. But I looked very grave and reserved, that is to say, demure, which was the proper move at this stage of the game, as played among the blackcoats. And Hot Nobless. 'As Mrs Jimson,' I said.

'Not being, ahem, in point of fact, legally speaking, ahem —'

'I quite agree, Mr Wilcher.'

'And yet, I should have thought – I feel sure, a woman of principle.'

'Oh,' I said, 'very much so. The best. Sara was quite ready to go to church. Always has been. The impediment was on the other side of the family. If I may say so.'

At this Mr W. sprang clean through the ceiling, turned several somersaults in mid air, sang a short psalm of praise and thanksgiving out of the Song of Solomon, accompanied on the shawm, and returned through the letter-box draped in celestial light. That is to say, he raised his right toe slightly from the carpet, said 'indeed' in mi-fa, and relaxed his ceremonial smile into an expression of tolerance. 'Indeed,' he repeated, this time in me-do, 'an impediment.'

'I had the misfortune to be married before,' I said, 'several times, in fact.'

'So that Mrs Monday was in no way to blame.'

'Not for not being married. Certainly not. By no means, never.'

'A truly religious woman,' said Mr W. using *vox humana.*

'Yes, you might say Sara had some religion, female religion.'

'I esteem Mrs Monday very highly,' he said then. He was now preparing for the general assault. 'Very highly indeed.' 'She always had a something,' I said, 'and so on.' 'A true woman, Mr Jimson.' 'You've only got to look at her.' 'The true old country stock.' 'Let us say breed.' 'Now, Mr Jimson, I have a suggestion to make to you,' charging down on me with all arms. Yes, a regular Boorjwarrior. London is full of them. Infuriated blackcoats. Lying low with some ambush with a dagger in one hand and a bomb in the other. And the fires of death and hell burning under their dickies. When you meet them, they're all clockwork bows and hems and how-de-do's, until they've got you where they want you, and then out come the claws, and bang, they're at your throat like a Bengal tiger.

Mr W.'s proposition was that if I came near Sara again or wrote to her for the money she owed me, he'd put me in charge; but on the other hand, if I would undertake to leave her unmolested, he was prepared to come to an arrangement.

'A financial one,' I said.

'Certainly.'

'You want to buy Sara – cash, I presume.'

'Nothing of the sort, sir.' And he burst into stars and rockets. For, of course, I'd dropped my match right on the spot where the gunpowder was kept. 'A most abominable suggestion. I have the deepest respect for Mrs Monday. My object, sir, is to protect her from a ruffian, sir, a blackguard. Which I intend to do, in any case, whether you accept my terms, or not.' And he folded his arms and stood on tiptoe and fairly crushed me with his glance. Or at least that was the intention.

'That's all right,' I said. 'So long as you don't expect me to protect you from Sara or versa vice. And the price is satisfactory.'

'A pound a week. And you will sign an undertaking not to write or communicate in any manner.'

'Thirty shillings for the whole property as a going concern.'

'I do not intend to bargain with a person of your sort. A pound is my highest offer. A pound or the police.'

And do what I would I couldn't get him above twenty-two and six. But to tell the truth men, like Wilcher, the real old blackcoat breed, out of Hellfire by the Times, get on my nerves. They frighten me. They're not normal. You never know what they'll do next. They're always fit for rape and murder, and why not, because they don't look upon you as human. You're a Lost Soul, or Bad Husband, or a Modern Artist, or a Good Citizen, or a Suspicious Character, or an Income Tax Payer. They don't live in the world we know, composed of individual creatures, fields and moons and trees and stars and cats and flowers and women and saucepans and bicycles and men; they're phantoms, spectres. And they wander screaming and gnashing their teeth, that is, murmuring to themselves and uttering faint sighs, in a spectrous world of abstractions, gibbering and melting into each other like a lot of political systems and religious creeds.

> All within is opened into the deeps of Eututhon Benython
> A dark and unknown night, indefinite, unmeasurable, without end,
> Abstract philosophy warring in enmity against Imagination.

I was glad to get away from that little black scorpion. Ringed with hellfire. I feel my hair rise still all over, where it used to be, when I think of him. No wonder they invented religion. Nothing but the heaviest dogma cast in the thickest metal can keep such demons, afreets and poltergeists bottled in their own juice, which is the only acid strong enough to disinfect their virtues.

29

Sara was still knocking pails and brooms about in the cellar, and I saw that she was trying to drown the voice of conscience with household noises, a common trick among the ladies. But it gave me an idea. If she can't hear herself, perhaps she won't hear me. And I went out very quietly into the passage and tried the first door.

But a woman doesn't need to hear somebody prowling through her domains uninvited; she has a special organ, situated just under the diaphragm, which detects him five miles away even when disguised as a relation by marriage. I had barely half opened the door, before crash went the broom, bang went the pail, and Sara was coming up the steps like a gas explosion.

'I was just looking round,' I said. 'Nice place you have here.' In fact, it was a dusty bare little room with nothing in it except one cane armchair, a new wheelbarrow, some matting on the floor, and a lot of empty beer bottles. 'The parlour.'

'It could be,' said Sara, sighing and panting. 'If they'd only let me have a bit of carpet and a soft chair.'

'Nice photograph on the mantelpiece – nice girl. Where did it come from?'

'It's me – it was in my parlour at Fred's. It's always been in my parlour. I used to have one in a silver frame, but somebody took it.'

'That silver frame. The one you gave me for your photograph. Well, Sara, to tell the truth, I picked it up again. I needed a little cash, and I thought you wouldn't mind.'

Sara took it like an old lady. She only drew in her lips and wrinkled her forehead. 'A good thing I had another copy,' she said. 'That's me in my wedding frock – the one I had when I married you. I mustn't say married, I suppose. But that's what I meant, God knows.'

'Of course it's you,' I said, 'now I look again. It's sunk in a bit, that's all. I couldn't forget that figure – a real figure. Ah, you were a woman, Sall, in the times when there were women who even looked like women. And I'll get that frame back for your picture.'

'Oh well,' said Sara, not believing me, 'I've got the photo, and it was a nice dress. I had a piece of the silk for a long time. I always had a feeling for it. But there, I was properly in love with you.'

'Or in love with getting married.'

And Sara didn't contradict me any more. She was too tired. 'Well,' she said, 'there was that, too, I daresay. What woman doesn't? But not because of what you thought, Gulley. No, it wasn't the bedding part of it. It was being your wife.'

'Anybody's wife.'

'Well, a home needs a man, I suppose, just like a cosy needs a teapot. And always I did like someone to do for. It's natural.'

'There's something boiling over,' for I'd had a good look round, and I knew the box wasn't in that room.

Sara listened and said, 'Bother it,' and hopped out quicker than you might expect. But she'd always had a dislike to things boiling over. And as she went into the kitchen, I skipped through the other door. Sure enough, the family bedroom. Italian brass bed with three knobs missing and most of the brass. Yellow cupboard with blisters. Little crooked table with a tin basin and a blue jug. Strip of wornout carpet in front of the fireplace. Christmas supplements pinned on the walls. Cherry Ripe. Christmas Eve, with snow and postman and little girl. Raphael Madonna. Smell of matrimony. Two burst hat-boxes on top of cupboard. Two boxes under bed. One solid wood bound with black iron strips. Old navigator's chest. Byles. One yellow tin, battered like crumpled glovepaper. Slavey's first trunk. Sara.

I knew that box. Sara had always kept her treasures in it. Old ribbons, old rags of velvet, old photographs, baby's first shoes, her mother's bible, a broken fan, a pair of stays (what a waist I had at seventeen) and bundles of letters, hotel bills (honeymoon), dance programmes and bits of yellow linen. Her bridal nightgown at the bottom, to be buried in. The last nest of an old bird. It was locked, of course. Sara always had it locked. But the lock was a woman's lock; half off its hinge and full of rust; the tongue was ready to jump off the hasp, at a touch. I had brought a little box-opener with me in case of having to open something, and I had the lid back in half a minute. A shawl on top. Then a pink silk dress, style of about 1900. And underneath that two great rolls of canvas, and a portfolio of drawings.

I spread out the canvases on the wall. The first was a sketch of Sara in a green dress, one of her old pre-war dresses with a full skirt. A knock in, nothing finished, except the hands and the bodice. But the other was a gem. The first study for the Bath. And in many ways better than the big one, fresher, more sensitive, more lively in the touch, and more character in the tones. More come and go. I was so pleased with it that I forgot all about Sara. Until she opened the door into my back, took one look at the open box and grabbed at the canvas. For a minute it was pull devil, pull Gulley. But then Sara suddenlly let go and the canvas fell down on the carpet. She said, 'Oh, Gulley, what's that?'

She'd seen the box-opener in my hand, and perhaps I'd waved it at her. But she was not so much frightened as shocked. She quite woke up all at once and forgot how old she was feeling.

'You weren't going to murder me?' she said. Then she put her hand to her side and leant against the bed-post. 'Oh dear,' she said, 'I'm too old. And then you looking like that. And looking in my box and taking my things.' 'They're not your things, Sara. They're mine, and I need them, too very badly.'

Sara gave a sigh so big, it was like a heartbreak. Except you knew that Sara's heart couldn't break. It was too soft. But she made the bed-frame creak, or perhaps it was her stays. And then she said, 'You with a jemmy, Gulley.'

I saw that she was changing her feelings. Sara could always change her feelings very quickly. And I said, 'It's not a jemmy. It's a box-opener.'

'Oh dear, what's the difference?'

'It's a box-opener when an honest man uses it and a jemmy when a thief uses it.'

'How can you laugh and make jokes when you were just going to murder me.'

She screwed up her cheeks and one and a half tears rolled down her cheeks, the half one out of the shut eye. It surprised me. And I sat down on the bed and put my arm round her as far as it would go. 'Come, Sall old girl. What's wrong? You know you hadn't any right to those pictures and both of us need the money.'

'Oh dear, it gave me such a shock when you looked at me like that. We're too old, Gulley. We oughtn't to go on like that at our age.'

'Well then, let's go off – there's twenty pounds for you and a bit for me, too – enough for a week at Brighton.'

The old lady took another one-eyed squint at the canvas and gave another screw to her cheeks. I was afraid she was going to cry again. But instead she let out a kind of groan and said, 'Wouldn't the other one do, Gulley?'

'The one in a dress? No, Sara. That wouldn't get five pounds. No, you can keep that one.'

'Well, Gulley,' and she gave an old woman's sigh; a long quiet one. 'I suppose you have more right to it than I have; and we don't want to quarrel any more at our age.'

'We never really quarrelled, Sall, we only differed.'

'And I was a good model when you painted that – you thought a lot of me then.'

'Well, look at you.'

'Yes, perhaps we did quarrel – but it was nice to be young.'

'We're not so old now.'

Sara shook her head. 'If you knew how old I feel, Gulley. Grey in my very bones.'

'Cheer up, Sall.' What with the poor old girl's eye, and her griefs, and her good sense about the picture, I was touched. And I gave her a kiss. A bit sideways because our noses got in the way. I hadn't kissed anybody since Rozzie died, which was nearly ten years past, so I'd forgotten to allow for the natural obstacles. 'You were always my best girl, Sall,' I said, 'and my best model. An inspiration to the eye and everything else. Look at that pair.'

Sara smiled and the pink came into her cheeks, under the purple. She shook her head. 'Ah, Gulley, you could always get what you wanted. But my figure wasn't so terribly bad, was it?'

'And they're not so bad now, I daresay,' I said.

'Not so bad as you might think,' said Sara with such a look as made me burst out laughing. She still had youth in her old bones.

'The model wife.'

'And you never saw me as I was, Gulley, I'd had five children before you painted me like that. Why, look at my waist. It was a nineteen when I first went out to service.'

'Silly girl, spoiling your shape.'

'Well, I do think you put a little bit on my hips, even then. I said so at the time. They're not my hips, Gulley. More like poor Rozzie's.' 'Of course, they're your hips, Sall. Why, that's where you were strong. I wish all the world could have seen those hips.' 'They weren't bad for shape, but you made them a little heavy.' 'So they ought to be heavy. The hearth stone of the house. The Church's one foundation. The Creator of civilization. The Mediterranean basin. The Keel of the world.' 'The blue curtain is nice.' 'Meaning that it shows up a nice line along the horizon.' 'The horizon, Gulley. Oh, you mean —' 'The left cheek.' 'Oh, you are awful,' said Sara, getting quite lively. 'But the colour, I didn't think I was so pink as that, unless I'd been sitting on the pebbles.' 'Why, it's a lovely skin, like a baby's.' 'Yes, it wasn't too bad then. When I went to have massage after my first, the nurse said she'd never seen such a skin. But you made my chin too long, Gulley. I know it's a bit thick, but gracious, you've made me look like the villain in Maria Martin.' 'I improved your nose though.' 'Funny that bit of white just there, how it brings it up,' said Sara, pointing with her toe at her breast. 'Yes,' I said, 'your left is your masterpiece.' 'Well, now you mention it, for a woman who'd nursed five and such suckers, too, it's a wonder I didn't come out like an old purse.' 'I did that bit between the arm and the breast rather well, it's a lovely bit that, the foothills —' 'You'll admit they were wonderful firm Gulley.' 'By God, firm as a Dutch cheese.' 'And wonderful white, too.' 'As curdled cream.' 'Well, do you know, Gulley, the monthly nurse used to stare at them till I was quite shy, and then she would say she'd never seen such sweet lovely shapes. And, of course, she'd seen thousands and thousands. You might say they were as common as turnips to a dairy farmer.' 'Look at the vein there, just a drag of the brush across the grain. Yes, I could handle the paint then.'

'That's what Mr Hickson says – he says you had a wonderful gift, but you never used it properly but once, when you did me. And you never did anything better than the Bath.' 'Anything more slick, you mean.' 'If you never did anything else but those you did of me, you'd be famous in history, that's what Mr Hickson told me.' 'If I never did anything else, Sall, I'd shoot myself for a lipstick merchant.' 'I'll never forget how you used to tear the clothes off my back and I never knew whether it was to put me down or to make me sit. You were mad to paint me, weren't you, Gulley?'

And there she was, the old cyclops, making a glad eye at her own image. The tear marks still on her cheek.

'I suppose you have this canvas out every night, Sall. It looks a bit dog-eared.'

She shook her head. 'I'd forgotten about it.'

'Tell me another, Sall, and I won't believe that one either.'

'I used to take a peep now and then, just to remember our happy times. But not since I came here. I've been too low.'

'And now it's doing you good. Why not, it does me a lot of good.'

'You won't say I wasn't a sweet armful for you, Gulley.'

'So you were and God bless you. He gave you all a woman could want.'

'And glad I was for your sake.'

'And all the others.'

'No, Gulley. For I never rejoiced with any but you. No, I never gloried in myself but when we were together.'

The old lady was getting so warm I thought she might argue.

'Come, Sall, I must go. I've got an appointment with an agent at one o'clock. And shall I send you your twenty pounds in notes or a money order.' I stooped to pick up the canvas.

But Sara stooped down, too, and took hold of it on the other side.

'Now, Sall,' I said. 'You're not going back on your word.'

'Wouldn't the other one do?' said Sara.

'No, it would not. No dealer would look at it. Be sensible, Sall. What good is the thing to you hidden away in your box? You're not such an old stupid that you'd rather go looking at yourself as you were twenty years ago than have twenty Jimmy o'goblins to play with.'

'Have you looked at the other one? It's very nice the way you've done the silk. It's really much nicer than this one.'

'Listen to the old trot. She wants to go on staring at herself still. She's still in love with herself.'

'Oh indeed, Gulley, it's not for pleasure. It makes me so sad I could cry.'

'Is there anything you care about in this world except yourself?' I said, for I was growing exasperated.

'Oh, Gulley, how can you ask? I was a true wife to you, and a true mother to your Tommy.' 'I was yourself, and so was Tommy. I was your best bed-warmer and Tommy was your heart cordial.' 'I nearly died when you left me,' 'Yes, as if you'd lost your left leg or your front teeth.' 'Well, you did what you liked with me, God knows. You broke my poor nose and I came back to you. And the times you pinched me and stuck pins in my poor behind, long ones, I wonder how I stood it. You were a cruel husband, Gulley.' 'You were a bad woman, Sall.' 'God knows I had my faults, but you shouldn't call me a bad woman, and even if you say I was bad, wasn't it all for your pleasure?' 'And you won't even give me back my own property – now when I need it.' 'Whatever you say, Gulley, I did make you happy, Gulley, often and often you said you were the happiest man in the world.' 'Come, Sall, wrap it up and let me get off.' 'Why, even the day you finished that, you were so mad after me' – I picked up the picture quickly and rolled it up under my arm. Sall gave a little cry, 'Oh, Gulley, you can't take it like that, all screwed up.' And I could see that she was nearly crying over her precious picture. I was sorry for her. This sketch, I thought, is the chief exhibit in the old museum. It's the treasure of the temple. She looks at it every day and says, 'What a girl I was, and what times I had. All the men after me. And no wonder. Look at my this and my that and my, etc.' Yes, it's a loss to the poor old dear. And so I gave her another squeeze or two. 'Oh, Gulley,' she said, 'you won't crack it, will you?' 'Crack it?' 'Crack the paint – let me do it up for you proper with a newspaper inside. As I used to. I wouldn't want your nice picture to get cracked.' 'My picture or your portrait,' I said. She made me laugh with her tricks. But I let her wrap the canvas in brown paper, which was just as well. For while she was tying it up in the bedroom, Byles came ramping in at the front door, and I was glad that he didn't catch us together.

As it was he just stood and looked at me. You could see the steam was turned on; and the wheels might move any minute. ''Ere,' he said at last, and lifted a fist like a coal scuttle.

'Good morning, Mr Byles,' I said. 'I was just calling on Mrs Monday, an old friend of the family.'

' 'Ere,' said Byles, and the wheels gave a jump. 'GET OUT,'

Sara slipped the parcel in my hand and I came away at once.

The Professor had actually been round that morning, while I was away, to ask for me. He was smelling out his fee. And I was just going off to Capel Mansions, to deliver the goods, when, by a piece of luck, I thought I would take another look at the canvas and see if it wouldn't be better on a stretcher. Amateurs like Beeder, and even dealers, often can't tell what a picture is worth, unless they see it on a stretcher.

So I unrolled my parcel. And there was nothing inside but four rolls of toilet paper done up in newspaper, I got such a surprise that I couldn't even swear.

Then, of course, I remembered that Sara had gone into the bedroom to look for string to tie up my parcel. And that she'd been some time about it. And I laughed. It was either that or wanting to cut the old woman's throat. And even to think of cutting Sara's throat always put me in rage. Because, I suppose, I'd got her in my blood, I'd been fond of her. And it's very highly dangerous to murder anyone you've been fond of, even in imagination. Throws all the functions out of gear. Blocks up your brain. Might easily blow the lid off.

I took a little walk along Greenbank and snuffed up the breeze. And I admired the view of the spring trees on the tow-path side, burning in the evening sun, like copper flames in a brass sky. Sun dirty old brass. And the river like brandy.

30

The next afternoon found me at Chatfield Buildings again. With a bigger box-opener. I wasn't annoyed with Sara, but I wanted to come to an arrangement. But just when I was making a reconnaissance at the front door, I had a special providence in the shape of a small dog which bit me in the leg. I'm used to dog bites. Dogs always bite the ragged. But I've never liked them. And when I turned round to fend off the dog, there was Byles about two yards away coming for me with a garden fork. He chased me about half a mile round the buildings, and he might have caught me if he hadn't wasted so much breath on telling me what he was going to do to me. As it was, I managed to dodge into another staircase and I sat in a lavatory, with the door bolted, for two hours, until it was dark enough to make my getaway. I wasn't going to take any risks with my new Fall. It would have been a crime.

It wouldn't have been wise to let the Professor know how Sara had diddled me. I wrote to tell him that the picture was at my agents, being stretched and cleaned, and I called the same evening to see Sir William and ask him to wait a few days for his masterpiece.

'Oh dear,' said the Professor when he met me in the hall. 'You're too late.'

'Too late?'

'They've gone to America, and they won't be back for three months.'

'Never mind,' I said, 'I'll use the time to find a frame. And I daresay Sir William wouldn't mind paying a hundred in advance.'

'I rather think,' said the Professor, 'Sir William will want to see the picture first.'

'In that case,' I said, 'I hold myself free to accept other offers. I believe Mr Hickson would make me a better offer.'

This worried the Professor a good deal, and he assured me that Sir William would certainly pay more than Hickson, if only I would wait.

The Professor was staying in the flat for the week-end. He had nowhere else to go until Monday when he was visiting an old friend in Devonshire. And nothing much to eat. For the Beeders had locked everything up except a piece of cheese and half a loaf of stale bread.

He was put out when I suggested staying with him. But when he found that I was prepared to do the catering, he became more hospitable.

'You might have the sofa in the studio,' he said, 'I'm sleeping in the drawing-room.'

'What about Sir William's bed?'

'The bedclothes have been locked up.'

'Never mind,' I said, 'I can make allowances while Sir William is away.'

Then I showed the Professor how to pawn his winter overcoat and with the proceeds I bought beer and bacon enough for two. The plan was to take the overcoat out of pawn as soon as I had the picture. So we lived in the land of Beulah on bread and cheese and bacon and bread and dripping and bacon, until the Monday. When his old friend called for him in a 40-50 Rolls to take him to Devonshire. The Professor's friends all seemed ready to give him every luxury when it suited their convenience, except clothes and money.

I was still in bed when the car came, and the Professor was worried. 'Excuse me, Mr Jimson,' he said, 'but I ought to lock up and take the key to the police.'

'Never mind,' I said. 'Give me the key and I'll attend to it. Don't keep your friends waiting.'

And, in fact, the friend was walking up and down in the studio, getting himself into a great state of impatience. Because his wife was waiting for him. The wife, I daresay, didn't like his friend the Professor very much; she was not prepared to wait very long for a gentleman with holes in his trousers.

'Come on, Alabaster,' he called, rushing out and in again. 'We've got a long way to go before lunch.'

'The Beeders are very particular,' said the Professor, quite pinched with agitation. 'They gave strict instructions. They naturally feel anxious about the safety of a unique collection like this.'

'They're quite right,' I said. 'Tell the porter to keep an eye on the door. Tell him that Mr Gulley Jimson will be responsible for handing over the key.'

The Professor was quite distracted. He was packing a cardboard box with the other socks, spare collar, notes on the Works of Gulley Jimson, toothbrush, etc. And every moment he ran to the door and said, 'Just coming, Sir Reginald,' and then he would run back to me. 'You'll be locking up this morning,' he said.

'Very likely,' I said. 'It depends on my poor stomach. But you can be sure I'll defend the place with my life. I look upon it as a sacred trust. And, of course, you must tell the porter that I'll give him the key.'

'Today,' said the Professor. And Sir Reginald was making noises like a horse that wants to win the Derby before the starting gate goes up.

The Professor kept on looking at me. But every time he looked I was looking at him. Straight in the eyes, sign of a clear conscience.

'Perhaps I'd better tell the police to call,' he said. 'You'd feel more comfortable, wouldn't you, Mr Jimson, if the police were in charge – less responsibility.'

'A good idea,' I said. 'Tell them that I'm in charge of the key, and will see to the locking up.'

'Are you coming, Alabaster?' cried Sir Reginald from outside. 'I can't stand your friend's pictures any longer – where did he get such trash?'

'Coming now,' said the Professor, quite horrified. 'Very well, Mr Jimson, I'll tell the porter, and the police, and you'll leave the key at the station. That will save you from all further anxiety.'

'Thank you,' I said. 'You're a good chap, Professor. For I do certainly feel a lot of responsibility. I like the Beeders and I appreciate their anxiety for all these fine things.'

'Yes,' said the Professor. 'Just coming, Sir Reginald. Here's the key then, Mr Jimson. And you'll be sure not to forget to close the windows and put on the burglar alarm, before you lock up.'

'Trust me,' I said. And Sir Reginald whisked him away, poor figment. So I took a late lunch on bread and cheese and smoked my pipe in the land of Beulah. And after I had opened the linen cupboard with a bit of stiff wire, I made up her ladyship's bed which seemed to be softer than Sir William's.

The porter and I had a little chat and a couple of gallons next morning at the Red Lion and he was so good as to call up the police for me, and to explain that I had been left in charge of the flat for the present, and took full responsibility for the property.

The porter had been very polite to me ever since he had discovered that I was a distinguished person. Now, when my boots flopped, he looked the other way; like a young lady when a baron shows a fly-button. He was most delicate in his feelings for the great. And beer. One of the old guard. A True Blue.

On the next morning after my bread and dripping on the mahogany, I took down the family portraits in the dining-room to see what the wall was like. For I hadn't forgotten my promise to Sir William of a mural above the sideboard. Tigers and orchids for a hundred guineas. The wall was not what I expected, and when I knocked in the tigers, lightly touched, with a piece of charcoal from her ladyship's box, they wouldn't stay on the shape. It was too square, like a backyard. It asked for hens and daisies.

But afterwards, when I took down the water-colours in the studio to have a look at the other walls, I made a discovery. A good wall is often ruined by pictures, and I have found most excellent material in unexpected places, for instance behind a collection of old Masters. And this was a gem. It was on the right side of the studio, near the entrance hall; framed between two doors and perfectly lighted by reflection from the ceiling. One of the sweetest walls I had ever seen. It made the remaining pictures look like fly-blows. I took them down and stacked them in the bathroom.

A good wall, as they say, will paint itself. And as I looked at this beautiful shape, I saw what it was for. A raising of Lazarus.

I jumped up at once and sketched the idea with a few touches of a pencil, where it wouldn't show behind the pictures. This gave me a parallelogram on a slant from top left to bottom right, the grave. And I saw it in burnt sienna with a glass-green Lazarus up the middle stiff as an ice man; cactus and spike grass all round, laurel green; a lot of yellow ochre feet in the top corner and bald heads in the bottom triangle – one small boy looking at a red beetle on a blue-green leaf. But it was the feet that jumped at me. The finest feet I'd ever seen, about four times life-size. I only had to put a line round 'em. Then I got out her ladyship's nice little colour box and rubbed on some body colour. It would all wash off. And I couldn't go wrong with those feet. They came up like music. Down on the left, in foreground, about a yard long and two feet high to the ankle bone – a yellow pair, long and stringy, with crooked nails; then a black pair, huge and strong with muscles like lianas; a child's pair, pink and round, with nails like polished coral; an odd pair, one thick and calloused, with knotty toes curled into the dust, one shrunk and twisted, its heel six inches from the ground, standing on its toes, a cripple's feet, full of resolution and pain; then a coffee-coloured pair with a bandage, an old woman's feet, flat, long, obstinate, hopeless, clinging to the ground with their bellies like a couple of discouraged reptiles, and gazing at the sky with blind broken nails; then a pair of Lord's feet, pink in gold sandals with trimmed nails and green veins, and one big toe raised impatiently.

When I fell down into a chair about tea-time and looked at those feet, a voice inside me said, They're good, good, good. Nobody has done better. The Works of Gulley Jimson. Jee-sus, Jimson, perhaps you are a genius. Perhaps the crickets are right.

And a masterpiece like that on the Beeders' wall. To be covered up by a lot of drawing-room pictures. The Hon. Mrs Teapot by Reynolds. Here's mud in your eye, your ladyship, and all down your left cheek. Lady Touch-me-not by Gainsborough, in one flitting, what soul in the eyes; the soul of a great baby. In milk and dill water. Poor sole, it's a flat life. One flatness on another. Flattery to flats.

But I'll get my feet on canvas, I thought. And I went into the kitchen for the teapot and the bread and jam. Lady Beeder had left only the tin teapot out. But I'd found a nice piece of Sèvres in a glass case in the studio. Tea out of tin. Not in the land of Beulah. And the Sèvres made good tea, though a bit on the simpering side. But there were only two slices of bread left, and when I'd eaten them, I was still hungry. I tried a few cupboard locks with a bent sardine key and opened two of 'em, but nothing inside except the best dinner plates and a lot of odd silver.

Then all at once I had an idea. To sell Lazarus to Sir William instead of the tigers. It was a better bargain for him. He'd get a masterpiece worth thousands for a hundred guineas, or, say, a hundred and fifty. And I could still make a copy on canvas.

And as for getting payment, I'd take an advance. In the only way open to me. Under the circumstances. Damme, I thought, looking at those feet, I'm giving him immortality. The glory he's tried to buy all his life. The Raising of Lazarus by Gulley Jimson, O.M., in the possession of Sir William Beeder. People will point at him in the street. One or two dealers, anyhow. Waiting for him to pop the hooks.

So off I went to the pop shop with the Sèvres teapot and a few apostle spoons. Two quid. And stood myself the best dinner I'd had in five years. No more scrimping and scramping, I said, for Gulley Jimson, O.M. His navel shall no longer shrink from the light. Not when he carries it in front of him

like the headlights of an express train. Puff, puff. That's the secret. Meet
the Professor. My publicity agent. And fetch another Aristotle, waiter. The
philosopher is full of drink. As well as meat.

But I played fair by Sir William. Always treat a patron well so long as
he keeps his bargain. And doesn't try to cheat you. By getting a masterpiece
that's going to be worth ten thousand pounds for a couple of hundred dirty
money and two of soft soap. I put the pawn tickets in an envelope and
wrote my account on the outside. Raising of Lazarus by Gulley Jimson
£157 10s., advance £2.

Next day I went out and ordered what I wanted, paints, brushes, trestles,
plank, canvas, and got down to making a real job of those feet. Of course,
they didn't seem to be so easy when it came to the details. I had to run
round for models. And the first negro I hired turned out all wrong, his feet
were so damned impudent that I had to make a separate study of them.
'How did you get such feet?' I asked him when we were having a rest
about dinner time. 'What kind of feet, sah?' For he was a sad and polite
sort of chap, six foot high, three foot wide, and full of consumption. 'Cheeky
feet.' 'I don't know, sah.' 'What do you do in life?' 'I been a steward, sah,
on a ship, sah.' 'So that's where it came out.' 'I no know how you mean,
sah.' 'It's got to come out somewhere when a chap waits on other chaps'
feeding. It's my belief,' I said, 'that if you took all the waiters' boots off,
their feet would make such rude remarks to the customers that nobody
would be able to enjoy his dinner.' 'Just how you say, sah,' said the poor
old Joe, and he swallowed another half glass of champagne. It was only
sec, but I hadn't time to get in some of the real stuff.

And when I got the feet I wanted, I couldn't get them to lie on the wall.
Those toes stuck out like a row of fists. And then the females. I hunted
three days for Sozie MacT., who used to have very good feet. But she'd got
married and gone to the devil. Been wearing women's shoes for five years
and more. Her feet were like something in a doctor's museum. And when
Bisson, a waster who calls himself a sculptor, lent me Carrie, the girl he
calls his model, for an afternoon he came with her and admired my Feet
so much and talked so much about the Idea of the Resurrection, that he
spoilt three days for me. I nearly scraped the whole thing off. On the third
day I was ready to jump out of the window or cut my throat. And on the
fourth Abel, who is a young friend of Bisson's, another sculptor, turned up
and asked me if he could borrow one end of the studio for a job he had in
hand; war memorial. A thin stooping young man, with a long crooked
nose, and blue eyes, shoulder blades like wings, a backbone like a dying
dog and enormous splay feet. His hands also were six sizes too big. He
didn't talk much and all he said about Lazarus was, 'The left black foot has
something.' I liked him. But I said I hadn't room for any bloody sculptors
with their dust in the same room where I was painting. Then I went out
to lunch and when I came back about six o'clock there were seven men

with a crane swinging a four-ton block of Hopton stone through my studio windows. They'd taken out the bars and piled all the furniture and carpets and cushions at one end of the room.

Bisson, Abel and three more of their gang were directing the work and when I told them to stop they didn't even hear me.

I ran into the middle of the floor and shouted, 'Hi, who lives here, you or me?'

'Lower away,' shouted Bisson, and the block began to come down on my head. Then Bisson, who is a big heavy man weighing seventeen stone, took me by the neck and the seat of my trousers and threw me on top of the furniture pile.

'Lower away, lower away,' he bawled. 'No, hold it.'

'Hold all!' Abel screamed, with his eyes coming out like blue snails and his hair standing out like a bottle-brush. 'Hold it, you . . . don't you see the block has three inches to drop? Do you want it to go through the floor and chip its edges? Here, you – get those rugs under. And the cushions.'

Down came the stone on top of all my precious rugs and fine cushions covered with priceless silk embroidery. And when I tried to grab off the last which was my favourite, Abel pushed me half across the room. But he hadn't even seen me. He was looking at the chains.

'Be careful of those chains, you . . . Don't let it swing. I've had stones ruined that way before by you . . .'

And nobody seemed to mind the way he cursed and swore. I suppose the workmen were used to sculptors. They knew that all real sculptors are insane; or they wouldn't have taken to sculpting.

'Damn it all, Bisson,' I said. 'Have you ever heard of the law? You can't come into an Englishman's house and treat it like this.'

'That's all right,' said Bisson. 'The porter won't know. He's round at the Red Lion with a friend of ours. And this is a commission. Abel's first real big chance. He's getting some real money for it, he'll make it all right about your pansy mats. That reminds me, if you want to get this stuff out of the way, I have the very man to store it for you.' He waved his hand at the pile of chairs and sofas. 'Keep it out of the dust. And you know what stone dust is.'

I always disliked Bisson. A big, cunning oaf. Born into money and tumbled young to the idea that the way to have a good time all his life and get away with murder was to be an artist. So he developed an artistic temperament at fifteen, stopped working, and came it over his people that he was a genius. At seventeen, he was playing at being an art student in Paris and keeping a couple of girls. At nineteen, he gave his first exhibition, imitations of Manet, etc. And at twenty-four, his second, imitations of the Cubists. Then he painted some walls in the style of Stanley Spencer, and did a little sculpture after Epstein and Henry Moore. But all with his left hand. Bisson never took any trouble about anything. He's never done a real job in his life. He doesn't mean to. He'd found out that it's more amusing to swindle, lie and swagger; to take advantage of his friends, and ruin the girls, who fall for his talk. They say he's driven three girls to suicide, and I believe he gets a kind of kick out of it. Makes him feel how impregnable he is. His very grin says, 'Nothing can touch me – I'm solid brass.'

But what is really annoying about Bisson is that he doesn't deceive himself. He knows he's a fraud. He knows he's getting away with it. And he enjoys the game. What I would wish Bisson, if I dared to hate him, is a complicated kidney disease, with chronic chordea. But I can't afford to hate him. He's too hateful. And I believe he knows that, too, the bastard.

When Bisson calmly proposed to throw all Sir William's furniture out of the house, I said, 'Look here, Bisson. This furniture is in my charge. It belongs to Sir William Beeder, who's an honoured friend of mine. I honour him especially because he is a generous and devoted friend of art. There are too few millionaires nowadays who spend money and even time on the encouragement of art, especially young artists, and I'm not going to see him victimized by any dirty phony blackguard who takes advantage of the bloody imbecility and good-natured innocence of the public to pass himself off for a real artist, who is trying to do a real job. I like you a lot, Bisson,' I said, 'but if you try to come it over me, I'll cut your tripe out with a push-razor, and that wouldn't suit your book. Where would you be without your stomach, etc.?'

'That's all right, my dear chap,' said Bisson, laughing and patting me on the shoulder. 'I know how you feel. I'd feel the same way myself. My idea was to avoid damage to the stuff. All this nice brocade won't be improved by Abel's mess.'

'That's true,' I said. 'But who is going to pay for storing it?'

'As for that,' said Bisson, 'you needn't pay. Do what I do when I want something well looked after for a few weeks. Pop it.'

'You can't pop sofas and chairs,' I said. 'I've tried. The only way to do business with stuffed furniture is to give a bill of sale and let the bailiffs find a market.'

'Nonsense,' said Bisson. 'You're out of touch. My friend is a real man of business – he'll do anything that's got money in it – but just as you like. Nice thing that of yours. Best thing you've done,' nodding at the Feet.

'I don't like 'em much,' I said. 'They've gone sour on me.'

'Sir William is lucky if he gets it for anything under five hundred,' said Bisson, who believes in flattery. It costs him nothing. 'A masterpiece. But don't mind me, let him do you if you like. You can afford to give your stuff away – I can't.' And he went off.

Afterwards, of course, I saw that his plan for storing the furniture was a good one. Especially as I was rather short of ready cash at the time. So I telephoned to Bisson's friend, and he came that same afternoon and arranged to remove all the articles that might suffer by Abel's dust. He offered even to lend me a reliable man to take the porter to the Red Lion during the removal. But I preferred to do that myself. It was a task requiring a certain capacity.

And Bisson's friend not only brought a pantechnicon for the goods, but paid on the nail, in notes. No ledger entries to perplex accountants. His prices were rather low, but then I wanted only a temporary advance.

As for Abel, as soon as the stone was on the floor, and even before the workmen had got the chains off it, he was chipping away with his hammer. He was a modern sculptor. He didn't believe in drawings. Just went for the stone and made it fly. And while he was at work, you could have fired off guns in his ear, he wouldn't have heard you. I couldn't have got rid of him if I had wanted to.

So I hung up a lot of sheets and eiderdowns across the middle of the room and went on with Lazarus. We never spoke to each other all day. I could hear him singing and whistling when the work was going well, and swearing when he was in desperation. And once when I threw a china dog through the glass door because I couldn't see the baby's feet any more, he came in and shouted at me, 'What the hell! Can't you let me alone?'

'Get out,' I said to him. 'You humbugging rock-knacker. Who asked you to come in?'

Then he came up close to me, poking out his chin. His eyes were like bottle-stoppers. He had his hammer in his hand, and I thought he was going to brain me. So I snatched up my palette knife and aimed it at his breast, 'My God,' I said, 'I'll stick you through like a chicken, you miserable chop-and-chance-it.'

'What's wrong with you?' he said, stopping and taking in his chin, eyes, etc.

'Nothing, God blast your soul,' for seeing him drop the hammer I thought I'd come it over him. 'Well,' he said, 'You've been throwing things.'

'What's that to you? They aren't your things. You seem to forget you're a guest.'

Then he took a look at the Feet and said, 'You haven't done much this week.'

'Mind your own business.'

'But you've done more than I have.'

'What,' I said. 'Are you stuck?'

'My God,' he said, 'it's the damnedest awfullest job I've ever done. I've ruined the finest piece of stone I ever saw. It's a bloody crime. Come and look before I cut my bloody throat.'

31

Now the truth was I was so sick of those feet that I could have knocked my head on the walls. It wasn't that they were hopeless. They still had some sense in them. I could still feel that there was something there. Something real. But it kept on fleeing away from us.

So I was glad of any excuse to break off work and I went off with Abel.

There was the usual mess. Dust, chips, half a bottle of stout on her ladyship's Bechstein. The model's clothes hanging on the crystal wall light and the model herself, a thick little blonde girl called Lolie, walking up and down and slapping herself with both hands to get back her circulation. Lolie has long hair and it was hanging down to her buttocks. Which was more than three-quarters of the woman, as she has the shortest legs in London.

'Isn't it good, Mr Jimson?' said Lolie. 'You tell him it's good.'

Abel paid no attention to her. He said to me, 'Look at that, Jimson. You see it was really a double block. A small one set into a big one at the corner. That was the character of the mass. Two levels on top – then the verticals of the small cube. Then the big block with the oblique left side . . .'

'Well,' I said. 'You've got that side all right.'

'I haven't touched that side,' he said, passing his hand over it as if stroking a horse. 'And I don't want to – it's a beauty. But come round here.'

He'd cut the little block into a woman's head and breasts and forearms. Forearms and breast on one horizontal plane. Head tilted sideways to get the cheek flat, and the hair flat down her back for the side of the stone. It was not bad for a young chap of thirty-four or so. 'That's not too bad,' I said. 'It's chunky.'

'Yes,' he said, 'but has it got the weight,' cupping his big hands like a pair of soup tureens. 'Can you feel her weight?'

'Heavier than the stone,' I said. 'Why, she looks about sixteen tons by herself – she's nearly as thick as Lolie.'

Lolie scratched herself with both hands at once, and said in a cross voice, 'It's coming on very nicely, and a nice subject, too. Earth mourning for her sons. But he never will listen to anything I say.'

'It's a bloody subject, of course,' said Abel. 'But I haven't bothered with the name. It was the town council planted that on me. One of them was educated. But we needn't worry about that.'

'It's time for tea,' said Lolie.

'Just turn round a bit, darling,' said Abel, 'yes, that's it.' And he turned her round by her shoulders. 'Look at that back. There's something there.'

And he passed the back of his great knuckly ham down her spine. 'If you forget it's meat.'

'Tell him he couldn't do it nicer, Mr Jimson,' said Lolie. 'He's only cross with it because he hasn't had his tea. That's what he wants. You tell him.'

'Look at what I've done with it – slop, just slop. Lost all the monumental. And that corner, oh my God . . .'

'Well,' I said, 'what did you mean – knocking that hole in the left side? What's it doing, that hole? What's it for?'

'Don't ask me,' he said, throwing his hammer on the floor and making a bit of the parquet jump right out of its socket. 'I thought I saw one of the dead there, sitting up with his head on his shoulder. I could feel him this morning, and this edge of the block is the line of his jaw and neck.'

'Well,' I said, 'I don't see why that shouldn't come out all right. You've got him square enough too. You could cut your fingers on his chin.'

'Yes, but what about the corner?' I saw a lying figure at the bottom, with a flat back giving the side plane. 'Excuse me, darling.' He took Lolie by the shoulders, pushed her to her knees and pressed her head down on her shoulder.

'Oh dear,' said Lolie, 'he'll only spoil it. And it was so nice. Oh dear, if only he'd had his tea at the proper time. But what's the good of talking?'

'You see,' said Abel, combing down Lolie's hair with a chisel. 'If you forget the flesh, the planes come right out,' and he moved his great flat paddles in the air as if rubbing them on a surface. 'Solid as rocks. And so I cut into the block above it, cut out the whole corner. But it went soft. And it goes on getting softer. However sharp you make the edges. And now I can't even see the next vertical. Got to be a vertical there. That's the whole character of the block. Must have another cube. For the blockiness. But Christ, look at it now – it's gone soft – it's rotten. You could put your bloody fingers through it like bad butter.' And he gave the stone a prod as if he really expected his finger to go through it.

'What I keep on saying,' said Lolie, 'some ammunition boxes. It's on the battlefield, isn't it? Earth surrounded by her dead. And you can't get anything squarer than ammunition boxes. But you better tell him, Mr Jimson – he won't listen to me. Not since I married him.'

'Why, darling,' said Abel, 'I have the highest regard for your taste. Just bend over a little further. That's it,' and he said to me, 'I thought I might do something with Lolie's head, by flattening it off a bit.'

'Oh dear,' said Lolie, 'why not a box? If you want a square edge. Oh dear, I wish you would have your tea.'

'My dear Lolie,' I said. 'You can't put a box of any kind in the middle of that group – any more than you could pin a bit of silk on a court portrait. It doesn't belong to the idea.'

'Not a real box,' said Lolie, shedding tears down towards her left ear. 'Oh dear, oh dear. He didn't have any lunch, not a real lunch. And now it's nearly six o'clock and no tea.'

'A box,' Abel said to me, 'has been suggested by that ass Bisson. But I pointed out to him that you couldn't have a manufactured cube among natural chunks, it wouldn't look solid. It would look like an empty drainpipe in a forest, or one of those toyshop pieces where you have a lot of men and cannons mixed up.'

'He ought to stop now, or he'll spoil it. Tell him to have some consideration for himself,' said Lolie, who had been turning blue with the evening breeze.

'You're right,' I said, for it was an interesting point. 'It's got to be all meat or it would stop being stone, can't have a change of idea in the middle of the block, not from meat to plank.'

'Tell him to cheer up,' said Lolie. 'All he wants is a cup of tea, and he'll feel better at once.'

'Why not a dead horse,' I said, 'with the face flat up the front and the neck slewed round?'

'That is an idea,' said Abel.

'A box is much better,' said Lolie. 'It won't take so long. Make it an iron box if you don't like wood.'

Abel was bending down sideways and looking through his hands.

'He thought of a box himself yesterday,' said Lolie. 'But he had a proper lunch yesterday.'

'Yes, darling,' said Abel, and he lifted her up from the ground. But one leg had gone dead and she couldn't stand. 'Just hop over there, dear, in the corner, and lie down on your side – yes, stretch out your legs and your arms, and twist up your neck. We want you to look like a dead horse.'

Lolie wiped her nose on her hand, which was all she had for the purpose, and lay down.

'I meant one that's been dead about a month,' I said. 'Not a bloated dead horse.'

'Just draw in your wind a bit, darling,' said Abel, pushing her stomach with the toe of his boot. 'We want to see your diaphragm.'

'Is that right?' said Lolie. 'Oh dear, he's so tired, Mr Jimson. He's just worn out – you can see he's ready to cry – he ought to be stopped, really he ought.'

'Not that way,' I said. 'Here, come next door and I'll cut it out in cheese.' So Abel came next door and I carved up a piece of cheese to show him my idea.

'It looks a bit made up,' he said. 'A bit as if you'd thought of it,' and we talked for a bit. Then we went out and had some beer at the Red Lion, and all at once I remembered Lolie.

'Lolie's changed a lot in the year,' I said. 'When I used to know her she looked like a pig, but now she looks more like a dog-faced baboon.'

'Yes.' Abel agreed. 'She's changed – on the whole it's for the better. Her jaw's grown out more and her features have lost importance. The whole effect is flatter, more compact. It's a good face considering what most faces are – a mass of piffling detail.'

'Paint her white and cut off her ears and she'd do for a milestone.'

'Hardly, I'm afraid. But you couldn't expect it. Not with skulls as they are. A wretched job.'

'And you've really married her.'

'Yes, really,' he said. 'I mean we went to the registry. Of course, my last wife may still be alive somewhere – I haven't had time to make enquiries. But Lolie has her lines, and I'm glad to get her.'

'Love at first sight.'

'That's it,' he said. 'As soon as I saw her I said, You attract me a lot. Take off, will you? So she stripped and – well, you've seen her. She's unique. Look here, Lolie, I said, you're practically made for me, but how much do you charge? Three bob an hour to a sculptor because of the dust, she said. I can't afford to pay anything, I said, but I'll marry you, and you can still sit in the mornings to anyone you like. I can carve all night.'

'And she accepted you.'

'Yes, she said she wanted to be settled. And she often makes four or five pounds in a good week. We do very well. It's been a great success. But as you see, we're both quiet people. Domesticated. We don't want to be rushing about amusing ourselves. Yes, there's nothing like marriage for an artist – if he can find the right woman, of course.'

'I found her once,' I said. 'And what a woman, Rubens and cream.' And I began to talk about Sara. So we went on chatting about Sara and Lolie, and boasting of the virtues of our wives, as married men do, until closing time.

But then we went back to the studio, and while Abel was using one of his chisels on a cupboard in the dining-room that looked like a cellarette, I walked through and found Lolie in Abel's end of the studio holding her face on the floor. She was blue and purple with cold and as stiff as a corpse.

'Hullo,' I said. 'You look cold, Lolie.'

'I didn't like to move – not when he's got something in his eye. He might say I'd spoilt everything.'

'You wouldn't be any good to me, that colour,' I said. 'But I suppose a sculptor isn't particular.'

Then Abel came in and said, 'Hullo, Lolie, what, have you been waiting here all the time?'

'You didn't tell me to put on.'

'Didn't I? I'm awfully sorry. Why, aren't you hungry? Get up and have some tea. No, here. Just a minute, there's something in the sag of that left shoulder,' and he began to chip away. He was chipping away all night. I heard him singing and whistling to himself, and when I went in at breakfast time I found him in the best of spirits. He was well away. Then we noticed that Lolie was crying, and when we asked her what was wrong, she said she was worried about Abel. He must be so tired, so we lifted her up and gave her a rub down with towels, and a cup of tea, and in ten minutes she was making breakfast for us.

'A girl in a thousand,' said Abel. 'She has the constitution of an elephant. She posed for me in the yard in December with three inches of snow on the ground. I didn't press her, but she insisted on it. And all she got was a chilblain on her nose which I never use, anyhow.'

And it was quite true that Lolie had a good constitution. Which is the chief thing in a wife. She posed for Abel all that day and most of the night. Until he couldn't hold a chisel or see out of his eyes.

Next day, of course, he struck another bad place; threw his hammer clean through Lady Beeder's long looking-glass; and disappeared. Lolie hunted him all over London. She used to come to me every night and say what a pity it was if he'd hanged himself again. 'But he's always so up and down. Oh dear, I do hate his downs. But there, everyone has his faults. And he's a good husband, I must say. Not like that Bisson, who knocks his girls about with an Indian club just for exercise.'

'I thought the carving was going rather well.'

'Did you?' said Lolie. 'I didn't. I think it's worse than the last. But all his stuff is rotten. Why, you wouldn't know me in any of them – I come out like a lot of bricks. But don't you tell him, whatever you do. He'll never learn, and it keeps him quiet. Poor old Abel,' she said sadly, 'I suppose he's about the rottenest sculptor that ever lived. But I think he's happy, don't you? I mean, as happy as a chap can be when he's got such bad health and never takes any regular meals.'

'I think he's happy,' I said. 'Now and then. But I don't suppose he knows it.'

'Oh, he likes sculpting,' said Lolie. 'Oh, I'm sure he does. He thinks a lot of me too, especially the back view. Oh, I'm sure he's happy.'

'As happy as a chap can be,' I said.

'I think so,' said Lolie doubtfully. 'Anyhow, in the ups. Oh, I know how to manage him when he has a new stone to hammer about and when he hasn't got his insomnia.'

'Did he hang himself before?'

'He started. But when his neck was beginning to stretch and just before he lost consciousness, he had an idea for a piece of modern gothic and knocked on the wall and the neighbours came in and cut him down.'

I didn't care for Lolie in her skin. She was a sculptor's shape, with no neck or waist and feet like ammunition boots. But I liked her dressed. Lolie's style is well known; bodies with buttons, long skirts, hats with feathers, in the old Phil May fashion. The fact is, as she told me, that as she had to have her hair long, and there was a lot of it, she put it up, and it didn't go with anything but a real hat. And as her legs were short and thick, she liked a long skirt. So she had taken to the style of 1890. And it suited her very well, with her pug face. Lolie dressed took me back to my youth when a woman was a female. Of course, she wasn't a real female, like Sara; she'd been brought up in the chromium-plate period and finished off with a synthetic spray. She didn't know sometimes whether she was a female or a dentist's chair. She used to say, 'Kids, not me, all that trouble for cannon fodder, not likely. Or just when you've worn yourself out on them they get saucy and tell you to lay off – it's time you were buried.'

To see her with a glass of beer down at the Eagle and her ostrich feathers shaking in the breeze of the gasworks made me feel like twenty again, in a curly bowler and chase-me trousers. But when I put my arm round Lolie, and squeezed her, she didn't giggle like a real old girl, or say 'Do give over,' or throw her eye at me, as Rozzie used to do, as much as to say, 'Go further and fare better,' she only took a sip of beer and went on talking about Abel's nerves. She was out of touch with life, Lolie; I mean, female life. And she couldn't expect to know any other.

But I liked going about with that bodice and those feathers, and we hunted all the pubs in the likely spots – Chelsea, Hampstead and Hammersmith. We even tried Elsinore.

I thought old Plant might be able to help us, as he knew a lot of dosses and their regulars.

Plant and I were not so friendly as we had been because he didn't like my going to the Beeders, and he wouldn't come to see me there or even take a loan from me.

'I'm sorry, Mr Jimson,' he said, 'but I like to be independent. And I never cared to run into debt.'

'Yes, but how are you going to live?' I said. I'd found him in the kitchen at Elsinore with no money and nothing to eat.

'They give me a bed now for doing a bit of scrubbing.'

As I looked at the old man I thought he was about twenty years older. He seemed eighty. 'Look here, Mr Plant,' I said, 'Elsinore is killing you. You weren't born for a doss. You've got to fight your way in life, the lower the harder, and you've never learnt how. You're too much of a philosopher and you're too light.'

But old Plantie just kept on shaking his head. 'It means something, Mr Jimson,' he said. 'It means something or it wouldn't happen like this.'

'And what means dinner?' I said.

'Oh well,' he said, 'they're very wasteful here, you'd be surprised all the bits of bread and bacon that get into the bucket. And hardly any of them seem to know how to get all the meat off a herring or a kipper. I don't do badly.'

And he wouldn't take a farthing from me. 'No,' he said. 'Excuse me, Mr Jimson, but I never liked debt.'

'Trouble with you, Plantie,' I said, 'is that you're too proud. You'd rather feed out of a dustbin than own you're wrong.'

'Wrong about what, Mr Jimson?'

'About the meaning of the world. The world doesn't mean anything to anybody except what the thrush said to the snail before she knocked it on the brick. GET ON OR GET OUT. LAZY BONES.'

But it was no good talking to Plantie. He was too far gone. And he couldn't even tell me if Abel had been that way, because he didn't seem to notice who came in or out. He sat in his corner all day, trying to find out what had happened to him, and why; until the boss came in and put a pail on his hook and a scrubbing-brush in his left hand; and then he went off to clean up the lavatories and the steps and the dustbins, just as if he were in a kind of dream.

But neither had anyone else seen Abel. Though he was easy to see with his eyes, his hair, his hands, his scarlet socks and green sandals. I began to think that he'd had an accident or even gone into the country.

But Lolie never lost hope. 'No,' she said, 'he wouldn't go into the country except just passing through on business, because he can't stand scenery. It reminds him of pictures. And I feel sure he hasn't drowned himself again. He left his tools behind.'

'Did he drown himself before?'

'Twice. First time he jumped off Westminster steps, but it turned out very well. Because the chap who fished him out had no lobes to his ears, and gave him an idea for an abstract bit of stuff he was doing, an urn or something; and the second time he put all his hammers in his pocket and jumped off Waterloo Bridge, but as soon as he hit the water, he got such a strong feeling of the horizontal that he shouted for the police. And he went straight home and did a thing called Plane Surface, which everybody thought was a joke. And between you and me, so it was. But it kept him happy for six weeks. And made a nice pastry board afterwards. Thank God he's chucked the abstract stuff,' said Lolie. 'He's still rotten, but he's not abstract any more.'

I was not surprised to hear that Lolie didn't admire the abstract; no more than if a coster's moke had told me it didn't take much interest in St Paul's dome.

'I suppose he doesn't need a model when he's doing the abstract?' I said.

'No, he only needs a woman. And the things it drives him to! A little more of the abstract and we'd both have gone potty. What is there to bite on in the abstract? You might as well eat triangles and go to bed with a sewing machine.'

Lolie was right about Abel. He met us in the street one day. on his way back to the flat. And he hadn't been in the country, He had spent the week in a drinking club down in Belgravia, drinking all night and sleeping it off all day. He hadn't had anything to eat but bread and cheese; his hair was full of flue off the floor and his beard was two inches long. His face was green, his eyes were crimson; and he had the shakes. But he was full of energy and enthusiasm. He had got a plastic notion. 'It's a feeling of declivity,' he said. 'I just had been sick,' he said, 'and I was looking at the bowl when it came to me, "That's what I've been feeling after – declivity." And I thought it was acclivity. You see, Jimson,' he said, waving his great hands as if he were wiping up a fishmonger's slab. 'I was trying to feel this thing upwards, against the grain, when all the time it was really downwards – like this. Here, Lolie, take off and I'll show him.'

And Lolie was so pleased to have her husband back that she began to take off in the street. I was glad to get her into the flat while she was still partly decent. And in two minutes Abel got Sir William's dining-table propped up on one edge against a pile of books, and Lolie hanging on the top edge by her arms and chin. 'I want the descending shapes,' he said, 'in a big way.'

He made such a noise, singing and swearing, for the next three days, that I couldn't think or feel. I thought I'd never be able to paint again. In fact, I was fairly driven out of the studio, and I would probably have given up the flat altogether if it hadn't been for young Barbon. I was coming out of the Red Lion one night, in a fog, when suddenly I saw a thin grey object in front of me, shaking in every inch. I thought it was the front of a cab-horse just about to fall off, when I heard Barbon's voice, 'Mr J-Jimson.'

'Why,' I said. 'It's you, Nosy. I thought you were a horse.'

'I've been waiting for you – I saw you through the window.'

'How are things? Are you working hard?'

'Very b-bad. I l-lost my s-scholarship, and I had to g-go for a clerk.'

'You go on for a clerk, Nosy. Steady pay and a dry life,'

'B-but I've g-got the s-s-sack.'

'What for?'

'I w-wasn't any g-good. I kept on being late.'

'Never you mind. You go for another clerk or office boy. Or kitchen man. You can always s-stay at home.'

'B-but, Mr J-Jimson, I c-can't go home any more. I c-can't tell my poor mother I g-got the s-sack.'

And in fact he had been going and coming home for a week pretending to be at the office. So I said, 'Look here, Nosy, I'm in funds just now. I've got a commission from Sir William Beeder for a wall decoration. Come along with me and I'll give you a job for a week or two till you get another clerkship. You can do secretarial work. Fetch my beer and answer the door. I'll give you a pound a week and your food. And you can go out for the beer.'

The poor boy couldn't thank me enough. And I put him into Sir William's bed the same night.

Of course, he thought the Feet were wonderful. He didn't know any better. But just by saying how wonderful they were, he got me criticizing them, and I thought I saw what was wrong. They were too low in tone. They wanted more jump. So I got started again. And forgot that Abel was in the same world, until he burst in upon me one afternoon with bloodshot eyes and his face and hair as white as a miller, and shouted, 'I've finished it, Gulley. It's done. For God's sake don't let me give it another touch. Come and take it away from me before I spoil it.'

'That's Lolie's job, isn't it? What's she for?'

'Lolie doesn't understand art,' said Abel. 'She was broken in with painters. Here, take my tools away while I telephone for the lorry.'

So I put his hammer and chisels into the fireplace while he telephoned for the lorry contractors and Bisson, and they swung out the group that afternoon through the same window, while Bisson and the porter tried a new pub further off. Abel, of course, was going with the lorry, to watch over his precious Earth mother on the road, and see her safely delivered.

And as soon as the stone was in the air, he came in with his suitcase, threw his tools inside, on top of his smock, and made a run for the stairs.

'Good-bye,' I said, touching up the negro's toenails. But he didn't hear me.

And just then it struck me that I hadn't seen Lolie. 'Where's Lolie?' I called. 'Stop him,' I said to Nosy. 'Catch him,' and I shouted after him, 'What have you done with Lolie?'

'Lolie,' he said. 'Lolie,' as if he'd never heard of Lolie. 'Oh my God, is that rain?' and he tried to rush past me.

'Here,' I said, catching him. 'What have you done with that girl?' For though I liked Lolie, I didn't want her left on my hands. I couldn't use a girl all the time. I was much too busy.

'Let me go,' he screamed. 'Do you want it to catch cold?'

'What catch cold?'

'The stone,' he said, 'it's not even covered.' And he tore himself clear. However, when he'd got the stone on the cart, and covered it up with wadding and canvas, he came to himself and apologized. 'I have to be careful of that block. Of course, some Hopton stone will stand up to an east wind and take no harm. But this is a delicate piece. Beautiful grain, as you saw, but no real stamina. However, it's going into a good home. Municipal entrance hall. Central heating, and so on. So it can afford to be a bit soft.'

'And what about Lolie?' I said.

'Yes, of course. Where the devil is she? I shall want her along.'

'I'm glad you can find some use for her,' I said with irony. I've never liked the way sculptors treat women, who are, after all, of considerable value to art, as essential raw material.

'Use for her,' said Abel. 'Why, I *need* her. Don't you make any mistake. I know what Lolie's good for. I *value* Lolie, especially when there's a stone to be looked after. She once nursed a block of Portland for me, through ten degrees of frost, in the middle of Salisbury Plain, when a lorry broke down. Put her own clothes on it. Saved it. And caught a pretty severe chill too. Luckily only on the inside. Yes,' he said, as we climbed the stairs, 'you can't do without women when you're dealing with a job like that. They have a special instinct. Maternal. I've never been sorry, not really sorry, that I married Lolie.'

So we went to find Lolie, and there she was, hanging on the dining-table like a side of pork, cold as wet meat. Abel was enraged. 'Damn it all,' he said, 'I told her I was finished. I told her to get down and put on and have a cup of tea before we started. Now she'll want it on the way. Lolie,' he shouted, 'Lolie darling.' But she didn't move. She'd passed out. I thought she was dead, and it was just going to upset me when Abel saw my trouble and consoled me. 'Don't worry, old chap. She'll come round. And she'll be all right in two ticks. Lolie is good stock – Bethnal Green. I'll just ring up the hospital, and if you don't mind sticking her in the ambulance, I'll be grateful. Oh my God, what's that?'

And he rushed off in terror that some wall or thunderbolt had fallen on his masterpiece.

So I sent for the ambulance and Nosy and I put Lolie in an old mattress cover and carried her downstairs. Nosy was shocked. 'It she all right?' he asked.

'Lolie's all right,' I said. 'She's attached for life. That's what she wants. To know where she is.' And we pushed her into the butcher's cart.

The diagnosis at the hospital was exposure, shock, displacement of the caudal vertebrae and malnutrition. I suppose the poor girl hadn't had a cup of tea for two or three days.

32

Abel's fussing about his lump of nonsense, and the trouble with Lolie, did not, as I had feared, put me off my work. In the next two days, I made a new thing of the Feet. Brought them up till they came right off the wall. And having got my key I decided to get on with the grave and Lazarus himself. That was a Sunday evening. I waited till eight o'clock that night, drawing. Then I was so tired I fell down. So I sent Nosy out to get two bottles of beer, a bottle of whisky, and a paper of fried fish and chips.

Nosy, as it happened, had to go some way off. Because we had run through our credit within the first half mile. In fact, I had been right out of petty cash for the last fortnight. Luckily Nosy had brought his post office savings book with him, three pounds four shillings, and I had been able to take over the three pounds as an advance on his salary.

And as I knew that Nosy was a great man for a bargain, and might be an hour on his shopping, I went up to the gallery and lay down on the floor for a doze. It wasn't by choice that I had taken to the floor-sleeping again. We had had to part with the beds only to raise current expenses. For the prices we were getting for furniture from Bisson's friend were so bad that though we had nothing left to pop except the kitchen stove and a tin jordan, we were not up to my advance. In fact, allowing for expenses, and assessing the Feet only at two hundred guineas, Sir William still owed me fifteen or twenty pounds.

I had taken to sleeping in the gallery because Bisson's friend had removed all the window curtains. Bisson's friend had been a bit hard at a bargain, but he was certainly good at business. One had to respect a man who understood his public duty so well. He had taken even the bathroom taps, and the chain out of the W.C., at a shilling for the taps and twopence for the chain.

No one could overlook me in the gallery. And I gradually built up a comfortable corner for myself there, with a spring mattress of crushed dailies shoved into some old sacks and a dozen *News of the World* wrapped up tight and tied with string, for a pillow. A permanent pillow is the luxury of home. You can get it fitted to your ear. And I was having a sweet nap, the kind of nap which comes to a man who has had a good day's work and sees another in front of him, when the studio door down below the gallery opened and waked me up.

Being in good spirits over the Feet, I was just going to call out some nonsense to Nosy about a fête of celebration when I heard Lady Beeder's voice say in a queer tone, 'But I don't understand.' You'd have thought the woman was coming out of an anaesthetic. Then a stranger cracked off, 'My God, it's one of those new daylight robberies – they've taken everything.'

'I should so like something to sit on,' said Lady Beeder, still faint.

'There isn't anything,' said the stranger. And I heard him running about. 'Yes, they've even taken up the linoleum.' And in fact Bisson's friend had given us only four and sixpence for two almost new pieces of best quality linoleum from the bathrooms. The ticket was in the envelope. 'They've taken the lot, Flora – all your beautiful collection. What a terrible thing. We must call the police at once. Where's the phone?' And he rushed to the corner next the door and began to ring up the house exchange and to shout, 'Hullo – police. Yes, put me on to the police. It's important – a big robbery.'

'But what is that on the wall?' Lady Beeder sighed. 'I don't understand.'

'I think they're meant for feet,' said Sir William. I peeped over the edge of the balustrade and there was Sir William dusting the packing-case I used for a table and pulling it forward for Lady Beeder to sit on. But she still kept gazing round her and then looking at the Feet. For you understand that the grave and Lazarus and the bald heads, so important to the composition, were only sketched in; so that the feet appeared rather prominent. 'Feet,' said Lady Beeder.

'Hullo, hullo. Yes, the police. My poor Flora. I can't say how sorry I am. It's a dreadful misfortune. Irremediable,' said the stranger, who was a little pink-nosed man with pince-nez glasses and a pinch-waist overcoat. 'One of the finest private collections in the country. So perfectly balanced. Quite unique. Hullo.'

'Looks a bit queer, I'm afraid,' said Sir William, in a reasonable voice. He was much more worried by Lady Beeder's demand for a chair. Because obviously he wanted to sit down himself. 'Do sit down, my dear. The box is only slightly dusty.'

'But where are we going to sleep?' said Lady Beeder. 'Really, I do so wish we could have known about this sooner.'

'It's come at an awkward time,' said Sir William, 'very awkward. But I could ring up Aunt Lucy. She's always delighted to have us.'

'A national calamity,' said Pinch-nose, who was fizzing with indignation, like a soda-water bottle. Probably he was a poor citizen, a Boorjay, perhaps even a writer of some kind. He had none of the Beeder's repose in the face of lost property. And again I said, 'God bless all Beeders. God bless the millionaires, who can forgive everything unless it bothers them too much.'

'Oh no, Bill,' said Lady Beeder, 'I really couldn't face being entertained.'

'Shall I try the Savoy?' said Sir William, going towards the telephone.

'Aren't the Mortons there? – they would be so terribly sorry for us.'

'Claridge's then – yes, excuse me, James.' And Sir William went to the phone.

'But the police – they're getting me the police,' said Pinch-nose. 'Every moment counts.'

'We really must have somewhere to sit, James,' said her ladyship, 'we can't live on packing-cases.'

And Sir William took the phone out of the little man's hand and said, 'Just a moment, James. Hullo, Claridge's, please. Never mind about the police just now. I want Claridge's. As soon as possible. It's rather urgent.'

And little pinch-waist was in such a fury and a fluster that he shouted he would call up the police from the public phone. And shot out of the room in a passion.

Now Sir William and Lady Beeder were behaving so well that I had half a mind to call down to them and explain the situation. That all the pawn tickets were in the empty tomato tin on the top of the bathroom door, where the mice wouldn't get them. But the little man had given me a fright with his shouts for the police. A dangerous type, as I could see and hear. Probably a hanger-on. One of those rats who take advantage of good-natured gentlemen and ladies like the Beeders. Full of parasitic bitterness and bum-suck spite.

So I decided to explain myself from a distance. Luckily Claridge's had a room for the Beeders, and Sir William at once rang up a taxi, and while he was putting Lady Beeder into the taxi, I went quietly out by the studio door, grabbed my mackintosh and overcoat, passed down the back stairs and followed Nosy towards the fried-fish shop.

I met him on the next corner and told him the necessary facts, that a quick move was essential. 'Preferably by country bus, from the central depot. No railway stations for me. They watch 'em in a case like this.'

'Whew – watch them?' said Nosy, who was greatly alarmed. He thought we were going to be arrested. 'It's all right,' I told him. 'We haven't got to be afraid of the police so much as the rain. I've got a bit of a cold in my head and a wet night in the rough might bring on my churchyard cough which is the worst of the five. How much money have you?'

'I have the fish and the chips, and the whew-whisky,' said Nosy, shivering with terror. 'And the change was ninepence and I've got a two-shilling bit.'

'And I have eightpence. We'll have to conserve our resources.' I held up my hand at the bus stop for a Victoria bus, and we went to the front seat on top. So that the conductor would take time to reach us. And I tried to put some heart into Nosy.

'It's not that we have done anything illegal,' I said, 'but there would have to be a legal investigation which would waste a lot of time. I'd be badgered to death by enquiries and solicitors when I ought to be at work. And then I might get irritated against the government. Which would be stupid. It's no good telling a government that an artist's time and peace of mind might be valuable to a nation, that is, of positive value, bringing in reputation and tourists and students and orders and friends and respect and allies and victories and security, and so on. It's no good telling it because it couldn't hear. It doesn't possess the necessary organ. It's no good running down the government,' I said, 'any more than swearing at a paralytic mule for having the habits appropriate to its condition.'

I admit that this language was injudicious; it's never wise to feel irritation against the lower animals, especially if they deserve it. But the truth was, that I was a trifle upset. For I kept on thinking, I'm getting on for seventy now, and I haven't the constitution I had at sixty. I'm in my prime as a painter, but how long will it last, ten, fifteen years at the outside. Old Mike Angelo was at his best at eighty-five, but then he went and died. No, I can't afford to waste my time in jug, or hospital. The very idea made me angry.

'No,' I said, 'that's the very biggest mistake anyone can make, to get annoyed with government. Because it's so easy.'

Just then the conductor reached us and I held out two pennies and said, 'Hammersmith, two, please. Like my brother-in-law, Ranken . . .'

'Hammersmith,' said the conductor. 'Why, you're going the wrong way.'

Some of the passengers smiled, and I was greatly confused. 'But this is a No. 11,' I said. 'I saw it on the outside.'

'Yes, but it's going the other way. See? Sorry, sir, You'd better wait at the next stop – on the other side.'

'Oh dear, I must have read it backwards.'

And we got off. And took another Victoria bus. 'My brother-in-law, Ranken,' I said, as we made for the top front seats, 'was an inventor, God help him.'

And he couldn't get anyone to take up his patents. So he used to curse the government and say that it was a lot of Boorjuice Blimps starving the inventive genius of the nation. 'All I want is a little progressive spirit – just a little – somewhere.'

'You can't get it,' I said, 'over the counter, not even in a special bottle. Progress isn't done by government or spirits, but by chaps. A few rich chaps gambling on their fancy and a few young chaps backing them up in order to give papa and mama a shock. It's just the same in art,' I said. 'What keeps it moving is not a big public shoving its little foot forward, but a little mosquito biting a big public behind. If you left the world to itself,' I said, 'it would die of fatty degeneration in about six weeks. It would lie down in the nice rich mudbank where it finds itself and close its eyes and stuff its ears and let itself be fed to death down a pipe-line. But God, not intending to lose a valuable pedigree hog that way, has sent the mosquito to give it exercise, and fever and the fear of death.'

'Fares, please,' said the conductor. He was quite worried when he found we were on the wrong bus. A nice chap like so many bus conductors, especially London conductors. He got down to show us where to find the stopping-place and which side of the road to look for a Hammersmith bus. And we had to wait in a queue till he was out of sight. It was only polite. Then we crossed the street to the country bus centre.

'B-but how are we going to p-pay for the tickets?' asked Nosy.

'That's the real difficulty,' I said, taking off my hat to wipe my anxious forehead. I was passing the queue at the time, as it happened, and several gentlemen put something into the hat. True, by a coincidence, I was simultaneously carrying a matchbox in my other hand.

And finding myself then at the top of the queue, which willingly made way for me, out of respect for my age or perhaps my appearance, distinguished by four days' beard and my habit of rolling my eyes and grinding my gums together, I took the opportunity of buying tickets for a considerable part of our way.

Providence had blessed us and we should have embarked at once, if Nosy at this moment, already slightly confused by the bustle of a great city, had not run into a policeman, and recoiled with such looks of horror and guilt, that the officer at once exclaimed, 'Here – what's this?'

But I quickly recognized the man. 'It's Tom Jones,' I said. 'How are you, officer?' 'Very well, thank you,' he said. 'But my name's not Jones.' 'No,' I said, 'but you gave me a shilling once for my kip when I was trying to sleep on a bench down by Millbank.' 'Did I?' he said, putting his hands together and grinding them a little. 'I thought I knew you. Well, how are things?' 'Not too good,' I said. 'Thank you all the same. But not too bad either. Me and my boy have got to get to Burlington tonight, and we've only got a shilling towards our breakfast. But it isn't raining yet. We could sleep rough.'

'The Burlington bus,' said the officer. And he took us down to the bus. Then having seen us get on and made sure that I wasn't telling the tale, he took out a shilling and gave it to me. 'Here you are. This will give you a kip.'

Nosy was much excited. He turned red in patches, like a bad case of scarlet fever, as usual when he was moved in his best feelings, and tears came to his eyes. 'How awfully k-k-k —'

'Yes,' I said, 'I hadn't quite expected that myself. But after all, one oughtn't to be surprised. My experience is that the police are pretty reliable, especially if they've ever done you a good turn before, or think they have.' 'D-didn't he help you before?' 'I don't know. Probably not. They all look the same to me in uniform. No, I rather think the chap who gave me a bob before was a sergeant with a red moustache. But that doesn't matter. Most officers have given something to an old bum like me. And naturally they take an interest in you afterwards. It's natural. Well,' I said, 'I honour policemen – as a class, they're nice chaps and a good deal better than the government deserves, but I suppose nobody gets his deserts.'

For the bus was shaking up my bones, and my rheumatism was beginning to shoot, and I was wondering what would happen to my palettes and colours and drawings; all my gear left behind at the Beeders'. I'm too old, I thought, to be poor. And too hardworking to be deprived of my tools and my studio. It's an outrage. And I said to Nosy, 'To accuse government of being selfish, cruel, blind, deaf and dumb, is simply stupid; because what else can you expect? What is a government, Nosy? It's a committee of committees and a committee hasn't even got trousers. It's only got a typist, and she's thinking of her young man and next Saturday afternoon at the pictures. If you gave a government imagination, it wouldn't know where to put it. It would pass it on to the cat or leave it out for the charwoman to be taken away with the tea leaves. The only good government,' I said, 'is a bad one in the hell of a fright; yes, what you want to do with government is to put a bomb under it every ten minutes and blow its whiskers off – I mean its sub-committees. And it doesn't matter if a few of its legs and arms go too, and it gets blown out of the window. Not that I've personally got a bad opinion of governments, as governments. A government is a government, that's all. You don't expect it to have the virtues of a gorilla because it doesn't belong to the same class. It's not a higher anthropoid. It has too many legs and hands. But if you blow off some of the old limbs, well, imagine. There you have a piece of government lying in the middle of Whitehall, and it says to itself, "This is most unusual. I distinctly heard a bang. I must inquire at once – yes, immediately – I must appoint a commission." So then it opens its eyes and looks at the crowd and says, "My God, what has happened, what are these creatures?" And the people say, "We're the people, you're the government, hurry up and do something for us." And the government says, "I'll have a committee on it at once." And the people say, "You haven't got any committees – they're all dead – you're the government." And the government says, "Haven't I got a secretary?" And the people shout, "No, we've just chopped her up with a rusty axe." "Or an office boy?" "No, we've pushed him down a drain."

'"But I can't be a government all by myself."

'"Yes you are, and you've got to do something."

'"But one man can't be a government, it isn't democratic."

'"Yes it is," the people say. "We've sent for another bomb. But you've got ten minutes still, so you'd better do something."

'So then the government looks round and thinks. It uses its imagination because it hasn't got any committee and because it hasn't got a secretary. It gets an idea all by itself, and it says, 'Jimini Christie, look at all these people. Look at their trousers and their gamps. What squalor. It seems that they aren't in the government." And then it makes a law that everyone is to get a steel-stick umbrella and a trouser-press free. And all the old clubmen who used to be in government say, it's impossible, it can't be done. The people won't stand it. But it is done, it is possible, and the people not only stand it, they ask for trousers as well, to put in the presses. And then the old clubmen themselves ask for new trousers and take it all as a matter of course. And then the bomb comes and the people blow that government into cottage pie and start again with committees. For the people is just as big a danger as the government. I mean, if you let it get on your mind. Because there's more of it. More and worse and bigger and emptier and stupider. One man is a living soul, but two men are an indiarubber milking machine for a beer engine, and three men are noises off and four men are an asylum for cretins and five men are a committee and twenty-five are a meeting, and after that you get to the mummy-house at the British Museum, and the Sovereign People and Common Humanity and the Average and the Public and the Majority and the Life Force and Statistics and the Economic Man, brainless, eyeless, wicked spawn of the universal toad sitting in the black bloody ditch of eternal night and croaking for its mate which is the spectre of Hell.'

33

For we were waiting for another bus to take us anywhere, somewhere down in Sussex, and it was as dark as the inside of a Cabinet Minister. 'Give me another drink,' I said to Nosy, 'I've got a chill on my bones.' And I took a little whisky out of the bottle. I hate whisky, it burns up the blood. But I didn't want to get irritated against the government, and especially the people. 'If I wasn't a reasonable man,' I said to Nosy, I should get annoyed with Governments and the People and the World, and so on. I should get into a state and wish that the dirty silly bitch had a nose so that I could kick it between the eyes. I should say that bugs have better manners and lice have more distinguished minds.' And then I began to say what I might have said about governments. And Nosy took me by the arm and steered me away from the lamp-post where the people were waiting. 'Someone might hear,' he said. 'Let them,' I said, and I was just going to tell them what I thought of the People, when I gave a stagger. Nosy caught hold of me. And I noticed my head was aching. And I thought, it's a stroke. So they've killed me after all – they've done worse than kill me. I daren't speak or move. In case I should find I was dumb or helpless. And I felt my indignation so hot and strong it was big enough to blow the stars out of their nail holes.

But I saw the danger in time. And I said, 'Hold me up, Nosy, and keep cool. No malice intended. Revenge has a green face, he feeds on corpses. The king on his throne must never groan. One jump from death to life. Is my face all right?'

'What is it, sir?' said Nosy. 'What do you mean?' For the lad was frightened. 'Is my face crooked?' I said. 'Like usual?' 'Yes, just like usual,' said Nosy, peering at me in the light of the lamp. 'And am I touching your nose?' I said putting out my finger at his nose. 'Yes, dat's by dose,' said Nosy, sneezing. Then I knew I was all right. 'A narrow escape,' I said. 'The government nearly got me that time.' 'Where are they?' said Nosy, looking fiercely at a chap in a bowler. 'They nearly knocked me off my pins,' I said. 'Put me into a temper. But by God, I beat 'em. Yes, there's spunk in the old louse.'

'I suppose it's only their job,' said Nosy. 'I mean the police.'

'I forgive 'em, Nosy. And tomorrow I shall forget 'em. To forgive is wisdom, to forget is genius. And easier. Because it's true. It's a new world every heartbeat. The sun rises seventy-five times a minute. After all, what is a people? It doesn't exist. Only individuals exist – lying low in their own rat-holes. As far apart as free drinks. Further because nothing can bring them into the same space. And what is a government individually, a hatful of prophets and murderers dreaming of bloody glories and trembling at the grin of the grave. I forgive it, the belly-ripping abortionist, the batter-brained, cake-handed, wall-eyed welsher, the club-foot trampler, the block-eared raper that would sell its sister for a cheer, the brick-faced hypocrite that would wipe art and artists off the face of the earth as it would skin an orange, and cut the balls off the genius of the Lord to make a tame gee-gee for the morning Park. I forgive it,' I said, as we got on to the bus. 'I forgive government, with all its works, because it can't rise out of its damnation, which is to be a figment.'

'That's rather strong,' said a gentleman in shammy gloves, opposite.

'A figment,' I said. 'A spectre living among a spectrous world – a satan in a mill.'

They were all looking at me as if I were cracked or religious, and so I said to them, 'I also stood in Satan's bosom and beheld its desolations.'

> A ruined man, a ruined building of God not made with hands
> Its plains of burning sand, its mountains of marble terrible
> Its pits and declivities flowing with molten ore and fountains
> Of pitch and nitre; its ruined palaces and cities and mighty works
> Its furnaces of affliction, in which his angels and emanations
> Labour with blackened visages among its stupendous ruins.

'Excuse me,' said the gentleman, 'but I don't hold with attacking the government. Mr Chamberlain seems to me —'

'Who is Mr Chamberlain?' I said, for I knew I had heard the name. Yes. In connection with orchids.

They were all very surprised. But respectful. Thinking I must be cracked. 'He is the Prime Minister. The Head of the Government.'

'God help him,' I said. 'He had better be the head of a mop, pushed by a lot of dead wood behind and nothing in front but loose dirt and flat-faced paving stones.'

'Moreover,' said the gentleman, putting his shammy gloves well forward on the top of his umbrella. And I could see what he was by birth and profession, a real old Boorjoe. Rusticus, Moreoverus. 'Moreover,' he said, 'it's my opinion that this is a good government – we need a strong government in these times. Strong for peace.' 'Here, here,' said a lady in pince-nez, sitting beside me with a man's portfolio. Lecturer. Boorjwas Pacificus Furiosouse. 'And not afraid to stand up to the warmongers in the army and navy and air force. Men like this Air Minister,' said the Boorjoe, and his gloves were quite fiery with indignation. 'Just provoking Germany with their aeroplanes and battleships,' said the lady, and enthusiastic cheers from a representative audience; that is, two grunts, and an approving sniff from a thin little woman opposite in goggles, with a little red nose and a basket of eggs on her knee; small farmer's wife.

'Thank God we *have* got a strong government,' said the lady, looking round to see if anyone dared to contradict her. 'Thank God you have,' I said. 'A government can't be too strong. I hope your government is a lot of devils. Or they won't have much chance against devils like you and me, ma'am. Look how we treat a government, worse than rats or bugs. The poor creature hasn't a real friend in the world. And the more it does for us, the worse we abuse it. Why, after a really long and glorious life, a government had better hang or shoot itself. And even the little boys in the street will spit on its coffin. There ought to be a branch of the Cruelty to Animals Society to protect governments, with special homes, of course, where the prevailing wind blows out to sea, and a lethal chamber. It's kinder to put them out of their misery before they retire. For of all the ungrateful spiteful cruel savages in the world, when it comes to dealing with governments, give me a Free and Sovereign People.'

'Speak for yourself,' said the egg woman.

'I can't speak for anyone else,' I said, 'I don't know the language.' And just then the bus stopped and the conductor told us our tickets wouldn't take us any further. So we got out, and there we were on a road in the middle of a forest. Through the forest we could see the sea. And the bus went off like a comet, like the flaming world. We were alone, and Nosy said in an alarmed voice, 'Where are we, Mr Jimson?'

'There,' I said.

'But where shall we sleep?'

'Here,' I said.

'But it's raining, Mr Jimson.'

'Not where I am,' I said. 'I've got my mackintosh and overcoat. Or if they aren't mine, they're Sir William's, which are better.'

'But, Mr Jimson, you know how you suffer in your chest.'

'You don't know how I suffered in London, neither did I,' I said. For the country was a bit of a surprise to me. It always is. And I hadn't seen a real wild tree for twelve years. I couldn't take my eyes off 'em, bulging out into the moon as solid as whales. By God, I thought, no one has seen a tree till this moment. And I believe I could paint it. And then again I felt that shape of the big fish and Churchill's hat. I felt an idea, a big one.

> Thou knowest, I said, that the ancient trees seen by their eyes, have fruit
> And knowest thou that trees and fruits flourish upon the earth
> To gratify senses unknown.
> In places yet unvisited by the voyager.

That is, until the voyager arrives. With the eye of imagination. And sees the strange thing. And throws a loop of creation around it.

'What we want is a place between the roots where leaves have drifted,' I said. 'This will do. No, don't touch 'em, don't turn 'em over. They'll be wetter underneath.'

'But your chest, Mr Jimson,' said the boy, playing the nurse of genius.

'Give me that bottle and go back to your mammy,' I said.

I spread out Sir William's overcoat and curled it round us. And put the mac on top, and we slept like birds till the morning, one eye open, and knowing all the time which way the wind blew, and how the clouds sailed. And came so wide awake at sunrise it was like flying off into the dirty sky.

There was Nosy rolling his eyes at the forest which was only a dozen trees round a petrol pump; with a villa opposite, and a parade down below, with some bathing-boxes and the sea coming in as grey as solder.

'We've got to get away from here,' he said.

'No,' I said, 'it's a good place. I've got to earn our living.' The beech over our heads had boughs so long it made my shoulders ache.

'But you haven't any paints, Mr Jimson.'

'Painting isn't a livelihood,' I said. 'Not if you paint anything worth the trouble. Give me a lift – my legs won't bend.'

So he got me up, all of a piece, and I took out the newspapers.

'There's a policeman,' he said.

'Never mind the police,' I said, for I wasn't going to let the government interfere with my notions. 'Go home to your mammy.'

'You don't want me to do that, Mr Jimson.'

But I didn't answer him. The wind in the leaves was removing my landmarks. A big idea, I felt it grow. The whale of an idea.

'A nice mess you've made of your life,' I said, 'throwing away that scholarship.'

It was drizzling rain and Nosy stood on one foot like a young horse, with the drops sticking to his nose and his ears flopped, meditating.

'Come on,' I said, jingling Tom Jones' shilling against three sixpences, 'I'm hungry.'

'I don't think it's a mess,' he said. 'It's only starting.'

'Wait till they jug you,' I said. 'Five years. And come out creeping or cracked. How much money have you got left?'

Still meditating, he put his red knobby boy's hand into his pocket and took out a shilling, fourpence halfpenny in coppers, a front stud and a Napoleon ten cent.

'The French copper will go in the machine for a packet of chocolate. We'll call it one-and-six,' I said, 'and you can charge it to expenses.'

'Perhaps it would be good for me,' he said.

'What would?' I said. For the waves kept breaking into my stiffness.

'Prison,' he said.

'My God,' I said, smelling the coffee outside a chromium restaurant. 'You ought to be a bath bun sitting on the road and waiting for the steam roller to expand your soul. Come on.' For the chromium restaurant was full of snotty girls with permanent waves, Deadheads. And the sea was on the move, rattling my shells and making jewels of my pebbles. Knocking away my fences. Strokes of the prophet.

I stood in the streams
Of Heaven's bright beams
My eyes more and more
Like a sea without shore
Continued expanding.
The Heavens commanding.

'I beg your pardon, Mr Jimson,' said Nosy.

'This looks a good place,' I said. Flyblown all over the window-panes and three night lorries at the door. Yes, two women that ought to be girls half dead with worry and work and grease and noise and desperation. That's the place. Back to the wall. Quality, quantity, or death. Spit on the floor and say your grace to the cabbage stumps.

So we went in and ate a meal. And when Nosy had forked down two rashers as thick as a bank door, two old eggs as strong as floor polish, half a loaf of bread and a half pound of marg., he said to me cheerfully, 'It's all experience.'

'So is a brick to a dead cat,' I said. 'The question is, what and what for?'

For I had eaten so much my wits were like drums and gave off only echoes.

'Prison,' he said.

'Yes,' I said, 'but a hatchet would be better to let some daylight into your loaf,' and I was so angry I was nearly rude to the boy. But then I thought, Keep cool. He's young. He's earnest. He's empty. He's like a new sawmill with nothing to cut – all buzz and bust. Ready to fly off its own steel, so I said, 'Have you thought how we're going to eat?'

'Yes, Mr Jimson – I'm sure you oughtn't to sleep in ditches.'

This surprised me. But there's a lot of child in a boy, and children are always practical. 'And what are you going to do for money?'

'I thought I'd get a job.'

'What kind of job?' I said.

'A navvy,' he said, 'or something like that.'

'For the experience,' I said.

'I thought perhaps it's what I need. To touch the bottom.'

'Navvies are not the bottom,' I said. 'Government is at the bottom. But they wouldn't have you. You can't get in on the ground floor without a scholarship.'

'Or an errand boy,' he said.

But I couldn't listen to him. The wind had come off my belly as sweet as an infant. The clouds had poured away. And as we went along the road the sky kept jingling my bells.

'This must be somewhere near Somewhere,' said Nosy, getting out of the way of a Rolls-Royce full of butcher's meat in pin stripes. Looking for larks in lounges, at three pounds a day. 'By the downs,' said Nosy.

700

'A wonderful place for larks,' I said. For there were two of them taking their first rise out of a sleepy morning.

> He leads the choir of day, trill, trill, trill, trill
> Mounting upon the wings of light into the great expanse
> And the awful sun
> Stands still upon the mountain looking on this little bird
> With eyes of soft humility and wonder, love and awe.

I said, 'That's better even than bacon. Talk of Nature. What is Nature to a man like old Billy Blake? To the imagination of genius. A door to glory.'

'There's a man following us,' said Nosy. 'He looks like a detective.'

'Very likely he is,' I said. 'Let him follow. Following is the government job. Ours is to lead the way. And you ought to be selling insurance. Nice safe work – in five years you would have your own Rolls-Royce.'

'I shouldn't want one.'

'Don't despise the good, the true and the beautiful.'

'I don't, but I want to be an artist.'

'Art is the biggest luxury of the lot,' I said, going into a post office. 'Like keeping alive. Which costs the earth.' I had one-and-fourpence over from the breakfast bill, and I bought a dozen postcards of the Burlington sights, the Promenade, the best churches, the piers. Good stuff. And six envelopes.

Nosy gazed at me with round eyes. But too polite to ask a question.

'Souvenirs,' I said. 'You wait at the corner here, and if you see a man with a blue face, ask him what's the time by his clock.' I put two cards in each envelope and stuck them up. A door to glory. The larks had stopped singing. Coming down, I supposed.

> A Memorable Fancy.
> How do you know but every bird that cuts the airy way
> Is an immense world of delight closed by your senses five.

Yes, I thought, fixing my eye on a superior pub. The angels must always be surprised when some man dives head-first into dirt, and then just by a twist of his imagination comes out again as clean as a comet with two wings bigger than the biggest in all heaven.

I had my eye on the saloon bar, and just then a young man came out.

Nice young man in a blue suit, with a dark-blue hat, and new shoes. But green silk socks. So I drew up level with him and let my arm touch his and all at once I showed him an envelope and gave him the wink and said, 'Want any postcards, mister? Beauties of Brighton. Nice new views. For artists only. Plain envelope.'

'No,' he said. 'Go away. How much?'

'Five bob to you, sir. They're worth five pounds to a real artist. Art photos.'

'Half a crown,' he said.

I turned away, but he said quickly, 'All right, you old blackguard, hand over.'

He gave me two florins and plucked away the envelope. It went into his pocket so quickly that it seemed to vanish in the air. The young man gave me a glance and said, 'You get off or I'll call a copper.'

I got off. I didn't trust that young man. But I was angry at the mean way he had swindled me. I hate the meanness of a man who throws away his self-respect for a bob. 'He thought I was a dirty old blackguard,' I told Nosy, 'and so he cheated me. There's a glimpse of human nature for you – a fellow that will make a shilling out of a dirty old blackguard.' And I was growing hot and furious when I saw how I was forgetting myself. 'I could kill that man,' I said, 'but why poison my wells with his nasty corpse?' So I went in and had a couple of pints and that man seen through the bottom of a pot seemed so small that I could dote upon him like any hair-leg of a flea. 'He was a fly-flat,' I said to Nosy. 'Poor little basket, he'll have but a hard life. Fly-flats fill all asylums and gaols and morgues and unions in the world. The flat is a flat, he keeps on the rails and carries only registered luggage. A fly man is a fly man, he spreads his wings and dives on his prey. But the fly-flat is a flat that thinks he's fly and even the worms bite him for the price of a workhouse coffin.'

Nosy kept on looking at me, and every time he looked he blushed.

'But the postcards were only twopence,' he said.

'So they were,' I said. 'Why did he give you four shillings for them?'

'Because I needed the money and you needed the money.'

'Was it charity?'

'No, it was commerce. Luxury trade. Due to the imagination. Ships, motors, wars, bankers, factories, swindles, taxes and ramps are all due to the imagination. For or against. A man who cuts a throat because of imagination is hanged by a judge who is appointed to keep imagination in order. If it wasn't for imagination,' I said, 'we shouldn't need any police or government. The world would be as nice and peaceful and uninteresting as a dead dog full of dead fleas. That's what I said to Ranken when he sold his patent regulator to a rich firm called Rackstraw, who were going to put it on the market. And then they found out that it wouldn't suit the market. "We're sorry, Mr Ranken," they said, "but your regulator is rather too sensitive – there is no demand at present for anything so delicate. Our customers prefer something cheaper, even if it doesn't do the work so well." And when Ranken told them how to make his regulator cheaper, by making a lot at once, they shook their heads and said that there wouldn't be a demand. "Then make a demand," said Ranken. "Advertise." But they put him off and put off the regulator too. They couldn't be bothered. Why should they? Old rich firm. Chief in Parliament, eldest son in the Guards, another on the county council.

'Ranken had a fit, and when my sister got him round again, he wanted to shoot old Rackstraw, who'd probably never heard of him. "Keep cool, old chap," I said. "Look at the bright side. They didn't put you in quod or burn you alive. That's what happens to most pioneers. And serve 'em right for upsetting people and business and old-established markets, which means private and domestic family affairs. And you've still got your imagination. You can go on inventing things. You don't have to make out with parliament and pedigree bulls and social importance like those poor devils the Rackstraws."'

'But excuse me,' said Nosy, who, like all good virtuous people, is a bit persistent. You might as well try to divert him as a colic. 'Those p-postcards.'

'Not at all,' I said. 'But I see what you mean. Now if you don't mind, will you go into that shop over there and ask them how much credit they'd allow you on a bottle of whisky for half a crown, taking due account of the Scotch rate of exchange?'

And I went out and sold another envelope to a serious-looking gentleman in a blue collar. But he had patent leather shoes with white insertions. He paid five bob without a word. And a fierce-looking woman in pince-nez gave me six. She was all in black, but the back of her neck was powdered and her umbrella had a monkey carved up the handle.

I had to buy some more cards. Before tea-time I was worth three pounds. But Nosy had got wise and he was upset.

'It's not fuffit for you, Mr Jimson,' he said. 'I'd rather do it myself.'

'You couldn't, Nosy,' I said. 'It needs an artist – it needs a lot of imagination. You weren't cut out for any of the arts and crafts. You were born for a government job, and since you missed that scholarship, your only hope is superior drapery. Service. To distribute frocks. The latest creations. The new world of female vision. The prophecies of Paquin and Molyneux against the golden calf – last year's short skirts. And the glory of the lord, that is, the new long skirts, eternally regenerated in Sion.'

My eye fell upon a long-faced young gentleman in a blue London suit, hand-sewn, crinkled all round the edges; with hand-made black shoes, black socks, an Eden hat. Very distinguished. Just coming out of a first-class hotel. You would have taken him for the highest aristocracy, big business, or Wimbledon tennis, if it hadn't been for his pink silk shirt, tie, and handkerchief to match, arranged in two points. I felt for my cards.

'Because the world of imagination,' I said to Nosy, 'is the world of eternity.' For, as Billy says, 'There exist in the eternal world the permanent realities of everything which we see reflected in the vegetable glass of Nature.' And, I thought, in the works of Gulley Jimson. Such as red Eves and green Adams, blue whales and spotted giraffes, twenty-three feet high. Lions, tigers, and all the dreams of prophets whose imagination sustains the creation, and recalls it from the grave of memory.

'Just get me an evening paper, Nosy,' I said. 'I want to see the Academy news, if any.' And as Nosy went into a paper shop, I said to the young duke, 'Excuse me, sir, but are you interested in art? I have here, at a great reduction, some of the finest reproductions of the photographic science. In plain envelope. Studies for students. Passed by censor. Latest lighting effects. For adults only. Half a guinea.'

'That's all right, old man,' he said, 'I was looking for you. Just step in here.' And he took me by the arm and pushed me up an alley. 'Fact is,' he said, 'I've had a complaint.'

'Have you?' I said. 'Well, look here.' And I opened an envelope and showed him my cards. Two local churches and a sunset over the sea. 'What's wrong with that?'

'Just what they told me,' he said. 'Why,' he said, taking me by the neck and giving me a poke in the stomach with his knee that nearly broke me in two. 'You dirty old crook – you son of a louse. What do you mean coming here on my pitch and swindling decent people with your filthy tricks. My God,' he said, giving me a kick on the kneecap that brought the tears of remorse to my eyes. 'You make me sick, you hound. Taking advantage of a lady that you aren't fit to speak to. I've a bloody good mind to set about you, if I wasn't afraid of dirtying my hands.' Then he kicked me up and kicked me down; kicked me in the guts and kicked me on the jaw; kicked me into the road and danced on me three or four times. His feet moved so fast one couldn't see them. At last Nosy came up, panting, and shouted for the police. The young gentleman then knocked Nosy down, kicked him five or six times a second for five seconds, and went away in a Daimler limousine, with a liveried chauffeur and a bunch of fresh flowers in the vase.

After that the police came and took me to hospital in an ambulance. And Nosy was waiting on the pavement when they carried me across. Purple with running behind and two black eyes where our honest friend had kicked him on the nose, but full of grief for the misfortunes of genius. The tears were creeping round the new nose, which was shaped like a logan-berry. 'You go back to Mammy,' I said to him, 'and ask her to forgive me.'

But he only shook his head, with looks of horror and despair. A terrible experience for Nosy. You could see he was suffering terribly and enjoying every minute of it.

When they put me to bed they found I had a broken nose, a broken arm, a broken collar bone, four broken ribs, three broken fingers, three or four square yards of serious contusions and a double rupture. The Sister thought I ought to die, the house surgeon thought I was dying, and the nurse was sure I ought to be going off before tea-time, as she hadn't a relief. And I was so angry that I might have done myself a serious injury, if I hadn't said to myself, Hold on, Gulley. Don't lose your presence of imagination. Wash out that blackguard till you're well again and get a new pair of boots.

With nails in them. Forgive and forget. Till you have him set. Remember that he had a certain amount of excuse for his actions. Give him his due, but not till you are ready with a crowbar. Don't get spiteful. Keep cool. It's the only way to handle a snake like that. Approach the matter in a judicious spirit, meet him with a friendly smile, and a couple of knuckledusters. Don't let him get on your nerves, that counts him one; but get on his face and push it through his backbone, that counts you one, two, three and an old age without regrets. Your only resort in a case like this is the Christian spirit. Because you haven't got anything else.

Then I began to feel better and when Nosy came to see me next afternoon, I made him buy me a penny note-book and a threepenny box of chalks. And my left hand began to draw things that surprised me. 'Yes,' I said, when I saw them, 'that's it.'

'What is it?' said Nosy, who happened to be looking over my shoulder.

'It,' I said. 'Yes, that is to say, a fact, a poke in the belly, well, it's got a feeling, hasn't it? – in fact, unless I'm much mistaken, it's something, almost itself by itself.'

34

Of course, while I was in hospital, Nosy went down hill. First down; and then up again. He began to show his true bent, which was for commerce. First he got a job as a dish-washer in a tea-shop, then he sold newspapers; then he was an errand boy in a grocery. Now, if he had gone into the postcard business under some arrangement with the gentleman who owned the local pitch, he could have made money, and set us both up again. But as I always said, Nosy had no imagination. He was born to be angel of grace.

And I was desperate for a few pounds, because I knew that I had the biggest idea of my life. It had begun from those trees on our first night in the country. Something bigger than the new Fall. A Creation. And I saw it about fifteen feet by twenty, the biggest thing I had ever seen. It would need a special studio, a special canvas, or wall; a full equipment of ladders, scaffolds, etc.; and buckets full of colour.

This thing grew on me all the time I was in hospital, till I dreamed blue whales, like gasometers; and red women growing out of the ground, with legs like Lolie's roots; and trees putting out their apples to the wind, like little breasts.

'We'll want about a thousand pounds, Nosy, to do the thing as it ought to be done,' I said. And Nosy, who was just as excited about the thing as I was, would say, 'We must s-save up.' He made me laugh.

'No,' I said, 'I'll write to Sir William.'

'W-what,' said Nosy, with his eyes popping.

'Why not,' I said. 'He's rich – he's a connoisseur – it's his job to support art. Yes, I'll ask him to finance us, a thousand down; and say another thousand on delivery.'

'But, the p-police,' said Nosy. 'What about all his things?'

'You don't understand millionaires, Nosy,' I said. 'A millionaire is nearly always wise. He doesn't let anything upset him. I remember when old Hickson was robbed by a blackguard of a dealer who sold him a fake. He made inquiries and found that it was no good running the man into court, because he had no money to pay damages. So he asked him to dinner and gave him the hint that he knew what he'd done and asked for a tip the next time the dealer saw a good thing going cheap. And Hickson got several good things through that dealer. Because he had the sense to cut his losses.

'"CUT YOUR LOSSES" MISTER GREEN, and start fair on Monday. That's pure Christianity.' 'And I bet you,' I said to Nosy, 'that Sir William will say to himself, there's no point in quarrelling with Jimson, even if he was a bit careless with my armchairs. I can't have the armchairs made new by being rude to him, but I might still get a good picture out of him, by being reasonable.' So I wrote:

Dear Sir William,

I was very sorry to be away when you returned home; and I should certainly have called long ago, if it had not been for ill health which has kept me in the nurse's hands for some weeks.

I daresay you noticed that I had carried out your kind and generous suggestion for a wall decoration. I believe the suggestion was for tigers in the dining-room. But as the wall there proved difficult, I designed a Lazarus for the Studio. I think you'll agree that the change has been advantageous to us both.

I should have liked to complete this work for you as soon as possible, subject to some friendly understanding about price, but I find myself unable to spare the time, as I am engaged on a work of major importance, to be called the Creation. It has been suggested that I should reserve this work for the State, and I have had very large private offers. But I am prepared to give you an option for a thousand guineas (1050,10, including stamp fee); completed work to cost 5000 guineas (5229, 19, with special stretcher, etc.) for the next seven days.

Please address care of my secretary,

H. Leslie Barbon, Esq.

14a, Dog Lane Mews,

Burlington-on-Sea.

Yours sincerely, my dear Sir William,

Gulley Jimson.

You have noticed that I sent the greater part of your furniture to store, to avoid damage during the painting, etc. The tickets were collected for safety in the safe deposit box on the top of the bathroom door, where you will find them in order. I feel myself entirely responsible for any damage, and I should like to be debited with such sums in view of a final settlement.

To this letter I received about a month later the following answer:

Dear Mr Jimson,

Sir William and Lady Beeder are at present in Cannes on a very necessary holiday. I forwarded your letter to Sir William, who has asked me say how much he has appreciated your kind offer, and your care for his furniture, etc. But he would still prefer an easel picture if possible, a study of the nude, in that inimitable brilliance of your Sara Monday period, to a mural. He fully understands the greater importance of the work proposed, but feels it unsulted to the modesty of his collection and his accommodation. He would be most gratified by a call from you on his return from abroad, of which however the date is at present uncertain.

I am yours most sincerely and respectfully,
A. W. Alabaster.

'There you are, Nosy,' I said. 'I told you Beeder was fit to be a millionaire and likely to stay one, too. If he uses the same Christian rule on the Stock Exchange as he does in art collecting.'

And as soon as I was out of the hospital, I made a dart for Capel Mansions. No one at home. But I dropped my card, giving for my address:

Elsinore House,
Ellam Lane, S.W.

It was raining bayonets and fish-hooks, and when I got to Elsinore about six, I was wet both down and up. And my winter cough, though more melodious than my dust cough or spring cough, is also more trouble. I hadn't really got the time for it. So I arrived in a bad mood, ripe for the devil. And the first devil I saw, who was a great bum with a face like a warthog, standing in the kitchen door, I said to him, 'Get out of my way, you son of something or something else.' And when he turned round to kill me, I let out a scream like an engine whistle. Bad for your throat, but it causes surprise and consternation among the savages. ''Ere,' he said, falling back two yards, 'I didn't touch ya.'

About sixteen other bums were crowding round and some of them had the idea of taking me up by the area and putting me in the dustbin. But others wanted to carry me up the stairs in order to throw me down the front steps. I voted with the dustbin party. But the stairs party won. Another victory for imaginative art. And they had just got me by the legs and arms face downwards, and were pushing the kitchen door open with my head, when suddenly I heard a voice I seemed to know saying, 'Here, stop that.' The bums protested that I was a union rat, and had no business in a place like Elsinore. But they stood me on my feet and there was a little old man in blue overalls with one hand and one hook. He had a pail in the hook and a brush in the hand. That's funny, I thought, Plantie had one hand and did out the lavatories. Then I saw it was Plantie, grown about forty years older; and Plantie saw that it was me.

'Mr Plant?' I said.

'Mr Jimson,' said Plantie, dropping the broom and giving me his left hand. 'Welcome, sir,' and he shook hands with me in a distinguished manner, 'This is a great pleasure – come in – come in.'

He towed me across the kitchen into the scullery and the bums got out of his way as if he had been royalty. Warthog actually carried his broom for him.

'Here you are,' said Plantie, pulling out a chair for me. 'And stay as long as you like.' To Warthog he did not condescend to speak. He merely pointed at a corner. Warthog, leaning very carefully the broom against the wall, said, 'Excuse me, Mr Plant, but if I could have the key.' Plantie didn't seem to hear. Warthog shuffled about a bit, and then tried again, 'Excuse me, Mr Plant –'

Plantie didn't even look at him. He waved his hook, and Warthog went out practically on tiptoe and shut the door behind him as gently as any chicken thief in the middle of the night.

'And how are you, Mr Jimson?' said Plantie. 'Pull up to the fire.' For he had a little fire in the copper grate.

He was smiling so pleasantly that I thought, 'He may be a bit broken down, but he's happy at last.'

'You look well, Mr Plant.'

'I'm pretty well, thank you, Mr Jimson.'

'Same job?'

'Same job.'

It was like an echo from the back of a church. And I thought that the old gentleman needed encouragement.

'And I can see who's king of the castle,' I said. 'By Gee and Jay, what a change. I congratulate you, Mr Plant. How did you do it?'

'Yes,' said Mr Plant, smiling at the fire. But he didn't seem much gratulated.

'You keep the key.'

Mr Plant bent his head sideways; an old man's nod. And went on smiling at the fire.

'And what happens if you don't think a chap is worthy of your lavatory.'

'He can always go to the public gents' down High Street.'

'About three-quarters of a mile and pay his penny. So that's how you got your hook in 'em, you old rascal,' I burst out laughing and clapped Mr Plant on the back. But Plant didn't laugh. He just had the same smile which didn't seem to be paying much attention.

'What they wanted was a philosopher to look after them,' I said. 'Why, that Warthog was almost human. It's a triumph, Mr Plant.'

Plantie was smiling at the ceiling. But he didn't seem to be noticing it.

'And how are you feeling, Mr Plant?'

'Very well, Mr Jimson. A bit older, of course. And that reminds me, there's some letters for you.'

And he went to his cupboard and brought out a packet of letters.

'Ha, ha,' I said. 'My fan mail – something from the Professor.' But they were all bills or circulars except one from Coker.

> The Boathouse,
> 22 Greenbank.
> 31/7/39.

I'd be obliged if you pay me what you owe which is five pounds thirteen and tenpence. If you can pay a pound a week to that nasty Leslie Barbon who's broken his mother's heart you can pay me.

> D. B. Coker.

I'm on the make from now on, and don't you forget it. This means that I want my money.

> To Mr Gulley Jimson, Esq.,
>   Common Lodging House,
>   Ellam Lane.

'A very nice mail,' I said. 'Tells you that you're not forgotten.'

'There's something else, too,' said Plantie, recollecting himself in the middle of some private thought. He took another dive into the cupboard and hooked out something like a sack of potatoes. 'Left here by a lady in a Rolls.'

The sack had a note tied to the neck by one corner. And when I read it I jumped in my boots for joy. The address was Gulley Jimson, Esq., Elsinore House, Ellam Lane, and the note: Sir William Beeder has asked me to remit these articles for you, and trusts that they are all in order. – M. B. M.

And inside the sack there was a colour box, two palettes, two tins of bully beef and a cardboard stay box marked, brushes and colours, and sealed with tape.

'Just like a millionaire,' I said. 'I wish there were more like Sir William, with a lot of chauffeurs, cooks, secretaries, and M. B. M.'s to look after them and carry out their kind Christian thoughts. God bless his millions.'

But when I opened the colour box, there was nothing in it, not even a palette knife; and when I opened the cardboard box, it contained two worn-out brushes, a lot of old squeezed-out, dried-up tubes, and three empty oil bottles. Somebody had got away with about twenty nearly new brushes, and three or four dozen new tubes of colours. 'Just like a millionaire,' I said. 'Surrounded by a lot of barefaced robbers. God bless him and to hell with M. B. M. Unless he or she only came in after someone else had had the pickings.'

'Dear me,' said Plantie, shaking his head. 'But there you are.'

He was still smiling and I was a bit annoyed so I said, 'It all means something.'

'Well, well,' said Plantie, as if he hadn't heard. So I thought it might be Spinoza again, and I said, 'A nice object of contemplation for the old tallyscoop.'

'Who?' said Plantie, smiling in the air and blinking his eyes. 'Who was that?'

'The glassy gazer – the old Popeye.'

But Plantie didn't seem to notice. And I thought perhaps he'd got over all his philosophies. Grown out of them. He'd stopped looking for a rabbit-hole and was feeling what you might call the nature of things, at last. Like my sister Jenny when her husband Ranken got his last knock. They were both very happy just then; the first time they'd been happy in their married lives because a keen young firm called Brouts had taken up the Ranken regulator. They were going to make regulators on a big scale in a special building, and Ranken drew some real money as manager of the department. But the South African war broke out and Brouts went smash. They had a lot of contracts with mines. Besides, they had been taking chances, giving a lot of credit and spending capital on developing new patents. An enterprising firm. Asking for trouble. And their stock, contracts, patents, etc., were bought up by one of the old steady companies which put the Regulator on the shelf. They hadn't any use for a flibberty-gibbet gadget which had ruined Brouts already. They were a good forty years behind the times building tried and trusty stuff for sound customers like the Admiralty and War Office.

The Rankens went bust for the third or fourth time. They had to pawn their clothes for food. And when Jenny came to borrow a few bob from me and to tell me the story, she didn't exactly smile. But she didn't cry either, as she'd done before; and blame the government, or the manufacturers, or her husband's enemies. She sat on my knee with her head on my shoulder, a comic sight, for Jenny, at thirty-two, looked like a worn-out char, and I was fresh from a casual ward; and she gave only one or two sighs. The kind they call heartfelt. But they really feel more than having your guts removed by the roots. And I said, 'Cheer up, old girl. Luck will turn.' But she shook her head. 'Why won't it turn?' 'It isn't just luck. 'What else?' 'I don't know – just things, I suppose.' So she'd got a dim idea at last. 'Well,' I said, 'to hell with things. Send them to the devil.' 'But Robert is so wretched – it's awful to see how he suffers. I didn't know anyone could suffer like that day and night – and not go mad. He'll kill himself – I know he will.' 'Never,' I said. 'Especially if he says so.' 'He's often threatened to do it, and he will.' 'The trouble with Robert is he won't face facts, things if you like. He wants them to come and lick his feet. But they can't – they can't lick. They can only fall about like a lot of loose rocks in a runaway train. Your Robert has got himself in a state, and now you're in a state.'

'How can I help it when he's so miserable.' And, of course, there wasn't any answer to that. Jenny was a good lover. She couldn't get out of loving Ranken just by wishing it. She could forgive things for knocking her about, but not for knocking Ranken about. You couldn't expect it. And so she went just as she had come. No one on earth could do anything for her. She was pushed right up against it, as they say.

It's the same with a lot of old people; even the ones that used to have a pass key to eternal joy. All at once you find that they are rather quiet and thoughtful. And a bit inattentive to glories and triumphs. Like Plantie in his present authority. I thought he didn't set much value on the courtly attentions of such as Warthog; and I thought even his smile didn't mean what it had meant before. Old men when they begin to hear the last trumpet, on the morning breeze, often have a kind of absentminded smile; like people listening. And these smiles are just politeness. They probably don't know whether they're laughing or crying, and perhaps they don't care so long as they're doing something or other. And they don't trouble much about what they're saying either, so long as it fills in the gaps of the conversation and expresses their general satisfaction at not being dead yet. So I didn't ask Plantie whether he was laughing at me or himself or anything else. I just went on keeping my own boiler warm, with my own feelings.

In fact, in spite of a certain rudeness in my cough, due to general indignation with the weather, and some anxiety about finance, I passed a very happy and peaceful evening with Plantie, in front of the copper fire. And a good night in a bed of chairs. For though I could not sleep, I had a good view, as Plantie pointed out, of the sky, through the top of the window, and the sky was like a cinema film gone mad. Great whirling heads and arms and noses, naked legs and trousered bottoms, guns, swords and top hats, rushing past all night. Sometimes you saw a lovely lady in a pose plastique, but before you could wink she had swelled out like a balloon, lost her leg or her head, and turned into an ammunition wagon galloping over the corpses.

Plantie himself didn't sleep either. Whenever I looked his way I could see his little eyes glinting as he stared at the ceiling. But what he was thinking of, I don't know. An old man's thoughts are an old man's secret, and no one else would even understand them. He only once spoke to me, when he heard the chairs creak and said, 'You all right, Mr Jimson?'

'I'm all right, Mr Plant. Why aren't you asleep?'

'I've had my sleep. I wondered how you were sleeping.'

'Like a top,' I said. For it saves a lot of trouble between friends to swear that life is good, brother. It leaves more time to live.

35

I didn't like Cokey's letter. It seemed to me that Coker might be turning dangerous. So I went down to the boat-shed next evening when Mrs Coker might be expected to be out at the late Saturday market, getting meat bargains, and took a peep through a side window. Nothing to be seen. But there was a sound like somebody pounding meat and cursing.

Now, when I had listened at the boat-shed, I could generally hear Mrs Coker's voice, grousing. A noise like the winter wind moaning softly through a broken jew's harp. But this sounded more like a wagon-load of railway irons being dragged along Pickleherring Street. It was more like Cokey in one of her old tempers. So at last I ventured to tap on the window.

'HULLO,' Cokey bawled. 'GET OFF, YOU! OR IT'LL BE THE WORSE. WHO IS IT?'

'Jimson.'

'That's a lie, anyhow,' said Cokey, and she pulled the curtain. 'Hullo, Mr Jimson,' she said, 'it's you, is it?'

'Where's your mother, Cokey?'

'Gone, thank God. But you can't come in here now, I'm too busy.'

I could see that Cokey was in her apron mood, full of temper.

'When can I come in, Cokey? I want to see you badly.'

'You can come in now if you'll keep your feet off the floor.'

So I went in, and there was Cokey with a cloth over her head, house cleaning. And a kid of about two months was sucking its big toe in a smart new cradle over by the bed.

'Hullo,' I said. 'All the family. And I must say you look well on it Cokey. Quite a figure.'

But Cokey was swearing at the dirt, at the broom, and the floor cracks and the job. 'Who would be a woman,' she said, 'chivvying dirt from morning to night, and changing nappies from night till morning. Yes', she said, when the kid put his toe into his eye instead of his mouth and gave a squeak. 'You little bastard, you're good enough now when it doesn't matter, but what about last night, I didn't get a wink.'

'Here,' I said. 'You oughtn't to throw it at her, Cokey. It's not her fault.'

'Her? Does it look like a girl. Use your lamps, Mr Jimson. A boy, you bet. It knew what was what. And as for throwing it at the kid, he doesn't know English yet. Not that he won't, all right. If I don't tell him, everyone else will, and good for him, too. Take him down a peg. He can't learn too soon that he's got to muck in with the rest of 'em.'

'Why, Cokey,' I said, 'I thought you'd be fond of a kid.'

'Oh yes,' said Cokey. 'I was waiting for the mother stuff. All I can say is Nature has done enough dirt on a woman without that. And don't you try it either,' she said to the kid. 'Don't you come it over me, you basket, or I'll leave you on the Union doorstep, like the Ellam Street girls do with their nasty little errors, that they don't even know who was their father –'

'Does Willie recognize his family?' I said.

'Mind your own business,' said Cokey. 'Willie has enough trouble with that slab-sided pork sucking the life out of him. And give me that dustpan. I don't know why I don't put myself in the river, with all the dirt. You'd think this bloody shed was a vacuum cleaner the way it sucks it up.'

'And a nice kid, too,' I said. 'Look at the crinkles on it, like new pork sausages.'

'Just like a man,' said Cokey. 'You didn't have to have it. And that old Plant telling me that God sent me a baby. I wish they'd send Plantie a baby. He didn't send me a husband, did he. It was Willie gave me a kid, and only because he didn't take enough trouble. Come up, you nuisance.' And she took the kid out of the cradle and pulled off its frock. To wash it. But I could see she made a good job of the washing. And the kid cooed away as if it was being tickled by the angels.

'A good kid,' I said.

'So it ought to be,' said Coker. 'It's enough trouble. The district nurse says this is the finest kid in six months and the best looked after – she wanted to put it in the Show. But I wasn't going to hear people say, "Look at the little bastard." '

'How could they tell?'

'Why, you've only got to look at him. Or at me when I'm round.'

'You ought to wear a ring. Why, all the girls down Ellam Street wear rings, whether they've got kids or whether they haven't.'

'Ellam Street girls can do what they like, the dirty bitches,' said Coker, giving the breast. 'I got my pride. Come up; Johnny, take a long pull at it. I haven't got any time to waste.'

'Don't put him in the Navy, that's all. It's an insult in the Navy.'

'Well, I don't blame 'em. I shouldn't like it myself. Go on, Johnny, bite it off. It's only your mother. That's it, stick in your nails, I'm only another bloody woman.'

'Open up a bit more, I want your chest,' I said, drawing away.

'Don't you draw me,' said Cokey. 'You've no right to see as much as you do. It's only because I'm too fed up to go in the scullery and you're just out of hospital. What you ought to do, Mr Jimson, if you had any sense, is stay here and let somebody see you got looked after properly, for once in a way. You look awful, strike me, you're enough to frighten a sexton. As for talk, let 'em talk. They've been talking about me for a year, that whore Coker and her bastard. Now they can add a lodger to that.'

'I should like that very much, Cokey. You're a nice girl, whatever anyone says. And I was needing a model.'

'A model. What do you take me for?'

'If I don't get a model and studio you won't get that money.'

'Don't you talk models to me or I'll answer back. But why can't you do your stuff here?'

'Too small, this is a big job. Biggest I ever did in my life.'

'There's an empty garage down Horsemonger Yard – they might let you use it for nothing.'

'I'll try it. I'm going to get a thousand for this picture, Cokey, and I'll give you fifty out of it. Guineas.'

'Never mind the guineas if you give me my five quid.'

'All right, Cokey. What about a pound a week, bed and board? Paid in advance. Put it in Johnny's savings bank.'

'I'll take that,' said Coker, 'I told you I was on the make. But when will you pay?'

'Next week. Or the week after.'

'A month in advance is enough,' said Coker, 'but I'd like to see it – don't you do me down, Mr Jimson, because I'm not taking sauce from anybody. I'm on the make from the first of April round to All Fools' Day. I've got to be, with this little handicap.'

And she went to get the supper. Grilled chops, mashed potatoes, and porter, bread, butter and cheese. I couldn't have done better.

'Thank you, Coker,' I said.

'It's all in the bill,' said Coker. 'You treat me fair, and I'll treat you fair.'

'And if you did want a little bit on account,' I said, 'you've only got to make Mrs Monday hand over that picture. I've a firm offer.'

'Now, that's enough. Time you were in bed, I should think, without any more nonsense.'

'I thought you wanted your money.'

'I'll get my money, but I don't need to be mixed up with any funny business. My character won't stand it. I'm lucky to have a job without one.'

And, in fact, after a few hours of Cokey in her new shape, I wondered if I was going to be as comfortable as I had expected. Cokey was a good housekeeper, and what they call a good mother. She kept her kid clean and fed it like a prize for the show. In fact, she was mad about the kid. It's always that way with a bastard, either all one thing, or all the other. And I would not say that Cokey's temper was worse. She used to smile sometimes, when the kid brought his wind up or hit himself on the nose. But she wasn't happy because she was not that sort. A million a year and a husband out of the films wouldn't have made Cokey happy. She took life too seriously. She was one of the Marthas. She was the salt of the earth, as they say, and too much salt makes a man dry. She did me good, but too much good and not the good I wanted. She sent me to bed at nine o'clock and when I tried to object that I wasn't sleepy, she pushed me about. 'I've no patience with you, you old bone,' she said, taking my clothes off as if I'd been another baby. 'You're not fit to be up at all, with that cough, much less running about the town after all sorts. You'll go to bed and stay there.'

It was no good arguing with the girl, and I let her lay me out in one of her nightdresses. 'You go to sleep,' she said, 'or it'll be the worse for you. I don't want a funeral on my hands as well as that basket waking me up four times a night for his pint.'

Cokey had gone behind the armchair to get ready for bed. But her shadow was running up the walls, and I said, 'I've got to do you, Cokey. You're just the woman I want. You've got a figure now. You used to be like a boiler, Venus de Silo, but now you've got a front.'

But it was no good talking to Coker. She was like all young mothers. She never heard anything anyone said, not to understand it. Her head was full of kid and glory.

I was glad to find that Coker was back at the bar; in the Feathers half day for the evening rush. 'It's a respectable house, the Feathers,' she said. 'So long as you're a respectable shape, they don't ask for a ring. Which I wouldn't wear. And the pram goes nicely in the snug.'

She gave me orders to stay in bed and took away my trousers. But as soon as she was round the corner with the pram, I was out and about. I didn't need my trousers, with my long overcoat and a pair of long socks well pulled up, and though the people looked, I might have been a squire in plus fours, going round his estate.

And I had to be out in the air. Even one day in bed was putting a cramp on my ideas, tucking them up in a tight parcel. My imagination was working inwards instead of outwards; it was fitting things into a pattern, instead of letting them grow together. If I stayed in the boat-shed for a week under Cokey, I said, I could say good-bye to my Creation – it would turn into a little square picture with four corners and a middle. However big I made it on the wall, it would be a piece of art work. A put-up job. A jigsaw of the back room. Whereas a real picture is a flower, a geyser, a fountain, it hasn't got a pattern but a Form. It hasn't got corners and middle but an Essential Being. And this picture of mine, the Creation, had to be a creation. A large event. And no one can feel largely except in the open air.

Indeed, I was afraid that already, what with Plantie and Cokey, I might have got so compressed that I couldn't do anything but think about ideas and colours from the outside. And Cokey was still sitting in my brain, like a lump of lead ballast in a balloon basket, even as I turned down below the willows. But as luck would have it, the day was clear, with a sky as bright and grey as London water. And as soon as I stretched my legs Cokey began to stretch her shadow out of the basket; until she grew into the air ten foot high and the shape of life itself, living. That's what I want, I said, the woman-tree, with something of Lolie about the roots. As round as a gasometer or Churchill's hat. Yes, Churchill's hat shall be a blue whale.

Suckling its calf. A whale with a woman's face, floating in the green sea. And the black ring in the middle shaped like a map of Australia shall just fit the old 'un who dreams it all for the first time. He shall be a grey-bearded old man, just like the nursery pictures; like something out of Blake but thicker, solider, and fitted more closely. He must fit the shape like a nut in the shell. But not too big. And the hollow rim of black, the cave of the eternal rock, should have a broken edge on which the she-whale rests while she nurses her calf. As for the yellow uprights, they'd better be giraffes, a hundred feet high, browsing off the top of the moon which should be covered with white flowers, the bigger the better. Yes, a thing like this wants to be so big that people when they see it will put up their umbrellas to keep the whale from falling on them. The whale wants to look as big as the Tower of London, and the giraffes must be bigger than life or they will look as small as photographs; at least thirty foot high on the canvas.

I was walking up Horsemonger Yard. I didn't believe in Cokey's garage, but I had nothing else to believe in. And when I found, to my surprise, that there was an empty garage to let, I wasn't surprised to see that it was a dirty old shed, about fifteen foot from floor to ridge with no walls at all. The sides were tin.

But I noticed a lot of boards up. Desirable site. Property coming down; and off the Yard, a little back alley I'd never seen before.

I always go up a back alley. May be a tree there or a girl sweeping out a yard. Moving herself in a nice way. It turned round sharp right. Six dustbins, a stable and an old chapel, Gothic windows, and a little tin vestry like a cupboard next the porch. Peeped in to have a look at the roof timbering and found a bare floor. Nothing inside but a few old tyres. Some rotten planks. A low lame pulpit like a dock. But what knocked me down was the east end *wall*. Twenty-five by forty. Windows bricked up and all smooth plaster round. Sent from God. Only wanted some plaster on the window bricks. Do it myself. And I thought, no, it can't be. It's another joke. They're having me on, I can hear them getting ready with the big, big laugh. My legs were trembling so much I had to sit down on the pulpit steps. I was all in a sweat. And I said to myself. No, Gulley, its a have. It's a catch. It's the old devil again. Don't you depend on anything. You got to be calm. You got to be free. But my legs kept on trembling and my heart went on beating. Jesus Christ, I thought, suppose it was true. Suppose it's meant for me. Oh for a drink. Four fingers of blue ruin and a chaser of rum. To put some armour-plating on my guts. I was getting worse instead of better. So I went out and knocked on the first gate. Young chap with forget-me-not eyes and a magenta chin put his banana out of the gate and said, 'Yerrrs.' I said, 'That old ruin there, who owns it?' 'Dunno.' 'What is it, anyhow?' 'Nothing. Used to be a garage, but now it's nothing. Dangerous building.' 'I should think so – you can see it stagger when the cats cough. Who looks after the rubbish.' 'Next door but one.' Next door but one was a little old man with grey eyes and one bandy leg. Nose like a pepper-pot, all over freckles. Said, 'Yes, I look after the chapel.' 'Condemned?' 'Why yes, but there's nothing wrong with it.' 'How much by the week on no notice either side.' 'Say a pound.' 'Say half a crown.' 'Couldn't do it under a pound.' 'For religious purposes.' 'What religion?' 'Low.' 'What sort?' 'Peculiar.' 'Ten shillings a week.' 'Three and six.' 'Split the difference.' 'Right oh, four and threepence. Here is a bob on account.' 'That's not the difference.' 'Ten shillings less three and six is six and six. Half of six and six is three and three, and I gave you a bob. That's four and three.' 'Here, wait a minute, Mister.' 'Name of Jimson, Gulley Jimson. That's a bargain. I'll go and get my traps.' 'But look here —'

I left him talking and made a dart for the boat-house. Coker had just come in with the pram and was abusing the kid. I snatched a chair in one hand and the frypan and my colour box in the other and flew. 'Hi,' said Coker. But I didn't stop. I was back in the chapel in five minutes. Put the chair in the middle of the floor, the colour box and the frypan in the pulpit. Old bandy leg put his pepper round the door. 'You can't come in – not at that money.' 'Yes, I can. I have. I've taken possession.' 'Out you go.' 'Too late, old boy. It's legal. Essential furniture. Cooking utensils and tools of trade. Look at 'em. You can't touch 'em. Send for the bailiff if you like. He'll tell you.' 'You're a rascal.' 'That's slander. You'll hear from my lawyers tomorrow. It's big damages to call a man a rascal.' 'There aren't any witnesses.' 'Are you going to deny it, you rascal?' 'Rascal. What about this rent.' 'Four and threepence.' 'You know that's not right.' 'You took my earnest.' 'It's a bad 'un, too. A French nickel.' 'My God, my lucky penny. Here, I want that back.' 'Why should I give it back.' 'Be a sport.' 'You be honest.' 'What did you think you wanted for the old dustbin.' 'Six shillings it came to.' 'I'll make it five for the sake of your great-grandchildren. But I warn you it's robbing God. You'll get no luck with it.' 'Make it five and sixpence, and I'll take my chance.' 'I see you're a Christian yourself.' 'Never mind what I am. What I want to see is your money.' 'You shall, old boy, but meanwhile I want time for meditation. I want to pray myself in.' 'I've half a mind to fetch a copper.' 'Is that what's wrong with you? What happened to the other half?' The old boy was cross and went out muttering like Ma Coker, but with a different neck action, more like a tortoise than a snake. I shut the door after him and pushed the bolt. Then measured up the floor. Twenty-five wide. And the timbering on the walls sound as Pharaoh's coffin. When I looked at the east wall, I saw my stuff on it. Finest job of my life. Twenty-five by forty. And I felt giddy. A bit too much for the old pipes. I sat down and laughed. And then I began to cry. Well, I said, you old hallacher, you've rolled into port at last. You've got your break. First the *idea* and then the wall. God has been good to you. That is to say, you've had a bit of luck. Two bits. And all the time, the forms were growing out of my egg like cracker snakes. Coker and Sara and

Lolie and Churchill's hat, white and red and blue, legs and arms and bottoms and a great black shape like a relief map of Iceland, with a white oval just by the north-east corner. God knows what it would have to stand for – he would give me the tip. But that black up against the reds made my angels sing. Oh Lord, I said, only let me fix that black shape and those fat reds before some damn fool talks to me about people or money or weather. And I had out my box and made a sketch on the side wall, four by three.

It's one thing to see or think you see a set of forms, and another to put it down. But this set came up nearly complete. Not a gap anywhere. No filling required. And as far as I could tell in the sketch, the shapes would fill the surface. But that, as every mural painter knows, is not very far. For the line that is as lively as spring steel in the miniature, may go as dead as apron string on the wall. And what is a living whole on the back of an envelope can look as flat and tedious as a holiday poster, when you draw it out full-size.

36

All at once I found it was dark.

And I was so hungry I could have eaten the frypan and tackled my gums with the handle. I put my box back in the pulpit, left my big brush in a cup of water, and slipped out by the vestry, leaving the front door bolted. In case Peppernose might try to make mischief. I closed the window from the outside, and there you were.

An evening by Randypole Billy. Green lily sky, orange flames over the West. Long flat clouds like copper angels with brass hair floating on the curls of the fire. River mint green and blood orange. Old man lying along the water with a green beard, one arm under head, face twisted up – vision of Thames among the pot-houses. I could use that, I thought – that blunt round shape like a copper St Paul's with a squeeze in the middle – like a teat with a long end. A bit flattened sideways – sweet as a baby's breath. Yes, it will come in just by the rock – the old un's cave. Yes, yes, just what I wanted. But not a cloud. Don't want solid cloud. How then. A dead branch. A rhino's horn. A gorilla's finger. Stump of a leg. And while I was eating sausage and mash with Walter Ollier at the Kosy Kot, it shot right out of the canvas like a bronze cannon. Here, I said to myself, how am I going to get a cannon into the Creation. When all at once it turned inside out and winked at me like a railway tunnel right through the canvas. A mole, it came to me at once. A mole for a good black. You've got to have a good black somewhere down in the right-hand corner, a mole with four hands – blind – feeling its way under the ground – and a man's face.

'Have another cup of coffee,' said Walter, who was doing the host. 'Thank you, Walter,' I said. 'But I suppose you couldn't lend me a hundred pounds.' 'I'm afraid it doesn't run to it,' said Walter. 'Not a hundred. Five I could.' 'No,' I said. 'I've got a big job on hand – and I need some capital.' 'A picture?' 'Yes, a picture.' 'I don't know,' said Walter, 'but seeing the government has got your picture up, I should have thought they might give you something on account.' 'You can't expect it of 'em,' I said. 'What does a government know about pictures?' 'They were glad to get yours.' 'But that was an old picture and they didn't know about it till they were told by the papers.' 'Well,' said Walter, 'I don't know about pictures, but if the papers know, why don't they tell the government to go after your new pictures.' 'But the papers don't know it, Walter. They won't know for another twenty or thirty years. A picture isn't like an illustration in a magazine. You can't get to know it by looking at it. First, you've got to get used to it – that takes about five years. Then you've got to know it, that takes ten years, then you learn how to enjoy it and that takes you the rest of your life. Unless you find out after ten years that it's really no good and you've been wasting your time over it. No, Walter, I've got a better bet than the government – a millionaire.' 'Better to call than write.' 'Takes too long – I've only got to phone and he'll fork out.' Walter looked at me round his nose; Walter, though army, has a navy nose, with a high bridge. 'Telephone?' he said, meaning in his polite way to warn me. 'Yes, telephone,' I said, 'I'm going to explain the situation to him.' 'What is the situation?'

'There's two, mine and his. His situation is a bit ticklish,' I said. 'He might get his throat cut.' 'Have some more coffee, Mr Jimson, do,' said Walter, turning quite red. I'd never seen him so brick. He was trying to keep me interested until he could discover some way of diverting my murderous intentions. 'It's good here, don't you think? At least I've always found it not too bad.' 'Thank you, Walter,' I said. 'I think I will. Mr Hickson is probably in his bath now, and he mightn't answer me personally.' 'Do you think he'll know about new pictures, like you said?' said Walter, waving to the waitress. 'I should think it might be better to try the government.' 'No,' I said, 'Mr Hickson never knew anything about my pictures – but he's a millionaire, and so he knows how to invest his money, or he wouldn't be a millionaire.' 'I wonder is he still a millionaire,' said Walter. 'I know they're getting a bit scarce. There's such a lot of people got a down on 'em.' 'Scarce as polecats,' I said. 'I've heard they're going to be stopped,' said Walter, 'though it's probably just the papers.' 'It's quite likely they'll stop themselves,' I said, 'they're a tough lot owing to the survival of the fittest – but even tigers and polar bears get discouraged when nobody loves them.' 'And what will happen to artists if there's no millionaires. Will art stop?' 'Not art – you can't stop art. But you can stop original art.' 'What happens then?' 'The people go on with the old stuff, and folk art and so on, until they get sick.' 'Sick of art?' 'Sick of everything. Though they don't know it. It's a kind of foot-and-mouth disease. The mouth gets very foul and the feet turn sideways, so that the patient is always going round to the pub, the same pub, of course. I'm told by experts that there's a lot of it in country districts where you only have old Masters to look at. Young chaps kind of waste away, and all at once they go and throw boiling water over a dog or cut a cow's tail off. In the end they get so full of spite and bile that they can't digest anything but whisky and politics, and finally they die in great misery.' 'So you're for the millionaires.' 'The more the better, Walter. In my view, everybody ought to be million-aires.' 'Money troubles are sometimes the worst kind,' said Walter. 'That's true,' I said. 'Look at me and look at Mr Hickson.' 'Has he a lot of trouble?' 'I've given him a lot to think about, and I'm going to give him more as soon as he's out of his bath.'

Walter gave a sort of jump and looked round as if for help. 'Have another go of sausage and mash, Mr Jimson?' 'No, thank you, Walter, it's about time for my call.' 'You're not going to call up Mr Hickson tonight, are you?' 'Certainly, Walter. The situation can't go on.' 'What is the situation really, Mr Jimson?'

'Well, Walter, I can tell you, because you're a friend; the situation is that I'm getting on in years and I shan't do much more painting. But I've still got my biggest work in me – a picture that will be famous for centuries. Yes, and it will give England something to be proud of, too, and let her look the nations in the face. She'll be able to say I bred Shakespeare and Milton, and Billy Blake, and Shelley and Wordsworth and Constable and Turner and Gulley Jimson. Only the trouble is, Walter, that it will take about five hundred pounds to make this picture, and twenty years to get it established – I mean respected. Of course, I'll be dead before that – a long time before, I should say, and that will be to the good, as far as this picture is concerned. It will establish my reputation. I shall become history, and history is respectable. Oxford and Cambridge study history. So you see, Walter, the job is to get this picture painted and keep it from being cut up or white-washed over or just left out in the rain until I've been dead a few years.' 'You'll want an attendant to keep the kids from doing it a mischief.' 'Yes, what I need is money – five hundred a year. And I'm going to get the first five hundred this evening.' 'On the telephone.' 'Yes,' I said. 'I don't know,' said Walter, 'but I never liked the telephone myself. I like writing letters.' 'Give me the telephone,' I said. 'It's quicker, and you can say what you like.'

When we got outside, Walter excused himself quickly, and went off at four miles an hour. This was half a mile quicker than his usual rate which is postman's regulations, three and a half. And I didn't waste time. I jumped into the next box and rang up Mr Hickson. A lady answered. 'Excuse me,' I said, 'I am speaking on behalf of the National Gallery, could I see Mr

Hickson?' 'Hold the line, please.' And almost at once a man's voice said, 'Hullo, Mr Hickson here.' He was disguising his voice; but I paid no attention. 'Mr Hickson,' I said, 'I am speaking on behalf of the National Gallery to tell you that it has come to their ears, through official but absolutely trustworthy channels, that the late Mr Gulley Jimson left behind him an extremely important work which ought to be the property of the nation.' 'Excuse me,' said the man, 'but is Mr Jimson dead?' 'Last week,' I said. 'That is the official account, but his secretary, Mr Barbon, will collect any money due.' 'That's a pity,' said Mr Hickson, 'because we've been looking for him with a view to the publication of a Life; in fact, the illustrations are in hand.' 'I shall make further inquiries,' I said, 'in case Mr Jimson's death should be a rumour.' 'I wish you would. My late uncle, as you know, left three of his pictures to the nation.' 'What late uncle?' 'Mr George Hickson.' 'But that's my Mr Hickson,' I said. And felt so queer that I nearly fell down in the box. 'You don't mean old Mr George Frederick Hickson is dead.' 'Three months ago.' 'I don't believe it,' I said. For I couldn't believe it. 'I shall want proof of that.' 'You can find it in *The Times* or apply to Somerset House. The will has been proved.' 'And who the devil are you?' 'Mr Philip Hickson, at your service.' 'Never heard of you,' I said. 'You may think it's funny to pull my leg, but you'd better be careful. Mr George Hickson was one of my oldest friends. I've known him for forty years and he was my earliest patron.' 'He's dead all right. The house is to be sold next week.' 'Why sold?' I said. 'It has the best room in London for showing pictures.' 'It's too big for any of us to keep up. The estate has been divided between seven of us, and the collections are to be sold. Except six pictures left to the nation.'

I thought a bit. I was so upset that my legs were shaking against my coat. Hickson gone. I couldn't believe it. It made me feel as lonely as a man who loses half his family in a shipwreck. 'I shall apply to Somerset House in due course,' I said at last, in a severe tone. 'And if it proves that this information about poor Mr Hickson is official, I shall have to look into things.' 'What things?' 'I suppose you know Mr Hickson owed Mr Jimson a considerable sum of money – nearly forty or fifty thousand pounds to be exact. A debt of honour, of course. So I daresay that a settlement could be arranged.' 'You're not Mr Jimson yourself, by any chance?' 'Certainly not, but I should feel bound to protect his memory against any hanky panky.' 'I'll inquire about the creditors, if you could hold the line.' But I did not hold the line. I wasn't to be caught a second time. I hit the receiver on the wall as hard as I could to give the rascal's drum a shock. And went out, leaving the door open.

But I didn't feel any better. I was so shaky in the legs that as soon as I was round the corner, I sat down on a step. 'I don't believe it,' I said. 'Hickson dead – why, he can't have been more than seventy. There's some dirty work at the bottom of this.' But I knew that Hickson was dead. I knew it just as a man knows when he's had his leg shot off, though he can still feel his corns. And it upset me. I felt as if the ground had given a yawn under my feet. I felt like that little dog in the story who ran out of Lombard Street to do his morning pee against the Bank of England and found it gone. Gone to nothing. Not even a hole in the ground. But nothing at all. Nothing even to bark at. What would be the good of a bark at nothing. Nothing. Because it would be nothing itself as soon as it went over the edge. I refuse to believe it, I said. But then I gave a great sigh and I found that I was crying. This cheered me up a little. Yes, real tears. I can't be so old, I said, if I can cry. There's sap in the old trunk yet. And I got up and hobbled home.

When Cokey saw me, she was shocked. She threw me into bed, with abuse. 'Look at you, you old bother, you've caught another chill. Going out like that.' 'No, Cokey,' I said, 'I've had a blow. I've lost my oldest friend. And it's damn nearly broken my nerve. If you were a real woman I'd throw myself on your breast and cry like a baby. You don't believe it, but I could. I never needed a woman more; not a female but a woman.' 'I'll give you something to cry about if you go off like that again.' Cokey didn't believe I had any real friends except herself. She had a lot of womanliness in her nature though she didn't indulge it.

37

Cokey did not let me out for three days. And by that time I couldn't even see my Wall. I might have been dead and coffined. But what could I do without money. I had no respect for myself, so Cokey paid no attention to my appeals. Luckily the fourth day was the fourteenth of the month, Rozzie's anniversary, and when I told Cokey that I had a grave to visit, she gave me my clothes.

And when I went to the florist's, I told him that I wanted a better wreath than usual. 'Make it a two-guinea one,' I said. 'In flowers,' said the florist. 'Yes, two guineas in flowers and three in the bill.' The florist looked sad out of respect. He felt that my grief was sincere. 'Bill to Mr Thomas Jimson?' he said. 'Yes,' I said, 'c/o Cox's Bank.' For Tom always paid for the wreath, and, in fact, he usually sent me a card to remind me of the date. 'Expenses are a bit higher this year,' I said, 'owing to the weather.'

The florist was an old friend of mine. 'It was three pounds eight last year,' he said. 'And the wreath was only a guinea and a half.'

'Last year included hotel expenses,' I said, for I was always very particular that Tom got a fair deal. 'Last year I had two windows blown out at the place where I was stopping – came to nine and sixpence.'

'And did the hotel make you pay?'

'It wasn't exactly an hotel, it was my studio, but I was stopping there at the time of the anniversary, so it came under expenses. That's all fair, I think —'

'Oh yes, sir, quite fair.' And he gave me a guinea change. So I took a taxi to the cemetery. I knew Tom liked to do the thing properly.

And when I had admired the grave which always had some nice daisies, and read the inscription, I was thinking of Rozzie and what a queer girl she was, all brass on the outside, and all bread-and-butter pudding within, when I looked up, and there was old Sara waddling down the path in her fusty blacks with a hat full of purple and violets, and a bunch of Michaelmas daisies and marigolds in her hand.

She had seen me already, and she was obviously afraid to come up. She went from side to side and her feet flopped out-ways without making any progress. Once she began to turn away. But at last she took hold of herself and gave herself a shake and came on like the old guard.

'Why, Gulley,' she panted, 'I never expected to see you here.'

'Or you wouldn't have come, you old thief. What about my picture?'

'Well, Gulley, it was a shame, and I never meant to play you a trick like that. But something came over me, and you know how it is with an old woman. It seemed like losing the last bit of those good times.'

'Why shouldn't I send the police to take my own property?'

'Is it your property, or ought the creditors to have it? Or Mr Hickson? I don't know.'

'You'd rather give it to anybody but me.'

'Oh no, Gulley. That's not so, and you know it's not.' And Sara was quite excited. Her nose turned purple; a sign that she was speaking the truth for once 'I'd rather you had it than anyone, and I'm sure you could have it now.'

At these words my heart jumped like a little ballet girl and the wreath jumped in my hand like a tambourine. 'What,' I said, 'you'll give it to me, the bath sketch.' And I saw three hundred sovereigns flash through the air like Phoebus horses followed by the Peculiar chapel, like a gypsy van.

'I would, indeed, if I could,' said Sara. 'But Byles's got it now. Locked up in his chest. He's got all my things, even my mother's bible. He says that it's valuable, and it will do to keep us when he retires from the council, and bury us.'

'What's valuable?'

'My mother's bible. He says it's an old one and worth a hundred pounds – though I know my mother only paid twelve and six at the S.P.C.A. But Byles thinks that all bibles are valuable.'

'And what about my picture, Sall?'

'He says it's worth five thousand pounds – only he doesn't like to sell it in case of the police. He says the police would be bound to think that we'd stolen it if we got all that money for it.'

I nearly dashed the wreath to the ground. I can stand a lot from Boorjays, God knows; but I could never bear the way they value pictures. Either they're worth nothing at all, or thousands. 'My God, Sara,' I said, 'five thousand for a sketch like that – I might get fifty for it, by special influence. No, if you want your burial money you'd better make Byles understand that I'm the only man who can pass off that daub as a masterpiece.'

'What is it really worth, Gulley?'

'I tell you, if I signed it, and polished it up a bit, I might get fifty – fifty pounds that is – from a friend, more out of charity than business.'

'I thought it might be worth more than that now that I'm in the Tate.'

'You in the Tate – oh, you mean Hickie's bath picture.'

'They say that one is worth thirty thousand pounds.'

'It will be, it will be. In a hundred years. It may be worth two thousand now.'

'Byles measured it up with his eye and it's five by eight, and this one is three and a half by two, which is nearly a sixth, he says. But, of course, I knew it didn't go by size.'

'No, it doesn't go by size any more than women. The biggest are often the smallest.'

'Well, Gulley, I would have given it to you – I'd give it to you now if I could – only for what you said. Thirty guineas, and that's only to bury me. For that nasty Doris ripped up my stays – will you believe the meanness of a woman like that who'd send a piece of her own sex to a pauper funeral – shovelled into the ground like an old can – look at the way you're holding that beautiful wreath. I'm sure there won't be a bloom left on it.'

I picked up the wreath and took Sara's arm. 'Come on, old girl, we're forgetting ourselves, and Rozzie.'

'You make me quite ashamed with that wreath,' said Sara. 'It must have cost two pounds.'

'Not too much for Rozzie,' I said.

'Oh, Gulley, you liked Rozzie better than you liked me.'

'Not a bit of it, Sall, I'd give you a five-pound wreath any day, if I had the money, wild roses with the thorns on.'

'Oh, Gulley, there you go.'

'The sweetest roses have the sharpest thorns, Sall. What are you going to do with that bunch, you'll need a vase?'

'A vase, I never thought to bring a vase. Last time I came this way I brought a pot of daffodils. I never came before on the funeral day, Gulley. I should have, but I never did. Not since the funeral itself.'

'Where we had a pint together.'

'Yes, you were at the funeral, too. But then, Rozzie was your real doting piece.'

I said nothing for fear of saying too much.

'Her legs were better,' said Sara with an old woman's cast in her eye, a back cast. 'If you like that kind of leg, like a custard glass; and her hair was lovely, for colour, that is – she never had too much of it.'

'The vases are over at the lodge, where the sexton lives.'

'Well, I suppose I'd better find some water for my daisies. Though they're nothing to your wreath. But Byles grew them on purpose.'

So we went along together to the lodge where the gardener kept some flowerpots and tin vases for visitors' flowers, and a stand-pipe. And while I picked out for Sara a vase without a hole in the bottom, she said, 'I'm glad you remembered Rozzie's day.'

'I haven't missed it once since the old girl died, except when prevented by circumstances.'

'You and Rozzie had a lot in common,' said Sara. 'Yes, you were closer to Rozzie than you were to me. The way you laughed together. But Rozzie had such wonderful spirits. Well, I always thought there was something in it. You always made so little of it.'

I put my face in a vase and lifted it up to the sky to see if there was a hole in the bottom and to hide any holes in my expression. Sara had a woman's eye for holes in the expression. She could see them when they weren't there; which comes to the same thing to a woman when she means to pin something on you.

'And all those wires from somebody called Robinson in Brighton with a box number,' said Sara.

'Here you are, my dear,' I said. 'The rustiest, but it seems to hold water. Come along, and I'll fill it for you.'

I didn't want to discuss Rozzie with Sara. For I knew she wouldn't be fair to Rozzie, and I was feeling tenderhearted about that ancient fireship.

38

Rozzie was the only girl in the world for me except Sara. They nearly finished me between them. The seven years when I had those two women on my mind and body were as good as fourteen penal. For each of them was a harem and you never knew which spouse you had to deal with.

Of course, I always liked big women. I suppose I was meant to be a sculptor or architect. And what attracted me to Rozzie in the first place was her size. She was bigger even than Sara in those days. It took several minutes to walk round her. You studied her from different aspects, like a public building. Something between St Paul's and the Brighton Pavilion. But though I may have had some idea of getting away with Rozzie, I didn't reckon to fall in love with her.

They say, of course, any woman can catch any man if she takes him at the right moment, on the bounce, in the air; going up or coming down. But Rozzie didn't try to catch me. When Sara refused me the first time, and I was suffering from temporary sanity, I went to Rozzie just round the corner and took her by as much as I could get hold of with my two arms and my teeth, and said, 'Rozzie, you've got to marry me, or something like that, or I'll cut both our bloody throats.'

Rozzie brushed me off like an earwig and said, 'I'd smack your face if I wasn't afraid of catching whatever it is. I'm Sara's friend, and don't you forget it. Do that again and I'll tell her.' But she said it very nicely. Rozzie was a nice girl. She couldn't be rough if she tried, in spite of her big fists.

'If you're Sara's friend,' I said, 'you'll be nice to me, because I'm going to cut my throat and that will upset Sara considerably. She's fond of me, though she doesn't know it.'

'Go on and cut,' said Rozzie. 'Sara and I want a good laugh.' But by this time I was sitting on her knee and making myself accustomed. And Rozzie didn't brush me off. I expected that smack every minute, but it didn't come. And Rozzie was so fierce in her look and rough in her tongue, that it was only after she was dead and I had time to think about her and to see her in the all round, that I realized she was all bark and no bite. Take off her clothes and she was like a port-wine jelly rabbit shelled out of the tin, a pink trembler; massive and shapely in the forms, but inclined to spread at the edges; firm to the eye, but soft to the touch. Deep but transparent; something like a lion, but not much.

Why did I fall in love with Rozzie? Most men fall in love because they want to; that's why they can't be stopped. But I didn't want to fall in love with either Sara or Rozzie. I wanted to get on with my work. I was the victim of circumstances.

Every billet has its bullet, there's a fatal woman waiting for every man. Luckily he doesn't often meet her. I was born six men and I had six fates, but thank God, I only met five of them. As a religious man, I fell for a Sunday school teacher, but I converted her to Christianity and she ran away with a primitive Communist. As a Briton I fell in love with Mrs Monday, the mother and the wife. I wanted to rest upon the domestic bosom. But she turned into a bride and wanted to rest on mine. As an artist, I fell in love with Sara, and her grand forms, but she was an artist herself, and she appreciated herself so much that she couldn't bear me to paint anyone or anything else.

But the man who fell in love with Rozzie was the poor little Peter Pan who wanted to creep back into his mother's womb and be safe and warm and comfortable for the rest of his life. Isolationist. With navel defence. Sure shield. And lo, Rozzie only wanted to creep into my stomach. She was the softie, the girl who never grew up, the rabbit that lived up a tree and sang to herself all day, the prayer: Oh God, don't let me know anything, or think anything or be anything. Because I know I never could. Don't let anything happen to me because I'm really much too young. Have pity on the silly little thing and don't ask her to make up her mind about anything, because she really couldn't. Just let her make jokes and drink and laugh —

Sara was a tyrant who tried to put me in a bottle and cork me up into a woman's cup of tea; and Rozzie was a slave who said, 'Beat me, eat me, but never, never ask me to make up my mind.'

Sara was an empress. It was a glory to have that woman, and to beat her. Alexander never felt bigger than me when I thumped that majestic meat upon the bone. Rozzie was a Leah, a concubine, a man tickler, the world's harem; she was the valley of peace and joy. She was a pillow for your head and a footstool for your rheumatism. But, of course, pillows and mattresses are not the sort of baggage a man wants to carry with him on a long journey. You could never get your own way with Sara. You might think so, but that was only her cunning. Life with Sara was all on the diplomatic scale, between the grand contracting parties. Sometimes we were noble allies and carried on the war together, sometimes we were enemies; but you were always yourself and Sara was always herself, and making love to Sara was a stormy joy, thunder and lightning. There was an exchange of powers, a flash and a bang; Jupiter and the cloud. You gave something and you took something.

But life with Rozzie was a doze beneath the palm trees; and loving her was like a shower of autumn leaves on a paddock. It left you bare.

Sara was a palace outside, but when you went in, you found yourself in a convalescent home. All clean and wholesome, h. and c., and indoor sanitation, regular meals by our resident dietitian, nothing to do but keep your nose clean and put your bottom in the chair that was meant for it. You respected yourself at Sara's. But Rozzie, who looked like something between Knightsbridge Barracks and Holloway Gaol, when you had dared to push at the iron gate, which collapsed like brown paper, was a club for retired gentlemen. I mean, gentlemen that had given up the job and didn't want to mind their manners any more. You could spit in the fender anywhere round Rozzie from the attics to the lounge, and eat sausage and mash in the gilded hall.

Sara was the everlasting trumpets, a challenge to battle and death. Rozzie was a cradle song, accompanied on the ocarina.

It was a pleasure to take things from Sara, even if you had to steal them; a double pleasure, because Sara liked giving; it was a joy to give things to Rozzie, because Rozzie liked presents. They gave her self-confidence. They made her feel that she was worth something. Sara never needed anyone to tell her what she was worth, she knew her value so well that I don't suppose she even thought of it. She never had any pride; and Rozzie was so particular that if only a man stared at her in the street, she would glare and swear for an hour afterwards; and say the rude things she would do to him if she caught him without his bathing drawers.

I still remember Rozzie's indignation when I unbuttoned her bodice. 'Here, what do you think you're up to?'

'I'm going to marry you, Rozzie, or the next best thing.' Then Rozzie raised her great knuckled butcher's fist and I ducked for the swing. But it didn't come. 'What do you take me for?' cried Rozzie. 'A bloody tart?'

'No,' I said, undoing another button. 'You're the nicest woman I ever wanted to meet.'

'Leave off,' said Rozzie. 'Get off, you —'

'I should like to get off,' I said. 'With you, Rozzie dear.' And Rozzie only said in a kind of perplexed tone. 'When you've finished with my bodice.'

But I hadn't finished, and as I went further, trembling all over and expecting to be knocked out of the window any minute, but getting madder and madder all the time, Rozzie's shouts changed into complaints and at last into appeals.

'No, Gulley, I never thought you would treat a girl like this – it's not right. I'm a decent woman, whatever you may think. I may have started behind the bar, but I always kept myself respectable —'

And at the end of it she was almost crying, as near crying as Rozzie could get. 'Oh, it's a shame, Gulley. I'm surprised at you, you nasty little man. And what's going to happen to me now? What will people think? Suppose I have a baby. My character will be dirt. And how am I going to meet Sara? My best oldest friend. I'd be ashamed —'

Rozzie had a conscience; Sara had a purpose and an object in life. Rozzie was a God-fearing heathen that never went to church in case of what might happen to her there; Sara was a God-using Christian that went to church to please herself and pick up some useful ideas about religion, hats and the local gossip.

Sara was a shot in the arm; she brought you alive one way or another; the very idea of Sara could always make me swear or jump or dance or sweat. Because of her damned independence and hypocrisy. When you knew Sara, you knew womankind, and no one who doesn't know womankind knows anything about the nature of Nature. But Rozzie was only a female and she never stirred up anything but love and pity. Sara was a menace and a tonic, my best enemy; Rozzie was a disease, my worst friend. Sara made a man of me and damn nearly a murderer; Rozzie might have turned me into a lop-eared crooner.

I remember the day I heard Rozzie was dying. I got a wire from her landlady in Brighton; I was down in Devonshire busy at a big job. But I told some lie to Sara and went right across England. Rozzie wasn't dying, but she was nearly dead. She'd given herself a miscarriage. I found her as white as a wall, all fallen away and flat as a cod on the slab. 'My God, Rozzie,' I said, 'what have you been doing?'

'I didn't want that kid,' said Rozzie, and she kept smiling all the time. 'Am I passing out?'

'No, but you nearly did, a nice mess that would have been.'

'Go on,' said Rozzie. 'A bit of all right for all concerned.'

'Don't talk like that, Rozzie. You know you don't mean it.'

'That's just what I do mean,' said Rozzie. 'Here, what am I good for? A bloody old burden – out of Barnums – or the back of a motor boat.'

'But Rozzie, what the hell. You aren't worrying about your character, are you. You aren't worrying about people looking at you. You've got a legal wedding ring, haven't you? You've got a right to a belly, you ought to be proud of yourself. Why, damn it all, it's a grand sight anyhow, a woman carrying.'

'Not this one,' said Rozzie. 'No, Gulley, I don't so much mind about the character – but what a fuss about nothing. And what's going to happen to the poor kid. It'll have a fine start with me for a mother. And you for a papa.'

'Damn it all, Rozzie, you'll be a splendid mother with your good nature, and as for me, I'm very fond of kids. And I shall be a better father than a lot of those boorjoes. I'm not going to hand over this kid to the schoolmasters and get rid of it under the pretence of education. No, I'm going to teach it myself. No reading and writing and arithmetic for my kid.' For I was really keen on education at that time. And I had the idea that if you could only prevent a kid learning to read, it couldn't pick up all the rubbish out of the newspapers and books, that spoils children's brains. My idea was to teach kids first of all to sing, since Nature starts 'em singing before they can talk; and then to draw; and then to swim and box, and then when they got a bit older and could do more brain work, to dance and make poetry in their heads. Also I was going to teach my kid to know all Blake's poetry and what it means and what is wrong with it, and then, if he was a boy, I should have gone on to Shakespeare and navigation, so that he could be a sailor and see some of the outside world, and keep away from culture and all the rest of it; or if a girl, Milton and cooking; so she might go into service and see some of the inside world.

But Rozzie was afraid of something. I don't know what. Responsibility or the judgement of Heaven. She felt that she had no right to a kid, or that the kid would be too much for her. 'You don't see me putting a kid to bed, and hearing its prayers.' 'Well damn it all, don't hear its prayers. Just teach it to sing something. Little lamb, who made thee, or Tiger, Tiger.' 'Go on, Gulley, I'd have to laugh and the kid would see I was playing the fool – kids are too bloody sharp.' 'Why, you damned old bag, you'll be so fond of this kid, you'll thank God for it.' 'It won't thank God for me, I'll be tight half the time.' 'Blast you, you don't get tight now, you old pudding. Why should you get tight because you've got a kid?' 'You know what kids are.' 'But I tell you you'll love a kid. It's natural – and of all the great lumps of nature I ever knew, you're the lumpiest.' 'That's what I'm afraid of.' 'What, having a kid.' 'Well, you know what it is, with mamas that get fond of their kids and then their kids wake up one fine day and say: Why should I have to go round with this common nasty fiery-faced old bitch – she'd ruin a Mary Pickford's chances.' 'Why, you old hurdy gurdy, why do you think it's going to be a girl?' 'A boy would be worse, he'd take to drink.'

It was a pleasure to get away from that great gutless Jill pudding, back to Sara, even though it was going back from peace and fun to the battlefield. Even though I could see all Rozzie's works going round like the wheels of a Greenwich clock and her face always told me the exact time; and Sara's face was only camouflage for the war factory. It was bracing to deal with a soldier again. You knew where you were, and you had some respect for yourself. And you could get on with your work.

But, of course, I never could put Rozzie off my mind any more than a nursing monkey can get its big baby off its back. I used to wake up in the night in a cold sweat and say, 'What's wrong? I wonder if Sara has poisoned me,' and then all at once I would feel that Rozzie had cut her throat, or jumped off the new pier, and I had no peace until I had wired. How I used to curse that great soft oaf, though not to herself. You couldn't curse at Rozzie in case she took it badly and did herself an injury. You can't put a backbone into a blancmange; if you try, you only cut it up. And after the boy was born, she was more than ever afraid; afraid to nurse it, afraid to wash it, afraid to touch it. I had to wash it myself until we got a good nurse. I might have wasted my life on Rozzie and that kid if it hadn't been for Sara. For that was the time I was maddest on Sara. Painting her and fighting her. Yes, Sara saved me for Rozzie. But what a life, making up lies all the time to keep Sara quiet while I dashed off to Brighton to see how young Tom was taking his bottle, and then making up arguments to keep Rozzie's conscience quiet and to stop her from throwing herself on Sara's bosom and confessing all. Never tell me that women haven't got a conscience. It's their most ticklish point, except a dozen others. Then back again to Sara in the blue horrors in case Rozzie should have wired or some kind friend written and exposed the system; and lost me my Sara, just when I was getting to understand her articulation.

I was down to six stone when Sara deserted me, and God knows what would have happened to my remains if it hadn't been for a nice young thing called Margaret, or Mud; a lady by education and a gentleman by birth, who had got the idea, thank heaven, after being thrown out of the College of Music, the Slade and the School of Dramatic Art, that she was born to be the wife of genius.

Mud got after me, and I let her catch me. She had an income. She could afford to indulge a thirst for glory. And a good wife she was until the money ran out and Hickson stopped my allowance; and her family threatened to run me in for bigamy.

Mud even squared Rozzie by taking over the boy. And after that, whenever I had the Rozzie feeling, I could run down to Brighton and have a drink with the old saloon front, and a laugh, and let her talk flow over me for a day or two; fruity as distilled bar-snug, rich as xxx. For no one I ever knew had such a give-away as Rozzie, she opened all the doors and windows, and you could walk about inside as if you were at home. And what a home; the complete female widow's museum.

When Rozzie fell under that bus, I suffered a loss which surprised me. I cried. Well, there I was, with my palette and brushes in one hand and the telegram in the other, choking; and Mud saying to me in that drawl which women always have when they haven't got any moral delicacy, 'But darling, she's not da-id – it only says, seriously injured.'

'She'll die,' I said. 'Boo-hoo. I know she'll die. I had it coming to me. Things were going altogether too well. And Rozzie will never make a fight for it. The poor bitch was murdered young – by her spots.'

'Her spots?'

'Yes, her complexion. She had spots, poor child, and so she had to marry a middle-aged publican who did the dirt on her for fifteen years – all sorts of dirt. No,' I said, 'Rozzie never had any guts – and she'll die like an express train, without stopping at the stations.'

And, of course, I was right. Rozzie died laughing at herself, so she shouldn't cry. She stopped crying young because, with her complexion, she had to keep her powder dry.

39

When I found the pump by the sexton's house, I gave Sara the vase and told her to hold on while I pumped. 'And look out for your feet,' I said. 'These churchyard pumps and standpipes are regular death traps. Too many mourners come here and get their feet wet, and then they are so overcome by grief they think it mean to change their stockings and the next thing is they're being measured for a wooden tow-piece in polished elm, with silver-plated handles.'

'Poor Rozzie never had even elm – a pauper's coffin.'

'What did Rozzie care so long as it didn't let in the draught. She never could bear a draught. That was the barmaid all over.'

'You knew her better than me, though we were such old friends. You liked Rozzie better than you did me.'

'Don't you believe it, Sara, you were my right hand.'

'Well, they often said Rozzie was another limb to you, but I wouldn't believe it.'

'Rozzie was a respectable girl, and I often wonder she didn't marry again.'

'So do I,' said Sara, 'and perhaps she ought to have been married again, though goodness knows I have no right to talk.'

'So you think Rozzie had her affairs,' I said.

'They say she had a baby.'

'They'd say anything,' and I took Sara's arm, as we wobbled back to the grave. 'You and I, Sall, are too old to worry about what they say.'

'So we are,' said Sara. 'I suppose it wasn't your baby, Gulley?'

'Me, what baby?' I said. 'When did all this happen?' I said. But I used the wrong voice, for Sara stopped and looked at me. 'Well,' she said, 'I never could have believed it, so that's what the operation was, she went into hospital for —'

'You mustn't blame Rozzie,' I said. 'She was the victim of circumstances.'

'Well, I should have guessed,' said Sara, as we walked on again. 'And so it was Rozzie you used to go off to.'

'Rozzie gave me a home when you threw me over.'

I thought Sara would fire up at this. For she always maintained that I deserted her, because I left the house before she did. Though the truth was, she had abandoned me, in spirit, about a month before.

But Sara was growing old and you never knew quite what new old thing would come up to her mind. 'You always liked her better for a randyvoo.'

It took me by surprise and I burst out, 'Now, what do you mean by that, Sara?' 'Well, for a holiday visit. She was so big and looked so fierce. You always liked to triumph over the sizeable ones, Gulley, being so little and light-bodied. Yes, I always thought you'd like to conquer over Rozzie, like a little bantam on a big midden.' 'Poor Rozzie, if you want to know, had no more spunk than a net of lard.' 'She was nervous of trains and dogs, certainly.' 'And everything else.' 'Not men, Gulley. She'd always know how to handle the men ever since she went into the "Case is Altered" at sixteen, a proper rough place, nothing but a beerhouse it was then.' 'Rozzie was meat for the first man that got hold of her.' But old Sara shook her head. 'She turned you round her finger, Gulley. But there, she always meant to get you away from me. And I hope you made her happy. I'm sure she deserved some happiness.'

'Dammit all, Sara,' I said, for I could not bear to see the old woman twisting everything about to suit herself. 'You don't believe that, and you know Rozzie was a loyal friend to you and to tell you the truth, she was very unhappy when the thing came about, she said she could never face you again.'

'I'm not blaming her,' said Sara, 'I'm sorry for her.'

'She was the honestest girl that ever knocked back a can,' I said, 'a true blue – it was the only good thing about her except perhaps her legs, and as for stealing me away from you, she had no idea of it. I did the stealing.'

We had reached the grave, and I read the inscription:

ROSINA BALMFORTH, BELOVED WIFE OF THE LATE
WILLIAM OKE BALMFORTH
BORN APRIL 2ND, 1881. DIED JUNE 14TH, 1928
BLESSED ARE THE POOR IN SPIRIT.

It brought up Rozzie in front of me, and by Jove my eyelids pricked. It was a high-shouldered stone, just like the poor old engine herself. I'd chosen it for Tom when he wanted to mark the grave. And I thought, Who will remember Rozzie when I go? Sara is immortal. She will live in the National Galleries of the world for ever, or at least for a few hundred years. But Rozzie is fading away already. I have to look twice before I can see those powdered cheeks, like over-ripe strawberries under a sprinkle of sugar; or hear that hoarse bookie's voice, full of good nature and resignation.

Yes, that was the attraction of the poor old barge; her despair. She seemed to say, I'm done for, but who cares. It's only another laugh on the house.

Rozzie was a desolation. You loved her like a ruin that has to be propped up and railed round to keep the dogs off. And she grew on you like the ivy and the drink, digging out your mortar with her great, knobby roost. Loving Rozzie was a special vice, like eating between meals.

'You don't tell me you had your own way with Rozzie,' said Sara. 'She could have eaten you at one bite, even without her front teeth. I mean her false ones. For you know her teeth were a weak point with poor Rozzie.'

'Why, Sara,' I said, 'if you will think badly of poor Rozzie, I can't help it. But I'm ashamed of you, standing here before her very grave – and I'm surprised at you because I didn't think you would be so mean.'

'I'm not thinking badly of Rozzie,' said Sara. 'Rozzie Balmforth was my best friend, and I'll never forget her good, kind heart.'

'Tom stands all my expenses and he'd like you to have something, Sara, so what about a half one to drink his health.'

But Sara didn't seem to hear me. She was waddling along so slowly that I had to stop for her. And when an old woman gets so slow as that, it means she's thoughtful of her latter end.

All at once she looked at me, quite sadly, and said, 'I suppose you'll be buried here, by Rozzie. Well, she gave you a boy.'

'To tell the truth, Sall, I don't want to be buried anywhere.'

'If you go with Rozzie, Gulley, I'd understand it. Indeed, I should, though there was a time I never dreamed you'd lie away from me.'

And I thought: Yes, poor old Sall, she's an old aged woman. She's fallen over the last step. Her mind is running on graves as only old women's minds do. Graves and buryings. Well, she always liked to make a home, and now it's the last home. Complete with husband.

'Come,' I said. 'You know there'll be room for you, Sall, wherever they earth me down.'

'I'd like that best,' said she, 'as God sees me. Well, isn't it natural. But, oh dear, I don't know if I can —'

'Ah, I forgot all the other claims, there's Monday and old Mr W. and Fred, as well as me. But why shouldn't we all come, Sara?'

'You may laugh, Gulley. But I wouldn't mind it. You can't have too many friends round you in that cold place.'

'Not laughing, Sall, I think it's a good idea.'

'But they all have their own places. And what I was thinking, Gulley, though it goes against my very soul, I oughtn't to lie with you now. I can't help it, but my duty is to poor Byles. He never had a house or a wife of his own these thirty years. And I promised him. That's what he said, "It will bury us both." '

She stopped again and I saw that this last quick turn was a tactical gambit of some kind. And she knew I knew. So we walked on arm-in-arm, feeling very kindly to each other in a graveyard way, and feeling each other's nature, too. For I said to myself: The old lady, full as she is of love, tears, regrets, grief and religion, is up to something; and I knew she was saying to herself, Dear Gulley, how awkward he is. It's as bad as catching eels to get him fixed to anything. And as usual Sara won the first round. I couldn't wait any longer, and I said, 'What will bury you both? I should have thought your family might be glad to do something.'

'Oh dear, my family – where is it? Phyllis, indeed – but where is she? – she may be buried herself. And Nancy with all her own troubles. I shouldn't like to come upon Nancy. I've been trouble enough to the poor thing already. No, it wasn't the family Byles meant.' And we walked on. Till I got impatient again, and burst out, 'You mean the picture, do you?' And I kept on squeezing her arm, but I had to tell myself not to pinch it or stick pins in the old carcase. For it would shock the old lady, at her age.

'Come on, Sall,' I said. 'Byles said that the picture, my picture, would bury you? And where do we go from there?'

'Though, indeed,' she said, making the usual Salleonic diversion on the left flank. 'I can't bear to think of that money lying wasted, just in a bit of canvas, and you getting no benefit.'

'Neither can I, Sall.'

'And you think I've kept it from you?'

'Come, Sall,' I said. For I saw the grand bombardment was about to begin. 'Come and have that drink and we'll work out what you're up to.'

'But the thing is, Byles is afraid to sell it in case there's questions asked. Why, that Doris might put Fred on to making a claim.'

'She might, indeed; you're quite right, Sara. Selling pictures that don't belong to you is a tricky business. It needs an expert to do a job like that.'

'And you know, Gulley, if we could get the money between us, I'd only want enough for a real funeral, and a bought grave and a stone. Well, perhaps I shouldn't ask for that, and you may say it's only a vanity. But oh dear, I don't know how it is, I can't get that pauper funeral out of my blood. It turns my very heart. And then to lie alone, among strangers – for ever and ever. No, it's too cruel for my old flesh.'

'Sall,' I said, pressing her arm, and I was pleased as you may think, 'if you can get that picture out of Byles, you shall have the best funeral money can buy – four coaches and an oak coffin. Two best funerals. And a stone six foot high with eight lines of poetry. That's four more than Tom did for Rozzie.'

'Oh, Gulley, may God bless you. You may have your laughs – but you don't throw a woman's weakness in her face. For you know that God made us so, and so we are, and we can't help it.'

The old lady was so warm that I was surprised. And I said to myself for about the hundredth time: Say what you like, women are a sex by themselves, so to speak.

'I shouldn't call it weakness, Sall, far from it,' I said. 'And as for being a woman, didn't I like you so. When it comes to a wife, give me a woman any day. A woman born and bred.'

So we took three more steps, waiting for each other to make the next move.

'But who would sell it for us?' said Sara, as if that little problem had just occurred to her.

'I would, Sall. Proud and pleased.'

'Oh dear, I'm afraid Byles would never agree to that.'

'What's your scheme, Sall?' For I saw that she had one.

'Well, I thought, we could go together to one of the Bond Street shops and they could send us a man.'

But that, of course, was just what I didn't want. Dealers. Publicity. All sorts of complications.

'Come, Sara,' I said. 'We don't want any third parties in this business. Contracts and bills and legal stuff. We're all friends together.'

'Yes, but I can't see any other way.'

'Give me the picture and I'll sell it this very morning.'

'I couldn't even get it. It's locked up in Byle's chest.'

'You don't trust me, Sara. Not even now, not with my own picture.'

'Oh, Gull, you know I do. It's Byles who's so mistrustful.'

We'd come to the main gate. And right opposite there was the usual pub you always see at a cemetery gate, for the mourners, quiet-looking place with a door as discreet as a coffin lid, and all as clean as a mortuary slab.

So I said, 'What about that drink, Sall?'

'Well,' said Sara, 'I shouldn't mind. I haven't to be home so soon because Byles is away.'

This made me jump in my skin. 'Mr Byles away,' I said. 'Yes, he's in hospital.' 'I thought he didn't like hospitals.' 'Neither he does, but he fell off a ladder and they picked him up unconscious. He didn't come round before he was in hospital.' 'I'm sorry about that, Sara, I hope he isn't badly hurt.' 'I hope not, and they say not, but you can't trust them, can you? You never know what they have in their minds.' 'Here we are, Sara – the Blue Posts.' And I went in and ordered a couple of pints, and sat Sara down to them in the bay window. 'Just a minute, Sall,' I said, 'while I see a man about a rose.' 'It's just inside the front door.' said Sara. 'Drink up,' I said. 'Don't wait for me, I take my time, on a cold evening like this.' And I went out quickly and hopped on to a bus. For I thought: Now's my chance if ever I had one. Byles away and Sara drowning her grief.

I stopped only at the ironmonger's to get a box-opener. And I was in the flat quicker than I had expected. But just as I worked the crow into Byles's chest, Sara put her head round the door. She had followed me home. Just like Sara to suspect me. And before I could creep under the bed she saw me and rushed down the passage, screaming, 'Police.'

I got a big fright. I didn't want the police. It might have meant five years. And five years would have finished me. I ran after Sara and grabbed her by the back of her skirt. But she still kept on screaming, 'Police.' So I gave her a little tap on the bonnet with the Iron Duke, to restore her to her senses; and a little push away from the window. Whereupon she fell down the cellar stairs into some dark hole. I said, for I was a bit surprised, 'What did you do that for?'

And to my relief she answered, 'Oh, Gulley, I never thought you would murder me.'

'Why,' I said, 'what about you, calling out police like that. You know I'd get five years if I went in again. And that would finish me.'

'Oh dear, oh dear,' said Sara, 'I never thought you would murder me. Oh dear, what a pity – what a waste.'

And I was just going down the steps to see if the old lady had broken something, when I heard a voice in the passage, by the front door, and saw a policeman coming in. I had a surprise. But by good luck he put his head into the parlour door, and before he got it back again, I nipped across into the kitchen, shut and bolted the door quietly behind me. Then I took a dive out of the window among the cabbage stalks and hopped over the back wall into a cottage garden at the other side. I never noticed my rheumatism.

The cottage was in a terrace. No way out. So I went in through a back kitchen and found a little girl washing up plates. I looked at her, and she looked at me. Her eyes were as big as tea cups.

'Good evening, my dear,' I said. 'I came about the gas – it's in the meter, isn't it? Do you mind if I get my mate, he's in the street?' The little girl didn't say anything. She just kept looking and wiping a plate round and round. She must have wiped that plate nearly through. I said, 'Thank you, my dear – that will suit very well'; and I went down the passage and let myself out, and made a quick move for the main road, where I could see traffic. I was back at the boat-shed before Cokey came in from washing-up the supper.

Nosy Barbon was waiting for me. He was in such a state of excitement that for a long time I couldn't get anything out of him but vibrations.

'Hold on, old chap,' I said. 'Take it easy.'

'B-beautiful,' he got out at last, 'm-marvellous.'

'What is?'

'The p-painting, your m-masterpiece, in the g-gallery. They've hung it in the m-m-middle, the B-bath, b-beautiful.'

He'd been at the Tate, looking at the Bath, and it had gone to his head, as it always did with weak heads at a first pull. Like champagne. Fizzy stuff.

'All right, old boy,' I said. 'Keep calm. Yes, it's not too bad. But beautiful is about the last word —'

'B-but there was a ch-chap c-copying it, but so b-badly, I thought I c-could do it b-better myself.'

'I daresay,' I said, and then I had an idea. 'My God, Nosy,' I said, 'our fortune's made.' I nearly cried. 'What's tomorrow. Don't say it's Sunday.' Thank God it wasn't Sunday. And before four o'clock the next afternoon I had the prettiest early Jimson you ever saw. Sketch for the Bath. Or rather, from the Bath, but bearing on its face all those indubitable marks which, as the crickets say, testify to that early freshness of vision and bravura of execution which can never be imitated by a hand which, in acquiring a mature decision of purpose, has lost, nevertheless, that *je ne sais quoi* without which perhaps no work of art is entitled to the name of genius. I dried it off too quick on Cokey's stove. Poor Sara had a blister on her behind when I took it round to Capel Mansions. But what did the Professor care? He wasn't buying a picture, but an early Jimson with an irrefutable pedigree.

When I asked him if he thought I had better take it to Bond Street, he nearly went down on his knees. He cabled to Sir William that very afternoon, and Sir William cabled back before dinner-time, fifty pounds, for a week's option. The rest to be paid on receipt of photographs, and a second report, from a cricket or preferably a critic of authority.

I made the option twenty-four hours; and Sir William, with true magnanimity, always ready to trust, when, on a large view, he had a good chance of a bargain, paid up at once.

40

I was so busy by that time that I forgot to cash the order. And Sir William, fearing that he had lost his promotion, wired the Professor to call. But when he called, we were all so busy that it was some time before we noticed him.

The old chapel was like a shipyard with noise, dust, ropes and scaffold poles; ladders and paint pots.

I had meant to paint direct on the wall. It was a wall twenty-five by forty; of common rough plaster, direct from the trowel; a sheer precipice of dirty grey, slightly varied by bird droppings and cobwebs at the top, and spit marks at the bottom, which made my fingers tingle for a No. 24 brush. I could have embraced that wall, less or more.

But Nosy objected so strongly that no one could have stood up to him without a complete suit of oilskins.

'But you can't paint direct on the wall,' he said. 'It's not g-good enough. You must p-paint on c-canvas or s-s-s-s—'

'Yes, but if I use ceiling-boards, I shall have to wait a fortnight to get them up.'

'B-but you *must* wait – till we've p-propped up the roof.'

'And what I think is that the damned old ruin will fall down by itself any day and then what will happen to your ceiling-boards? For me to paint a wall on any building,' I said, 'is as good as asking it to catch fire, or get struck by lightning, or fall down. And as this thing I'm doing is the biggest I've done yet, it will probably bring up an earthquake, or a European war, and wreck half the town.'

But Nosy was horrified by such talk. His nose turned pink, it seemed to swell up with distress. This was due to the pressure of his feelings which were so strong that at first he couldn't get them out, and then they came all together like a dust shoot. 'B-but that's why you m-must wait. You m-mustn't take any risks, Mr J-Jimson, with a p-picture like this. You've no right to take such a risk.' 'No right, Nosy. Damn it all, it's my own picture, isn't it?' 'Y-yes. N-no, I m-mean, it's a n-national picture, it's a w-world m-masterpiece. Y-yes, it belongs to the w-world, to p-posterity.' 'Pup-posterity will probably not give a damn for pictures except the movies.' 'N-no, p-please, Mr J-Jimson, this is a s-serious matter. You've no *right* to take the risk. Until the roof is p-propped.' 'Not on your life, Nosy, I'm starting now right away.' 'But the whole thing may fall down.' 'It will fall down.' 'And then all your w-work will be lost for ever.' 'That's it, Nosy, but there'll still be a lot of bloody fools painting pictures, even wall pictures. You can't stop art by dropping bricks on its head.' 'You know that no one is painting anything as good as yours, not g-great pictures.' 'How do you know they're great, Nosy?' 'Why,' said Nosy, quite shocked. 'Nobody can help knowing it. You've only got to see them.' 'You haven't seen this one yet.' 'This is the greatest of them all – you know it is.' 'You'll never be any bloody good as an artist, Nosy, you were born for the Church or big business. Faith rather than works. You ought to be a rising Ford or an early Christian. And to hell with the lions. You can't please everybody.'

But the truth was that I myself was a bit roused up by the Creation. I had it on my mind. I hadn't really had any proper sleep or meals for a week, since the first lovely money fell from Heaven, via Beeder, into my pocket. I used to wake up at night shivering all over and thinking the vampires were eating my toes; but it was only the Creation sticking its great beak into me. I used to laugh all at once and jump up in the street, several feet or inches into the air, so that the kids threw orange peel at me and the girls drew back their skirts and looked round for a policeman to remove the offensive rubbish; but it was only because I felt cold hands down my back, hands of Creation. In fact, I'm not surprised that, in those days, Cokey thought I was slightly touched, and used to run after me with bottles of stout, woolly combinations and rubber water-bottles. For I slept on the job, like every good general, and according to Cokey, the chapel, being built only for hellfire religion, had no damp-course.

'Look here, Nosy,' I said, 'there's something in what you s-say about the —'

'S-s-s—' said Nosy, who couldn't even wait for me to speak. 'And if you can get them up before tomorrow night, I'll spend the time on the cartoons.'

The reason why I couldn't wait, of course, was Sara. In case the police were after me. And another five years, even two years in chokey, would finish me off. So I was in a bit of a hurry to get my stuff on the wall. 'I'll give you twenty-four hours, Nosy,' I said, 'to put your ceiling-boards up – but I can't wait longer than that. It's more than my life is worth.'

'Can I pay overtime?' said Nosy, the lance-corporal of industry 'It will save in the end.' 'Pay what you like. Money no object,' I said; and he went to use his influence. He used it so well that the ceiling-boards and three plasterers arrived that afternoon. Also a wagon-load of scaffold poles, ladders, cement, rope, buckets, trestles, and paint. A school friend of Nosy's called Jorks, who, like all schoolboys, understood electricity, went into the roof and joined some new wires on to the old chapel cable, so that we were able to hang down dozens of big lights, which made the whole place as bright as a restaurant. And two other boys from Ellam Street, called Muster and Toogood, who, being real London boys, were interested in ships, ropes, knots and blocks, set up a rigging in the east end from which they swung a couple of painter's cradles. That is to say, boxes with one side knocked out, in which one could sit and paint.

In fact, the whole job would have been finished by next evening, except Nosy's props, if it had not been for the usual accidents. First, a gentleman came from some committee or council to say the place wasn't safe and to give me notice. 'But we're making it safe,' I said. 'And it's my business premises. You can't turn a man out of his business premises. I've got a three-years' lease.' 'That wouldn't be valid, I'm afraid, against the council's order,' said the gentleman, who had a blue knitted waistcoat and a red face with smile, gold spectacles, fat nose and expression; full of committee politeness.

'Why do you want me to go?' I said, 'Because the place isn't safe,' said the gentleman. 'I don't mind,' I said. 'But it might fall down and kill you,' he said. 'I appreciate your kind feelings,' I said. 'But I won't hold you responsible.' 'So you really intend to defy the council's orders,' he said. 'Oh no,' I said. 'I'm a law-abiding citizen. I'll stay quietly.' 'You understand,' he said, 'that the matter can't rest here.' 'You c-can't do that,' said Nosy, appearing suddenly in a state of considerable excitement. We both looked at him with surprise and disapproval. 'What?' said the gentleman. 'What can't we do?' I said. 'It's a s-scandal,' said Nosy. 'D-don't you understand that this Mr J-Jimson is Mr Gulley J-Jimson? *The* Mr J-Jimson.' 'Certainly,' said the gentleman. 'That's just what we do understand.'

'You hear him,' said Nosy to me, throwing off a heat-wave like a radiator. 'It's b-because you're Gulley Jimson.' 'That's all right, Nosy,' I said, patting his arm. 'Go home and sleep it off. No one's noticed anything yet.'

'We'll appeal to the nation,' Nosy shouted.

'Certainly,' said the nice gentleman, smiling gaily. 'That's often done. When we wanted to turn some old almshouses into a garage the year before last, there was a national appeal. They collected over a thousand pounds to buy us out. But it all blew over in a week. And you can see the pumps there now. A lovely station, brings us in about a thousand a year in reduction of rates.'

'You d-dare,' Nosy shouted, getting more and more furious. 'You d-dare. Don't you unders-stand it would be in history? P-people would c-curse you for thousands of years.' 'That's all right by the council,' said the councillor, charming and friendly. 'The council don't mind about history because it won't be there. But it will be here on the appointed date, to do its duty by the public. Good evening, Mr Jimson.' 'Good evening, Mr Councillor. My respects to the family.' And I was just in time to prevent Nosy from rushing at the gentleman and perhaps doing him a fatal injury. Fatal to the Creation.

'Are you mad, Nosy? His person is sacred. He is democracy in its best trousers.'

'B-boorjaw b-brute,' said Nosy, waving his arms. 'They want to stop the whole thing, b-because they don't like your s-stuff.'

'Don't be s-silly, Nosy,' I said. 'He was quite a nice chap, that chap. Doing his duty by the ratepayers.'

'But it's a pup-plot,' shouted Nosy, 'They're all talking about it. They d-don't want your p-picture here – near the s-school.'

'Don't you du-dare to talk to me about pup-plots,' I said, losing my temper, just like Nosy. For talk of plots against me or anyone else is what I can't bear. 'Don't you dare,' I said. 'It's the wickedest, dirtiest thing you could do – you might ruin me for life. Why, a chap I knew had a plot against him, he was a chap who sold matches and they wanted to get him off his pitch. And somebody told him about it and he started writing to the papers. And making speeches against the government, and then he knocked a policeman's helmet off. And now he's in an asylum. And what's more, he's not really enjoying life.'

'B-but —' said Nosy. I took him firmly by the arm and interrupted quickly. 'You ought to go and apologize to that poor councillor.' 'But he does want to stop you,' said Nosy, turning pickled-cabbage colour. 'And why not?' I said severely, 'if he doesn't like my painting. To paint a picture that a chap doesn't like – a great big picture like this that anyone might see – is very inconsiderate. It is really an insult. It's just as if I stood out here in the road and shouted that I didn't like his waistcoat; or his manners; that his nose was all wrong; or his face ridiculous. Anyone has a right to defend his own waistcoat. That's what freedom means. So go away, Nosy, and don't try to put these wild ideas in my head or, by Gee and Jay, I won't let you paint.'

This settled Nosy. And I knew how to manage the council. When dealing with men like that you have to TRUST IN THE LORDS – for there's no one else. I sent a note to the Professor telling him that all my influence was necessary, and forgot the council. So that it did not really upset me at all. It did not stop the work. But the other hitch was serious. It could not be overlooked. We had labour trouble, and I couldn't blame it. When the carpenter began to nail up his battens, several bricks fell on his head, a large beam detached itself from the wall and hung in the air, tiles flew off the roof; and finally a two-inch crack appeared in the north side of the chapel.

The workmen then left the place and said they would not go back because it wasn't safe for them. And Nosy was inclined to the view that it was not safe for my picture, until his famous props arrived.

But in this crisis I remembered Nelson. I put a roll of paper to my nose, directed it at the crack, and said, 'I cannot see any crack. And as for being safe, is it likely that I should entrust my life work to a building that is just going to fall down?'

And while the workmen were discussing this argument, I went to Jorks and said, 'They say this building is going to fall down and I rather think it may. So what. I vote to carry on.' 'So do I,' said Jorks, who was a red-faced boy with a big mouth and a short nose. 'I've got a plan for another dozen lights right down the middle. It will take some doing though.' 'So it will,' I said. 'It will probably break your neck.' 'Yes,' said Jorks, turning up his eyes towards the roof. 'Everything is absolutely rotten up there.' 'That's what I say,' I said. 'What's all this fuss about a brick or two when the roof is only supported by the dirt on the cobwebs?' 'Don't you worry. I can do it,' said Jorks. 'I've got it all planned out.' 'You go ahead,' I said, 'and don't let anyone interfere with you.' The end of it was that the workmen propped up the wall and carried on. 'We didn't ought to do it, mister,' they said. 'This place is a fair death trap, but seeing that it's in a good cause.' 'The cause of art,' I said. 'No, sir, but we hear you've had trouble with the council.' 'The council told me to get out.' 'Well, sir, we shouldn't like to let you down against the council.' And they worked all night. British to the core.

The boards were up by next morning, the cracks were filled with putty, and the roof was secured by several more electric wires. Of course, a certain amount of debris was still coming down, and Nosy was still disturbed in his mind.

'It will f-fall any m-minute,' he said, 'and then w-what about your picture?' 'Yes, I was going to speak about that, Nosy, we have to transfer about six hundred sketches and a couple of dozen cartoons on to the wall by Saturday.' 'S-s-s—' 'Yes, Saturday.' 'Why S-s-s—' 'Because we haven't got time to waste. Especially if this damn place is falling down, which seems not improbable as it has actually started to do so, and what I want is about a dozen first-class assistants. Girls from the Polytechnic art class would do.' 'But the place is d-dangerous,' said Nosy. 'They might all g-get killed.' 'That's one of the reasons why I think they'll enjoy the job,' I said. 'It's dangerous, and the other reasons are it's dirty and it's painty.' 'And it's art,' said Nosy. 'I shouldn't say anything about that,' I said, 'to an art class. Better stick to the danger, the dirt and the paint.' And, in fact, before tea-time that day we had offers from twenty-five girls and four boys, the whole class, from which I picked twelve of the middle faces. My rule is, middle faces for the best graft. Pretty ones may be more sensible, but they are always lazy; plain ones may be more earnest, but they are particular. The result was that the Professor found us busy. The plasterers and carpenters were still working on the bottom boards, while Nosy and I, on a thirty-five-foot scaffold, were painting at the top. Jorks and Muster, with a six-foot straight-edge, a level, two art-school angles and a plumb line, were stuck on painter's ladders, fifteen feet below, ruling the plaster into foot squares. On which the ten girls and the two art school boys were knocking in the first lines from the cartoons. Cokey, who had just arrived with the basket, the day's shopping, and six bottles of stout, in the perambulator, was sweeping. Cokey began every afternoon's work, first by cursing us all round for making such a dirt, and then by sweeping and dusting all the dust off the floor into the air again.

There was also a good deal of noise. Jorks was singing, Muster was whistling, the girls were talking-laughing, talking-coughing, giggling, talking and abusing the boys for dropping paint on their heads; the three plasterers and the carpenters were hammering, talking, whistling and singing; Nosy was sneezing and I was trying to make Cokey understand that all the dust she was raising would stick to my paint. That is to say, I was shouting as loud as I could. And I will admit that I wanted to shout, for standing on the top of a scaffold in front of a good new wall always goes to my head. It is a sensation something between that of an angel let out of his cage into a new sky and a drunkard turned loose in a royal cellar.

And after all, what nobler elevation could you find in this world than the scaffold of a wall painter – in this world? No admiral on the bridge of a new battleship designed by the old navy could feel more pleased with himself than Gulley, on two planks, forty feet above dirt level, with his palette table beside him, his brush in his hand, and the draught blowing up his trousers; when he cleared for action.

41

It was just then that I saw, through the clouds of Cokey's dust and the plasterer's smoke, and the kettle's steam, the Professor picking his way among ropes and poles and beds and buckets, followed by Sir William Beeder and half a dozen other people in whom I could perceive, even from the roof, marks of the highest distinction. Such as clothes from Bond Street, and intelligent expressions from the best finishing schools.

In fact, as soon as I set eyes on them I knew who they must be. The Lords. My Influence. Which had been growing very fast since Hickson's death got my name in the papers. The Professor, in fact, had been writing to me or calling on me most every day since the sale, to discover more early Jimsons, or to get details about my life. For the Life and Works of Gulley Jimson was on the way. A publisher had been found public spirited enough to immortalize my genius, on a guarantee of all expenses from Hickson's executors, who still had several Jimsons to dispose of; and from Sir William, who was, of course, a rising man among collectors, and really deserved to have his name handed up, or down, to posterity.

That deputation, in fact, so expensive and important, gave me such pleasure that I nearly fell off my legs. Yes, I thought, this is indeed a triumph – it reminds me of history, of old Punch's visits to the artist's studio. I might be dead already. Why haven't I a velvet jacket and a beard?

And I began to think better of myself. For my opinion of myself had been rising for the last week. This was due partly to regular meals, no doubt, and the best of everything, but also, I admit, to the Professor. It is very encouraging to be written up, even by a writer. And the Professor was in good form. He'd spent his fifty guineas rake-off on a complete new outfit down to socks, shirts and pyjamas. He was a new cricket and a cricket full of chirp. He sang to me so sweetly about myself that I began to soften towards my own pretensions.

So, seeing my dear Professor and the Lords come to the rescue, I was not so much surprised as delighted. A rapid glow, resembling a measles rash, broke out all over my body. And I said to myself: This is not only fame; it is self-satisfaction. I shall now be able to leave off my winter vest, at least for the summer.

'Who are they?' said Nosy, glaring down with doglike suspicion, in his nose. 'Fans,' I said carelessly. 'Never mind them. Attend to your job. And just look what you've been doing.'

For he had been painting the whale's nose in the wrong place. 'Look at what you're doing, Nosy. Look at the sketch, you great looby.' 'B-but a whale d-doesn't have a face on the b-back of its head.' 'Yes it does. My whale does. It must.' 'B-but I c-can't just s-stick it on.' 'Oh, my God, that's just what you've got to do. Stick it on like a mask on the side of a gasometer. If you don't, that whale will be a corpse, it won't have reality. It won't live, it will just be a bloody illustration out of a whale book.'*

Nosy was a bad apprentice, because he was in such a state of enthusiasm that he couldn't see straight or hold a brush steady. 'Come, Nosy,' I said. 'You've got to take a pull at yourself. Keep cool. You can't paint in a frenzy – you have to do some hard brainwork – you've got to concentrate in about fourteen places at once. You've got to think with your eyes, fingers, ears, nose, stomach, all available limbs, any brain that may have been left over from school, and the end of your tongue. Many good painters do their best work with their tongues. Oh my God, look at you!' for he was putting in a high light on the whale's nose. 'My God, do you want that great pecker to come right off the wall?'

'I c-can p-paint it out.'

'No, you can't pup-paint it out – not on a wall, or the paint will lose all its wall quality – and the oil will float instead of going in, and the whole damn thing will shine like poor old Sara's nose over a fish kettle. You'll have to bring the tone up to it – it's a good thing you didn't put it in lighter. My God, don't you see the effect of that great black jib up there?' For I may say this beak was giving me a sensation of considerable pleasure. It was my pride and joy.

And I forgot about the Jimson fans until I turned round, some time later, to spit, and there they were, right in the line of fire. Entangled, and now quite brought to amid the debris, they raised their noses into the air with expressions so intelligent and smiles so full of delighted appreciation that anyone but Nosy could have seen that they didn't know quite what was happening or where they were. And all the boys and girls looked at them with contempt and disgust, because for the moment they were as good as artists. Even the plasterers, who are a domesticated and civilized race of man, looked at the visitors with contempt and disgust. Because the influence

---

* A description of this composition will be found in the Appendix to the 'Life and Works of Gulley Jimson,' published in 1940, soon after Jimson's lamented death, with illustrations from the Hickson collection. But as Mr Alabaster points out in his scholarly introduction, it is on works in his earlier manner, such as the first Lady in her Bath, that this artist must depend for any permanent niche in the history of art.

of a piece of wall art forty-five by twenty-five is stronger than X-rays. It has profound and often permanent effects upon the character up to a distance of twenty-five yards. One of my early walls, only twelve by fifteen, turned a foxhunter into an etcher. Bang. Afterwards he cut his throat. He hadn't the constitution for etching. Too risky. Couldn't throw his heart over the bullfinches.

'Oh, my G-god,' said Nosy, 'look at the b-bloody p-people, just when we were g-getting s-s-s-started.'

'Chuck a pot of paint on 'em, Nosy,' and Jorky, just below, shouted out to Muster who was only ten feet away, 'Hi, look behind at what the dog's brought in.'

Muster, who is a bit of a prig, said, 'The Philistines be upon us, gentlemen.' And the girls all laughed so scornfully that icicles formed upon Cokey's tea-kettle.

Only Cokey, who was in her county suit and, being a young mother, was impervious to all influences of any kind, behaved herself like a lady. She went up to the gang of dukes and asked them if they knew where they were going. 'This is a private studio,' she said. 'Who asked you to come barging in?'

Alabaster then presented himself, introduced the rest, and Cokey came along to the ladders and bawled up to me, 'Mister Jimson, come down and have your tea and talk to this lot. They say they're real people.'

'Tell 'em to wait, Cokey,' I said. For I was knocking in the old man's forehead, and it was going along very well, a shining pink dome against the brown cave of the rocks. The outside of the cave against the whale's back took up the pink, but in a jagged line which I had brought up against the sky; to cut the horizon. And I saw that the sky itself would have to be as smooth as cream. Not flat but deepening in tone very quickly towards the top edge. Like the sea in a bad Japanese print.

'Tell 'em to go away,' shouted Jorky. Muster and the girls, who were so covered with plaster and paint drippings that they looked like little Easter cakes, sprinkled with hundreds and thousands. Happy as angels in the thought that it would take them a week to get the dirt out of their hair and their finger-nails; that they were suffering in the noble cause of wall painting. 'Tell them to go away,' they shrilled. 'Who are they anyhow? Some dirt off the streets.' But the party, being real ladies and gentlemen, looked still more delighted and intelligent. One very pretty lady in the front row even began to point out the beauties of the scene to her gentleman friend, or spouse, or duke, aiming her slender finger at the nearest carpenter's back and exclaiming in a voice of ecstasy, 'Don't you love that bit – how marvellous where it curves into the blue – what atmosphere.'

And I forgot them again. Until a few minutes later, there was a crisis among the girls. About the tenth that hour. Madgie, the mouse on the extreme left, began to cry out loudly. 'Oh, Mr Jimson, oh, sir, oh please, I can't bear it.'

Jorky, Muster and the other girls at once broke into cries of derision and wrath respectively. Girls are very savage against girls who fall down on a job. 'Hold on,' I shouted. 'Hold up, Madgie, don't do anything rash. Poppa's coming,' and I slid down the ladders at top speed. Just in time to prevent the young biped from bursting into tears. 'Oh, Mr Jimson, sir. I *can't* see how it goes. It's got all wrong, and it won't join up, and I'm sure somebody's made a terrible mistake.' 'Somebody's made a terrible mistake, have they? Well, my dear, that's not what nobody wouldn't expect. Let's have a look at your sketch. I see, square No. 6, portrait of a fish with feet; and where's No. 6 on the wall, I don't see No. 6; I see No. 9.'

'Oh, Mr Jimson, oh what an ass I am, I'd got it upside down!' And all the boys and girls burst into cries of rage or disgust. 'Go home, Madgie.'

'Take it away, Madgie, you mucker.'

'Why did she come, that girl?'

'Throw her out, the thing.'

But the girl herself did not mind in the least. Owing to the influence of the wall, she was invulnerable. Like a young mother, even like Cokey. She hummed to herself while she rubbed out her pencil lines and started again, right side up. 'Oh thank you, Mr Jimson.'

'Don't mention it, Madgie. It might happen to anybody almost – history relates that Michael Angelo often got his squares wrong – numbers were invented by Arabs who hate art,' and it was at this moment that the Professor touched my sleeve and hastily called my attention to the Princess, the Duke, etc. And they were so rich, so nice, and already so dusty that I could not be unkind to them. '*How* do you do?' I said. 'How *do* you do, Duke?' 'How do *you* do, Princess?' 'How do you *do*, Mr Smith?'

'Mr Alvin Smith, the multimillionaire,' the Professor murmured in my ear. And I shook hands again with Mr Smith, twice. And gave him the famous Gulley Jimson smile. A special unlimited edition.

'We have been admiring your marvellous picture,' said the Princess. 'It's quite the biggest I've ever seen.'

'Yes,' I said. 'Though some of it is bigger than others.'

'And what does it represent?' said the Duke. 'Though perhaps I shouldn't ask such a question.'

It was indeed the sort of question a fan should never ask. But fortunately for his grace, I was in a condescending and gracious mood.

'Don't apologize,' I said, 'I don't usually expect to be asked questions like that, of course, but I don't mind telling you, as a friend, anything that might be satisfactory.'

'Then we should so much like to know what it means,' said the duchess.

'It means, Duchess,' said I, with my best social manner, which I believe is not unworthy of a President of the Salon or the memory of Charles Peace in the dock, 'you will be sorry to hear, getting up at seven o'clock every morning. I have to use all the light available. But joking apart, a surface like that is something and it covers an area, for instance, of 1,000 square feet, and will involve the use of sixteen gallons of paint, three dozen brushes, and over twenty pounds' worth of scaffolding, ladders; that means a lot of money.'

'We understood,' said the Professor, 'that the subject was to be the Creation.'

'Very likely,' I said. 'That is a good idea, or whatever you call it. Hi, Jorks' – for I saw that the boy was getting above himself. 'Don't drop that paint on the girls – accidents can't be helped, but that viridian is expensive, we can't afford to throw it about —'

'And what's the price,' said Mr Smith, 'in dollars? Finished, delivered and ready for erection.'

'I'm sorry to disappoint you, Mr Smith,' I said, in that kindly manner which is peculiarly the secret of the great. 'But I cannot accept your kind and generous offer. As a patriot yourself you will, I'm sure, understand those feelings of patriotism which have forced me to decide that a British masterpiece, of this importance, ought not to leave the country. And I intend, in fact, to offer it to the nation. Of course, for a suitable price. But I don't anticipate any difficulty about that,' I said, smiling confidentially at the princess, who cried, 'Dear Mr Jimson, I do so agree with you.'

'Of course, I must make some conditions,' I said. 'A work this size is not suitable to a public gallery. It really needs a cathedral. You will say, no doubt, that none of the existing cathedrals would be able to give the necessary lighting. And, in fact,' I said, removing, with an open-hearted gesture, several more inhibitions, including my electric chest protector, cricket-proof waistcoat, etc., 'my idea was really a special building somewhere near Trafalgar Square. I don't know what your own plans are,' I said, and the whole party murmured that noise which means, according to circumstances, either homage to Art or how long it seems till dinner.

'I don't wish to seem to dictate,' I said, 'but such a building, thoroughly modern in style, would really be cheaper in the long run. Lighted by daylight bulbs. Open day and night. Preferably with attendants in the royal livery. I particularly want the red-coats to bring up the greens. Also, if I may intrude on what is, after all, your business, I suggest free drinks should be provided while the pubs are closed. Limited, of course. Let us say, to a pint for each visitor.'

'Free drinks?' said Sir William. 'You mean at the national expense.' I was relieved to see that none of the party felt the least surprise at my suggestion. I warmed to them. They were undoubtedly, taken all round, the most cultivated, that is to say, the richest people I had ever met.

And abandoning not only my waistcoat but my plot-proof dicky and friend-defying shirt, I admitted candidly that my idea was to get people interested in the supreme works of the native genius. 'For,' I pointed out, 'you could not expect them to come, in large numbers, without some *quid pro quo*. And if they didn't come, my work would be wasted.'

'I think that is a very good idea,' said the princess, who was a darling in first-class practice, 'a lovely idea, to educate the masses.'

'That hadn't occurred to me,' I said, and I was now quite recklessly exposed. 'My intention was more to give brewery shares a fillip, for I've noticed that any rise in brewery shares means a great increase in art appreciation – and art-patrons – buyers, in fact.'

Nosy had now come down the ladders and was moving about on the outskirts of the group. He had a suspicious look about the eyes and nose, and I knew he was still suffering from persecution mania. But I was not even annoyed. I smiled like Jove upon the ministering ganymedes, and said laughing, 'You mightn't see the connection at first sight, but there it is. A fact of experience. When shares go up, pictures sell. There is a rush for spiritual nourishment. But why I want to see steady national support for the market is because it takes time to make a patron. The first generation of profiteers are often, to put it frankly, merely human, what in England we call plain men. That is to say, chaps of whom you can't say anything except that they are good for nothing else, but are very pleased with themselves on that account. It's only in the next generation that you get the real collectors – the men of intelligence, sincerity, industry, perseverance, guts and scholarship – men who are really educated, that is, who know that they don't know anything that matters about anything that matters, and have learned where to find the experts who do.' And, out of that innocent trustfulness so often observed among the truly great, throwing away the last of my garments (and thus perhaps revealing some minor details discreet historians would prefer hidden) I laughed again and said to the Duke, 'But that, of course, hah-ha, is a special art.'

'And what experts do you recommend?'

'Dealers,' I said. 'Most decidedly. If you want a good spec, ask the dealers. It stands to reason, if you want the best eggs, you don't ask advice from the hens. Hens are prejudiced. You go to a reputable shop. It's the same with pictures. But of course you must choose a living dealer. Some, unfortunately, are mortal. And it's not always easy to tell that they have passed over merely by their expressions. For really successful collecting you want, as the poets say, a nose.'

The Professor had withdrawn a little and was making a note of my conversation. A pleased smile cricketed across his lower features. What an art biogrubber loves is a subject that talks. Because then he can fill up the gaps between the reproductions and the dates; and sell the thing as a Work at a guinea, instead of a catalogue at sixpence. And if the filling is polite conversation, which is rude nonsense, so much the better, because the readers will feel that it's given them their money's worth, and they won't have to bother with the reproductions.

'That's why,' I said, 'art reached such a high state of cultivation among the ancient Hittites, and in modern New York, so I've heard, appreciation is growing so rapidly that —'

'Ha-ha,' said the duke, who had the nose of a true aristocrat, a Solomon; and then instantly, with the practical art of a courtier, or first-class head waiter, became grave. 'But excuse me, Mr Jimson, we came upon a mission.'

'Yes,' said the Professor, quickly putting up his diary between his heart and his pocket-book, and giving it a little pat of affection. 'These ladies and gentlemen are among your chief admirers, Mr Jimson —'

I saw that he was coming to business, and I hastened to give them a lead, before they committed themselves, unwittingly, to something I could not approve. 'There are really,' I said, 'only two alternatives, either to buy the council out, and perhaps one or two adjoining sites, so as to give this building a more worthy approach. Or to transport the east wall, as it stands, to some central position in the city, and place it in a new building. I daresay you would prefer the second,' I said, 'but I myself am quite indifferent. Trafalgar Square, Millbank, have their attractions, but provided that proper surroundings and attendance could be secured, I should be quite happy to see the picture stay here, at least for my life-time.'

Nosy was shaking his head at me, and now exclaimed, 'Bubbubbub —'

'That is fairly obvious,' I said, frowning to show him that I had control of the situation.

'I hope, indeed, that it will stay here for your life-time,' said the duke. 'And meanwhile we have a request, which I hope will please you.'

'It must be a full length, duke,' said the princess.

'A full length, for three hundred guineas, or, if exhibited in the Royal Academy, four hundred guineas. But we do not insist on the Academy.'

'I think you will realize, Mr Jimson,' said the Professor, smiling his new beige smile, 'that this is a great compliment to your position in the art world. Of course, this deputation would be glad if you could see your way to send the portrait to the Academy, but they don't insist.'

'A portrait?' I said.

'Didn't you get my letter?' said the Professor.

'Very likely,' I said. 'I've had three or four in the last month.'

'These gentlemen and ladies,' said the Professor, 'who are members of the London Association of Loamshire Bumpkins (or something like that), are delegated to make a presentation to their founder, General Rollo Rumchin (or thereabouts) of his portrait, in oils. And when they approached me for advice —'

'It would be a great honour, Mr Jimson,' said the duke, turning to me.

'I know you won't refuse me, as a Loamshire man yourself,' said the princess, darling me.

'So kind,' said the duchess, with an endearing smile.

And I simply didn't know what to say. The tears were standing to my eyes; either of gratitude or some other feeling. Probably I should have made them a little speech expressing my sense of obligation, and so on, if Cokey hadn't been discovered boiling over in the corner by the stove.

Cokey boils over all at once, like a porridge pot. It may be due to the straight sides. 'I don't know about you,' she sizzled, 'but I can't wait any longer – I've got to open in ten minutes – anyone who wants tea can make it fresh. This is poison.' And off she went.

Cokey's indignation caused a panic to the highest ladder. For Cokey, at the afternoon opening, was Queen of the Feathers and it didn't matter how old you were if she didn't choose to serve. You were under age; and it was outside.

Muster, Toogood and the girls fell off the scaffold so quickly that I had to shout, 'All brushes for washing, all pots to be handed in – look sharp, Jorky, on the door.' And while I was getting control of the work, I didn't notice what happened to the deputation. I had a notion afterwards that I saw the duke being swept into the vestry with several old brooms and a few odd lengths of rope, but if so, he is there still. His bones are whitening among the plaster buckets. Another victim of art. But the path to the National Gallery is paved with Academy dukes.

42

By good luck, it was an interesting sunset. The sky was extremely hollow; as hollow as a hat. And nicely graded from a dirty gold, westwards, like well-fried bacon; through leek-green and bottle-green to a real Life Guards blue, on the east. No clouds. And the air extremely clear. It was so clear that you couldn't have painted it, you could only stretch your mind in it. And this, of course, is a great pleasure, when one has been cramped by conversation and easy politeness. It was giving me the greatest benefit, and would certainly have removed any slight stiffness remaining after my recent accident, which would have seemed almost as comic as it was, if it had not been for Nosy, who rushed up to me in the street and told me that the deputation had been got at.

'What do you mean?' I said sadly. 'Got at. What a strange expression.'

'They were s-seen,' said Nosy, hissing in my ear like a snake, like the old serpent. 'Madgie saw them out of the window talking to the man in a blue waistcoat.'

'Asking their way,' I said. 'And I'm not surprised in this part of town.'

'But you wrote to Mr Alabaster asking him to do something about the council, and he never said anything.'

'He hadn't a chance to say anything,' I said. But, of course, Nosy's argument was a strong one.

'They've got at him,' said Nosy, 'behind your back.'

Now this was the very voice of the original serpent. It is only too easy to believe that something is going on behind one's back; because, of course, it always is. But I was too tired to murder Nosy on the spot. I said to him only in a mild voice, 'Well, Nosy, you know very well the Professor doesn't like the Creation. Nobody does. Nobody, that is, who is over twenty-five and has any money. You can't expect them to like a picture like that. It's dangerous. It's an act of aggression. It's really equivalent to going into a man's garden and putting dynamite under his wife. Or trying to kidnap his children. Many a man has lost his children like that – on account of some picture which has carried them away. No,' I said, 'if there is a plot, it's a fair and reasonable plot. And I won't have you abusing my friends, Nosy, even if they are enemies. When you are as old as I am,' I said severely, 'you'll take my tip, "BE FRIENDS WITH YOUR FRIENDS." It may not be prudent, and it is often difficult. But it is better for the liver, lights, and kidneys. After all, friendship has one great advantage; if you don't like your friends, you can always avoid them, and they won't mind. Not if there is really good feeling on both sides.'

Just then we came to the Feathers, and seeing Alfred's old white cat coming out at the door, I caught her and carried her in. I wanted some kindness. And no one is more kind than a cat. Her own kind. But she jumped out of my arms on to Madgie's neck, and then before Madgie could even scream, melted into the convivial atmosphere, always very thick at the Feathers.

And I recalled myself to the duties of enjoyment. 'Now girls,' I said, 'remember the law. No one in here under eighteen. Don't forget you're eighteen.'

And they sang back like little canaries, 'You needn't tell us, Mr Jimson. We've been here before.' 'And no ports,' I said. 'I don't believe in ports for young girls. Beer was good enough for Queen Elizabeth, and it's good enough for little pieces that ought to be in bed with a feeding bottle.' 'Oh, Mr Jimson, you do go on so.' 'Sixteen half cans, Alfred, and minerals to choice. How goes it, Walter?' For there was Postie Ollier and all his crowd. 'Seventeen half cans, Alfred. Take it out of that,' and I gave him a pound. 'Had a winner, Mr Jimson?' 'That sort of thing, Alfred.' For I didn't want a lot of explanation. I wanted a rest.

The cat appeared on the counter. Came up from somewhere without a sound, like a demon on the magic-lantern. And walked across. She didn't look anywhere but she never touched a puddle. Keeping herself to herself. Tiger, tiger, burning bright.

'Here's luck, Mr Jimson,' 'Mud in your eye, Bert. Cheeroh, Walter.'

I thought we were going to have a good evening. I wasn't sure, but I was feeling I hoped so. When all at once a little old man with a crooked leg and long red nose like a badly scraped carrot came up to me and began to shout and wave his fists. He had a friend with him, a fat short man in a black coat, with black hair over his eyes, and a moustache like a seal, who tried to push him away.

'How do you do?' I said. 'Pleased to meet you.' And I tried to shake hands with them both. 'Telling me all those lies,' bawled the old man. 'Which ones?' I said. 'About you were hiring my chapel for religious purposes.'

I looked again and I saw the old man was Pepper Pot, but his nose had changed colour in the electric light, like a Michaelmas daisy. And I felt depressed. I didn't want to be tactful any more. I wanted a rest. 'Yes,' I said, 'religion. Religious art.' 'What, that wicked muck. Religious?' 'I hope so. But, of course, I can't be sure.'

Bert was tickling the old cat under the ear. Sometimes she liked being tickled. But tonight, I was glad to see she paid no attention. She just went on moving through the forests of Bert, Ollier and me.

Pepper was making a speech, very loud. 'He can't be sure,' he said. 'Well, we can. We've got eyes. We *know* it's muck.'

'No,' I said, 'I can't really be sure. Not just now. I'm tired.'

'And let me tell you,' bawled Pepper, getting triumphant when he saw he was winning. 'I've put in an information against you, at the magistrate's. For blasphemy and obskeenity. So you needn't waste any more paint on the dirty muck.'

'No; I needn't,' I said, sighing so deeply that I blew half my beer away with the froth. For I couldn't help feeling that plots were going on. And I didn't want to feel them just then. 'But I think I'll get it down all the same,' I said. 'Somehow I like to get it down – get it out of my system.' 'The police'll do that for you,' Pepper screamed, warming up a bit. 'And get you out, too.'

At this Nosy rushed up to Pepper and tried to shout something. But all that came out was 'S-s-s—' He changed the shape of his face and tried something else, like 'M-m-m—' Then he changed his face again, burst into tears, and hit Pepper on the pot.

'Outside,' said Cokey, and before anyone could wink an eye, she had taken Nosy by the collar and thrown him into the road. Then she went behind the counter again and said to me, 'And you be careful, you two, or you'll go the same way.'

And there was dead silence for about a minute. Tribute of respect to Cokey.

'Seems a pity, when you have a tenant, Mr Herne,' said Ollier. 'I don't care,' shouted Pepper Pot. 'I'm not a bum. I put religion before rent. I stop at godless wasters that call themselves artists.' 'Modern artists,' said the seal in a quiet voice, as if he were afraid to find himself so brave. 'Modern artists,' screamed Pepper Pot, foaming like a Bass, 'fakers that can't even draw right and twist up God's works so you wouldn't know them. Blasphemy. Spitting in the face of the Lord.' 'I see what you mean,' I said. 'Ya,' said Pepper Pot, turning puce all over and shaking his can at me. He was getting hotter all the time with his own fire. 'Ya. You can talk. But you've done for yourself. They'll take your dirty picture away and burn it.'

Cokey came through the slab again and took him by the collar. 'Here, what have I done?' he shouted. 'I warned you,' said Cokey. 'I didn't hit anybody,' said Pepper Pot. 'You can't shout in this bar,' said Cokey, throwing him into the street. And then she went back again and said to me, 'But you be careful, Mr Jimson.' 'I'll be careful, miss.' For if Cokey had been princess in the Eagle, she was Queen of the Feathers. Because of the basket. But one girl's error is another's glory. Depends where she wears it, I suppose.

'Mr Herne is a true Christian,' said the seal, looking round as if he would fight us all, if he had to. But he hoped that he wouldn't. 'That's it,' I said, 'a good chap, loyal to his principles.'

The old cat came back again and sat down by my can. I suppose she had remembered that I hadn't tried to interfere with her. But she didn't look at me. Stretched out one arm towards the whisky bottles, like a salute. And gave her wrist a lick. Cherishing herself. A cat is a nice idea. Classical. Big lines and good detail. And she knows it, too. All over.

The seal was still telling the crowd how Mr Herne as a young Christian had broken the windows of the Education Officer. 'Yes,' I said, 'I honour such men. People with real principles. Ready to lay down their rent for their religion. Warriors of the old faith or even of the one before.'

'Warriors all right, all right,' said Bert. 'Too many about if you ask me.'

'Any news since last time,' said one of the boys. 'Not much,' said Alfred. 'Things don't look too good in Poland.' 'They didn't look too good last time.' 'You'll have something,' I said to the seal. He was a friend of Pepper Pot, and I felt a sort of kindness for Pepper Pot. Because of his nose and his bad leg and his bad temper and his age. He was probably older than I was, poor devil. 'Nineteen half cans, Alfred. Gents and ladies, give it a name. This is an anniversary with me.' 'Anniversary of what, Mr Jimson?' 'Same day last year.' 'You get a lot of anniversaries that way,' said Bert. 'It's practically all anniversaries at my age,' I said, and while Alfred and Coker were making the handles jump, I felt such a sigh come up that I thought I had had too much beer. But I remembered Pepper Pot in time and recognized it as grief for mortal things. Yes, I thought, I'll never finish that wall – I may just manage the whale. But no. Probably not. The roof will fall in and break my skull. Or probably not. It will be something I didn't expect. But it's certain about the whale.

For my experience is that life is full of big certainties and small surprises. You can usually tell that the knock is coming; but the details are unexpected. You get it on the right ear instead of the jaw. Look at the Rankens. Everyone knew they couldn't last much longer after the last disaster. And they were quite right. But when the crash came, it was quite clever. It wasn't Jenny that left Robert, but Robert that left Jenny. He went back to his wife who'd come into some money, just enough to make some more working models and take out some more patents. For a new and improved regulator. And it was Jenny, instead of Robert, who put her head in a gas oven. I suppose, after all, she hadn't his resources. He had his new governor to think about. He'd always had his governors and regulators to think about. But she'd only had Robert, and when he went off she had nothing and no idea of anything. We can't all be inventors. And a good thing, too.

'To you, Mr Jimson.' 'To you, Bert, with flowers.'

'I don't like it,' said one of the boys. 'Looks to me as if Poland was having trouble.'

'Chap in my paper, he's an expert, says that war is full of surprises.' 'It is,' I said, 'and also peace.' 'This bloody war,' said Bert. 'Which one?' I said. 'Haven't you heard about the war, Mr Jimson?' said Muster politely. 'Yes, of course,' I said. 'But I thought it had stopped a little bit after the Peace Conference.' 'It stopped for a time,' said Bert, 'but now they've got it started again all right, all right, and it's going something beautiful.' 'Who's the enemy, Kaiser Bill?' 'No, Kaiser Adolf.' 'It's Germany again, is it?' 'What they call the Nazis, Mr Jimson.'

The old cat put up its nose to my can, and then quickly pulled it back and shook its whiskers. 'Look at her,' said Bert laughing. 'Particular, ain't she? Hi, puss. Have one on the house.' The cat turned its head away with a dignity you can't get in humans. They try too hard. And they're so sympathetic. They feel what other people are trying to do to them even when they aren't doing anything.

'Puss, pussy,' said Bert. He dipped his finger in the beer and offered it to her. 'Pussy.' And he laughed because she was putting him down, before the crowd. Bert is sensitive about his public position. In publics. A regular bachelor.

'She can't hear you,' said Alfred. 'She has been stone deaf ever since she had the distemper.'

'It's the Nazis, is it?' I said. 'Yes, I know all about them. They're against modern art.' 'And lipstick,' said Madgie. 'And examinations,' said Muster. 'They don't believe in examinations.' 'Hear, hear,' said Jorky, 'I never could pass examinations myself.' 'What do they have instead?' asked a girl in spectacles, with some of my green paint on her nose. Right off the eternal sea. 'Character,' said Muster. 'What's character?' 'What the boss thinks of you,' said Bert. 'Hitler is a boss, and no mistake.' 'They say it's his blue eyes got the girls.' 'Go on,' said Bert, 'They didn't start the war because of Hitler's blue eyes.' 'Well, he's got something, too – he gives 'em ideas.'

'Puss, puss,' said Bert, but the cat stretched itself and then jumped off the counter. Disappeared without a sound. What a shoulder, what loins. What a movement. The flying tiger.

'That cat has a lot of character,' said Alfred.

'Yes, you can see it's her own,' I said. Bert gave Pussy up and knocked his can on the counter, standing no more nonsense. 'What I say is: why did they start it? They know they can't win. Not against the French army and our navy.'

'Because of modern art,' I said, 'Hitler never could put up with modern art. It's against his convictions. His game was water-colour in the old coloured-water style. Topographical.' 'I believe you, old son,' said Bert, meaning that he didn't. 'All wars are due to modern art.' 'Well,' said Ollier, 'I have heard that the Nazis are against modern art. But I don't know about the Kaiser.' 'The Kaiser couldn't stand modern art.' 'Well then, Mr Jimson, what about Kruger,' 'Kruger was all against modern art. He stood by the Bible, which is the oldest kind of art. And what he'd been brought up to.' 'Well, what about the Spanish Armada?' 'The Armada was all against modern art and the new prayer book.' 'According to that,' said Bert, 'it's got a lot to answer for.' 'Of course it has,' I said, feeling as flat as the floor which was also worn into knobs and holes. 'That's the trouble. It's a disturbing influence. Every time a new lot of kids get born, they start some new art. Just to have something of their own. If it isn't a new dance band it's a new religion. And the old lot can't stand it. You couldn't expect it at their age. So they try to stop it, and then there's another bloody war.' 'What do you go in for it then for?' 'I can't help it, gentlemen, it's like the drink. I shouldn't have let it get hold of me. But I was born very young, and I grew up with little experience of the world. Yes, gentlemen, until I was twenty-five I didn't really know the dangers of my position, that is to say, I was practically on my own, you might say,' and I drank my beer out of an empty can, Right under Cokey's nose. To use a figure of speech. For since I had paid Cokey her money, she had had a sort of kindness for me, and sometimes gave me a pint on the house.

But she didn't even see that I was dry. She was scratching her left cheek with her left little finger-nail, the county one, and frowning at the air. Her mind was in the snug, trying to make sure the basket was still asleep; or examining his features to see if he was likely to be a Prime Minister. Works of imagination. Cokey had grown a bit absentminded these days. She used to be worried to fiddlestrings because her face was out of drawing, and now she was worried to fiddlestrings in case the kid was taking after her. And I thought, she's got something to live for, Cokey, and it will kill her by the painful method patented for lucky mothers. She'll be a hag in five years, and she'll never die till she's dead. She's forgotten herself already, poor bitch, and what a load off her mind.

I lifted my can upside down and licked the edge. Cokey took it from me and filled it. But without looking. All in a dream. And every wrinkle in her forehead said, Oh, these men.

'Thank you, miss,' I said. 'Bless your heart, etc.'

'You be careful with your etcs.,' said Cokey. 'This is a respectable house.' But she didn't put any kick into it. She was listening towards the snug door. And there were at least two more listening wrinkles in her forehead, vertical ones. The ones that make you look old. But no good warning her. What would she care.

'The Lady Mayoress of somewhere says she wouldn't give a cup of tea to a wounded soldier,' said Bert.

'Why not?'

'She's against war.'

'I didn't make the war,' said a soldier, young chap. 'Blimey, you can have the war. And let me get back to my job.'

'What's your job, old man?' 'Never you mind,' said the soldier. 'Here, you want to know a lot, don't you? Perhaps you'd like to see my birthmark.' 'I was only asking.'

The soldier went out and tried to bang the door. But it was a swing door. You can't bang a pub door. The pubs know a lot, almost as much as the churches. They've got a tradition.

'That's young Simpson in our office,' said Walter. 'He's just married and feels a bit sore about the war coming on just now.'

'On purpose, you might say.'

'What's he so private about his job for?'

'I don't know. He's like that, Simpson.'

The cat mewed at the door. Then it suddenly appeared on the counter, winding its way among the pots like a white serpent. Three of the girls stroked it in turn, but it didn't even look. It's coming to me, I thought. And it stopped and looked at me. Made a point. With one paw in the air. Then it looked through me for about thirty seconds or half an hour. I looked at the cat and the cat looked through me. I wasn't even in the way.

'Puss, puss,' Bert said, tickling her suddenly. A surprise attack. She jumped on Alfred's shoulder, went down half his back and sailed away to the whisky shelf. The individual cat. The private beauty.

'Getting a bit restless at sunset,' Alfred said.

'Spring time,' said Bert.

'No use to Pussy,' said Alfred. 'He's an It. Just nature it must be. She likes being round in the dark.'

'It,' said Bert. 'If it's an It. What do you call it she for?'

'Well, I'm fond of poor old Snow.'

'She doesn't seem to think much of you, Alfred.'

'I can't say that she does. She's a character, I can tell you. You can't tell what's going on inside her.' 'Probably cat,' I said, 'or that's what I should think.'

The seal had been looking at me for a long time out of the sides of his eyes. Now he made a big effort as if he were going to jump through the ceiling, and said in a small voice, 'A lot of people think modern art is at the bottom of a lot of this trouble we're always having.' 'They're quite right,' I said. 'It is. Right at the bottom.'

And I was on the point of bursting into tears when Mr Moseley came in and knocked on the counter with a half-crown. His face was as red as red ink; and he had a complete new colour scheme, all in browns. Brown suit, the colour of old ale. Golden brown tie like lager. Brown boots shining like china beer handles. Guinness socks. And a new brown bowler, the colour of bitter beer, over his left eye.

It cheered me up. I like a man who takes all that trouble for the public good. 'Good evening, Mr Moseley,' I said. But he didn't see me or hear me, any more than the cat.

'Twenty half can, Alfred, and a double whisky for Mr Moseley, Miss Coker, if you please.'

But I was feeling absentminded. What is it, I thought. Moseley's boots or Pepper Pot. And all at once I saw Hitler's blue eyes fixed on me. So that's it, I thought. Yes, that's what the whale's wanted all the time. Pale sky-blue in slate, to pick up the sky. Pretty large, too. But what a lot of trouble.

'Here's looking to you, Mr Jimson.' 'Here's luck.' 'Here's mud.' 'Here's hoping.'

Shaped like tipcats, I thought. Wide open. But it will mean a lot of work. And if the roof is going to fall on my napper —

'Cheerio,' said Bert, 'chin, chin.' 'Your very good health, sir.' 'Thank you gentlemen, and ladies.' 'But what I want to know is,' said Bert, 'what's the cause of wars, I mean the cause of all these wars.' 'Fighting,' said Mr Moseley. 'You've said it, Mr Moseley,' said Alfred. 'But what's the cause of fighting,' said Bert. 'Fighting,' said Mr Moseley. 'You've said it, Mr Moseley,' said Alfred.

'But what I want to know,' said the girl with eternity on her nose, 'how are we going to stop people fighting.' 'You fight 'em,' said Mr Moseley. 'You've said it, Mr Moseley,' said Alfred.

'Twenty-one half cans,' I said, 'and another double for Mr Moseley, miss.'

But the beer had no more taste than liquid. Those eyes wouldn't let me alone. Yes, I said, I can see you. Curves as sharp as blades. And the right eye extended a bit to the left, so that the point would come up very nearly to the right side of the whale's face, which is against the white cloud. Or through it, to break the line there. Gives you a kind of cut in the side of the hat. But no, a bit too clever. That whale has got to be sincere – it's got to be an honest young cow.

I felt something brush my trouser leg and then the cat was sitting right in front of me, like a Landseer lion; but with one paw curled up. She half closed her eyes, and sat like marble. And I looked at her, deaf, castrated cat. What did she care? She never knew what she was missing. The only individual cat in the world. Universal cat.

I knocked my can on the wood; respectfully.

'No, I won't serve you any more,' said Coker. 'You've had enough.' 'But this is my birthday.' 'Yesterday was your birthday, too, and you had too much. Every day seems to be your birthday.' 'Yes, every day's my birthday. Often twice a day. Due to art.' 'Art has a lot to answer for, all right, all right,' said Bert. 'Yes, and it doesn't answer. It only keeps on.' 'Keeps on?' 'Keeps on what?' 'Keeping on.'

I drank up Green-nose's beer while she was wiping her spectacles. And sighed most of it back again. I was very low. That damned creation was pestering me. To get those eyes, those marble mountains down. Before they were lost. But I wasn't a kid. I wasn't to be caught with a milky finger. I've had some. I knew what happened when you began changing things on the wall – a lot of nasty new problems, no end of worry and work.

Green-nose took up her own can and found it was empty. Then she put it down again, hollowed her back, and gave her hair a pat. You could see she was pleased. She didn't like beer, I suppose, any more than the girls who were taking minerals. But had more sense of duty. Ambition, learning to be an art teacher. Senior school. Elementary would take lemonade and teach wash-drawing. And she'll tell the little lads and lassies about when she worked with Gulley Jimson, and when they grow up, they'll all say, 'Oh yes, Gulley Jimson, he's one of the old gang. The pre-wars. Stale stuff. Dead as Julius Caesar.'

The news had started again. We were having it every hour. And Bert said, 'Another raid on Warsaw, poor old Warsaw.' 'They say it's a nice town,' said Madgie. 'Got a famous gallery,' said Muster, 'but I suppose that's gone up already.' 'Not the pictures,' said Bert, shocked. 'Why, they'd be old Masters.' Bert is very conservative. 'They'd look after those.' 'Yes,' said the seal, 'they're valuable. They've got beauty. Done by real artists.' The seal spoke quite loud, and looked me in the face. And I saw he hated my guts. It gave me a shock. '*Real* artists,' he said. 'They're not by modern artists.' There was nothing to say to that, so I gave him a friendly nod. To wish him luck. The individual seal. In a world all made of seal. The heart of sealdom.

> What the hammer, what the chain,
> In what furnace was thy brain?
> What the anvil? What dread grasp
> Dare its deadly terror clasp?

Concentrated seal. Winding like a black tiger through its own forest, with teeth of china and gold.

> When the stars threw down their spears
> And watered Heaven with their tears
> Did he smile his work to see?
> Did he who made the lamb make thee?

I drank Bert's beer while he was proving that the old Masters in Warsaw couldn't have come to any harm. Because the Poles were lovers of art; and besides, the director of an art gallery would get it in the neck if he let old valuable masters be bombed.

That beard, I thought, the old man's beard will be a much more important shape if the values come up; the range of tones will be bigger. Yes, I'll have a lot to play with there – I'll make it the biggest beard in history – an eternal beard. And that green shine will pick up the greens of the sea, it will sing very nicely among the pink rocks. And I began to feel hot again. I'd certainly caught something.

The wireless had got on to the police notices, and all at once it read out, Mrs Monday, the victim of a murderous attack on the tenth of last month, died today. Before she died, she became conscious for a short time, and she was able to give the following description of her assailant.

Bert was getting so angry that nobody was attending to the wireless except Cokey, and I saw her looking at me. But I felt so queer, I couldn't pretend not to be.

And all at once Cokey turned off the wireless. I don't suppose she knew anything, It was just on suspicion, or something. Cokey, I thought, going quietly towards the door, is almost a woman. No one knows how she knows what she does know, But it's definitely horse meat.

As I slipped out, something like a fiery comet whizzed past my left ear and I saw old Snow land in the light in front of me; all four feet at once. And then with one spring, in every joyful lovely muscle, ascend into Heaven; or the garden wall.

43

Having retired unobtrusively from social prominence, I went home. That is to say, I climbed the ladders, right up to the light platform, switched on the top light, got out in the swing, and began to paint the whale's eyes. And every now and then I gave Jorky's patent rope a pull and wheeled along a bit further. Till I was swinging about in the air, thirty feet from the ground, like an angel.

And as soon as those eyes took shape and I put in the pupils, they got me. They were so something, I don't know what. There they were, gazing at me like all the grief and glory in the world, about a yard long and a foot high, and they brought the tears to my eyes. Boo-hoo, I cried, putting a little more cobalt on the shadow side; and I didn't know whether I was more upset about Sara or the whale. And the more those eyes took shape, the more I felt sure that I had got something good; straight from the stable. The cut in the outline was just what the mass wanted. Of course, a shape like the right eye, bang among the dark purple, jumped like the moon.

I'm raising up some nasty difficulties, I said, with a great sob, probably for Sara. But who cares. Boo-hoo. There's no doubt I'm damned upset about Sara, worse even than about poor old Hickie. It's quite surprising. I feel as if I'd lost my right leg or even my left leg, which is, on the whole, the best one. Of course, that's just what she always wanted me to feel, the old succubus. Getting after me with all her hooks. So I ought to tell her to go to the devil. And I sharpened up the whale's upper eyelid. But what's the good when I feel like this. Yes, she knew how to dig herself in. She knew how to get on a man's brain – stomach rather, or liver, or whatever this pain is. And stay there. Boo-hoo, there's a tear on my palette. Who would have thought I could cry a tear as big as a halfpenny. At sixty-eight, for a battered old helmet like Sara Monday. Who would have thought that at my age and experience she could take me by the throat like this, and choke me. Boo-hoo. The whale looked at me with such something or other that I couldn't contain myself. The tears ran down my nose, and I said, It's a masterpiece. Perhaps. And as for the old 'un's legs, I shall have to make them as solid as rock, solider – yes, I've got a lot of work to do in the next twenty-four hours.

And I painted like six students at once. But under certain difficulties. For Sara kept interfering with my inside and upsetting my respiration, and the cradle was playing tricks. I hadn't been able to find Jorky's stay ropes, and so the whole machine kept swinging about. Sometimes when I had mixed a colour and was going to put it on the wall, I found myself trying to paint the air. In fact, the cradle kept turning round and turning back again, and then it began to jump up and down. And once it swung slowly in a circle like the big wheel, until I was upside down. Here, I said, there's something wrong – this is against gravity – it's illegal – I must have got a touch of the old trouble: delayed beer, or perhaps Alfred put some alcohol in it.

But I felt my wrist and it was as hot as a breakfast kipper.

'Yes,' said Sara. 'It's a fever. Just like when I felt your pulse at Bournemouth on the first Saturday we were on our honeymoon. You ought to be in bed.' 'Hullo, Sara,' I said. 'What are you doing out there in the middle of nothing? Mind you don't fall off.' 'Don't worry about me,' said Sara. 'I know how to look after myself. It's you you've got to worry about. You're damned ill.' 'You're going downhill with that Byles, Sara. I never heard

you swear before. It's not like you.' 'No,' said Sara. 'It's not. You put that
in my mouth.' 'I beg your pardon, Sall,' I said, 'I forgot you were dead.'
'Yes, I'm dead, and that shows how ill you are. You've got a temperature,
Gulley – you must be delirious to see me like this. Get down like a sensible
man, do, and go to bed.' 'I haven't time, Sall. I've got a lot to do before
tomorrow evening. Be a good girl and let me alone.' 'I should never forgive
myself if I let you catch your death on that silly bit of wood.' 'Go along,
Sall. Go back to your nice warm grave. I should have thought you'd be
glad to be dead.' 'Oh, Gulley, how can you speak so? It was a cruel thing
for you to push me down the stairs and break my back.' 'I didn't mean to
murder you.' 'Come now, Gulley, you can't swear to that.' 'Well, I was a
bit annoyed – with you calling police and trying to get me put away for
the rest of my life. Worse than murder, that would have been.' 'I didn't
mean for the police to come, I'm sure that policeman had no business round
the flat.' 'Come, Sara, you won't swear you didn't want to get rid of me.'
'Oh dear,' said Sara. 'How do I know? I was so worried and torn in half.
Goodness knows I wanted you to have your rightful share, Gulley. But I
wanted to have my little bit of funeral money, too, for Byles and me, just
to bury us and keep us from a cold-hearted grave.' 'Come, Sara, you know
I'd always have buried you. And as for being dead, you're not missing
much at your age. With no money and that brute knocking you about.'
'Don't you call him a brute, Gulley. I wish there were no worse than poor
Byles. His temper may be a bit short, but he's been a true friend to me in
my old age.' 'You were happy with your Byles. You could be happy with
anyone, Sall, anyone in trousers.' 'Oh dear, what's happiness got to do
with it? You are the only one I ever loved, Gulley.' 'Why was that? I've
often wondered. Because you needed me more? I certainly kept you busy,
didn't I, I was a full-time occupation.' 'Oh, dear, the times I've laid awake
wondering what to do with you – I couldn't even cry my heart was so sore.
Yes, Gulley, you broke my heart as well as my poor nose and my poor
back.' 'And yet you always say it was a good time.' 'A lovely time.' 'We
weren't happy, but we were all alive.' 'Oh dear, Gulley, but why weren't
we happy? You know we could have been. Well, weren't we suited to each
other? Did you ever like any other woman half as much? Why, even to
pester me, or think about me when I wasn't there.' 'That's right, Sara.'
'Oh, you properly doted on me, Gulley, didn't you?' 'Sometimes, Sall.' 'And
that's why you hit me on the nose, didn't you, Gulley. Because you didn't
like me being on your mind. You didn't like not to be free, did you?' 'No, I
wasn't a meal for any old wife. And I had work to do. Now, Sall, you go
away. You get off. I've got a job on – the biggest job of my life. And I've
got to finish it before they hang me.' 'You might as well talk to me as
pretend you're doing any good with that brush. Why, half the times you
don't know where you're putting the colours. And you can't tell blue from
green either, in this light.' 'But I'm getting in the forms and the tones, and

I've no time to waste. Just look at this wall – two years' work and I'll be lucky if I get twenty-four hours for it.' 'Twenty-four hours. You won't get one at this rate. Why, you're killing yourself. You're as hot as a stove. You're trembling all over. You can't go on like this at sixty-eight. You'll be falling off the ropes in another minute – oh, you make me cry.' And she did actually begin to cry, big tears rolled down her cheeks, each with a full moon on the left side, coming through a Gothic window. Crying for me, or perhaps I was crying for myself.

'And what for, I'd like to know,' she said. 'What for did you spoil all our happiness with your worrying about your painting? – whether you ought to make this blue and that green. When we might have been so happy.' 'It was a nuisance, wasn't it?' I said, putting in a nice sharp edge on the rocks where they cut against the whale, light ochre on the blue purple. I had to sharpen this up because of the new eyes. 'A nuisance to you.' 'And yourself, Gulley. Well, I mustn't say it, but I used to say to myself, if it makes him so miserable, it seems a pity. And he with such a gift for enjoying himself.' 'You're quite right, Sara. Art has been my misfortune.' 'It'll be your death unless you come down off that swing.' 'I shouldn't be surprised.' 'Now then, Gulley dear, be sensible for once. Just let me put you to bed and call that nice girl to tuck you up and keep you warm.' 'I don't sleep with Cokey, Sall.' 'Better if you did, it would do you good only to have her there, like King Solomon in the Bible. And as for me, you needn't mind me, Gulley. I shouldn't be jealous. I used to be jealous of all your girls, I admit, and of poor old Rozzie. But if I could give you a nice girl just to keep your old bones warm, I'd do it this minute.' 'I believe you would, you old rascal. You never had any morals.' 'Indeed, Gulley, you know I was brought up strict. As my mother said, a girl can't have too many good principles when she's going into service, and goodness knows, when I was a young maid, I had plenty. But I don't know how it is, when you grow old, they get worn out of you, like lumps in a mayonnaise sauce. When you're old, you're all for smoothness.' 'All for making the best of what's left.' 'Come now, sweetheart, you'll be sensible, won't you? Get down and wrap yourself up.' 'Sall, my dear, I'd like to please you, but I'm busy. Remember what happened when you interfered with me before. Go and mother your Byles or your Fred or your Dicky. They'll make you happy.' 'Happy. You make me laugh, and you make me cry. Happy, well, how could a woman be happy getting her teeth knocked out. Oh dear, those teeth, they were the last of my vanities.' 'Why did you stay with him then, Sara?' 'Oh dear, whatever would that man have done without me. So down as he was, about getting old and losing his job. And couldn't sew a button on for himself with his hands so shaky.' 'Fred did without you.' 'And did you ever see him since I left? Quite fallen in. Oh, he's missed me, poor Fred. And that woman wouldn't do the right thing by him if she could – too spiteful in her nature. And little Dicky back in hospital for his chest. Oh dear, these last months, I've lain awake night after night, for that poor little lamb. And now there's you.' 'I'm all right, Sall. You've only got to look at me, full of jump.' 'Oh dear, aren't I looking and grieving? Don't I know that you know that you're done for. Come, dearie, give it up. Listen to your Sara. Didn't I give you comfort and peace often and often when you were fit to be tied with worrying about your greens and your blues and the rest of your nonsense? Yes, even though you did hit me on the nose, weren't you glad to come into my arms after, yes, with the very blood on your pyjamas, and think you were back with your mother again.' 'There you go, Sall, you old bluemange, you've thrown away your stays at last and taken the whole world to your bosom.' 'Well, I go on asking myself, why can't people be happy, poor dears? Why do they have to go moiling and toiling and worrying each other? Life's too short.' 'Now, Sara, old girl, if you don't mind —' 'And you don't really want me?' 'Not just now, my dear.' 'And aren't you sorry I'm dead?' 'Well, look at me, my dear, boo-hoo, with the tears running down my nose, real tears. A genuine grief. Yes, I'm sorry you're dead, my dear, and that I'm done for. But after all, we mustn't get too upset, must we? It's the way things are.' 'Oh dear, oh dear, I ought to know what life is.' 'Yes,' I said, putting another touch on the old 'un's nose, to give it more elevation. 'Practically A MATTER OF LIFE AND DEATH, you might say, or thereabouts.'

44

Then I must have dozed a bit, for when I waked up, it was daylight, a wonderful top light which made that whale look at me as if I loved her. A world's sweetheart, I said. Love her for yourself and what does it matter what she does with the milkman.

'Good morning, sir,' said an archangel. But when I looked up I saw he was wearing a policeman's helmet and had Gabriel with him, in a green hat. They had opened a skylight and were standing outside on a cloud or a ladder.

'I suppose,' I said, 'you've come about Sara Monday.'

'Sara Monday,' said the policeman. 'What do you know about Sara Monday?'

'Nothing,' I said, 'I didn't do it.'

'Do what?' said the policeman.

I saw the trap and answered, 'What you think I did. Not if she told you herself. The description is all wrong.'

The policeman took out his note-book and said, 'If you mean Mrs Monday who died yesterday in hospital —'

'That's her,' I said. 'What about her?'

'The description she gave is – wait a minute.' And he turned over some papers and read out, 'A man of about six foot high, with red hair and moustache, dressed like a seaman. Spoke with a foreign accent. An anchor tattooed on his right hand. Large blue scar as if from gunpowder on left cheek.'

I began to laugh. I was surprised. But I thought, just like Sara. To diddle a man with her last breath.

The policeman kept looking at me. 'You say this description's wrong?' 'Yes,' I said, 'the bit about the six foot high.' 'How do you know?' 'How could an old woman tell – probably he was only about five foot ten.' 'Did you know Mrs Sara Monday?' 'More or less, we'd met – we knew each other sometimes – we were acquainted in a way —' And then I carelessly gave Jorky's rope a pull and glided away about fifteen feet so that I could get a general idea of the whole situation. It wasn't as bad as I had expected. But the old 'un's left leg was showing too much activity, and, of course, the whale had far too high a value. Yes, I said, I'll have to keep that girl in her place and the only way to do that is to make the place bigger than the girl – the sea will have to roar upon the shore a little darker and the giraffes must elevate their horns to more surprising brassiness in the upper register.

A lot of talk was going on down below. There was quite an orchestra. I distinguished Cokey, like a kettledrum, Nosy like a cracked oboe, Jorky like a viola, and four or five of the girls like a glockenspiel of tea cups.

Yes, I thought, chrome on the giraffes will sing very nicely with the whale's nose, and I called out to Nosy for a tube of chrome. And he ran up the ladder. But when I stretched out my hand towards the platform, I heard a voice say 'Mr Jimson.'

'No,' I said, 'I'm painting.' 'My name is Godman,' he said; or perhaps it was Manley. 'I represent the Borough Council.' So I looked at him, and it was the angel in the green hat.

'Excuse me,' he said, 'I am the borough engineer, and my orders are to demolish this building as unsafe.' 'That is impossible,' I said, 'it's against my agreement.' 'What agreement?' 'I have the council's undertaking not to demolish it till next month – that gives me three weeks.' Then I pulled at the rope and glided away ten feet, towards the whale's right eye. Yes, I thought, she's got something, and I've got something; and began to work on the baby which was taking its milk at her right breast. I wasn't satisfied with the expression in its eye. A sucking baby has a round blank eye. The inward-gazing eye of a mystic which contemplates eternal joy.

The light was getting better all the time. But there was a lot of dust. 'Not so much of it, Cokey,' I shouted. 'Cleanliness is next to Godliness, and just now we're on the real job.' But when I looked round I saw that the dust wasn't coming from Cokey but from a cascade of bricks which were falling off the back wall. A couple of young walruses were standing on the top of it with picks and knocking it down so fast that it seemed to be melting under their feet. 'Take care, you chaps,' I said, 'I wouldn't guarantee any of that brick wall – very impressionist stuff, much of it.' But they didn't even hear me. Enjoying themselves too much. A couple of walruses on duty in full uniform, with knee-straps and wrist-straps and belt-straps, don't like to be talked to by the common herd.

Most of the roof at that end had also disappeared. Which greatly improved the light. I got on to the old 'un, and seeing Nosy on the platform about five feet on my right I shouted to him for the crimson lake. Nosy was also shouting, for what with the bricks and tiles coming down and the men rumbling and the boys and girls underneath arguing with the councillors, the noise was getting noisy. 'No,' I said, 'I know what you think, that the old 'un is too much like Santa Claus on a cracker box. But that's what I want, Nosy. That's how I feel him. When you get to the bottom you're very near the top. Well, look at Renoir's children. Next door to the Christmas supplements. But no tricks – no cleverness – no an't I smart, an't I slick. That's what we don't want. That's what we've got to dodge – that's the jaws of death – and it champs up a couple of promising young geniuses every two minutes. Yes, my pet,' I said to the whale, 'nobody can call you slick, you've got a figure like a barrel of stout, and now I notice it, your right eye is twice the size of your left eye. Why did I do that?'

A large red object came between me and the whale's left breast, and when I looked I saw it was a fireman's ladder. There was a fireman coming up, so I shook down a little green paint from the eternal sea on him and he went back again.

Nosy and Jorky on the platform were arguing with the councillor, and I told them to stop. 'Don't get excited,' I said, 'or you'll do something that he'll be glad of, like breaking his neck. It's no good getting irritated against the bureaucracy,' I said. 'That's giving it best, and it doesn't deserve it. Hit it on the conk – forget it for it knows not what it does. No more than you do. You've got to take people as you find yourself and give your best attention to something else.' I told them, or perhaps I only thought I told them, because I was thinking, What it wants in the top left corner is a lively passage in a strong green. Say a field of cabbage. Yes, curly kale. After all, curly kale, as a work of the imagination, beats Shakespeare. The green, the tender, the humorous imagination. When the old 'un dreamt curly kale, he smiled in his beard.

Nosy and Jorky were fighting three councillors and two policemen. And I remonstrated with them. 'Don't go on like that, boys. You'll end by creating a disturbance in your tempers, you'll spoil your appetites, which in children takes the place of a rational power. Besides,' I said, but speaking in a quiet voice, to save my breath, because nobody was listening to me, 'it's unnecessary to make all this fuss. Remember that dukes and millionaires are among my fans and that I've got four pictures in the national collections.

In fact, I shall write to *The Times* myself as soon as I've got a moment. Don't you worry about the Council. They may take out a few bricks from the back wall, and the tiles off the roof, but that's an old trick. It's often done to remove bad tenants with too many children or bugs or wall painters. Notice that they haven't touched the beams or the side walls. Because they daren't. Essential structure. If they killed me, I could run them in for damages. I've had some before, and I've never paid any attention. It's what you call the pischological attack. Everybody goes in for pischology these days. It started in Genesis, and it reached the government about 1930. But when anyone gives you pischology, you can always give it 'em back. Pay no attention. Look at me, here I am, and here I sit.'

My platform began to waggle up and down and I nearly put a splash of chrome on the whale's eye. 'Hi,' I said, 'don't do that. It's not safe. A wall isn't a canvas. You can't scrape.'

And just then the whale smiled. Her eyes grew bigger and brighter and she bent slowly forward as if she wanted to kiss me. I had a shock. I was touched, of course, to see this affection in a favourite child, but I thought I must be dreaming again. 'My dear girl,' I said, 'my petsie – do be careful – remember your delicate constitution.'

And all at once the smile broke in half, the eyes crumpled, and the whole wall fell slowly away from my brush; there was a noise like a thousand sacks of coal falling down the Monument, and then nothing but dust; a regular fog of it. I couldn't believe it, and no doubt I was looking a little surprised with my brush in my hand, and my mouth open, because when the dust began to clear I saw through the cloud about ten thousand angels in caps, helmets, bowlers and even one top hat, sitting on walls, dustbins, gutters, roofs, window sills and other people's cabbages, laughing. That's funny, I thought, they've all seen the same joke. God bless them. It must be a work of eternity, a chestnut, a horse-laugh.

Then I perceived that they were laughing at me. And I should have got up and bowed if my swing had been steady enough. But it was waggling more than ever.

'Hi,' I said. 'Don't do that. I'll come quietly.' For I didn't want to cause any trouble. I wanted a new studio quickly. I wanted to get that whale straight down again before I lost the feeling of her.

But, of course, they couldn't hear me because of the amusement. And all at once the swing turned right over and I fell off into a blanket held by six art enthusiasts or friends of democracy.

Unluckily I cricked my back or neck or something, and I did not fully understand what was going forward until I found myself in a police ambulance with a peculiar sensation in my arms and legs and a slight headache. Nosy was there, too, with his face so much out of shape that at first I took him for somebody else after a serious accident. There were also, sitting in a row on the opposite cot, Jorky, a nun and a policeman. Jorky had an eye closed and his mouth was under his ear. He was whistling so sideways that it seemed like cheek. And probably it was. The nun was holding my wrist and looking professional.

'Excuse me, officer,' I said, 'but this is illegal. You can't arrest a house-holder for doing art, not on his own premises.'

'Please don't talk,' said the nun. 'You are very ill.'

'Right,' I said. 'Not a word, mother.'

Nosy, who was now and then letting out a sob or perhaps a swear, grabbed my other hand. 'It's a c-crime,' he said.

'No,' I said. 'It was a resolute act of anti-aggression.'

'Pulled down all my lights,' said Jorky, 'without even asking.'

'But they'll pay for it,' said Nosy.

'No they won't,' I said. 'They'll get another good laugh and a considerable deal of self-satisfaction at the clever way they handled an awkward situation.'

'You must not excite yourself,' said the nun. 'It's very dangerous.'

'I haven't broken my neck, have I?' For I wanted to scratch myself, and I couldn't manage it.

'No, you have broken a blood vessel.'

'So that's it,' I said. 'The stroke at last. It only shows that you've got to be careful. Or that it doesn't make much difference, anyway.'

'Oh, sir,' said Nosy, he had a tear-drop on the end of what had been his nose. 'I c-can't bear it.'

'Yes, you can,' I said. 'Take a deep breath, hold your thumbs, count up to fifty and USE LARGE MAPS.'

'It's not fair,' said Nosy. 'They're all against you.'

'There you go,' I said, 'getting up a grievance. Which is about the worst mistake anyone can make, especially if he has one. Get rid of that sense of justice, Nosy, or you'll feel sorry for yourself, and then you'll soon be dead – blind and deaf and rotten. Get a job, get that grocery, get a wife and some kids, and spit on that old dirty dog, the world. Why, I can tell you, as a friend, if it goes no further, that I once had a sense of justice myself, when I was very young. I resented seeing my mother scrub the floor while her worsers went to take the air in Heaven-sent bonnets and shining two-horse chariots that were a glory to the Lord. Works of passion and imagination. Even when I was a young man older than you, I didn't like being kicked up the gutter by cod-eyed money-changers warm from the banquets of reason, the wine of the masters, and the arms of beauty, that houri of paradise. I was a bit inclined to think it a raw deal. Yes, even the celebrated Gulley Jimson, the darling of fortune, much caressed by all classes except the ones that never heard of him, might have turned a bit nasty and given the dirty dog best, if it hadn't been for his fairy godmother sending him a wall. Walls have been my salvation, Nosy, not forgetting the new types of plaster board. Walls and losing my teeth young, which prevented me from biting bus conductors and other idealists. But especially walls. And above all that wall which is now no more. Yes, I have been privileged to know some of the noblest walls in England, but happy fortune reserved the best for my last – the last love of my old age. In form, in surface, in elasticity, in lighting, and in that indefinable something which is, as we all know, the final beauty of a wall, the very essence of its being, Pepper-nose's wall was the crowning joy of my life. I can never forget the way it took the brush. Yes, boys, I have to thank God for that wall. And all the other walls. They've been good to me. The angel, in fact, that presided at my birth – her name was old Mother Groper or something like that – village midwife. Worn-out tart from the sailor's knocking shop. Said, little creature born of joy and mirth. Though I must admit that poor Papa was so distracted with debt and general misery that I daresay he didn't know what he was doing. And poor Mamma, yes, she was glad to give him what she could, if it didn't cost anything and didn't wear out the family clothes. And I daresay she was crying all the time for pity of the poor manny, and herself, too. Go love without the help of anything on earth; and that's real horse meat. A man is more independent that way, when he doesn't expect anything for himself. And it's just possible he may avoid getting in a state.'

'Please don't talk,' said the nun. 'That's all right, mother,' I said, 'they can't hear me because of the noise of the traffic and because they aren't listening. And it wouldn't make any difference if they did. They're too young to learn, and if they weren't they wouldn't want to.' 'It's dangerous for you to talk, you're very seriously ill.' 'Not so seriously as you're well. How don't you enjoy life, mother. I should laugh all round my neck at this minute if my shirt wasn't a bit on the tight side.' 'It would be better for you to pray.' 'Same thing, mother.'